". . . *The Unknown Ajax* will provide the reader with wonderful entertainment from first page to last."

— *Chicago Sunday Tribune*

"Miss Heyer well knows just how long to beat her batter to keep suspense building, and in this book she adds a soupcon of surprise at the end to make the whole piquant. . . . She tells a lively story and imparts a good deal of incidental historical background."

— *Christian Science Monitor*

"(Hugh) is a hero to match with the author's best . . . there is plenty of action, all of it treated with amusement rather than awe and some of it handled as downright farce. . . ."

— *New York Herald Tribune*

"Miss Heyer is a witty writer and an expert at this kind of story."

— *New Yorker*

"The Regency Period is peculiarly Miss Heyer's own . . ."

— *Saturday Review*

Georgette Heyer

THE UNKNOWN AJAX

ACE BOOKS

A Division of Charter Communications Inc.
1120 Avenue of the Americas
New York, N. Y. 10036

The Unknown Ajax,
Copyright © 1959 by Georgette Heyer

First Ace Printing, 1970
Second Ace Printing, 1972

An ACE Book
by arrangement with G. P. Putnam's Sons.

Printed in the U.S.A.

I

Silence had reigned over the dining-room since his lordship, midway through the first course, had harshly commanded his widowed daughter-in-law to spare him any more steward's room gossip. As Mrs. Darracott had merely been recounting to her daughter the tale of her activities that day the snub might have been thought unjust, but she accepted it, if not with equanimity, with a resignation born of custom, merely exchanging a droll look with her daughter, and directing one of warning at her handsome young son. The butler glanced menacingly at the younger of the two footmen, but the precaution was unnecessary: Charles had not been employed at Darracott Place above six months, but he was not such a whopstraw as to make the least noise in the performance of his duties when his lordship was out of humour. That was the way Chollacombe described as knaggy an old gager as ever Charles had had the ill-fortune to serve. Stiff-rumped, that's what he was, always nabbing the rust, or riding grub, like he had been for months past.

Charles had thought himself lucky to have been taken on at Darracott Place, but he wasn't going to stay above his twelve-month, not if he knew it! It might suit James, being Kentish born, to work in a great, rambling house stuck down miles from anywhere, in a marsh flat and bare enough to give anyone a fit of the blue devils, and with never a soul, outside the Family, coming next or nigh it, but when Charles went after another place he was going to London. Let alone he was always one for a bit of life, you could earn extra gelt in London, for there were always errands to be run, or notes to be delivered, and you got a shilling every time you were sent off to execute such commissions. If messages had to be carried in the country it stood to reason they were taken by one of the grooms; while as for the throng of open-fisted guests his Dad had told him it would be his duty to wait upon—well, a houseful of guests might have been what his Dad was used to in his

5

day but it wasn't what they was used to at Darracott Place!

Such visions as Charles had indulged when he had first blessed his good fortune at being hired to fill the post of second footman in a nobleman's establishment! A proper take-in that had been, and so he would tell his Dad! Dad, honourably retired from employment as butler to a Gentleman of Fashion, had assured him that to be hired to serve in a lord's country seat did not mean that he would be immured in rural fastness throughout the year. My lord (said Dad) would certainly retire to Kent during the winter months; but at the beginning of the Season he would remove to his London house; and at the end of the Season (said Dad) the chances were that he would hire a house in Brighton for the summer months. And from time to time, of course, he would be absent, visiting friends in other parts of the country, during which periods his servants would enjoy a great deal of leisure, and might even be granted leave to go on holiday.

But nothing like that had happened at Darracott Place since Charles had first entered its portals. My lord, whose grim mouth and arctic stare could set stronger knees than Charles's knocking together, remained in residence all the year round, neither entertaining nor being entertained. And no use for anyone to tell Charles that this was because the Family was in mourning for Mr. Granville Darracott and his son, Mr. Oliver, both drowned off the coast of Cornwall in an ill-fated boating expedition: Charles might only have been second footman at Darracott Place for a couple of months when that disaster occurred, but no one could gammon him into thinking that my lord cared a spangle for his heir. If you were to ask him, Charles would say that my lord cared for no one but Mr. Richmond: he certainly couldn't abide Mr. Matthew Darracott, who was the last of his sons left alive; while as for Mr. Claud, who was the younger of Mr. Matthew's two sons, it was as much as anyone could do not to burst out laughing to see my lord look at him as if he was a cockroach, or a bed-bug. Nor, though he didn't look at him like that, could you think he cared a groat for Mr. Vincent neither; while as for poor Mrs. Darracott, as kind a lady as you'd find anywhere, even if she was a bit of a prattle-box, it seemed like she had only to open her mouth for my lord to give her one of his nasty set-downs. He didn't, it was true, do that to Miss Anthea, but that was probably because Miss Anthea wasn't scared of him, like her Ma, and would maybe give as good as she got: it wasn't because he was fond of her, as you'd think her granddad would be. It wouldn't be Miss Anthea as would coax him out of his sullens; it would be Mr. Richmond.

But Richmond, his grandfather's darling, after one thoughtful glance cast under his lashes at that uncompromising countenance appeared to lose himself in his own reflections. Some pickled crab, which he had not touched, had been removed with a damson pie; and his sister saw, peeping round the massive silver epergne that almost obscured him from her view, that he had eaten no more than a spoonful of this either. Since he had partaken quite liberally of two of the dishes that had made up the first course she was undismayed by anything other than her grandfather's failure to notice his present abstention. In general Lord Darracott would have bullied Richmond into eating the pie, imperfectly concealing his anxious affection for the youth, whose earlier years had been attended by every sort of ailment, under a hectoring manner, to which Richmond, docile yet unafraid, would submit.

As little as Charles the footman did Anthea, or Mrs. Darracott, or even Richmond understand the cause of his lordship's brooding ill-humour; rather less than Charles did any one of these three believe that it sprang from grief at the death of his eldest son. His lordship had both disliked and despised Granville; yet when the news of that fatal accident had reached Darracott Place he had been for many minutes like a man struck to stone; and when he had recovered from the first shock he had horrified his son Matthew, and Lissett, his man of business, by saying several times over, and in a voice of icy rage: "Damn him! Damn him! Damn him!" They had almost feared for his reason, and had stood staring at him with dropped jaws until he had violently ordered them out of his sight. Matthew had never dared to enquire what extraordinary circumstances had provoked this outburst, and his lordship neither offered an explanation nor again referred to the matter. Only a black cloud seemed to descend on him, rendering him more unapproachable than ever, and so brittle-tempered that Mrs. Darracott quite dreaded having to address him, and even Richmond several times had his head bitten off.

Dinner was always a protracted meal; tonight it seemed interminable; but at last it came to an end. As the servants began to remove the covers, Mrs. Darracott picked up her reticule, and rose.

His lordship's hard, frowning eyes lifted; he said curtly: "Wait!"

"Wait, sir?" faltered Mrs. Darracott.

"Yes, wait!" he repeated impatiently. "Sit down! I have something to say to you!"

She sank back on to her chair, looking at once bewildered and apprehensive. Anthea, who had risen with her, remained standing, her head turned towards her grandfather, her brows a little raised. He paid no heed to her; his eyes were on the two footmen, and it was not until they had left the room that he spoke again. So forbidding was his expression that Mrs. Darracott, in growing trepidation, began to search wildly in her mind for some forgotten error of ommission or commission. Chollacombe softly shut the door on the heels of his subordinates, and picked up the port decanter from the sideboard; he perceived that his master's hands were clenching and unclenching on the arms of his chair, and his heart sank: there had been a storm brewing all day, and it was going to burst now over their heads.

But when my lord again spoke it was as though it cost him an effort. He said: "You will be good enough, Elvira, to inform Flitwick that I expect my son and his family here tomorrow. Make what arrangements you choose!"

She was so much surprised that she was betrayed into uttering an unwise exclamation. "Good gracious! Is *that* all? But what in the world—I mean, I hadn't the least notion——"

"What brings them here, sir?" asked Anthea, intervening to draw her grandfather's fire.

He looked for a moment as though he were about to utter one of his rough snubs, but after a slight pause he answered her. "They are coming because I've sent for them, miss!" He paused again, and then said: "You may as well know now as later! I've sent for my heir as well."

At these bitterly uttered words Chollacombe nearly dropped the decanter.

"Sent for your heir *as well?*" repeated Richmond. "But my uncle Matthew is your heir, Grandfather—isn't he?"

"No."

"Then who is, sir?" demanded Anthea.

"A weaver's brat!" he replied, his voice vibrant with loathing.

"Oh, *dear!*" said Mrs. Darracott, breaking the stunned silence that succeeded his lordship's announcement.

The hopeless inadequacy of this exclamation dragged

a choke of laughter out of Anthea, but it caused his lordship's smouldering fury to flare up. "Is that all you have to say? Is that all, woman? You are a wet-goose—a widgeon—a—take yourself off, and your daughter with you! Go and chatter, and marvel, and bless yourselves, but keep out of my sight and hearing! By God, I don't know how I bear with you!"

"No, indeed!" said Anthea instantly. "It is a great deal too bad, sir! Mama, how could you speak so to one so full of compliance and good nature as my grandfather? So truly the gentleman! Come away at once!"

"That's what you think of me, is it, girl?" said his lordship, a glint in his eyes.

"Oh, no!" she responded, dropping him a curtsy. "It's what I *say*, sir! You must know that my featherheaded Mama has taught me to behave with all the propriety in the world! To tell you what I *think* of you would be to sink myself quite below reproach! Come, Mama!"

He gave a bark of laughter. "Tongue-valiant, eh?"

She had reached the door, which Chollacombe was holding open, but she looked back at that. "Try me!"

"I will!" he promised.

"Oh, Anthea, *pray——!*" whispered Mrs. Darracott, almost dragging her from the room. She added, as Chollacombe closed the door behind them: "My love, you *should* not! You know you should not! What, I ask you, would become of us if he were to cast us off?"

"Oh, he won't do that!" replied Anthea confidently. "Even he must feel that once in a lifetime is enough for the performance of *that* idiocy! I collect that the *weaver's son* is the offspring of the uncle we are never permitted to mention? Who is he, and what is he, and—oh, come and tell me all about it, Mama! You know we have leave to marvel and chatter as much as we choose!"

"Yes, but I don't know anything," objected Mrs. Darracott, allowing herself to be drawn into one of the saloons that opened on to the central hall of the house. "Indeed, I never knew of his existence until your grandfather threw him at my head in that scrambling way! And I consider," she added indignantly, "that I behaved with perfect propriety, for I took it with composure, and I'm sure it was enough to have cast me into strong hysterics! He would have been well-served if I had fallen senseless at his feet. I was never more shocked!"

A smile danced in her daughter's eyes, but she said with

9

becoming gravity: "Exactly so! But a well-bred ease of manner, you know, is quite wasted on my grandfather. Mama, when you ruffle up your feathers you look like a very pretty partridge!"

"But I am not wearing feathers!" objected the widow. "Feathers for a mere family evening, and in the country, too! It would be quite ineligible, my love! Besides, you should not say such things!"

"No, very true! It was the stupidest comparison, for whoever saw a partridge in purple plumage? You look like a turtle-dove, Mama!"

Mrs. Darracott allowed this to pass. Her mind, never tenacious, was diverted to the delicate sheen of her gown. She had fashioned it herself, from a roll of silk unearthed from the bottom of a trunk stored in one of the attics, and she was pardonably pleased with the result of her skill. The design had been copied from a plate in the previous month's issue of *The Mirror of Fashion*, but she had improved upon it, substituting some very fine Brussels lace (relic of her trousseau) for the chenille trimming of the illustration. Her father-in-law might apostrophize her as a wet-goose, but even he could scarcely have denied (had he had the least understanding of such matters) that she was a notable needlewoman. She was also a very pretty woman, with a plump, trim figure, large blue eyes, and a quantity of fair hair which was partially concealed under a succession of becoming caps. From the moment when she had detected a suspicion of sagging under her jaw she had made her caps to tie beneath her chin or (more daringly) her ear; and the result was admirable. She was neither learned nor intelligent, but she contrived to dress both herself and her daughter out of a meagre jointure, supplying with her clever fingers what her purse could not buy; and she had never, during the twelve years of her widowhood, allowed either her father-in-law's snubs or the frequent discomforts of her situation to impair the amiability of her disposition. Her temper being cheerful, and the trend of her mind optimistic, she seldom fretted over the major trials which were beyond her power to mend. Her daughter, of whom she was extremely fond, was twenty-two years of age and still unwed; her spirited young son, whom she adored, was kept kicking his heels in idleness to serve his grandfather's caprice; but although she recognized that such a state of affairs was deplorable she could not help feeling that *something* would happen to make all right, and was able, without much difficulty, to put such dismal thoughts aside, and to expend her anxiety on lesser and more remedial problems.

Anthea's quizzing remark brought one of these to her mind. Smoothing a crease from the purple-bloom satin, she said very seriously: "You know, dearest, it will be excessively awkward!"

"What will be awkward? The weaver's son?"

"Oh, him——! No, poor boy—though of course it *will* be! I was thinking of your Aunt Aurelia. I am persuaded she will expect to see us in mourning. You know what a high stickler she is for *every* observance! She will think it very odd of us to be wearing colours—even improper!"

"Not at all!" replied Anthea coolly. "By the time my grandfather has demanded to be told what cause *she* has to wear mourning for my uncle and my cousin, and has made her the recipient of his views on females rigging themselves out to look like so many crows, she will readily understand why you and I have abstained from that particular observance."

Mrs. Darracott considered this rather dubiously. "Well, yes, but there is no *depending* on your grandfather. I think we should at least wear black ribbons."

"Very well, Mama, we will wear whatever you choose—at least. *I* will do so if *you* will stop teasing yourself about such fripperies and tell me about the weaver's son, and the uncle who must not be mentioned."

"But I don't know anything!" protested Mrs. Darracott. "Only that he was the next brother to poor Granville, and quite your grandfather's favourite son. Your papa was used to say that that was what enraged Grandpapa so particularly, though for my part I can't believe that he held him in the slightest affection! Never, never could I bring myself to disown *my* son! Not though he married a *dozen* weaver's daughters!"

"Oh, I think we should be obliged to disown him if he married a dozen of them, Mama!" Anthea said, laughing. "It would be quite excessive, and so embarrassing! Oh, no, don't frown at me! It don't become you, and I won't fun any more, I promise you! Is that what my uncle did? Married a weaver's daughter?"

"Well, that's what I was told," replied Mrs. Darracott cautiously. "It all happened before I was married to your papa, so I am not perfectly sure. Papa wouldn't have spoken of it only that there was a notice of Hugh's death published in the *Gazette,* and he was afraid I might see it, and make some remark."

"When did he die, Mama?"

"Now that I *can* tell you, for it was the very year I was married, and had just come back from my honeymoon to live here. It was in 1793. He was killed, poor man. I can't remember the name of the place, but I do know it was in Holland. I daresay we were engaged in a war there, for he was a military man. And I shouldn't be at all astonished, Anthea, if *that* is what makes your grandfather so determined Richmond shan't enter the army. I don't mean Hugh's being killed, but if he had not been a military man he would never have been stationed in Yorkshire, and, of course, if he had not been stationed there he would never have met that female, let alone have become so disastrously entangled. I believe she was a very low, vulgar creature, and lived in Huddersfield. I must own that it is not at all what one would wish for one's son."

"No, indeed!" Anthea agreed. "What in the world can have possessed him to do such a thing? And he a Darracott!"

"Exactly so, my love! The most imprudent thing, for he cannot have supposed that your grandfather would forgive such a shocking misalliance! When one thinks how he holds up his nose at quite respectable persons, and never visits the Metropolis because he says it has grown to be full of mushrooms, and once-a-week beaux——! I must say, I never knew anyone who set himself on such a high form. And then to have his son marrying a weaver's daughter! *Well!*"

"And to be obliged in the end to receive her son as his heir!" said Anthea. "No wonder he has been like a bear at a stake all these months! Did he know, when my uncle and Oliver were drowned, how it was? Was that what made him so out of reason cross? Why has he waited so long before breaking it to us? Why—— Oh, how provoking it is to think he won't tell us, and we dare not ask him!"

"Perhaps he will tell Richmond," suggested Mrs. Darracott hopefully.

"No," Anthea said, with a decided shake of her head. "Richmond won't ask him. Richmond never asks him questions he doesn't wish to answer, any more than he argues with him, or runs counter to him."

"Dear Richmond!" sighed Mrs. Darracott fondly. "I am sure he must be the best-natured boy in the world!"

"Certainly the best-natured grandson," said Anthea, a trifle dryly.

"Indeed he is!" agreed her mother. "Sometimes I quite marvel at him, you know, for young men are not in general so tractable and goodhumoured. And it is *not* that he lacks spirit!"

"No," said Anthea. "He doesn't lack spirit."

"The thing is," pursued Mrs. Darracott, "that he has the sweetest disposition imaginable! Only think how good he is to your grandfather, sitting with him every evening, and playing chess, which must be the dullest thing in the world! I wonder, too, how many boys who had set their hearts on a pair of colours would have behaved as beautifully as he did, when your grandfather forbade him to think of such a thing? I don't scruple to own to you, my love, that I was in a quake for days, dreading, you know, that he might do something foolish and hot-headed. After all, he *is* a Darracott, and even your uncle Matthew was excessively wild when he was a young man." She sighed. "Poor boy! It was a sad blow to him, wasn't it? It quite wrung my heart to see him so restless, and out of spirits, but thank heaven *that* is all over now, for I couldn't have borne it if your grandfather had agreed to let him join! I daresay it was just a boyish fancy—but Richmond has such good sense!"

Anthea looked up, as though she would have spoken; but she apparently thought better of the impulse, and closed her lips again.

"Depend upon it," said Mrs. Darracott comfortably, "he will never think of it again, once he has gone to Oxford. Oh dear, how we shall miss him! I don't know what I shall do!"

The crease which had appeared between Anthea's brows deepened. She said, after a moment's hesitation: "Richmond has no turn for scholarship, Mama. He has failed *once*, and for my part I think he will fail again, because he doesn't wish to succeed. And here we are in September, so that he will be more than nineteen by the time he *does* go to Oxford—*if* he goes—and he will have spent another year here, with nothing to do but to——"

"Nothing of the sort!" interrupted Mrs. Darracott, bristling in defence of her idol. "He will be *studying!*"

"Oh!" said Anthea, in a colourless voice. She glanced uncertainly at her mother, again hesitated, and then said: "Shall I ring for some working-candles, Mama?"

Mrs. Darracott, who was engaged in darning, with exquisite stitches, the torn needlepoint lace flounce to a petticoat, agreed to this; and in a very short space of time both ladies were deedily employed: the elder with her needle, the younger with some cardboard, out of which she was making a reticule, in the shape of an Etruscan vase. This was in accordance with the latest mode; and, if *The Mirror of Fashion* were to be believed, any ingenious lady could achieve the desired result without the smallest difficulty. "Which confirms me in the melancholy suspicion that I am quite lacking in ingenuity, besides having ten thumbs," remarked Anthea, laying it aside as Chollacombe brought the tea-tray into the room.

"I think it will look very elegant when you have painted it, my love," said Mrs. Darracott consolingly. She looked up, and saw that Richmond had followed the butler into the room, and her face instantly became wreathed in smiles. "Oh, Richmond! You have come to take tea with us! How charming this is!" A thought occurred to her; her expression underwent a ludicrous change; she said apprehensively: "Does your grandfather mean to join us, dearest?"

He shook his head, but there was a gleam of mischief in his eyes, which did not escape his sister. His mother, less observant, said in a relieved tone: "To be sure, he rarely does so, does he? Thank you, Chollacombe: nothing more! Now, sit down, Richmond, and *tell us!*"

"What, about the weaver's son? Oh, I can't! Grandpapa snapped my nose off, so we played backgammon, and I won, and then he said I might take myself off, because he wants to talk to *you*, Mama!"

"You *are* a detestable boy!" remarked Anthea. "Mama take care! you will spill that! Depend upon it, he only means to throw a great many orders at your head about the manner in which we are to entertain the heir."

"Yes," agreed Mrs. Darracott, recovering her complexion. "Of course! I wonder if I should go to him immediately, or whether——"

"No, you will first drink your tea, Mama," said Anthea firmly. "Did he tell you *nothing* about our unknown cousin, Richmond?"

"Well, only that he's a military man, and was in France, with the Army of Occupation, when my uncle Granville was drowned, and that he has written that he will visit us the day after tomorrow."

"That must have been the letter James brought from the

receiving office, then!" exclaimed Mrs. Darracott. "Well, at least he can *write!* Poor young man! I can't but pity him, though I perfectly appreciate how provoking it is for us all that he should have been born. Still, even your grandfather can't blame him for that!"

"For shame, Mama! You are under-rating my grandfather in the most disrespectful way! Of course he can!"

Mrs. Darracott could not help laughing at this, but she shook her head at her too-lively daughter as well, saying that she ought not to speak so saucily of her grandfather. After that she finished drinking her tea, begged Richmond not to go to bed before she returned from the ordeal before her, and went away to the library.

Anthea got up to fill her cup again. She glanced down at Richmond, sunk into a deep chair and smothering a yawn. "You look to be three parts asleep. Are you?"

"No—yes—I don't know! I had one of my bad nights, that's all. Don't cosset me—and, for God's sake, don't say anything to Mama!"

"What a fortunate thing that you've warned me!" said Anthea, sitting down in her mother's vacated chair. "I was just about to run after Mama, before procuring a composer for you."

He grinned at her. "Pitching it *too* rum!" he murmured. "I wonder what Grandpapa *does* want to say to Mama?"

"I don't know, but I hope he may say it with civility! How *could* you stand there, and let him speak to her as he did at dinner, Richmond?"

"Well, *I* can't stop him! What's more, I've more sense than to rip up at him as *you* did! It only puts Mama into a quake, when she thinks he may fly into a passion with you or me: you should know that!"

"He doesn't like one the less for squaring up to him," she said. "I will allow him *that* virtue: I don't know that he has any other."

"He may not like *you* less, but you're a female: the cases are different."

"I don't think so. He liked Papa far more than he liked Uncle Granville or Uncle Matthew, but I can't tell you how often they were at outs. I daresay you might not remember, but——"

"Oh, don't I just!" he interrupted. "Grandpapa abusing Papa like a pickpocket, Papa as mad as Bedlam, the pair of them brangling and brawling to be heard all over the house——! *Not remember?* I don't remember anything half as well! Too well to court the same Turkish treatment that Papa got: you may be sure of *that!*"

She looked curiously at him. "But you're not afraid of him, are you?"

"No, I'm not afraid of him, but I detest the sort of riot and rumpus he kicks up when he's in a rage. Besides, it doesn't answer: you'll get nothing out of Grandpapa if you come to cuffs with him. I'll swear he gives me more than ever he gave Papa!"

She reflected that this was true. Lord Darracott, who grudged every groat he was obliged to spend on anything but his own pleasure, pandered to his favourite grandson's every extravagant whim. If coaxing did not move him, it was seldom that Richmond failed to bring him round his thumb by falling into a fit of despondency. That was how Richmond had come by the beautiful headstrong colt he had himself broken and trained. He had coaxed in vain. "Do you think I'll help you to break your neck, boy?" had demanded his lordship. Richmond had not persisted, and even so clearsighted a critic as his elder sister had been unable to accuse him of sulkiness. He was as docile as ever, as attentive to his grandfather, and quite uncomplaining. But he made it very evident that his spirits were wholly cast down; and within a week his dejection, besides throwing Mrs. Darracott into high fidgets, had won the colt for him. Anything, said Lord Darracott, was better than to have the boy so languid and listless.

It had been to cajole him out of silent despair at being told that under no circumstances would my lord buy him a pair of colours that his yacht had been bestowed on him. Suddenly Anthea wondered if the possession of a sailing vessel had been what he had all the time desired. She turned her eyes towards him, and said abruptly: "Do you still wish for a military career, Richmond?"

He had picked up one of the weekly journals from the table at his elbow, and was glancing through it, but he looked up quickly at that, his expressive eyes kindling. "I don't care for anything else!"

"Then——"

"You needn't go on! Why don't I persist? Why don't I do this—or that—or the other? Because I know when my grandfather can't be persuaded by anything I could do or say! That's why! I'm under age—and if you are thinking that I might run off and take the King's shilling, it's the sort of hubble-bubble notion a female *would* get into her head!

That's not how I wish to join! I—oh, stop talking about it! I *won't* talk about it! It's over and done with! I daresay I shouldn't have liked it, after all!"

He turned back to his journal, hunching an impatient shoulder, and Anthea said no more, knowing that it would be useless. She was deeply troubled, however, and not for the first time. He was spoilt, and wilful, but she loved him, and was wise enough to realize that his faults sprang from his upbringing, and were to be laid at Lord Darracott's door.

He had been a sickly, undersized baby, succumbing to every childish ailment: not at all the sort of grandson that might have been expected to occupy Lord Darracott's heart. His lordship, indeed, had paid scant heed to him until it was forcibly borne in upon him that the frail scrap whom he despised was possessed of a demon of intrepidity. But from the day when a terrified groom had carried into the house a baby who screamed: "Put me down, put me down! I *can* ride him! I *can!*" and had learned from this trembling individual that his tiny grandson had (by means unknown and unsuspected) got upon the back of one of his own hunters and put this great, rawboned creature at the gate that led out of the stableyard, he had adored Richmond. There had been no bones broken, but the child had been stunned by the inevitable fall, and shockingly bruised. "Let me go!" he had commanded imperiously. "I *will* ride him, I will, I will, I *will!*"

Nothing could have made a greater hit with my lord. Himself a man of iron nerve, he was at once surprised and exultant to discover in the weakling of the family a fearlessness that matched his own. There was no more talk of puling brats or miserable squeeze-crabs: thenceforward little Richmond figured in his grandfather's conversation as a right one, game as a pebble; and my lord, who had suffered scarcely a day's illness in his life, very soon became more morbidly anxious about the state of his darling's health than was Richmond's fond mama. Poor Mrs. Darracott, labouring for six years under the stigma of being a doting idiot who cosseted her whelp to death, suddenly, and to her considerable bewilderment, underwent a transformation, changing, almost overnight, into an unnatural parent to whose callous neglect every one of her son's ailments could be attributed. She bore the slur with fortitude, too thankful for my lord's change of heart to resent the injustice to herself. She had dreaded the day when she would be forced to

17

send her delicate son to Eton, but when that day dawned it had been my lord, not she, who had decreed that Richmond must be educated at home. At the time, Anthea, four years older than her brother, had been as glad as she that Richmond was not to be subjected to the rigours of boarding-school; it was not until several years had passed that she realized, looking back, that by the time he was eleven Richmond had largely outgrown his delicacy of constitution. Today, a little more than eighteen years old, he was certainly a thin youth, but he seemed to have no other weakness than a tendency towards insomnia. As a child, the slightest stir in his room had jerked him wide-awake, and this idosyncrasy had remained with him, causing him to choose for his own a bedchamber as far removed from the main body of the house as was possible; to bolt his door; and to forbid his solicitous family to come near him once he had retired for the night. None of them ever did so, but it was only Anthea who suspected that the prohibition sprang from a strong dislike of being teased by offers of hot bricks, drops of laudanum, supporting broths, or saline draughts, rather than from an inability to drop off to sleep again once he had been roused. No one, she thought (but privately), who suffered from disturbed nights could be as energetic as Richmond.

He was certainly looking heavy-eyed this evening, yawning from time to time, as he flicked over the pages of the journal; but as he had begun to bring his hunters into condition, and had spent the morning at trotting exercise, following this up by soundly beating his sister in several games of battledore-and-shuttlecock, before going off to shoot rabbits in a turnip-field, it would have been surprising had he not looked weary at the end of the day.

He glanced up presently from the journal, as a thought occurred to him, and said, with a gleam of decidedly impish amusement: "I wouldn't be in that fellow's shoes for a fortune, would you?"

"Our unknown cousin? No, indeed I wouldn't! If he's not up to the rig, Grandpapa will behave abominably, and we shall all be put to the blush. What do you think he will be like, Richmond? It seems to me that if he's a military man he can't be *very* vulgar. Unless—Good God, he isn't just a common soldier, is he?"

"Rifleman. No, of course he—Lord, I never thought of that!" said Richmond, in an awed tone. He grinned appreciatively. "Well, if that *is* the way of it it *will* mean the devil to pay, won't it? I wonder if my uncle knows what Grandpapa has in store, or whether—Vincent, too! I'll tell you what Anthea, I don't give a fig for Uncle Matthew, but I think it's a curst shame that Vincent should be cut out by this mushroom!"

She did not answer, for at that moment Mrs. Darracott came back into the room.

II

It was instantly apparent to her children that Mrs. Darracott had not been summoned by her father-in-law to discuss such trivialities as the arrangements to be made for the reception of his heir. She was looking slightly dazed; but when Anthea asked her if my lord had been unkind, she replied in a flustered way: "No, no! *Nothing* like that! Well, that is to say—Except for—Not that I regarded it, for it was nothing out of the ordinary, and I hope I know better than to take a pet over a trifle. I must own, too, that I can't be astonished at his being vexed to death over this business. It is excessively awkward! However, he doesn't lay the blame at *my* door: you mustn't think that!"

"I should think not indeed!" exclaimed Anthea, between amusement and indignation. "How could he possibly do so?"

"No, very true, my love!" agreed Mrs. Darracott. "I thought that myself, but it did put me on the fidgets when Richmond said he wanted to see me, because, in general, you know, things I never even heard about turn out to be my fault. However, as I say, it wasn't so today. Now, where did I put my thimble? I must finish darning that shocking rent before your aunt arrives tomorrow."

"No, that you shan't!" declared Anthea, removing the work-box out of her mother's reach. "You are big with news, Mama!"

"I am sure I haven't the least guess why you should think so. And you shouldn't say things like that! It is most improper!"

"But not by half as improper as to try to bamboozle your children! Now, Mama, you know you can't do it! *What* has Grandpapa disclosed to you? Instantly tell us!"

"Nothing at all!" asserted the widow, looking ridiculously guilty. "Good gracious, as though he ever told me anything! How can you be so absurd?"

"Now, that is trying it on much too rare and thick!" said Richmond accusingly.

"Foolish boy! You are as bad as your sister, and what your poor papa would think of you both, if he could hear you, I'm sure I don't know! And you ought to be in bed, Richmond! You look worn to a bone!"

At this, her masterful offspring converged upon her, Anthea sinking down on to a stool at her feet, and Richmond perching on the arm of her chair.

"And *we* don't know what poor Papa would think of you for shamming it so, dearest!" said Anthea. "Grandpapa has told you all about the weaver's son. Confess!"

"No, no, I promise you he hasn't! He told me nothing about him—well, nothing to the purpose! Only when I ventured to ask him if it had not been a great shock to him to learn of the young man's existence, he said he had known of it for ever. My dears, would you have believed it? It seems that poor Hugh wrote to tell your grandfather of *this* Hugh's birth, twenty-seven years ago! And not a word has he uttered to a soul until today! Unless, of course, he disclosed the truth to Granville, but I am positive he never did so, for your aunt Anne and I were the closest friends, and she must have told me, if she had known anything about it. Oh dear, poor soul, I wonder how she does? I wonder how it will answer, living with her daughter and her son-in-law? To be sure, Sir John Caldbeck seemed a most amiable man, and I daresay *anything* was preferable to Anne than continuing here—though I always used to think that Grandpapa was by far more civil to her than——"

"Yes, Mama," interrupted Anthea. "But all this is fair and far off, you know! So Grandpapa has known from the start how it was, has he? We needn't marvel that he said nothing about it while my Uncle Granville and Oliver were alive, but how can he have allowed my Uncle Matthew to suppose all these months that he was now the heir to the barony? It is a great deal too bad, besides being quite crackbrained! Did he hope the young man might be dead? He can't, surely, have forgotten him!"

"Well, I fancy, from something he said to me just now, that he had the intention of disinheriting him, if it might be done, only from some cause or another—but I don't precisely understand about settlements, so—Or do I mean an entail? No, I don't *think* it was that, and naturally I shouldn't dream of asking your grandfather to explain, for nothing

20

provokes him more than to be asked questions, though why it should I can't conjecture!"

"I didn't know one *could* cut out the heir to one's title," objected Richmond.

"It seems to be established that Grandpapa, at all events, cannot," said Anthea.

"Sequestration!" suddenly and triumphantly exclaimed Mrs. Darracott. "That was the word! I thought very likely it would come back to me, for very often things do, and sometimes, which always seems extraordinary to me, in the middle of the night! Well, that was it, only it can't be done, and so Grandpapa feels that there is nothing for it but to make the best of this young man."

"Did he say that, Mama?" asked Anthea incredulously.

"Yes, he did," nodded Mrs. Darracott. "Well, it was what he *meant!*"

"But what did he *say?*" demanded Richmond.

"Oh, I can't recall exactly what he said! Only he seems to think he might go off at any moment, though why he should I can't imagine, for I never knew anyone so hearty! In fact, it wouldn't surprise me if he—Well, never mind that! Dear me, I have forgotten what I was about to say!"

"It wouldn't surprise you if he outlived us all," supplied Anthea helpfully.

"Certainly not!" stated Mrs. Darracott, blushing. "Such a thought never entered my head!"

"Lord, what a rapper!" remarked Richmond, palliating this undutiful criticism by hugging her briefly. "You're trying to cut a wheedle, but if you think you can turn *us* up sweet, you're a goose, Mama!"

"Richmond!"

"How many more times is Mama to tell you not to speak to her so saucily?" interpolated Anthea severely.

"You are two very silly, impertinent children!" said Mrs. Darracott, trying not to laugh. "And what your Aunt Aurelia will think of you, if you talk in that improper style, makes me quite sick with apprehension!"

"We won't," promised Anthea. "We will remember that a want of conduct in us reflects directly upon you, love, and we will behave with all the propriety in the world."

"If she stops trying to gammon us," amended Richmond.

"Oh, that is understood! *How* does Grandpapa mean to make the best of our new cousin, Mama?"

"Well, my dears," responded the widow, capitulating, "he seems to think that it will be necessary to lick the unfortunate young man into shape. At least, that's what he said."

"Unfortunate young man indeed!"

"I own, one can't but feel a great deal of compassion for him, yet it can't be denied that it *is* a severe trial for your grandfather to know that he must be succeeded by quite a *vulgar* person. I should be very much vexed myself, and heaven knows I don't set half the store by my consequence that your grandfather does! Oh dear, how uncomfortable it will be! I did hope, when I learned that he is a military man, that he might be quite gentlemanlike, but your grandfather says that the army has grown so large, on account of the war's having dragged on for such a time, that it is full of what he calls shabby-genteel officers—though how he should know that, when he never stirs from home, is more than I can tell! And to make it worse the poor man is in the wrong sort of regiment."

"What?" ejaculated Richmond, kindling. "He's in the 95th! A Light Division man! I should like to know what is wrong with that!"

"Well, dearest, I don't know anything about such matters myself, but Grandpapa spoke of its being newfangled, which, of course, would account for his not liking it."

"If that's the way my grandfather means to talk he'll make more of a Jack-pudding of himself than ever this cousin could, even if he is a rum 'un!" declared Richmond hotly. "Of all the antiquated, top-lofty——"

"Well, don't put yourself in a passion!" recommended his sister. "You cannot suppose that anything other than a cavalry regiment, or the 1st Foot Guards, would do for a Darracott!"

"Balderdash!" said Richmond. "I don't mean I wouldn't wish for a cavalry regiment myself, but if I can't—*couldn't*—join one, I'd as lief be a Light Bob as anything else. And if Grandpapa says something slighting—oh, lord, I shan't know where to look! I wonder if this man marched to Talavera? Do you know that——" He broke off, seeing his mother look quickly up at him, a stricken expression in her face. "Oh, well!" he said, shrugging. "It's of no consequence—only I do hope to God Grandpapa doesn't make a cake of himself! Go on, Mama! How is our cousin to be licked into shape? Does my grandfather mean to undertake the task himself? The wretched victim will seize the first opportunity that offers of escaping from the home of his fathers!"

"Oh, no!" Mrs. Darracott said. "That is—no, I am persuaded your grandfather doesn't mean—He said something about Vincent's being able to *hint* him into the established mode."

"Vincent! He won't do it!" said Richmond positively.

"No, well—well, at least your grandfather seems to feel that we ought, all of us, to use the young man kindly!" Mrs. Darracott perceived that both her children were regarding her with a mixture of surprise and disbelief, and her colour rose. She began to rearrange the Paisley shawl she wore draped round her shoulders, and said, rather too airily: "I am sure it is greatly to his credit, and not at all what one would have expected! Poor young man! Your cousin, I mean, not Grandpapa! I daresay he will feel sadly out of place here, and we must try to make him welcome. I shall certainly do so, and I hope you will, too, dearest Anthea. Grandpapa is—is particularly anxious that you should make yourself agreeable to him. Indeed, I don't know why you should not! Not that I mean . . ." Aware that two pairs of fine grey eyes were fixed on her face, she found herself unable to finish this sentence, and tried hurriedly to begin another. "Dear me, how late it is! Anthea, my love,——"

"Mama!" uttered Anthea accusingly. "If you don't tell me precisely what it was that my grandfather said to you I'll go to the library and ask him!"

This dreadful threat threw Mrs. Darracott into instant disorder. She scolded a little, wept a little, asseverated that my lord had said nothing at all, and ended by divulging to her children that my lord had conceived the happy notion of bringing about a match between his shabby-genteel heir and his only unmarried granddaughter. "To keep him in the *Family!*" she explained earnestly.

That was all that was needed to send Richmond into shouts of laughter. His sister, in general a girl with a lively sense of the ridiculous, found herself easily able to withstand the infection of his laughter. She waited in ominous silence until his mirth abated, and then, transferring her gaze from him to her mother, asked with careful restraint: "Does it ever occur to you, Mama, that my grandfather is a lunatic?"

"*Frequently!*" Mrs. Darracott assured her. "That is—oh, dear, what am I saying? Of course not! Perhaps he is a trifle *eccentric!*"

"Eccentric! He's a mediaeval bedlamite!" said Anthea, not mincing matters. "Upon my word, this is beyond everything!"

"I was afraid you would not quite like it," agreed her mother unhappily. "Now, Richmond——! You will be in whoops if you don't take care! Foolish boy! There is nothing to laugh at!"

"Let him go into whoops, Mama! They may *choke* him!"

Mrs. Darracott was shocked by this unfeeling speech, but thought it wisest, after one glance at Anthea's stormy face, to beg Richmond to go away. He did go, but it was a moment or two before Anthea's wrath abated. She had jumped up from the footstool, and now took several turns about the room in a hasty, impetuous way which filled Mrs. Darracott with foreboding. However, she soon recovered her temper, and, although still incensed, was presently able to laugh at herself. "I should know better than to fly up into the boughs for anything that detestable old man could say or do! I beg your pardon, Mama, but it puts me in such a rage when he behaves as though he were the Grand Turk, and we a parcel of slaves——! So I am to marry the weaver's son, am I? I collect that *I* have nothing to say in the matter: has the weaver's son? Has he been informed of the fate that awaits him?"

"Oh, no! That is—I *did* venture to suggest to your grandfather—But he said—you know his way!—that the poor young man would do as he was bid!"

"And he will!" said Anthea. "That's to say, he'll try! Wretched, wretched man! I pity him with all my heart! He will be miserably ill-at-ease, miserably out of place, and will arrive to find himself under fire! Grandpapa will overawe him within five minutes! Mama, it is *infamous!* Did you tell my grandfather that I shouldn't consent to such a scheme?"

"Well—well, I didn't say *that*, precisely!" confessed Mrs. Darracott, in acute discomfort. "To own the truth, my love, I was so much taken-aback that——"

"Then I will, and immediately!" declared Anthea, going towards the door.

She was halted by a small, anguished shriek. "Anthea, I forbid you—I implore you!—He would be so angry! He will say that he told me not to say one word to you about it, and he *did!*"

Anthea could not be impervious to this appeal. She paused; and, pursuing her advantage, Mrs. Darracott said: "My dearest, you have so much good sense! I know you will consider carefully before you—Not that I would urge you to marry him if you felt you couldn't like him! I promise you

I would never, never—But what will you *do*, Anthea? Oh, my dearest child, I'm cast into despair whenever I think of it! You are two-and-twenty, and how can you hope to receive a respectable offer, when you never meet anyone but the Family, or go anywhere, or—And here is your grandfather saying that you frittered away your chances when he was so obliging as to frank you to a London Season, and so you must now be content with a husband of his choosing!"

"During my one Season," said Anthea, in a level tone, "I received two offers of marriage. One came from a widower, old enough, I conjecture to have been my father. The other was from young Oversley, who, besides being next door to a moonling, had the fixed intention of continuing under his parents' roof. Between Grandpapa and Lady Aberford I am persuaded there wasn't the difference of a hair! I haven't watched the trials you've been made to endure only to stumble into the same snare, Mama!"

"No, and heaven knows, dear child, I must be the last person alive to wish to see you in such a situation," sighed Mrs. Darracott.

"I could, I think, have developed a *tendre* for Jack Froyle," said Anthea reflectively. "But he, you know, was obliged to hang out for a rich wife, and thanks to the improvidence for which the Darracotts are so justly famed my portion can't be called anything but paltry. Does Grandpapa consider that circumstance when he talks of the chances I have frittered away?"

"No, he doesn't!" replied Mrs. Darracott, with unaccustomed bitterness. "But *I* do, and it utterly sinks my spirits! That's why I can't help thinking that perhaps you ought not to set your face against this scheme of your grandfather's. Not, until you have met your cousin, at all events, my love! Of course, if he should prove to be impossible—only, you know, he *is* a Darracott on *one* side!"

"The side I should like the least!" said Anthea.

"Yes, but—but you would be *established!*" Mrs. Darracott pointed out. "Even if the young man is a coxcomb, which I do pray he is not, *your* position as Lady Darracott would be one of the first respectability. Anthea, I cannot bear to see you dwindle into an old maid!"

Anthea could not help laughing at this impassioned utterance, but Mrs. Darracott was perfectly serious, saying very earnestly: "How can you help but do so when no eligible gentleman ever *sees* you? Dear Anne was used to say that when Elizabeth and Caroline were off her hands she would invite you to stay in London, because she entered into all my sentiments on that head; but now that your uncle Granville is dead, and she has gone away into Gloucestershire, it would be useless to depend on her. Aurelia has still two daughters of her own to bring out, and although I *could* write to my brother——"

"On no account in the world!" exclaimed Anthea. "My uncle is the most amiable soul alive, but I would far rather dwindle into an old maid than stay for as much as two days with my aunt Sarah! Besides, I don't think she could be prevailed upon to invite me."

"No, nor do I: she is the most disagreeable woman! So what, I ask you, is to become of you? When Grandpapa dies we shall be obliged to leave Darracott Place, you know. We shall be reduced to seeking *lodgings*, very likely in some dreadful back-slum, and eat black-pudding, and turn our dresses, and——"

A peal of laughter interrupted this dismal catalogue. "Stop, stop, Mama, before you fall into an incurable fit of the blue-devils! We shall do nothing of the sort! With *your* skill in dressmaking, and *my* turn for making elegant reticules, we shall set up as mantua-makers. In Bath, perhaps, on Milsom Street: not a large establishment, but an excessively modish one. Shall we call it Darracott's, to enrage the Family, or would it be more tonnish to call ourselves Elvira? Yes, I'm persuaded we should make a hit as Elvira! Within a year every woman of fashion will patronize us, because we shall charge the most exorbitant prices, which will convince the world that we *must* be top-of-the-trees!"

Mrs. Darracott, while deprecating such a nonsensical idea, could not help being strongly attracted by it. Anthea encouraged her to enlarge upon the day-dream; and soon had the satisfaction of seeing her volatile parent restored to her usual optimism. Not until they retired to bed was the unknown cousin again mentioned. He came into Mrs. Darracott's mind as she picked up her candle, and she ventured to beg Anthea not to speak of the matter to her grandfather. She was much relieved when Anthea, kissing her, and giving her shoulder a reassuring pat, replied: "No, I shan't say anything to Grandpapa. I am sure it would be quite useless!"

Mrs. Darracott, much cheered, was able then to go to bed with a quiet mind. She was too deeply occupied with household cares on the following morning to have a thought to spare for any other problems than which bedchamber it would be proper to allot to the heir; how best to hide from Lady Aurelia that there was not a linen sheet in the house which had not been darned; and whether the undergroom would be able to purchase in Rye enough lobsters to make, when elegantly dressed, a handsome side-dish for the second course at dinner that day. She, and Mrs. Flitwick too, would have been glad to know for how many days my lord had invited five guests to stay at Darracott Place, but neither considered for as much as a minute the eligibility of applying to him for information on this head. Nothing but a rough answer could be expected. My lord would be unable to understand what difference it could make to anyone. He would also be unable to understand why the addition of five persons to his household should make any appreciable difference to the cost of maintaining his establishment. As he would, at the same time, cut up very stiff indeed if fewer than seven or eight dishes were provided for each course, the task of catering to his satisfaction was one of the labours of Hercules. "For, ma'am," (as Mrs. Flitwick sapiently observed) "I dare not for my life tell Godney to use up the mutton in a nice haricot, or toss up some oysters in an escallop: his lordship will want everything to be of the best."

It soon transpired that there was one thing which his lordship did not want to be of the best. When Mrs. Darracott asked him if he wished Poor Granville's bedchamber to be prepared for the reception of his successor, his reply was explosive and unequivocal, and carried the rider that the weaver's brat would think himself palatially housed if put to sleep in one of the attics.

The first of the guests to arrive were Mr. Matthew Darracott and Lady Aurelia. They came in their own travelling-carriage, drawn by a single pair of horses; and they reached Darracott Place shortly after noon, having left town the day before, and rested for the night at Tonbridge.

Of my lord's four sons, Matthew, the third, was the one who had caused him the least trouble and expense. His youthful peccadilloes had been of a venial nature, committed either in emulation of his elder brothers, or at their instigation. He had been the first to marry; and from the day that he led Lady Aurelia Holt to the altar his career had been at once blameless and successful. It had been a very good match, for although Lady Aurelia was not beautiful her fortune was respectable, and her connections excellent. She had also a forceful personality, and it was not long before Matthew, weaned from the Whiggish heresies in which he had been reared, found himself (under the aegis of his father-in-law) with his foot firmly set on the first rung of the political ladder. His progress thereafter had been steady; and although it seemed unlikely that he would ever achieve the topmost rungs of the ladder it was only during the brief reign of "All the Talents" that he was out of office; and although there were those who did not scruple to stigmatize his continued employment as jobbery, no one could deny that he discharged his duties with painstaking honesty.

His political apostasy notwithstanding, it might have been expected that so worthy a son would have occupied the chief place in his father's affection. Unfortunately Lord Darracott was bored by virtue, and contemptuous of those whom he could bully. Matthew had always been the meekest of his sons, and although his marriage had rendered him to some extent independent of his father, he still accorded him a sort of nervous respect, obeying his periodic and imperious summonses with anxious promptitude, and saying yes and amen to his lordship's every utterance. His reward for this filial piety was to be freely apostrophized as a pudding-heart, with no more pluck in him than a dunghill cock. Since his conduct was largely governed by the precepts of his masterful and rigidly correct wife, my lord was able to add, with perfect truth, that he lived under the sign of the cat's foot.

What Lady Aurelia thought of my lord no one knew, for she had been reared in the belief that the head of a family was entitled to every observance of civility. So far as outward appearances went, she was a dutiful daughter-in-law, neither arguing with his lordship, nor encouraging Matthew to rebel against his autocratic commands. Simple-minded persons, such as Mrs. Rupert Darracott, were continually astonished by Matthew's divergence, on all important issues, from his father's known prejudices; but Lord Darracott was not a simple-minded person, and he was well-aware that however politely Lady Aurelia might defer to him it would be her dictates Matthew would obey in major matters. In consequence, he held her in equal respect and dislike, and never lost an opportunity to plant what he hoped would be a barb in her flesh.

According to Granville, whose own son had found little

28

favour in his grandfather's eyes, it was with this amiable intention that my lord encouraged Vincent in a career which his parents were known to think ruinous. More charitable persons suspected that in Vincent my lord saw a reflection of his own youth; but, as Granville once bitterly remarked, it was strange, if that were so, that my lord's feeling for him fell far short of the doting fondness he lavished on Richmond.

It must have been apparent to the most casual observer that Matthew Darracott was labouring under a strong sense of ill-usage. He was rather a stout man, not quite as tall as his father, or any of his brothers, and with a chubby countenance. When he was pleased he looked what nature had intended him to be: a placid man with a kindly, easy-going disposition; but when harassed his expression changed to one of peevishness, a frown dragging his brows together, and a pronounced pout giving him very much the look of a thwarted baby.

As he climbed down from the carriage, he saw that Chollacombe was waiting by the open door of the house. Leaving James, the footman, to assist Lady Aurelia to alight, he trod up the shallow terrace-steps, exclaiming: "This is a damned thing, Chollacombe! Where's my father?"

"His lordship went out with Mr. Richmond, sir, and is not yet come in," replied the butler.

"Has that fellow—*I* don't know what he calls himself!— Has he arrived here?"

"No, sir. You are the first to arrive. As you no doubt know, Mr. Matthew, we are expecting Mr. Vincent and Mr. Claud also, but——"

"Oh, them!" said Matthew, dismissing his sons with an impatient shrug.

By this time he had been joined by his wife. She never reproved him in public, and she did not now so much as glance at him, but said majestically: "Good-day, Chollacombe. I hope I see you well?"

"Very well, thank you, my lady. Mrs. Darracott is in the Green Saloon, I fancy. Perhaps your ladyship would——"

He broke off, for at that moment Mrs. Darracott came hurrying across the hall. "Oh, Matthew! My dear Aurelia! How glad I am to see you! I did not expect you would be so early—but so delightful!"

"We lay at Tonbridge," said Lady Aurelia, presenting her cheek to her sister-in-law. "I do not care to travel above thirty or forty miles at a stretch: it does not agree with my constitution."

"No, it is very disagreeable!" agreed Mrs. Darracott. "The road from Tonbridge, too, is so horridly rough! I am sure——"

"Elvira!" interrupted Matthew, thrusting his hat into James's hand, "what do you know about this appalling business?"

"Oh, my dear Matthew, *nothing!* That is, only—— But won't you come into the Green Saloon? Unless you would wish to take off your bonnet and pelisse, Aurelia? I will take you upstairs—not that there is any *need* to escort you, for you must feel yourself to be quite as much at home as I am."

This, however, her ladyship disclaimed, saying graciously that she considered herself a guest in the house, her sister-in-law being its unquestionable mistress. Mrs. Darracott, though privately thinking that there was a good deal of question about it, accepted this, and the two ladies went upstairs, leaving Matthew to get what information he could from Chollacombe. But as the butler knew very little more than he did, the only tidings he was able to glean were that the heir was not expected to arrive until the following day, and that my lord was (if Chollacombe might venture to say so) a trifle out of humour.

"Ay, I'll be bound he is!" said Matthew. "Well, it is enough to put a saint out of temper! What's more, I shouldn't wonder at it if the fellow's an impostor!"

Chollacombe thought it prudent to return no answer to this; so, after fidgeting about the hall for a few moments, Matthew took himself off, saying that if my lord was out riding with Mr. Richmond he might as well go down to the stables to meet him on his return.

In the event, he reached the main stableyard to find that his father had already returned, and in time to see the two sturdy coach-horses being taken out of the shafts of Matthew's travelling-carriage. He himself was bestriding a neatish bay cover-hack, but Richmond, as his uncle resentfully perceived, had just dismounted from the back of a high-bred hunter which probably cost my lord anything from three to five hundred guineas.

"So you've arrived, have you?" said my lord, by way of paternal greeting. "I might have known this paltry turn-out was yours! What did you give for that pair of commoners?"

"I don't recall—but they are not commoners, sir! Pure-bred Welsh, I assure you!" responded Matthew, nettled.

"Cleveland machiners!" said his lordship, with a bark of sardonic mirth. "You've been burnt, my boy! If ever I knew such a slow-top!" He pointed his whip at Richmond's hunter. "Now, *there's* a horse of the right stamp! Breed in every inch of him, perfect fencer, flying or standing!"

"Hardly the right stamp for carriage-work, sir!" said Matthew. "A goodlooking horse, however, and carries a good head." He held out his hand to Richmond, adding kindly: "Well, my boy? And how are you?"

"Pretty stout, sir, thank you," replied Richmond, shaking hands with him. "I hope you are well? And my aunt, of course. Is my cousin with you?"

The note of eagerness did not escape Matthew; he smiled faintly. "No, neither of them. I collect, thought, that you meant Vincent: I expect he will arrive presently."

"You may be sure that he will!" interpolated his lordship, dismounting, and handing over his bridle to the waiting groom. He then looked his son over, remarked that he was becoming as fat as a flawn, and strode off towards the house, imperatively commanding Richmond to follow him.

But Richmond, who disliked being made to stand by in acute embarrassment while my lord insulted his son, had already slipped away into a wing of the stables, and it was Matthew who, swallowing his resentment, caught up with my lord. "Father, I must ask you—indeed, I must insist——"

My lord stopped, and turned, his grasp on his riding-whip tightening. "Oh? So you must insist, must you? Go on!"

"Well, I must say that I think you owe me—well, that an explanation is due to me!" amended Matthew sulkily.

"If you think you'll get any explanation out of me, other than what I choose to tell you, muffin-face, you're a bigger clunch than I knew! What I choose to tell you I have told you, and it's all that concerns you!"

"No, sir!" said Matthew resolutely. "That don't fit! You don't like me; you didn't wish for me to step into your shoes; but when—after what happened in June—I was your heir: no question about it!"

"You were not."

"No! As it now appears, and if this fellow who has sprung up out of nowhere is not an impostor! And that, sir, is something even you will own I've a right to ask!"

"He is not an impostor."

"I beg your pardon, but what proof have you of that? For my part I think it damned smoky, Father! If the fellow is my brother's son I should like to know why he never approached you before! Upon my word, a very neat thing this is! If he had had the impudence to put forward his so-called claim to *me,* I'd have set Lissett to enquire into his credentials, and you may depend upon it we should soon have found that it was nothing more than an attempt to run a rig! Well, I've seen Lissett, and he tells me you didn't desire him to do any such thing, but merely to write a letter informing the rascal you would receive him here. Now, Father——"

"Damn you, when I want your advice I'll ask you for it!" broke in his lordship roughly. "I'm not in my dotage yet! I've known for twenty-seven years that this cocktail existed!"

"Good God!" gasped Matthew. "Known for—— And never *told* us?"

"Why should I have told you?" demanded his father. "D'ye think I was proud of a weaver's spawn? D'ye think I ever imagined I should be succeeded by a whelp I thought never to set eyes on? As for approaching me—laying claims —you're fair and far off! He never did so! He's coming here because I've sent for him—and he's taken his time about coming!" he added grimly. "If you've seen Lissett, no doubt he told you that the fellow's a soldier. *I've* known that these five years and more."

"Do you mean to say you've followed his career?" asked Matthew incredulously.

"No, I don't! I never gave the whelp a thought. Old Barnwood ran against him when he was out in the Peninsula, and had the curst brass to come up to me in Brook's, and ask me if I knew I'd a grandson in the 95th. I damned his eyes for it, meddling busybody!"

Matthew said slowly: "So when my brother was drowned you knew! And yet you—— For God's sake, sir, why didn't you tell me *then?* Why——"

"Because I hoped he might be dead, chucklehead, or that there might be some way of keeping him out of my shoes!" replied Lord Darracott, his face working. "Well, he's not dead, and there's no way of keeping him out! When I'm booked, he'll be the head of the family, but I'm not booked yet, and, by God, I'll see to it he's been licked into shape before I get notice to quit!"

Vincent was the first of Matthew's two sons to reach Darracott Place, driving himself in a curricle to which were har-
nessed three magnificent black geldings, random-tandem;
and by the time that Richmond, who had been on the
watch for him, let out a halloo, and exclaimed: "Here's my
cousin at last! Oh, he's driving unicorn! He's the most
complete hand!" even Mrs. Darracott, with whom Vincent
was no favourite, felt a certain measure of relief. In her
view, Vincent was a dangerous blade, with a viperous
tongue, and a deplorable influence over her impressionable
young son; but after spending three hours in an atmosphere
of deepening gloom, she would have been much inclined
to have welcomed the arrival of Beelzebub himself. My
lord having shut himself up in the library, it had fallen
to her lot to entertain his guests: an exercise which consisted of lending a sympathetic ear to Matthew's complaints,
rhetorical questions, and dire forebodings. Not a very arduous task, it might have been thought; but Mrs. Darracott
(like her son) was impressionable, and long before Matthew had talked himself into a more cheerful frame of mind
the depression which hung over him had communicated itself to her, quite sinking her spirits, and exhausting her vi-
tality. Every effort to introduce another topic of conversation than the blighting of Matthew's prospects failed: he
returned mechanical answers only, and at the first opportunity returned to the grievance that possessed his mind.

Anthea too was glad to know that Vincent had arrived.
She had not been subjected to so severe a strain as her
mother, but she had been obliged, after Lady Aurelia had
rested for an hour on her bed to recover from the rigours
of her journey, to escort that rather formidable lady on a
stately and prolonged tour of the gardens. In her youth,
Lady Aurelia had been an enthusiastic gardener; since her
marriage she had had no other home than a tall, narrow
house in Mayfair, but she had forgotten none of the botani-
cal lore so zealously acquired, and was perfectly ready to
place it at the disposal of the various friends and relations
whom it was her custom to visit (often for weeks at a time)
during the summer months. She never uttered an adverse
criticism, but her hostesses had been known to uproot whole
borders only because she had said, with flat civility, "Very
pretty"; and her way of ignoring the presence of a weed
could cover the hardiest with shame. Anthea, no horticul-

turist, had much to endure, but she was spared the trials her mother was forced to undergo. Beyond stating, in a voice totally devoid either of sympathy or interest, that her husband was sadly put out by the appearance on the scene of the rightful heir, Lady Aurelia made no reference whatsoever to the event which filled the minds of the Darracotts. She did not say it, but no one blessed with a modicum of intelligence could have doubted that to an Earl's daughter the succession to a mere barony was a matter of indifference.

Her peregrinations had brought her within sight of the avenue which led from the crumbling stone entrace-gates to the north front of the house, when Vincent's natty curricle swept into view. The arrival of her eldest-born seemed to be a matter of equal indifference to her, but she raised no objection to Anthea's suggestion that they should go to meet him.

Before they had reached the avenue, Richmond had bounded out of the house, and was standing beside the curricle, smiling a little shyly up at his magnificent cousin. "What a hand you are! I have been watching for you this hour and more!"

The Corinthian in the curricle looked down at him, his brows lifting in exaggerated surprise. "But, my dear boy, you surely cannot have supposed that even *I* could accomplish more than sixty-two miles in less than five hours? Our beloved Regent, I would remind you, took four-and-a-half hours on his memorable dash to Brighton, and *that* road, you know, was vastly superior to this, even in those archaic times. Or did you think that my eagerness to reach the home of my ancestors—*not,* I apprehend, to be one day my own—would set me on the road before I had swallowed my breakfast?"

Richmond laughed. "No! Oh, lord, what a curst thing it is!—*you* to be cut out by this miserable fellow from Yorkshire! But what's this new quirk, Vincent? You were always used to drive that bang-up team of grays in your curricle! Is it now the high kick of fashion to drive—unicorn, do you call it?"

"Yes,—or Sudden Death," replied Vincent, transferring the reins into the hands of his groom. "And *no,* little cousin, you may *not* drive them. We have had enough sudden deaths in the family."

From no one but Vincent would Richmond have tolerated such a form of address, but a cousin, nearly ten years his senior, who, in addition to being carelessly kind to him, was a buck of the first cut, might bestow whatever opprobrious epithet upon him which happened to occur to him. He protested, but with a grin; and before Vincent could roast him into defending hotly his ability to drive any number of horses, Lady Aurelia and Anthea had come up to the group.

"Well, Vincent!" said Lady Aurelia.

He had climbed down from the curricle, and he now swept off his beaver, bowed, and with incomparable grace kissed first her hand, and then her cheek. "My dear Mama! Ah, and my dear cousin Anthea as well! A double pleasure!"

"And so unexpected!" she retorted, shaking hands with him.

His eyes glinted at her. "I never expect to find each time I come here that you are in greater beauty than the last time I saw you. It is really quite remarkable."

She was not in the least disconcerted by this, but only laughed, and said: "Yes, and I so stricken in years! Remarkable indeed! Where is your brother? Did you chance to see him on the road?"

"Now, that puts me in mind of something that causes me to feel the gravest concern!" he exclaimed. "I *did* see him—in fact, I passed him, driving, as I thought, to an inch. How it can have come about I can't conceive, unless it might be that at the fatal moment my attention was diverted by the new lining he has had made for his chaise (maiden's blush I believe that particular shade of pink is called), but I very much fear that I may have ditched him."

Richmond burst into a crow of joy. "Lord, what a famous lark! I wish I might have seen it! Hunting the squirrel!"

"No, no, how can you say such a thing?" protested Vincent, in a pained voice. "How often have I told you that such tricks as that are not at all the thing? I wonder if I can be losing my precision of eye?"

"A stupid and ill-natured prank," pronounced Lady Aurelia, with measured severity. "If I find that Claud has sustained any injury I shall be excessively displeased."

"Then I do most sincerely trust he has escaped injury, Mama. Unfortunately, a sharp bend in the road almost immediately hid the scene from my view, so I can give you no very certain information on that head. But never mind! Crimplesham is following me, with my luggage, you know, and I am sure we may depend upon him to render my

35

brother all the assistance in his power. What is the time? Should I, do you think, present myself to my grandfather at once, or— No, I perceive that it lacks only ten minutes to five. I have brought my evening-dress with me, but it will take me quite an hour to dress without Crimplesham's aid. You *do* still dine at six, I daresay? Such a depressing habit I find it! And my anxiety about Claud to make it worse! Poor fellow! But he shouldn't have urged his postboys to hold the road when I wished to give him the go-by: really, I think he almost deserves to sustain some injury for being so foolish!"

When Mrs. Darracott learned of this episode, which she very soon did, from Richmond, who could not keep such a good story to himself, she was much shocked. It all went to show, she told Anthea, that everything she had ever felt about Vincent had been correct: he showed an unsteadiness of character which she would be very sorry to see in any son of hers; his temper was jealous; he was idle and expensive; and, unless she much mistook the matter (which was not at all likely), he had such libertine propensities as must cause his poor father to suffer the gravest anxiety. Or, she amended, the penance she had undergone that afternoon still fresh in her memory, they would have done so if Matthew had the smallest regard for anything but his own troubles. As for the stoic calm with which Lady Aurelia had received the news of what might well prove to have been a serious accident, *that*, said Mrs. Darracott, was something that quite passed her understanding. Had any son of *hers* been overturned into a ditch she would have had the horses put-to immediately, and dashed to his rescue. She was extremely attached to Lady Aurelia, but it was impossible to forbear the thought that if Claud were to be presently borne into the house with his neck broken it would be a judgment on her.

But no judgment fell on Lady Aurelia. Claud, arriving at Darracott Place half-an-hour later, had sustained no injury, except to his temper. This, however, had been seriously impaired, and he complained so bitterly and at such length of the usage to which he had been subjected that his father lost patience, and said testily: "Oh, that's enough, that's enough! Vincent forced your near wheels into the ditch, and it cost you twenty minutes to haul the chaise back on to the road! Very vexing, but no harm done! If you're at outs with Vincent, go and plant him a facer! Don't come whining to me, like a sickly girl!"

Even Richmond, who wholeheartedly despised Claud, felt that this advice was unkind. His dislike of all forms of violence apart, Claud was both slighter and shorter than his brother: no match for him under any circumstances. He said, with pardonable indignation: "Dash it, he'd throw me out of the window!"

"Well, go away and change your dress!" said Matthew. "It won't be Vincent, but your grandfather, who will throw you out of the window if you keep him waiting for his dinner!"

This dreadful warning had the effect of sending Claud out of the room with much the mien and speed of a coursing hare. His father and Richmond both laughed, but Mrs. Darracott was moved to say that she thought the boy had been very unkindly treated.

"Oh, pooh!" replied Matthew impatiently. "If he had ever had one half the tricks played on him which *I* had to endure when I was a lad it would have been the better for him! Besides, it's his own fault, with his silly daintification, and his finicking ways. *I* don't blame Vincent for making game of him!"

It was on the tip of her tongue to say that making rough game of a younger brother was conduct quite unbecoming in a man of eight-and-twenty, but Matthew had begun to pout, and so she refrained, knowing as well as everyone else that the ill-will Vincent bore Claud was to some extent shared by him, and did not spring in either of them from any particular dislike of Claud's dandyism.

Five years separated the brothers. In appearance they were not unalike, each having the aquiline nose and rather sunken eye which made them unmistakeable Darracotts; but Claud was by far the better-looking, his features being more delicate, his complexion less swarthy, and his countenance unmarred by the deep, almost sneering lines that characterized both Vincent and Lord Darracott. In general, Claud's expression was one of slightly vacuous amiability; Vincent's was sardonic, and frequently unpleasant.

In all but their features they were dissimilar. Vincent had a reckless intrepidity which drove him into all manner of dangerous exploits; Claud, though not (he hoped) henhearted, felt not the smallest impulse to ride straight at the worse oxer in the county, or to take the shine (at the risk of his neck) out of every other top-sawyer on the road; while as for putting on the gloves with Gentleman Jackson, there was almost nothing he less wished to do. But he was

37

not without ambition. It was his ardent desire to become just such a leader of Fashion, such an arbiter of Taste, as Mr. Brummell had been, until so short a time ago. He grudged Vincent none of his fame as a member of the Corinthian set; it would not have gratified him in the least to be hailed as an out-and-outer, a regular dash, or a right cool fish: his heart was set on becoming the chief Pink of the Ton.

This ambition found no favour at all in the eyes of his parents, and would, indeed, have been impossible to realize had not a stroke of amazing good fortune befallen Claud. Hardly had he reached his majority when the maternal uncle after whom he had been named died, and left him the heir to a comfortable independence. Nothing then stood between him and the achievement of his goal but a want of genius. Try as he would he could neither create a new quirk of fashion, nor hit upon some original eccentricity which would make him instantly famous. He was obliged to exaggerate the prevailing mode, and to adopt as his own the tricks and mannerisms of other and more ingenious dandies, and somehow these expedients did not quite answer the purpose.

Vincent, of course, recognized every one of these plagiarisms, but what would have amused him in a young brother no plumper in the pocket than he was himself became a matter for bitter contempt when Claud inherited an easy competence. Vincent, with nothing but his allowance and the erratic generosity of his grandfather to depend on, lived precariously on the edge of Dun Territory. He was a gamester, and his luck had more than once saved him from being run quite off his legs; but he had several times been out-of-town, as the saving was; and he was no stranger to an obliging individual known to every gentleman seeking to raise the wind as Old Tens-in-the-Hundred. Envy and resentment changed his indifference to Claud into rancorous dislike. He was irritated by everything Claud did, whether it was wasting his blunt on the relining of his private chaise, or being such a muckworm as to travel behind job-horses. Nothing short of seeing Claud rolled-up would soften his dislike, and of that there was small likelihood: Claud's fortune was genteel rather than handsome, but he had no taste for gaming or racing, and, like his mother, he knew how to hold household.

It was an added source of exasperation in Vincent to know that his tongue had no power to wound Claud. Nothing short of being tipped into a ditch stirred Claud to resentment; and if he thought about Vincent at all it was with no other emotion than a sort of mild surprise. None of his brother's hazardous exploits awoke in his breast a spark of envy or of emulation: he envied Vincent only his splendid shoulders, and the incomparable blacking which made his boots shine like mirrors. Unfortunately both these desirable possessions were beyond his reach. Nature had seen fit to add drooping shoulders to his willowy form; and the secret of the blacking was locked in Crimplesham's bosom. Buckram and wadding could supply what Nature had withheld, but neither guile nor bribery would ever win from Crimplesham the least clue to his secret.

If it cost Claud a pang to know that Vincent's Hessians outshone his own, this was nothing to the rage and the despair that filled his valet's soul. Nor was the hostility that flourished between the brothers comparable to the feelings of jealousy, hatred, and contempt which filled the hearts of their valets. If Crimplesham excelled in the arts of polishing boots, and keeping buckskins in perfect order, Polyphant's genius lay in his skill with an iron, and his flair for evolving new and intricate modes of tieing a neckcloth, or dashing styles for his master's curled and pomaded locks. He believed himself to be by far the more expert valet, and it galled him beyond endurance to know that, while Crimplesham's one excellence was apparent to all, his own talents must inevitably go to his master's credit. Few people would suspect any aspirant to high fashion of entrusting the arrangement of his hair, or of his neckcloth, to his valet; none would suppose that any gentleman would black his own boots.

By the time Claud hurried into his bedchamber, Polyphant had unpacked his portmanteaux, and had even found time to press the creases from a longtailed coat of superfine, and a pair of black satin knee-breeches. These Claud eyed with disfavour, uttering a protest: "No, I'll be damned if I'll wear that rig here! Dash it, it ain't the thing, Polyphant!"

"No, sir, and well do I know it!" agreed Polyphant, in a feeling voice. "The proper mode, of course, would be pantaloons, since it is hardly feasible to suppose you will be taking a look-in at Almack's." He ventured to point this pleasantry with a titter, but it did not answer; and upon Claud's demanding peevishly how the devil he could take a look-in at Almack's in September, and from Darracott Place, he at once banished the smile from his face, and said: "No, sir. Very true. But it *might* be wise to consider his lordship's prejudice. Not that I would presume to dictate. I *did* venture to enquire of his lordship's man if the custom of wearing knee-breeches every evening still obtains at Darracott Place. He assured me that it *does,* sir."

The sinister nature of this warning was not lost on Claud, and he said no more. It vexed him very much to be obliged to present himself to his family in a costume so out-dated as to amount to a sartorial solecism, but he had his reward in that he incurred no censure from his grandfather other than the comprehensive disapproval contained in that gentleman's greeting. "Twiddle-poop!" said his lordship, as Claud minced up to him to make his bow, and thereafter paid no heed to him.

Dinner, in Mrs. Darracott's view (for her expectations had not been high), passed off very well. No lobsters had been obtainable, but Godney had procured some partridges, which, with some dried salmon, cleverly dressed in a case, quite made up this deficiency, and drew praise from Matthew, who was known to be a *gourmet;* and although the family reunion could hardly have been described as convivial it was not rendered hideous by any explosion of wrath from Lord Darracott.

When the gentlemen rose from the table, my lord, recommending his son, and his younger grandsons, to join the ladies, bore Vincent off to the library, saying, as soon as they had reached this sanctuary: "Your father's as sick as a horse over this business."

"And who shall blame him?" returned Vincent. "I'm not chirping merry about it myself, you know, sir, and I should suppose that *you* are not thrown into transports precisely."

"No, by God!" His lordship poured brandy into two glasses, tossed off the contents of his own, and refilled it. "I did my best to keep the fellow out, but the trap's down. Got to lick him into shape."

"I feel sure you'll manage to do so, sir. How old is he?"

"Much your own age: seven-and-twenty."

"If he is as old as that, he's irreclaimable," said Vincent cynically.

"We'll see that!" snapped his lordship. After a moment he added grudgingly: "He won't eat with his knife, at all events. He's a military man: one of these new regiments, but still——!"

"A military man! Oh, I was expecting a yokel in homespuns! Er—commissioned, sir?"

"Major," replied Lord Darracott shortly.

Vincent's eyes opened wide at that. "The devil he is!" For a moment his expression was inscrutable; then he gave a short laugh, and said: "Well, it's to be devoutly hoped that he's up to the rig, for you can scarcely send a Major back to school, sir!"

"Can't I?" said my lord, looking grimmer than ever. "This whipstraw is my grandson, I'll have you remember! He'll dance to my piping, or I'll send him packing!"

"Am I to understand, sir, that you have the intention of *keeping* him here?" demanded Vincent.

"Yes, if he behaves himself. I want him under my eye. The thing turns out not as badly as I feared, but there are plenty of rum 'uns with military titles these days, and this fellow was reared the Lord knows how—in a weaver's hovel, I daresay! If I'd known—if I'd ever dreamt——!" He broke off, his hands clenching and unclenching as they always did when his rage threatened to master him. He glanced under his craggy brows at Vincent. "Well! Between us we should be able to give him a new touch!"

"Between us?" repeated Vincent. "My dear sir, I would do much to oblige you, but bear-leading a cousin I heartily wish at the devil is a feat quite beyond me."

"I didn't say you were to bear-lead him. You're an idle, extravagant dog, but your ton is good: you'll serve as a model for him to copy!"

"If I had had the remotest guess that that was why I was invited I shouldn't have come!" said Vincent.

"Oh, yes, you would!" retorted his lordship. "And, what's more, jackanapes, you'll stay for precisely as long as I choose, unless you have a fancy for paying your own debts in future!" He observed, with satisfaction, that he had at once infuriated and silenced his grandson, and smiled derisively. "Ay, that's where the shoe pinches, isn't it? Scorched again?"

Regaining command over his temper, Vincent replied coolly: "Oh, no! Just a trifle cucumberish! I own it will suit me pretty well to remain here for the next few weeks—until the quarter, you know!"

"The allowance your father gives you won't bring *you* round," remarked his lordship.

"No, sir, but the first October meeting may!" countered Vincent.

"I wish I may see it! Well, I didn't send for you only for

that. Since I can't keep the fellow out of the family you'd best meet him at the outset, all of you!"

"*All* of us?" said Vincent. "Are we to have the rare felicity of seeing my aunts here, sir? Not to mention their numerous progeny, and——"

"Don't be impertinent, sir!" barked his lordship.

Vincent, who knew very well that he was perfectly indifferent to his three married daughters, and, indeed, to all his female descendants, bowed meekly. My lord glared at him for a moment, and then said: "I don't care how soon the rest of 'em take themselves off, but I want you here." He paused, frowning. "It's the boy!" he said abruptly. "I'm not going to have that fellow putting ideas into his head: I've had trouble enough over that silly business!"

Vincent raised his brows. "Richmond?"

"Ay, Richmond. It's gone off now, but he was devilish set on joining, six months ago. Fell into flat despair when I told him I wouldn't have it. Well, as I say, the notion seems to have gone off, and I don't want him to start moping and pining again. He's a good boy, but he's got an odd kick in his gallop, you know. For two pins he'd hang on this fellow's lips—make a hero of him, I daresay! Well, he won't do that while you're here."

"Won't he?" said Vincent. "Er—what do I do if I find him talking to our unwanted cousin? Take him by the ear, and haul him off?"

A sardonic smile curled his lordship's mouth. "You won't have to. Think I don't know what he makes of *you?* Whistle him to heel, and you'll have him following like a tantony-pig!"

The prospect of having an eager stripling following him like a tantony-pig was not one which Vincent could bring himself to contemplate with enthusiasm, but he said nothing, reflecting that it would probably be unnecessary to do more than keep Richmond in a string. There would be no difficulty about that, for it was true enough that the boy liked and admired him. He would almost certainly take his tone from his Corinthian cousin, for to win his approval, to emulate his sporting prowess, had always been the top of his desire.

As though he had read Vincent's mind, Darracott said: "He won't sit in your pocket. Won't tease you either. But while you're here, and he thinks there's a chance you may take him off to see a mill, or some cocking, or teach him how to handle the reins in form, he'll pay precious little heed to anyone else."

Vincent nodded. "Very well, sir: I'll engage to charm him away from this—— What *is* the fellow's name?"

Darracott's face twitched; he replied shortly: "Same as his father's. Signs himself Hugo. Don't know why, and don't like it."

"Oh, you've had letters from him, have you, sir?"

"I haven't. He wrote to Lissett—a damnable scrawl!"

A smile flickered in Vincent's eyes for an instant, but he swiftly lowered his lids. My lord's own handwriting would have led no one to suppose that he was a man of birth, far less of education; but it would plainly be unwise even to hint as much. Instead, Vincent asked: "Did he—er—put forward his claims, as my father appears to believe?"

"No, I'll grant him that: he didn't. Never gave a sign of life till I told Lissett to write to him. Seems not to have known he was the heir, unless he was shamming it. Very likely! He wrote that he was sorry to hear of Granville's death. Gammon!"

"Oh, mere civility!"

"Ay! So I might have thought if he hadn't added that he didn't see what was to be done about the business, but would as lief not step into his uncle's shoes! Dry-boots!"

"Oh, that is pitching it very much too rum!" agreed Vincent. "Demonstrably an underbred person: we can do nothing for him!"

"*You* may not; *I* shall! I don't deny I thought myself done-up at the start, but I've never been out-jockeyed yet, and I fancy I've hit on a way to button it up tolerably well. The fellow shall marry Anthea."

Vincent had been idly twirling his quizzing-glass on the end of its riband, but he was so much startled by this announcement that he let it drop, and gave an audible gasp. "Marry *Anthea?*"

"Yes, lobcock!" said his lordship testily. "Why not?"

Vincent drew a breath. "I can think of a score of reasons why *not,* but it seems that I must indeed be a lobcock, since I can't think of one why he *should!* How very humiliating! I've always believed myself to be a man of reasonable intelligence."

"You're as muttonheaded as the rest of 'em! It's the best way out of a curst hobble. He ain't likely to form a more eligible connection——"

Up went Vincent's brows again. "A Darracott of Darracott?" he said.

"A half-bred Darracott!" my lord said savagely. "Ten to one he'd choose a commoner like himself, if I gave him his head! Well, I won't do it! No, and I won't have him making a figure of himself in what passes in these days for the ton! I'll have him leg-shackled as soon as I can, and depend on Anthea for the rest! She'll do the trick: she doesn't want for sense, and she doesn't want for spirit either. She's a girl of rank and character, and he may think himself lucky if she takes him."

"Certainly he may! And what may *she* think *her*self, sir?"

"She may think the same. She's not a pea-goose, like her mother! She had her chance, and a pretty penny that cost me! Either she frittered it away, or she didn't take: *I* don't know. I do know that Oversley offered for her, and she wouldn't have him. If she don't want to end up an ape-leader she'll take her cousin, and make the best of him."

"Which," Vincent told Anthea on the following day, "leads me to hope, for your sake, my poor girl, that this intrusive relation of ours is married already."

"Yes, but what an uproar there would be! Has Grandpapa informed everyone of this splendid match he has made for me? It is too abominable! However, I imagine you can none of you suppose me to be so meek and dutiful as to acquiesce in such a scheme!"

"If *I* thought that, my love, I should feel constrained to marry you myself."

"Is that a declaration?" she demanded.

"Certainly not! I *don't* think it."

"I wish it had been!" she said longingly. "How unhandsome of you! When you know how few pleasures come in my way, you might have granted me the indulgence of refusing you!"

He laughed, but said, a certain gleam in his eyes: "I wonder if you would?"

She met his look without a trace of embarrassment, a good deal of amusement in her face. "Dear Vincent, with enthusiasm! You must never marry. Don't, I do earnestly beg of you, allow yourself to be taken in by any lure thrown out to you! You cannot hope to find a lady who will like you better than you like yourself."

He was nettled, but made a quick recover. "Not *like*, sweetest cousin: *appreciate!*"

She only smiled; and, as a few drops of rain had begun

to fall, turned towards the house. As they entered it, they were met by Matthew, who was looking peevish. He exclaimed: "It's to be hoped this fellow don't dawdle on the road! Your grandfather may say he doesn't want to clap eyes on him, but here he is, fretting and fuming already! and it's barely past noon! *I* don't expect him to show a minute before three o'clock!"

By three o'clock, however, there was still no sign of Major Darracott, and my lord was fast working himself into a passion. He strode into one of the saloons, with his watch in his hand, and demanded explosively what the devil could be keeping the fellow. Since no one knew, no one answered, whereupon he asked if they were a set of dumb mutes.

"Mute, but not of malice," murmured Vincent. "Claud, where is your cousin?"

"Which cousin?" enquired Claud.

This instantly brought him under fire. He was apostrophized as an impudent young idiot, and warned not to try his grandfather's patience too far. He looked very much startled, and protested earnestly that nothing was more remote from his intention. "Not such an idiot as that, sir!" he said, with a placating but nervous smile.

My lord, regarding him with loathing, said awfully: "It's my belief you're queer in your attic!" His gaze swept to Lady Aurelia, tatting, by the window, and he added with relish: "He must take after your family, my dear. We Darracotts never bred a mooncalf yet!"

"Very likely," responded Lady Aurelia.

My lord, balked, stood fulminating, and Claud, who had been turning the question put to him over in his mind, suddenly said: "Oh, *that* cousin! Well, I'll tell you!" He discovered that everyone but his mother was staring at him in surprise, and blushed, saying modestly: "I may not be a clever cove, but I can answer *that*. Well, what I mean is, nothing has happened to him. I don't precisely know where he is, mind, though I've a notion about that, too." He looked round the circle with mild pride, and enunciated triumphantly: "Tonbridge! Won't be here for another three hours. More, if the postboys lose the way, which I daresay they will. Dashed difficult place to find, this. Lost the way myself once."

After this burst of loquacity he subsided. His grandfather, a most alarming expression on his face, was still struggling for words with which to annihilate him when Lady Aurelia intervened, saying calmly: "No doubt you are right. Indeed, I see no reason to expect the young man before dinner-time."

"Oh, you don't, ma'am?" said his lordship, abandoning Claud for a worthier prey. "Then let me tell you that my orders to Lissett were that the fellow should be sent off post not an instant later than eight o'clock! He will have to learn that when I give an order I expect it to be obeyed to the letter!"

"It seems reasonable to prophesy that he will," remarked Vincent, as the door shut with a decided slam behind his lordship.

"Oh, dear!" sighed Mrs. Darracott. "Since your grand-father seems to *want* him, I do wish he hadn't chosen to be late! I can't help feeling that we shall have a very un-comfortable evening."

By twenty minutes to six, the Major still not having ar-rived, my lord was in a mood of cold rage, as surly (as Claud confided to Richmond) as a butcher's dog. The ladies of the party had not yet come down from their respective bedchambers, but the gentlemen had prudently changed their dress in good time, and dutifully assembled in the Green Saloon. My lord tugged the bell-rope, his brow black, and upon the butler's coming into the room, told him that dinner was to be served punctually at six o'clock.

"Very good, my lord," Chollacombe said, "but——"

"You heard me!"

It was apparent from Chollacombe's raised head, and straining expression, that he had also heard something else. He said: "Yes, my lord. But I fancy the Major has arrived."

"Bring him in here immediately!" commanded his lord-ship.

Chollacombe bowed, and left the room, carefully shutting the door. An indistinguishable murmur of voices penetrated to the saloon, as though an argument had sprang up.

"Wants to change his dress first," said Claud, explaining the pause, and nodding wisely. "Very understandable. I would myself."

"Whipper-snapper!" said my lord.

The door was opened again. "Major Darracott!" announced Chollacombe.

The Major trod resolutely over the threshold, and there stopped, pulled up short by the battery that confronted him. Five pairs of eyes scanned him with varying degrees of astonishment, hostility, and criticism. He looked round, his own, very blue orbs holding a comical expression of dismay, and a deep flush creeping up under his tan. Three of the gentlemen had levelled their quizzing-glasses at him; and one, whom he judged to be his grandfather, was scowling at him from under a beetling brow.

For a nerve-racking minute no one spoke, or moved. Surprise was, in fact, responsible for this frozen immobility, but only Richmond's widening gaze and Claud's dropped jaw betrayed this.

The Darracotts were a tall race, but the man who stood on the threshold dwarfed them all. He stood six foot four in his stockinged feet, and he was built on noble lines, with great shoulders, a deep barrel of a chest, and powerful thighs. He was much fairer than his cousins, with tightly curling brown hair, cut rather shorter than was fashionable, and a ruddy complexion. His nose had no aquiline trend: it was rather indeterminate; and this, with his curly locks and his well-opened and childishly blue eyes, gave him an air of innocence at variance with his firm-lipped mouth and decided chin. He looked to be amiable; he was certainly bashful, but for this there was every excuse. He had been ushered into a room occupied by five gentlemen attired in raiment commonly worn only at Court, or at Almack's Assembly Rooms, and he was himself wearing leathers and topboots, and a serviceable riding-coat, all of which were splashed with mud.

"Good God!" muttered Matthew, breaking the silence.

"So you've shown at last, have you?" said Lord Darracott. "You're devilish late, sir!"

"I am a trifle late," acknowledged the culprit. "I'm sorry for it, but I missed the way, and that delayed me."

"Thought as much!" said Claud.

"Well, don't stand there like a stock!" said Darracott. "This is your uncle Matthew, and the others are your cousins: Vincent—Claud—Richmond!"

Considerably unnerved by his reception, the Major took an unwary step forward, and very nearly fell over an unnoticed stool in his path. Vincent said, in Richmond's ear, not quite under his breath: *"The lubber Ajax!"*

47

If the Major heard him, he gave no sign of having done so. Matthew caught the words, and uttered a short laugh, which he changed, not very convincingly, into a cough. The Major, recovering his balance, advanced towards Lord Darracott, who waved him, slightly impatiently, to his uncle. He turned, half putting out his hand, but Matthew, not moving from his stand before the empty fireplace, only nodded to him, and said: "How do you do?"

The Major made no attempt to shake hands with the rest of the company, but when he had exchanged formal bows with Vincent and Claud, Richmond, whose colour was also considerably heightened, stepped forward, with his hand held out, saying with a little stammer: "How—how do you do, Cousin Hugh?"

His hand was lost in the Major's large clasp. "Now, which of my cousins are you?" asked the Major, smiling kindly down at him.

"I'm Richmond, sir."

"Nay!" protested the Major. "Don't call me sir! I'd as lief you didn't call me Cousin Hugh either. I was christened Hugh, but I've never answered to anything but Hugo all my life."

Lord Darracott broke in on this. Having by this time had time to assimilate the fact that Hugo's clothes were freely bespattered with mud, he demanded to know the reason. Hugo released Richmond's hand, and turned his head towards his grandfather. "Well, you've had some rain down here, sir. I should not have come in till I'd got rid of my dirt, but I wasn't given any choice in the matter," he explained.

"Chaise overturn?" enquired Claud, not without sympathy.

Hugo laughed. "No, it wasn't as bad as that. I didn't come by chaise."

"Then how did you come?" asked Matthew. "From the look of you one would say that you had ridden from town!"

"Ay, so I did," nodded Hugo.

"*Ridden?*" gasped Claud. "Ridden all the way from London?"

"Why not?" said Hugo.

"But—— Dash it, you can't do things like that!" Claud said, in a shocked tone. "I mean to say—no, really, coz! Your luggage!"

"Oh, that!" replied Hugo. "John Joseph had all I need, loaded on my spare horse—my groom, I mean—my private groom!"

"How very original!" drawled Vincent. "I rarely travel by chaise myself, but I confess it had never before occurred to me to turn any of my cattle into pack-horses."

"Nay, why should it?" returned the Major goodhumouredly. "Maybe you've never been obliged to travel rough. I don't think I've gone in a chaise above two or three times in my life."

Lord Darracott stirred restlessly in his chair, gripping its arms momentarily. "No doubt! You are not obliged to travel rough, as you term it, now! My orders were that a chaise was to be hired for you, and I expect my orders to be obeyed!"

"Ay, I'm that road myself," agreed Hugo cheerfully. "Your man of business was mighty set on arranging the journey for me. He said it was what you'd told him to do, so there's no sense in blaming him. And not much sense in blaming me either," he added, on a reflective note. He smiled down at his seething progenitor. "I'm much obliged to you, sir, but there's no need for you to worry your head over me: I've looked after myself for a good few years now."

"*Worry my head*——? Richmond! Ring the bell! You, sir! Did you bring your valet, or haven't you one?"

"Well, no," confessed the Major apologetically. "I used to have a bâtman, of course, but, what with one thing and another, I haven't had time to think about hiring a personal servant since I came home."

"*No valet?*" repeated Claud, gazing at him incredulously. "But how to you manage? I mean to say, packing—your boots—your neckcloths——!"

"Hold your tongue!" said his father, in an undervoice.

"If you had been listening," interpolated Vincent severely, "you would have heard our cousin say that he has been in the habit of looking after himself. Except when he had a bâtman, that is."

"Ay, but I'm a poor hand at packing," said Hugo, shaking his head over this shortcoming.

"How much longer is dinner to be kept waiting?" demanded Lord Darracott. "Ring that damned bell again, Richmond! What the devil does Chollacombe mean by—— Oh, you're there, are you? Have Major Darracott taken up to his room, and tell someone to wait on him! We shall dine in twenty minutes from now!"

Claud was moved to protest, his sympathy roused by the plight of anyone who was expected to dress for dinner in twenty minutes. "Make it an hour, sir! Well, *half* an hour, though I must say it's coming it a bit strong to ask the poor fellow to scramble into his clothes in that short time!"

"No, no, twenty minutes will be long enough for me!" said Hugo hastily, a wary eye on his lordship. "If I'm not down then, don't wait for me!"

Chollacombe, ushering him out of the saloon, and softly closing the door behind him, said: "I will take you up myself, sir. I understand you haven't brought your valet with you, so his lordship's man has unpacked your valise!"

"Much obliged to him!" said Hugo, following him to the broad, uncarpeted oak staircase. "It seems as if Mr. Lissett ought to have warned me not to show my front here without a jack-a-dandy London valet at my heels."

"Yes, sir. Being as his lordship is, as they say, rather a high stickler. Not but what Grooby—that's his lordship's man, sir—will be very happy to wait on you. We were very much attached to the Captain, if I may venture to say so."

"My father? I never knew him: he was killed when I was just three years old. I'm afraid I don't favour him much."

"No, sir. Though you do remind me a little of him." The butler paused, and then said with great delicacy, as they reached the upper hall: "I hope you won't think it a liberty, sir, but if there *should* be anything you might wish to know —his lordship being a trifle twitty at times, and not one to make allowances—I beg you won't hesitate to ask me! Quite between ourselves, sir, of course."

"I won't," promised Hugo, a twinkle in his eye.

"It is sometimes hard to know the ways of a house when one is strange to it," said Chollacombe. "*Anybody* might make a mistake! Indeed, I well remember that I was obliged to give my Lord Taplow a hint, when he stayed here on one occasion. He was a friend of Mr. Granville's: quite in the first style of elegance, but he had a habit of unpunctuality which would have put his lordship out sadly. This way, if you please, sir. We have put you in the West Wing."

"It's to be hoped I don't lose myself," remarked Hugo, following him through an archway into a long gallery. "If ever I saw such a place!"

"It *is* rather large, sir, but I assure you there are many that are far larger."

"Nay!" said Hugo astonished.

"Oh, yes, indeed, sir! This is your bedchamber. I should

perhaps tell you that Mr. Richmond sleeps at the end of the gallery, and must not on any account be disturbed."

"Why not?" enquired Hugo.

"Mr. Richmond suffers from insomnia, sir. The least sound brings him broad awake."

"What, a lad of his age?" exclaimed Hugo.

"Mr. Richmond's constitution is not strong," explained Chollacombe, opening the door into a large, wainscoted room, hung with faded blue damask, and commanding a distant view of the sea beyond the Marsh. "This is Grooby, sir. His lordship dines in fifteen minutes, Grooby."

The valet, an elderly man of somewhat lugubrious mien, bowed to the Major, and said in a voice of settled gloom: "I have everything ready for you, sir. Allow me to assist you to take off your coat!"

"If you want to assist me, pull off my boots!" said Hugo. "And never mind handling them with gloves! If I'm to be ready in fifteen minutes, I shall have to be pretty wick, as we say in Yorkshire."

Grooby, kneeling before him, as he sat with his legs stretched out, had already drawn one muddied boot half off, but he paused, and looked up, saying earnestly: *"Don't,* Master Hugh!"

"Don't what?" asked Hugo, ripping off his neckcloth, and tossing it aside.

"Say what they do in Yorkshire, sir. Not if you can avoid it! I'm sure I ask your pardon, but you don't know his lordship like I do, and you want to be careful, sir—*very* careful!"

The blue eyes looked down at him for an inscrutable moment. "Ay," Hugo drawled. "Happen you're reet!"

The valet heaved a despairing sigh, and returned to his task. The boots off, he would have helped Hugo to remove his coat, but Hugo kindly but firmly put him out of the room, saying that he could dress himself more speedily if left alone. He shut the door on Grooby's protests, let his breath go in a long *Phew!* and began, very speedily indeed, to strip off his coat and breeches.

When he presently emerged from his room, he found Grooby hovering in the gallery. Grooby said that he had waited to escort him back to the saloon, in case he should have forgotten his way; but it was evident, from the expert eye he ran over his protégé's attire, that his real purpose was to assure himself that no sartorial solecism had been committed. It was a pity, but not a solecism, that the Ma-

51

jor had not provided himself with knee-smalls, but his long-tailed coat was by Scott, and well-enough; his linen was decently starched; and his shoe-strings ironed. He favoured a more modest style than was fashionable, wearing no jewelry, sporting no inordinately high collar, and arranging his neckcloth neatly, but with none of the exquisite folds that distinguished the tie of a dandy or a Corinthian. Grooby regretted the absence of a quizzing-glass and a fob, but on the whole he was inclined to think that so large a man was right to adopt a plain mode.

The Major entered the saloon one minute before the stipulated time, thereby winning a measure of approval from his grandfather. Lord Darracott's brows shot up; he said: "Well, at all events you're not a dawdler! I'll say that for you. Make your bow to your aunts, and your cousin! Lady Aurelia, Mrs. Darracott, you'll allow me to present Hugh to you; Anthea, you'll look after your cousin: show him the way about!"

The Major, receiving a formal bow from a Roman-nosed matron in a turban, and the smallest of stiff curtsies from a tall girl who looked at him with quelling indifference, turned his eyes apprehensively towards the third lady. Mrs. Darracott, her heart wrung (as she afterwards explained to her daughter), smiled at him, and gave him her hand. "How do you do?" she said. "I am so happy to meet you! So vexed, too, that I wasn't dressed quite in time to welcome you when you arrived. Not but what that might have made it worse for you—I mean, so many strange new relations! I daresay you must be perfectly bewildered."

He did not kiss her hand, but he shook it warmly, and thanked her, smiling down at her so gratefully that she almost wished she had braved my lord's displeasure, and placed Hugo instead of Matthew beside her at the dinner-table.

She and Chollacombe had arranged the table, and an arduous labour it had been, necessitating the use of a slate and much chalk. The result was not ideal, but, as Chollacombe very sensibly pointed out, the ideal was not to be achieved with a party of nine persosn, all of them related, and too many of them brothers. In this unexceptionable way Chollacombe was able to convey to Mrs. Darracott the unwisdom of placing Claud within Vincent's orbit. She perfectly understood him; and he perfectly understood that when she said that his lordship would certainly wish to have Vincent on his left hand she meant that she was not going to expose the hapless newcomer to the full force of his lordship's trenchant conversation. In the end, though the table was necessarily uneven, with Lady Aurelia, Richmond, and Claud on one side, and Vincent, Anthea, Hugo, and Matthew on the other, Claud was as far removed as was possible from Vincent, Hugo from Lord Darracott, and Anthea had been placed between Hugo and Vincent, in which position she must willy-nilly shield Hugo from Vincent's tongue.

The arrangement was not entirely happy, however, as Mrs. Darracott soon perceived; for although Vincent was keeping his grandfather amused, and Richmond was nobly trying to entertain his aunt, Matthew divided his attention equally between herself and his plate; and Anthea, determined to cold-shoulder her intended-suitor at the outset, replied to his tentative attempts to engage her interest with icy civility, and in a manner that did not encourage him to persevere. Mrs. Darracott, scandalized by such a display of gaucherie, tried several times to catch her daughter's eye, but never once succeeded.

Hugo, with a hostile uncle on his left and a frozen damsel on his right, meekly ate his dinner, and took stock of as many of his relations as came within his view. Of these the most attractive were Mrs. Darracott, and Richmond, who was not quite obscured from Hugo's sight by the epergne in the centre of the table. Hugo thought he seemed a friendly boy: a trifle resty, perhaps; light at hand, like so many high-spirited but spoilt youngsters. He was talking to his aunt: a most alarming female, Hugo thought, eyeing her in awe, and admiring Richmond's address. Then Richmond chanced to turn his head away from Lady Aurelia, and, seeing that his cousin was looking at him, he smiled shyly. Yes, a nice lad: worth a dozen of the Tulip beside him! Not that Hugo had the least objection to the fops of Society. Being blessed with a vast tolerance he was able to regard Claud with amusement, enjoying the extravagances and the affectations which exasperated Lord Darracott and Matthew. Claud was wearing a coat which represented the highest kick of fashion, and had come (he said) straight from the hands of Nugee. His father told him that it made him look ridiculous, which of course it did, with its wasp-waist, and its shoulders built up into absurd peaks, but there was no need to comb the lad's hair in public; and certainly no need for that brother of his to have said that he couldn't help but look ridiculous.

Hugo ventured to steal a glance at the unyielding profile on his right. Not a beauty, his cousin Anthea, but she was pretty enough, and not just in the common style. Her figure was tall and graceful, and she had remarkably fine eyes, with long, curling lashes; but she looked to be a disagreeable girl, every bit as contemptuous as the appalling old windsucker at the head of the table.

He was debating within himself how soon he would be able to escape from the home of his ancestors when he found that he was being addressed by his uncle, who told him, rather sharply, that Mrs. Darracott was speaking to him.

She had, in fact, seized the excuse afforded by Lord Darracott's asking Richmond some question, across Lady Aurelia, to try to draw into conversation the poor young man who was being, she felt, shamefully neglected. She wanted to know if he had found all he needed in his bedchamber, and to tell him, with a motherly smile, that he had only to ask her, or the housekeeper, if there was anything he wished for. He thanked her, but assured her that there was nothing: he would be very comfortable.

Claud, satisfied that his grandfather's attention was being engaged by Vincent, shook his head. "You won't," he said. "Couldn't be. I don't know where they've put you, but it don't signify: there ain't a comfortable room in the house."

"Nonsense!" said Matthew impatiently.

"Why, you said so yourself, sir!" exclaimed Claud. "What's more, you always say it. The last time you had to come down here you said——"

"Oh, be quiet!" interrupted his father. "It is a very old house, and naturally——"

"Yes, and falling to bits," corroborated Claud.

Matthew, eyeing him almost with dislike, said: "That remark, my good boy, is as false as it is foolish!"

"Well, if it ain't falling to bits you can't deny it's being eaten to bits," said Claud, quite unabashed. "The last time I had to come here, I was kept awake half the night by rats chewing the wainscoting."

"Oh, not *rats*, Claud!" protested Mrs. Darracott. "Only a mouse! Not but what it's perfectly true that the house does need repairing, while as for the linen, and some of the hangings, I declare I feel positively *ashamed!* Well, you know what it is, Matthew! Nothing I can say will induce your father—— However, we won't talk of that now! Though I do sometimes feel that if I have to spend another winter here, which, of course, I shall, I shall be *crippled* with rheumatism! None of the windows fits as it should, and the draught *whistles* through the house!"

"More like a hurricane," said Claud. He nodded at Hugo. "*You'll* find it out, coz. Of course, it's summer now, so it ain't so bad, but you wait for the winter! Take my advice, and don't let 'em light a fire in your room: all the bedroom chimneys smoke, so you're worse off than before."

"Not *all* of them!" said Mrs. Darracott. "At least, not very *much!* Only when the wind is in the wrong quarter. I do hope—for it has begun to get so chilly in the evening now that Mrs. Flitwick is having a fire kindled in *your* room, Hugh! Oh, dear, I wonder if the wind *is* in the wrong quarter?"

"Nay, don't fidget yourself on my account, ma'am!" Hugo said, laughing. "I'm not so nesh as my cousin! I've been used to sleep in a room that had a fire in the middle of the floor, and not so much as a vent to take off the smoke, so it will need more than a puff or two blown down the chimney to make me uncomfortable."

His voice, which was a deep one, had a carrying quality. His words were heard by everyone in the room, and were producitive of a sudden, shocked silence. He glanced innocently round the table, and added: "A mud floor, of course."

"How—how horrid for you!" said Mrs. Darracott faintly.

Chollacombe, with great presence of mind, refilled the Major's glass at this moment, contriving, as he did so, to give him a warning nudge. The Major, not susceptible to hints, said cheerfully: "Oh, it was noan so bad! I was glad to have a roof over my head in those days!"

Mrs. Darracott looked wildly round for help, and received it from an unexpected quarter.

"Don't look so dismayed, my dear aunt!" said Vincent. "The locality of this dismal dwelling-place was not, as I apprehend, Yorkshire, but Spain."

"Portugal," corrected Hugo, as impervious to insult as to hints.

"Most interesting!" pronounced Lady Aurelia majestically. "No doubt you have seen a great deal of the world during the course of your military service?"

"I have and-all!" agreed Hugo.

"The billeting arrangements in the Peninsula," stated her ladyship, "left much to be desired."

"Ay, sometimes they did, but at others, think on, they

were better nor like," said Hugo reflectively. "After Toulouse I shared quarters with the Smiths in a château, and lived like a prince. That was in France, of course. A château," he explained, "is what the Frogs call a castle—though it wasn't a castle, not by any means. You might call it a palace."

"Our ignorance is now enlightened," murmured Vincent.

"We all know what a château is!" snapped Lord Darracott.

"Ay, you would, of course," said Hugo, on a note of apology. "Eh, but I thought myself in clover! I'd never been in such a place before—except when I was in prison, but you can't reetly count that."

James, the first footman, let a fork slide from the plate he had just removed from the table, but Charles, deftly nipping away the plate before Lady Aurelia, maintained his equilibrium. James was shocked, but Charles was storing up these revelations with glee. A rare tale to recount to his Dad, so niffy-naffy as he was about the Quality! Properly served out was old Stiff-Rump, with a jail-bird for his grandson!

"What?" thundered his lordship, glaring at his heir. "Do you tell me that you have been in prison?"

"Ay, but it wasn't for long, sir," replied Hugo. "Of course, I was nobbut a lad then, and it seemed a terrible thing to me. I had the fever, too, mortal bad!"

Claud, perceiving that the rest of the company was deprived of speech, made a gallant attempt to respond. "Nasty thing, jail-fever," he said chattily. "Not had it myself, but so they tell me! Very glad you recovered from it, coz!"

"It was being transported set me to reets," said Hugo. "A rare, tedious voyage we had of it, but——"

"Transported?" interjected his lordship, gripping the arms of his chair till his knuckles shone. "You were transported, sir?"

"We all were," said Hugo. "The most of us three parts dead with fever, and that ashamed——! Eh, it doesn't bear thinking on! Such a voyage as it was, too! Close on five months it was before we landed, for the transport I was on carried away its rudder in a gale, and we ran four hundred miles out of our course before the *Swallow* towed us into Falmouth, and then we had to sail on to the Downs before they'd let us ashore."

A delightful chuckle broke from Richmond. "I thought

that was it! You are the most complete hand, Cousin Hugo!"

"I collect," said Matthew coldly, "that when you speak of having been imprisoned, and—er—transported, you mean that you were a prisoner-of-war?"

"Why, what did you think I meant?" asked Hugo, much astonished.

"You must forgive us!" said Vincent, leaning forward to speak to him across Anthea. "The thought that you had been imprisoned for poaching, perhaps, did, I fancy, occur to some of us."

"Nay! I've always been respectable!" countered Hugo.

At this point, Anthea, who had been surprised into turning her head to stare at him, lowered her eyes rather swiftly to her plate again, and took her underlip between her teeth. Matthew, far more conscious than his parent of the presence of the servants, said, with a tolerable assumption of amusement: "You are, as Richmond says, a complete hand. From the length of time your voyage lasted I am led to suppose that you took part in our ill-fated expedition to South America?"

"That's reet," nodded Hugo. "I joined as soon as I left— as soon as I was seventeen. I was gazetted to the 1st Battalion just in time to set sail with Whitelock. A rare piece of good fortune I thought it, but all I got out of it was a fever that mighty near carried me off, and a horse. I paid three dollars for him, I remember. Eh, but I was a Johnny Raw! I could have had him for two."

"Did you take part in the assault on Buenos Ayres?" asked Richmond.

"I wouldn't, myself, call it an assault," replied Hugo.

"A disgracefully mismanaged affair!" said Matthew.

"Ay, we suffered a bad back-cast. Our people wrote up that General Whitelock was a coward, or a traitor, or maybe both, on all the street-corners in Montevideo, but, myself, I think he was no more than a sackless hodgobbin." He drank off his wine, and grinned. "The men used to drink success to grey-beards but bad luck to white locks," he disclosed.

"And then?" Richmond prompted.

Hugo smiled at him. "Oh, then I was packed off home, on sick furlough, for there was nothing of me left but skin and bone!"

"Poor boy!" said Mrs. Darracott, her motherly instincts stirred. "How shocked your mama must have been! But I am persuaded she soon nursed you back to health."

"Nay, my mother died a year before I joined," he answered.

"Oh, *poor* boy!" she exclaimed, braving her father-in-law's displeasure. "But perhaps you have other relatives?"

"I'd my grandfather," he said. "Mother was all the children he had. Happen it was Yorkshire air and good Yorkshire food that plucked me up."

"Were you at Corunna?" asked Richmond.

Hugo nodded; but before Richmond could beg for further information Lord Darracott intervened, saying harshly that he desired to hear no talk about the war at his dinnertable. Hugo, accepting this snub with what appeared to be unshakeable placidity, then retired from the conversation, to discuss with an excellent appetite a large helping of apple pie.

The rest of the meal passed without incident. For perhaps the first time in all the years she had lived at Darracott Place it was with reluctance that Mrs. Darracott gave the signal for the departure of the ladies from the board. Her compassion had been roused, and it went to her heart to leave her enormous but hapless nephew to the mercy of his hostile male relations.

In the event, it was not Hugo but Claud who drew my lord's fire. When the cloth had been removed, it was the custom of the house that not only decanters of port and madeira should be set before his lordship, but that three jars of snuff should also be placed on the table. My lord was a connoisseur; he mixed his own sort, but provided for his guests Old Bureau, King's Martinique, and Hardman's '37. He invited no one but Vincent to help himself from his gold box, and was amused rather than offended when that elegant young man, declining the honour, drew out a box of his own, and snapped it open with a flick of his thumb, saying: "Try some of mine, sir! I shall value your opinion."

"Mixed it yourself, did you?" said his lordship. He helped himself to a pinch, and inhaled it critically. "Too much Brazill" he said. "Why don't you come to me for a recipe? All the same, you young——" He broke off suddenly, his gaze fixed in wrath and stupefaction on Claud, who had produced a small silver shovel and a haresfoot from his pocket, and was preparing, in happy unconsciousness of the baleful stare bent upon him, to scoop some snuff out of the jar in front of him. "What the devil——?" demanded his lordship, in such stridulous accents that Claud, startled, looked up, and promptly dropped his little shovel. "Well?" said his lordship. "Well, popinjay?"

"Put that thing away, you young fool!" said Matthew, in a vexed undervoice. "Making a figure of yourself——!"

"I ain't making a figure of myself!" returned Claud indignantly. "Assure you, sir! Quite the go! You take the snuff in the shovel, to save dabbling your fingers, and if you spill any on your coat you brush it off in a trice with the hares-foot, like——"

"I'll have no such infernal foppery in my house!" declared his lordship. "Good God, that any grandson of mine should find nothing better to do than to spend his time thinking what extravagant folly he can next commit!"

"My dear sir, you are blaming the innocent!" said Vincent. "The guilty person is Thingwall: the Trig-and-Trim dandy, you know. That's one of his tricks. It is the tragedy of Claud's life that he has never yet been able to hit upon a new quirk of fashion, but is always obliged to copy other men."

"Well, *you* needn't sneer!" retorted Claud, flushing. "You only started driving pickaxe in the Park because Brading did so!"

"Not at all, brother. Brading followed *my* lead."

"That's enough, that's enough!" interposed Matthew, removing the snuff-jar from Claud's reach, and pushing it towards Hugo. "Help yourself, if you like this sort!"

"Nay, I don't like it," Hugo said. "I'd rather blow a cloud which is a habit I got into in Spain."

"It is not a habit you will indulge in here!" said Lord Darracott. "Smoking is a filthy and a disgusting misuse of tobacco: intolerable!"

"Well, I was never one to beat squares," said Hugo equably. "I'll smoke my cigars in the garden, and that road we won't fratch."

"Won't do what?" asked Claud, interested.

"Fratch—quarrel! It's what we say in Yorkshire," explained Hugo.

"Possibly not in the first circles, however, so don't copy it, Claud," said Vincent coldly. "Permit me to point out to you, cousin, that you are chased."

Hugo, finding the port at his elbow, begged pardon, filled his glass, and passed the decanter on, his demeanour one of unruffled amiability.

Breakfast at Darracott Place was not served until eleven o'clock, early risers being obliged to sustain nature until that hour on a cup of chocolate and a slice of bread-and-butter, brought to their bed-chambers. The custom was not an unusual one; in many country houses of ton noon was the appointed hour for the first meal of the day; but to a soldier, accustomed to much earlier hours, it was both strange and unacceptable. Major Darracott, awaking betimes from a night of untroubled repose, thrust back the curtains that shrouded the four-poster in which he lay, and pulled his watch from under the pillows. The tidings it conveyed were unwelcome enough to make him utter a despairing groan, and sink back, resolutely closing his eyes in an attempt to recapture sleep. After spending half-an-hour in this barren endeavour, he abandoned it, linked his hands under his head, and lay for a time with his eyes fixed abstractedly on the line of light seeping through the join of the curtains drawn across the windows, and his mind roving over the events of the previous evening. What he thought of them no spy could have guessed, for even in solitude his countenance afforded no clue to whatever thoughts might be revolving behind the blankness of his eyes. There was something rather bovine about its immobility: Vincent had already told his grandfather that he lived in momentary expectation of seeing his ox-like cousin chew the cud.

It had been a daunting evening, judged by any standards. When the gentlemen had risen from the dining-table, Vincent had challenged Richmond to a game of billards, and Richmond, instantly accepting the challenge, had gone off with him, his quick flush betraying his gratification. The rest of the male company had gone upstairs to join the ladies in the long drawing-room, his lordship having apparently decided that even an evening spent amongst females was preferable to one spent alone, or closeted with his son in the library. Only two females were discovered in the drawing-room. Mrs. Darracott, inviting Hugo to a chair beside her own, explained, a little nervously, that Anthea had the head-ache, and had gone to bed. It seemed for an instant as though my lord would have uttered some blistering censure, but although his brow was black he refrained, with what was plainly an effort, from making any comment. Seating himself in a wing-chair, he fell into conversation with his son, while Lady Aurelia, who had abandoned her tatting for some tapestry-work, handed Claud a tangle of coloured wools, and desired him, with much the air of one providing a child with a simple puzzle, to unravel the various strands. He was perfectly ready to oblige her, and even, having subjected her work to a critical scrutiny, to offer her some very good advice on the accomplishment of the design.

Mrs. Darracott, meanwhile, was doing what lay within her power to make Hugo feel at home, considerably hampered by the knowledge that his lordship, lending only half an ear to Matthew, was listening to all that was said.

What my lord had learned by this means had not been very much, but one piece of information he had gleaned which had put him into a better temper: Hugo seemed to have no maternal relations living—or, at all events, none of whom he took account. His grandfather, he told Mrs. Darracott, in reply to her sympathetic question, had been dead for several years; he supposed, rather vaguely, that there were those who could call cousins with him, but the connection must of necessity be remote. No, he didn't think he had ever met them; the only member of his mother's family whom he remembered was Great-aunt Susan, who had been used to live with them when he was a child. She had been a spinster, but he thought Grandfather had had other sisters.

Lord Darracott was so much cheered by this that he had presently asked Hugo if he played chess. Upon Hugo's replying doubtfully that he knew what the moves were but hadn't played since he was a boy, he had said bluntly: "You couldn't give me a game, then. What can you play? Piquet? Backgammon?"

"Ay, or whist," offered Hugo.

"Play whist, do you?" said his lordship. "Very well, I'll try you in a rubber or two. Aurelia, you won't object to making up a table? Ring the bell, Hugh!"

The Major, with an uneasy apprehension that the form of whist played by a number of generally impecunious young officers belonging to a regiment that boasted very few bucks and blades of Society was likely to fall considerably short of his lordship's standard, tried to draw back from the engagement; but his suggestion that he should watch, while Mrs. Darracott, or Claud, took his place, found no favour at all. His lordship said that Mrs. Darracott was fit for nothing but casino, and that he would be damned if he played with Claud, who had no head for cards, or, indeed, anything else. So Hugo had been obliged to take his seat at the card-table, with his grandfather for partner. They played only for chicken-stakes, and it was not long before Hugo found that his apprehension had been well-grounded. He was forced to endure many sharp scolds for stupidity; and later, when the billiard-players came into the drawing-room, the severe imposition of having his hand overlooked by Vincent. He seized the earliest opportunity of relinquishing his seat to Vincent. No opposition had been raised, my lord merely saying "Well, you're no card-player!" and recommending him to watch his cousin's play. He had preferred, however, to slip away when my lord's attention was devoted to the play of a difficult hand, and to enjoy the solace of one of his cigars on the terrace. Here he had presently been joined by Richmond. "I thought you had come out to blow a cloud!" Richmond had said.

"Now, if you're framing to squeak beef on me——!" he had responded.

Richmond had chuckled. "You'd be in the suds, cousin! So would I be, if you were to squeak beef on me! Grandpapa thinks I've gone to bed. He wouldn't like it above half if he knew—— That is, he don't want me to ask you about the war in the Peninsula, or—— But never mind that! I wanted to tell you—you might not know—he—he doesn't *understand!*" He had raised his handsome young face, pallid in the moonlight, and had blurted out: "About the Light Division, I mean! He—he only thinks of the Guards, and the Cavalry! He may say—oh, I don't know, but *pray* don't take it amiss!"

"Nay," Hugo had said reassuringly. "I won't take it amiss! Why should I? I've nothing to say against the Gentlemen's Sons, or the Cavalry either—some of 'em!"

"No. Well, I wanted just to warn you!" Richmond had confided. "He's quite antiquated, you know, and, of course, he does ride devilish rusty—though not with me, so perhaps I ought not to say it, only——"

"There's no need for you to be fatched, lad: my Grandfather Bray was just such a cobby old fellow!"

"Oh!" Richmond had sounded rather taken-aback. "*Was* he? I mean—— Yes, I see! But there's Vincent, too, and——" He paused, knitting his brows. "I don't know why he was in such a bad skin tonight, but in general he—he is a bang-up fellow, you know! What they call Top-of-the-Trees! A regular out-and-outer! You should see him with a four-in-hand!"

"Happen I will."

"Yes, of course. Do you drive yourself, cousin?"

"Nay, I'm no Nonesuch!"

Richmond had been disappointed, but he had said quickly: "No, you haven't had the opportunity——" He had broken off short, and although no colour could live in the moonlight Hugo had known that a vivid flush had flooded his cheeks. He had stammered: "I don't mean—I meant only that you have been doing other things! Things m-more worth the doing! I wish you will tell me, if it isn't a dead bore, about your campaigns!"

Yes, Hugo thought, reviewing that interlude, a nice lad, young Richmond; but what such an ardent colt was doing hobbled at Darracott Place was a puzzle. If ever a lad was mad after a pair of colours! He had said that his grandfather had set his face against the granting of this desire, but he didn't look to be the sort of lad to submit docilely to the decree of even so absolute an autocrat as old Darracott. If my lord didn't take care, thought Hugo, casting off the bedclothes, and swinging his feet to the ground, he would have the lad chin-deep in mischief.

Dismissing Richmond from his mind, he strode to the window, and pulled back the curtains, and stood for a minute or two, leaning his hands on the sill, and looking out. The sprawling house was built on a slight elevation, in parkland which stretched for a considerable distance to the south and east, but merged rapidly into thick woods on the northern and western fronts. Below Hugo's window, a part of the gardens, which appeared to be extensive though not in very trim order, lay between the house and the park; and the Military Canal and, beyond it, the Welland Marsh stretched into a distance still shrouded in morning mist. The day was fresh but fair; it beckoned compellingly; and within a very short space of time Hugo, fortified by a thick ham sandwich and a pint of Kentish ale, supplied to him by a pleasantly fluttered kitchenmaid, had set out for an exploratory ramble round the park.

He returned by way of the stables, which were situated to the west of the house. They had been built to accommodate many more horses than now stood in the stalls, and were ranged round several cobbled yards. Only two of these seemed to be in use; in the others weeds were pushing up between the cobbles, and rows of shut doors, the paint on them blistered and cracked with age, lent a melancholy air of decay to the scene.

The Major found his groom, a middle-aged Yorkshireman of stocky built and dour countenance, severely repelling the mischievous advances of a plump damsel in a print frock and a mob cap. To judge by the grin on the face of one of the stableboys, who had paused, bucket in hand, to listen to her sallies, she was full of liveliness and wit; but when she saw Hugo coming across the yard she fell into a twitter of embarrassment, dropped a hasty curtsy, and ran away.

"Set up a flirt already, have you?" remarked Hugo. "I'm surprised at you, John Joseph, at your time of life!"

"That giglet!" snorted his servitor. "I' bahn to take t'gray to the stithy, Mester Hugo: he's got a shoe loose, like I told you."

"How's Rufus?"

"Champion!"

"Good! I'll take a look at him. All well with you, John Joseph?"

"I'm suited," responded John Joseph stolidly. He cast an upward sidelong glance at his master's face, and added in a rougher tone: "Tha knows we mun be suited, Mester Hugo, choose how!"

The blue eyes gave nothing away, but there was a hint of mulishness about the Major's firm lips. "Maybe! We'll see!"

"Tha's quality-make, like t'gaffer used to say," urged John Joseph. "Nay then, sir——! If tha's bahn to be a lord, think on——"

"I am thinking," Hugo answered. He smiled. "Hold thy gab John Joseph!"

"*Mester Hugo!* If t'gaffer could hear thee——!"

"I'd get a bang on the lug. But——"

"Sneck up!" commanded his henchman. "Here comes his lordship, and Mester Richmond! I mun fettle t'tits."

With these words he withdrew into the stable, just as Lord Darracott and Richmond, who had been out at exercise, dismounted.

"Ha! Glad to see you're up and about!" said his lordship. "I've no patience with young fellows who lie abed till all hours. Another morning you may come out with me: no use suggesting it to you last night: you'll need to rest your horses. I'll take a look at 'em."

"Ay, sir, do! They're neither of them the equal of this

64

fellow," said Hugo, patting the neck of Richmond's colt, "but the bay's a prime fencer, and strong in work. He has need to be!"

"H'm! Pity you're so big!" commented his lordship. "What do you ride? Seventeen stone?"

"All of that," admitted Hugo. "Eh, lad, you've got a proper high-bred 'un here!"

"Do you like him?" Richmond asked eagerly. "He's young —pretty green still, but a perfect mover! I broke him myself."

Lord Darracott, leaving Richmond to show off his treasure, went into the stable, and was soon heard putting curt questions to John Joseph. It seemed doubtful that he would find John Joseph's answers intelligible, but he apparently understood enough to satisfy him, for when he presently emerged he rather surprisingly told Hugo that he had a good man there, who knew his work. He bestowed moderate praise on Rufus, the big bay, but dismissed the Andalusian with the loose shoe as a clumsy-looking brute, high in flesh. Richmond having gone off to confer with his groom, his lordship commanded Hugo to accompany him back to the house. "I've a good deal to say to you," he informed him. "I'll see you in the library after breakfast."

Few members of his family would have sat down to breakfast with much appetite after such a pronouncement as this, but although a slightly wary expression came into Hugo's eyes his appetite remained unimpaired, and he was soon consuming an extremely hearty meal. The fact that his cousin Anthea had chosen to seat herself on the opposite side of the table troubled him not at all. Glancing dispassionately at her, he was able to verify his first impression that she was a pretty girl, with remarkably fine eyes, and a good deal of countenance. It seemed a pity that she should be so cold and inanimate when a little vivacity would have done so much to improve her.

Neither Vincent nor Claud was an early riser, and each incurred censure for walking into the breakfast-parlour when the meal was nearly over. Vincent, never in his sunniest mood before breakfast, furiously resented the scold he received, but betrayed this only by his thinned lips and a certain glitter in his eyes. Claud, on the other hand, was unwise enough to excuse himself. Owing to the stupidity of his man, the carelessness of the laundress, and the inexplicable whims of Fate, which decreed that although one might sometimes achieve a desired result at the first attempt, at others success would elude one until one was exhausted, it had taken him three quarters of an hour to tie his neckcloth. The style he had chosen was the Mailcoach, and as it was as bulky as it was wide he bore all the appearance of having bound a compress round a sore throat, as his brother took care to inform him.

"Jack-at-warts!" said his lordship bitterly.

Everyone waited for him to develop this theme, but he said no more, merely staring fixedly at Claud under such lowering brows that that unfortunate exquisite became so much discomposed that he took an unwary gulp of tea and scalded his mouth.

"I have it!" suddenly announced his lordship, grimly triumphant. "I'll set you to work!"

"Eh?" ejaculated Claud, alarmed.

"You are a Bartholomew baby, a park-saunterer, a good-for-nothing Jack Straw!" said his fond grandfather.

"Well, I shouldn't put it like that myself, sir," said Claud, "but I daresay you're right. Well, what I mean is, no use setting me to work: I couldn't!"

"A smock-faced wag-feather!" pursued my lord inexorably. "Your only talent is for àlamodality!"

"Well, there you are, sir!" Claud pointed out.

"A certain sort of something!" mocked Vincent.

"*That's* what I'll turn to good account!" said his lordship. "You can teach Hugh how to pass himself off with credit! Give him a new touch! Rid him of that damned brogue! You don't know much, but you've moved in the first circles all your life, and you do know the established model!"

"Father! Really——!" Matthew exclaimed.

"Cousin Hugo doesn't need any touch that Claud could give him!" declared Richmond, scarlet-faced.

Hugo, who had continued throughout this embarrassing dialogue to eat his way through several slices of cold beef, looked up from his plate to smile amiably, and to say, with a marked Yorkshire drawl: "Nay, I'd be fain to learn how to support the character of a gentleman. I've a fancy to be up to the knocker, and I'll be well-suited to be put in the way of it. And I should think," he added handsomely, "that our Claud could teach me better nor most."

"Exactly so!" said Vincent. "*An assinego may tutor thee!*"

"To support the character of a gentleman!" exclaimed Anthea, unexpectedly entering the lists. "In this house, cousin, unless you will be content with my brother, you will search in vain for a model!"

"You keep your tongue, miss!" said his lordship, without any particular animosity.

"Anthea, *pray——!*" whispered Mrs. Darracott.

"Oh, have you changed your mind?" asked Vincent, levelling his quizzing-glass at Anthea. A provocative smile curled his lip; he said silkily: "*Shall the elephant Ajax carry it thus,* my sweet life?"

Her eyes blazed, and Hugo, considerably surprised, intervened, saying in his deep, slow voice: "Nay then! Don't fratch over me! I don't know what I'm to carry, but I'm agreeable to be called an elephant: it won't be for the first time! They call me Gog Darracott in the regiment, but when I was a lad it was more often *tha great lump!* There's no need for any fuss and clart on my account: I've a broad back."

"It must at all events be acknowledged that you have an amiable temper," said Matthew, pushing back his chair. "You will excuse me, Elvira, if you please! I must go up to see how her ladyship does. She passed an indifferent night, and has the head-ache this morning."

Mrs. Darracott replied suitably, and Matthew left the room. He was shortly followed by Lord Darracott, who went away, commanding Hugo not to keep him waiting. Hugh, who had just received his third cup of tea from Mrs. Darracott, said that he would follow him when he had finished his breakfast, a reply which struck Claud as being so foolhardy that he was moved to utter an earnest warning. "Better go at once!" he said. "No sense in putting him in a bad skin, coz! Very likely to regret it!"

"Nay, what could he do to me?" said Hugo, dropping sugar into his cup.

"That you will discover," said Vincent dryly. "You will also discover the pains and penalties that attach to the position of heir."

"Happen I've discovered a few already," drawled Hugo.

Claud coughed delicately. "Rather fancy you mean *perhaps,* coz!"

"Ay, so I do!" agreed Hugo. "I'm much obliged to you."

"The spectacle of Claud entering upon his new duties, though not unamusing, is not one which I can support at this hour of the day," said Vincent. "Do you mind postponing any further tuition until I have withdrawn from the room?"

"Ah!" retorted Claud, with an odious smirk. "You're

piqued because m'grandfather didn't ask *you* to hint Hugh into the proper model!"

This quite failed to ruffle Vincent. "He did," he answered. "I was persuaded, however, that it would prove to be a task beyond my poor power, and declined the office." He saw that, while his target remained unmoved, Richmond was looking at him with a troubled frown between his eyes. He smiled slightly at the boy, and said, as he rose from the table: "What I *am* going to do is to teach Richmond how to point his leaders."

Richmond had been shocked by Vincent's conduct, but this was an invitation not to be resisted. His brow cleared; he jumped up, exclaiming: "No! Do you mean it? You're not hoaxing me, are you?"

"No, but perhaps I should have said I mean to *try* to teach you."

"Brute!" Richmond said, laughing. He thought he saw how to turn this cut to good account, and said ingenuously: "Vincent is always out of reason cross before breakfast, Cousin Hugo! Snaps all our noses off!"

"Well, if you ask me," said Claud, as soon as the door was shut again, "he's got a devilish nasty tongue in his head any hour of the day! Takes after the old gentleman." He looked at his large cousin, and shook his head. "*You* may think it's a fine thing to be the heir: got a strong notion m'father liked it pretty well, too. All I can say is, I'm dashed glad *I'm* not. Y'know, coz, if you've finished your tea, I'd as lief you went off to see what m'grandfather wants. There's no saying but what he may blame me for it if you keep him waiting."

Thus adjured, Hugo went in search of Lord Darracott, and found him (after peeping into three empty saloons) seated at his desk in the library. There was a pen in his hand, but the ink had dried on it, and he was staring absently out of the bay window. He turned his head when he heard the door open, and said: "Oh, so here you are! Shut the door, and come over here! You can take that chair, if it will bear you!"

It creaked, but gave no sign of immediate collapse under Hugo's weight, so he disposed himself comfortably in it, crossed one booted leg over the other, and awaited his grandfather's pleasure with every outward semblance of placidity.

For several moments his lordship said nothing; but sat

looking at him morosely. "You don't favour your father!" he said at last.

"No," agreed the Major.

"Well, I daresay you're none the worse for that! You are his son: there's no doubt about it!" He put down his pen, and pushed aside the papers on his desk, something in the gesture seeming to indicate that with them he was pushing aside his memories. "Got to make the best of it!" he said. "When I'm booked, you'll step into my shoes. I don't mean to wrap the matter up in clean linen, and I'll tell you to your head that that's not what I wanted, or ever dreamed would come to pass!"

"No," said the Major again, sympathetically. "It's been a facer to the both of us."

Lord Darracott stared at him. "A facer for me, but a honey-fall for you, young man!"

The Major preserved a stolid silence.

"And don't tell me you'd as lief not step into your uncle's shoes!" said Lord Darracott. "You'll find me a hard man to bridge, so cut no wheedles for my edification!" He paused, but the Major still had nothing to say. His lordship gave a short laugh. "If you thought you'd turn me up sweet by writing that flim-flam to Lissett you mistook your man! I detest maw-worms, and that's what you sounded like to me! I do you the justice to say you haven't the look of a maw-worm, so maybe it was your notion of civility. Let me have no more of it!" He waited again for any answer the Major might like to make, but, getting none, snapped: "Well, have you a tongue in your head?"

"I have," responded Hugo, "but I was never one to give my head for washing."

"You're not such a fool as you look," commented his lordship. "Whether you've enough sense to learn what every other Darracott has known from the cradle we shall see. That's why I sent for you."

"It's why I came, think on," said Hugo reflectively. "My father being killed almost before I was out of long coats, there was no one to tell me anything about my family, and barring I'd a lord for grandfather I didn't know anything."

"You're blaming me, are you? Very well! If I had known that there would ever have been the smallest need for you to know anything about me, or mine, I should have sent for you when your father died, and had you reared under my eye."

"Happen my mother would have had something to say to that," remarked Hugo.

"There's nothing to be gained by discussing the matter now. When your father married against my wish he cut himself off from his family. I don't scruple to tell you, for you must be well aware of it, that in marrying a weaver's daughter—however virtuous she may have been!—he did what he knew must ruin him with me!"

"Ay, they were pluck to the backbone, the pair of 'em," nodded Hugo. "What with you on the one hand, and Granddad on t'other, they must have had good bottom, seemingly." He smiled affably upon his lordship. "I never heard that they regretted it, though Granddad always held to it that no good would come of the match. Like to like and Nan to Nicholas was *his* motto."

"Are you telling me, sir, that the fellow *objected* to his daughter's marrying my son?" demanded Lord Darracott.

"Oh! he wasn't at all suited with it!" replied Hugo. "Let alone my father was Quality-make, he was too much of a care-for-nobody for Granddad: caper-witted, he called him. Shutful with his brass, too, which used to put Granddad, by what I'm told, into a rare passion. But Granddad's bark was worse than his bite, and he came round to the marriage in the end. It's a pity you never met him: you'd have agreed together better nor you think."

Lord Darracott, almost stunned, sought in vain for words with which to dispel this illusion. Before he could find them, Hugo had added thoughtfully: "You put me in mind of him now-and-now, particularly when you start ringing a peal over someone. However, you didn't send for me to talk about Granddad, so likely I'm wasting your time, sir."

"I wish to hear nothing about your granddad, as you call him, or your mother, or the life you led when you were a boy!" declared his lordship, his face still alarmingly suffused with colour. "Understand me, that period is never to be mentioned! I recommend you to put it out of your mind! It shouldn't be difficult; you've been a serving officer for the past ten years, and must have other things to talk of. I collect that there are no longer any ties binding you to Yorkshire, and that circumstance I cannot but regard as fortunate. I'll be plain with you: since I can't keep you from succeeding me I mean to see you licked into shape before I stick *my* spoon in the wall."

"Nay, we can't tell but what I'll break my neck over a

70

rasper, or go off in the smallpox," interposed Hugo, in a heartening tone.

"Where the devil did you learn to hunt?" exclaimed his lordship.

"In Portugal."

"Oh!" His lordship sat for a minute or two digesting this. "Well, that's more than I hoped for!" he said presently. "You'll be able to hunt from here: it's humbug country, but you'll see plenty of sport. *I* used to hunt in the shires, but I'm getting too old for it now. Sold my lodge in Leicestershire some years ago. Just as well I did! I should have had that nick-or-nothing boy of mine coming to grief over those fences, sure as a gun!"

"I've a fancy to hunt in the shires myself," confessed Hugo. "In fact——"

"Oh, you have, have you? Then you'd best rid yourself of it!" interrupted his lordship sardonically. "Behave yourself, and I'll make you a respectable allowance, but it won't run to the Quorn or the Pytchley, so don't think it!"

"Nay, I wasn't thinking it!" replied Hugo, looking a little startled. "Nor of your making me an allowance neither, sir. I'm much obliged to you, but I don't want that: I've plenty of brass."

Lord Darracott was amused. "Ay, your pockets are well-lined because you've just had the prize-money for the Peninsula and Waterloo paid to you. I know all about that, and no doubt it seems a fortune to you. You'll change your ideas a little when you've learnt the ways of *my* world."

"My grandfather left me some brass too," said Hugo diffidently.

"What you choose to do with your grandfather's savings is no concern of mine: spend them as you wish! For your support, you'll look to me—and you'll be glad enough to do so before you're much older! You are going to live in a different style to any you've been accustomed to, and you wouldn't find yourself able to strike a balance on a weaver's savings, however thrifty he may have been. Let me hear no more on that subject!"

"No," said Hugo meekly.

"Well, that brings me to what I have to say to you," said his lordship. "You're my heir, and you've all to learn, and I choose that you shall learn it under my roof. For the present you'll remain here—at all events until you've lost that damned, north-country accent! Later I'll let your uncle introduce you into Society, but the time for that's not yet.

71

This is your home, and here you'll stay. Which reminds me that you must sell out, if you haven't already done so."

"I have," said Hugo.

The craggy brows drew together. "Taking a lot for granted, weren't you?"

"Well," Hugo drawled, "there was a lot I *could* take for granted, sir."

"What if I hadn't chosen to acknowledge you?"

"Nay, I hadn't thought of that," confessed Hugo.

"Don't be too pot-sure!" said his lordship, by no means pleased. "I could still send you packing! And make no mistake about it: if I find you intolerable I'll do it!"

A flicker of relief shone for an instant in the Major's eyes, but he said nothing.

"However, you're better than I expected," said his lordship, mollified by this docility. "I daresay something can be made of you. Watch your cousins, and take your tone from them! I don't mean Claud—though no one would ever mistake him for other than a gentleman, mooncalf though he is! —but the other three. Vincent's an idle, extravagant dog, but his ton is excellent—what they call nowadays top-of-the-trees! You may take him for your model—and I'll see to it you don't copy his extravagance! No use looking to him to set you right when you make mistakes, however: he won't do it, because he's as sulky as a bear over the whole business. I could force him to take you in hand, but I shan't: I don't want the pair of you coming to cuffs. That's why I've told Claud to give you a new touch. Between 'em, he and Anthea can teach you pretty well all you need to know. *She* was born and bred here, knows all the ways of the place, all our history, every inch of my land! Not married, are you?"

"Married!" ejaculated Hugo, taken-aback. "Lord, no, sir!"

"No, I didn't think you could be," said his lordship. "I recommend you to get on terms with your cousin Anthea. She doesn't want for sense, and she's a spirited, lively girl, and would make you an excellent wife, if she took a fancy to you. I shall say no more on that head at present, however. Time enough to be looking to the future when you're better acquainted. What you can do at the moment is to go over the house with her: get her to tell you about the family! Ring the bell!"

The Major rose, and obeyed this peremptory behest. He also mopped his brow.

"I'm going to send for her," said his lordship. "She can take you up to the picture-gallery for a start."

The Major, showing alarm for the first time, tried to protest, but was cut short. "Ay, I know that throws you into a stew! You haven't been in the way of doing the pretty, and you're as shy as be-damned: you needn't tell me! You'll have to get the better of that, and you may as well begin at once. Chollacombe, desire Miss Darracott to come to me here immediately!"

The Major, attempting no further remonstrance, ran a finger inside a neckcloth grown suddenly too tight, and awaited in considerable trepidation the arrival of his cousin Anthea.

VI

It was some little time before Anthea obeyed the summons to the library, but Lord Darracott, contrary to the Major's expectation, showed no sign of putting himself in a passion. He occupied himself with giving his grandson a few hints on the best ways of fixing his interest with females in general and his cousin in particular; and when Anthea did at last enter the room, greeted her quite genially, saying: "Ah, here you are, my dear! Where the devil have you been hiding yourself?"

She put up her brows. "I have merely been with my mother, sir. We are rather busy this morning."

"Well, never mind that!" said his lordship. "I want you to show your cousin round the house. Tell him its history! He don't know anything about the family, and that won't do. You can take him up to the picture-gallery, and let him see a few of his ancestors."

"I am persuaded, sir, that that is a task Chollacombe is longing to perform. He would be delighted to instruct my cousin."

"Don't argue with me, girl, but do as I bid you!" snapped his lordship.

"Nay, if my cousin's throng——"

"And don't you think you can argue with me either!" said his lordship. "You'll do as you're told, the pair of you!"

The Major hesitated, but Anthea said coolly: "Very well, Grandpapa. Will you come with me, if you please, Cousin Hugo?"

The Major, with something of the air of one nerving himself to lead a forlorn hope, bowed, and accompanied her out of the room. But once beyond Lord Darracott's sight and hearing he said apologetically: "There's no sense in fratching with the old gentleman, but if you're throng this morning I can look after myself well-enough, cousin."

"When you have lived in this house for a few days you will have discovered that it is wisest to obey Grandpapa," she returned, leading the way towards the staircase. "Certainly in small matters. Unless, of course, you have a fancy for the sort of brangling *he* delights in?"

"Nay, I'm a peaceable man."

"So I have observed," she said. "I don't know how you contrived to keep your temper at the breakfast-table. I could have wished that you hadn't."

"Well, it wouldn't be proper for me to start a fight with my grandfather."

"It would be very proper for you to start one with Vincent, however!"

He smiled, but shook his head. "Hard words break no bones. Seemingly, I've put Vincent's nose out of joint, so it's natural he should be nattered. Happen he'll come about."

She did not speak again until they had reached the upper hall. She paused then, at the head of the stairs, and asked abruptly: "Has Grandpapa told you that he means to keep you here?"

"Ay, but chance it happens that he can't abide me he'll send me packing," he replied cheerfully.

"Do you—are you going to submit to his tyranny?"

"Well, there you have me," he said, rubbing his nose with a large forefinger, and slightly wrinkling his brow. "It won't do for me to be at outs with him, so it's likely I'll have to submit to him."

She glanced up at him rather searchingly. "I see!"

"While I'm under his roof," added Hugo. "The odds are that won't be for long."

She walked across the hall, and into a large saloon, whose chairs and pendant chandelier were all muffled in holland covers. "The State apartments," she announced. "So-called because Queen Elizabeth once occupied them for a sennight. Tradition has it that she contrived, hunting in *forse* and in the chase, to denude the park of deer. I've forgotten what it cost our noble ancestor to entertain her: some fabulous sum, and all to no avail, for she quarrelled violently with his lady, and is said to have left Darracott

74

Place in a dudgeon. That, by the way, is a portrait of our noble ancestor," she added, nodding to the picture over the fireplace. "Very Friday-faced, not to say hangdog, but that might have been because of the Queen's visit."

"I should say myself that the poor fellow suffered from a colicky disorder," replied Hugo. "He has the look of it. Sallow as a Nabob!"

She laughed, and led him on into an antechamber. "Very likely! We are now approaching the Queen's Bedchamber. You will notice her cipher over the bedstead. The hangings are all original, but pray don't touch them! The silk is quite rotten."

The Major stood looking round at faded and tarnished magnificence. "Eh, but it's a shame!" he said. "Why has it all been let go to ruin? It queers me that a man as proud as his lordship shouldn't keep his house in better order!"

"Well, it won't *queer* you when you are rather better acquainted with him," she replied. "His pride is of a peculiar order, and is not in the least diminished by debts or encumbered estates. Did you suppose yourself to be inheriting fortune as well as title? You will be sadly disappointed!"

"I can see that. But that colt your brother has wasn't bought for a song, and here's the old gentleman wishing to make me an allowance!"

She stared at him. "He must do that, of course. As for Richmond's colt, there's always money to pay for what *he* has set his heart on. Vincent is another who can in general get what he wants from Grandpapa. Next to Richmond, he is Grandpapa's favourite. Have you looked your fill at our past grandeur? We have now only to go through the room allotted to the maids-of-honour—quite unremarkable, as you perceive—and we have reached the picture-gallery. There is a stairway at the far end which was originally the principal one. The present Grand Stairway is of later date."

"If ever I saw such a rabbit-warren!" he remarked.

"Exactly so, but I advise you not to say that within Grandpapa's hearing." She walked over to the first of six large window-embrasures, and stood looking out through the latticed panes, with her back turned to the Major. "Before I show you our forebears, cousin, there is something I wish to say. No, not that: something I feel myself obliged to say! You may think it odd of me—even improper! —but I have a notion you are not quite as stupid as you would like us to believe. I daresay you may understand why it is that I find myself in the very awkward position of being forced to put myself, and you too, to the blush. I know Grandpapa well enough to be tolerably certain that he has ordered you to make me an offer." She turned her head as she spoke, her colour a little heightened, but her eyes meeting the Major's squarely. "If he has not already done so, he will. But I think he has. Am I right?"

"He didn't precisely do that," replied Hugo cautiously.

"He will. I hope you will summon up the courage to refuse to obey that particular command. Pray believe that nothing would induce *me* to obey it! If that seems to you uncivil, I beg your pardon, but——"

"Nay, I'm reet glad to hear you say it!" he responded ingenuously.

Her eyes narrowed in sudden amusement. "I was persuaded you would be. I must warn you, however, that there will be—oh, the devil to pay, and every sort of pressure brought to bear on you——! You don't know! He has ways of forcing us all to knock under: you may find yourself in a fix over it!"

"I may do that," he acknowledged, "but I'll be far if I make you an offer at his or any other man's bidding!" He added hastily, as she broke into laughter: "The thing is, I'm by way of being promised already! Othergates, of course, it would be different."

"Good God! Did you tell Grandpapa so?"

"I've not told him *yet*," owned Hugo sheepishly.

"You were afraid to!"

"Nay, it was just that it wasn't, seemingly, the reet moment for telling him!" he protested.

She was looking scornful. "It never will be the right moment. You *were* afraid!"

"Well, you weren't so brave yourself, not to tell him you wouldn't marry me," he pointed out.

"Yes, I was!" she retorted. "I would have told him so that instant I knew what he meant to do! I didn't do so because—oh, you don't understand! For me the case is quite otherwise!"

"Ay, it would be," he agreed.

"Well, it is, so you need not speak in that detestable way! Whenever I come to cuffs with Grandpapa it's Mama who suffers for it, and she has enough to bear without being blamed for my sins! That's why I asked you *not* to offer for me, so that Grandpapa couldn't say it was my fault, or bully Mama into urging me to accept you. Heaven knows your shoulders are big enough, but I see you are just like the rest, and dare not square up to him!"

The huge creature before her, looking the picture of guilt, said feebly: "It wasn't that-a-way. The thing is, I'm in a bit of a hobble. It wouldn't do for me to tell my grandfather I was promised, not before I was sure of it myself."

"But aren't you sure of it?" she asked, a good deal astonished.

"Well," he temporized, once more rubbing his nose, "I am and I'm not. There's been nothing *official,* as you might say. It's—it's been kept secret betwixt the pair of us. It was just before the last campaign, you see, and I was recalled in such a bang that there was no time to do aught but get my baggage together, and be off. What's more there was no knowing but what I might have been killed, so it was thought best to keep it secret. And I haven't been home since."

"Good God, have you been engaged for two years?" she exclaimed.

"Better nor that," he said. "It was in the spring of '15 that it happened, and now we're in September. It seems to me I ought to make sure she hasn't changed her mind before I speak to the old gentleman, and so far I haven't been home."

"But she must have written to you!"

"Er—no," said Hugo, much discomposed. "She—well, there were reasons why she couldn't do that!"

A dreadful suspicion occurred to Anthea. "Cousin do you mean—is she a—a lady of Quality?"

The Major shook a miserable head.

"*Can't* she write?" Anthea asked, in a hushed voice.

"No," confessed the Major.

Feeling a trifle weak, Anthea sat down on the window-seat. "Cousin, this is—this is positively *terrible!* You can have no notion——! What's to be done?"

"If you think I *ought* to tell the old gentleman——"

"No, no!" she said quickly. "On no account in the world! Of course, I see now why you didn't say you wouldn't offer for me! He would have been bound to have asked you why not, and—I beg your pardon for being so uncivil about that! *No one* could be brave enough to make *that* disclosure to him! But what are you going to do?"

The Major had the grace to look a little conscience-stricken. He said vaguely that he hadn't yet made up his mind.

"I can't think how you dared to come here at all," said

Anthea, knitting her brows. "To be sure, you didn't know what Grandpapa was like, but you *must* have known that he would never tolerate *that* sort of marriage! In fact, it was because he is afraid that you might wish to marry someone he would think unworthy that he made this odious scheme to marry you to me. Cousin, you're not in a hobble! you're in the *suds!*"

The Major, who, by this time, had had the satisfaction of seeing that his judgment had not been at fault when he had decided that animation would greatly improve Miss Darracott, ventured to approach her, and to sit down. "I am and-all!" he agreed ruefully.

"He won't receive her, you know," Anthea said. "It is useless to think he might come about. He never forgave your father, and *he* was his favourite son."

"Nay, I wouldn't bring her here."

"That's all very well, but you can't expect the poor girl to wait for years and years to be married!" objected Anthea. "Besides, surely you would not like that yourself! If you're thinking that Grandpapa may die soon, I must tell you that I don't think there's the least chance of it: he's old, but not at all decrepit, you know!"

"Oh, no, I should think he's good for a piece yet!" Hugo agreed. "But I'm not going to stay here for years and years."

"He thinks you are," she said doubtfully.

"Ay, but that's just one of the daft notions he takes into his head. There's no sense in stirring coals, so I didn't tell him he'd got the wrong sow by the ear. Happen he'll think it a good shuttance when I do tell him I'm off."

"But how will you do?" she asked. "It's he who holds the purse-strings, remember! I assure you he wouldn't hesitate to draw them tight."

He laughed. "Nay, he doesn't hold my purse-strings!"

"Ah, no! How stupid of me! You have your profession, and can afford to snap your fingers under his nose! Oh, how much I envy you!" She heaved a short sigh, but smiled immediately after, and said: "Did you come to look us over only? How long do you mean to stay?"

"Well, that depends," he said. "When I got the letter that told me the way things had fallen out, it fairly sent me to grass, for, not knowing anything about my family, I'd no notion how close to the succession I stood. Nothing will persuade my grandfather I wasn't happy as a grig to be succeeding him—though why he should have thought any-one would want to inherit a house that's falling to ruin,

78

let alone encumbered estates, and a sackful of debts, has me fairly capped—but the truth is I wasn't at all suited, and the first thing that came into my head was to see if there wasn't a way out. That wouldn't fadge, however, so——" He paused, considering. "Well, I made up my mind to it that I'd have to come here, whether or no."

"I can understand that you didn't wish to do that while Grandpapa was alive."

"No," he admitted. "But if I've to step into the old gentleman's shoes, soon or late, it'll be as well I shouldn't be strange to the place, or the people. So when Lissett wrote to tell me I was to come here I did come. I don't say I wouldn't as lief have sent word his lordship might go to hell—eh, that slipped out! I'm reet sorry!"

"Don't give it a thought!" said Anthea cordially. "I never before heard such beautiful words, I promise you!"

He smiled, but shook his head. "I'd have caught cold at that. What's more, if his lordship and my father were at outs, that's no concern of mine. My other grandfather had more rumgumption than any man I've ever known, and he always would have it that my father came by his deserts. He didn't hold with a man's marrying out of his own order, and, taking it by and large, I'd say he was in the reet of it. What with him on the one side, hammering it into me I was Quality-born, and Grandfather Darracott here looking at me as if I was a porriwiggle, I don't know *what* I am!"

She went into a peal of laughter. "Oh, what is it? Porriwiggle?"

He grinned. "It's what we call a tadpole."

That made her laugh more than ever. She said, wiping her eyes: "No, I don't think anyone would liken you to a tadpole, cousin! Tell me about the girl you are going to marry! Is she pretty?"

"I don't know if you'd say she was pretty. She—she has golden hair—corn-gold, you know—and blue eyes, with long lashes that curl. She has a straight little nose, and a mouth like a bow, and—and a complexion like strawberries and cream!" replied Hugo rhapsodically.

"I should say she was a beauty!" Anthea said, slightly taken aback.

"She has a good figure too," added Hugo, dwelling with obvious pleasure on the vision he had conjured up.

"In that case I think you should lose no time in posting north—though it is probably too late already. Such a paragon *cannot* be wearing the willow!"

"I'm not afraid of that. I forgot to tell you that she's not one to break her promise."

She eyed him suspiciously. "What is her name?"

"Amelia," responded Hugo, adding after a reflective moment: "Melkinthorpe."

Anthea rose. "Well, I wish you very happy. Meanwhile, we haven't yet looked at the ancestors. We must do so, you know, for Grandpapa is quite likely to ask you searching questions about them. Chiefly you must study the Van Dyck: here it is! Ralph Darracott, who was killed at Naseby; his wife, Penelope—she was pretty, wasn't she?—holding Charles Darracott in her lap. There's another one of Charles in later life, a Lely, over here."

The Major, having subjected Charles Darracott to a critical scrutiny, remarked that he knew what he thought of him.

"Very likely," said Anthea. "His son, however, was extremely virtuous, as you may see for yourself. He was succeeded by his nephew, Ralph II. I daresay you may have been thinking that our ancestors were rather commonplace, but Ralph II, I assure you, made quite a noise in the world."

"He would," said Hugo, regarding Ralph with disfavour.

"Yes, he was a beau of the first stare. His waistcoats were copied by all the smarts of his day; he had fought three duels, and killed his man, before he was five-and-twenty; and he is generally supposed to have murdered his first wife, either by throwing her out of the window, or by driving her to throw herself out of the window. Grandpapa, of course, holds by the latter theory, but the country-people know better. Her ghost walks, you know."

"What, here?"

Anthea laughed. "No, don't be alarmed! This stirring event took place before Ralph became Lord Darracott. When he came into the country, which was seldom, he resided at the Dower House. He is said to have incarcerated his wife there, and to have ridden all the way from London one stormy night, and murdered her. Then he galloped away again, and shortly afterwards married his second wife. There can really be *no* doubt of the truth of this legend, for the sound of his horse's hooves are frequently heard in the dead of night. He came to a violent end, like so many of our illustrious family."

"I should think he ended on the gallows, that road," observed the Major.

"Nothing so vulgar!" replied Anthea. "He was murdered."

"Who murdered him?"

"They never discovered that. His body was found in the Home Wood, and from some cause or another he had so many enemies that it was thought the deed might have been committed by almost anyone."

"And does his ghost walk?"

"No, happily it doesn't: we are quite free of spectres here, at the Place! The portrait you are looking at now is of Lucinda Darracott. She married an Attlebridge, but that likeness was taken when she was eighteen. Several minor poets made her the subject of lyrics, but in later life she grew sadly stout. And here, cousin, we have my grandfather, surrounded by his progeny, his wife, and two dogs. The urchin leaning against his chair is your papa; mine is the infant being dandled by Grandmama. The coy damsel with the posy is Aunt Mary—Lady Chudleigh; beside her, Aunt Sarah, now Mrs. Wenlock; and the pretty one admiring my papa is Aunt Caroline, Lady Haddon. Your uncle Granville is the youth with one hand on his hip, and his riding-whip in the other; and the chubby lad is my uncle Matthew."

Hugo dutifully gazed upon this conversation piece, but made no comment. His eye was attracted by a kit-kat hanging beside it, and he exclaimed: "That's good!"

"Richmond? Yes, it's very like," she agreed. "Mr. Lonsdale painted it a year ago. There's a miniature of him also, but Grandpapa keeps that in his own room."

He stood looking up at the portrait. "Eh, he's a handsome lad!" he remarked. "Full of gig, too. What does the old gentleman mean to do with him?"

"I don't know."

He glanced down at her, and saw that the amusement had faded from her face. "Seemingly, the lad's army-mad?"

"My grandfather will never permit him to join, however."

"That's a pity. I never knew any good to come of setting a lad's nose to the wrong grindstone."

"Oh, that won't happen either!" she answered. "The likelihood is that he will be kept kicking his heels here. My grandfather dotes on him, you see."

"Nay, if he dotes on him he'll let him have his way!"

"How little you know Grandpapa! His affection for Richmond is perfectly selfish: he likes to have Richmond with him, and so it will be. The excuse is that Richmond's constitution is sickly. He is as tough as whiteleather, in fact, but his childhood was sickly, and that is enough for Grandpapa. Do you wish to look at any more portraits, or have you had your fill?"

"I was forgetting that you're throng this morning," he apologized. "I've had my fill, and I'm reet grateful to you."

"I'll take you down the old stairway," she said, moving towards the door at the end of the gallery. "This end of the house is not used nowadays, but you might care to see it. It's the original house, but when the third Granville Darracott started building he added so much that the earlier part became nothing more than a wing. Take care how you tread on these stairs! Much of the timber is rotten."

He came down cautiously behind her, but paused on the half-landing to look about him, at dampstained walls, dry wood, and crumbling plaster. "It'll take some brass to put this in order!" he remarked.

"Money? Oh, it would cost a fortune, if it could be done at all! I daresay no one would think it worth it, for none of the rooms are handsome, and most of the panelling is sadly worm-eaten. It has been going to rack for nearly a hundred years." She showed him one or two of the parlours bare save for lumber, and he shook his head, pursing his lips in a silent whistle. She smiled. "Does it throw you into gloom? The only time anyone gives it a thought is when the windows are all cleaned. We can get back to the main part of the house through this door, if you don't object to going past the kitchens and the scullery."

When they reached the main hall of the house again their arrival coincided with that of Vincent and Richmond, who had just come in from the stables. Richmond was looking pleased, for although he had had to endure some stringent criticisms on his handling of the ribbons his Corinthian cousin had said that at least he had good light hands. Vincent, wearing a blue Bird's Eye neckcloth, and a coat with shoulder-capes past counting, rarely looked pleased, and just now looked bored. He was bored. He was quite fond of Richmond, but teaching a stripling how to drive a team in style was a task he found wearisome. He had offered the lesson of impulse, because it had nettled him to see Richmond so much inclined to take Hugo's part against himself; and it annoyed him still more to know that he could be nettled by such a trivial matter. There was a pronounced crease between his brows as he set his hat down on a table, and began to draw off his gloves, and it deepened as he looked at Hugo and Anthea.

"How did you acquit yourself?" Anthea asked her brother. "Was your teacher odious or kind?"

"Oh, odious!" replied Richmond, laughing. "I'm a mere whipster, with no more precision of eye than a farm-hand, but at least I didn't overturn the phaeton!"

Vincent, whose penetrating glance little escaped, put up his glass and levelled it at the hem of Anthea's dress. "It seems unlikely," he said, "but one might almost be led to infer that you had been sweeping the carpets, dear Anthea, or even clearing ash out of the grates."

She looked down, and gave an exclamation of annoyance. "How vexatious! I thought I had taken such pains to hold my skirt up, too! No, we have not yet been reduced quite to that: I have been showing the East Wing to our cousin here, and the floors are filthy."

"The East Wing?" said Richmond. "What the devil for? There's nothing to be seen there!"

"Oh, Grandpapa desired me to take him to the picture-gallery, and when we had reached the end of it I thought it a good opportunity to show him the original part of the house. He certainly ought to see it, but I'm sorry I did take him there now, for I must change my dress again."

"You don't mean to say you dragged poor Cousin Hugo all over that tumbledown barrack?"

"No, of course not. I let him see the parlours, that's all—and quite enough to bring on a fit of the dismals, wasn't it, cousin?"

"Well, it's melancholy to see the place falling into ruin," Hugo admitted. "Still, I'd like to go all over it one day."

"You had better not," Richmond advised him. "The last time I went to rummage amongst the lumber for something I wanted I nearly put my leg through a rotten floor-board in one of the attics. At all events, don't venture without me! I'll show you over, if you're set on it. Then, if you go through the floor, and break a limb, I can summon all the able-bodied men on the estate to come and carry you to your room!"

"It 'ud take a tidy few," agreed Hugo, grinning.

"Why this desire to inspect a ruin?" enquired Vincent. "Pride of prospective possession, or do you perhaps mean to restore it, in due course?"

"Nay, I don't know," Hugo said vaguely.

"Obviously you don't. The cost of restoring it—a singularly useless thing to do, by the by!—would very soon run you off your legs."

"Happen you're reet," said Hugo amicably. "I'm just by way of being interested in our first-ends. It's early days to be making plays."

"Just so!" said Vincent, with so much meaning in his voice that Richmond intervened quickly, asking Hugo if he had seen the Van Dyck.

"He means the portrait of the first Ralph Darracott," explained Vincent smoothly.

"An unnecessary piece of information, Vincent!" said Anthea.

"Ay, so it is," nodded Hugo. "Now, wait a piece, while I cast my mind back! Ay, I have it! That was the picture of the gentleman with the long curls. What's more," he added, with naïve pride in this feat of memory, "it's the one my cousin told me I must look at particularly. Van Dyck would be the man who painted it. I've heard of him before, think on."

Richmond hurried into speech. "I don't know much about pictures myself, or care for them, but I like Ralph I. He was a great gun! Most of our ancestors were either ramshackle fellows, or dead bores. Did Anthea tell you about the second Ralph? Not that she knows the half of it! If ever there was a loose fish——! A regular thatchgallows!"

"Yes!" Anthea interrupted. "And isn't it *mortifying* to reflect on the number of Darracotts who look like him? *You* favour the first Ralph, and so did Oliver, a little; but Uncle Granville, and Papa, and Aunt Caroline, and Grandpapa himself are clearly descended from Ralph II, while as for Vincent——"

"—you have only to place a powdered wig on his head and no one would know them apart," supplied Vincent. "Thank you, my love! I must derive what consolation I may from the knowledge that at least I resemble *one* of my forebears!"

At this point a welcome interruption occurred. Claud, hearing voices in the hall, came out of one of the saloons, and, addressing himself to Hugo, said severely: "Been looking for you all over!"

"What's amiss?" Hugo asked.

"Just what I expected!" said Claud. "Didn't I tell you the odds were my grandfather would blame me if you was to vex him? Dash it if he hasn't told me he shall hold me responsible for you!"

"Ee, that's bad!" said Hugo, shaking his head. "If I were

84

you, I'd make off back to London as fast as ever I could, lad."

Claud looked a little doubtful. "Well, I *could* do that," he admitted. "At least—— No, it wouldn't fadge. Don't want my father to take a pet, and he would, because *he* don't want to offend the old man. There's another thing, too."

He paused, and it was evident from his darkling brow that he was brooding over a serious affront. His brother, halfway up the stairs, stood looking down at him contemptuously. "Don't keep us in suspense!" he begged. "What inducement has been held out to you?"

"He didn't hold out any inducement. No inducement he could hold out. *I* haven't swallowed a spider! *I* don't haunt Pontius Pilate's doorstep! *I* don't have to hang on my grandfather's sleeve!" He perceived that Vincent had turned and was about to descend the stairs again, and temporized. "Well, what I mean is, I haven't yet! No saying when I *might* have to, of course!"

"Fighting shy, brother?" said Vincent.

"I'm not fighting at all," replied Claud frankly. "I don't say I wouldn't like to see someone plant you a facer because I would, but I don't care for boxing myself, never did! Besides, I'm not up to your weight."

"Remember that, and don't crow so loudly, little dunghill-cock!" said Vincent, resuming his progress upstairs.

"One of these days," said Claud, as soon as Vincent was out of earshot, "somebody will do Vincent a mischief!"

"Gammon!" retorted Richmond. "It was you who stirred the coals, not Vincent! Cutting at him like that!"

"Well, I've been vexed to death!" said Claud. "I don't mind it when my grandfather comes the ugly. I don't mind his cursing me. I don't mind it when he says I've got no brains. I don't mind his calling me a fribble, or a popinjay, or a Bartholomew baby. But when he tells me I look like a demi-beau—*a demi-beau!*——"

"Claud!" breathed Anthea, deeply shocked. "He did not say *that?*"

"Oh, yes, he did! To my face! Said he didn't want Hugh tricked out to look like me, too. Said I could mend Hugh's speech, but he wouldn't have me teaching him to look like a counter-coxcomb! That to *me!* He must be queer in his attic!"

"Depend upon it, that's it!" she said. "If I were you I wouldn't stay another day where you have been so insulted!"

"Well, I am going to stay!" replied Claud. "I'll make him eat it, dashed if I won't! *He* wants Hugo to model himself on Vincent. A nice cake Hugo would make of himself if he started aping the Corinthian set!"

"I would and-all," said Hugo, who was listening to this with his shoulders propped against the wall, his arms folded across his great chest, and an appreciative grin on his face.

"Of course you would! You can't wear a Bird's Eye Wipe, and fifteen capes, and a Bit-of-Blood hat unless you're a top-sawyer, and you ain't! Told us you weren't! What's more, you couldn't wear a coat like that one of Vincent's even if you were, because you're a dashed sight too big already. You'd have all the street-urchins clamouring to know where the Fair was going to be held. You put yourself in my hands! *I'll* turn you out in new trim—show you the proper mode—all in print—no finery, but up to the nines!"

Hugo shook his head. "Nay," he said mournfully, "you can't make a silk purse out of a sow's ear, lad."

"Dashed if I don't have a touch at it! Yes, and don't say *nay*, or call me *lad!*"

"Nay then!" expostulated Hugo, opening his innocent eyes wide.

VII

If the Major nursed a hope that his elegant cousin's determination to give him a new touch would not survive his wrath he was soon obliged to abandon it. A crusading spirit had entered Claud's bosom, and before the day was out he had succeeded in cornering the Major, whom he found writing a letter in one of the smaller saloons. He had given much thought to a difficult problem, and he had decided that the first step must be a bolt to the village, where he would himself superintend the choice of hats, boots, gloves, knee-smalls, neckcloths, waistcoats, and shirts; and summon his own tailor to bring his pattern-card to his lodging in Duke Street. Gathering from this programme that a bolt to the village signified a visit to the Metropolis, the Major declined the threat. He was of the opinion that Lord Darracott would cup up extremely stiff if such a plan were even mooted.

"Thought of that too," countered Claud. "Say you have the toothache! I'll offer to drive to London with you, and take you to a good tooth-drawer. No need to tell the old gentleman I'm going to rig you out in style."

The Major said that he thought his lordship had too much know to be bamboozled; and Claud made the disheartening discovery that his pupil was as obstinate as he was amiable, and so woodheaded that although he listened to what was said to him he seemed to be incapable of taking it in. He agreed that to present a good appearance was of the first importance; when it was pointed out to him that the points of his shirt-collars were so moderate as to be positively dowdy he said he had been afraid that was so from the start; when told that Nugee or Stultz would turn him out in smarter style than Scott, he nodded; but whenever he had been worked up to the point (as Claud thought) of making the necessary alterations to his attire it became apparent that either he had not been attending, or had failed to grasp the meaning of what had been said to him.

"Cast your ogles over me!" Claud adjured. "Don't want to boast, but I assure you this rig of mine is precise to a pin!"

"Ay, you're as fine as fivepence," said Hugo, obediently looking him over.

"Well, I flatter myself this coat is an excellent hit. I don't say it would do for you, because you haven't the figure for it. Not but what you could wear a Cumberland corset, you know. Just to nip you in at the waist!"

"That 'ud be the thing," agreed Hugo.

"No need to broaden the shoulders, but a bit of wadding at the top of the sleeve would give 'em a modish peak."

"So it would!"

"The sleeves must be gathered at the shoulder, too."

"Ay, they'd have to be."

"And the tails made longer. Then, with a set of silver buttons—basket-work, I think; a natty waistcoat, and pantaloons of stockinette—*not* nankeen, or Angola!—well, you see what I mean, coz?"

"I'd look champion."

"You'd look as neat as wax," said Claud. "Or trim as a trencher. *Not* champion!"

"I'd look as neat as wax," said Hugo tractably.

"Take my advice, and let Nugee make your coats! Vincent goes to Schweitzer and Davidson for his sporting toggery, and I rather fancy Weston made the coat he wore last night, but Nugee is the man for my money. Or Stultz. I'll tell you what! Have a coat from each of 'em!"

"Nay, I've enough coats already," said Hugo.

"Dash it, haven't I been telling you for ever that they won't do?" demanded Claud, in pardonable exasperation.

"Ay, you have, and I'm fairly nappered I didn't meet you before I let Scott take my measurements," said Hugo sadly.

A worse set-back was in store for the Pink of the Ton. When he pointed out to the Major that two cloak-bags and a portmanteau could not, by any stretch of the imagination, provide adequate accommodation for the number of shirts any aspirant to fashion must carry with him, he was, in his own phrase, floored by his pupil's simple rejoinder that he had been informed that when staying in the country he might with perfect propriety make good the deficiencies of bucolic launderers with a Tommy.

"A tommy?" gasped Claud, his eyes starting from their sockets. "*A false shirt-front?*"

"Ay, that's it," nodded Hugo. "Only in the country, of course!"

A shudder ran through Claud's frame. "No, no! Well, what I mean is—— Dash it, coz!—*No!*"

Encountering only a blank stare from the Major, Claud was moved to order Richmond's man, Wellow, who was looking after Hugo, to render up to him any Tommies he might have found. Wellow naturally repeated this extraordinary command to his own master, with the result that when Richmond rode out with Anthea and Hugo next morning he warmly congratulated Hugo on having successfully bubbled Claud.

"Bubbled Claud? How did I do that?" asked Hugo.

"No, no, cousin, you won't bubble *me!* Telling him you meant to eke out your shirts with Tommies! The silly gudgeon bade Wellow hand 'em over to him. Wellow thought he must be touched, for of course you have none."

"There, now, I knew there was something I'd forgot to pack!" said Hugo.

"Yes, and you have also forgotten that since Grooby unpacked your luggage, and Wellow is waiting on you, everyone in the house knows that the Major's linen is of the finest," remarked Anthea.

"Now, that I *am* glad to hear, because I took care to buy the best," confided Hugo.

She cast a somewhat amused glance at him, but said

nothing. Riding on the other side of the big bay, Richmond said diffidently: "You don't mean to let Claud rig you out, do you?"

"Eh, but I'm sorely tempted!" said Hugo. "I'd look gradely! That is, I would if I wore some kind of a corset, and that's where the water sticks, for I'm one who likes to be comfortable."

"A corset?" exclaimed both his companions in chorus.

"To nip me in round the waist," he explained.

"Of all the impudence!" said Richmond. "You've a better figure than Claud!" He hesitated, and then said, with a slight stammer: "As a matter of fact—if you won't take it amiss!—my grandfather says you look more the gentleman than Claud does!"

The Major showed no signs of offence, but he did not seem to be much elated either. "Well, if he said our Claud looked like a counter-coxcomb that's not praising me to the skies," he observed.

"Praising one to the skies is not one of Grandpapa's weaknesses," said Anthea. "You look what you are, cousin: a soldier! I don't know how it is, but there is always a certain neatness that distinguishes them."

"That's due to Scott," he replied. "There wasn't much neatness about me, or any of us, barring poor Cadoux, in my Peninsular days. You'll hear people talk about our jack-a-dandy green uniforms, but, Lord, you should have seen 'em by the time we got to Madrid!"

That was quite enough for Richmond, who at once began to ply his cousin with questions about his campaigns. The Major replied to them in his goodnatured way, but either because he was not a loquacious person, or because he had been forbidden to encourage Richmond's interest in military matters, he was not as forthcoming as his young cousin had hoped he might be. Sometimes he was even a little disappointing, for when he was begged to describe the march to Talavera, or the battle of Salamanca, the only things he seemed to remember about the march were one or two ludicrous incidents in which he cut a comical but unheroic figure; and all he had to say about the battle was that the Light Bobs had had very little to do in it. Richmond, persevering, asked him if it had always been his ambition to become a soldier. His own romantic ardour glowed in his eyes, but the Major's reply was again disappointing. "Nay, I never thought of it when I was a lad. All I ever wanted to do was to get under everyone's feet in the mill, or to run off up to the moors instead of minding my book."

"What made you join?" enquired Anthea. "Was it because your father had been a soldier, perhaps?"

"There wasn't much else I *could* do," he explained. "It was this road, you see: I never framed to be a scholar, so it was no use thinking of the Church, or the Law; and as for tewing in the mill, my grandfather wouldn't hear of it, because I was a gentleman's son. So, as I'd no fancy for the navy, it had to be the army."

It was evident that this prosaic speech daunted Richmond. He said "Oh!" in a flattened tone, and relapsed for some time into silence.

He had accompanied the Major and his sister on their ride at Anthea's request. Lord Darracott had told her at the breakfast-table that she might usefully employ herself in making her cousin acquainted with the Darracott land: an attempt to throw them together so blatant that she could only be thankful that she had had the resolution to declare herself to the Major. More from a desire to be revenged on her grandfather than from reluctance to be tête-à-tête with Hugo, she had instantly invited Richmond to accompany her. In this she had been supported by Mrs. Darracott, whose notions of propriety, though constantly outraged by the careless Darracotts, were too nice to allow her to regard with complaisance the spectacle of her daughter's jauntering about the countryside with a strange man (be he never so much her cousin) for her only escort. Richmond, hoping to be regaled with stirring tales of war, had agreed willingly to go; and although the Major had disappointed him he was too well-mannered a boy to make an excuse to leave the small party, or to betray that he thought talk about boundaries, enclosures, rights-of-way, advowsons, leases, and crops a dead bore. He had never had much interest in such matters, and knew far less about them than his sister; so his contributions to the task of instructing the heir were largely confined to a description of the various forms of sport to be obtained in the neighbourhood.

The northern boundary to the estates being considerably nearer to the house than any other, they had set out in that direction. A nursery joke had had to be explained to Hugo. "And after that, which?" Richmond had asked his sister. "Kent or Sussex?"

"Kent," she had decided; and then, flashing a smile at

Hugo: "We have a foot in each county, you know. Here, we are in Kent, and it was here that the first Darracott—well, the first that was ever in England!—settled. There's nothing left of the old Saxon manor, but it was certainly on the site of the present house. Darracott tradition has it that he was a person of consequence, but *we*—Richmond, and Vincent, and I—take leave to doubt that, because the original manor was quite small. That's why the house lies so close to the northern boundary. It was much later that the family crept over into Sussex. Today, that part of Grandpapa's lands is the most important, because of the rents, you know; but although Darracott Place has been pulled down, and rebuilt, and enlarged a great many times, no reigning Darracott has ever had the temerity to remove from the original site. *That* would be flying in the face of tradition! an unpardonable crime!"

So they had ridden towards the Weald, into more wooded country, and then eastward, above the Rother levels, for a little way, before dropping down again to the Marsh, and crossing the Military Canal at Appledore. The Marsh stretched before them, smiling and lush in the September sunshine, yet with a suggestion of eery loneliness about it which made the Major exclaim, under his breath: "Eh, it's a queer place!"

Just beyond Fairford, a cluster of alleys round a church, they had reined in their horses, so that the few landmarks could be more easily pointed out. Anthea had directed Hugo's attention to the tower of Lydd Church, visible some six miles to the south-east, but although he bestowed a cursory glance on it his interest was claimed by the expanse of reclaimed land that lay between Lydd and Rye. Seen from the slight elevation on which Darracott Place had been built, the Marsh had appeared to be quite flat, with nothing but intersecting dykes, and, here and there, a few willows and thornbushes to relieve its tame monotony. His eye had been attracted by Rye, perched so unexpectedly high above the Marsh, and reminding him, in the distance, of the Point of Cassilhas, near Lisbon, where there had been a military hospital (in which he had languished for several painful weeks), and on the top of just such another steep, isolated hill a convent had been built. Now, standing on the edge of the Marsh, he perceived that it was not quite flat, but sloped slightly upwards towards the dunes that hid the sea from his sight. A road meandered erratically across it, but there was no traffic to be seen, and not so much as a shepherd's cot afforded any sign of human habitation. There seemed to be no living things on the Marsh but sheep, gulls, a moorhen seeking safety in the rushes, and somewhere, sounding its unmistakeable note, a peewit. The scene was peaceful, but it was not tame. As Anthea looked enquiringly at Hugo, he spoke the thought that came into his mind: "Do you meet flay-boggards, if you venture out when the light goes?"

"I don't *think* so," replied Anthea cautiously.

He glanced down at her, and laughed. "Where's our Claud to set me right? Hobgoblins is what I should have said! This is just where I'd look for them."

To Anthea and Richmond, born and bred on the edge of the Marsh, this was ridiculous. Richmond said: "Hobgoblins? You don't believe in them, do you, cousin?"

"Nay, I'm not so sure I don't since I've come into these parts," said Hugo, shaking his head. "I'll take care to turn my coat inside out, if ever I come here after nightfall, for fear of being pixie-led."

Richmond laughed; but Anthea said: "Does it seem to you an uncanny place? My aunt Anne hated it: she used to say it was sullen land, full of evil sea-spirits, but she was very fanciful! It isn't uncanny—not a bit!—even though it was once at the bottom of the sea! Innings have been made all along this stretch of coast, you know, as far as Saxon times. People say it's unhealthy—aguish—and I own that those who live on the Marsh are peculiarly subject to fits of ague. That's why Darracott Place is almost the last of the great houses still remaining here: in general, the lords of the district removed to the uplands. Not the Darracotts, however! You may depend on that!"

"Unless *you* do so, Cousin Hugo?" interpolated Richmond. "My uncle Granville was used to say he would leave Darracott Place, and live in one of the manors on the Sussex side. Northiamway."

"Yes! When he was at outs with Grandpapa!" retorted Anthea. "He would never have done it! Even had he really wished to abandon the Place, only think of the cost!" She smiled at Hugo, dancing lights in her eyes. "Did you fancy, cousin, that you had seen the worst of your family? I assure you, you have seen it at its best! When my uncle was alive, and he lived here, with all his family, brangles and brawls between him and my grandfather were the rule rather than the exception. He was inclined to be sickly, which Grandpapa took as an affront; and no matter what ailed him he always said that it was due to the horrid, marish situation of the house. You may imagine Grandpapa's wrath!"

"Well, what slum it was!" said Richmond scornfully. "Grandpapa knew he only got the notion out of an old book my aunt found, and was for ever quoting! It was enough to put anyone out of temper, for there wasn't a word of truth in it! Something about the Marsh being grievous in winter——"

"*Evil* in winter, grievous in *summer*, and never good," Anthea amended. "Also that Kent has three steps, Wealth without health—that's our part! Wealth *and* health—which is the Weald; and the third which *affordeth health only, and no Wealth*."

"Which proves it was a fudge!" said Richmond. "*We* haven't wealth!"

"Ay, but there's wealth here right enough," said Hugo, his gaze roving over the scene before him. "The land's carrying more sheep to the acre than I ever saw. How many do you reckon on?"

"From six to twelve—but that's over Romney Marsh too," Anthea replied. "The farmers think it a bad year if the Marshes don't yield four thousand packs. I believe it's good wool, but I don't know much about it, because we don't keep sheep ourselves, of course. The pasturage and the arable lands are leased."

"I don't know much about it either," said Hugo, "but I've seen the fleeces in grease, in the market, and listened to a deal of talk. It's short-staple wool, isn't it? Carding wool, that is?"

"I haven't the least notion," replied Anthea frankly. "In fact, I don't know what carding wool is. Tell me!"

"Nay, I'd likely tell you wrong, for I was never very sure in my own mind between wools and worsteds. Long-staple makes the worsteds: combing wool, they call it. Lincoln and Leicestershire is where it mostly comes from. The Southdown is the best of the carding wools: it mills well. I know that much, but when it comes to qualities I'm at a stand. Pitlock's the first of the wools, and Fine of the worsteds, and Abb's pretty well the last of 'em both, but I'd be done up if you were to ask me what comes betwixt the first and the last. As for stapling, if I pored over the lot for a sennight as like as not I'd mistake Breech for Prime at the back-end of the week!"

She was interested, and would have questioned him further, but Richmond, attending with only half an ear, interrupted her to say: "Oh, never mind the sheep! I'll tell you what's to be had in abundance here besides those silly creatures, and that's hares! Only wait until January—from then until March is when they run strongest—and we'll show you some famous sport! There's excellent duck-shooting, too, if you care for it."

"Do you course your hares?" Hugo asked. "I've done a lot of that in the Peninsula."

"No, we hunt them with harriers. You'll soon see! The young hounds will be entered in a week or two. They hunt leverets at this season, of course: it teaches them their business, but the real sport is after Christmas. Do you know, an old Jack will give you almost as good a run as a fox? The doe doubles and turns shorter, but a Jack will very likely travel a four or even five mile point."

There was no more talk of wool or agriculture after that. As they rode gently along the track, Anthea let her mare drop behind a little, well-aware that once two gentlemen were fairly launched into sporting-talk neither would have a word to spare for a mere female. She occasionally rode to hounds herself, but she was by no means hunting-mad, and descriptions of great runs, of the wiles by which hares would baffle hounds, of the rival merits of the big Sussex-bred hound, and the faster, rough-coated harrier, very soon bored her. She preferred to follow the gentlemen at her leisure, and to occupy herself with her own thoughts.

These were largely concerned with her new cousin. She found him baffling. At first sight, he had appeared to her to be stupid: an overgrown gapeseed, slow of speech, and short of wit; either too woodheaded to understand the malicious shafts that had been aimed at him, or too meek to resent them. When she had first taken up the cudgels in his defence, she had yielded to the promptings, not of pity for a humble creature unable to defend himself, but of exasperation. High-spirited herself, and never afraid to answer a challenge, it had vexed her that Hugo should allow Vincent to make a butt of him. Her swift retort had been intended to furnish him with an example; it had won no response from him: he had merely looked surprised; but just as she had decided that he was too blockish to be worth a thought she had seen the twinkle in his eye, and had realized that however meek and yielding his disposition might be he was not lacking in intelligence. Her curiosity roused, she had been covertly studying him ever since. By the time she had conducted him through the picture-gallery she had revised her first opinion of his character, and given free room in her brain to the suspicion that her ox-like cousin had a strong (and possibly reprehensible) sense of humour. Final judgment was suspended, but of one thing there was no doubt: Major Darracott was as kind as he was goodtempered. As she rode behind him and Richmond, catching snatches of their talk, her heart warmed to him. In his place, Vincent, after a very short space of time, would have grown bored with the outpourings of a stripling; he would never have taken the trouble to draw Richmond out, as Hugo was doing. It would be no bad thing, Anthea thought, if Richmond were to transfer his allegiance from Vincent to Hugo. The Corinthian might prove dangerous to a worshipful young cousin; the Major, her instinct told her, could be trusted to do him no harm.

By the time she had arrived at this conclusion the road that zig-zagged through the Marsh on its way to New Romney and Hythe had been reached. She called out laughingly: "Whoa there! How much farther do you mean to go in this direction, you wool-gatherers?"

They halted; and Hugo, turning Rufus about, walked him back a few paces to meet Anthea. He said, smilingly, as she came up to him: "We've been chewing the bacon so hard we forgot you! I'm sorry!"

His simplicity pleased her; she smiled back at him, saying: "Odious creatures! Do you wish to go on, or shall we turn back?"

"I'll do as you bid me," he replied. "Richmond has been telling me about his boat. He wants to show her to me, but he may do that another day."

"No, why?" said Richmond. "I've got her beached only a mile from here. We have plenty of time to take a look at her."

"Perhaps your sister's tired," suggested Hugo.

"Not she! Come along, Anthea!"

"Very well, but you'll swear a solemn oath that you will *only* take a look! I know you!"

"Nonsense! I'll just make sure all's snug. We shan't be late for dinner, if that's what's in your mind. Now, coz, over the ditch and into Sussex!"

He led the way at a brisk canter. The pastures were poor near the coast, with furze bushes growing out of the sand, and the grass giving place to marrams. The dunes were

95

soon reached; the horses scrambled up, the sand sliding away under their hooves; and the sea (as it seemed to Hugo) burst suddenly into view.

Big Rufus, checking at the top of the path between two towering dunes, snorted, and put his ears forward. "Nay then!" the Major admonished him reproachfully. "Pluck up, lad! Tha's seen the sea afore, think on!"

Anthea, already awaiting him on the shore, said, as the bay came slithering down the steep slope: "Ah, Yorkshire-bred, I collect?"

He met her quizzical look with one of his most guileless stares. "Nay, it's this road," he explained confidentially. "He was nobbut a young 'un when I came by him, and a smattering of Spanish was all he knew. He learned his English from John Joseph, sithee!"

"I must make John Joseph's acquaintance," she said. "How useful he must be to you!"

He eyed her speculatively. "Ay, he is and-all!"

"I daresay he has been with you for a great many years?"

"Since I was a lad," he corroborated.

"I thought as much. You'd be at a loss without him, wouldn't you, cousin?"

There was a dancing mockery in her eyes, a lurking smile in his. Before he could reply, Richmond, who had been listening impatiently to this passage, said: "This is the place I told you about, Cousin Hugo. Look, you may see the stakes holding the nets quite plainly! The season's drawing to a close now, but at its height, when they pull in the Keddle nets, the whole of the foreshore is covered with mackerel. But don't let's stand dawdling here! The Gap where I've got the *Seamew* beached is a little way along, towards Camber."

"Lead on, then!" said Hugo. "It seems to me an unhandy place, though. How do you get to your boat?"

"I ride, of course: it's a mile closer than Rye, you know."

"What happens to your horse while you're at sea?" asked Hugo, slightly mystified.

"Oh, I stable him in Camber! There's an inn," said Richmond briefly. "As a matter of fact, it's handier for me to run the *Seamew* into Mackerel Gap during the summer, when I might want to take her out any day, because Jem Hordle lives at Camber. He's my crew! When I have her moored in Rye harbour, someone must take a messege to Jem before I can set sail: she's too big for one man to sail."

He had turned his head, to answer Hugo over his shoulder, but Anthea, looking ahead, said suddenly: "Good God, here comes that tiresome Preventive officer! I never knew anyone so ubiquitous! What on earth is he doing here, I wonder?"

"The Lord only knows!" replied Richmond, watching the approach of the Customs' Riding-officer with disfavour.

"Well, for heaven's sake be civil to the poor man!" she begged. "The last time I encountered him was when I was with Grandpapa, and he was so ill-advised as to accost us. He got so badly snubbed that I'm persuaded he thinks now that we are all of us in league with the free-traders."

"I wish I had been there!" Richmond said, grinning.

"I would have yielded my place to you with pleasure. Grandpapa is never more embarrassing than when he becomes high in the instep.—Good-day to you, Mr. Ottershaw!"

The Riding-officer, a rather tight-lipped young man, with eyes of a hard, shallow grey, pulled his horse up, and raised his hand in a stiff salute. "Good-day, ma'am."

"Whither away, Lieutenant?" enquired Richmond. "Not looking for tubs amongst the sandhills, are you? *I've* never come upon any there!"

The Lieutenant replied in a flat tone that matched his rigid back and unsmiling countenance: "No, sir. I am riding to Lydd. I see you have your boat beached in Mackerel Gap."

"Yes, I'm taking my cousin down to see her. Lieutenant Ottershaw—Major Darracott, of the 95th!"

"Sir!" said the Lieutenant, bringing his hand up again to the salute.

Hugo touched his hat in acknowledgment, and said, with a smile: "Land-guard?" The Lieutenant bowed slightly. "I'm told that's no sinecure on this coast."

"No, sir," said the Lieutenant, with a good deal of emphasis. "But we may see a change presently!"

"Yes, you've established a famous blockade, haven't you?" remarked Richmond. "What with Customs' cruisers, and Revenue cutters you should have the Channel swept clear before the year's out."

"The task of stamping out the illicit trade, sir, would be rendered easier if the rascals who engage in it met with less sympathy from those who live in these counties."

"And if the duties were less extortionate there would be no trade to be stamped out!" retorted Richmond. "It's all the fault of the Government—and a pretty set of leatherheads they are! The remedy is under their noses, but instead of cutting the duties they squander fortunes on Preventive measures!"

"Nay, that's no answer," interposed Hugo. "The law may be daft, but it has to be obeyed." He looked at Ottershaw, and said pleasantly: "I'm from the West Riding myself. They used to say there was plenty of smuggling went on at the ports, but I never knew much about it."

"If it were only the ports!" said Ottershaw bitterly.

"Ay, you've a job on here, with the French coast so near. I wouldn't want it—with the countryside hostile. I know what *that* means."

"Why, were the Spaniards hostile?" asked Richmond. "I thought——"

"They weren't hostile to us, but to the French they were." He nodded at the Riding-officer. "What you need is a Division here, and I doubt if that would answer either. Myself, I'd say it was a job for the navy."

"The Admiralty, sir, is now in control of the coast blockade, and the force patrolling the Channel is under the command of a very able and zealous officer. I am happy to say that running the blockade is becoming every night a more dangerous enterprise."

"Lord, yes!" said Richmond. "It's getting to be dangerous to put out to sea at all! I was overhauled myself last week by one of the sloops. What the commander thought I was doing, God knows! For two pins, I daresay, he'd have fired a shot across my bows. He wanted to know who I was, where I came from, where I was bound for, why I didn't heave-to at once—which I thought I had done, but it turned out that I hadn't obeyed his signal. The only wonder is I wasn't put in irons.

"A strict watch is being kept on all vessels, sir, and it is the duty of those engaged on the coastal guard to pay particular heed to any vessel that appears to be behaving suspiciously. Failing to obey a naval signal would naturally give rise to grave suspicion—though in your case, as I collect the officer soon realized, this was groundless."

Having uttered this severe speech, the Lieutenant took his leave, punctiliously saluting, and then riding off without a word or a smile.

"Did you ever see such a pompous whipstraw?" said Richmond scornfully.

The Major looked meditatively at him. "Happen he's nattered," he drawled. "Seemingly, he doesn't like you, lad."

"I don't think he likes any of us," said Anthea. "That's Grandpapa's fault! He was odiously haughty to the poor man—and you may depend upon it that the Preventives have a pretty shrewd notion that all the brandy we have at the Place is run."

"It is, is it?" said Hugo. "That would account for it, then."

VIII

There was not very much time left for as minute an inspection of Richmond's boat as its owner would have liked. He would certainly have made the whole party late for dinner had he found a kindred spirit in Hugo; but Hugo, although he uttered suitable comments when the vessel's various perfections were pointed out to him, knew little about boats or sailing, and was quite ready to leave the shore as soon as Anthea grew impatient. Richmond was again disappointed. It would have been unreasonable to have expected a man brought up in an inland town to be as knowledgeable as he was himself, but he detected a lack of enthusiasm in his cousin which was hard to understand, until Hugo disclosed that whenever he went to sea he was sick. Richmond, like most excellent sailors, was much inclined to think seasickness largely imaginative: no one need be ill who did not think he would be. He responded with a sympathy as spurious as Hugo's admiration of the *Seamew*'s lines, and tried not to think the worse of him.

Hugo was not deceived. When he set off for home with Anthea, Richmond having left them to visit his boatman in Camber, he shook his head, saying sadly: "I've sunk myself beneath reproach."

Anthea laughed. "Yes, but you may easily make a recover, you know! You have only to unbutton a trifle, and tell him about your adventures in the Peninsula, to win his worship."

"Nay, I'm no figure for worship!"

"You are a soldier, however, and he's army-mad. Do you dislike talking about your campaigns? I wished you would have told us more, but it seemed as if you didn't care to."

"I'd tell him anything he wants to know, but it wouldn't be the right thing for me to do, when your mother and his lordship don't wish it."

"I wondered if that was why you said so little. Grandpapa you need not heed; and Mama—well, I think you shouldn't heed her either! Poor love, she would be quite dismayed if Richmond should succeed in winning Grandpapa over, but she would soon become reconciled, I promise you. She has the happiest disposition! For myself, I believe nothing else will do for Richmond. I wish it were not so, but we have *none* of us the right to push him into some occupation he doesn't care for! You said that yourself, cousin!"

"Ay, so I did, but that's just my opinion. If his lordship asked me for it, I'd give it to him, but he won't, and I've no business to encourage Richmond to go against him, nor to offer advice that's not wanted." He smiled ruefully, and added: "It's bad enough for him to have me foisted on to him without my meddling in what's no concern of mine! A fine trimming he would give me, if I was to be so presumptuous, and small blame to him! From what I can see, Vincent is the only one he might listen to. If the lad wants someone to help him, why doesn't he ask Vincent? Seemingly Vincent's fond of him, so it's likely he'd be willing to try what he could do."

"Nothing is more *un*likely!" replied Anthea. "Vincent, my dear Hugo, is fond of no one but himself. As for thinking that he would run the risk of offending Grandpapa, merely to oblige Richmond, he would stare at such a notion!"

He offered no comment on this, but said, after a short pause: "It queers me to know why Richmond's so set on the army. I should have thought he'd be mad for the navy, with his liking for sailing."

"Yes, so should I," she agreed. "But it has always been the army with him, and if you ask him why he doesn't wish to become a sailor he says that it's a nonsensical question, and that being partial to sailing is not at all the same thing as wishing to embrace the navy as a profession."

"Happen he's right. Though to hear him talk about that boat of his—— What did he call it? a yawl?"

"Yes, or a yacht, though she's too big for a yacht, I think."

"What did he want with a boat that size?" asked Hugo curiously. "I should have thought a little one he could handle himself would have been more to his taste."

"I daresay it would, in some ways, but it wouldn't have been to Grandpapa's taste," she explained. "And I must do him the justice to own that if he gave Richmond a yacht at all he was right to give him one he couldn't handle alone! I don't mean he doesn't know how, but you can never tell when he will take it into his head to run some foolish risk. You see, he *enjoys* doing dangerous things. You can't think what agonies of apprehension we have had to suffer!"

"Ay, no doubt he'd be prime for any lark, and the more risk the better. It would be well if he were put into harness."

"Yes," she agreed. "Yet sometimes I wonder—you see, he has never been in harness, as you call it. Papa died when he was very young, and Grandpapa has always indulged him so much that there has never been anyone to say him nay. He had two tutors, but only the first of them tried to make him obedient. His reign was consequently short, and his successor, speedily perceiving how things were, prudently acquiesced in all Grandpapa's ideas. It was a fortunate circumstance that Richmond liked him well enough not to wish for another in his place, so he was never so naughty with him as he had been with Mr. Crewe. I'm afraid he didn't learn very much, however!"

"Well, I was never bookish myself," Hugo said. "It's a pity the lad wasn't bridled when he was a little chap, but there's no need that I can see for you to be much worried. His lordship may indulge him, but he snaps out his orders to him just as he does to everyone else. I'd say myself that the lad is remarkably docile: there's many that would kick in his shoes."

"Richmond never argues with Grandpapa. He—yes, I suppose he *is* docile. He always does what Grandpapa wishes, and it is perfectly true, what Mama says: that he is sweet-tempered, never gets into a miff, or the sulks! Only—you may *think* he has yielded, but all the time, I believe, he means to have his own way, and, in general, he gets it!"

"Then maybe he'll get his way, over this business of a pair of colours," said Hugo, in a comfortably matter-of-fact voice.

She shook her head. "Not over that. He told me so himself. He said that there was nothing he could do or say to make Grandpapa change his mind. I wish——" She stopped, surprised and a little vexed to find herself talking so unguardedly to one who was a stranger. "But I must not run on! If we don't make haste, cousin, we shall have a peal rung over us for being late for dinner!"

She urged her mare into a canter, and the Major followed suit, saying, however: "Ay, so we shall. What's more, there's no knowing but what I might repeat what you say to me."

She blushed vividly. "Oh——! No, I'm persuaded you would not!"

"You can't tell that. If I was to have a fit of gabbing——"

"I should be much astonished!" she retorted. "You are not precisely *garrulous*, you know!"

"The thing is that I have to mind my tongue," he explained. "It's what you might call a handicap to conversation."

"Ah, to be sure! How stupid of me! But you have been minding it so well that I must be forgiven for not remembering how hard it is for you to speak the King's English!"

"Ay!" he said, with simple pride. "I have and-all, haven't I? I was taking pains, you see."

They had reached one of the gates that led into the park, and she waited for him to open it for her, eyeing him with a little speculation and a good deal of amusement. "Just as you did when you first arrived! You managed beautifully, and for such a long time, too! You deserve the greatest credit, for, I assure you, no one would have guessed you came from Yorkshire until we were halfway through dinner, when you suffered a sudden relapse—and grew rapidly worse."

He heaved a dejected sigh. "Came all-a-bits, didn't I? It's that road with me when I'm scared."

"But you contrived to conceal *that* from us," said Anthea encouragingly. "You didn't look to be in the least scared."

"You don't know how I looked: you never lifted your eyes from your plate!" he retorted.

"Nevertheless I was very well able to see how you looked," she said firmly. "I must tell you that you don't look scared *now*, though I realize, of course, that you must be. You haven't caught sight of a—a flay-boggard, have you?"

"It's not that," he said. "I'm thinking what a hirdum-durdum there'll be if the old gentleman is kept waiting for his dinner. It has me in fair sweat, so just you leave quizzing me, lass, and come through this gate!"

She obeyed, but said: "*What* did you call me?"

"It slipped out!" he said hastily. He shut the gate, and added, with all the air of one extricating himself neatly from a difficult situation: "We always call a cousin lass in Yorkshire—if she's a female. Of course, it would be lad, if I was talking to Richmond."

"That," said Anthea, with severity, "is a shocking bouncer, sir!"

"You're reet: it is!" he said, stricken.

She could not help laughing, but she said, as they fell into a canter again: "Instead of trying to bamboozle me, cousin, you had better consider how to get out of the fix you're in. You cannot talk broad Yorkshire for ever!"

"Nay, it wouldn't be seemly," he agreed. "I'll have to get shut of it, won't I?"

"Exactly so!"

"Happen our Claud will bring the thing off!" he said hopefully.

Since her feelings threatened to overcome her, it was perhaps fortunate that a peremptory hail at that moment interrupted them. Lord Darracott, accompanied by Vincent, was also riding home through the park. He came at a brisk trot, as erect in the saddle as his grandson, and demanded to be told where Anthea and Hugo had been. His manner would not have led the uninitiated to suppose that his humour was benign, but Anthea saw at once that he was pleased; and whatever timidity assailed Hugo at having questions barked at him he seemed well able to conceal. Not all of his answers were satisfactory, since he knew very little about the subjects that were of paramount importance to landowners; but although his ignorance made Lord Darracott impatient, and he asked several questions which were naïve enough to exasperate his irascible progenitor, his lordship was not wholly dissatisfied. Indeed, it was generally felt, when he later announced that something might yet be made of Hugh, that he had begun to look upon his heir with an almost approving eye.

Escaping from his rigorous grandparent, the Major went upstairs to change his dress. Sounds of altercation assailed his ears as he approached his bedchamber; and when he reached it, and stood in the open doorway, he found that it had suffered an invasion.

Two gentlemen of the same calling, but of different cut, were confronting one another in a manner strongly suggestive of tomcats about to join battle. Each wore the habit of a private servant; but whereas the elder of the two, a middle-aged man of stocky build and rigid countenance, was meticulous in his avoidance of any ornament or touch of colour to relieve the sobriety of his raiment, the younger not only sported a pin in his neckcloth, but added an even more daring note to his appearance by wearing a striped waist-coat which only the most indulgent of masters would have tolerated. As the Major paused, in some astonishment, on the threshold, he said, in mincing accents: "Vastly obliging of you, Mr. Crimplesham, I am sure! Quite a condesension indeed!"

"Do not name it, Mr. Polyphant!" begged Crimplesham. "We are all put on this earth to help one another, and knowing as I do what a labour it is to you to get a gloss on to a pair of boots—something that *passes* for a gloss, I should say—it quite went to my heart to think of you wearing yourself out over a task that wouldn't take up more than a couple of minutes of *my* time. It is just a knack, Mr. Polyphant, which some of us have and others don't."

"And very right you were to cultivate it, Mr. Crimplesham! I vow and declare I would have done the same if I'd had only the one talent!" said Polyphant. "For, as I have often and often remarked, an over-polished boot may present a flash appearance, but it *does* draw the eye away from badly got-up linen!"

"As to that, Mr. Polyphant, I'm sure I can't say, but *nothing*, I do promise you, will distract the attention from a spot of iron-mould on a neckcloth!"

"I will have you know, Mr. Crimplesham," said Polyphant, trembling violently, "that it was a spot of soup!"

"Well, Mr. Polyphant, you should know best, and whatever it was no one feels for your mortification more than I do, for, as I said to Mr. Chollacombe, when the matter was being talked of in the Room, if *I* had been so careless as to let Mr. Vincent Darracott go down to dinner wearing a neckcloth that wasn't perfectly fresh I could never have held up my head again."

"When Mr. Claud Darracott left my hands, Mr. Crimplesham, that neckcloth was spotless!" declared Polyphant, pale with fury. "If Mr. Chollacombe says other, which I do not credit, being as only a perjured snake would utter those lying words——"

"What the devil are you doing in my quarters?" demanded the Major, bringing the altercation to an abrupt end.

This deep-voiced interruption was productive of a sudden transformation. The disputants turned quickly towards the door, guilt and dismay in their countenances, but only for an instant was the Major permitted a glimpse of these, or any other, emotions. Before he had advanced one step into the room, all trace of human passion had vanished, and he was confronted by two very correct gentlemen's gentlemen, who received him with calm and dignity, and, after bowing in a manner that paid deference to his quality without diminishing their own consequence, deftly relieved him of his hat, his whip, and his gloves.

"If you will permit me, sir!" said Crimplesham, nipping the hat from the Major's hand. "Having been informed that you have not brought your man with you, I ventured, sir, to give your boots a touch, young Wellow, though a painstaking lad, being but a rustic, and quite ignorant of the requirements of military gentlemen."

"If you will permit *me*, sir!" said Polyphant, possessing himself of the whip and the gloves. "You will pardon the intrusion, sir, I trust, being as my master, Mr. Claud Darracott, desired me to offer my services to you."

"I'm much obliged to you both, but I don't need either of you," said the Major, pleasantly, but in a tone that was unmistakeably dismissive.

There was nothing for his would-be attendants to do but to bow in acceptance of his decree, and leave the room. Crimplesham held the door, and made a polite gesture to his rival to precede him. Before he had time to consider what devilish stratagem might lie beneath the courtesy from one whose position in the hierarchy of the servants' hall was superior to his own, Polyphant had tripped out of the room, bestowing on Crimplesham, as he passed him, a gracious bow, and a smile of such condescension as was calculated to arouse the bitterest passions in his breast.

But herein he showed himself to be of lesser calibre than Crimplesham, who returned his smile with one of quiet triumph, and gently closed the door on his heels.

"Shall I pull off your boots before I go, sir?" he asked, coming back into the centre of the room, and drawing forward a chair for the Major to sit in. "Wellow, I fancy, is laying out Mr. Richmond's evening-dress, and you would hardly wish to make use of the jack."

The Major, having, indeed, no desire to use the jack, submitted, wondering, as he watched Crimplesham take a pair of gloves from his pocket and put them on, what was at the back of this very superior valet's determination to wait on him.

Two circumstances had in fact combined to overcome Crimplesham's regard for his own dignity: he had a score to pay off, and a nephew to establish suitably. Of these, the first operated the more powerfully upon him, but it was only the second which he disclosed to the Major. Whatever might be the differences between himself and his master, no living soul would ever learn from his lips that the smallest disharmony marred their relationship. To complain, as less lofty valet's might, that his employer was exacting, impatient, often impossible to please, and always inconsiderate, would serve only to lower his own consequence. The truth was that he was frequently at silent loggerheads with Vincent, who neither tried nor wished to endear himself to his servants. When a suitable opportunity offered, Crimplesham had every intention of changing masters; but this was not a step to be taken lightly. Vacancies in the ranks of those who ministered to the leaders of high fashion occurred infrequently, and nothing could more fatally damage a valet's reputation than to leave the service of a noted Corinthian for that of a kinder but less worthy master. Vincent was as thankless as he was exacting, but he did Crimplesham great credit, and through him Crimplesham was steadily acquiring the renown he craved. He had not yet attained the ultimate peak, when (he allowed himself to hope) aspirants to fashion would employ every sort of wile to lure him away from his master; but he was already well-known for his unequalled skill with a boot. The fantasies Vincent performed on his necklcoths sprang from his own genius, but the high gloss on his Hessians that excited the envy of his acquaintance he owed to Crimplesham, and not willingly would he part with him. Crimplesham was perfectly well-aware of that, so when any serious affront was offered him he was able to punish Vincent without fear of dismissal. He was not in Vincent's confidence, but he had no doubt at all that it would very much annoy him to learn that his cousin's footwear had received treatment at the hands of his own expert.

"A beautiful pair, sir," he said, tenderly setting them down. "Hoby, of course, as anyone that *knows* a boot can see at a glance. It quite goes to one's heart to see them mishandled. Not that Wellow doesn't do his best, according to his lights, but I fear he will never rise above Bayly's Blacking."

"What do you use?" enquired Hugo. "Champagne? Above my touch!"

"I have a recipe of my own, sir," replied Crimplesham, putting him in his place. "The care of a gentleman's boots is quite an Art, as I don't doubt you are aware." He picked up one of the stretchers and inserted it carefully into the boot. "You are, if I may be permitted to say it, sir, particular as to your boots. It occurs to me—but possibly you have made your arrangements already!"

For a surprised moment Hugo wondered whether Crimplesham was about to offer him his services, but in this he showed his ignorance of the world of ton: had he been the heir to a dukedom Crimplesham would not for an instant have contemplated an engagement so prejudicial to his career. Nothing that even the great Robinson, who had been Mr. Brummell's valet, could do would avail to turn a man of the Major's size and powerful build into a Tulip of Fashion.

"If you haven't yet engaged a valet, sir, I venture to think that I might be able to put my hand on just such a one as might suit you," Crimplesham said. "A nephew of my own, sir, whose name occurs to me because he has previously been employed by a military gentleman like yourself. A conscientious young man, sir, and one for whom I can vouch. Should you desire to interview him I should be happy to arrange it—without, of course, wishing to put myself forward unbecomingly."

"I'll think about it," promised Hugo, adding, as a discreet knock sounded on the door: "Yes, come in!"

The door opened to admit Polyphant, profuse in apologies for intruding upon the Major, but imperfectly concealing the jubilation that filled his soul. Mr. Vincent had rung his bell three times, he explained, with spurious concern, and was now demanding to have Crimplesham sent instantly to his room. "So I ventured to inform him of it, sir, feeling sure you would pardon me. *Very* put-out, Mr. Vincent is, though, of course, I explained to him that Crimplesham was assisting *you* with your toilet, sir!"

"Well, you'd better make haste and go to him," Hugo advised Crimplesham. "You can tell him I kept you."

"It will not be necessary, sir," replied Crimplesham calmly. He rose unhurriedly from his knees, and carried the top-boots over to the wall, setting them down very precisely. "You need not wait, Polyphant," he said, to that gentleman's speechless fury. "Since you have been so kind as to bring me Mr. Vincent's message, perhaps you will inform him that I shall be with him directly." He met Polyphant's goggling stare with a faint, bland smile before nodding dismissal to him, and turning away.

It was almost more than flesh and blood could bear. A severe struggle took place in Polyphant's breast before his more primitive self yielded to the dictates of propriety, and he withdrew again from the room.

Crimplesham then satisfied himself that the Major's evening attire was correctly laid out for him, begged him to give his shoes a final rub with a handkerchief, to remove any possible fingermarks, and bowed himself out in good order.

This episode had more than one repercussion, for not only did it make Vincent late for dinner, which all concerned in it had foreseen, but it very much vexed Claud, and decided Hugo to lose no more time in engaging a valet of his own.

Claud, learning from Polyphant that Crimplesham's services had been preferred, was deeply mortified, and took a pet, for which, as he was all too ready to explain, there was every justification. He had taken on himself the onerous task of giving his cousin a new touch; he had devoted the whole of one afternoon to the problem of how best to achieve a respectable result when confronted by a subject who refused to purchase a new coat; and when, having reached the decision that a more modish style in neckcloths would make a vast improvement to Hugo's appearance, he had gone his length, giving up several of his own neckcloths for Hugo's use, and changing his dress for dinner hours too early, so that Polyphant might be free to instruct Hugo in the art of arranging these, his only reward had been to have his self-sacrificing flung in his face.

"Nay, I never did that!" protested Hugo.

"Flung in my face!" repeated Claud. "I dashed well exhausted myself trying to think how to do the trick. Yes, and I was ready to go through stitch with it, even when I realized I should have to lend you some of my own neckcloths, because yours are all too paltry! I made Polyphant take three of my new muslin ones, so that he could turn you out in a Mathematical tie, for it can't be done with a cloth less than two foot wide, and I know dashed well you've nothing except what serves for that miserable Osbaldeston which you keep on wearing! And even so," he added, somewhat inconsequently, but with immense bitterness, "it couldn't have been anything but a shabby affair, because your shirt-points ain't high enough."

"Happen it's all for the best!" suggested Hugo.

"I'll be damned if it is! And don't say happen when you mean perhaps! Best, indeed! When you've put Polyphant into the hips, sending him off and letting that impudent fellow of Vincent's wait on you!"

That made the Major laugh. "Nay, that's doing it much too brown! You're not going to tell me that that niminy-piminy fribble was pining to waste his talents on me!"

"I should rather think not!" retorted Claud. "Why, it took me the better part of an hour to coax him into it! And the chances are I shouldn't have done it then if I hadn't hit on the idea of telling him it didn't signify, because not even he could make you look elegant! Naturally that put him on his mettle. Well, he saw what a triumph it would be! I'm not surprised he's got a fit of the blue-devils, but I'll tell you this, coz!—I resent it! *You* may think it a chuck-farthing matter, but that's just what it ain't! When Polyphant gets moped there's no saying what he may do. Why, the last time he fell into a fit of dejection he handed me a Joliffe Shallow to wear in the Park! I've a dashed good mind to wash my hands of you!"

"Perhaps you should," agreed Hugo sympathetically. "It's plain I'm a hopeless case. You know, I warned you you couldn't make a silk purse out of a sow's ear."

But a gleam had come into Claud's lack-lustre eye. His frown lifted; he ejaculated: "By Jupiter, I will, though! Well, what I mean is, it *can* be done! Just proved it!"

"Who has?" asked Hugo, all at sea.

"You have! You said *perhaps!* Said it to the manner born, what's more! In the very nick of time, because I don't mind telling you I'd lost heart. Well, if it don't all go to *show!*"

"Ee, I was always a great gowk!" said Hugo, suffering another bad relapse.

When Vincent entered the saloon it was ten minutes past six, and he was greeted, inevitably, by a demand from his grandfather to know what the devil had been keeping him. There was a deep cleft between his brows, but he replied languidly: "Accept my apologies, sir! I regret infinitely that I have been obliged to keep you waiting, but I cannot—I really *cannot!*—be expected to scramble into my clothes, under any circumstances whatsoever. Certainly not to suit my cousin's convenience, which, I must own, is not an object with me."

"I don't know what the devil you're talking about!" said his lordship irritably. "I'll thank you to——"

"Nay, but I do," intervened Hugo guiltily. "I'm reet sorry, lad!"

"Not *reet,* and not *lad!*" begged Claud.

"You have your uses, brother," observed Vincent.

"Now, that will do!" said Matthew sharply. "Let us have one evening free from bickering between you two!"

"You are mistaken, sir: I am profoundly grateful to Claud."

"Profoundly ill-tempered!" said Matthew.

"It's my blame," said Hugo remorsefully. "You can't wonder at his being kickish, for he's been ringing and ringing for his man, and all the time the silly fellow was letting me keep him by me to pull off my boots."

"What, the great Crimplesham?" cried Richmond incredulously. "No! What the deuce can have possessed him?"

"Overweening conceit, I imagine: a desire to impress me with his skill in creating something out of nothing." Vincent's hard, insolent eyes flickered over Hugo's person. "*Vaulting ambition . . . !*"

"You are offensive, Vincent," said Anthea, in a low voice, and with a look of contempt. "If you had as much elegance of mind as of person——!"

"Impossible, dearest cousin!" he retorted.

"It is a severe mortification to reflect how often I am put to the blush by your want of conduct, Vincent," said Lady Aurelia, in a tone of dispassionate censure.

"You are too unkind, Mama! My dear Hugh, pray make the fullest use of Crimplesham! Your need, after all, is greater than mine. How could I be so selfish as to grudge him to you?"

"Nay, I don't know," drawled Hugo amiably.

Lord Darracott put a summary end to the discussion, as Chollacombe came into the room to announce dinner. "I've had enough of this damned folly!" he said. "One of you—you, Richmond!—may write to Lissett for me by tomorrow's post, and tell him to send down a valet for your cousin. Let me hear no more about it!"

"I'm much obliged to you," said Hugo mildly, "but there is no need for our Richmond to trouble himself."

Lord Darracott paused on his way to the door to glare at him. "I say you are to have a valet, and a valet you will have!"

"Oh, I'll do that, sir!" replied Hugo. "It's just that I've a fancy to engage one for myself."

"You should have done so before you came here!"

"I should, of course," Hugo agreed.

"You're a fool!" snapped his lordship. "Where do you imagine you will find one here?"

"Well, I think I'll give Crimplesham's nephew a trial," said Hugo. "That is, if my cousin Vincent's got no objection."

"It is a matter of indifference to me," shrugged Vincent.

It was not, however, a matter of indifference to Claud. Waiting only until his grandfather had walked out of the room behind the ladies of the party, he said indignantly: "Well, if that's not the outside of enough! *Crimplesham's nephew!*"

"Why, what's wrong with him?" enquired Hugo.

"Everything's wrong with him! For one thing, we don't know anything about the fellow, and for another thing, Polyphant won't like it. Yes, and now I come to think of it I'm dashed if *I* like it! Here am I, fagging myself to death with thinking how to bring you up to the knocker, lending you some of my best neckcloths, let alone Polyphant to put you in the way of arranging them, and first you set Polyphant's back up by sending him off, and allowing Crimplesham to help you to dress, and now you've settled to hire a valet without a word to me! Dashed well tipping me a rise!"

"No, no, I never settled it until a minute ago!" protested Hugo. "Now, don't flusk at me! I'm engaging in no flights with you, or anyone, if I can avoid it. Come in to dinner before the old gentleman starts putting himself in a passion!"

They entered the dining-room in time to forestall this disaster. My lord, just about to take his seat at the head of the table, had indeed turned his frowning eyes towards the door, but he made no comment. To Mrs. Darracott's relief, he seemed to be in one of his more mellow moods, which was surprising, since he had undergone the unusual experience of having his will crossed. She had quaked for Hugo, knowing how intolerant of opposition my lord was; she had even shaken her head warningly at him, but the poor young man had not grasped the meaning of her signal, merely smiling at her in a childlike way that showed how far he was from appreciating the perils of his situation. It was a thousand pities, she thought, that he should be so very slow-witted, and so prone to allow his origins to show themselves in his speech, for in all other respects he seemed to be an excellent person. Mrs. Darracott, in fact, was developing a marked kindness for the hapless heir. Her mettlesome daughter might say what she chose in condemnation of what she called his want of spirit, but for her part Mrs. Darracott had no fault to find with an amiable temper and a docile disposition. In her view there were already far too many persons at Darracott Place endowed with spirit. No good had ever yet come from thwarting the head of the house, she thought, remembering with an inward shudder the devastating battles that had been fought when Granville and Rupert had been alive. Nor would any good that she could perceive come from Hugo's joining issue with Vincent. In wit, he was no match for Vincent; and if it came to blows (as she had the liveliest apprehension that it would) the resulting situation, whichever of them won the encounter, would be such as she preferred not to contemplate.

It was surprising that my lord had allowed Hugo to countermand his order to Richmond, for although the matter might have been thought too trivial for argument his autocracy was becoming every day more absolute, and his temper more irritable. Lady Aurelia said that these were signs of senility, but Mrs. Darracott was unable to draw much comfort from this pronouncement. His lordship was certainly eighty years of age, but anyone less senile would have been hard to find. His energy would have shamed many a younger man; and no one, seeing him ride in after a hard day's hunting, would have supposed him to be a day over fifty.

Perhaps it was Hugo's horsemanship which had saved him from having his nose snapped off. My lord had watched him riding home across the park with Anthea, and there was no doubt that he had been agreeably surprised, for he had told Matthew that at all events the fellow had an excellent seat, and (unless he much mistook the matter) good, even hands. Mrs. Darracott recognised this as praise of a high order, and ventured to indulge the hope that Hugo was beginning to insinuate himself into his grandsire's good graces. She saw my lord look at Hugo several times as he sat talking to Anthea; it would have been too much to have said that there was kindness in his expression, but she fancied that there was a certain measure of approval.

Unfortunately this was short-lived. With the withdrawal of the ladies, and the removal of the cloth from the table, Hugo's fortunes fell once more into eclipse. "I can let you have some cognac, if you want it," my lord said to Matthew, who had moved round the table to take his wife's vacated chair. "Tell Chollacombe to put some up for you!"

"Take care, sir!" said Vincent warningly. "I feel reasonably sure that what you are offering my father paid no duty at any port."

"Of course it didn't!" replied his lordship. "Do you take me for a slow-top?"

"Far from it!" smiled Vincent. "You are awake upon every suit, sir. I apprehend, however, that there is an enemy in our midst." He turned his head to look at Hugo, a mocking challenge in his eyes. "You are opposed to the trade, are you not, coz?"

It was Richmond who betrayed discomfiture, not Hugo. Richmond flushed hotly, and kept his eyes lowered, wishing that he had not confided in Vincent; Hugo replied cheerfully: "If you mean the free trade, yes: I am."

Lord Darracott, bending a fierce stare upon him, barked: "Oh, you are, are you? And what the devil do you think you know about it?"

"Not much," Hugo answered.

"Then keep your tongue between your teeth!"

"Oh, I'll do that reet enough!" Hugo said reassuringly. He bestowed an affable smile upon Vincent, and added: "Chance it happens you were thinking I might inform against you——"

"Inform!" exclaimed Matthew. "Good God, what maggot have you got into your head? You don't, I trust, imagine that your grandfather—any of us!—is in league with smugglers?"

"Nay, I'd never think such a thing of you, sir!" said Hugo, shocked.

Matthew's colour mounted a little. "You may be very sure—— My department has nothing to do with the Customs: I daresay I know as little about smuggling as you do!"

"Now, don't you start shamming it!" interrupted his father. "I'm not in league with the free-traders, and I'm not in league with the tidesmen either, but by God, sir, if I had to choose between 'em I'd support the Gentlemen! That's the name they go by here: more worthy of it, too, than these damned Excisemen! A shuffling set! Mawworms, most of 'em, feathering their nests! I can tell you this; for every petty seizure that's made there are a dozen cargoes winked at!"

"Oh, well, no, Father!" said Matthew uneasily. "It's not as bad as that! I don't deny that there have been cases, perhaps—— The pay is bad, and the rewards not large enough, you see, Hugh."

"I thought you knew nothing about it?" jeered his lordship.

"Some things are common knowledge, sir."

"Yes, and everyone knows that at many of the regular ports they bring the cargoes in as openly as you please, and how much is declared and how much is slipped through is just a matter of—oh, arrangement between the Revenue officer and the captains of the vessels!" said Richmond.

"Nay, lad, what difference does that make?" said Hugo. "Dishonesty amongst the Preventives doesn't alter the case."

"Of course it doesn't!" Matthew said, rather shortly. "Free-trading is to be deplored—no one denies that!—but while the duties remain at their present level, particularly on such commodities as tea and tobacco and spirits, the temptation to evade——"

"While duties remain at their present level," interrupted his lordship grimly, "the Board of Customs will get precious little support for its land-guard. Land-guard! Much hope they have of stopping the trade! By God, it puts me out of all patience when I hear that more and more money is being squandered on so-called Prevention! Now we are to have special coastguards, or some such tomfoolery! I'll lay you any odds the rascals will run the goods in under their noses."

"Oh, I should think undoubtedly," agreed Vincent. "I am not personally acquainted with any of the Gentlemen—at least, not to my knowledge—but I have the greatest admiration for persons so full of spunk. I am unhappily aware that they have more pluck than I have."

Richmond laughed; but Matthew said in a displeased voice: "I wish you will not talk in that nonsensical style! A very odd idea of you Hugh will have!"

"Oh, no, do you think so, Papa? *Have* you an odd idea of me, cousin? Or any idea of me?"

Hugo shook his head. "Nay, I'm not judging you," he said gently.

Matthew stared at him for a moment, and then gave a reluctant laugh. "Well, there's for you, Vincent!"

"As you say, sir. Something in the nature of a half-armed stop. Do enlighten my ignorance, cousin! Does your very proper dislike of the Gentlemen arise from—er—an innate respectability, or from some particular cause, connected, perhaps, with the wool-trade?"

"There's no owling done now!" Richmond objected.

"What's owling?" asked Claud, with a flicker of interest.

"Oh, smuggling wool out of the country! But that was when there was a law against exporting wool, and ages ago, wasn't it, Grandpapa? There used to be a great deal of it done all along the coast."

"I wasn't thinking of that," said Hugo. "There were two things smuggled out of the country, and into France, while we were at war with Boney, that did more harm than owling."

"Why, what?" demanded Richmond, frowning.

"Guineas, and information. Did you never hear tell of the guinea boats that were built in Calais? It was before your time, and before mine too, but it was English gold that kept the First Empire above hatches. Boney used to encourage English smugglers. He came by a deal of information that didn't make our task any the easier."

Richmond looked rather daunted; but Lord Darracott said testily: "No doubt! Possibly we too came by information through the same channel. Do you imagine yourself to be the only person here who thinks smuggling a bad thing? We all think it! It sprang from a damned bad cause, and until that's removed it will go on, and so it may for anything I'll do to stop it! Don't you talk to me about the rights and wrongs of it! Bad laws were made to be broken!"

He stopped, his hands clenching on the arms of his chair, for a chuckle had escaped Hugo. Vincent put up his glass, and eyed his cousin through it. "I do trust you mean to share the joke with us?" he said.

"I was just thinking what a pudder we'd be in, if every Jack rag of us set about breaking all the laws we weren't suited with," explained Hugo, broadly grinning. "Donnybrook Fair would be nothing to it, that road!"

IX

Richmond, knowing that his indiscreet confidence to Vincent was largely to blame for Hugo's fall from grace, tried gallantly to intervene; but it was Claud who saved Hugo from annihilation. To everyone's surprise, he suddenly said: "Well, Hugo's right! No question about it!" He looked up to discover that a singularly baleful stare from his grandfather's hard eyes was bent upon him, and blenched a little. "Well, what I mean is," he said manfully, though in a less decided tone, "no harm in buying run brandy, though I shouldn't do it myself, because I don't like brandy above half. The thing is you don't know where it's going to stop. Not the brandy. Running it."

"I collect that *some* meaning lies behind these cryptic utterances," remarked Vincent. "Or am I indulging optimism too far?"

"Much too far!" said Lord Darracott gratingly.

"No, you ain't!" retorted Claud, stung. "What's more, if you'd as much know as you think you have, you wouldn't ask me what I mean, because it's as plain as a pikestaff!"

"Is that to my address?" demanded his lordship ominously.

"No, no, sir! Good God, no!" said Claud hastily. "Talking to my brother! Besides, you *do* know what I mean: you told us all about it yourself! Hawkhurst Gang!"

"The Hawkhurst Gang!" ejaculated his lordship, and fell suddenly into silence.

"Yes, of course no one wants—— But that was *years* ago!" Richmond said. "Nothing like that happens nowadays!"

"It could, though," said Claud. "Never thought about it much before, but now I do come to think about it I'm dashed if I don't think it's bound to happen!"

"Nonsense!" snapped his lordship.

"Well, Father——" said Matthew hesitantly, "one must hope, of course—but I own that there is a great deal of sense in what Claud says." He looked across the table at Hugo, and said: "The Hawkhurst Gang was a pernicious set of ruffians—smugglers, you understand—that held a rule of terror over the countryside when your grandfather was a boy. They committed every sort of atrocity, and were so strong in numbers—how many men was it they were able to muster within an hour, Father?"

"I forget," returned his lordship shortly.

"Five hundred," supplied Richmond. "And they used to have regular battles with rival gangs!"

"They indulged in far worse practices than that, my boy," said Matthew dryly.

"Yes, I know—murdering people, and torturing any they thought had informed against them—horrid! It went on for years, too. I wish I had been alive then!"

"Wish you'd been alive then?" echoed Claud. The height of his collar made it impossible for him to turn his head, so he was obliged to slew his body round in his chair to obtain a view of Richmond, seated beside him. "Well, of all the jingle-brained things to say!"

"No, because only think what sport it would have been! None of us—I don't mean only ourselves, but everyone like us!—seems to have made the least push to get the better of the gang, and of course the Government did nothing but what was paltry, but I'll swear the country people only wanted someone to lead them! Arms, too, but we could have supplied them with arms, and made them into—what do you call those irregular troops that fought in Spain, Hugo?"

"Guerrilleros," Hugo responded, regarding him with a lurking twinkle. "So that's what you'd have enjoyed, is it?"

Richmond blushed, but his eyes still glowed. "Well, you must own it—it would have been something like!"

Hugo shook his head. "Nay, lad, what it would have been like is something you've never seen."

"Oh, you mean burning ricks, and laying the country waste, but *that* wouldn't happen! I daresay the gang would have tried to burn our houses, but we should have kept watch—yes, and laid ambushes, too!"

"Well, if that's your notion of comfort it ain't mine!" said Claud. "Dashed if I don't think you've got windmills in your head!"

Lord Darracott thrust back his chair, and rose. "I wish to hear no more from any of you!" he said harshly. "I don't know which puts me the more out of patience, Hugh's damned morality, or your nonsense, Richmond! Matthew, I want a word with you! The rest of you may join the ladies."

He then stalked out of the room, and Vincent, getting up, said: "That I take to be a command. Shall we go?"

His lordship was not seen again that evening, but shortly before the tea-tray was brought in Matthew joined the drawing-room party, all of whom, with the exception of Vincent, who was absent, were gathered round a card-table. As Matthew entered the room, his wife laid her hand face upwards on the table, to the accompaniment of a chorus of indignant protests, which she acknowledged with a small, triumphant smile.

"Dash it, Mama, that makes it five times you've looed the board!"

"Oh, Aurelia, you *wretch!*"

"Aunt! That was my forlorn hope! You've left me without a feather to fly with!"

"Well! you are all very merry!" said Matthew. "Silver-loo, eh?"

"No, *copper*-loo, sir," replied Richmond. "We were too fly to be hooked in to play silver-loo with my aunt!"

"Aha! so you have been physicking them, have you, my dear?"

"I should rather think she has!" said Claud. "If she don't loo the board outright, you may depend upon it she holds Pam!"

"Except when Hugo has it! Hugo, if you've saved your groats *again*——!"

"No, not this time. My luck is nothing to her ladyship's. Do you always hold such cards, ma'am?"

"I am, in general, very fortunate," said Lady Aurelia. She gathered up her fan and her reticule, and said graciously: "Well, that was very diverting! You would have stared, I daresay, Matthew, had you seen us being so foolish, and cutting such jokes!"

Matthew had never known his wife to cut jokes, or to behave foolishly, but he accepted this without a blink, saying that he was glad she had been so well entertained. He then looked round the room, and asked, with a slight frown, what had become of Vincent. To this she replied with majestic unconcern that she had no notion, but it was to be inferred from the subsequent folding of her lips that she was displeased.

"Begged to be excused," said Claud. "Beneath his touch to play copper-loo."

"Stupid fellow!" Matthew said, his frown deepening.

He did not mention Vincent again until he was alone with Lady Aurelia. He found her ladyship attired in a voluminous dressing-gown, reading a volume of sermons, as was her invariable custom, while her maid brushed her hair. She raised her eyes, and after a moment's dispassionate study of his face, placed a marker in her book, laid it down, and dismissed the maid.

"Well, Matthew?"

He was fidgeting about the room, and at first seemed to have nothing of much moment to say; but after making several desultory remarks, to which she responded with accustomed patience, he disclosed the real purpose of his visit by saying that he wished she would speak to Vincent.

"It would be useless," she replied.

"He is behaving abominably!" Matthew said angrily. "I am vexed to death! If anyone has a right to resent Hugh's presence it is I—though I trust I have too much dignity to conduct myself towards him as Vincent does! It is a fortunate circumstance that Hugh is a muttonhead, and doesn't know when Vincent is cutting at him, but sooner or later Vincent will go too far, and a pretty uproar there will be!"

"I do not consider Hugh a muttonhead, nor do I think he is unaware of Vincent's hostility."

He stared at her. "I cannot imagine why you should say so, ma'am! For my part, he seems to me little better than a dummy! It is always so with these clumsy giants: beef-witted! When I think of the future—that oaf in my father's shoes!—I declare I don't know how to support my spirits! But as for coming the ugly, as Vincent does—— Upon my word, he will be well served if Hugh does take offence! That is——" He paused, looking harassed, but Lady Aurelia said nothing, and after a minute he burst out with the true cause of his anxiety. "I do not conceal from you, Aurelia, that my mind misgives me! There is no saying what might come of it, if a quarrel were to spring up between those two! Vincent is capable of anything: he is my father over again!"

She considered this calmly, before saying: "There is a want of conduct in him that vexes me very much, but I cannot suppose that he would go so far as to force such a quarrel upon his cousin as I collect you have in mind, my dear Matthew."

It was what he had in mind, but he exclaimed instantly: "Good God, I hope not indeed! It does not bear thinking of!" He took a hasty turn about the room. "I wish I knew what to do for the best! I don't understand Vincent: I have frequently been shocked by the reckless things he will do. His temper, too! Then the feeling he seems to have for this place: one would imagine he had always expected to inherit it, but that is absurd! And—— But I will not say all I feel upon this occasion!"

"You are afraid that Vincent may force a duel on his cousin," she said relentlessly. "I cannot think it possible. If he did so, it could only be with the intention of putting a period to Hugh's life, and that, my dear sir, would be such an infamous act as I am persuaded no son of ours would be capable of performing."

"No, no, of course not!" he said. "Good God, I should hope—Aurelia, my father told me this evening that he wishes Vincent to remain here for a week or two! I had had no notion that anything like that was in the air, and I cannot like it. I ventured to suggest to my father that it would be wiser to let Vincent go, but you know what he is! He will never listen to one word of advice. Indeed, he is becoming so—— However, I do not mean to discuss *that!* But I don't deny that I am excessively uneasy, and could almost wish it were not necessary for me to be in London next week. However little *intention* Vincent may have of bringing things to a—a fatal conclusion, I cannot rid myself of the apprehension that a quarrel might flare up; and I do not scruple to tell *you*, ma'am, that I do not feel that any dependence may be placed on my father's nipping anything of that nature in the bud. In fact, the suspicion flashed across my mind—— But that's nonsense, of course! You will not regard it, I beg!"

"Certainly not," she replied. "I believe you are overanxious, and although I place no more reliance than you do upon your father's behaving as he ought I am strongly of the opinion that we may place every reliance on Major Hugh Darracott's good sense. Of the amiability of his disposition even you can have no doubt. I have observed him narrowly, and have been agreeably surprised. He is a man of principle; his temper is equable; his manners perfectly gentlemanlike and unaffected. The only fault I perceive in him is a tendency to levity, but——"

"*Levity?*" broke in Matthew.

"If it escaped your notice, my dear sir, that his atrocious brogue overcame him only when it had been made deplorably plain to him that his family held him in contempt, I can only say that it did not escape mine."

"You mean to tell me—— No, I don't believe it! He slips into it when he forgets to guard his tongue! If he *is* shamming it—— Well, upon my word, what infernal impudence!"

"I am no friend to levity, but I cannot but acknowledge that in taking his family's hostility in good part he showed himself to be a man of considerable forbearance," said her ladyship repressively.

He coloured, and looked discomfited. Lady Aurelia satisfied that her words had gone home, continued in precisely the same composed tone: "As to Vincent, though I do not anticipate any such issue as you have suggested, I daresay it would be wiser for me to remain at Darracott Place, instead of returning with you to Mount Street."

His expression changed to one of relief. "Should you dislike it, ma'am? I own, *I* should be easier in my mind, for although you may say Vincent does not listen to you I am tolerably certain that while you are at hand he will take care to keep within bounds. But I don't mean to press you:

it is not an object with my father to make his guests comfortable!"

"My dear sir, I hope my mind is stronger than you believe it to be! I do not suffer from an excess of sensibility. I have never allowed your father's odd humours to sink my spirits, and it would be a strange thing if I did so now, after nearly thirty years. I am perfectly willing to remain, particularly so because Elvira has twice expressed her wish that I should stay to support her through this very awkward time."

"Ay, no doubt she must be dreading your departure! I hadn't thought of that, but I promise you I pity her with all my heart! She is thrown into high fidgets by no more than a rough word from my father. If she could school herself to be a little less in alt she would go on better with him, but her understanding I have never thought superior. I only wish you may not find it a bore to be continually with her!"

"You may be easy on that head. We have the habit of easy intercourse, and if she has little force of mind she is always so good-natured and attentive that you need entertain no fears that I shall not be comfortable."

With these words, Lady Aurelia picked up her book again, and Matthew, interpreting this as a sign that the audience was at an end, imprinted a salute upon her cheek, and took himself off to his own room.

Hugo, meanwhile, had been strolling up and down the terrace, and enjoying the solace of one of his forbidden cigars. His countenance was thoughtful; and when he presently sat down on the parapet there was the hint of a crease between his brows. He remained there for some little time, staring abstractedly before him; but presently some small sound caught his attention, and he turned his head to look searchingly across the shadowed garden below. The moonlight was faint, obscured by broken clouds, but he was able to discern a vague figure striding across the lawn towards the house. He remained motionless, and in another minute or two recognized Vincent. It was not until Vincent had reached the foot of the shallow stone steps that he perceived his cousin. He paused, looking up, and said: "Ah! Ajax! Taking the air, or is it possible you were waiting for me?"

"Just blowing a cloud," replied Hugo, lifting his hand to show the butt of the cigar between his fingers.

"A filthy habit—if you don't object to my saying so?"

"Nay, why should I?"

Vincent mounted the steps leisurely. "Who am I to instruct you? I daresay you know why you should *not*, at all events."

"Oh, yes, I know that!" Hugo said serenely.

"Your compliance is only equalled by your amiability—and I find both insupportable."

"There's no need to tell me that. I'm sorry for it, but happen you'd find me insupportable whatever I did."

"Almost undoubtedly. I find virtue a dead bore. I have very little myself. I don't know how it is, but the virtuous are invariably dull, which I can't bring myself to pardon."

Hugo's deep chuckle sounded. "Nay then! You're trying to hoax me! To think of you calling me virtuous! You'll have me blushing like a lass!" He pitched the butt of his cigar into one of the flowerbeds below. When he turned again towards Vincent he spoke in a different tone, and with less than his usual drawl. "Sithee, Vincent! Squaring with me won't help either of us. I'd be very well suited if you were in my shoes, but there's no way of bringing that about, and naught for either of us to do but make the best of it."

"Yes, you wrote as much to my grandfather, didn't you?" Vincent said. "A mistake! It didn't turn him up sweet at all. He's a hard man to gammon, and that, you know, was doing it much too brown."

Hugo heaved a despairing sigh. "You're as daft as he is! I can understand that you should think it a grand thing to inherit all this, for you've known it your life long, and I don't doubt it's home to you. It's not home to me, and why any of you should have got it stuck in your heads that I'd want to be saddled with a place that's falling to ruin I'll be damned if I know!"

"To *you*, I feel sure, it must seem a sad, rubbishing place—almost a hovel, in fact!"

"Nay, I didn't mean to offend you! It's a fine old house, but it's like everything else I've seen: there's been no brass spent on it for many a day, and it'll take a mountain of brass to set it to rights. As for the land, I've a notion there's something more than brass needed, and that's better management. I can see I'll have a hard job on, and one to which I wasn't bred. Eh, it's more like a mill-stone tied round my neck than a honey-fall!"

"And the title, of course, means nothing to you!"

"I'd as lief be without it," admitted Hugo.

122

"Humdudgeon! Are you really such a Jack Adams as to think I'll swallow that?"

"Suit yourself!" Hugo answered. "If that's the way it is with you, there's no good talking."

"None whatsoever—for you would certainly be unable to understand what it means to be Darracott of Darracott Place! You do not appear to me even to understand that I dislike you!"

"Oh, I understand that!" Hugo said, with another chuckle. "If there were any cliffs here you'd be ettling to push me over the edge, wouldn't you?"

"The temptation would be almost irresistible, but I hardly think I should go to those lengths. Let us say that if you tottered on the verge I shouldn't pull you back from it!" Vincent retorted.

"It 'ud be a daft thing for you to do, think on," said Hugo reflectively. "You'd go over with me, choose how!"

X

Major Darracott spent the next week acquainting himself as best he might with his future inheritance. He received no assistance and very little encouragement from his grandfather, his tentative suggestion that my lord enlighten his ignorance being met with a crushing snub. My lord had not enjoyed the novel experience of being left without a word to say, nor was he accustomed to meet with disagreement in the bosom of his family. His sons and his grandsons, and even his spirited granddaughter, had learnt the wisdom of refraining from argument, in general receiving his more dogmatic utterances in silence, and never forcing him into the position of being obliged to defend the indefensible. Such divergent opinions as they might have held remained unuttered, under which arrangement they were at liberty, for anything his lordship cared, to differ from him as much as they chose. It had come, therefore, as a shock to him when Hugo (an upstart, as near to being misbegotten as made no odds), instead of keeping to himself his shabby-genteel notions of morality had not only owned to them without hesitation when challenged, but had had the effrontery to maintain them in the teeth of his grandfather's disapprobation. That he had taken little part in the resultant argument in no way alleviated my lord's anger. What he had said had served to compel Matthew, uneasily conscious of his office, to support him. My lord was indifferent to Claud's revolt, but Matthew's defection had infuriated him. Forgetting that it was not Hugo, but Vincent, who had tossed the bone of dissension into their midst, he saw Hugo as an impudent make-bait, too full of north-country bumptiousness to realize that he had nothing to do but to hold his peace amongst the relatives who had magnanimously admitted him to a place within their ranks. Far from conducting himself with becoming humility he had, in his maddeningly simple way, exposed the weakness of his grandfather's case; and, to crown his iniquity, he had recognized and laughed at the absurdity of an aphorism hastily uttered as a clincher to a losing argument.

The hostility which the Major's style in the saddle had done something to diminish flamed up again; and when he expressed a desire to be instructed in the extent and management of the estates he was seen as an encroaching mushroom, a burr, and an irreclaimable commoner, and was informed that his cousin Anthea would tell him as much as it was needful for him to know. My lord added that if he thought he would be allowed to put a finger in a pie not yet his own he would soon learn his mistake.

It had not been Anthea's intention to gratify her grandsire by devoting any appreciable part of her time to the entertainment or the education of Major Darracott. She had not disliked her one expedition in his company: indeed, she had enjoyed it, for she had discovered him to be likeable and amusing. But she had detected in him a certain audacity which set her on her guard, and made her determined to keep him (in a perfectly friendly way) at arm's length. Had he tried to advance himself in her good graces, or to coax her to ride with him, she would have hardened her heart, and abandoned him to Claud; but the Major committed neither of these imprudences. When Mrs. Darracott, her earlier scruples forgotten, suggested that Anthea should take him to see some view, or picturesque village, he said that he did not wish to be a nuisance to his cousin, who must not feel it to be her duty to entertain him when, no doubt, she had many more important tasks on hand.

Unlike her mother, who thought the Major's meekness very touching, Anthea regarding him with a good deal of suspicion. She could detect nothing but humble deference in his smile, but she was finding it increasingly difficult to believe that he was either meek or biddable. His countenance was certainly goodhumoured, and his blue eyes guileless, but about his firm-lipped mouth and decided chin there was not a trace of weakness or of humility; and although he was unassertive, making no attempt to force his way into the family circle, or to take an uninvited part in any conversation, this modesty carried with it very little suggestion of bashfulness. It had more than once occurred to Anthea that he had a good deal of quiet assurance. He could scarcely be unaware of the hostility with which he was regarded by at least three members of the household; a shy man, she thought, must have been flustered by the knowledge that his every word and movement came under critical survey; but she had yet to see him betray any sign of nervousness. It was significant, too, that the servants, usually quick to take their tone from their betters, treated him with respect, and served him with every appearance of willingness. It might have been expected that he should have the habit of command, but Anthea could not discover that he did command: he merely requested.

"The servants all like him," Mrs. Darracott told her. "Mrs. Flitwick was saying so to me only this morning, and I am not at all surprised, for I am sure everyone must like him—except, of course, your grandfather and Vincent, which doesn't signify, because they never like anyone! He is the kindest creature!"

"I can see that you like him, at all events, Mama!"

"Yes, my love, I do like him. I should be a positive monster if I didn't, for I don't think I ever met anyone so considerate. Only think of his mending the casement in my bedchamber, just because I told him how disobliging and cross old Rudge is, saying he will do it when he has time to spare, and never making the least push to do anything except what Glossop, or your grandfather, orders him to do!"

"If he borrowed Rudge's tools, there is *one* servant who doesn't like him!"

"Nothing of the sort!" said Mrs. Darracott. "I own, I was very much afraid Rudge would take a pet, but—would you believe it, love?—he came up to my room while Hugo was at work on the window, and actually apologized to me! He wanted to finish the job, but Hugo wouldn't have it, so, to my amazement, he stayed to help Hugo, telling him all the time what he *ought* to do, and shaking his head over it, but not in the least disagreeably! And he asked me if there was anything else that needed attention, so I mentioned the loose board in your room, and he has promised he will nail it down this very afternoon! Say what you will, Anthea, he never would have done so for *me*: he didn't want Hugo to think he was disobliging, which, of course, he *is!*" She looked a little anxiously at her daughter, and ventured to say: "I wish you will take pity on him, my dear! Poor boy, he must feel quite wretched, with your grandfather treating him so unkindly, and Matthew very little better, while as for Vincent— Well, I only hope he comes by his deserts!"

So Anthea took pity on her cousin. He did not look at all wretched, although he admitted that he was in disgrace with his grandfather, and, to some extent, he thought, with his uncle.

"Yes, we heard all about it," she said. "You put my uncle in a fix, you know, for while, on the one hand, he did not wish to vex Grandpapa, on the other, he felt himself to be obliged, as a member of the Government, to condemn the free-traders. My aunt, however, considers that you feel just as you ought, and honours you for it!"

"Now, if you're going to roast me——!"

"Nothing of the sort! She says you are pretty-behaved, and don't want for sense. High praise, I assure you!"

"She frightens me to death," he confided.

She turned her head, and surveyed him thoughtfully. "Will you think me very uncivil if I say that I don't believe you, cousin?"

"Ay, I shall and-all!" he replied promptly.

Her eyes laughed, but she said: "Then I will merely say that you are what Richmond calls a complete hand. Does Vincent frighten you too?"

"He has me all of a twitter."

"I shouldn't wonder at it if he thinks so!" she said, with some tartness. "I wish you will stop shamming it, and tell me how much longer you mean to endure his insolence!"

"Nay, it doesn't worry me," he said, smiling.

"It should! It puts me in such a rage when he cuts at you, and you do *nothing* to stop him!"

"Now, why?"

"Because he would be all the better for a sharp set-down!"

"Happen he'll get one, but it won't be from me."

She rode on in silence for a few moments, but presently said: "It—it is so *spiritless* of you!"

"I know it is," he said, with a mournful shake of his head. "Downright malten-hearted, that's me!"

"Yes, but I don't think you are! Well, how could you be? You are a soldier!"

"Ay, and a terrible time I had of it, keeping in the rear," he said failling into reminiscent vein. "When I wasn't being a Belem-ranger—that's what we—*they!*—used to call the fellows who were always going off to hospital in Lisbon, you know——"

"No doubt that's how you became a Major!" she interrupted.

"No, you're out there: I had my majority by purchase, of course. Mind you, if it hadn't been for the losses we suffered at Waterloo——"

"If you mean to continue in this style," she exclaimed, reining in her mare, "I shall go home immediately!"

"I was being modest," he explained. "It wouldn't become me to tell you what a devil of a fellow I was. However, since I see you've guessed it, I'll own that Hector was nothing to me. You'd have thought I was one of the Death or Glory boys!"

"Well, what I think now is that you are the most shameless prevaricator I ever encountered!" retorted Anthea.

"Eh, there's no pleasing you!" he said, heaving a despondent sigh. "Now I've perjured myself to no purpose at all!"

"You are perfectly ridiculous!" she told him, choking on a laugh. "It would please me—though what you do is quite your own affair, and no concern of mine!—to see Vincent taken at fault for once in his life!"

He rubbed his nose meditatively. "Ay, I can see it would, and that's where the water sticks, lass! Now, just you tell me what you'd have me do!"

"Good heavens, make it plain to him you'll stand no more of it!"

"And how will I do that?"

"You have a tongue in your head! If I were in your shoes, I'd give as good as I got!"

He smiled. "I don't doubt you would. But, setting aside I've no taste for fratching, if that didn't answer I'd be in a bit of a hobble, wouldn't I?" She looked frowningly at him, and his smile broadened. "Ay, I know what's in your head. I'd look champion, coming to handyblows with a man two or three stone lighter than I am, and a good three inches shorter!"

"I hadn't thought of that," she admitted. "What a dead bore it must be to you, being so very large!"

"Ay, it's a reet handicap," he agreed gravely. "If I'd been a reasonable size I could have kicked up all sorts of riot and rumpus. I daresay I'd have been a prime favourite with everyone by this time."

She laughed. "Well, I must own I, at least, shouldn't blame you if you knocked Vincent down! I see, of course, that you won't do it—unless, perhaps, he hit you first? I believe he is a very good boxer."

He grinned at the hopeful note in her voice. "Nay, why should he? If you're thinking I might provoke him to it, I'm sorry to disoblige you, but my name's Darracott—not Captain Hackum!"

"No, no, of course I wouldn't wish you to do that! In fact, I trust you won't, because there's no saying, with Vincent—— Well, never mind! Let us go on, shall we?"

"Where are you taking me?" he asked, trotting beside her down the narrow lane.

"Into Sussex. We extend for some way across the county border. I'll make you known to one or two of Grandpapa's tenants. You may depend upon it they are all agog to see you! They won't show it, however, so don't be dismayed if they seem unfriendly. Sussex people are suspicious of *foreigners!* Your father was well liked, though: that will stand you in good stead! My Uncle Granville was not, and nor is Grandpapa—for reasons that will soon become apparent to you if they are not so already."

It had been apparent to the Major for several days that his grandfather was a bad landlord; by the time they turned their horses' heads homewards, after a tour that had included visits to two tenant-farmers of long-standing, and a brief survey of two farms leased on short tenancies, he had a more exact knowledge of the condition of his inheritance.

Wondering what he made of it (for his countenance was inscrutable), Anthea said, breaking a long silence: "Well?"

He glanced down at her, and smiled. "I'm sorry: I was in the clouds!"

"What were you thinking, Hugo?"

"I was wishing I knew more about husbandry—and wondering what the deuce I'm going to do."

"I doubt if you'll be permitted to do anything," she said frankly. "Unless you can contrive to bring Grandpapa round your thumb, and I never knew anyone do that except Richmond. Besides, what could you do?"

"It wouldn't be a question of bringing him round my thumb, though the Lord knows it would be a ticklish business to do the thing without setting up his back. I'd be loth to do that, for he's an old man, and my grandfather besides."

"Do you wish to manage the estates?" she asked, in a little perplexity. "I thought—something you said made me think you didn't mean to remain here while Grandpapa is alive."

"I don't know what I mean to do," he said. "I didn't think to stay, but there's work crying out to be done here, and though I'm not the man to do it I can't hoax myself into believing that it isn't a matter of duty to make a push to set things to rights."

"Hugo," she said earnestly, "to set things to rights will mean putting money into the land instead of wringing the last groat out of it, and that you'll never persuade Grandpapa to do! Do, pray, talk to Glossop before you do anything rash!"

"Is he your steward? I can't talk to him behind my grandfather's back, but I shan't do anything rash, I promise you. It's too soon for me to do aught but feel my way, at any hand." He saw that she was looking rather anxious, and smiled reassuringly down at her. "Nay, lass, I'm not one to go full-fling at anything! If I *don't* feel my way, I'll be off!"

"But I thought—that is, Grandpapa told us that you had sold out? How will you do, if you don't remain here?"

"I'll do well-enough," he replied, with a chuckle. "I've some brass of my own. My grandfather Bray left me what he had—his savings, you might call it. That's what his lordship calls it, at all events."

Her brow cleared. "Oh, in that case——! I didn't know, and was afraid you might, having sold out, be dependent upon Grandpapa. Hugo, take my advice, and don't let yourself be bullied into staying at the Place! I've lived here all my life, and I've seen what it *does* to people! There's never any peace, there never was! Grandpapa quarrels with everyone: I think he enjoys it. Not only with the family, you understand, but with *everyone!* That's why you'll rarely see a guest at the Place, and never a morning visitor. He is not on terms even with the Vicar! When you have lived with us for a little longer, you'll understand. We are all so fretted and rubbed that our tempers will be as bad as Grandpapa's in the end: I know mine will! Not Mama's, but it is worse for her, because she has more sensibility than I have, poor love, and is very nervous. But if you had known the family when my father and my uncle Granville were alive——! I assure you, you would take care not take up residence under the same roof as Grandpapa, for even *your* temper would crack under the strain!"

He smiled, but said: "I daresay it would. I haven't been here many days yet, but I know already that I couldn't live with his lordship, and I don't mean to try. And that puts me in mind of something! Who lives in the Dower House?"

"No one, at present. No one but Spurstow, that is. He was Great-aunt Matty's butler, and when she died Grandpapa said he might remain at the Dower House, to look after it until it should be inhabited again."

"And who was Great-aunt Matty?" he enquired.

"Oh, she was Grandpapa's sister! When Grandpapa was married, she and our *great*-grandmother removed to the Dower House. Great-grandmother died before I was born, and Aunt Matty continued there until *she* died—oh, nearly two years ago now! She was very eccentric, and she looked exactly like a witch, and was used to mutter to herself. Richmond and I were terrified of her, when we were children, but fortunately she hated to be visited, so that it was only very occasionally that we were obliged to go to the Dower House. She always sat in one room, and kept the blinds drawn in the others, and had *dozens* of the most odious cats. It used to be one of Richmond's worst nightmares, that he was shut up in that dark house, with cats' eyes staring at him wherever he looked, and poor Jane Darracott's ghost creeping up behind him!"

"I'd forgotten the ghost. Is that why the house stands empty?"

"Well, yes, in a way it is. My Uncle Granville wished to live there, after Aunt Matty died, but Aunt Anne said that she would as lief do anything in the world as set foot inside the house. She's very fanciful, suffers nervous disorders—distempered freaks, Grandpapa calls them! But I believe the real cause of the scheme's coming to nothing was that the house was found to be in shocking repair, and, of course, Grandpapa refused to waste any money on it. When Grandpapa practises economy it is always at the expense of his family, never his own! Are you thinking that you might live there? I warn you, it is rat-ridden, ghost-ridden, and damp into the bargain! Spurstow says the roof leaks in several places."

"It sounds champion!" he remarked. "Don't tell me it hasn't dry rots as well, for I wouldn't believe you!"

"Very likely, I should think." She threw him a mischievous glance. "And to add to your comfort, there is said to be an underground passage, leading from the cellars to the Place, in which (could you but find it) you would discover the bones of several persons who were so unfortunate as to have fallen out with one—or possibly more—of our ancestors."

"That adds a cosy touch," he agreed. "Ralph II?"

"No, we were obliged to abandon that notion," she said regretfully. "It seems to be established that the passage was walled up long before his time. However, the son of the Darracott who came over with the Conqueror we understand to have been a *shockingly* loose screw, so we are much inclined to think it was he who hid the bodies of his enemies in it."

"Ay, a passage would be just the place anyone would choose," he nodded. "And, if you've done trying to make an April-gowk out of me, I'd be glad to know why you're so set on holding me off from the house?"

She laughed. "Oh, I'm not! I merely thought it right to warn you!"

"Eh, that was kind!" he said appreciatively. "Of course, I'd be wasting my time if I tried to find the passage, wouldn't I?"

"Well, we wasted ours, when we were children," she admitted, "but if you mean to say that you don't believe there is a passage I shall take it in very bad part. Its existence is one of our more cherished traditions! There's a reference to it somewhere in our archives. Unfortunately, no hint of its precise locality is vouchsafed, and when Oliver ventured to suggest to Grandpapa that we might discover it with the aid of a pickaxe or two, the notion, from some cause or another, found no favour with him! He did own that in ancient times there had been a passage, but although we—that is, Oliver, and Caro, and Eliza, and Vincent, and Claud, and I—thought it could be put to *excellent* use, he quite failed to enter into our sentiments!"

"I'm not so sure that I blame him!"

She gurgled. "I wish you might have seen his face when Claud and I said that it was his duty to find the bones of our murdered foes, and give them decent burial! You see, we were the youngest, and we became wholly confused by the tales the others made up! I think the bones were Oliver's contribution to the legend, and to this day I'm not perfectly sure how much belongs to the original legend, and how much was added by the boys. I must say I wish you may persuade Grandpapa to let you have the Dower House (although I fear you won't!), so that you might do a little excavation, and confirm our ancient tradition! I'll take you to see it tomorrow, if you would like it."

The Dower House was situated only some four hundred yards to the north-east of Darracott Place, from which it was hidden by a belt of trees, and a tangle of overgrown bushes. A carriage-drive gave access to it from a narrow lane, but Anthea took the Major there by way of a foot-path through the wood, and entered the garden at the side of the house. A ditch surmounted by a black-thorn hedge enclosed the grounds, which seemed, at first glance, to consist almost wholly of a shrubbery run riot. Holding open a wicket-gate, which squeaked on its rusty hinges, Hugo glanced round, remarking that it looked a likely place for a ghost. Anthea, disentangling the fringe of her shawl from the encroaching hedge, agreed to this, and at once took him to see what she called the fatal window. It was at the back of the house, and faced south-east, on to what Hugo took to be a wilderness but which was, she assured him, a delightful pleasure-garden. "If you look closely, you will see that there are several rose-beds, and a sun-dial," she said severely. "The lawn, perhaps, needs mowing."

"It does, doesn't it?" said Hugo, eyeing the rank grass with disfavour. "Myself, I'd have it ploughed up and re-sown, but I daresay it's in keeping with the rest as it is."

"Well, I warned you how it would be. *That* is the window. The room was originally the best bedchamber, but after the accident—if it wasn't a murder—none of the subsequent tenants cared to sleep in it, so it was reserved for the accommodation of guests."

"Ay, it would be. It must go to his lordship's heart to think he hasn't a haunted room at the Place: I don't doubt I'd have found myself in it if there had been one. Is this where the lady walks?"

"Oh, she walks all round the house, and in it, too, according to some! Very few of Aunt Matty's servants ever stayed for long with her, but I never heard that they *saw* the ghost. They used to complain that they heard strange noises, but I fancy they wouldn't have made anything of that if they hadn't been warned by the villagers. None of *them* would dream of coming near the house after dark, of course."

She led the way, as she spoke, towards the front of the house. Here the trees grew so close to the building that a branch of one giant elm almost brushed the roof, seeing which, Hugo said decidedly: "I'd have that down for a start. Eh, but it's a fine old house!"

"I suppose it is," Anthea replied, with a certain lack of enthusiasm. "It is older than the Place, I know, and said to be a good example of that style of ancient stone-building, but it has always seemed to me a dreadfully gloomy house."

"If all that ivy were stripped away, and the bushes uprooted, and some of the trees felled, it wouldn't be gloomy. I allow there's no prospect on this side, but there should be as good a one, or better, as there is from the Place, on the garden side, once a clearance was made."

"Is that what you would do?"

He nodded. "I would, if I meant to live here. I've a strong notion that we have only to let in some light and air to lay that ghost of yours."

"But this is iconoclasm!" she exclaimed. "Lay the Darracott spectre? For shame! Have you no respect for tradition?"

He looked quizzically down at her. "Nay, that's a matter of up-bringing," he said. "I wasn't reared to respect Darracott tradition. Come to think of it, I doubt if I'd respect a ghost that scared the servants out of my house, whatever way I'd been reared. Can we go inside?"

"Certainly—unless Spurstow has gone out, and left the doors locked," she responded. "If he is in, he won't accord us a very warm welcome, but don't be dismayed! He has grown to be as eccentric as ever Aunt Matty was, and regards all visitors in the light of hostile invaders, but he won't repel us with violence! He has lived for thirty years here, so you can't wonder at it that he should be a trifle crusty."

"So he's not afraid of the ghost?"

"Oh, no! He holds poor Jane in great contempt—like you!"

"Do *you* believe she haunts the place?" Hugo asked, walking beside her up the weed-grown drive towards the house.

She hesitated. "N-no. At least—I don't believe it at this moment, in broad sunlight, but—no, I shouldn't care to come here at night! It isn't only the villagers who have seen things: Richmond has, too."

"Has he, indeed? What did he see?"

"A female form. He couldn't imagine who it was at first. He says he went towards her, and suddenly she vanished. Ugh!"

"Well, if that's all she does she's welcome to haunt the place," said the Major prosaically.

They trod up two worn stone steps into the flagged porch; but as Anthea grasped the rusted iron bell-pull the door was opened by a grizzled man in a frieze coat. He looked the visitors over morosely, bade Anthea a grudging good-morning, and said that he had seen her coming up the drive, and supposed that she must be wanting something.

"Yes, I want to show the house to Major Darracott," she replied cheerfully.

"If you'd have sent me word, Miss Anthea, you were coming here this day-morning I'd have had it ready to be shown," said Spurstow, with considerable severity. "The rooms are all shut up, as well you know. You'll have to bide while I get my keys."

With these quelling words, he admitted them into the hall, and left them there while he went off, grumbling under his breath, to his own quarters. When he presently returned he found that the Major, having opened the shutters covering the windows at the back of the hall, was standing in rapt contemplation of the Cromwellian staircase, while Miss Darracott, holding her flounced skirt gathered in one hand, looked with a wry face at the dusty floor.

"It's not my fault, miss," said Spurstow, forestalling criticism. "You shouldn't ought to have come without you gave me warning."

"I can see I shouldn't!" she retorted. "But I have come, and I mean to take Major Darracott over the house, even though it be *knee*-deep in dust, so you may as well make up your mind to it."

This forthright speech appeared rather to please than to exacerbate the retainer. He gave a sour smile, and, with only a passing reference to the troublesome characteristics displayed by Miss Darracott in childhood, unlocked the door leading into the dining-parlour, and opened the shutters.

It would not have surprised Anthea if the Major's wish to inspect the Dower House had deserted him long before their tour of the ground-floor had been completed. Dirty panes and encroaching ivy darkened the rooms; there were several patches of damp on the walls; most of the ceilings were ominously blackened above the old-fashioned fireplaces; every room smelled of must; and a final touch of melancholy was added by the furniture, which had been huddled together in the middle of each room, and covered with newspapers, old sheets, and scraps of sackcloth.

"I warned you what it would be like!" she told Hugo.

"Ay, it's in bad repair, but it could be put to rights," he answered.

"That could be done, but it will always be a dark, gloomy house."

"Nay, if the ivy were stripped from it, and all those bushes cleared away, you'd never recognize it," he said. "The best of the rooms face to the south-east, but the sun's shut out by trees and shrubs."

"Miss Matty, sir," observed Spurstow, in hostile accents, "wouldn't have the sun shining in, and fading the carpets."

"Maybe she wouldn't, but she wasn't reared on the edge of the moors," returned Hugo. "I'm not used to be shut in: I want room to breathe, and never mind the carpets!"

A disapproving sniff was the only answer vouchsafed to this. Spurstow then conducted the unwelcome visitors to the upper floor, and volunteered no further remark until Anthea, showing Hugo Jane Darracott's bedchamber, asked whether her ghost had been seen there. He said repressively that he took no account of ghosts.

"The Major takes no account of them either," said Anthea. "He thinks I'm telling him a Banbury story, but the house *is* haunted, isn't it?"

"Folks say so," Spurstow replied. "I never did, miss. I'm not one to talk, and I don't scare easy. I've lived here thirty years and more, and it's done me no harm. I don't take any notice."

Anthea gave an involuntary shiver, but the Major said: "Any notice of what?"

Spurstow looked at him under his brows. "Aught I hear," he said.

"What *do* you hear?" enquired Anthea.

"Nothing, miss. It doesn't worry me," he said. "Time was when I'd get up out of my bed, thinking there was someone got into the house, but it was all foolishness: you can search from the cellars to the attics, but you'll see naught. Leastways, I never did. Its only footsteps, when all's said."

"Oh!" said Anthea rather faintly. "Only footsteps!"

"Now, you don't want to listen to the silly stories folks tell, Miss Anthea!" said Spurstow roughly. "The rest's naught but the wind in the trees, or an owl, maybe. There are nights when it sounds like someone was moaning outside

135

here pitiful, but lor' bless you, miss, the wind can make queer noises! I don't heed it!"

Repressing an impulse to glance over her shoulder, Anthea moved rather closer to the Major, unexpectedly grateful for the presence of so large and solid a body. He looked down at her, and smiled reassuringly. "That makes another good reason for pushing the woodland back from the house," he remarked. "As for the footsteps, I'd have in the rat-catcher!"

His eyes were on Spurstow as he spoke, but that worthy said nothing. There was nothing acquiescent in his silence, however; his expression was that of one who might, had he chosen to do so, have made further and more alarming disclosures; and Anthea could only be glad that nothing more remained to be seen of the house than the cellars and the servants' quarters. The Major obligingly disclaimed any interest in these, so they went downstairs again, followed by Spurstow, who broke his silence to inform them that whenever it rained the roof leaked in a dozen places. If they had gone up into the attics, he said, they would have seen the buckets placed there to catch the drips.

On this depressing note they departed, Spurstow, slightly mellowed by the *douceur* bestowed upon him by the Major, holding open the door for them, and even going so far as to say that they would always be welcome.

"If we were welcome, I'd be sorry for anyone that was unwelcome," remarked Hugo, as they retraced their steps to the wicket-gate. "Did you say he'd been the old lady's butler?"

"Yes, but he was never trained to be a butler. Aunt took him out of the stables, because none of the butlers she hired from London ever stayed with her above a month. She didn't care about his manners, and I must own that he was amazingly faithful to her, and, I think, fond of her, in his rough way. She let him do just as he pleased, and, of course, when she took to living in one room he managed everything, and never cheated her out of a groat, what's more. He was born and bred on the estate, and his father and grandfather before him, but even Grandpapa wouldn't have wondered at it if he had feathered his nest at Aunt Matty's expense. She left him an annuity, but only quite a small one, which was why, I suppose, he was willing to stay on alone in the Dower House. I wouldn't have done so for a fortune! Didn't he make your blood run cold when he said it was *only footsteps?* Just as though that made everything right! *I* thought it made everything ten times eerier, didn't you?"

"Ay, he did it very well," agreed Hugo.

She looked quickly up at him. "Did it very well? Do you mean he was trying to frighten us? It didn't seem so to me. He made so little of it! He even said the wind was to blame for the moaning noise."

Hugo chuckled. "So he did! If you could have seen your own face, lass! Not that I think it was you he was trying to scare away. What I did think was that as soon as he suspected I'd a notion of living in the Dower House myself he did all he could to set me against it."

She knit her brows. "Yes, I suppose that's possible," she said, after considering for a minute or two. "Unless you hired him with the house, which is not very likely, he would be obliged to leave, and I daresay— No, it can't be that! The house was known to be haunted long before he came to it!"

"If it was half as badly haunted as he'd have us believe, our great-grandmother wouldn't have gone to live there in the first place, let alone have stayed there till she died!" replied Hugo. "Nay, lass! Spurstow wants to keep people away from it. That might be because he's afraid of being turned out: I'm not saying it isn't, but what I suspect is that he's got some other reason—and a havey-cavey one at that!—for scaring the people roundabout here with his talk of footsteps and pitiful moanings!"

"But Richmond *saw* the ghost!" she argued. "One or two of the villagers have seen it, too, though not as clearly as he did. Old Buttermere said it was a white *thing*, that glided over the ground, and vanished into the shrubbery."

"And a very good place for it to vanish, too," said Hugo, wholly unimpressed. "Give me a sheet, and a night without too much moonlight, and I'll engage to do the same!"

"And the form Richmond mistook for a living person?"

"If Richmond came up here expecting to see the ghost of Jane Darracott," he suggested, after a moment, "and in fact saw that old rascal, draped in a sheet, the likelihood is that his imagination took hold of him, and made him ready to swear he'd seen a deal more than he *did* see. It's a queer thing, imagination—and I'd say Richmond's was a lively one."

She thought this over, saying at the end of her cogitations: "Well, if you are right, Hugo, I daresay I can guess why Spurstow wishes to keep everyone away from the

Dower House. Indeed, I wonder that it shouldn't have occurred to any of us! Depend upon it, the house is being used by free-traders!"

XI

The Major received this suggestion without any visible signs of surprise or disapproval; but after turning it over in his mind, he said: "I don't know much about smuggling, but I should have thought the Dower House would have been too far from the coast to be of use."

"No, why? It's not much more than ten miles, and you may be sure that those who carry the run goods inland know the Marsh so well that they can find their way on the darkest of nights. They must wish to store the goods as far from the shore as they may, because the land-guard keep their strictest watch on the dwellings nearest to the coast, but they can't go very far, on account of the darkness. The goods are landed on moonless nights, you see: the *darks* is what they call them."

"Ay, they'd have to be. Do the smuggling vessels sail close in to the shore, or do the landsmen row out to them?"

"Well, I don't know precisely. I think they very often land their cargoes in creeks, and gaps, but sometimes, I believe, they cast the goods overboard at high tide. I remember once, when I was a child, that the tide-waiters captured a cargo of tea which had been thrown overboard. It was packed in oilskin bags, made to look like mackerel pots, my nurse told me. She knew a great deal about the trade: I expect her brothers had to do with it."

He could not help grinning at her cheerful unconcern, but he was somewhat startled, and said incredulously: "Your nurse's brothers were smugglers?"

"Not *master*-smugglers, but hired to help carry the goods up from the shore," she explained. "They worked on their father's farm, and were perfectly respectable, I assure you!"

"Nay!" he protested.

She smiled. "Well, quite as respectable as their fellows at all events. You don't understand, Hugo! In Kent and Sussex almost everyone has to do with smuggling in some way or another. The farm labourers hire themselves out as porters, and the farmers themselves sometimes lend their horses, and nearly always allow their barns to be used as hiding-places. We, of course, don't have any dealings with smugglers, but if we found ankers in one of our outhouses

138

we shouldn't say a word about it. No one would! Why, Grandpapa told us once how a cargo of brandy was stored in Guldeford Church, with the Vicar knowing all about it, and saying from the pulpit that there would be no service on the following Sunday because the roof needed repair! Grandpapa could tell you hundreds of stories about smuggling: he used to do so when we were children, and he was in a good humour: we thought it a high treat!"

"I'll be bound you did," Hugo said.

She detected a little dryness in his voice, and said, with a touch of impatience: "I collect you think it very shocking! I daresay it may be, but it is not so regarded in Kent. When Grandpapa was a young man, he says there was scarcely a magistrate to be found who would commit a man charged with smuggling."

"So that made all right," he nodded.

"No, of course it didn't! I only meant—well, to show you why we don't think it such a dreadful crime as you do!"

"Nay, you don't know what I think," he said, smiling down at her.

"You will not be much liked here if you show yourself to be at enmity with the Gentlemen," she warned him.

"That's bad," he said, gravely shaking his head.

She said no more then, but the subject came up again later in the day, when Richmond asked Hugo how he had fared at the Dower House. It was Anthea who answered, exclaiming: "Richmond, do you think that odious old man is trying to keep everyone away from the house?"

"Yes, of course he is!" he replied, laughing. "You know he hates visitors! Besides, if we took to paying him visits, he'd be obliged to bestir himself, and scrub the floors. Was he crusty?"

"Yes, and worse! He made my blood run cold, with his talk of footsteps, and moaning, and *paying no heed to the things he hears!* I began to have that horrid feeling that there was something behind me. If Hugo hadn't been there, I should have picked up my skirts and fled!"

"Humdudgeon!" scoffed Richmond. "In broad daylight?"

"Well, it ain't humdudgeon," intervened Claud. "I know just what she means, and a dashed nasty feeling it is! It happened to me once, walking up the lane here. Couldn't get it out of my head there was something following me. Made my flesh creep, because it was getting dark, and not a soul about."

"Did you run?" asked Anthea, quizzing him.

"I should dashed well think I did run!" he replied. "It was a devilish great black boar that had got loose. Never had such a fright in my life! Yes, it's all very well for you to laugh, but they're dangerous things, boars."

"I'd prefer to have a boar behind me than a ghost," said Anthea. "At least it would be a *live* thing!"

"Well, if you think a live boar behind you would be better than a dead one, it's easy to see you've never been chased by one!" said Claud, with some feeling. "And as for ghosts, you ought to know better than to believe in 'em! They don't exist."

"Oh, don't they?" struck in Richmond. "Would you be willing to spend the night in the grounds of Dower House?"

"You know, Richmond, you've got the most uncomfortable notions of anyone I ever met," said Claud. "Dashed if I don't think you're a trifle queer in your attic! A nice cake I'd make of myself, prowling round the Dower House all night!"

"But wouldn't you be afraid to, Claud?" Anthea asked. "*Truly*, wouldn't you?"

"Of course I'd be afraid to! I'd be bound to catch a chill, for it stands to reason I couldn't keep on walking for ever, and I'd be lucky if it didn't turn to an inflammation of the lung. I'm not afraid of seeing a ghost, if that's what you mean. I know dashed well I shouldn't."

"Don't be too sure of that!"

Claud bent a sapient eye upon his young cousin. "Well, I am sure of it. And don't you take a notion into your head that I ain't up to slum, my boy, because I am! What I should see, if I was such a nodcock as to spend the night at the Dower House, would be you, capering about in your nightshirt, with a pillowcase over your head. I don't doubt I'd see *that!*"

Richmond laughed, but said emphatically: "Not I! Anywhere else I'd be happy to try if I couldn't hoax you, but not at the Dower House! Once is enough, thank you!"

Hugo, who had been glancing through the latest edition of the *Morning Post* to reach Darracott Place, lowered the journal at this, and looked at Richmond with a twinkle in his eye. "Seemingly you're the only person who ever saw the poor lady plainly," he remarked. "What did she look like, lad?"

"I didn't see her plainly enough to be able to answer that," Richmond returned. "Besides, she was gone in a flash."

"But you did see a female form, didn't you?" Anthea asked.

"Yes, I thought it was someone from the village, when I first caught sight of it, but there wasn't much light, of course, and——"

"A misty form?" interrupted Claud.

"Yes. That is——"

"Did it shimmer?"

"Lord, I don't know! There was no time to see whether it did or not: one moment it was there, and the next it had melted into the shrubbery."

"Thought as much!" said Claud, with a satisfied air. "I get it myself. In fact, it runs in the family. There's only one thing for it, and that's mercury. You take my advice, young Richmond, and the next time you see things slipping away when you look at them ask my Aunt Elvira for a Blue Pill! Surprised she doesn't give 'em to you, because it's as plain as a pikestaff you're as liverish as Vincent!"

Vincent, entering the room in time to hear this comparison, interrupted Richmond's indignant refutal, saying, as he shut the door: "Am I liverish? I wonder if you could be right? I thought it was boredom. What have you been doing to earn this stigma, bantam?"

The matter was explained to him by Richmond and Anthea in chorus. Hugo had returned to the *Morning Post,* and Claud had lost interest, his mind being occupied suddenly by a more important matter. As Vincent strolled forward, Claud's gaze was dragged irresistibly to his gleaming Hessians, and he fell into a brown study, wondering if their magical gloss could have been produced by a mixture of brandy and beeswax, and if it had ever occurred to Polyphant to experiment with this entirely original recipe. He tore his eyes away from the Hessians, and found that Vincent was looking mockingly down at him.

"Even I do not know, brother," Vincent said gently. "I hope you haven't wasted any blunt on champagne? It isn't that."

Claud was pardonably annoyed. "If you want to know what I was thinking——"

"I do know," interpolated Vincent. "I beg your pardon, Anthea! You were saying?"

"I was saying—no, Claud, don't answer him! it's precisely what he wants you to do!—I was saying that whatever Richmond may, or may not, have seen, I think the Dower House

141

is haunted," stated Anthea. "I had the horridest feeling, all the time I was there!"

Hugo, who was seated sideways on the window seat, with the *Morning Post* spread before him, raised his head, and said, with a grin: "No wonder, if you let that old humbug bamboozle you into believing him!"

"You're not going to tell me that Spurstow said the place was haunted?" demanded Richmond. "Because I'll swear he never did so! He doesn't give a rush for any ghost! I happen to know, too, that when they ask him questions about it, down at the Blue Lion, he turns surly, and won't answer. Why should he take it into his head to start talking about it to you?"

"Hugo thought he was trying to frighten him. And I must say, Hugo, it does seem as though you might be right!"

"Fiddle!" said Richmond. "Why should he want to frighten Hugo?"

"Happen he thought I'd too much interest in the place," suggested Hugo, turning a sheet of his journal.

"Hugo said that he would like to strip all the ivy off, and clear away those thick shrubs," explained Anthea. "I wonder? You know, it's perfectly true that he tries to keep everyone away. It hadn't previously occurred to me that he might be hiding something, because Aunt Matty never would see visitors either, but when Hugo put it into my head—Richmond, could he be using the Dower House as a hiding-place for run cargoes?"

"He *could* be," Richmond replied, "but I don't advise you to accuse him of it. He'll take it very unkind, and start prosing about having been thirty years in service and never a stain on his reputation. Ash told me he went right up in the bows when that clunch, Ottershaw, set a watch on the Dower House."

"Good God, did he do so?" exclaimed Anthea. "I never knew that! When was it?"

"Oh, soon after Ottershaw was sent here! Just after Christmas, wasn't it?"

"Dear me, what stirring events seem to take place when I am not here to be beguiled by them!" remarked Vincent. "What made Ottershaw suspect Spurstow?"

"His face, I should think," said Claud. "Anyone would!"

"The Preventives always suspect haunted houses," said Richmond, ignoring the interruption. "Ottershaw's a bigger sapskull than the man we had before! He came up to see my grandfather about it!" He grinned at Vincent, his eyes alight with mischief. "You ask Chollacombe how Grand-papa liked it!"

"I am sure he disliked it very much," said Vincent, flicking open his snuff-box. "I have every sympathy with him. A gross impertinence: Spurstow has been in Grandpapa's service all his life."

"But was that all the reason Ottershaw had?" demanded Anthea. "Merely that the Dower House is haunted?"

Richmond shrugged. "No use asking me: *I'm* not in the fellow's confidence. All I know is that he had the place watched. Spurstow discovered it, of course, and nabbed the rust. He went off to Rye, ran Ottershaw to earth in the Ship, and asked him what the devil he meant by it. I wasn't there myself, but I'm told there was a rare kick-up. Ottershaw lost his temper, because Spurstow challenged him to go back with him and search the Dower house, and of course, he dared not to it without a warrant, unless he had Grandpapa's permission, which he most certainly had *not!*"

"And did Spurstow's display of righteous indignation allay suspicion?" enquired Vincent, restoring his snuff-box to his pocket, and dusting his sleeve with his handkerchief.

"Well, it wouldn't allay my suspicion!" said Claud. "If any such gallows-faced cove came and talked to me about his spotless reputation, I'd give him in charge! Too smoky by half! Depend upon it, he's got run goods hidden all over the house!"

"If that's so, how did he get them there?" retorted Richmond. "Each time the Preventives have got wind of a big run Ottershaw has posted dragoons in the lane, and they've never seen or heard a thing! There's no other way of getting to the house, except by the gate that leads out of the shrubbery into our grounds, and that couldn't possibly be used. For one thing, it squeaks loud enough to be heard half-a-mile away, and, for another, a man posted outside the main-gate, in the lane, couldn't help but see if anyone came out of the shrubbery."

"True," agreed Vincent. "Assuming, of course, that he was a stout-hearted fellow, and maintained his post—which I doubt. From what I know of the inhabitants of this unre-generate locality, I should suppose that they could be counted on to fortify the dragoon for his vigil with some pretty choice ghost-stories."

"Yes, of course they do," grinned Richmond. "Ash—he's the

buffer at the Blue Lion, you know—says the men hate that duty like the devil. According to him, they've seen more ghosts at the Dower House than we ever dreamed of! I don't suppose they do stay too close to the gate, but it makes no odds as long as they keep the lane covered: any pack-train would have to come that way. The best of it is that while Ottershaw concentrated his forces there, the night of a big run, the train was miles to the west, and got through without catching so much as a whiff of a Preventive!"

Vincent looked rather amused. "You are remarkably well-informed! Where do you come by all this information, little cousin?"

Richmond laughed. "My boatman, of course! Lord, you don't imagine anything happens along the coast that Jem Hordle doesn't know about, do you?"

"I had forgotten your boatman. Is he one of the fraternity?"

"I haven't asked him. You should know better than to think one puts *that* sort of a question to one's boatman!"

"To be sure I do! How could I be so stupid?"

"I'll tell you something, young Richmond!" said Claud suddenly. "You're a dashed sight too caper-witted! If you don't take care you'll be made to look no-how. Ought to be sure of your boatman! What's more, you oughtn't to beach that yawl of yours where anyone could launch her, and not a soul the wiser. A rare mess you'd find yourself in if she was caught bringing in run goods, and it's all the world to a handsaw that that's just what *will* happen one of these nights!"

"I fail to see why Richmond should find himself in a rare mess because his boat was stolen and put to improper purposes, even though I'm spell-bound by your eloquence," said Vincent. "Have you undertaken to bear-lead him as well as Hugo, by the way?"

"You needn't be anxious, Claud!" Richmond interposed, a confident little smile playing about his mouth. "Jem would no more take my boat out without my leave than he'd rob me of my watch, and he wouldn't let anyone else do so either."

Claud, an expression of deep scepticism on his face, looked as though he had more to say, but as his father came into the room at that moment, the subject was allowed to drop.

Matthew, on the eve of his departure from Darracott Place, made another attempt to persuade Vincent to follow his example. He failed, for the very simple reason that Vincent's financial embarrassments made it desirable not only that he should oblige his grandfather, but that he should be put to no living-expenditure until quarter-day came to relieve his situation. But as Vincent was well aware that Matthew strongly resented Lord Darracott's capricious custom of bestowing on his grandsons handsome sums which he grudged to his own son, he did not present Matthew with this explanation to remain where he was plainly bored to death. In fact, he presented him with no explanation at all, a circumstance which sent Matthew back to London in a mood of anxious foreboding only partially allayed by his dependence on his lady's ability to control what he felt to be an increasingly dangerous situation. "My dear sir," Vincent said, "it would be so unkind—really quite barbarous!—to leave my grandfather without support in this hour of trial. I could not think of it! But do, I beg of you, remove Claud!"

But Matthew very properly ignored this request, and Claud too remained at Darracott Place. He received no encouragement from his host, nor could anyone feel that a rural existence held the slightest charm for him. Still less was it felt that he entertained any very real hope of reforming his large cousin, for his first enthusiasm had not survived the several checks he had received, and although he frequently censured Hugo's dialectical lapses, and occasionally made an attempt to coax him into a more fashionable mode, it was certainly not to educate him that he remained in Kent. The truth was that his grandfather's summons had made it necessary for him to refuse an invitation to make one of a very agreeable houseparty in quite another part of the country, so that he found himself in the position of having nowhere to go for several weeks, a return to his lodgings in Duke Street at this season being clearly ineligible. He would not have chosen to stay for any length of time at Darracott Place, but he was not bored, as was his more energetic and very much more dashing brother. Notwithstanding his sartorial ambition, Claud's tastes were simple; and since the self-imposed strain of cutting a notable figure in the world of fashion was extremely exhausting he was really quite glad to spend a few weeks in the country, on what he referred to as a repairing lease. He was able to try the effect of various daring new quirks of fashion without having his pleasure marred by the dread of being thought by the high sticklers to have gone a little too far; for although he met with much adverse criticism in the bosom of his family this was so ill-informed as to have no power to discompose him. His grandfather's notions were Gothic; his father had never aspired to a place amongst the smarts; Richmond was a callow youth, knowing nothing whatsoever about matters of taste and ton; and Vincent's contempt sprang so obviously from jealousy that he was able to ignore it. Criticism from Hugo would naturally have been beneath contempt, but Hugo never criticized his appearance: he regarded each new extravagance with awe and admiration, only once being betrayed into the expression of something in the nature of a protest. "Eh, lad, you're never going to Rye in that rig?" he exclaimed involuntarily, when Claud came down the stairs wonderfully attired for this projected expedition.

"Certainly he is," said Vincent, who had unfortunately come out of the library at that moment. "Claud, my dear coz, likes nothing better than to preen himself under the admiring gaze of the local population. Don't try to deter him! So much endeavour deserves *some* recognition, after all, and when he goes on the strut in London he can never be perfectly sure that the attention he attracts is as admiring as he hoped it would be."

Since he had, with his usual acumen, stated the exact truth, Claud was roused to fury, and would have favoured him with some pithy criticisms of the style he had chosen to affect that morning had not Hugo intervened, saying, as he gently but irresistibly thrust him out of the house: "Nay, if you start a flight we shan't get to Rye at all!"

Fuming, Claud climbed up into the waiting curricle, the reins gathered in one elegantly gloved hand; Hugo got up beside him; Claud told the groom to stand away from the heads of the staid pair of horses borrowed from his grandfather's stable; and drove off, sped on his way by an earnest entreaty from Vincent, who had strolled out of the house to watch his departure, not to put his cousin in the ditch. This shaft, however, fell wide of the target, for Claud, though by no means a Nonesuch, was well-able to handle the reins in form. He instantly proved this by taking the first bend in the avenue in style, a feat which quite restored him to good-humour, since he knew Vincent to be watching him.

The road to Rye was rough, the post-road being in almost as bad a state of repair as the lane which led to it, but the journey was accomplished without mishap; and in

deal ruffled; and when he discovered a serious scratch on the shining leather he came near to losing his temper. "It's no use asking me how old the place is, because I don't know, and what's more I dashed well don't care!" he said testily. "Don't stand there gaping at it! Just look at this boot of mine! Do you realize I've only had this pair a couple of months? Now they're ruined, all because nothing will do for you but to go prowling about this ramshackle town!"

"I shouldn't worry," said Hugo, with only the most cursory glance at the damaged boot. "I daresay Polyphant will know what to do. Can we get into this place?"

"No, we can't, and as for not worrying, anyone can see *you* wouldn't, but I'll have you to know——" He stopped, suddenly, and, as Hugo turned his head to look enquiringly at him, ejaculated in an altered tone: "By Jupiter, I believe that's—— No, it ain't, though!—Yes, by Jupiter, it *is!*"

With this disjointed utterance he made his way across the street, sweeping off his hat, and executing a superb bow to a blushing damsel in a print dress, and a straw bonnet tied over a mop of yellow curls, who was coming down the street with a basket over one mittened arm. "La, Mr. Darracott, to think of meeting you!" she said coyly, dropping him a curtsy. "And me on my way to the chandler's, never dreaming you was in the town! Well, I do declare!"

"Allow me to carry your basket!" begged Claud gallantly.

"How can you, Mr. Darracott? As though I'd think of such a thing!"

"At least you won't refuse me the pleasure of escorting you!" said Claud.

Perceiving that the lady had no intention of refusing him this pleasure, the Major seized the opportunity to make good his escape, tolerably confident that Claud would be happily engaged in flirtation for some time to come. The yellow-haired charmer spoke in far from refined accents, but the Major felt no surprise at his elegant cousin's effusive behaviour, for he had discovered Claud two days previously, trysting with the blacksmith's pretty daughter. Claud's disposition was mildly amorous, but as he was terrified of falling a victim to a matchmaking mama he rarely attempted to flirt with girls of his own order, indulging instead in a form of innocuous dalliance (which made his more robust brother feel very unwell) with chambermaids, milliners' apprentices, village maidens, or, in fact, any personable young female of humble origin who was ready to encourage his attentions without for a moment imagining that these were serious.

So the Major deserted him with a clear conscience, and explored the town by himself. At the end of Watchbell Street he fell into conversation with a venerable citizen, who gave him much interesting information about Rye's history, not all of which was apocryphal, and directed him to the Flushing Inn, which was the scene of the murderous butcher's last drink before his execution. The Major thanked him, but preferred to visit the church, after which he wandered on until he found himself at the end of the town, in front of the ancient Ypres Tower, which provided Rye with its jail. Close by it the town-wall had been breached to allow those wishing to reach the quay below to do so by way of the Baddyng Steps. The Major walked towards the steps, and reached them just as Lieutenant Ottershaw arrived, somewhat out of breath, at the top of them.

The Lieutenant stared for a moment, and then saluted the Major, who greeted him pleasantly, and said, looking over the low wall at the precipitous slope of the hill: "A stiff climb!"

The Lieutenant agreed to this monosyllabically, and hesitated, as though he were in two minds whether to continue on his way, or to linger. Hugo settled the matter for him by nodding towards the rugged jail, and saying: "I take it that must have been a mediaeval Martello Tower. I've been talking to one of the inhabitants of the town, and from what I could gather—but my ear's not used yet to the Sussex tongue!—the Frogs made a habit of raiding Rye."

"Yes, sir, I believe they did land here on more than one occasion. Is it your first visit?"

"Ay, it is. I was never in Sussex, think on, before I came to stay with my grandfather. I don't know Kent either, beyond what I saw when I was at Shorncliffe, and that wasn't much. Are you a native of these parts?"

"No, sir. I was born in London, but my father's people were from Yorkshire," disclosed the Lieutenant.

"No, is that so? Ee, lad, that's gradely! Is ta from t'West Riding?" exclaimed Hugo broadly.

The Lieutenant's severe countenance relaxed into a reluctant grin. "No, sir—North Riding, not far from York. I was never in Yorkshire myself, though."

Hugo shook his head over this, and by dint of a few friendly questions succeeded in thawing some of the ice in which the Riding officer seemed to wish to encase himself. Ottershaw ventured, in his turn, to enquire after Hugo's military service; and in a very short while had relaxed sufficiently to perch beside him on the wall, listening with keen interest to what he had to say about the war in the Peninsula, and allowing himself to be beguiled into talking a little about his own career. It was evident that he had chosen his profession as the next best to joining the army; he spoke of it in a defensive manner, as though he suspected Hugo of despising it; whereupon Hugo said, with his slow smile: "From all I can discover, yours is a harder job than any I ever met with, and a thankless one, too."

Ottershaw gave a short laugh. "It's thankless enough! I don't care for that, but these people—in Kent and Sussex both: there's nothing to choose between 'em!—well, sir, they say Cornish folk are double-faced, but I'll swear they're nothing to what I've met with here! You saw that barrel-bellied fellow who doffed his hat to me a minute ago, and smiled all over his oily face? To hear him talk you'd think he ought to have been a Preventive himself, while as for the way he begs me to come and take my pot-luck at his house whenever I choose——" He broke off, his jaw hardening. "One of these days that's what I will do—when I'm sure I'll find pot-luck there!" he said. He jerked his thumb over his shoulder. "There's a tavern down there, on the quay—the Ypres: I was coming away from it when I met you. I *know* it's a smugglers' haunt, and I'll take my affidavit there's no one they want to see inside it less than me, but I've never been there yet but what the rascally ale-draper that owns it is all smiles and welcome! He thinks he's tipping me a rise, but I'll catch him redhanded if it's the last thing I do! I'll tell you this, sir: the whole town's abandoned to smuggling! Ay, and the Mayor, and the jurat, winking at what goes on under their noses!"

"Where does the stuff come from?" asked the Major.

Ottershaw shrugged. "Most of it from Guernsey: that's the biggest *entrepôt;* but some of it is run straight over from roundabout Calais."

"Don't they get intercepted at sea?"

"Sometimes, but, to make the naval patrol effective, double—three times!—the number of vessels is needed. Even then—with the whole coast to be watched, and the tricks that are employed being past counting—I doubt if it could be done. It's not only a matter of false bulkheads, and suchlike, sir. There's no question but that the smuggling craft slip through time and again because they get signals warning them where there's a Revenue cruiser or a sloop lurking, from vessels no one would suspect." He nodded to where a fishing smack was drawing clear of the harbour. "That craft, for instance. She may be innocent, but the chances are that if she sights a patrol-boat some damned hoverer will have her bearings before nightfall." He paused, as though deliberating, and then said: "You can't signal every craft you see to heave-to, sir, let alone board them. People don't like it—very naturally, if they're going about an honest business, such as that smack out there may be, or perhaps cruising for pleasure, as Mr. Richmond Darracott does."

"They wouldn't, of course," agreed the Major.

"However, there's one thing you can be sure of," said Ottershaw. "The blockade's in charge of a man who means to stamp out smuggling, no matter how many people he offends. Ay, and so does the Government! Time was when they were pretty lukewarm in London, but since the war ended there's been so much smuggling done that if it isn't stopped things will get to be as bad as ever they were when the Hawkhurst Gang was ruling Sussex. That's something that those who protect the *Gentlemen,* as they call them, maybe don't realize, but it'll be as well for them—and I name no names!—if they——"

His voice died in mid-sentence, and the Major saw his jaw drop, and his gaze become fixed, a sort of fascinated awe in his eyes. Considerably surprised, the Major looked round to discover what he had seen to strike him to sudden silence, and beheld his cousin Claud advancing towards him.

XII

Since he had parted from Hugo, Claud had acquired a buttonhole of enormous size, which added the final touch to an appearance startling enough to excuse Lieutenant Ottershaw's stupefaction. It was seldom that any gentleman honoured Rye by sauntering through its streets in the long-tailed coat, the pantaloons, and the Hessians that were fashionable for a lounge down Bond Street, or a promenade in Hyde Park; and even in these modish haunts Claud's costume must have been remarkable, for his pantaloons (with which he hoped to set a fashion) were neither of a sober biscuit hue, nor of a more dashing yellow, but of a clear and delicate lilac; his neckcloth was of inordinate size, and had a large amethyst pin stuck in its folds; his hat, the very latest product of Baxter's inventive genius, was so revolutionary in design as to cause even its wearer to feel some qualms, for instead of being the bell-topped and rough beaver favoured by town-dwellers, or the more countrified shallow, it bore a marked resemblance to a tapering chimney-pot. But even more stunning than his hat, or his pantaloons, was the long cloak of white drab, lined with lilac silk, which hung in graceful folds from his shoulders. It was not the custom of gentlemen to wear cloaks over anything but evening-dress; but it had occurred to Claud, studying his reflection once before setting out for Almack's Assembly Rooms, that there was something peculiarly becoming in a well-cut and silk-lined cloak. The idea of designing one suitable for day-wear had flashed into his mind, and he had instantly suggested it to Polyphant. Polyphant had not seemed to care for it, but although he usually allowed Polyphant to guide his taste he had been so much taken with this flower of his own brain that after brooding over it for several weeks he laid it before the more adventurous of his tailors. "Yes, sir. For a masquerade?" had said Mr. Stultz, rather dauntingly.

But Claud had not allowed himself to be daunted; and when he subsequently showed his cloak to two of his particular friends they were loud in their expressions of envy and approval. He had not yet worn it in London, but its effect on Rye had been very encouraging, and he rather thought he would venture to try it on the ton at the start of the Little Season.

Lieutenant Ottershaw found his voice. "Is that—is that Mr. *Claud* Darracott, sir?" he asked.

"Yes," replied the Major. "It is!"

The Lieutenant drew a long breath. "I'm glad I've seen him," he said simply. "I've heard a lot about him, but I didn't believe the half of it."

Having come within range, Claud put his glass, the better to scrutinize his cousin's companion. The Lieutenant, fascinated by an eye thus hideously magnified, could not drag his gaze from it, and was only released from its spell when Claud let the glass fall, and addressed himself to Hugo, in fretful accents. "Dash it, coz! Been searching for you all over! Even took a look-in at the church. If I hadn't thought to ask pretty well everyone I met if they'd seen a mountain moving about on legs I might be hunting for you still!"

"I've been chewing the bacon with Lieutenant Ottershaw here," replied Hugo.

"How-de-do?" murmured Claud, groping for his glass again. He raised it, a puzzled frown on his brow, and levelled it at the Lieutenant's blue and white uniform. "Naval?" he said doubtfully.

"Customs' Land-Guard, sir," said the Lieutenant stiffly.

"Thought you wasn't wearing naval rig," said Claud. "Never know one uniform from another, but those breeches didn't seem right. Well, what I mean is, don't wear 'em in the navy, do they? Silly thing to do, because it stands to reason —*Customs' Land-Guard,* did you say?"

The Lieutenant, growing stiffer every minute, made him a slight bow. "I am a Riding-officer, sir."

"That accounts for the breeches," said Claud, glad to have this point cleared up. "Had me in a puzzle. Very happy to have met you, but trust you'll forgive me if I drag my cousin away: got a nuncheon waiting for us at the George!"

"You remind me that I also must be on my way, sir," responded Ottershaw. He then bowed again, saluted Hugo, and strode off.

"If ever I met such a ramshackle fellow!" said Claud severely. "Hobnobbing with a dashed tidesman! Next you'll be arm-in-arm with the beadle!"

"You're mighty high in the instep all at once!" remarked Hugo.

"No, I ain't: no all at once about it! Never rubbed shoulders with a Preventive in my life! Not the thing! I'll tell you what, coz: if you don't take care you'll have people wondering if you're hand-in-glove with the fellow, and you'll be in bad loaf. Take my word for it!"

"And if I were thought to be hand-in-glove with the free-traders? I collect that would be all right and regular?"

"Nothing of the sort!" retorted Claud crossly. "What you ought to do is to have nothing to say to any of 'em. I don't wish that tidesman of yours any harm—in fact, I hope he may prosper, though I shouldn't think he would, because he looked like a clunch to me. The point is, catching free-traders ain't my business, and it ain't yours either. And another thing! If my grandfather knew you'd formed that sort of an acquaintance he'd very likely go off in an apoplexy!"

Having uttered this warning, and even enlarged on it over the excellent ham pie provided for nuncheon at the George, it was with considerable exasperation that Claud heard his incorrigible cousin, some hours later, describing his encounter with Lieutenant Ottershaw to an audience that included not only Lord Darracott, but Vincent as well. This foolish lapse took place at the dinner-table, and just when everything, in Claud's judgment, was going on particularly well. When the port had been set on the mahogany, his lordship had bethought him of his heir's expedition to Rye, and had asked him, in a mood of rare geniality, if he had been pleased with the town. Upon Hugo's responding that he had been both pleased and interested, and would like to know much more about its history than he had been able to glean in one visit, he had nodded approvingly; and it had needed only one question from Hugo to set him talking about the town. As far as Claud was concerned, it was a dead bore, but he was glad to see Hugo getting on terms with his grandfather, feeling vaguely that a great deal of credit was due to himself; and he did his best to promote further discussion by requesting my lord to tell Hugo the true facts about the murderous butcher. Happily unaware of having irritated my lord, who had been describing the original island-town, he then retired into his own thoughts, and paid no more heed to the conversation until his attention was recalled by Vincent's saying idly: "Didn't you tell me once, sir, that one of the cottages in Trader's Passage has a secret way down to the Strand, or some such thing?"

"That's what Ottershaw is trying to find, I daresay," remarked Richmond. "He's supposed to be stationed at Lydd, but he's for ever prowling about Rye. You didn't see him there, did you, Cousin Hugo?"

"Oh, yes, I saw him!" Hugo replied. He refilled his glass, and passed the decanter on to Vincent, and added: "I met him at the top of the steps by the Ypres Tower."

Beginning to feel a trifle uneasy, Claud directed a look at him that was meant to convey a warning that any further disclosure should be sedulously avoided. He succeeded in catching his cousin's eye, and so was startled and exacerbated when Hugo said, quite unnecessarily: "He said he had been at the Ypres Tavern."

"Accosted you, did he?" said his lordship. "Intolerable Jack Straw! I hope you gave him a sharp set-down?"

"Nay, he didn't accost me: I accosted him," said Hugo. "I wouldn't call him a Jack Straw, either."

"What the devil possessed you to do so?" demanded his lordship, a frown gathering. "I wish you will remember that you're a Darracott, sir, and learn to keep a proper distance! The fellow's an infernal coxcomb!"

"I expect my cousin didn't realize that," said Vincent suavely.

"You're right: I didn't," replied Hugo. "I'd say myself that he's a stiff-necked lad, and devilish punctilious."

"Full of starch, and muttonheaded into the bargain!" said Richmond.

"Nay, I wouldn't run away with that notion," said Hugo, meeting Richmond's eyes, and holding them. "He's not as muttonheaded as you think, lad."

"What makes you say so?"

"Some of the things he told me," Hugo replied. He lowered his eyes to the glass in his hand, contemplating the play of the candlelight on the port. "There's not much he doesn't know about smuggling ways, seemingly, and not much that escapes him. I've met his sort before: I'd take care how I tried to cut a wheedle with him."

"I feel sure you are right," said Vincent. "I cannot believe that you would cut a successful wheedle with anyone."

A little chuckle shook the Major, but he said regretfully: "Nay, I'm too gaumless."

"Can none of you find anything of more interest to discuss?" demanded his lordship contemptuously. "I wish you will inform me what you find to interest you in an Exciseman?"

"Speaking for myself," answered Vincent, "nothing whatsoever, sir. Should you object to it if I were to take that sprig——" he nodded at Richmond—"to see how Cribb's latest pupil shapes in the ring? He's matched to fight Tom Bugle at Sevenoaks, for twenty guineas a side, and shows off, Cribb tells me, in excellent style. If he's not levelled in the first round, it should be a good contest: stopping and hitting the order of the day—no hugging, or hauling, and nothing shy."

"You may take him, if he cares to go," replied his lordship. "*I've* no objection, though no doubt your aunt will raise a dust."

"No, she won't, Grandpapa! Not if I have *your* leave!" Richmond said impetuously. "Besides, I'm not a child! When is it to be, Vincent? How shall we do? I've never seen a real match—only a few turn-ups, with tremendous milling, but no science."

He could talk of nothing else. His grandfather listened to him indulgently, Vincent with weary resignation, and

Claud not at all. It seemed to occur to no one but Hugo, watching him curiously, that his eager excitement was that of a schoolboy rather than a youth on the threshold of manhood. He was transformed, his big, expressive eyes sparkling, his cheeks a little flushed; and it was evident that he looked forward as much to spending two nights away from his home as to the treat of watching a fight under the aegis of a patron of the Fancy. As soon as his grandfather left the dining-room, he went off to cajole his mother into viewing the project with complaisance, reminding Hugo of a spirited colt kicking up his heels in sheer exuberance.

"I wonder what can have possessed me?" said Vincent, a look of ineffable boredom on his face. "My only hope now is that my Aunt Elvira may be moved to beg me not to take her nestling to watch such a horrid, brutal exhibition: I should not dream of doing so against her wishes."

"Well, it beats me why he should be so devilish full of gig about it, but I call it dashed shabby if you run sly, when you've cast him into transports!" said Claud disapprovingly.

"Yes, that reflection quite sinks my spirits," agreed Vincent. "If only I had known that he _would_ be cast into transports!"

"Didn't you? And you so all-alive!" said Hugo.

Vincent looked at him, his brows lifting haughtily.

"No saying what Richmond will do!" said Claud, intervening in some haste. "Odd sort of a boy. Often thought so!"

"There's not one of you that has thought about him at all," said Hugo. "Eh, Vincent, can't you see that what's cast him into transports is being let off his chain for a piece? The only odd thing about him is that he's much too biddable for such a high-couraged lad!"

"The subject holds very little more interest for me than that of Excisemen, but I feel sure you are right."

"You'd have more hair than wit if you didn't," replied Hugo, smiling. "I've had to do with a score of lads of Richmond's age! You may take it that I know what I'm saying when I tell you that if he's kept for much longer dancing attendance on his grandfather he'll be getting up to mischief."

"How very dreadful!" said Vincent sardonically.

"That's what I'm thinking," replied Hugo. "He's got a deal of energy, and no more worldly sense than a lass not out of the schoolroom. He wants always to be _doing_, but

157

what he's got his heart set on he's been forbidden to think of, and the chances are there'll be the devil to pay, because you're brewing trouble when you try to keep randy, hey-go-mad lads of his cut in leading-strings."

"May I suggest that instead of wasting your eloquence on me you shoud bestow your advice—no doubt excellent!—on my grandfather?"

"Good God, no!" exclaimed Claud, horrified. "Don't you do any such thing, Hugo! Assure you—wouldn't answer the purpose at all! In fact, far otherwise!"

"Nay, what right have I to interfere?" Hugo said.

"For once, cousin, I am entirely in accord with you," remarked Vincent.

"Happen we've neither of us any right, but if I'd known the lad from his cradle, and he looked up to me, as he does to you, I'd make a push to help him. Why don't you do it, instead of throwing your tongue at me in a way that'll do you no good nor me any harm?"

"*Happen,*" Vincent retorted. "I lack the effrontery!"

"Nay, you don't lack that!" said Hugo, with his deep chuckle.

Vincent stiffened, his eyes narrowing; for a moment the issue seemed to be in the balance; and then he shrugged, and walked out of the room.

As had been foreseen, Mrs. Darracott was strongly opposed to the projected scheme for her son's entertainment. She held prize-fighting in abhorrence, and seemed to be equally divided in her mind between dislike of Richmond's being taken into low, vulgar company, and fear that he had only to witness an encounter to be fired with emulation. It was useless for Lady Aurelia to tell her that she need be under no apprehension, since gentlemen did not engage in prize-fighting: between prize-fighting and boxing she was unable to perceive the least difference; and, in any event, he had been subject, as a child, to severe nose-bleedings, which would very likely be brought on again if he were to sustain a blow in the face.

"But, Mama, indeed, I don't think he has the least wish to be a boxer!" Anthea said coaxingly. "After all, Oliver didn't box, did he? And he was for ever going off to see a fight!"

She broke off suddenly, with a comical look of dismay, as it occurred to her that this comparison was not entirely felicitous.

"*Well!*" uttered Mrs. Darracott, her plump bosom swelling

with indignation. "If you wish to see your brother—your *only* brother!—return in the perfectly *disgusting* condition——"

"I don't, I don't!" interrupted Anthea, trying not to laugh. "Now, Mama——!"

"I am no friend to the sport in any form," announced Lady Aurelia, "but in this instance, my dear Elvira, you need not fidget yourself. Recollect that Richmond will be in his cousin's charge! Depend upon it, Vincent will take good care of him."

Good manners compelled Mrs. Darracott to hold her peace, but it was with difficulty that she refrained from retort, as Anthea presently explained to Hugo.

"I daresay she wouldn't have cared so very much, if Richmond had not been going with Vincent," she said. "Not that she would have *liked* it, for she never could. Indeed, I don't see how *anyone* could, except that men seem to like the most peculiar things. There is no understanding it at all!"

"That's true," he agreed. "Time and again I've wondered what maggots gets into lasses' heads to make them wild after summat that seems to me plain daft!"

"Very possibly! But at least *we* don't like cocking, and prize-fighting, and wrestling, and getting odiously foxed!" she countered, with spirit.

"We're a terrible set!" he said, much struck.

"Yes, but some of you, I own, are worse than others," she conceded handsomely. "I was used to think you were all detestable, but that, of course, was because I had only met the men of my own family. I still think *them* detestable—well, perhaps not Claud, and certainly not Richmond, though he's only a boy—but the rest of them—ugh!"

"Well, that's sent me to grass, choose how!" said Hugo, in a dejected voice.

She stared at him for a moment, and then burst out laughing. "I didn't mean you! You know I didn't! I never think of you as one of the family."

"That's the worst you've said yet!"

"On the contrary! Not—but what you are detestable too, but in your own fashion!" said Anthea. "Now, do, pray, be serious! Do you think there can be any harm in Richmond's going to this horrid fight with Vincent?"

"None at all," he replied.

"No, nor do I, but Mama has it fixed in her head that Vincent may lead Richmond into his own way of life. I am not very sure I know what that is, precisely, but Mama

159

seems to think it quite shocking, which I can readily believe. But, in fairness to Vincent, I should perhaps tell you that Mama is *not* to be depended on when she speaks of him, for she holds him in the greatest aversion."

"She needn't be in a worry," he said, smiling a little. "Vincent won't lead Richmond into any way of life at all!"

"Well, I wish you will tell Mama so!" she said. "She is in such a fret over it! Since Grandpapa has said he may go I don't think Richmond will attend to her, but it must spoil his pleasure if he knows he is making her unhappy! At least——" She paused, considering this. "Well, I should think it would, wouldn't you?"

"No," he replied frankly. "But if you wish me to do so I'll talk to your mama, and gladly! Eh, lass, what nonsense it is! All this uproar about Richmond's going to watch a prize-fight, as though he were eight years old instead of past eighteen! There's not one lad in a hundred would have thought he must have his grandfather's permission, and none at all that would have breathed a word about it to his mother! Lord, by the time I was Richmond's age I'd fought my first campaign in South America, and was on my way to Sweden, with Sir John Moore! I wasn't thought to be so very young when I joined, either."

She looked up into his face, her eyes searching it rather anxiously. "It *is* unnatural, isn't it, the life Richmond leads? I didn't question it at first: you see, I know very little about the world! Except for one Season in London, and going to stay now and then with one or other of my aunts, I've hardly ever been away from this place. Of course I knew that Oliver wasn't brought up as Richmond has been, but that only made me think how fortunate it was that Grandpapa loved Richmond too much to part with him, because Oliver was for ever getting into trouble! I don't know what he did, except that it was always very expensive, and put my Uncle Granville into a passion, as well as Grandpapa, but I *do* know that he was a *loose* fish, because I once heard my uncle tell him so, and I daresay you know what *that* means!"

"Yes, love," said Hugo, smiling very kindly at her. "I know right enought, but happen you'd better not say it!"

"Oh, no! It sounds most improper! I wouldn't say it to anyone but—Hugo, how dare you call me *love?*"

"Did I do that?" he asked incredulously.

"You know very well you did! What is more, it is by far more improper than anything *I* said!"

Micronite filter.
Mild, smooth taste.
For all the right reasons.
Kent.

America's quality cigarette.
King Size or Deluxe 100's.

Micronite filter.
Mild, smooth taste.
For all the right reasons.
Kent.

© Lorillard 1972

Regular or Menthol.

"It must have slipped out," said Hugo feebly. "It's a common expression in the north!"

"Like *lass*, no doubt! And if you think, sir, that just because I grew fagged to death with telling you not to call me that, you are at liberty to call me anything else that comes into your head——"

"No, ma'am!" he intervened hastily. He shook his head in self-condemnation. "I wasn't minding my tongue. The instant our Claud's not by to give me a nudge it's down with my apple-cart again! Eh, but it's downright disheartening!"

"And d-don't call me m-ma'am either!" said Anthea, in a hopelessly unsteady voice.

He heaved a disconsolate sight. "I thought it would please you—Cousin Anthea!"

"You did *not*! You are an abominable person, Hugo! You've done nothing but make a May-game of us all ever since you set foot inside the house, while as for the whiskers you tell——!"

"Not *whiskers*, Cousin Anthea!" he pleaded.

"Whiskers!" she repeated firmly. "Besides acting the dunce——"

"Nay, I was always terribly gawky!"

"—and talking broad Yorkshire on the least provocation!"

"But I told you how it is with me!"

"You did! You said you couldn't help but do so whenever you are scared, and if that wasn't a whisker I never heard one! Well! If you spent your time hoaxing them all in your regiment I shouldn't wonder at it if you were *compelled* to sell out!" said Anthea, nodding darkly.

"Worse!" said the woebegone sinner before her. "I was hoping you wouldn't discover it, but there! I might have known——"

"Hugo——! You—you——"

He laughed. "Yes, Cousin Anthea?"

"Where did you go to school?" demanded Anthea sternly.

"That's a long time ago," he objected. "There's so much has happened to me since then——"

"More whiskers!" said Anthea, casting up her eyes.

"Well, it was—it was a school not so very far from London," he disclosed, looking sheepish.

"Eton?"

"Nay, lass!" he exclaimed shocked. "What would I have been doing at a place like that?"

"Wearing your tutor to death, I should think. But now

161

I come to think of it I know you can't have been at Eton, for you must have met Vincent there. Harrow?"

He looked at her for a moment, and then grinned, and nodded.

"And why have you told no one that you were there?"

"Well, no one asked me," he replied. "If it comes to that, Claud hasn't told me he was at Eton!"

"No, but he hasn't done his best to make you think he was educated at a charity school!"

"Now, what have I ever said——"

"Hugo, you deliberately tried to talk like your groom! They *cannot* have allowed you to do so at Harrow!"

He smiled. "No, but I was very broad in my speech before I went there, and I had it in my ears in the holidays, so that I've never really lost it. My grandfather—not this one!——"

"*I* know!" she interpolated. "T'gaffer!"

There was an appreciative twinkle in his eye. "Ay, t'gaffer! Well, he spoke good Yorkshire all his life, but I got skelped for doing it—being Quality-make! But I do use Yorkshire expressions now-and-now—when the occasion calls for them! And in the regiment—cutting a joke, you know!"

"Yes, I understand *that!* Like Richmond saying things in the broadest Sussex—he does it beautifully, and so did Oliver! Only Grandpapa disliked it, and made them stop doing it. He said it would get to be a habit, and I must own it became very tedious. But *you*, Hugo, talked Yorkshire to hoax us!"

"It wasn't exactly that," he said. "I'd no notion of hoaxing anybody when I came here, but when I saw the way you were all of you pretty well expecting me to eat with my knife—eh, lass, I couldn't resist!"

"How anyone who looks as you do can be so mad-brained——!" she marvelled. "If ever I hear of you in Newgate I shall know you owed your downfall to a prank you couldn't resist going into full-fling!"

"I'll be lucky if it's no worse," he said pessimistically. "Granddad was used to say I'd end on the gallows, all for the sake of cutting a joke. Mind you, I didn't think to find myself in the suds over this, because I hadn't been in the house above an hour before I was wondering how soon I could escape! I'd no more notion of remaining here than of flying to the moon."

"What will you do?" she asked.

"Oh, I'll bring myself home!" he said cheerfully.

"You do mean to remain, then?"

"If I get what I want."

"The Dower House?"

"Nay, that's a small matter! I'll tell you what it is one of these days, but I'm not so very sure I can get it yet, so happen I'll do best to keep it to myself."

"Well, I wouldn't tell anyone!" she exclaimed.

"The thing is you might say I'd no hope of getting it," he explained. An odd little smile came into his eyes as he saw her puzzled frown. "I'd be all dashed down in a minute," he said, shaking his head. "That would never do!"

XIII

If the Major did not succeed in wholly reconciling Mrs. Darracott to Richmond's expedition, he did contrive, with the aid of much tact and patience, to convince her that to protest against it would only serve to make Richmond feel that he was tied to her apron-strings. Perceiving from her suddenly thoughtful expression that he had struck home, he enlarged gently upon this theme; but it soon became apparent that while she could be persuaded to agree (with a sigh) that Richmond must be allowed to spread his wings, any suggestion that she should support his ambition to enter upon a military career threw her instantly on the defensive. In a rush of volubility, she explained why this was not to be thought of, her reasons ranging over a wide field which began with the delicacy of Richmond's constitution, and ended with the clinching statement that Lord Darracott would not hear of it. Not being one (as he himself phrased it) to fling his cap after lost causes, he let the matter rest, devoting his energies instead to the task of soothing her fear that Vincent was imbued with a sinister determination to corrupt the morals of his young cousin. To do this without setting up her back by the least hint that few things would bore Vincent more than to be obliged to sponsor Richmond into his own or any other social circle called for no little ingenuity; and it spoke volumes for Hugo's adroit handling of the situation that Mrs. Darracott should later have told her daughter that no one would ever know what a comfort dear Hugo was to her. She added that he was like a son to her; and, upon Anthea's objecting that only fifteen years lay between them, replied, with great dignity, that in mediaeval times it would not have been considered remarkable had she become a mother at an even earlier age.

So Richmond was allowed to set forth for Sevenoaks with no other manifestation of maternal concern than a few injunctions to be sure that his bed at the Crown had been well aired before he got between possibly damp sheets; to wrap himself up while watching the fight (because however warm he might suppose himself to be nothing could be more depended upon to give him a chill than sitting about in the open air); to go to bed in good time; to remember that buttered crab and roast pork were alike fatal to his digestion; to resist any attempts made by persons unnamed to lead him into excess; to be careful always to have a clean handkerchief in his pocket; and, finally, not to forget to thank his cousin for the treat.

Blithely promising to bear all these sensible instructions in mind, Richmond kissed his anxious parent farewell, climbed up into the phaeton, and proceeded without loss of time to forget all about them. However, as he returned two days later not a penny the worse for his hazardous adventure, Mrs. Darracott remained in ignorance of his perfidy, and was even able (though with the utmost reluctance) to give Vincent credit for having taken every care of the delicate treasure entrusted to his charge.

Meanwhile, the absence of his two favourites left Lord Darracott with no other male companion (for Claud could not be said to count) than his heir: a circumstance which prevailed upon him not only to take Hugo on a tour of his estates, but also to embark on the disagreeable task of putting him in possession of a great many financial details which he would have preferred to have kept to himself. Treading warily, Hugo listened, and made few comments. His lordship would have been furious had he demanded explanations, which, since the estate was settled, he had every right to do; but when Hugo asked no questions that could be construed as criticism he was not in the least grateful for this forbearance, but bitterly contemptuous, informing Lady Aurelia later that he did not know what he had done to be cursed with a blubberheaded commoner for his heir. She could have furnished him with several reasons, but she remained true to her traditions, hearing him out in high-bred silence, and merely remarking, at the end of his tirade, that for her part she did not consider Major Darracott to be at all deficient in understanding, however meagre might be his scholastic attainments.

The Major emerged from these sessions with his grandsire undismayed, and with one object attained: my lord's steward had been formally presented to him, and he had been advised to ask this melancholy individual to furnish him with such further information as he might desire.

Glossop, regarding the neophyte without enthusiasm, said, with mechanical civility, that he would be happy to be of service to him. Hugo responded with equal civility and even less enthusiasm, his own observations having given him the poorest opinion of Mr. Glossop's capability. It was not long, however, before each discovered that he had done the other less than justice. The steward's laodicean attitude rose not from ineptitude but from despair; and the Major's ignorance was offset by a shrewdness which awoke in Glossop's breast a faint gleam of hope that the repairs and improvements he had long since ceased to urge upon Lord Darracott might some day be undertaken.

The return of Vincent and Richmond from Sevenoaks coincided with the arrival at Darracott Place of Crimplesham's nephew. He was a solemn-eyed and conscientious young man, the eldest of a numerous family. His mother, a widow of long-standing, sped him on his way with anxious exhortations to prove himself worthy of her dear brother's exceeding kindness; his uncle received him with rather stronger exhortations to the same effect; and by the time he was conducted to his new master's presence he was so nervous that he could hardly speak. The Major's size did nothing to soothe his alarm, nor did his uncle's introductory speech add to his self-esteem. No one could have gathered from it that he had the smallest pretension to call himself a valet. His uncle trusted that the Major would make allowance for his lack of experience; and the best he seemed able to say of him was that he believed him to be honest and hard-working. It would not have surprised the unhappy young man if the Major had then and there dismissed him; but the Major dismissed Crimplesham instead, which did something to restore his sinking spirits. Upon being asked his name, he said: "Ferring, sir," and ventured to raise his eyes to his employer's face. The Major smiled kindly, and said: "Eh, don't look so dejected! If your uncle's spoken the truth about you, we'll deal very well together. I don't want a valet who will try to turn me into a Bond Street Beau, and I don't want a dry-nurse either. You'll keep my gear in good order, and make yourself useful in a general way, but you won't shave me, or brush my hair for me, and if I find you waiting to put me to bed we'll fall out!"

Ferring grinned shyly at him, and said that he would do his best to give satisfaction. By the time he had laid out the Major's evening-dress, hauled off his boots, helped him out of his coat, and rendered him as much assistance in dressing as he would accept, he had registered a silent vow to exert himself to the utmost in his determination to make himself indispensable to a master who seemed to him to approach very nearly to the ideal. When he went down to the Servants' Hall he was blissfully looking forward to an honourable and comfortable future; and when his formidable uncle yielded precedence to him at the table his cup almost overflowed. He was a modest young man, and would willingly have taken the lowliest place, but when Mrs. Flitwick invited him to a seat beside her, opposite no less a personage than Grooby, his lordship's own valet, he realized that he had leapt magically into a position of consequence, and his elation was only tempered by regret that his mother was not present to see his triumph.

He would have been distressed had he known what heart-burnings his elevation had caused his uncle to suffer, for he was deeply grateful to him. It had not occurred to Crimplesham, when he recommended Ferring to the Major, that he was placing his nephew above himself; and when the odious Polyphant maliciously pointed this circumstance out to him his first impulse had been to claim precedence over Ferring on the score of their relationship. But however lax they might be in the dining-room, in the Hall the hierarchy was strictly observed. There could be no question that the heir's valet ranked above Mr. Vincent's, and Crimplesham was a stickler on points of etiquette. Moreover, although he had no doubt that Ferring would yield precedence to him, he had also no doubt that he would yield it to Polyphant too. Having weighed the matter carefully, he decided that the most dignified course for him to pursue, and the one that would most annoy his rival, would be to insist on Ferring's going before him, with a smile that would indicate at once appreciation of a humorous situation, and sublime indifference to his own position at the board. Having carried out this programme, he had the consolation of knowing that he had not only annoyed Polyphant, but had disappointed him as well. This was satisfactory, and even more so was the very proper way Ferring responded to several spiteful remarks addressed

166

to him by Polyphant. He was civil, as became his years, but his smile was abstracted, conveying the irritating impression that his mind was otherwise. This happened to be the exact truth, but as Crimplesham did not know it he continued to be very well pleased with him, and even suspected that the boy had more intelligence than he had hitherto supposed.

By the end of the week, Ferring had completely identified himself with the Major's interests, and had consolidated his position by winning the qualified approval of John Joseph, who informed his master somewhat grudgingly that the lad was better nor like, and (although born south of the Trent, which was to be deplored) certainly preferable to the Major's late bâtman: a hapless creature, to whom John Joseph referred as *that gauming, clouterly gobbin we had wi' us in Spain.*

The major let this pass. He was seated on a horse-block, smoking a cigarillo, a circumstance that prompted John Joseph to inform him that it was a favourite perch of Miss Anthy's. "Ee, she's a floutersome lass!" he said, with a dry chuckle, and a wag of his grizzled head. "Eyeable, too," he added, with a sidelong glance at Hugo.

The Major let this pass too, his countenance immovable. After a pause, John Joseph asked bluntly: "What's tha bahn to do, Mester Hugo? Tha knows I'm not one to frump, but chance it happens tha's framing to bide here I winna be so very well suited."

"No, I'm thinking I might set up for myself at the Dower House," said the Major.

"Nay then! By what that slamtrash that lives there tells me, it's flue-full of boggarts!"

"Oh, so he's been telling you ghost-stories too, has he? Tell me now, John Joseph, what do you think of him?"

"He's a reet hellion!" replied John Joseph promptly. "Ee, Mester Hugo, what gaes on here? Seck a meedless set they are in these parts as I never saw! Ay, and not to take pack-thread, sir, t'gaffer up yonder——" He jerked his thumb in direction of the house—"nigh as bad as the rest! Sithee, tha knows t'Blue Lion, Mester Hugo?"

Hugo nodded. "Yes, I know it: it's the inn in the village. Well?"

"I've been there whiles, playing off my dust, and neighbouring wi' t'tapper. Seemingly there's some kind of scuggery afoot at that Dower House."

"Smuggling?"

"Ay, that's what I think mysen, nor it wouldn't surprise me. There's nowt 'ud surprise me in these flappy, slibber-slabber south-country folk! I'd be reet fain to be shut of every Jack rag of 'em! Hooseever, that's not to be, so no use naffing. Mester Hugo, if tha's shaping to wink at smuggling, like t'rest o' t'gentry hereabouts——"

"Don't be a clodhead, John Joseph! Are the Preventives still suspicious of Spurstow? I know they had dragoons watching the Dower House, but I was told they never had sight or sound of run goods being carried into it."

"Nor they hadn't, sir, but when t'new young gadger came into these ungodly parts he got it into his head, seemingly, that uncustomed goods were being brung up from t'coast and stored in t'Dower House. They run t'boats in pick-nights, and mun store t'goods until t'moon's up. They carry 'em on to London then. By what t'tapper's let fall—and a reet clash-me-saunter he is when he gets to be nazy, which he does at-after he's swallowed nobbut a driver's pint!—there's hidden ways hereabouts. Leastways, that's what they call 'em, but they're nobbut t'owd roads, sunk-like."

"Is there a watch kept on moonlight nights, to see if anything is taken *out* of the house?"

"Nay, that 'ud be sackless, Mester Hugo! Hark-ye-but, if there's nowt carried in there'll be nowt carried out! There's nobbut a half-squadron o' dragoons quartered twixt here and t'North Foreland, besides t'gadgers—and noan so many of them, by what I learn—and there's plenty of other places need a watch kept on 'em. But I'll tell you summat, sir!"

He paused, nodding. Hugo waited patiently, and after a few moments, during which he seemed to be chewing the cud of his own reflections, John Joseph said: "T'young Riding-officer's more frack than t'owd one, and since t'last run, when him and them dragoons was made April-gowks of, chasing after nobbut a few loads o' faggots, Peasmarsh way, while t'run was carried off, it were rumoured, not so very far from here, I'll take my accidavy he's got his eye fixed on Spurstow again. Happen he's not so sickened on watching the Dower House as he makes out, for there's them as is ready to swear they seen him up t'lane now-and-now. There's been no dragoons stationed thereabouts this while back, and no manner o' good gin there had been, for Clotton—him as is his lordship's head groom—tells me they'd got so that they took every bush for a boggart, and reet laughable it was one night when a couple of 'em—nobbut ignorant lads!—came sticklebutt into t'Blue Lion, frining and

168

faffling that there was a flaysome thing jangling round t'Dower House, and wailing fit to freeze t'blood in a body's veins. At-after that t'sergeant went up there, wi' another chap, neither of 'em being flaid o' boggarts." He smiled dourly. "They say in t'village t'sergeant weren't very well suited wi' what he saw and heard. Hooseever, he challenged t'boggart, but it vanished into t'shrubbery, and he didna care to gae after it, chance it happened Spurstow went frumping to t'owd lord that he'd been trespassing."

"Spurstow himself, with a sheet draped round him!" said Hugo. "Well, I thought as much."

"Nay, hold thee a minute, Mester Hugo! Tha's out there: it weren't Spurstow. That's sure, because Spurstow stuck his head out o' t'window, calling out to know who was there, and tha knows there's no road he could have got back into t'house from t'shrubbery without t'sergeant would have seen him, let alone he'd no time to do it."

"Oh!" said Hugo slowly. He was silent for a minute, and then looked thoughtfully at John Joseph, and said: "Keep your eyes and your ears open, will you, John Joseph?"

"Ay—and my tongue between my teeth. Happen it's nobbut a silly lad playing tricks, Mester Hugo."

"Happens it is," Hugo agreed. "I think I'll go up to the Dower House myself one night."

John Joseph grunted. "Tha'll need to bide a spirt, till t'moon's up a bit. I'll gae wi' ye."

"The devil you'll not! Do you think I'm afraid of ghosts?"

"Nay, it's no ghost, sir!"

"I'll go alone, thank you, John Joseph."

Several days elapsed before the waxing moon afforded enough light to make a midnight visit to the grounds of the Dower House practicable, and when the Major did go he saw nothing more alarming than Spurstow, who came out of the house (he said) to discover who was prowling about the gardens. As the Major had strolled all round the house in full view of its windows, and knew that even in the dim light his great size made him easily recognizable, he doubted this statement, but he replied in his pleasant way that he was sorry if he had alarmed Spurstow. "I came up to see this ghost of yours, but it seems to be shy of me."

"You shouldn't ought to listen to what they'll tell you in the village, sir. It's all foolishness! Leastways, *I've* never seen it!" Spurstow said, in a surly tone.

"I'll go bail, you haven't!" replied the Major, amused.

He mentioned his expedition to none but Anthea. She regarded him in frank admiration, exclaiming: "All by yourself? Weren't you nervous? Just the *least* bit nervous?"

"Nay, I was as brave as a lion!" he assured her.

She laughed, but said: "Well, I must own I think you were! And you didn't see or hear anything horrid?"

"No, but I wasn't expected," he said. "Another time maybe I might see something."

"You mean you believe that there's no ghost, only Spurstow? If it is so, he'll never dare to try to hoax *you*—not when he knows you weren't afraid to walk all round the house in the middle of the night! What are you hoping to do? To find if smugglers do use the Dower House, or to lay the ghost?"

"Well, I'd like to do that," he answered.

"To be sure! Miss Melkinthorpe would wish it laid, of course!"

"Who's she?" asked Hugo, taken off his guard.

She opened her eyes at him. "But, my dear cousin——! Miss *Amelia* Melkinthorpe!"

"Miss Amel——" He broke off abruptly, and Anthea was glad to perceive that he had the grace to blush. "Oh! *Her!*"

She said, in a shocked voice: "You cannot, surely, have forgotten her?"

"Ay, but I had," he confessed, rubbing his nose. "I'm that road, you see: out of sight, out of mind!"

Miss Darracott realized, with considerable indignation, that the Major had yielded once more to the promptings of his worser self, and said, somewhat ominously: "Indeed?"

He nodded, meeting her smouldering gaze with one of his blandest looks. "Ay. Mind you, I wouldn't forget a lass I'd formed a *lasting* passion for!" He sighed. "The trouble is I mistook my own heart. Of course, she being so beautiful, it's no wonder I was carried away."

"I should suppose her to have all Yorkshire at her feet," said Anthea. "I remember thinking, when you described her to me, that she must be the loveliest creature imaginable! Almost too lovely to be true, in fact. There is something so particularly ravishing about brown eyes, and black curls, isn't there?"

"Nay!" he said reproachfully. "That was another one! Amelia's got *blue* eyes, and *golden* curls."

She choked.

"The thing is, she wouldn't be the right kind of wife for

170

me when I get to be a peer. She wouldn't wish to leave Huddersfield, either—on account of her mother."

"Her mother," said Anthea encouragingly, "could come to live with you."

"No, that won't fit. She's bedfast," explained the Major, ever-fertile.

Anthea strove with herself.

"Besides, we shouldn't suit. And there's no use thinking his lordship would take to her, because he wouldn't."

"*Surely*, cousin, you cannot mean to *jilt* her?" said Anthea, in accents of reprobation.

"Nay, it wouldn't be seemly," he agreed. "I'll just have to dispose of her, as you might say."

"Good God! *Murder* her?"

"There's no need to be in a quake," he said reassuringly. "No one will ever know!'"

"If only—oh, if *only* I could do to you what I *long* to do!" exclaimed Anthea. "If you were but a *few* inches shorter—!"

He said hopefully: "Nay, don't let that fatch you, love! It'll be no trouble at all to lift you up: in fact, there's nothing I'd like better!"

Furiously blushing, she retorted: "I didn't mean that I wished to *kiss* you!"

He heaved a despondent sigh. "I was afraid you didn't," he said, sadly shaking his head. "I was reet taken-aback, but I thought to myself: Come now, lad! She'd never raise your hopes only to cast you down! So——"

"Cousin Hugo, you are *outrageous!*" said Anthea, in a shaking voice.

Horrified, he replied: "You're reet; I am, love! I need someone to take me in hand, and that's the truth! Of course, if Amelia had been a different sort of a lass—more after your style!—she'd have been just the one to undertake me, but——"

"Cousin Hugo!" interrupted Anthea, feeling that it was high time he was brought to book, "you may bamboozle everyone else, but you won't bamboozle *me!*"

"Do you think I don't know that, love?" he said, smiling at her in a very disturbing way.

"You invented Amelia Melkinthorpe because you were afraid you might find yourself obliged to offer for me!" continued Anthea, prudently ignoring this interpolation. "And if you think——"

"Nay, you're fair and far off, lass!"

"Am I? Then perhaps, cousin, you will tell me why you *did* invent her? Not," she added scathingly, "that I shall believe a word of it!"

"Are you telling me I'm a liar?" demanded Hugo, insulted.

"Yes!" responded Anthea doggedly.

"I thought you were," said Hugo, relapsing with disconcerting suddenness into dejection.

Miss Darracott, realizing with bitter resentment that she was quite unable to control her own voice, averted her gaze, and took her quivering underlip firmly between her teeth.

Much encouraged, the abandoned creature before her said confidentially: "It was this road, love! By the time you took me up to the picture-gallery my spirits were so low and oppressed by all th 'black looks I'd had cast on me, and I was feeling that lonely—eh, I was never more miserable in my life!"

"F-Fiddle!" uttered Anthea, shaken but staunch.

"I won't deny the old gentleman threw me into a terrible quake when he told me the scheme he had in his mind," pursued Hugo, making a clean breast of it. "It seemed to me there was only one thing for it: to shab off as fast I could before I found myself gapped! For of all the proud, disagreeable females——"

"Yes, but I—— You know v-very well why I——"

"The way you sat there beside me at the dinner-table, never so much as looking at me!" he said reminiscently. "And not a word to be got from you but *Yes,* and *No,* except once, when you said *Indeed!* I thought you were reet cruel. There I was, scared out of my wits——"

"You weren't! You were *not!*"

"—scared out of my wits," he repeated firmly, "and my heart in my shoes, and you weren't even civil to me, let alone friendly!"

"You need not th-think I don't know you are m-merely trying to overset me! You didn't care a rush for any of us!"

"However, when you told me how it was," he continued, still lost in reminiscence, "I saw I'd been mistaken in you. That was the first time you smiled at me. Ee, lass, you've got a lovely smile! Happen you don't know the way it starts in your eyes, giving them such a mischievous look as——"

"That will do!" interposed Anthea, rigorously suppressing a strong desire to encourage him to develop this agreeable theme.

"I was only trying to explain how I came to invent Amelia!" he said in an injured voice. "The thing was that when you smiled at me it set me cudgelling my brains to hit on some way I could get you to stop thinking you had to keep me at a distance, which I could see you'd be bound to do, the way his lordship was trying to throw us together, unless I could put it into your head that there was no reason why you should."

"Is it possible that you have the—the *audacity* to suppose that you can make me believe that I had only to smile to make you wish to marry me?" demanded Anthea, justly incensed.

"Nay, I never said that!" he protested. "All I wanted was a friend! In fact," he added, with the air of one brilliantly inspired, "it was Hobson's Choice! I don't say I wouldn't liefer have made up to my Aunt Aurelia, mind, but——"

"*Will* you stop behaving in this odious fashion?" begged Anthea, in sore straits. "You are *utterly* without conduct, or—or propriety of taste! You would be very well-served if you did find yourself riveted to me! I promise you, you'd come home by weeping cross!"

"Ay, I know I would," he agreed. "A dog's life I'd lead, with you riding rough-shod over me, as I don't doubt you would, seeing that you're such a shrew, but——"

"Exactly so! So why, pray, do you wish to be married to me?" said Anthea, pouncing on opportunity.

"Eh, lass, I thought you knew!" he answered, his eyes round with surprise. "To please his lordship, of course!"

Miss Darracott's feelings threatened to overcome her. None of the rejoinders that rose to her lips seemed adequate to the occasion; she stared up in seething impotence at her tormentor; saw that he was watching her with an appreciative and extremely reprehensible twinkle in his eyes; and decided that the only way to deal with him was to pay him back in his own coin. So she said, with really very creditable calm: "I need scarcely tell you that that is an object with me too, but try as I will I can't bring myself to the sticking-point."

"Come now, love, never say that!" he responded, in heartening accents. "To be sure, there's a lot of me to swallow but you're too game to be beaten on any suit!"

She shook her head. "There's not *enough* of you to swallow," she said. "I must tell you that my disposition, besides being shrewish, is mercenary. I am determined to marry a man of fortune. *Large* fortune!"

"Oh, I've plenty of brass!" he assured her.

"I am only interested in gold," she said loftily. "Furthermore, I have no fancy for living in the Dower House."

"Well, I can offer you a house in Yorkshire, if you think you could fancy that. I was meaning to sell it, but——"

"Have you really a house in Yorkshire?" she asked suspiciously.

"Of course I have!"

"There's no *of course* about it!" she said, with asperity. "You tell such shocking whiskers that not the slightest dependence can be placed on anything you say! Where is this house?"

"On the edge of the moor, by Huddersfield. That's the trouble. When my grandfather gave up the old house, next to the mill, and we went to live at Axby House, it was right in the country, but the town's been growing and growing, and it will grow still faster now the war's over, and more and more machines are being invented, and put to use. I hardly recognized the place when I came home at the end of the war in the Peninsula. I don't think you'd like it, love."

"No, not at all. I should want a house in London—in the best part, of course!"

"Oh, we'll have *that!*" he replied cheerfully.

"We shan't have anything of the sort—I mean, we *shouldn't* —because my Uncle Matthew has the town-house!"

"Well, there's more than one house to be had in town!"

"Dear me, yes! How could I be so stupid? I might have known you meant to purchase a handsome establishment!"

"I was thinking of hiring one, myself."

"No, no, only think how shabby! Next you will say that you don't intend to have more than one house in the country!"

"Nay, I shan't say that! I want one in Leicestershire."

"Oh, in that case there's no more to be said, for I've set *my* heart on one in the moon!"

"You don't mean that, love! Nay then, you can't have thought!" he expostulated. "It's much too far from town!"

An involuntary laugh escaped her, but she said: "I might have known you'd have an answer! Do you think we have now talked enough nonsense?"

"I'm not talking nonsense, lass. I'd give you the whole of the moon if I could, and throw in the stars for good measure," he said, taking her hand, and kissing it. "You couldn't be content with less?"

174

"You—you *are* talking nonsense!" she said, feeling suddenly breathless, and more than a little startled. She was inexperienced in the art of flirtation, but it had certainly occurred to her on various occasions that in this her large cousin had the advantage of her. His methods (judged by such knowledge as she had acquired during one London Season) were original, but that he might be entertaining serious intentions she had not consciously considered. Nor had she looked into her own heart. She had accepted him, after her first mistrust, as a delightfully easy companion who had kept her in a ripple of amusement: not the hero of her vague imaginings, but a simple solid creature, wholly to be trusted. She now realized, with a sense of shock, that this enormous and apparently guileless intruder had taken the grossest advantage of her innocence, advancing by imperceptible but rapid stages from the position of a stranger to be treated with circumspection to that of the close friend in whom she could safely confide, and who was, for some obscure reason, indispensable to her comfort. Any belief she might have had in the existence of the beautiful Miss Melkinthorpe had admittedly been of short duration, but the thought of marrying the Major herself had not, until this moment, entered her head. It was clearly necessary to temporize. Withdrawing her hand from his, she said, in a rallying tone: "Recollect that we have been acquainted for less than a month! You cannot, cousin, have fallen—formed an attachment in so short a time!"

"Nay, love, don't be so daft!" he expostulated. "There's no sense in saying I can't do what I *have* done!"

Miss Darracott, an intelligent girl, now perceived that in harbouring for as much as an instant the notion of marrying a man who fell so lamentably short of the ideal lover she was an irreclaimable ninnyhammer. Ideal lovers might differ in certain respects, but in whatever mould they were cast not one of them was so unhandsome as to make it extremely difficult for one not to giggle at their utterances. This hopelessly overgrown and unromantic idiot must be given a firm set-down. Resolutely lifting her eyes to his face, and summoning to her aid a smile which was (she hoped) satirical, but not so unkind as to wound him, she said: "You are being quite absurd, my dear cousin! Pray say no more!"

"Never?"

She transferred her gaze to the topmost button of his coat. If anything had been wanting to convince her that he was quite unworthy of her regard, he had supplied it by putting a pistol to her head in this unchivalrous way. She wished very much that she had not committed the imprudence of looking up into his face, but how, she wondered indignantly, could she have guessed that anyone so incurably frivolous would look so anxious? Any female of sensibility must shrink from inflicting pain upon a fellow-creature, but how did one depress pretension without hurting the sinner, or rendering him unnecessarily despondent?

On the whole, she could only be thankful that the Major, apparently realizing that he had fallen into error, spared her the necessity of answering him. He said ruefully: "If ever there was a cod's head, his name is Hugo Darracott! Don't look so fatched, love! Forget I said it! I know it was too soon!"

Grateful to him for his quick understanding of her dilemma, Miss Darracott decided, with rare forbearance, to overlook the impropriety of his putting his arm round her, as she spoke, and giving her a hug. "*Much* too soon!" she answered.

His arm tightened momentarily; he dropped a kiss on the top of her head, but this she was also able to ignore, for he then said, in a thoughtful voice which conveyed to her the reassuring intelligence that he had reverted to his usual manner: "Now, where will I come by a book on etiquette? You wouldn't know if his lordship's got one in the library, would you, love?"

Her colour somewhat heightened, she disengaged herself from his embrace, saying: "No, but I shouldn't think so. He has one about ranks and dignities and orders of precedency: is that what you mean?"

"Nay, that's no use to me! I want one that'll tell me how to behave correctly."

"I am well-aware that you are trying to roast me," said Anthea, resigned to this fate, "and also that you don't stand in any need of a book on etiquette—though one on *propriety* wouldn't come amiss!"

"I'm not trying to roast you!" declared Hugo. "I want to know how long you must be acquainted with a lass before it's polite to propose to her!"

XIV

Any fears lurking in Anthea's mind that the Major's premature declaration might be productive of some awkwardness between them were very swiftly put to rout. Except for a certain warmth in his eyes, when they rested on her, she could detect no change in his demeanour. She was devoutly thankful, for she knew that her grandfather was closely watching the progress of a courtship he had instigated.

It was perhaps fortunate that his lordship's attention should have been diverted by the repercussions of quite another sort of courtship. The blacksmith, a brawny individual, imbued with what his lordship considered revolutionary notions, had not only taken exception to Claud's elegant trifling with his daughter, but had seized the opportunity afforded by that rather too accommodating damsel to pay off an old score against his lordship. To Claud's startled dismay, the elder Ackleton waylaid my lord when he was riding home through the village, and lodged an accusation against his least favourite grandson, referring to him darkly as a serpent, who had stung his daughter, and hinting (without, however, much conviction) at reprisals of an obscure but dreadful nature. My lord, whose native shrewdness had earned for him the reputation in the neighbourhood of being a deep old file, was neither credulous of the story, nor alarmed by the threats. He might be eighty years of age, and considered by his family to be verging on senility, but he was perfectly capable of dealing with far more determined efforts at blackmail, and he disposed of the blacksmith in a few forceful and well-chosen words, which included a recommendation to that disconcerted gentleman to take care the fair Eliza did not end her adventurous career in the nearest Magdalen. Since this interview took place in the middle of the village street it very soon became common property, and was the occasion of much merriment, and many exchanges, when neither the elder Ackleton nor his even more formidable son was within earshot, of damaging rumours about Eliza's way of life. His lordship was not popular, but the Ackletons were cordially disliked by all but their few cronies, Eliza being thought by the respectable to be a disgrace to the community, and the two male members of the family not only scandalizing decent folk with their hazy but seditious political opinions, but alienating all sorts by their invariable pugnacity when they had had a cup too much. No one was hardy enough to betray the least knowledge of the encounter outside the forge, but the sudden silence that fell on the company in the taproom of the Blue Lion, when the father and son walked in that evening left neither of them in any doubt of what the subject of the interrupted discussion had been. The elder Ackleton, after vainly trying to pick out a quarrel with anyone willing to oblige him, was bowled out by a toothless and decrepit Ancient, who took infuriating advantage of his years and infirmity, and asked the raging blacksmith, with a shrill cackle of mirth, if he had had comely speech with his lordship that morning. Encouraged by a smothered guffaw, he wagged his hoary head and stated his readiness to back the old lord to make the smith and a dozen like him look la-amentable blue.

The smith, realizing that the weight of public opinion was against him, stayed only to inform the Ancient what his fate would have been had he been some seventy years younger before slamming his tankard down, and departing. It would have been as well if he had taken his son with him, instead of leaving him to drink himself into a pot-valiant condition, in the company of a like-minded young man, whose reckless statements of what he would do if he stood in Ned's shoes strengthened his resolve to draw Mr. Claud Darracott's cork at the earliest opportunity. By the time an astonishing quantity of heavy wet and several glasses of jackey had been drunk, the propensity of the entire aristocracy and gentry for grinding the faces of the poor under their heels discussed, and the date of a revolution modelled after the French pattern settled, Ned Ackleton was determined to seek out Mr. Claud Darracott immediately, and Jim Booley, applauding this bold decision, announced his intention of accompanying him. The landlord, contemptuously watching the manner of their departure, gave it as his opinion that the courage of neither would be sufficient to carry him beyond the gates of Darracott Place. In uttering this prophecy, however, he failed to make allowance for the invigorating effect of companionship. The harbingers of the revolution reached the house itself before Booley realized that it would be improper for him to take any active part in a quarrel which was no concern of his. He began to feel that it might, perhaps, be wiser if Ned were to postpone drawing Mr. Claud Darracott's cork until such time as he should meet him in some rather more suitable locality. But Ned was made of sterner stuff; and although the effects of liquor had to some extent worn off he had ranted himself into a state of mental intoxication which made him even more belligerent. Rejecting with scorn his friend's uneasy suggestion that it might be wiser to seek an entrance at the scullery-door, he tugged violently at the bell hanging beside the main door, and followed this up by hammering the great iron knocker in a ferocious style that caused Mr. Booley to retreat several paces, urgently advising him to *adone-do!*

This craven attitude, far from damping Ned's ardour, whipped up his courage, which had faltered a little for a moment and gave him an added incentive to force his way into the house. Booley should see that he was a man of his word; and Booley was not going to be given a chance to undermine his friend's prestige by spreading through the village a story of flight at the last moment.

Charles, the footman, opened the door. Startled by so thunderous a demand for admittance, he did so rather cautiously, which incensed Ned. Commanding him to get out of the way, he barged his way into the house, demanding, in stentorian accents, to be led immediately to Claud, whose character, appearance, and licentious villainy he described in terms which made Charles's eyes start from their sockets. Charles was of unheroic stature, but he knew his duty, and he was no coward. He did his best to hustle Ned out of the house, and was sent reeling backwards, bringing down a chair in his fall.

All this commotion brought Chollacombe and James hurrying to the scene. Ned, his appetite whetted, invited them to come on, promising them some home-brewed as a reward, but before either could accept the invitation three more persons entered on the stage. The first was Lord Darracott, who came stalking out of the library, demanding to know what the devil was going on; the second was Major Darracott, in his shirtsleeves; and the third, also in his shirtsleeves, and still holding a billiard-cue in his hand, was the hapless cause of the whole affair.

Ned put up his fists menacingly as Lord Darracott advanced towards him, but there was something about that tall, gaunt figure which made him give ground, even though he uttered a blustering threat to mill his lordship down if he tried to interfere with him.

"You drunken scum!" said his lordship, with awful deliberation. "How dare you bring your filthy carcase into my house? Outside!"

Ned spat a foul epithet at him.

"That's enough! You've had your marching orders! I'll give you precisely fifteen seconds to get yourself through that door."

Ned jumped, and looked round, but he was hardly more startled than the rest of the company. No one at Darracott

Place had heard the Major speak in that voice before. It brought a gleam into Lord Darracott's eyes, and a grim smile to his lips, and it made Ned drop his fists instinctively. But just as he was about to retreat he caught sight of Claud, and he threw caution to the winds. Before he could wreak his vengeance on Claud's willowy person, Major Darracott must be swept from his path. The Major was large, but large men were notoriously slow, and could be bustled. Ned, himself a big man, and with thews of iron, went in with a rush, to mill him down before he could get upon his guard, and was sent crashing to the floor by a nicely delivered punch from something more nearly resembling a sledge-hammer than a human fist.

The Major, standing over him, waited with unruffled calm for him to recover sufficiently from the stupefying effect of this punch to struggle to his feet again. When Ned got upon his hands and knees he apparently judged it to be necessary to assist him to leave the premises, which he did in an expeditious fashion that struck terror into the heart of Mr. Booley, faithfully awaiting the return of his friend from his punitive expedition.

The Major, having hurled the unbidden guest forth, turned, and came back into the hall, nodding to James, who was holding open the door, and saying with his customary amiability: "That's all: shut the door now!"

Lord Darracott, surveying him with something approaching approval, said: "I'm obliged to you!" and went back into the library.

He was better-pleased than he chose to betray, for without supposing that there was anything very remarkable in the Major's ability to floor Ned Ackleton he liked the neatness with which he had done it, and was agreeably surprised to see that for all his great size Hugo could move with unexpected swiftness. When Vincent presently came in he described the episode to him, saying: "Well, he's not such a clumsy oaf as I'd thought: I'll say that for him. Showed to advantage. Good foot-work, too."

Vincent was not much impressed, but he congratulated Hugo on his exploit with an air of exaggerated admiration. "I wish I had been privileged to witness the encounter," he said. "I hear you rattled in, game as a pebble, coz; stopped your opponent's plunge in first-rate style; and ended by throwing in a classic hit."

"Wonderful, it was!" replied Hugo, shaking his head. "Ay, you missed a high treat! He was no more than half-sprung, mind you, and not very much more than a couple of stone lighter than I am, so I did well, didn't I?"

That drew a reluctant laugh from Vincent. "My grandfather seems to think so. I'm told the fellow is much fancied as a fighter in these parts, but I collect you're not yourself a novice?"

"I can box," Hugo admitted, "but it's not often I do. I'm too big."

Everyone was pleased with Hugo's conduct except the Ackletons, both of whom were popularly held to be planning a hideous revenge; and Claud, who had no doubt on whom such a revenge would be wreaked, and considered that Hugo would have done better to have detained Ned at Darracott Place until he could have been induced to have listened to reason. Claud knew himself to be innocent of the charge brought against him, and great was his indignation when he discovered that his grandfather not only believed in his innocence on no grounds at all, but thought the worse of him for it. In high dudgeon he declared his intention of leaving Darracott Place immediately, and might actually have done so had not his lordship said, crashing his fist down on the table before him, that, by God, he should do no such thing!

"No grandson of mine shall turn-tail while I'm in the saddle!" he announced. "I wouldn't let you shab off, you pudding-hearted fribble, if you *had* given that light-skirt a slip on the shoulder!"

What Lady Aurelia thought about it no one knew, for she never mentioned the matter, and nothing could be learned from her countenance or her demeanour. One or two jibes addressed to her by Lord Darracott were met with such blank stares of incomprehension that even he seemed to be daunted; and Mrs. Darracott confessed to her daughter that she for one doubted whether her ladyship knew anything at all about the affair.

Several days passed before Hugo paid his second nocturnal visit to the Dower House, wet weather making the sky too cloudy for observation. But on the first clear evening he strolled up the path to the wicket-gate into the shrubbery shortly before midnight, a cigar between his teeth. The gate shrieked on its rusty hinges; the beaten track that led to the house was sodden; and the leaves of the bushes were very wet, damping the Major's coat as he brushed past them.

A slight reconnaissance showed him that the shrubbery

was intersected by several paths, once, no doubt, when the hedges were clipped, and gravel strewn underfoot, furnishing the inhabitants of the Dower House with an agreeable promenade on windy days. The hedges had not been trimmed for years, however, and the place had become a wilderness, the various paths so overgrown as sometimes to be difficult to follow. The Major, making his way out of it to the path at the side of the house, thought it would afford an excellent retreat for any ghost finding itself hard-pressed.

The moon was not yet half-full, and its light was a little fitful, clouds occasionally obscuring its face; but it was possible to make out the way, and even to discern objects at some distance. The house showed no light at any window, so it was to be inferred that Spurstow was either in bed and asleep or had put up the shutters in the kitchen-quarters as well as everywhere else in the house. Having walked round the building, Hugo trod across the rank grass that had once been a shaven lawn and took up his position in the shadow of a tree standing on the edge of the carriage-drive.

He had not very long to wait. The wind that fretted the tree-tops was hardly more than a whisper, but the stillness was broken after a short time by the screech of an owl in the woods, followed almost immediately by a long drawn-out wail that rose to a shriek, and died away in a sobbing moan, eerie in the night-silence. The next instant a vague, misty figure appeared round the angle of the house, and flitted into the shrubbery.

The Major, unperturbed by these manifestations, threw away the butt of his cigar, and strode towards the shrubbery. A hasty movement behind him made him check, and turn quickly, searching with narrowed eyes the deep shadows cast by the bushes by the gates. Someone, who had been concealed by these, started forward. The Major saw the moonlight gleam on the barrel of a pistol, and, a moment later, recognized Lieutenant Ottershaw. Ottershaw, paying no heed to him, began to run across the grass, with the obvious intention of plunging into the shrubbery, but two long strides brought the Major between him and his goal, and obliged him to check.

"Nay, lad, I wouldn't do that, if I were you," Hugo said placidly.

"Did you see?" Ottershaw shot at him. "After that ghastly—that damned scream—someone in a sheet! Well, I'm going to discover who it is!"

"I saw," Hugo said. "But happen you'd best take care what you're about. You can't go ghost-hunting in a private garden, you know."

"That was no ghost!" Ottershaw said violently. "*You* know that, sir! I watched you: you never so much as jumped when that scream sounded! If you'd believed it was a ghost——"

"Oh, no! I didn't, of course."

"No! And why did you come here if it wasn't to discover who's playing tricks to keep people away from this place? I don't believe you're in it, but——"

"In what?" interposed Hugo.

The Lieutenant hesitated. "In what I know to be an attempt to drive *me* off!" he answered rather defiantly. "I've had my suspicions of this house ever since I came here, and I'm as sure as any man may be that it's one of the smugglers' chief storehouses!"

"No, I'm not in anything like that," said Hugo.

"No, sir, I never supposed you could be. But——"

"If I were you, I'd put up that pistol, Mr. Ottershaw," said Hugo. "Were you meaning to challenge the ghost with it? You'd catch cold if you did, you know. It's no crime that I ever heard of to caper about rigged up as a boggard."

The Lieutenant did restore the pistol to its holster, but he was angry, and said very stiffly: "Very well, sir! But I will tell you plainly that I believe that—apparition!—to have been none other than Mr. Richmond Darracott!"

"Ay, so do I," agreed Hugo.

Ottershaw peered up at his face, trying in the uncertain light to read its expression. He sounded a little nonplussed. "*You* think that?"

"Why, yes!" Hugo said. "I think he's trying to make a May-game of you, and, if you want to know, I also think there's little he'd like better than for you to hold him up. Eh, lad, don't be so daft! It would be all over the county before the cat could lick her ear! Your commander wouldn't thank you for making a laughing-stock of yourself, and if you were to interfere with Richmond the dust you'd raise would be nothing to the dust his lordship would kick up!"

"Oh, I'm well aware of that!" replied Ottershaw bitterly. "I look for nothing but obstruction from *that* quarter! I may say—from any member of your family, sir! I'd risk being made a laughing-stock if I could catch Richmond Darracott at his tricks—as I might have done, but for you!"

"Now, what good would that do you?" asked the Major.

"I daresay you'd like to give him a sharp lesson not to get up to this kind of bobbery at your expense, but you'd regret it if you did. You'd be better advised to pay no heed to him: he'd soon tire of the sport if you laughed at him—and got your men to do the same!"

"So you think he does it for sport, do you, sir?"

"Of course I do!" said the Major. "It's just the sort of thing a mischievous lad would do—particularly if he thought you were a trifle over-zealous."

Ottershaw was silent for a moment. Then he said curtly: "I'll say goodnight to you, sir. I should not have spoken so freely, perhaps, but since I have done so there can be little point in concealing what I make no doubt you have guessed: I believe Mr. Richmond Darracott to be hand-in-glove with these pernicious smugglers! I have no wish—it is not the wish of the Board of Customs—to incur the ill-will of persons of Lord Darracott's consequence, but I shall take leave to warn you that no such consideration would deter me—or, I should add, would be expected to deter me!—in the performance of what I might consider to be my duty!"

"Very proper," approved the Major, a note of amusement in his voice. "But, if you don't despise a word of advice from one who's older than you, and maybe more experienced, you'll make very sure you're right in your suspicions before you go tail over top into action. It's one thing to sympathize with smuggling, but quite another to be engaged in the trade, if that's what you're suggesting. You've been having the devil of a time of it here, and seemingly it's made you think that everyone who don't help you must be mixed up in the business himself. You'll end with windmills in your head that road—if you haven't 'em already!—let alone finding yourself in bad loaf with that Board of yours."

"Is that a threat, sir?" demanded Ottershaw, standing very erect.

"Nay, it's a friendly warning," replied Hugo. "Don't you make a pigeon of yourself! Goodnight!"

The Lieutenant clicked his heels together, bowed, and strode off. Hugo watched him go, and then began to retrace his own footsteps. When he reached the wicket-gate, he studied it thoughtfully for a moment. It would have been no difficult feat to have vaulted over it, but having satisfied himself on this head he merely opened it, and walked through, impervious to its protesting shriek.

He had left his bedroom candle and his tinder-box on a

table by the side-door through which he had left the house, and after kindling a light, and bolting the door, he made his way up one of the secondary staircases with which Darracott Place was lavishly provided. This one served the wing in which his own and Richmond's bedchambers were situated; and when he reached the head of it he went without hesitation to Richmond's door, and knocked on it. Eliciting no response, he turned the handle, only to find that the door was locked. He knocked again, this time imperatively, and was rewarded by hearing Richmond call out: "Who is it?"

"Hugo. I want to speak to you," he replied.

There was the sound of an impatient exclamation, followed by the rattle of curtain-rings along a rod, and a creak which indicated that Richmond had got out of bed. The key turned in the well-oiled lock, and the door was pulled open.

"What the devil do you want?" Richmond said crossly. "I thought you knew I hate to be disturbed at night!"

"I do," said Hugo. "It had me in a bit of a puzzle to understand why, too. Nay, don't stand there holding the door! I'm coming in, and it's not a bit of use scowling at me. You can get back into bed, and we're going to have a talk, you and I."

"At this hour?" Richmond ejaculated. "I'll be damned if I do!"

"I don't know about that, but I do know that I'll toss you into bed if you don't do as you're bid," responded Hugo, wresting the door from his hold and shutting it. He held up the candlestick, and looked round. The room was a large one, with a four-poster bed standing out into it. A glance showed Hugo that the curtains had been thrust back from one side, and the bedclothes flung off. Not far from it, a chair stood, with a coat thrown carelessly on to it. Hugo's gaze alighted on this, and travelled to where a pair of breeches and a shirt lay untidily on the floor. "You did undress in a hurry, didn't you?" he said.

Richmond, climbing into bed again, linked his hands behind his head, and said, with a yawn: "I wish you will say what you want, and go away! I shan't get a wink of sleep now: I never can, if I'm wakened."

Hugo set his candle down on the table beside the bed, and lightly clasped the other which stood there. He said, smiling: "Nay, lad, I don't think you were asleep: your candle's still warm."

"I suppose I had just dropped off. That's worse! O God, *must* you sit on the bed?"

Hugo paid no heed to this complaint (for which there was some justification, as his weight bore the springs down ominously), but said: "Richmond, my lad, you've not been to sleep at all, and those clothes you've just stripped off weren't the ones you were wearing at dinner, so let's have no more humbug! Not half an hour ago you were playing hide-and-seek over at the Dower House! And from the hasty way you got between sheets I think you'd a shrewd notion you'd be receiving a visit from me."

Richmond's eyes gleamed under his down-dropped lids. "Oh, have you seen the ghost, cousin?"

"No."

Richmond chuckled. "Didn't I hoax you? I made sure I should! What made you suspect—— Oh, I suppose it was what Claud said!"

"You didn't hoax anyone, and it wasn't me you were trying to hoax, was it?"

"Of course it was! I saw you set out, and guessed what you meant to do, so I followed you. Didn't you think I made a good ghost? *I* think I did!"

"Nay, you didn't follow me. You were there before me," replied Hugo. "You came round the corner of the house, and you couldn't have crossed the path between the shrubbery and the house unbeknownst to me."

"But I could get into the garden from the shrubbery, and keep under cover there until the house shut me from your view."

"Ay, you could have done that," agreed Hugo. "Did Spurstow tell you that I visited the place before, on the same errand?"

Richmond laughed. "Of course!"

"And that Ottershaw was watching the house himself?"

"No, *is* he?"

"Come, lad, you knew that!"

"How should I know it?" Richmond countered.

"Probably because Spurstow told you; and if it wasn't he I've a notion you've other sources of information. Between the pair of you, you've scared Ottershaw's men, but when you set out to scare him you made a back-cast, Richmond: he wasn't scared, and he wasn't deceived. If I hadn't stopped him he might well have caught you."

"Not he! Much good would it have done him if he had, too!"

"So I told him," said Hugo. "It would have done him no good, but it would have done you no good either."

"Why, is there a law against bamboozling Excisemen?" asked Richmond, opening his eyes wider.

Hugo looked rather gravely down at him. "For what purpose?"

"Oh, just kicking up a lark!"

"Is that why you did it?"

"Yes, of course: why else should I do it?" Richmond said impatiently.

"That's what I don't know, lad, but I think you're too old to be kicking up that sort of a lark."

The impish gleam had faded from Richmond's dark eyes; the look he shot at Hugo was one of smouldering resentment. "Maybe! What the devil else have I to do? In any event, what concern is it of yours? I wish you will go away!"

"Happen I will, when you stop trying to stall me off, and give me a plain answer," Hugo replied, a little sternly. "I've a notion you're in dangerous mischief. If I'm right, you're likely to find yourself floored at all points, for Ottershaw's not the clodhead you think him. Don't play off your cajolery on me, but tell me the truth! Have you embroiled yourself in the smuggling trade?"

Richmond sat up with a jerk. "Well, upon my word——! What next will you ask me? Just because I cut a lark with that stiff-rumped Exciseman you seem to think I'm as good as rope-ripe! Why should I take to free-trading, pray?"

"For sport," replied Hugo, smiling faintly. "Because it's a dead bore to have nothing to do but mind your book—which I've yet to see you do!—and dance attendance on your grandfather. I own, the life you're made to lead would be out of cry to me, as it is to you. If you're helping to run contraband goods, it's because you like the adventure, not for gain." His smile broadened as he saw Richmond glance strangely at him. "Well, has that hit the needle?"

Richmond lay down again, this time on his side, pillowing his cheek on his hand. "Lord, no! I played ghost for sport. Famous sport it was, too! You should have seen those cowhearted dragoons huddling together! I made 'em take to their heels once. However, if Ottershaw's rumbled me there's no sense in continuing. I won't do it again: are you satisfied?"

Hugo shook his head. "Not quite. What makes you lock your door every night?"

"How do you know that I do?" Richmond countered quickly, up in arms.

"Eh, there's no secret about it! Everyone in the house knows it. You take precious good care no one should come near you once you've gone to bed, don't you?"

"Yes, and you've been told why!"

"I've been told that if you're roused you don't drop off to sleep again, and I think—not to take packthread, you young gull-catcher!—that that's humdudgeon!"

Richmond gave a little chuckle. "Oh, no! Not wholly! But there are nights when I don't sleep much. If you must know, when that happens I can't lie counting the minutes: I get up, and go out, if there's moonlight. And sometimes I go out with Jem Hordle, fishing. Well, that's why I take care no one shall come tapping at my door! If my mother knew, or Grandpapa—Lord, what a clutter there would be! They want to keep me wrapped in lambswool: you know that! As for taking the *Seamew* out at night—particularly since my uncle and Oliver were drowned—if either of them so much as suspected I did that—oh, I'd be so watched and guarded I should run mad!"

Hugo said nothing for a moment or two, but sat looking down at Richmond with a slight frown in his eyes. The explanation was reasonable, but he thought the boy was on the defensive, watching him from under his lashes, a guarded look on his face, a hint of tautness about him.

It was Richmond who broke the silence, saying sweetly: "May I try now if I can go to sleep, cousin?"

"I suppose so," Hugo answered, getting up. He hesitated, and then said: "You've told me you're not meddling in contraband, and I hope that was the truth, because if it wasn't you won't be the only one to fall all-a-bits. You've listened to a deal of loose talk about free-trading, lad, but if it were to come out that you'd had a hand in such dealings there's no one who would be more over-powered than your grandfather."

"Oh, go to the devil!" snapped Richmond, with a spurt of temper. "You needn't be afraid! Do you mean to tell him that you think I'm a free-trader? I wish I may be present! No, I don't, though: I hate brangles! As for what I choose to do when I can't sleep, you've no right to scold: you're not my guardian, or—or even head of the family—yet!"

"Nay, did I do that?" asked Hugo, mildly surprised.

There was an angry flush on Richmond's cheek, but it

faded. He muttered: "No—I beg pardon! But I can't endure —oh, well, it's no matter!"

Hugo picked up his candlestick, saying, with his slow grin: "Can't endure to be interfered with, eh? It's high time you learned discipline, you meedless colt—military discipline! I'm not the head of the family, but happen I'll help you to that pair of colours, if you don't bring yourself to ruin before I've a chance to do it."

Richmond smiled wryly. "Thank you! You can't do it, however. When I'm of age—oh, talking pays no toll! I shall be at Oxford then, I daresay."

"I doubt it! In the meantime, lad, tread the line-way, and never mind if it's a bore. I mislike the cut of that Riding-officer. He's mighty suspicious of you, and though I wouldn't say he was down to every move on the board, he's by no means the sapskull you think him."

A little, confident smile curled Richmond's mouth. "He's been outjockeyed again and again—by what I've heard."

"Ay, and he's not the man to cry craven," said Hugo significantly. "He don't love you, Richmond, and if he thought he could bowl you out he'd do it."

"But he can't."

"I hope he can't, but chance it happens that you find yourself in a hobble, don't throw your cap after it, but come to me! I've been in more than one tight squeeze in my time."

"Much obliged to you!" Richmond murmured. "It's mid-summer moon with you, you know, but I'm persuaded you mean it kindly! *Do* go to bed, Hugo! I'm so *very* sleepy!"

XV

Richmond did not look, on the following morning, as though he could have been as sleepy as he said he was when Hugo left him. He went riding as usual before breakfast, but when his mother and his grandfather saw him each perceived immediately that he was heavy-eyed, and a little pale. He was subjected to a cross-fire of anxious solicitude on the one hand and rigorous interrogation on the other, and bore it with such patience that Hugo marvelled at his restraint. His eyes met Hugo's once, in a look ridiculously compound of defiance and entreaty. He won no response, but derived considerable reassurance from his large cousin's expression, which was one of bovine stupidity. Since he did not think that Hugo was at all stupid, he interpreted this as a sign that he had no immediate intention of disclosing the previous night's events to Lord Darracott, and did not again glance in his direction.

That swift, challenging look had not, however, escaped his sister's notice, and at the earliest opportunity she commanded Hugo to explain its meaning. Even less than Richmond was she beguiled by his air of childlike incomprehension. She said severely: "And pray don't stare at me as though you were a moonling!"

"Nay, love, that's not kind!" protested the Major, much hurt. "I know I'm not needle-witted, but I'm not a *moonling!*"

"You're the slyest thing in nature!" his love informed him with great frankness. "But I myself am pretty well up to snuff, so don't think to tip *me* a rise, if you please! You'll make wretched work of it."

Shocked by this forthright speech, he said: "Eh, you mustn't talk like that, lass! You'll be setting folks in a regular bustle! That's a very ungenteel thing to say: even *I* know that!"

"Forgive me, cousin!" she begged, primming up her mouth. "I meant, of course, that it is useless to think you can *deceive* me!"

"That's much more seemly," he said approvingly.

"Yes, but I now find myself at a loss to know how to advise you, in polite language, not to draw herrings across the track in the vain hope that you'll persuade me to run counter!" she retorted.

"Oh, I'd never be able to do that!"

"Well, I'm happy to know you're awake upon *that* suit, at all events!" She looked up into his face, smiling a little wistfully. "Don't quiz me, Hugo! Why did Richmond look at you like that? As if he was afraid of you—afraid you were going to say something he didn't wish you to! Tell me what it was—*pray* tell me, Hugo!"

He possessed himself of her hands, and held them clasped together against his chest. Smiling reassuringly down at her, he said: "Now, what's made you so hot in the spur, love? And just what sort of a queer nabs do you think I am?"

"Oh, no, no, I don't think that!" she said quickly.

"Well, I'd be a *very* queer nabs if I'd a secret with Richmond, and blabbed it to you!" he replied. "Nay then! don't look so fatched! All Richmond was afraid of was that I might say something, in my clumsy way, which he'd as lief wasn't said before his mother and the old gentleman.

190

And I can't say I blame him," he added reflectively. "To hear the pair of them talk you'd think he was eight years old instead of eighteen!"

She nodded. "Yes, I know that. Do I seem a dreadful pea-goose? I daresay I am!"

"You do and-all!" he told her lovingly.

"What a truly detestable creature you are!" she remarked. "I collect Richmond was not tossing restless in his bed, but was not, in fact, in his bed at all, but I promise you I don't mean to enquire where he was, because from anything I have ever heard one should never, if one wishes to retain the least respect for them, enquire what gentlemen do when they have contrived to escape from their female relatives."

Charmed by this large-mindedness, the Major said, with simple fervour: "I *knew* you'd make a champion wife, love!"

"On the contrary! My husband will live under the cat's foot."

"I'm very partial to cats," offered the Major hopefully.

She smiled, but drew her hands away, shaking her head at him. "My own belief is that you are a gazetted flirt!"

"Oh, is it?" he retorted. "If that's so I'll be off and ask my Aunt Elvira's leave to pay my addresses to you without any more ado!"

"I shall warn her to hint you away—not that I have much hope that a mere hint will serve, because you are quite without conduct or delicacy, and altogether a most improper person!"

Cordially agreeing with this reading of his character, the Major ventured to remind her that it was her duty, as seen by her grandfather, to reclaim him.

"I am persuaded it would be a hopeless task," she replied firmly. "What's more, I know very well that all this nonsensical talk is what Richmond calls a *fling*, to lead me away from what I wish to say to you. Don't joke me any more, but tell me——" She broke off, knitting her brows.

"Tell you what, love?"

"I don't know. That is, it is so hard to put it into words! Lately—before you came here—I have felt uneasy about Richmond. I can't precisely tell why, except that he was in such flat despair when Grandpapa ordered him to put the thought of a military career out of his head. He wasn't sullen, or rebellious—he never is, you know!—but dawdling, and languid, not caring for anything very much, his spirits low, and depressed—Mama was afraid he would fall into a lethargy! And then, all at once, and for no reason that I

191

could perceive, he became *alive* again. He has a great deal of reserve, but one can always tell by his eyes: they are so very speaking! Mama says that when they are bright it is a sign that he is in good health, but it's not so—not wholly! When he was a little boy, and in dangerous mischief, they used to look alight, just as I've seen them again and again in these past months. Once, when I went for a sail with him and Jem in the *Seamew,* a gale blew up, and we had the narrowest of escapes from foundering. *I* was never so frightened in my life—well, it was the *horridest* thing!—but Richmond *enjoyed* it! He had that look: his eyes positively blazing—smiling, too, in the most *inhuman* way! It was as though he liked fighting the waves, and being in the greatest peril, which Jem afterwards told me we were!"

Hugo nodded. "Ay, he would: he's that road. It's excitement he likes, and it leads him into dare-devilry, because he's bored, and too full of energy for the loitering life he leads. I've met his like before. Don't fret, lass! He's only a colt yet—a resty, high-couraged colt that needs exercise, and breaking to bridle. He puts me in mind of a friend of mine: just such a wiry, craze care-for-nobody, but the best duty-officer I ever knew. By hedge or by stile we must bring his lordship round to the notion of a Hussar regiment for the lad."

"If one could!" she sighed. "He thinks Richmond will outgrow that ambition—has done so already, perhaps."

"He'll learn his mistake," the Major said dryly. "If he won't yield now, with a good-grace, he'll suffer a bad back-cast the moment the lad comes of age, and joins as a volunteer. You may lay your life that's what he'll do, and his lordship wouldn't be very well suited with *that!*"

"No, indeed! Or any of us!" she exclaimed. "But he's not nineteen yet, and sometimes I feel such an apprehension that he may do something reckless, or even outrageous, because he's not used to being crossed, besides never counting the cost before he plunges into the most hare-brained scrapes! You may say I'm indulging crotchets, but when he looked at you today it flashed across my mind that he is in a scrape, and that you know what it is. Do you, Hugo?"

"Nay, I'm not in his confidence," he replied.

She scanned his face searchingly but to no avail. "When he shot that look at you I knew that he didn't go to bed when he said goodnight to us, and it was plain that you knew *that* at least."

He laughed. "Don't fidget yourself, love! He took it into his head to try if he could play a prank on me, young varmint!"

She looked relieved, but not wholly convinced. After thinking it over for a moment, she said: "I think he does sometimes slip out of the house when we believe him to be in bed. I went to his room once, in the middle of the night, because Mama had the toothache, and remembered that she had given her bottle of laudanum to him when he had a bad tic. I knocked and knocked on his door, and even called to him, but he didn't answer me, and I thought then that he wasn't there. But when I told him about it in the morning he said that he had taken a few drops of laudanum himself, which had made him sleep like the dead."

"Well, that's very possible," Hugo answered.

"Yes, only—one can't but own that the Darracotts all have a—a certain unsteadiness of character—if you know what I mean!"

"I know just what you mean, and the Darracotts have not *all* that particular unsteadiness of character!"

She smiled. "Well, I *hope* not! But after Claud's escapade——"

"So that's what's put you into the hips!" he interrupted. "You may be easy! I fancy we'll receive no drunken invasion on our Richmond's account. I'd a notion myself he might be in mischief, but he's told me it's not so. Think no more of it, love!"

She said gratefully: "If Richmond knows your eye is on him I shouldn't think he'd dare plunge into a scrape. I am *very* much obliged to you!"

He had the satisfaction of seeing the worried look vanish from her face; but the reassurance he had conveyed to her was no reflection of his own state of mind. He found himself in a quandary; for while, on the one hand, the task of informing Lord Darracott of his discovery and his suspicion was naturally repugnant to him, and certainly fatal to his future relationship with Richmond, on the other, he was unable to persuade himself that Richmond's word might be accepted without reservation. He had come away from his interview with the boy considerably disquieted, and at a loss to know what course to pursue. He was too much a stranger to be able to win Richmond's confidence, and even doubted whether Richmond gave his confidence to anyone. He had thought from the outset that Richmond was oddly aloof. The reason had not been far to seek, but it had not been until he came to grips with him that he realized how impenetrable was the barrier behind which Richmond dwelled. An impulse to encourage Anthea to question him herself had no sooner occurred to him than he had rejected it. Richmond, in his judgement, was neither young enough nor old enough to tolerate the interference of a sister. There seemed to be nothing for it (since his uneasy suspicion rested on no solid foundation) but to watch Richmond unobtrusively, and to hope that the knowledge that there was one member of the household at least who was on the alert would make him chary of pursuing any unlawful form of amusement.

A third course swiftly presented itself. Vincent, encountering him on his way home from one of his tours of the estate with my lord's bailiff, elected to ride back to the house with him, and said as soon as Glossop had parted company with the cousins: "I hear you've laid the Darracott ghost, coz. Poor Richmond! But I think he should have known better than to have entertained the least hope of shaking your stolidity."

"So he told you, did he?" Hugo said slowly.

"But of course!" Vincent returned, his brows lifting in mockery. "He may have misjudged *you*, but he knows *me* well enough not to dream of withholding such an excellent story from me."

"I should have thought of that before," said Hugo. He turned his head, the hint of his disarming grin on his countenance. "You were in the right of it: *dull, brainless Ajax* fairly hits me off! Happen you're the only one amongst us with the power to bring that lad to his senses. Did he tell you all that passed between us last night?"

"He didn't withhold the cream of the jest from me, if that's what you mean," replied Vincent, with his glinting smile.

"Remember I'm blockish!" said Hugo. "What was the cream of it, by your reckoning?"

"Do you know, dear cousin, there have been moments when I have wondered whether I was a trifle out in my first judgment of you? How comforting it is to meet with reassurance on this head! The cream of the jest was the conclusion you jumped to, in your somewhat ingenuous fashion—if I may be permitted so to describe it!"

Quite unmoved by the studied offensiveness of this answer, Hugo asked straitly: "Has it never occurred to you that there's something devilish smoky about that halfling's docility? He doesn't want for spirit: he's full of spunk, and as meedless as be-damned besides!"

"I am afraid I have never given the matter a thought," said Vincent, smothering a yawn.

"Give it one now, then! You may be too well-accustomed to the state of affairs here to be struck by what must fairly stagger anyone coming, as I did, as a stranger amongst you. I told you once that I've had more experience of lads than you, and I'll tell you now that I hadn't been here above a sennight before I hadn't a doubt but that our Richmond was playing some kind of double game, though what it might be I hadn't a notion, until I got into conversation with that Riding-officer. I'd have had to be twice as blockish as I am not to have realized that there was more behind his hostility to Richmond than resentment at the treatment he'd met with at his lordship's hands. I'm bound to own that the suspicion that gave me seemed too cock-brained to be entertained—until I'd added one thing to another, and, in particular, the sort of loose talk the lad had listened to all his life: not one of you, seemingly, having enough sense to see the daft risk you were running! The blame's to be laid chiefly at his lordship's door, but you're no floss-head, and you've known the lad from his cradle! Nay then, Vincent! Did it never occur to you he was touchwood, needing no more than a spark to set him ablaze?"

"No," said Vincent, very gently. "But do, pray, continue! You mustn't think I'm am not enjoying it. I am, in fact, *much rapt in this,* and—er—apprehend *immediately The unknow Ajax.* The passage, which I've mauled a little, continues: *Heavens, what a man is there!*—But perhaps it would be uncivil to complete the line, and for me to be uncivil to the future head of my family would not do at all."

The Major regarded him with tolerant amusement, remarking placidly: "For one who doesn't want for sense you waste a mort of time milking the pigeon! You'll pick no quarrel with me, so you may as well stop trying to make me nab the rust, and attend to what's of much more moment. Richmond wasn't playing ghost last night for my benefit: he wanted to scare Ottershaw away from the Dower House, if he could do it. He knows now he can't, and I believe him when he says he won't cut the caper again. If I didn't, I'd have no choice but to lay the whole matter before his lordship, which is the last thing I want to do. Ottershaw had his pistol in his hand when I halted him.

Whether he'd have used it is another pair of shoes: I think not, but it won't do to run the risk of it."

"If it comforts you, you may know that I have already told Richmond that, however amusing the repercussion of his exploit may have been, such pranks are really quite unworthy of him," said Vincent languidly.

"It would comfort me much more if I felt I could leave the matter in your hands. Richmond won't confide in me: it's not to be expected he should."

"But he has—unless I have misinformed—given you his assurance that he is not engaged in any such nefarious occupation as smuggling," interpolated Vincent, in a voice of silk.

"Ay, he's done that," admitted Hugo. He was silent for a moment, gazing meditatively ahead, between his horse's ears. A rather rueful smile crept into his eyes. "I've no reason to doubt his word, and the Lord knows it goes against the pluck with me to do so, but I think he lied to me."

"I cannot supply you with any reason for doubting him, but I can, and will, supply you with one—possibly incomprehensible to you, but nevertheless to be relied on—for accepting his word," said Vincent, his eyes hard and contemptuous. "Richmond, my dear coz, was born into, and reared in, an order of society whose members do not commonly give lying assurances, or engage in criminal pursuits. However much *you* may have been misled by what you term the *loose talk* so reprehensibly indulged in by my grandfather, it is as inconceivable that Richmond should confuse *sympathy* with *participation* as that he, a Darracott, would entertain for one instant the thought that he might join a gang of such vulgar persons as free-traders. I trust I have made myself plain?"

"You've done that, right enough," Hugo replied. "I don't know if you believe what you say, or if you say it because you dislike me too much to think of aught else; and any road it doesn't make a ha'porth of odds: you don't mean to lift a finger to save a lad who thinks the world and-all of you from bringing himself to ruin! You've made me a fine, top-lofty speech about Richmond's birth and rearing: his birth's well-enough, but his rearing was as bad as it could be! Sithee, Vincent, you know that! I know it too. When you were at Eton, I was at Harrow, and what hadn't been clouted into me by my granddad I learned there." He paused, and the twinkle came back into his eyes. "And there wasn't so very much to learn either!" he added. "Reet vulgar he

196

was, my granddad, but worth a score of any Darracott I've yet laid eyes on!"

"Harrow——!" murmured Vincent, in the grip of cold fury. "To be sure, our opinion of Harrow was never very high, but —ah, well!"

Hugo chuckled. "Nor ours of Eton, think on! Ee, if you haven't got me talking as you do yourself! Sneck up, and ask yourself how much you'd have learnt if you'd been reared as Richmond was!"

They had ridden into the stableyard by this time, and as their grooms had already come out to take charge of the horses Vincent's sense of ton prevented him from making any reply which he considered to be worthy of the occasion. He was silent therefore, but his groom, catching a glimpse of his face, would have given a month's pay to have been privileged to know what the Major had said to put him in the devil's own passion.

He strode out of the yard without vouchsafing a word either to his cousin or to his servant; and after exchanging a few observations with John Joseph, and, to that severe critic's disapproval and the grinning delight of several stableboys, admonishing Rufus in the broadest dialect for his want of manners in demanding with every sign of equine impatience the sugar he knew very well would be bestowed upon him, the Major followed him, in his leisurely way, to the house.

The post had been brought up from the receiving-office during his absence, and a thick letter, addressed to himself, and stamped Post Paid, lay on the table by the door. He had just broken the wafer that sealed it, and spread open three closely written sheets, when Chollacombe came into the hall to tell him that my lord desired to see him in the library as soon as might be convenient to him. The Major, already perusing the lengthy communication sent him by one who subscribed himself as his attached friend and obedient servant, Jonas Henry Poulton, acknowledged this message with an abstracted grunt, neither looking up from the letter in his hand, nor evincing the smallest disposition to make all speed to his grandfather's presence. Any one of his cousins would have recognized the civil form in which the message was phrased as the cloak spread by Chollacombe over a peremptory (and possibly explosive) command; but nothing would ever avail, thought Chollacombe despairingly, to teach Mr. Hugh the wisdom of obeying such summonses with all possible dispatch. He coughed deprecatingly, and said: "His lordship, sir, is anxious to see you, I fancy."

The Major nodded. "Yes, very well! I heard you. I'll go to him as soon as I've changed my clothes. Send Ferring up to my room, will you, Chollacombe?"

Chollacombe sighed, but attempted no remonstrance. For his own part, the Major's invariable custom of putting off his riding-habit as soon as he came in from the stables met with his fullest approval, but my lord, he knew well, had no particular objection to the aroma inseparable from horses, and every objection to being kept waiting for as long as five minutes. He went away, knowing from experience how useless it would be to remind the Major of this circumstance, or to hint to him that my lord was sadly out of temper.

The Major discovered this for himself when he walked into the library some twenty minutes later. When last seen by him my lord had been unusually amiable; his brow was now thunderous, and he showed, by the nervous twitch of his fingers, and the throb of the pulse beside his grim, thin-lipped mouth, that something had happened to cast him into the worst of ill-humours. He was standing with his back to the fireplace, and he greeted his huge grandson with a fierce scowl, and a barked demand to know where the devil he had been.

"Over into Sussex, sir," replied the Major, shutting the door. "Was there something you wanted me to do? I'm sorry."

Lord Darracott seemed to be exerting himself to curb his temper. He did not answer the Major, but said abruptly: "I sent for you because I've had a letter from your uncle Matthew. I don't know what maggot's in his head, or where he came by the information he has sent me. He's a damned fool, and always was! Anyone could gull him!"

The Major, though of the opinion that Matthew had rather more common-sense than any other member of the family, allowed this unflattering estimate to pass without comment, and waited with patience and equanimity for my lord to reach the kernel of whatever piece of information had raised his ire.

Lord Darracott, hungry for legitimate prey, glared more menacingly than before; and, failing to unnerve his grandson into committing the imprudence of answering him, snapped, with bitter loathing: "Dummy!" The gambit eliciting no more than a twinkle in the Major's guileless blue eyes, he expressed, not for the first time, his burning desire to be told why Fate had seen fit to afflict him with a gapeseed for his heir; and came, at last, to the meat of the matter. "My son writes to inform me that that fellow—your maternal grandfather!—was the head of some curst firm or other—I don't know anything about such things!—that goes by the name of Bray & Poulton. Is that so?"

The Major nodded. "Ay, that's so. He was its founder. Uncle Jonas Henry is the head of it now, but at the first-end, when he was a little lad, he was just one of the piece-ners—they're the children that keep the frames filled, or join the cardlings for the slubbers——"

"Uncle?" interrupted his lordship. "You told me you had none!"

"Nay, he's no kith of mine," replied Hugo soothingly. "It was what I used to call him when I was a lad myself, and he the best weaver in the Valley. He was a prime favourite with my granddad, but it wasn't until near the back-end of his life that Granddad took him into partner-ship—having no one but me to succeed him, who hadn't been bred to the wool trade."

"Are you telling me, sir, that your maternal grandfather was a mill owner?" thundered my lord.

"Why, yes!" replied Hugo, smiling. "That's what he rose to be, though he started as a weaver, like his father before him. He was as shrewd as he could hold together, my granddad—a reet knowing one!"

Stunned by this disclosure, it was several moments be-fore his lordship was able to command his voice enough to utter: "A man of substance?"

"Ay, he was well to pass," replied the Major. "You might say that he addled a mort of brass in his day, tewing and toiling—which he did to the end, think on! It wasn't often you wouldn't have found him at the mill, wearing his brat, even when he'd got to be one of the stiffest men in the whole of the West Riding. His brass wasn't come-by easily, either," he added. "It was make and scrape with him before he'd addled enough to get agate—not that he was what we call sneck-drawn, in the north. It was just that he knew how to hold household, like any good Yorkshireman." He paused, perceiving that my lord was staring at him in mingled incredulity and wrath, and added, in a tone of kindly ex-planation: "That wasn't the way he made his fortune, of course: it was only the start of it. He was flue-full of mother-wit: the longestheaded man I ever knew, and with

199

a longsight to match it, what's more! Fly shuttles were invented before he was born, of course, but it wasn't until he was five years old that the first of the power-looms was put into use—and precious few liking it overly much! He saw it when he was a piecener himself: he told me once that that was the start of his life. Seemingly, he had never any other notion in his head from that time on but what was tied up with machines. He was one of the first to buy Cartwright's loom—not the one they use now: that didn't come till a matter of a dozen years later; but a queer old machine you'd think even-down antiquated today. All that was long before I was born or thought of: by the time I was out of short coats such things weren't considered new-fangled any more, and the mill, which the better part of Huddersfield said Granddad had run mad to build, was doing fine!" He smiled, and said apologetically: "Nay, I might as well talk Spanish to you, sir, mightn't I?" His smile broadened to a grin. "And if any wool-man could hear me explaining the trade to you he'd laugh himself into stitches, think on! You could floor me with any one of a dozen questions, for all I know is little more than I picked up, running about the mill when my grandfather's back was turned. The thing was that in the old days there was no such thing as a mill, where the packs went in at one door, as you might say, and came out of another as cloths—serges, kerseymeres, friezes, and the like. Cartwright set up a factory in Doncaster, where weaving and spinning both were done; but Granddad went one better nor that—levelling at the moon, they used to say—until they saw that old, ramshackle mill growing and growing! Today, the name of Bray is known to the trade the world over."

This intelligence did not appear to afford Lord Darracott the smallest gratification. He said, in the voice of one goaded to exasperation: "I know nothing about mills, and care less! Answer me this, sir! Is it true, what your uncle writes me—that you inherited a *fortune* from Bray?"

"Well," replied the Major cautiously, "I don't know just what you'd call a fortune, sir. I'd say myself I was pretty well-inlaid."

"Don't come any niffy-naffy, shabby-genteel airs over me!" barked his lordship. "Tell me without any damned round-aboutation how much you're worth!"

The Major rubbed his nose. "Nay, that's what I can't do!" he confessed.

"You can't, eh? I guessed as much! Trust Matthew to exaggerate out of all recognition! *Why* can't you?"

"I don't know myself, sir," said Hugo, making a clean breast of it.

"What the devil do you mean by that, idiot?" demanded his lordship. "Presumably you know what your grandfather left you!"

"Oh, I know what his private fortune was, reet enough!" said Hugo. "It's invested mostly in the Funds, and brings in between fifteen and sixteen thousand pounds a year; but that's not the whole of it. I've a sizeable share in the mill over and above that. I can't tell you what that may be worth to me. Times have been bad lately, what with Luddite riots, and the depression that followed close on the Peace. The harvests were bad last year, too: my uncle Jonas Henry wrote me that in Yorkshire wheat rose to above a guinea the bushel. However, things seem to be on the mend now, so——"

"Are you telling me that Bray cut up to the tune of *half a million?*" said my lord, in a strange voice.

"It would be about that figure—apart from the mill," Hugo agreed.

Lord Darracott was shaken by a sudden gust of rage: "How dared you, sir, deceive me?" he exclaimed.

"Nay then! I never did so," Hugo reminded him. "It was in this very room that I told you I'd plenty of brass."

"I remember! I supposed you to be referring to prizemoney—as you knew!"

Hugo smiled down at him. "And I told you that my other grandfather had left his brass to me. You said I might do what I pleased with my granddad's savings, but that you wanted to hear no more of them or him. So I didn't tell you any more, for, to own the truth, sir, I was better suited, at that time, to keep my tongue between my teeth until I'd had time to look about me. What's more," he added reminiscently, "I wasn't ettling to remain here above a sennight—particularly when you told me you had it all settled I was to wed my cousin Anthea. Eh, it was a wonder I didn't take to my heels there and then!"

Lord Darracott stared at him, his lips tightly gripped together, and his eyes smouldering. He did not speak, but after a moment went to the wing-chair on one side of the fireplace, and sat down, his hands grasping its arms. The Major sat down too, saying: "Happen it's as well my uncle wrote to you, for it's time we reached an understanding. It

201

chances that I'd a letter myself by today's post, from Uncle Jonas Henry." He chuckled. "Seemingly he's as throng as he can be, and a trifle hackled with me for loitering here. I shall have to post off to Huddersfield next week, sir—and a bear-garden jaw I'll get when I arrive there, if I know Jonas Henry!"

Lord Darracott said, with an effort: "Have the goodness to tell me whether you mean to return, or to stay there!"

"Nay, that's for you to say, sir."

The fierce old eyes flashed. "It appears I have no hold over you!"

The Major considered him, not unsympathetically. "Well, that's true enough, of course, but don't fatch yourself over it, sir! If you're thinking of the brass, I'll tell you to your head it makes no difference: you'd have had no hold over me any road. But all the brass in the world wouldn't help me to cross this threshold if you didn't choose to let me."

His lordship gave a contemptuous snort of unmirthful laughter, but said in a milder tone: "Well, what do you mean to do?"

"Unless you dislike it, I'd choose, once I've settled my affairs, and talking things over with Jonas Henry—I'm by way of being his sleeping partner, you see—to come back. I'd be very well suited if you'd let me have the Dower House. That's assuming you wish me to take up my quarters here. If not—well, there's my grandfather's house above Huddersfield, or I might buy a house in the Shires, perhaps. Time enough to decide what I'll do—and maybe it won't be for me to decide, either."

Lord Darracott looked intently at him. "Am I to understand you mean to marry Anthea?"

"If she'll have me," said the Major simply.

"She should be flattered! In these hurly-burly times I don't doubt your fortune will make you acceptable to any female. I dare swear every matchmaking mother in town will cast out lures to you: you have only to throw the handkerchief," said my lord sardonically.

"Well, as I'm doing no throwing of handkerchiefs we'll never know if you're right. Myself, I shouldn't think it, but there's no sense in breaking squares over what won't come to pass. If my cousin won't have me—eh, that doesn't bear thinking about!"

"H'm! You seem to have become wondrous great with her!" remarked his lordship. "Does she know what your circumstances are?"

"Well, I told her, but she didn't believe a word of it," replied Hugo. "And what she's going to say when she finds I wasn't trying to bamboozle her has me in the devil of a quake!" he confessed.

His lordship returned no answer to this, but said presently, keeping his eyes fixed on the Major's face: "What's your purpose in wishing to live here while I'm above ground?"

"Much what yours was, when you sent for me, sir. Since I must succeed you, it will be as well your people should know me, and I them. I've the devil of a lot to learn, too, about the management of estates, for that's something that's never come in my way." He paused, returning my lord's gaze very steadily. "All to one, they're in bad shape, sir, so happen it's a good thing I've plenty of brass."

"Ah!" My lord's hands clenched on the arms of his chair. "We come to it at last, do we? I don't need you to tell me my land's in bad heart! I know better by far than you what is crying out to be done, and what it would cost to do it! But if you think to make yourself master here in my time, you may take your *brass*, as you call it, to hell with you!"

"Nay, that's foolishness, sir!" Hugo remonstrated. "I've no wish to be master here, for I'd make wretched work of it, as ignorant as I am. But soon or late it will be my fortune that sets matters to rights, and I'd liefer it was soon. If I put money into the place, I'll not be kept in the dark about any question that properly concerns me, so it's likely we'll fratch now-and-now; but I'll be no more master than Glossop is. I'd be the junior partner."

"I'll brook no interference from you or anyone with what's my own!" declared his lordship. "You'd like to make me your pensioner, wouldn't you? I'll see you damned first!"

"There's nothing I'd like less," replied Hugo. "And what you do with your own is none of my business. But what's done with settled estates you won't deny is very much my business." He saw his grandfather stiffen; and said, smiling a trifle wryly: "You bade me talk without roundaboutation, sir! I'm not such a dummy that I can't see for myself that there have been things done the trustees never knew of, for they'd not have consented to what's nothing more nor less than waste."

"Are you threatening me?" demanded his lordship.

Hugo shook his head. "Lord, no, sir! I don't doubt it was forced on you. I'm neither threatening, nor asking questions. I'll set things to rights—and keep 'em so! That's all."

"It is, is it?" said his lordship, eyeing him with grim

humour. "I begin to think that you're a damned, encroaching, managing fellow, Hugh!"

Hugo chuckled. "Ay, but happen you'll grow accustomed to me, for you need someone to manage for you, other than your bailiff." He got up, and stood for a moment or two, looking down with a lurking twinkle at his lordship's brooding countenance. "You sent for me to lick me into shape, sir, because you couldn't stomach the thought that a regular rum 'un would step into your shoes, if naught was done to teach him how to support the character of a gentleman. Well, it may be that I'm not quite such a Jack Pudding as I let you think. I own, it was a ramshackle thing to do, but when I saw how there wasn't one amongst you that didn't believe I'd been reared in a hovel I could no more resist trying how much I could make you swallow than I could stop drawing breath! But by what road you thought I came by a commission in such a regiment as mine, if I'd been an unlettered rustic, the lord only knows! I was no more bookish than Richmond, but I got my schooling at Harrow, sir! However, when it comes to the management of large estates, I'm no better than a raw recruit—and that's what I'm hoping you mean to teach me."

A gleam shone in his lordship's eyes. "At the end of which time you'll be ruling the roast, I collect!"

"Nay, if I'm here at all I'll be leg-shackled, and no spirit left in me!" replied the Major. "Never you fear, sir! A terrible shrew she is, the lass I've set my heart on!"

XVI

The first person to learn the news was Vincent, entering the library not ten minutes after Hugo had left it. His mood was far from sunny; and when his grandfather told him bluntly that so far from being a penniless weaver's brat his cousin was the grandson of a wealthy mill owner, and plump enough in the pocket to be able to buy an Abbey, he stared at him for a full minute, his eyes glittering, and his mouth thin with bitterness. When he at last spoke, it was with his usual languor, but in a voice that had a cutting edge to it. "So!" he said. He drew out his snuff-box, and took a pinch. "I felicitate you, sir!"

Lord Darracott gave a sardonic grunt, but said: "So you may! He's prepared to drop his blunt to bring the place about."

Vincent flicked a grain of snuff from his sleeve. "Handsome of him! Does he happen to have the smallest notion how much blunt he will be obliged to drop to restore the Darracott fortune, I wonder?"

"He seems to have a good many more notions than I knew!" replied his lordship harshly. "He may or he may not have that one, and he's not likely to care: he won't easily break his back! He's worth half a million at the least computation."

"Half a million——!" Vincent ejaculated. His mouth smiled unpleasantly. "*That mongrel cur, Ajax!*"

His lordship laughed shortly. "Ironic, ain't it? Damn his effrontery! He as good as told me I'd rendered myself open to an action at law!"

"You do not surprise me at all, sir: I always thought you were over-sanguine in believing he could be brought up to the rig."

"Oh, he was within his rights!" said his lordship unexpectedly. "It put me out of temper, but I'm not sure I don't like him the better for showing fight. He needn't think he's going to rule the roast, however!"

"I devoutly trust you may be able to hold your own, sir, but I must confess that I find it difficult to perceive how, if he pays for it, he is to be prevented from ruling the roast."

"You'll perceive how soon enough, if I have any inching attempts made to unsaddle me!" said his lordship tartly. "To do him justice, he told me he'd no such intention. Said he'd prefer to be my junior partner, if you please!"

"*Timeo Danaos . . . !*" Vincent murmured.

"Don't be a fool! He may have hoaxed us all, impudent dog! but he's no shuffler. It's a pity he was ever born, but I'll say this for him: he's the only one amongst you that ain't a blood-sucker!" He added, on a note of satisfaction: "He means to marry Anthea, too, so that takes *her* off my hands."

"Yes, that has been very obvious," answered Vincent. "I must certainly be the first to congratulate her on her good fortune!"

Since he encountered her in the hall, on her return from a carriage-drive with Mrs. Darracott, he was not only the first to congratulate her on her good fortune, but the first to inform her of it. She lifted her brows, asking him what he meant. He replied, with exaggerated surprise: "But, my dearest cousin, what could I possibly mean? How could

205

you think I should be backward in offering you my felicitations on your forthcoming marriage?"

Her smile was quite as satirical as his. "Am I about to be married? I did not know it."

"Then I have been not backward but premature, which is much worse—quite unworthy of me, indeed! Between such old friends as we are, however, the *convenances* need not be too strictly regarded. Dear Anthea, *don't*, I do most earnestly counsel you, let such a prize slip through your fingers! Believe me, once he shows his front in town there will be girls past counting on the catch for him! I would not, on any account, play fast and loose, though I feel sure you do it charmingly. One does not—if one is a Darracott!—play fast and loose with a fortune!"

She began to look genuinely amused. "Ah, I understand you now! When do you mean to stop allowing Hugo to hoax you? I was used to think you the most knowing one in the family, too!"

"Did you, my sweet? That comforts me, for I was used to think so myself, until I discovered that I must yield priority to you."

"Vincent, what *are* you talking about?" she asked patiently.

"Why, Hugo's fortune, of course!" he said, opening his eyes at her.

She burst out laughing. "He hasn't got a fortune! Vincent, you goose!"

"What a day of surprises this is!" he remarked. "Do you know, I never dreamed you were possessed of such large ideas? For myself, I should be content with a *quarter* of a million pounds!"

"I should think you might indeed be! You don't imagine, surely, that Hugo has a quarter of a million pounds?"

"No, no, nothing so paltry! Half a million at the *least!*"

She was still amused, but a puzzled frown gathered on her brow. "I hope you mean to tell me why you are trying to gammon me!" she said. "In general, I understand you pretty well, but this fling is quite beyond me. If Hugo told you he had a huge fortune——"

"I shouldn't have believed him, of course," he interrupted. "The news, dear Anthea, came from my father, and I can't feel that he was gammoning us. It would be quite unlike him, you know."

The smile had vanished from her lips; she stared incredulously, growing a little pale. "It's not true!"

"Oh, weren't you aware of it? I am disappointed: I was thinking you the only provident member of the family! Yes: half a million, in the Funds. Quite a genteel fortune! Then there is his share in the mill—not, perhaps so genteel, but I daresay you won't despise it."

"I don't believe it!" she exclaimed impetuously. "My uncle must have been mistaken—or you are trying to roast me!"

He looked at her, his brows raised. "Do you know, I begin to think you really were unaware of your good fortune?" he said.

She returned no answer, but stood perfectly still, an expression of shocked dismay in her eyes. He laughed, and sauntered away; and for a full minute she remained at the foot of the staircase, one gloved hand tightly gripping the carved baluster. Recovering slightly from her stupor, she set her foot on the first stair, and then, on a sudden impulse, turned back, determined to find the Major immediately, and to confront him with what she still suspected to be a hoax.

She ran him presently to earth in one of the smaller saloons, engaged in writing a soothing reply to his partner's letter. "So here you are!" she exclaimed. "I have been searching all over for you! You will please explain to me, *at once,* how Vincent came by this—this cock-and-bull story he has just told me!"

He looked round, his pen in hand, and said admiringly: "Eh, you do look pretty, love!"

Since the flower-trimmed silk bonnet tied under her chin with a broad satin ribbon was of her own making, this tribute would, at any other time, have been very acceptable. At the present moment, however, she had no thought to spare for such frivolities, and retorted with asperity: "Never mind how I look! Vincent says—Hugo, it isn't true, is it? You *haven't* a large fortune, have you?"

"Nay, lass!" he said, in a tone of pained remonstrance. "I *told* you I had!"

She gazed at him, flushed and horrified. "I thought you were funning! I never *dreamed——!* Oh, how *could* you?" she said passionately.

He laid the pen down, and got up, and went towards her. "Oh, it was none of my doing!" he assured her. "Granddad addled it, and, having no other chick or child, he just left it to me."

"*Half a million pounds?*" she said, in tones of revulsion.

"Something like that," he nodded.

"Oh, how—how *horrible!*" she uttered, putting out her hands to thrust him away.

"Nay, love, I thought you'd be pleased!" he expostulated.

"Pleased?"

"Of course I did! Why, you told me yourself you meant to marry a man of large fortune! Mind, I was a trifle shocked to find you were so mercenary, but——"

"You knew very well I was joking you! I would never have said such a thing if I'd had the least notion—— Oh, how abominable you are!" she said indignantly.

"Now, how was I to know that? The way you stood there, telling me only a house in the best part of town would do for you, and saying I was sneck-drawn to be thinking of hiring one instead of buying it—well, I was fairly taken-aback!" he said, shaking his head.

"Then I marvel at it that you still wished to offer for me!" she said, quite unable to refrain from retort.

"Well," he confessed, looking sheepish, "I'd gone so far I couldn't for the life of me see how to hedge off."

After a moment's severe struggle with herself, Miss Darracott said bitterly: "I should have known better! I might have guessed you were only waiting for the chance to say something outrageous! Well, you can hedge off now, sir!"

"It's too late, lass," he said, with a heavy sigh. "I'd have everyone saying I'd conducted myself reet shabbily."

"That needn't trouble you! I will engage to make it very plain to all that I refused your obliging offer! As for people saying you had behaved shabbily, what, pray, do you think they would say of me, if I married you? Cream-pot love is what they'd say! Vincent is doing so already! He—he thinks I knew the truth from the start, and—and set my cap at you, just because I wished to be wealthy! And I don't!" declared Miss Darracott, much agitated.

Perceiving that she was having great difficulty in finding her handkerchief in the recesses of her reticule, the Major very kindly gave her his own. She took it, casting a wet but darkling glance at him, angrily dried her eyes, and informed him, in a slightly husky voice, that she never cried but when she was enraged.

"If ever I met such a naggy lass!" observed the Major, recovering his handkerchief, and contriving, at the same time, to put his arms round her. "Now, don't cry, love! We can soon set things to rights! How much money would you *like* to have?"

"Don't be absurd!" begged Anthea, making a half-hearted

effort to push him away. "What I should like is of no consequence whatsoever!"

"Ay, but it is. It won't do for me to get rid of my fortune without knowing how much of it you want me to keep," he said reasonably.

"Get rid of it?" She lifted her head to stare at him. "Would you—if I asked you to?"

He smiled down at her. "Well, it wouldn't be a particle of use to me if you didn't marry me. The only thing that fatches me a trifle is that I've promised my grandfather to let him have what's needed to set this place in order. Of course, I *could* make him a present of it, to play at ducks and drakes with, which I don't doubt he would: but setting aside that it would drive me daft to see him doing it, if I've to step into his shoes one day it'll be just as well if I'm able to stand the nonsense. Besides, I'll have to support an establishment of my own—and it's no use asking me to set you up in a weaver's cottage, love, because there's reason in all things, and I won't do it! It would be well enough if I were a small man, but to be obliged to duck my head every time I went through the doorway wouldn't suit me at all. What's more," he added thoughtfully, "I'd be bound to fill the place up more than you'd like."

"Are you *never* serious?" asked Anthea despairingly.

"I was trying to hit on a way out of the difficulty," he explained, injured.

"You were trying to make me laugh—and don't waste your breath denying it!"

"I wouldn't call it a *laugh* exactly," said the Major diffidently. "It's more of a *gurgle*, if you know what I mean. Yes, *that's* it!"

"Any female who was so idiotish as to marry you would be driven to madness within one week!" declared Anthea.

"I know she would," he agreed. "That's why I'll not live in a cottage with you, love."

"Hugo, this is no laughing matter!" she said. "I feel quite *dreadfully* about it!"

"I can see you do, but why you should has me in a puzzle. If you're nattered by what Vincent says——"

"What Vincent says is what everyone else will say, or, at any rate, think!" she interrupted. "I daresay I should myself. They'll say I *caught* you before you'd had time to meet other, and far more eligible females! Indeed, I shouldn't wonder at it if they said you had been *entrapped* into marrying me—which is perfectly true, because Grandpapa

209

sent for you with that end in view! Hugo, you might marry *anyone!* I think you should go to town, and—and look about you! At least no one could say then that you were allowed no opportunity to make your own choice."

"Nay, I can't do that!" he said hastily. "It would be downright foolhardy, and that's something we Light Bobs don't hold with. I'm not going next or nigh London till I'm safely wed."

"*Now* what are you going to say?" asked Anthea, in a resigned tone.

"I see I'll have to make a clean breast of it," said the Major, with every sign of shamefaced reluctance. "The thing is, love, that my grandfather tells me that the instant I show my front in town I'll have all the matchmaking mothers hunting me down. I wouldn't know what to do, for I'm not accustomed to that sort of thing, never having had lures cast out to me before, besides being a bashful kind of a man. It wouldn't be cousinly of you to abandon me. In fact," he added, rapidly developing a strong sense of ill-usage, "it would be reet cruel, seeing how I put myself in your hands, just as I was bid."

"I would give much to see you fleeing in terror from a matchmaking mother," remarked Anthea wistfully. "Or, indeed, from anyone. But as you are utterly brazen——"

"Nay!"

"... and *much* in need of a set-down——"

"I'm not in need of that, lass, for I'm getting one," he interpolated ruefully.

"No, no!—— At least—— Oh, dear, I daresay it sounds foolish to you, and I know I told you I was mercenary, but I'm *not,* Hugo! Only think how it would appear to everyone! As though I had been determined before ever I saw you not to let your odious fortune slip through my hands!"

He patted her consolingly. "You needn't worry about that, love. When people see you wearing the same bonnet for years on end they'll never think you married me for my fortune."

"As nothing would induce me to wear the same bonnet for years on end——"

"You'll have to," he said simply. "I'm a terrible nip-farthing. Sare-baned, we call it. It'll take a deal of coaxing to get as much as a groat out of me. I hadn't meant to tell you, but I wouldn't want to take advantage of you, and if you were thinking I'm not one to cut up stiff over the bills, or——"

"If you knew what I was thinking you'd never hold up your head again!" she told him. "You seem to forget that you wished to purchase the moon for me!"

"Nay, I don't forget that! The thing is I can't purchase it, so there was no harm in saying it. Now, if I'd said I'd like to give you a diamond necklace, or some such thing, you might have taken me up on it. I remembered that just in time to stop myself," he explained, apparently priding himself on his forethought.

"I should like very much to have a diamond necklace," said Anthea pensively.

"Wouldn't a paste one do as well?" he asked, in a voice of great uneasiness.

She had been so sure that he would fall into the trap that she was taken, for an instant, off her guard, and looked up at him with such a startled expression on her face that his deep chuckle escaped him, and he lifted her quite to her feet, and kissed her.

Scandalized by such impropriety, Miss Darracott commanded him to set her down immediately, on pain of never being spoken to by her again. This threat cowed him into obedience, and Miss Darracott, considerably flushed and ruffled, was just about to favour him with her opinion of his conduct when Claud walked into the room, thus saving his large cousin from annihilation.

Claud had come in search of him, the news of his affluence having by this time reached him. He could scarcely have been more delighted had he himself suddenly inherited a fortune, for he instantly perceived that now more than ever would Hugo need a guiding hand, particularly in the choice of a suitable town residence, and its furnishings. He had a great turn for such matters, and had, indeed, so unerring an eye for colour, and such exquisite taste in decoration, that his advice was frequently sought by ladies of high fashion who desired to bestow a new touch on their drawing-rooms. Since he lived modestly in two rooms in Duke Street, there was little scope for his genius in his own abode: a circumstance which made him look forward with intense pleasure to the prospect of being able to lavish his skill not merely on a drawing-room or a saloon, but on an entire house, from attics to basement. "It'll be something like!" he assured Hugo. "Just you leave it to me, old fellow! No need for you to worry yourself over it! You dub up the possibles, and I'll lay 'em out to the best advantage. Yes, and don't, on any account, enter into a treaty for a house behind my back! You'd be diddled, as sure as check, because it stands to reason you can't know your way about in London. Anthea don't know either, so it's no use thinking you can leave it to her. As likely as not she'd land you in Russell Square, all amongst the Cits and the bankers, or Upper Grosvenor Street, miles from anywhere."

This was a little too much for Miss Darracott. "Have no fear!" she said coldly. "Indeed, I can't conceive why you should suppose I should wish to choose a house for Hugo!"

"Dash it, you're going to marry him, aren't you?" said Claud. "We all know *that!*"

"You know nothing of the sort!" she declared hotly. "The only thing you know is that Grandpapa desires it, and if you imagine that I care a rush for——"

"No, dash it!" interrupted Claud. "Never thought about the old gentleman at all! Well, what I mean is, it's as plain as a pikestaff! You can't go about smelling of April and May, the pair of you, and then expect to gull people into thinking you don't mean to get riveted! A pretty set of gudgeons you must think we are!"

"That's dished me!" said the Major fatalistically.

"I'll tell you what!" said Claud, engrossed in his vicarious schemes, "we'll take a holt to the village next week, and see what's to be had! No reason why you and my Aunt Elvira shouldn't come too, Anthea. You can put up at——"

"Nay, we'll do no such thing!" intervened Hugo, in some haste. "I'm off to Huddersfield next week."

Anthea, making a dignified exit, looked back involuntarily. "Going away! Oh—oh, are you? Will you be making a long stay in Yorkshire?"

"Not a day longer than I must," replied Hugo, smiling at her so warmly that she felt herself blushing, and retired in shaken order.

In all but one quarter, the news of Hugo's wealth was very well received, Ferring, in particular, becoming so puffed-up that his uncle felt obliged to snub him severely. My lord came to dinner in a mood of unprecedented amiability; and Mrs. Darracott told her affronted daughter that fortune was the one thing needed to make dear Hugo wholly acceptable.

"Mama, how can you!" exclaimed Anthea.

"Well, my love, it is a great piece of nonsense to pretend that life is not very much more comfortable when one can command its elegancies, and always be beforehand with the world, because it is!" replied Mrs. Darracott, with one of her disconcerting flashes of common-sense. "I liked Hugo from the outset, but although I very soon perceived that he was just the man to make you happy, I *could* not wish you to marry him when I believed it meant that you would be obliged to live here, dependent on your grandfather! But he has been telling me about his scheme to refurbish up the Dower House, if you should not dislike it—and I can't think why you should, dearest, for he says the ghost is nothing more than Spurstow, trying to keep everyone away, which wouldn't surprise me in the least, for I always disliked that man, and even if there is a ghost it cannot possibly be more disagreeable to live with than your grandfather! *I* should not find it so, at all events, and only think, Anthea! dear Hugo wishes me to live there too! Of course I said I should not, but I was very much affected: indeed, I cried a little!" She paused, to dry the tears that were again rolling down her cheeks. "He couldn't have been kinder if he had been my own son!" she disclosed. "You must not suppose I wasn't *devoted* to your poor Papa, my dear, but no one could call him a *dependable* man, and oh, what a *comfort* it is to one to have a creature like Hugo to turn to! Say what you will, my love, there is something *about* very big, quiet men! So ridiculous, too!" she added, with a rather shaky laugh. "He says if you won't marry him he will want me more than ever to live at the Dower House, to keep house for him! I was obliged to laugh, though naturally I gave him a scold for talking such nonsense. And although I wouldn't press you for the world, my dearest child, I did tell him that nothing could make me happier than to see you married to him—and it is of no use to take a pet, because if you are not in love with him, all I can say is that you are a most shocking *flirt*, which I should be sorry to think of any child of mine! And as for not marrying him because he is much wealthier than we knew, I never heard anything so absurd in my life!"

Miss Darracott made no attempt to defend herself; but, revolted by the knowledge that the better part of her family was apparently waiting in hourly expectation of receiving the news of her betrothal, she roundly informed her suitor next day that nothing would induce her to gratify a set of persons whom she very improperly described as vulgar, prying busybodies.

The Major received this declaration with perfect equanimity, even going so far as to say that he would be very well suited to postpone the announcement of the engagement until (as he phrased it) they were shut of his Uncle Matthew's family. "That won't be long after I get back from Huddersfield, from what my Aunt Aurelia was saying t'other evening. I'll have to go there, love, because when I was recalled, before Waterloo, I'd no time to do more than pitch all my affairs back into Jonas Henry's lap, as you might say. Ay, and that puts me in mind of another thing! He hired Axby House from me when my grandfather died, and I've a notion he'd be glad if I'd sell it to him outright. Now, tell me, love: shall I do it, or have you a fancy for it?"

"I think you should do exactly as you wish."

"Nay, love!" expostulated the Major.

"I only meant that—well, how could I have a fancy for a house I've never seen?" said Anthea. "Though I own I *should* like to see that place where you were born."

"Well, I wasn't born at Axby House, so that settles it," said the Major cheerfully. "Tell me another thing! Do you think Richmond would care to go with me?"

She looked quickly at him. "Richmond! Why, Hugo?"

He said, with one of his most innocent stares: "Just for company. Happen he'd be interested to see something more of the country than he's yet had the chance to."

"I should think he would like very much to go, but I do *not* think that that's what you have in your head," she said shrewdly. "I know you don't mean to tell me what it is, so I shan't waste my breath in trying to persuade you to do so. I only wish you may prevail upon Grandpapa to let Richmond go with you, but I very much doubt that you will. He is suspicious of you, Hugo: did you know that? He is afraid you may foster Richmond's military ambition."

He nodded. "Yes, I know that, and he's in the right of it, think on! I'm going to do more than that, odd-come-shortly —and that's another reason, love, why you should marry me!"

This was an opening not to be ignored. "You mean, I collect," said Anthea thoughtfully, "that you won't help Richmond unless I do marry you."

"No, love," responded the Major gently, "I'm not holding a pistol to your head. I'll do what I can for Richmond in any event, but I'd be standing in a far better position if I were his brother-in-law, and not merely one of his cousins."

She drew an audible breath. "What a delightful thing it is to know that if I'm such a wet-goose as to marry you I shall be able to depend on having a husband who won't hesitate to take the wind out of my eye every time I try to get a point the better of him!" she remarked. "And let me tell you," she added, with strong indignation, "that that wounded look doesn't move me in the least, because nothing will make me believe you didn't know very well that I was trying to roast you!"

XVII

Richmond's first reaction to the invitation to accompany his cousin to Yorkshire was a sparkling look of surprised pleasure. This was followed almost immediately, however, by a slight withdrawal. He said, stammering a little: "Thank you! I should be very happy—I should like to—but—I don't know! It might not be possible: Grandpapa . . ."

"Nay, that won't fadge!" said Hugo, with a grin. "You can bring Grandpapa round your thumb if you wish to!"

Richmond laughed, but shook his head. "Not always! When do you mean to set out?"

"On Wednesday next, but if that doesn't do for you I could change the date," replied Hugo obligingly.

"Not till Wednesday! Oh!" Richmond said. He glanced up, feeling his cousin's inscrutable blue gaze to be fixed on him, and coloured, saying quickly: "That should give me time to bring him round my thumb! Thank you! I'd like to go with you—if I can do it."

It seemed to Hugo that his hesitation had its root in something other than doubt of winning Lord Darracott's consent, but what this could be was difficult to guess. Had the moon been on the wane Hugo would have suspected that he had engaged himself to pick up, from the *Seamew*, a dropped cargo; but smuggling craft did not put to sea on moonlit nights, and it would be several days yet before the moon reached the full. If there was a run cargo lying concealed in the Dower House, it seemed improbable that Richmond should consider it necessary to take any part in its removal. The possibility that he might prefer the excitement of such a venture to an expedition into Yorkshire did occur to the Major, but he discarded it: Richmond had been within ames-ace of jumping at the chance offered him, and his subsequent hesitation had clearly been due to an undisclosed afterthought.

The Major knew better than to question him. Richmond had made it plain that he was not going to confide in him;

and to persist in interrogating him would serve no other purpose than to arouse his hostility. Hostility had certainly flickered for a minute in his eyes during the session in his bedchamber; and it seemed unpleasantly probable that Richmond, regarding his cousin as a foe to beware of, was only waiting until he should be out of the way to prosecute whatever illicit undertaking it was that he had on hand.

This unwelcome suspicion was not quite laid to rest by the discovery that Richmond had at least told Lord Darracott of the offered treat. Telling his lordship and coaxing him were two very different things: Richmond was bound to tell him, but in what manner he had done it Hugo could not know. If he had used any cajolery his efforts had not so far met with success. When his lordship was alone with his elder grandsons that evening, the ladies of the party, and also Richmond, who rarely kept late hours, having retired to bed, he bent one of his more intimidating stares upon the Major and demanded to be told what the devil he meant by inviting Richmond to go with him on a tedious journey that was certain to knock him up.

"I don't think it would knock him up, sir," replied Hugo, with the imperturbability which had by this time ceased to surprise his cousins.

"Much you know!" barked his lordship. "Your way of travel won't do for Richmond, let me tell you!"

"Never fear!" said Hugo, an appreciative twinkle in his eye. "I'll be travelling post, and it's no matter to me how many times I break the journey: I won't let the lad be knocked-up!"

Balked at this point, his lordship delivered himself of a diatribe against posting-houses, all of which, he appeared to believe made it their invariable custom to seek, by every means at their disposal, to render their patrons' visit not only uncomfortable, but generally fatal.

Listening in great astonishment to these strictures, Claud was moved to protest. "No, no, sir!" he said earnestly. "Assure you——! Not a word of truth in it! Daresay it may have been like that in your day, but it ain't so now! Ask anyone! No reason at all to think young Richmond would be put between damp sheets, or given bad fish to eat! What's more, if you ask me, it would take more than a journey by stage-coach, let alone one in a post-chaise-and-four, to knock *him* up!"

"I don't ask you—fribble!" snapped his lordship, rounding on him, with the speed of a whiplash. "You may keep your tongue between your teeth!"

"Yes, sir—happy to!" uttered Claud dismayed. "No wish to offend you! Thought you might like to be set right!"

"Thought *I* might like to be set right?"

"No, no! Spoke without thinking!" said Claud hastily. "I know you don't!"

"There's no need for any fratching about it," interposed Hugo. "I'd be glad of the lad's company, I'll see he takes no harm, I think he'd enjoy it, and that's all there is to it."

His deep, unperturbed voice seemed to exercise a soothing effect upon Lord Darracott. After glaring at Claud for a moment he turned away from him, to inform Hugo, disagreeably, but in a milder tone, that Richmond would find nothing whatsoever to interest him in such a place as Huddersfield. Driven out of this position, as he very soon was, he once more lost his temper, and said, gripping the arms of his chair: "Very well, sir, if you will have it, you may! The less Richmond sees of you the better I shall be pleased! I've had trouble enough with him without wishing for more! Before you came here, to set him off again, he was in a fair way to forgetting a crack-brained notion he took into his head that nothing would do for him but to join the army. *I* knew it was merely a silly, boy's fancy he'd soon recover from, but I'm not running the risk of letting you stir him up, so don't think it!"

Hugo stood looking down at him impassively; but it was Vincent who spoke. He had been listening with an expression on his face of sardonic amusement, but at this point he said, unexpectedly: "I fear, sir, that such an attempt on my cousin's part would be a work of supererogation. To judge by the confidences made to me when I took Richmond to Sevenoaks he has by no means forgotten that crackbrained notion. He was, in fact, a dead bore on the subject."

Lord Darracott stared at him. "He was, was he? Well, if he hasn't recovered yet, he will presently! I'll never give my consent, do you hear me? Good God, *that* weakly boy? As well kill him outright!"

Forgetting caution, Claud said incredulously: "What, is Richmond weakly? I'd never have thought it! Well, what I mean is, he don't seem to me to be happy unless he's careering all over the county on one of his wild horses, or walking for miles after a few wretched pigeons, or tossing about in that boat of his! I should think the army would suit him down to the ground, for they always seem to be drilling, or manoeuvring, or doing something dashed un-restful, and that's just what Richmond is—unrestful!"

"*Will* you hold your tongue?" said his lordship violently.

"It goes against the grain with me to agree with Claud," drawled Vincent, "but honesty compels me to own that there is much in what he says, sir."

"So you're in this, are you?" said his lordship, danger-ously. "What the devil do you imagine it has to do with you?"

"Nothing at all, sir: I am merely curious. Forgive me if the question is impertinent, but have you any other reason than Richmond's supposed sickliness for holding a military career in abhorrence?"

"One of them should be obvious to you!" flashed his lordship. "I had a son who embraced a military career!"

"Well, if that don't cap the globe!" gasped Claud. "No, dash it, sir——!"

"Nay, I've a broad back! Sneck up!" said Hugo, rather amused.

"Really, I had no intention of being so maladroit!" sighed Vincent. "I fancy—but I am wretchedly ignorant on the subject of military customs!—that it is seldom that junior offi-cers ally themselves with the daughters of—er—wealthy mill owners." He smiled wryly at his grandfather. "Now, don't, I implore you, sir, put me under the obligation of apolo-gizing to Hugo for drawing down your fire upon his head, for I should dislike it excessively! Is it permissible to ask what you do mean to do with Richmond?"

"No! Nor need you trouble yourself over the boy!" said his lordship curtly. "I'll take care of his future!"

"I am sure you will," said Vincent. "But the thought that he might perhaps—er—take care of it himself, does just faintly occur to me."

"Richmond is under age! By the time he's twenty-one he will have forgotten he ever so much as thought of the army! Depend upon it, it's nothing more than a trumpery, boy's wish to peacock about in a jack-a-dandy Hussar regiment! I knew that as soon as he blurted out that it was a Hussar regiment he had in his mind. Well, I'm not squandering a thousand pounds, or whatever the sum is, on a cornetcy which the silly boy would wish to God he'd never asked me for by the time he'd spent a month in the army!"

"It would be very expensive," agreed Vincent. "We have one amongst us, however, so full of—er—juice, as to be able to stand the nonsense, if he chose to do it." He turned his head to survey Hugo. "*Would* you choose to do it?" he enquired.

It was not the moment Hugo would have selected for the broaching of so ticklish a subject, but he nodded. The result was much what he had foreseen. Lord Darracott's wrath boiled over. It was to Hugo that he addressed himself, but so menacing was his mien, and so unbridled his tongue, that Claud, fearful that he might become the next target, edged his way to the door and, opening it with great stealth, made good his escape.

Hugo, reminding Vincent irresistibly of a rock battered by the waves, waited, with an unmoved countenance, for his lordship's eloquence to expend itself. All he said, at the end of a comprehensive denunciation, was: "Well, it wouldn't be seemly if I were to start a flight with you, sir, so happen I'd best say goodnight! I'd buy a cornetcy for Richmond tomorrow, if I were his guardian, but as I'm not there's no reason that I can see why you should be at the housetop." He then smiled amiably upon his seething grandsire, nodded to Vincent, and went unhurriedly out of the room.

Lord Darracott, exhausted by his passion, remained silent for several minutes, leaning back in his chair; but presently, as his breathing grew steadier, he turned his head to look at Vincent, still seated at his graceful ease on the sofa. "Since you've elected to remain here, you may tell me, you treacherous young hound, what the devil you meant by turning against me!" he said, in a rather spent voice. "How *dared* you, sir?"

"My dear sir, I have numerous vices, but no one has yet accused me of running shy!" replied Vincent coolly. "Nor have I turned against you. Far from it, in fact!"

"Don't lie to me! You know very well what my sentiments are on *that* subject! Why did you encourage that—that upstart to think his damned fortune gave him the right to meddle with Richmond?"

"I *was* maladroit, wasn't I? I can only set it down to inexperience: I can't recall that I ever before attempted to play the rôle of disinterested benevolence. I own I made sad work of it, but do acquit me, sir, of encouraging the elephant Ajax! My opinion of his intellect is not high, but he is not so blockish as to suppose that it is within his power to meddle with Richmond's future."

"So you were being benevolent, were you?" said his lordship, on a jeering note. "And since when have you cared the snap of your fingers for Richmond's future?"

A slight frown appeared between Vincent's brows. "I don't know that I do care for it, sir. I have a certain amount of affection for him, but, I confess, it wouldn't prompt me to concern myself in his affairs if I could be perfectly sure that frustrating the only ambition he appears to have would not lead to trouble."

"Balderdash!" said his lordship impatiently. "What put that rubbishing notion into your head?"

"It was put there by your damned upstart, and pray don't imagine that I accepted it readily! No one is more violently irritated by him than I am, believe me, sir!"

"I might have guessed it was he! Much he knows about it!"

Vincent's frown deepened. "Yes, that was more or less what I told him, but the disagreeable truth is that I have a reluctant suspicion that he may be right. He could scarcely have attained his present rank, one presumes, without acquiring considerable experience of striplings of Richmond's age."

"He knows nothing whatsoever about Richmond, whatever he may know of any other boy! I should like to know what trouble he thinks could possibly befall *my* grandson!" said his lordship contemptuously. "Damme, I thought you'd more wit than to be nose-led by Hugh! I know his cut! I'd be willing to lay you any odds that his notion of trouble is the sort of scrape I don't doubt Richmond will tumble into, just as you did, and I did, and every one of my sons did! It won't worry me, but I haven't any shabby-genteel moralities, as you may be sure he has! Damn his infernal impudence! I'll have him know that Richmond's a gentleman! Ay, and a grandson to be proud of, too! There's not one of you that can match him for pluck, for he don't know what fear is! He has the best disposition of any of you, too, *and* the best looks! Let me hear no more from you! *Hugh* to think he knows the boy better than I do——! By God, it passes the bounds of effrontery!"

"Certainly," said Vincent. "But I am afraid I have expressed myself inaccurately. It is only fair that I should tell you that Hugo cast no slur on Richmond's character. The trouble he has in mind is the sort of dangerous—mischief—a green and headstrong boy might plunge into because he was bored, reckless—as we all know Richmond is!—and too much disappointed to care what risks he ran." He glanced frowningly at Lord Darracott, and then lowered his eyes to the snuff-box he was holding. "Rather a surprising youth,

220

Richmond," he said slowly. "I collect *you* didn't know that he hasn't by any means forgotten his ambition; *I* certainly didn't, until I took him to watch that fight. I can only suppose that he was a trifle carried away, for he has never before favoured me with his confidence. I am quite sure he later regretted it, which makes me wonder how much any of us know about him."

"Well, don't wonder any more!" said his lordship brusquely. "Why the devil should he confide in you? I know all I need to about him, and I'll thank you to mind your own business!"

Vincent shrugged, and got up. "As you wish, sir. I am clearly unequal to the rôle I so foolishly assumed, but I do hope it may be chalked up somewhere to my credit that I did at least attempt it."

"Oh, don't talk such fustian!" exclaimed his lordship irritably. "Go away before I lose my patience with you!"

"Consider me gone, sir!" Vincent replied.

He went out of the room as he spoke, and walked slowly across the hall to the staircase. Before he had reached it, Hugh came into the house through the still unbolted main door. At sight of him, a shade of annoyance came into Vincent's eyes, but he said lightly: "Ah, still indulging your lamentable taste for cigars, I collect!" He hesitated, and then, as Hugo said nothing, added, with a wry grimace: "I am afraid, coz, that I did more harm than good—or, at any rate, that you think so!"

"I do," said Hugo, just a trifle grimly. "And I'm wondering which of the two it was that you meant to do."

"Strange as it may seem to you—it seems very strange to me!—my intentions were admirable. I actually had not the smallest desire to set you at outs with my grandfather, and even less to thrust a spoke into your wheel, which is what I can't deny I have done."

"There's little chance he'll let Richmond go with me to Yorkshire, if that's what you mean," answered Hugo.

"It is precisely what I mean. I perceive that I shall be obliged, after all, to offer you an apology."

"Nay, I'll make shift to do without it. Will you keep your eye on that lad while I'm away?" said Hugo bluntly.

"Yes, coz, I will—if only to prove you wrong in your suspicion! By the way, I wouldn't, if I were you, mention it to my grandfather!"

"That's the last thing I'll do!" said Hugo.

"Very prudent! Goodnight!" said Vincent, beginning to

221

mount the stairway. At the first landing, he paused, and looked down at Hugo, saying smoothly: "I wonder how it was that we contrived, before your arrival, to rub along tolerably well, and certainly without falling into disaster? I must confess myself to be wholly at a stand to account for it."

"Well, that's something that has me in a puzzle too!" retorted Hugo, a sudden grin putting the unusual gravity of his countenance to flight.

Vincent raised his brows in faint surprise. "Your trick, cousin!" he acknowledged, and went on up the stairs.

By the time a somewhat depleted breakfast-party met next morning, everyone at Darracott Place knew that the previous day had ended with a Scene of no common order, for those, like Richmond, whose rooms were so remote from the library as to put them out of the reach of even such a powerful voice as Lord Darracott's had the pleasing intelligence conveyed to them with their cups of chocolate and cans of hot water. Mrs. Darracott, whose room was situated immediately above the library, carried the news to Lady Aurelia, together with a moving description of the nervous spasms which had subsequently made it impossible for her to close her eyes all night. Her appearance bore such eloquent testimony in support of her story that Lady Aurelia, though herself made of sterner stuff, said kindly: "Very disagreeable!"

"No one seems to know what provoked Lord Darracott, but my woman had it from Charles that Hugo *slammed* out of the house in a terrible rage—though that I do *not* believe, because I must have heard the door slam had he done so, and in any event Chollacombe told me himself that Hugo merely went out to smoke a cigar, which he always does—not that I knew it, and I own I wish he would not, for I *cannot* like smoking, even if it's dear Hugo! However, that has nothing to do with it, and for my part I don't believe that Hugo was in a rage, for there was never a sweeter-tempered, more truly amiable creature born, and when one considers— but I shall not speak of *that*, for I am sure we have talked it over often enough, and enter into each other's sentiments *exactly!* But what makes me quite ill with apprehension, Aurelia, is that there seems to be no doubt at all that it was Hugo Lord Darracott quarrelled with! But why? What, I ask you, can Hugo possibly have done or said to provoke my lord? There were just the three of them, when we had gone up to bed, and it can't have been Claud, because

222

James told Mrs. Flitwick that he came out of the library *long* before the end of the quarrel; and it can't have been Vincent, because he stayed with my lord, after Hugo had left the room, and *after* my lord stopped shouting. So it *must* have been dear Hugo! And what *utterly* sinks my spirits is that my woman met Grooby coming away from Lord Darracott's room this morning, and knew, the instant she set eyes on him, that things are as bad as they could possibly be, instead of having blown over, as very often they do, and my lord in the *worst* of humours! So I sent for some coffee, and a slice of bread-and-butter, to my bedchamber, not that I could swallow a morsel, for *nothing* will prevail upon me to go down to the breakfast-room while everyone is at outs! *But*," concluded the widow, with sudden resolution, "if Lord Darracott has dared to endanger my only daughter's happiness, he will have Me to reckon with, for where my children are concerned I can be as brave as a Lioness, Aurelia, even at the breakfast-table!"

Lady Aurelia, whose invariable custom it was to partake of a far more substantial breakfast in bed, saw nothing to object to in this, and nodded her head. After considering the matter, she pronounced, in a very regal way: "I will see Claud."

But Claud, summoned to his august parent's room before he had finished dressing, was far too peevish to be of any material assistance. Attired in a dressing-gown of rich silk, he was much more concerned with the style of neckcloth most proper to be worn with a frock-coat, and a daring waistcoat of Polyphant's design, than with a quarrel from which he had managed to escape, and only wished to forget. He was inclined to be indignant with his mother for having sent for him on frivolous grounds; and, finding that she was determined to get to the bottom of what seemed to him a very trivial affair, extricated himself without hesitation or compunction by advising her to apply to Vincent for information, since he was the instigator of the quarrel. Before he could make good his retreat, however, he was incensed and appalled by a command to go immediately to Vincent's room, and to inform him that his mama desired to have speech with him before he went down to breakfast. Since it was the time-honoured practice of the brothers to sacrifice each other in such situations as now confronted Claud, it was not fear of Vincent's wrath at finding himself betrayed which prompted Claud to despatch Polyphant on the errand, but the knowledge that not even a messenger bearing gifts of great price would meet with anything but the rudest of receptions from Vincent at this hour of the morning.

The events of the previous evening having put Vincent in the worst of tempers, it was in anything but a propitious mood that he presently visited Lady Aurelia, nor did the measured speech with which she favoured him soften his humour. Her ladyship, disclaiming any desire either to know the gist of the quarrel, or to listen to excuses, informed him, without passion or waste of words, that if his cousin and his grandfather were set at loggerheads through his agency he would fall under her deepest displeasure. That, she said, was all she wished to say to him; and as Vincent was well-aware that her fortune, and not his father's humbler portion, was the source of his own allowance, it was quite unnecessary for her to say more. Pale with anger, he bowed stiffly, and replied in a voice of ice: "I do not propose to burden you, ma'am, with an account of what occurred last night, nor can I deny that some unfortunate words of mine were the cause of my grandfather's attack on my cousin. It was not, however, my intention to instigate a quarrel, as I trust I made plain to my cousin. I have only to add that you need be under no apprehension that my dislike of Hugo would, under any circumstances, prompt me to make mischief between him and my grandfather."

"Your character, Vincent, is in many ways unsatisfactory, but I have never found you untruthful," said her ladyship. "I have no hesitation in accepting your assurance, therefore. Pray close the door carefully behind you! the catch is defective."

After this, it was not surprising that Vincent, instead of putting in an appearance at the breakfast-table, strode off to the stables, and worked off the worst of his spleen by riding at a slapping pace to Rye, where the George provided him with a belated but excellent breakfast.

The breakfast-party at Darracott Place was thus reduced to four persons, Anthea having left the room before Claud entered it. Conversation did not flourish. Lord Darracott wore a forbidding scowl, and, beyond nodding curtly to Richmond, paid no attention to anyone; Richmond, as yet uninitiated into the cause of the quarrel, was looking anxious, and scarcely spoke; Claud, after one glance at his grandfather, confined his utterances to what was strictly necessary; and Hugo, finding his companions disinclined for conversation, placidly consumed his customary and sustaining meal.

It was not until he was about to rise from the table that Lord Darracott broke his silence. Addressing himself to Richmond, he demanded to know how long it was since he had visited his tutor. Without waiting for an answer, he said that Richmond had been idle for weeks, and must now resume regular hours of study.

"Yes, Grandpapa. But am I not to go with Hugo?" Richmond asked.

"No, certainly not! You need not look glum, for you would find nothing to interest you in Huddersfield, and a great deal to disgust you!"

"The mills would interest me," Richmond said. "I know how sheep are sheared, but I don't know what is done to the fleeces to turn them into cloth, but Hugo says I may see every bit of it, if I like. *Pray* let me go, Grandpapa!"

"I said no, and I meant it!" interrupted his lordship, more peremptorily than it was his custom to speak to Richmond. "I am astonished that you could wish to interest yourself in a cloth mill! You have nothing to do with mills, or any other such things, and you will oblige me by not mentioning the subject again!" He then turned towards Hugo, and said: "As for you, I do not know what your purpose is in travelling to Yorkshire, but I trust you mean to dispose of whatever may be your interest in your grandfather's business. It is extremely repugnant to me to think that a Darracott, and my heir, should owe any part of his subsistence to it!"

He did not wait for an answer, which was fortunate, since Hugo showed no sign of giving him one, but stalked out of the room.

Claud, who had listened to him in open-mouthed astonishment, exclaimed: "Dashed if I don't think he's begun to get queer in his attic! Well, what I mean is, hubble-bubble! I don't set up as one of these clever coves, but I've got more sense in my knowledge-box than to say such an addlebrained thing as that! Seems to me it don't make a ha'porth of difference whether you keep the dashed mill, or whether you don't, because that's where all your gingerbread came from, whichever way you look at it. And don't you tell me it's repugnant to him to have you coming down with the derbies, because all I've got to say to that is, *Gammon!*"

Hugo did not reply. He was watching Richmond, who had gone over to the window, and was staring out, his gaze unfocused. He looked dejected, and Hugo said: "I'm sorry, lad, but happen I'll be able to take you another time."

Richmond turned his head. "Yes, of course. I hope you will, for I should like very much to go with you. Was it that which made him angry last night? He didn't like it, when I told him you'd asked me to go, but he didn't rip up at me. Why did he fly into a passion all at once, and quarrel with you?"

"Nay, the Lord only knows!" said Hugo.

"Well, that's a hummer, if ever I heard one!" said Claud. "We all know what made him quarrel with you! It was Vincent's doing, of course. Sort of thing he would do, what's more!"

"*Vincent?*" Richmond said.

"That's it," nodded Claud. "If he hadn't stirred the coals, it wouldn't have happened, and I daresay the old gentleman would have let you go with Hugo, but once he'd flung the cat amongst the pigeons the trap was down."

"He didn't mean to stir the coals," interposed Hugo, seeing the look of bewildered chagrin on Richmond's face. "He certainly took the wrong sow by the ear, but what he wanted to do was to try whether he couldn't get his lordship to listen to reason about *you*, lad."

"Well, if that's what you think, you don't know Vincent!" said Claud. "Yes, I wish I may see Vincent trying to help Richmond, or anyone else, for that matter! A fine way to help him, asking you whether you'd be willing to purchase a cornetcy for him! Why, even a regular flat would have seen what he was trying to do!"

Richmond caught his breath, his eyes flying to Hugo's face. "Oh, no! You wouldn't—would you?"

Hugo smiled at him. "Yes, of course I would, but I may not be able to do it until you're of age. You needn't fear I won't make a push to bring his lordship round to the notion, but it'll be best if you, and Vincent, too, leave it to me to choose my own time for coming to grips with him."

Those ridiculously expressive eyes were fairly blazing; Richmond said impetuously: "I'll do anything you say! Hugo, do you *mean* it? If I'd *known*——! I didn't think there was the least hope, because even when I'm of age I shan't be able to purchase it for myself, and all I thought I could do was to join as a volunteer, which I would, only I want a cavalry regiment m-more than anything else in the world! Hugo, will you *lend* me the purchase-price? I shan't be able to pay it back for years, because my father didn't leave any-

226

thing but debts, and Mama's own fortune is very small, but in the end, of course, it will come to me, so——"

"Whoa, lad!" begged Hugo, laughing at this tumbled entreaty. "You keep out of mischief, and I'll make you a present of it for your twenty-first birthday!"

Richmond tried to speak, failed, swallowed convulsively, and managed to jerk out: "Thank you! I c-can't—— You don't *know* what it means to me! Even if I have to wait—go to Oxford—it doesn't signify! It was thinking there wasn't any *hope——! Well, I—— Well, *thank you!*" he ended, in a rush. He bestowed a shy, tremulous smile upon his benefactor, and, his feelings threatening to overcome him, ran out of the room.

Claud, who had been regarding him with the sort of mild wonder he might have felt upon being confronted with a freak at Bartholomew Fair, sighed, and shook his head. "What did I tell you?" he said. "It wouldn't surprise me if it turns out *he's* a trifle queer in his attic too. I don't say he won't look bang-up to the knocker in Hussar rig, because, now I come to think of it, it's just the thing for him, but it's my belief he don't care a rush what kind of a uniform he'll have to sport."

"Nay, do you think *I'm* queer in my attic?" expostulated Hugo.

"*Think?* I dashed well know you are! In fact," said Claud frankly, "it's my belief you were *born* with rats in your upper storey!"

XVIII

Lord Darracott's bleak mood lasted throughout the day, but since Richmond appeared to have accepted his harsh decree with perfect serenity, and neither repulsive looks nor snubbing replies produced any change whatsoever in Hugo's demeanour, he had become so far mollified, by the time he sat down to dinner on the following evening, as to be able to bring himself to address several remarks to Hugo, and even, once, to agree with what he said, besides demanding of Lady Aurelia, with a near approach to geniality, whether they were to enjoy their usual rubber or two of whist. This was generally felt to be a sign that the storm (provided that no one offered him any provocation) was over; and although Anthea could have thought of a more agreeable way of passing the evening, and Vincent considered that playing whist for chicken-stakes was a dead bore, neither hesitated to acquiesce in this scheme for his lordship's entertainment, though both wished heartily that it had not developed into a ritual. Lord Darracott had been a hardened gamester in his day, but, unlike Vincent, he cared as much for the play as for the stake, and all that was needed for his enjoyment was a reasonable degree of luck, and three other players who could be relied on not to provoke him by stupidity, inattention, slowness of wit, or, in fact, any of the faults that characterized such indifferent card-players as Mrs. Darracott, and Hugo.

Any apprehension that Richmond's unmistakeable air of elation would make his lordship suspicious the Major was soon able to banish from his mind. His lordship's egotism was of too sublime an order to allow of his having the smallest perception; and since a long and unquestioned reign over his family had convinced him that submission to his commands and prohibitions was inevitable, he saw nothing remarkable in a docility that anyone else must have deemed so unnatural as to give rise to serious alarm. If he thought at all of the warning Vincent had tried to convey to him, it was with contempt. No doubt of his infallibility troubled him; no misgiving that the high courage in which he gloried was incompatible with docility ever so much as occurred to him: Richmond was the product of his own, untrammelled training; he had perceived at the outset he was worthy of attention; so it would have seemed to him very extraordinary had the boy not grown up to be as near perfection as made no odds.

Vincent, perceiving more clearly than anyone the absolute nature of his lordship's belief, remarked to Hugo, with something of a snap: "It is devoutly to be hoped there's no truth in your suspicion, coz, for I shudder to think of what the consequences might be if Richmond were to tumble off the pedestal our misguided progenitor built for him to sit on!"

Hugo nodded.

"I tried to give him a hint, you know. I might as well have spared my breath."

"Eh, you shouldn't have done that!" Hugo said.

"Oh, have no fear! I seem to have made a slip-slop of the whole affair, but I am not quite chuckleheaded! I gave him no hint of the particular mischief I had in mind," replied Vincent, with a short laugh. "I collect, by the way, that you've promised Richmond that cornetcy. I trust it may give him something other to think of than smuggling—if he does think of smuggling!"

"That's what I trust, too," said Hugo. "I told him he should have it if he kept out of mischief, and I'm hopeful we'll have no more need to fatch ourselves, for there's no question at all about it: he was thrown into such transports he could hardly speak!"

"I am aware. You have certainly become his beau ideal!"

"Nay, there's no hope of that," said Hugo despondently. "I'll never be able to take the shine out of you, for I'm no top-sawyer, and I'm sick everytime I go to sea."

Vincent laughed, but a faint flush stained his cheeks, and he said sharply: "Good God, do you think I care? Not the snap of my fingers!"

Having had ample time to become acquainted with his demon of jealousy, Hugo heaved a profound sigh of relief, and said: "Eh, I'm glad to hear you say that! The way you're never happy but what you have the lad at your heels, let alone the pleasure it is to you to listen to his chatter, I thought you'd be reet miserable!"

This response succeeded as well as any could; but although Vincent smiled in genuine amusement, he was still furious with himself for that instant's self-betrayal, and his temper, already exacerbated, was not improved. He had never felt more than tolerance for Richmond; and the boy's admiration had amused rather than gratified him. Had he arrived at Darracott Place to find that Richmond had outgrown his youthful hero-worship it would not have troubled him in the least; but when he saw Richmond's eyes turn away from him towards Hugo, and realized that, instead of following his lead, Richmond had drawn a little aloof from him, he fell a prey to a jealousy which none knew better than he to be irrational. Between this bitter envy of his brother and cousin whose financial circumstances rendered them independent of Lord Darracott; resentment that his own, very different, circumstances made it necessary for him to serve his grandfather's caprice; and dislike of the usurper whose arrival on the scene had led to a great many disagreeable results, he was so much chafed that to keep his temper under control imposed a severe strain upon him. Pride, quite as much as prudence, demanded that he should preserve an attitude of languid indifference, but so coldly civil was his manner to Hugo that that usually immovable giant was considerably surprised when, two evenings later, he came quickly into the billiard-room, and said, in a voice from which all affectation had vanished: "Hugo, where's Richmond? Have you seen him?"

Claud, startled into miscueing, exclaimed indignantly: "Damn you, Vincent, what the devil do you mean by bursting in here when you know dashed well we're playing? Anyone would take you for a cawker instead of the Go you think you are! *Look* what you've made me do!"

Vincent paid not the smallest heed to him; his frowning eyes remained fixed on the Major's face; he said: "He's not in his room."

The Major met that hard, anxious stare without any sign of emotion. He returned it, in fact, with a blankess that might well have led Vincent to suppose that he was wholly lacking in comprehension. After a moment, he said calmly: "Nay, it's too early."

"It's eleven o'clock."

"As late as that?" Hugo seemed to consider this, but shook his head. "No, I don't think it. Not while everyone's still up."

"Then where is he?"

Claud, who had been listening to this exchange with gathering wrath, demanded, in the voice of one goaded beyond endurance: "Who the devil cares where he is? Dash it, have you got a drop in the eye? Bouncing in when I'm in the middle of a break, just to ask Hugo where young Richmond is! If you want him, rub off, and find him for yourself! *I* don't want him, and Hugo don't want him either, and, what's more, we don't want you!"

"Oh, be quiet!" snapped Vincent impatiently.

"Well, if that don't beat the Dutch!" gasped Claud.

"Nay, keep your tongue, lad, will you?" Hugo interposed. "I've not seen Richmond since we left the dining-room. I thought he went up to the drawing-room with you."

"Yes, he did. He took up a book, when we began to play whist, but went off to bed very early. I don't know what the time may have been: it was considerably before Chollacombe brought in the tea-tray—possibly half-past nine, or thereabouts. I thought nothing of it: he'd been yawning his head off, and my aunt kept on urging him to go to bed. I can't say I paid much heed, beyond wishing that he *would* go, instead of insisting that he wasn't tired, for I found the pair of them extremely distracting. In fact, I was on the point of suggesting that he should either stop yawning or do what he was told, when my grandfather took the words out of my mouth, and ordered him off to bed."

He paused, knitting his brows. His incensed brother exclaimed: "*No!* Ordered him off to bed, did he? Never heard such an interesting story in my life—wouldn't have missed it for a fortune! Well, if I were you, I'd go off to bed too, because if you're not top-heavy you're in pretty queer stirrups, take my word for it! Very likely you'll have thrown out a rash by tomorrow."

"Damn the young dry-boots!" Vincent said suddenly, ignoring the interruption. "I'll teach him to make a bleater of me!"

"You think it was a hoax?"

"Not at the time, but I do now. Rather more up to snuff than I knew, my little cousin Richmond! If he'd made an excuse to retire, I should have been suspicious, and he knew that. I asked him yesterday if he was in mischief—it's wonderful, the harm I do every time I try to do good!"

Hugo was slightly frowning. "It doesn't fit," he said. "Not at that hour! He couldn't be as crazy! Eh, Vincent, think of the risk he'd be running! Are you sure he wasn't in his room when you went to find him?"

"I am very sure he wasn't. His door was locked, and I must have wakened him, had he been asleep, but there wasn't a sound to be heard within the room. Why should Richmond hesitate to answer me?"

"Well, *I* can tell you that!" said Claud. "What's more, I wish I'd locked *this* door!"

Hugo laid down his cue, and strode over to one of the windows, and flung back the heavy curtain. "Cloudy. Looks like rain," he said. "He told me that he sometimes takes his boat out at night, fishing. You know more than I do about sea-fishing: would he be likely to do so tonight?"

"God knows!" replied Vincent, shrugging. "I shouldn't, myself, because it doesn't amuse me to get soaked to the skin. Nor should I choose to go sailing when the light is uncertain. But I'm not Richmond. *Does* he sail at night? I wonder why he never told me?"

"He might have been afraid you'd put a stop to it."

"I should have supposed there was more fear that *you* would, but that didn't prevent his telling you."

"He told me when I asked him why he always locked his door. I didn't believe him, but it might have been true."

"It might, but—Hugo, I don't like the sound of it! What the devil is the confounded brat up to?"

"I'm damned if I know!" said Hugo.

"Well, if ever I met a more buffleheaded pair of silly

231

gudgeons——!" exclaimed Claud disgustedly. "Dash it, if young Richmond's gone out, it's as plain as a pikestaff what he's up to! And I must say it's coming to something if he can't slip off for a bit of fun and gig without you two trying to nose out what game he's flying at, and raising all this dust! Anyone would think, to listen to you, that he'd gone off to rob the Mail!" He found that he was being stared at by both his auditors, and added with considerable asperity: "And don't stand there goggling at me as if you'd never heard of a young chub having a petticoat-affair, because that's doing it a dashed sight too brown!"

"Good God, I wonder if you could be right?" said Vincent. He looked at Hugo. "I didn't think—but it might be so, I suppose."

Hugo shook his head. "No. There's not a sign of it. He's not that road yet. You'd know it, if he'd started in the petticoat-line."

"Dashed if I can make out what's the matter with you both!" said Claud. "Why can't you leave the wretched boy alone? He won't come to any harm! Why should he?"

"Hugo thinks he's in a string with a gang of smugglers," said Vincent curtly.

"*What?*" gasped Claud. "Thinks *Richmond*—— No, dash it! Of all the crack-brained notions I ever heard——! *You* don't believe that, Vincent!"

"I don't know what I believe!" said Vincent, jerking the curtain across the window again, in a way that betrayed his disquiet. "I do know *one* thing, and that's that I'll have the truth out of Richmond when he comes in!"

"Well, if you mean to ask him if he's joined a gang of smugglers, I hope he draws your cork! I call it a dashed insult! You can't go about saying things like that just because he's gone out on the spree!"

"There's more to it than that," Hugo said. "Ottershaw's watching him like a cat at a mouse-hole, and he'd not do that if he hadn't good reason to suspect him. He's got no proof yet, or we'd know it, but—eh, I wish the lad would come in!"

Claud's eyes started almost from their sockets. "Are you talking about that Riding-officer I found you gabbing to at Rye? Suspects Richmond? You can't mean that!"

"Ay, but I do mean it," replied Hugo grimly. "There's little would suit him better than to catch the lad redhanded—make no mistake about that!"

232

"He wouldn't dare! No, no! Dash it, Hugo—a Darracott of Darracott?"

"That won't weigh with him, if Richmond walks into a trap he's set. Plague take the lad! I warned him that Ottershaw's not the clodhead he thinks him, but he's as pot-sure as he's meedless!" He checked himself, and said, after a moment. "Well, talking will pay no toll!"

"Just so!" said Vincent. "Perhaps you'll tell me what *will* pay toll!"

"Ask me that when I know where the lad is! There's only one thing I can think of to do at this present: I'll walk up to the Dower House—ghost-catching! Happen I might get some kind of a kenning—and if I find the place is being watched, at the least we'll know they've not got wind of the lad yet, for it's there that they look for him!" He glanced at Vincent. "If I'm asked for here, you'll have to cut some kind of a wheedle for me: we don't want to raise a breeze! What are they doing, upstairs? Have my aunts gone to bed yet?"

"They hadn't, when I left the room, though my Aunt Elvira was about to go. She said something about a sore throat, and feeling a cold coming on, so no doubt she'll have retired by now. Anthea went off to find Mrs. Flitwick —something about a posset she knows how to brew!—so it's more than likely she's in the kitchen-quarters. Does she know?"

"No, and I don't mean she shall! Fob her off, if she should come in here! I take it his lordship's still up?"

"Since he and my mother were engaged in playing over again every hand about which they had—er—disagreed, you may take it that they will both be up for some time to come," replied Vincent sardonically.

"Well, if that's what they're doing, they won't be heeding aught else. I'll be off," Hugo said, turning to pick up his coat.

Even as he spoke, the door opened, and Anthea came hurriedly into the room, her face as white as paper. "Hugo!" she uttered breathlessly. "Please come—please come *quickly!* I—I *need* you!"

Two strides brought him to her. He saw that she was trembling, and grasped her shoulders. "Steady, lass! What is it? Nay, there's no need to fear your cousins! Out with it, now! Is it Richmond?"

She nodded, and said, trying to command her voice: "He's hurt—bleeding dreadfully! John Joseph says—not fa-

233

tally, but I don't know! They were cutting his coat off, when I came running to find you——"

"Who were?" he interrupted.

"John Joseph, and Polyphant. Chollacombe is there too, and Mrs. Flitwick. We—she and I—went to the pantry, you see, and that's how—John Joseph had carried him there. He w-wasn't conscious, and his face—his face was *black,* Hugo! At first, I—I couldn't think who it was! He had on a smock——"

"Oh, my God——!" exclaimed Vincent. "It's true, then! *Now* what do you propose we should do, cousin?"

"Find out how badly the lad's hurt!" Hugo answered. "Come, love! no vapours! We're not grassed yet!"

"No—oh, no!" she said, following him from the room. "I won't fail! It was only the shock of—— Hugo, he—he must have been *smuggling!* I c-can't *believe* it! *Richmond!*"

"Keep mum for that just now, love!" he replied. "Happen we'll bring him about."

He was striding down the broad corridor that led from the hall to the kitchen-quarters, and she had almost to run to keep up with him. "We must, Hugo, we *must!* John Joseph says you'll know how to do it. He's washed the soot from Richmond's face, and Mrs. Flitwick bundled that dreadful smock up, and took it away under her apron, to burn it immediately. They were so *good,* Hugo! They did *everything*—even Polyphant!"

They had reached the door leading to the kitchen-wing, and as Hugo thrust it open, Vincent, hard on his heels, demanded: "How many of the servants know about this? Is the entire household attending to Richmond?"

"No, only those three—and Chollacombe, I think."

He uttered an impatient exclamation under his breath, but by this time Hugo had entered the pantry, and Anthea, squeezing her way in, between his massive form and the door-post, paid no heed.

Richmond, who was lying on the flagged floor, had come round. He was being supported by John Joseph, kneeling behind him, while Polyphant was waving some burnt feathers under his nose, and Chollacombe, looking very much shaken, stood rather helplessly behind Polyphant, holding a glass of brandy in his hand. Richmond's coat had been cut off, and his shirt ripped away from his left arm and shoulder. Claud, managing to obtain a glimpse into the room over Vincent's shoulder, recoiled, shuddering, from a scene which did, indeed, resemble a shambles. There seemed

234

to be blood everywhere he looked, even on his valet's immaculate raiment, and as he invariably felt queasy if he only cut his finger, he could scarcely be blamed for his hasty retreat.

John Joseph looked up under his brows at the Major, saying dourly: "Tha'll do well to bestir thysen, Mester Hugo, if we bahn to bring t'lad out of this scuddle! Happen t'gadgers will be banging on t'door in a piece, so, if tha wants to be any hand afore, think quick!"

"How badly is he hit?" Hugo asked, putting Polyphant out of his way, and bending over Richmond.

"Nay, it's noan so bad, but seemingly t'bullet's lodged." He shifted Richmond slightly, and raised the folded dish-cloth he was holding over an ugly wound high up on Richmond's shoulder. It began to bleed again, but sluggishly. Hugo saw that the blood was coming mostly from the torn flesh; and a brief scrutiny satisfied him that the bullet, which seemed to have ripped its way at an oblique angle into the shoulder, had not penetrated deeply enough to touch any vital parts. He said cheerfully: "Well, that's the first thing to be dealt with. But we'll have him where I can get to work on him. Nay, Anthea, a little bloodletting won't kill him! One of you bring lights in the morning-room —you, Polyphant! I'll want a bowl of hot water, plenty of lint, if you have it, and the brandy: take it along there, Chollacombe! Now then, you young good-like-naught!" He stooped, as he spoke, and, without apparent effort, lifted Richmond up in his arms.

Richmond, still dazed and faint, muttered: "Dragoons, I think. Two of them. Couldn't see clearly—light bad. In the Home Wood. Must have rumbled me."

"Out of the way, Vincent!" Hugo said, bearing his burden to the door.

"Wait, you fool!" Vincent said. "The boy's got to be hidden! You can't take him into the morning-room! If there were dragoons in our grounds they must have a warrant to search: we may have them upon us at any moment! They mustn't find him here, like this!"

"Nay, we'll have him in better shape to be looked at. Don't be a dafthead, man! If it's Richmond they want, the lad must be here, where he should be! There's no hiding him: you had as well hand him over to Ottershaw without more ado! We must think of a better way out of the mess than that. Nay, sneck up, Vincent! you're wasting time, and it may be we've very little of it at our disposal."

Vincent fell back, but said angrily: "What can we possibly do but hide him? He's led them straight to this house, dripping blood all the way, I don't doubt, the damned little idiot, and what can we do but get him away?—out of the country, if we can!"

"I'm sorry—they were guarding the Dower House," Richmond said, very faint still, but in a rather stronger voice. "No light in the window. That's Spurstow's signal. Hugo said come to him—in a tight squeeze. I was nearly caught, not far from Peasmarsh. *Very* tight squeeze!"

Hugo lowered him into a chair by the table in the middle of the morning-room, but kept a supporting arm round him, stretching out a hand for the brandy Chollacombe was still holding. He put the glass to Richmond's lips, and made him swallow the draught. His face was quite calm, but a little graver than usual; he glanced round, taking note of the bowl of water Anthea had set down on the table, of the lint, and the torn sheets Mrs. Flitwick was assembling; and said, his eyes coming to rest on his groom: "How do you come into this, John Joseph? Were you seen with Mr. Richmond?"

"Nay, I was nobbut taking a stroll, and smoking my pipe. I heard t'shot, but I never saw hair nor hide of any dragoon, nor gadger neither."

"I shook them off. Only got a glimpse of me," Richmond said, wincing under Hugo's hands. "Thought I could reach the house, but I suppose I was losing blood all the way. Found I couldn't see—began to feel too giddy——" He broke off, setting his teeth, as Hugo began to swab the wound.

"That's reet enough, Mester Hugo. I saw him come stackering round t'corner of t'ould barn up yonder, and I brung him in nighest-about, and washed t'soot off his face first thing."

"That's good; they'll search through the woods before they come here," said Hugo, not lifting his eyes from his task. "Get back to your own quarters now, John Joseph: I don't want you mixed up in this. Tell me, Richmond: why did they shoot at you?"

"I didn't halt, when one of them shouted out. Couldn't, because—no time to get rid of—the smock," Richmond gasped jerkily. "Blacked my face, too—*Hugo!*"

"I'm sorry, lad, but I've got to pack this wound as tight as I can, or we'll fall all-abits. There was no coming to cuffs?"

"No. I didn't know they were there, till I heard them

shout. Then I ran for it, dodging—this way and that. Know the wood better than they do—didn't need much light."

"Ottershaw wasn't there," Hugo decided. "He'd have given no order for shooting, and he won't be suited when he knows you *were* shot at."

Vincent, who was holding Richmond's arm in a firm grip, glanced up at the Major, saying: "If they didn't catch the boy with smuggled goods, they've no case against him. As for shooting at him—in his own grounds, too!—we might use that to scotch the whole business, if it weren't for the smock, and the black face. You damned young fool, what possessed you to put on that rig?"

"Had to put myself out of twig—didn't want to be recognized. Before, I've always put off my disguise at the Dower House. Tonight, couldn't. I think—Ottershaw guessed it—some time ago. I knew he was on a hot scent. That's why I took the risk of getting the goods away as soon as it was dark. It seemed the only chance—hoped there'd be no watch so early. I didn't want to fall back on—my other plan—but—had to—because——"

"Hold him, Hugo! he's going off again!" Vincent said quickly, releasing Richmond's arm to snatch up the decanter of brandy.

"No wish to be troublesome," said Claud, in an ominously faint voice, "but I think I'll take a drop myself! Can't stand the sight of blood: never could! Willing to do anything in my power, but I can't and I won't come near the table till you take that bowl away, so I'll be obliged to you if you'll bring a glass over to me, Vincent. Not you, Polyphant! There's blood all over your coat!"

Vincent glanced towards him, where he sat limply on the sofa, his handkerchief pressed to his mouth, and exclaiming contemptuously: "For God's sake, don't be so lily-livered, you miserable man-milliner! Anyone would think, to look at you, that *you'd* been wounded! Hell and the devil, he *is* going faint!" He relinquished the glass he had just filled into Hugo's hand, and swiftly crossed the room to render rough and ready treatment to his younger brother, thrusting his head down between his knees, and holding it there despite protests from his victim, who tried feebly to free himself, but was only rescued by Anthea's intervention. She begged Vincent to let him go, so that he could lie flat on the sofa, and recover at leisure. "Take the smelling-salts, Claud, and shut your eyes! You *mustn't* faint!" she told him urgently. "Chollacombe, pray fetch another glass directly!"

Richmond, meanwhile, was recovering his colour a little. He swallowed some of the brandy, and murmured: "Not going to go off again. Better now. Give me a moment! It was only—hurts like the devil—what you're doing!"

"It's got to be done, lad, if I'm to bring you off. I've no time to do more than stop the bleeding the best way I can, and it's bound to hurt like the devil, for I'm packing it tightly, and you've a bullet lodged there, you know. Come, now, swallow another mouthful, and you'll be champion!"

Richmond obeyed. He was lying relaxed against Hugo's arm, and he looked up at him, saying: "I lied to you. I had to. It was *my* responsibility: I couldn't leave them in the lurch! I *had* to see all safe. I was in command, you see, because it was my scheme."

The Major looked down at him, slightly smiling. "Happen you'll shape to be a good officer, after all," he said. "Lean forward again now: I've nearly done."

"Go on! I've got him," Vincent said. "I'm damned if I know what we do next, though! You're not going to try to convince the Excisemen he's been with us all the evening, are you? If we could get rid of the bloodstains here, in the house, which we've no hope of doing, the tracks will lead them to the side-door, as soon as there's light enough for them to be followed." He felt Richmond writhe, and his hold on him tightened. "Keep still! You're very well-served if it does hurt: I've no sympathy to waste on you! How you can have been such a crass fool as to have gone out on the damned disreputable business tonight, after all that Hugo said to you, after assuring me you weren't in mischief, inspires me with only one desire, and that's to wring your worthless neck!"

"I *had* to! The casks were still here!"

"Still *where?*" Vincent said sharply.

"Here. In the passage. Ever since the last run."

"*What* passage?" Vincent demanded, looking down at him in sudden, astonished suspicion. He could not see his face, however, for a pang of exquisite anguish had made Richmond gasp, and lean his forehead against his supporting arm. Vincent stared down at the top of his dark head. "Are you trying to tell me you've found the secret passage?"

Richmond managed to utter: "Yes. *This* end. Spurstow found—the other—ages ago."

He stopped, quite unable to continue speaking for several moments. Vincent glanced quickly up at Hugo, but Hugo's attention seemed to be fixed wholly on what he was doing.

Vincent, violently irritated, was obliged to choke back an impatient demand to know whether he was listening.

He was certainly the only one of those present to remain unmoved. Mrs. Flitwick, letting the scissors fall from her fingers, ejaculated: "Lawk-a-mussy on us, whatever do you mean, Master Richmond?"

"Richmond, you didn't?" Anthea said, quite incredulous.

"The boy's raving! Doesn't know what he's saying!" pronounced Claud, who had sat up with a jerk.

"Yes, I do. Not difficult—once we'd cleared—the blockage," Richmond said thickly. "Roof had fallen in—not far from the other entrance. Think it must be—where there's that dip—in the ground——"

"Never mind that!" interrupted Vincent.

"No. Well—Spurstow only used it—to store—the run cargoes—till I found out—and knew—must be the passage—and made him—help to clear the blockage. Devil of a task, but managed to do it. Easy, after that. Only had to work out—where the other entrance must have been. In the old part of the house, of course. Cellars. Bricked up. Only fear was—might be heard when we broke through. Servants' quarters—too close to the old wing. But bad thunderstorm one night—did it then!"

"Well, I'll be damned!" said Claud, who had been listening, open-mouthed, to these revelations. "You know, there's no getting away from it!—Young Richmond's a hell-born babe, all right and tight, but, by Jupiter, he's a bit of a dab!"

"A bit of a dab to use this house as a smuggler's store?" said Vincent, in a voice of scathing contempt.

"I'm not a hell-born babe!" Richmond lifted his head. "It's no worse than letting them use the barn by the Five Acre—which they've always done! *Grandpapa* wouldn't say so!"

"My God——!" Vincent's eyes again went to Hugo's face, but he was still not attending. "Listen, you young sapskull!" Vincent said harshly. "Can you see no difference between that and becoming yourself a smuggler?"

"Oh! Well,—yes, but I didn't think it was so very bad. I only did it for the sport of it! I don't *benefit* by it—and in any event—when Grandpapa said he would never let me be a soldier—I didn't care about anything anymore! You wouldn't understand. It doesn't signify."

"Master Richmond, Master *Richmond!*" said Chollacombe, tears of dismay in his eyes. "*Never* did I think to hear——"

"No sense in talking like that!" snapped Mrs. Flitwick.

239

"A judgment—that's what it is! A judgment on those as should have known better, and nothing will make me say different!"

"Sticking-plaster!" interrupted Hugo imperatively.

Polyphant, who had constituted himself his assistant, started, and said hurriedly: "Yes, sir—immediately! I beg pardon, I am sure! I allowed myself to be distracted, but it shall not occur again! And the scissors! Mrs. Flitwick, the scissors!—Good gracious me, ma'am—— Ah, I have them!"

Richmond, wincing as Hugo began to cover his handiwork as tightly as he could with strips of the sticking-plaster, said: "Any way—I did it! Ottershaw was always suspicious of Spurstow. Began to watch the Dower House whenever he got word a run was expected. Made it devilish difficult—to use the place. That's how—I came into it. Saw how I could make Ottershaw look as blue as—as megrim. I did, too. He don't know now—how the kegs were got into the Dower House. We ran them up here, from the coast, and took them the rest of the way through the passage. But I never had them *kept* at this end of the passage! Or let them be taken away from here—until tonight, when—nothing else I could do. Knew I might have to, so had it all—trig and trim. Ponies in the Park. Had the kegs carried there: too dangerous to bring 'em up to the house. Only thing was—knew Ottershaw was hot on my scent—couldn't be sure he wasn't keeping some kind of a watch on this place too, so—had to lay a false scent. That's why we did the thing—so early. Ottershaw's grown too—fly to the time of day. Had to make him think it *must* be the real run, and we'd hoped to get away before any watch was set on the place. He did." Richmond's head was up, and his sister, gazing at him in horror, saw the glow in his eyes. "It was the best chase of them all—my last!" he said, an exultant little smile on his pale lips. "You don't *know*——! If only I hadn't taken it for granted I was safe on our own ground!—I ought to have known, but I'd shaken off the pursuit, and never dreamed there'd be anyone watching for my return *here*. I've never come back before except by the passage. Jem said I'd be taken at fault one day, but he's got no stomach at all for a close-run thing. He didn't like it even when we took up the casks in broad daylight once—pulling in mackerel-nets! Swore he'd never go out with me again, but *I* knew no Exciseman would think anyone would dare do that, so it wasn't really very dangerous." A tiny laugh broke from him. "We were hailed by a naval cutter: you should have seen

Jem's face! But the kegs were hidden under the mackerel—we'd got the *Seamew* spilling over with them! I offered to sell 'em to the lieutenant aboard the cutter: just joking him! —and of course we came off safe!"

Claud, who had been listening with his eyes starting from their sockets, drew a long breath. "When I think of the way we've been living here, never dreaming we'd be a dashed sight safer in a powder-magazine——! Well, at least there's *one* good thing! No need to be afraid he'll go to Newgate! Well, what I mean is, he's stark, staring mad! Ought to have put him into Bedlam years ago!"

"Not mad!" Vincent said. "Rope-ripe!"

"There!" said the Major, pressing down his last strip of sticking-plaster. "Cut, Polyphant! I fancy that will do the trick."

"*Beautiful*, sir!" said Polyphant, carefully snipping off the dangling end of the plaster. "A really *prime* piece of work, if I may be permitted to say so!"

"We'll hope it may hold, anyhow. If it doesn't, we shall all of us end in Newgate!"

"That," said Vincent acidly, "is extremely likely unless we are able to think what next is to be done! If you can drag your mind away from this damned young scoundrel's wound, perhaps you'll apply it to *that* problem, for it is quite beyond my poor capabilities to solve!"

"Then happen you'll find that *Ajax shall cope the best!*" retorted the Major, with a grin. "Now then! we must bustle about a little. The dragoons will have gone to report to Ottershaw, but for aught we know they may not have had to go far, so just do what I'm going to tell you, every one of you, without asking why, or arguing about it! Mrs. Flitwick, I want you out of the way until we're rid of Excisemen: the fewer people to be mixed up in this the better. So you may stay out of sight, and don't say a word to anyone about what's been happening! Chollacombe, I want a couple of packs of cards, another brandy-glass, and the clothes you stripped from Mr. Richmond—yes, I mean that, so off with you! Anthea, love, slip away to the billiard-room, and fetch Claud's and my coats, will you? Nay, pluck up, lass! We're going to save Richmond's groats, never you fear!"

She nodded, trying to smile, and hurried away.

"Claud," said the Major, a twinkle in his eye, "I want every stitch of clothing you've got on, except your drawers! Go on, lad, don't stand gauping at me, or we'll have Anthea

241

back before we've made you respectable again! It's you that got fired at, not Richmond, and I want your clothes for him!"

"Here, I say, no!" exclaimed Claud, appalled. "If you think I'll put on Richmond's clothes—dash it, even if they weren't soaked in blood I wouldn't like it, and——"

"Get your shoes off, and be quick about it!" interrupted Vincent, advancing upon him. "If you don't, I'll knock you out and strip you myself! *Hurry!*"

The look on his face was so alarming that Claud sat down hastily to untie his exquisitely ironed shoestrings. No sooner were his shoes and striped socks off than Vincent jerked him to his feet, ripped off his neckcloth, and began to unbutton his waistcoat, commanding him to do the same to his breeches. Over his shoulder, he said: "I make you my compliments, Hugo! But *why* was Claud skulking in the wood? I see that no Exciseman in his right senses could possibly think him engaged in smuggling but we must have some reason to account for his running away when challenged!"

"Nay, lay!" said the Major reproachfully, tossing Richmond's rent and blood-soaked shirt on to the floor. "You've got a short memory! He thought it was the Ackletons, lying in wait to rend him limb from limb, of course! Happen it gave him such a fright that he didn't hear just what they were shouting—nothing about halting in the name of the King, for instance!—and when they took to firing at him, what could he do but run for his life? Let alone he'd no weapon, he was in a very ticklish situation—having been trysting with that prime article of virtue the Ackletons forbade him ever to look at again!"

"I'll be *damned* if I have anything to do with a story like that!" declared Claud indignantly. "Why, I'd never be able to show my face here again!"

"Why should you want to?" said Vincent, who was shaking with laughter. "It's magnificent, Hugo! Here, Polyphant, take these, and give me Mr. Richmond's! Claud, there's no need to *look* at Richmond's breeches: all you have to do is to step into them: I'll even pull 'em up for you! They'll be a tight fit, but you won't have to sit down in them: we'll stretch you out on the sofa!"

Claud, bullied and hustled into his cousin's obnoxious breeches, was so much incensed that he became quite scarlet in the face as he informed his relatives, in impassioned accents, that nothing would induce him to take part in the proposed drama. "I ain't handy with my fists, and I don't like turn-ups, but I ain't a rum 'un, and I'm damned if I'll have you two cooking up a story like that about me! Not if you were to offer me a fortune!"

"No one will offer you a fortune, brother," said Vincent, pushing him on to the sofa, and picking up one of Richmond's boots. "Pull this on!—all you will be offered, if you don't do as you're bid, is a facer heavy enough to send you to sleep while we exhibit you to the Excisemen."

"Think, lad!" Hugo interposed. "If we're to hoax Ottershaw, we must have a tale that's got some likelihood to it, for he'll not swallow it readily!"

"*Likelihood?*" gasped. Claud. "Well, of all the——"

"Nay, how should he know whether you're a right one, or a pudding-heart?" said Hugo hastily. "What, you may depend upon it, he *does* know, is what happened to Ackleton, the night he came up here, and the silly way he's been blustering ever since about what he'll do to you, if he gets the chance. Knowing that much for truth, he'll find it hard to disbelieve the rest surely enough to put our tale to the test—for he knows well that if he were to make a false accusation against Richmond there'd be the devil to pay, and no pitch hot for him!" He paused, and then, as Claud still looked mutinous, added: "It's no matter if you're made to look foolish, Claud. If we can't conceal the truth from Ottershaw, it's not only Richmond who'll be laid low, but every Darracott amongst us."

Richmond said suddenly: "*No!* You can't ask Claud to do that! *I* wouldn't—I *couldn't!*"

"That we believe!" retorted Vincent. "It is possible, however, that Claud cares more for our name than you have given us reason to suppose *you* do! Come, Claud! what odds does it make to you if a parcel of hicks laughs at you?" He added, rather unfortunately: "They've been laughing at you for years!"

The astonished gratification with which Claud had listened to the first part of this speech changed rapidly. A mulish look came into his face, and he was just about to deliver himself of a flat refusal to sacrifice himself for the sake of any family of which his brother was a member, when Polyphant, engaged in tieing the neckcloth round Richmond's neck, saved the situation by saying: "If I may take the liberty, Mr. Vincent, I venture to say—with the greatest deference, sir!—that Mr. Claud is equal to *anything!*"

Claud wavered. Anthea came back into the room at that

moment, and was not unnaturally staggered to find him sketchily attired in her brother's bloodstained breeches, and topboots. The reason for this peculiar transformation was briefly explained to her, whereupon she instantly threw herself into the obviously necessary task of persuading Claud to immolate himself. Without allowing him an opportunity to speak, she thanked him with so much warmth as to make it extremely hard for him to disabuse her mind of its apparent conviction that he had consented. By the time she had marvelled at his nobility, prophesied the reverence with which he would for ever afterwards be regarded by them all, and declared her positive belief in his ability to carry the thing off to admiration, Claud had become so far reconciled to the scheme as to raise no further objection to it.

Polyphant, who had come into his own with the necessity of arraying Richmond in his borrowed plumage, then called upon the Major to assist him in the task of getting him into Claud's coat. It was plain that he was revelling in the affair, but only he knew the cause of his elation; and none could have guessed that while his nimble fingers coped with shoestrings, buttons, and neckcloth, his mind was filled with the vision of himself triumphant beyond his wildest dreams over the odious Crimplesham. Crimplesham might never learn just what had taken place on this fateful evening, but Crimplesham would know, like everyone else, that there had been very strange goings-on from which he had been rigorously excluded, with such insignificant persons as the footmen, while his rival had been in the thick of it, the trusted confidant of even his own master. And if Crimplesham tried to discover what had happened, Polyphant had every intention of proving himself worthy of the trust reposed in him by replying that his lips were sealed, which would undoubtedly infuriate Crimplesham very much indeed.

"Now, sir!" he said, with the authority of one who knew himself to be an expert, "if you will be so obliging as to do precisely what I shall request you to do, I trust I shall be able to manage to put Mr. Richmond into both waistcoat and coat—you will observe that I have placed one within the other—without causing him to feel too much discomfort, and without disturbing *your* handiwork, sir. From you, Mr. Richmond, I wish for no assistance at all. Do not attempt, I most earnestly implore you, to shrug your sound shoulder into the garment! You will please to leave it *en-*

tirely to me. Fortunately, you are of slighter build than Mr. Claud: indeed, we must hope that the Riding-officer is not a person of *ton* (if you will pardon the jest!), and so will not think your coat sadly ill-fitting, must we not?"

Talking chattily all the time, he began to ease Richmond into the coat. Claud, watching him with a jaundiced eye, expressed his conviction that he was going about it in quite the wrong way; but the Major meekly obeyed such instructions as he was given; and by the time Chollacombe came into the room the difficult feat had been performed with a competence that drew a *Well-done!* from the Major. Polyphant bowed his acknowledgment, saying that he would now slip upstairs to collect one of Mr. Claud's black silk socks. "For it occurs to me, sir, that a few snips with the scissors will make it a tolerable mask, and we must not forget, must we, that Mr. Richmond's face was blackened? So you will pardon me if I now absent myself for a very few moments!"

He then departed, sped on his way by a bitter recommendation from his master to ruin a few more of his garments while he was about it.

The Major picked up his own coat, and had just shrugged himself into it when Anthea, whose hearing was very acute, caught the sound of hoof-beats, and said sharply: "Listen! Hugo, they're coming!"

"Well, we could have done with another few minutes, but happen we'll make shift without them," he responded calmly. "Vincent, go up to the drawing-room before they start knocking on the door—or, if his lordship's come down to the library, join him there! You've been writing letters—anything you choose!—and you've not been next or nigh the rest of us. Keep Ottershaw brangling with the old gentleman: that oughtn't to be difficult! I must see Claud bandaged up, and the scene well set, and then I'll part, but *make me tell you* why I want to speak privately to you! Quick, man! Here they are!" He fairly thrust Vincent from the room, and turned to Chollacombe. "Not in too much of a hurry to open the door to them!" he warned him. "You're not expecting any such visitors, so you may look as surprised as you please, but take you you look affronted too! Treat them just as you would any vulgar person who came here asking impertinent questions—not that I think they'll ask you any. All I want of you is that you shall bear it in mind that Mr. *Claud* has met with an accident, which is no business of any Exciseman, and that Mr. *Richmond* and I have been playing cards here all the evening. Don't take them straight to his lordship: shut them into the Green Saloon, and say you'll inform his lordship! Mr. Vincent will take care he don't refuse to see them. Once you've taken them to the drawing-room, don't show yourself again!"

"Have no fear, sir!" said Chollacombe. "I trust I know how to depress the pretensions of such persons who know no better than to hammer on the door of a gentleman's residence in *that* ill-mannered fashion!"

The knocker had certainly been somewhat violently plied, and the effect of this solecism on Chollacombe was all that the Major could have desired. At one moment a very shaken old man, he stiffened at the next into the personification of outraged dignity, and, with a slow and stately tread, left the room, and proceeded down the broad passage that led through an archway into the central hall.

Hugo shut the door, and cast a swift, measuring look at Richmond, seated at the table, and resting his left arm on it. Richmond was very pale, but his eyes were alert, and he met his cousin's searching glance with a confident smile. "I shall do!" he said.

"Ay, you'll do, you scamp! Give him some more brandy, love!" said the Major, picking up the bowl of reddened water, and setting it down on the floor beside the sofa.

"I shall be foxed if I drink any more," Richmond warned him.

"I want you to be foxed, lad—just about half-sprung! Not so drunk that you'll say what you shouldn't, but drunk enough to look as if you might be. That'll be reason enough why you should stay sprawling in your chair." He turned his head as the door opened, and for an instant it seemed to Anthea that he stiffened. But it was only Polyphant who entered the room, with his tripping gait, and delicately dropped a maltreated sock beside the horrid pile of Richmond's clothing. The Major said: "I'm more obliged to you than I can say, Polyphant. The moment the coast is clear, off with you! I don't want you to get tangled up in this business, so stand out now—and thank you!"

"Sir!" said Polyphant, exalted by the realization that his moment was upon him, "any other command you may see fit to give me I shall obey with alacrity, but never, never shall it be said that a Polyphant deserted his master in his hour of need, or flinched in the face of danger!"

"Well, if that's how you feel, you can dashed well move that disgusting bowl out of my sight!" said his master tartly.

XIX

It was not quite fifteen minutes later that the Major entered the drawing-room; and he knew before he opened the door that the task of prolonging the interview between his grandfather and Lieutenant Ottershaw had imposed no very severe strain upon Vincent's ingenuity. It even seemed improbable that he had found it necessary to take any steps at all to achieve his aim, for his lordship had plainly taken instant umbrage when informed that the Lieutenant had come armed with a warrant, and was in fine fighting fettle.

The scene was not quite what the Major had hoped it might be. It included two persons with whom he could well have dispensed: Lady Aurelia was still seated at the card-table; and Mrs. Darracott, attired in a dressing-gown, was standing beside her chair, her pretty countenance flushed, and her expression one of strong indignation. Lord Darracott was also seated at the card-table, his chair pushed back a little from it, and one leg crossed over the other. Before him, very stiff, stood the Lieutenant; standing in front of the fireplace was Vincent; and a stalwart Sergeant of dragoons had taken up a discreet position in the background. His mien was one of stern stolidity, but although his appearance was formidable to the uninitiated the Major was not uninitiated, and one glance was enough to inform him that Sergeant Hoole, while doggedly determined to do his duty, was very far from sharing the Lieutenant's conviction that he had as good a right to force his way into a nobleman's house as into a common person's humbler dwelling.

The Sergeant was indeed wishing himself otherwhere. At no time (as the Major well knew) did he relish being placed at the orders of the Board of Customs; and when it came to being obliged to accompany a mere Riding-officer into the presence of a fierce old gentleman who reminded him forcibly of his own Colonel, he disliked it very much indeed, for it was quite evident to him, if not to Lieutenant Ottershaw (who was not by any means *his* notion of an officer), that the old lord was not one with whom it was at all safe to take what he felt increasingly sure was a gross liberty.

The Lieutenant was not entirely at his ease either, but

he was upheld by a Calvinistic sense of duty, and he was not so much awed by Lord Darracott's manner as resentful of it. He had convinced his superiors that an application for the warrant he had exhibited to his lordship was fully justified, but the attitude of the Board had been cautious and reluctant, and he knew that a mistake on his part would lead to consequences disastrous to his career. He was determined to execute the warrant, but how to do it, if Lord Darracott remained obstinate in opposing him, was unexpectedly difficult to decide. Nor had he been prepared for the presence of two ladies, one of whom was a Roman-nosed dowager of quelling aspect, and the other his quarry's mother.

Mrs. Darracott's entrance had followed hard upon his own, and was due, not to any apprehension that her son might stand in need of her protection, but to her conviction that the arrival of visitors at so late an hour could only mean that Matthew Darracott had returned to his ancestral home; and since this would entail such domestic duties as the making up of his bed, and the provision of a suitable supper, she very naturally wished to assure herself, before setting all these matters in train, that it was indeed he who had arrived. When she had entered the drawing-room to find her father-in-law berating a complete stranger, she would have retreated in haste, had his lordship not caught sight of her, and commanded her to come in, and listen to what the stranger (whom he described as an insolent whipstraw) was having the infernal impudence to say about her son. She seemed at first to be quite bewildered by the charge laid at Richmond's door, but by the time Hugo came into the room she had passed from bewilderment to sparkling indignation.

Hugo's entrance was a masterpiece of clumsy stealth. He opened the door cautiously, and having first looked round the edge of it, ventured to advance a few steps into the room, fixedly regarding his cousin Vincent. It was apparent to those who had observed his entrance that he wished to attract Vincent's attention, and also that he was in a condition generally described as a little bit on the go. His appearance was not quite as neat as it might have been, and a singularly foolish smile dwelled on his lips. The Sergeant surveyed him dispassionately; his aunts, both of whom were facing towards the door, in considerable surprise; and Vincent, putting up his quizzing-glass, with languid contempt. This had the effect of making his lordship and Lieutenant

Ottershaw look round, at which moment the Major sought, by dint of a wink, and a tiny jerk of his head towards the door, to convey to his cousin the information that he desired private speech with him.

Ottershaw, instantly on the alert, watched him suspiciously; my lord, irritated by his peculiar behaviour, said impatiently: "Oh, it's you, is it? Don't stand there like a moonling! What do you want?"

"Nay, I didn't know you'd company!" said the Major sheepishly.

"I have not what you choose to call company! What the devil's the matter with you, sir?"

"Oh, there's naught the *matter!*" Hugo hastened to assure him. "I just wondered whether my cousin was here!"

"And now that you know that I am here, in what way can I serve you?" said Vincent, with smooth mockery.

"Oh, it's nothing of importance!" replied Hugo unconvincingly. He then became aware of Lieutenant Ottershaw, and exclaimed: "Ee, lad, I didn't see it was you! What brings you here this late?"

"Unlike you, sir, I am here on a matter of considerable importance!" replied Ottershaw curtly. "Perhaps *you* can——"

"Eh, I'm sorry!" Hugo said, conscience-stricken. "I shouldn't have come cluntering in on you!" Addressing himself to his grandfather, he added, apologetically: "I didn't know there was anyone with you, sir! I'll take myself off! Vincent lad, if you're not throng, I'd be glad if you'd spare me a minute: got something to tell you! It's just a private matter—nothing of consequence!"

Vincent regarded him with a faint, supercilious smile. "A trifle castaway, coz? I should be interested to know what you can possibly have to say to me of a private nature, but it happens that I am, as you put it, extremely throng. Oh, don't look so discouraged! I'll join you presently—if I must!"

"Nay, it won't do presently: it's what you might call urgent!" said the Major desperately.

"Oh, for God's sake——!" exploded Lord Darracott. "You're disguised, sir! You can take yourself off—and if you'll take this fellow whom you're so devilish pleased to see with you I shall be obliged to you! And as for you, sir," he said, rounding on Ottershaw, "I'll see you damned before I'll let you search my house!"

"Search the house?" repeated the Major, his eyes round

with astonishment. "Whatever do you want to do that for, lad?"

"I have no wish to search the house!" said Ottershaw. "As I have already informed Lord Darracott, I am here to see Mr. Richmond Darracott, and that, sir, I am going to do! If his lordship doesn't want his house to be searched, perhaps you can convince him that his only course is to produce Mr. Richmond! He seems strangely reluctant so to do, and I warn you——"

"You impertinent jack-at-warts, how dare you——"

"Nay, don't start fratching!" begged the Major. He looked at Ottershaw, and shook his head. "You know, lad, you should know better than to come up here at this time of night! It's no way to go about things. What's more, you've no need to be in a pelter because our Richmond's been playing tricks on you: I gave him a rare dressing, the night you and I watched him capering about in a sheet, and got the whole of it out of him, the young rascal! There'll be no more of it: take my word for it! Eh, but you shouldn't let yourself be hoaxed so easily, lad!"

The Lieutenant, stiff as a ramrod, held out his warrant. "Perhaps, sir, you would like to read this! I am not here to enquire into any *hoax!*"

Hugo chuckled, but took the warrant, and perused it, apparently deriving considerable enjoyment from it. But he shook his head again, as he handed it back to Ottershaw, and said: "You've made a bad mistake, lad, but if you're set on making a reet cod's head of yourself there's nowt I can do to stop you!"

During this exchange, Lord Darracott, glancing at Vincent, had encountered from Vincent's hard eyes a steady look. It held his own suddenly arrested gaze perhaps for five seconds; and then dropped. Vincent drew out his snuff-box, tapped the lid, and opened it, and delicately helped himself to a pinch, raising it to one sharp-cut nostril. As he inhaled, his eyes lifted again to his grandfather's face, fleetingly this time, but still holding that curiously enigmatic expression. It was on the tip of Lord Darracott's tongue to demand what the devil he meant by staring at him, but he refrained. It was unfamiliar, that hard stare, and it disturbed him; it was almost insolent, but Vincent was never insolent to him. His lordship, grasping that Vincent must be trying to convey a warning to him, but having as yet no clue to what it could be, curbed his tongue, and turned his angry gaze upon his heir.

The Major, as everyone could see, was looking harassed, and rubbing his nose. He cast an eloquent glance at Vincent, who promptly responded to it, saying in a resigned tone: "Well, what is it, cousin? Don't keep me in suspense any longer, I beg of you! It is quite obvious that you have something of great moment to disclose, but why you are making such a mystery of it—dear me, how stupid of me! You appear to be so well-acquainted with Lieutenant—er—Ottershaw, is it not?—that it had not occurred to me that——"

"Nay, I don't mind *him!*" interrupted the Major ingenuously. "The thing is——" He gave a foolish laugh, and again rubbed his nose. "Eh, I've made a reet jumblement of it!" He turned once more to the Lieutenant, who was by this time almost quivering with rampant suspicion, and said confidentially: "Sithee, lad, the fact is, it'll be a deal better if you shab off now, and come back tomorrow!"

"For you, sir, no doubt! But I have no inten——"

"It'll be better for you too, think on!" remarked the Major, with a reflective grin. "You'll get precious little sense out of our Richmond tonight, lad!" He added hastily, and with a wary glance at Mrs. Darracott: "At this hour of the night, I mean! Now, I'm not saying you can't see him, because if you've a warrant to do it——"

"Hugo!" uttered Mrs. Darracott, unable to contain herself another instant. "This—this person is accusing my son of being a—a common *smuggler!*"

His grin broadened. "I'd give a plum to see him at it!" he said. "Nay then, ma'am, don't be nattered! The Lieutenant's got a bee in his head, but I'm bound to say it was Richmond who put it there, so it's not the Lieutenant you should be giving a scold to, but Richmond, the hey-go-mad young scamp that he is! If ever I met such a whisky-frisky, caper-witted lad! Anything for a bit of fun and gig! that's his motto! You can't but laugh at him, but one of these days he'll find himself in the suds, and all for the sake of some silly hoax! Happen it wouldn't do him any harm if he did get a bit of a fright, but we don't want any more upsets——"

"How dare you say Richmond is a scamp?" broke in Mrs. Darracott, bristling. "He is nothing of the sort! He has never given me a *moment's* anxiety, and as for his being what you call a caper-witted, I have not the least guess what can have put such a notion into your head!"

"No, dear aunt, of course you haven't!" said Vincent. He sighed wearily. "I wondered if that was it. You have all

251

my sympathy, Lieutenant—even though I must own I am devoutly thankful that you, and not I, have been his latest victim."

"Vincent!" she cried indignantly. "Of all the ill-natured, false things to say! You know very well——"

"Be quiet!" interrupted his lordship harshly. "I will not endure any more of this nonsense! The boy doesn't tell you what pranks he gets up to, ma'am, or me either! I've no doubt he plays all manner of tricks—all boys do so!—but let no one dare to tell me he has ever gone one inch beyond the line!" He glared at Ottershaw as he spoke, his breathing a little quickened, his face very grim.

"Eh, I know that, sir!" Hugo assured him, apparently taking this to himself. "Now, there's no need for anyone to go giddy over the lad! And no need for you to think our Richmond's being hidden from you, Ottershaw, just because his lordship don't like getting visits at midnight from Riding-officers, and being told he's to produce his grandson slap! Nor because I told you you'd do better to go away—which doesn't mean that the lad's not here! He's here reet enough, but there are reasons why you've not just nicked the nick in choosing your time! The fact is there's been a bit of an upset——"

"Why the devil couldn't you have said so before?" demanded Vincent. "What sort of an upset?"

"Nay, I can't explain it now! All I want——"

"Major Darracott!" suddenly interrupted the Lieutenant, "you are perhaps not aware that your cuff-band is blood-stained!"

The Major looked quickly at his wrist, and then directed a quelling glance at Ottershaw. "Ay, well—never mind that! It's of no consequence!"

"I must ask you to tell me, sir, how you come to have blood on your cuff, when you appear to have sustained no injury!"

He was somewhat taken aback by the Major's response. Looking at him with a fulminating eye, the Major said, under his breath: "Sneck up, will you, *dafthead?*"

"Hugo, *no!*" Mrs. Darracott cried involuntarily, starting forward. "*Richmond—?* Not Richmond, Hugo, not Richmond! It isn't true—it couldn't be true!"

"No, no, it's got nothing to do with Richmond!" said Hugo, in exasperated accents, adding bitterly to the Lieutenant: "*Now* see what you've done!"

"Whom *has* it to do with?" demanded Vincent. "Come, out with it!"

"If you *must* have it, our Claud's met with an accident!" said Hugo, in a goaded voice. He looked at Lady Aurelia, and said apologetically: "I didn't mean to say it in front of you, ma'am, and, what's more, Claud'll be reet angry with me for doing it! There's no cause for alarm, mind, but happen if you'd go down to the morning-room, Vincent——"

"I will certainly go down. What happened? Did he cut himself?"

"Nay, it's not exactly a *cut*," replied the Major evasively. Lady Aurelia rose. She had scarcely taken her eyes from the Major from the moment that he entered the room, as he was perfectly well aware, but it was impossible to interpret that steady gaze. She said, with her accustomed calm: "I will accompany you, Vincent."

"Well, I wouldn't do that, if I were you," said Hugo. "He'd as lief you didn't: he doesn't want a fuss made, you see!"

"You would do better to remain where you are, Aurelia!" said his lordship, his voice a little strained. "Depend upon it, he's done something foolish, which he doesn't wish us to know! Elvira, I wish you will go back to bed, instead of standing there like a stock!"

"I will *not* go to bed!" declared Mrs. Darracott, with startling resolution. "If this *insulting* young man is determined to see my son, he *shall* see him! I will take you to him myself, sir, and when you have seen that he is precisely where I told you he was—in bed and asleep!—I shall expect an apology from you! An *abject* apology! Come with me, if you please!"

"Nay, ma'am, I'll take him!" offered Hugo hastily.

"Thank you, I prefer to take him myself!" she said.

Ottershaw, glancing uncertainly from one face to the other, encountered yet another of the Major's fulminating looks. This time it was accompanied by an unmistakeable sign to him not to go with Mrs. Darracott. He began to feel baffled. He had not expected to find that Major Darracott was in any way entangled in Richmond's crimes, but he had very soon realized his mistake. He was a good deal shocked, even sorry, for it was abundantly plain that the Major was desperately trying to fob him off. Then, just as he had decided that the Major was recklessly aiding Richmond to escape from his clutch, it seemed as if it was not from him that this large and somewhat clumsy intriguer was trying to conceal something, but from Lady Aurelia, and Mrs. Darracott. That had puzzled Ottershaw; the signal that had just been made he found quite incomprehensible, for it almost seemed as if what the Major was trying to conceal could scarcely have anything to do with Richmond. Frowning, he stood listening to the Major's efforts to get rid of Mrs. Darracott. It suddenly occurred to him that perhaps he was only anxious to spare her the shock of witnessing her son's inevitable exposure. If that were so, Ottershaw was very willing to further the scheme. He said: "If you will take me to Mr. Darracott's room, sir, there is no need for Mrs. Darracott to come with us."

"That is for me to decide!" said Mrs. Darracott, flushed and very bright-eyed. "*I*, and no one else, will take you, sir!"

The Major gave it up. "Nay, he's not *in* his room!" he disclosed. "He's downstairs." Looking extremely guilty, he said: "Seemingly, my grandfather ordered him off to bed, but—well, he came downstairs instead! We've been playing piquet."

"Major Darracott, do you tell me that he has been with you all the evening?" demanded Ottershaw. "Take care how you answer me, sir! I have very good reason to suppose that Mr. Richmond Darracott, until less than an hour ago, was not in the house at all!"

"Nay, you can't have," replied the Major. "He's been with me ever since he was sent off to bed—and, what's more, he'd no thought of leaving the house, for he's having such a run of luck as I never saw! Pretty well ruined me, the young devil!"

"Well!" exclaimed Mrs. Darracott. "I must say, Hugo, I think it was very wrong of you to encourage Richmond to sit up late when you *know* how bad it is for him! And as for gambling with him—— Well, I shall say nothing *now*, except that I didn't think it of you!" Her voice broke, and tears started to her eyes as she directed a look of wounded reproach at Hugo. He hung his head, looking very like an overgrown schoolboy detected in crime. Mrs. Darracott, the top of whose head perhaps reached the middle of his chest, said with cold severity: "You will now oblige me by going downstairs again, and desiring Richmond to come to me here immediately!"

The expression of dismay on Hugo's face lured Lieutenant Ottershaw into banishing doubt. Certainly betrayed him into abandoning the dogged deliberation which made him formidable; the light of triumph was in his eye as he said, on a challenging note: "Well, sir?"

"Nay, I can't do that! I mean—I don't think——" Hugo stammered, looking wildly round for succour. "Well,—well, for one thing—happen he won't care to leave our Claud!" His guileless blue eyes, meeting Ottershaw's in seeming horror, took due note of the fact that that dangerously levelheaded young man had at last allowed himself to be coaxed into an unaccustomed state of cocksure excitement. He said, as one driven from his last defensive position: "The fact is—he's just a bit on the go!"

"Do you mean that Richmond is *drunk?*" cried Mrs. Darracott. "Oh, how *could* you? I thought you were so kind, and good, and *trustworthy!*"

"In that case, Major Darracott, *I* will go to *him!*" said Ottershaw. "You are sure, no doubt, that Mr. Richmond Darracot is drunk, and not *wounded?*"

"No, no, *he's* not——" Hugo checked himself suddenly, an arrested look on his face. "Now, wait a minute!" he said. "*Wounded,* did you say?"

"The Lieutenant, coz," interposed Vincent, "was good enough to inform us, before you came upstairs, that Richmond had been shot by one of the men under his command, not an hour since. He appears—perhaps fortunately!—to have been misinformed, but I am strongly of the opinion that an enquiry into the incident is called for."

The Sergeant stared woodenly before him. "Upon being commanded to halt, in the name of the King, the pris—gentle —the individual in question, instead of obeying——"

"*Shot?*" interrupted Hugo. He turned his eyes towards Ottershaw. "In the wood, up yonder was it?"

"Yes, sir, in the wood, up yonder! He was challenged——"

"Were there—*two* men posted in the wood?" asked Hugo, in a very odd voice.

The Lieutenant stared at him, suspicious and puzzled. "Yes, sir, two dragoons! They——"

"And was—Mr. Richmond Darracott—wearing a *mask,* by any chance?" enquired Hugo, a look of unholy awe in his eyes.

"His face was *blackened,* sir!"

"Well, happen it may have looked like that," said Hugo, very unsteadily, "but it was only—a sock, with a c-couple of holes c-cut in it!"

At this point his command over himself deserted him, and, to the utter bewilderment both of Ottershaw and of

Sergeant Hoole, he went off into a roar of laughter. Feeling much the same sensations as a man might have felt who, believing the ice to be solid, suddenly found it cracking all round his feet, Ottershaw saw the Major helpless in the grip of his mirth: slapping his thigh; trying to speak, and failing to utter more than two unintelligible words before becoming overpowered again; mopping his eyes; and finally collapsing into a large armchair, as though too weak with laughter to remain on his feet.

Watching this masterly performance with every sign of hauteur, Vincent said, as soon as his cousin's paroxysms began to abate: "I think, my dear Mama, that, if Richmond's condition in any way approaches Hugo's, you would perhaps be well advised—and my aunt too!—not to come down to the morning-room."

She replied at once: "You need be under no apprenension: I have the greatest dislike of inebriety! Unless you should find your brother in a worse case than I consider probable, I have no intention of coming—or, if I can prevail upon her to listen to me, of allowing your aunt to do so either!"

"Your good sense, Mama, is always to be relied upon!" he said, with his glinting smile, and graceful bow. His glance flickered to his grandfather's face, set like a mask, its harsh lines deeply graven, the fierce eyes fixed in a rather dreadful stare on Hugo. Vincent could only hope that the silence which had fallen upon him would not strike the Lieutenant as strangely unlike him.

The Lieutenant's attention was concentrated on Hugo, who managed to utter, in choked but remorseful accents: "Ee, I'm sorry! Nay, it's no laughing matter, but—oh, Lord, it's better nor like! far, far better nor like!" He gave a final wipe to eyes that so much rubbing had artisitically reddened, and looked at Ottershaw. He gave a gasp, and said imploringly: "Don't look at me like that, lad, or you'll start me off again! You come with me, and I'll sh-show you—what you've done!" He got up, now grinning broadly. "Happen you'd better come too, Vincent, but there's no need for anyone else!" He saw Lord Darracott rise stiffly to his feet, and said: "Nay, stay where you are, sir! Richmond will be fit to murder me if he knows I let it out to you that he's had a cup too much!"

"I am coming!" said his lordship gratingly, and, with a repelling gesture, stalked towards the door.

"Yes, and so am I!" declared Mrs. Darracott.

"One moment, Elvira!" interposed Lady Aurelia, firmly grasping her wrist.

"Phew!" breathed Hugo, as he left the drawing-room in the wake of the Sergeant, and closed the door behind him. "It's to be hoped your mother will be able to hold her, Vincent!"

"My mother is no stupider than the rest of us, I assure you. Is he badly castaway?"

"Well, he was in fairly prime and plummy order when I came away," confessed Hugo. "I wish you will make a push to head his lordship off! I'd as lief not get the boy into trouble."

"I'll try, but it's unlikely I shall succeed," Vincent replied.

As he ran lightly downstairs, after his grandfather, Hugo laid a restraining hand on the Lieutenant's shoulder, saying "Wait! Give him a chance to divert the old gentleman! It'll be the better for you if you do, I can tell you. Eh, lad, I can't but laugh about it, but this is a bad business!"

The Sergeant silently agreed with him. It had seemed at one moment as though Lieutenant Ottershaw's conviction was about to be proved, but the Major's laughter had killed that hope stone-dead. No man, in Sergeant Hoole's opinion, who stood on the brink of exposure as an aider and abettor of criminals could go off into a fit of laughter like that: it stood to reason he couldn't, any more than he could talk to his cousin, like he'd just done, as though it didn't matter a rush who might be listening. Which was a sure sign it didn't, thought the Sergeant, hoping that this jingle-brained Riding-officer he'd been sent to assist wasn't going to make bad worse, and that the haughty young gentleman would succeed in keeping his lordship away.

Lieutenant Ottershaw had not so entirely abandoned hope as the Sergeant, but his state was the more to be pitied, since he did not know what to think, and much less what to do. Until the arrival of Major Darracott upon the scene, everything had gone according to his expection, with Richmond's family on the defensive; incredulous, belligerent, trying to overawe him, but powerless to divert him from his stern purpose. He had known himself to be master of that situation, for although it might be difficult to handle, it was perfectly straightforward. But within a very few minutes of the Major's entrance it had undergone a bewildering change, always eluding his grasp. He had an uneasy feeling that he had been lured away from the road into a maze; yet he could not, trying to think it over, see at what point he had lost his way; or reasonably blame the Major for that loss. The Major had certainly attempted by every means he could think of to evade the necessity of producing Richmond, but his efforts had been extremely clumsy, causing him to flounder from one position to another, and finally to capitulate. Or so it had seemed, until the moment of his discomfiture, when, instead of being dejected, he had burst into a roar of laughter. Ottershaw, already puzzled by the contradictory nature of his antics, had suffered a shock from which he had not yet recovered. He needed time in which to regain his balance, and to think the whole episode over coolly and carefully; and he felt that he was being rushed. But again it was impossible to blame the Major. Not that leisurely giant but himself had been the one to insist that he should instantly be taken to Richmond. His brain was in a turmoil, with a nagging, unwelcome thought constantly recurring: if Richmond really was drunk, and not wounded, there was nothing in the least contradictory in the Major's behaviour. He had all the time been trying to shield Richmond from his mother and his grandfather, not from the avenging hand of the law. This explanation of conduct which had seemed extraordinary was so simple, and so instantly unravelled every knot in the tangled skein, that the Lieutenant was obliged to cling doggedly to the only certainty remaining: Richmond *had* been wounded, and no matter what the Major did he could not conceal the damning evidence against him.

The Lieutenant said abruptly, as he began to descend the stairs beside Major Darracott: "It will perhaps save time, sir, if I inform you that I have seen with my own eyes the blood on the steps leading to one of the side-doors into this house."

His eyes were fixed on the Major's profile, on the watch for the tiniest sign of dismay. The Major grinned. "I don't know about the steps, but you ought to see the pantry!" he replied. The grin faded, and he shook his head. "Nay, it's all very well, but you've made a rare mess of it, lad! The Lord only knows what the afterclap may be now, for there's more to it than you've any idea of—or I either, think on, at the start of it. I tried my best to tip you the wink, but not a bit of heed would you pay to me!" He turned his head to look down at the Lieutenant, saying, with a quizzical smile: "You know, lad, I'd have something to say to any subaltern of mine who charged tail over top into a quagmire the way you do! Happen we might have hushed it up, between the pair of us, if I could have brought you to your bearing. Eh, I don't know, though, for it's a reet scaddle, and how to button it up is beyond me!" He sighed ruefully. "I could have kept his lordship from finding our Richmond as drunk as a drum, at any hand, if you hadn't insisted on seeing him, you dafthead! You may say it's my blame for letting him get shot in the neck, but the fact is I was dipping rather deep myself. Well, I daresay you know how it is, when you're playing cards! you don't pay any heed to aught else. It's my belief it was as much excitement as brandy that made him top-heavy, too," he added reflectively, "but it's likely to be the devil of a task to persuade his lordship to believe that. And that's what worries me most, because it's taken the lad the Lord knows how long to coax my grandfather to let him have his way, and join the army, and if he flies into one of his passions there's no saying that he won't take back his consent, for it went clean against the pluck with him to give it."

"Going into the army!" exclaimed the Lieutenant, thunder-struck.

"Seventh Hussars," said Hugo. "He's been mad after a cavalry regiment pretty well since he was breeched, seemingly. Well, that's no concern of yours, of course—except that if he gets a nay-say from his lordship now he'll be so crazy with disappointment that happen he really *will* take to smuggling!"

As far as the Sergeant was concerned, that settled it. Descending the stairs behind his superiors, he had absorbed the Major's ruminations with a steadily growing conviction that Mr. Ottershaw had allowed himself to be properly slumguzzled—which, now he came to think of it, was what he'd thought in the first place, because whoever heard of a high-up young gentleman leading a gang of smugglers? There was no sense to it; but these Riding-officers got so that they took to thinking anyone might be a smuggler. The Sergeant wondered uneasily what dire consequences would befall him, if the terrible old lord came the ugly. It wasn't his blame that they'd been hunting an elephant in the moon; on the other hand, no one was going to blame Mr. Ottershaw for what was done by a bottleheaded, addle-brained recruit too raw to be trusted with a pop-gun, let alone a carbine. As far as Sergeant Hoole could see, the only hope of bringing themselves home lay in this lumping great Major, who was the only one of these Darracotts who seemed to be kindly disposed. And ten to one, thought the Sergeant bitterly, Mr. Ottershaw would set up *his* back next.

Reaching the foot of the stairs, after setting a leisurely pace that gave Vincent time to put his grandfather in possession of enough of the truth to prevent his bringing all to ruin by some unwitting blunder, Hugo led the way across the great hall to the corridor that gave access to the morning-room, and to the servants' quarters beyond it. Here Vincent had overtaken his lordship, and rapidly explained the situation to him. As soon as the rest of the party appeared, he said: "Very well, sir: as you wish!" and, turning, grimaced, for the benefit of Lieutenant Ottershaw, and slightly shrugged his shoulders.

Hugo would have much preferred to be rid of Lord Darracott, but since his lordship was obviously determined to take part in the approaching scene he could only make the best of it, and hope that Ottershaw was too slightly acquainted with him to think his silence remarkable, or to recognize the stricken look behind the fierceness in his eyes. He said cheerfully, his own eyes twinkling: "We've got him in here, this smuggler of yours. It's a fortunate thing he's too weak from loss of blood to be dangerous, for it would take a battalion to hold him othergates! He's a terrible ruffian!"

With these encouraging words, he walked into the room, and held the door wide for his companions. Over his shoulder, he said, with his deep chuckle: "Pluck up, lad! It was all a mistake, and not Ned Ackleton who shot you. It was Excisemen—and here they are!"

XX

The scene which met the Lieutenant's suspicious but startled gaze was lurid enough to astonish even Hugo, who had had no time to do more than sketch for his players the nature of the rôles allotted to them, before he was obliged to leave them. The stage had then been by no means set; but one swift glance round the room now was enough to satisfy him that his subordinates had more than obeyed his rapid instructions: they had surpassed themselves.

Not the most uninformed of observers could have failed to realize that something must have happened to interrupt two persons in the middle of a game of cards, even if the obvious cause of the interruption had been hidden from sight. Richmond was seated at the table in the middle of the room, with his cards stacked and laid face downwards before him; but opposite him a hand had been flung down in such careless haste that two of the cards which composed it had fallen on to the floor. A silver tray, with the stopper of the decanter lying in it, had been placed on the table; and beside Richmond a litter of bank-notes and scraps of paper bore eloquent testimony to the run of luck he must have been enjoying. The candles in the wall-sconces behind him had been lit, but since the branched candelabra, which must presumably have stood on the table, had been seized, and set down on a chair by the sofa, to provide Anthea and Polyphant with more light for their activities, no direct light fell upon his face. Nearly all the available light was, in fact, concentrated round the sofa, on which, supported by Polyphant, standing behind him, reclined Claud, the focal point of the scene.

His aspect was ghastly. From the waist upward he was naked except for the bandages which Anthea, kneeling beside him, had apparently just finished winding round him; as much of his chest as could be seen was smeared with blood; his left arm, which dangled uselessly, its limply crooked fingers brushing the carpet, was horribly covered with bloodstains; his head lolled on his right shoulder; his countenance, thanks to the thoughtfulness of his valet, who had brandished before his eyes the gruesome dishclout which had been used by John Joseph to stanch the flow of blood from Richmond's wound, was of a sickly hue; and his breathing was accompanied by a series of faint but alarming moans. The chair which had been dragged up to serve as a stand for the candelabra also accommodated an empty glass, a bottle of smelling-salts, and a bowl containing a revolting collection of used swabs. A larger bowl, half-full of reddened water, and the almost empty brandy-decanter stood on the floor within Anthea's reach, together with a heap of lint and torn-up linen; and the final macabre touch was provided by the rent and blood-boltered garments which no one had apparently found time even to bundle out of sight.

Hugo, realizing that his accomplices, not content with such meagre tokens of bloodshed as his neat work on Richmond's wound had afforded them, must have collected from the pantry every cloth and rag which had been used there, surveyed the scene with deep appreciation; but the Lieutenant brought up short on the threshold by the sight of so unexpected a shambles, was badly jolted; and the Sergeant, craning his neck to look over his shoulder, was perfectly appalled.

As soon as Hugo opened the door, Anthea exclaimed, without looking round, or pausing in her task of bandaging the sufferer: "At *last!* What on *earth* can have kept you so long?" but at his frivolously worded announcement, she cast an exasperated glance at him over her shoulder, saying in the voice of one perilously near the limit of her endurance: "For heaven's sake, don't start cutting idiotic jokes! I've had enough to bear from Richmond already! There's nothing *funny* about what's happened, and as for all your fine talk about it's not being serious, either you know nothing whatsoever about it, or you're as odiously drunk as Richmond—which wouldn't surprise me in the least!— Do you think that's tight enough, Polyphant?"

"Nay, I wasn't joking you! Our Claud was shot by a dragoon, lass!"

"To be sure!" she snapped, inserting a pin carefully into the end of her bandage. "Nothing could be more likely! Don't put yourself to the trouble of explaining what a dragoon was doing in our wood, for I've something better to do than to listen to quite unamusing, ill-timed nonsense!" She brought the point of her pin through several thicknesses of the bandage, and said: "I think that should hold it firmly, Polyphant. You can lay him down now. Oh, dear, how dreadfully white he is! Perhaps my aunt *ought* to be sent for—Hugo, did you find Vincent? is he com——" She broke off abruptly, for she had turned to ask this question, and now perceived Lieutenant Ottershaw. She stared at him, looked towards Hugo, looked again at the Lieutenant. "But—— Good God, what in heaven's name——? Hugo, if this is *your* doing——"

"Now, how could it be my doing?" he expostulated, helping her to rise to her feet.

She pressed a hand to her temple. "Oh, I don't know, but—— No, I suppose it couldn't be! But after that Banbury story about dragoons in the Home Wood—I beg your pardon, Mr. Ottershaw, but I am so much distracted—— Oh, Vincent, thank God you've come!"

Vincent, firmly putting the Lieutenant out of the way, had managed to enter the room. "Now, what is all this about Claud having met with an accident?" he began, breaking off abruptly, however, as he allowed his eyes to travel past Anthea to the sofa. "Good God!" he ejaculated. *"Claud——!"*

Polyphant, zealously waving the vinaigrette under his master's nose, said: "He will be better directly, sir, I promise you. He keeps swooning off, but if only we can keep him still and quiet—— It's the loss of blood, sir: I thought we should never be able to—— *That's* better, sir!—— He's coming round, Mr. Vincent! If someone would pour out a little brandy—just a drop or two!—and we could manage to make him swallow it——"

"Ay, that'll pull him together!" agreed Hugo. "Eh, he does look poorly! Where's the brandy?"

For the next few minutes, no one paid the smallest heed either to Ottershaw, or to the Sergeant, except Lord Darracott, who frustrated the Sergeant's instinctive attempt to retreat from this shocking scene, by thrusting him violently into the room, saying as he did so: *"Will* you make way for your betters, oaf?" which terrified him into edging his way along the wall to the corner of the room into which Ottershaw had already been manoeuvred. No one had asked the Lieutenant to move as far from the centre of the room as he could, but Claud's revival spurred his anxious relatives into so much activity that he was obliged to retire into the corner to get out of the way. For all the notice that was besowed upon him, while the rival merits of brandy and hartshorn were hotly argued, a sling was made to hold up Claud's left arm, his temples were dabbed with lavender-water, his right hand chafed, his brow fanned, and brandy held to his unwilling lips, he might as well have been invisible: and if he had not been a very dogged young man he would have yielded to the Sergeant's whispered suggestion that they should both of them slip away quiet-like without any loss of time.

To the surprise and the relief of his fellow-conspirators, who had feared he might prove the weak link in their chain, Claud, perhaps because he found himself for the first time in his life the star round which the other members of the family revolved, came artistically to his senses, and, seizing the cue afforded by Lord Darracott's demanding to be told how the devil he had come to be shot, at once took command of the scene, in a manner that won even his brother's admiration. Punctuating his utterances with winces, stifled groans, and dramatic pauses during which he stiffened into rigidity, with his eyes closed, and his lower lip clenched between his teeth, he disclosed that he had been set upon by two Bedlamites, both of whom had jumped out from behind a bush, roaring at him like a couple of ferocious wild beasts, and one of whom had fired at him. "Knew at once!" he said, shuddering at the memory. "Ackletons!"

The Sergeant cast a doubtful glance at Lieutenant Ottershaw, for, in his opinion, this had a false ring. His men, as he frequently informed them, put him forcibly in mind of many things, ranging from gapeseeds, hedge-birds, slushbuckets, and sheep-biters, to beetles, tailless dogs, and dead herrings, but none of them, least of all the two raw dragoons in question, had ever reminded him of a ferocious wild beast. Field-mice, yes, he thought, remembering the sad loss of steel in those posted to watch the Dower House; but if the young gentleman had detected any resemblance to ferocious wild beasts in his assailants, the Sergeant was prepared to take his Bible oath they had not been the baconbrained knock-in-the-cradles he had posted (much against his will) within the grounds of Darracott Place.

But Sergeant Hoole had never, until this disastrous evening, set eyes on Mr. Claud Darracott. Lieutenant Ottershaw had beheld that Pink of the Ton picking his delicate way across the cobbles in Rye, clad in astonishing but unquestionably modish raiment, and holding a quizzing-glass up to his eye with one fragile white hand, and it did not strike him as remarkable that this Bartholomew baby should liken two over-zealous dragoons to wild beasts.

"Did you recognize them, Claud?" Vincent asked.

Claud feebly shook his head, as it rested on one of the sofa-cushions, and instantly contracted his features in an expression of acute anguish, drawing a hissing breath, and ejaculating: "O God!—No, how could I? Too dark to recognize anyone at that distance. Besides,—only saw them for a minute. Dash it!—you don't suppose I stopped to ask 'em for their visiting-cards, do you? Knew it was the Ackletons. Couldn't have been anyone else!"

"As I apprehend the matter, it might well have been somebody else," said Vincent.

Claud opened his eyes, and regarded him with disfavour. "Well, it mightn't!" he said. "I daresay half the county may want to murder *you*, but——" He broke off, recalling his injury, and groped with his right hand. "Vinaigrette!" he uttered, in failing accents. "Polyphant!"

"Don't *agitate* him, Vincent!" begged Anthea, as Polyphant hastened to his master's side. "It must have been a terrible experience for him, poor Claud! And how he contrived to escape from those murderous bullies, and to struggle to the house, bleeding as dreadfully as he must have been, I can't imagine! I think it shows the greatest determination!"

"Yes, indeed, cousin: most creditable! But I think you have not exactly understood how the case stands. We have every reason to suppose that Claud was not attacked by the Ackletons, but by a couple of dragoons, precisely as Hugo told you."

"But that's nonsensical!" she exclaimed.

Lord Darracott, who, after one glance at Richmond, had stalked over to the fireplace behind him, and taken up a position there, with his hands gripped behind his back, said in a voice of suppressed passion: "Is that what you call it, girl? Preventives posted in my grounds without my knowledge or consent, one of my grandsons accused of being a common felon, another fired upon—*fired upon!*—because he don't choose to account for himself to a couple of loutish dragoons——"

"*What?*" interrupted Claud, once more opening his eyes. "Dragoons? *Dragoons?*"

His lordship swept on remorselessly. "My house broken into at midnight, warrants thrust at me by a damned jack-at-warts with no more conduct than wit——"

"What's a common felon?" suddenly demanded Richmond. He had been lounging in his chair, with his left arm on the table, an empty glass loosely held in his hand, his right hand dug into his pocket, and his gaze fixed on nothing in particular, but he now judged it to be time to demonstrate to Lieutenant Ottershaw that he was in no way incapacitated. His left arm was not entirely powerless: if the elbow was supported, he could make slight movements with his forearm, and he knew that he still had the use of that hand. He was in considerable discomfort, any strain on his hurt shoulder was exquisitely painful, and he had lost enough blood to weaken him to the point of hovering on the brink of collapse; but none of these ills had the power to daunt him, or to subdue the fearless spirit that responded with alacrity to the spur of danger, and found a strange enjoyment in flirting with disaster. It had flickered and sunk for an instant when a single, fleeting glance at his grandfather's face had brought home to him the enormity of what he had done, but only for an instant. Somewhere, at the back of his mind, lurked shame, repentance, grief for an

265

old man's agony, but there would be time enough later to think of such things: no time now, when disaster, so often defeated, was grinning at him in triumph. Richmond Darracott, pluck to the backbone, grinned back at disaster, gaily accepting a grim challenge.

He sat up. " 'Nother thing!" he pronounced, staring frowningly at the Lieutenant. "That's Ottershaw! What's he doing here?"

The Lieutenant, watching him with narrowed eyes, took a few steps into the room, and replied: "I am here to see *you,* sir!"

"See me," repeated Richmond, slurring his sibilants. His gaze remained fixed on the Lieutenant's face, frowning in an effort of concentration. Suddenly, to that serious-minded officer's discomfited surprise, his eyes began to dance, and a mischievous smile curled his lips. He giggled.

"Be silent, Richmond!" commanded Lord Darracott. "You're drunk!"

"But I don't understand!" complained Anthea, looking helplessly round. "*Why* should you want to see my brother, sir? At this hour, too? *Why* did dragoons shoot Claud? Why—— Oh, for goodness sake, *tell* me, somebody, before I go into strong hysterics, which, I warn you, I shall, at any moment!"

"Nay, lass, it's naught but a storm in a teacup!" said Hugo soothingly. "There's no need to be in a worry!"

She rounded on him. "No need to be in a worry, when I find Richmond in this *odious* condition, and Claud bleeding to death?"

"None regrets the accident to Mr. Claud Darracott more than I, ma'am," said the Lieutenant. "It is a mistake which——"

"It is a mistake which is going to cost you dear!" interrupted Lord Darracott.

As Richmond Darracott responded to the challenge of danger, so did Lieutenant Ottershaw to that of threats. Where the injury to Claud was concerned (if such an injury existed), he knew himself to be standing on thin ice, but he answered at once: "I would remind you, my lord, that it is the absolute duty of any person, when commanded to halt in the King's name——"

"Help me up!" commanded Claud, making ineffectual efforts to heave himself on to his sound elbow.

"Take care!" cried Anthea, hurrying back to the sofa. "No, no, Claud, pray be still! Vincent—Polyphant!"

"Help me up!" repeated Claud. "Dash it—can't—talk to

that fellow—like this! Going to sit up! Going to—sit up—if it kills me!"

"Keep still, brother!" Vincent said, pressing him down again. "*I* will talk to the fellow—have no fear of *that!*"

"There are some questions I wish to put to Mr. Claud Darracott," said Ottershaw, "but—*if* he has sustained serious injury, I will refrain until his condition is less precarious. Perhaps Mr. *Richmond* Darracott will be so good as to answer a question I wish to put to *him?*"

"*If* I've sustained—— *If?*" gasped Claud. "Let me up, Vincent! By God, if you don't——"

"Gently, lad! You shall sit up!" intervened Hugo. "Better let him have his way!" he added, to Vincent. "And as for you, Ottershaw, just keep quiet for a few moments, will you?"

"Hugo, if that bandage were to slip——!" Anthea said, in an urgent undervoice.

Sergeant Hoole, surreptitiously wiping the sweat from his brow, tried in vain to catch the Lieutenant's eye. Dicked in the nob, that's what he was! As though anyone couldn't see that the young chap wasn't bandaged, let alone he was as drunk as an artillery-man, sitting there, giggling to himself. As for the other young gentleman, a nice set-out it would be if he was to start bleeding again, all through Mr. Ottershaw not believing his own eyes! Why, there was blood all over everywhere! The gentleman was as green as a leek too: if they didn't take care he'd go off again.

"Quick, Polyphant! Brandy!" said Vincent, as Claud, tenderly raised against a bank of cushions, allowed his head to loll on to his shoulder again.

Richmond, when he saw both Ottershaw's and the Sergeant's eyes fixed on the fainting Claud, got both his elbows on the table, and, lifting his left hand with his right, dropped his chin on both. In this position, and keeping his weight on his right elbow, he watched Ottershaw, mockery in his eyes, an impish grin on his lips; and when the Lieutenant, as though feeling himself to be under scrutiny, turned his head to look at him, he said: "*I* know why you shot Claud!"

"Oh, I wish you'd go to bed, Richmond!" exclaimed his sister exasperatedly. "Things are bad enough without you to make them worse! Mr. Ottershaw did *not* shoot Claud!"

"Yes, he did," insisted Richmond. "You think I'm castaway, but I'm not. *I* can carry my wine! All the Darracotts can carry their wine. He shot Claud because Hugo wouldn't let him shoot me!" He chuckled. "Silly clunch!"

"The Darracotts do not appear to be able to carry their brandy with any very notable success," remarked Vincent dryly.

"Tell me, sir!" said Ottershaw, looking at Richmond very hard. "*Why* should I have wanted to shoot you?"

If he thought to disconcert Richmond by his searching stare, he was disappointed: those dark, gleaming eyes were brimful of wicked laughter. "Because I made the dragoons run away!" Richmond let his clasped hands drop to the table, and bowed his head over them, idiotically giggling.

Vincent regarded him with raised brows, and then said to Hugo: "I wonder what gave rise to that—admittedly enchanting!—delusion? I fear we shall never know."

"Nay, it's simple enough! The dragoons were set to keep watch on the Dower House, and they weren't very well suited with that duty—eh, Sergeant?"

"Well, sir . . ."

Hugo's eyes twinkled. "Eh, Sergeant, *you* know, and *I* know—the things we both know!"

The Sergeant smiled gratefully at him. "Yes, sir!" he said, feeling that all might not be lost if this Major would take command. He'd thought him a queer sort of a gentleman at first, but he was what the Sergeant called a right officer: any soldier could tell that, he thought.

Richmond lifted his head. "Ran all the way to the Blue Lion!" he disclosed. "Only me! Not a ghost." He stopped giggling, and frowned. "*Not* a silly clunch. Forgetting!" He looked vaguely round, his eyes coming finally to rest on the Lieutenant. He smiled in a friendly way. "*You* weren't frightened. My cousin said you weren't. Mustn't hoax you any more. Might get shot, like Claud. That's what Hugo says. *I* dunno!"

Vincent cast up his eyes. "So far as I understand these cryptic utterances, I collect that my extremely tiresome young cousin has been playing at being a hobgoblin—with, apparently, disintegrating results. Very improper! But it in no way explains why my brother became a target, Mr. Ottershaw. Perhaps you would care to enlighten me?"

"If your brother was shot, sir, the reason was that he was mistaken for Mr. Richmond Darracott!"

Claud, listening to this with dropped jaw, said, in a

dazed voice: "*I was shot, because I was—* Dash it, I don't look like Richmond!"

"You are of much the same height and build, sir, and I had good reason to believe that he was abroad tonight."

"But you can't shoot at everyone who's the same height and build as my cousin! Besides, what's it got to do with you if he was abroad? Never heard anything to equal it in my life! You must be mad!" said Claud, stunned.

"He's got it firmly fixed in his head that our Richmond is mixed up with the free-traders," explained Hugo.

"Well, that proves he's mad. If my head weren't swimming so— What I mean is—nothing to do with *me*, if he was mixed up with them! Silly notion, anyway. And when I think——" He put up a hand to his shoulder, cautiously feeling it, and wincing. "I don't know what you've done to me," he said fretfully, to his valet. "It's too tight. Devilish uncomfortable!"

"Pray do not touch it, sir! I implore you, sir, do not try to shift those bandages!"

"Something sticking into me," muttered Claud, closing his eyes again.

"Yes, sir, but it was necessary to bind a thick pad over the wound," said Polyphant soothingly. "We fear that the bullet may be deeply lodged, so you must not——"

"What!" Claud's eyes flew open. "You mean to tell me I've got a bullet in me?"

"It'll be dug out, never fear!" Hugo consoled him.

"Oh, *no!*" moaned Claud.

"Mr. Darracott, I have two questions which I shall be obliged if you will answer! That will not, I trust, exhaust you! Why were you wearing a mask, and why did you run away when commanded to halt in the King's name?"

"Take this fellow away!" begged Claud feebly. "A bullet lodged in me! It may be *fatal!* And all the fellow can do is to stand there, asking me questions! How was I to know what they were shouting? Next you'll say I should have begged pardon and asked them to speak more clear— Polyphant, *where* is the bullet lodged? I am feeling very low."

"And the mask, sir?" demanded Ottershaw inexorably.

"Very low *indeed!* Shouldn't wonder if I fainted away again. Dashed if I'll answer you! No concern of yours!"

"Were you wearing a mask, Claud?" said Vincent, looking amused. "Now, I wonder if I could hazard a guess? Rather a late hour for a ramble in the wood, was it not?

Unless you wished for some reason to go by the shortest way to the village—or to meet someone, not far from—perhaps—the smithy?"

"You go to the devil!" said Claud sulkily. "And you can take that nosy tidewatcher with you!"

"I wonder if any of my cattle want shoeing? I feel sure they do. I have a positively burning curiosity to see that game-pullet of yours, Claud. But I shan't wear a mask, however savage her brother may be. What Hugo can do, I can!"

"Leave the poor lad alone!" said Hugo reprovingly, but with a grin. He laid his fingers on Claud's limp wrist for a minute. "Yes, I think the sooner we get him to bed the better it will be."

"If I may say so, I am entirely of your mind, sir!" said Polyphant. "Knowing Mr. Claud's constitution as I do, I shall make bold to say that he will be in a high fever if we do not procure for him a little *quiet!*"

Hugo nodded, and looked at Ottershaw. "Well, lad, you've had your wish, and kicked up a rare scrow-row into the bargain, but happen it's time you took your leave now," he said, not unkindly, but with a certain authority in his deep voice.

The Lieutenant stared up into his face, his eyes hard and searching, his lips tightly compressed. For several moments he did not speak: to the Darracotts the moments seemed hours. The Sergeant cleared his throat, and moved towards the door, but Ottershaw paid no heed. He could read nothing in Hugo's calm face but slight amusement, nor did those very blue eyes waver. Could any man appear so totally unconcerned unless he was as innocent as the Major looked? Some, perhaps, but this enormous, simple creature——? Nothing could have been clumsier than his efforts to keep Richmond's mother and grandfather in ignorance of his condition; his naïve attempts at deception had been the big, good-natured, stupid man he appeared to be. But was he? There was no subtlety in his face, as there was in Vincent Darracott's; his eyes were sometimes grave, and sometimes twinkling, but they were the eyes of a child: they gazed innocently upon the world, there was no thought behind them.

The Lieutenant glanced at Richmond. It struck him that Richmond was too pale; paler, surely, than he had been a few minutes earlier? His eyes narrowed, intently watching the boy. It was useless to question him: if he was drunk his answers would be valueless; if he was pretending to be drunk he could make them so. He was leaning forward, both his arms on the table, foolishly trying to stand the stopper of the decanter on end, using both hands impartially. It was incredible that he could sit like that, vacantly smiling, if he had a bullet lodged in him; it was incredible that he should be sitting in that chair at all under such circumstances: surely he must have swooned from sheer weakness? But he was certainly growing paler.

"Vincent!"

The Major's voice was lowered. Ottershaw's suspicious eyes went instantly to his face, but Hugo was no longer looking at him, he was looking at Richmond, a rather rueful smile on his lips. He glanced towards Vincent, and significantly directed his attention to Richmond, saying, in an undervoice: "From the looks of it, he'll be casting up his accounts before he's much older. Better get him to bed."

"Damn the brat!" said Vincent. "Inevitable, of course! He will in all probability cast 'em up as soon as he gets to his feet. What a singularly disagreeable evening this has been, to be sure!"

He went up to the table as he spoke, and grasped Richmond's left arm, just above the elbow, as though to pull him to his feet. "Come along, bantam!" he said. "Bedtime!"

Richmond hiccuped. "I don't want to go to bed."

"One moment!" Ottershaw said suddenly, obedient to an insistent, inner prompting. "Before you retire, Mr. Richmond, oblige me, please, by removing your coat!"

XXI

"Well, upon my word!" cried Anthea, as though she could no longer restrain herself. "Mr. Ottershaw, are you indeed mad, or merely determined to insult us! I never heard of anything so outrageous in my life! Who are you to throw orders about in this house? Pray how *many* people have been fired on tonight?"

Uncertainty, chagrin, the intangible feeling that he was being fooled to the top of his bent, were making the Lieutenant lose his temper. He snapped back accusingly: "Only *one*, Miss Darracott!"

She stared at him, her eyes blazing. "Only—— Why, you—you *impertinent* idiot! Do you know what you are saying? Do you seriously imagine that *I*—my grandfather—my cousins —all of us, in fact: every member of the household!—are engaged in the smuggling trade?"

271

"No! But that you are engaged in protecting Mr. Richmond Darracott, *yes!*" he said recklessly.

"Don't be so daft, Ottershaw!" said Hugo quietly.

Anthea paid no heed, but gave a scornful, angry laugh, and said: "Well, I hope *you* know how my brother has contrived to become a smuggler without anyone's being the wiser, for I can assure you I don'tl When I think of the way every single soul at Darracott Place fusses and cossets him—— Oh, what is the use of talking to you? You are out of your senses!" She swung round towards Lord Darracott, demanding impetuously: "Grandpapa, how much more of this do you mean to endure?"

"Let him go his length, my girl!" he replied. "The farther the better! Do you think *I* mean to stop him tieing the noose round his own neck? I don't, pea-goose!"

Sergeant Hoole stepped forward, laying a hand on the Lieutenant's arm. "Sir!" he uttered imploringly. "Begging your pardon, but——"

Ottershaw shook him off, and the voice within his brain that urged him not to let these Darracotts outjockey him was growing every second more insistent. Rather pale, but with his jaw outthrust, he said: "If Mr. Richmond Darracott is unhurt, why should he hesitate to remove his coat, so that I may be convinced by the evidence of my own eyes that it is so?"

Hugo, who had bent over Claud, adjusting the sling that supported his left arm, straightened himself, saying: "Oh, for God's sake, take your coat off, Richmond, and your waistcoat too! Let's be done with this business!"

Richmond might be pale, but his eyes, tremendously alive, gave the lie to the drawn look on his face, not a trace of fear in them. He gave a gleeful chuckle, and pointed a derisive finger at the Major. "*Who* said I couldn't bamboozle the Exciseman? *Who* said he was too fly to the time of day to be hoaxed by a *silly schoolboy?* I've *done* it! Vincent, do you know what Hugo——"

"I'm going to say something more, when you're sober enough to attend to me," said Hugo, somewhat grimly. "Happen you won't find that so amusing! In the meantime, we've had more than enough of your hoax, so take your coat off, and let me have no argument about it!"

Richmond's laughter was quenched. He looked resentfully at his large cousin, saying sulkily: "I don't know why I need do as *you* say. I don't care for what *you* think. Nothing to do with you!"

"Help him off with it, Vincent!" said Hugo curtly.

At this point Claud, who had opened his eyes some few minutes previously, demanded, in bewildered accents: "What the devil does that fellow want with Richmond's coat? Dash it, he *is* mad!"

"Don't fatch!" said Hugo. "He thinks it's Richmond that was shot, and not you at all, so the easiest way to prove him wrong——"

"Thinks—thinks *I* wasn't shot?" gasped Claud, galvanized into struggling up on to his right elbow. "Oh, so that's what you think, is it, you murderous lunatic? Then let me tell you——"

"You young fool, keep still! *Claud——!*" exclaimed Hugo, taking two hasty strides to the head of the sofa, as Claud, with every sign of one exerting a superhuman effort, dragged himself up from the cushions, panting, and making unavailing attempts to speak. "Nay then, lad! Gently now!" he begged, his arms round Claud. "You'll do yourself an injury, you silly lad! You mustn't——"

"Don't you talk to me!" raged Claud, between laboured breaths. "If you think—— *Ow——!*"

The anguish throbbing in this sharp cry was so real that even Vincent was startled, while Anthea could almost have exclaimed Bravo! Ottershaw, who had been paying no heed to him, but keeping his eyes fixed on Richmond, just about to let Vincent pull off his coat, turned involuntarily.

"Hugo, you—you——!"

"Nay, lad, it's your own fault!" protested Hugo. "Stop wriggling about like——"

"You put your great, clumsy hand right on—— Oh—ah—ugh——!" moaned Claud, reduced again to *extremis.*

"Brandy, Polyphant!" Hugo said, his anxious gaze on Claud's face. He shifted him slightly, and stretched out an imperative hand. "Or the salts! Anything, only give it to me quickly!"

A tiny, perfectly spontaneous shriek escaped Anthea. "Hugo——! Your *hand!*" she stammered, her dilating eyes riveted to it.

"Good God!" ejaculated Vincent involuntarily.

Hugo looked round, surprised at Anthea, and then at his own bloodstained palm. "Oh, my God!" he uttered, swiftly glancing down at Claud's back, which only he was in a position to see.

"*Sir——!*" exclaimed Polyphant reproachfully, and darting forward to snatch up some lint from the pile on the floor.

273

"No, no, let me, sir! I beg pardon, but *pray* don't—— Just hold him, if you please! Oh, dear, oh, dear! Miss Anthea, the longest strip of linen you can find—or knot two together —anything! Don't move, Mr. Claud! I implore you, sir, *don't move!*"

Since no one in the room had seen the Major pick up several of the blood-soaked swabs from the bowl still standing on the chair beside the sofa, and close his hand on them, it was hardly surprising that the sight of his horridly reddened palm should have come as a shock to the rest of his family. Had Lieutenant Ottershaw not been far too much shocked himself to think of studying the expressions on the faces of his companions, one glance must have satisfied him that the Darracotts were honestly horrified.

Anthea was the first to recover her wits, and to rush to the sofa, scolding distractedly; Vincent was swift to follow suit. Both blamed Hugo for having handled the drooping Claud with abominable clumsiness; my lord joined in, directing his menaces, however, towards Lieutenant Ottershaw, for being the real cause of this fresh disaster; and the Sergeant, prompted by real dismay, and a very lively dread of the consequences, seized the opportunity provided by all this commotion to represent to Ottershaw, with all the eloquence at his command, that any more attempts to exacerbate the Darracots would only bring them both to ruin.

It was at this moment that Lady Aurelia entered the room, and, halting on the threshold, demanded, in a voice which, without being raised to any vulgar pitch, easily penetrated the hubbub: "*What*, may I ask, is the meaning of this *extraordinary* scene?"

Such was the effect of her commanding eye, and air of surprise assurance, that Lieutenant Ottershaw found himself to his subsequent fury, adding his voice to those of Anthea and Vincent, in an attempt to present her ladyship with the explanation she desired.

She seemed to grasp the gist of what was told her with all the rapidity of a powerful intelligence; and, considerably before the various accounts had been brought to their conclusions, paralysed the company by uttering, in icy yet ominous accents: "Be silent, if you please! I have heard enough!"

She then swept forward to the sofa, Anthea, Vincent, and the Major giving way instinctively before her, and bent over Claud, feeling his brow, and his wrist. Magnificently ignoring everyone else, she exchanged a few words with Polyphant, who had remained devoutly at the head of the sofa; and, upon Claud's venturing to open his eyes sufficiently to cast a doubtful, slightly nervous glance up at her, said with calm kindness: "You will keep perfectly still, my son: do you understand me? You have no need to trouble yourself about anything, for Mama is here, and will make you better directly."

She then turned, and looked round the room, with all the lofty contempt natural to the descendant of eleven Earls, all of whom, if not otherwise distinguished, had been remarkable for the high-handed and very successful way with which they had dealt with inferior persons, and overridden all opposition to their domestic decrees. No one saw these august personages range themselves at Lady Aurelia's back, but (as her appreciative elder son afterwards asserted) no one could doubt that they had all of them hurried to the support of so worthy a daughter.

"I do not know," she stated, in a tone of dispassionate censure, "why I have been obliged to come downstairs to discover for myself the precise nature of Claud's injury, but I do not attempt to conceal from you that I am excessively displeased. *Your* conduct, Vincent, I consider particularly reprehensible, for it was on the understanding that you would instantly apprise me of it, if you found your brother's injury to be of a serious character, that I allowed myself to be persuaded to remain upstairs. Neither you nor Anthea, whom I must deem to have been gravely at fault, are so stupid as to have supposed that the *accident* was of a *trifling* nature. I shall say no more to *you*, Hugo, than that I trust you will in future refrain from making well-meaning but foolish attempts to conceal from some other female in my position the very dangerous state in which one of her children may be lying. Pray do not answer me! I have neither the time nor the desire to listen to excuses or apologies. You will all of you, with the exception of Polyphant, be so good as to leave this room immediately. Vincent, since I apprehend that Richmond is disgracefully inebriated, you will please assist him to his bed-chamber. I do not presume to dictate to *you*, my lord, but since there is nothing for you to do here I am persuaded you will be very much more comfortable in your library." Her eyes next fell on Lieutenant Ottershaw, and after considering him for a moment or two in a way that made the Sergeant feel profoundly thankful that her gaze had swept past him, said, without the slightest change of intonation: "You, I believe, are the author of this outrage. I collect that you are in the service of the Board of Customs. I shall be obliged to you if you will furnish me with your name, and style."

The Lieutenant's colour was considerably heightened, but he replied with commendable readiness: "My name is Ottershaw, ma'am—Thomas Ottershaw, and I am a Riding-officer of the Customs' Land-Guard. Allow me to assure your ladyship that, while I do not seek to disclaim responsibility for whatever injury Mr. Darracott has suffered, my explicit order was that no shot was to be fired, other than a warning shot over the head of any person failing to obey a summons to halt in the King's name. I regret very much that an accident should have occurred, but I must take leave to inform your ladyship of the circumstances which led——"

"Pray say no more!" she interrupted. "I am neither deaf nor slow of understanding, and since I was present when you made known to his lordship the precise nature of your errand any further explanation would be superfluous. Let me make it plain to you that whatever may be my opinion of the accusation you then made, I am not concerned with my nephew's affairs, but with the attack upon my son. I have nothing further to add, except that I shall immediately lay the matter before my husband. No doubt he will know what action to take. As a mere female, I cannot consider myself competent to deal with such an affair. I will not detain you any longer. If you have anything further to do in this house, pray desire Major Darracott to conduct you to some other room!"

Wtih these measured words, she turned to Polyphant, and began to question him on the exact nature of Claud's injury, wholly ignoring her stunned audience.

The Major, a phlegmatic man, was the first to recover from the shattering effect of this encounter with a mere female, and he acted with great promptitude and good sense, saying meekly: "Yes, ma'am! I will do so immediately," and thrusting the Lieutenant out of the room. Sergeant Hoole, holding the door for them, needed no urging to follow, the manner of his exit suggesting that only a rigid adherence to discipline restrained him from preceding his superiors.

No one moved or spoke for several moments, the actors in the conspiracy remaining as though frozen, nearly all of them looking towards the door, intently listening. Then Lord Darracott sank into a chair beside the fire, and with shaking hands grasped its arms, his countenance grey, and his eyes staring straight before him, fixed and sightless. Lady Aurelia glanced at him, and then away from him, as though averting her gaze from some indecent spectacle. As Claud sat up, saying: "Well, thank the lord that's over!" she lifted a warning finger, and said: "Do not abandon your position until we are assured that those men have departed! Since you have all of you chosen to pursue a line of conduct as criminal as it is grossly improper, I must beg you to maintain the imposture!"

Claud sank back obediently, but said: "Dash it, Mama, if you think we *chose*—— Besides, I should like to know what *you* were doing! Well, what I mean is——"

"I know exactly what you mean, Claud. Pray do not imagine that my participation in this disgraceful affair in any way alters my sentiments!" said her ladyship severely.

"You are quite superb, Mama," said Vincent. "May I make you my heartfelt compliments on a performance that will ever command my admiration? Your entrance I can only describe as a clincher."

"I have the greatest objection to cant terms," responded her ladyship. "I trust I may have *expedited* the departure of the Preventive officer, but I must suppose, from what I have seen of your powers of what I can only call deception, that you would have done very well without my intervention."

"Hugo did it," Anthea said, with a wavering smile. "It was all Hugo. We didn't know what to do. Even Vincent didn't. We just—did what Hugo told us." She dashed a hand across her eyes, adding: "It was the *pageant of Ajax!* Not that I mean the others weren't wonderful too, *particularly* Claud! Claud, that shriek you gave almost persuaded me to believe you *had* suffered a spasm of anguish!"

"Oh, it did, did it?" said Claud bitterly. "I should rather think it might! Hugo jabbed a pin into me!" He eyed his relatives with disfavour. "Yes, I daresay you think it's devilish funny, but when *I* see Hugo next—— Well, dash it, I knew what he wanted me to do, because he told me, when he pretended to be arranging this damned sling, and there was no need to stick pins into me! When I think of the things I've had to do this night, let alone being smeared all over with young Richmond's blood—— Yes, and how much longer have I got to lie here, swaddled up in bandages which are dashed uncomfortable, besides——"

"You have my sympathy, brother, but Mama is, as usual,

right. It will not do for any of us to be caught off our guard. I have no real apprehension—the hideous experiences of the past hour have taught me that our cousin's bovine countenance is, to say the least of it, misleading—but we will take no eleventh-hour risks. I wonder what glib lies he is telling that unfortunate Exciseman now?"

"It is a very distressing reflection that any gentleman of birth—and particularly one whose military rank is distinguished—should have been obliged to lend himself to so disreputable a business," pronounced her ladyship, with undiminished severity. "It is, however, to his credit that he appears at least to know what is his duty to his *Family*, and although I am far from approving of his conduct I cannot deny that I regard his arrival at Darracott Place as the greatest piece of good fortune that has befallen the Family for very many years. As to whether the Family is deserving of its good fortune—*that* is a subject upon which I prefer to remain silent!"

This measured speech not unnaturally reduced its auditors to speechless discomfort; and when Hugo presently came back into the room, he found his actors so apparently petrified into the positions in which he had left them that he grinned, and said: "Eh, you look just like a set of waxworks!"

"Not waxworks, coz: puppets!" retorted Vincent. "What unnatural antics must we next perform?"

"Hugo, have they gone?" Anthea asked anxiously.

"Oh, yes, they've gone, lass!" He smiled cordially upon Lady Aurelia. "Thanks to you, ma'am! I'm reet grateful to you. Nay, till you came in there was no deciding which was the best actor amongst the lot of you! Myself, I couldn't make up my mind between Claud and Richmond, but, eh, when you took command, there was——"

"Yes, dear cousin," interrupted Anthea firmly, "we are well aware that everyone, except you, acted to admiration, but what we are desirous of knowing is how you contrived to rid us of Ottershaw."

"Oh, there was no difficulty about that, lass, once her ladyship's guns had broken the square!" he assured her. "You might say that I'd nothing to do but to harass the retreat."

"I might, but it is very unlikely that I shall," she retorted. "Hugo, are we *safe*?"

"Nay, love, don't look so fatched! We shall be safe enough,

278

once we've tied up a few knots, which we'll do easily, never fear!" he assured her.

"Did you succeed in convincing that damned, obstinate tide-watcher?" demanded Vincent.

"Nay, I'm not one to level at the moon. Happen he'll suspect to the end of his days that he was made a May-game of, poor lad! But what with her ladyship setting him in a quake, and me telling him that you'd so much influence, ma'am, that if he'd caught our Richmond red-handed you'd have seen to it the whole business was hushed-up, he didn't know which way to turn. He's no turn-tail, but he knew well he'd exceeded his commission, and when he saw I knew it too, there was naught he could do but retire—the position being untenable, as you might say! I don't know much about Preventive work, but I do know that unless they find a smuggler in actual possession of run goods the Preventives are pretty well ham-strung—even when they've been nose-led after a decoy-train of rascals rigged out in smocks to deceive them, and leading a string of ponies carrying nothing more than loads of faggots. They know full well they've been bamboozled, but it's no crime to carry faggots across the country in the middle of the night, so the poor devils have naught to do but own themselves gapped. Well, it was plain enough that, whatever Ottershaw *had* seen, he hadn't seen our Richmond in possession of anything other than a load of devilry. All he was doing tonight was trying to catch the lad, or at any road to discover how he was contriving to flit in and out of the Dower House, no matter how strong a guard was set on it. He'd no more intention of executing that warrant than he had of getting the lad shot. Once that had happened, he may have felt there was naught to do but go through stitch with the business, or he may have gambled on the chance that if he found the lad here, wounded, he could scare him into making a confession. If he couldn't do that, he knew he'd be taken at fault, so you can't but allow he's got plenty of courage. I must say, it went to my heart to cheat him, poor lad! However, a back-cast won't harm him, for he didn't handle the business well, and happen he'll do better in future." His rueful grin dawned. "It was a reet shame," he confessed. "I gave him a dressing, just as I would any skelterbrained subaltern that had plunged stickle-butt into trouble all because he was too pot-sure, and that took the last bit of fight out of him. So I told him when he was fairly down that I knew it was our Richmond's mischief that had led him into the hobble, and I'd do my best to bring him safely home, and no one the wiser as long as he kept his tongue between his teeth. So we'll hope that's buttoned the thing up, which there's no reason to think it won't—once he knows *that* young scamp's not here any longer to plague the life out of him."

There was a tiny pause, several pairs of eyes instinctively turning towards Lord Darracott. He gave no sign of having heard what Hugo had said, still sitting immobile, and staring straight ahead. Anthea glanced from him to Richmond, no longer tense, but sitting rather limply, his right elbow on the table, and his brow dropped on to his hand; her eyes travelled to Vincent, reading the look of strain on his face; and suddenly she began to laugh rather tremulously, realizing that the only one whose nerves were not in some way or other disordered from the ordeal they had passed through was the one on whom the success of an enterprise fraught with peril had depended, and thinking how ridiculous it was that he should rejoin his shattered accomplices as placidly as though he had done nothing more than escort two harmless morning-callers to the door. She saw that he was looking at her in mild surprise, and said: "Oh, Hugo, Hugo! I don't know what to say to you!"

"Well, we've no time to waste on any more talk now, love, so happen that's just as well," he replied matter-of-factly. "We must dispose of Richmond's clothes, and clear up all this mess. Nay, then, Polyphant! don't stand gauping! There's work to be done!"

Polyphant, who had indeed been standing staring at him, gave a start, and recalled his scattered wits. "Yes, sir—to be sure! I fear I was indulging in reflection—I will remove the bowls first, and then Mr. Claud will be comfortable again!"

"You'll find the swabs I squeezed in my hand behind the sofa cushions," Hugo warned him. "Vincent, will you see all these clothes disposed of? I've been trying to decide what had best be done with Richmond, and it seems to me that we'll have to put him to bed in Claud's room, for that wound of his must be attended to, and since it's Claud who's supposed to be the wounded one we mustn't have any bloodstains anywhere but on his sheets. Now, there's no need to start shuddering, lad! I'm not asking you to sleep on them!"

"No, and it wouldn't be any use if you did ask me to!" Claud informed him, pausing in his struggles to unwind the bandages from round his slim person. "Dashed if I ever met such a fellow as you are!"

"How seldom it is that I find myself in accord with you, brother!" remarked Vincent. He looked at Hugo, and said, with a wry smile: "You irritate me intensely, you know. I have little doubt that you always will, but if ever I should get into a tight corner I do hope to God you will be at hand to pull me out of it, coz!"

"Never mind throwing the hammer at me!" replied Hugo, unmoved by this tribute. "If you want to throw it at anyone, throw it at Claud, because he's the one who saved our groats!" His eyes were on Richmond, and he went to him, saying: "I think I'll carry you up to bed, lad, before I do aught else."

Richmond lifted his head with an effort. The fire had gone out of his eyes, and with the passing of danger the spirit that had upheld him so indomitably had sunk, allowing his physical weakness at last to overcome him. He managed to smile, and to say, in the thread of a voice: "A close-run thing . . . ! Thank you—so very grateful—so *sorry*, Hugo— Grandpapa . . ."

Hugo caught him, as he collapsed, and lifted him up in his arms. "Eh, poor lad, I ought to have got him to bed sooner, instead of standing there chattering!" he said remorsefully. "Anthea, run upstairs to see if the coast is clear, will you, love?" He looked at Lady Aurelia. "I take it you warned his mother, ma'am?"

"Certainly," she replied. "She was cast into very natural affliction, and dared not come down to this room for fear that her agitation might overcome her, and so betray you all, but I left her in Mrs. Flitwick's care, and have no doubt that she will be more composed by now."

"I'm very much obliged to you, ma'am," he said. "Breaking it to her was the thing I dreaded most."

"An unpleasant task," she agreed. "I am happy to have been able to relieve you of it, for, however little I may *approve* of your conduct this evening I must own myself to be deeply grateful to you for all that you have done, and, I may add, very conscious of the magnanimity you have shown."

"Nay——!" begged the Major, reddening.

She said graciously: "You have no need to blush, my dear Hugo. I do not mean to flatter you, and will only say that I have from the beginning of our acquaintance believed you to be a most estimable young man. I have little doubt that when you have overcome your tendency to levity you will do very well at Darracott Place."

Fortunately, since Hugo was showing signs of acute embarrassment, Anthea had by this time come back into the room, to report that it was safe to carry Richmond upstairs. Lord Darracott rose stiffly from the chair into which he had sunk, and looked at Hugo, saying, as though the words were forced from him: "I am obliged to you, Hugh."

"There's no need for that, sir," Hugo replied cheerfully. "The young scamp's as near to being my brother-in-law as makes no odds—though happen I'd have better not to have said that, because, now I come to think of it, you've not accepted my offer yet, have you, love?"

"*More* levity?" she murmured.

He grinned. "You're reet: I'm past praying for! Come, now, lead the way, lass!" He saw that Lord Darracott was looking at Richmond's white, unconscious face, and paused for a moment, and said gently: "He's got spunk, you know, sir."

His lordship's grim mouth twisted. "Yes," he said, turning away. "He was always—full of pluck. Take him up to his mother!"

It was some considerable time later that Hugo came downstairs again. Claud had retired to bed, but Lord Darracott and Vincent were still up, seated in the library. As Hugo came into the room, Vincent looked up with a flickering smile. "Well? How is that abominable brat?"

"Oh, he's nicely!" Hugo replied. "He won't be very comfortable till he's had the bullet dug out of him—and that's something he won't enjoy, think on—but it would take more than one bullet to daunt *him!* I won't deny that he's caused a deal of trouble—eh, if ever a lad wanted a good skelping——! but I can't but like young devils as full of gaiety as he is."

"Yes, excellent bottom," Vincent agreed, getting up, and walking across the room to a side-table. "I owe you an apology, Ajax: you warned me, and I paid no heed. I'm sorry. Had I attended to you, I might have averted the singularly nerve-racking events we have survived this night, thanks, I admit,—and you have no notion how much it costs me to do so!—to your unsuspected genius for—er—diddling the dupes! Accept my compliments, and allow me to offer you some brandy! Unless the very word has, for reasons which I need not, I feel, explain to you, become re-

282

pulsive to you, I am persuaded you must stand in urgent need of it."

Hugo grinned, as he took the glass Vincent was holding out to him, but said quite seriously: "Well, it nattered me at the time that you wouldn't heed me, but I'm not so sure now that it would have made any difference if you had. The best thing about this business is that, while that cargo was hidden in this passage of ours, it didn't matter to Richmond how close the hounds were: it was his doing that they were stored there, and nothing anyone could have said would have turned him from what he saw to be his duty. You heard him, Vincent: he said he couldn't leave his men in the lurch, because it was his scheme, and he was in command. Never mind the rest!—that's the stuff out of which a damned good officer is made!" He looked down at his grandfather. "You don't like roundaboutation, sir, and nor do I. I told Ottershaw that Richmond had won your consent to his joining, and I'm looking to you to make my word good. Will you let me purchase a cornetcy for him?"

There was a long silence. Vincent broke it. "You have no choice, sir."

"Do as you will!" his lordship said harshly. "That any grandson of mine could—and, of you all, *Richmond!*——"

"It's no wish of mine to fratch with you over what's done, and can't be mended," interrupted Hugo, "but ask yourself, sir, whose fault it was that a lad of his cut, crazy with disappointment, and hearing nothing but praise of smuggling all his life, was brought to this pass?"

"I have said you may do as you will! I am not answerable to you for Richmond's upbringing!"

"Not to me, but to him, sir."

Lord Darracott threw him a strange glance, and lowered his eyes again. After a slight pause, Vincent said: "And so, coz?"

"If it's left to me, I'd like to see the boy in the Seventh Hussars. I've several good friends in the regiment, who'll need no urging to keep an eye on a lad who bears my name."

"That, cousin," murmured Vincent, *"is the most unkindest cut of all!* Proceed!"

"Nay, I didn't mean it so! For the rest, we've settled it between us—my aunts and I—that it will be best to get the lad away from here, and Claud too, at first light, before the servants are up and about. It will be easily done, and accounted for: your mother wants her own doctor to deal with Claud, and Richmond goes to help her with him on the journey. John Joseph will drive them to Tonbridge in her ladyship's own carriage, and see to the hiring of a postchaise there to carry them on to London. I've promised my Aunt Elvira I'll take her to London myself as soon as I get back from the north, but it won't do for her to join Richmond too soon, for we don't want to set tongues wagging."

"Have you induced her to let him go without her? Good God!"

"She'll do nothing to hinder us from doing what's best for him, little though she may like it. She knows your mother will take good care of him, too."

"Your staff work is admirable, coz. Why, by the way, does Richmond go to succour Claud while I remain here?"

"No one will wonder at that, lad! Claud's in no state for fratching!"

"*Touché!*" Vincent acknowledged, throwing up a hand. "You don't feel that I ought to drive myself to town in the wake of the chaise, as—er—rearguard?"

"I don't," replied Hugo. "You and I, lad, have got work to do here! Something must be done about that secret passage. If we can do no more, between the pair of us, than block it, as it was when Richmond first saw it, we'll do that."

"What an enchanting prospect!" said Vincent faintly. "How right you are—*damn* you!"

Hugo chuckled, but addressed his grandfather. "There's one thing more, sir. That young good-like naught of yours won't rest until he's seen you. He knows well the blow he's dealt you. He bade me tell you so."

Lord Darracott rose from his chair. "I'll go to him," he said curtly.

Hugo moved to the door, to open it for him. His lordship paused for a moment before he went out, passing a hand across his brow. "I suppose you will do what's necessary. There will be many things—his boat, his horses—I'm too tired tonight, but I'll discuss it with you tomorrow. Goodnight!"

"Goodnight, sir," Hugo replied. He shut the door, and came back into the room. "Happen I'd best do something to put him in a passion tomorrow," he said thoughtfully. "It won't do to let him fall into a lethargy."

"You will, cousin, you will!" Vincent said, with his mocking smile. "I own, however, that I shall greet the familiar storm-signs with positive relief."

Ten minutes later, Anthea was saying much the same thing. "I never thought I *could* be sorry for Grandpapa," she told her cousins, "but I am, and, what's more, I had rather by far have him cross than stunned!"

"Have no fear!" said Vincent. "Ajax is already considering how best to enrage him."

She smiled, but said: "Well, anything would be preferable to having him so quiet and crushed. He didn't utter one word of reproach to Richmond. But what almost sank me to the floor was his saying to Mama that she had much to forgive him! It was precisely what she had been saying to me, except that she said she never *would* forgive him, so you may imagine my astonishment when she burst into tears on his chest! As a matter of fact I nearly burst into tears myself."

"Dear me, what a lachrymose scene!" remarked Vincent. "I shall go to bed to fortify myself for the inevitable reaction—not to mention the exhausting labours I shall no doubt be expected to undertake in that accursed passage. To think how much I once wanted to discover it, and how much I wish now that it never had been discovered!" He went to the door, and opened it, looking back to say: "My dislike of you is rapidly growing, Ajax: I shouldn't make the smallest attempt to drag you back from that cliff-edge!"

"What cliff-edge?" enquired Anthea, as Vincent left the room.

"Just a joke, lass. Eh, you look tired out!"

"I am tired out, but I couldn't go to bed without coming to thank you, Hugo. I—oh, Hugo, I can't believe yet that it wasn't a nightmare!" she said, walking straight into his arms, and hugging as much of him as she could.

He received her with great willingness, enfolding her in a large and comforting embrace. "Well, that's all it was, think on," he said. "Now, don't *you* start to cry, lass!"

"I won't," she promised. She took his face between her hands, smiling up at him, and saying: "*Noble Ajax, you are as strong, as valiant, as wise, no less noble, much more gentle, and altogether more tractable!*"

"Nay then, love!" expostulated the Major. "Don't be so daft!"

Regency Romances
by Elizabeth Renier
and Sheila Bishop

Just 75c each

064352	Blade of Justice Renier
175216	Durable Fire Bishop
228601	Favorite Sister Bishop
344101	House of Granite Renier
344549	House of Water Renier
363358	If This Be Love Renier
583559	No Hint of Scandal Bishop
658625	Penelope Devereux Bishop
757088	Second Husband Bishop
767400	A Singing in the Woods Renier
791368	Sweet Nightingale Bishop
807305	Tomorrow Comes The Sun Renier
859108	Valley of Secrets Renier
980334	Woman from the Sea Bishop

Available wherever paperbacks are sold or use this coupon.

ace books, (Dept. MM) Box 576, Times Square Station
New York, N.Y. 10036

Please send me titles checked above.

I enclose $.................Add 15¢ handling fee per copy.

Name ....

Address ....

City...................... State.............. Zip.........

Please allow 4 weeks for delivery.   12-72-28C

The Novels of
Dorothy Eden
Just 95c Each

079301	Bride by Candlelight
079731	Bridge of Fear
081836	The Brooding Lake
092569	Cat's Prey
123539	Crow Hollow
133827	The Daughters of Ardmore Hall
141838	The Deadly Travellers
141887	Death is a Red Rose
225425	Face Of An Angel
474031	The Laughing Ghost
484287	Listen to Danger
578039	The Night of the Letter
678532	The Pretty Ones
760710	Shadow Of A Witch
769729	Sleep in the Woods
771238	The Sleeping Bride
866012	The Voice of the Dolls
885541	Whistle for the Crows
943928	Yellow is for Fear

Available wherever paperbacks are sold or use this coupon.

ace books, (Dept. MM) Box 576, Times Square Station
New York, N.Y. 10036

Please send me titles checked above.

I enclose $.................Add 15¢ handling fee per copy.

Name ....

Address ....

City..................... State.............. Zip........
Please allow 4 weeks for delivery.   5 C

GEORGETTE HEYER

026013	April Lady	75c
028910	Arabella	75c
048322	Bath Tangle	95c
110015	A Civil Contract	95c
816413	Cotillion	95c
248260	The Foundling	95c
253013	Friday's Child	95c
302414	The Grand Sophy	75c
698910	The Quiet Gentleman	75c
713016	The Reluctant Widow	75c
778324	Sprig Muslin	75c
793513	Sylvester Or, the Wicked Uncle	75c
816413	The Toll Gate	95c
846667	The Unknown Ajax	95c
861112	Venetia	75c

Table A.2 Cumulative Normal Distribution (continued)

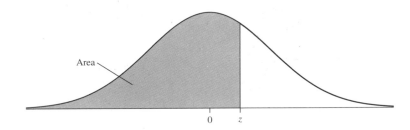

z	0.00	0.01	0.02	0.03	0.04	0.05	0.06	0.07	0.08	0.09
0.0	.5000	.5040	.5080	.5120	.5160	.5199	.5239	.5279	.5319	.5359
0.1	.5398	.5438	.5478	.5517	.5557	.5596	.5636	.5675	.5714	.5753
0.2	.5793	.5832	.5871	.5910	.5948	.5987	.6026	.6064	.6103	.6141
0.3	.6179	.6217	.6255	.6293	.6331	.6368	.6406	.6443	.6480	.6517
0.4	.6554	.6591	.6628	.6664	.6700	.6736	.6772	.6808	.6844	.6879
0.5	.6915	.6950	.6985	.7019	.7054	.7088	.7123	.7157	.7190	.7224
0.6	.7257	.7291	.7324	.7357	.7389	.7422	.7454	.7486	.7517	.7549
0.7	.7580	.7611	.7642	.7673	.7704	.7734	.7764	.7794	.7823	.7852
0.8	.7881	.7910	.7939	.7967	.7995	.8023	.8051	.8078	.8106	.8133
0.9	.8159	.8186	.8212	.8238	.8264	.8289	.8315	.8340	.8365	.8389
1.0	.8413	.8438	.8461	.8485	.8508	.8531	.8554	.8577	.8599	.8621
1.1	.8643	.8665	.8686	.8708	.8729	.8749	.8770	.8790	.8810	.8830
1.2	.8849	.8869	.8888	.8907	.8925	.8944	.8962	.8980	.8997	.9015
1.3	.9032	.9049	.9066	.9082	.9099	.9115	.9131	.9147	.9162	.9177
1.4	.9192	.9207	.9222	.9236	.9251	.9265	.9279	.9292	.9306	.9319
1.5	.9332	.9345	.9357	.9370	.9382	.9394	.9406	.9418	.9429	.9441
1.6	.9452	.9463	.9474	.9484	.9495	.9505	.9515	.9525	.9535	.9545
1.7	.9554	.9564	.9573	.9582	.9591	.9599	.9608	.9616	.9625	.9633
1.8	.9641	.9649	.9656	.9664	.9671	.9678	.9686	.9693	.9699	.9706
1.9	.9713	.9719	.9726	.9732	.9738	.9744	.9750	.9756	.9761	.9767
2.0	.9772	.9778	.9783	.9788	.9793	.9798	.9803	.9808	.9812	.9817
2.1	.9821	.9826	.9830	.9834	.9838	.9842	.9846	.9850	.9854	.9857
2.2	.9861	.9864	.9868	.9871	.9875	.9878	.9881	.9884	.9887	.9890
2.3	.9893	.9896	.9898	.9901	.9904	.9906	.9909	.9911	.9913	.9916
2.4	.9918	.9920	.9922	.9925	.9927	.9929	.9931	.9932	.9934	.9936
2.5	.9938	.9940	.9941	.9943	.9945	.9946	.9948	.9949	.9951	.9952
2.6	.9953	.9955	.9956	.9957	.9959	.9960	.9961	.9962	.9963	.9964
2.7	.9965	.9966	.9967	.9968	.9969	.9970	.9971	.9972	.9973	.9974
2.8	.9974	.9975	.9976	.9977	.9977	.9978	.9979	.9979	.9980	.9981
2.9	.9981	.9982	.9982	.9983	.9984	.9984	.9985	.9985	.9986	.9986
3.0	.9987	.9987	.9987	.9988	.9988	.9989	.9989	.9989	.9990	.9990
3.1	.9990	.9991	.9991	.9991	.9992	.9992	.9992	.9992	.9993	.9993
3.2	.9993	.9993	.9994	.9994	.9994	.9994	.9994	.9995	.9995	.9995
3.3	.9995	.9995	.9995	.9996	.9996	.9996	.9996	.9996	.9996	.9997
3.4	.9997	.9997	.9997	.9997	.9997	.9997	.9997	.9997	.9997	.9998
3.5	.9998	.9998	.9998	.9998	.9998	.9998	.9998	.9998	.9998	.9998
3.6	.9998	.9998	.9999	.9999	.9999	.9999	.9999	.9999	.9999	.9999
3.7 or more	.9999									

Table A.3 Critical Values for the Student's *t* Distribution

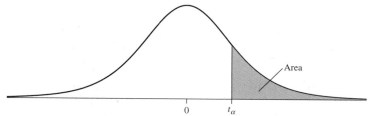

Degrees of Freedom	Area in Right Tail									
	0.40	0.25	0.10	0.05	0.025	0.01	0.005	0.0025	0.001	0.0005
1	0.325	1.000	3.078	6.314	12.706	31.821	63.657	127.321	318.309	636.619
2	0.289	0.816	1.886	2.920	4.303	6.965	9.925	14.089	22.327	31.599
3	0.277	0.765	1.638	2.353	3.182	4.541	5.841	7.453	10.215	12.924
4	0.271	0.741	1.533	2.132	2.776	3.747	4.604	5.598	7.173	8.610
5	0.267	0.727	1.476	2.015	2.571	3.365	4.032	4.773	5.893	6.869
6	0.265	0.718	1.440	1.943	2.447	3.143	3.707	4.317	5.208	5.959
7	0.263	0.711	1.415	1.895	2.365	2.998	3.499	4.029	4.785	5.408
8	0.262	0.706	1.397	1.860	2.306	2.896	3.355	3.833	4.501	5.041
9	0.261	0.703	1.383	1.833	2.262	2.821	3.250	3.690	4.297	4.781
10	0.260	0.700	1.372	1.812	2.228	2.764	3.169	3.581	4.144	4.587
11	0.260	0.697	1.363	1.796	2.201	2.718	3.106	3.497	4.025	4.437
12	0.259	0.695	1.356	1.782	2.179	2.681	3.055	3.428	3.930	4.318
13	0.259	0.694	1.350	1.771	2.160	2.650	3.012	3.372	3.852	4.221
14	0.258	0.692	1.345	1.761	2.145	2.624	2.977	3.326	3.787	4.140
15	0.258	0.691	1.341	1.753	2.131	2.602	2.947	3.286	3.733	4.073
16	0.258	0.690	1.337	1.746	2.120	2.583	2.921	3.252	3.686	4.015
17	0.257	0.689	1.333	1.740	2.110	2.567	2.898	3.222	3.646	3.965
18	0.257	0.688	1.330	1.734	2.101	2.552	2.878	3.197	3.610	3.922
19	0.257	0.688	1.328	1.729	2.093	2.539	2.861	3.174	3.579	3.883
20	0.257	0.687	1.325	1.725	2.086	2.528	2.845	3.153	3.552	3.850
21	0.257	0.686	1.323	1.721	2.080	2.518	2.831	3.135	3.527	3.819
22	0.256	0.686	1.321	1.717	2.074	2.508	2.819	3.119	3.505	3.792
23	0.256	0.685	1.319	1.714	2.069	2.500	2.807	3.104	3.485	3.768
24	0.256	0.685	1.318	1.711	2.064	2.492	2.797	3.091	3.467	3.745
25	0.256	0.684	1.316	1.708	2.060	2.485	2.787	3.078	3.450	3.725
26	0.256	0.684	1.315	1.706	2.056	2.479	2.779	3.067	3.435	3.707
27	0.256	0.684	1.314	1.703	2.052	2.473	2.771	3.057	3.421	3.690
28	0.256	0.683	1.313	1.701	2.048	2.467	2.763	3.047	3.408	3.674
29	0.256	0.683	1.311	1.699	2.045	2.462	2.756	3.038	3.396	3.659
30	0.256	0.683	1.310	1.697	2.042	2.457	2.750	3.030	3.385	3.646
31	0.256	0.682	1.309	1.696	2.040	2.453	2.744	3.022	3.375	3.633
32	0.255	0.682	1.309	1.694	2.037	2.449	2.738	3.015	3.365	3.622
33	0.255	0.682	1.308	1.692	2.035	2.445	2.733	3.008	3.356	3.611
34	0.255	0.682	1.307	1.691	2.032	2.441	2.728	3.002	3.348	3.601
35	0.255	0.682	1.306	1.690	2.030	2.438	2.724	2.996	3.340	3.591
36	0.255	0.681	1.306	1.688	2.028	2.434	2.719	2.990	3.333	3.582
37	0.255	0.681	1.305	1.687	2.026	2.431	2.715	2.985	3.326	3.574
38	0.255	0.681	1.304	1.686	2.024	2.429	2.712	2.980	3.319	3.566
39	0.255	0.681	1.304	1.685	2.023	2.426	2.708	2.976	3.313	3.558
40	0.255	0.681	1.303	1.684	2.021	2.423	2.704	2.971	3.307	3.551
50	0.255	0.679	1.299	1.676	2.009	2.403	2.678	2.937	3.261	3.496
60	0.254	0.679	1.296	1.671	2.000	2.390	2.660	2.915	3.232	3.460
80	0.254	0.678	1.292	1.664	1.990	2.374	2.639	2.887	3.195	3.416
100	0.254	0.677	1.290	1.660	1.984	2.364	2.626	2.871	3.174	3.390
200	0.254	0.676	1.286	1.653	1.972	2.345	2.601	2.839	3.131	3.340
z	0.253	0.674	1.282	1.645	1.960	2.326	2.576	2.807	3.090	3.291
	20%	50%	80%	90%	95%	98%	99%	99.5%	99.8%	99.9%
					Confidence Level					

Essential
STATISTICS

William Navidi
Colorado School of Mines

Barry Monk
Macon State College

Mc
Graw
Hill

Connect
Learn
Succeed™

ESSENTIAL STATISTICS

Published by McGraw-Hill, a business unit of The McGraw-Hill Companies, Inc., 1221 Avenue of the Americas, New York, NY 10020. Copyright © 2014 by The McGraw-Hill Companies, Inc. All rights reserved. Printed in the United States of America. No part of this publication may be reproduced or distributed in any form or by any means, or stored in a database or retrieval system, without the prior written consent of The McGraw-Hill Companies, Inc., including, but not limited to, in any network or other electronic storage or transmission, or broadcast for distance learning.

Some ancillaries, including electronic and print components, may not be available to customers outside the United States.

This book is printed on acid-free paper.

3 4 5 6 7 8 9 0 QVS/QVS 1 0 9 8 7 6 5 4

ISBN 978–0–07–353499–2
MHID 0–07–353499–4

ISBN 978–0–07–760069–3 (Annotated Instructor's Edition)
MHID 0–07–760069–X

Senior Vice President, Products & Markets: *Kurt L. Strand*
Vice President, General Manager, Products & Markets: *Marty Lange*
Vice President, Content Production & Technology Services: *Kimberly Meriwether David*
Director of Development: *Rose Koos*
Managing Director: *Ryan Blankenship*
Brand Manager: *Holly Rhodes*
Director of Digital Content Development: *Emilie J. Berglund*
Developmental Editor: *Ashley Zellmer*
Marketing Managers: *Tim Cote/Kevin Ernzen/John Osgood/Peter A. Vanaria*
Lead Project Manager: *Peggy J. Selle*
Senior Buyer: *Laura Fuller*
Senior Media Project Manager: *Sandra M. Schnee*
Manager, Creative Services: *Michelle D. Whitaker*
Senior Designer: *Laurie B. Janssen*
Cover Image: © *Jezper / Alamy*
Content Licensing Specialist: *Lori Hancock*
Compositor: *Cenveo Publisher Services*
Typeface: *10/12 Times LT Std Roman*
Printer: *Quad/Graphics*

All credits appearing on page or at the end of the book are considered to be an extension of the copyright page.

Library of Congress Cataloging-in-Publication Data

Navidi, William Cyrus, author.
    Essential statistics / William Navidi, Colorado School of Mines [and] Barry Monk, Macon State College.—1 [edition].
        pages cm
    Includes index.
    ISBN 978–0–07–353499–2—ISBN 0–07–353499–4 (hard copy : alk. paper)   1. Mathematical statistics–Textbooks.   I. Monk, Barry (Barry J.), author.   II. Title.
    QA276.12.N386   2014
    519.5–dc23

                                                                                              2012020800

www.mhhe.com

*T*o Catherine, Sarah, and Thomas

—*William Navidi*

*T*o Shaun, Mom, and Dad

—*Barry Monk*

About the Authors

William Navidi   is a professor of Applied Mathematics and Statistics at the Colorado School of Mines in Golden, Colorado. He received a Bachelor's degree in Mathematics from New College, a Master's degree in Mathematics from Michigan State University, and a Ph.D. in Statistics from the University of California at Berkeley. Bill began his teaching career at the County College of Morris, a two-year college in Dover, New Jersey. He has taught mathematics and statistics at all levels, from developmental through the graduate level. Bill has written two Engineering Statistics textbooks for McGraw-Hill. In his spare time, he likes to play racquetball.

Barry Monk   is an Associate Professor of Mathematics and serves as the Department Chair of Mathematics at Macon State College in Macon, Georgia. Barry received a Bachelor of Science in Mathematical Statistics, a Master of Arts in Mathematics specializing in Optimization and Statistics, and a Ph.D. in Applied Mathematics, all from the University of Alabama. Barry has been teaching Introductory Statistics since 1992 in the classroom and online environments. He received the Best Performing Teacher Award from the State of Georgia's core curriculum online, eCore. Barry has a minor in Creative Writing and is a skilled jazz pianist.

Brief Contents

Preface   vi
Index of Applications   xxv

CHAPTER 1   Basic Ideas   1

CHAPTER 2   Graphical Summaries of Data   35

CHAPTER 3   Numerical Summaries of Data   87

CHAPTER 4   Probability   147

CHAPTER 5   Discrete Probability Distributions   193

CHAPTER 6   The Normal Distribution   225

CHAPTER 7   Confidence Intervals   287

CHAPTER 8   Hypothesis Testing   337

CHAPTER 9   Inferences on Two Samples   399

CHAPTER 10   Tests with Qualitative Data   453

CHAPTER 11   Correlation and Regression   479

Preface

This book is designed for an introductory course in statistics. The mathematical prerequisite is basic algebra. In addition to presenting the mechanics of the subject, we have endeavored to explain the concepts behind them, in a writing style as straightforward, clear, and engaging as we could make it. As practicing statisticians, we have done everything possible to ensure that the material presented is accurate and correct. We believe that this book will enable instructors to explore statistical concepts in depth yet remain easy for students to read and understand.

To achieve this goal, we have incorporated a number of useful pedagogical features:

Features

- **Check Your Understanding Exercises:** After each concept is explained, one or more exercises are immediately provided for students to be sure they are following the material. These exercises provide students with confidence that they are ready to go on, or alert them to the need to review the material just covered.

- **Explain It Again:** Many important concepts are reinforced with additional explanation in these marginal notes.

- **Real Data:** Statistics instructors universally agree that the use of real data engages students and convinces them of the usefulness of the subject. A great many of the examples and exercises use real data. Some data sets explore topics in health or social sciences, while others are based in popular culture such as movies, contemporary music, or video games.

- **Integration of Technology:** Many examples contain screenshots from the TI-84 Plus calculator, MINITAB, and Excel. Each section contains detailed, step-by-step instructions, where applicable, explaining how to use these forms of technology to carry out the procedures explained in the text.

- **Interpreting Technology:** Many exercises present output from technology and require the student to interpret the results.

- **Write About It:** These exercises, found at the end of each chapter, require students to explain statistical concepts in their own words.

- **Case Studies:** Each chapter begins with a discussion of a real problem. At the end of the chapter, a case study demonstrates applications of chapter concepts to the problem.

Flexibility

We have endeavored to make our book flexible enough to work effectively with a wide variety of instructor styles and preferences. We cover both the *P*-value and critical value approaches to hypothesis testing, so instructors can choose to cover either or both of these methods.

Instructors differ in their preferences regarding the depth of coverage of probability. A light treatment of the subject may be obtained by covering Section 4.1 and skipping the rest of the chapter. More depth can be obtained by covering Section 4.2.

Supplements

Supplements, including online homework, videos, and PowerPoint presentations, play an increasingly important role in the educational process. As authors, we have adopted a hands-on approach to the development of our supplements, to make sure that they are consistent with the style of the text and that they work effectively with a variety of instructor preferences. In particular, our online homework package offers instructors the flexibility to choose whether the solutions that students view are based on tables or technology, where applicable.

William Navidi
Barry Monk

Setting the Standard for Introductory Statistics

In Navidi/Monk, *Essential Statistics,* we are setting the standard by incorporating the *clarity* students need while maintaining the **statistical accuracy** instructors want, with superior technology integration and digital assets built simultaneously with the text. You will find that the combination of Bill and Barry's years of experience with statistics in the classroom, authorship, and the online teaching environment result in a clear, approachable Introductory Statistics text with precise language and statistics, sound technology integration, and superior digital content. The diamond is to the jewelry industry as Navidi/Monk is to Introductory Statistics… **setting the standard**, a brilliant reflection of what students and instructors need today.

The following outline accents the prominence of the themes of **clarity, quality, and accuracy** throughout Navidi/Monk, *Essential Statistics:*

Clarity

- **Check Your Understanding:** After each concept is explained, one or more exercises are immediately provided for students to be sure they are following the material. These exercises provide students with confidence that they are ready to go on, or alter them to the need to review the material just covered.

- Marginal notes, such as **Explain It Again,** reinforce important concepts throughout the text.

- The authors use a **clear and concise writing style,** providing explanations of concepts and ideas in a conversational tone that students can understand.

Quality

- **Exercise sets** provide a variety of exercises, ranging in difficulty from basic to more challenging exercises. Many exercises reinforce basic skills, while incorporating large numbers that require students to apply concepts to real situations. Real data is utilized throughout the exercise sets to explore areas such as health, social science, or pop culture.

- **Examples** within the text have clear and detailed solutions, and are relevant and interesting to students, while incorporating real data.

- **Technology** is incorporated strategically throughout. Many of the examples in the text present solutions generated by technology. In addition, the authors provide exercises that present technology displays and require students to interpret the results, which encourages conceptual understanding of the material. At the end of each section, the procedures covered in the section are explained, step-by-step with accompanying screenshots, for the TI-84 Plus graphing calculator, MINITAB, and Microsoft Excel.

Accuracy

- Both authors have degrees in Statistics with more than 40 years of experience in teaching and conducting research in statistical methods.

- The authors played a key role in developing the supplements to maintain the same style and voice as the text.

- Feedback and guidance from statistics instructors through reviews, focus groups, and symposia provided the authors and editors with clear direction to ensure the text was meeting the needs of both students and instructors.

Setting the Standard for Clarity Through...

A Logical Organization and Presentation of Concepts

▶ **Objectives** are referenced at the beginning of each section and reintroduced in the margins as they are being discussed to serve as a reminder to students.

> **SECTION 5.1** Random Variables
>
> **Objectives**
> 1. Distinguish between discrete and continuous random variables
> 2. Determine a probability distribution for a discrete random variable
> 3. Describe the connection between probability distributions and populations
> 4. Construct a probability histogram for a discrete random variable
> 5. Compute the mean of a discrete random variable
> 6. Compute the variance and standard deviation of a discrete random variable

▶ **Concepts** are developed in bite-sized pieces, with each concept building upon previous concepts.

> **Objective 3** Describe the connection between probability distributions and populations
>
> **Connection Between Probability Distributions and Populations**
> Statisticians are interested in studying samples drawn from populations. Random variables are important because when an item is drawn from a population, the value observed is the value of a random variable. The probability distribution of the random variable tells how frequently we can expect each of the possible values of the random variable to turn up in the sample. Example 5.5 presents the idea.

A Focused Emphasis on the Comprehension and Understanding of Concepts

▶ **Check Your Understanding** exercises are incorporated throughout each section and allow students to work through complex material one concept at a time. As a result, students can verify that they are grasping the material as they read through the section, rather than waiting until the end of the section exercises to find out.

> **Check Your Understanding**
>
> 5. There are 5000 undergraduates registered at a certain college. Of them, 478 are taking one course, 645 are taking two courses, 568 are taking three courses, 1864 are taking four courses, 1357 are taking five courses, and 88 are taking six courses. Let X be the number of courses taken by a student randomly sampled from this population. Find the probability distribution of X.

▶ **Explain It Again** margin notes reintroduce a potentially confusing concept or definition in simplified terms, shortly after it has been presented in the narrative. These timely refreshers ensure that students fully understand the concept before moving on.

> **Explain It Again**
>
> **A probability distribution describes a population:** We can think of a probability distribution as describing a population. The probability of each value represents the proportion of population items that have that value.

▶ **Caution** boxes are found throughout the margins. They signal students to stop and take note of important information in order to avoid making mistakes as they continue in the section.

> **CAUTION**
>
> Confidence intervals constructed using technology may differ from those constructed by hand due to rounding. The differences are never large enough to matter.

A Clear and Concise Writing Style

The authors focused on developing a clear and concise writing style and accomplished this by:

▶ Incorporating **clear explanations** and definitions in an approachable manner.

> **"**The text is written in a voice that talks to students rather than at students. This approach lends itself to the readability of the text for students.**"**
> —Todd Hendricks, Georgia Perimeter College-Newton Campus

▶ Writing in a **conversational tone** that is clear and to the point.

> **"**The Navidi/Monk textbook is a little more conversational in tone and has explanations in language closer to 'teacher talk'. This makes the chapter easier to read and more student friendly.**"**
> —Jada Hill, Richland College

A Clean and Easy-to-Follow Layout

▶ Pages are **uncluttered and easy to follow,** allowing students to navigate through text in an efficient manner. The margins are thoughtfully used to reference or highlight important, relevant information, without being overused.

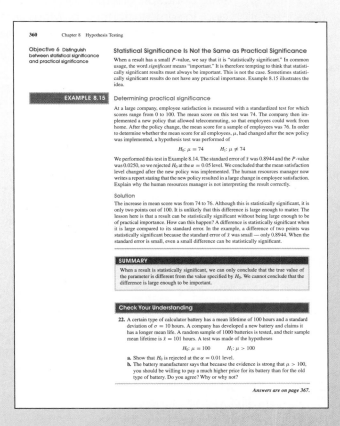

Setting the Standard for Quality Through...

Comprehensive and Diverse Exercise Sets

Exercise sets provide a variety of exercise types, ranging in difficulty from basic to more challenging exercises.

▶ **Practicing the Skills** exercises allow students to practice the basic concepts presented in the section.

▶ **Extending the Concepts** exercises require students to synthesize concepts discussed in the current section and, in some instances, previous sections, to ensure that they can apply what they've learned to new situations.

▶ Throughout the text, the authors focus on ensuring that the exercises are *modern and relevant*, with the intent of keeping students engaged.

▶ Exercises with *self-contained data* are included when possible, allowing students to complete their computation without having to reference data found on a different page. Students are then asked to *interpret* the data to ensure that they have full understanding of the concept.

Practicing the Skills

11. Find the P-value for the following values of the test statistic t, sample size n, and alternate hypothesis H_1. If you use Table A.3, you may specify that P is between two values.
   a. $t = 2.336$, $n = 5$, H_1: $\mu > \mu_0$
   b. $t = 1.307$, $n = 18$, H_1: $\mu \neq \mu_0$
   c. $t = -2.864$, $n = 51$, H_1: $\mu < \mu_0$
   d. $t = -2.031$, $n = 3$, H_1: $\mu \neq \mu_0$

12. Find the P-value for the following values of the test statistic t, sample size n, and alternate hypothesis H_1. If you use Table A.3, you may specify that P is between two values.
   a. $t = -1.584$, $n = 19$, H_1: $\mu \neq \mu_0$
   b. $t = -2.473$, $n = 41$, H_1: $\mu < \mu_0$
   c. $t = 1.491$, $n = 30$, H_1: $\mu \neq \mu_0$
   d. $t = 3.635$, $n = 4$, H_1: $\mu > \mu_0$

Extending the Concepts

33. **Using z instead of t:** When the sample size is large, some people treat the sample standard deviation s as if it were the population standard deviation σ, and use the standard normal distribution rather than the Student's t distribution, to find a critical value. Assume that a right-tailed test will be made with a sample of size 100 from a normal population, using the $\alpha = 0.05$ significance level.
   a. Find the critical value under the assumption that σ is known.
   b. In fact, σ is unknown. How many degrees of freedom should be used for the Student's t distribution?
   c. What is the probability of rejecting H_0 when it is true if the critical value in part (a) is used? You will need technology to find the answer.

Working with the Concepts

49. **Facebook:** A study by the Web metrics firm Hitwise showed that in August 2008, the mean time spent per visit to Facebook was 19.5 minutes. Assume the standard deviation is $\sigma = 8$ minutes. Suppose that a simple random sample of 100 visits in August 2009 has a sample mean of $\bar{x} = 21.5$ minutes. A social scientist is interested in knowing whether the mean time of Facebook visits has increased.
   a. State the appropriate null and alternate hypotheses.
   b. Compute the value of the test statistic.
   c. State a conclusion. Use the $\alpha = 0.05$ level of significance.

---

21. **Weight loss:** In a study to determine whether counseling could help people lose weight, a sample of people experienced a group-based behavioral intervention, which involved weekly meetings with a trained interventionist for a period of six months. The following data are the numbers of pounds lost for 14 people, based on means and standard deviations given in the article.

| 18.2 | 24.8 | 3.9 | 20.0 | 17.1 | 8.8 | 13.4 |
| 17.3 | 33.8 | 29.7 | 8.5 | 31.2 | 19.3 | 15.1 |

Source: *Journal of the American Medical Association* 299:1139–1148

   a. Following is a boxplot for these data. Is it reasonable to assume that the conditions for performing a hypothesis test are satisfied? Explain.

   b. If appropriate, perform a hypothesis test to determine whether the mean weight loss is greater than 10 pounds. Use the $\alpha = 0.05$ level of significance. What do you conclude?

Clear and Easy-to-Follow Examples

▶ The authors provide students with **interesting and relevant examples** that include clear instruction on how to work through the problem.

> **EXAMPLE 8.8**   Performing a hypothesis test with the critical value method
>
> The Energy Information Administration reported that the mean price of a gallon of regular grade gasoline in the city of Los Angeles in July 2010 was $3.15. A recently taken simple random sample of 50 gas stations in Los Angeles had an average price of $3.10 for a gallon of regular grade gasoline. Assume that the standard deviation of prices is $0.15. An economist is interested in determining whether the mean price is less than $3.15. Use the critical value method to perform a hypothesis test at the $\alpha = 0.05$ level of significance.
>
> **Solution**
>
> We first check the assumptions. We have a simple random sample, the sample size is large ($n > 30$), and the population standard deviation σ is known. The assumptions are satisfied.
>
> **Step 1: State H_0 and H_1.** The null hypothesis says that the mean price is $3.15. Therefore, we have

▶ Solutions to examples are broken down into **easy-to-follow steps** that allow students to digest the material.

> **EXAMPLE 8.16**   Perform a hypothesis test
>
> In a recent medical study, 76 subjects were placed on a low-fat diet. After 12 months, their sample mean weight loss was $\bar{x} = 2.2$ kilograms, with a sample standard deviation of $s = 6.1$ kilograms. Can we conclude that the mean weight loss is greater than 0? Use the $\alpha = 0.05$ level of significance.
> Source: *Journal of the American Medical Association* 297:969–977
>
> **Solution**
>
> We first check the assumptions. We have a simple random sample. The sample size is 76, so $n > 30$. The assumptions are satisfied.
>
> **Step 1: State H_0 and H_1.** The issue is whether the mean weight loss μ is greater than 0. So the null and alternate hypotheses are
>
> $$H_0: \mu = 0 \qquad H_1: \mu > 0$$
>
> Note that we have a right-tailed test, because we are particularly interested in whether the diet results in a weight loss.

Superior Technology Integration

▶ In each section, examples of how to use the TI-84 Plus graphing calculator, Microsoft Excel, and MINITAB to solve problems are provided.

Step 1. Press **STAT** and highlight the **TESTS** menu.
Step 2. Select **ZInterval** and press **ENTER** (Figure A). The ZInterval menu appears.
Step 3. For **Inpt**, select the **Stats** option and enter the values of σ, $\bar{x}$, and n. For Example 8.4, we use $\sigma = 15$, $\bar{x} = 67.30$, and $n = 100$.
Step 4. In the **C-Level** field, enter the confidence level. For Example 8.4, we use 0.98 (Figure B).
Step 5. Highlight **Calculate** and press **ENTER** (Figure C).

Note that if the raw data are given, the **ZInterval** command may be used by selecting **Data** as the **Inpt** option and entering the location of the data as the **List** option (Figure D).

Figure A

Figure B

Figure C

Figure D

▶ The authors incorporate exercises that require students to **view a technology display and interpret the results.** This encourages conceptual understanding of the material being presented.

59. Interpreting calculator display: The following TI-84 Plus display presents the results of a hypothesis test.

a. What are the null and alternate hypotheses?
b. What is the value of the test statistic?
c. What is the *P*-value?
d. Do you reject H_0 at the $\alpha = 0.05$ level?
e. Do you reject H_0 at the $\alpha = 0.01$ level?

Setting the Standard for Accuracy

Pledge to Accuracy

As textbook publishers, we at McGraw-Hill acknowledge the importance that is placed on accuracy, in both the textbook and the supplements that accompany a textbook. With this in mind, we've taken the following steps to ensure that *Essential Statistics* has been developed with accuracy at the forefront of our efforts:

Written by Statisticians with Decades of Experience

Both William (Bill) Navidi and Barry Monk have backgrounds in Statistics. Bill received his Ph.D. in Statistics from the University of California at Berkeley. Barry received his Master of Arts in Mathematics specializing in Optimization and Statistics, and a Ph.D. in Applied Mathematics from the University of Alabama.

Collectively, the authors have over 40 years of experience in the field of Statistics, in both teaching and conducting research.

Author-Developed Supplements

The authors helped to develop a multitude of supplements that are available with *Essential Statistics*. By creating supplements with author involvement, we ensure that a consistent and accurate voice is maintained from the textbook to each individual resource.

▶ **Connect Statistics Hosted by ALEKS Corp.®**   Barry Monk served as Lead Digital Contributor in the development of the stepped-out solutions and guided feedback for the algorithms found in McGraw-Hill's online homework platform—Connect Statistics Hosted by ALEKS Corp. In this way, the authors ensured that each algorithm stayed true to its original intent and maintained the same "voice" used throughout the text.

▶ **Graphing Calculator, Microsoft Excel, and MINITAB Manuals**   The authors oversaw the creation of the Graphing Calculator, Microsoft Excel, and MINITAB manuals, which provide students with detailed guidance on how to utilize each type of technology to solve problems. Examples from the text are referenced, and the author proofread each manual to ensure that a voice consistent with the text was maintained.

▶ **Student and Instructor Solution Manuals**   Both manuals were derived from author approved stepped-out solutions approved by the author to be included in Connect Statistics Hosted by ALEKS Corp.

▶ **Lecture and Exercise Videos**   The authors produced lecture videos that introduce concepts, definitions, formulas, and problem-solving procedures to help students comprehend topics presented throughout the text. They also created exercise videos that show students how to work through selected exercises from the text, following the solution methodology employed in the text.

▶ **PowerPoint Presentations**   Lecture PowerPoints, created with input from the authors, walk through key concepts that would be presented in an in-class lecture setting.

▶ **McGraw-Hill LearnSmart**   The authors developed content for McGraw-Hill LearnSmart, an adaptive learning system designed to help students learn faster, study more efficiently, and retain more knowledge for greater success. LearnSmart assesses a student's knowledge of course content through a series of adaptive questions. It pinpoints concepts the student does not understand and maps out a personalized study plan for success. This innovative study tool also has features that allow instructors to see exactly what students have accomplished and a built-in assessment tool for graded assignments.

Feedback from Statistics Instructors

Paramount to the development of *Essential Statistics* was the invaluable feedback provided by the instructors from around the country who reviewed the manuscript over the course of the 4 years the text was in development.

▶ Over 150 instructors reviewed the manuscript from the first draft through the final manuscript, providing feedback to the authors at each stage of development.

▶ Laurel Tech accuracy checked every worked example and exercise in the text numerous times, both in the final phase of the manuscript and in the page proof stages.

▶ Focus groups and symposia were conducted with instructors from around the country to provide feedback to editors and the authors to ensure the direction of the text was meeting the needs of students and instructors.

A Special Thanks to All of the Symposia and Focus Group Attendees Who Helped Shape Essential Statistics

Andrea Adlman, *Ventura College*

Diane Benner, *Harrisburg Area Community College*

Denise Brown, *Collin County College-Spring Creek*

Don Brown, *Macon State College*

Mary Brown, *Harrisburg Area Community College*

Gerald Busald, *San Antonio College*

Robert Cappetta, *College of DuPage*

Joe Castillo, *Broward College*

Ivette Chuca, *El Paso Community College*

James Condor, *State College of Florida*

Hema Deshmukh, *Mercyhurst College*

Charles Wayne Ehler, *Anne Arundel Community College*

Franco Fedele, *University of West Florida*

Robert Fusco, *Broward College*

Wojciech Golik, *Lindenwood University*

Tim Grant, *Southwestern Illinois College*

Todd Hendricks, *Georgia Perimeter College*

Mary Hill, *College of DuPage*

Steward Huang, *University of Arkansas-Fort Smith*

Laura Iossi, *Broward College*

Maryann Justinger, *Erie Community College–South Campus*

Joseph Karnowski, *Norwalk Community College*

Esmarie Kennedy, *San Antonio College*

Lynette Kenyon, *Collin College–Plano*

Raja Khoury, *Collin College–Plano*

Alexander Kolesnik, *Ventura College*

Holly Kresch, *Diablo Valley College*

Dan Kumpf, *Ventura College*

Erica Kwiatkowski-Egizio, *Joliet Junior College*

Corey Manchester, *Grossmont Community College*

Penny Morris, *Polk State College*

Cindy Moss, *Skyline College*

Kris Mudunuri, *Long Beach City College*

Linda Myers, *Harrisburg Area Community College*

Ronald Palcic, *Johnson County Community College*

Blanche Presley, *Macon State College*

Ahmed Rashed, *Richland College*

Ginger Rowell, *Middle Tennessee State University*

Sudipta Roy, *Kanakee Community College*

Laura Shick, *Clemson University*

Larry Shrewsbury, *Southern Oregon University*

John Trimboli, *Macon State College*

Jo Tucker, *Tarrant County College*

Dave Vinson, *Pellissippi State Community College*

Daniel Wang, *Central Michigan University*

Acknowledgments

We are indebted to many people for contributions at every stage of development. Colleagues and students who reviewed the evolving manuscript provided many valuable suggestions. In particular, John Trimboli contributed exercises and helped to develop the technology manuals, Don Brown assisted with the PowerPoint slides, and Mary Wolfe helped create the supplemental video presentations. Ashlyn Munson contributed a number of exercises, and Tim Chappell played an important role in the development of our digital content.

The staff at McGraw-Hill has been extremely capable and supportive. Project Manager Peggy Selle was always patient and helpful. Emilie Berglund was superb in directing the development of our digital content. We owe a debt of thanks to Kevin Ernzen, for his creative marketing and diligence in spreading the word about our book. We appreciate the guidance of our editors, Ryan Blankenship, Adam Fischer, Michelle Smith, and Ashley Zellmer, whose input has considerably improved the final product.

William Navidi
Barry Monk

Manuscript Review Panels

Over 150 instructors reviewed the various drafts of manuscript to give feedback on content, design, pedagogy, and organization that was used to guide the direction of the text.

Alisher Abdullayev, *American River College*
Andrea Adlman, *Ventura College*
Olcay Akman, *Illinois State University*
Raid Amin, *University of West Florida*
Diana Asmus, *Greenville Technical College*
John Avioli, *Christopher Newport University*
Robert Bass, *Gardner-Webb University*
Robbin Bates-Yelverton, *Park University*
Lynn Beckett-Lemus, *El Camino College*
Diane Benner, *Harrisburg Area Community College*
Abraham Biggs, *Broward College*
Wes Black, *Illinois Valley Community College*
Gregory Bloxom, *Pensacola State College*
Donna Brouilette, *Georgia Perimeter College*
Allen Brown, *Wabash Valley College*
Denise Brown, *Collin County Community College*
Don Brown, *Macon State College*
Mary Brown, *Harrisburg Area Community College*
Jennifer Bryan, *Oklahoma Christian University*
William Burgin, *Gaston College*
Gerald Busald, *San Antonio College*
David Busekist, *Southeastern Louisiana University*
Lynn Cade, *Pensacola State College*
Elizabeth Carrico, *Illinois Central College*
Connie Carroll, *Guilford Technical Community College*
Joseph Castillo, *Broward College*

Linda Chan, *Mount San Antonio College & Pasadena City College*
Ayona Chatterjee, *University of West Georgia*
Chand Chauhan, *Indiana University Purdue University Fort Wayne*
Pinyuen Chen, *Syracuse University*
Askar Choudhury, *Illinois State University*
Lee Clendenning, *State College Gainesville*
James Condor, *State College of Florida-Manatee*
Natalie Creed, *Gaston College*
John Curran, *Eastern Michigan University*
John Daniels, *Central Michigan University*
Larry Dumais, *American River College*
Christina Dwyer, *State College of Florida-Manatee*
Wayne Ehler, *Anne Arundel Community College*
Mark Ellis, *Central Piedmont Community College*
Franco Fedele, *University of West Florida*
Art Fortgang, *Southern Oregon University*
Thomas Fox, *Cleveland State Community College*
Robert Fusco, *Broward College*
David Garth, *Truman State University*
Sharon Giles, *Grossmont Community College*
Carrie Grant, *Flagler College*
Delbert Greear, *Gainesville State College*
Jason Greshman, *Nova Southeastern University*
David Gurney, *Southeastern Louisiana University*

Chris Hail, *Union University-Jackson*

Phillip Harris, *Illinois Central College*

James Harrington, *Adirondack Community College*

Matthew He, *Nova Southeastern University*

Mary Beth Headlee, *State College of Florida-Manatee*

James Helmreich, *Marist College*

Todd Hendricks, *Georgia Perimeter College-Newton Campus*

Jada Hill, *Richland College*

Mary Hill, *College of DuPage*

William Huepenbecker, *Bowling Green State University-Firelands*

Patricia Humphrey, *Georgia Southern University*

Nancy Johnson, *State College of Florida-Manatee*

June Jones, *Macon State College*

Maryann Justinger, *Erie Community College-South Campus*

Joseph Karnowski, *Norwalk Community College*

Joseph Kazimir, *East Los Angeles College*

Esmarie Kennedy, *San Antonio College*

Lynette Kenyon, *Collin College*

Gary Kersting, *North Central Michigan College*

Raja Khoury, *Collin College*

Heidi Kiley, *Suffolk County Community College-Selden*

Daniel Kim, *Southern Oregon University*

Ann Kirkpatrick, *Southeastern Louisiana University*

John Klages, *County College of Morris*

Karon Klipple, *San Diego City College*

Alex Kolesnik, *Ventura College*

Erica Kwiatkowski-Egizio, *Joliet Junior College*

William Langston, *Finger Lakes Community College*

Jiawei Liu, *Georgia State University*

Fujia Lu, *Endicott College*

Timothy Maharry, *Northwestern Oklahoma State University*

Aldo Maldonado, *Park University*

Kenneth Mann, *Catawba Valley Community College*

James Martin, *Christopher Newport University*

Erin Martin-Wilding, *Parkland College*

Amina Mathias, *Cecil College*

Mark McFadden, *Montgomery County Community College*

Karen McKarnin, *Allen Community College*

Penny Morris, *Polk Community College*

B. K. Mudunuri, *Long Beach City College-CalPoly Pomona*

Linda Myers, *Harrisburg Area Community College*

Miroslaw Mystkowski, *Gardner-Webb University*

Shai Neumann, *Brevard Community College*

Karen Orr, *Roane State Community College*

Richard Owens, *Park University*

Irene Palacios, *Grossmont College*

Luca Petrelli, *Mount Saint Mary's University*

Blanche Presley, *Macon State College*

Robert Prince, *Berry College*

Richard Puscas, *Georgia Perimeter College*

Ramaswamy Radhakrishnan, *Illinois State University*

Leela Rakesh, *Central Michigan University*

Gina Reed, *Gainesville State College*

Andrea Reese, *Daytona State College-Daytona Beach*

Jason Rosenberry, *Harrisburg Area Community College*

Yolanda Rush, *Illinois Central College*

Loula Rytikova, *George Mason University*

Vicki Schell, *Pensacola State College*

Carol Schoen, *University of Wisconsin-Eau Claire*

Pali Sen, *University of North Florida*

Rosa Seyfried, *Harrisburg Area Community College*

Larry Shrewsbury, *Southern Oregon University*

Abdallah Shuaibi, *Truman College*

Rick Silvey, *University of Saint Mary*

Russell Simmons, *Brookhaven College*

Peggy Slavik, *University of Saint Mary*

Karen Smith, *University of West Georgia*

Pam Stogsdill, *Bossier Parish Community College*

Susan Surina, *George Mason University*

Victor Swaim, *Southeastern Louisiana University*

Scott Sykes, *University of West Georgia*

John Trimboli, *Macon State College*

Barbara Tucker, *Tarrant County College South East*

Steven Forbes Tuckey, *Jackson Community College*

Christopher Turner, *Pensacola State College*

Dave Vinson, *Pellissippi State Community College*

Joseph Walker, *Georgia State University*

Xiaohong Wang, *Central Michigan University*

Jason Willis, *Gardner-Webb University*

Fuzhen Zhang, *Nova Southeastern University*

Yichuan Zhao, *Georgia State University*

Deborah Ziegler, *Hannibal LaGrange College*

Bashar Zogheib, *Nova Southeastern University*

Stephanie Zwyghuizen, *Jamestown Community College*

Connect Statistics Hosted by ALEKS Corp.

Built By Today's Educators, For Today's Students

Fewer clicks means more time for you...

Change assignment dates right from the home page.

Teaching multiple sections? Easily move from one to another.

Edit, print, and view assignments in just one click.

...and your students.

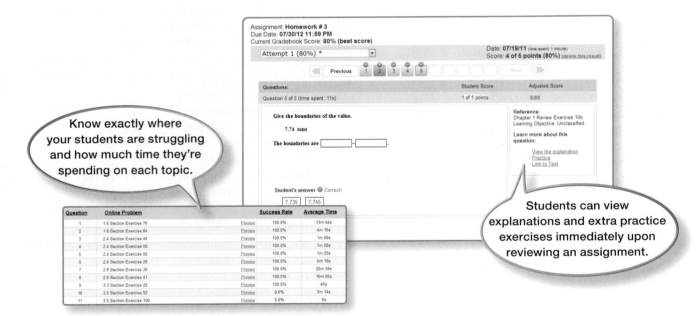

Know exactly where your students are struggling and how much time they're spending on each topic.

Students can view explanations and extra practice exercises immediately upon reviewing an assignment.

Quality Content For Today's Online Learners

Online Exercises were carefully selected and developed to provide a seamless transition from textbook to technology.

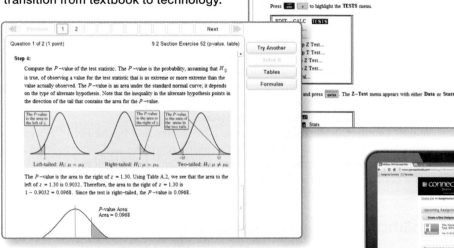

For consistency, the guided solutions match the style and voice of the original text as though the author is guiding the students through the problems.

Multimedia eBook includes access to a variety of media assets and a place to highlight and keep track of class notes

ALEKS Corporation's experience with algorithm development ensures a commitment to accuracy and a meaningful experience for students to demonstrate their understanding with a focus towards online learning.

The ALEKS® Initial Assessment is an artificially intelligent (AI), diagnostic assessment that identifies precisely what a student knows. Instructors can then use this information to make more informed decisions on what topics to cover in more detail with the class.

ALEKS is a registered trademark of ALEKS Corporation.

Supplements

Multimedia Supplements

Connect   www.connectstatistics.com

McGraw-Hill's Connect is a complete online homework system for mathematics and statistics. Instructors can assign textbook-specific content from over 40 McGraw-Hill titles as well as customize the level of feedback students receive, including the ability to have students show their work for any given exercise. Assignable content includes an array of videos and other multimedia tools along with algorithmic exercises, providing study tools for students with many different learning styles.

Within Connect, a diagnostic assessment tool powered by ALEKS® is available to measure student preparedness and provide detailed reporting and personalized remediation. Connect also helps ensure consistent assignment delivery across several sections through a course administration function and makes sharing courses with other instructors easy.

LearnSmart   www.mhlearnsmart.com

McGraw-Hill LearnSmart is an adaptive learning system designed to help students learn faster, study more efficiently, and retain more knowledge for greater success. In statistics, concepts drive the math and LearnSmart's conceptual probes help improve students' understanding of lectures and online homework assignments. LearnSmart assesses a student's knowledge of course content through a series of adaptive questions. It pinpoints concepts the student does not understand and maps out a personalized study plan for success. This innovative study tool also has features that allow instructors to see exactly what students have accomplished and a built-in assessment tool for graded assignments.

ALEKS   www.aleks.com

ALEKS® ALEKS (Assessment and LEarning in Knowledge Spaces) is a dynamic online learning system for mathematics education, available over the Web 24/7. ALEKS assesses students, accurately determines their knowledge, and then guides them to the material that they are most ready to learn. With a variety of reports, Textbook Integration Plus, quizzes, and homework assignment capabilities, ALEKS offers flexibility and ease of use for instructors.

- ALEKS uses artificial intelligence to determine exactly what each student knows and is ready to learn. ALEKS remediates student gaps and provides highly efficient learning and improved learning outcomes.
- ALEKS is a comprehensive curriculum that aligns with syllabi or specified textbooks. When it is used in conjunction with McGraw-Hill texts, students also receive links to text-specific videos, multimedia tutorials, and textbook pages.
- Textbook Integration Plus allows ALEKS to be automatically aligned with syllabi or specified McGraw-Hill textbooks with instructor-chosen dates, chapter goals, homework, and quizzes.
- ALEKS with AI-2 gives instructors increased control over the scope and sequence of student learning. Students using ALEKS demonstrate a steadily increasing mastery of the content of the course.
- ALEKS offers a dynamic classroom management system that enables instructors to monitor and direct student progress toward mastery of course objectives.

ALEKS Prep for Statistics

ALEKS Prep for Statistics can be used during the beginning of the course to prepare students for future success and to increase retention and pass rates. Backed by two decades of National Science Foundation–funded research, ALEKS interacts with students much as a human tutor, with the ability to precisely assess a student's preparedness and provide instruction on the topics the student is ready to learn.

ALEKS Prep for Statistics

- Assists students in mastering core concepts that should have been learned prior to entering the present course.
- Frees up lecture time for instructors, allowing more time to focus on current course material and not review material.
- Provides up to six weeks of remediation and intelligent tutorial help to fill in students' individual knowledge gaps.

TEGRITY   http://tegritycampus.mhhe.com

Tegrity Campus is a service that makes class time available all the time by automatically capturing every lecture in a searchable format for students to review when they study and complete assignments. With a simple one-click start and stop process, you capture all computer screens and corresponding audio. Students replay any part of any class with easy-to-use browser-based viewing on a PC or Mac.

Educators know that the more students can see, hear, and experience class resources, the better they learn. With Tegrity Campus, students quickly recall key moments by using Tegrity Campus's unique search feature. This search helps students efficiently find what they need, when they need it, across an entire semester of class recordings. Help turn all your students' study time into learning moments immediately supported by your lecture.

To learn more about Tegrity, watch a 2-minute Flash demo at

http://tegritycampus.mhhe.com

Electronic Textbook

CourseSmart is a new way for faculty to find and review eTextbooks. It's also a great option for students who are interested in accessing their course materials digitally and saving money. CourseSmart offers thousands of the most commonly adopted textbooks across hundreds of courses from a wide variety of higher education publishers. It is the only place for faculty to review and compare the full text of a textbook online, providing immediate access without the environmental impact of requesting a print exam copy. At CourseSmart, students can save up to 50% off the cost of a print book, reduce the impact on the environment, and gain access to powerful Web tools for learning including full text search, notes and highlighting, and email tools for sharing notes between classmates. **www.CourseSmart.com**

MegaStat®

MegaStat® is a statistical add-in for Microsoft Excel, handcrafted by J. B. Orris of Butler University. When MegaStat is installed, it appears as a menu item on the Excel menu bar and allows you to perform statistical analysis on data in an Excel workbook.

Computerized Test Bank (CTB) Online (instructors only)

The computerized test bank contains a variety of questions, including true/false, multiple-choice, short-answer, and short problems requiring analysis and written answers. The testing material is coded by type of question and level of difficulty. The Brownstone Diploma® system enables you to efficiently select, add, and organize questions, such as by type of question or by level of difficulty. It also allows for printing tests along with answer keys as well as editing the original questions, and it is available for Windows and Macintosh systems. Printable tests and a print version of the test bank can also be found on the website.

Videos

Author-produced lecture videos introduce concepts, definitions, formulas, and problem-solving procedures to help students better comprehend the topic at hand. Exercise videos illustrate the authors working through selected exercises, following the solution methodology employed in the text. These videos are closed-captioned for the hearing-impaired, are subtitled in Spanish, and meet the Americans with Disabilities Act Standards for Accessible Design.

SPSS Student Version for Windows

A student version of SPSS statistical software is available with copies of this text. Consult your McGraw-Hill representative for details.

Instructor's Solution Manual

Derived from author-approved Connect solutions, this manual contains detailed solutions to all of the problems in the text.

Guided Student Notes   Guided notes provide instructors with the framework of day-by-day class activities for each section in the book. Each lecture guide can help instructors make more efficient use of class time and can help keep students focused on active learning. Students who use the lecture guides have the framework of well-organized notes that can be completed with the instructor in class.

Data Disc   Data sets from selected exercises have been pre-populated into MINITAB, TI-Graph Link, Excel, SPSS, and comma-delimited ASCII formats for student and instructor use. These files are available on the text's website as well as on the Data CD included with the text.

MINITAB 14 Manual

With guidance from the authors, this manual includes material from the book to provide seamless use from one to the other, providing additional practice in applying the chapter concepts while using the MINITAB program.

TI-84 Plus Graphing Calculator Manual

This friendly, author-influenced manual teaches students to learn about statistics and solve problems by using this calculator while following each text chapter.

Excel Manual

This workbook, specially designed to accompany the text by the authors, provides additional practice in applying the chapter concepts while using Excel.

Print Supplements

Annotated Instructor's Edition (instructors only)

The Annotated Instructor's Edition contains answers to all exercises. The answers to most questions are printed in blue next to each problem. Answers not appearing on the page can be found in the Answer Appendix at the end of the book.

Student's Solution Manual

Derived from author-approved Connect solutions, this manual contains detailed solutions to all odd-numbered text problems and answers to all Quizzes, Reviews, and Case Study problems found at the end of each chapter.

Contents

Index of Applications   xxv

CHAPTER **1** **Basic Ideas   1**

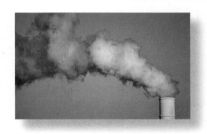

1.1 Sampling   2
1.2 Types of Data   12
1.3 Design of Experiments   18
1.4 Bias in Studies   26
   Chapter 1 Summary   30
   Chapter Quiz   30
   Review Exercises   31
   Case Study   32

CHAPTER **2** **Graphical Summaries of Data   35**

2.1 Graphical Summaries for Qualitative Data   36
2.2 Frequency Distributions and Their Graphs   48
2.3 More Graphs for Quantitative Data   63
2.4 Graphs Can Be Misleading   74
   Chapter 2 Summary   80
   Chapter Quiz   80
   Review Exercises   81
   Case Study   85

CHAPTER **3** **Numerical Summaries of Data   87**

3.1 Measures of Center   88
3.2 Measures of Spread   104
3.3 Measures of Position   124
   Chapter 3 Summary   140
   Chapter Quiz   140
   Review Exercises   141
   Case Study   144

CHAPTER **4** Probability 147

4.1 Basic Ideas 148
4.2 The Addition Rule and the Rule of Complements 157
4.3 Conditional Probability and the Multiplication Rule 166
4.4 Counting 178
Chapter 4 Summary 186
Chapter Quiz 187
Review Exercises 188
Case Study 190

CHAPTER **5** Discrete Probability Distributions 193

5.1 Random Variables 194
5.2 The Binomial Distribution 208
Chapter 5 Summary 218
Chapter Quiz 219
Review Exercises 220
Case Study 221

CHAPTER **6** The Normal Distribution 225

6.1 The Standard Normal Curve 226
6.2 Applications of the Normal Distribution 240
6.3 Sampling Distributions and the Central Limit Theorem 251
6.4 The Central Limit Theorem for Proportions 258
6.5 The Normal Approximation to the Binomial Distribution 265
6.6 Assessing Normality 271
Chapter 6 Summary 281
Chapter Quiz 282
Review Exercises 283
Case Study 284

CHAPTER **7** Confidence Intervals 287

7.1 Confidence Intervals for a Population Mean, Standard Deviation Known 288
7.2 Confidence Intervals for a Population Mean, Standard Deviation Unknown 306
7.3 Confidence Intervals for a Population Proportion 317
7.4 Determining Which Method to Use 329
Chapter 7 Summary 332
Chapter Quiz 332
Review Exercises 333
Case Study 335

CHAPTER **8** Hypothesis Testing   337

8.1 Basic Principles of Hypothesis Testing   338

8.2 Hypothesis Tests for a Population Mean, Standard Deviation Known   343

8.3 Hypothesis Tests for a Population Mean, Standard Deviation Unknown   367

8.4 Hypothesis Tests for Proportions   380

8.5 Determining Which Method to Use   391

Chapter 8 Summary   393
Chapter Quiz   394
Review Exercises   395
Case Study   397

CHAPTER **9** Inferences on Two Samples   399

9.1 Inference About the Difference Between Two Means: Independent Samples   400

9.2 Inference About the Difference Between Two Proportions   418

9.3 Inference About the Difference Between Two Means: Paired Samples   433

Chapter 9 Summary   446
Chapter Quiz   447
Review Exercises   448
Case Study   451

CHAPTER **10** Tests with Qualitative Data   453

10.1 Testing Goodness-of-Fit   453

10.2 Tests for Independence and Homogeneity   462

Chapter 10 Summary   473
Chapter Quiz   473
Review Exercises   474
Case Study   476

CHAPTER **11** Correlation and Regression   479

11.1 Correlation   480

11.2 The Least-Squares Regression Line   492

11.3 Inference on the Slope of the Regression Line   503

11.4 Inference About the Response   519

Chapter 11 Summary   526
Chapter Quiz   527
Review Exercises   528
Case Study   531

Appendix A Tables   A-1

Appendix B TI-84 PLUS Stat Wizards   B-1

Answers to Selected Exercises (Student edition only)   SA-1

Answers to Selected Exercises (Instructor's edition only)   IA-1

Index   I-1

Index of Applications

Agricultural/gardening/farming applications

effect of herbicide on bean plants, 450
egg diameters, 274
farmland area versus total land area, 485
fertilizer types and vegetable/fruit yields, 25, 342, 416
seed germination probabilities, 270
tree heights, 250
volume of trees versus diameters, 528
weights of Hereford bulls, 255–256
weights of pumpkins, 330

Archaeological applications

ages of skeletons, 474
mummy's curse at King Tut's tomb, 415

Automotive/motor vehicle applications

age of driver and accident locations, 423–424
auto insurance risk categories, 156
break pad lifetime, 437–438, 444
car battery lifetimes, 283
car color possibilities, 178–179
car inspection failures, 217
car repair estimates, 273
car repair probabilities, 164–165, 177, 214–215, 270
cars and light trucks sold, 41
commuting to work, 137
driver's license exam attempts, 188
drivers test scores, 121
effect of temperature on truck emissions, 444
emissions test failures, 392
fuel efficiency of convertibles and sports cars, 118
gas mileage, 31, 257, 333, 339–340, 433–434
gas mileage of Hummer H2, 316
gas prices in selected countries and cities, 100, 118, 347–348
highway mileage ratings for compact cars, 85
license plate possibilities, 179, 185
new car sales by brand name, 47
octane rating for gasoline, 334
particulate emissions frequencies at high altitudes, 66–67, 139, 334, 430
particulate emissions frequencies at sea level, 139
particulate emissions frequencies per gallon of fuel, 62, 71
paved streets versus number of cars in cities, 527
percentage of cars going faster than 75 mph, 251
percent of small cars sold from random selection, 163
premium gas effect on maintenance costs, 447–448
probability for low air pressure in tires, 205
probability of purchasing black SUV, 177
rental car makes, mode of, 94
retail prices for BMW autos, 61, 71
satisfaction with new car, 264
speed of cars and noise of street, 517–518, 524
tire lifetimes, 250
tires and fuel economy, 445
weight of trucks and fuel economy, 528

Aviation applications

delayed flight probabilities, 217
departure and arrival delays in U.S., 527
getting a seat on airline, 270–271
noisy airport effect on health, 30
types of aircraft landing at small airport, 38

Behavioral study applications

age at which children first form words, 315
counseling to help people lose weight, 378
enjoyment of competitive situations, 386
holiday shopping behavior, 448
hours spent sleeping, 334–335
low-fat and low-carb diet effectiveness, 415
nicotine patch to quit smoking, 389
phonics instruction for children, 315
rats in maze, 60
reaction time after drinking alcohol, 438–439
smoking prohibition in public, 471
weight loss diet, 366–369, 380, 415

Beverage applications

active breweries in selected states, 99–100, 119
amounts of beverage in cans, 299, 378–379
carbohydrates in espresso beverages, 138
coffee maker prices, 141
drinking and driving, 11, 101
reaction time after drinking alcohol, 438–439
salaries of college professors versus beer consumption, 486
volume of beverage in a can, 250

Biology/life science applications

birth weights of newborn babies, 121, 249
blood types of humans, 44, 188, 217
body mass index and diabetes, 416
butterfly lifespan versus wingspan, 491, 502, 517, 524
cholesterol levels for adults, 257, 430
days of week when children likely to be born, 456
diastolic blood pressure, 248–249
fish lengths, 249
fish weights, 280, 342
flounder lengths, 137, 409
half-life of drugs in human body, 316
height and length of forearm, 528
height and weight for adult males, 123, 124

heights for adult females, 124, 241
heights of adult male humans, 244, 251
heights of fathers and sons, 517, 524
heights of male college students, 59–60
heights of mothers and daughters, 527
lengths of newborn babies, 116
pregnancy lengths in humans, 242–243
rats in maze, 60
systolic blood pressure, 115
waist size of men aged 20–29, 335
weight of mice, 299
weights of baby boys, 217–218, 249, 270, 303, 339, 378
weights of baby girls, 315
weights of chickens, 249
weights of large dogs, 342
weights of male college students, 66

Business applications

adults who work two jobs, 263
advertising spending, 101, 143
age discrimination at work, 471
amount of money saved by U.S. residents, 78
annual earnings of family practitioners, 378
annual income, 139, 448
annual income of college graduates, 304–305
annual returns for selected investment stocks, 120
annual salaries and raises, 103
auto insurance risk categories, 156
banking hours survey, 29
bus schedule changes, 11
CD sales decline, 77–78, 83–84
cell phone features, 11
coffee maker prices, 141
commercials on TV, 283
companies planning to increase workforce, 328
compensations for chief executives, 316
computer sales growth, 78
computer use at work, 420–421
corporate profits, 142, 144
credit card annual interest rates, 333
credit scores, 378
day and night shift choices, 185
delivery trucks load weights, 283
digital music sales growth, 83–84
digital music sales retail values, 84
Dow Jones industrial average by year, 68–69
ease of finding new job, 221
electricity costs, 123, 249
email spam received at company computers, 388
executive salaries, 388–389
federal income tax mean amounts, 257, 283
federal support amounts for arts programs, 141–142
firms with more than 15 employees, 324
flextime choices, 448

fuel efficiency of convertibles and sports cars, 118

gas mileage, 31, 257, 333, 339–340, 433–434

gas prices in selected countries and cities, 100, 118, 347–348

gender and management jobs, 177

HDTV prices, 316

health insurance benefits, 327

house prices in selected metropolitan areas, 100–101, 364

income tax for high incomes, 458–459

inflation rate versus unemployment rate, 531–532

insurance premium prices, 203–204, 207

Internet monthly costs, 121

job interview probabilities, 169, 176, 183–184

job satisfaction, 354–355, 360, 396

job security, 46

life insurance ages and policy charges, 190–191

magazine subscription rates, 101

magnitude of stock market drop, 78

marketing survey questions, 17–18, 323

mortgage interest rates, 315–316, 490, 501–502

music sales by type, 47

new car sales by manufacturer, 47

new product rating survey, 472

nonfarm workers who are government employees, 263

number of days between bills mailed out and payment made, 121, 156

on-site day care, 11

percentage not paying income tax, 264

percentage of people owning a business, 393

plasma TV vendor market shares, 82

profit expected value, 203

purchase return rates at clothing store, 220

quality control, 11, 144, 176–177, 207

retail prices for BMW autos, 61

salaries of recent college graduates, 282

sales commissions, 449

sales of computer types, 38

service occupation and gender, 177

social networks for job recruiting, 389

starting salaries, 141

start-up business becoming profitable or not, 188, 207

stock prices, 101, 102, 120, 142, 304, 390, 395

stressful jobs, 218, 270

tall men as business executives, 353–354

technology firm salaries, 62, 71

time employed in present job, 314

time needed to complete tasks, 280

travel time of business trips, 342

unemployment rate in U.S. by year, 72

utility company survey, 30

visitors to popular websites, 40

weekly earnings, 264

workers who changed jobs in past 6 months, 328

Chemicals/chemistry applications

carbon monoxide concentration, 317

computer chip coatings, 142

half-life of drugs in human body, 316

Computer applications. *See* Electronics/computer applications

Construction/home improvement/home purchases and sales applications

concrete block testing, 328

concrete expansion over time, 518, 525

concrete strength, 444

house prices in selected metropolitan areas, 100–101, 120

rivet lengths, 143

size of house and selling price, 480–482, 492–493, 495–498

square feet of U.S. homes, 393

Crime applications

effectiveness of police department, 29

illegal music downloads, 263

murder rate by population numbers in U.S. cities, 61

number of police versus number of crimes, 491

taxicabs and crime, 25

violent crime rates, 461

Earth sciences applications

geyser eruption timetable, 61

silver ore amounts in rocks, 62

Education/school applications

Advanced Placement tests taken and their scores, 220–221

age at which children first form words, 315

age of college student randomly chosen, 162

ages of students at public high school, 202

age versus education level, 491

annual income of college graduates, 304–305

arithmetic teaching method effectiveness, 365

attitudes toward school, 304

choosing books to study from, 185

choosing required courses, 189

college enrollment of males and females, 72–73

college graduates working at home, 327

college seniors finding jobs, 324

college tuition and fees, 378

computer programming class for middle school, 305

computer programming teaching method, 426

computer use in math classes, 403–404

confidence in educational institutions, 156

course choice probabilities, 188

daily student absences, 129, 131, 133, 476

dropout rates of boys and girls, 177

dropouts and GED attainment, 177

drug use in high school, 29, 69

educational attainment, 46

educational level and income, 500

education level of women, 475

education levels and gender of persons over 25, 168–169

effectiveness of math skills improvement program, 334

effect of hip-hop on music education, 322

electronic-based assignments and homework, 31

enrollment and acceptance probabilities, 271

exam grade percentiles, 250–251

exam score median/mean, 90, 123

executive committee selection for student government, 166–168, 185

extracurricular activities of college freshmen, 197

Facebook use in college, 283, 395

females as business majors, 189

final grades of randomly chosen students, 163, 165, 188

freshmen majoring in STEM disciplines, 263–264

gender bias in college admissions, 476–478

GPA for random sample of college students, 305, 365

grade and gender probabilities, 165

grade distribution, 461

heights of selected students, 59–60, 103

homework assignment scores, 103

hours of sleep per night for freshmen, 316

hours spent on hybrid college course, 315

hours spent studying, 81, 141, 250

impression of online learning courses, 314

improving SAT scores with coaching, 343–345, 348–349

IQ test scores, 294, 299, 342

listening to music while studying, 187

math and reading assessment, 484–485, 495

math SAT test scores, 257, 303, 327, 364, 366

math skills of second-graders, 363–364

mean age of college students, 255

multiple choice exam questions, 179, 207, 216–217

number of text messages sent by high school students, 95, 111–112

numbers enrolled in grades 1 through 8, 206–207

numbers of courses taken in college, 198

numbers of pets of school children, 62

numbers of siblings of school children, 62, 94

parents saving for children's college, 393

parking on campus, 11

percentage of elementary students being girls, 283

percentage of students graduating, 263

percentile exam scores, 138

percent of students not completing homework, 82

phonics instruction for children, 315

placement exam for college, 277

probability of attending college, 170, 217, 268–269

probability of choosing math major, 153, 329

quality of cafeteria food in college, 221

quartile exam scores, 138

quiz scores, 82–83

reading improvement, 11, 436

reading levels of fourth-graders, 221

reading proficiency of elementary school children, 327

reading program enrollment, 431

reading scores on test, 280

reading skills improvement, 320
salaries of college professors versus beer consumption, 486
SAT writing scores and years of study in English, 529
semester pretest and end test, 448
shoe size versus vocabulary scores, 486
standardized test scores, 136–137, 339
starting salaries of recent college graduates, 282, 341
student loan debt, 263
student satisfaction with college, 390
students with runny nose or sore throat, 165
study time for some college majors, 463–464
teacher salaries, 393
time spent watching TV, 294
true/false exam questions, 156, 179, 201, 216, 462
vocabulary size and student heights, 25
vocabulary teaching method effectiveness, 298
weights of male college students, 66
years of education for adults, 355

Elderly individuals applications

heart attacks by gender and age, 189
height and age of older men, 364
hospital survey, 11
longevity and life insurance, 32
sleep apnea in ages over 65, 327

Electronics/computer applications

ages of video gamers, 46, 389
BlackBerry smartphone prices, 303–304
CD sales decline, 77–78, 83–84
cell phone features, 11
cell phone ringtones, 16
cell phone usage exclusively by year, 81
computer chip coatings, 142
computer chips manufactured on cheaper machines, 432
computer crash frequencies, 375, 416
computer memory choices, 179
computer password possibilities, 185, 188
computer prices, 140
computer programming teaching method, 426
computer purchase types, 165
computer sales growth, 78
computer speeds, 444
cost of cable TV, 389
customers who plan to buy another Android, 326
dampness and electrical connections, 317, 328, 426–427
defective cell phone batteries, 164, 219–220
defective circuits, 205
defective components, 392, 430–431
defective computer chips, 262, 322
defective pixels in computer monitor, 199, 201–202
digital music sales growth, 83–84
digital music sales retail values, 84
electronic component repairs, 334
email spam received at company computers, 388
frequency of backing up hard drives, 46
Google as primary search engine, 164, 217, 270, 389

illegal music downloads, 263
Internet monthly costs, 121
Internet usage, 415
iPod sales by year, 45
lifetime of electronic components, 304
music sales by type, 47
number of children with cell phones, 389
online news site visiting, 47
plasma TV vendor market shares, 82
playback times of MP3 players, 98–99, 138
playlist selection probabilities, 176
popular Facebook applications, 99
product and delivery satisfaction of e-store, 29
reconstructing table after printer failure, 475
recycled silicon wafers, 144–145
sales of computer types, 38
technology firm salaries, 62, 71
teenagers playing video games on cell phones, 263
time cell phone keeps a charge, 333
top ten PC games, 17
video games sold, 44, 45
video running times, 282
virus and worm probabilities, 165
visitors to popular websites, 40

Entertainment applications. *See also Gambling applications*

ages of Grammy award winners, 257
cable news watching, 397
CD sales decline, 77–78
choosing marbles in a jar, 188
coin toss, 152
critical strikes in *World of War* computer game, 327
effect of video games on music education, 319–322
Facebook rating by students, 380–382
female audience for movie, 261
German child and recognizing SpongeBob, 155, 177
Google as primary search engine, 164
Internet usage, 415
Modern Warfare 2 game, 214
movie running times, 315
percentage of teenagers playing video games, 389
playback times of MP3 players, 98–99, 138
pool ball ordering, 188
popular Facebook applications, 99
recreation fee increase, 11
roller coaster design, 257
target shooting probabilities, 177
television viewing habits, 11
theaters showing *Night at the Museum,* 527
time spent per visit to Facebook, 363
time spent playing video games, 60–61
time spent watching TV, 378
top-grossing movies, 17, 71–72
top-rated TV programs, 99, 119–120
top ten PC games, 11
YouTube video viewing times, 314–315

Environmental applications

air pollution and respiratory problems, 25, 32–33
ambient temperature and evaporation rate of water, 518

ammonium contamination of water wells, 251
benzene in water at gas field, 395, 406–407, 416
carbon dioxide emissions per person, 490, 501
carbon monoxide concentration, 317
cost of environmental restoration, 333–334
days of excessive air pollution, 206
effect of temperature on truck emissions, 444
geyser eruption timetable, 61
global warming, 16
hazardous waste sites, 137
humidity and ozone levels, 519, 525
interest in environmental issues, 389
lead in drinking water, 327, 364–365
leaking underground storage tanks, 335
mercury pollution in lake, 393
ozone pollution and lung function, 425–426
PCB contamination of rivers, 334
pollution from new wood stoves, 335–336

Exercise applications. *See Sports/exercise/fitness applications*

Farming applications. *See Agricultural/gardening/farming applications*

Food applications

active breweries in selected states, 99–100, 119
caffeine content of coffee, 342
calories in fat, 510, 519–522
calories in hamburgers from fast-food restaurants, 98, 135
calories in protein, 517, 524
cereal box weights, 258, 295–297, 315, 339, 340–341
cracker box weights, 396
dessert choices, 188
eating fruits and vegetables and developing colon cancer, 25
egg and milk prices, 489, 500
food expenditures in U.S., 44, 73, 79–80
ice cream flavors, 185
menu test marketing by restaurants, 176
mineral content of kale, 316
mineral content of spinach, 315
number of dinner customers at restaurant, 379
pizza topping choices, 185
sugar content of syrup, 396

Gambling applications

annual income before and after winning lottery, 91–92, 103
betting on horses, 185
blackjack, 186
card drawing, 172–174
choosing marbles in a jar, 188
coin toss, 152, 155, 156, 170, 174–176, 187, 195, 209–210, 216, 259–260, 266–268, 271
Colorado Lottery Lotto, 186
craps betting, 207, 221
die rolling, 156, 157, 164, 172, 175, 188, 216, 251–252, 455–456, 462, 473

Georgia Cash-4 Lottery, 150
Georgia Fantasy Lottery, 186
lottery, 177, 207, 221, 461
pool ball ordering, 188
Powerball fairness, 461, 475–476
raffle, 11
roulette wheel spinning, 155, 156, 202–203
slot machine playing, 188
Texas hold'em card game, 185–186

Gardening applications.
See **Agricultural/gardening/
farming applications**

Genetics/gender applications

age at which women first marry, 79
birth order and intelligence, 415
birth rate of women aged 15–44, 84
DNA locations on chromosome, 472
dominant or recessive gene possibilities, 176
education levels and gender of persons over
    25, 168–169
gender and management jobs, 177
gender bias in college admissions, 476–478
gender probabilities for children in family,
    151, 196–197
gene combination possibilities, 185
height relative to gender of humans, 124
inheriting cystic fibrosis, 151–152
live births to women by age, 55
Mendel's laws of heredity, 215, 270
number of children a woman has, 198–199
percentage of elementary students being
    girls, 283
political party and gender, 165
prize winners and gender possibilities, 183
probability that newborn baby is boy,
    153–154
service occupation and gender, 177
sickle-cell anemia probabilities, 221
weights of boys versus girls, 416
women never married, by age group, 79

**Health/healthcare
applications.** *See also*
**Medical/medical research/
alternative medicine
applications**

asthma patients in hospitals, 157
blood pressure in males and females, 137
blood pressure probabilities, 196, 218, 270
calories in hamburgers from fast-food
    restaurants, 98, 135
carbohydrates in espresso beverages, 138
childhood obesity, 430
cholesterol levels in men, 430
cholesterol levels in women, 137
choosing a doctor, 389
cold medication effectiveness, 25
coronary bypass surgery and age, 217
days with pain before seeking treatment, 206
drug concentration in bloodstream over time,
    280
eating fruits and vegetables and developing
    colon cancer, 25
exercise and heart rate, 450
FEV for 10-year-old boys, 364
fluoridation and tooth decay, 31
formaldehyde and respiratory problems, 25

headache drug testing, 11
heavy weights of children, 364
heights of U.S. women aged 20–29, 98
hospital survey, 11
lead in drinking water, 327, 364–365
living to certain age intervals, 190–191
longevity and life insurance, 32
low-fat and low-carb diet effectiveness, 415
nicotine patch to quit smoking, 389
noisy airport effect on health, 30
ozone pollution and lung function, 425–426
pain reliever effectiveness, 24, 422
percentage of adults visiting a doctor, 262
percentage of adults with high blood
    pressure, 264
pulse rate measuring, 272
radiation and lung cancer, 24
reasons for hospital admissions, 45
respiratory health and air pollution, 22, 24
restaurant health inspections, 415
smoking/drinking and liver cancer, 22
smoking prohibition in public, 471
smoking-related deaths, 157
stressful jobs, 218
systolic blood pressure, 115
trust placed in doctors, 81–82
types of health insurance, 166
weight loss diet, 366–369, 380, 415

Library/book applications

ages of library patrons, 165
best fiction books, 16
book arrangements on shelf, 189–190
choosing books to study from, 185
favorite news sources, 102
favorite type of book of library patrons, 102
magazine subscription rates, 101
online dictionary lookups, 17
patrons buying book and paying with credit
    card, 188
reading improvement, 11
time required to review submissions for
    publication, 121
travel magazine subscriptions, 47

Life sciences applications.
See **Biology/life sciences
applications**

Manufacturing applications

accuracy of can/bag-filling machines, 311,
    378–379
accuracy of laboratory scale, 295, 444
assembly line failure rates, 474
assembly line quality, 475
battery lifetimes, 110, 143, 258, 294 283,
    360
battery testing, 107–108
calibration of scales, 342, 364
ceramic tiles with surface defects, 264
computer chips manufactured on cheaper
    machines, 432
defective components/items, 177, 189, 199,
    205, 207, 280, 284, 392, 448
drill lifetimes, 333
drying time of paint versus an additive, 529
efficient precision manufacturing, 250, 304
flaws in aluminum parts, 165
impurities in aluminum cans, 280

lightbulb lifetimes, 283, 311
oven thermostat testing, 272
quality control, 144, 176–177, 207
recycled silicon wafers, 144–145
rivet lengths, 143
shoe leather testing, 274
steel rod length sampling, 300
strength of aluminum cans, 284–285
time cookies spend in store before being
    bought, 333

**Medical/medical research/
alternative medicine
applications.** *See also* **Health/
healthcare applications**

annual earnings of family practitioners, 378
antifungal drug testing, 379
beryllium disease, 471
blood pressure drug testing, 408–409,
    439–440
blood pressure measuring, 491, 502, 517,
    524
cholesterol levels and age, 519, 525
choosing a doctor, 389
cold medication effectiveness, 25
colonoscopy to prevent cancer, 431
coronary bypass surgery and age, 217
disease testing outcome probabilities, 178
DNA locations on chromosome, 472
drug concentration in bloodstream over time,
    280, 379
drugs to lower cholesterol, 303, 444–445
drugs to prevent heart attack, 430, 467–468
eating fruits and vegetables and developing
    colon cancer, 25
exercising and blood pressure, 24–25
FEV for 10-year-old boys, 364
foot temperatures and diabetes, 490, 501
generic drug testing, 371–372
half-life of drugs in human body, 316
headache drug testing, 11
heart attacks by gender and age, 189
heart rates of babies with nonsmoking/
    smoking mothers, 25
house size and recovery from heart attacks,
    25
improvement after surgery at hospitals, 475
inheriting cystic fibrosis, 151–152
kidney transplants for ages under 18, 264
knee replacements resulting in
    complications, 327–328
lengths of hospital stay, 365–366
lengths of newborn babies, 116
medications administered by syringe, 283
new drug testing, 408–409, 439–440,
    443–444
new versus standard treatment for heart
    failure, 451–452
pain reliever effectiveness, 24, 316, 443–444
patient safety in hospitals, 72
random sampling of bypass surgery patients,
    300
recovery time after surgery, 90–91, 143, 415,
    450
reducing volume of stomach to cure
    diabetes, 389
Salk polio vaccine trials, 26
sickle-cell anemia probabilities, 221

side effects from medical procedure, 284
sleep apnea in ages over 65, 327
starting salaries for physicians, 392
stent use requiring additional treatment, 395
surgery time for hip replacement, 315
systolic blood pressure, 115, 408–409
trust placed in doctors, 81–82

Miscellaneous applications
age and residence probabilities, 171
ages of residents of selected town, 102, 121
annual income before and after winning lottery, 91–92, 103
annual incomes, 139, 448
apartment rent, 143, 257, 339, 396–397
children who own cell phones, 327, 431
committee member choosing, 181, 185
credit card charges, 305
customer spending at restaurant, 339, 342
days with pain before seeking treatment, 206
elevator design, 258
event attendees and random selection for prizes, 182–183
event probabilities, 155
Facebook use in college, 283
false fire alarms by month, 461
family size, 471
favorite news sources, 102
federal support amounts for arts programs, 141–142
free T-shirts to randomly sampled students, 174
frequency of first digits in probabilities, 221–223
hours spent on Internet for ages 18–22, 310
hours spent relaxing each day, 206
hours spent sleeping, 334–335
hours watching TV, 253
household electric bills, 249
household energy efficiency, 528
household income mean and median, 98, 103
household income versus energy consumed, 529
households that reduce water consumption, 333
households with dog or cat as pet, 188
households with DVR, 210–213
households with TV sets, 257
income of parents and IQs of their children, 500
IQ score percentiles, 245
job security, 46
ladies' shoe sizes, 393
languages spoken at home, 47
lightbulb selection, 183
listening to songs in random order, 189
mall shopping, 11
mean annual income, 258
mean population of U.S., 316–317
measuring a tennis ball, 142–143
Mensa IQ scores, 245
menu test marketing by restaurants, 176
music sales by type, 47
mutually exclusive events, 164
new parking structure survey, 333
number of boys in family, 200–201, 474
number of children a woman has, 156–157, 198–199

number of children with cell phones, 389
number of customers in line at checkout, 205
number of dinner customers at restaurant, 379
number of occupants in carpool, 205–206
number of PCs in households, 303
number of people in households, 305
number of teenagers sending text messages, 206, 217
number of TV sets in household, 396
numbers of cars in households, 197
numbers of children of U.S. presidents, 67
numbers of pets in families, 219
numbers of pets of school children, 62
numbers of siblings of school children, 62
numbers who read daily newspaper, 382–383
on-site day care, 11
opinion survey, 11
owners and renters among town population, 152–153
percentage not paying income tax, 264
percentage of population aged 65 and over, 112–113
personal incomes per capita of U.S. states, 102
populations of largest U.S. cities, 130
poverty rates for children in Colorado, 82
prize-winning at fast-food restaurant, 260
proportions living in geographic regions of U.S., 461–462
random-digit and landline dialing for surveys, 29
recycled newspaper collection amounts, 273
refrigerator prices, 379
refugees admitted to U.S., 41–42
sentence completion choices, 186
sizes of households, 395–396
smoke detector probabilities, 174
soap weights, 144
spending habits survey, 11
technology firm salaries, 62
time employed in present job, 314
time for fluorescent bulb to reach brightness, 242
traffic light color probabilities, 164
types of employment for U.S. residents, 39
types of occupation and educational level, 161
unemployment rate in U.S. by year, 72
vacancy rate in apartments, 72
visitors to popular websites, 40
YouTube video viewing times, 314–315

Motor vehicles applications. See Automotive/motor vehicles applications

Nuclear applications
hazardous waste sites, 137
nuclear power survey, 29
nuclear reactors in selected countries, 138
radon level in homes, 249

Political applications
abortion voting preferences, 462
ages at death of British monarchs, 83
ages at death of U.S. presidents, 83
Congress' handling of economy, 29
did Congress accomplish more/less/same, 42

economic conditions survey, 16, 328
effectiveness of women in government, 329
election reform survey, 29
electoral votes cast by states, 74
federal budget spending, 44–45
government funding for arts and culture, 489, 500–501
health-care survey, 32
heights of U.S. presidents, 316
interest in environmental issues, 389
Literary Digest election polling, 29
military spending in U.S., 72
number of words in inaugural addresses, 61–62, 138
numbers of children of U.S. presidents, 67
numbers of female and male senators, 79
numbers of freshmen elected to U.S. House, 83
optimism about economic status, 431, 462, 472–473
political party and gender, 165, 176
satisfaction with presidential candidates, 328
support for bond issue, 154
voter preferences, 11, 270, 283–284, 390
voter sampling, 174, 187, 216, 262, 270, 322–323
voting for bonds, 448–450
voting for government support for higher education, 158–160
voting for mayor/governor, 155, 390, 448

Psychological applications
enjoyment of competitive situations, 386
multiple-choice questions order, 29, 179, 207, 216–217
rats in maze, 60, 275
true/false exam questions, 156, 179, 201, 216
visual and auditory reaction times, 518, 525

Safety applications
cell phone usage and driving, 31
drinking and driving, 11, 101
effectiveness of police department, 29
patient safety in hospitals, 72
seat belt effectiveness, 29
smoking prohibition in public, 471
smoking-related deaths, 157

School applications. See Education/school applications

Sociological applications
age at which women first marry, 79
ages of video gamers, 46
birth rate of women aged 15–44, 84
Facebook rating by students, 380–382
interest in educational issues related to museum visiting, 471
Internet usage, 415
job satisfaction, 156
languages spoken at home, 47
opinion survey, 11
populations of continents, 46
poverty rates for children in Colorado, 82
refugees admitted to U.S., 41–42
social networks for job recruiting, 389
spending habits survey, 11
tall men as business executives, 353–354

tattoos in ages 18–29, 389
time spent watching TV, 378
women never married, by age group, 79

Sports/exercise/fitness applications

ages of tennis and golf tournament winners, 71
baseball pitching, 156
baseball runs scored, 395
baseball salaries, 73–74, 131–132, 138–139
batting averages, 60
bench press weights lifted, 447
bowling score probabilities, 177
bowling scores, 103, 282
drag racer stopping probabilities, 189
exercise and heart rate, 450
exercising and blood pressure, 24–25

football player weights/heights, 101, 118–119, 489–490, 501
football turnover margin and wins, 528–529
gold medals won by Michael Phelps, 98
gold medals won by U.S. in Olympics, 73
lifeguard duty roster choices, 181
measuring a tennis ball, 142–143
Olympic athletes representing U.S. and Canada, 162–163
proportion of people who watched Super Bowl, 334
running a race outcomes, 179–180
soccer goals scored, 207
weight of person versus weightlifting capacity, 498

Travel applications

commuting distances, 258
distances traveled to work, 62, 258, 378

traffic congestion worsening, 333
traffic speed at intersection, 409
travel magazine subscriptions, 47

Weather applications

annual precipitation/rainfall, 116, 125, 134–135, 335
daily rainfall, 328
daily temperatures, 71, 72, 130
mean temperature, 122
monthly rainfall, 127, 139
quartile rainfall, 127–128
rain probabilities, 189, 220, 221
snowfall amounts, 73, 129, 431
temperature ranges, 105, 256–257
temperature variance, 106–107
warming trends in Washington, D.C., 397–398
wind speeds in San Francisco, 137

Basic Ideas

Introduction

How does air pollution affect your health? Over the past several decades, scientists have become increasingly convinced that air pollution is a serious health hazard. The World Health Organization has estimated that air pollution causes 2.4 million deaths each year. The health effects of air pollution have been investigated by measuring air pollution levels and rates of disease, then using statistical methods to determine whether higher levels of pollution lead to higher rates of disease.

Many air pollution studies have been conducted in the United States. For example, the town of Libby, Montana, was the focus of a recent study of the effect of particulate matter — air pollution that consists of microscopic particles — on the respiratory health of children. As part of this study, parents were asked to fill out a questionnaire about their children's respiratory symptoms. It turned out that children exposed to higher levels of particulate pollution were more likely to exhibit symptoms of wheezing, as shown in the following table.

Level of Exposure	Percentage with Symptoms
High	8.89%
Low	4.56%

The rate of symptoms was almost twice as high among those exposed to higher levels of pollution. At first, it might seem easy to conclude that higher levels of pollution cause symptoms of wheezing. However, drawing accurate conclusions from information like this is rarely that simple. The case study at the end of this chapter will present more complete information and will show that additional factors must be considered.

SECTION 1.1 | Sampling

Objectives

1. Construct a simple random sample
2. Determine when samples of convenience are acceptable
3. Describe stratified sampling, cluster sampling, systematic sampling, and voluntary response sampling
4. Distinguish between statistics and parameters

In the months leading up to an election, polls often tell us the percentages of voters that prefer each of the candidates. How do pollsters obtain this information? The ideal poll would be one in which every registered voter were asked his or her opinion. Of course, it is impossible to conduct such an ideal poll, because it is impossible to contact every voter. Instead, pollsters contact a relatively small number of voters, usually no more than a couple of thousand, and use the information from these voters to predict the preferences of the entire group of voters.

The process of polling requires two major steps. First, the voters to be polled must be selected and interviewed. In this way the pollsters collect information. In the second step, the pollsters analyze the information to make predictions about the upcoming election. Both the collection and the analysis of the information must be done properly for the results to be reliable. The field of statistics provides appropriate methods for the collection, description, and analysis of information.

DEFINITION

Statistics is the study of procedures for collecting, describing, and drawing conclusions from information.

The polling problem is typical of a problem in statistics. We want some information about a large group of individuals, but we are able to collect information on only a small part of that group. In statistical terminology, the large group is called a **population**, and the part of the group on which we collect information is called a **sample**.

DEFINITION

- A **population** is the entire collection of individuals about which information is sought.
- A **sample** is a subset of a population, containing the individuals that are actually observed.

Explain It Again

Why do we draw samples?
It's usually impossible to examine every member of a large population. So we select a group of a manageable size to examine. This group is called a **sample**.

Ideally, we would like our sample to represent the population as closely as possible. For example, in a political poll, we would like the proportions of voters preferring each of the candidates to be the same in the sample as in the population. Unfortunately, there are no methods that can guarantee that a sample will represent the population well. The best we can do is to use a method that makes it very likely that the sample will be similar to the population. The best sampling methods all involve some kind of random selection. The most basic, and in many cases the best, sampling method is the method of **simple random sampling**.

Objective 1 Construct a simple random sample

Simple Random Sampling

To understand the nature of a simple random sample, think of a lottery. Imagine that 10,000 lottery tickets have been sold, and that 5 winners are to be chosen. What is the fairest way to choose the winners? The fairest way is to put the 10,000 tickets in a drum, mix them thoroughly, then reach in and draw 5 tickets out one by one. These 5 winning tickets are a simple random sample from the population of 10,000 lottery tickets. Each ticket is equally likely to be one of the 5 tickets drawn. More importantly, each collection of 5 tickets that can be formed from the 10,000 is equally likely to comprise the group of 5 that is drawn.

DEFINITION

A **simple random sample** of size n is a sample chosen by a method in which each collection of n population items is equally likely to make up the sample, just as in a lottery.

Since a simple random sample is analogous to a lottery, it can often be drawn by the same method now used in many lotteries: with a computer random number generator. Suppose there are N items in the population. We number the items 1 through N. Then we generate a list of random integers between 1 and N, and choose the corresponding population items to make up the simple random sample.

EXAMPLE 1.1

Choosing a simple random sample

There are 300 employees in a certain company. The Human Resources department wants to draw a simple random sample of 20 employees to fill out a questionnaire about their attitudes toward their jobs. Describe how technology may be used to draw this sample.

Solution

Step 1: Make a list of all 300 employees, and number them from 1 to 300.
Step 2: Use a random number generator on a computer or a calculator to generate 20 random numbers between 1 and 300. The employees who correspond to these numbers make up the sample.

EXAMPLE 1.2

Determining whether a sample is a simple random sample

A physical education professor wants to study the physical fitness levels of students at her university. There are 20,000 students enrolled at the university, and she wants to draw a sample of size 100 to take a physical fitness test. She obtains a list of all 20,000 students, numbered from 1 to 20,000. She uses a computer random number generator to generate 100 random integers between 1 and 20,000, then invites the 100 students corresponding to those numbers to participate in the study. Is this a simple random sample?

Solution

Yes, this is a simple random sample because any group of 100 students would have been equally likely to have been chosen.

EXAMPLE 1.3

Determining whether a sample is a simple random sample

The professor in Example 1.2 now wants to draw a sample of 50 students to fill out a questionnaire about which sports they play. The professor's 10:00 A.M. class has 50 students. She uses the first 20 minutes of class to have the students fill out the questionnaire. Is this a simple random sample?

Solution

No. A simple random sample is like a lottery, in which each student in the population has an equal chance to be part of the sample. In this case, only the students in a particular class had a chance to be in the sample.

EXAMPLE 1.4

In a simple random sample, all samples are equally likely

To play the Colorado Lottery Lotto game, you must select six numbers from 1 to 42. Then lottery officials draw a simple random sample of six numbers from 1 to 42. If your six numbers match the ones in the simple random sample, you win the jackpot. Sally plays the lottery and chooses the numbers 1, 2, 3, 4, 5, 6. Her friend George says that this isn't a good choice, since it is very unlikely that a random sample will turn up the first six numbers. Is he right?

Solution

No. It is true that the combination 1, 2, 3, 4, 5, 6 is unlikely, but every other combination is equally unlikely. In a simple random sample of size 6, every collection of six numbers is equally likely (or equally unlikely) to come up. So Sally has the same chance as anyone to win the jackpot.

EXAMPLE 1.5

Using technology to draw a simple random sample

Use technology to draw a simple random sample of five employees from the following list.

1. Dan Aaron	11. Johnny Gaines	21. Jorge Ibarra	31. Edward Shingleton
2. Annie Bienh	12. Carlos Garcia	22. Maurice Jones	32. Michael Speciale
3. Oscar Bolivar	13. Julio Gonzalez	23. Jared Kerns	33. Andrew Steele
4. Dominique Bonnaud	14. Jacqueline Gordon	24. Kevin King	34. Neil Swain
5. Paul Campbell	15. James Graves	25. Frank Lipka	35. Sherry Thomas
6. Jeffrey Carnahan	16. Ronald Harrison	26. Carl Luther	36. Shequiea Thompson
7. Joel Chae	17. Andrew Huang	27. Laverne Mitchell	37. Barbara Tilford
8. Dustin Chen	18. Anthony Hunter	28. Zachary Quesada	38. Jermaine Tryon
9. Steven Coleman	19. Jonathan Jackson	29. Donnell Romaine	39. Lizbet Valdez
10. Richard Davis	20. Bruce Johnson	30. Gary Sanders	40. Katelyn Yu

Solution

We will use the TI-84 Plus graphing calculator. The step-by-step procedure is presented in the Using Technology section on page 9. We begin by choosing a **seed**, which is a number that the calculator uses to get the random number generator started. Display (a) shows the seed being set to 21. (The seed can be chosen in almost any way; this number was chosen by looking at the seconds display on a digital watch.) Display (b) presents the five numbers in the sample.

(a)   (b)

The simple random sample consists of the employees with numbers 27, 39, 30, 35, and 17. These are Laverne Mitchell, Lizbet Valdez, Gary Sanders, Sherry Thomas, and Andrew Huang.

CAUTION

If you use a different type of calculator, a different statistical package, or a different seed, you will get a different random sample. This is perfectly all right. So long as the sample is drawn by using a correct procedure, it is a valid random sample.

Check Your Understanding

1. A pollster wants to estimate the proportion of voters in a certain town who are Democrats. He goes to a large shopping mall and approaches people to ask whether they are Democrats. Is this a simple random sample? Explain.

2. A telephone company wants to estimate the proportion of customers who are satisfied with their service. They use a computer to generate a list of random phone numbers, and call those people to ask them whether they are satisfied. Is this a simple random sample? Explain.

Answers are on page 12.

Objective 2 Determine when samples of convenience are acceptable

Samples of Convenience

In some cases, it is difficult or impossible to draw a sample in a truly random way. In these cases, the best one can do is to sample items by some convenient method. A sample obtained in such a way is called a **sample of convenience**.

> **DEFINITION**
>
> A **sample of convenience** is a sample that is not drawn by a well-defined random method.

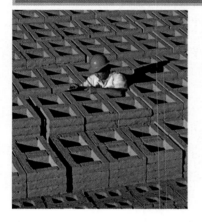

EXAMPLE 1.6

Drawing a sample of convenience

A construction engineer has just received a shipment of 1000 concrete blocks, each weighing approximately 50 pounds. The blocks have been delivered in a large pile. The engineer wishes to investigate the crushing strength of the blocks by measuring the strengths in a sample of 10 blocks. Explain why it might be difficult to draw a simple random sample of blocks. Describe how the engineer might draw a sample of convenience.

Solution

To draw a simple random sample would require removing blocks from the center and bottom of the pile, which might be quite difficult. One way to draw a sample of convenience would be to simply take 10 blocks off the top of the pile.

Problems with samples of convenience

The big problem with samples of convenience is that they may differ systematically in some way from the population. For this reason, samples of convenience should not be used, except in some situations where it is not feasible to draw a random sample. When it is necessary to draw a sample of convenience, it is important to think carefully about all the ways in which the sample might differ systematically from the population. If it is reasonable to believe that no important systematic difference exists, then it may be acceptable to treat the sample of convenience as if it were a simple random sample. With regard to the concrete blocks, if the engineer is confident that the blocks on the top of the pile do not differ systematically in any important way from the rest, then he may treat the sample of convenience as a simple random sample. If, however, it is possible that blocks in different parts of the pile may have been made from different batches of mix, or may have different curing times or temperatures, a sample of convenience could give misleading results.

> **CAUTION**
>
> Don't use a sample of convenience when it is possible to draw a simple random sample.

> **SUMMARY**
>
> - A sample of convenience may be acceptable when it is reasonable to believe that there is no systematic difference between the sample and the population.
> - A sample of convenience is not acceptable when it is possible that there is a systematic difference between the sample and the population.

Objective 3 Describe stratified sampling, cluster sampling, systematic sampling, and voluntary response sampling

Some Other Sampling Methods
Stratified sampling

In **stratified sampling**, the population is divided into groups, called **strata**, where the members of each stratum are similar in some way. Then a simple random sample is drawn from each stratum. Stratified sampling is useful when the strata differ from one another, but the individuals within a stratum tend to be alike.

EXAMPLE 1.7

Drawing a stratified sample

A company has 1000 employees, of whom 800 are full-time and 200 are part-time. The company wants to survey 50 employees about their opinions regarding benefits. Attitudes toward benefits may differ considerably between full-time and part-time employees. Why might it be a good idea to draw a stratified sample? Describe how one might be drawn.

Solution

If a simple random sample is drawn from the entire population of 1000 employees, it is possible that the sample will contain only a few part-time employees, and their attitudes will not be well represented. For this reason, it might be advantageous to draw a stratified sample. To draw a stratified sample, one would use two strata. One stratum would consist of the full-time employees, and the other would consist of the part-time employees. A simple random sample would be drawn from the full-time employees, and another simple random sample would be drawn from the part-time employees. This method guarantees that both full-time and part-time employees will be well represented.

> **Explain It Again**
>
> **Example of a cluster sample:**
> Imagine drawing a simple random sample of households, and interviewing every member of each household. This would be a cluster sample, with the households as the clusters.

Cluster sampling

In **cluster sampling**, items are drawn from the population in groups, or clusters. Cluster sampling is useful when the population is too large and spread out for simple random sampling to be feasible. Cluster sampling is used extensively by U.S. government agencies in sampling the U.S. population to measure sociological factors such as income and unemployment.

EXAMPLE 1.8

Drawing a cluster sample

To estimate the unemployment rate in a county, a government agency draws a simple random sample of households in the county. Someone visits each household and asks how many adults live in the household, and how many of them are unemployed. What are the clusters? Why is this a cluster sample?

Solution

The clusters are the groups of adults in each of the households in the county. This a cluster sample because a simple random sample of clusters is selected, and every individual in each selected cluster is part of the sample.

> **Explain It Again**
>
> **The difference between cluster sampling and stratified sampling:**
> In both cluster sampling and stratified sampling, the population is divided into groups. In stratified sampling, a simple random sample is chosen from each group. In cluster sampling, a random sample of groups is chosen, and every member of the chosen groups is sampled.

Systematic sampling

Imagine walking alongside a line of people and choosing every third one. That would produce a **systematic sample**. In a systematic sample, the population items are ordered. It is decided how frequently to sample items; for example, one could sample every third item, or every fifth item, or every hundredth item. Let k represent the sampling frequency. To begin the sampling, choose a starting place at random. Select the item in the starting place, along with every kth item after that.

Systematic sampling is sometimes used to sample products as they come off an assembly line, in order to check that they meet quality standards.

EXAMPLE 1.9

Describe a systematic sample

Automobiles are coming off an assembly line. It is decided to draw a systematic sample for a detailed check of the steering system. The starting point will be the third car, then every fifth car after that will be sampled. Which cars will be sampled?

Solution

We start with the third car, then count by fives to determine which cars will be sampled. The sample will consist of cars numbered 3, 8, 13, 18, and so on.

Voluntary response sampling

Voluntary response samples are often used by the media to try to engage the audience. For example, a news commentator will invite people to log on to a website to express an opinion, or a radio announcer will invite people to call the station to say what they think. How reliable are voluntary response samples? To put it simply, *voluntary response samples are never reliable*. People who go to the trouble to volunteer an opinion tend to have stronger opinions than is typical of the population. In addition, people with negative opinions are often more likely to volunteer their responses than those with positive opinions.

Figures 1.1–1.4 illustrate several valid methods of sampling.

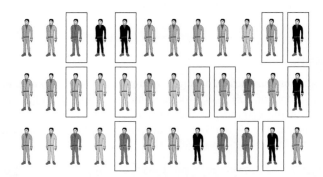

Figure 1.1 Simple random sampling

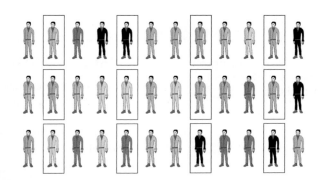

Figure 1.2 Systematic sampling

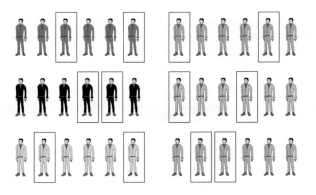

Figure 1.3 Stratified sampling

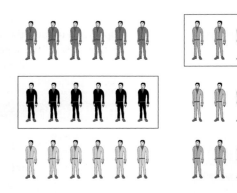

Figure 1.4 Cluster sampling

Check Your Understanding

3. A radio talk-show host invites listeners to send an email to express their opinions on an upcoming election. More than 10,000 emails are received. What kind of sample is this?

4. Every ten years, the U.S. Census Bureau attempts to count every person living in the United States. To check the accuracy of their count in a certain city, they draw a sample of census districts (roughly equivalent to a city block) and recount everyone in the sampled districts. What kind of sample is formed by the people who are recounted?

5. A public health researcher is designing a study of the effect of diet on heart disease. The researcher knows that the diets of men and women tend to differ, and that men are more susceptible to heart disease. To be sure that both men and women are well represented, the study comprises a simple random sample of 100 men and another simple random sample of 100 women. What kind of sample do these 200 people represent?

6. A college basketball team held a promotion at one of its games in which every twentieth person who entered the arena won a free basketball. What kind of sample do the winners represent?

Answers are on page 12.

Simple random sampling is the most basic method

Simple random sampling is not the only valid method of random sampling. But it is the most basic, and we will focus most of our attention on this method. From now on, unless otherwise stated, the terms *sample* and *random sample* will be taken to mean *simple random sample*.

Objective 4 Distinguish between statistics and parameters

Statistics and Parameters

We often use numbers to describe, or summarize, a sample or a population. For example, suppose that a pollster draws a sample of 500 likely voters in an upcoming election, and 68% of them say that the state of the economy is the most important issue for them. The quantity "68%" describes the sample. A number that describes a sample is called a **statistic**.

> **DEFINITION**
>
> A **statistic** is a number that describes a sample.

Now imagine that the election takes place, and that one of the items on the ballot is a proposition to raise the sales tax to pay for the development of a new park downtown. Let's say that 53% of the voters vote in favor of the proposition. The quantity "53%" describes the population of voters who voted in the election. A number that describes a population is called a **parameter**.

> **DEFINITION**
>
> A **parameter** is a number that describes a population.

EXAMPLE 1.10 ## Distinguishing between a statistic and a parameter

Which of the following is a statistic and which is a parameter?

a. 57% of the teachers at Central High School are female.

b. In a sample of 100 surgery patients who were given a new pain reliever, 78% of them reported significant pain relief.

Solution

a. The number 57% is a parameter, because it describes the entire population of teachers in the school.

b. The number 78% is a statistic, because it describes a sample.

USING TECHNOLOGY

We use Example 1.5 to illustrate the technology steps.

TI-84 PLUS

Drawing a simple random sample

Step 1. Enter any nonzero number on the HOME screen as the seed.

Step 2. Press **STO >**

Step 3. Press **MATH**, select **PRB**, then **1: rand**, and then press **ENTER**. This enters the seed into the calculator memory. See Figure A, which uses the number 21 as the seed.

Step 4. Press **MATH**, select **PRB**, then **5: randInt** Then enter **1, N, n**, where **N** is the population size and **n** is the desired sample size. In Example 1.5, we use **N** = 40 and **n** = 5 (Figure B).

Step 5. Press **ENTER**. The five values in the random sample for Example 1.5 are **27, 39, 30, 35, 17** (Figure C).

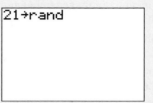

Figure A   **Figure B**

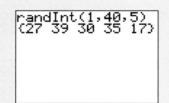

Figure C

MINITAB

Drawing a simple random sample

Step 1. Click **Calc**, then **Random Data**, then **Integer...**

Step 2. In the **Generate _____ rows of data** field, enter twice the desired sample size. For example, if the desired sample size is 10, enter 20. The reason for this is that some sample items may be repeated, and these will need to be deleted.

Step 3. In the **Store in column(s)** field, enter **C1**.

Step 4. Enter **1** for the **Minimum value** and the population size **N** for the **Maximum value**. We use **Maximum value** = 40 for Example 1.5. Click **OK**.

Step 5. Column **C1** of the worksheet will contain a list of randomly selected numbers between **1** and **N**. If any number appears more than once in **Column C1**, delete the replicates so that the number appears only once. For Example 1.5, our random sample begins with **16, 14, 30, 28, 17, ...** (Figure D).

↓	C1
1	16
2	14
3	30
4	28
5	17
6	13
7	4
8	8
9	6
10	15
11	35
12	5

Figure D

EXCEL

Drawing a simple random sample

Step 1. In **Column A**, enter the values **1** through the population size **N**. For Example 1.5, **N** = 40.

Step 2. In **Column B**, next to each value in **Column A**, enter the command **=rand( )**. This results in a randomly generated number between 0 and 1 in each cell in **Column B**.

Step 3. Select all values in **Columns A** and **B** and then click on the **Data** menu and select **Sort**.

Step 4. In the **Sort by** field, enter **Column B** and select **Smallest to Largest** in the **Order** field. Press **OK**. **Column A** now contains the random sample. Our random sample begins with **17, 12, 28, 20, 6, ...** (Figure E).

	A	B
1	17	0.919798
2	12	0.833304
3	28	0.105403
4	20	0.863496
5	6	0.820379
6	11	0.514735
7	36	0.051148
8	19	0.756971
9	39	0.826555
10	26	0.315564
11	8	0.119579
12	30	0.329793

Figure E

SECTION 1.1 Exercises

Exercises 1–6 are the Check Your Understanding exercises located within the section.

Understanding the Concepts

In Exercises 7–12, fill in each blank with the appropriate word or phrase.

7. The entire collection of individuals about which information is sought is called a _____.

8. A _____ is a subset of a population.

9. A _____ is a type of sample that is analogous to a lottery.

10. A sample that is not drawn by a well-defined random method is called a _____.

11. A _____ sample is one in which the population is divided into groups and a random sample of groups is drawn.

12. A _____ sample is one in which the population is divided into groups and a random sample is drawn from each group.

In Exercises 13–16, determine whether the statement is true or false. If the statement is false, rewrite it as a true statement.

13. A sample of convenience is never acceptable.

14. In a cluster sample, the population is divided into groups, and a random sample from each group is drawn.

15. Both stratified sampling and cluster sampling divide the population into groups.

16. One reason that voluntary response sampling is unreliable is that people with stronger views tend to express them more readily.

Practicing the Skills

In Exercises 17–20, determine whether the number described is a statistic or a parameter.

17. In a recent poll, 57% of the respondents supported a school bond issue.

18. The average age of the employees in a certain company is 35 years.

19. Of the students enrolled in a certain college, 80% are full-time.

20. In a survey of 500 high-school students, 60% of them said that they intended to go to college.

Exercises 21–24 refer to the population of animals in the following table. The population is divided into four groups: mammals, birds, reptiles, and fish.

Mammals		Birds	
1. Aardvark	6. Lion	11. Flamingo	16. Hawk
2. Buffalo	7. Zebra	12. Swan	17. Owl
3. Elephant	8. Pig	13. Sparrow	18. Chicken
4. Squirrel	9. Dog	14. Parrot	19. Duck
5. Rabbit	10. Horse	15. Pelican	20. Turkey

Reptiles		Fish	
21. Gecko	26. Python	31. Catfish	36. Shark
22. Iguana	27. Turtle	32. Tuna	37. Trout
23. Chameleon	28. Tortoise	33. Cod	38. Perch
24. Rattlesnake	29. Alligator	34. Salmon	39. Guppy
25. Boa constrictor	30. Crocodile	35. Goldfish	40. Minnow

21. **Simple random sample:** Draw a simple random sample of eight animals from the list of 40 animals in the table.

22. Another sample: Draw a sample of eight animals by drawing a simple random sample of two animals from each group. What kind of sample is this?

23. Another sample: Draw a simple random sample of two groups of animals from the four groups, and construct a sample of 20 animals by including all the animals in the sampled groups. What kind of sample is this?

24. Another sample: Choose a random number between 1 and 5. Include the animal with that number in your sample, along with every fifth animal thereafter, to construct a sample of eight animals. What kind of sample is this?

In Exercises 25–36, identify the kind of sample that is described.

25. Parking on campus: A college faculty consists of 400 men and 250 women. The college administration wants to draw a sample of 65 faculty members to ask their opinion about a new parking fee. They draw a simple random sample of 40 men and another simple random sample of 25 women.

26. What's on TV? A pollster obtains a list of all the residential addresses in a certain town, and uses a computer random number generator to choose 150 of them. The pollster visits each of the 150 households and interviews all the adults in each household about their television viewing habits.

27. Cruising the mall: A pollster walks around a busy shopping mall, and approaches people passing by to ask them how often they shop at the mall.

28. Don't drink and drive: Police at a sobriety checkpoint pull over every fifth car to determine whether the driver is sober.

29. Tell us your opinion: A television newscaster invites viewers to log on to a website to state their opinions on a proposed bill on immigration policy. More than 50,000 people express their opinions in this way.

30. Reading program: The superintendent of a large school district wants to test the effectiveness of a new program designed to improve reading skills among elementary school children. There are 30 elementary schools in the district. The superintendent chooses a simple random sample of 5 schools, and institutes the new reading program in those schools. A total of 4700 children attend these five schools.

31. Customer survey: All the customers who entered a store on a particular day were given a survey to fill out concerning their opinions of the service at the store.

32. Raffle: Five hundred people attend a charity event, and each buys a raffle ticket. The 500 ticket stubs are put in a drum and thoroughly mixed, and 10 of them are drawn. The 10 people whose tickets are drawn win a prize.

33. Hospital survey: The director of a hospital pharmacy chooses at random 100 people age 60 or older from each of three surrounding counties to ask their opinions of a new prescription drug program.

34. Bus schedule: Officials at a metropolitan transit authority want to get input from people who use a certain bus route about a possible change in the schedule. They randomly select five buses during a certain week and poll all riders on those buses about the change.

35. How much did you spend? A retailer samples 25 receipts from the past week by numbering all the receipts, generating 25 random numbers, and sampling the receipts that correspond to these numbers.

36. Phone features: A cell phone company wants to draw a sample of 600 customers to gather opinions about potential new features on upcoming phone models. The company draws a random sample of 200 from customers with Blackberry phones, a random sample of 100 from customers with LG phones, a random sample of 100 from customers with Samsung phones, and a random sample of 200 from customers with other phones.

Working with the Concepts

37. You're giving me a headache: A pharmaceutical company wants to test a new drug that is designed to provide superior relief from headaches. They want to select a sample of headache sufferers to try the drug. Do you think that it is feasible to draw a simple random sample of headache sufferers, or will it be necessary to use a sample of convenience? Explain your reasoning.

38. Pay more for recreation? The director of the recreation center at a large university wants to sample 100 students to ask them whether they would support an increase in their recreation fees in order to expand the hours that the center is open. Do you think that it is feasible to draw a simple random sample of students, or will it be necessary to use a sample of convenience? Explain your reasoning.

39. Voter preferences: A pollster wants to sample 500 voters in a town to ask them who they plan to vote for in an upcoming election. Describe a sampling method that would be appropriate in this situation. Explain your reasoning.

40. Quality control: Products come off an assembly line at the rate of several hundred per hour. It is desired to sample 10% of them to check whether they meet quality standards. Describe a sampling method that would be appropriate in this situation. Explain your reasoning.

41. On-site day care: A large company wants to sample 200 employees to ask their opinions about providing a day care center for the employees' children. They want to be sure to sample equal numbers of men and women. Describe a sampling method that would be appropriate in this situation. Explain your reasoning.

42. The tax man cometh: The Internal Revenue Service wants to sample 1000 tax returns that were submitted last year to determine the percentage of returns that had a refund. Describe a sampling method that would be appropriate in this situation. Explain your reasoning.

Extending the Concepts

43. Draw a sample: Imagine that you are asked to determine students' opinions at your school about a potential change in library hours. Describe how you could go about getting a sample of each of the following types: simple random sample, sample of convenience, voluntary response sample, stratified sample, cluster sample, systematic sample.

44. A systematic sample is a cluster sample: Explain how a systematic sample is actually a type of cluster sample.

Answers to Check Your Understanding Exercises for Section 1.1

1. No; this sample consists only of people in the town who visit the mall.

2. Yes; every group of n customers, where n is the sample size, is equally likely to be chosen.

3. Voluntary response sample

4. Cluster sample

5. Stratified sample

6. Systematic sample

SECTION 1.2 | Types of Data

Objectives

1. Understand the structure of a typical data set
2. Distinguish between qualitative and quantitative variables
3. Distinguish between ordinal and nominal variables
4. Distinguish between discrete and continuous variables

Objective 1 Understand the structure of a typical data set

Data Sets

In Section 1.1, we described various methods of collecting information by sampling. Once the information has been collected, the collection is called a **data set**. A simple example of a data set is presented in Table 1.1, which shows the major, final exam score, and grade for several students in a certain statistics class.

Table 1.1 Major, Final Exam Score, and Grade for Several Students

Student	Major	Exam Score	Grade
1	Psychology	92	A
2	Business	75	B
3	Communications	82	B
4	Psychology	72	C
5	Art	85	B

Table 1.1 illustrates some basic features that are found in most data sets. Information is collected on **individuals**. In this example, the individuals are students. In many cases, individuals are people; in other cases, they can be animals, plants, or things. The characteristics of the individuals about which we collect information are called **variables**. In this example, the variables are major, exam score, and grade. Finally, the values of the variables that we obtain are the **data**. So, for example, the data for individual #1 are Major = Psychology, Exam score = 92, and Grade = A.

Check Your Understanding

1. A pollster asks a group of six voters about their political affiliation (Republican, Democrat, or Independent), their age, and whether they voted in the last election. The results are shown in the following table.

Voter	Political Affiliation	Age	Voted in Last Election?
1	Republican	34	Yes
2	Democrat	56	Yes
3	Democrat	21	No
4	Independent	28	Yes
5	Republican	61	No
6	Independent	46	Yes

a. How many individuals are there?
b. Identify the variables.
c. What are the data for individual #3?

Answers are on page 18.

Objective 2 Distinguish between qualitative and quantitative variables

Qualitative and Quantitative Variables

Variables can be divided into two types: qualitative and quantitative. **Qualitative variables**, also called **categorical variables**, classify individuals into categories. For example, college major and gender are qualitative variables. **Quantitative variables** are numerical and tell how much or how many of something there is. Height and score on an exam are examples of quantitative variables.

Explain It Again

Another way to distinguish qualitative from quantitative variables: Quantitative variables are counts or measurements, whereas qualitative variables are descriptions.

SUMMARY
- Qualitative variables classify individuals into categories.
- Quantitative variables tell how much or how many of something there is.

EXAMPLE 1.11

Distinguishing between qualitative and quantitative variables

Which of the following variables are qualitative and which are quantitative?

a. A person's age
b. A person's gender
c. The mileage (in miles per gallon) of a car
d. The color of a car

Solution

a. Age is quantitative. It tells how much time has elapsed since the person was born.
b. Gender is qualitative. It consists of the categories "male" and "female."
c. Mileage is quantitative. It tells how many miles a car will go on a gallon of gasoline.
d. Color is qualitative.

Objective 3 Distinguish between ordinal and nominal variables

Ordinal and Nominal Variables

Qualitative variables come in two types: **ordinal variables** and **nominal variables**. An ordinal variable is one whose categories have a natural ordering. The letter grade received in a class, such as A, B, C, D, or F, is an ordinal variable. A nominal variable is one whose

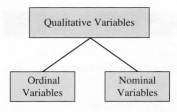

Figure 1.5 Qualitative variables come in two types: ordinal variables and nominal variables.

categories have no natural ordering. Gender is an example of a nominal variable. Figure 1.5 illustrates how qualitative variables are divided into nominal and ordinal variables.

SUMMARY

- Ordinal variables are qualitative variables whose categories have a natural ordering.
- Nominal variables are qualitative variables whose categories have no natural ordering.

EXAMPLE 1.12   **Distinguishing between ordinal and nominal variables**

Which of the following variables are ordinal and which are nominal?

- **a.** State of residence
- **b.** Gender
- **c.** Letter grade in a statistics class (A, B, C, D, or F)
- **d.** Size of soft drink ordered at a fast-food restaurant (small, medium, or large)

Solution

- **a.** State of residence is nominal. There is no natural ordering to the states.
- **b.** Gender is nominal.
- **c.** Letter grade in a statistics class is ordinal. The order, from high to low, is A, B, C, D, F.
- **d.** Size of soft drink is ordinal.

Objective 4 Distinguish between discrete and continuous variables

Discrete and Continuous Variables

Quantitative variables can be either **discrete** or **continuous**. Discrete variables are those whose possible values can be listed. Often, discrete variables result from counting something, so the possible values of the variable are 0, 1, 2, and so forth. Continuous variables can, in principle, take on any value within some interval. For example, height is a continuous variable because someone's height can be 68, or 68.1, or 68.1452389 inches. The possible values for height are not restricted to a list. Figure 1.6 illustrates how quantitative variables are divided into discrete and continuous variables.

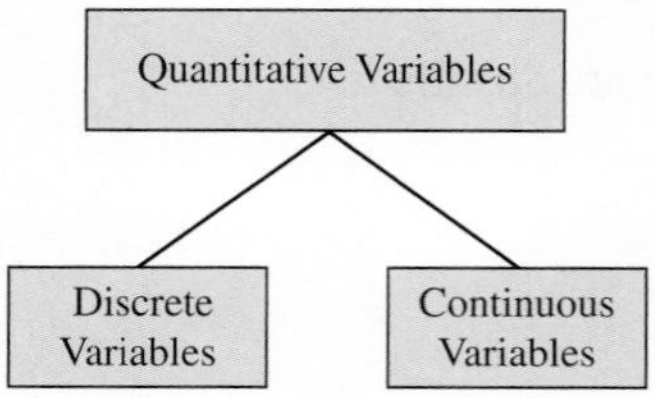

Figure 1.6 Quantitative variables come in two types: discrete variables and continuous variables.

SUMMARY

- Discrete variables are quantitative variables whose possible values can be listed. The list may be infinite — for example, the list of all whole numbers.
- Continuous variables are quantitative variables that can take on any value in some interval. The possible values of a continuous variable are not restricted to any list.

EXAMPLE 1.13   Distinguishing between discrete and continuous variables

Which of the following variables are discrete and which are continuous?

- **a.** The age of a person at his or her last birthday
- **b.** The height of a person
- **c.** The number of siblings a person has
- **d.** The distance a person commutes to work

Solution

a. Age at a person's last birthday is discrete. The possible values are 0, 1, 2, and so forth.

b. Height is continuous. A person's height is not restricted to any list of values.

c. Number of siblings is discrete. The possible values are 0, 1, 2, and so forth.

d. Distance commuted to work is continuous. It is not restricted to any list of values.

Check Your Understanding

2. Which are qualitative and which are quantitative?
  a. The number of patients admitted to a hospital on a given day
  b. The model of car last sold by a particular car dealer
  c. The name of your favorite song
  d. The seating capacity of an auditorium

3. Which are nominal and which are ordinal?
  a. The names of the streets in a town
  b. The movie ratings G, PG, PG-13, R, and NC-17
  c. The winners of the gold, silver, and bronze medals in an Olympic swimming competition

4. Which are discrete and which are continuous?
  a. The number of female members of the U.S. House of Representatives
  b. The amount of water used by a household during a given month
  c. The number of stories in an apartment building
  d. A person's body temperature

Answers are on page 18.

SECTION 1.2 Exercises

Exercises 1–4 are the Check Your Understanding exercises located within the section.

Understanding the Concepts

In Exercises 5–10, fill in each blank with the appropriate word or phrase.

5. The characteristics of individuals about which we collect information are called _____.

6. Variables that classify individuals into categories are called _____.

7. _____ variables are always numerical.

8. Qualitative variables can be divided into two types: _____ and _____.

9. A _____ variable is a quantitative variable whose possible values can be listed.

10. _____ variables can take on any value in some interval.

In Exercises 11–14, determine whether the statement is true or false. If the statement is false, rewrite it as a true statement.

11. Qualitative variables describe how much or how many of something there is.

12. A nominal variable is a qualitative variable with no natural ordering.

13. A discrete variable is one whose possible values can be listed.

14. A person's height is an example of a continuous variable.

Practicing the Skills

In Exercises 15–24, determine whether the data described are qualitative or quantitative.

15. Your best friend's name

16. Your best friend's age

17. The number of touchdowns in a football game

18. The title of your statistics book

19. The number of files on a computer

20. The waist size of a pair of jeans

21. The ingredients in a recipe

22. Your school colors

23. The makes of cars sold by a particular car dealer

24. The number of cars sold by a car dealer last month

In Exercises 25–32, determine whether the data described are nominal or ordinal.

25. The categories Strongly disagree, Disagree, Neutral, Agree, and Strongly agree on a survey

26. The names of the counties in a state

27. The shirt sizes of Small, Medium, Large, and X-Large

28. I got an A in statistics, a B in biology, and C's in history and English.

29. This semester, I am taking statistics, biology, history, and English.

30. I ordered a pizza with pepperoni, mushrooms, olives, and onions.

31. In the track meet, I competed in the high jump and the pole vault.

32. I finished first in the high jump and third in the pole vault.

In Exercises 33–38, determine whether the data described are discrete or continuous.

33. The amount of caffeine in a cup of Starbucks coffee

34. The distance from a student's home to his school

35. The number of steps in a stairway

36. The number of students enrolled at a college

37. The amount of charge left in the battery of a cell phone

38. The number of patients who reported that a new drug had relieved their pain

Working with the Concepts

39. **Ringtones:** Following are the ten top-selling ringtones for the year 2009:

     1. Kings of Leon — Sex on Fire
     2. Lady Gaga — Poker Face
     3. Black Eyed Peas — I Gotta Feeling
     4. Cheryl Cole — Fight for This Love
     5. Alexandra Burke Featuring Flo Rida — Bad Boys
     6. Black Eyed Peas — Meet Me Halfway
     7. Black Eyed Peas — Boom Boom Pow
     8. Flo Rida — Right Round
     9. Lady Gaga Featuring Colby Odonis — Just Dance
     10. The Killers — Human

     Source: www.ringtones-direct.com

     Are these data nominal or ordinal?

40. **More ringtones:** In the year 2009, six different artists had ringtones among the top ten. Following are the number of ringtones in the top ten for each artist.

Black Eyed Peas	3
Lady Gaga	2
Flo Rida	2
Kings of Leon	1
Cheryl Cole	1

     Are these data discrete or continuous?

41. **How's the economy?** A poll conducted by the American Research Group in December 2008 asked individuals their views on how the economy will be a year from now. Respondents were given four choices: Better than today, Same as today, Worse than today, and Undecided. Are these choices nominal or ordinal?

42. **Global warming:** A Pew poll conducted in October 2010 asked people how serious a problem global warming is. Of those who responded, 32% thought it was very serious, 31% thought it was somewhat serious, 16% thought it was not too serious, 18% thought it was not a problem, and 3% didn't know. Are these percentages qualitative or quantitative?

43. **Read any good books lately?** According to *Time* magazine, some of the best fiction books in 2008 were:

     Lush Life by Richard Price
     2666 by Roberto Bolaño
     Anathem by Neal Stephenson
     Unaccustomed Earth by Jhumpa Lahiri
     American Wife by Curtis Sittenfeld

     Are these data nominal or ordinal?

44. Watch your language: According to Merriam-Webster Online, the ten words that received the highest intensity of lookups in 2008 were:

1. bailout	6. trepidation
2. vet	7. precipice
3. socialism	8. rogue
4. maverick	9. misogyny
5. bipartisan	10. turmoil

Are these data nominal or ordinal?

45. Top ten PC games: In October 2008, Nielsen Media published the following data about the top ten PC games:

Game Title	Publisher	Percentage of Gaming Audience	Average Minutes Played per Week
1. World of Warcraft	Blizzard Entertainment	12.509	546
2. Warcraft III: Reign of Chaos	Blizzard Entertainment	1.890	328
3. Half-Life 2	Vivendi Games	1.917	288
4. Spore	Electric Entertainment	2.234	268
5. Bookworm	PopCap Games	3.074	133
6. Cake Mania 3	Sandlot Games	4.260	138
7. Virtual Villagers: The Secret City	Wild Games	1.567	204
8. Chessmaster Challenge	PlayFirst	8.856	47
9. Halo: Combat Evolved	Microsoft Game Studios	2.005	165
10. Build-a-Lot 2: Town of the Year	HipSoft LLC	1.661	183

Source: Nielsen Media Research

a. Which of the columns represent qualitative variables?
b. Which of the columns represent quantitative variables?
c. Which of the columns represent nominal variables?
d. Which of the columns represent ordinal variables?

46. At the movies: The following table provides information about the top-grossing movies for the years 1995–2010.

Year	Movie Title	Creative Type	MPAA Rating	Ticket Sales (millions)	Tickets Sold (millions)
1995	*Batman Forever*	Super hero	PG-13	184.0	42.3
1996	*Independence Day*	Science fiction	PG-13	306.1	69.3
1997	*Men in Black*	Science fiction	PG-13	250.1	54.5
1998	*Titanic*	Dramatization	PG-13	443.3	94.5
1999	*Star Wars Ep. I: The Phantom Menace*	Science fiction	PG	430.4	84.7
2000	*How the Grinch Stole Christmas*	Kids fiction	PG	253.4	47.0
2001	*Harry Potter and the Sorcerer's Stone*	Fantasy	PG	291.6	51.5
2002	*Spider-Man*	Super hero	PG-13	403.7	69.5
2003	*Finding Nemo*	Kids fiction	G	339.7	56.3
2004	*Shrek 2*	Kids fiction	PG	436.5	70.3
2005	*Star Wars Ep. III: Revenge of the Sith*	Science fiction	PG-13	380.3	59.3
2006	*Pirates of the Caribbean: Dead Man's Chest*	Fantasy	PG-13	423.3	64.6
2007	*Spider-Man 3*	Super hero	PG-13	336.5	48.9
2008	*The Dark Knight*	Super hero	PG-13	531.0	74.0
2009	*Transformers: Revenge of the Fallen*	Science fiction	PG-13	402.1	53.6
2010	*Toy Story 3*	Kids fiction	G	415.0	52.6

Source: http://www.the-numbers.com/

a. Which of the columns represent qualitative variables?
b. Which of the columns represent quantitative variables?
c. Which of the columns represent nominal variables?
d. Which of the columns represent ordinal variables?

Extending the Concepts

47. What do the numbers mean? A survey is administered by a marketing firm. Two of the people surveyed are Brenda and Jason. Three of the questions are as follows:

   i. Do you favor the construction of a new shopping mall?
     (1) Strongly oppose   (2) Somewhat oppose   (3) Neutral   (4) Somewhat favor   (5) Strongly favor
   ii. How many cars do you own?

iii. What is your marital status?
      (1) Married   (2) Single   (3) Divorced   (4) Domestically partnered   (5) Other
  a. Are the responses for question (i) nominal or ordinal?
  b. On question (i), Brenda answers (2) and Jason answers (4). Jason's answer (4) is greater than Brenda's answer (2). Does Jason's answer reflect more of something?
  c. Jason's answer to question (i) is twice as large as Brenda's answer. Does Jason's answer reflect twice as much of something? Explain.
  d. Are the responses for question (ii) qualitative or quantitative?
  e. On question (ii), Brenda answers 2 and Jason answers 1. Does Brenda's answer reflect more of something? Does Brenda's answer reflect twice as much of something? Explain.
  f. Are the responses for question (iii) nominal or ordinal?
  g. On question (iii), Brenda answers (4) and Jason answers (2). Does Brenda's answer reflect more of something? Does Brenda's answer reflect twice as much of something? Explain.

Answers to Check Your Understanding Exercises for Section 1.2

1. a. 6   **b.** Political affiliation, Age, and Voted in last election
   c. Political affiliation = Democrat, Age = 21,
        Voted in last election = no
2. a. Quantitative   **b.** Qualitative   **c.** Qualitative
   d. Quantitative

3. a. Nominal   **b.** Ordinal   **c.** Ordinal
4. a. Discrete   **b.** Continuous   **c.** Discrete
   d. Continuous

SECTION 1.3   Design of Experiments

Objectives

1. Distinguish between a randomized experiment and an observational study
2. Understand the advantages of randomized experiments
3. Understand how confounding can affect the results of an observational study
4. Describe various types of observational studies

Objective 1 Distinguish between a randomized experiment and an observational study

Experiments and Observational Studies

Will a new drug help prevent heart attacks? Does one type of seed produce a larger wheat crop than another? Does exercise lower blood pressure? To illustrate how scientists address questions like these, we describe how a study might be conducted to determine which of three types of seed will result in the largest wheat yield.

- Prepare three identically sized plots of land, with similar soil types.
- Plant each type of seed on a different plot, choosing the plots at random.
- Water and fertilize the plots in the same way.
- Harvest the wheat, and measure the amount grown on each plot.
- If one type of seed produces substantially more (or less) wheat than the others, then scientists will conclude that it is better (or worse) than the others.

The following terminology is used for studies like this.

> **DEFINITION**
>
> The **experimental units** are the individuals that are studied. These can be people, animals, plants, or things. When the experimental units are people, they are sometimes called **subjects**.

In the wheat study just described, the experimental units are the three plots of land.

> **DEFINITION**
>
> The **outcome**, or **response**, is what is measured on each experimental unit.

In the wheat study, the outcome is the amount of wheat produced.

> **DEFINITION**
>
> The **treatments** are the procedures applied to each experimental unit. There are always two or more treatments. The purpose is to determine whether the choice of treatment affects the outcome.

In the wheat study, the treatments are the three types of seed.

In general, studies fall into two categories: **randomized experiments** and **observational studies**.

> **DEFINITION**
>
> A **randomized experiment** is a study in which the investigator assigns the treatments to the experimental units at random.

The wheat study described above is a randomized experiment. In some situations, randomized experiments cannot be performed, because it isn't possible to randomly assign the treatments. For example, in studies to determine how smoking affects health, people cannot be assigned to smoke. Instead, people choose for themselves whether to smoke, and scientists observe differences in health outcomes between groups of smokers and nonsmokers. Studies like this are called **observational studies**.

> **DEFINITION**
>
> An **observational study** is one in which the assignment to treatment groups is not made by the investigator.

When possible, it is better to assign treatments at random and perform a randomized experiment. As we will see, the results of randomized experiments are generally easier to interpret than the results of observational studies.

Objective 2 Understand the advantages of randomized experiments

Randomized Experiments

In July 2008, an article in *The New England Journal of Medicine* (359:339–354) reported the results of a study to determine whether a new drug called raltegravir is effective in reducing levels of virus in patients with human immunodeficiency virus (HIV). A total of 699 patients participated in the experiment. These patients were divided into two groups. One group was given raltegravir. The other group was given a placebo. (A placebo is a harmless tablet, such as a sugar tablet, that looks like the drug but has no medical effect.) Thus there were two treatments in this experiment, raltegravir and placebo.

The experimenters had decided to give raltegravir to about two-thirds of the subjects and the placebo to the others. To determine which patients would be assigned to which group, a simple random sample consisting of 462 of the 699 patients was drawn; this sample constituted the raltegravir group. The remaining 237 patients were assigned to the placebo group.

It was decided to examine subjects after 16 weeks and measure the levels of virus in their blood. Thus the outcome for this experiment was the number of copies of virus per milliliter of blood. Patients were considered to have a successful outcome if they had fewer than 50 copies of the virus per milliliter of blood. In the raltegravir group, 62% of the subjects had a successful outcome, but only 35% of the placebo group did. The conclusion was that raltegravir was effective in lowering the concentration of virus in HIV patients. We will examine this study, and determine why it was reasonable to reach this conclusion.

The raltegravir study was a randomized experiment, because the treatments were assigned to the patients at random. What are the advantages of randomized experiments? In a perfect study, the treatment groups would not differ from each other in any important way except that they receive different treatments. Then, if the outcomes differ among the groups, we may be confident that the differences in outcome must have been caused by differences in treatment. In practice, it is impossible to construct treatment groups that are exactly alike. But randomization does the next best thing. In a randomized experiment, any differences between the groups are likely to be small. In addition, the differences are due only to chance.

Because the raltegravir study was a randomized experiment, it is reasonable to conclude that the higher success rate in the raltegravir group was actually due to raltegravir.

SUMMARY

In a randomized experiment, if there are large differences in outcomes among the treatment groups, we can conclude that the differences are due to the treatments.

EXAMPLE 1.14

Identifying a randomized experiment

To assess the effectiveness of a new method for teaching arithmetic to elementary school children, a simple random sample of 30 first graders was taught with the new method, and another simple random sample of 30 first graders was taught with the currently used method. At the end of eight weeks, the children were given a test to assess their knowledge. What are the treatments in this study? Explain why this is a randomized experiment.

Solution

The treatments are the two methods of teaching. This is a randomized experiment because children were assigned to the treatment groups at random.

Double-blind experiments

We have described the advantages of assigning treatments at random. It is a further advantage if the assignment can be done in such a way that neither the experimenters nor the subjects know which treatment has been assigned to which subject. Experiments like this are called **double-blind** experiments. The raltegravir experiment was a double-blind experiment, because neither the patients nor the doctors treating them knew which patients were receiving the drug and which were receiving the placebo.

DEFINITION

An experiment is **double-blind** if neither the investigators nor the subjects know who has been assigned to which treatment.

Experiments should be run double-blind whenever possible, because when investigators or subjects know which treatment is being given, they may tend to report the results differently. For example, in an experiment to test the effectiveness of a new pain reliever, patients who know they are getting the drug may report their pain levels differently than those who know they are taking a placebo. Doctors can be affected as well; a doctor's diagnosis may be influenced by a knowledge of which treatment a patient received.

In some situations, it is not possible to run a double-blind experiment. For example, in an experiment that compares a treatment that involves taking medication to a treatment that involves surgery, both patients and doctors will know who got which treatment.

EXAMPLE 1.15

Determining whether an experiment is double-blind

Is the experiment described in Example 1.14 a double-blind experiment? Explain.

Solution

This experiment is not double-blind, because the teachers know whether they are using the new method or the old method.

Randomized block experiments

The type of randomized experiment we have discussed is sometimes called a **completely randomized experiment**, because there is no restriction on which subjects may be assigned which treatment. In some situations, it is desirable to restrict the randomization a bit. For example, imagine that two reading programs are to be tested in an elementary school that has children in grades 1 through 4. If children are assigned at random to the programs, it is possible that one of the programs will end up with more fourth graders while the other one will end up with more first graders. Since fourth graders tend to be better readers, this will give an advantage to the program that happens to end up with more of them. This possibility can be avoided by randomizing the students within each grade separately. In other words, we randomly assign exactly half of the students within each grade to each reading program.

This type of experiment is called a **randomized block experiment**. In the example just discussed, each grade constitutes a block. In a randomized block experiment, the subjects are divided into blocks in such a way that the subjects in each block are the same or similar with regard to a variable that is related to the outcome. Age and gender are commonly used blocking variables. Then the subjects within each block are randomly assigned a treatment.

Observational Studies

Recall that an observational study is one in which the investigators do not assign the treatments. In most observational studies, the subjects choose their own treatments. Observational studies are less reliable than randomized experiments. To see why, imagine a study that is intended to determine whether smoking increases the risk of heart attack. Imagine that a group of smokers and a group of nonsmokers are observed for several years, and during that time a higher percentage of the smoking group experiences a heart attack. Does this prove that smoking increases the risk of heart attack? No. The problem is that the smoking group will differ from the nonsmoking group in many ways other than smoking, and these other differences may be responsible for differences in the rate of heart attacks. For example, smoking is more prevalent among men than among women. Therefore, the smoking group will contain a higher percentage of men than the nonsmoking group. It is known that men have a higher risk of heart attack than women. So the higher rate of heart attacks in the smoking group could be due to the fact that there are more men in the smoking group, and not to the smoking itself.

Objective 3 Understand how confounding can affect the results of an observational study

Confounding

The preceding example illustrates the major problem with observational studies. It is difficult to tell whether a difference in the outcome is due to the treatment or to some other difference between the treatment and control groups. This is known as **confounding**. In the preceding example, gender was a **confounder**. Gender is related to smoking (men are more likely to smoke) and to heart attacks (men are more likely to have heart attacks). For this reason, it is difficult to determine whether the difference in heart attack rates is due to differences in smoking (the treatment) or differences in gender (the confounder).

Explain It Again

Another way to describe a confounder: A confounder is something other than the treatment that can cause the treatment groups to have different outcomes.

SUMMARY

A **confounder** is a variable that is related to both the treatment and the outcome. When a confounder is present, it is difficult to determine whether differences in the outcome are due to the treatment or to the confounder.

How can we prevent confounding? One way is to design a study so that the confounder isn't a factor. For example, to determine whether smoking increases the risk of heart attack, we could compare a group of male smokers to a group of male nonsmokers, and a group of female smokers to a group of female nonsmokers. Gender wouldn't be a confounder here, because there would be no differences in gender between the smoking and nonsmoking groups. Of course, there are other possible confounders. Smoking rates vary among ethnic groups, and rates of heart attacks do, too. If people in ethnic groups that are more susceptible to heart attacks are also more likely to smoke, then ethnicity becomes a confounder. This can be dealt with by comparing smokers of the same gender and ethnic group to nonsmokers of that gender and ethnic group.

Designing observational studies that are relatively free of confounding is difficult. In practice, many studies must be conducted over a long period of time. In the case of smoking, this has been done, and we can be confident that smoking does indeed increase the risk of heart attack, along with other diseases. If you don't smoke, you have a much better chance to live a long and healthy life.

SUMMARY

In an observational study, when there are differences in the outcomes among the treatment groups, it is often difficult to determine whether the differences are due to the treatments or to confounding.

EXAMPLE 1.16

Determining the effect of confounding

In a study of the effects of blood pressure on health, a large group of people of all ages were given regular blood pressure checkups for a period of one year. It was found that people with high blood pressure were more likely to develop cancer than people with lower blood pressure. Explain how this result might be due to confounding.

Solution

Age is a likely confounder. Older people tend to have higher blood pressure than younger people, and older people are more likely to get cancer than younger people. Therefore people with high blood pressure may have higher cancer rates than younger people, even though high blood pressure does not cause cancer.

Check Your Understanding

1. To study the effect of air pollution on respiratory health, a group of people in a city with high levels of air pollution and another group in a rural area with low levels of pollution are examined to determine their lung capacity. Is this a randomized experiment or an observational study?

2. It is known that drinking alcohol increases the risk of contracting liver cancer. Assume that in an observational study, a group of smokers has a higher rate of liver cancer than a group of nonsmokers. Explain how this result might be due to confounding.

Answers are on page 26.

Objective 4 Describe various types of observational studies

Types of Observational Studies

There are two main types of observational studies: cohort studies and case-control studies. Cohort studies can be further divided into prospective, cross-sectional, and retrospective studies.

Cohort studies

In a **cohort study**, a group of subjects (the cohort) is studied to determine whether various factors of interest are associated with an outcome.

In a **prospective** cohort study, the subjects are followed over time. One of the most famous prospective cohort studies is the Framingham Heart Study. This study began in 1948 with 5209 men and women from the town of Framingham, Massachusetts. Every two years, these subjects are given physical exams and lifestyle interviews, which are studied to discover factors that increase the risk of heart disease. Much of what is known about the effects of diet and exercise on heart disease is based on this study.

Prospective studies are among the best observational studies. Because subjects are repeatedly examined, the quality of the data is often quite good. Information on potential confounders can be collected as well. Results from prospective studies are generally more reliable than those from other observational studies. The disadvantages of prospective studies are that they are expensive to run, and that it takes a long time to develop results.

In a **cross-sectional** study, measurements are taken at one point in time. For example, in a study published in the *Journal of the American Medical Association* (300:1303–1310), I. Lang and colleagues studied the health effects of bisphenol A, a chemical found in the linings of food and beverage containers. They measured the levels of bisphenol A in urine samples from 1455 adults. They found that people with higher levels of bisphenol A were more likely to have heart disease and diabetes.

Cross-sectional studies are relatively inexpensive, and results can be obtained quickly. The main disadvantage is that the exposure is measured at only one point in time, so there is little information about how past exposures may have contributed to the outcome. Another disadvantage is that because measurements are made at only one time, it is impossible to determine a time sequence of events. For example, in the bisphenol A study just described, it is possible that higher levels of bisphenol A cause heart disease and diabetes. But it is also possible that the onset of heart disease or diabetes causes levels of bisphenol A to increase. There is no way to determine which happened first.

In a **retrospective** cohort study, subjects are sampled after the outcome has occurred. The investigators then look back over time to determine whether certain factors are related to the outcome. For example, in a study published in *The New England Journal of Medicine* (357:753–761), T. Adams and colleagues sampled 9949 people who had undergone gastric bypass surgery between 5 and 15 years previously, along with 9668 obese patients who had not had bypass surgery. They looked back in time to see which patients were still alive. They found that the survival rates for the surgery patients were greater than for those who had not undergone surgery.

Retrospective cohort studies are less expensive than prospective cohort studies, and results can be obtained quickly. A disadvantage is that it is often impossible to obtain data on potential confounders.

One serious limitation of all cohort studies is that they cannot be used to study rare diseases. Even in a large cohort, very few people will contract a particular rare disease. To study rare diseases, case-control studies must be used.

Case-control studies

In a **case-control** study, two samples are drawn. One sample consists of people who have the disease of interest (the cases), and the other consists of people who do not have the disease (the controls). The investigators look back in time to determine whether a particular factor of interest differs between the two groups. For example, S. S. Nielsen and colleagues conducted a case-control study to determine whether exposure to pesticides is related to brain cancer in children (*Environmental Health Perspectives*, 118:144–149). They sampled 201 children under the age of 10 who had been diagnosed with brain cancer, and 285 children who did not have brain cancer. They interviewed the parents of the children to estimate the extent to which the children had been exposed to pesticides. They did not find a clear relationship between pesticide exposure and brain cancer. This study could not have been conducted as a cohort study, because even in a large cohort of children, very few will get brain cancer.

Case-control studies are always retrospective, because the outcome (case or control) has occurred before the sampling is done. Case-control studies have the same advantages and disadvantages as retrospective cohort studies. In addition, case-control studies have the advantage that they can be used to study rare diseases.

Check Your Understanding

3. In a study conducted at the University of Southern California, J. Peters and colleagues studied elementary school students in 12 California communities. Each year for 10 years, they measured the respiratory function of the children and the levels of air pollution in the communities.
   a. Was this a cohort study or a case-control study?
   b. Was the study prospective, cross-sectional, or retrospective?

4. In a study conducted at the University of Colorado, J. Ruttenber and colleagues studied people who had worked at the Rocky Flats nuclear weapons production facility near Denver, Colorado. They studied a group of workers who had contracted lung cancer, and another group who had not contracted lung cancer. They looked back at plant records to determine the amount of radiation exposure for each worker. The purpose of the study was to determine whether the people with lung cancer had been exposed to higher levels of radiation than those who had not gotten lung cancer.
   a. Was this a cohort study or a case-control study?
   b. Was the study prospective, cross-sectional, or retrospective?

Answers are on page 26.

SECTION 1.3   Exercises

Exercises 1–4 are the Check Your Understanding exercises located within the section.

Understanding the Concepts

In Exercises 5–10, fill in each blank with the appropriate word or phrase.

5. In a _____ experiment, subjects do not decide for themselves which treatment they will get.

6. In a _____ study, neither the investigators nor the subjects know who is getting which treatment.

7. A study in which the assignment to treatment groups is not made by the investigator is called _____.

8. A _____ is a variable related to both the treatment and the outcome.

9. In a _____ study, the subjects are followed over time.

10. In a _____ study, a group of subjects is studied to determine whether various factors of interest are associated with an outcome.

In Exercises 11–16, determine whether the statement is true or false. If the statement is false, rewrite it as a true statement.

11. In a randomized experiment, the treatment groups do not differ in any systematic way except that they receive different treatments.

12. A confounder makes it easier to draw conclusions from a study.

13. In an observational study, subjects are assigned to treatment groups at random.

14. Observational studies are generally more reliable than randomized experiments.

15. In a case-control study, the outcome has occurred before the subjects are sampled.

16. In a cross-sectional study, measurements are made at only one point in time.

Practicing the Skills

17. To determine the effectiveness of a new pain reliever, a randomly chosen group of pain sufferers is assigned to take the new drug, and another randomly chosen group is assigned to take a placebo.
    a. Is this a randomized experiment or an observational study?
    b. The subjects taking the new drug experienced substantially more pain relief than those taking the placebo. The research team concluded that the new drug is effective in relieving pain. Is this conclusion well justified? Explain.

18. A medical researcher wants to determine whether exercising can lower blood pressure. At a health fair, he measures the blood pressure of 100 individuals, and interviews them about their exercise habits. He divides the individuals into two categories: those whose typical level of exercise is low, and those whose level of exercise is high.
    a. Is this a randomized experiment or an observational study?

b. The subjects in the low-exercise group had considerably higher blood pressure, on the average, than subjects in the high-exercise group. The researcher concluded that exercise decreases blood pressure. Is this conclusion well justified? Explain.

19. A medical researcher wants to determine whether exercising can lower blood pressure. She recruits 100 people with high blood pressure to participate in the study. She assigns a random sample of 50 of them to pursue an exercise program that includes daily swimming and jogging. She assigns the other 50 to refrain from vigorous activity. She measures the blood pressure of each of the 100 individuals both before and after the study.

a. Is this a randomized experiment or an observational study?

b. On the average, the subjects in the exercise group substantially reduced their blood pressure, while the subjects in the no-exercise group did not experience a reduction. The researcher concluded that exercise decreases blood pressure. Is this conclusion well justified? Explain.

20. An agricultural scientist wants to determine the effect of fertilizer type on the yield of tomatoes. There are four types of fertilizer under consideration. She plants tomatoes on four plots of land. Each plot is treated identically except for receiving a different type of fertilizer.

a. What are the treatments?

b. Is this a randomized experiment or an observational study?

c. The yields differ substantially among the four plots. Can you conclude that the differences in yield are due to the differences in fertilizer? Explain.

Working with the Concepts

21. Air pollution and colds: A scientist wants to determine whether people who live in places with high levels of air pollution get more colds than people in areas with little air pollution. Do you think it is possible to design a randomized experiment to study this question, or will an observational study be necessary? Explain.

22. Cold medications: A scientist wants to determine whether a new cold medicine relieves symptoms more effectively than a currently used medicine. Do you think it is possible to design a randomized experiment to study this question, or will an observational study be necessary? Explain.

23. Taxicabs and crime: A sociologist discovered that regions that have more taxicabs tend to have higher crime rates. Does increasing the number of taxicabs cause the crime rate to increase, or could the result be due to confounding? Explain.

24. Recovering from heart attacks: In a study of people who had suffered heart attacks, it was found that those who lived in smaller houses were more likely to recover than those who lived in larger houses. Does living in a smaller house increase the likelihood of recovery from a heart attack, or could the result be due to confounding? Explain.

25. Eat your vegetables: In an observational study, people who ate four or more servings of fresh fruits and vegetables each day were less likely to develop colon cancer than people who ate little fruit or vegetables. True or false:

a. The results of the study show that eating more fruits and vegetables reduces your risk of contracting colon cancer.

b. The results of the study may be due to confounding, since the lifestyles of people who eat large amounts of fruits and vegetables may differ in many ways from those of people who do not.

26. Vocabulary and height: A vocabulary test was given to students at an elementary school. The students' ages ranged from 5 to 11 years old. It was found that the students with larger vocabularies tended to be taller than the students with smaller vocabularies. Explain how this result might be due to confounding.

27. Secondhand smoke: A recent study compared the heart rates of 19 infants born to nonsmoking mothers with those of 17 infants born to mothers who smoked an average of 15 cigarettes a day while pregnant and after giving birth. The heart rates of the infants at one year of age were 20% slower on the average for the smoking mothers.

a. What is the outcome variable?

b. What is the treatment variable?

c. Was this a cohort study or a case-control study?

d. Was the study prospective, cross-sectional, or retrospective?

e. Could the results be due to confounding? Explain.

Source: *Environmental Health Perspectives* 118:a158–a159

28. Pollution in China: In a recent study, Z. Zhao and colleagues measured the levels of formaldehyde in the air in 34 classrooms in the schools in the city of Taiyuan, China. On the same day, they gave questionnaires to 1993 students aged 11–15 in those schools, asking them whether they had experienced respiratory problems (such as asthma attacks, wheezing, or shortness of breath). They found that the students in the classrooms with higher levels of formaldehyde reported more respiratory problems.

a. What is the outcome variable?

b. What is the treatment variable?

c. Was this a cohort study or a case-control study?

d. Was the study prospective, cross-sectional, or retrospective?

e. Could the results be due to confounding? Explain.

Source: *Environmental Health Perspectives* 116:90–97

Extending the Concepts

29. **The Salk Vaccine Trial:** In 1954, the first vaccine against polio, known as the Salk vaccine, was tested in a large randomized double-blind study. Approximately 750,000 children were asked to enroll in the study. Of these, approximately 350,000 did not participate, because their parents refused permission. The children who did participate were randomly divided into two groups of about 200,000 each. One group, the treatment group, got the vaccine, while the other group, the control group, got a placebo. The rate of polio in the treatment group was less than half of that in the control group.
    a. Is it reasonable to conclude that the Salk vaccine was effective in reducing the rate of polio?
    b. Polio is sometimes difficult to diagnose, as its early symptoms are similar to those of the flu. Explain why it was important for the doctors in the study not to know which children were getting the vaccine.
    c. Perhaps surprisingly, polio was more common among upper-income and middle-income children than among lower-income children. The reason is that lower-income children tended to live in less hygienic surroundings. They would contract mild cases of polio in infancy while still protected by their mother's antibodies, and thereby develop a resistance to the disease. The children who did not participate in the study were more likely to come from lower-income families. The rate of polio in this group was substantially lower than the rate in the placebo group. Does this prove that the placebo caused polio, or could this be due to confounding? Explain.

30. **Another Salk Vaccine Trial:** Another study of the Salk vaccine, conducted at the same time as the trial described in Exercise 29, used a different design. In this study, approximately 350,000 second graders were invited to participate. About 225,000 did so, and the other 125,000 refused. All of the participating second graders received the vaccine. The control group consisted of approximately 725,000 first and third graders. They were not given any placebo, so no consent was necessary.
    a. Was this a randomized experiment?
    b. Was it double-blind?
    c. The treatment group consisted of children who had consent to participate. The control group consisted of all first and third graders. It turned out that the results of this study seriously underestimated the effectiveness of the vaccine. Use the information provided in Exercise 29(c) to explain why.

Answers to Check Your Understanding Exercises for Section 1.3

1. Observational study
2. People who smoke may be more likely to drink alcohol than people who do not smoke. Therefore, it might be possible for smokers to have higher rates of liver cancer without it being caused by smoking.

3. **a.** Cohort study **b.** Prospective
4. **a.** Case-control study **b.** Retrospective

SECTION 1.4 | **Bias in Studies**

Objectives

1. Define bias
2. Identify sources of bias

Objective 1 Define bias

Defining Bias

No study is perfect, and even a properly conducted study will generally not give results that are exactly correct. For example, imagine that you were to draw a simple random sample of students at a certain college to estimate the percentage of students who are Democrats. Your sample would probably contain a somewhat larger or smaller percentage of Democrats than the entire population of students, just by chance. However, imagine drawing many simple random samples. Some would have a greater percentage of Democrats than in the population, and some would have a smaller percentage of Democrats than in the population. But on the average, the percentage of Democrats in a simple random sample will be the same as the percentage in the population. A study conducted by a procedure that produces the correct result on the average is said to be **unbiased**.

Now imagine that you tried to estimate the percentage of Democrats in the population by selecting students who attended a speech made by a Democratic politician. On the average, studies conducted in this way would overestimate the percentage of Democrats in the population. Studies conducted with methods that tend to overestimate or underestimate the true value are said to be **biased**.

DEFINITION

- A study conducted by a procedure that produces the correct result on the average is said to be **unbiased**.
- A study conducted by a procedure that tends to overestimate or underestimate the true value is said to be **biased**.

Objective 2 Identify sources of bias

Identifying Sources of Bias

In practice, it is important to design studies to have as little bias as possible. Unfortunately, some studies are highly biased, and the conclusions drawn from them are not reliable. Here are some common types of bias.

Voluntary response bias

Recall that a voluntary response survey is one in which people are invited to log on to a website, send a text message, or call a phone number, in order to express their opinions on an issue. In many cases, the opinions of the people who choose to participate in such surveys do not reflect those of the population as a whole. In particular, people with strong opinions are more likely to participate. In general, voluntary response surveys are highly biased.

Self-interest bias

Many advertisements contain data that claim to show that the product being advertised is superior to its competitors. Of course, the advertiser will not report any data that tend to show that the product is inferior. Even more seriously, many people are concerned about a trend for companies to pay scientists to conduct studies involving their products. In particular, physicians are sometimes paid by drug companies to test their drugs and to publish the results of these tests in medical journals. People who have an interest in the outcome of an experiment have an incentive to use biased methods.

Social acceptability bias

People are reluctant to admit to behavior that may reflect negatively on them. This characteristic of human nature affects many surveys. For example, in political polls it is important for the pollster to determine whether the person being interviewed is likely to vote. A good way to determine whether someone is likely to vote in the next election is to find out whether they voted in the last election. It might seem reasonable to ask the following question:

"Did you vote in the last presidential election?"

The problem with this direct approach is that people are reluctant to answer "No," because they are concerned that not voting is socially less acceptable than voting. Here is how the Pew Research Center asked the question in a 2010 poll:

"In the 2008 presidential election between Barack Obama and John McCain, did things come up that kept you from voting, or did you happen to vote?"

People are more likely to answer this version of the question truthfully.

Leading question bias

Sometimes questions are worded in a way that suggests a particular response. For example, a political group that supports lowering taxes sent out a survey that included the following question:

"Do you favor decreasing the heavy tax burden on middle-class families?"

The words "heavy" and " burden" suggest that taxes are too high, and encourage a "Yes" response. A better way to ask this question is to present it as a multiple choice:

"What is your opinion on decreasing taxes for middle-class families?
Choices: Strongly disagree, Somewhat disagree, Neither agree nor disagree, Somewhat agree, Strongly agree."

Nonresponse bias

People cannot be forced to answer questions or to participate in a study. In any study, a certain proportion of people who are asked to participate refuse to do so. These people are called **nonresponders**. In many cases, the opinions of nonresponders tend to differ from the opinions of those who do respond. As a result, surveys with many nonresponders are often biased.

Sampling bias

Sampling bias occurs when some members of the population are more likely to be included in the sample than others. For example, samples of convenience almost always have sampling bias, because people who are easy to sample are more likely to be included. It is almost impossible to avoid sampling bias completely, but modern survey organizations work hard to keep it at a minimum.

A Big Sample Size Doesn't Make Up for Bias

A sample is useful only if it is drawn by a method that is likely to represent the population well. If you use a biased method to draw a sample, then drawing a big sample doesn't help; a big nonrepresentative sample does not describe a population any better than a small nonrepresentative sample. In particular, voluntary response surveys often draw several hundred thousand people to participate. Although the sample is large, it is unlikely to represent the population well, so the results are meaningless.

Check Your Understanding

1. Eighty thousand people attending a professional football game filled out surveys asking their opinions on using tax money to upgrade the football stadium. Seventy percent said that they supported the use of tax money. Then a pollster surveyed a simple random sample of 500 voters, and only 30% of the voters in this sample supported the use of tax money. The owner of the football team claims that the survey done at the football stadium is more reliable, because the sample size was much larger. Is he right? Explain.

2. A polling organization placed telephone calls to 1000 people in a certain city to ask them whether they favor a tax increase to build a new school. Two hundred people answered the phone, and 150 of them opposed the tax. Can you conclude that a majority of people in the city oppose the tax, or is it likely that this result is due to bias? Explain.

Answers are on page 29.

SECTION 1.4   Exercises

Exercises 1 and 2 are the Check Your Understanding exercises located within the section.

Understanding the Concepts

In Exercises 3–5, fill in each blank with the appropriate word or phrase.

3. _____ are highly unreliable in part because people who have strong opinions are more likely to participate.

4. People who are asked to participate in a study but refuse to do so are called _____ .

5. A large sample is useful only if it is drawn by a method that is likely to represent the _____ well.

In Exercises 6–8, determine whether the statement is true or false. If the statement is false, rewrite it as a true statement.

6. The way that a question in a survey is worded rarely has an effect on the responses.

7. Surveys with many nonresponders often provide misleading results.

8. Large samples usually give reasonably accurate results, no matter how they are drawn.

Practicing the Skills

In Exercises 9–16, specify the type of bias involved.

9. A bank sent out questionnaires to a simple random sample of 500 customers asking whether they would like the bank to extend its hours. Eighty percent of those returning the questionnaire said they would like the bank to extend its hours. Of the 500 questionnaires, 20 were returned.

10. To determine his constituents' feelings about election reform, a politician sends a survey to people who have subscribed to his newsletter. More than 1000 responses are received.

11. An e-store that sells cell phone accessories reports that 98% of its customers are satisfied with the speed of delivery.

12. The e-store in Exercise 11 sends a survey out to a random sample of 1000 recent customers, asking whether they are satisfied with the products they received. Ninety percent of those returning questionnaires indicated that they were satisfied. A total of ten customers returned the questionnaire.

13. A television newscaster invites viewers to email their opinions about whether the U.S. Congress is doing a good job in handling the economy. More than 100,000 people send in an opinion.

14. A police department conducted a survey in which police officers interviewed members of their community to ask their opinions on the effectiveness of the police department. The police chief reported that 90% of the people interviewed said that they were satisfied with the performance of the police department.

15. In a study of the effectiveness of wearing seat belts, a group of people who had survived car accidents in which they had not worn seat belts reported that seat belts would not have helped them.

16. To estimate the prevalence of illegal drug use in a certain high school, the principal interviewed a simple random sample of 100 students and asked them about their drug use. Five percent of the students acknowledged using illegal drugs.

Working with the Concepts

17. Nuclear power, anyone? In a survey conducted by representatives of the nuclear power industry, people were asked the question: "Do you favor the construction of nuclear power plants in order to reduce our dependence on foreign oil?" A group opposed to the use of nuclear power conducted a survey with the question: "Do you favor the construction of nuclear power plants that can kill thousands of people in an accident?"
   a. Do you think that the percentage of people favoring the construction of nuclear power plants would be about the same in both surveys?
   b. Would either of the two surveys produce reliable results? Explain.

18. Who's calling, please? Random-digit dialing is a sampling method in which a computer generates phone numbers at random to call. In recent years, caller ID has become popular. Do you think that caller ID increases the bias in random digit dialing? Explain.

19. Who's calling, please? Many polls are conducted over the telephone. Some polling organizations choose a sample of phone numbers to call from lists that include landline phone numbers only, and do not include cell phones. Do you think this increases the bias in phone polls? Explain.

20. Order of choices: When multiple-choice questions are asked, the order of the choices is usually changed each time the question is asked. For example, in the 2008 presidential election, a pollster would ask one person "Who do you prefer for president, Barack Obama or John McCain?" For the next person, the order of the names would be reversed: "John McCain or Barack Obama?" If the choices were given in the same order each time, do you think that might introduce bias? Explain.

Extending the Concepts

21. *Literary Digest* poll: In the 1936 presidential election, Republican candidate Alf Landon challenged President Franklin Roosevelt. The *Literary Digest* magazine conducted a poll in which they mailed questionnaires to more than 10 million voters. The people who received the questionnaires were drawn from lists of automobile owners and people with telephones. The magazine received 2.3 million responses, and predicted that Landon would win the election in a landslide with 57% of the vote. In fact, Roosevelt won in a landslide with 62% of the vote. Soon afterward, the *Literary Digest* folded.
   a. In 1936 most people did not own automobiles, and many did not have telephones. Explain how this could have caused the results of the poll to be mistaken.
   b. What can be said about the response rate? Explain how this could have caused the results of the poll to be mistaken.
   c. The *Literary Digest* believed that its poll would be accurate, because it received 2.3 million responses, which is a very large number. Explain how the poll could be wrong, even with such a large sample.

Answers to Check Your Understanding Exercises for Section 1.4

1. No. The sample taken at the football stadium is biased, because football fans are more likely to be sampled than others. The fact that the sample is big doesn't make it any better.

2. No. There is a high degree of nonresponse bias in this sample.

Chapter 1 Summary

Section 1.1: Most populations are too large to allow us to study each member, so we draw samples and study those. Samples must be drawn by an appropriate method. Simple random sampling, stratified sampling, cluster sampling, and systematic sampling are all valid methods. When none of these methods are feasible, a sample of convenience may be used, so long as it is reasonable to believe that there is no systematic difference between the sample and the population.

Section 1.2: Data sets contain values of variables. Qualitative variables place items in categories, whereas quantitative variables are counts or measurements. Qualitative variables can be either ordinal or nominal. An ordinal variable is one for which the categories have a natural ordering. For nominal variables, the categories have no natural ordering. Quantitative variables can be discrete or continuous. Discrete variables are ones whose possible values can be listed, whereas continuous variables can take on values anywhere within an interval.

Section 1.3: Scientists conduct studies to determine whether different treatments produce different outcomes. The most reliable studies are randomized experiments, in which subjects are assigned to treatments at random. When randomized experiments are not feasible, observational studies may be performed. Results of observational studies may be hard to interpret, because of the potential for confounding.

Section 1.4: Some studies produce more reliable results than others. A study that is conducted by a method that tends to produce an incorrect result is said to be biased. Some of the most common forms of bias are voluntary response bias, self-interest bias, social acceptability bias, leading question bias, nonresponse bias, and sampling bias.

Vocabulary and Notation

bias 26	leading question bias 27	sample of convenience 5
biased 27	nominal variable 13	sampling bias 28
case-control study 23	nonresponders 28	seed 4
categorical variable 13	nonresponse bias 28	self-interest bias 27
cluster sample 6	observational study 19	simple random sample 3
cohort study 23	ordinal variable 13	social acceptability bias 27
completely randomized experiment 21	outcome 19	statistic 8
confounder 21	parameter 8	statistics 2
confounding 21	population 2	strata 5
continuous variable 14	prospective study 23	stratified sample 5
cross-sectional study 23	qualitative variable 13	subject 18
data 12	quantitative variable 13	systematic sample 6
data set 12	randomized block experiment 21	treatment 19
discrete variable 14	randomized experiment 19	unbiased 27
double-blind 20	response 19	variable 12
experimental unit 18	retrospective study 23	voluntary response bias 27
individual 12	sample 2	voluntary response sample 7

Chapter Quiz

1. Provide an example of a qualitative variable and an example of a quantitative variable.

2. Is the name of your favorite author a qualitative variable or a quantitative variable?

3. True or false: Nominal variables do not have a natural ordering.

4. _____ variables are quantitative variables that can take on any value in some interval.

5. True or false: Ideally, a sample should represent the population as little as possible.

6. A utility company sends surveys to 200 of its customers in such a way that 100 surveys are sent to customers who pay their bills on time, 50 surveys are sent to customers whose bills are less than 30 days late, and 50 surveys are sent to customers whose bills are more than 30 days late. Which type of sample does this represent?

7. A sample of convenience is _____ when it is reasonable to believe that there is no systematic difference between the sample and the population. (*Choices:* acceptable, not acceptable)

8. The manager of a restaurant walks around and asks selected customers about the service they have received. Which type of sample does this represent?

9. True or false: An experiment where neither the investigators nor the subjects know who has been assigned to which treatment is called a double-blind experiment.

10. A poll is conducted of 3500 households close to major national airports, and another 2000 that are not close to an airport, in order to study whether living in a noisier environment results in health effects. Is this a randomized experiment or an observational study?

11. In a study, 200 patients with skin cancer are randomly divided into two groups. One group receives an experimental drug and the other group receives a placebo. Is this a randomized experiment or an observational study?

12. In a randomized experiment, if there are large differences in outcomes among treatment groups, we can conclude that the differences are due to the _____.

13. In analyzing the course grades of students in an elementary statistics course, a professor notices that students who are seniors performed better than students who are sophomores. The professor is tempted to conclude that older students perform better than younger ones. Describe a possible confounder in this situation.

14. True or false: The way that questions are worded on a survey may have an effect on the responses.

15. A radio talk show host invites listeners to call the show to express their opinions about a political issue. How reliable is this survey? Explain.

Review Exercises

1. Qualitative or quantitative? Is the number of points scored in a football game qualitative or quantitative?

2. Nominal or ordinal? Is the color of an MP3 player nominal or ordinal?

3. Discrete or continuous? Is the area of a college campus discrete or continuous?

4. Which type of variable is it? A theater concession stand sells soft drink and popcorn combos that come in sizes small, medium, large, and jumbo. True or false:
 a. Size is a qualitative variable.
 b. Size is an ordinal variable.
 c. Size is a continuous variable.

In Exercises 5–8, identify the kind of sample that is described.

5. Website ratings: A popular website is interested in conducting a survey of 400 visitors to the site in such a way that 200 of them will be under age 30, 150 will be aged 30–55, and 50 will be over 55.

6. Favorite performer: Viewers of a television show are asked to vote for their favorite performer by sending a text message to the show.

7. School days: A researcher selects 4 of 12 high schools in a certain region and surveys all of the administrative staff members in each school about a potential change in the ordering of supplies. Which type of sample does this represent?

8. Political polling: A pollster obtains a list of registered voters and uses a computer random number generator to choose 100 of them to ask which candidate they prefer in an upcoming election.

9. Fluoride and tooth decay: Researchers examine the association between the fluoridation of water and the prevention of tooth decay by comparing the prevalence of tooth decay in countries that have fluoridated water with the prevalence in countries that do not.
 a. Is this a randomized experiment or an observational study?
 b. Assume that tooth decay was seen to be less common in countries with fluoridated water. Could this result be due to confounding? Explain.

10. Better gas mileage: A taxi company in a large city put a new type of tire with a special tread on a random sample of 50 cars, and the regular type of tire on another random sample of 50 cars. After a month, the gas mileage of each car was measured.
 a. Is this a randomized experiment or an observational study?
 b. Assume that one of the samples had noticeably better gas mileage than the other. Could this result be due to confounding? Explain.

11. Cell phones and driving: To determine whether using a cell phone while driving increases the risk of an accident, a researcher examines accident reports to obtain data about the number of accidents in which a driver was talking on a cell phone.
 a. Is this a randomized experiment or an observational study?
 b. Assume that the accident reports show that people were more likely to have an accident while talking on a cell phone. Could this result be due to confounding? Explain.

12. Turn in your homework: The English department at a local college is considering using electronic-based assignment submission in its English composition classes. To study its effects, each section of the class is divided into two groups at random. In one group, assignments are submitted by turning them in to the professor on paper. In the other group, assignments are submitted electronically.
 a. Is this a randomized experiment or an observational study?
 b. Assume that the electronically submitted assignments had many fewer typographical errors, on average, than the ones submitted on paper. Could this result be due to confounding? Explain.

In Exercises 13–15, explain why the results of the studies described are unreliable.

13. Which TV station do you watch? The TV columnist for a local newspaper invites readers to log on to a website to vote for their favorite TV newscaster.

14. **Longevity:** A life insurance company wants to study the life expectancy of people born in 1950. The company's actuaries examine death certificates of people born in that year to determine how long they lived.

15. **Political opinion:** A congressman sent out questionnaires to 10,000 constituents to ask their opinions on a new health-care proposal. A total of 200 questionnaires were returned, and 70% of those responding supported the proposal.

Write About It

1. Describe the difference between a stratified sample and a cluster sample.

2. Explain why it is better, when possible, to draw a simple random sample rather than a sample of convenience.

3. Describe circumstances under which each of the following samples could be used: simple random sample, a sample of convenience, a stratified sample, a cluster sample, a systematic sample.

4. Suppose that you were asked to collect some information about students in your class for a statistics project. Give some examples of variables you might collect that are: ordinal, nominal, discrete, continuous.

5. Quantitative variables are numerical. Are some qualitative variables numerical as well? If not, explain why not. If so, provide an example.

6. What are the primary differences between a randomized experiment and an observational study?

7. What are the advantages of a double-blind study? Are there any disadvantages?

8. Provide an example of a study, either real or hypothetical, that is conducted by people who have an interest in the outcome. Explain how the results might possibly be misleading.

9. Explain why each of the following questions is leading. Provide a more appropriate wording.
   a. Should Americans save more money or continue their wasteful spending?
   b. Do you support more funding for reputable organizations like the Red Cross?

Case Study: Air Pollution And Respiratory Symptoms

Air pollution is a serious problem in many places. One form of air pollution that is suspected to cause respiratory illness is particulate matter (PM), which consists of tiny particles in the air. Particulate matter can come from many sources, most commonly ash from burning, but also from other sources such as tiny particles of rubber that wear off of automobile and truck tires.

The town of Libby, Montana, was recently the focus of a study on the effect of PM on the respiratory health of children. Many houses in Libby are heated by wood stoves, which produce a lot of particulate pollution. The level of PM is greatest in the winter when more stoves are being used, and declines as the weather becomes warmer. The study attempted to determine whether higher levels of PM affect the respiratory health of children. In one part of the study, schoolchildren were given a questionnaire to bring home to their parents. Among other things, the questionnaire asked whether the child had experienced symptoms of wheezing during the past 60 days. Most parents returned the questionnaire within a couple of weeks. Parents who did not respond promptly were sent another copy of the questionnaire through the mail. Many of these parents responded to this mailed version.

Table 1.2 presents, for each day, the number of questionnaires that were returned by parents of children who wheezed, the number returned by those who did not wheeze, the average concentration of particulate matter in the atmosphere during the past 60 days (in units of micrograms per cubic meter), and whether the questionnaires were delivered in school or through the mail.

We will consider a PM level of 17 or more to be high exposure, and a PM level of less than 17 to be low exposure.

1. How many people had high exposure to PM?

2. How many of the high-exposure people had wheeze symptoms?

3. What percentage of the high-exposure people had wheeze symptoms?

4. How many people had low exposure to PM?

5. How many of the low-exposure people had wheeze symptoms?

6. What percentage of the low-exposure people had wheeze symptoms?

7. Is there a large difference between the percentage of high-exposure people with wheeze and the percentage of low-exposure people with wheeze?

8. Explain why the percentage of high-exposure people with wheeze is the same as the percentage of school-return people with wheeze.

Table 1.2

Date	PM Level	Number of People Returning Questionnaires	Number Who Wheezed	School/Mail
3/5/07	19.815	3	0	School
3/6/07	19.885	72	9	School
3/7/07	20.006	69	5	School
3/8/07	19.758	30	1	School
3/9/07	19.827	44	7	School
3/10/07	19.686	31	1	School
3/11/07	19.823	38	3	School
3/12/07	19.697	66	5	School
3/13/07	19.505	42	4	School
3/14/07	19.359	31	1	School
3/15/07	19.348	19	4	School
3/16/07	19.318	3	1	School
3/17/07	19.124	2	0	School
4/12/07	14.422	10	1	Mail
4/13/07	14.418	9	1	Mail
4/14/07	14.405	8	0	Mail
4/15/07	14.141	3	0	Mail
4/16/07	13.910	4	0	Mail
4/17/07	13.951	2	0	Mail
4/18/07	13.545	2	0	Mail
4/20/07	13.326	3	0	Mail
4/22/07	13.154	2	0	Mail

9. Explain why the percentage of low-exposure people with wheeze is the same as the percentage of mail-return people with wheeze.

10. As the weather gets warmer, PM goes down because wood stoves are used less. Explain how this causes the mode of response (school or mail) to be related to PM.

11. It is generally the case in epidemiologic studies that people who have symptoms are often eager to participate, while those who are unaffected are less interested. Explain how this may cause the mode of response (school or mail) to be related to the outcome.

12. Rather than send out questionnaires, the investigators could have telephoned a random sample of people over a period of days. Explain how this might have reduced the confounding.

Graphical Summaries of Data

Introduction

Are cars becoming more fuel efficient? Increasing prices of gasoline, along with concerns about the environment, have made fuel efficiency an important concern. To determine whether recently built cars are getting better mileage than older cars, we will compare the U.S. Environmental Protection Agency highway mileage ratings for model year 2009 cars with the mileages for model year 2000 cars. The following tables present the results, in miles per gallon.

Highway Mileage Ratings for 2000 Compact Cars							
28	21	30	33	24	29	30	38
27	23	27	34	21	27	38	28
29	21	31	31	32	23	36	28
27	32	31	30	26	23	40	28
27	27	34	28	34	28	38	27
29	27	33	24	31	33	27	28
26	26	31	16	28	30	30	24
37	35	30	33	31	32		

Highway Mileage Ratings for 2009 Compact Cars						
30	30	27	15	14	17	28
26	25	34	29	26	25	33
35	35	25	30	25	25	25
21	17	18	17	21	18	25
34	33	18	18	27	28	30
25	26	31	30	35	29	29
25	29	28	26	28	26	26
25	30	19	22	26	29	

Source: www.fueleconomy.gov

It is hard to tell from the lists of numbers whether the mileages have changed much between 2000 and 2009. What is needed are methods to summarize the data, so that their most important features stand out. One way to do this is by constructing graphs that allow us to visualize the important features of the data. In this chapter, we will learn how to construct many of the most commonly used graphical summaries. In the case study at the end of the chapter, you will be asked to use graphical methods to compare the mileages between 2000 cars and 2009 cars.

SECTION 2.1 | Graphical Summaries for Qualitative Data

Objectives

1. Construct frequency distributions for qualitative data
2. Construct bar graphs
3. Construct pie charts

Objective 1 Construct frequency distributions for qualitative data

Frequency Distributions for Qualitative Data

How do retailers analyze their sales data to determine which items are most popular? Table 2.1 presents a list compiled by a computer retailer. Four types of computers are sold: desktops, laptops, notebooks, and tablets. The list contains the types of computers sold to the last 50 customers.

Table 2.1 Types of Computers Sold

Tablet	Laptop	Laptop	Laptop	Laptop
Laptop	Laptop	Notebook	Desktop	Laptop
Notebook	Desktop	Laptop	Laptop	Laptop
Laptop	Notebook	Notebook	Desktop	Laptop
Desktop	Laptop	Tablet	Notebook	Tablet
Notebook	Notebook	Tablet	Laptop	Desktop
Laptop	Laptop	Laptop	Laptop	Desktop
Desktop	Notebook	Laptop	Desktop	Laptop
Desktop	Tablet	Desktop	Laptop	Laptop
Desktop	Tablet	Notebook	Tablet	Laptop

Table 2.1 is typical of data in raw form. It is a big list, and it's hard to gather much information simply by looking at it. To make the important features of the data stand out, we construct summaries. The starting point for many summaries is a frequency distribution.

DEFINITION

- The **frequency** of a category is the number of times it occurs in the data set.
- A **frequency distribution** is a table that presents the frequency for each category.

EXAMPLE 2.1 | Construct a frequency distribution

Construct a frequency distribution for the data in Table 2.1.

Solution

To construct a frequency distribution, we begin by tallying the number of observations in each category and recording the totals in a table. Table 2.2 presents a frequency distribution for the computer sales data. We have included the tally marks in this table, but in practice it is permissible to omit them.

Table 2.2 Frequency Distribution for Computer Sales

Type of Computer	Tally	Frequency
Desktop	LHT LHT I	11
Laptop	LHT LHT LHT LHT III	23
Notebook	LHT IIII	9
Tablet	LHT II	7

It's a good idea to perform a check by adding the frequencies, to be sure that they add up to the total number of observations. In Table 2.2, the frequencies add up to 50, as they should.

Relative frequency distributions

A frequency distribution tells us exactly how many observations are in each category. Sometimes we are interested in the proportion of observations in each category. The proportion of observations in a category is called the **relative frequency** of the category.

> **DEFINITION**
>
> The **relative frequency** of a category is the frequency of the category divided by the sum of all the frequencies.
>
> $$\text{Relative frequency} = \frac{\text{Frequency}}{\text{Sum of all frequencies}}$$

We can add a column of relative frequencies to the frequency distribution. The resulting table is called a **relative frequency distribution**.

> **DEFINITION**
>
> A **relative frequency distribution** is a table that presents the relative frequency of each category. Often the frequency is presented as well.

EXAMPLE 2.2

Constructing a relative frequency distribution

Construct a relative frequency distribution for the data in Table 2.2.

Solution

We compute the relative frequencies for each type of computer in Table 2.2 by using the following steps.

Step 1: Find the total number of observations by summing the frequencies.

$$\text{Sum of frequencies} = 11 + 23 + 9 + 7 = 50$$

Step 2: Find the relative frequency for the first category, desktop computers.

$$\text{Relative frequency for desktop} = \frac{11}{50} = 0.22$$

Step 3: Find the relative frequencies for the remaining categories.

$$\text{Relative frequency for laptop} = \frac{23}{50} = 0.46$$

$$\text{Relative frequency for notebook} = \frac{9}{50} = 0.18$$

$$\text{Relative frequency for tablet} = \frac{7}{50} = 0.14$$

Table 2.3 on page 38 presents a relative frequency distribution for the data in Table 2.2.

Table 2.3 Relative Frequency Distribution for Computer Sales

Type of Computer	Frequency	Relative Frequency
Desktop	11	0.22
Laptop	23	0.46
Notebook	9	0.18
Tablet	7	0.14

Check Your Understanding

1. The following table lists the types of aircraft for the landings that occurred during a day at a small airport. ("Single" refers to single-engine and "Twin" refers to twin-engine.)

Types of Aircraft Landing at an Airport

Twin	Single	Helicopter	Turboprop	Twin	Single
Turboprop	Jet	Jet	Turboprop	Turboprop	Single
Jet	Single	Single	Twin	Twin	Turboprop
Helicopter	Single	Single	Single	Twin	Single
Jet	Twin	Twin	Single	Twin	Twin

  a. Construct a frequency distribution for these data.
  b. Construct a relative frequency distribution for these data.

Answers are on page 47.

Objective 2 Construct bar graphs

Bar Graphs

A **bar graph** is a graphical representation of a frequency distribution. A bar graph consists of rectangles of equal width, with one rectangle for each category. The heights of the rectangles represent the frequencies or relative frequencies of the categories. Example 2.3 shows how to construct a bar graph for the computer sales data in Table 2.3.

EXAMPLE 2.3

Constructing bar graphs

Construct a frequency bar graph and a relative frequency bar graph for the computer sales data in Table 2.3.

Solution

Step 1: Construct a horizontal axis. Place the category names along this axis, evenly spaced.

Step 2: Construct a vertical axis to represent the frequency or the relative frequency.

Step 3: Construct a bar for each category, with the heights of the bars equal to the frequencies or relative frequencies of their categories. The bars should not touch and should all be of the same width.

Figure 2.1(a) presents a frequency bar graph, and Figure 2.1(b) presents a relative frequency bar graph. The graphs are identical except for the scale on the vertical axis.

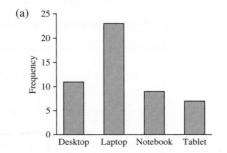
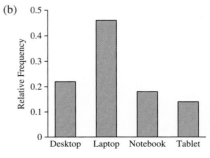

Figure 2.1 (a) Frequency bar graph. (b) Relative frequency bar graph.

Pareto charts

Sometimes it is desirable to construct a bar graph in which the categories are presented in order of frequency or relative frequency, with the largest frequency or relative frequency on the left and the smallest one on the right. Such a graph is called a **Pareto chart**. Pareto charts are useful when it is important to see clearly which are the most frequently occurring categories.

EXAMPLE 2.4

Constructing a Pareto chart

Construct a relative frequency Pareto chart for the data in Table 2.3.

Solution

Figure 2.2 presents the result. It is just like Figure 2.1(b) except that the bars are ordered from tallest to shortest.

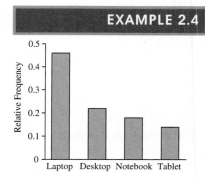

Figure 2.2 Pareto chart for the computer sales data

EXAMPLE 2.5

Horizontal bars

The bars in a bar graph may be either horizontal or vertical. Horizontal bars are sometimes more convenient when the categories have long names.

Constructing bar graphs with horizontal bars

The following relative frequency distribution categorizes employed U.S. residents by type of employment in the year 2009. Construct a relative frequency bar graph.

Type of Employment	Relative Frequency
Farming, forestry, fishing	0.007
Manufacturing, extraction, transportation, and crafts	0.203
Managerial, professional, and technical	0.373
Sales and office	0.242
Other services	0.176

Source: CIA — *The World Factbook*

Solution

The bar graph follows. We use horizontal bars, because the category names are long.

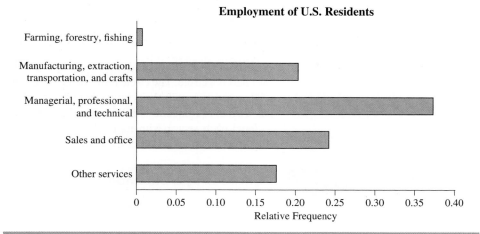

Side-by-side bar graphs

Sometimes we want to compare two bar graphs that have the same categories. The best way to do this is to construct both bar graphs on the same axes, putting bars that correspond to the same category next to each other. The result is called a **side-by-side bar graph**.

As an illustration, Table 2.4 presents the number of visitors, in millions, to several popular websites in February 2009 and in February 2010.

Table 2.4 Number of Visitors, in Millions

Website	February 2009	February 2010
Facebook	65	125
Google	126	137
YouTube	70	93
Microsoft Network (MSN)	37	38
Yahoo	66	66

Source: mostpopularwebsites.net

We would like to visualize the changes in the numbers of visitors between 2009 and 2010. Figure 2.3 presents the side-by-side bar graph. The bar graph clearly shows that Facebook's traffic grew enormously between 2009 and 2010, while the growth in traffic to the other websites was much less pronounced.

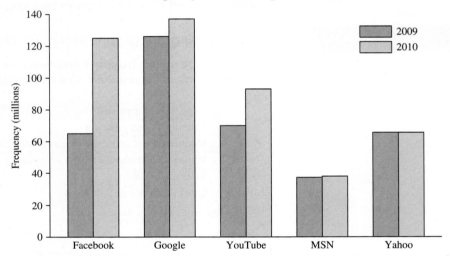

Figure 2.3 Side-by-side bar graph for the number of visitors to various websites

Objective 3 Construct pie charts

Pie Charts

A **pie chart** is an alternative to the bar graph for displaying relative frequency information. A pie chart is a circle. The circle is divided into sectors, one for each category. The relative sizes of the sectors match the relative frequencies of the categories. For example, if a category has a relative frequency of 0.25, then its sector takes up 25% of the circle. It is customary to label each sector with its relative frequency, expressed as a percentage. Example 2.6 illustrates the method for constructing a pie chart.

EXAMPLE 2.6   Constructing a pie chart

Construct a pie chart for the computer sales data in Table 2.3.

Solution

For each category, we must determine how large the sector for that category must be. Since there are 360 degrees in a circle, we multiply the relative frequency of the category by 360 to determine the number of degrees in the sector for that category. For example, the relative frequency for the Desktop category is 0.22. Therefore, the size of the sector for this category is $0.22 \cdot 360° = 79°$. Table 2.5 presents the results for all the categories.

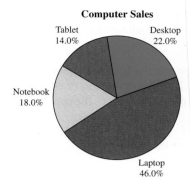

Figure 2.4 Pie chart for the computer data in Table 2.5

Table 2.5 Sizes of Sectors for Pie Chart of Computer Sales Data

Type of Computer	Frequency	Relative Frequency	Size of Sector
Desktop	11	0.22	79°
Laptop	23	0.46	166°
Notebook	9	0.18	65°
Tablet	7	0.14	50°

Figure 2.4 presents the pie chart.

Constructing pie charts by hand is tedious. However, many software packages, such as MINITAB and Excel, can draw them. Step-by-step instructions for constructing a pie chart in MINITAB and Excel are presented in the Using Technology section on page 43.

Check Your Understanding

2. The following table presents a frequency distribution for the number of cars and light trucks sold in the month of May 2008.

Type of Vehicle	Frequency
Small car	334,053
Midsize car	338,328
Large car	12,920
Luxury car	109,961
Minivan	85,157
SUV	124,507
Pickup truck	174,523
Cross-over truck	217,516

Source: *The Wall Street Journal*

   a. Construct a bar graph.
   b. Construct a relative frequency distribution.
   c. Construct a relative frequency bar graph.
   d. Construct a pie chart.

3. The following bar graph presents the number of refugees admitted to the United States between October 2004 and October 2005 from each of the top six countries.

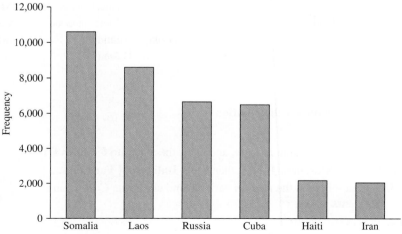

Source: CIA — *The World Factbook*

   a. Which country provided the greatest number of refugees?
   b. Someone says that Cuba provided more refugees than Haiti and Iran together. Is this correct? Explain how you can tell.

    c. Approximately how many refugees came from Russia?

    d. Approximately how many more refugees came from Somalia than from Laos?

4. In October 2010, the Gallup poll asked a sample of people the following question: "Do you think Congress has accomplished more this year, less this year, or about the same as it has in the past few years?" The following pie chart presents the percentages of people who gave each response.

Did Congress Accomplish More, Less, or the Same?

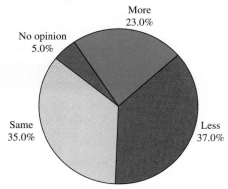

    a. Which was the most common response?

    b. What percentage of people said that Congress has accomplished the same or less than in the past few years?

    c. True or false: More than half of the people surveyed said that Congress accomplished as much or more this year than in the past few years.

Answers are on page 48.

USING TECHNOLOGY

We use the data in Table 2.6 to illustrate the technology steps. Table 2.6 lists 20 responses to a survey question about the reason for visiting a local library.

Table 2.6

Study	Meet someone	Check out books	Meet someone	Check out books
Study	Study	Meet someone	Check out books	Check out books
Meet someone	Check out books	Study	Study	Check out books
Check out books	Study	Study	Meet someone	Study

MINITAB

Constructing a frequency distribution

Step 1. Name your variable *Reason*, and enter the data into **Column C1**.

Step 2. Click on **Stat**, then **Tables**, then **Tally Individual Variables...**

Step 3. Double-click on the *Reason* variable and check the **Counts** and **Percents** boxes.

Step 4. Press **OK** (Figure A).

Tally for Discrete Variables: Reason

Reason	Count	Percent
Check out books	7	35.00
Meet someone	5	25.00
Study	8	40.00
N=	20	

Figure A

Constructing a bar graph

Step 1. Name your variable *Reason*, and enter the data into **Column C1**.

Step 2. Click on **Graph**, then **Bar Chart**. If given raw data as in Table 2.6, select **Bars Represent: Counts of Unique Values**. For the **Bar Chart type**, select **Simple**. Click **OK**. (If given a frequency distribution, select **Bars Represent: Values from a Table**.)

Step 3. Double-click on the *Reason* variable and click on any of the options desired.

Step 4. Press **OK** (Figure B).

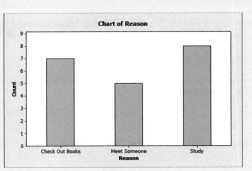

Figure B

Constructing a pie chart

Step 1. Name your variable *Reason*, and enter the data into **Column C1**.

Step 2. Click on **Graph**, then **Pie Chart**. If given raw data as in Table 2.6, select **Chart Raw Data**, and click **OK**. (If given a frequency distribution, select **Chart Values from a Table**.)

Step 3. Double-click on the *Reason* variable and click on any of the options desired.

Step 4. Press **OK** (Figure C).

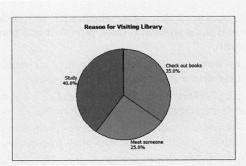

Figure C

EXCEL

Constructing a frequency distribution

Step 1. Enter the data in **Column A** with the label *Reason* in the topmost cell.

Step 2. Select **Insert**, then **Pivot Table**. Enter the range of cells that contain the data in the **Table/Range** field and click **OK**.

Step 3. In **Choose fields to add to report**, check Reason.

Step 4. Click on *Reason* and drag to the **Values** box. The result is shown in Figure D.

Row Labels	Count of Reason
Check out books	7
Meet someone	5
Study	8
Grand Total	**20**

Figure D

Constructing bar graphs and pie charts

Step 1. Enter the categories in **Column A** and the frequencies or relative frequencies in **Column B**.

Step 2. Highlight the values in **Column A** and **Column B**, and select **Insert**. For a bar graph, select **Column**. For a pie chart, select **Pie**.

SECTION 2.1 Exercises

Exercises 1–4 are the Check Your Understanding exercises located within the section.

Understanding the Concepts

In Exercises 5–8, fill in each blank with the appropriate word or phrase.

5. In a data set, the number of items that are in a particular category is called the _____ .

6. In a data set, the proportion of items that are in a particular category is called the _____ .

7. A _____ is a bar graph in which the bars are ordered by size.

8. A _____ is represented by a circle in which the sizes of the sectors match the relative frequencies of the categories.

In Exercises 9–12, determine whether the statement is true or false. If the statement is false, rewrite it as a true statement.

9. In a frequency distribution, the sum of all frequencies is less than the total number of observations.

10. In a pie chart, if a category has a relative frequency of 30%, then its sector takes up 30% of the circle.

11. The relative frequency of a category is equal to the frequency divided by the sum of all frequencies.

12. In bar graphs and Pareto charts, the widths of the bars represent the frequencies or relative frequencies.

Practicing the Skills

13. The following bar graph presents the average amount a U.S. family spent, in dollars, on various food categories in a recent year.

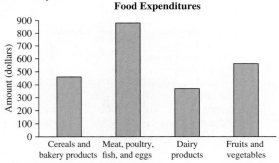

Food Expenditures

Source: Consumer Expenditure Survey

a. On which food category was the most money spent?

b. True or false: On the average, families spent more on cereals and bakery products than on fruits and vegetables.

c. True or false: Families spent more on animal products (meat, poultry, fish, eggs, and dairy products) than on plant products (cereals, bakery products, fruits, and vegetables).

14. The most common blood typing system divides human blood into four groups: A, B, O, and AB. The following bar graph presents the frequencies of these types in a sample of 150 blood donors.

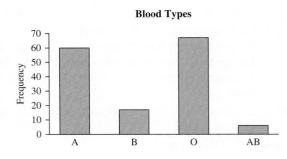

Blood Types

a. Which is the most frequent type?

b. True or false: More than half of the individuals in the sample had type O blood.

c. True or false: More than twice as many people had type A blood as had type B blood.

15. Following is a pie chart that presents the percentages of video games sold in each of four rating categories.

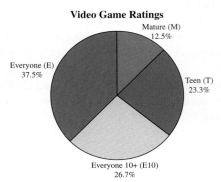

Video Game Ratings

Mature (M) 12.5%

Everyone (E) 37.5%

Teen (T) 23.3%

Everyone 10+ (E10) 26.7%

Source: Entertainment Software Association

a. Construct a relative frequency bar graph for these data.

b. Construct a relative frequency Pareto chart for these data.

c. In which rating category are the most games sold?

d. True or false: More than twice as many T-rated games are sold as M-rated games.

e. True or false: Fewer than one in five games sold is an M-rated game.

16. Following is a pie chart that presents the percentages of the U.S. federal budget that were spent in various categories in the fiscal year 2009.

U.S. Federal Spending - Fiscal Year 2009

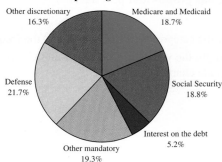

Other discretionary 16.3%

Medicare and Medicaid 18.7%

Defense 21.7%

Social Security 18.8%

Other mandatory 19.3%

Interest on the debt 5.2%

Source: Office of Management and Budget

a. Construct a relative frequency bar graph for these data.
b. Construct a relative frequency Pareto chart for these data.
c. In which category was the largest amount spent?
d. Social Security, Medicare and Medicaid, and interest on the debt are considered to be mandatory spending because they fulfill promises previously made by the government. Including other mandatory spending with these categories, what percentage of the spending was mandatory?

Working with the Concepts

17. iPod sales: The following frequency distribution presents the number of iPods sold (in thousands) in each quarter of each year from 2007 to 2010.

Quarter	Number Sold (in thousands)
Jan.–Mar. 2007	10,549
Apr.–Jun. 2007	9,815
Jul.–Sep. 2007	10,200
Oct.–Dec. 2007	22,121
Jan.–Mar. 2008	10,644
Apr.–Jun. 2008	11,011
Jul.–Sep. 2008	11,052
Oct.–Dec. 2008	22,727
Jan.–Mar. 2009	11,013
Apr.–Jun. 2009	10,215
Jul.–Sep. 2009	10,177
Oct.–Dec. 2009	20,970
Jan.–Mar. 2010	10,885
Apr.–Jun. 2010	9,410
Jul.–Sep. 2010	9,050
Oct.–Dec. 2010	19,446

Source: Wikipedia

a. Construct a frequency bar graph.
b. Construct a relative frequency distribution.
c. Construct a relative frequency bar graph.
d. True or false: The four quarters with the largest sales were all October to December.

18. Popular video games: The following frequency distribution presents the numbers of copies sold in 2009 (through November) for each of the ten best-selling video games.

Game	Platform	Sales (millions of units)
Call of Duty: Modern Warfare 2	Xbox 360	4.2
Wii Fit with balance board	Wii	3.5
Wii Sports Resort with MotionPlus	Wii	2.4
Mario Kart Wii with wheel	Wii	2.2
Wii Play with remote	Wii	2.1
Halo 3: ODST	Xbox 360	2.0
Pokemon Platinum	DS	1.9
Call of Duty: Modern Warfare 2	PS3	1.9
Madden NFL 10	Xbox 360	1.5
New Super Mario Bros. Wii	Wii	1.4

Source: NPD Group

a. Construct a frequency bar graph.
b. Construct a relative frequency distribution.

c. Construct a relative frequency bar graph.
d. True or false: More than 20% of the games sold were Call of Duty: Modern Warfare 2.

19. More iPods: Using the data in Exercise 17:
a. Construct a frequency distribution for the total number of iPods sold in each of the four quarters Jan.–Mar., Apr.–Jun., Jul.–Sep., and Oct.–Dec.
b. Construct a frequency bar graph.
c. Construct a relative frequency distribution.
d. Construct a relative frequency bar graph.
e. Construct a pie chart.
f. True or false: More than half of iPods were sold between October and December.

20. Popular platforms: Using the data in Exercise 18:
a. Construct a frequency distribution that presents the total sales for each of the platforms among the top ten games.
b. Construct a frequency bar graph.
c. Construct a relative frequency distribution.
d. Construct a relative frequency bar graph.
e. Construct a pie chart.
f. True or false: More than half the games sold among the top ten were Wii games.

21. Hospital admissions: The following frequency distribution presents the five most frequent reasons for hospital admissions in U.S. community hospitals in a recent year.

Reason	Frequency (in thousands)
Congestive heart failure	990
Coronary atherosclerosis	1400
Heart attack	744
Infant birth	3800
Pneumonia	1200

Source: Agency for Health Care Policy and Research

a. Construct a frequency bar graph.
b. Construct a relative frequency distribution.
c. Construct a relative frequency bar graph.
d. Construct a relative frequency Pareto chart.
e. Construct a pie chart.
f. The categories coronary atherosclerosis, congestive heart failure, and heart attack refer to diseases of the circulatory system. True or false: There were more hospital admissions for infant birth than for diseases of the circulatory system.

22. **World population:** Following are the populations of the continents of the world (not including Antarctica) in the year 2000.

Continent	Population (in millions)
Africa	800
Asia	3676
Oceania	31
Europe	731
North America	485
South America	348

Source: U.S. Census Bureau

a. Construct a frequency bar graph.
b. Construct a relative frequency distribution.
c. Construct a relative frequency bar graph.
d. Construct a relative frequency Pareto chart.
e. Construct a pie chart.
f. True or false: In the year 2000, more than half of the people in the world lived in Asia.
g. True or false: In the year 2000, there were more people in Europe than in North and South America combined.

23. **Ages of video gamers:** The Nielsen Company estimated the numbers of people in various gender and age categories who used a video game console. The results are presented in the following frequency distribution.

Gender and Age Group	Frequency (in millions)
Males 2–11	13.0
Females 2–11	10.1
Males 12–17	9.6
Females 12–17	6.2
Males 18–34	16.1
Females 18–34	11.6
Males 35–49	10.4
Females 35–49	9.3
Males 50+	3.5
Females 50+	3.9

Source: The Nielsen Company

a. Construct a frequency bar graph.
b. Construct a relative frequency distribution.
c. Construct a relative frequency bar graph.
d. Construct a pie chart.
e. True or false: More than half of video gamers are male.
f. True or false: More than 40% of video gamers are female.
g. What proportion of video gamers are 35 or over?

24. **How secure is your job?** In a survey, employed adults were asked how likely they thought it was that they would lose their jobs within the next year. The results are presented in the following frequency distribution.

Response	Frequency
Very likely	741
Fairly likely	859
Not too likely	3789
Not likely	9773

Source: General Social Survey

a. Construct a frequency bar graph.
b. Construct a relative frequency distribution.
c. Construct a relative frequency bar graph.
d. Construct a pie chart.
e. True or false: More than half of the people surveyed said that it was not likely that they would lose their job.
f. What proportion of the people in the survey said that it was very likely or fairly likely that they would lose their job?

25. **Back up your data:** In a survey commissioned by the Maxtor Corporation, U.S. computer users were asked how often they backed up their computer's hard drive. The following frequency distribution presents the results.

Response	Frequency
More than once per month	338
Once every 1–3 months	424
Once every 4–6 months	212
Once every 7–11 months	127
Once per year or less	311
Never	620

Source: The Maxtor Corporation

a. Construct a frequency bar graph.
b. Construct a relative frequency distribution.
c. Construct a relative frequency bar graph.
d. Construct a pie chart.
e. True or false: More than 30% of the survey respondents never back up their data.
f. True or false: Less than 50% of the survey respondents back up their data more than once per year.

26. **Education levels:** The following frequency distribution categorizes U.S. adults aged 18 and over by educational attainment in the year 2007.

Educational Attainment	Frequency (in thousands)
None	870
1–4 years	2,100
5–6 years	3,774
7–8 years	5,244
9 years	4,329
10 years	5,588
11 years	11,833
High school graduate	70,108
Some college but no degree	42,349
Associate's degree (occupational)	9,597
Associate's degree (academic)	8,641
Bachelor's degree	39,824
Master's degree	13,756
Professional degree	3,113
Doctoral degree	2,496

Source: U.S. Census Bureau

a. Construct a frequency bar graph.
b. Construct a relative frequency distribution.
c. Construct a relative frequency bar graph.
d. Construct a frequency distribution with the following categories: 8 years or less, 9–11 years, High school graduate, Some college but no degree, College degree (Associate's or Bachelor's), Graduate degree (Master's, Professional, or Doctoral).
e. Construct a pie chart for the frequency distribution in part (d).
f. What proportion of people did not graduate from high school?

27. Music sales: The following frequency distribution presents the number of units sold for categories of physical and digital music in the years 2007 and 2008. The Mobile category refers to ringtones and other music downloaded to a mobile device. The category "Other" includes CD singles, cassettes, DVDs, and download albums.

	Sales (in millions)	
Type of Music	**2007**	**2008**
CDs	511	385
Download single	810	1033
Mobile	362	338
Other	117	50

Source: Recording Industry Association of America

a. Construct a relative frequency distribution for the 2007 sales.
b. Construct a relative frequency distribution for the 2008 sales.
c. Construct a side-by-side relative frequency bar graph to compare the sales in 2007 and 2008.
d. True or false: More than half of all sales in 2008 were download singles.

28. Bought a new car lately? The following table presents the number of vehicles sold in the United States by several manufacturers in March 2009 and March 2010.

Manufacturer	2009	2010
General Motors	154,069	188,011
Ford	124,744	178,188
Chrysler LLC	101,001	92,623
Toyota	132,802	186,863
Honda	88,379	108,262
Nissan	66,634	95,468

Source: *The Wall Street Journal*

a. Construct a relative frequency distribution for the 2009 sales.
b. Construct a relative frequency distribution for the 2010 sales.
c. Construct a side-by-side relative frequency bar graph to compare the sales in 2009 and 2010.
d. True or false: For every manufacturer, sales were higher in 2010 than in 2009.

29. What are you reading? The following frequency distribution presents the number of subscriptions to four popular travel magazines in the spring of 2008.

Magazine	Subscribers (in thousands)
A.F.'s Budget Travel	620
Condé Nast Traveler	796
National Geographic Traveler	670
Travel & Leisure	956

Source: Mediaweek

a. Construct a frequency bar graph.
b. Construct a relative frequency distribution.
c. Construct a relative frequency bar graph.
d. Construct a pie chart.
e. What proportion of subscriptions are to *Travel & Leisure*?

30. The latest news: According to the Pew Research Center, there were 199 online news sites with more than 500,000 monthly unique visitors in 2009. The following table presents the number of sites in each of several categories.

Type of Site	Frequency
Newspaper	95
Online only	66
Magazine	11
Local TV	10
Other	17

Source: The Pew Research Center

a. Construct a frequency bar graph for these data.
b. Construct a relative frequency distribution.
c. Construct a relative frequency bar graph.
d. Construct a pie chart.
e. What proportion of online sites are associated with newspapers?

Extending the Concepts

31. Native languages: The following frequency distribution presents the number of households (in thousands) categorized by the language spoken at home, for the cities of New York and Los Angeles in the year 2006. The Total column presents the numbers of households in both cities combined.

Language	New York	Los Angeles	Total
English	3982	1384	5366
Spanish	1884	1539	3423
Other Indo-European	998	244	1242
Asian and Pacific Island	546	277	823

Source: U.S. Census Bureau

a. Construct a frequency bar graph for each city.
b. Construct a frequency bar graph for the total.
c. Construct a relative frequency bar graph for each city.
d. Construct a relative frequency bar graph for the total.
e. Explain why the heights of the bars for the frequency bar graph for the total are equal to the sums of the heights for the individual cities.
f. Explain why the heights of the bars for the relative frequency bar graph for the total are not equal to the sums of the heights for the individual cities.

Answers to Check Your Understanding Exercises for Section 2.1

1. a.

Aircraft	Frequency
Twin	9
Single	10
Helicopter	2
Turboprop	5
Jet	4

b.

Aircraft	Frequency	Relative Frequency
Twin	9	0.300
Single	10	0.333
Helicopter	2	0.067
Turboprop	5	0.167
Jet	4	0.133

Continued on page 48

Answers to Check Your Understanding Exercises for Section 2.1 (continued)

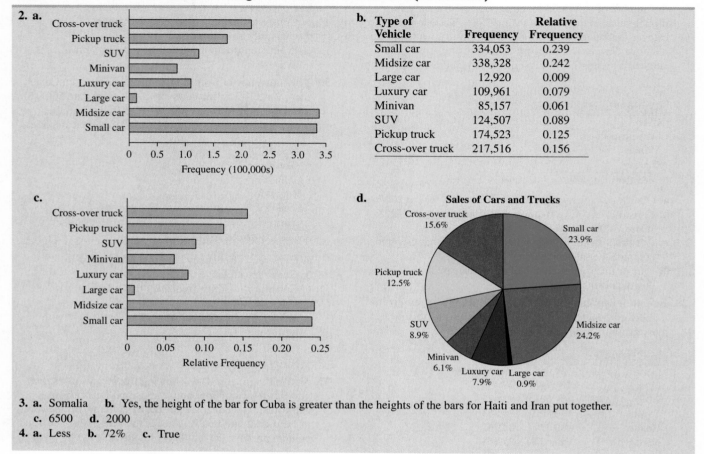

2. a.

b.

Type of Vehicle	Frequency	Relative Frequency
Small car	334,053	0.239
Midsize car	338,328	0.242
Large car	12,920	0.009
Luxury car	109,961	0.079
Minivan	85,157	0.061
SUV	124,507	0.089
Pickup truck	174,523	0.125
Cross-over truck	217,516	0.156

3. a. Somalia   **b.** Yes, the height of the bar for Cuba is greater than the heights of the bars for Haiti and Iran put together.
c. 6500   **d.** 2000
4. a. Less   **b.** 72%   **c.** True

SECTION 2.2	Frequency Distributions and Their Graphs

Objectives

1. Construct frequency distributions for quantitative data
2. Construct histograms
3. Determine the shape of a distribution from a histogram

Objective 1 Construct frequency distributions for quantitative data

Frequency Distributions for Quantitative Data

How much air pollution is caused by motor vehicles? This question was addressed in a study by Dr. Janet Yanowitz at the Colorado School of Mines. She studied the emissions of particulate matter, a form of pollution consisting of tiny particles, that has been associated with respiratory disease. The emissions for 65 vehicles, in units of grams of particles per gallon of fuel, are presented in Table 2.7.

Table 2.7 Particulate Emissions for 65 Vehicles

1.50	0.87	1.12	1.25	3.46	1.11	1.12	0.88	1.29	0.94	0.64	1.31	2.49
1.48	1.06	1.11	2.15	0.86	1.81	1.47	1.24	1.63	2.14	6.64	4.04	2.48
1.40	1.37	1.81	1.14	1.63	3.67	0.55	2.67	2.63	3.03	1.23	1.04	1.63
3.12	2.37	2.12	2.68	1.17	3.34	3.79	1.28	2.10	6.55	1.18	3.06	0.48
0.25	0.53	3.36	3.47	2.74	1.88	5.94	4.24	3.52	3.59	3.10	3.33	4.58

To summarize these data, we will construct a frequency distribution. Since these data are quantitative, there are no natural categories. We therefore divide the data into **classes**. The classes are intervals of equal width that cover all the values that are observed. For example, for the data in Table 2.7, we could choose the classes to be 0.00–0.99, 1.00–1.99, and so forth. We then count the number of observations that fall into each class, to obtain the class frequencies.

<table>
<tr><td>**EXAMPLE 2.7**</td></tr>
</table>

Construct a frequency distribution

Construct a frequency distribution for the data in Table 2.7, using the classes 0.00–0.99, 1.00–1.99, and so on.

Explain It Again

Frequency distributions for quantitative and qualitative data: Frequency distributions for quantitative data are just like those for qualitative data, except that the data are divided into classes rather than categories.

Solution

First we list the classes. We begin by noting that the smallest value in the data set is 0.25 and the largest is 6.64. We list classes until we get to the class that contains the largest value. The classes are 0.00–0.99, 1.00–1.99, 2.00–2.99, 3.00–3.99, 4.00–4.99, 5.00–5.99, and 6.00–6.99. Since the largest number in the data set is 6.64, these are enough classes.

Now we count the number of observations that fall into each class. The first class is 0.00–0.99. We count nine observations between 0.00 and 0.99 in Table 2.7. The next class is 1.00–1.99. We count 26 observations in this class. We repeat this procedure with classes 2.00–2.99, 3.00–3.99, 4.00–4.99, 5.00–5.99, and 6.00–6.99. The results are presented in Table 2.8. This is a frequency distribution for the data in Table 2.7.

Table 2.8 Frequency Distribution for Particulate Data

Class	Frequency
0.00–0.99	9
1.00–1.99	26
2.00–2.99	11
3.00–3.99	13
4.00–4.99	3
5.00–5.99	1
6.00–6.99	2

We can also construct a relative frequency distribution. As with qualitative data, the relative frequency of a class is the frequency of that class, divided by the sum of all the frequencies.

DEFINITION

The **relative frequency** of a class is given by

$$\text{Relative frequency} = \frac{\text{Frequency}}{\text{Sum of all frequencies}}$$

<table>
<tr><td>**EXAMPLE 2.8**</td></tr>
</table>

Construct a relative frequency distribution

Construct a relative frequency distribution for the data in Table 2.7, using the classes 0.00–0.99, 1.00–1.99, and so on.

Solution

The frequency distribution is presented in Table 2.8. We compute the sum of all the frequencies:

$$\text{Sum of all frequencies} = 9 + 26 + 11 + 13 + 3 + 1 + 2 = 65$$

We can now compute the relative frequency for each class. For the class 0.00–0.99, the frequency is 9. The relative frequency is therefore

$$\text{Relative frequency} = \frac{\text{Frequency}}{\text{Sum of all frequencies}} = \frac{9}{65} = 0.138$$

Table 2.9 is a relative frequency distribution for the data in Table 2.7. The frequencies are shown as well.

Table 2.9 Relative Frequency Distribution for Particulate Data

Class	Frequency	Relative Frequency
0.00–0.99	9	0.138
1.00–1.99	26	0.400
2.00–2.99	11	0.169
3.00–3.99	13	0.200
4.00–4.99	3	0.046
5.00–5.99	1	0.015
6.00–6.99	2	0.031

Choosing the classes

In Examples 2.7 and 2.8, we chose the classes to be 0.00–0.99, 1.00–1.99, and so on. There are many other choices we could have made. For example, we could have chosen the classes to be 0.00–1.99, 2.00–3.99, 4.00–5.99, and 6.00–7.99. As another example, we could have chosen them to be 0.00–0.49, 0.50–0.99, and so on, up to 6.50–6.99. We now define some of the terminology that we will use when discussing classes.

DEFINITION

- The **lower class limit** of a class is the smallest value that can appear in that class.
- The **upper class limit** of a class is the largest value that can appear in that class.
- The **class width** is the difference between consecutive lower class limits.

CAUTION

The class width is the difference between the lower limit and the lower limit of the next class, not the difference between the lower limit and the upper limit.

Class limits should be expressed with the same number of decimal places as the data. The data in Table 2.7 are rounded to two decimal places, so the class limits for these data are expressed with two decimal places as well.

EXAMPLE 2.9   **Find the class limits and widths**

Find the lower class limits, the upper class limits, and the class widths for the relative frequency distribution in Table 2.9.

Solution

The classes are 0.00–0.99, 1.00–1.99, and so on, up to 6.00–6.99. The lower class limits are therefore 0.00, 1.00, 2.00, 3.00, 4.00, 5.00, and 6.00. The upper class limits are 0.99, 1.99, 2.99, 3.99, 4.99, 5.99, and 6.99.

We find the class width for the first class by subtracting consecutive lower limits:

$$\text{Class width} = \text{Lower limit for second class} - \text{Lower limit for first class}$$
$$= 1.00 - 0.00$$
$$= 1.00$$

Similarly, we find that all the classes have a width of 1.

When constructing a frequency distribution, there is no one right way to choose the classes. However, there are some requirements that must be satisfied:

Requirements for Choosing Classes

- Every observation must fall into one of the classes.
- The classes must not overlap.
- The classes must be of equal width.
- There must be no gaps between classes. Even if there are no observations in a class, it must be included in the frequency distribution.

The following procedure will produce a frequency distribution whose classes meet these requirements.

Procedure for Constructing a Frequency Distribution for Quantitative Data

Step 1: Choose a class width.

Step 2: Choose a lower class limit for the first class. This should be a convenient number that is slightly less than the minimum data value.

Step 3: Compute the lower limit for the second class by adding the class width to the lower limit for the first class:

Lower limit for second class = Lower limit for first class + Class width

Step 4: Compute the lower limits for each of the remaining classes, by adding the class width to the lower limit of the preceding class. Stop when the largest data value is included in a class.

Step 5: Count the number of observations in each class, and construct the frequency distribution.

EXAMPLE 2.10

Constructing a frequency distribution

Construct a frequency distribution for the data in Table 2.7, using a class width of 1.50.

Solution

Step 1: The class width is given to be 1.50.

Step 2: The smallest value in the data is 0.25. A convenient number that is smaller than 0.25 is 0.00. We will choose 0.00 to be the lower limit for the first class.

Step 3: The lower class limit for the second class is $0.00 + 1.50 = 1.50$.

Step 4: Continuing, the lower limits for the remaining classes are

$$1.50 + 1.50 = 3.00$$
$$3.00 + 1.50 = 4.50$$
$$4.50 + 1.50 = 6.00$$
$$6.00 + 1.50 = 7.50$$

Since the largest data value is 6.64, every data value is now contained in a class.

Step 5: We count the number of observations in each class to obtain the following frequency distribution.

Frequency Distribution for Particulate
Data Using a Class Width of 1.5

Class	Frequency
0.00–1.49	28
1.50–2.99	18
3.00–4.49	15
4.50–5.99	2
6.00–7.49	2

1. Using the data in Table 2.7, construct a frequency distribution with classes of width 0.5.

Answer is on page 63.

Computing the class width for a given number of classes

In Example 2.10, the first step in computing the frequency distribution was to choose a class width. Sometimes we begin by choosing an approximate number of classes instead. In these cases, we compute the class width as follows:

Step 1: Decide approximately how many classes to have.

Step 2: Compute the class width as follows:

$$\text{Class width} = \frac{\text{Largest data value} - \text{Smallest data value}}{\text{Number of classes}}$$

Step 3: Round the class width to a convenient value. It is usually better to round up.

Once the class width is determined, we proceed just as in the case where the class width is given. We choose a lower limit for the first class by choosing a convenient number that is slightly less than the minimum data value. We then compute the lower limits for the remaining classes, count the number of observations in each class, and construct the frequency distribution. Note that the actual number of classes may differ somewhat from the chosen number, because the class width is rounded and because the lower limit of the first class will generally be less than the smallest data value.

EXAMPLE 2.11   Computing the class width

Find the class width for a frequency distribution for the data in Table 2.7, if it is desired to have approximately seven classes.

Solution
Step 1: We will have approximately seven classes.

Step 2: The smallest data value is 0.25 and the largest is 6.64. We compute the class width:

$$\text{Class width} = \frac{6.64 - 0.25}{7} = 0.91$$

Step 3: We round 0.91 up to 1, since this is the nearest convenient number. We will use a class width of 1.

A reasonable choice for the lower limit of the first class is 0. This choice will give us the frequency distribution in Table 2.8.

Objective 2 Construct histograms

Histograms

Once we have a frequency distribution or a relative frequency distribution, we can put the information in graphical form by constructing a **histogram**. Histograms based on frequency distributions are called **frequency histograms**, and histograms based on relative frequency distributions are called **relative frequency histograms**. Histograms are related to bar graphs and are appropriate for quantitative data. A histogram is constructed by drawing a rectangle for each class. The heights of the rectangles are equal to the frequencies or the relative frequencies, and the widths are equal to the class width. The left edge of each rectangle corresponds to the lower class limit, and the right edge touches the left edge of the next rectangle.

EXAMPLE 2.12   Construct a histogram

Table 2.10 presents a frequency distribution and the relative frequency distribution for the particulate emissions data.

Construct a frequency histogram based on the frequency distribution in Table 2.10. Construct a relative frequency histogram based on the relative frequency distribution in Table 2.10.

Table 2.10 Frequency and Relative Frequency Distributions for Particulate Data

Class	Frequency	Relative Frequency
0.00–0.99	9	0.138
1.00–1.99	26	0.400
2.00–2.99	11	0.169
3.00–3.99	13	0.200
4.00–4.99	3	0.046
5.00–5.99	1	0.015
6.00–6.99	2	0.031

Solution

We construct a rectangle for each class. The first rectangle has its left edge at the lower limit of the first class, which is 0.00, and its right edge at the lower limit of the next class, which is 1.00. The second rectangle has its left edge at 1.00 and its right edge at the lower limit of the next class, which is 2.00, and so on.

For the frequency histogram, the heights of the rectangles are equal to the frequencies. For the relative frequency histogram, the heights of the rectangles are equal to the relative frequencies.

Figure 2.5 presents a frequency histogram, and Figure 2.6 presents a relative frequency histogram, for the data in Table 2.10. Note that the two histograms have the same shape. The only difference is the scale on the vertical axis.

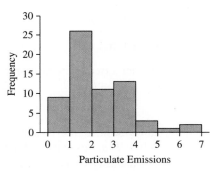

Figure 2.5 Frequency histogram for the frequency distribution in Table 2.10

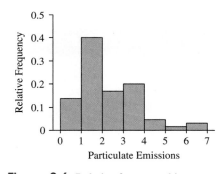

Figure 2.6 Relative frequency histogram for the relative frequency distribution in Table 2.10

How should I choose the number of classes for a histogram?

There are no hard-and-fast rules for choosing the number of classes. In general, it is good to have more classes rather than fewer, but it is also good to have reasonably large frequencies in some of the classes. The following two principles can guide the choice:

- Too many classes produce a histogram with too much detail, so that the main features of the data are obscured.
- Too few classes produce a histogram lacking in detail.

Figures 2.7 and 2.8 on page 54 illustrate these principles. Figure 2.7 presents a histogram for the particulate data where the class width is 0.1. This narrow class width results in a large number of classes. The histogram has a jagged appearance, which distracts from the overall shape of the data. On the other extreme, Figure 2.8 presents a histogram for these

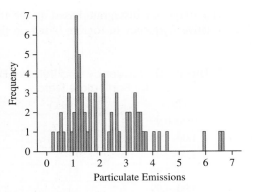

Figure 2.7 The class width is too narrow. The jagged appearance distracts from the overall shape of the data.

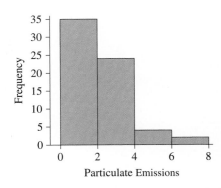

Figure 2.8 The class width is too wide. Only the most basic features of the data are visible.

data with a class width of 2.0. The number of classes is too small, so only the most basic features of the data are visible in this overly simple histogram.

Choosing a large number of classes will produce a narrow class width, and choosing a smaller number will produce a wider class width. It is appropriate to experiment with various choices for the number of classes, in order to find a good balance. The following guidelines are helpful.

Guidelines for Selecting the Number of Classes

- For many data sets, the number of classes should be at least 5 but no more than 20.
- For very large data sets, a larger number of classes may be appropriate.

EXAMPLE 2.13

Constructing a histogram with technology

Use technology to construct a frequency histogram for the emissions data in Table 2.7 on page 48.

Solution

The following figure shows the histogram constructed in MINITAB. Note that MINITAB has chosen a class width of 0.5. With this class width, there are two empty classes. These show up as a gap that separates the last two rectangles on the right from the rest of the histogram.

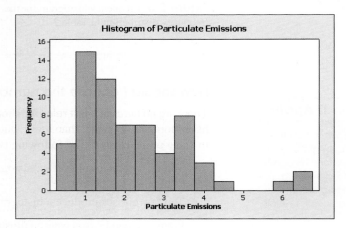

Step-by-step instructions for constructing histograms with the TI-84 Plus and with MINITAB are given in the Using Technology section on pages 57 and 58.

2. Following is a frequency distribution that presents the number of live births to women aged 15–44 in the state of Wyoming in a recent year.

Distribution of Births by Age of Mother

Age	Frequency
15–19	795
20–24	2410
25–29	2190
30–34	1208
35–39	499
40–44	109

Source: Wyoming Department of Health

 a. List the lower class limits.
 b. What is the class width?
 c. Construct a frequency histogram.
 d. Construct a relative frequency distribution.
 e. Construct a relative frequency histogram.

Answers are on page 63.

Open-ended classes

It is sometimes necessary for the first class to have no lower limit or for the last class to have no upper limit. Such a class is called **open-ended**. Table 2.11 presents a frequency distribution for the number of deaths in the United States due to pneumonia in a recent year for various age groups. Note that the last age group is "85 and older," an open-ended class.

Table 2.11 Deaths Due to Pneumonia

Age	Number of Deaths
5–14	69
15–24	178
25–34	299
35–44	875
45–54	1872
55–64	3099
65–74	6283
75–84	17,775
85 and older	27,758

Source: U.S. Census Bureau

When a frequency distribution contains an open-ended class, a histogram cannot be drawn.

Histograms for discrete data

When data are discrete, we can construct a frequency distribution in which each possible value of the variable forms a class. Then we can draw a histogram in which each rectangle represents one possible value of the variable. Table 2.12 on page 56 presents the results of a hypothetical survey in which 1000 adult women were asked how many children they had. Number of children is a discrete variable, and in this data set, the values of this variable are 0 through 8. To construct a histogram, we draw rectangles of equal width, centered at the values of the variables. The rectangles should be just wide enough to touch. Figure 2.9 on page 56 presents a histogram.

Table 2.12 Women with a Given Number of Children

Number of Children	Frequency
0	435
1	175
2	222
3	112
4	38
5	9
6	7
7	0
8	2

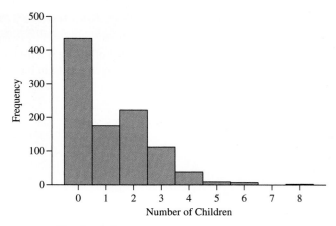

Figure 2.9 Histogram for data in Table 2.12

Objective 3 Determine the shape of a distribution from a histogram

Shapes of Histograms

The purpose of a histogram is to give a visual impression of the "shape" of a data set. Statisticians have developed terminology to describe some of the commonly observed shapes. A histogram is **symmetric** if its right half is a mirror image of its left half. Very few histograms are perfectly symmetric, but many are approximately symmetric. A histogram is **skewed** if one side, or tail, is longer than the other. A histogram with a long right-hand tail is said to be **skewed to the right**, or **positively skewed**. A histogram with a long left-hand tail is said to be **skewed to the left**, or **negatively skewed**. These terms apply to both frequency histograms and relative frequency histograms. Figure 2.10 presents some histograms for hypothetical samples. As another example, the histogram for particulate concentration, shown in Figure 2.5, is skewed to the right.

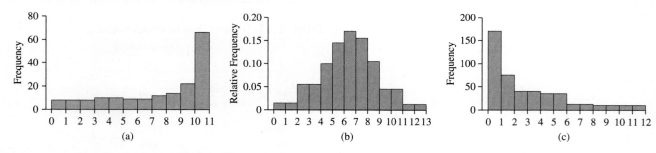

Figure 2.10 (a) A histogram skewed to the left. (b) An approximately symmetric histogram. (c) A histogram skewed to the right.

The examples in Figure 2.10 are straightforward to categorize. In real life, the classification is not always clear-cut, and people may sometimes disagree on how to describe the shape of a particular histogram.

Modes

A peak, or high point, of a histogram is referred to as a **mode**. A histogram is **unimodal** if it has only one mode, and **bimodal** if it has two clearly distinct modes. In principle, a histogram can have more than two modes, but this does not happen often in practice. The histograms in Figure 2.10 are all unimodal. Figure 2.11 presents a bimodal histogram for a hypothetical sample.

As another example, it is reasonable to classify the histogram for particulate emissions, shown in Figure 2.5, as unimodal, with the rectangle above the class 1–2 as the only mode. While some might say that the rectangle above the class 3–4 is another mode, most would agree that it is too small a peak to count as a second mode.

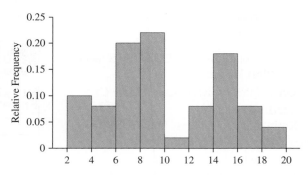

Figure 2.11   A bimodal histogram

Check Your Understanding

3. Classify each of the following histograms as skewed to the left, skewed to the right, or approximately symmetric.

a.

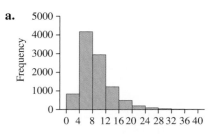

b.

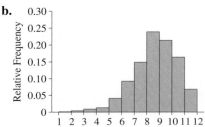

c.

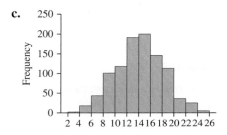

4. Classify each of the following histograms as unimodal or bimodal.

a.

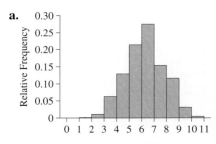

b.

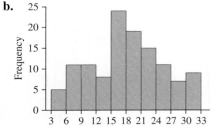

c.

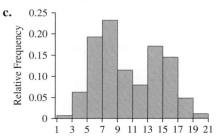

Answers are on page 63.

USING TECHNOLOGY

We use the data in Table 2.7 to illustrate the technology steps.

TI-84 PLUS

Entering Data

Step 1. We will enter the data into **L1** in the data editor. First, to clear out any data that may be in the list, press **STAT**, then **4: ClrList**, then enter **L1** by pressing **2nd, L1** (Figure A). Then press **ENTER**.

Step 2. Enter the data into **L1** in the data editor by pressing **STAT** then **1: Edit**. For the data in Table 2.7, we begin with **1.5, .87, 1.12, 1.25, 3.46, ...** (Figure B).

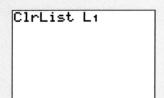

Figure A

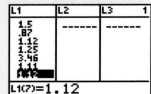

Figure B

Constructing a Histogram

Step 1. Press **2nd, Y=** to access the STAT PLOTS menu
and select **Plot1** by pressing **1**.

Step 2. Select **On** and the histogram icon (Figure C).

Step 3. Press **WINDOW** and:
- Set **Xmin** to the lower class limit of the first
class. We use 0 for our example.
- Set **Xmax** to the lower class limit of the class
following the one containing the largest data
value. We use 7.
- Set **Xscl** to the class width. We use 1.
- Set **Ymin** to 0.
- Set **Ymax** to a value greater than the largest
frequency of all classes. We use 30.

Step 4. Press **GRAPH** to view the histogram (Figure D).

Figure C

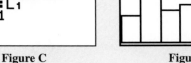

Figure D

MINITAB

Constructing a Histogram

Step 1. Name your variable *Particulate Emissions* and
enter the data from Table 2.7 into Column **C1**.

Step 2. Click on **Graph**. Select **Histogram**. Choose the
Simple option. Press **OK**.

Step 3. Double-click on the *Particulate Emissions*
variable and press **OK** (Figure E).

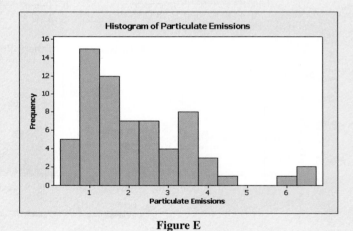

Figure E

EXCEL

Constructing a Histogram

Step 1. Enter the *Particulate Emissions* data from Table 2.7 in **Column A**.

Step 2. Press **Data**, then **Data Analysis**. Select **Histogram** and click **OK**.

Step 3. Enter the range of cells that contain the data in the **Input Range** field and check the **Chart Output** box.

Step 4. Click **OK**.

SECTION 2.2   Exercises

Exercises 1–4 are the Check Your Understanding exercises located within the section.

Understanding the Concepts

In Exercises 5–8, fill in each blank with the appropriate word or phrase.

5. When the right half of a histogram is a mirror image of the left half, the histogram is _____ .

6. A histogram is skewed to the left if its _____ tail is longer than its _____ tail.

7. A histogram is _____ if it has two clearly distinct modes.

8. The _____ of a category is the number of times it appears in the data set.

In Exercises 9–12, determine whether the statement is true or false. If the statement is false, rewrite it as a true statement.

9. In a frequency distribution, the class width is the difference between the upper and lower class limits.

10. The number of classes used has little effect on the shape of the histogram.

11. There is no one right way to choose the classes for a frequency distribution.

12. A mode occurs at the peak of a histogram.

Practicing the Skills

In Exercises 13–16, classify the histogram as skewed to the left, skewed to the right, or approximately symmetric.

13.

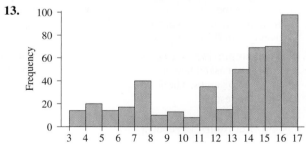

14.

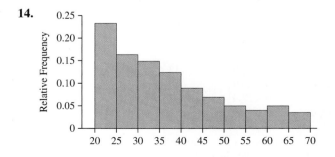

15.

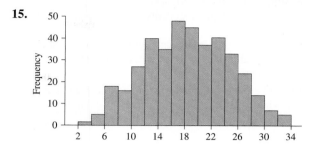

16.

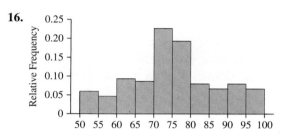

In Exercises 17 and 18, classify the histogram as unimodal or bimodal.

17.

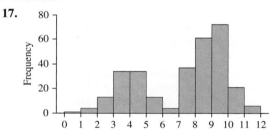

18.

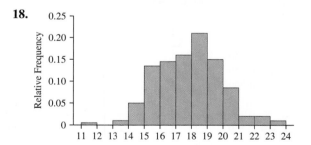

Working with the Concepts

19. **Student heights:** The following frequency histogram presents the heights, in inches, of a random sample of 100 male college students.

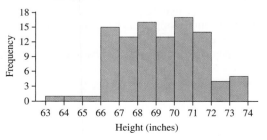

a. How many classes are there?
b. What is the class width?
c. Which class has the highest frequency?
d. What percentage of students are more than 72 inches tall?
e. Is the histogram most accurately described as skewed to the right, skewed to the left, or approximately symmetric?

20. **Trained rats:** Forty rats were trained to run a maze. The following frequency histogram presents the numbers of trials it took each rat to learn the maze.

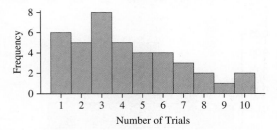

a. What is the most frequent number of trials?
b. How many rats learned the maze in three trials or less?
c. How many rats took nine trials or more to learn the maze?
d. Is the histogram most accurately described as skewed to the right, skewed to the left, or approximately symmetric?

21. **Batting average:** The following frequency distribution presents the batting averages of Major League Baseball players who had 300 or more plate appearances during the 2010 season.

Batting Average	Frequency
0.180–0.199	3
0.200–0.219	8
0.220–0.239	22
0.240–0.259	72
0.260–0.279	80
0.280–0.299	47
0.300–0.319	28
0.320–0.339	6
0.340–0.359	2

Source: sports.espn.go.com

a. How many classes are there?
b. What is the class width?
c. What are the class limits?
d. Construct a frequency histogram.
e. Construct a relative frequency distribution.
f. Construct a relative frequency histogram.
g. What percentage of players had batting averages of 0.300 or more?
h. What percentage of players had batting averages less than 0.220?

22. **Batting average:** The following frequency distribution presents the batting averages of Major League Baseball players in both the American League and the National League who had 300 or more plate appearances during the 2010 season.

Batting Average	American League Frequency	National League Frequency
0.180–0.199	2	1
0.200–0.219	4	4
0.220–0.239	14	8
0.240–0.259	34	38
0.260–0.279	35	45
0.280–0.299	21	26
0.300–0.319	15	13
0.320–0.339	3	3
0.340–0.359	2	0

Source: sports.espn.go.com

a. Construct a frequency histogram for the American League.
b. Construct a frequency histogram for the National League.
c. Construct a relative frequency distribution for the American League.
d. Construct a relative frequency distribution for the National League.
e. Construct a relative frequency histogram for the American League.
f. Construct a relative frequency histogram for the National League.
g. What percentage of American League players had batting averages of 0.300 or more?
h. What percentage of National League players had batting averages of 0.300 or more?
i. Compare the relative frequency histograms. What is the main difference between the distributions of batting averages in the two leagues?

23. **Time spent playing video games:** A sample of 200 college freshmen was asked how many hours per week they spent playing video games. The following frequency distribution presents the results.

Number of Hours	Frequency
1.0 – 3.9	25
4.0 – 6.9	34
7.0 – 9.9	48
10.0 – 12.9	29
13.0 – 15.9	23
16.0 – 18.9	17
19.0 – 21.9	13
22.0 – 24.9	7
25.0 – 27.9	3
28.0 – 30.9	1

a. How many classes are there?
b. What is the class width?

c. What are the class limits?

d. Construct a frequency histogram.

e. Construct a relative frequency distribution.

f. Construct a relative frequency histogram.

g. What percentage of students play video games less than 10 hours per week?

h. What percentage of students play video games 19 or more hours per week?

24. Murder, she wrote: The following frequency distribution presents the number of murders (including negligent manslaughter) per 100,000 population for each U.S. city with population over 250,000 in the year 2008.

Murder Rate	Frequency
0.0 – 4.9	16
5.0 – 9.9	23
10.0 – 14.9	21
15.0 – 19.9	3
20.0 – 24.9	6
25.0 – 29.9	2
30.0 – 34.9	2
35.0 – 39.9	1
40.0 – 44.9	0
45.0 – 49.9	1
50.0 – 54.9	0
55.0 – 59.9	0
60.0 – 64.9	1

Source: Federal Bureau of Investigation

a. How many classes are there?

b. What is the class width?

c. What are the class limits?

d. Construct a frequency histogram.

e. Construct a relative frequency distribution.

f. Construct a relative frequency histogram.

g. What percentage of cities had murder rates less than 20 per 100,000 population?

h. What percentage of cities had murder rates of 40 or more per 100,000 population?

25. BMW prices: The following table presents the manufacturer's suggested retail price (in $1000s) for 2008 base models and styles of BMW automobiles.

28.8	52.0	34.5	49.5	53.8	46.2	50.4
34.9	58.8	36.4	76.6	56.5	54.8	52.4
33.1	54.4	35.6	83.7	64.95	52.5	39.1
32.7	37.4	76.8	83.9	63.0	44.6	34.6
41.2	79.9	100.3	36.7	46.8	39.3	43.0
124.1	106.1	42.7	49.8	41.2	43.5	115.0
38.6	40.7					

Source: www.edmunds.com

a. Construct a frequency distribution using a class width of 10, and using 20 as the lower class limit for the first class.

b. Construct a frequency histogram from the frequency distribution in part (a).

c. Construct a relative frequency distribution using the same class width and lower limit for the first class.

d. Construct a relative frequency histogram.

e. Are the histograms unimodal or bimodal?

f. Repeat parts (a)–(d), using a class width of 20, and using 20 as the lower class limit for the first class.

g. Do you think that class widths of 10 and 20 are both reasonably good choices for these data, or do you think that one choice is much better than the other? Explain your reasoning.

26. Geysers: The geyser Old Faithful in Yellowstone National Park alternates periods of eruption, which typically last from 1.5 to 4 minutes, with periods of dormancy, which are considerably longer. The following table presents the durations, in minutes, of 60 dormancy periods that occurred during the period January 21–25, 2010.

91	99	99	83	99	85	90	96	88	93
88	88	92	116	59	101	90	71	103	97
82	91	89	89	94	94	61	96	66	105
90	93	88	92	86	93	95	83	90	99
89	94	90	95	93	105	96	92	101	91
94	92	94	86	88	99	90	99	84	92

a. Construct a frequency distribution using a class width of 5, and using 55 as the lower class limit for the first class.

b. Construct a frequency histogram from the frequency distribution in part (a).

c. Construct a relative frequency distribution using the same class width and lower limit for the first class.

d. Construct a relative frequency histogram.

e. Are the histograms skewed to the left, skewed to the right, or approximately symmetric?

f. Repeat parts (a)–(d), using a class width of 10, and using 50 as the lower class limit for the first class.

g. Do you think that class widths of 5 and 10 are both reasonably good choices for these data, or do you think that one choice is much better than the other? Explain your reasoning.

27. Hail to the chief: There have been 56 presidential inaugurations in U.S. history. At each one, the president has made an inaugural address. Following are the number of words spoken in each of these addresses.

1425	135	2308	1729	2158	1175	1209	3217
4467	2906	1125	1172	3838	8445	4776	996
3319	2821	3634	698	1128	1337	2480	2978
1681	4388	2015	3967	2217	985	5433	1802
1526	3318	4059	3801	1883	1807	1340	559
2242	2446	2449	1355	1437	2130	1668	1087
2463	2546	2283	1507	2170	1571	2073	2406

Source: www.infoplease.com

a. Construct a frequency distribution with approximately five classes.

b. Construct a frequency histogram from the frequency distribution in part (a).

c. Construct a relative frequency distribution using the same classes as in part (a).

d. Construct a relative frequency histogram from this relative frequency distribution.

e. Are the histograms skewed to the left, skewed to the right, or approximately symmetric?

f. Construct a frequency distribution with approximately nine classes.

g. Repeat parts (b)–(d), using the frequency distribution constructed in part (f).

h. Do you think that five and nine classes are both reasonably good choices for these data, or do you think that one choice is much better than the other? Explain your reasoning.

28. **Technology salaries:** The following table presents the annual salaries for the employees of a small technology firm.

91,808	118,625	131,092	60,763
36,463	37,187	45,870	50,594
98,302	123,973	182,255	59,186
44,889	164,861	71,082	69,695
28,098	157,110	50,461	98,132
49,742	25,339	24,164	107,878
136,690	129,514	99,254	57,468

a. Construct a frequency distribution with approximately nine classes.

b. Construct a frequency histogram from this frequency distribution.

c. Construct a relative frequency distribution using the same classes.

d. Construct a relative frequency histogram from this relative frequency distribution.

e. Are the histograms skewed to the left, skewed to the right, or approximately symmetric?

f. Construct a frequency distribution with approximately four classes.

g. Repeat parts (b)–(d), using the frequency distribution constructed in part (f).

h. Do you think that four and nine classes are both reasonably good choices for these data, or do you think that one choice is much better than the other? Explain your reasoning.

29. **Brothers and sisters:** Thirty students in a first-grade class were asked how many siblings they have. Following are the results.

1	1	2	1	2	3	7	1	1	5
1	1	3	0	1	1	1	2	5	0
0	1	2	2	4	2	2	3	3	4

a. Construct a frequency histogram.

b. Construct a relative frequency histogram.

c. Are the histograms skewed to the left, skewed to the right, or approximately symmetric?

30. **Pets:** Thirty students in a second-grade class were asked how many pets their family has. Following are the results.

1	0	0	1	1	2	0	1	2	1
1	2	2	0	1	0	1	1	3	1
1	5	2	1	1	4	0	1	1	2

a. Construct a frequency histogram.

b. Construct a relative frequency histogram.

c. Are the histograms skewed to the left, skewed to the right, or approximately symmetric?

31. **No histogram possible:** A company surveyed 100 employees to find out how far they travel in their commute to work. The results are presented in the following frequency distribution.

Distance in Miles	Frequency
0.0 – 4.9	18
5.0 – 9.9	26
10.0 – 14.9	15
15.0 – 19.9	13
20.0 – 24.9	12
25.0 – 29.9	9
30 or more	7

Explain why it is not possible to construct a histogram for this data set.

32. **Histogram possible?** Refer to Exercise 31. Suppose you found out that none of the employees traveled more than 34 miles. Would it be possible to construct a histogram? If so, construct a histogram. If not, explain why not.

Extending the Concepts

33. **Silver ore:** The following histogram presents the amounts of silver (in parts per million) found in a sample of rocks. One rectangle from the histogram is missing. What is its height?

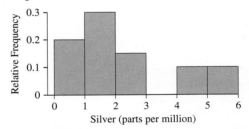

34. **Classes of differing widths:** Consider the following relative frequency distribution for the data in Table 2.7, in which the classes have differing widths.

Class	Frequency	Relative Frequency
0.00–0.99	9	0.138
1.00–1.49	19	0.292
1.50–1.99	7	0.108
2.00–2.99	11	0.169
3.00–3.99	13	0.200
4.00–6.99	6	0.092

a. Compute the class width for each of the classes.

b. Construct a relative frequency histogram. Compare it to the relative frequency histogram in Figure 2.6, in which the classes all have the same width. Explain why using differing widths gives a distorted picture of the data.

c. The *density* of a class is the relative frequency divided by the class width. For each class, divide the relative frequency by the class width to obtain the density.

d. Construct a histogram in which the height of each rectangle is equal to the density of the class. This is called a *density histogram.*

e. Compare the density histogram to the relative frequency histogram in Figure 2.6, in which the classes all have the same width. Explain why differing class widths in a density histogram do not distort the data.

Answers to Check Your Understanding Exercises for Section 2.2

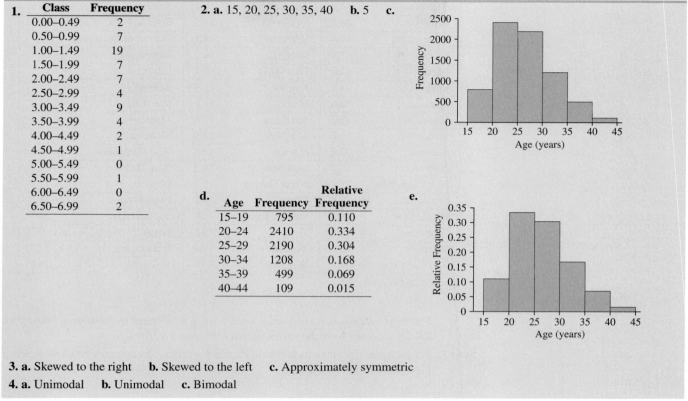

1.

Class	Frequency
0.00–0.49	2
0.50–0.99	7
1.00–1.49	19
1.50–1.99	7
2.00–2.49	7
2.50–2.99	4
3.00–3.49	9
3.50–3.99	4
4.00–4.49	2
4.50–4.99	1
5.00–5.49	0
5.50–5.99	1
6.00–6.49	0
6.50–6.99	2

2. a. 15, 20, 25, 30, 35, 40   **b.** 5   **c.**

d.

Age	Frequency	Relative Frequency
15–19	795	0.110
20–24	2410	0.334
25–29	2190	0.304
30–34	1208	0.168
35–39	499	0.069
40–44	109	0.015

e.

3. a. Skewed to the right   **b.** Skewed to the left   **c.** Approximately symmetric

4. a. Unimodal   **b.** Unimodal   **c.** Bimodal

SECTION 2.3   More Graphs for Quantitative Data

Objectives
1. Construct stem-and-leaf plots
2. Construct dotplots
3. Construct time-series plots

Histograms and other graphs that are based on frequency distributions can be used to summarize both small and large data sets. For small data sets, it is sometimes useful to have a summary that is more detailed than a histogram. In this section, we describe some commonly used graphs that provide more detailed summaries of smaller data sets. These graphs illustrate the shape of the data set, while allowing every value in the data set to be seen.

Objective 1 Construct stem-and-leaf plots

Stem-and-Leaf Plots

Stem-and-leaf plots are a simple way to display small data sets. For example, Table 2.13 on page 64 presents the U.S. Census Bureau projection for the percentage of the population aged 65 and over for each state and the District of Columbia in the year 2010.

In a stem-and-leaf plot, the rightmost digit is the leaf, and the remaining digits form the stem. For example, the stem for Alabama is 14, and the leaf is 1. We construct a stem-and-leaf plot for the data in Table 2.13 by using the following three-step process:

Step 1: Make a vertical list of all the stems in increasing order, and draw a vertical line to the right of this list. The smallest stem in Table 2.13 is 8, belonging to Alaska, and the largest is 17, belonging to Florida. The list of stems is shown in Figure 2.12(a) on page 64.

Step 2: Go through the data set, and for each value, write its leaf next to its stem. For example, the first value is 14.1, for Alabama. We write a "1" next to the stem 14.

Table 2.13 Percentage of Population Aged 65 and Over, by State

Alabama	14.1	Alaska	8.1	Arizona	13.9
Arkansas	14.3	California	11.5	Colorado	10.7
Connecticut	14.4	Delaware	14.1	District of Columbia	11.5
Florida	17.8	Georgia	10.2	Hawaii	14.3
Idaho	12.0	Illinois	12.4	Indiana	12.7
Iowa	14.9	Kansas	13.4	Kentucky	13.1
Louisiana	12.6	Maine	15.6	Maryland	12.2
Massachusetts	13.7	Michigan	12.8	Minnesota	12.4
Mississippi	12.8	Missouri	13.9	Montana	15.0
Nebraska	13.8	Nevada	12.3	New Hampshire	12.6
New Jersey	13.7	New Mexico	14.1	New York	13.6
North Carolina	12.4	North Dakota	15.3	Ohio	13.7
Oklahoma	13.8	Oregon	13.0	Pennsylvania	15.5
Rhode Island	14.1	South Carolina	13.6	South Dakota	14.6
Tennessee	13.3	Texas	10.5	Utah	9.0
Vermont	14.3	Virginia	12.4	Washington	12.2
West Virginia	16.0	Wisconsin	13.5	Wyoming	14.0

Source: U.S. Census Bureau

The next value is 8.1 for Alaska, so we write a "1" next to the stem 8. When we are finished, we have the result shown in Figure 2.12(b).

Step 3: For each stem, arrange its leaves in increasing order. The result is the stem-and-leaf plot, shown in Figure 2.12(c).

```
 8 |                      8 | 1                    8 | 1
 9 |                      9 | 0                    9 | 0
10 |                     10 | 7 2 5               10 | 2 5 7
11 |                     11 | 5 5                 11 | 5 5
12 |                     12 | 0 4 7 6 2 8 4 8 3 6 4 4 2     12 | 0 2 2 3 4 4 4 4 6 6 7 8 8
13 |                     13 | 9 4 1 7 9 8 7 6 7 8 0 6 3 5   13 | 0 1 3 4 5 6 6 7 7 7 8 8 9 9
14 |                     14 | 1 3 4 1 3 9 1 1 6 3 0         14 | 0 1 1 1 1 3 3 3 4 6 9
15 |                     15 | 6 0 3 5             15 | 0 3 5 6
16 |                     16 | 0                   16 | 0
17 |                     17 | 8                   17 | 8
    (a)                       (b)                      (c)
```

Figure 2.12 Steps in the construction of a stem-and-leaf plot

Rounding data for a stem-and-leaf plot

Table 2.14 presents the particulate emissions for 65 vehicles. The first digits range from 0 to 6, and we would like to construct a stem-and-leaf plot with these digits as the stems. The problem is that this leaves two digits for the leaf, but the leaf must consist of only one digit. The solution to this problem is to round the data so that there will be only one digit for the leaf. Table 2.15 presents the particulate data rounded to two digits.

Table 2.14 Particulate Emissions for 65 Vehicles

1.50	0.87	1.12	1.25	3.46	1.11	1.12	0.88	1.29	0.94	0.64	1.31	2.49
1.48	1.06	1.11	2.15	0.86	1.81	1.47	1.24	1.63	2.14	6.64	4.04	2.48
1.40	1.37	1.81	1.14	1.63	3.67	0.55	2.67	2.63	3.03	1.23	1.04	1.63
3.12	2.37	2.12	2.68	1.17	3.34	3.79	1.28	2.10	6.55	1.18	3.06	0.48
0.25	0.53	3.36	3.47	2.74	1.88	5.94	4.24	3.52	3.59	3.10	3.33	4.58

Table 2.15 Particulate Emissions for 65 Vehicles, Rounded to Two Digits

1.5	0.9	1.1	1.3	3.5	1.1	1.1	0.9	1.3	0.9	0.6	1.3	2.5
1.5	1.1	1.1	2.2	0.9	1.8	1.5	1.2	1.6	2.1	6.6	4.0	2.5
1.4	1.4	1.8	1.1	1.6	3.7	0.6	2.7	2.6	3.0	1.2	1.0	1.6
3.1	2.4	2.1	2.7	1.2	3.3	3.8	1.3	2.1	6.6	1.2	3.1	0.5
0.3	0.5	3.4	3.5	2.7	1.9	5.9	4.2	3.5	3.6	3.1	3.3	4.6

We now follow the three-step process to obtain the stem-and-leaf plot. The result is shown in Figure 2.13.

```
0 | 355669999
1 | 011111122223333344455566689
2 | 11124556777
3 | 0111334555678
4 | 026
5 | 9
6 | 66
```

Figure 2.13 Stem-and-leaf plot for the data in Table 2.15

Split stems

Sometimes one or two stems contain most of the leaves. When this happens, we often use two or more lines for each stem. The plot is then called a **split stem-and-leaf plot**. We will use the data in Table 2.16 to illustrate the method. These data consist of scores on a final examination in a statistics class, arranged in order.

Table 2.16 Scores on a Final Examination

58	66	68	70	70	71	71	72	73	73
75	76	78	78	79	80	80	80	81	82
82	82	82	83	84	86	86	86	87	88
89	89	89	90	92	93	95	97		

Figure 2.14 presents a stem-and-leaf plot for these data, using the stems 5, 6, 7, 8, and 9.

```
5 | 8
6 | 68
7 | 001123356889
8 | 000122223466678999
9 | 02357
```

Figure 2.14 Stem-and-leaf plot for the data in Table 2.16

Most of the leaves are on two stems, 7 and 8. For this reason, the stem-and-leaf plot does not reveal much detail about the data. To remedy this situation, we will assign each stem two lines on the plot instead of one. Leaves with values 0–4 will go on the first line, and leaves with values 5–9 will go on the second line. So, for example, we will do the following with the stem 7:

```
7 | 001123356889        will become        7 | 0011233
                                           7 | 56889
```

The split stem-and-leaf plot is shown in Figure 2.15 on page 66. Note that every stem is given two lines, even those that have only a few leaves. Each stem in a split stem-and-leaf plot must receive the same number of lines.

CAUTION

In a split stem-and-leaf plot, each stem must be given the same number of lines.

```
5 |
5 | 8
6 |
6 | 68
7 | 0011233
7 | 56889
8 | 0001222234
8 | 66678999
9 | 023
9 | 57
```

Figure 2.15 Split stem-and-leaf plot for the data in Table 2.16

Check Your Understanding

1. **Weights of college students:** The following table presents weights in pounds for a group of male college freshmen.

136	163	157	195	150	149	151	155	163	145
124	124	156	148	195	192	133	129	160	158
166	155	171	157	182	124	160	172	161	143

a. List the stems for a stem-and-leaf plot.
b. For each item in the data set, write its leaf next to its stem.
c. Rearrange the leaves in numerical order to create a stem-and-leaf plot.

Answers are on page 74.

Back-to-back stem-and-leaf plots

When two data sets have values similar enough that the same stems can be used, we can compare their shapes with a **back-to-back stem-and-leaf plot**. In a back-to-back stem-and-leaf plot, the stems go down the middle. The leaves for one of the data sets go off to the right, and the leaves for the other go off to the left.

EXAMPLE 2.14

Constructing a back-to-back stem-and-leaf plot

In Table 2.15, we presented particulate emissions for 65 vehicles. In a related experiment carried out at the Colorado School of Mines, particulate emissions were measured for 35 vehicles driven at high altitude. Table 2.17 presents the results. Construct a back-to-back stem-and-leaf plot to compare the emission levels of vehicles driven at high altitude with those of vehicles driven at sea level.

Table 2.17 Particulate Emissions for 35 Vehicles Driven at High Altitude

8.9	4.4	3.6	4.4	3.8	2.4	3.8	5.3	5.8	2.9	4.7	1.9	9.1
8.7	9.5	2.7	9.2	7.3	2.1	6.3	6.5	6.3	2.0	5.9	5.6	5.6
1.5	6.5	5.3	5.6	2.1	1.1	3.3	1.8	7.6				

Solution

Figure 2.16 presents the results. It is clear that vehicles driven at high altitude tend to produce higher emissions.

High Altitude		Sea Level
	0	3 5 5 6 6 9 9 9 9
9 8 5 1	1	0 1 1 1 1 1 2 2 2 2 3 3 3 3 4 4 5 5 5 6 6 6 8 8 9
9 7 4 1 1 0	2	1 1 1 2 4 5 5 6 7 7 7
8 8 6 3	3	0 1 1 1 3 3 4 5 5 5 6 7 8
7 4 4	4	0 2 6
9 8 6 6 6 3 3	5	9
5 5 3 3	6	6 6
6 3	7	
9 7	8	
5 2 1	9	

Figure 2.16 Back-to-back stem-and-leaf plots comparing the emissions in vehicles driven at high altitude with emissions from vehicles driven at sea level

Objective 2 Construct dotplots

Dotplots

A **dotplot** is a graph that can be used to give a rough impression of the shape of a data set. It is useful when the data set is not too large, and when there are some repeated values. As an example, Table 2.18 presents the number of children of each of the presidents of the United States and their wives.

Table 2.18 Numbers of Children of U.S. Presidents and Their Wives

0	2	10	2	5	3	6	2	2	4	1
5	4	15	3	4	5	3	2	3	4	2
6	0	0	0	8	3	3	6	2	4	2
0	4	6	4	7	2	0	1	2	6	

Figure 2.17 presents a dotplot for the data in Table 2.18. For each value in the data set, a vertical column of dots is drawn, with the number of dots in the column equal to the number of times the value appears in the data set. The dotplot gives a good indication of where the values are concentrated, and where the gaps are. For example, it is immediately apparent from Figure 2.17 that the most frequent number of children is 2, and only four presidents had more than 6. (John Tyler holds the record with 15.)

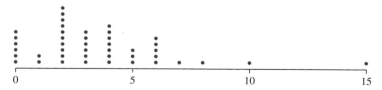

Figure 2.17 Dotplot for the data in Table 2.18

EXAMPLE 2.15 Constructing a dotplot with technology

Use technology to construct a dotplot for the exam score data in Table 2.16 on page 65.

Solution

The following figure shows the dotplot constructed in MINITAB. Step-by-step instructions for constructing dotplots with MINITAB are given in the Using Technology section on page 70.

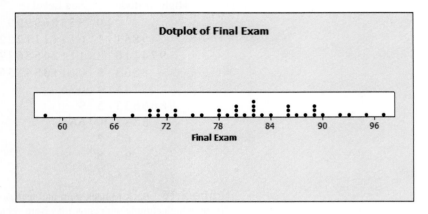

Objective 3 Construct time-series plots

Time-Series Plots

A **time-series plot** may be used when the data consist of values of a variable measured at different points in time. As an example, we consider the Dow Jones Industrial Average, which reflects the prices of 30 large stocks. Table 2.19 presents the closing value of the Dow Jones Industrial Average at the end of each year from 2000 to 2009.

Table 2.19 Dow Jones Industrial Average

Year	Average
2000	10,786.85
2001	10,021.50
2002	8,341.63
2003	10,453.92
2004	10,783.01
2005	10,717.50
2006	12,463.15
2007	13,264.82
2008	8,776.39
2009	10,428.05

Source: www.1stock1.com/1stock1_139.htm

In a time-series plot, the horizontal axis represents time, and the vertical axis represents the value of the variable we are measuring. We plot the values of the variable at each of the times, then connect the points with straight lines. Example 2.16 shows how.

EXAMPLE 2.16 Constructing a time-series plot

Construct a time-series plot for the data in Table 2.19.

Solution
Step 1: Label the horizontal axis with the times at which measurements were made.
Step 2: Plot the value of the Dow Jones Industrial Average for each year.
Step 3: Connect the points with straight lines.

The result is shown in Figure 2.18. It is clear that the average declined from 2000 to 2002, generally increased from 2002 to 2007, dropped sharply in 2008, and increased in 2009.

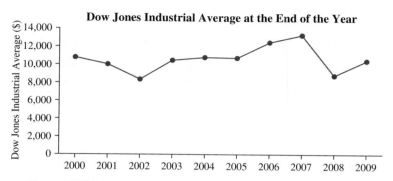

Figure 2.18 Time-series plot for the Dow Jones Industrial Average

Check Your Understanding

2. The Centers for Disease Control and Prevention surveyed U.S. high school students every two years to determine the percentage who said they had used marijuana one or more times. The following time-series plot presents the results.

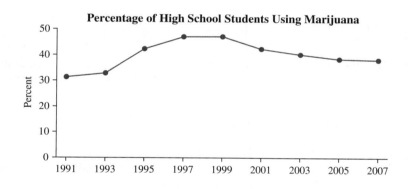

a. During what time period was marijuana use among high school students the highest?

b. True or false: At one time, more than half of all high school students reported using marijuana.

c. During what periods of time was marijuana use increasing? During what periods of time was it decreasing?

d. True or false: Marijuana use among high school students in 2007 was lower than it had been since 1991.

Answers are on page 74.

USING TECHNOLOGY

We use the data in Table 2.16 to illustrate the technology steps.

MINITAB

Constructing a stem-and-leaf plot and dotplot

Step 1. Name your variable *Final Exam* and enter the data from Table 2.16 into **Column C1**.

Step 2. Click on **Graph**. Select **Stem-and-Leaf** or **Dotplot**. For **Dotplot**, choose the **Simple** option. Press **OK**.

Step 3. Double-click on the *Final Exam* variable and press **OK**. (See Figures A and B.)

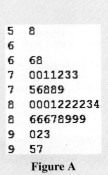

Figure A

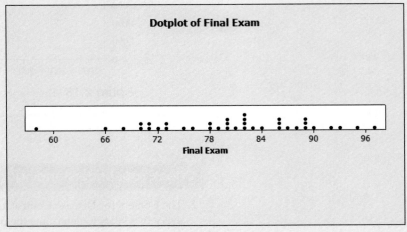

Figure B

SECTION 2.3 Exercises

Exercises 1 and 2 are the Check Your Understanding exercises located within the section.

Understanding the Concepts

In Exercises 3–6, fill in each blank with the appropriate word or phrase.

3. In a stem-and-leaf plot, the rightmost digit of each data value is the _____ .

4. In a back-to-back stem-and-leaf plot, each of the two data sets plotted must have the same _____ .

5. A _____ is useful when the data consist of values measured at different points in time.

6. In a time-series plot, the horizontal axis represents _____ .

In Exercises 7–10, determine whether the statement is true or false. If the statement is false, rewrite it as a true statement.

7. Stem-and-leaf plots and dotplots provide a simple way to display data for small data sets.

8. In a stem-and-leaf plot, each stem must be a single digit.

9. In a dotplot, the number of dots in a vertical column represents the number of times a certain value appears in a data set.

10. In a time-series plot, the vertical axis represents time.

Practicing the Skills

11. Construct a stem-and-leaf plot for the following data.

| 57 | 20 | 27 | 16 | 11 | 12 | 29 | 39 | 45 | 52 | 58 | 15 |
| 46 | 27 | 22 | 21 | 15 | 50 | 16 | 45 | 20 | 55 | 12 | 31 |

12. Construct a stem-and-leaf plot for the following data, in which the leaf represents the hundredths digit.

5.03	4.99	4.95	5.01	4.99	5.03	4.91	5.25	4.80
5.24	4.94	5.04	5.17	4.81	5.22	4.92	5.05	4.89
5.19	5.17	5.25	5.14	5.10	4.94	5.19	4.99	

13. List the data in the following stem-and-leaf plot. The leaf represents the ones digit.

3	0 0 1 2
3	5 6 7 7 9
4	2 3 4
4	5 6 7 7 7 7 8 8 9
5	0 1 1 1 2 2 2 2 4
5	6 7 8 8 9
6	1 3
6	

14. List the data in the following stem-and-leaf plot. The leaf represents the tenths digit.

```
14 | 4 6 8 9
15 | 1 2 2 4 5 7 7 8
16 | 0 1 1 1 2 3 7 7 9
17 |
18 | 2 3 8
```

15. Construct a dotplot for the data in Exercise 11.

16. Construct a dotplot for the data in Exercise 12.

Working with the Concepts

17. BMW prices: The following table presents the manufacturer's suggested retail price (in $1000s) for 2008 base models and styles of BMW automobiles.

28.8	52.0	34.5	49.5	53.8	46.2	50.4
34.9	58.8	36.4	76.6	56.5	54.8	52.4
33.1	54.4	35.6	83.7	64.95	52.5	
39.1	32.7	37.4	76.8	83.9	63.0	
44.6	34.6	41.2	79.9	100.3	36.7	
46.8	39.3	43.0	124.1	106.1	42.7	
49.8	41.2	43.5	115.0	38.6	40.7	

Source: www.edmunds.com

   a. Round the data to the nearest whole number (round .5 up) and construct a stem-and-leaf plot, using the numbers 2 through 12 as the stems.

   b. Repeat part (a), but split the stems, using two lines for each stem.

   c. Which stem-and-leaf plot do you think is more appropriate for these data, the one in part (a) or the one in part (b)? Why?

18. How's the weather? The following table presents the daily high temperatures for the city of Macon, Georgia, in degrees Fahrenheit, for the winter months of January and February, 2010.

54	43	45	42	42	47	54	38	39	42
50	51	54	58	68	57	63	71	69	73
59	48	47	71	58	56	58	68	60	46
44	59	50	63	47	49	49	51	58	52
45	50	41	43	59	50	48	52	60	67
70	72	63	60	46	49	56	58	63	

   a. Construct a stem-and-leaf plot, using the digits 3, 4, 5, 6, and 7 as the stems.

   b. Repeat part (a), but split the stems, using two lines for each stem.

   c. Which stem-and-leaf plot do you think is more appropriate for these data, the one in part (a) or the one in part (b)? Why?

19. Air pollution: The following table presents amounts of particulate emissions for 65 vehicles. These data also appear in Table 2.15.

1.5	0.9	1.1	1.3	3.5	1.1	1.1	0.9	1.3	0.9	0.6	1.3	2.5
1.5	1.1	1.1	2.2	0.9	1.8	1.5	1.2	1.6	2.1	6.6	4.0	2.5
1.4	1.4	1.8	1.1	1.6	3.7	0.6	2.7	2.6	3.0	1.2	1.0	1.6
3.1	2.4	2.1	2.7	1.2	3.3	3.8	1.3	2.1	6.6	1.2	3.1	0.5
0.3	0.5	3.4	3.5	2.7	1.9	5.9	4.2	3.5	3.6	3.1	3.3	4.6

   a. Construct a split stem-and-leaf plot in which each stem appears twice, once for leaves 0–4 and again for leaves 5–9.

   b. Compare the split stem-and-leaf plot to the plot in Figure 2.13. Comment on the advantages and disadvantages of the split stem-and-leaf plot for these data.

20. Technology salaries: The following table presents the annual salaries for the employees of a small technology firm. Round each number to the nearest thousand, and then construct a stem-and-leaf plot.

91,808	118,625	131,092	60,763
36,463	37,187	45,870	50,594
98,302	123,973	182,255	59,186
44,889	164,861	71,082	69,695
28,098	157,110	50,461	98,132
49,742	25,339	24,164	107,878
136,690	129,514	99,254	57,468

21. Tennis and golf: Following are the ages of the winners of the men's Wimbledon tennis championship and the Master's golf championship for the years 1968 through 2010.

Ages of Wimbledon Winners

29	30	26	27	25	27	21	31	20	21	22
23	24	22	29	24	25	17	18	22	22	21
24	22	22	21	22	23	26	25	26	27	28
31	21	21	22	23	24	25	22	27	24	

Ages of Master's Winners

39	29	38	33	32	36	38	35	33	27	42
27	23	31	28	26	32	27	46	28	30	31
32	33	32	35	28	43	38	23	41	33	37
25	26	32	31	29	33	31	28	39	39	

   a. Construct back-to-back split stem-and-leaf plots for these data sets.

   b. How do the ages of Wimbledon champions differ from the ages of Master's champions?

22. Pass the popcorn: Following are the running times (in minutes) for the 15 top-grossing movies rated PG or PG-13, and the 15 top-grossing movies rated R, for the weekend of April 2–4, 2010.

Movies Rated PG or PG-13	
Clash of the Titans (2010)	110
Tyler Perry's Why Did I Get Married Too?	121
How to Train Your Dragon	90
The Last Song	108
Alice in Wonderland (2010)	108
The Bounty Hunter	106
Diary of a Wimpy Kid	91
The Ghost Writer	128
Avatar	162
Our Family Wedding	90
Remember Me	113
Percy Jackson & The Olympians: The Lightning Thief	120
The Blind Side	120
Tooth Fairy	102
Sherlock Holmes	129

Source: Box Office Mojo

Movies Rated R

Hot Tub Time Machine	100
She's Out of My League	105
Shutter Island	136
Green Zone	115
Greenberg	107
Repo Men	111
Chloe	96
Crazy Heart	111
Cop Out	110
The Crazies	101
The Book of Eli	118
Brooklyn's Finest	125
The Runaways	105
A Prophet (Un prophète)	149
The Last Station	112

Source: Box Office Mojo

a. Construct back-to-back stem-and-leaf plots for these data sets.
b. Do the running times of R-rated movies differ greatly from the running times of movies rated PG or PG-13, or are they roughly similar?

23. **More weather:** Construct a dotplot for the data in Exercise 18. Are there any gaps in the data?

24. **Safety first:** Following are the numbers of hospitals in each of the 50 U.S. states plus the District of Columbia that won Patient Safety Excellence Awards. Construct a dotplot for these data and describe its shape.

2	15	0	1	4	3	3	0	5	3	5
0	1	15	10	4	7	7	0	8	5	1
4	4	4	11	4	8	4	4	1	13	8
0	0	0	8	0	12	2	0	17	0	10
1	0	3	10	1	10	0				

Source: Health Grades, Inc., March 2010

25. **Looking for a job:** The following table presents the U.S. unemployment rate for each of the years 1986 through 2009.

Year	Unemployment	Year	Unemployment
1986	7.0	1998	4.5
1987	6.2	1999	4.2
1988	5.5	2000	4.0
1989	5.3	2001	4.7
1990	5.6	2002	5.8
1991	6.8	2003	6.0
1992	7.5	2004	5.5
1993	6.9	2005	5.1
1994	6.1	2006	4.6
1995	5.6	2007	4.6
1996	5.4	2008	5.8
1997	4.9	2009	9.3

Source: National Bureau of Labor Statistics

a. Construct a time-series plot of the unemployment rate.
b. For which periods of time was the unemployment rate increasing? For which periods was it decreasing?

26. **Vacant apartments:** The following table presents the percentage of U.S. residential rental units that were vacant during each quarter from 2006 through 2009.

Quarter	Vacancy Rate	Quarter	Vacancy Rate
Mar. 2006	9.5	Mar. 2008	10.1
Jun. 2006	9.6	Jun. 2008	10.0
Sep. 2006	9.9	Sep. 2008	9.9
Dec. 2006	9.8	Dec. 2008	10.1
Mar. 2007	10.1	Mar. 2009	10.1
Jun. 2007	9.5	Jun. 2009	10.6
Sep. 2007	9.8	Sep. 2009	11.1
Dec. 2007	9.6	Dec. 2009	10.7

Source: Current Population Survey, U.S. Census Bureau

a. Construct a time-series plot for these data.
b. From December 2007 through December 2009, the U.S. economy was in a recession. What was the trend in the vacancy rate during this time period?

27. **Military spending:** The following table presents the amount spent, in billions of dollars, on national defense by the U.S. government every other year for the years 1947 through 2009. The amounts are adjusted for inflation, and represent 2009 dollars.

Year	Spending	Year	Spending
1947	108.6	1979	296.3
1949	98.5	1981	335.9
1951	170.0	1983	401.2
1953	359.7	1985	451.3
1955	285.3	1987	479.5
1957	284.8	1989	481.7
1959	293.7	1991	403.2
1961	289.5	1993	409.5
1963	304.4	1995	366.9
1965	280.3	1997	351.8
1967	375.1	1999	348.5
1969	400.2	2001	370.1
1971	347.3	2003	472.8
1973	307.2	2005	546.4
1975	292.8	2007	574.6
1977	285.6	2009	675.1

Source: Center for Strategic Budget Analysis

a. Construct a time-series plot for these data.
b. The plot covers six decades, from the 1950s through the decade of 2000–2009. During which of these decades did national defense spending increase, and during which decades did it decrease?
c. The United States fought in the Korean War from 1950 to 1953. What effect did this have on military spending during that period?
d. During the period 1965–1968, the United States steadily increased the number of troops in Vietnam from 23,000 at the beginning of 1965 to 537,000 at the end of 1968. Beginning in 1969, the number of Americans in Vietnam was steadily reduced, with the last of them leaving in 1975. How is this reflected in the national defense spending from 1965 to 1975?

28. **College students:** The following table presents the numbers of male and female students (in thousands) enrolled in college in the United States as undergraduates for each of the years 1990 through 2008.

Year	Male	Female	Year	Male	Female
1990	5380	6579	2000	5778	7377
1991	5571	6868	2001	6004	7711
1992	5583	6955	2002	6192	8065
1993	5484	6840	2003	6227	8253
1994	5422	6840	2004	6340	8441
1995	5401	6831	2005	6409	8555
1996	5421	6906	2006	6514	8671
1997	5469	6982	2007	6728	8876
1998	5446	6991	2008	7123	9372
1999	5559	7122			

Source: National Center for Educational Statistics

a. Construct a time-series plot for the male enrollment; then on the same axes, construct a time-series plot for the female enrollment.

b. Which is growing faster, male enrollment or female enrollment?

29. Let's eat: The following time-series plot presents the amount spent, in billions of dollars, on food by U.S. residents for the years 1992 through 2008.

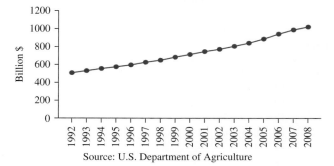

Source: U.S. Department of Agriculture

a. Estimate the amount spent on food in 1996.

b. Estimate the amount by which food expenditures increased between 2000 and 2008.

c. True or false: The amount spent in 2008 is approximately twice as much as the amount spent in 1992.

d. True or false: The amount spent increased every year from 1992 to 2008.

30. Going for gold: The following time-series plot presents the number of Summer Olympic events in which the United States won a gold medal in each Olympic year from 1948 to 2008.

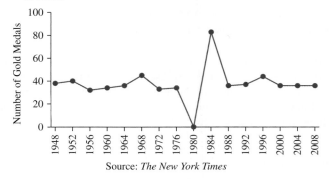

Source: *The New York Times*

a. In one year, the United States did not participate in Summer games that were held in Moscow, in protest of the invasion of Afghanistan by the Soviet Union. Which year was this?

b. In 1984, the Soviet Union did not participate in the Summer games held in Los Angeles, citing "undisguised threats" against their athletes. Estimate the number of gold medals won by the United States in that year.

c. Other than 1980 and 1984, has the number of gold medals won by the United States been generally increasing, generally decreasing, or staying about the same?

31. Let's go skiing: The following time-series plot presents the number of inches of snow falling in Denver each year from 1882 through 2009.

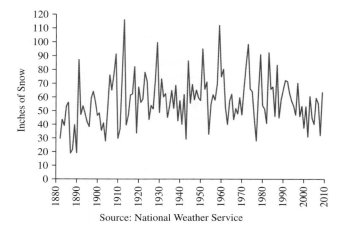

Source: National Weather Service

a. Estimate the largest annual snowfall ever recorded in Denver.

b. Was the year of the largest annual snowfall closest to 1900, 1910, or 1920?

c. Was the amount of snowfall in the years 2000–2009 greater than, less than, or about equal to the snowfall in most other decades?

d. True or false: The year with the least snowfall ever recorded in Denver was in the 1800s.

e. True or false: It usually snows more than 80 inches per year in Denver.

32. Baseball salaries: The following time-series plot presents the average salary of Major League Baseball players for the years 1989–2008.

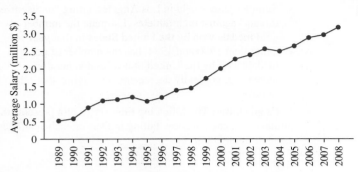

a. What is the first year that the average salary was more than one million dollars?

b. In 1994, the players went on strike, and the last two months of the season were canceled. In 2003, a new labor agreement was reached that penalized teams that paid unusually high salaries. How did these events affect the average salary?

Extending the Concepts

33. Elections: In U.S. presidential elections, each of the 50 states casts a number of electoral votes equal to its number of senators (2) plus its number of members of the House of Representatives. In addition, the District of Columbia casts three electoral votes. Following are the numbers of electoral votes cast for president for each of the 50 states and the District of Columbia in the election of 2008.

9	3	10	6	55	9	7	3	3
27	15	4	4	21	11	7	6	8
9	4	10	7	12	17	10	6	11
3	5	5	4	15	5	31	15	3
7	7	21	4	8	3	11	34	5
3	13	11	5	10	3			

a. Construct a split stem-and-leaf plot for these data, using two lines for each stem.

b. Construct a frequency histogram, with the classes chosen so that there are two classes for each stem.

c. Explain why the stem-and-leaf plot and the histogram have the same shape.

Answers to Check Your Understanding Exercises for Section 2.3

1. a.

12
13
14
15
16
17
18
19

b.

12	4494
13	63
14	9583
15	70156857
16	330601
17	12
18	2
19	552

c.

12	4449
13	36
14	3589
15	01556778
16	001336
17	12
18	2
19	255

2. a. 1997–1999   **b.** False   **c.** Increasing 1991–1997; decreasing 1999–2007   **d.** False

---

SECTION 2.4 | Graphs Can Be Misleading

Objectives

1. Understand how improper positioning of the vertical scale can be misleading
2. Understand the area principle for constructing statistical graphs
3. Understand how three-dimensional graphs can be misleading

Statistical graphs, when properly used, are powerful forms of communication. Unfortunately, when graphs are improperly used, they can misrepresent the data and lead people to draw incorrect conclusions. We discuss here three of the most common forms of misrepresentation: incorrect position of the vertical scale, incorrect sizing of graphical images, and misleading perspective for three-dimensional graphs.

Objective 1 Understand how improper positioning of the vertical scale can be misleading

Positioning the Vertical Scale

Table 2.20 is a distribution of the number of passengers, in millions, at Denver International Airport in each year from 2002 to 2008.

Table 2.20 Passenger Traffic at Denver International Airport

Year	Number of Passengers (in millions)
2002	35.7
2003	37.5
2004	42.4
2005	43.4
2006	47.3
2007	49.9
2008	51.2

Source: Wikipedia

In order to get a better picture of the data, we can make a bar graph. Figures 2.19 and 2.20 present two different bar graphs of the same data. Figure 2.19 presents a clear picture of the data. We can see that the number of passengers has been rising gradually over the years. Now imagine that someone was eager to persuade us that passenger traffic had been increasing rapidly over the years. If they were to show us Figure 2.19, we wouldn't be convinced. So they might show us a misleading picture like Figure 2.20 instead. Figure 2.20 gives the impression of a truly dramatic increase.

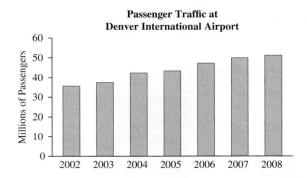

Figure 2.19 The bottom of the bars is at zero. This bar graph gives a correct impression of the data.

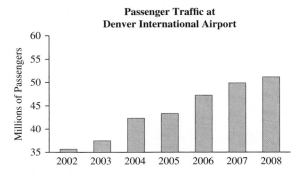

Figure 2.20 The bottom of the bars is not at zero. This bar graph exaggerates the differences between the bars.

Figures 2.19 and 2.20 are based on the same data. Why do they give such different impressions? The reason is that the baseline (the value corresponding to the bottom of the bars) is at zero in Figure 2.19, but not at zero in Figure 2.20. This exaggerates the differences between the bars. For example, in Figure 2.20, the bar for the year 2007 is more than 10 times as long as the bar for the year 2002, but the actual increase in passenger traffic is much less than that.

This sort of misleading information can be created with time-series plots as well. Figures 2.21 and 2.22 present two different time-series plots of the data. In Figure 2.21, the

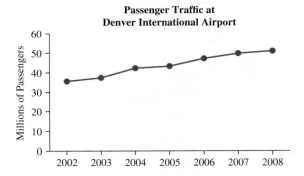

Figure 2.21 The baseline is at zero. This plot gives an accurate picture of the data.

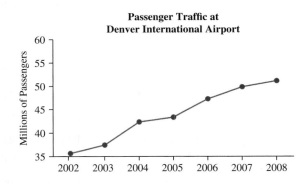

Figure 2.22 The baseline is not at zero. This plot exaggerates the rate of increase.

baseline is at zero, so an accurate impression is given. In Figure 2.22, the baseline is larger than zero, so the rate of increase is exaggerated.

> When a graph or plot represents how much or how many of something, check the baseline. If it isn't at zero, the graph may be misleading.

Objective 2 Understand the area principle for constructing statistical graphs

The Area Principle

We often use images to compare amounts. Larger images correspond to greater amounts. To use images properly in this way, we must follow a rule known as the **area principle**.

The Area Principle

When amounts are compared by constructing an image for each amount, the **areas** of the images must be proportional to the amounts. For example, if one amount is twice as much as another, its image should have twice as much area as the other image.

When the area principle is violated, the images give a misleading impression of the data.

Bar graphs, when constructed properly, follow the area principle. The reason is that all the bars have the same width; only their height varies. Therefore, the areas of the bars are proportional to the amounts. For example, Figure 2.23 presents a bar graph that illustrates a comparison of the cost of jet fuel in 2000 versus 2008. In 2000, the cost of jet fuel was $0.90 per gallon, and in 2008 it had risen to $3.16 per gallon.

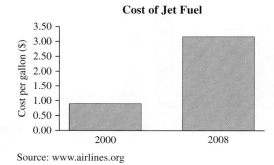

Source: www.airlines.org

Figure 2.23 Price per gallon of jet fuel in 2000 and 2008. The bar graph accurately represents the difference.

The bars in the bar graph differ in only one dimension — their height. The widths are the same. For this reason, the bar graph presents an accurate comparison of the two prices. The price in 2008 is about 3.5 times as much as the price in 2000, and the area of the bar for 2008 is about 3.5 times as large as the area of the bar for 2000.

Unfortunately, people often mistakenly vary both dimensions of an image when making a comparison. This exaggerates the difference. Following is a comparison of the cost of jet fuel in the years 2000 and 2008 that uses a picture of an airplane to illustrate the difference.

Cost of Jet Fuel

2000   2008

The pictures of the planes make the difference appear much larger than the correctly drawn bar graph does. The reason is that both the height and the width of the airplane have been increased by a factor of 3.5. Thus, the area of the larger plane is more than 12 times the area of the smaller plane. This graph violates the area principle, and gives a misleading impression of the comparison.

Check Your Understanding

1. The population of country A is twice as large as the population of country B. True or false: If images are used to represent the populations, both the height and width of the image for country A should be twice as large as the height and width of the image for country B.

2. If the baseline of a bar graph or time-series plot is not at zero, then the differences may appear to be _____ than they actually are. (*Choices: larger, smaller*)

Answers are on page 80.

Objective 3 Understand how three-dimensional graphs can be misleading

Three-Dimensional Graphs and Perspective

Figure 2.23 presented a bar graph that presented an accurate picture of the prices of jet fuel in the years 2000 and 2008. Newspapers and magazines often prefer to present three-dimensional bar graphs, because they are visually more impressive. Unfortunately, in order to make the tops of the bars visible, these graphs are often drawn as though the reader is looking down on them. This can make the bars look shorter than they really are.

Figure 2.24 presents a three-dimensional bar graph of the sort often seen in publications. The data are the same as in Figure 2.23: The price in 2000 is $0.90, and the price in 2008 is $3.16. However, because you are looking down on the bars, they appear shorter than they really are.

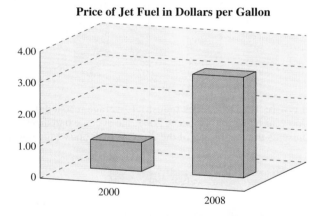

Figure 2.24   Price per gallon of jet fuel in 2000 and 2008. The bars appear shorter than they really are, because you are looking down at them.

Beware of three-dimensional bar graphs. If you can see the tops of the bars, they may look shorter than they really are.

SECTION 2.4   Exercises

Exercises 1 and 2 are the Check Your Understanding exercises located within the section.

Understanding the Concepts

In Exercises 3 and 4, fill in each blank with the appropriate word or phrase.

3. A plot that represents how much of something there is may be misleading if the baseline is not at _____ .

4. The area principle says that when images are used to compare amounts, the areas of the images should be _____ to the amounts.

Working with the Concepts

5. CD sales decline: Sales of CDs have been declining for several years as more music is downloaded over the Internet. Following are two bar graphs that illustrate the decline in CD sales. (Source: Recording Industry Association of America)

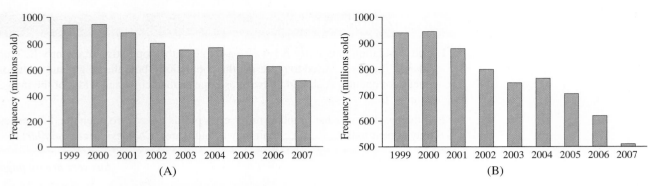

(A)   (B)

Choose one of the following options, and explain why it is correct:
(i) Graph A presents an accurate picture, and graph B exaggerates the decline.
(ii) Graph B presents an accurate picture, and graph A understates the decline.

6. **Computer sales:** Worldwide sales of computers have been increasing every year. The following bar graph and time-series plot both present a picture of the increase for the years 2005–2008. (The value for 2008 is a projection.) Which of the two graphs presents the more accurate picture? Why? (Source: IDC Worldwide Quarterly PC Tracker)

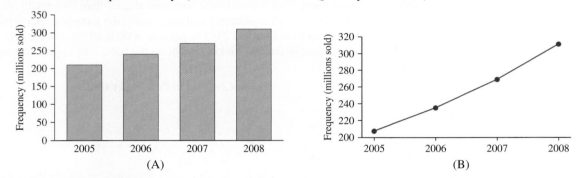

(A)   (B)

7. **Stock market crash:** The Dow Jones Industrial Average reached its highest level ever on October 9, 2007, when it closed at $14,164.53. One year later, on October 9, 2008, the average had dropped almost 40%, to $8,579.19. Which of the following graphs accurately represents the magnitude of the drop? Which one exaggerates it?

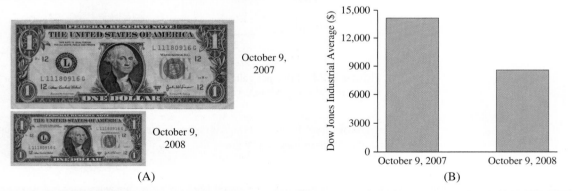

(A)   (B)

8. **Save your money:** In August 2008, U.S. residents saved a total of $184 billion. In August 2009, that amount approximately doubled, to $392 billion. Which of the following graphs compares these totals more accurately, and why? (Source: Bureau of Economic Analysis)

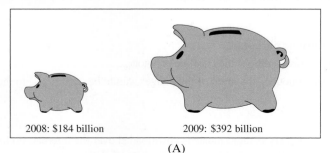

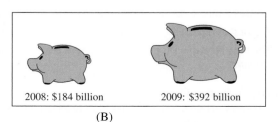

(A)   (B)

9. **Tying the knot:** Data compiled by the U.S. Census Bureau suggests that the percentage of women who have never been married has increased over time. The following bar graph presents the percentages of women who had never married in the years 1970 and 2003. Does the bar graph present an accurate picture of the increase, or is it misleading? Explain.

Percentage of Women Never Married, by Age Group and Year

10. **Age at marriage:** Data compiled by the U.S. Census Bureau suggests that the age at which women first marry has increased over time. The following time-series plot presents the average age at which women first marry for the years 1950–2000. Does the plot present an accurate picture of the increase, or is it misleading? Explain.

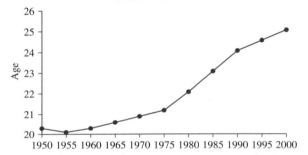

11. **Female senators:** Of the 100 members of the United States Senate in 2010, 83 were men and 17 were women. The following three-dimensional bar graph attempts to present this information.

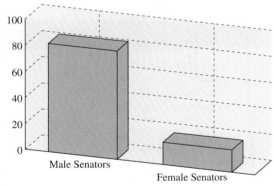

   a. Explain how this graph is misleading.
   b. Construct a graph (not necessarily three-dimensional) that presents this information accurately.

12. **Food expenditures:** Both of the following time-series plots present the percentage of income spent on food by U.S. residents for the years 1992 through 2008. (Source: U.S. Department of Agriculture)

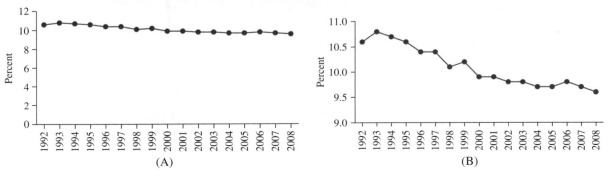

Which of the following statements is more accurate, and why?
 (i) The percentage of income spent on food decreased considerably between 1992 and 2008.
 (ii) The percentage of income spent on food decreased slightly between 1992 and 2008.

Extending the Concepts

13. **Manipulating the y-axis:** For the data in Table 2.20:
    a. Construct a bar graph in which the y-axis is labeled from 0 to 100.
    b. Compare this bar graph with the bar graphs in Figures 2.19 and 2.20. Does this bar graph tend to make the difference seem smaller than the other bar graphs do?
    c. Which of the three bar graphs do you think presents the most accurate picture of the data? Why?

Answers to Check Your Understanding Exercises for Section 2.4

1. False   2. Larger

Chapter 2 Summary

Section 2.1: The first step in summarizing qualitative data is to construct a frequency distribution or relative frequency distribution. Then a bar graph or pie chart may be constructed. Bar graphs may illustrate either frequencies or relative frequencies. Side-by-side bar graphs may be used to compare two qualitative data sets that have the same categories.

Section 2.2: Frequency distributions and relative frequency distributions are also used to summarize quantitative data. Histograms are graphical summaries that illustrate frequency distributions and relative frequency distributions, allowing us to visualize the shape of a data set. Histograms can show us whether a data set is skewed or symmetric, unimodal or bimodal.

Section 2.3: Stem-and-leaf plots and dotplots are useful summaries for small data sets. They have an advantage over histograms: They allow every point in the data set to be seen. Back-to-back stem-and-leaf plots can be used to compare the shapes of two data sets. Time-series plots illustrate how the value of a variable has changed over time.

Section 2.4: To avoid constructing a misleading graph, be sure to start the vertical scale at zero. When images are used to compare amounts, the area principle should be followed. This principle states that the areas of the images should be proportional to the amounts. Three-dimensional bar graphs are often misleading, because the bars look shorter than they really are.

Vocabulary and Notation

area principle 76	lower class limit 50	side-by-side bar graph 39
back-to-back stem-and-leaf plot 66	mode 56	skewed 56
bar graph 38	negatively skewed 56	skewed to the left 56
bimodal 56	open-ended class 55	skewed to the right 56
class 49	Pareto chart 39	split stem-and-leaf plot 65
class width 50	pie chart 40	stem-and-leaf plot 63
dotplot 67	positively skewed 56	symmetric 56
frequency 36	relative frequency 37	time-series plot 68
frequency distribution 36	relative frequency distribution 37	unimodal 56
frequency histogram 52	relative frequency histogram 52	upper class limit 50
histogram 52		

Chapter Quiz

1. Following is the list of letter grades for students in an algebra class: A, B, F, A, C, C, A, B, D, F, D, A, A, B, C, F, B, D, C, A, A, A, F, B, C, A, C. Construct a frequency distribution for these data.

2. Construct a relative frequency distribution for the data in Exercise 1.

3. Construct a frequency bar graph for the data in Exercise 1.

4. Construct a pie chart for the data in Exercise 1.

5. The first class in a relative frequency distribution is 2.0–4.9, and there are six classes. Find the remaining five classes. What is the class width?

6. True or false: A histogram can have more than one mode.

7. A sample of 100 students was asked how many hours per week they spent studying. The following frequency distribution shows the results. Construct a frequency histogram for these data.

Number of Hours	Frequency
1.0 – 4.9	14
5.0 – 8.9	34
9.0 – 12.9	29
13.0 – 16.9	15
17.0 – 20.9	8

8. Construct a relative frequency histogram for the data in Exercise 7.

9. List the data in the following stem-and-leaf plot. The leaf represents the ones digit.

1	1 1 5 5 9 9 9
2	2 2 3 5 7 8
3	0 0 8
4	4 5 7 8
5	0 1 3 3 5 6 8

10. Following are the prices (in dollars) for a sample of coffee makers.

19   22   29   68   35   37   28   22   41   39   28

Construct a stem-and-leaf plot for these data.

11. Following are the prices (in dollars) for a sample of espresso makers.

99   50   31   65   50   99   70   40   25   56   30   77

Construct a stem-and-leaf plot for these data.

12. Construct a back-to-back stem-and-leaf plot for the data in Exercises 10 and 11.

13. Construct a dotplot for the data in Exercise 10.

14. The following table presents the percentage of Americans who use a cell phone exclusively, with no landline phone, for the years 2005–2009. Construct a time-series plot for these data.

Time Period	Percent
January–June 2005	6.7
July–December 2005	7.7
January–June 2006	9.6
July–December 2006	11.8
January–June 2007	12.6
July–December 2007	14.5
January–June 2008	16.1
July–December 2008	18.4
January–June 2009	21.1

Source: National Health Interview Survey

15. According to the area principle, if one amount is twice as much as another, its image should have _____ as much area as the other image.

Review Exercises

1. Trust your doctor: The General Social Survey recently surveyed people to ask, "How much would you trust your doctor to put your health above costs?" The following relative frequency bar graph presents the results.

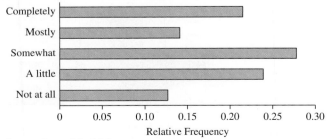

Source: General Social Survey

  a. Which was the most frequently given answer?
  b. True or false: Less than one-fourth of the respondents said that they trusted their doctor completely.
  c. True or false: More than half of the respondents said that they trusted their doctor either a little or not at all.
  d. A total of 2719 people responded to this question. True or false: More than 500 of them said that they completely trusted or mostly trusted their doctor.

2. **Plasma TVs:** The following relative frequency distribution presents the market share for several plasma TV vendors in the fourth quarter of 2007.

TV Vendor	Market Share (percent)
Panasonic	37.1
Samsung	19.7
LG Electronics	12.7
Hitachi	6.5
Vizio	5.5
Philips	5.2
Pioneer	4.6
Others	8.7

Source: www.itfacts.biz

  a. Construct a relative frequency bar graph.
  b. Construct a pie chart.
  c. True or false: The top two vendors have more than 50% of the market share between them.

3. **Poverty rates:** The following table presents the percentage of children who lived in poverty in several Colorado counties in 2000 and in 2008.

County	Percent in 2000	Percent in 2008
Adams	11.4	18.7
Arapahoe	7.3	13.7
Boulder	8.0	9.3
Denver	20.8	27.3
El Paso	10.4	15.7
Jefferson	6.2	11.2

Source: Colorado Childrens' Campaign

  a. Construct a side-by-side bar graph for these data.
  b. True or false: The poverty rate was higher in 2008 than in 2000 for each of the counties.
  c. Which county had the greatest increase?

4. **Do your homework:** The National Survey of Student Engagement asked a sample of college freshmen how often they came to class without completing their assignments. Following are the results:

Response	Percent
Never	35
Sometimes	48
Often	12
Very often	5

  a. Construct a relative frequency bar graph.
  b. Construct a pie chart.
  c. True or false: More than half of the students reported that they sometimes come to class without completing their assignments.

5. **Quiz scores:** The following frequency histogram presents the scores on a recent statistics quiz in a class of 50 students.

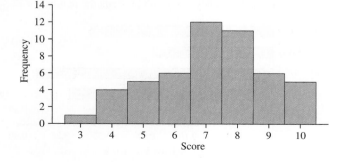

  a. What is the most frequent score?
  b. How many students scored less than 6?
  c. What percentage of students scored 10?
  d. Is the histogram more accurately described as unimodal or as bimodal?

6. **House freshmen:** Newly elected members of the U.S. House of Representatives are referred to as "freshmen." The following frequency distribution presents the number of freshmen elected in each of the past 50 elections, from 1912 to 2010.

Number of Freshmen	Frequency
20 – 39	2
40 – 59	13
60 – 79	10
80 – 99	13
100 – 119	7
120 – 139	3
140 – 159	1
160 – 179	1

Source: Library of Congress

  a. How many classes are there?
  b. What is the class width?
  c. What are the class limits?
  d. Construct a frequency histogram.
  e. Construct a relative frequency distribution.
  f. Construct a relative frequency histogram.

7. **More freshmen:** For the data in Exercise 6:
  a. In what percentage of elections were 100 or more freshmen elected?
  b. In what percentage of elections were fewer than 60 freshmen elected?

8. **Royalty:** Following are the ages at death for all English and British monarchs since 1066.

59	40	67	58	56	28	41	49	65	68
43	64	33	46	35	49	40	12	32	52
55	15	42	69	58	48	54	67	51	49
67	76	81	67	71	81	68	70	77	56

  a. Construct a frequency distribution with approximately eight classes.
  b. Construct a frequency histogram based on this frequency distribution.
  c. Construct a relative frequency distribution with approximately eight classes.
  d. Construct a relative frequency histogram based on this frequency distribution.

9. **More royalty:** Construct a stem-and-leaf plot for the data in Exercise 8.

10. **Presidents:** Following are the ages at deaths for all U.S. presidents.

67	83	90	73	85	68	78	80	53	65
71	79	56	77	64	74	66	49	63	57
70	67	58	71	60	57	67	72	60	63
46	90	78	88	64	81	93	93		

  a. Construct a frequency distribution with a class width of 5 and a lower limit of 45 for the first class.
  b. Construct a frequency histogram based on this frequency distribution.
  c. Construct a relative frequency distribution with a class width of 5 and a lower limit of 45 for the first class.
  d. Construct a relative frequency histogram based on this frequency distribution.

11. **Royalty and presidents:** For the data in Exercises 8 and 10:
  a. Construct a back-to-back stem-and-leaf plot.
  b. Construct a back-to-back stem-and-leaf plot with split stems.
  c. Which plot do you think is more appropriate for these data?

12. **Dotplot:** Construct a dotplot for the data in Exercise 10.

13. **Music sales:** In recent years, sales of digital music (downloads) have been increasing, while sales of physical units (CDs, cassettes, and others) have been declining. The following table presents the number of units sold (in millions) for both digital and physical music formats in each of the years 2004–2008.

Year	Digital	Physical
2004	143.9	814.1
2005	383.1	748.7
2006	625.3	648.2
2007	868.4	543.9
2008	1112.3	401.8

Source: Recording Industry Association of America

a. Construct a time-series plot for digital sales. On the same axes, construct a time-series plot for physical sales.

b. Describe the trends in sales for digital and physical music formats.

14. **More music:** Refer to Exercise 13. Although physical formats sell fewer units than digital formats, their retail value is higher — CDs typically sell for $15 or more, while a download single typically costs a dollar or less. The following table presents the total number of music units, in millions, sold in each year from 2004 through 2008, and the total retail value, in millions of dollars, of the sold units.

Year	Units Sold	Retail Value
2004	958.0	12,345
2005	1301.8	12,296
2006	1588.5	11,758
2007	1774.3	10,372
2008	1852.5	8,480

Source: Recording Industry Association of America

a. Construct a time-series plot for units sold.

b. Construct a time-series plot for total retail value.

c. Explain why the total retail value has been decreasing while the total units sold has been increasing.

15. **Rising birth rate:** The following time-series plots both present the number of births per 1000 women aged 15–44 for the years 2000–2008. Which statement is more accurate? Explain your reasoning.

(i) The birth rate rose dramatically between 2001 and 2007.

(ii) The birth rate rose slightly between 2001 and 2007.

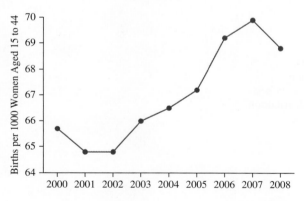 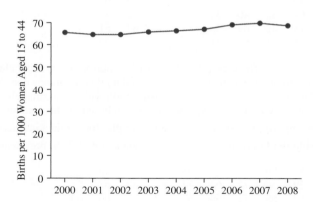

Source: Pew Research Center

Write About It

1. Explain why the frequency bar graph and the relative frequency bar graph for a data set have a similar appearance.

2. In what ways do frequency distributions for qualitative data differ from those for quantitative data?

3. Provide an example of a data set whose histogram you would expect to be skewed to the right. Explain why you would expect the histogram to be skewed to the right.

4. Time-series data are discrete when observations are made at regularly spaced time intervals. The time-series data sets in this section are all discrete. Time-series data are continuous when there are observations at extremely closely spaced intervals that are connected to provide values at every instant of time. An example of continuous time-series data is an electrocardiogram. Provide some examples of time-series data that are discrete and some that are continuous.

5. Find examples of graphs in newspapers, magazines, or on the Internet that are misleading in some way. Explain how they are misleading. Then find some that present accurate comparisons and explain why you believe they are accurate.

Case Study: Do Late-Model Cars Get Better Gas Mileage?

In the chapter introduction, we presented gas mileage data for 2000 and 2009 model year compact cars. We will use histograms and back-to-back stem-and-leaf plots to compare the mileages between these two groups of cars. The following tables present the mileages, in miles per gallon.

Highway Mileage Ratings for 2000 Compact Cars							
28	21	30	33	24	29	30	38
27	23	27	34	21	27	38	28
29	21	31	31	32	23	36	28
27	32	31	30	26	23	40	28
27	27	34	28	34	28	38	27
29	27	33	24	31	33	27	28
26	26	31	16	28	30	30	24
37	35	30	33	31	32		

Highway Mileage Ratings for 2009 Compact Cars							
30	30	27	15	14	17	28
26	25	34	29	26	25	33
35	35	25	30	25	25	25
21	17	18	17	21	18	25
34	33	18	18	27	28	30
25	26	31	30	35	29	29
25	29	28	26	28	26	26
25	30	19	22	26	29	

Source: www.fueleconomy.gov

1. Construct a frequency distribution for the 2000 cars with a class width of 1.
2. Explain why a class width of 1 is too narrow for these data.
3. Construct a relative frequency distribution for the 2000 cars with a class width of 2, where the first class has a lower limit of 15.
4. Construct a histogram based on this relative frequency distribution. Is the histogram unimodal or bimodal? Describe the skewness, if any, in these data.
5. Construct a frequency distribution for the 2009 cars with an appropriate class width.
6. Using this class width, construct a relative frequency distribution for the 2009 cars.
7. Construct a histogram based on this relative frequency distribution. Is the histogram unimodal or bimodal? Describe the skewness, if any, in these data.
8. Compare the histogram for the 2000 cars with the histogram for the 2009 cars. Which cars tend to have higher gas mileage?
9. Construct a back-to-back stem-and-leaf plot for these data, using two lines for each stem. Which do you think illustrates the comparison better, the histograms or the back-to-back stem-and-leaf plot? Why?

Numerical Summaries of Data

Introduction

How do manufacturers increase quality and reduce costs? Companies continually consider new ideas to produce higher-quality, lower-cost products. To determine whether a new idea can lead to higher quality or lower cost, data must be collected and analyzed.

The following tables on page 88 present data produced by a manufacturer of computer chips, as described in the book *Statistical Case Studies for Industrial Process Improvement* by V. Czitrom and P. Spagon. Computer chips contain electronic circuits and are sealed with a thin layer of silicon dioxide. For the manufacturing process to work, the thickness of the layer must be carefully controlled. The manufacturer considered using recycled silicon wafers rather than new ones. Recycled wafers are much cheaper, so if the idea were feasible, it would lead to a reduction in cost. It must be determined whether the thicknesses of the oxide layers for recycled wafers are similar to those for the new wafers. The following tables present thickness measurements (in tenths of a nanometer) from some test runs.

New								
90.0	92.2	94.9	92.7	91.6	88.2	92.0	98.2	96.0
91.1	89.8	91.5	91.5	90.6	93.1	88.9	92.5	92.4
96.7	93.7	93.9	87.9	90.4	92.0	90.5	95.2	94.3
92.0	94.6	93.7	94.0	89.3	90.1	91.3	92.7	94.5

Recycled								
91.8	94.5	93.9	77.3*	92.0	89.9	87.9	92.8	93.3
92.6	90.3	92.8	91.6	92.7	91.7	89.3	95.5	93.6
92.4	91.7	91.6	91.1	88.0	92.4	88.7	92.9	92.6
91.7	97.4	95.1	96.7	77.5*	91.4	90.5	95.2	93.1

*Measurement is in error due to a defective gauge.

It is difficult to determine by looking at the tables whether the thicknesses tend to differ between new and recycled wafers. To interpret these data sets, we need to summarize them in ways that will reveal the important features. Histograms, stem-and-leaf plots, and dotplots are graphical summaries of data sets. While graphs are excellent tools for visualizing the important features of a data set, they have limitations. In particular, graphs often cannot measure a feature precisely; for precise descriptions, we need to use numbers.

In this chapter, we will learn about several of the most commonly used numerical summaries of data. Some of these describe the center of the data; these are called **measures of center**. Others describe how spread out the data values are; these are called **measures of spread**. Still others, called **measures of position**, specify the proportion of the data that is less than a given value.

In the case study at the end of the chapter, you will be asked to use some of the summaries introduced in the chapter to help determine which type of wafer will produce better results.

SECTION 3.1 | Measures of Center

Objectives

1. Compute the mean of a data set
2. Compute the median of a data set
3. Compare the properties of the mean and median
4. Find the mode of a data set
5. Approximate the mean with grouped data

Objective 1 Compute the mean of a data set

The Mean

How do instructors determine your final grade? It's the end of the semester, and you have just finished your statistics class. During the semester, you took five exams, and your scores were 78, 83, 92, 68, and 85. Your instructor must find a single number to give a summary of your performance. The quantity he or she is most likely to use is the **arithmetic mean**, which is often simply called the **mean**. To find the mean of a list of numbers, add the numbers, then divide by how many numbers there are.

EXAMPLE 3.1

Computing the mean

Find the mean of the exam scores 78, 83, 92, 68, and 85.

Explain It Again

The mean and the average: Some people refer to the mean as the "average." In fact, there are many kinds of averages; the mean is just one of them.

Solution

Step 1: Add the numbers.
$$78 + 83 + 92 + 68 + 85 = 406$$
Step 2: Divide the sum by the number of observations. There were five observations. Therefore, the mean is
$$\text{Mean} = \frac{406}{5} = 81.2$$

In Example 3.1, we rounded the mean to one more decimal place than the data. We will follow this practice in general.

SUMMARY

We will round the mean to one more decimal place than the data.

Notation for the mean

Computing a mean involves adding a list of numbers. It is useful to have some notation that will allow us to discuss lists of numbers in general.

When we wish to write down a list of n numbers without specifying what the numbers are, we often write $x_1, x_2, ..., x_n$. To indicate that we are adding these numbers, we write $\sum x$. (The symbol Σ is the uppercase Greek letter sigma.)

NOTATION

- A list of n numbers is denoted $x_1, x_2, ..., x_n$.
- $\sum x$ represents the sum of these numbers: $\sum x = x_1 + x_2 + \cdots + x_n$

Sample means and population means

Often, we wish to compute the mean of values sampled from a population. If $x_1, x_2, ..., x_n$ is a sample, then the mean is called the **sample mean** and is denoted with the symbol $\bar{x}$. Sometimes we need to discuss the mean of all the values in a population. The mean of a population is called the **population mean** and is denoted by μ (the Greek letter mu).

DEFINITION

If $x_1, ..., x_n$ is a sample, the **sample mean** is

$$\bar{x} = \frac{x_1 + x_2 + \cdots + x_n}{n} = \frac{\sum x}{n}$$

If $x_1, ..., x_N$ is a population, the **population mean** is

$$\mu = \frac{x_1 + x_2 + \cdots + x_N}{N} = \frac{\sum x}{N}$$

How the mean measures the center of the data

The mean is a **measure of center**. Figure 3.1 presents the exam scores in Example 3.1 on a number line, and shows the position of the mean. If we imagine each data value to be a weight, then the mean is the point at which the data set would balance.

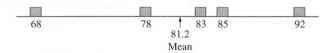

Figure 3.1 The mean is the point where the data set would balance, if each data value were represented by an equal weight.

A misconception about the mean

Some people believe that the mean represents a "typical" data value. In fact, this is not necessarily so. This is shown in Example 3.1, where we computed the mean of five exam scores and obtained a result of 81.2. If, like most exams, the scores are always whole numbers, then 81.2 is certainly not a "typical" data value; in fact, it could not possibly be a data value.

Objective 2 Compute the median of a data set

The Median

The basic idea behind the **median** is simple: We try to find a number that splits the data set in half, so that half of the data values are less than the median and half of the data values are greater than the median. The procedure for computing the median differs, depending on whether the number of observations in the data set is even or odd.

Procedure for Computing the Median

Step 1: Arrange the data values in increasing order.

Step 2: Determine the number of data values, n.

Step 3: *If n is odd:* The median is the middle number. In other words, the median is the number in position $\frac{n+1}{2}$.

If n is even: The median is the average of the middle two numbers. These are the numbers in positions $\frac{n}{2}$ and $\frac{n}{2} + 1$.

In Example 3.1, we found the mean of five exam scores. In Example 3.2, we will find the median.

EXAMPLE 3.2

Computing the median

Find the median of the exam scores 78, 83, 92, 68, and 85.

Solution

Step 1: We arrange the data values in increasing order to obtain

$$68 \quad 78 \quad 83 \quad 85 \quad 92$$

Step 2: There are $n = 5$ values in the data set, so n is odd.

Step 3: The middle number is 83, so the median is 83.

EXAMPLE 3.3

Computing the median

One of the goals of medical research is to develop treatments that reduce the time spent in recovery. Eight patients undergo a new surgical procedure, and the number of days spent in recovery for each is as follows.

$$20 \quad 15 \quad 12 \quad 27 \quad 13 \quad 19 \quad 13 \quad 21$$

Find the median time spent in recovery.

Solution

Step 1: We arrange the numbers in increasing order to obtain

$$12 \quad 13 \quad 13 \quad 15 \quad 19 \quad 20 \quad 21 \quad 27$$

Step 2: There are $n = 8$ numbers in the data set, so n is even.

Step 3: The middle two numbers are 15 and 19. The median is the average of these two numbers.

$$\text{Median} = \frac{15 + 19}{2} = 17$$

The median time spent in recovery is 17 days.

Using technology to compute the mean and median

In practice, technology is often used to compute means and medians, as Example 3.4 shows.

EXAMPLE 3.4

Using technology to compute the mean and median

Use technology to compute the mean and median of the recovery times in Example 3.3.

Solution

Enter the data into **L1**, then use the **1-Var Stats** command. Figure 3.2 presents the TI-84 Plus display. The mean is $\bar{x} = 17.5$ and the median (denoted "Med") is 17. Step-by-step instructions for computing the mean and median with the TI-84 Plus are presented in the Using Technology section on page 96.

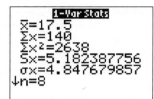
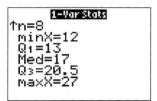

Figure 3.2 TI-84 Plus display showing the mean and median for the data in Example 3.3

Figure 3.3 presents MINITAB output. The mean and median are highlighted in red. Step-by-step instructions for computing the mean and median in MINITAB are presented in the Using Technology section on page 96.

Variable	N	Mean	SE Mean	StDev	Minimum	Q1	Median	Q3	Maximum
Time	8	17.5	1.832	5.182	12.00	13.00	17.00	20.25	27.00

Figure 3.3

Objective 3 Compare the properties of the mean and median

Comparing the Properties of the Mean and Median

Both the mean and the median are frequently used as measures of center. It is important to know how their properties differ.

The mean is more influenced by extreme values than the median is

One important difference between the mean and the median is that the formula for the mean uses every value in the data set, but the formula for the median depends only on the middle number or the middle two numbers. This is particularly important for data sets in which one or more numbers are unusually large or unusually small. In most cases, these extreme values will have a large influence on the mean, but little or no influence on the median. Example 3.5 illustrates this principle.

EXAMPLE 3.5

Determining that the mean is more influenced by extreme values than the median is

Five families, named Smith, Jones, Gonzales, Brown, and Jackson, live in an apartment building. Their annual incomes, in dollars, are 25,000, 31,000, 34,000, 44,000, and 56,000. The Smith family, whose income is 25,000, wins a million-dollar lottery, so their income increases to 1,025,000. Find the mean and median income both before and after the Smiths win the lottery. Which measure of center is more influenced by the large number, the mean or the median?

Solution

We compute the mean and median before the lottery win. The mean income is

$$\text{Mean} = \frac{25,000 + 31,000 + 34,000 + 44,000 + 56,000}{5} = 38,000$$

The median is the middle number:

$$\text{Median} = 34,000$$

After the lottery win, the mean is

$$\text{Mean} = \frac{1{,}025{,}000 + 31{,}000 + 34{,}000 + 44{,}000 + 56{,}000}{5} = 238{,}000$$

To find the median, we arrange the numbers in order, obtaining

$$31{,}000 \quad 34{,}000 \quad 44{,}000 \quad 56{,}000 \quad 1{,}025{,}000$$

The median is the middle number:

$$\text{Median} = 44{,}000$$

The extreme value of 1,025,000 has influenced the mean quite a lot, increasing it from 38,000 to 238,000. In comparison, the median has been influenced much less, increasing only from 34,000 to 44,000.

Because the median is not much influenced by extreme values, we say that the median is **resistant**.

DEFINITION

A statistic is **resistant** if its value is not affected much by extreme values (large or small) in the data set.

We can summarize the results of Example 3.5 as follows.

SUMMARY

The median is resistant, but the mean is not.

The mean and median can help describe the shape of a data set

The mean and median measure the center of a data set in different ways. The mean is the point at which a data set balances (see Figure 3.1). The median is the middle number, so that half of the data values are less than the median and half are greater. It turns out that when a data set is symmetric, the mean and median are equal.

When a data set is skewed, however, the mean and median are often quite different. When a data set is skewed to the right, there are some large values in the right tail. Because the median is resistant while the mean is not, the mean is generally more affected by these large values than the median is. Therefore, for a data set that is skewed to the right, the mean is often greater than the median.

Figure 3.4 illustrates the idea. For most data sets that are skewed to the left, the mean will be to the left of, or less than, the median. For most data sets that are skewed to the right, the mean will be to the right of, or greater than, the median. When a data set is approximately symmetric, the balancing point is near the middle of the data, so the mean and the median will be approximately equal.

> **CAUTION**
>
> The relationship between the mean and median and the shape of the data set holds for most data sets, but not all.

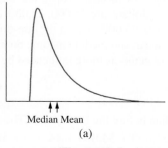 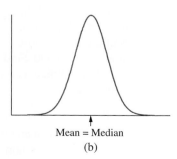 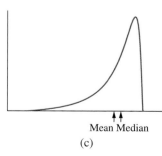

Median Mean   Mean = Median   Mean Median
(a)   (b)   (c)

Figure 3.4 (a) When a data set is skewed to the right, the mean is generally greater than the median. (b) When a data set is approximately symmetric, the mean and median will be approximately equal. (c) When a data set is skewed to the left, the mean is generally less than the median.

SUMMARY

In most cases, the shape of a histogram reflects the relationship between the mean and median as follows:

Shape	Relationship Between Mean and Median
Skewed to the right	Mean is noticeably greater than median
Approximately symmetric	Mean is approximately equal to median
Skewed to the left	Mean is noticeably less than median

For an exception to this rule, see Exercise 64.

Which is a better measure of center, the mean or the median?

The short answer is that neither one is better than the other. They both measure the center in different, but appropriate, ways. When the data are highly skewed or contain extreme values, some people prefer to use the median, because the median is more representative of a typical value. However, the mean is still an appropriate measure of center, and is sometimes preferable, even when the data are highly skewed (see Exercises 53 and 54).

The following table summarizes the features of the mean and median.

	Advantages	Disadvantages
Mean	Takes every value into account	Highly influenced by extreme values: not resistant
Median	Not much influenced by extreme values: resistant	Depends only on middle value or middle two values

Check Your Understanding

1. Compute the mean and median of the following sample:
   74 87 36 97 60 58 46

2. Compute the mean and median of the following sample:
   69 17 75 96 74 80

3. Someone surveys the families in a certain town and reports that the mean number of children in a family is 2.1. Someone else says that this must be wrong, because it is impossible for a family to have 2.1 children. Comment.

4. A data set has a mean of 6 and a median of 4. Would you expect this data set to be skewed to the right or skewed to the left?

5. A data set has a mean of 5 and a median of 7. Would you expect this data set to be skewed to the right or skewed to the left?

Answers are on page 104.

Critical thinking about the mean and median

We can compute the mean and median for any list of numbers. However, they do not always produce meaningful results. The mean and median are useful for numbers that measure or count something. They are not useful for numbers that are used simply as labels. Example 3.6 illustrates the idea.

EXAMPLE 3.6

Determining whether the mean and median make sense

Following is information about the five starting players on a certain college basketball team:

Their heights, in inches, are 74, 76, 79, 80, and 82.

Their uniform numbers are 15, 32, 4, 43, and 26.

Will we obtain meaningful information by computing the mean and median height? How about the mean and median uniform number? Explain.

Solution

The mean and median height are meaningful, because heights are measurements.

The mean and median uniform numbers are not meaningful, because these numbers are just labels. They don't measure or count anything.

Objective 4 Find the mode of a data set

The Mode

In Section 2.2, we defined a mode to be the highest point of a histogram. There is another definition of this term. The **mode** of a data set is the value that appears most frequently.

EXAMPLE 3.7

Finding the mode

Ten students were asked how many siblings they had. The results, arranged in order, were

$$0 \quad 1 \quad 1 \quad 1 \quad 1 \quad 2 \quad 2 \quad 3 \quad 3 \quad 6$$

Find the mode of this data set.

Solution

The value that appears most frequently is 1. Therefore, the mode of this data set is 1.

Explain It Again

The mode isn't really a measure of center: The mode is sometimes classified as a measure of center. However, this isn't really accurate. The mode can be the largest value in a data set, or the smallest, or anywhere in between.

When two or more values are tied for the most frequent, they are all considered to be modes. If no value appears more than once, we say that the data set has no mode.

> **SUMMARY**
> - The mode of a data set is the value that appears most frequently.
> - If two or more values are tied for the most frequent, they are all considered to be modes.
> - If no value appears more than once, we say that the data set has no mode.

Computing the mode for qualitative data

The mean and median can be computed only for quantitative data. The mode, on the other hand, can be computed for qualitative data as well. For qualitative data, the mode is the most frequently appearing category.

EXAMPLE 3.8

Finding the mode for qualitative data

Following is a list of the makes of all the cars rented by an automobile rental company on a particular day. Which make of car is the mode?

Honda	Toyota	Toyota	Honda	Ford
Chevrolet	Nissan	Ford	Chevrolet	Chevrolet
Honda	Dodge	Ford	Ford	Toyota
Chevrolet	Toyota	Toyota	Toyota	Nissan

Solution

The most frequent category is "Toyota," which appears six times. Therefore, the mode is "Toyota."

Check Your Understanding

6. Find the mode or modes, if they exist:
   a. The sample is 3, 6, 0, 1, 1, 8, 0, 1, 1.
   b. The sample is 4, 7, 4, 1, 6, 5, 6.
   c. The sample is 4, 8, 5, 9, 6, 3.

Answers are on page 104.

Objective 5 Approximate the mean with grouped data

Approximating the Mean with Grouped Data

Sometimes we don't have access to the raw data in a data set, but we are given a frequency distribution. In these cases we can approximate the mean. We use Table 3.1 to illustrate the method. This table presents the number of text messages sent via cell phone by a sample of 50 high school students. We will approximate the mean number of messages sent.

Table 3.1 Number of Text Messages Sent by High School Students

Number of Text Messages Sent	Frequency
0–49	10
50–99	5
100–149	13
150–199	11
200–249	7
250–299	4

We present the method for approximating the mean with grouped data.

Procedure for Approximating the Mean with Grouped Data

Step 1: Compute the midpoint of each class. The midpoint of a class is found by taking the average of the lower class limit and the lower limit of the next larger class. For the last class, there is no next larger class, but we use the lower limit that the next larger class would have.

Step 2: For each class, multiply the class midpoint by the class frequency.

Step 3: Add the products Midpoint × Frequency over all classes.

Step 4: Divide the sum obtained in Step 3 by the sum of the frequencies.

EXAMPLE 3.9

Approximating the mean with grouped data

Compute the approximate mean number of messages sent, using Table 3.1.

Solution

The calculations are summarized in Table 3.2.

Step 1: Compute the midpoints: For the first class, the lower class limit is 0. The lower limit of the next class is 50. The midpoint is therefore

$$\frac{0 + 50}{2} = 25$$

We continue in this manner to compute the midpoint of each class. Note that for the last class, we average the lower limit of 250 with 300, which is the lower limit that the next class would have.

Step 2: Multiply the midpoints by the frequencies as shown in the column in Table 3.2 labeled "Midpoint × Frequency."

Step 3: Add the products Midpoint × Frequency, to obtain 6850.

Step 4: The sum of the frequencies is 50. The mean is approximated by $6850/50 = 137$.

Table 3.2 Calculating the Mean Number of Text Messages Sent by High School Students

Class	Midpoint	Frequency	Midpoint × Frequency	
0–49	25	10	25 × 10 = 250	
50–99	75	5	75 × 5 = 375	
100–149	125	13	125 × 13 = 1625	$\text{Mean} \approx \dfrac{6850}{50} = 137$
150–199	175	11	175 × 11 = 1925	
200–249	225	7	225 × 7 = 1575	
250–299	275	4	275 × 4 = 1100	
		Sum = 50	Sum = 6850	

USING TECHNOLOGY

We use Example 3.1 to illustrate the technology steps.

TI-84 PLUS

Computing the mean and median

Step 1. Enter the data into **L1** in the data editor by pressing **STAT** then **1: Edit**. For Example 3.1, we use **78, 83, 92, 68, 85** (Figure A).

Step 2. Press **STAT** and highlight the **CALC** menu.

Step 3. Select **1-Var Stats** and press **ENTER**. The **1-Var Stats** command is now shown on the home screen.

Step 4. Enter the list name **L1** next to the **1-Var Stats** command by pressing **2nd**, then **L1** (Figure B).

Step 5. Press **ENTER**. The descriptive statistics are displayed on the screen (Figures C and D).

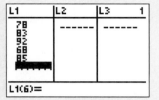

Figure A

Figure B

Using the TI-84 PLUS Stat Wizards (see Appendix B for more information)

Step 1. Enter the data into **L1** in the data editor by pressing **STAT** then **1: Edit**. For Example 3,1, we use **78, 83, 92, 68, 85** (Figure A).

Step 2. Press **STAT** and highlight the **CALC** menu.

Step 3. Select **1-Var Stats** and press **ENTER**. Enter **L1** next to the **List** field. Keep the **FreqList** field blank.

Step 4. Select **Calculate** and press **ENTER**. The descriptive statistics are displayed on the screen (Figures C and D).

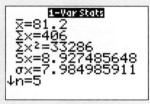

Figure C

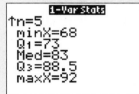

Figure D

MINITAB

Computing the mean and median

Step 1. Enter the data in **Column C1**. For Example 3.1, we use **78, 83, 92, 68, 85**.

Step 2. Click on **Stat**, then **Basic Statistics**, then **Display Descriptive Statistics...** .

Step 3. Enter **C1** in the **Variables** field.

Step 4. Click **Statistics** and select the desired statistics. Press **OK**.

Step 5. Press **OK** (Figure E).

Descriptive Statistics: C1

Variable	Mean	SE Mean	StDev	Minimum	Q1	Median	Q3	Maximum
C1	81.20	3.99	8.93	68.00	73.00	83.00	88.50	92.00

Figure E

EXCEL

Computing the mean and median

Step 1. Enter the data in **Column A**. For Example 3.1, we use **78, 83, 92, 68, 85**.

Step 2. Select **Data**, then **Data Analysis**. Highlight **Descriptive Statistics** and press **OK**.

Step 3. Enter the range of cells that contain the data in the **Input Range field** and check the **Summary Statistics** box.

Step 4. Press **OK** (Figure F).

	A	B
1	*Column1*	
2		
3	Mean	81.2
4	Standard Error	3.992493
5	Median	83
6	Mode	#N/A
7	Standard Deviation	8.927486
8	Sample Variance	79.7
9	Kurtosis	0.715308
10	Skewness	-0.59281
11	Range	24
12	Minimum	68
13	Maximum	92
14	Sum	406
15	Count	5

Figure F

SECTION 3.1   Exercises

Exercises 1–6 are the Check Your Understanding exercises located within the section.

Understanding the Concepts

In Exercises 7–10, fill in each blank with the appropriate word or phrase.

7. The _____ is calculated by summing all data values and dividing by how many there are.

8. The _____ is a number that splits the data set in half.

9. The median is resistant because it is not affected much by _____.

10. The _____ is the value in the data set that appears most frequently.

In Exercises 11–14, determine whether the statement is true or false. If the statement is false, rewrite it as a true statement.

11. Every data set contains at least one mode.

12. The mean is resistant.

13. For most data sets that are skewed to the right, the mean is less than the median.

14. A mode is always a value that is in the data set.

Practicing the Skills

15. Find the mean, median, and mode for the following data set:

    12   27   26   27   25

16. Find the mean, median, and mode for the following data set:

    −20   15   21   −20   19

17. Find the mean, median, and mode for the following data set:

    28   −31   28   0   31   −23

18. Find the mean, median, and mode for the following data set:

    83   98   22   89   99   98

In Exercises 19–22, use the given frequency distribution to approximate the mean.

19.
Class	Frequency
0–9	13
10–19	7
20–29	10
30–39	9
40–49	11

20.
Class	Frequency
0–15	2
16–31	14
32–47	6
48–63	13
64–79	15

21.
Class	Frequency
0–49	17
50–99	26
100–149	14
150–199	34
200–249	26
250–299	8

22.
Class	Frequency
0–19	18
20–39	11
40–59	6
60–79	6
80–99	10
100–119	5

23. Which is the correct mean and median for the following histogram?

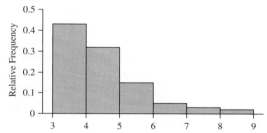

   (i)   Mean is 4.6; median is 5.0
   (ii) Mean is 4.5; median is 4.2
   (iii) Mean is 3.5; median is 4.3
   (iv) Mean is 5.6; median is 5.3

24. Which is the correct mean and median for the following histogram?

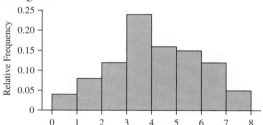

   (i)   Mean is 3.6; median is 4.8
   (ii) Mean is 4.8; median is 3.6
   (iii) Mean is 3.5; median is 3.1
   (iv) Mean is 4.2; median is 4.1

25. Which is the correct mean and median for the following histogram?

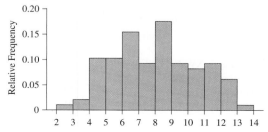

(i) Mean is 8.0; median is 8.1
(ii) Mean is 8.5; median is 6.5
(iii) Mean is 7.0; median is 8.3
(iv) Mean is 6.2; median is 6.1

26. Which is the correct mean and median for the following histogram?

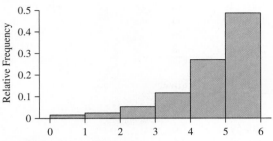

(i) Mean is 3.0; median is 4.1
(ii) Mean is 4.2; median is 3.2

(iii) Mean is 4.4; median is 5.0
(iv) Mean is 4.3; median is 4.1

27. Find the mean, median, and mode of the data in the following stem-and-leaf plot. The leaf represents the ones digit.

1	2
2	0779
3	78
4	13

28. Find the mean, median, and mode of the data in the following stem-and-leaf plot. The leaf represents the ones digit.

0	8
1	16
2	3559
3	0

Working with the Concepts

29. **Mean and median income:** The U.S. Census Bureau reports that in the year 2008, the mean household income was $68,424 and the median was $50,303. If a histogram were constructed for the incomes of all households in the United States, would you expect it to be skewed to the right, skewed to the left, or approximately symmetric? Explain.

30. **Mean and median height:** The National Center for Health Statistics reports that in 2008, the mean height for U.S. women aged 20–29 was 64.3 inches, and the median was 64.2 inches. If a histogram were constructed for the heights of all U.S. women aged 20–29, would you expect it to be skewed to the right, skewed to the left, or approximately symmetric? Explain.

31. **Hamburgers:** An ABC News story reported the number of calories in hamburgers from six fast-food restaurants: McDonald's, Burger King, Wendy's, Hardee's, Sonic, and Dairy Queen. The results are

$$250 \quad 290 \quad 230 \quad 310 \quad 310 \quad 350$$

a. Find the mean number of calories.
b. Find the median number of calories.

32. **Great swimmer:** In the 2008 Olympic Games, Michael Phelps won eight gold medals in swimming. Following are the events he won, along with his margin of victory, in seconds.

Event	Margin of Victory
100m Butterfly	0.01
200m Freestyle	1.89
200m Butterfly	0.67
200m Individual medley	2.29
400m Individual medley	2.32
4 × 100m Freestyle	0.08
4 × 200m Freestyle	4.74
4 × 100m Medley	0.30

a. What was the mean margin of victory?
b. What was the median margin of victory?
c. Assume the margin of victory in the 200m freestyle was incorrectly entered as 18.9. Which would increase more, the mean or the median? Explain why.

33. **Playback time:** The following table presents the playback time (in hours) of a sample of 20 MP3 players.

Brand & Model	Playback Time	Brand & Model	Playback Time
Samsung YP-T10	29	SanDisk Sansa View	35
Samsung YP-P2	25	Philips GoGear SA5245BT	40
Creative ZEN	23	Archos 405	13
iRiver SPINN MP4 Player	21	Creative ZEN X-Fi with Wireless LAN	38
Sony Walkman NWZ- S738FBNC	47	Apple iPod Nano	34
Apple iPod Touch	46	Archos 105	23
Sony Walkman NWZ-E438F	66	Sony Walkman NWZ-A828	42
Sony Walkman NWZ-A729	43	Creative Mozaic	38
Creative ZEN X-Fi	35	SanDisk Sansa Fuze	29
Sony Walkman NWZ-S638F	47	Samsung YP-S3	25

Source: *Consumer Reports*

a. Find the mean playback time.
b. Find the median playback time.
c. Find the mode or modes, if any.
d. Would you expect the playback times to be skewed to the left, skewed to the right, or approximately symmetric? Explain.

34. **Facebook applications:** The following table presents the number of monthly users for the 25 most popular Facebook applications as of December 2008.

Application	Monthly Users (millions)	Application	Monthly Users (millions)
Super Wall	21.4	Birthday Calendar	4.6
Causes	16.6	Pieces of Flair	4.6
Top Friends	15.3	SuperPoke!	4.5
Slide FunSpace	11.6	Pass a Drink	4.4
Bumper Sticker	7.5	Likeness	4.0
Texas HoldEm Poker	7.1	Who Has the Biggest Brain?	3.7
We're Related	6.9	Birthday Cards	3.6
Movies	6.3	Are YOU Interested?	3.5
(Lil) Green Patch	6.0	Word Challenge	3.5
iLike	5.7	Snowball Fight!	3.4
Compare People	5.4	Geo Challenge	3.4
Hug Me	5.4	Mobile	3.1
Pet Society	4.7		

Source: www.allfacebook.com

a. Find the mean number of monthly users.
b. Find the median number of monthly users.
c. Would you expect these data to be skewed to the right, skewed to the left, or approximately symmetric? Explain.

35. **What's your favorite TV show?** The following tables present the ratings for the top 20 prime-time shows for the 1997–1998 and 2007–2008 seasons. The rating is the percentage of households with TV sets that watched the program.

Top Rated TV Programs: 1997–1998

Program	Rating
Seinfeld	21.7
ER	20.4
Veronica's Closet	16.6
Friends	16.1
Monday Night Football	15.0
Touched by an Angel	14.2
60 Minutes	13.8
Union Square	13.6
CBS Sunday Movie	13.1
Frasier	12.0
Home Improvement	12.0
Just Shoot Me	11.9
Dateline NBC — Tuesday	11.5
Dateline NBC — Monday	11.4
The Drew Carey Show	11.1
20/20 — Friday	10.9
N.Y.P.D. Blue	10.8
Primetime Live	10.8
The X-Files	10.6
Law and Order	10.2

Source: www.classictvhits.com

Top Rated TV Programs: 2007–2008

Program	Rating
American Idol — Tuesday	16.1
American Idol — Wednesday	15.9
Dancing With the Stars — Monday (2007)	14.0
Dancing With the Stars — Tuesday (2007)	12.7
Dancing With the Stars — Monday (2008)	12.6
Dancing With the Stars — Tuesday (2008)	11.8
Desperate Housewives	11.6
CSI	10.6
House — Tuesday	10.5
Grey's Anatomy	10.4
Sunday Night Football	9.7
CSI: Miami	9.2
House — Monday	9.2
NCIS	9.2
Survivor: China	9.0
Without a Trace	8.8
The Moment of Truth	8.8
Two and a Half Men	8.5
60 Minutes	8.4
Criminal Minds	8.2

Source: Nielsen Media Research

a. Find the mean and median ratings for 1997–1998.
b. Find the mean and median ratings for 2007–2008.
c. The total number of TV channels increased considerably between 1998 and 2008. Some media experts believe that the audience is now spread out over more channels so that ratings are not as high as they used to be. Do the results of parts (a) and (b) support this claim? Explain.

36. **Beer:** The following table presents the number of active breweries for samples of states located east and west of the Mississippi River.

| East | | West | |
State	Number of Breweries	State	Number of Breweries
Connecticut	18	Alaska	17
Delaware	10	Arizona	31
Florida	47	California	305
Georgia	22	Colorado	111
Illinois	52	Iowa	21
Kentucky	13	Louisiana	6
Maine	38	Minnesota	41
Maryland	23	Montana	30
Massachusetts	40	South Dakota	5
New Hampshire	16	Texas	37
New Jersey	20	Utah	15
New York	76		
North Carolina	46		
South Carolina	14		
Tennessee	19		
Vermont	20		

Source: http://www.beerinstitute.org/

a. Find the mean number of breweries for states east of the Mississippi.
b. Find the mean number of breweries for states west of the Mississippi.
c. Find the median number of breweries for states east of the Mississippi.
d. Find the median number of breweries for states west of the Mississippi.
e. Does one region have a lot more breweries per state than the other, or are they about the same?
f. The sample of western states happens to include California. Remove California from the sample of western states, and compute the mean and median for the remaining western states.
g. How does the removal of California affect the comparison of the number of breweries between eastern and western states?

37. **Gas prices:** The following table presents the average price, in U.S. dollars per gallon, of unleaded regular gasoline in several countries in the years 2001 and 2007.

Country	2001	2007
Australia	1.71	3.85
Canada	1.72	3.59
China	1.22	2.29
Germany	3.40	6.88
Japan	3.27	4.49
Mexico	2.20	2.40
South Korea	3.76	6.21
Taiwan	2.02	3.20
United States	1.46	2.80

Source: U.S. Department of Energy

a. Find the mean and median gas price for 2001.
b. Find the mean and median gas price for 2007.
c. Which increased more between 2001 and 2007, the mean or the median?

38. **House prices:** The following table presents prices, in thousands of dollars, of single-family homes for 24 of the 25 largest metropolitan areas in the United States for the third quarter of 2007 and the third quarter of 2008 (information for Detroit was unavailable).

Metro Area	2007	2008	Metro Area	2007	2008
Atlanta, GA	175.3	151.3	New York, NY	476.1	452.5
Baltimore, MD	291.4	279.2	Philadelphia, PA	243.0	241.1
Boston, MA	414.7	373.4	Phoenix, AZ	255.5	185.1
Chicago, IL	286.4	250.8	Pittsburgh, PA	127.7	122.7
Cincinnati, OH	145.3	136.0	Portland, OR	299.7	278.6
Cleveland, OH	132.7	116.4	Riverside, CA	375.1	227.2
Dallas, TX	153.7	150.2	St. Louis, MO	150.5	142.7
Denver, CO	254.1	225.1	San Diego, CA	589.3	377.3
Houston, TX	155.8	160.2	San Francisco, CA	824.2	615.7
Los Angeles, CA	602.9	391.4	Seattle, WA	394.7	350.0
Miami, FL	346.3	287.8	Tampa, FL	218.3	173.4
Minneapolis, MN	229.6	205.1	Washington, DC	438.0	332.7

Source: National Realtors Association

   a. Find the mean and median price for 2007.
   b. Find the mean and median price for 2008.
   c. In general, house prices decreased from 2007 to 2008. Which decreased more, the mean or the median?

39. Heavy football players: Following are the weights, in pounds, for offensive and defensive linemen on the New York Giants National Football League team at the beginning of the 2008 season.

Offense:	315	253	255	319	252	300	327	303	299	310	317	302
Defense:	304	309	306	305	265	270	264	317	255	274	261	296

   a. Find the mean and median weight for the offensive linemen.
   b. Find the mean and median weight for the defensive linemen.
   c. Do offensive or defensive linemen tend to be heavier, or are they about the same?

40. Stock prices: Following are the closing prices of Google stock for each trading day in June and July 2010.

June					
482.37	493.37	505.60	498.72	485.52	484.78
474.02	487.01	488.50	483.19	497.99	501.27
500.08	500.03	488.56	486.25	482.05	475.10
472.68	472.08	454.26	444.95		

July					
439.49	436.55	436.07	450.20	456.56	467.49
475.83	489.20	491.34	494.02	459.61	466.18
481.59	477.50	484.81	490.06	488.97	492.63
484.35	484.99	484.85			

   a. Find the mean and median price in June.
   b. Find the mean and median price in July.
   c. Does there appear to be a substantial difference in price between June and July, or are the prices about the same?

41. Commercial break: Following are the amounts spent (in billions of dollars) on media advertising in the United States by a sample of ten companies in 2008.

3.2	2.4	2.2	2.0	1.4	1.4	1.3	1.2	1.2	1.0

Source: TNS Media Intelligence

   a. Find the mean amount spent on advertising.
   b. Find the median amount spent on advertising.
   c. How many modes are there? Find them.
   d. If the amount of 3.2 was incorrectly listed as 32, how would this affect the mean? How would it affect the median?

42. Magazines: The following data represent the annual costs in dollars, of a sample of 22 popular magazine subscriptions.

14.98	9.97	20.99	7.97	9.99	11.97	116.99	14.95	11.97	16.00	9.97
17.98	38.95	14.98	14.98	16.00	24.99	14.98	10.99	18.00	12.99	11.99

Source: http://magazines.com

   a. Find the mean annual subscription cost.
   b. Find the median annual subscription cost.
   c. What is the mode?
   d. Which value in this data set is most accurately described as an extreme value?
   e. How would the mean, median, and mode be affected if the extreme value were removed from the list?

43. Don't drink and drive: The Insurance Institute for Highway Safety reported that there were 3958 fatalities among drivers in auto accidents in 2008. Following is a frequency distribution of their ages.

Age	Number of Fatalities
11–20	339
21–30	1544
31–40	844
41–50	686
51–60	413
61–70	132

Source: Insurance Institute for Highway Safety

   a. Approximate the mean age.
   b. The first class consists of ages 11 through 20, but most drivers are at least 16 years old. Does this tend to make the approximate mean too large or too small? Explain.

44. Age distribution: The ages of residents of Banks City, Oregon, are given in the following frequency distribution.

Age	Frequency
0–9	283
10–19	203
20–29	217
30–39	256
40–49	176
50–59	92
60–69	21
70–79	23
80–89	12
90–99	3

Source: U.S. Census Bureau

a. Approximate the mean age.

b. Assume all three people aged 90–99 were in fact 90 years old. Would this tend to make the approximate mean too large or too small? Explain.

45. Income: The personal income per capita of a state is the total income of all adults in the state, divided by the number of adults. The following table presents the personal income per capita (in thousands of dollars) for each of the 50 states and the District of Columbia.

32	40	33	30	42	41	54	41	61	38	33	39	31	40	34	35	37
31	35	34	46	49	35	41	29	34	32	36	40	42	49	31	47	34
35	35	34	35	39	39	31	34	33	37	31	37	41	38	30	36	43

Source: U.S. Bureau of Economic Analysis

a. What is the mean state income?

b. What is the median state income?

c. Based on the mean and median, would you expect the data to be skewed to the left, skewed to the right, or approximately symmetric? Explain.

d. Construct a frequency histogram. Do the results agree with your expectation?

46. Stock prices: The following table presents the stock prices for a sample of 43 companies at the close of business on Friday, September 11, 2009.

26.10	23.47	31.03	22.30	69.98	60.42	1.65	32.54	21.69	16.25	11.76
7.33	28.42	31.46	29.30	83.96	27.34	34.17	55.18	16.97	16.07	4.61
54.39	48.41	50.72	23.56	75.23	58.80	60.58	15.59	51.51	172.16	54.99
16.60	55.64	24.86	3.77	24.39	26.66	77.32	51.35	9.34	14.67	

a. Find the mean and median of the stock prices.

b. Based on the mean and median, would you expect that a histogram would be skewed to the left, skewed to the right, or approximately symmetric? Explain.

c. Construct a frequency histogram. Do the results agree with your expectation?

47. Read any good books lately? The following data represent the responses of 24 library patrons when asked about their favorite type of book. Which type of book is the mode?

Biography	Fiction	Biography	Historical	Fiction	Biography
Fiction	Nonfiction	Fiction	Fiction	Historical	Biography
How-to guide	Nonfiction	How-to guide	Nonfiction	Historical	Nonfiction
Fiction	Fiction	How-to guide	How-to guide	Biography	How-to guide

48. Sources of news: A sample of 32 U.S. adults was surveyed and asked, "Do you get most of your information about current events from newspapers, magazines, the Internet, television, radio, or some other source?" The results are shown below. What is the mode?

Television	Internet	Television	Other	Newspapers	Internet	Television	Radio
Magazines	Newspapers	Other	Radio	Radio	Internet	Other	Television
Internet	Magazines	Other	Television	Internet	Newspapers	Newspapers	Internet
Newspapers	Other	Television	Newspapers	Television	Magazines	Television	Television

Source: General Social Survey

49. How many numbers? A data set has a median of 17, and six of the numbers in the data set are less than 17. The data set contains a total of n numbers.
  a. If n is odd, and exactly one number in the data set is equal to 17, what is the value of n?
  b. If n is even, and none of the numbers in the data set are equal to 17, what is the value of n?

50. How many numbers? A data set has a median of 10, and eight of the numbers in the data set are less than 10. The data set contains a total of n numbers.
  a. If n is odd, and exactly one of the numbers in the data set is equal to 10, what is the value of n?
  b. If n is even, and two of the numbers in the data set are equal to 10, what is the value of n?

51. What's the score? Jermaine has entered a bowling tournament. To prepare, he bowls five games each day and writes down the score of each game, along with the mean of the five scores. He is looking at the scores from one day last week and finds that one of the numbers has accidentally been erased. The four remaining scores are 201, 193, 221, and 187. The mean score is 202. What is the missing score?

52. What's your grade? Addison has been told that her average on six homework assignments in her history class is 85. She can find only five of the six assignments, which have scores of 91, 72, 96, 88, and 75. What is the score on the lost homework assignment?

53. Mean or median? The Smith family in Example 3.5 had the good fortune to win a million-dollar prize in a lottery. Their annual income for each of the five years leading up to their lottery win are as follows:

$$15,000 \quad 18,000 \quad 20,000 \quad 25,000 \quad 1,025,000$$

  a. Compute the mean annual income.
  b. Compute the median annual income.
  c. Which provides a more appropriate description of the Smiths' financial position, the mean or the median? Explain.

54. Mean or median? The incomes in a certain town of 1000 households are strongly skewed to the right. The mean income is $60,000, and the median income is only $40,000. The town is going to impose a 1% income tax, and the town council wants to estimate how much revenue will be generated. Which is the more relevant measure of center for the town council, the mean income or the median income? Explain.

55. Properties of the mean: Make up a data set in which the mean is equal to one of the numbers in the data set.

56. Properties of the median: Make up a data set in which the median is equal to one of the numbers in the data set.

57. Properties of the mean: Make up a data set in which the mean is *not* equal to one of the numbers in the data set.

58. Properties of the median: Make up a data set in which the median is *not* equal to one of the numbers in the data set.

59. The midrange: The **midrange** is a measure of center that is computed by averaging the largest and smallest values in a data set. In other words,

$$\text{Midrange} = \frac{\text{Largest value} + \text{Smallest value}}{2}$$

Is the midrange resistant? Explain.

60. Mean, median, and midrange: A data set contains only two values. Are the mean, median, and midrange all equal? Explain.

Extending the Concepts

61. Changing units: A sample of five college students have heights, in inches, of 65, 72, 68, 67, and 70.
  a. Compute the sample mean.
  b. Compute the sample median.
  c. Convert each of the heights to units of feet, by dividing by 12.
  d. Compute the sample mean of the heights in feet. Is this equal to the sample mean in inches divided by 12?
  e. Compute the sample median of the heights in feet. Is this equal to the sample median in inches divided by 12?

62. Effect on the mean and median: Four employees in an office have annual salaries of $30,000, $35,000, $45,000, and $70,000.
  a. Compute the mean salary.
  b. Compute the median salary.
  c. Each employee gets a $1000 raise. Compute the new mean. Does the mean increase by $1000?
  d. Each employee gets a 5% raise. Compute the new mean. Does the mean increase by 5%?

63. Nonresistant median: Consider the following data set:

$$0 \quad 0 \quad 1 \quad 1 \quad 1 \quad 1 \quad 1 \quad 1 \quad 2 \quad 2 \quad 8 \quad 8 \quad 9 \quad 9 \quad 9 \quad 9 \quad 9 \quad 9 \quad 10 \quad 10$$

  a. Show that the mean and median are both equal to 5.
  b. Suppose that a value of 26 is added to this data set. Which is affected more, the mean or the median?
  c. Suppose that a value of 100 is added to this data set. Which is affected more, the mean or the median?
  d. It is possible for an extreme value to affect the median more than the mean, but if the value is extreme enough, the mean will be affected more than the median. Explain.

64. Exception to the skewness rule: Consider the following data set:

$$0\ 0\ 0\ 0\ 0\ 0\ 0\ 0\ 0\ 0\ 1\ 1\ 1\ 1\ 1\ 1\ 1\ 1\ 2\ 2\ 2\ 3$$

  a. Compute the mean and median.
  b. Based on the mean and median, would you expect the data set to be skewed to the left, skewed to the right, or approximately symmetric? Explain.
  c. Construct a frequency histogram. Does the histogram have the shape you expected?

Answers to Check Your Understanding Exercises for Section 3.1

1. Mean is 65.4; median is 60.

2. Mean is 68.5; median is 74.5.

3. The mean does not have to be a value that could possibly appear in the data set.

4. Skewed to the right

5. Skewed to the left

6. a. 1   **b.** 4 and 6   **c.** No mode

SECTION 3.2 | Measures of Spread

Objectives

1. Compute the range of a data set
2. Compute the variance of a population and a sample
3. Compute the standard deviation of a population and a sample
4. Approximate the standard deviation with grouped data
5. Use the Empirical Rule to summarize data that are unimodal and approximately symmetric
6. Use Chebyshev's Inequality to describe a data set
7. Compute the coefficient of variation

Would you rather live in San Francisco or St. Louis? If you had to choose between these two cities, one factor you might consider is the weather. Table 3.3 presents the average monthly temperatures, in degrees Fahrenheit, for both cities.

Table 3.3 Temperatures in San Francisco and St. Louis

	Jan	Feb	Mar	Apr	May	Jun	Jul	Aug	Sep	Oct	Nov	Dec
San Francisco	51	54	55	56	58	60	60	61	63	62	58	52
St. Louis	30	35	44	57	66	75	79	78	70	59	45	35

Source: National Weather Service

To compare the temperatures, we will compute their means.

$$\text{Mean for San Francisco} = \frac{51+54+55+56+58+60+60+61+63+62+58+52}{12}$$
$$= 57.5$$

$$\text{Mean for St. Louis} = \frac{30+35+44+57+66+75+79+78+70+59+45+35}{12}$$
$$= 56.1$$

The means are similar: 57.5° for San Francisco and 56.1° for St. Louis. Does this mean that the temperatures are similar in both cities? Definitely not. St. Louis has a cold winter and a hot summer, while the temperature in San Francisco is much the same all year round.

Another way to say this is that the temperatures in St. Louis are more spread out than the temperatures in San Francisco. The dotplots in Figure 3.5 illustrate the difference in spread.

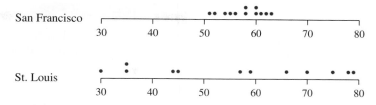

Figure 3.5 The monthly temperatures for St. Louis are more spread out than those for San Francisco.

The mean does not tell us anything about how spread out the data are; it only gives us a measure of the center. It is clear that the mean by itself is not adequate to describe a data set. We must also have a way to describe the amount of spread. Dotplots allow us to visualize the spread, but we need a numerical summary to measure it precisely.

Objective 1 Compute the range of a data set

The Range

The simplest measure of the spread of a data set is the range.

> **DEFINITION**
>
> The **range** of a data set is the difference between the largest value and the smallest value.
>
> $$\text{Range} = \text{Largest value} - \text{Smallest value}$$

EXAMPLE 3.10

Compute the range of a data set

Compute the range of the temperature data for San Francisco and for St. Louis, and interpret the results.

Solution

The largest value for San Francisco is 63 and the smallest is 51. The range for San Francisco is $63 - 51 = 12$.

The largest value for St. Louis is 79 and the smallest is 30. The range for St. Louis is $79 - 30 = 49$.

The range is much larger for St. Louis, which indicates that the spread in the temperatures is much greater there.

Although the range is easy to compute, it is not often used in practice. The reason is that the range involves only two values from the data set — the largest and the smallest. The measures of spread that are most often used are the variance and the standard deviation, which use every value in the data set.

Objective 2 Compute the variance of a population and a sample

The Variance

When a data set has a small amount of spread, like the San Francisco temperatures, most of the values will be close to the mean. When a data set has a larger amount of spread, more of the data values will be far from the mean. The **variance** is a measure of how far the values in a data set are from the mean, on the average. We will describe how to compute the variance of a population.

The difference between a population value, x, and the population mean, μ, is $x - \mu$. This difference is called a **deviation**. Values less than the mean will have negative deviations, and values greater than the mean will have positive deviations. If we were simply to add the deviations, the positive and the negative ones would cancel out. So we square the deviations to make them all positive. Data sets with a lot of spread will have many large squared deviations, while those with less spread will have smaller squared deviations. The average of the squared deviations is the **population variance**.

DEFINITION

Let $x_1, ..., x_N$ denote the values in a population of size N. Let μ denote the population mean. The **population variance**, denoted by σ^2, is

$$\sigma^2 = \frac{\sum (x - \mu)^2}{N}$$

We present the procedure for computing the population variance.

Procedure for Computing the Population Variance

Step 1: Compute the population mean μ.

Step 2: For each population value x, compute the deviation $x - \mu$.

Step 3: Square the deviations, to obtain quantities $(x - \mu)^2$.

Step 4: Sum the squared deviations, obtaining $\sum (x - \mu)^2$.

Step 5: Divide the sum obtained in Step 4 by the population size N to obtain the population variance σ^2.

In practice, variances are usually calculated with technology. It is a good idea to compute a few by hand, however, to get a feel for the procedure.

EXAMPLE 3.11

Computing the population variance

Compute the population variance for the San Francisco temperatures.

Solution

The calculations are shown in Table 3.4.

Step 1: Compute the population mean:

$$\mu = \frac{51 + 54 + 55 + 56 + 58 + 60 + 60 + 61 + 63 + 62 + 58 + 52}{12} = 57.5$$

Step 2: Subtract μ from each value to obtain the deviations $x - \mu$. These calculations are shown in the second column of Table 3.4.

Table 3.4 Calculations for the Population Variance in Example 3.11

x	$x - \mu$	$(x - \mu)^2$
51	−6.5	$(-6.5)^2 = 42.25$
54	−3.5	$(-3.5)^2 = 12.25$
55	−2.5	$(-2.5)^2 = 6.25$
56	−1.5	$(-1.5)^2 = 2.25$
58	0.5	$0.5^2 = 0.25$
60	2.5	$2.5^2 = 6.25$
60	2.5	$2.5^2 = 6.25$
61	3.5	$3.5^2 = 12.25$
63	5.5	$5.5^2 = 30.25$
62	4.5	$4.5^2 = 20.25$
58	0.5	$0.5^2 = 0.25$
52	−5.5	$(-5.5)^2 = 30.25$

$$\mu = 57.5 \qquad \sum (x - \mu)^2 = 169$$

$$\sigma^2 = \frac{169}{12} = 14.083$$

Step 3: Square the deviations. These calculations are shown in the third column of Table 3.4.

Step 4: Sum the squared deviations to obtain

$$\sum(x - \mu)^2 = 169$$

Step 5: The population size is $N = 12$. Divide the sum obtained in Step 4 by N to obtain the population variance σ^2.

$$\sigma^2 = \frac{\sum(x - \mu)^2}{N} = \frac{169}{12} = 14.083$$

In Example 3.11, note how important it is to make all the deviations positive, which we do by squaring them. If we simply add the deviations without squaring them, the positive and negative ones will cancel each other out, leaving 0.

Check Your Understanding

1. Compute the population variance for the St. Louis temperatures. Compare the result with the variance for the San Francisco temperatures, and interpret the result.

Answer is on page 123.

The sample variance

When the data values come from a sample rather than a population, the variance is called the **sample variance**. The procedure for computing the sample variance is a bit different from the one used to compute a population variance.

CAUTION

The sample variance will *never* be negative. It will be equal to zero if all the values in a sample are the same. Otherwise, the sample variance will be positive.

DEFINITION

Let $x_1, ..., x_n$ denote the values in a sample of size n. The **sample variance**, denoted by s^2, is

$$s^2 = \frac{\sum(x - \bar{x})^2}{n - 1}$$

The formula is the same as for the population variance, except that we replace the population mean μ with the sample mean $\bar{x}$, and we divide by $n - 1$ rather than N.

We present the procedure for computing the sample variance.

Explain It Again

Another formula for the sample variance: An alternate formula for the sample variance is

$$s^2 = \frac{\sum x^2 - n\bar{x}^2}{n - 1}$$

This formula will always give the same result as the one in the definition.

Procedure for Computing the Sample Variance

Step 1: Compute the sample mean $\bar{x}$.

Step 2: For each sample value x, compute the difference $x - \bar{x}$. This quantity is called a deviation.

Step 3: Square the deviations, to obtain quantities $(x - \bar{x})^2$.

Step 4: Sum the squared deviations, obtaining $\sum(x - \bar{x})^2$.

Step 5: Divide the sum obtained in Step 4 by $n - 1$ to obtain the sample variance s^2.

EXAMPLE 3.12

Computing the sample variance

A company that manufactures batteries is testing a new type of battery designed for laptop computers. They measure the lifetimes, in hours, of six batteries, and the results are 3, 4, 6, 5, 4, and 2. Find the sample variance of the lifetimes.

Solution

The calculations are shown in Table 3.5.

Step 1: Compute the sample mean:

$$\bar{x} = \frac{3+4+6+5+4+2}{6} = 4$$

Step 2: Subtract $\bar{x}$ from each value to obtain the deviations $x - \bar{x}$. These calculations are shown in the second column of Table 3.5.

Table 3.5 Calculations for the Sample Variance in Example 3.12

x	$x - \bar{x}$	$(x - \bar{x})^2$
3	-1	$(-1)^2 = 1$
4	0	$0^2 = 0$
6	2	$2^2 = 4$
5	1	$1^2 = 1$
4	0	$0^2 = 0$
2	-2	$(-2)^2 = 4$

$$\bar{x} = 4 \qquad\qquad \sum (x - \bar{x})^2 = 10$$

$$s^2 = \frac{10}{6-1} = 2$$

Step 3: Square the deviations. These calculations are shown in the third column of Table 3.5.

Step 4: Sum the squared deviations to obtain

$$\sum (x - \bar{x})^2 = 10$$

Step 5: The sample size is $n = 6$. Divide the sum obtained in Step 4 by $n - 1$ to obtain the sample variance s^2.

$$s^2 = \frac{\sum (x - \bar{x})^2}{n - 1} = \frac{10}{6 - 1} = 2$$

Why do we divide by $n - 1$ rather than n?

It is natural to wonder why we divide by $n - 1$ rather than n when computing the sample variance. When computing the sample variance, we use the sample mean to compute the deviations $x - \bar{x}$. For the population variance, we use the population mean for the deviations $x - \mu$. Now it turns out that the deviations using the sample mean tend to be a bit smaller than the deviations using the population mean. If we were to divide by n when computing a sample variance, the value would tend to be a bit smaller than the population variance. It can be shown mathematically that the appropriate correction is to divide the sum of the squared deviations by $n - 1$ rather than n.

The quantity $n - 1$ is sometimes called the **degrees of freedom** for the sample standard deviation. The reason is that the deviations $x - \bar{x}$ will always sum to 0. Thus, if we know the first $n - 1$ deviations, we can compute the nth one. For example, if our sample consists of the four numbers 2, 4, 9, and 13, the sample mean is

$$\bar{x} = \frac{2 + 4 + 9 + 13}{4} = 7$$

The first three deviations are

$$2 - 7 = -5, \quad 4 - 7 = -3, \quad 9 - 7 = 2$$

The sum of the first three deviations is

$$-5 + (-3) + 2 = -6$$

We can now determine that the last deviation must be 6, in order to make the sum of all four deviations equal to 0. When we know the first three deviations, we can determine the fourth one. Thus, for a sample of size 4, there are 3 degrees of freedom. In general, for a sample of size n, there will be $n - 1$ degrees of freedom.

Objective 3 Compute the standard deviation of a population and a sample

The Standard Deviation

There is a problem with using the variance as a measure of spread. Because the variance is computed using squared deviations, the units of the variance are the squared units of the data. For example, in Example 3.12, the units of the data are hours, and the units of variance are squared hours. In most situations, it is better to use a measure of spread that has the same units as the data. We do this simply by taking the square root of the variance. The quantity thus obtained is called the **standard deviation**. The standard deviation of a sample is denoted s, and the standard deviation of a population is denoted σ.

DEFINITION

- The **sample standard deviation** s is the square root of the sample variance s^2.

$$s = \sqrt{s^2}$$

- The **population standard deviation** σ is the square root of the population variance σ^2.

$$\sigma = \sqrt{\sigma^2}$$

EXAMPLE 3.13

CAUTION

Don't round off the variance when computing the standard deviation.

Computing the standard deviation

The lifetimes, in hours, of six batteries (first presented in Example 3.12) were 3, 4, 6, 5, 4, and 2. Find the standard deviation of the battery lifetimes.

Solution

In Example 3.12, we computed the sample variance to be $s^2 = 2$. The sample standard deviation is therefore

$$s = \sqrt{s^2} = \sqrt{2} = 1.414$$

EXAMPLE 3.14

Computing standard deviations with technology

Compute the standard deviation for the data in Example 3.13.

Solution

Following is the display from the TI-84 Plus.

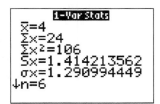

The TI-84 Plus calculator denotes the sample standard deviation by **Sx**. The display shows that the sample standard deviation is equal to 1.414213562. The calculator does not know whether the data set represents a sample or an entire population. Therefore, the display also presents the population standard deviation, which is denoted σx.

Check Your Understanding

2. Find the sample variance and standard deviation for the following samples.
   a. 2   2   1   5   4   5   0   1
   b. 22   27   13   53   47   50

3. Find the population variance and standard deviation for the population values 7, 3, 2, 5, 4, 9, 6, 3.

Answers are on page 123.

Recall: A statistic is resistant if its value is not affected much by extreme data values.

The standard deviation is not resistant

Example 3.15 shows that the standard deviation is *not* resistant.

EXAMPLE 3.15

Show that the standard deviation is not resistant

In Example 3.14, we found that the sample standard deviation for six battery lifetimes was $s = 1.414$. The six lifetimes were 3, 4, 6, 5, 4, and 2. Assume that the battery with a lifetime of 6 actually had a lifetime of 20, so that the lifetimes are 3, 4, 20, 5, 4, and 2. Compute the standard deviation.

Solution

Following is the display from the TI-84 Plus.

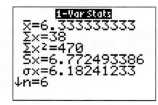

Including the extreme value of 20 in the data set has increased the sample standard deviation from 1.414 to 6.772. Clearly, the standard deviation is not resistant.

Objective 4 Approximate the standard deviation with grouped data

Approximating the Standard Deviation with Grouped Data

Sometimes we don't have access to the raw data in a data set, but we are given a frequency distribution. In Section 3.1, we learned how to approximate the sample mean from a frequency distribution. We now show how to approximate the standard deviation.

We use Table 3.6 to illustrate the method. Table 3.6 presents the number of text messages sent via cell phone by a sample of 50 high school students. In Section 3.1, we computed the approximate sample mean to be $\bar{x} = 137$. We will now approximate the standard deviation.

Table 3.6 Number of Text Messages Sent by High School Students

Number of Text Messages Sent	Frequency
0–49	10
50–99	5
100–149	13
150–199	11
200–249	7
250–299	4

We present the procedure for approximating the standard deviation from grouped data.

Procedure for Approximating the Standard Deviation with Grouped Data

Step 1: Compute the midpoint of each class. The midpoint of a class is found by taking the average of the lower class limit and the lower limit of the next larger class. Then compute the mean as described in Section 3.1.

Step 2: For each class, subtract the mean from the class midpoint to obtain Midpoint − Mean.

Step 3: For each class, square the difference obtained in Step 2 to obtain (Midpoint − Mean)^2, and multiply by the frequency to obtain (Midpoint − Mean)^2 × Frequency.

Step 4: Add the products (Midpoint − Mean)^2 × Frequency over all classes.

Step 5: Compute the sum of the frequencies n. To compute the *population* variance, divide the sum obtained in Step 4 by n. To compute the *sample* variance, divide the sum obtained in Step 4 by $n − 1$.

Step 6: Take the square root of the variance obtained in Step 5. The result is the standard deviation.

EXAMPLE 3.16

Computing the standard deviation for grouped data

Compute the approximate sample standard deviation of the number of messages sent, using the data given in Table 3.6.

Solution

The calculations are summarized in Table 3.7.

Table 3.7 Calculating the Variance and Standard Deviation of the Number of Text Messages

Class	Midpoint	Frequency	Mean	Midpoint − Mean	(Midpoint − Mean)^2 × Frequency
0–49	25	10	137	−112	12544 × 10 = 125,440
50–99	75	5	137	−62	3844 × 5 = 19,220
100–149	125	13	137	−12	144 × 13 = 1,872
150–199	175	11	137	38	1444 × 11 = 15,884
200–249	225	7	137	88	7744 × 7 = 54,208
250–299	275	4	137	138	19044 × 4 = 76,176

Sum = 50   Sum = 292,800

$$\text{Variance} = \frac{292{,}800}{50 − 1} = 5975.51020 \qquad \text{Standard deviation} = \sqrt{5975.51020} = 77.3014$$

Step 1: Compute the midpoints: For the first class, the lower class limit is 0. The lower limit of the next class is 50. The midpoint is therefore

$$\frac{0 + 50}{2} = 25$$

We continue in this manner to compute the midpoints of each of the classes. Note that for the last class, we average the lower limit of 250 with 300, which is the lower limit that the next class would have. We computed the sample mean in Example 3.9 in Section 3.1. The sample mean is $\bar{x} = 137$.

Step 2: For each class, subtract the mean from the class midpoint as shown in the column labeled "Midpoint − Mean."

Step 3: For each class, square the difference obtained in Step 2 and multiply by the frequency as shown in the column labeled "(Midpoint − Mean)^2 × Frequency."

Step 4: Add the products (Midpoint − Mean)^2 × Frequency over all classes, to obtain the sum 292,800.

Step 5: The sum of the frequencies is 50. Since we are considering the data to be a sample, we subtract 1 from this sum to obtain 49. The sample variance is 292,800/49 = 5975.51020.

Step 6: The sample standard deviation is $\sqrt{5975.51020} = 77.3014$.

Objective 5 Use the Empirical Rule to summarize data that are unimodal and approximately symmetric

The Empirical Rule

Many histograms have a single mode near the center of the data, and are approximately symmetric. Such histograms are often referred to as *bell-shaped*. Other histograms are strongly skewed; these are not bell-shaped. When a data set has a bell-shaped histogram, it is often possible to use the standard deviation to provide an approximate description of the data using a rule known as the **Empirical Rule**.

The Empirical Rule

When a population has a histogram that is approximately bell-shaped, then

- Approximately 68% of the data will be within one standard deviation of the mean. In other words, approximately 68% of the data will be between $\mu - \sigma$ and $\mu + \sigma$.
- Approximately 95% of the data will be within two standard deviations of the mean. In other words, approximately 95% of the data will be between $\mu - 2\sigma$ and $\mu + 2\sigma$.
- All, or almost all, of the data will be within three standard deviations of the mean. In other words, all, or almost all, of the data will be between $\mu - 3\sigma$ and $\mu + 3\sigma$.

CAUTION

The Empirical Rule should not be used for data sets that are not approximately bell-shaped.

The Empirical Rule holds for many bell-shaped data sets. Figure 3.6 illustrates the Empirical Rule.

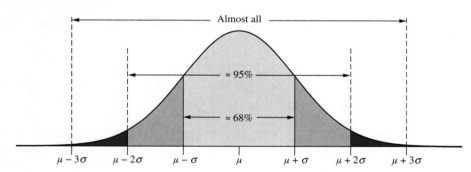

Figure 3.6 The Empirical Rule. Approximately 68% of the data values are between $\mu - \sigma$ and $\mu + \sigma$, approximately 95% are between $\mu - 2\sigma$ and $\mu + 2\sigma$, and almost all are between $\mu - 3\sigma$ and $\mu + 3\sigma$.

EXAMPLE 3.17

Using the Empirical Rule to describe a data set

Table 3.8 presents the percentage of the population aged 65 and over in each state and the District of Columbia. Figure 3.7 presents a histogram of these data. Compute the mean and standard deviation, and use the Empirical Rule to describe the data.

Table 3.8 Percentage of People Aged 65 and Over in Each of the 50 States and District of Columbia

14.1	8.1	13.9	14.3	11.5	10.7	14.4	14.1	11.5	17.8	14.0
10.2	14.3	12.0	12.4	12.7	14.9	13.4	13.1	12.6	15.6	
12.2	13.7	12.8	12.4	12.8	13.9	15.0	13.8	12.3	12.6	
13.7	14.1	13.6	12.4	15.3	13.7	13.8	13.0	15.5	14.1	
13.6	14.6	13.3	10.5	9.0	14.3	12.4	12.2	16.0	13.5	

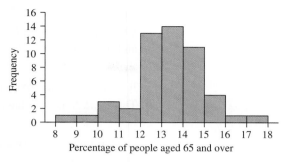

Figure 3.7 Histogram for the data in Table 3.8

Solution

Step 1: Figure 3.7 shows that the histogram is approximately bell-shaped, so we may use the Empirical Rule.

Step 2: We use the TI-84 Plus to compute the mean and standard deviation. The display is shown here.

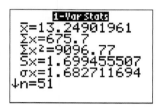

Note that the 51 entries (corresponding to 50 states plus the District of Columbia) are an entire population. Therefore we will interpret the quantity $\bar{x} = 13.24901961$ produced by the TI-84 Plus as the population mean μ, and we will use $\sigma = 1.682711694$ for the standard deviation.

Step 3: We compute the quantities $\mu - \sigma$, $\mu + \sigma$, $\mu - 2\sigma$, $\mu + 2\sigma$, $\mu - 3\sigma$, and $\mu + 3\sigma$.

$$\mu - \sigma = 13.24901961 - 1.682711694 = 11.57$$

$$\mu + \sigma = 13.24901961 + 1.682711694 = 14.93$$

$$\mu - 2\sigma = 13.24901961 - 2(1.682711694) = 9.88$$

$$\mu + 2\sigma = 13.24901961 + 2(1.682711694) = 16.61$$

$$\mu - 3\sigma = 13.24901961 - 3(1.682711694) = 8.20$$

$$\mu + 3\sigma = 13.24901961 + 3(1.682711694) = 18.30$$

We conclude that the percentage of the population aged 65 and over is between 11.57 and 14.93 in approximately 68% of the states, between 9.88 and 16.61 in approximately 95% of the states, and between 8.20 and 18.30 in almost all the states.

The Empirical Rule can be used for samples as well as populations. When we work with a sample, we use $\bar{x}$ in place of μ and s in place of σ.

EXAMPLE 3.18

Using the Empirical Rule to describe a data set

A sample of size 200 has sample mean $\bar{x} = 50$ and sample standard deviation $s = 10$. The histogram is approximately bell-shaped.

a. Find an interval that is likely to contain approximately 68% of the data values.

b. Approximately what percentage of the data values will be between 30 and 70?

Solution

a. We use the Empirical Rule. Approximately 68% of the data will be between $\bar{x} - s$ and $\bar{x} + s$. We compute

$$\bar{x} - s = 50 - 10 = 40 \qquad \bar{x} + s = 50 + 10 = 60$$

It is likely that approximately 68% of the data values are between 40 and 60.

b. The value 30 is two standard deviations below the mean, since

$$\bar{x} - 2s = 50 - 20 = 30$$

and the value 70 is two standard deviations above the mean, since

$$\bar{x} + 2s = 50 + 20 = 70$$

Therefore, it is likely that approximately 95% of the data values are between 30 and 70.

EXAMPLE 3.19

Determining whether the Empirical Rule is appropriate

Following is a histogram for a data set. Should the Empirical Rule be used?

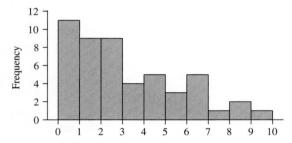

Solution

No. The distribution is skewed, rather than bell-shaped. Therefore, the Empirical Rule should not be used.

Check Your Understanding

4. A data set has a mean of 20 and a standard deviation of 3. A histogram is shown here. Is it appropriate to use the Empirical Rule to approximate the proportion of the data between 14 and 26? If so, find the approximation. If not, explain why not.

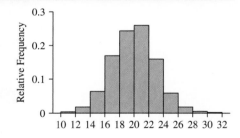

5. A data set has a mean of 50 and a standard deviation of 8. A histogram is shown here. Is it appropriate to use the Empirical Rule to approximate the proportion of the data between 42 and 58? If so, find the approximation. If not, explain why not.

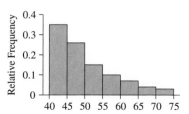

Answers are on page 123.

Objective 6 Use Chebyshev's Inequality to describe a data set

Chebyshev's Inequality

When a distribution is bell-shaped, the Empirical Rule gives us an approximation to the proportion of data that will be within one or two standard deviations of the mean. **Chebyshev's Inequality** is a rule that holds for any data set.

Chebyshev's Inequality

In any data set, the proportion of the data that will be within K standard deviations of the mean is at least $1 - 1/K^2$. Specifically, by setting $K = 2$ or $K = 3$, we obtain the following results:

- At least 3/4 (75%) of the data will be within two standard deviations of the mean.
- At least 8/9 (88.9%) of the data will be within three standard deviations of the mean.

EXAMPLE 3.20

Using Chebyshev's Inequality

As part of a public health study, systolic blood pressure was measured for a large group of people. The mean was $\bar{x} = 120$ and the standard deviation was $s = 10$. What information does Chebyshev's Inequality provide about these data?

Solution

We compute:

$$\bar{x} - 2s = 120 - 2(10) = 100 \qquad \bar{x} + 2s = 120 + 2(10) = 140$$
$$\bar{x} - 3s = 120 - 3(10) = 90 \qquad \bar{x} + 3s = 120 + 3(10) = 150$$

We conclude:

- At least 75% of the people had systolic blood pressures between 100 and 140.
- At least 88.9% of the people had systolic blood pressures between 90 and 150.

Comparing Chebyshev's Inequality to the Empirical Rule

Both Chebyshev's Inequality and the Empirical Rule provide information about the proportion of a data set that is within a given number of standard deviations of the mean. An advantage of Chebyshev's Inequality is that it applies to any data set, whereas the Empirical Rule applies only to data sets that are approximately bell-shaped. A disadvantage of Chebyshev's Inequality is that for most data sets, it provides only a very rough approximation. Chebyshev's Inequality produces a minimum value for the proportion of the data that will be within a given number of standard deviations of the mean. For most data sets, the actual proportions are much larger than the values given by Chebyshev's Inequality.

Check Your Understanding

6. A group of elementary school students took a standardized reading test. The mean score was 70 and the standard deviation was 10. Someone says that only 50% of the students scored between 50 and 90. Is this possible? Explain.

7. A certain type of bolt used in an aircraft must have a length between 122 and 128 millimeters in order to be acceptable. The manufacturing process produces bolts whose mean length is 125 millimeters with a standard deviation of 1 millimeter. Can you be sure that more than 85% of the bolts are acceptable? Explain.

Answers are on page 123.

Objective 7 Compute the coefficient of variation

The Coefficient of Variation

The coefficient of variation (CV for short) tells how large the standard deviation is relative to the mean. It can be used to compare the spreads of data sets whose values have different units.

> ### DEFINITION
>
> The **coefficient of variation** is found by dividing the standard deviation by the mean.
>
> $$CV = \frac{\sigma}{\mu}$$

EXAMPLE 3.21   Computing the coefficient of variation

National Weather Service records show that over a 30-year period, the annual precipitation in Atlanta, Georgia, had a mean of 49.8 inches with a standard deviation of 7.6 inches, and the annual temperature had a mean of 62.2 degrees Fahrenheit with a standard deviation of 1.3 degrees. Compute the coefficient of variation for precipitation and for temperature. Which has greater spread relative to its mean?

Solution

The coefficient of variation for precipitation is

$$\text{CV for precipitation} = \frac{\text{Standard deviation of precipitation}}{\text{Mean precipitation}} = \frac{7.6}{49.8} = 0.153$$

The coefficient of variation for temperature is

$$\text{CV for temperature} = \frac{\text{Standard deviation of temperature}}{\text{Mean temperature}} = \frac{1.3}{62.2} = 0.021$$

The CV for precipitation is larger than the CV for temperature. Therefore, precipitation has a greater spread relative to its mean.

Note that we cannot compare the standard deviations of precipitation and temperature because they have different units. It does not make sense to ask whether 7.6 inches is greater than 1.3 degrees. The CV is unitless, however, so we can compare the CVs.

> ### Check Your Understanding
>
> **8.** Lengths of newborn babies have a mean of 20.1 inches with a standard deviation of 1.9 inches. Find the coefficient of variation of newborn lengths.

Answer is on page 123.

USING TECHNOLOGY

TI-84 Plus

Computing the sample standard deviation

The TI-84 PLUS procedure to compute the mean and median, described on page 96, will also compute the standard deviation.

MINITAB

Computing the sample standard deviation

The MINITAB procedure to compute the mean and median, described on page 96, will also compute the standard deviation.

EXCEL

Computing the sample standard deviation

The EXCEL procedure to compute the mean and median, described on page 96, will also compute the standard deviation.

SECTION 3.2 Exercises

Exercises 1–8 are the Check Your Understanding exercises located within the section.

Understanding the Concepts

In Exercises 9–12, fill in each blank with the appropriate word or phrase.

9. If all values in a data set are the same, then the sample variance is equal to _____.

10. The standard deviation is the square root of the _____.

11. For a bell-shaped data set, approximately _____ of the data will be in the interval $\mu - \sigma$ to $\mu + \sigma$.

12. Chebyshev's Inequality states that for any data set, the proportion of data within K standard deviations of the mean is at least _____.

In Exercises 13–16, determine whether the statement is true or false. If the statement is false, rewrite it as a true statement.

13. The variance and standard deviation are measures of center.

14. The range of a data set is the difference between the largest value and the smallest value.

15. In a bell-shaped data set with $\mu = 15$ and $\sigma = 5$, approximately 95% of the data will be between 10 and 20.

16. For some data sets, Chebyshev's Inequality may be used but the Empirical Rule should not be.

Practicing the Skills

17. Find the sample variance and standard deviation for the following sample:
    17   40   24   18   16

18. Find the sample variance and standard deviation for the following sample:
    59   25   12   29   16   8   26   30   17

19. Find the sample variance and standard deviation for the following sample:
    15   9   5   12   9   21   4   24   18

20. Find the population variance and standard deviation for the following population:
    16   6   18   3   25   22

21. Find the population variance and standard deviation for the following population:
    20   8   11   23   27   29   62   4

22. Find the population variance and standard deviation for the following population:
    26   25   29   23   14   20   12   18   24   31   22   32

23. Approximate the sample variance and standard deviation given the following frequency distribution:

Class	Frequency
0–9	13
10–19	7
20–29	10
30–39	9
40–49	11

24. Approximate the sample variance and standard deviation given the following frequency distribution:

Class	Frequency
0–15	2
16–31	14
32–47	6
48–63	13
64–79	15

25. Approximate the population variance and standard deviation given the following frequency distribution:

Class	Frequency
0–49	17
50–99	26
100–149	14
150–199	34
200–249	26
250–299	8

26. Approximate the population variance and standard deviation given the following frequency distribution:

Class	Frequency
0–19	18
20–39	11
40–59	6
60–79	6
80–99	10
100–119	5

27. The following TI-84 Plus display presents some population parameters.

```
1-Var Stats
x̄=32
Σx=480
Σx²=15900
Sx=6.210590034
σx=6
↓n=15
```

a. Assume the population is bell-shaped. Approximately what percentage of the population values are between 26 and 38?
b. Assume the population is bell-shaped. Between what two values will approximately 95% of the population be?
c. If we do not assume that the population is bell-shaped, at least what percentage of the population will be between 20 and 44?

28. The following TI-84 Plus display presents some population parameters.

```
1-Var Stats
x̄=134
Σx=2680
Σx²=359620
Sx=5.12989176
σx=5
↓n=20
```

a. Assume the population is bell-shaped. Approximately what percentage of the population values are between 124 and 144?

b. Assume the population is bell-shaped. Between what two values will approximately 68% of the population be?

c. If we do not assume that the population is bell-shaped, at least what percentage of the population will be between 119 and 149?

29. The following TI-84 Plus display presents some sample statistics.

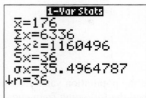

a. Assume that a histogram of the sample is bell-shaped. Approximately what percentage of the sample values are between 104 and 248?

b. Assume that a histogram for the sample is bell-shaped. Between what two values will approximately 68% of the sample be?

c. If we do not assume that the histogram is bell-shaped, at least what percentage of the sample values will be between 68 and 284?

30. The following TI-84 Plus display presents some sample statistics.

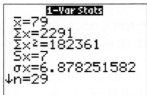

a. Assume that a histogram of the sample is bell-shaped. Approximately what percentage of the sample values are between 72 and 86?

b. Assume that a histogram for the sample is bell-shaped. Between what two values will approximately 95% of the sample be?

c. If we do not assume that the histogram is bell-shaped, at least what percentage of the sample values will be between 65 and 93?

Working with the Concepts

31. Gas prices: The following table presents the average price, in U.S. dollars per gallon, of unleaded regular gasoline in several countries in the years 2001 and 2007.

Country	2001	2007
Australia	1.71	3.85
Canada	1.72	3.59
China	1.22	2.29
Germany	3.40	6.88
Japan	3.27	4.49
Mexico	2.20	2.40
South Korea	3.76	6.21
Taiwan	2.02	3.20
United States	1.46	2.80

Source: U.S. Department of Energy

a. Find the sample standard deviation of the gas prices for 2001.

b. Find the sample standard deviation of the gas prices for 2007.

c. Gas prices increased between 2001 and 2007. Did the spread in gas prices increase as well?

32. Sports car or convertible? The following table presents the fuel efficiency, in miles per gallon, for a sample of convertibles and a sample of sports cars.

Convertible Model	MPG	Sports Model	MPG
Volkswagen Eos	25	BMW 135i	23
Mini Cooper	25	Mazda3 Mazdaspeed	24
Saab 9-3	24	Subaru Impreza WRX STi	21
BMW 328i	21	Mazda RX-8	18
Toyota Camry Solara	21	Mitsubishi Lancer Evolution	21
Volvo C70	21	Volkswagen GTI	25
Ford Mustang V6	20	Honda Civic Si	27

Source: *Consumer Reports*

a. Find the sample standard deviation of the mileage for the sample of convertibles.

b. Find the sample standard deviation of the mileage for the sample of sports cars.

c. Which sample has greater spread?

33. Heavy football players: Following are the weights, in pounds, for samples of offensive and defensive linemen in the National Football League at the beginning of the 2010 season.

Offense:	335	301	307	252	260	307	325	310	305	305	264	325
Defense:	284	290	286	355	305	295	297	325	310	297	314	348

a. Find the sample standard deviation for the weights for the offensive linemen.
b. Find the sample standard deviation for the weights for the defensive linemen.
c. Is there greater spread in the weights of the offensive or the defensive linemen?

34. Beer: The following table presents the number of active breweries for samples of states located east and west of the Mississippi River.

East		West	
State	**Number of Breweries**	**State**	**Number of Breweries**
Connecticut	18	Alaska	17
Delaware	10	Arizona	31
Florida	47	California	305
Georgia	22	Colorado	111
Illinois	52	Iowa	21
Kentucky	13	Louisiana	6
Maine	38	Minnesota	41
Maryland	23	Montana	30
Massachusetts	40	South Dakota	5
New Hampshire	16	Texas	37
New Jersey	20	Utah	15
New York	76		
North Carolina	46		
South Carolina	14		
Tennessee	19		
Vermont	20		

Source: http://www.beerinstitute.org/

a. Compute the sample standard deviation for the number of breweries east of the Mississippi River.
b. Compute the sample standard deviation for the number of breweries west of the Mississippi River.
c. Compute the range for each data set.
d. Based on the standard deviations, which region has the greater spread in the number of breweries?
e. Based on the ranges, which region has the greater spread in the number of breweries?
f. The sample of western states happens to include California. Remove California from the sample of western states, and compute the sample standard deviation for the remaining western states. Does the result show that the standard deviation is not resistant? Explain.
g. Compute the range for the western states with California removed. Is the range resistant? Explain.

35. What's your favorite TV show? The following tables present the ratings for the top 20 prime-time shows for the 1997–1998 season and for the 2007–2008 season. The rating is the percentage of households with TV sets that watched the program.

Top Rated TV Programs: 1997–1998		Top Rated TV Programs: 2007–2008	
Program	**Rating**	**Program**	**Rating**
Seinfeld	21.7	*American Idol* — Tuesday	16.1
ER	20.4	*American Idol* — Wednesday	15.9
Veronica's Closet	16.6	*Dancing With the Stars* — Monday (2007)	14.0
Friends	16.1	*Dancing With the Stars* — Tuesday (2007)	12.7
Monday Night Football	15.0	*Dancing With the Stars* — Monday (2008)	12.6
Touched by an Angel	14.2	*Dancing With the Stars* — Tuesday (2008)	11.8
60 Minutes	13.8	*Desperate Housewives*	11.6
Union Square	13.6	*CSI*	10.6
CBS Sunday Movie	13.1	*House* — Tuesday	10.5
Frasier	12.0	*Grey's Anatomy*	10.4
Home Improvement	12.0	*Sunday Night Football*	9.7
Just Shoot Me	11.9	*CSI: Miami*	9.2
Dateline NBC — Tuesday	11.5	*House* — Monday	9.2
Dateline NBC — Monday	11.4	*NCIS*	9.2
The Drew Carey Show	11.1	*Survivor: China*	9.0
20/20 — Friday	10.9	*Without a Trace*	8.8
N.Y.P.D. Blue	10.8	*The Moment of Truth*	8.8
Primetime Live	10.8	*Two and a Half Men*	8.5
The X-Files	10.6	*60 Minutes*	8.4
Law and Order	10.2	*Criminal Minds*	8.2

Source: www.classictvhits.com   Source: Nielsen Media Research

a. Find the population standard deviation of the ratings for 1997–1998.
b. Find the population standard deviation of the ratings for 2007–2008.
c. Compute the range for the ratings for both seasons.
d. Based on the standard deviations, did the spread in ratings increase or decrease over the two seasons?
e. Based on the ranges, did the spread in ratings increase or decrease over the two seasons?

36. **House prices:** The following table presents prices, in thousands of dollars, of single-family homes for 24 of the 25 largest metropolitan area in the United States for the third quarter of 2007 and the third quarter of 2008 (information for Detroit was unavailable).

Metro Area	2007	2008	Metro Area	2007	2008
Atlanta, GA	175.3	151.3	New York, NY	476.1	452.5
Baltimore, MD	291.4	279.2	Philadelphia, PA	243.0	241.1
Boston, MA	414.7	373.4	Phoenix, AZ	255.5	185.1
Chicago, IL	286.4	250.8	Pittsburgh, PA	127.7	122.7
Cincinnati, OH	145.3	136.0	Portland, OR	299.7	278.6
Cleveland, OH	132.7	116.4	Riverside, CA	375.1	227.2
Dallas, TX	153.7	150.2	St. Louis, MO	150.5	142.7
Denver, CO	254.1	225.1	San Diego, CA	589.3	377.3
Houston, TX	155.8	160.2	San Francisco, CA	824.2	615.7
Los Angeles, CA	602.9	391.4	Seattle, WA	394.7	350.0
Miami, FL	346.3	287.8	Tampa, FL	218.3	173.4
Minneapolis, MN	229.6	205.1	Washington, DC	438.0	332.7

Source: National Realtors Association

a. Find the population standard deviation for 2007.
b. Find the population standard deviation for 2008.
c. In general, house prices decreased from 2007 to 2008. Did the spread in house prices decrease as well, or did it increase?

37. **Stock prices:** Following are the closing prices of Google stock for each trading day in June and July 2010.

June					
482.37	493.37	505.60	498.72	485.52	484.78
474.02	487.01	488.50	483.19	497.99	501.27
500.08	500.03	488.56	486.25	482.05	475.10
472.68	472.08	454.26	444.95		

July					
439.49	436.55	436.07	450.20	456.56	467.49
475.83	489.20	491.34	494.02	459.61	466.18
481.59	477.50	484.81	490.06	488.97	492.63
484.35	484.99	484.85			

a. Find the population standard deviation for the prices in June.
b. Find the population standard deviation for the prices in July.
c. Financial analysts use the word *volatility* to refer to the variation in prices of assets such as stocks. In which month was the price of Google stock more volatile?

38. **Stocks or bonds?** Following are the annual percentage returns for the years 1990–2009 for three categories of investment: stocks, Treasury bills, and Treasury bonds. Stocks are represented by the Dow Jones Industrial Average.

Year	Stocks	Bills	Bonds	Year	Stocks	Bills	Bonds
1990	−4.34	7.55	6.24	2000	−6.18	5.76	16.66
1991	20.32	5.61	15.00	2001	−7.10	3.67	5.57
1992	4.17	3.41	9.36	2002	−16.76	1.66	15.12
1993	13.72	2.98	14.21	2003	25.32	1.03	0.38
1994	2.14	3.99	−8.04	2004	3.15	1.23	4.49
1995	33.45	5.52	23.48	2005	−0.61	3.01	2.87
1996	26.01	5.02	1.43	2006	16.29	4.68	1.96
1997	22.64	5.05	9.94	2007	6.43	4.64	10.21
1998	16.10	4.73	14.92	2008	−33.84	1.59	20.10
1999	25.22	4.51	−8.25	2009	18.82	0.14	−11.12

Source: Federal Reserve

a. The standard deviation of the return is a measure of the risk of an investment. Compute the population standard deviation for each type of investment. Which is the riskiest? Which is least risky?
b. Treasury bills are short-term (1 year or less) loans to the U.S. government. Treasury bonds are long-term (30-year) loans to the government. Finance theory states that long-term loans are riskier than short-term loans. Do the results agree with the theory?
c. Finance theory states that the more risk an investment has, the higher its mean return must be. Compute the mean return for each class of investment. Do the results follow the theory?

39. Time to review: The following table presents the time taken to review articles that were submitted for publication to the journal *Technometrics* during a recent year. A few articles took longer than 9 months to review; these are omitted from the table. Consider the data to be a population.

Time (Months)	Number of Articles
0.0–0.9	45
1.0–1.9	17
2.0–2.9	18
3.0–3.9	19
4.0–4.9	12
5.0–5.9	14
6.0–6.9	13
7.0–7.9	22
8.0–8.9	11

a. Approximate the variance of the times.
b. Approximate the standard deviation of the times.

40. Age distribution: The ages of residents of Banks City, Oregon, are given in the following frequency distribution. Consider these data to be a population.

Age	Frequency
0–9	283
10–19	203
20–29	217
30–39	256
40–49	176
50–59	92
60–69	21
70–79	23
80–89	12
90–99	3

Source: U.S. Census Bureau

a. Approximate the variance of the ages.
b. Approximate the standard deviation of the ages.

41. Drivers test: The GMAC Insurance company reported that the mean score on the 2009 National Drivers Test was 76.6 with a standard deviation of 2.7 points. The test scores are approximately bell-shaped. Estimate the percentage of participants in the test who had scores between
a. 68.5 and 84.7
b. 73.9 and 79.3
c. Between what two values will approximately 95% of the scores be?

42. Pay your bills: In a large sample of customer accounts, a utility company determined that the average number of days between when a bill was sent out and when the payment was made is 32 with a standard deviation of 7 days. Assume the data to be approximately bell-shaped.
a. Between what two values will approximately 68% of the numbers of days be?
b. Estimate the percentage of customer accounts for which the number of days is between 18 and 46.
c. Estimate the percentage of customer accounts for which the number of days is between 11 and 53.

43. Newborn babies: A study conducted by the Center for Population Economics at the University of Chicago studied the birth weights of 621 babies born in New York. The mean weight was 3234 grams with a standard deviation of 871 grams. Assume that birth weight data are approximately bell-shaped. Estimate the number of newborns who weighed between
a. 2363 grams and 4105 grams
b. 1492 grams and 4976 grams

44. Internet providers: In a survey of 600 homeowners with high-speed Internet, the average monthly cost of a high-speed Internet plan was $64.20 with standard deviation $11.77. Assume the plan costs to be approximately bell-shaped. Estimate the number of plans that cost between
a. $40.66 and $87.74
b. $52.43 and $75.97

45. Empirical Rule OK? The following histogram presents a data set with a mean of 4.5 and a standard deviation of 2. Is it appropriate to use the Empirical Rule to approximate the proportion of the data between 0.5 and 8.5? If so, find the approximation. If not, explain why not.

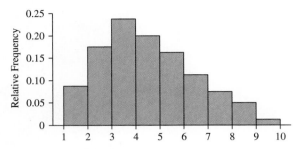

46. Empirical Rule OK? The following histogram presents a data set with a mean of 62 and a standard deviation of 17. Is it appropriate to use the Empirical Rule to approximate the proportion of the data between 45 and 79? If so, find the approximation. If not, explain why not.

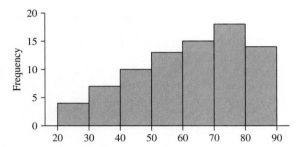

47. Empirical Rule OK? The following histogram presents a data set with a mean of 35 and a standard deviation of 9. Is it appropriate to use the Empirical Rule to approximate the proportion of the data between 26 and 44? If so, find the approximation. If not, explain why not.

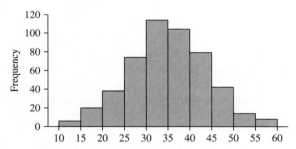

48. Empirical Rule OK? The following histogram presents a data set with a mean of 16 and a standard deviation of 2. Is it appropriate to use the Empirical Rule to approximate the proportion of the data between 12 and 20? If so, find the approximation. If not, explain why not.

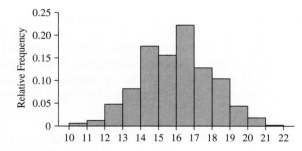

49. What's the temperature? The temperature in a certain location was recorded each day for two months. The mean temperature was 62.4°F with a standard deviation of 3.1°F. What can you determine about these data by using Chebyshev's Inequality with $K = 2$?

50. **Price of electricity:** The Energy Information Administration records the price of electricity in the United States each month. In January 2010, the average price of electricity was 10.54 cents per kilowatt-hour. Suppose that the standard deviation is 2.1 cents per kilowatt-hour. What can you determine about these data by using Chebyshev's Inequality with $K = 3$?

51. **Possible or impossible?** A data set has a mean of 20 and a standard deviation of 5. Which of the following might possibly be true, and which are impossible?
    a. Less than 50% of the data values are between 10 and 30.
    b. Only 1% of the data values are greater than 35.
    c. More than 15% of the data values are less than 5.
    d. More than 90% of the data values are between 5 and 35.

52. **Possible or impossible?** A data set has a mean of 50 and a standard deviation of 10. Which of the following might possibly be true, and which are impossible?
    a. More than 10% of the data values are negative.
    b. Only 5% of the data values are greater than 70.
    c. More than 20% of the data values are less than 30.
    d. Less than 75% of the data values are between 30 and 70.

53. **Standard deviation and mean:** For a list of positive numbers, is it possible for the sample standard deviation to be greater than the mean? If so, give an example. If not, explain why not.

54. **Standard deviation equal to 0?** Is it possible for the sample standard deviation of a list of numbers to equal 0? If so, give an example. If not, explain why not.

55. **Height and weight:** A National Center for Health Statistics study states that the mean height for adult men in the United States is 69.4 inches with a standard deviation of 3.1 inches, and the mean weight is 194.7 pounds with a standard deviation of 68.3 pounds.
    a. Compute the coefficient of variation for height.
    b. Compute the coefficient of variation for weight.
    c. Which has greater spread relative to its mean, height or weight?

56. **Test scores:** Scores on a statistics exam had a mean of 75 with a standard deviation of 10. Scores on a calculus exam had a mean of 60 with a standard deviation of 9.
    a. Compute the coefficient of variation for statistics exam scores.
    b. Compute the coefficient of variation for calculus exam scores.
    c. Which has greater spread relative to their mean, statistics scores or calculus scores?

Extending the Concepts

57. **Mean absolute deviation:** A measure of spread that is an alternative to the standard deviation (SD) is the **mean absolute deviation** (MAD). For a data set containing values $x_1, \ldots, x_n$, the mean absolute deviation is given by

$$\text{Mean absolute deviation} = \frac{\sum |x - \bar{x}|}{n}$$

    a. Compute the mean $\bar{x}$ for the data set 1, 3, 4, 7, 9.
    b. Construct a table like Table 3.5 that contains an additional column for the values $|x - \bar{x}|$.
    c. Use the table to compute the SD and the MAD.
    d. Now consider the data set 1, 3, 4, 7, 9, 30. Compute the SD and the MAD for this data set.
    e. Which measure of spread is more resistant, the SD or the MAD? Explain.

Answers to Check Your Understanding Exercises for Section 3.2

1. The variance of the St. Louis temperatures is 291.9. This is greater than the variance of the San Francisco temperatures, which indicates that there is greater spread in the St. Louis temperatures.

2. a. Variance is 3.7143; standard deviation is 1.9272.
   b. Variance is 281.8667; standard deviation is 16.7889.

3. Variance is 4.8594; standard deviation is 2.2044.

4. Approximately 95% of the data values are between 14 and 26.

5. The Empirical Rule should not be used because the data are skewed.

6. No. The interval between 50 and 90 is the interval within two standard deviations of the mean. At least 75% of the data must be between 50 and 90.

7. Yes. The interval between 122 and 128 is the interval within three standard deviations of the mean. At least 8/9 (88.9%) of the data must be between 122 and 128.

8. 0.0945

SECTION 3.3 | **Measures of Position**

Objectives

1. Compute and interpret z-scores
2. Compute the percentiles of a data set
3. Compute the quartiles of a data set
4. Compute the five-number summary for a data set
5. Understand the effects of outliers
6. Construct boxplots to visualize the five-number summary and outliers

Objective 1 Compute and interpret z-scores

The z-Score

Who is taller, a man 73 inches tall or a woman 68 inches tall? The obvious answer is that the man is taller. However, men are taller than women on the average. Let's ask the question this way: Who is taller relative to their gender, a man 73 inches tall or a woman 68 inches tall? One way to answer this question is with a **z-score**.

The z-score of an individual data value tells how many standard deviations that value is from its population mean. So, for example, a value one standard deviation above the mean has a z-score of 1. A value two standard deviations below the mean has a z-score of -2.

DEFINITION

Let x be a value from a population with mean μ and standard deviation σ. The **z-score** for x is

$$z = \frac{x - \mu}{\sigma}$$

EXAMPLE 3.22 | **Computing and interpreting z-scores**

A National Center for Health Statistics study states that the mean height for adult men in the United States is $\mu = 69.4$ inches, with a standard deviation of $\sigma = 3.1$ inches. The mean height for adult women is $\mu = 63.8$ inches, with a standard deviation of $\sigma = 2.8$ inches. Who is taller relative to their gender, a man 73 inches tall, or a woman 68 inches tall?

Solution

We compute the z-scores for the two heights:

$$z\text{-score for man's height} = \frac{x - \mu}{\sigma} = \frac{73 - 69.4}{3.1} = 1.16$$

$$z\text{-score for woman's height} = \frac{x - \mu}{\sigma} = \frac{68 - 63.8}{2.8} = 1.50$$

The height of the 73-inch man is 1.16 standard deviations above the mean height for men. The height of the 68-inch woman is 1.50 standard deviations above the mean height for women. Therefore, the woman is taller, relative to the population of women, than the man is, relative to the population of men.

---

z-scores and the Empirical Rule

z-scores work best for populations whose histograms are approximately bell-shaped — that is, for populations for which we can use the Empirical Rule. Recall that the Empirical Rule says that for a bell-shaped population, approximately 68% of the data will be within one standard deviation of the mean, approximately 95% will be within two standard deviations, and almost all will be within three standard deviations. Since the z-score is the number of standard deviations from the mean, we can easily interpret the z-score for bell-shaped populations.

z-Scores and the Empirical Rule

When a population has a histogram that is approximately bell-shaped, then

- Approximately 68% of the data will have z-scores between -1 and 1.
- Approximately 95% of the data will have z-scores between -2 and 2.
- All, or almost all, of the data will have z-scores between -3 and 3.

The z-score is less useful for populations that are not bell-shaped. For example, in some skewed populations there will be no values with z-scores greater than 1, while in others, values with z-scores greater than 1 occur frequently. We can't be sure how to interpret z-scores when the population is skewed. It is best, therefore, to use z-scores only for populations that are approximately bell-shaped. See Exercise 39 for an illustration.

Objective 2 Compute the percentiles of a data set

Percentiles

The weather in Los Angeles is dry most of the time, but it can be quite rainy in the winter. The rainiest month of the year is February. Table 3.9 presents the annual rainfall in Los Angeles, in inches, for each February from 1965 to 2006.

Table 3.9 Annual Rainfall in Los Angeles During February

Year	Rainfall	Year	Rainfall	Year	Rainfall	Year	Rainfall
1965	0.23	1976	3.71	1987	1.22	1998	13.68
1966	1.51	1977	0.17	1988	1.72	1999	0.56
1967	0.11	1978	8.91	1989	1.90	2000	5.54
1968	0.49	1979	3.06	1990	3.12	2001	8.87
1969	8.03	1980	12.75	1991	4.13	2002	0.29
1970	2.58	1981	1.48	1992	7.96	2003	4.64
1971	0.67	1982	0.70	1993	6.61	2004	4.89
1972	0.13	1983	4.37	1994	3.21	2005	11.02
1973	7.89	1984	0.00	1995	1.30	2006	2.37
1974	0.14	1985	2.84	1996	4.94		
1975	3.54	1986	6.10	1997	0.08		

There is a lot of spread in the amount of rainfall in Los Angeles in February. For example, in 1984 there was no measurable rain at all, while in 1998 it rained more than 13 inches.

In Section 3.1, we learned how to compute the mean and median of a data set, which describe the center of a distribution. For data sets like the Los Angeles rainfall data, which exhibit a lot of spread, it is useful to compute measures of positions other than the center, to get a more detailed description of the distribution. **Percentiles** provide a way to do this. Percentiles divide a data set into hundredths.

DEFINITION

For a number p between 1 and 99, the **pth percentile** separates the lowest $p\%$ of the data from the highest $(100 - p)\%$.

There are several methods for computing percentiles, all of which give similar results. We present a fairly straightforward method here.

Procedure for Computing the Data Value Corresponding to a Given Percentile

Step 1: Arrange the data in increasing order.

Step 2: Let n be the number of values in the data set. For the pth percentile, compute the value

$$L = \frac{p}{100} \cdot n$$

Step 3: *If L is a whole number*, then the pth percentile is the average of the number in position L and the number in position $L + 1$.

If L is not a whole number, round it *up* to the next higher whole number. The pth percentile is the number in the position corresponding to the rounded-up value.

EXAMPLE 3.23

Computing a percentile

Compute the 30th percentile of the Los Angeles rainfall data.

Solution

Step 1: Table 3.10 presents the data in increasing order.

Step 2: There are $n = 42$ values in the data set. For the 30th percentile, we take $p = 30$ and compute

$$L = \frac{30}{100} \cdot 42 = 12.6$$

Step 3: Since $L = 12.6$ is not a whole number, we round it *up* to 13. The 30th percentile is the number in the 13th position. From Table 3.10 we can see that the 30th percentile is 1.22.

CAUTION

Always round L *up*. Do not round down.

Table 3.10 Annual Rainfall in Los Angeles During February, in Increasing Order

Year	Rainfall	Year	Rainfall	Year	Rainfall	Year	Rainfall
1984	0.00	1982	0.70	1990	3.12	1993	6.61
1997	0.08	1987	1.22	1994	3.21	1973	7.89
1967	0.11	1995	1.30	1975	3.54	1992	7.96
1972	0.13	1981	1.48	1976	3.71	1969	8.03
1974	0.14	1966	1.51	1991	4.13	2001	8.87
1977	0.17	1988	1.72	1983	4.37	1978	8.91
1965	0.23	1989	1.90	2003	4.64	2005	11.02
2002	0.29	2006	2.37	2004	4.89	1980	12.75
1968	0.49	1970	2.58	1996	4.94	1998	13.68
1999	0.56	1985	2.84	2000	5.54		
1971	0.67	1979	3.06	1986	6.10		

Computing the percentile corresponding to a given data value

Sometimes we are given a value from a data set, and wish to compute the percentile corresponding to that value. Following is a simple procedure for doing this.

Procedure for Computing the Percentile Corresponding to a Given Data Value

Step 1: Arrange the data in increasing order.

Step 2: Let x be the data value whose percentile is to be computed. Use the following formula to compute the percentile:

$$\text{Percentile} = 100 \cdot \frac{(\text{Number of values less than } x) + 0.5}{\text{Number of values in the data set}}$$

Round the result to the nearest whole number.

EXAMPLE 3.24

Computing the percentile corresponding to a given data value

In 1989, the rainfall in Los Angeles during the month of February was 1.90. What percentile does this correspond to?

Solution

Step 1: Table 3.10 presents the data in increasing order.

Step 2: There are 42 values in the data set. There are 17 values less than 1.90. Therefore,

$$\text{Percentile} = 100 \cdot \frac{17 + 0.5}{42} = 41.7$$

We round the result to 42. The value 1.90 corresponds to the 42nd percentile.

Objective 3 Compute the quartiles of a data set

Quartiles

There are three percentiles, the 25th, the 50th, and the 75th, that are used more often than the others. These percentiles divide the data into four parts, each of which contains approximately one quarter of the data. For this reason, these three percentiles are called **quartiles**.

Explain It Again

The second quartile is the same as the median: The second quartile, Q_2, divides the data in half. Therefore, Q_2 is the same as the median.

DEFINITION

Every data set has three quartiles:

- The **first quartile**, denoted Q_1, is the 25th percentile. Q_1 separates the lowest 25% of the data from the highest 75%.
- The **second quartile**, denoted Q_2, is the 50th percentile. Q_2 separates the lower 50% of the data from the upper 50%. Q_2 is the same as the median.
- The **third quartile**, denoted Q_3, is the 75th percentile. Q_3 separates the lowest 75% of the data from the highest 25%.

To compute the first and third quartiles, simply compute the 25th and 75th percentiles as explained previously. The easiest way to compute the second quartile is to compute the median as explained in Section 3.1.

EXAMPLE 3.25

Computing quartiles

Find the first and third quartiles for the Los Angeles rainfall data, presented in Table 3.9.

Solution

The first quartile is the same as the 25th percentile and the third quartile is the same as the 75th percentile. We follow the steps to compute the data values corresponding to the 25th and 75th percentiles.

Step 1: The sorted data are presented in Table 3.10.

Step 2: There are $n = 42$ rainfall values in the data set. For the first quartile, we follow the procedure for computing the 25th percentile. We first compute

$$L = \frac{25}{100} \times 42 = 10.5$$

Step 3: Since $L = 10.5$ is a not whole number, we round it up to 11. The first quartile, Q_1, is the number in the 11th position. From Table 3.10, we see that this number is 0.67. So $Q_1 = 0.67$.

Step 4: For the third quartile, we compute

$$L = \frac{75}{100} \times 42 = 31.5$$

Step 5: Since 31.5 is not a whole number, we round it up to 32. The third quartile, Q_3, is the value in the 32nd position. From Table 3.10, we see that $Q_3 = 5.54$.

Figure 3.8 presents a dotplot of the Los Angeles rainfall data set with the quartiles indicated. The quartiles divide the data set into four parts, with approximately 25% of the data in each part. Recall that the median is the same as the second quartile. Since there are 42 values in this data set, the median is the average of the 21st and 22nd values when the data are arranged in order. From Table 3.10, we can see that the median is 2.95.

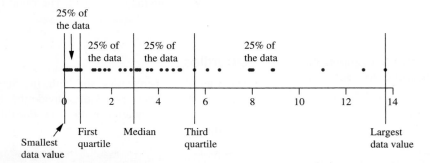

Figure 3.8 The quartiles of the Los Angeles rainfall data set

EXAMPLE 3.26

Using technology to compute quartiles

Use technology to compute the first and third quartiles for the Los Angeles rainfall data, presented in Table 3.9.

Solution

Figure 3.9 presents MINITAB output. The quartiles are highlighted in red. Note that the values produced by MINITAB differ slightly from the results obtained in Example 3.25, because MINITAB uses a slightly different procedure than the one we describe here. The MINITAB procedure for computing the mean and median will also compute the quartiles. Step-by-step instructions are presented in the Using Technology section on page 96.

Variable	N	Mean	SE Mean	StDev	Minimum	Q1	Median	Q3	Maximum
Rainfall	42	3.749	0.559	3.624	0.000	0.643	2.950	5.680	13.680

Figure 3.9

Check Your Understanding

1. Following are final exam scores, arranged in increasing order, for 28 students in an introductory statistics course.

58	59	62	64	67	68	69	71	73	74	74	75	76	76
76	77	78	78	78	82	82	84	86	87	87	88	91	97

   a. Find the first quartile of the scores.
   b. Find the third quartile of the scores.
   c. Fred got a 73 on the exam. On what percentile is this score?
   d. Students whose scores are on the 80th percentile or above will get a grade of A. Louisa got an 88 on the exam. Will she get an A?

2. For the years 1869–2007, the 90th percentile of annual snowfall in Central Park in New York City was 50.1 inches. Approximately what percentage of years had snowfall less than 50.1 inches?

Answers are on page 139.

Objective 4 Compute the five-number summary for a data set

The Five-Number Summary

The five-number summary of a data set consists of the median, the first quartile, the third quartile, the minimum value, and the maximum value. These values are generally arranged in order.

DEFINITION

The **five-number summary** of a data set consists of the following quantities:

| Minimum | First quartile | Median | Third quartile | Maximum |

EXAMPLE 3.27

Constructing a five-number summary

Table 3.11 presents the number of students absent in a middle school in northwestern Montana for each school day in January 2008. Construct the five-number summary.

Table 3.11 Number of Absences in January 2008

Date	Number Absent	Date	Number Absent	Date	Number Absent
Jan. 2	65	Jan. 14	59	Jan. 23	42
Jan. 3	67	Jan. 15	49	Jan. 24	45
Jan. 4	71	Jan. 16	42	Jan. 25	46
Jan. 7	57	Jan. 17	56	Jan. 28	100
Jan. 8	51	Jan. 18	45	Jan. 29	59
Jan. 9	49	Jan. 21	77	Jan. 30	53
Jan. 10	44	Jan. 22	44	Jan. 31	51
Jan. 11	41				

Solution

Step 1: We arrange the numbers in increasing order. The ordered numbers are:

 41 42 42 44 44 45 45 46 49 49 51 51 53 56 57 59 59 65 67 71 77 100

Step 2: The minimum is 41 and the maximum is 100.

Step 3: We use the methods described in Example 3.25 to compute the first and third quartiles. The first quartile is $Q_1 = 45$, and the third quartile is $Q_3 = 59$.

Step 4: We use the method described in Section 3.1 to compute the median. The median is 51.

Step 5: The five-number summary is

$$41 \quad 45 \quad 51 \quad 59 \quad 100$$

Objective 5 Understand the effects of outliers

Outliers

An **outlier** is a value that is considerably larger or considerably smaller than most of the values in a data set. Some outliers result from errors; for example a misplaced decimal point may cause a number to be much larger or smaller than the other values in a data set. Some outliers are correct values, and simply reflect the fact that the population contains some extreme values.

> **CAUTION**
>
> Do not delete an outlier unless it is certain that it is an error.

When it is certain that an outlier resulted from an error, the value should be corrected or deleted. However, if it is possible that the value of an outlier is correct, it should remain in the data set. Deleting an outlier that is not an error will produce misleading results.

EXAMPLE 3.28

Determining whether an outlier should be deleted

The temperature in a downtown location in a certain city is measured for eight consecutive days during the summer. The readings, in degrees Fahrenheit, are 81.2, 85.6, 89.3, 91.0, 83.2, 8.45, 79.5, and 87.8. Which reading is an outlier? Is it certain that the outlier is an error, or is it possible that it is correct? Should the outlier be deleted?

Solution

The outlier is 8.45, which is much smaller than the rest of the data. This outlier is certainly an error; it is likely that a decimal point was misplaced. The outlier should be corrected if possible, or deleted.

EXAMPLE 3.29

Determining whether an outlier should be deleted

The following table presents the populations, as of July 2009, of the five largest cities in the United States.

City	Population in millions
New York	8.4
Los Angeles	3.8
Chicago	2.9
Houston	2.3
Phoenix	1.6

Source: U.S. Census Bureau

Which value is an outlier? Is it certain that the outlier is an error, or is it possible that it is correct? Should the outlier be deleted?

Solution

The population of New York, 8.4 million, is an outlier because it is much larger than the other values. This outlier is not an error. It should not be deleted. If it were deleted, the data would indicate that the largest city in the United States is Los Angeles, which would be incorrect.

The interquartile range

The interquartile range (IQR for short) is a measure of spread that is often used to detect outliers. The IQR is the difference between the first and third quartiles.

> **DEFINITION**
>
> The **interquartile range** is found by subtracting the first quartile from the third quartile.
>
> $$IQR = Q_3 - Q_1$$

The IQR method for finding outliers

In Examples 3.28 and 3.29, we determined the outlier just by looking at the data and finding an extreme value. In many cases, this is a good way to find outliers. There are some formal methods for finding outliers as well. The most frequently used method is the **IQR method**.

The IQR Method for Finding Outliers

Step 1: Find the first quartile, Q_1, and the third quartile, Q_3, of the data set.

Step 2: Compute the interquartile range.

$$IQR = Q_3 - Q_1$$

Step 3: Compute the **outlier boundaries**. These boundaries are the cutoff points for determining outliers.

$$\text{Lower outlier boundary} = Q_1 - 1.5\,IQR$$
$$\text{Upper outlier boundary} = Q_3 + 1.5\,IQR$$

Step 4: Any data value that is less than the lower outlier boundary or greater than the upper outlier boundary is considered to be an outlier.

EXAMPLE 3.30   Detecting outliers

Use the IQR method to determine which values, if any, in the absence data in Table 3.11 are outliers.

Solution

Step 1: In Example 3.27, we computed the first and third quartiles: $Q_1 = 45$ and $Q_3 = 59$.

Step 2: $IQR = Q_3 - Q_1 = 59 - 45 = 14$

Step 3: The outlier boundaries are:

$$\text{Lower outlier boundary} = 45 - 1.5(14) = 24$$
$$\text{Upper outlier boundary} = 59 + 1.5(14) = 80$$

Step 4: There are no values in the data set less than the lower boundary of 24. There is one value, 100, that is greater than the upper boundary of 80. Thus there is one outlier, 100.

Check Your Understanding

3. Table 3.12 presents the 2008 payrolls (in millions of dollars) for each of the 30 Major League Baseball teams.

Table 3.12 2008 Payrolls for Major League Baseball Teams

Team	Payroll	Team	Payroll	Team	Payroll
New York Yankees	209	St. Louis Cardinals	101	Texas Rangers	68
Detroit Tigers	139	Toronto Blue Jays	99	Baltimore Orioles	67
New York Mets	138	Philadelphia Phillies	98	Arizona Diamondbacks	66
Boston Red Sox	133	Houston Astros	89	Minnesota Twins	62
Chicago White Sox	121	Milwaukee Brewers	81	Kansas City Royals	58
Los Angeles Angels	119	Cleveland Indians	79	Washington Nationals	55
Chicago Cubs	119	San Francisco Giants	77	Pittsburgh Pirates	49
Los Angeles Dodgers	119	Cincinnati Reds	74	Oakland Athletics	48
Seattle Mariners	118	San Diego Padres	74	Tampa Bay Rays	44
Atlanta Braves	102	Colorado Rockies	69	Florida Marlins	22

Source: CBS Sports

a. Construct the five-number summary.
b. Find the IQR.
c. Find the upper and lower outlier boundaries.
d. Which values, if any, are outliers?

Answers are on page 139.

Objective 6 Construct boxplots to visualize the five-number summary and outliers

Boxplots

A **boxplot** is a graph that presents the five-number summary along with some additional information about a data set. There are several kinds of boxplots. The one we describe here is sometimes called a **modified boxplot**.

Procedure for Constructing a Boxplot

Step 1: Compute the first quartile, the median, and the third quartile.
Step 2: Draw vertical lines at the first quartile, the median, and the third quartile. Draw horizontal lines between the first and third quartiles to complete the box.
Step 3: Compute the lower and upper outlier boundaries.
Step 4: Find the largest data value that is less than the upper outlier boundary. Draw a horizontal line from the third quartile to this value. This horizontal line is called a **whisker**.
Step 5: Find the smallest data value that is greater than the lower outlier boundary. Draw a horizontal line (whisker) from the first quartile to this value.
Step 6: Determine which values, if any, are outliers. Plot each outlier separately.

EXAMPLE 3.31   Constructing a boxplot

Construct a boxplot for the absence data in Table 3.11.

Solution

Step 1: In Example 3.27, we computed the median to be 51 and the first and third quartiles to be $Q_1 = 45$ and $Q_3 = 59$.
Step 2: We draw vertical lines at 45, 51, and 59, then horizontal lines to complete the box, as follows:

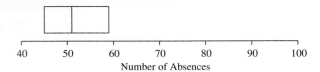

Number of Absences

Step 3: We compute the outlier boundaries as shown in Example 3.30:

$$\text{Lower outlier boundary} = 45 - 1.5(14) = 24$$

$$\text{Upper outlier boundary} = 59 + 1.5(14) = 80$$

Step 4: The largest data value that is less than the upper boundary is 77. We draw a horizontal line from 59 up to 77, as follows:

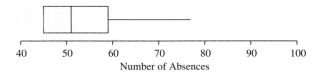

Number of Absences

Step 5: The smallest data value that is greater than the lower boundary is 41. We draw a horizontal line from 45 down to 41, as follows:

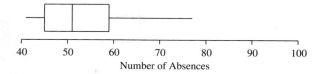

Step 6: We determine, as shown in Example 3.30, that the value 100 is the only outlier. We plot this point separately, to produce the boxplot shown in Figure 3.10.

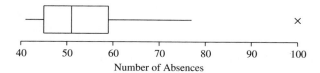

Figure 3.10 Boxplot for the absence data in Table 3.11

Check Your Understanding

4. Construct a boxplot for the payroll data in Table 3.12.

Answer is on page 139.

Determining the shape of a data set from a boxplot

In Section 2.2, we learned how to determine from a histogram whether a data set is symmetric or skewed. In many cases, a boxplot can give us the same information. For example, in the boxplot for the absence data (Figure 3.10), the median is closer to the first quartile than to the third quartile, and the upper whisker is longer than the lower one. This indicates that the data are skewed to the right.

Figure 3.11 presents a histogram of the absence data. The skewness is clearly apparent.

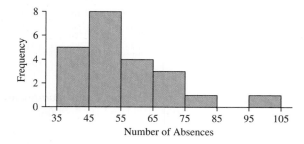

Figure 3.11 Histogram for the absence data in Table 3.11

Determining Skewness from a Boxplot

- If the median is closer to the first quartile than to the third quartile, or the upper whisker is longer than the lower whisker, the data are skewed to the right.
- If the median is closer to the third quartile than to the first quartile, or the lower whisker is longer than the upper whisker, the data are skewed to the left.
- If the median is approximately halfway between the first and third quartiles, and the two whiskers are approximately equal in length, the data are approximately symmetric.

Figures 3.12–3.14 illustrate the way in which boxplots reflect skewness and symmetry.

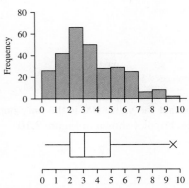

Figure 3.12 Skewed to the right

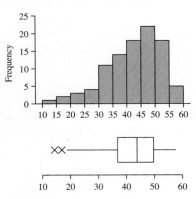

Figure 3.13 Skewed to the left

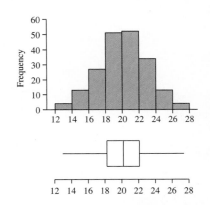

Figure 3.14 Approximately symmetric

Comparative boxplots

Boxplots do not provide as much detail as histograms do regarding the shape of a data set. However, they provide an excellent method for comparing data sets. We can plot two or more boxplots, one above another, to provide an easy visual comparison.

As an example, Table 3.13 presents the rainfall in Los Angeles each February for the years 1923–1964. We would like to compare these data with the February rainfall for the years 1965–2006, which was presented in Table 3.9.

Table 3.13 Annual Rainfall in Los Angeles During February: 1923–1964

Year	Rainfall	Year	Rainfall	Year	Rainfall	Year	Rainfall
1923	0.75	1934	2.04	1945	3.34	1956	0.59
1924	0.03	1935	2.23	1946	1.52	1957	1.47
1925	0.53	1936	7.25	1947	0.86	1958	6.46
1926	2.70	1937	7.87	1948	1.29	1959	3.32
1927	9.03	1938	9.81	1949	1.41	1960	2.26
1928	1.43	1939	1.13	1950	1.67	1961	0.15
1929	2.15	1940	5.43	1951	1.48	1962	11.57
1930	0.45	1941	12.42	1952	0.63	1963	2.88
1931	3.25	1942	1.05	1953	0.33	1964	0.00
1932	5.33	1943	3.07	1954	2.98		
1933	0.00	1944	8.65	1955	0.68		

Figure 3.15 presents **comparative boxplots** for February rainfall during the years 1923–1964 and 1965–2006.

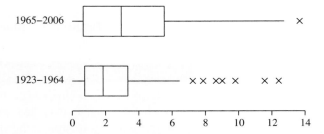

Figure 3.15   Comparative boxplots for February rainfall in Los Angeles, 1923–1964 and 1965–2006

We can see that both the box and the upper whisker for 1965–2006 extend farther to the right than the corresponding elements for 1923–1964. This tells us that 1965–2006 was, on the whole, rainier than 1923–1964. We can also see that both the box and upper whisker for 1965–2006 are longer than the corresponding elements for 1923–1964. This tells us that the rainfall was more variable during 1965–2006. Finally, the upper whisker is longer than the lower whisker in both boxplots. This tells us that both rainfall data sets are skewed to the right. Finally, we note that there were several outliers in 1923–1964, but only one in 1965–2006.

USING TECHNOLOGY

Table 3.14 lists the number of calories in 11 fast-food restaurant hamburgers. We use these data to illustrate the technology steps.

Table 3.14 Number of Calories in Fast-Food Hamburgers

840	1090	680	950	1070	860
940	1285	900	1120	720	

TI-84 PLUS

Computing Quartiles

The procedure used to compute the mean and median, presented on page 96, will also compute the quartiles. The quartiles for the data in Table 3.14 are shown in Figure A.

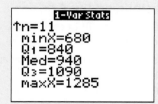

Figure A

Drawing Boxplots

Step 1. Enter the data from Table 3.14 into **L1** in the data editor.

Step 2. Press **2nd, Y=** to access the STAT PLOTS menu and select **Plot1** by pressing **1**.

Step 3. Select **On** and the boxplot icon in the lower left. Press **ENTER** (Figure B).

Step 4. Press **ZOOM** and then **9: ZoomStat** (Figure C).

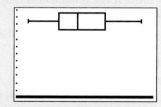

Figure B   **Figure C**

MINITAB

Computing Quartiles

The MINITAB procedure used to compute the mean and median, described on page 96, will also compute the quartiles. The quartiles for the data in Table 3.14 are shown in Figure D.

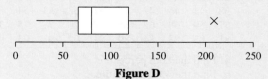

Figure D

Drawing Boxplots

Step 1. Enter the data from Table 3.14 into **Column C1**.

Step 2. Click on **Graph** and select **Boxplot**. Choose the **One Y, Simple option** and press **OK**.

Step 3. Double-click on **C1** and press **OK**.

EXCEL

Computing Quartiles

Step 1. Enter the data from Table 3.14 in Column **A**.

Step 2. Select the **Insert Function** icon f_x and highlight **Statistical** in the category field.

Step 3. Highlight **QUARTILE.EXC** and press **OK**. Enter the range of cells that contain the data from Table 3.14 in the **Array** field. In the **Quart** field, enter **1** for Q_1, **2** for Q_2, or **3** for Q_3.

Step 4. Click **OK**.

SECTION 3.3 Exercises

Exercises 1–4 are the Check Your Understanding exercises located within the section.

Understanding the Concepts

In Exercises 5–8, fill in each blank with the appropriate word or phrase.

5. _____ divide the data set approximately into quarters.

6. The median is the same as the _____ quartile.

7. The quantity $Q_3 - Q_1$ is known as the _____.

8. A value that is considerably larger or smaller than most of the values in a data set is called an _____.

In Exercises 9–12, determine whether the statement is true or false. If the statement is false, rewrite it as a true statement.

9. The third quartile, Q_3, separates the lowest 25% of the data from the highest 75%.

10. The 25th percentile is the same as the first quartile.

11. The five-number summary consists of the minimum, the first quartile, the mode, the third quartile, and the maximum.

12. In a boxplot, if the lower whisker is much longer than the upper whisker, then the data are skewed to the left.

Practicing the Skills

13. A population has mean $\mu = 7$ and standard deviation $\sigma = 2$.
    a. Find the z-score for a population value of 5.
    b. Find the z-score for a population value of 10.
    c. What number has a z-score of 2?

14. A population has mean $\mu = 25$ and standard deviation $\sigma = 4$.
    a. Find the z-score for a population value of 16.
    b. Find the z-score for a population value of 31.
    c. What number has a z-score of 2.5?

In Exercises 15 and 16, identify the outlier. Then tell whether the outlier seems certain to be due to an error, or whether it could conceivably be correct.

15. A rock is weighed five times. The readings in grams are 48.5, 47.2, 4.91, 49.5, and 46.3.

16. A sociologist samples five families in a certain town and records their annual income. The incomes are $34,000, $57,000, $13,000, $1,200,000, and $62,000.

17. For the data set

| 37 | 82 | 20 | 25 | 31 | 10 | 41 | 44 | 4 | 36 | 68 |

   a. Find the first and third quartiles.
   b. Find the IQR.
   c. Find the upper and lower outlier boundaries.
   d. List all the values, if any, that are classified as outliers.

18. For the data set

| 15 | 7 | 2 | 4 | 4 | 3 | 4 | 3 | 4 | 25 | 4 | 9 | 3 |
| 12 | 2 | 8 | 3 | 2 | 2 | 6 | 7 | 3 | 10 | 4 | 5 | 4 |

   a. Find the first and third quartiles.
   b. Find the IQR.
   c. Find the upper and lower outlier boundaries.
   d. List all the values, if any, that are classified as outliers.

19. For the data set

2	2	2	2	5	7	8	8	9	9	14	14
14	16	19	20	21	22	22	24	24	27	32	33
33	33	34	34	35	35	35	37	38	38	38	40
40	40	41	42	46	47	48	48	48	48	48	49

   a. Find the 58th percentile.
   b. Find the 22nd percentile.
   c. Find the 78th percentile.
   d. Find the 15th percentile.

20. For the data set

1	5	8	8	8	11	13	14	15	15	16	17
20	23	24	25	25	26	26	29	31	34	35	35
38	44	45	47	47	51	53	53	54	55	55	57
57	59	60	62	65	69	70	75	75	76	78	79
81	83	83	84	89	91	92	93	93	96	96	99

   a. Find the 80th percentile.
   b. Find the 43rd percentile.
   c. Find the 18th percentile.
   d. Find the 65th percentile.

Working with the Concepts

21. **Standardized tests:** In 2008, the mean score on the ACT test was 21.1 and the standard deviation was 5.0. The mean score on the SAT mathematics test was 515 and the standard deviation was 116. The distributions of both scores were approximately bell-shaped.

a. Find the z-score for an ACT score of 25.

b. Find the z-score for an SAT math score of 650.

c. Which score is higher, relative to its population of scores?

d. Jose's ACT score had a z-score of 1.98. What was his ACT score?

e. Emma's SAT score had a z-score of −1.5. What was her SAT score?

22. A fish story: The mean length of one-year-old spotted flounder, in millimeters, is 126 with standard deviation of 18, and the mean length of two-year-old spotted flounder is 162 with a standard deviation of 28. The distribution of flounder lengths is approximately bell-shaped.

a. Anna caught a one-year-old flounder that was 150 millimeters in length. What is the z-score for this length?

b. Luis caught a two-year-old flounder that was 190 millimeters in length. What is the z-score for this length?

c. Whose fish is longer, relative to fish the same age?

d. Joe caught a one-year-old flounder whose length had a z-score of 1.2. How long was this fish?

e. Terry caught a two-year-old flounder whose length had a z-score of −0.5. How long was this fish?

Source: *Turkish Journal of Veterinary and Animal Science*, 29:1013–1018

23. Blood pressure in men: The three quartiles for systolic blood pressure in a sample of 3179 men were $Q_1 = 108$, $Q_2 = 116$, and $Q_3 = 127$.

a. Find the IQR.

b. Find the upper and lower outlier boundaries.

c. A systolic blood pressure greater than 140 is considered high. Would a blood pressure of 140 be an outlier?

Source: *Journal of Human Hypertension*, 16:305–312

24. Blood pressure in women: The article referred to in Exercise 23 reported that the three quartiles for systolic blood pressure in a sample of 1213 women between the ages of 20 and 29 were $Q_1 = 100$, $Q_2 = 108$, and $Q_3 = 115$.

a. Find the IQR.

b. Find the upper and lower outlier boundaries.

c. A systolic blood pressure greater than 140 is considered high. Would a blood pressure of 140 be an outlier?

25. Hazardous waste: Following is a list of the number of hazardous waste sites in each of the 50 states of the United States in a recent year. The list has been sorted into numerical order.

0	1	2	2	3	5	6	9	9	9
9	9	11	12	12	12	12	12	13	13
14	14	14	14	15	15	15	16	19	19
20	21	25	26	29	30	32	32	32	38
40	48	49	49	52	67	86	97	97	116

Source: U.S. Environmental Protection Agency

a. Find the first and third quartiles of these data.

b. Find the median of these data.

c. Find the upper and lower outlier boundaries.

d. Are there any outliers? If so, list them.

e. Construct a boxplot for these data.

f. Describe the shape of this distribution.

g. What is the 30th percentile?

h. What is the 85th percentile?

i. The state of Georgia has 16 hazardous waste sites. What percentile is this?

26. Cholesterol levels: The National Health and Nutrition Examination Survey (NHANES) measured the serum HDL cholesterol levels in a large number of women. Following is a sample of 40 HDL levels (in milligrams per deciliter) that are based on the results of that survey. They have been sorted into numerical order.

27	28	30	32	34	36	37	37	37	37
37	40	45	47	48	49	53	53	54	56
57	58	61	62	63	63	64	64	64	65
66	70	72	73	73	74	80	80	81	84

Source: NHANES

a. Find the first and third quartiles of these data.

b. Find the median of these data.

c. Find the upper and lower outlier boundaries.

d. Are there any outliers? If so, list them.

e. Construct a boxplot for these data.

f. Describe the shape of this distribution.

g. What is the 20th percentile?

h. What is the 67th percentile?

i. One woman had a cholesterol level of 58. What percentile is this?

27. Commuting to work: Jamie drives to work every weekday morning. She keeps track of the time it takes, in minutes, for 35 days. The results follow.

15	17	17	17	17	18	19
19	19	19	19	19	20	20
20	20	20	21	21	21	21
21	21	21	21	21	22	23
23	24	26	31	36	38	39

a. Find the first and third quartiles of these data.

b. Find the median of these data.

c. Find the upper and lower outlier boundaries.

d. Are there any outliers? If so, list them.

e. Construct a boxplot for these data.

f. Describe the shape of this distribution.

g. What is the 14th percentile?

h. What is the 87th percentile?

i. One day, the commute time was 31 minutes. What percentile is this?

28. Windy city by the bay: Following are wind speeds (in mph) for 29 randomly selected days in San Francisco.

13.4	23.1	27.2	31.8	36.3	40.3	14.1	24.6
27.7	32.6	38.1	40.9	18.3	25.2	29.7	33.6
38.7	44.2	20.8	26.8	30.1	34.5	40.2	46.8
22.9	26.9	30.8	35.8	40.3			

a. Find the first and third quartiles of these data.

b. Find the median of these data.

c. Find the upper and lower outlier boundaries.

d. Are there any outliers? If so, list them.

e. Construct a boxplot for these data.

f. Describe the shape of this distribution.

g. What is the 40th percentile?

h. What is the 10th percentile?

i. One day, the wind speed was 30.1 mph. What percentile is this?

29. Caffeine: Following are the number of grams of carbohydrates in 12-ounce espresso beverages offered at Starbucks.

| 14 | 43 | 38 | 44 | 31 | 27 | 39 | 59 | 9 | 10 | 54 |
| 14 | 25 | 26 | 9 | 46 | 30 | 24 | 41 | 26 | 27 | 14 |

Source: www.starbucks.com

a. Find the first and third quartiles of these data.
b. Find the median of these data.
c. Find the upper and lower outlier boundaries.
d. The beverage with the most carbohydrates is a Peppermint White Chocolate Mocha, with 59 grams. Is this an outlier?
e. The beverages with the least carbohydrates are an Iced Skinny Flavored Latte, and a Cappuccino, each with 9 grams. Are these outliers?
f. Construct a boxplot for these data.
g. Describe the shape of this distribution.
h. What is the 31st percentile?
i. What is the 71st percentile?
j. There are 38 grams of carbohydrates in an Iced Dark Cherry Mocha. What percentile is this?

30. Nuclear power: The following table presents the number of nuclear reactors as of December 31, 2007, in each country that had one or more reactors.

Country	Number of Reactors	Country	Number of Reactors
Argentina	2	Mexico	2
Armenia	1	Netherlands	1
Belgium	7	Pakistan	2
Brazil	2	Romania	2
Bulgaria	2	Russia	31
Canada	18	Slovakia	5
China	11	Slovenia	1
Czech Republic	6	South Africa	2
Finland	4	Spain	8
France	59	Sweden	10
Germany	17	Switzerland	5
Hungary	4	Taiwan	6
India	17	Ukraine	15
Japan	55	United Kingdom	19
South Korea	20	United States	104
Lithuania	1		

Source: International Atomic Energy Agency

a. Find the first and third quartiles of these data.
b. Find the median of these data.
c. Find the upper and lower outlier boundaries.
d. Which countries are outliers?
e. Construct a boxplot for these data.
f. Describe the shape of this distribution.
g. What is the 45th percentile?
h. What is the 88th percentile?
i. India has 17 nuclear reactors. What percentile is this?

31. Playback time: Following are the playback times (in hours) for a sample of 20 MP3 players.

| 29 | 25 | 23 | 21 | 47 | 46 | 66 | 43 | 35 | 47 |
| 35 | 40 | 13 | 38 | 34 | 23 | 42 | 38 | 29 | 25 |

Source: *Consumer Reports*

a. Find the first and third quartiles of these data.
b. Find the median of these data.
c. Find the upper and lower outlier boundaries.
d. Are there any outliers? If so, list them.
e. Construct a boxplot for these data.
f. Describe the shape of this distribution.
g. What is the 35th percentile?
h. What is the 70th percentile?
i. The Apple iPod Nano has a playback time of 34 hours. What percentile is this?

32. Hail to the chief: There have been 56 presidential inaugurations in U.S. history. At each one, the president has made an inaugural address. Following are the number of words spoken in each of these addresses.

1425	135	2308	1729	2158	1175	1209	3217
4467	2906	1125	1172	3838	8445	4776	996
3319	2821	3634	698	1128	1337	2480	2978
1681	4388	2015	3967	2217	985	5433	1802
1526	3318	4059	3801	1883	1807	1340	559
2242	2446	2449	1355	1437	2130	1668	1087
2463	2546	2283	1507	2170	1571	2073	2406

Source: www.infoplease.com

a. Find the first and third quartiles of these data.
b. Find the median of these data.
c. Find the upper and lower outlier boundaries.
d. The two shortest speeches were 135 words, by George Washington in 1793, and 559 words, by Franklin Roosevelt in 1945. Are either of these outliers?
e. The two longest speeches were 8445 words, by William Henry Harrison in 1841, and 5433 words, by William Howard Taft in 1909. Are either of these outliers?
f. Construct a boxplot for these data.
g. Describe the shape of this distribution.
h. What is the 15th percentile?
i. What is the 65th percentile?
j. Barack Obama used 2406 words in his inauguration speech in 2009. What percentile is this?

33. Bragging rights: After learning his score on a recent statistics exam, Ed bragged to his friends: "My score is the first quartile of the class." Did Ed have a good reason to brag? Explain.

34. Who scored the highest? On a final exam in a large statistics class, Tom's score was the tenth percentile, Dick's was the median, and Harry's was the third quartile. Which of the three scores was the highest? Which was the lowest?

35. Baseball salaries: In 2008, the Philadelphia Phillies won the World Series to become the champions of Major League Baseball. The New York Yankees, who had been expected to do well, did not qualify for the playoffs. Following are the salaries, in millions of dollars, of the players on each of these teams.

Phillies							
14.2	10.0	8.6	8.0	8.0	7.8	6.4	6.0
5.5	5.0	3.3	3.0	2.4	1.7	1.4	0.90
0.90	0.60	0.50	0.48	0.45	0.44	0.43	0.42
0.42	0.40	0.39	0.39	0.39			

Yankees							
28.0	23.4	21.6	16.0	16.0	15.0	13.1	13.0
13.0	11.0	11.0	5.9	4.0	3.8	3.0	1.9
1.8	1.2	1.2	0.73	0.50	0.46	0.41	0.40
0.40	0.39	0.39	0.39	0.39	0.39		

a. Find the median, the first quartile, and the third quartile of the Phillies' salaries.

b. Find the median, the first quartile, and the third quartile of the Yankees' salaries.

c. Find the upper and lower outlier bounds for the Phillies' salaries.

d. Find the upper and lower outlier bounds for the Yankees' salaries.

e. Construct comparative boxplots for the two data sets. What conclusions can you draw?

36. **Automotive emissions:** Following are levels of particulate emissions for 65 vehicles driven at sea level, and for 35 vehicles driven at high altitude.

Sea Level									
1.5	0.9	1.1	1.3	3.5	1.1	1.1	0.9	1.3	0.9
0.6	1.3	2.5	1.5	1.1	1.1	2.2	0.9	1.8	1.5
1.2	1.6	2.1	6.6	4.0	2.5	1.4	1.4	1.8	1.1
1.6	3.7	0.6	2.7	2.6	3.0	1.2	1.0	1.6	3.1
2.4	2.1	2.7	1.2	3.3	3.8	1.3	2.1	6.6	1.2
3.1	0.5	0.3	0.5	3.4	3.5	2.7	1.9	5.9	4.2
3.5	3.6	3.1	3.3	4.6					

High Altitude						
8.9	4.4	3.6	4.4	3.8	2.4	3.8
5.3	5.8	2.9	4.7	1.9	9.1	8.7
9.5	2.7	9.2	7.3	2.1	6.3	6.5
6.3	2.0	5.9	5.6	5.6	1.5	6.5
5.3	5.6	2.1	1.1	3.3	1.8	7.6

a. Find the median, the first quartile, and the third quartile of the sea-level emissions.

b. Find the median, the first quartile, and the third quartile of the high-altitude emissions.

c. Find the upper and lower outlier bounds for the sea-level emissions.

d. Find the upper and lower outlier bounds for the high-altitude emissions.

e. Construct comparative boxplots for the two data sets. What conclusions can you draw?

Extending the Concepts

37. **The vanishing outlier:** Seven families live on a small street in a certain town. Their annual incomes (in $1000s) are 15, 20, 30, 35, 50, 60, and 150.

a. Find the first and third quartiles, and the IQR.

b. Show that 150 is an outlier.

A big new house is built on the street, and the income (in $1000s) of the family that moves in is 200.

c. Find the first and third quartiles, and the IQR of the eight incomes.

d. Are there any outliers now?

e. Explain how adding the value 200 to the data set eliminated the outliers.

38. **Beyond quartiles and percentiles:** If we divide a data set into four approximately equal parts, the three dividing points are called quartiles. If we divide a data set into 100 approximately equal parts, the 99 dividing points are called percentiles. In general, if we divide a data set into k approximately equal parts, we can call the dividing points k-tiles. How would you find the ith k-tile of a data set of size n?

39. **z-scores and skewed data:** Table 3.9 presents the February rainfalls in Los Angeles for the period 1965–2006.

a. Show that the mean of these data is $\mu = 3.749$ and the standard deviation is $\sigma = 3.5808$.

b. Show that the z-score for a rainfall of 0 (rounded to two decimal places) is $z = -1.05$.

c. Show that the z-score for a rainfall of 7.5 (rounded to two decimal places) is $z = 1.05$.

d. What percentage of the years had rainfalls of 0?

e. What percentage of the years had rainfalls of 7.5 or more?

f. The z-scores indicate that a rainfall of 0 and a rainfall of 7.5 are about equally extreme. Is a rainfall of 7.5 really as extreme as a rainfall of 0, or is it less extreme?

g. These data are skewed to the right. Explain how skewness causes the z-score to give misleading results.

Answers to Check Your Understanding Exercises for Section 3.3

1. a. 70   b. 83   c. 30th   d. Yes

2. 90%

3. a. 22   66   80   119   209   b. 53
   c. Lower outlier bound is -13.5; upper bound is 198.5.
   d. 209 is the only outlier.

4.

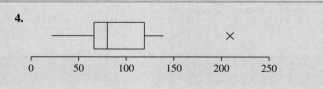

Chapter 3 Summary

Section 3.1: We can describe the center of a data set with the mean or the median. When a data set is skewed to the left, the mean is generally less than the median, and when a data set is skewed to the right, the mean is generally greater than the median. The mode of a data set is the most frequently occurring value.

Section 3.2: The spread of a data set is most often measured with the standard deviation. For data sets that are unimodal and approximately symmetric, the Empirical Rule can be used to approximate the proportion of the data that lies within a given number of standard deviations of the mean. Chebyshev's Inequality, which is valid for all data sets, provides a lower bound for the proportion of the data that lies within a given number of standard deviations of the mean. The coefficient of variation (CV) measures the spread of a data set relative to its mean. The CV provides a way to compare spreads of data sets whose values are in different units.

Section 3.3: For bell-shaped data sets, the z-score gives a good description of the position of a value in a data set. Quartiles and percentiles can be used to describe the positions for any data set. Quartiles are used to compute the five-number summary, which consists of the minimum value, the first quartile, the median, the third quartile, and the maximum value. Outliers are values that are considerably larger or smaller than most of the values in a data set. Boxplots are graphs that allow us to visualize the five-number summary, along with any outliers. Comparative boxplots allow us to visually compare the shapes of two or more data sets.

Vocabulary and Notation

$\sum x = x_1 + \cdots + x_n$ 89	mean 88	population variance σ^2 106
arithmetic mean 88	mean absolute deviation (MAD) 123	quartile 127
boxplot 132	measure of center 88	range 105
Chebyshev's Inequality 114	measure of position 88	resistant 92
coefficient of variation (CV) 116	measure of spread 88	sample mean $\bar{x}$ 89
comparative boxplots 134	median 90	sample standard deviation s 109
degrees of freedom 108	mode 94	sample variance s^2 107
deviation 105	modified boxplot 132	second quartile Q_2 127
Empirical Rule 112	outlier 130	standard deviation 109
first quartile Q_1 127	outlier boundaries 131	third quartile Q_3 127
five-number summary 129	percentile 125	variance 105
interquartile range (IQR) 130	population mean μ 89	whisker 132
IQR method 131	population standard deviation σ 109	z-score 124

Important Formulas

Sample mean:
$$\bar{x} = \frac{\sum x}{n}$$

Coefficient of variation:
$$CV = \frac{\sigma}{\mu}$$

Population mean:
$$\mu = \frac{\sum x}{N}$$

z-score:
$$z = \frac{x - \mu}{\sigma}$$

Range:
Range = largest value − smallest value

Interquartile range:
IQR = $Q_3 - Q_1$ = third quartile − first quartile

Population variance:
$$\sigma^2 = \frac{\sum (x - \mu)^2}{N}$$

Lower outlier boundary:
$$Q_1 - 1.5 \, IQR$$

Sample variance:
$$s^2 = \frac{\sum (x - \bar{x})^2}{n - 1}$$

Upper outlier boundary:
$$Q_3 + 1.5 \, IQR$$

Chapter Quiz

1. Of the mean, median, and mode, which must be a value that actually appears in the data set?

2. The prices (in dollars) for a sample of personal computers are: 550, 700, 420, 580, 550, 450, 690, 390, 350. Calculate the mean, median, and mode for this sample.

3. If a computer with a price of $2000 were added to the list in Exercise 2, which would be affected more, the mean or the median?

4. In general, a histogram is skewed to the left if the _____ is noticeably less than the _____ .

5. A sample of 100 students was asked how many hours per week they spent studying. The following frequency table shows the results:

Number of Hours	Frequency
1.0–4.9	14
5.0–8.9	34
9.0–12.9	29
13.0–16.9	15
17.0–20.9	8

  a. Approximate the mean time this sample of students spent studying.
  b. Approximate the standard deviation of the time this sample of students spent studying.

6. A sample has a variance of 16. What is the standard deviation?

7. Each of the following histograms represents a data set with mean 20. One has a standard deviation of 3.96 and the other has a standard deviation of 2.28. Which is which? Fill in the blanks: Histogram I has a standard deviation of _____ and histogram II has a standard deviation of _____ .

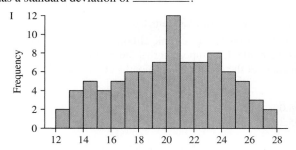
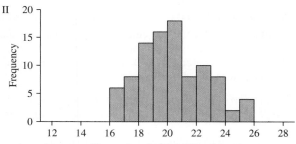

In Exercises 8–11, suppose that the mean starting salary of social workers in a specific region is $37,480 with a standard deviation of $1,400.

8. Assume that the histogram of starting salaries is approximately bell-shaped. Approximately what percentage of the salaries will be between $34,680 and $40,280?

9. Assume it is not known whether the histogram of starting salaries is bell-shaped. Fill in the blank: At least _____ percent of the salaries will be between $34,680 and $40,280.

10. John's starting salary is $38,180. What is the z-score of his salary?

11. Find the coefficient of variation of the salaries.

12. True or false: If a student's exam grade is on the 55th percentile, then approximately 45% of the scores are below his or her grade.

13. The five-number summary for a sample is 7, 18, 35, 62, 85. What is the IQR?

14. The prices (in dollars) for a sample of coffee makers are:

        19   22   29   68   35   37   28   22   41   39   28

  a. Find the first and third quartiles.
  b. Find the upper and lower outlier boundaries.
  c. Are there any outliers? Of so, list them.

15. Construct a boxplot for the data in Exercise 14.

Review Exercises

1. Support your local artist: Following are the annual amounts of federal support (in millions of dollars) for National Endowment for the Arts programs for the years 2000 to 2006.

Year	Amount
2000	85.2
2001	94.0
2002	98.6
2003	101.0
2004	105.5
2005	108.8
2006	112.8

Source: National Endowment for the Arts

a. Find the mean annual amount of federal aid from 2000 to 2006.

b. Find the median annual amount of federal aid from 2000 to 2006.

2. **Corporate profits:** The following table presents the profit, in billions of dollars, for the year 2007 for each of the 15 largest U.S. corporations in terms of revenue.

Corporation	Profit	Corporation	Profit
Wal-Mart	12.7	Bank of America	15.0
Exxon Mobil	40.6	AT&T	12.0
Chevron	18.7	Berkshire Hathaway	13.2
General Motors	−38.7	J.P. Morgan Chase	15.3
ConocoPhillips	11.9	American International Group	6.2
General Electric	22.2	Hewlett-Packard	7.2
Ford Motor	−2.8	IBM	10.4
Citigroup	3.6		

Source: *Fortune*

a. Find the mean profit.

b. Find the median profit.

c. Are these data skewed to the right, skewed to the left, or approximately symmetric? Explain.

3. **Computer chips:** A computer chip is a wafer made of silicon that contains complex electronic circuitry made up of microscopic components. The wafers are coated with a very thin coating of silicon dioxide. It is important that the coating be of uniform thickness over the wafer. To check this, engineers measured the thickness of the coating, in millionths of a meter, for samples of wafers made with two different processes.

Process 1:	90.0	92.2	94.9	92.7	91.6	88.2	92.0	98.2	96.0
Process 2:	76.1	90.2	96.8	84.6	93.3	95.7	90.9	100.3	95.2

a. Find the mean of the thicknesses for each process.

b. Find the median of the thicknesses for each process.

c. If it is desired to obtain as thin a coating as possible, is one process much better than the other? Or are they about the same?

4. **More computer chips:** Using the data in Exercise 3:

a. Find the sample variance of the thicknesses for each process.

b. Find the sample standard deviation of the thicknesses for each process.

c. Which process appears to be better in producing a uniform thickness? Explain.

5. **Stock prices:** Following are the closing prices of Microsoft stock for each trading day in September and October 2010.

September						October					
23.90	23.94	24.29	23.96	23.93	24.01	24.38	23.91	24.35	24.43	24.53	24.57
23.85	25.11	25.03	25.12	25.33	25.22	24.59	24.83	25.34	25.23	25.54	25.82
25.43	25.15	24.61	24.43	24.78	24.73	25.10	25.31	25.42	25.38	25.19	25.90
24.68	24.50	24.49				26.05	26.28	26.67			

a. Find the mean and median price in September.

b. Find the mean and median price in October.

c. Does there appear to be a substantial difference in price between September and October? Or are the prices about the same?

6. **More stock prices:** Using the data in Exercise 5:

a. Find the population standard deviation of the prices in September.

b. Find the population standard deviation of the prices in October.

c. Financial analysts use the word *volatility* to refer to the variation in stock prices. Was the volatility for the price of Microsoft stock greater in September or October?

7. **Measure that ball:** Each of 16 students measured the circumference of a tennis ball by two different methods:

A: Estimate the circumference by eye.

B: Measure the circumference by rolling the ball along a ruler.

The results (in centimeters) are given below, in increasing order for each method:

A:	18.0	18.0	18.0	20.0	22.0	22.0	22.5	23.0	24.0	24.0	25.0	25.0	25.0	25.0	26.0	26.4
B:	20.0	20.0	20.0	20.0	20.2	20.5	20.5	20.7	20.7	20.7	21.0	21.1	21.5	21.6	22.1	22.3

a. Compute the sample standard deviation of the measurements for each method.

b. For which method is the sample standard deviation larger? Why should one expect this method to have the larger standard deviation?

   c. Other things being equal, is it better for a measurement method to have a smaller standard deviation or a larger standard deviation? Or doesn't it matter? Explain.

8. Time in surgery: Records at a hospital show that a certain surgical procedure takes an average of 162.8 minutes with a standard deviation of 4.9 minutes. If the data are approximately bell-shaped, between what two values will about 95% of the data fall?

9. Rivets: A machine makes rivets that are used in the manufacture of airplanes. To be acceptable, the length of a rivet must be between 0.9 centimeter and 1.1 centimeters. The mean length of a rivet is 1.0 centimeter, with a standard deviation of 0.05 centimeter. What is the maximum possible percentage of rivets that are unacceptable?

10. How long can you talk? A manufacturer of cell phone batteries determines that the average length of talk time for one of its batteries is 470 minutes. Suppose that the standard deviation is known to be 32 minutes and that the data are approximately bell-shaped. Estimate the percentage of batteries that have z-scores between -1 and 1.

11. Paying rent: The monthly rents for apartments in a certain town have a mean of $800 with a standard deviation of $150. What can you determine about these data by using Chebyshev's Inequality with $K = 3$?

12. Advertising costs: The amounts spent (in billions) on media advertising in the United States for a sample of categories in 2008 are presented in the following table.

Advertising Category	Amount Spent on Advertising
Automotive	12.8
Financial services	9.6
Local services	8.6
Telecom	8.4
Miscellaneous retail	8.3
Direct response	7.3
Food & candy	6.0
Personal care products	6.0
Restaurants	5.6
Travel & tourism	5.2

Source: TNS Media Intelligence

   a. Find the mean amount spent on advertising.
   b. Find the median amount spent on advertising.
   c. Find the sample variance of the advertising amounts.
   d. Find the sample standard deviation of the advertising amounts.
   e. Find the first quartile of the advertising amounts.
   f. Find the third quartile of the advertising amounts.
   g. Find the 40th percentile of the advertising amounts.
   h. Find the 65th percentile of the advertising amounts.

13. Matching: Match each histogram to the boxplot that represents the same data set.

a.

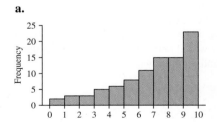

b.

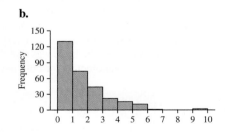

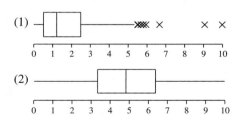

c.

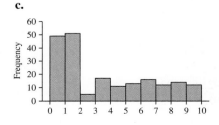

d.

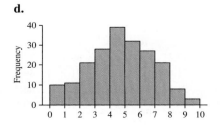

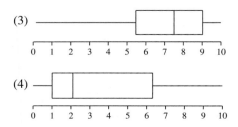

14. **Weights of soap:** As part of a quality control study aimed at improving a production line, the weights (in ounces) of 50 bars of soap are measured. The results are shown below, sorted from smallest to largest.

11.6	12.6	12.7	12.8	13.1	13.3	13.6	13.7
13.8	14.1	14.3	14.3	14.6	14.8	15.1	15.2
15.6	15.6	15.7	15.8	15.8	15.9	15.9	16.1
16.2	16.2	16.3	16.4	16.5	16.5	16.5	16.6
17.0	17.1	17.3	17.3	17.4	17.4	17.4	17.6
17.7	18.1	18.3	18.3	18.3	18.5	18.5	18.8
19.2	20.3						

a. Find the first and third quartiles of these data.
b. Find the median of these data.
c. Find the upper and lower outlier boundaries.
d. Are there any outliers? If so, list them.
e. Construct a boxplot for these data.

15. **More corporate profits:** Using the data in Exercise 2:
a. Find the first and third quartiles of the profit.
b. Find the median profit.
c. Find the upper and lower outlier boundaries.
d. Are there any outliers? If so, list them.
e. Construct a boxplot for these data.

Write About It

1. The U.S. Department of Labor annually publishes an Occupational Outlook Handbook, which reports the job outlook, working conditions, and earnings for thousands of different occupations. The handbook reports both the mean and median annual earnings. For most occupations, which is larger, the mean or the median? Why do you think so?

2. Explain why the Empirical Rule is more useful than Chebyshev's Inequality for bell-shaped distributions. Explain why Chebyshev's Inequality is more useful for distributions that are not bell-shaped.

3. Does Chebyshev's Inequality provide useful information when $K = 1$? Explain why or why not.

4. Is Chebyshev's Inequality true when $K < 1$? Is it useful? Explain why or why not.

5. Percentiles are values that divide a data set into hundredths. The values that divide a data set into tenths are called deciles, denoted $D_1, D_2, ..., D_9$. Describe the relationship between percentiles and deciles.

Case Study: Can Recycled Materials Be Used In Electrical Devices?

Electronic devices contain electric circuits etched into wafers made of silicon. These silicon wafers are sealed with an ultrathin layer of silicon dioxide, in a process known as oxidation. This can be done with either new or recycled wafers.

In a study described in the book *Statistical Case Studies for Industrial Process Improvement* by V. Czitrom and P. Spagon, both new and recycled wafers were oxidized, and the thicknesses of the layers were measured to determine whether they tended to differ between the two types of wafers. Recycled wafers are cheaper than new wafers, so the hope was that they would perform at least as well as the new wafers. Following are 36 thickness measurements (in tenths of a nanometer) for both new and recycled wafers.

New								
90.0	92.2	94.9	92.7	91.6	88.2	92.0	98.2	96.0
91.1	89.8	91.5	91.5	90.6	93.1	88.9	92.5	92.4
96.7	93.7	93.9	87.9	90.4	92.0	90.5	95.2	94.3
92.0	94.6	93.7	94.0	89.3	90.1	91.3	92.7	94.5

Recycled								
91.8	94.5	93.9	77.3*	92.0	89.9	87.9	92.8	93.3
92.6	90.3	92.8	91.6	92.7	91.7	89.3	95.5	93.6
92.4	91.7	91.6	91.1	88.0	92.4	88.7	92.9	92.6
91.7	97.4	95.1	96.7	77.5*	91.4	90.5	95.2	93.1

*Measurement is in error due to a defective gauge.

1. Construct comparative boxplots for the thicknesses of new wafers and recycled wafers.

2. Identify all outliers.

3. Should any of the outliers be deleted? If so, delete them and redraw the boxplots.

4. Identify any outliers in the redrawn boxplots. Should any of these be deleted? Explain.

5. Are the distributions of thicknesses skewed, or approximately symmetric?

6. Delete outliers as appropriate, and compute the mean thickness for new and for recycled wafers.

7. Delete outliers as appropriate, and compute the median thickness for new and for recycled wafers.

8. Delete outliers as appropriate, and compute the standard deviation of the thicknesses for new and for recycled wafers.

9. Suppose that it is desired to use the type of wafer whose distribution has less spread. Write a brief paragraph that explains which type of wafer to use and why. Which measure is more useful for spread in this case, the standard deviation or the interquartile range? Explain.

Probability

Introduction

How likely is it that you will live to be 100 years old? The following table, called a **life table**, can be used to answer this question.

United States Life Table, Total Population

Age Interval	Proportion Surviving	Age Interval	Proportion Surviving
0–10	0.99123	50–60	0.94010
10–20	0.99613	60–70	0.86958
20–30	0.99050	70–80	0.70938
30–40	0.98703	80–90	0.42164
40–50	0.97150	90–100	0.12248

Source: Centers for Disease Control and Prevention

The column labeled "Proportion Surviving" presents the proportion of people alive at the beginning of an age interval who will still be alive at the end of the age interval. For example, among those currently age 20, the proportion who will still be alive at age 30 is 0.99050, or 99.050%. With an understanding of some basic concepts of probability, one can use the life table to compute the probability that a person of a given age will still be alive a given number of years from now. Life insurance companies use this information to determine how much to charge for life insurance policies. In the case study at the end of the chapter, we will use the life table to study some further questions that can be addressed with the methods of probability.

This chapter presents an introduction to probability. Probability is perhaps the only branch of knowledge that owes its existence to gambling. In the seventeenth century, owners of gambling houses hired some of the leading mathematicians of the time to calculate the chances that players would win certain gambling games. Later, people realized that many real-world problems involve chance as well, and since then the methods of probability have been used in almost every area of knowledge.

SECTION 4.1 | Basic Ideas

Objectives

1. Construct sample spaces
2. Compute and interpret probabilities
3. Approximate probabilities by using the Empirical Method

At the beginning of a football game, a coin is tossed to decide which team will get the ball first. There are two reasons for using a coin toss in this situation. First, it is impossible to predict which team will win the coin toss, because there is no way to tell ahead of time whether the coin will land heads or tails. The second reason is that in the long run, over the course of many football games, we know that the home team will win about half of the tosses, and the visiting team will win about half. In other words, although we don't know what the outcome of a single coin toss will be, we do know what the outcome of a long series of tosses will be — they will come out about half heads and half tails.

A coin toss is an example of a **probability experiment**. A probability experiment is one in which we do not know what any individual outcome will be, but we do know how a long series of repetitions will come out. Another familiar example of a probability experiment is the rolling of a die. A die has six faces; the faces have from one to six dots. We cannot predict which face will turn up on a single roll of a die, but, assuming the die is evenly balanced (not loaded), we know that in the long run, each face will turn up one-sixth of the time.

The **probability** of an event is the proportion of times that the event occurs in the long run. So, for a "fair" coin, that is, one that is equally likely to come up heads as tails, the probability of heads is 1/2 and the probability of tails is 1/2.

DEFINITION

The **probability** of an event is the proportion of times the event occurs in the long run, as a probability experiment is repeated over and over again.

The South African mathematician John Kerrich carried out a famous study that illustrates the idea of the long-run proportion. Kerrich was in Denmark when World War II broke out and spent the war interned in a prisoner-of-war camp. To pass the time, he carried out a series of probability experiments, including one in which he tossed a coin 10,000 times and recorded each toss as a head or a tail.

Figure 4.1 summarizes a computer-generated re-creation of Kerrich's study, in which the proportion of heads is plotted against the number of tosses. For example, it turned out that after 5 tosses, 3 heads had appeared, so the proportion of heads was $3/5 = 0.6$. After 100 tosses, 49 heads had appeared, so the proportion of heads was $49/100 = 0.49$. After 10,000 tosses, the proportion of heads was 0.4994, which is very close to the true probability of 0.5. The figure shows that the proportion varies quite a bit within the first few tosses, but the proportion settles down very close to 0.5 as the number of tosses becomes larger.

The fact that the long-run proportion approaches the probability is called the **law of large numbers**.

Explain It Again

Law of large numbers: The law of large numbers is another way to state our definition of probability.

Law of Large Numbers

The **law of large numbers** says that as a probability experiment is repeated again and again, the proportion of times that a given event occurs will approach its probability.

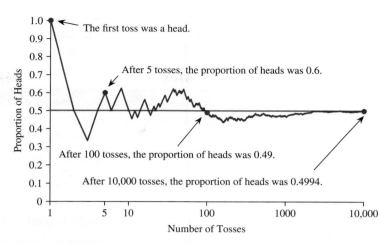

Figure 4.1   As the number of tosses increases, the proportion of heads fluctuates around the true probability of 0.5, and gets closer to 0.5. The horizontal axis is not drawn to scale.

Objective 1 Construct sample spaces

Probability Models

To study probability formally, we need some basic terminology. The collection of all the possible outcomes of a probability experiment is called a **sample space**.

> **DEFINITION**
>
> A **sample space** contains all the possible outcomes of a probability experiment.

EXAMPLE 4.1

Describe sample spaces

Describe a sample space for each of the following experiments.

    a. The toss of a coin
    b. The roll of a die
    c. Selecting a student at random from a list of 10,000 students at a large university
    d. Selecting a simple random sample of 100 students from a list of 10,000 students

Solution

    a. There are two possible outcomes for the toss of a coin: Heads and Tails. So a sample space is {Heads, Tails}.
    b. There are six possible outcomes for the roll of a die: the numbers from 1 to 6. So a sample space is {1, 2, 3, 4, 5, 6}.
    c. Each of the 10,000 students is a possible outcome for this experiment, so the sample space consists of the 10,000 students.
    d. This sample space consists of every group of 100 students that can be chosen from the population of 10,000 — in other words, every possible simple random sample of size 100. This is a huge number of outcomes; it can be written approximately as a 6 followed by 241 zeros. This is larger than the number of atoms in the universe.

We are often concerned with occurrences that consist of several outcomes. For example, when rolling a die, we might be interested in the possibility of rolling an odd number. Rolling an odd number corresponds to the collection of outcomes {1, 3, 5} from the sample space {1, 2, 3, 4, 5, 6}. In general, a collection of outcomes of a sample space is called an **event**.

> **DEFINITION**
>
> An **event** is an outcome or a collection of outcomes from a sample space.

Once we have a sample space for an experiment, we need to specify the probability of each event. This is done with a **probability model**. We use the letter "P" to denote probabilities. So, for example, if we toss a coin, we denote the probability that the coin lands heads by "P(Heads)."

DEFINITION

A **probability model** for a probability experiment consists of a sample space, along with a probability for each event.

Notation: If A denotes an event, the probability of the event A is denoted $P(A)$.

Objective 2 Compute and interpret probabilities

Probability models with equally likely outcomes

In many situations, the outcomes in a sample space are equally likely. For example, when we toss a coin, we usually assume that the two outcomes "Heads" and "Tails" are equally likely. We call such a coin a *fair* coin. Similarly, a fair die is one in which the numbers from 1 to 6 are equally likely to turn up. When the outcomes in a sample space are equally likely, we can use a simple formula to determine the probability of events.

Explain It Again

Fair and unfair: A fair coin or die is one for which all outcomes are equally likely. An unfair coin or die is one for which some outcomes are more likely than others.

Computing Probabilities with Equally Likely Outcomes

If a sample space has n **equally likely outcomes,** and an event A has k outcomes, then

$$P(A) = \frac{\text{Number of outcomes in } A}{\text{Number of outcomes in the sample space}} = \frac{k}{n}$$

EXAMPLE 4.2

Compute the probability of an event

A fair die is rolled. Find the probability that an odd number comes up.

Solution
The sample space has six equally likely outcomes: $\{1, 2, 3, 4, 5, 6\}$. The event of an odd number has three outcomes: $\{1, 3, 5\}$. The probability is

$$P(\text{odd number}) = \frac{3}{6} = \frac{1}{2}$$

EXAMPLE 4.3

Compute the probability of an event

In the Georgia Cash-4 Lottery game, a winning number between 0000 and 9999 is chosen at random, with all the possible numbers being equally likely. What is the probability that all four digits of the winning number are the same?

Solution
The outcomes in the sample space are the numbers from 0000 to 9999, so there are 10,000 equally likely outcomes in the sample space. There are 10 outcomes for which all the digits are the same: 0000, 1111, and so on up to 9999. The probability is

$$P(\text{all four digits the same}) = \frac{10}{10,000} = 0.001$$

The law of large numbers states that the probability of an event is the long-run proportion of times that the event occurs. An event that never occurs, even in the long run, has a probability of 0. This is the smallest probability an event can have. An event that occurs every time has a probability of 1. This is the largest probability an event can have.

Explain It Again	SUMMARY
Rules for the value of a probability: A probability can never be negative, and a probability can never be greater than 1.	The probability of an event is always between 0 and 1. In other words, for any event A, $0 \leq P(A) \leq 1$. If A cannot occur, then $P(A) = 0$. If A is certain to occur, then $P(A) = 1$.

EXAMPLE 4.4   Computing probabilities

A family has three children. Denoting a boy by B and a girl by G, we can denote the genders of these children from oldest to youngest. For example, GBG means the oldest child is a girl, the middle child is a boy, and the youngest child is a girl. There are eight possible outcomes: BBB, BBG, BGB, BGG, GBB, GBG, GGB, and GGG. Assume these outcomes are equally likely.

    a. What is the probability that there are two girls?

    b. What is the probability that all three children are of the same gender?

Solution

    a. Of the eight equally likely outcomes, the three outcomes BGG, GBG, and GGB correspond to having two girls. Therefore,

$$P(\text{Two girls}) = \frac{3}{8}$$

    b. Of the eight equally likely outcomes, the two outcomes BBB and GGG correspond to having all children of the same gender. Therefore,

$$P(\text{All three have same gender}) = \frac{2}{8} = \frac{1}{4}$$

Check Your Understanding

1. In Example 4.4, what is the probability that the youngest child is a boy?

2. In Example 4.4, what is the probability that the oldest child and the youngest child are of the same gender?

Answers are on page 157.

EXAMPLE 4.5   Constructing a sample space

Cystic fibrosis is a disease of the mucous glands whose most common sign is progressive damage to the respiratory system and digestive system. This disease is inherited, as follows. A certain gene may be of type A or type a. Every person has two copies of the gene — one inherited from the person's mother, one from the person's father. If both copies are a, the person will have cystic fibrosis. Assume that a mother and father both have genotype Aa, that is, one gene of each type. Assume that each copy is equally likely to be transmitted to their child. What is the probability that the child will have cystic fibrosis?

Solution

Most of the work in solving this problem is in constructing the sample space. We'll do this in two ways. First, the tree diagram in Figure 4.2 on page 152 shows that there are four possible outcomes. In the tree diagram, the first two branches indicate the two possible outcomes, A and a, for the mother's gene. Then for each of these outcomes there are two branches indicating the possible outcomes for the father's gene. An alternate method is to construct a table like Table 4.1 on page 152.

Table 4.1

Mother's Gene	Father's Gene	Child's Genotype
A	A	AA
A	a	Aa
a	A	aA
a	a	aa

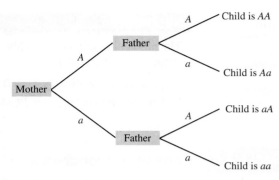

Figure 4.2 Tree diagram illustrating the four outcomes for the child's genotype

We can use either the table or the tree to list the outcomes. Listing the mother's gene first, the four outcomes are AA, Aa, aA, and aa. For one of the four outcomes, aa, the child will have cystic fibrosis. Therefore, the probability of cystic fibrosis is 1/4.

Check Your Understanding

3. A penny and a nickel are tossed. Each is a fair coin, which means that heads and tails are equally likely.
  a. Construct a sample space containing equally likely outcomes. Each outcome should specify the results for both coins.
  b. Find the probability that one coin comes up heads and the other comes up tails.

Answers are on page 157.

Sampling from a population is a probability experiment

In Section 1.1, we learned that statisticians collect data by drawing samples from populations. Sampling an individual from a population is a probability experiment. The population is the sample space, and the members of the population are equally likely outcomes. For this reason, the ideas of probability are fundamental to statistics.

EXAMPLE 4.6 ### Computing probabilities involving sampling

There are 10,000 families in a certain town. They are categorized by their type of housing as follows.

Own a house	4753
Own a condo	1478
Rent a house	912
Rent an apartment	2857

A pollster samples a single family at random from this population.

  a. What is the probability that the sampled family owns a house?
  b. What is the probability that the sampled family rents?

Solution

  a. The sample space consists of the 10,000 households. Of these, 4753 own a house, so the probability that the sampled family owns a house is

$$P(\text{Owns a house}) = \frac{4753}{10,000} = 0.4753$$

b. The number of families who rent is $912 + 2857 = 3769$. Therefore, the probability that the sampled family rents is

$$P(\text{Rents}) = \frac{3769}{10,000} = 0.3769$$

In practice, of course, the pollster would sample many people, not just one. In fact, statisticians use the basic ideas of probability to draw conclusions about populations by studying samples drawn from them. In later chapters of this book, we will see how this is done.

Unusual events

As the name implies, an unusual event is one that is not likely to happen — in other words, an event whose probability is small. There are no hard-and-fast rules as to just how small a probability needs to be before an event is considered unusual, but 0.05 is commonly used.

Explain It Again

Unusual events: The cutoff value for the probability of an unusual event can be any small value that seems appropriate for a specific situation. The most commonly used value is 0.05.

> **SUMMARY**
>
> An **unusual event** is one whose probability is small.
>
> Sometimes people use the cutoff 0.05; that is, they consider any event whose probability is less than 0.05 to be unusual. But there are no hard-and-fast rules about this.

EXAMPLE 4.7	**Determine whether an event is unusual**

In a college of 5000 students, 150 are math majors. A student is selected at random, and turns out to be a math major. Is this an unusual event?

Solution
The sample space consists of 5000 students, each of whom is equally likely to be chosen. The event of choosing a math major consists of 150 students. Therefore,

$$P(\text{Math major is chosen}) = \frac{150}{5000} = 0.03$$

Since the probability is less than 0.05, then by the most commonly applied rule, this would be considered an unusual event.

Objective 3 Approximate probabilities by using the Empirical Method

Approximating Probabilities with the Empirical Method

The law of large numbers says that if we repeat a probability experiment a large number of times, then the proportion of times that a particular outcome occurs is likely to be close to the true probability of the outcome. The **Empirical Method** consists of repeating an experiment a large number of times, and using the proportion of times an outcome occurs to approximate the probability of the outcome.

EXAMPLE 4.8	**Approximate the probability that a baby is a boy**

Explain It Again

The Empirical Method is only approximate: The Empirical Method does not give us the exact probability. But the larger the number of replications of the experiment, the more reliable the approximation will be.

The Centers for Disease Control and Prevention reports that in the year 2002, there were 2,057,979 boys and 1,963,747 girls born in the United States. Approximate the probability that a newborn baby is a boy.

Solution
We compute the number of times the experiment has been repeated:

$$
\begin{array}{rl}
 2{,}057{,}979 & \text{boys} \\
+1{,}963{,}747 & \text{girls} \\
\hline
= 4{,}021{,}726 & \text{births}
\end{array}
$$

The proportion of births that are boys is

$$\frac{2{,}057{,}979}{4{,}021{,}726} = 0.5117$$

We approximate $P(\text{Boy}) \approx 0.5117$.

Example 4.8 is based on a very large number (4,021,726) of replications. The law of large numbers says that the proportion of outcomes approaches the true probability as the number of replications becomes large. For a number this large, we can be virtually certain that the proportion 0.5117 is very close to the true probability; in fact, we can be virtually certain that the true probability of having a boy is not 0.5 as many believe, but is actually greater than 0.5.

Check Your Understanding

4. There are 100,000 voters in a city. A pollster takes a simple random sample of 1000 of them and finds that 513 support a bond issue to support the public library, and 487 oppose it. Estimate the probability that a randomly chosen voter in this city supports the bond issue.

Answer is on page 157.

USING TECHNOLOGY

TI-84 PLUS

Simulating 100 rolls of a die

Step 1. Press **MATH**, scroll to the **PRB** menu, and select **5: randInt(**

Step 2. Enter **1**, comma, **6**, comma, and then the number of rolls you wish to simulate (100). Close the parentheses (Figure A).

Step 3. To store the data in **L1**, press **STO**, then **2nd, 1**, then **ENTER** (Figure B).

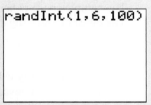

Figure A

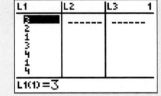

Figure B

MINITAB

Simulating 100 rolls of a die

Step 1. Click **Calc**, then **Random Data**, then **Integer**.

Step 2. Enter **100** as the number of rows of data.

Step 3. Enter **C1** in the **Store in column(s)** field.

Step 4. Enter **1** as the **Minimum value** and **6** as the **Maximum value**.

Step 5. Click **OK**.

EXCEL

Simulating 100 rolls of a die

Step 1. Click on a cell in the worksheet and type **=RANDBETWEEN(1, 6)**. Press **ENTER**.

Step 2. Copy and paste the formula into cells for the number of rolls you wish to simulate (100).

SECTION 4.1   Exercises

Exercises 1–4 are the Check Your Understanding exercises located within the section.

Understanding the Concepts

In Exercises 5–8, fill in each blank with the appropriate word or phrase.

5. If an event cannot occur, its probability is _____.

6. If an event is certain to occur, its probability is _____.

7. The collection of all possible outcomes of a probability experiment is called a _____.

8. An outcome or collection of outcomes from a sample space is called an _____.

In Exercises 9–12, determine whether the statement is true or false. If the statement is false, rewrite it as a true statement.

9. The law of large numbers states that as a probability experiment is repeated, the proportion of times that a given outcome occurs will approach its probability.

10. If A denotes an event, then the sample space is denoted by $P(A)$.

11. The Empirical Method can be used to calculate the exact probability of an event.

12. For any event A, $0 \leq P(A) \leq 1$.

Practicing the Skills

In Exercises 13–18, assume that a fair die is rolled. The sample space is $\{1, 2, 3, 4, 5, 6\}$, and all the outcomes are equally likely.

13. Find $P(2)$.

14. Find $P(\text{Even number})$.

15. Find $P(\text{Less than 3})$.

16. Find $P(\text{Greater than 2})$.

17. Find $P(7)$.

18. Find $P(\text{Less than 10})$.

19. A fair coin has probability 0.5 of coming up heads.
    a. If you toss a fair coin twice, are you certain to get one head and one tail?
    b. If you toss a fair coin 100 times, are you certain to get 50 heads and 50 tails?
    c. As you toss the coin more and more times, will the proportion of heads approach 0.5?

20. Roulette wheels in Nevada have 38 pockets. They are numbered 0, 00, and 1 through 36. On each spin of the wheel, a ball lands in a pocket, and each pocket is equally likely.
    a. If you spin a roulette wheel 38 times, is it certain that each number will come up once?
    b. If you spin a roulette wheel 3800 times, is it certain that each number will come up 100 times?
    c. As the wheel is spun more and more times, will the proportion of times that each number comes up approach 1/38?

In Exercises 21–24, assume that a coin is tossed twice. The coin may not be fair. The sample space consists of the outcomes $\{HH, HT, TH, TT\}$.

21. Is the following a probability model for this experiment? Why or why not?

Outcome	HH	HT	TH	TT
Probability	0.55	0.42	0.31	0.25

22. Is the following a probability model for this experiment? Why or why not?

Outcome	HH	HT	TH	TT
Probability	0.36	0.24	0.24	0.16

23. Is the following a probability model for this experiment? Why or why not?

Outcome	HH	HT	TH	TT
Probability	0.09	0.21	0.21	0.49

24. Is the following a probability model for this experiment? Why or why not?

Outcome	HH	HT	TH	TT
Probability	0.33	0.46	−0.18	0.4

Working with the Concepts

25. **How probable is it?** Someone computes the probabilities of several events. The probabilities are listed on the left, and some verbal descriptions are listed on the right. Match each probability with the best verbal description. Some descriptions may be used more than once.

Probability	Verbal Description
(a) 0.50	i. This event is certain to happen.
(b) 0.00	ii. This event is as likely to happen
(c) 0.90	as not.
(d) 1.00	iii. This event may happen, but it isn't
(e) 0.10	likely.
(f) −0.25	iv. This event is very likely to happen,
(g) 0.01	but it isn't certain.
(h) 2.00	v. It would be unusual for this event
	to happen.
	vi. This event cannot happen.
	vii. Someone made a mistake.

26. **Do you know SpongeBob?** According to a survey by Nickelodeon TV, 88% of children under 13 in Germany recognized a picture of the cartoon character SpongeBob SquarePants. What is the probability that a randomly chosen German child recognizes SpongeBob?

27. **Who will you vote for?** In a survey of 500 likely voters in a certain city, 275 said that they planned to vote to reelect the incumbent mayor.
    a. What is the probability that a surveyed voter plans to vote to reelect the mayor?
    b. Interpret this probability by estimating the percentage of all voters in the city who plan to vote to reelect the mayor.

28. Job satisfaction: In a poll conducted by the General Social Survey, 497 out of 1769 people said that their main satisfaction in life comes from their work.
   a. What is the probability that a person who was polled finds his or her main satisfaction in life from work?
   b. Interpret this probability by estimating the percentage of all people whose main satisfaction in life comes from their work.

29. True–false exam: A section of an exam contains four true–false questions. A completed exam paper is selected at random, and the four answers are recorded.
   a. List all 16 outcomes in the sample space.
   b. Assuming the outcomes to be equally likely, find the probability that all the answers are the same.
   c. Assuming the outcomes to be equally likely, find the probability that exactly one of the four answers is "True."
   d. Assuming the outcomes to be equally likely, find the probability that two of the answers are "True" and two of the answers are "False."

30. A coin flip: A fair coin is tossed three times. The outcomes of the three tosses are recorded.
   a. List all eight outcomes in the sample space.
   b. Assuming the outcomes to be equally likely, find the probability that all three tosses are "Heads."
   c. Assuming the outcomes to be equally likely, find the probability that the tosses are all the same.
   d. Assuming the outcomes to be equally likely, find the probability that exactly one of the three tosses is "Heads."

31. Empirical Method: A coin is tossed 400 times and comes up heads 180 times. Use the Empirical Method to approximate the probability that the coin comes up heads.

32. Empirical Method: A die is rolled 600 times. On 85 of those rolls, the die comes up 6. Use the Empirical Method to approximate the probability that the die comes up 6.

33. Pitching: During a stretch of the 2009 baseball season, Colorado Rockies pitcher Ubaldo Jimenez threw 2825 pitches. Of these, 1912 were fastballs, 228 were curveballs, 457 were sliders, and 228 were changeups.
   a. What is the probability that Ubaldo Jimenez throws a fastball?
   b. What is the probability that Ubaldo Jimenez throws a breaking ball (curve or slider)?

34. More pitching: Pitcher Mark Buehrle of the Chicago White Sox threw 3103 pitches during part of a recent season. Of these, 1286 were thrown with no strikes on the batter, 946 were thrown with one strike, and 871 were thrown with two strikes.
   a. What is the probability that a Mark Buehrle pitch is thrown with no strikes?
   b. What is the probability that a Mark Buehrle pitch is thrown with fewer than two strikes?

35. Risky drivers: An automobile insurance company divides customers into three categories: good risks, medium risks, and poor risks. Assume that of a total of 11,217 customers, 7792 are good risks, 2478 are medium risks, and 947 are poor risks. As part of an audit, one customer is chosen at random.

   a. What is the probability that the customer is a good risk?
   b. What is the probability that the customer is not a poor risk?

36. Pay your bills: A company audit showed that of 875 bills that were sent out, 623 were paid on time, 155 were paid up to 30 days late, 78 were paid between 31 and 90 days late, and 19 remained unpaid after 90 days. One bill is selected at random.
   a. What is the probability that the bill was paid on time?
   b. What is the probability that the bill was paid late?

37. Roulette: A Nevada roulette wheel has 38 pockets. Eighteen of them are red, eighteen are black, and two are green. Each time the wheel is spun, a ball lands in one of the pockets, and each pocket is equally likely.
   a. What is the probability that the ball lands in a red pocket?
   b. If you bet on red on every spin of the wheel, you will lose more than half the time in the long run. Explain why this is so.

38. More roulette: Refer to Exercise 37.
   a. What is the probability that the ball lands in a green pocket?
   b. If you bet on green on every spin of the wheel, you will lose more than 90% of the time in the long run. Explain why this is so.

39. Get an education: The General Social Survey asked 32,201 people how much confidence they had in educational institutions. The results were as follows.

Response	Number
A great deal	10,040
Some	17,890
Hardly any	4,271
Total	32,201

   a. What is the probability that a sampled person has either some or a great deal of confidence in educational institutions?
   b. Assume this is a simple random sample from a population. Use the Empirical Method to estimate the probability that a person has a great deal of confidence in educational institutions.
   c. If we use a cutoff of 0.05, is it unusual for someone to have hardly any confidence in educational institutions?

40. How many kids? The General Social Survey asked 46,349 women how many children they had. The results were as follows.

Number of Children	Number of Women
0	12,656
1	7,438
2	11,290
3	7,143
4	3,797
5	1,811
6	916
7	522
8 or more	776
Total	46,349

a. What is the probability that a sampled woman has two children?

b. What is the probability that a sampled woman has fewer than three children?

c. Assume this is a simple random sample of U.S. women. Use the Empirical Method to estimate the probability that a U.S. woman has more than five children.

d. Using a cutoff of 0.05, is it unusual for a woman to have no children?

41. Hospital visits: According to the Agency for Healthcare Research and Quality, there were 409,706 hospital visits for asthma-related illnesses in the year 2008. The age distribution was as follows.

Age Range	Number
Less than 1 year	7,866
1–17	103,040
18–44	79,659
45–64	121,728
65–84	80,649
85 and up	16,764
Total	409,706

a. What is the probability that an asthma patient is between 18 and 44 years old?

b. What is the probability that an asthma patient is 65 or older?

c. Using a cutoff of 0.05, is it unusual for an asthma patient to be less than one year old?

42. Don't smoke: The Centers for Disease Control and Prevention reported that there were 443,000 smoking-related deaths in the United States in a recent year. The numbers of deaths caused by various illnesses attributed to smoking are as follows:

Illness	Number
Lung cancer	128,900
Ischemic heart disease	126,000
Chronic obstructive pulmonary disease	92,900
Other	95,200
Total	443,000

a. What is the probability that a smoking-related death was the result of lung cancer?

b. What is the probability that a smoking-related death was the result of either ischemic heart disease or other?

Extending the Concepts

Two dice are rolled. One is red and one is blue. Each will come up with a number between 1 and 6. There are 36 equally likely outcomes for this experiment. They are ordered pairs of the form (Red die, Blue die).

43. Find a sample space: Construct a sample space for this experiment that contains the 36 equally likely outcomes.

44. Find the probability: What is the probability that the sum of the dice is 5?

45. Find the probability: What is the probability that the sum of the dice is 7?

46. The red die has been rolled: Now assume that you have rolled the red die, and it has come up 3. How many of the original 36 outcomes are now possible?

47. Find a new sample space: Construct a sample space containing the outcomes that are still possible after the red die has come up 3.

48. New information changes the probability: Given that the red die came up 3, what is the probability that the sum of the dice is 5? Is the probability the same as it was before the red die was observed?

49. New information doesn't change the probability: Given that the red die came up 3, what is the probability that the sum of the dice is 7? Is the probability the same as it was before the red die was observed?

Answers to Check Your Understanding Exercises for Section 4.1

1. 0.5

2. 0.5

3. a.

Penny	Nickel
H	H
H	T
T	H
T	T

b. 0.5

4. 0.513

SECTION 4.2	The Addition Rule and the Rule of Complements

Objectives

1. Compute probabilities by using the General Addition Rule
2. Compute probabilities by using the Addition Rule for Mutually Exclusive Events
3. Compute probabilities by using the Rule of Complements

If you go out in the evening, you might go to dinner, or to a movie, or to both dinner and a movie. In probability terminology, "go to dinner and a movie" and "go to dinner or a movie" are referred to as **compound events**, because they are composed of combinations of other events — in this case the events "go to dinner" and "go to a movie."

DEFINITION

A **compound event** is an event that is formed by combining two or more events.

In this section, we will focus on compound events of the form "*A* or *B*." We will say that the event "*A* or *B*" occurs whenever *A* occurs, or *B* occurs, or both *A* and *B* occur. We will learn how to compute probabilities of the form $P(A \text{ or } B)$.

DEFINITION

$P(A \text{ or } B) = P(A \text{ occurs or } B \text{ occurs or both occur})$

Table 4.2 presents the results of a survey in which 1000 adults were asked whether they favored a law that would provide more government support for higher education. In addition, each person was asked whether he or she voted in the last election. Those who had voted were classified as "Likely to vote" and those who had not were classified as "Not likely to vote."

Table 4.2

	Favor	**Oppose**	**Undecided**
Likely to vote	372	262	87
Not likely to vote	151	103	25

Table 4.2 is called a **contingency table**. It categorizes people with regard to two variables: whether they are likely to vote, and their opinion on the law. There are six categories, and the numbers in the table present the frequencies for each category. For example, we can see that 372 people are in the row corresponding to "Likely to vote" and the column corresponding to "Favor." Thus, 372 people were likely to vote and favored the law. Similarly, 103 people were not likely to vote and opposed the law.

EXAMPLE 4.9   Compute probabilities by using equally likely outcomes

Use Table 4.2 to answer the following questions:

a. What is the probability that a randomly selected adult is likely to vote and favors the law?

b. What is the probability that a randomly selected adult is likely to vote?

c. What is the probability that a randomly selected adult favors the law?

Solution

We think of the adults in the survey as outcomes in a sample space. Each adult is equally likely to be the one chosen. We begin by counting the total number of outcomes in the sample space:

$$372 + 262 + 87 + 151 + 103 + 25 = 1000$$

To answer part (a), we observe that there are 372 people who are likely to vote and favor the law. There are 1000 people in the survey. Therefore,

$$P(\text{Likely to vote and Favor}) = \frac{372}{1000} = 0.372$$

To answer part (b), we count the total number of outcomes corresponding to adults who are likely to vote:

$$372 + 262 + 87 = 721$$

There are 1000 people in the survey, and 721 of them are likely to vote. Therefore,

$$P(\text{Likely to vote}) = \frac{721}{1000} = 0.721$$

To answer part (c), we count the total number of outcomes corresponding to adults who favor the law:

$$372 + 151 = 523$$

There are 1000 people in the survey, and 523 of them favor the law. Therefore,

$$P(\text{Favor}) = \frac{523}{1000} = 0.523$$

Objective 1 Compute probabilities by using the General Addition Rule

The General Addition Rule

EXAMPLE 4.10

Compute a probability of the form *P(A* or *B)*

Use the data in Table 4.2 to find the probability that a person is likely to vote or favors the law.

Solution

We will illustrate two approaches to this problem. In the first approach, we will use equally likely outcomes, and in the second, we will develop a method that is especially designed for probabilities of the form $P(A \text{ or } B)$.

Approach 1: To use equally likely outcomes, we reproduce Table 4.2 and circle the numbers that correspond to people who are either likely voters or who favor the law.

	Favor	**Oppose**	**Undecided**
Likely to vote	(372)	(262)	(87)
Not likely to vote	(151)	103	25

There are 1000 people altogether. The number of people who either are likely voters or favor the law is

$$372 + 262 + 87 + 151 = 872$$

Therefore,

$$P(\text{Likely to vote or Favor}) = \frac{372 + 262 + 87 + 151}{1000} = \frac{872}{1000} = 0.872$$

Approach 2: In this approach we will begin by computing the probabilities $P(\text{Likely to vote})$ and $P(\text{Favor})$ separately. We reproduce Table 4.2; this time we circle the numbers that correspond to likely voters and put rectangles around the numbers that correspond to favoring the law. Note that the number 372 has both a circle and a rectangle around it, because these 372 people are both likely to vote and favor the law.

	Favor	**Oppose**	**Undecided**
Likely to vote	[(372)]	(262)	(87)
Not likely to vote	[151]	103	25

There are $372 + 262 + 87 = 721$ likely voters and $372 + 151 = 523$ voters who favor the law. If we try to find the number of people who are likely to vote or who favor the law by adding these two numbers, we get $721 + 523 = 1244$, which is too large (there are only 1000 people in total). This happened because there are 372 people who are both likely voters and who favor the law, and these people are counted twice. We can still solve the problem by adding 721 and 523, but we must then subtract 372 to correct for the double counting. We illustrate this reasoning, using probabilities.

$$P(\text{Likely to vote}) = \frac{721}{1000} = 0.721$$

$$P(\text{Favor}) = \frac{523}{1000} = 0.523$$

$$P(\text{Likely to vote AND Favor}) = \frac{372}{1000} = 0.372$$

$$
\begin{aligned}
P(\text{Likely to vote OR Favor}) &= P(\text{Likely to vote}) + P(\text{Favor}) \\
&\quad - P(\text{Likely to vote AND Favor}) \\
&= \frac{721}{1000} + \frac{523}{1000} - \frac{372}{1000} \\
&= \frac{872}{1000} = 0.872
\end{aligned}
$$

The method of subtracting in order to adjust for double counting is known as the General Addition Rule.

Explain It Again

The General Addition Rule: Use the General Addition Rule to compute probabilities of the form $P(A \text{ or } B)$.

The General Addition Rule

For any two events A and B,

$$P(A \text{ or } B) = P(A) + P(B) - P(A \text{ and } B)$$

EXAMPLE 4.11

Compute a probability by using the General Addition Rule

Refer to Table 4.2. Use the General Addition Rule to find the probability that a randomly selected person is not likely to vote or is undecided.

Solution

Using the General Addition Rule, we compute

$P(\text{Not likely to vote or Undecided})$

$\quad = P(\text{Not likely to vote}) + P(\text{Undecided}) - P(\text{Not likely to vote and Undecided})$

There are $151 + 103 + 25 = 279$ people not likely to vote out of a total of 1000. Therefore,

$$P(\text{Not likely to vote}) = \frac{279}{1000} = 0.279$$

There are $87 + 25 = 112$ people who are undecided out of a total of 1000. Therefore,

$$P(\text{Undecided}) = \frac{112}{1000} = 0.112$$

Finally, there are 25 people who are both not likely to vote and undecided. Therefore,

$$P(\text{Not likely to vote and Undecided}) = \frac{25}{1000} = 0.025$$

Using the General Addition Rule,

$$P(\text{Not likely to vote or Undecided}) = 0.279 + 0.112 - 0.025 = 0.366$$

Check Your Understanding

1. The following table presents numbers of U.S. workers, in thousands, categorized by type of occupation and educational level.

Type of Occupation	Non-College Graduate	College Graduate
Managers and professionals	17,564	31,103
Service	15,967	2,385
Sales and office	22,352	7,352
Construction and maintenance	12,511	1,033
Production and transportation	14,597	1,308

Source: Bureau of Labor Statistics

   a. What is the probability that a randomly selected worker is a college graduate?

   b. What is the probability that the occupation of a randomly selected worker is categorized either as Sales and office or as Production and transportation?

   c. What is the probability that a randomly selected worker is either a college graduate or has a service occupation?

Answers are on page 166.

Objective 2 Compute probabilities by using the Addition Rule for Mutually Exclusive Events

Mutually Exclusive Events

Sometimes it is impossible for two events both to occur. For example, when a coin is tossed, it is impossible to get both a head and a tail. Two events that cannot both occur are called **mutually exclusive**. The term *mutually exclusive* means that when one event occurs, it excludes the other.

DEFINITION

Two events are said to be **mutually exclusive** if it is impossible for both events to occur.

Explain It Again

Meaning of mutually exclusive events: Two events are mutually exclusive if the occurrence of one makes it impossible for the other to occur.

We can use **Venn diagrams** to illustrate mutually exclusive events. In a Venn diagram, the sample space is represented by a rectangle, and events are represented by circles drawn inside the rectangle. If two circles do not overlap, the two events cannot both occur. If two circles overlap, the overlap area represents the occurrence of both events. Figures 4.3 and 4.4 illustrate the idea.

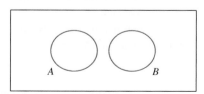

Figure 4.3 Venn diagram illustrating mutually exclusive events

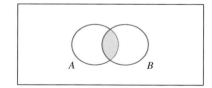

Figure 4.4 Venn diagram illustrating events that are not mutually exclusive

EXAMPLE 4.12

Determine whether two events are mutually exclusive

In each of the following, determine whether events *A* and *B* are mutually exclusive:

   a. A die is rolled. Event *A* is that the die comes up 3, and event *B* is that the die comes up an even number.

   b. A fair coin is tossed twice. Event *A* is that one of the tosses is a head, and event *B* is that one of the tosses is a tail.

Solution

a. These events are mutually exclusive. The die cannot both come up 3 and come up an even number.

b. These events are not mutually exclusive. If the two tosses result in HT or TH, then both events occur.

Check Your Understanding

2. A college student is chosen at random. Event A is that the student is older than 21 years, and event B is that the student is taking a statistics class. Are events A and B mutually exclusive?

3. A college student is chosen at random. Event A is that the student is an only child, and event B is that the student has a brother. Are events A and B mutually exclusive?

Answers are on page 166.

If events A and B are mutually exclusive, then $P(A \text{ and } B) = 0$. This leads to a simplification of the General Addition Rule.

The Addition Rule for Mutually Exclusive Events

If A and B are mutually exclusive events, then

$$P(A \text{ or } B) = P(A) + P(B)$$

In general, three or more events are mutually exclusive if only one of them can happen. If $A, B, C, \ldots$ are mutually exclusive, then

$$P(A \text{ or } B \text{ or } C \text{ or } \ldots) = P(A) + P(B) + P(C) + \cdots$$

EXAMPLE 4.13 **Compute a probability by using the Addition Rule for Mutually Exclusive Events**

In the 2008 Olympic Games, a total of 11,028 athletes participated. Of these, 596 represented the United States, 332 represented Canada, and 85 represented Mexico.

a. What is the probability that an Olympic athlete chosen at random represents the United States or Canada?

b. What is the probability that an Olympic athlete chosen at random represents the United States, Canada, or Mexico?

Solution

a. These events are mutually exclusive, because it is impossible to compete for both the United States and Canada. We compute $P(\text{U.S.})$ and $P(\text{Canada})$.

$$P(\text{U.S. or Canada}) = P(\text{U.S.}) + P(\text{Canada})$$

$$= \frac{596}{11,028} + \frac{332}{11,028}$$

$$= \frac{928}{11,028}$$

$$= 0.08415$$

b. These events are mutually exclusive, because it is impossible to compete for more than one country. Therefore

$$P(\text{U.S. or Canada or Mexico}) = P(\text{U.S.}) + P(\text{Canada}) + P(\text{Mexico})$$

$$= \frac{596}{11{,}028} + \frac{332}{11{,}028} + \frac{85}{11{,}028}$$

$$= \frac{1013}{11{,}028}$$

$$= 0.09186$$

Check Your Understanding

4. In a statistics class of 45 students, 11 got a final grade of A, 22 got a final grade of B, and 8 got a final grade of C.
   a. What is the probability that a randomly chosen student got an A or a B?
   b. What is the probability that a randomly chosen student got an A, a B, or a C?

Answers are on page 166.

Objective 3 Compute probabilities by using the Rule of Complements

Complements

If there is a 60% chance of rain today, then there is a 40% chance that it will not rain. The events "Rain" and "No rain" are **complements**. The complement of an event A is the event that A does not occur.

DEFINITION

If A is any event, the **complement** of A is the event that A does not occur. The complement of A is denoted A^c.

Explain It Again

The complement occurs when the event doesn't occur: If an event does not occur, then its complement occurs. If an event occurs, then its complement does not occur.

Two important facts about complements are:

1. Either A or A^c must occur. For example, it must either rain or not rain.
2. A and A^c are mutually exclusive; they cannot both occur. For example, it is impossible for it to both rain and not rain.

In probability notation, fact 1 says that $P(A \text{ or } A^c) = 1$, and fact 2 along with the Addition Rule for Mutually Exclusive Events says that $P(A \text{ or } A^c) = P(A) + P(A^c)$. Putting them together, we get

$$P(A) + P(A^c) = 1$$

Subtracting $P(A)$ from both sides yields

$$P(A^c) = 1 - P(A)$$

This is the Rule of Complements.

The Rule of Complements

$$P(A^c) = 1 - P(A)$$

EXAMPLE 4.14 Compute a probability by using the Rule of Complements

According to the *Wall Street Journal*, 42% of cars sold in May 2008 were small cars. What is the probability that a randomly chosen car sold in May 2008 is not a small car?

Solution

$$P(\text{Not a small car}) = 1 - P(\text{Small car}) = 1 - 0.42 = 0.58$$

SECTION 4.2 Exercises

Exercises 1–4 are the Check Your Understanding exercises located within the section.

Understanding the Concepts

In Exercises 5–8, fill in each blank with the appropriate word or phrase.

5. The General Addition Rule states that
$P(A \text{ or } B) = P(A) + P(B) - \underline{\qquad}$.

6. If events A and B are mutually exclusive, then
$P(A \text{ and } B) = \underline{\qquad}$.

7. Given an event A, the event that A does not occur is called the _____ of A.

8. The Rule of Complements states that $P(A^c) = \underline{\qquad}$.

In Exercises 9–12, determine whether the statement is true or false. If the statement is false, rewrite it as a true statement.

9. The General Addition Rule is used for probabilities of the form $P(A \text{ or } B)$.

10. A compound event is formed by combining two or more events.

11. Two events are mutually exclusive if both events can occur.

12. If an event occurs, then its complement also occurs.

Practicing the Skills

13. If $P(A) = 0.75$, $P(B) = 0.4$, and $P(A \text{ and } B) = 0.25$, find $P(A \text{ or } B)$.

14. If $P(A) = 0.45$, $P(B) = 0.7$, and $P(A \text{ and } B) = 0.65$, find $P(A \text{ or } B)$.

15. If $P(A) = 0.2$, $P(B) = 0.5$, and A and B are mutually exclusive, find $P(A \text{ or } B)$.

16. If $P(A) = 0.7$, $P(B) = 0.1$, and A and B are mutually exclusive, find $P(A \text{ or } B)$.

17. If $P(A) = 0.3$, $P(B) = 0.4$, and $P(A \text{ or } B) = 0.7$, are A and B mutually exclusive?

18. If $P(A) = 0.5$, $P(B) = 0.4$, and $P(A \text{ or } B) = 0.8$, are A and B mutually exclusive?

19. If $P(A) = 0.35$, find $P(A^c)$.

20. If $P(B) = 0.6$, find $P(B^c)$.

21. If $P(A^c) = 0.27$, find $P(A)$.

22. If $P(B^c) = 0.64$, find $P(B)$.

23. If $P(A) = 0$, find $P(A^c)$.

24. If $P(A) = P(A^c)$, find $P(A)$.

In Exercises 25–30, determine whether events A and B are mutually exclusive.

25. A: Sophie is a member of the debate team; B: Sophie is the president of the theater club.

26. A: Jayden has a math class on Tuesdays at 2:00; B: Jayden has an English class on Tuesdays at 2:00.

27. A sample of 20 cars is selected from the inventory of a dealership. A: At least 3 of the cars in the sample are red; B: Fewer than 2 of the cars in the sample are red.

28. A sample of 75 books is selected from a library. A: At least 10 of the authors are female; B: At least 10 of the books are fiction.

29. A red die and a blue die are rolled. A: The red die comes up 2; B: The blue die comes up 3.

30. A red die and a blue die are rolled. A: The red die comes up 1; B: The total is 9.

In Exercises 31 and 32, find the complements of the events.

31. A sample of 225 Internet users was selected.
    a. More than 200 of them use Google as their primary search engine.
    b. At least 200 of them use Google as their primary search engine.
    c. Fewer than 200 of them use Google as their primary search engine.
    d. Exactly 200 of them use Google as their primary search engine.

32. A sample of 700 cell phone batteries was selected.
    a. Exactly 24 of the batteries were defective.
    b. At least 24 of the batteries were defective.
    c. More than 24 of the batteries were defective.
    d. Fewer than 24 of the batteries were defective.

Working with the Concepts

33. **Traffic lights:** A commuter passes through two traffic lights on the way to work. Each light is either red, yellow, or green. An experiment consists of observing the colors of the two lights.
    a. List the nine outcomes in the sample space.
    b. Let A be the event that both colors are the same. List the outcomes in A.
    c. Let B be the event that the two colors are different. List the outcomes in B.
    d. Let C be the event that at least one of the lights is green. List the outcomes in C.
    e. Are events A and B mutually exclusive? Explain.
    f. Are events A and C mutually exclusive? Explain.

34. **Dice:** Two fair dice are rolled. The first die is red and the second is blue. An experiment consists of observing the numbers that come up on the dice.
    a. There are 36 outcomes in the sample space. They are ordered pairs of the form (Red die, Blue die). List the 36 outcomes.
    b. Let A be the event that the same number comes up on both dice. List the outcomes in A.
    c. Let B be the event that the red die comes up 6. List the outcomes in B.
    d. Let C be the event that one die comes up 6 and the other comes up 1. List the outcomes in C.
    e. Are events A and B mutually exclusive? Explain.
    f. Are events A and C mutually exclusive? Explain.

35. **Car repairs:** Let E be the event that a new car requires engine work under warranty and let T be the event that the car requires transmission work under warranty. Suppose that $P(E) = 0.10$, $P(T) = 0.02$, and $P(E \text{ and } T) = 0.01$.

a. Find the probability that the car needs work on either the engine, the transmission, or both.

b. Find the probability that the car needs no work on the engine.

36. Sick computers: Let V be the event that a computer contains a virus, and let W be the event that a computer contains a worm. Suppose $P(V) = 0.15$, $P(W) = 0.05$, and $P(V \text{ and } W) = 0.03$.

a. Find the probability that the computer contains either a virus or a worm or both.

b. Find the probability that the computer does not contain a virus.

37. Computer purchases: Out of 800 large purchases made at a computer retailer, 336 were personal computers, 398 were laptop computers, and 66 were printers. As part of an audit, one purchase record is sampled at random.

a. What is the probability that it is a personal computer?

b. What is the probability that it is not a printer?

38. Visit your local library: On a recent Saturday, a total of 1200 people visited a local library. Of these people, 248 were under age 10, 472 were aged 10–18, 175 were aged 19–30, and the rest were more than 30 years old. One person is sampled at random.

a. What is the probability that the person is less than 19 years old?

b. What is the probability that the person is more than 30 years old?

39. How are your grades? In a recent semester at a local university, 500 students enrolled in both Statistics I and Psychology I. Of these students, 82 got an A in statistics, 73 got an A in psychology, and 42 got an A in both statistics and psychology.

a. Find the probability that a randomly chosen student got an A in statistics or psychology or both.

b. Find the probability that a randomly chosen student did not get an A in psychology.

40. Statistics grades: In a statistics class of 30 students, there were 13 men and 17 women. Two of the men and three of the women received an A in the course. A student is chosen at random from the class.

a. Find the probability that the student is a woman.

b. Find the probability that the student received an A.

c. Find the probability that the student is a woman or received an A.

d. Find the probability that the student did not receive an A.

41. Sick children: There are 25 students in Mrs. Bush's sixth-grade class. On a cold winter day in February, many of the students had runny noses and sore throats. After examining each student, the school nurse constructed the following table.

	Sore Throat	No Sore Throat
Runny Nose	6	12
No Runny Nose	4	3

a. Find the probability that a randomly selected student has a runny nose.

b. Find the probability that a randomly selected student has a sore throat.

c. Find the probability that a randomly selected student has a runny nose or a sore throat.

d. Find the probability that a randomly selected student has neither a runny nose nor a sore throat.

42. Flawed parts: On a certain day, a foundry manufactured 500 cast aluminum parts. Some of these had major flaws, some had minor flaws, and some had both major and minor flaws. The following table presents the results.

	Minor Flaw	No Minor Flaw
Major Flaw	20	35
No Major Flaw	75	370

a. Find the probability that a randomly chosen part has a major flaw.

b. Find the probability that a randomly chosen part has a minor flaw.

c. Find the probability that a randomly chosen part has a flaw (major or minor).

d. Find the probability that a randomly chosen part has no major flaw.

e. Find the probability that a randomly chosen part has no flaw.

43. Senators: The following table displays the 100 senators of the 112th U.S. Congress on January 5, 2011, classified by political party affiliation and gender.

	Male	Female	Total
Democrat	39	12	51
Republican	42	5	47
Independent	2	0	2
Total	83	17	100

A senator is selected at random from this group. Compute the following probabilities.

a. The senator is a male Republican.

b. The senator is a Democrat or a female.

c. The senator is a Republican.

d. The senator is not a Republican.

e. The senator is a Democrat.

f. The senator is an Independent.

g. The senator is a Democrat or an Independent.

44. Health insurance: A poll was taken of 121,973 people in the United States aged 15–44 to determine their health insurance status. The participants were classified by gender and by type of insurance coverage. The results were as follows.

Type of Insurance	Male	Female	Total
Private	41,209	42,658	83,867
Medicaid	3,432	6,092	9,524
Other	769	1,140	1,909
Uninsured	15,108	11,565	26,673
Total	60,518	61,455	121,973

Source: Centers for Disease Control and Prevention

A person is selected at random. Compute the following probabilities.

a. The person is male and has private health insurance.
b. The person is female or has private insurance.
c. The person is uninsured.
d. The person is not uninsured.
e. The person has private insurance.
f. The person has Medicaid.
g. The person has private insurance or Medicaid.

Extending the Concepts

45. Mutual exclusivity is not transitive: Give an example of three events A, B, and C, such that A and B are mutually exclusive, B and C are mutually exclusive, but A and C are not mutually exclusive.

46. Complements: Let A and B be events. Express $(A \text{ and } B)^c$ in terms of A^c and B^c.

Answers to Check Your Understanding Exercises for Section 4.2

1. a. 0.342 **b.** 0.361 **c.** 0.469

2. No

3. Yes

4. a. 0.733 **b.** 0.911

SECTION 4.3 Conditional Probability and the Multiplication Rule

Objectives

1. Compute conditional probabilities
2. Compute probabilities by using the General Multiplication Rule
3. Compute probabilities by using the Multiplication Rule for Independent Events
4. Compute the probability that an event occurs at least once

Objective 1 Compute conditional probabilities

Conditional Probability

Approximately 15% of adult men in the United States are more than six feet tall. Therefore, if a man is selected at random, the probability that he is more than six feet tall is 0.15. Now assume that you learn that the selected man is a professional basketball player. With this extra information, the probability that the man is more than six feet tall becomes much greater than 0.15. A probability that is computed with the knowledge of additional information is called a **conditional probability**; a probability computed without such knowledge is called an **unconditional probability**. As this example shows, the conditional probability of an event can be much different than the unconditional probability.

EXAMPLE 4.15 Compute an unconditional probability

Joe, Sam, Eliza, and Maria have been elected to the executive committee of their college's student government. They must choose a chairperson and a secretary. They decide to write each name on a piece of paper and draw two names at random. The first name drawn will be the chairperson and the second name drawn will be the secretary. What is the probability that Joe is the secretary?

Table 4.3 is a sample space for this experiment. The first name in each pair is the chairperson and the second name is the secretary.

Table 4.3 Twelve Equally Likely Outcomes

(Joe, Sam)	(Sam, Joe)	(Eliza, Joe)	(Maria, Joe)
(Joe, Eliza)	(Sam, Eliza)	(Eliza, Sam)	(Maria, Sam)
(Joe, Maria)	(Sam, Maria)	(Eliza, Maria)	(Maria, Eliza)

There are 12 equally likely outcomes. Three of them, (Sam, Joe), (Eliza, Joe), and (Maria, Joe), correspond to Joe's being secretary. Therefore, $P(\text{Joe is secretary}) = 3/12 = 1/4$.

EXAMPLE 4.16

Compute a conditional probability

Suppose that Eliza is the first name selected, so she is chairperson. Now what is the probability that Joe is secretary?

Solution

We'll answer this question with intuition first, then show the reasoning. Since Eliza was chosen to be chairperson, she won't be the secretary. That leaves Joe, Sam, and Maria. Each of these three is equally likely to be chosen. Therefore, the probability that Joe is chosen as secretary is 1/3. Note that this probability differs from the probability of 1/4 calculated in Example 4.15.

Now let's look at the reasoning behind this answer. The original sample space, shown in Table 4.3, had 12 outcomes. Once we know that Eliza is chairperson, we know that only three of those outcomes are now possible. Table 4.4 highlights these three outcomes from the original sample space.

Table 4.4

(Joe, Sam)	(Sam, Joe)	(Eliza, Joe)	(Maria, Joe)
(Joe, Eliza)	(Sam, Eliza)	(Eliza, Sam)	(Maria, Sam)
(Joe, Maria)	(Sam, Maria)	(Eliza, Maria)	(Maria, Eliza)

Of the three possible outcomes, only one, (Eliza, Joe), has Joe as secretary. Therefore, given that Eliza is chairperson, the probability that Joe is secretary is 1/3.

Example 4.16 asked us to compute the probability of an event (that Joe is secretary) after giving us information about another event (that Eliza is chairperson). A probability like this is called a **conditional probability**. The notation for this conditional probability is

$$P(\text{Joe is secretary} \mid \text{Eliza is chairperson})$$

We read this as "the conditional probability that Joe is secretary, given that Eliza is chairperson." It denotes the probability that Joe is secretary, under the assumption that Eliza is chairperson.

DEFINITION

The **conditional probability** of an event B, given an event A, is denoted $P(B \mid A)$.

$P(B \mid A)$ is the probability that B occurs, under the assumption that A occurs.

We read $P(B \mid A)$ as "the probability of B, given A."

The General Method for computing conditional probabilities

In Example 4.16, we computed

$$P(\text{Joe is secretary} \mid \text{Eliza is chairperson}) = \frac{1}{3}$$

Let's take a closer look at the answer of 1/3. The denominator is the number of outcomes that were left in the sample space after it was known that Eliza was chairperson. That is,

$$\text{Number of outcomes where Eliza is chairperson} = 3$$

The numerator is 1, and this corresponds to the one outcome in which Eliza is chairperson and Joe is secretary. That is,

$$\text{Number of outcomes where Eliza is chairperson and Joe is secretary} = 1$$

Therefore, we see that

P(Joe is secretary | Eliza is chairperson)

$$= \frac{\text{Number of outcomes where Eliza is chairperson and Joe is secretary}}{\text{Number of outcomes where Eliza is chairperson}}$$

We can obtain another useful method by recalling that there were 12 outcomes in the original sample space. It follows that

$$P(\text{Eliza is chairperson}) = \frac{3}{12}$$

and

$$P(\text{Eliza is chairperson and Joe is secretary}) = \frac{1}{12}$$

We now see that

$$P(\text{Joe is secretary} \mid \text{Eliza is chairperson}) = \frac{P(\text{Eliza is chairperson and Joe is secretary})}{P(\text{Eliza is chairperson})}$$

This example illustrates the General Method for computing conditional probabilities, which we now state.

The General Method for Computing Conditional Probabilities

The probability of B given A is

$$P(B \mid A) = \frac{P(A \text{ and } B)}{P(A)}$$

Note that we cannot compute $P(B \mid A)$ if $P(A) = 0$.

When the outcomes in the sample space are equally likely, then

$$P(B \mid A) = \frac{\text{Number of outcomes corresponding to } (A \text{ and } B)}{\text{Number of outcomes corresponding to } A}$$

EXAMPLE 4.17   **Use the General Method to compute a conditional probability**

Table 4.5 presents the number of U.S. men and women (in millions) 25 years old and older who have attained various levels of education as of March 2007.

Table 4.5 Number of Men and Women with Various Levels of Education (in millions)

	Not a high school graduate	High school graduate	Some college, no degree	Associate's degree	Bachelor's degree	Advanced degree
Men	14.0	29.6	15.6	7.2	17.5	10.1
Women	13.7	31.9	17.5	9.6	19.2	9.1

Source: U.S. Census Bureau

A person is selected at random.

a. What is the probability that the person is a man?

b. What is the probability that the person is a man with a bachelor's degree?

c. What is the probability that the person has a bachelor's degree, given that the person is a man?

Solution

a. Each person in the study is an outcome in the sample space. We first compute the total number of people in the study. We'll do this by computing the total number of men, then the total number of women.

Total number of men $= 14.0 + 29.6 + 15.6 + 7.2 + 17.5 + 10.1 = 94.0$

Total number of women $= 13.7 + 31.9 + 17.5 + 9.6 + 19.2 + 9.1 = 101.0$

There are 94.0 million men and 101.0 million women. The total number of people is $94.0 + 101.0 = 195.0$ million. We can now compute the probability that a randomly chosen person is a man.

$$P(\text{Man}) = \frac{94.0}{195.0} = 0.4821$$

b. The number of men with bachelor's degrees is found in Table 4.5 to be 17.5 million. The total number of people is 195.0 million. Therefore

$$P(\text{Man with a Bachelor's degree}) = \frac{17.5}{195.0} = 0.08974$$

c. We use the General Method for computing a conditional probability.

$$P(\text{Bachelor's degree}|\text{Man}) = \frac{P(\text{Man with a Bachelor's degree})}{P(\text{Man})} = \frac{17.5/195.0}{94.0/195.0} = 0.1862$$

Check Your Understanding

1. A person is selected at random from the population in Table 4.5.
   a. What is the probability that the person is a woman who is a high school graduate?
   b. What is the probability that the person is a high school graduate?
   c. What is the probability that the person is a woman, given that the person is a high school graduate?

Answers are on page 178.

Objective 2 Compute probabilities by using the General Multiplication Rule

The General Multiplication Rule

The General Method for computing conditional probabilities provides a way to compute probabilities for events of the form "A and B." If we multiply both sides of the equation by $P(A)$ we obtain the General Multiplication Rule.

Explain It Again

The General Multiplication Rule: Use the General Multiplication Rule to compute probabilities of the form $P(A \text{ and } B)$.

The General Multiplication Rule

$$P(A \text{ and } B) = P(A)P(B \mid A)$$

or, equivalently,

$$P(A \text{ and } B) = P(B)P(A \mid B)$$

EXAMPLE 4.18

Use the General Multiplication Rule to compute a probability

Among those who apply for a particular job, the probability of being granted an interview is 0.1. Among those interviewed, the probability of being offered a job is 0.25. Find the probability that an applicant is offered a job.

Solution

Being offered a job involves two events. First, a person must be interviewed; then, given that the person has been interviewed, the person must be offered a job. Using the General Multiplication Rule, we obtain

$$P(\text{Offered a job}) = P(\text{Interviewed})P(\text{Offered a job} \mid \text{Interviewed})$$
$$= (0.1)(0.25)$$
$$= 0.025$$

Check Your Understanding

2. In a certain city, 70% of high school students graduate. Of those who graduate, 40% attend college. Find the probability that a randomly selected high school student will attend college.

Answer is on page 178.

Objective 3 Compute probabilities by using the Multiplication Rule for Independent Events

Independence

In some cases, the occurrence of one event has no effect on the probability that another event occurs. For example, if a coin is tossed twice, the occurrence of a head on the first toss does not make it any more or less likely that a head will come up on the second toss. Example 4.19 illustrates this fact.

EXAMPLE 4.19   Coin tossing probabilities

A fair coin is tossed twice.

> **a.** What is the probability that the second toss is a head?
> **b.** What is the probability that the second toss is a head given that the first toss is a head?
> **c.** Are the answers to (a) and (b) different? Does the probability that the second toss is a head change if the first toss is a head?

CAUTION

Do not confuse independent events with mutually exclusive events. Two events are independent if the occurrence of one does not affect the probability of the occurrence of the other. Two events are mutually exclusive if the occurrence of one makes it impossible for the other to occur.

Solution

> **a.** There are four equally likely outcomes for the two tosses. The sample space is {HH, HT, TH, TT}. Of these, there are two outcomes where the second toss is a head. Therefore, $P(\text{Second toss is H}) = 2/4 = 1/2$.
> **b.** We use the General Method for computing conditional probabilities.
>
> $$P(\text{Second toss is H} \mid \text{First toss is H})$$
> $$= \frac{\text{Number of outcomes where first toss is H and second is H}}{\text{Number of outcomes where first toss is H}} = \frac{1}{2}$$
>
> **c.** The two answers are the same. The probability that the second toss is a head does not change if the first toss is a head. In other words,
>
> $$P(\text{Second toss is H} \mid \text{First toss is H}) = P(\text{Second toss is H})$$

In the case of two coin tosses, the outcome of the first toss does not affect the second toss. Events with this property are said to be **independent**.

DEFINITION

Two events are **independent** if the occurrence of one does not affect the probability that the other event occurs.

If two events are not independent, we say they are **dependent**.

In many situations, we can determine whether events are independent just by understanding the circumstances surrounding the events. Example 4.20 illustrates this.

EXAMPLE 4.20

Determine whether events are independent

Determine whether the following pairs of events are independent:

a. A college student is chosen at random. The events are "being a freshman" and "being less than 20 years old."

b. A college student is chosen at random. The events are "born on a Sunday" and "taking a statistics class."

Solution

a. These events are not independent. If the student is a freshman, the probability that the student is less than 20 years old is greater than for a student who is not a freshman.

b. These events are independent. If a student was born on a Sunday, this has no effect on the probability that the student takes a statistics class.

When two events, A and B, are independent, then $P(B \mid A) = P(B)$, because knowing that A occurred does not affect the probability that B occurs. This leads to a simplified version of the Multiplication Rule.

Explain It Again

The Multiplication Rule for Independent Events: Use the Multiplication Rule for Independent Events to compute probabilities of the form $P(A$ and $B)$ when A and B are independent.

The Multiplication Rule for Independent Events

If A and B are independent events, then

$$P(A \text{ and } B) = P(A)P(B)$$

This rule can be extended to the case where there are more than two independent events. If A, B, C, ... are independent events, then

$$P(A \text{ and } B \text{ and } C \text{ and } \ldots) = P(A)P(B)P(C) \cdots$$

EXAMPLE 4.21

Using the Multiplication Rule for Independent Events

According to recent figures from the U.S. Census Bureau, the percentage of people under the age of 18 was 23.5% in New York City, 25.8% in Chicago, and 26.0% in Los Angeles. If one person is selected from each city, what is the probability that all of them are under 18? Is this an unusual event?

Solution

There are three events: person from New York is under 18, person from Chicago is under 18, and person from Los Angeles is under 18. These three events are independent, because the identity of the person chosen from one city does not affect who is chosen in the other cities. We therefore use the Multiplication Rule for Independent Events. Let N denote the event that the person from New York is under 18, and let C and L denote the corresponding events for Chicago and Los Angeles, respectively.

$$P(N \text{ and } C \text{ and } L) = P(N) \cdot P(C) \cdot P(L) = 0.235 \cdot 0.258 \cdot 0.260 = 0.0158$$

The probability is 0.0158. This is an unusual event, if we apply the most commonly used cutoff point of 0.05.

Distinguishing mutually exclusive from independent

Although the mutually exclusive property and the independence property are quite different, in practice it can be difficult to distinguish them. The following diagram can help you to determine whether two events are mutually exclusive, independent, or neither.

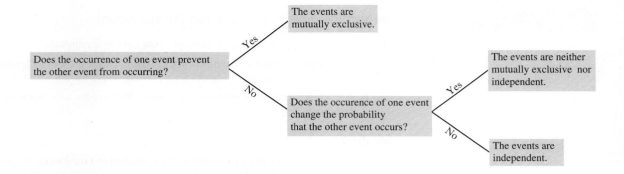

Check Your Understanding

3. Two dice are rolled. Each comes up with a number between 1 and 6. Let A be the event that the number on the first die is even, and let B be the event that the number on the second die is 6.
   a. Explain why events A and B are independent.
   b. Find $P(A)$, $P(B)$, and $P(A \text{ and } B)$.

Answers are on page 178.

Sampling with and without replacement

When we sample two items from a population, we can proceed in either of two ways. We can replace the first item drawn before sampling the second; this is known as **sampling with replacement**. When sampling with replacement, it is possible to draw the same item more than once. The other option is to leave the first item out when sampling the second one; this is known as **sampling without replacement**. When sampling without replacement, it is impossible to sample an item more than once.

   When sampling with replacement, each draw is made from the entire population, so the probability of drawing a particular item on the second draw does not depend on the first draw. In other words, when sampling with replacement, the draws are independent. When sampling without replacement, the draws are not independent. Examples 4.22 and 4.23 illustrate this idea.

EXAMPLE 4.22   Sampling without replacement

A box contains two cards marked with a "0" and two cards marked with a "1" as shown in the following illustration. Two cards will be sampled without replacement from this population.

$$\boxed{\; \boxed{0} \quad \boxed{0} \quad \boxed{1} \quad \boxed{1} \;}$$

   a. What is the probability of drawing a $\boxed{1}$ on the second draw given that the first draw is a $\boxed{0}$?
   b. What is the probability of drawing a $\boxed{1}$ on the second draw given that the first draw is a $\boxed{1}$?
   c. Are the first and second draws independent?

Solution

   a. If the first draw is a $\boxed{0}$, then the second draw will be made from the population $\boxed{\; \boxed{0} \quad \boxed{1} \quad \boxed{1} \;}$. There are three equally likely outcomes, and two of them are $\boxed{1}$. The probability of drawing a $\boxed{1}$ is 2/3.

b. If the first draw is a $\boxed{1}$, then the second draw will be made from the population $\boxed{0}$ $\boxed{0}$ $\boxed{1}$. There are three equally likely outcomes, and one of them is $\boxed{1}$. The probability of drawing a $\boxed{1}$ is 1/3.

c. The first and second draws are not independent. The probability of drawing a $\boxed{1}$ on the second draw depends on the outcome of the first draw.

EXAMPLE 4.23

Sampling with replacement

Two items will be sampled with replacement from the population in Example 4.22. Does the probability of drawing a $\boxed{1}$ on the second draw depend on the outcome of the first draw? Are the first and second draws independent?

Solution

Since the sampling is with replacement, then no matter what the first draw is, the second draw will be made from the entire population $\boxed{0}$ $\boxed{0}$ $\boxed{1}$ $\boxed{1}$. Therefore, the probability of drawing a $\boxed{1}$ on the second draw is $2/4 = 0.5$ no matter what the first draw is. Since the probability on the second draw does not depend on the outcome of the first draw, the first and second draws are independent.

The population in Examples 4.22 and 4.23 was very small — only four items. When the population is large, the draws will be nearly independent even when sampled without replacement, as illustrated in Example 4.24.

EXAMPLE 4.24

Sampling without replacement from a large population

A box contains 1000 cards marked with a "0" and 1000 cards marked with a "1" as shown in the following illustration. Two cards will be sampled without replacement from this population.

$$\boxed{1000\ \boxed{0}\text{'s} \qquad 1000\ \boxed{1}\text{'s}}$$

a. What is the probability of drawing a $\boxed{1}$ on the second draw given that the first draw is a $\boxed{0}$?

b. What is the probability of drawing a $\boxed{1}$ on the second draw given that the first draw is a $\boxed{1}$?

c. Are the first and second draws independent? Are they approximately independent?

Solution

a. If the first draw is a $\boxed{0}$, then the second draw will be made from the population $\boxed{999\ \boxed{0}\text{'s} \qquad 1000\ \boxed{1}\text{'s}}$. There are 1999 equally likely outcomes, and 1000 of them are $\boxed{1}$. The probability of drawing a $\boxed{1}$ is $1000/1999 = 0.50025$.

b. If the first draw is a $\boxed{1}$, then the second draw will be made from the population $\boxed{1000\ \boxed{0}\text{'s} \qquad 999\ \boxed{1}\text{'s}}$. There are 1999 equally likely outcomes, and 999 of them are $\boxed{1}$. The probability of drawing a $\boxed{1}$ is $999/1999 = 0.49975$.

c. The probability of drawing a $\boxed{1}$ on the second draw depends slightly on the outcome of the first draw, so the draws are not independent. However, because the difference in the probabilities is so small (0.50025 versus 0.49975), the draws are approximately independent. In practice, it would be appropriate to treat the two draws as independent.

Example 4.24 shows that when the sample size is small compared to the population size, then items sampled without replacement may be treated as independent. A rule of thumb is that the items may be treated as independent so long as the sample comprises less than 5% of the population.

SUMMARY

- When sampling with replacement, the sampled items are independent.
- When sampling without replacement, if the sample size is less than 5% of the population, the sampled items may be treated as independent.
- When sampling without replacement, if the sample size is more than 5% of the population, the sampled items cannot be treated as independent.

Check Your Understanding

4. A pollster plans to sample 1500 voters from a city in which there are 1 million voters. Can the sampled voters be treated as independent? Explain.

5. Five hundred students attend a college basketball game. Fifty of them are chosen at random to receive a free T-shirt. Can the sampled students be treated as independent? Explain.

Answers are on page 178.

Objective 4 Compute the probability that an event occurs at least once

Solving "at least once" problems by using complements

Sometimes we need to find the probability that an event occurs **at least once** in several independent trials. We can calculate such probabilities by finding the probability of the complement and subtracting from 1. Example 4.25 illustrates the method.

EXAMPLE 4.25

Find the probability that an event occurs at least once

A fair coin is tossed five times. What is the probability that it comes up heads at least once?

Solution
The tosses of a coin are independent, since the outcome of a toss is not affected by the outcomes of other tosses. The complement of coming up heads at least once is coming up tails all five times. We use the Rule of Complements to compute the probability.

$$P(\text{Comes up heads at least once})$$
$$= 1 - P(\text{Comes up tails all five times})$$
$$= 1 - P(\text{First toss is T and Second toss is T and} \ldots \text{and Fifth toss is T})$$
$$= 1 - P(\text{First toss is T})P(\text{Second toss is T}) \cdots P(\text{Fifth toss is T})$$
$$= 1 - \left(\frac{1}{2}\right)^5$$
$$= \frac{31}{32}$$

Check Your Understanding

6. An office has three smoke detectors. In case of fire, each detector has probability 0.9 of detecting it. If a fire occurs, what is the probability that at least one detector detects it?

Answer is on page 178.

Determining Which Method to Use

We have studied several methods for finding probabilities of events of the form $P(A$ and $B)$, $P(A$ or $B)$, and $P(\text{At least one})$. The following diagram can help you to determine the correct method to use for calculating these probabilities.

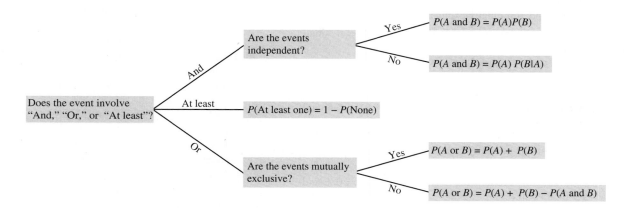

SECTION 4.3   Exercises

Exercises 1–6 are the Check Your Understanding exercises located within the section.

Understanding the Concepts

In Exercises 7–10, fill in each blank with the appropriate word or phrase.

7. A probability that is computed with the knowledge of additional information is called a _____ probability.

8. The General Multiplication Rule states that $P(A$ and $B) = $ _____.

9. When sampling without replacement, if the sample size is less than _____ % of the population, the sampled items may be treated as independent.

10. Two events are _____ if the occurrence of one does not affect the probability that the other event occurs.

In Exercises 11–14, determine whether the statement is true or false. If the statement is false, rewrite it as a true statement.

11. $P(B \mid A)$ represents the probability that A occurs under the assumption that B occurs.

12. If A and B are independent events, then $P(A$ and $B) = P(A)P(B)$.

13. When sampling without replacement, it is possible to draw the same item from the population more than once.

14. When sampling with replacement, the sampled items are independent.

Practicing the Skills

15. Let A and B be events with $P(A) = 0.4$, $P(B) = 0.7$, and $P(B \mid A) = 0.3$. Find $P(A$ and $B)$.

16. Let A and B be events with $P(A) = 0.6$, $P(B) = 0.4$, and $P(B \mid A) = 0.4$. Find $P(A$ and $B)$.

17. Let A and B be events with $P(A) = 0.2$ and $P(B) = 0.9$. Assume that A and B are independent. Find $P(A$ and $B)$.

18. Let A and B be events with $P(A) = 0.5$ and $P(B) = 0.7$. Assume that A and B are independent. Find $P(A$ and $B)$.

19. Let A and B be events with $P(A) = 0.8$, $P(B) = 0.1$, and $P(B \mid A) = 0.2$. Find $P(A$ and $B)$.

20. Let A and B be events with $P(A) = 0.3$, $P(B) = 0.5$, and $P(B \mid A) = 0.7$. Find $P(A$ and $B)$.

21. Let A, B, and C be independent events with $P(A) = 0.7$, $P(B) = 0.8$, and $P(C) = 0.5$. Find $P(A$ and B and $C)$.

22. Let A, B, and C be independent events with $P(A) = 0.4$, $P(B) = 0.9$, and $P(C) = 0.7$. Find $P(A$ and B and $C)$.

23. A fair coin is tossed four times. What is the probability that all four tosses are heads?

24. A fair coin is tossed four times. What is the probability that the sequence of tosses is HTHT?

25. A fair die is rolled three times. What is the probability that the sequence of rolls is 1, 2, 3?

26. A fair die is rolled three times. What is the probability that all three rolls are 6?

In Exercises 27–30, assume that a student is chosen at random from a class. Determine whether the events A and B are independent, mutually exclusive, or neither.

27. A: The student is a freshman.
    B: The student is a sophomore.

28. A: The student is on the basketball team.
    B: The student is more than six feet tall.

29. A: The student is a woman.
    B: The student belongs to a sorority.

30. *A*: The student is a woman.
   B: The student belongs to a fraternity.

31. Let *A* and *B* be events with $P(A) = 0.25$, $P(B) = 0.4$, and $P(A \text{ and } B) = 0.1$.
   a. Are *A* and *B* independent? Explain.
   b. Compute $P(A \text{ or } B)$.
   c. Are *A* and *B* mutually exclusive? Explain.

32. Let *A* and *B* be events with $P(A) = 0.6$, $P(B) = 0.9$, and $P(A \text{ and } B) = 0.5$.
   a. Are *A* and *B* independent? Explain.
   b. Compute $P(A \text{ or } B)$.
   c. Are *A* and *B* mutually exclusive? Explain.

33. Let *A* and *B* be events with $P(A) = 0.4$, $P(B) = 0.5$, and $P(A \text{ or } B) = 0.6$.
   a. Compute $P(A \text{ and } B)$.
   b. Are *A* and *B* mutually exclusive? Explain.
   c. Are *A* and *B* independent? Explain.

34. Let *A* and *B* be events with $P(A) = 0.5$, $P(B) = 0.3$, and $P(A \text{ or } B) = 0.8$.
   a. Compute $P(A \text{ and } B)$.
   b. Are *A* and *B* mutually exclusive? Explain.
   c. Are *A* and *B* independent? Explain.

35. A fair die is rolled three times. What is the probability that it comes up 6 at least once?

36. An unfair coin has probability 0.4 of landing heads. The coin is tossed four times. What is the probability that it lands heads at least once?

Working with the Concepts

37. Job interview: Seven people, named Anna, Bob, Chandra, Darlene, Ed, Frank, and Gina, will be interviewed for a job. The interviewer will choose two at random to interview on the first day. What is the probability that Anna is interviewed first and Darlene is interviewed second?

38. Shuffle: Charles has six songs on a playlist. Each song is by a different artist. The artists are Usher, Ke$ha, Lady Gaga, Eminem, the Black Eyed Peas, and Ludacris. He programs his player to play the songs in a random order, without repetition. What is the probability that the first song is by Lady Gaga and the second song is by Eminem?

39. Let's eat: A fast-food restaurant chain has 600 outlets in the United States. The following table categorizes them by city population size and location, and presents the number of restaurants in each category. A restaurant is to be chosen at random from the 600 to test market a new menu.

Population	Region			
of city	NE	SE	SW	NW
Under 50,000	30	35	15	5
50,000–500,000	60	90	70	30
Over 500,000	150	25	30	60

   a. Given that the restaurant is located in a city with a population over 500,000, what is the probability that it is in the Northeast?
   b. Given that the restaurant is located in the Southeast, what is the probability that it is in a city with a population under 50,000?

   c. Given that the restaurant is located in the Southwest, what is the probability that it is in a city with a population of 500,000 or less?
   d. Given that the restaurant is located in a city with a population of 500,000 or less, what is the probability that it is in the Southwest?
   e. Given that the restaurant is located in the South (either SE or SW), what is the probability that it is in a city with a population of 50,000 or more?

40. U.S. senators: The following table displays the 100 senators of the 112th U.S. Congress on January 5, 2011, viewed by political party affiliation and gender.

	Male	Female	Total
Democrat	39	12	51
Republican	42	5	47
Independent	2	0	2
Total	83	17	100

A senator is selected at random from this group.
   a. What is the probability that the senator is a woman?
   b. What is the probability that the senator is a Republican?
   c. What is the probability that the senator is a Republican and a woman?
   d. Given that the senator is a woman, what is the probability that she is a Republican?
   e. Given that the senator is a Republican, what is the probability that the senator is a woman?

41. Genetics: A geneticist is studying two genes. Each gene can be either dominant or recessive. A sample of 100 individuals is categorized as follows.

	Gene 2	
Gene 1	**Dominant**	**Recessive**
Dominant	56	24
Recessive	14	6

   a. What is the probability that in a randomly sampled individual, gene 1 is dominant?
   b. What is the probability that in a randomly sampled individual, gene 2 is dominant?
   c. Given that gene 1 is dominant, what is the probability that gene 2 is dominant?
   d. Two genes are said to be in linkage equilibrium if the event that gene 1 is dominant is independent of the event that gene 2 is dominant. Are these genes in linkage equilibrium?

42. Quality control: A population of 600 semiconductor wafers contains wafers from three lots. The wafers are categorized by lot and by whether they conform to a thickness specification, with the results shown in the following table. A wafer is chosen at random from the population.

Lot	Conforming	Nonconforming
A	88	12
B	165	35
C	260	40

a. What is the probability that a wafer is from Lot A?

b. What is the probability that a wafer is conforming?

c. What is the probability that a wafer is from Lot A and is conforming?

d. Given that the wafer is from Lot A, what is the probability that it is conforming?

e. Given that the wafer is conforming, what is the probability that it is from Lot A?

f. Let E_1 be the event that the wafer comes from Lot A, and let E_2 be the event that the wafer is conforming. Are E_1 and E_2 independent? Explain.

43. Stay in school: In a recent school year in the state of Washington, there were 326,000 high school students. Of these, 159,000 were girls and 167,000 were boys. Among the girls, 7800 dropped out of school, and among the boys, 10,300 dropped out. A student is chosen at random.

a. What is the probability that the student is male?

b. What is the probability that the student dropped out?

c. What is the probability that the student is male and dropped out?

d. Given that the student is male, what is the probability that he dropped out?

e. Given that the student dropped out, what is the probability that the student is male?

44. Management: The Bureau of Labor Statistics reported that 64.5 million women and 74.6 million men were employed. Of the women, 25.8 million had management jobs, and of the men, 25.0 million had management jobs. An employed person is chosen at random.

a. What is the probability that the person is a female?

b. What is the probability that the person has a management job?

c. What is the probability that the person is female and has a management job?

d. Given that the person is female, what is the probability that she has a management job?

e. Given that the person has a management job, what is the probability that the person is female?

45. GED: In a certain high school, the probability that a student drops out is 0.05, and the probability that a dropout gets a high-school equivalency diploma (GED) is 0.25. What is the probability that a randomly selected student gets a GED?

46. Working for a living: The Bureau of Labor Statistics reported that in 2008, the probability that a randomly chosen employed adult worked in a service occupation was 0.17, and given that a person was in a service occupation, the probability that the person was a woman was 0.57. What is the probability that a randomly chosen employed person was a woman in a service occupation?

47. New car: At a certain car dealership, the probability that a customer purchases an SUV is 0.20. Given that a customer purchases an SUV, the probability that it is black is 0.25. What is the probability that a customer purchases a black SUV?

48. Do you know Squidward? According to a survey by Nickelodeon TV, 88% of children under 13 in Germany recognized a picture of the cartoon character SpongeBob

SquarePants. Assume that among those children, 72% also recognized SpongeBob's cranky neighbor Squidward Tentacles. What is the probability that a German child recognized both SpongeBob and Squidward?

49. Target practice: Laura and Philip each fire one shot at a target. Laura has probability 0.5 of hitting the target, and Philip has probability 0.3. The shots are independent.

a. Find the probability that both of them hit the target.

b. Given that Laura hits the target, the probability is 0.1 that Philip's shot hits the target closer to the bull's-eye than Laura's. Find the probability that Laura hits the target and that Philip's shot is closer to the bull's-eye than Laura's shot is.

50. Bowling: Sarah and Thomas are going bowling. The probability that Sarah scores more than 175 is 0.4, and the probability that Thomas scores more than 175 is 0.2. Their scores are independent.

a. Find the probability that both score more than 175.

b. Given that Thomas scores more than 175, the probability that Sarah scores higher than Thomas is 0.3. Find the probability that Thomas scores more than 175 and Sarah scores higher than Thomas.

51. Defective components: A lot of 10 components contains 3 that are defective. Two components are drawn at random and tested. Let A be the event that the first component drawn is defective, and let B be the event that the second component drawn is defective.

a. Find $P(A)$.

b. Find $P(B \mid A)$.

c. Find $P(A \text{ and } B)$.

d. Are A and B independent? Explain.

52. More defective components: A lot of 1000 components contains 300 that are defective. Two components are drawn at random and tested. Let A be the event that the first component drawn is defective, and let B be the event that the second component drawn is defective.

a. Find $P(A)$.

b. Find $P(B \mid A)$.

c. Find $P(A \text{ and } B)$.

d. Are A and B independent? Is it reasonable to treat A and B as though they were independent? Explain.

53. Lottery: Every day, Jorge buys a lottery ticket. Each ticket has probability 0.2 of winning a prize. After seven days, what is the probability that Jorge has won at least one prize?

54. Car warranty: The probability that a certain make of car will need repairs in the first six months is 0.3. A dealer sells five such cars. What is the probability that at least one of them will require repairs in the first six months?

Extending the Concepts

Exercises 55–58 refer to the following situation:

A medical test is available to determine whether a patient has a certain disease. To determine the accuracy of the test, a total of 10,100 people are tested. Only 100 of these people have the disease, while the other 10,000 are disease free. Of the disease-free people, 9800 get a negative result, and 200 get a positive result. The 100 people with the disease all get positive results.

55. Find the probability: Find the probability that the test gives the correct result for a person who does not have the disease.

56. Find the probability: Find the probability that the test gives the correct result for a person who has the disease.

57. Find the probability: Given that a person gets a positive result, what is the probability that the person actually has the disease?

58. Why are medical tests repeated? For many medical tests, if the result comes back positive, the test is repeated. Why do you think this is done?

59. Mutually exclusive and independent? Let A and B be events. Assume that neither A nor B can occur; in other words, $P(A) = 0$ and $P(B) = 0$. Are A and B independent? Are A and B mutually exclusive? Explain.

60. Still mutually exclusive and independent? Let A and B be events. Now assume that $P(A) = 0$ but $P(B) > 0$. Are A and B always independent? Are A and B always mutually exclusive? Explain.

61. Mutually exclusive and independent again? Let A and B be events. Now assume that $P(A) > 0$ and $P(B) > 0$. Is it possible for A and B to be both independent and mutually exclusive? Explain.

Answers to Check Your Understanding Exercises for Section 4.3

1. **a.** 0.164   **b.** 0.315   **c.** 0.519

2. 0.28

3. **a.** The outcome on one die does not influence the outcome on the other die.

   b. $P(A) = 1/2$; $P(B) = 1/6$; $P(A \text{ and } B) = 1/12$

4. Yes, because the sample is less than 5% of the population.

5. No, because the sample is more than 5% of the population.

6. 0.999

SECTION 4.4 | Counting

Objectives

1. Count the number of ways a sequence of operations can be performed
2. Count the number of permutations
3. Count the number of combinations

When computing probabilities, it is sometimes necessary to count the number of outcomes in a sample space without being able to list them all. In this section, we will describe several methods for doing this.

Objective 1 Count the number of ways a sequence of operations can be performed

The Fundamental Principle of Counting

The basic rule, which we will call the **Fundamental Principle of Counting**, is presented by means of the following example:

EXAMPLE 4.26   Using the Fundamental Principle of Counting

A certain make of automobile is available in any of three colors — red, blue, or green — and comes with either a large or small engine. In how many ways can a buyer choose a car?

Solution

There are 3 choices of color and 2 choices of engine. A complete list is shown in the tree diagram in Figure 4.5, and in the form of a table in Table 4.6. The total number of choices is $3 \cdot 2 = 6$.

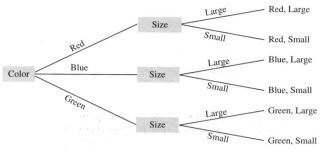

Figure 4.5 Tree diagram illustrating the six choices of color and engine size

Table 4.6 Six Outcomes for the Color and Engine Size

	Large	**Small**
Red	Red, Large	Red, Small
Blue	Blue, Large	Blue, Small
Green	Green, Large	Green, Small

To generalize Example 4.26, if there are m choices of color and n choices of engine, the total number of choices is mn. This leads to the **Fundamental Principle of Counting**.

The Fundamental Principle of Counting

If an operation can be performed in m ways, and a second operation can be performed in n ways, then the total number of ways to perform the sequence of two operations is mn.

If a sequence of several operations is to be performed, the number of ways to perform the sequence is found by multiplying together the numbers of ways to perform each of the operations.

EXAMPLE 4.27 Using the Fundamental Principle of Counting

License plates in a certain state contain three letters followed by three digits. How many different license plates can be made?

Solution

There are six operations in all: choosing three letters and choosing three digits. There are 26 ways to choose each letter and 10 ways to choose each digit. The total number of license plates is therefore

$$26 \cdot 26 \cdot 26 \cdot 10 \cdot 10 \cdot 10 = 17,576,000$$

Check Your Understanding

1. When ordering a certain type of computer, there are three choices of hard drive, four choices for the amount of memory, two choices of video card, and three choices of monitor. In how many ways can a computer be ordered?

2. A quiz consists of three true-false questions and two multiple-choice questions with five choices each. How many different sets of answers are there?

Answers are on page 186.

Objective 2 Count the number of permutations

Permutations

The word *permutation* is another word for *ordering*. When we count the number of permutations, we are counting the number of different ways that a group of items can be ordered.

EXAMPLE 4.28 Counting the number of permutations

Five runners run a race. One of them will finish first, another will finish second, and so on. In how many different orders can they finish?

Solution

We use the Fundamental Principle of Counting. There are five possible choices for the first-place finisher. Once the first-place finisher has been determined, there are four remaining choices for the second-place finisher. Then there are three possible choices for the third-place finisher, two choices for the fourth-place finisher, and only one choice for the fifth-place finisher. The total number of orders of five individuals is

$$\text{Number of orders} = 5 \cdot 4 \cdot 3 \cdot 2 \cdot 1 = 120$$

We say that there are 120 permutations of five individuals.

In Example 4.28, we computed a number of permutations by using the Fundamental Principle of Counting. We can generalize this method, but first we need some notation.

DEFINITION

For any positive integer n, the number $n!$ is pronounced "n factorial" and is equal to the product of all the integers from n down to 1.

$$n! = n(n-1)\ldots(2)(1)$$

By definition, $0! = 1$.

In Example 4.28, we found that the number of permutations of five objects is $5!$. This idea holds in general.

The number of permutations of n objects is $n!$.

Sometimes we want to count the number of permutations of a part of a group. Example 4.29 illustrates the idea.

EXAMPLE 4.29   Counting the number of permutations

Ten runners enter a race. The first-place finisher will win a gold medal, the second-place finisher will win a silver medal, and the third-place finisher will win a bronze medal. In how many different ways can the medals be awarded?

Solution

We use the Fundamental Principle of Counting. There are 10 possible choices for the gold-medal winner. Once the gold-medal winner is determined, there are nine remaining choices for the silver medal. Finally, there are eight choices for the bronze medal. The total number of ways the medals can be awarded is

$$10 \cdot 9 \cdot 8 = 720$$

In Example 4.29, three runners were chosen from a group of ten, then ordered as first, second, and third. This is referred to as a **permutation** of three items chosen from ten.

DEFINITION

A **permutation** of r items chosen from n items is an ordering of the r items. It is obtained by choosing r items from a group of n items, then choosing an order for the r items.

Notation: The number of permutations of r items chosen from n is denoted $_nP_r$.

In Example 4.29, we computed $_nP_r$ by using the Fundamental Principle of Counting. We can generalize this method by using factorial notation.

The number of permutations of r objects chosen from n is

$$_nP_r = n(n-1)\cdots(n-r+1) = \frac{n!}{(n-r)!}$$

EXAMPLE 4.30   Counting the number of permutations

Five lifeguards are available for duty one Saturday afternoon. There are three lifeguard stations. In how many ways can three lifeguards be chosen and ordered among the stations?

Solution
We are choosing three items from a group of five and ordering them. The number of ways to do this is

$$_5P_3 = \frac{5!}{(5-3)!} = \frac{5!}{2!} = \frac{5\cdot4\cdot3\cdot2\cdot1}{2\cdot1} = 5\cdot4\cdot3 = 60$$

In some situations, computing the value of $_nP_r$ enables us to determine the number of outcomes in a sample space, and thereby compute a probability. Example 4.31 illustrates the idea.

EXAMPLE 4.31   Using counting to compute a probability

Refer to Example 4.30. The five lifeguards are named Abby, Bruce, Christopher, Donna, and Esmeralda. Of the three lifeguard stations, one is located at the north end of the beach, one in the middle of the beach, and one at the south end. The lifeguard assignments are made at random. What is the probability that Bruce is assigned to the north station, Donna is assigned to the middle station, and Abby is assigned to the south station?

Solution
The outcomes in the sample space consist of all the choices of three lifeguards chosen from five and ordered. From Example 4.30, we know that there are 60 such outcomes. Only one of the outcomes has Bruce, Donna, Abby, in that order. Thus, the probability is $\frac{1}{60}$.

EXAMPLE 4.32   Using counting to compute a probability

Refer to Example 4.31. What is the probability that Bruce is assigned to the north station, Abby is assigned to the south station, and either Donna or Esmeralda is assigned to the middle station?

Solution
As in Example 4.31, the sample space consists of the 60 permutations of three lifeguards chosen from five. Two of these permutations satisfy the stated conditions: Bruce, Donna, Abby; and Bruce, Esmeralda, Abby. So the probability is $\frac{2}{60} = \frac{1}{30}$.

Check Your Understanding

3. A committee of eight people must choose a president, a vice president, and a secretary. In how many ways can this be done?

4. Refer to Exercise 3. Two of the committee members are Ellen and Jose. Assume the assignments are made at random,
   a. What is the probability that Jose is president and Ellen is vice president?
   b. What is the probability that either Ellen or Jose is president and the other is vice president?

Answers are on page 186.

Objective 3 Count the number of combinations

Combinations

In some cases, when choosing a set of objects from a larger set, we don't care about the ordering of the chosen objects; we care only which objects are chosen. For example, we may not care which lifeguard occupies which station; we might care only which three lifeguards are chosen. Each distinct group of objects that can be selected, without regard to order, is called a **combination**. We will now show how to determine the number of combinations of r objects chosen from a set of n objects. We will illustrate the reasoning with the result of Example 4.30. In that example, we showed that there are 60 permutations of 3 objects chosen from 5. Denoting the objects A, B, C, D, E, Table 4.7 presents a list of all 60 permutations.

Table 4.7 The 60 Permutations of 3 Objects Chosen from 5

ABC	ABD	ABE	ACD	ACE	ADE	BCD	BCE	BDE	CDE
ACB	ADB	AEB	ADC	AEC	AED	BDC	BEC	BED	CED
BAC	BAD	BAE	CAD	CAE	DAE	CBD	CBE	DBE	DCE
BCA	BDA	BEA	CDA	CEA	DEA	CDB	CEB	DEB	DEC
CAB	DAB	EAB	DAC	EAC	EAD	DBC	EBC	EBD	ECD
CBA	DBA	EBA	DCA	ECA	EDA	DCB	ECB	EDB	EDC

Explain It Again

When to use combinations: Use combinations when the order of the chosen objects doesn't matter. Use permutations when the order does matter.

The 60 permutations in Table 4.7 are arranged in 10 columns of 6 permutations each. Within each column, the three objects are the same, and the column contains the 6 different permutations of those three objects. Therefore, each column represents a distinct combination of 3 objects chosen from 5, and there are 10 such combinations. Table 4.7 thus shows that the number of combinations of 3 objects chosen from 5 can be found by dividing the number of permutations of 3 objects chosen from 5, which is $\dfrac{5!}{(5-3)!}$, by the number of permutations of 3 objects, which is 3!. In summary:

The number of combinations of 3 objects chosen from 5 is $\dfrac{5!}{3!(5-3)!}$

The number of combinations of r objects chosen from n is often denoted by the symbol $_nC_r$. The reasoning above can be generalized to derive an expression for $_nC_r$.

The number of combinations of r objects chosen from a group of n objects is

$$_nC_r = \frac{n!}{r!(n-r)!}$$

EXAMPLE 4.33

Counting the number of combinations

Thirty people attend a certain event, and 5 will be chosen at random to receive prizes. The prizes are all the same, so the order in which the people are chosen does not matter. How many different groups of 5 people can be chosen?

Solution

Since the order of the 5 chosen people does not matter, we need to compute the number of combinations of 5 chosen from 30. This is

$$_{30}C_5 = \frac{30!}{5!(30-5)!}$$

$$= \frac{30 \cdot 29 \cdot 28 \cdot 27 \cdot 26}{5 \cdot 4 \cdot 3 \cdot 2 \cdot 1}$$

$$= 142{,}506$$

EXAMPLE 4.34

Using counting to compute a probability

Refer to Example 4.33. Of the 30 people in attendance, 12 are men and 18 are women.

    a. What is the probability that all the prize winners are men?

    b. What is the probability that at least one prize winner is a woman?

Solution

    a. The number of outcomes in the sample space is the number of combinations of 5 chosen from 30. We computed this in Example 4.33 to be $_{30}C_5 = 142{,}506$. The number of outcomes in which every prize winner is a man is the number of combinations of five men chosen from 12 men. This is

$$_{12}C_5 = \frac{12!}{5!(12-5)!} = \frac{12 \cdot 11 \cdot 10 \cdot 9 \cdot 8}{5 \cdot 4 \cdot 3 \cdot 2 \cdot 1} = 792$$

The probability that all prize winners are men is

$$P(\text{All men}) = \frac{792}{142{,}506} = 0.0056$$

    b. This asks for the probability of at least one woman. We therefore find the probability of the complement; that is, we find the probability that none of the prize winners are women. The probability that none of the prize winners are women is the same as the probability that all of the prize winners are men. In part (a), we computed $P(\text{All men}) = 0.0056$. Therefore,

$$P(\text{At least one woman}) = 1 - P(\text{All men}) = 1 - 0.0056 = 0.9944$$

EXAMPLE 4.35

Using counting to compute a probability

A box of lightbulbs contains eight good lightbulbs and two burned-out bulbs. Four bulbs will be selected at random to put into a new lamp. What is the probability that all four bulbs are good?

Solution

The order in which the bulbs are chosen does not matter; all that matters is whether a burned-out bulb is chosen. Therefore, the outcomes in the sample space consist of all the combinations of four bulbs that can be chosen from 10. This number is

$$_{10}C_4 = \frac{10!}{4!(10-4)!} = \frac{3{,}628{,}800}{24 \cdot 720} = 210$$

To select four good bulbs, we must choose the four bulbs from the eight good bulbs. The number of outcomes that correspond to selecting four good bulbs is therefore the number of combinations of four bulbs that can be chosen from eight. This number is

$$_{8}C_4 = \frac{8!}{4!(8-4)!} = \frac{40{,}320}{24 \cdot 24} = 70$$

The probability that four good bulbs are selected is therefore

$$P(\text{Four good bulbs are selected}) = \frac{70}{210} = \frac{1}{3}$$

Check Your Understanding

    5. Eight college students have applied for internships at a local firm. Three of them will be selected for interviews. In how many ways can this be done?

6. Refer to Exercise 5. Four of the eight students are from Macon State College. What is the probability that all three of the interviewed students are from Macon State College?

Answers are on page 186.

USING TECHNOLOGY

TI-84 PLUS

Evaluating a factorial

Step 1. To evaluate $n!$, enter n on the home screen.
Step 2. Press **MATH**, scroll to the **PRB** menu, and select **4: !**
Step 3. Press **ENTER**.

Permutations and combinations

Step 1. To evaluate $_nP_r$ or $_nC_r$, enter n on the home screen.
Step 2. Press **MATH** and scroll to the **PRB** menu.
  - For permutations, select **2: nPr** and press **ENTER** (Figure A).
  - For combinations, select **3: nCr** and press **ENTER**.
Step 3. Enter the value for r and press **ENTER**.

The results of $_{12}P_3$ and $_{12}C_3$ are shown in Figure B.

| **Figure A** | **Figure B** |

EXCEL

Evaluating a factorial

Step 1. To evaluate $n!$, click on a cell in the worksheet and type **=FACT(n)** and press **ENTER**. For example, to compute **12!**, type **=FACT(12)** and press **ENTER**.

Permutations

Step 1. To evaluate $_nP_r$, click on a cell in the worksheet and type **=PERMUT(n,r)**. Press **ENTER**.

Combinations

Step 1. To evaluate $_nC_r$, click on a cell in the worksheet and type **=COMBIN(n,r)**. Press **ENTER**.

SECTION 4.4 Exercises

Exercises 1–6 are the Check Your Understanding exercises located within the section.

Understanding the Concepts

In Exercises 7 and 8, fill in the blank with the appropriate word or phrase:

7. If an operation can be performed in m ways, and a second operation can be performed in n ways, then the total number of ways to perform the sequence of two operations is _____.

8. The number of permutations of 6 objects is _____.

In Exercises 9 and 10, determine whether the statement is true or false. If the statement is false, rewrite it as a true statement.

9. In a permutation, order is not important.

10. In a combination, order is not important.

Practicing the Skills

In Exercises 11–16, evaluate the factorial.

11. 9!   **12.** 5!   **13.** 0!
14. 12!   **15.** 1!   **16.** 3!

In Exercises 17–22, evaluate the permutation.

17. $_7P_3$ **18.** $_8P_1$ **19.** $_{35}P_2$

20. $_5P_4$ **21.** $_{20}P_0$ **22.** $_{45}P_5$

In Exercises 23–28, evaluate the combination.

23. $_9C_5$ **24.** $_7C_1$ **25.** $_{25}C_3$

26. $_{10}C_9$ **27.** $_{12}C_0$ **28.** $_{50}C_{50}$

Working with the Concepts

29. Pizza time: A local pizza parlor is offering a half-price deal on any pizza with one topping. There are eight toppings from which to choose. In addition, there are three different choices for the size of the pizza, and two choices for the type of crust. In how many ways can a pizza be ordered?

30. Books: Josephine has six chemistry books, three history books, and eight statistics books. She wants to choose one book of each type to study. In how many ways can she choose the three books?

31. Playing the horses: In horse racing, one can make a trifecta bet by specifying which horse will come in first, which will come in second, and which will come in third, in the correct order. One can make a box trifecta bet by specifying which three horses will come in first, second, and third, without specifying the order.
- **a.** In an eight-horse field, how many different ways can one make a trifecta bet?
- **b.** In an eight-horse field, how many different ways can one make a box trifecta bet?

32. Ice cream: A certain ice cream parlor offers 15 flavors of ice cream. You want an ice cream cone with three scoops of ice cream, all different flavors.
- **a.** In how many ways can you choose a cone if it matters which flavor is on the top, which is in the middle, and which is on the bottom?
- **b.** In how many ways can you choose a cone if the order of the flavors doesn't matter?

33. License plates: In a certain state, license plates consist of four digits from 0 to 9 followed by three letters. Assume the numbers and letters are chosen at random. Replicates are allowed.
- **a.** How many different license plates can be formed?
- **b.** How many different license plates have the letters S-A-M in that order?
- **c.** If your name is Sam, what is the probability that your name is on your license plate?

34. Committee: The Student Council at a certain school has ten members. Four members will form an executive committee consisting of a president, a vice president, a secretary, and a treasurer.
- **a.** In how many ways can these four positions be filled?
- **b.** In how many ways can four people be chosen for the executive committee if it does not matter who gets which position?
- **c.** Four of the people on Student Council are Zachary, Yolanda, Xavier, and Walter. What is the probability that Zachary is president, Yolanda is vice president, Xavier is secretary, and Walter is treasurer?
- **d.** What is the probability that Zachary, Yolanda, Xavier, and Walter are the four committee members?

35. Day and night shifts: A company has hired 12 new employees, and must assign 8 to the day shift and 4 to the night shift.
- **a.** In how many ways can the assignment be made?
- **b.** Assume that the 12 employees consist of six men and six women and that the assignments to day and night shift are made at random. What is the probability that all four of the night-shift employees are men?
- **c.** What is the probability that at least one of the night-shift employees is a woman?

36. Keep your password safe: A computer password consists of eight characters. Replications are allowed.
- **a.** How many different passwords are possible if each character may be any lowercase letter or digit?
- **b.** How many different passwords are possible if each character may be any lowercase letter?
- **c.** How many different passwords are possible if each character may be any lowercase letter or digit, and at least one character must be a digit?
- **d.** A computer is generating passwords. The computer generates eight characters at random, and each is equally likely to be any of the 26 letters or 10 digits. Replications are allowed. What is the probability that the password will contain all letters?
- **e.** A computer system requires that passwords contain at least one digit. If eight characters are generated at random, what is the probability that they will form a valid password?

37. It's in your genes: Human genetic material (DNA) is made up of sequences of the molecules adenosine (A), guanine (G), cytosine (C), and thymine (T), which are called *bases*. A *codon* is a sequence of three bases. Replicates are allowed, so AAA, CGC, and so forth are codons. Codons are important because each codon causes a different protein to be created.
- **a.** How many different codons are there?
- **b.** How many different codons are there in which all three bases are different?
- **c.** The bases A and G are called *purines*, while C and T are called *pyrimidines*. How many different codons are there in which the first base is a purine and the second and third are pyrimidines?
- **d.** What is the probability that all three bases are different?
- **e.** What is the probability that the first base is a purine and the second and third are pyrimidines?

38. Choosing officers: A committee consists of ten women and eight men. Three committee members will be chosen as officers.
- **a.** How many different choices are possible?
- **b.** How many different choices are possible if all the officers are to be women?
- **c.** How many different choices are possible if all the officers are to be men?
- **d.** What is the probability that all the officers are women?
- **e.** What is the probability that at least one officer is a man?

39. Texas hold 'em: In the game of Texas hold 'em, a player is dealt two cards (called hole cards) from a standard deck of

52 playing cards. The order in which the cards are dealt does not matter.

a. How many different combinations of hole cards are possible?

b. The best hand consists of two aces. There are four aces in the deck. How many combinations are there in which both cards are aces?

c. What is the probability that a hand consists of two aces?

40. Blackjack: In single-deck casino blackjack, the dealer is dealt two cards from a standard deck of 52. The first card is dealt face down and the second card is dealt face up.

a. How many dealer hands are possible if it matters which card is face down and which is face up?

b. How many dealer hands are possible if it doesn't matter which card is face down and which is face up?

c. Of the 52 cards in the deck, four are aces and 16 others (kings, queens, jacks, and tens) are worth 10 points each. The dealer has a blackjack if one card is an ace and the other is worth 10 points; it doesn't matter which card is face up and which card is face down. How many different blackjack hands are there?

d. What is the probability that a hand is a blackjack?

41. Lottery: In the Georgia Fantasy 5 Lottery, balls are numbered from 1 to 39. Five balls are drawn. To win the jackpot, you must mark five numbers from 1 to 39 on a ticket, and your numbers must match the numbers on the five balls. The order does not matter. What is the probability that you win?

42. Lottery: In the Colorado Lottery Lotto game, balls are numbered from 1 to 42. Six balls are drawn. To win the jackpot, you must mark six numbers from 1 to 42 on a ticket, and your numbers must match the numbers on the six balls. The order does not matter. What is the probability that you win?

Extending the Concepts

43. Sentence completion: Let A and B be events. Consider the following sentence:

If A and B are ____(i)____ , then to find ____(ii)____ , ____(iii)____ $P(A)$ and $P(B)$.

Each blank in the sentence can be filled in with either of two choices, as follows:

(i) independent, mutually exclusive
(ii) $P(A \text{ and } B)$, $P(A \text{ or } B)$
(iii) multiply, add

a. In how many ways can the sentence be completed?

b. If choices are made at random for each of the blanks, what is the probability that the sentence is true?

Answers to Check Your Understanding Exercises for Section 4.4

1. 72	**4. a.** 1/56 **b.** 1/28
2. 200	**5.** 56
3. 336	**6.** 1/14

Chapter 4 Summary

Section 4.1: A probability experiment is an experiment that can result in any one of a number of outcomes. The collection of all possible outcomes is a sample space. Sampling from a population is a common type of probability experiment. The population is the sample space, and the individuals in the population are the outcomes. An event is a collection of outcomes from a sample space. The probability of an event is the proportion of times the event occurs in the long run, as the experiment is repeated over and over again. A probability model specifies a probability for every event.

An unusual event is one whose probability is small. There is no hard-and-fast rule about how small a probability has to be for an event to be unusual, but 0.05 is the most commonly used value. The Empirical Method allows us to approximate the probability of an event by repeating a probability experiment many times and computing the proportion of times the event occurs.

Section 4.2: A compound event is an event that is formed by combining two or more events. An example of a compound event is one of the form "A or B." The General Addition Rule is used to compute probabilities of the form $P(A \text{ or } B)$. Two events are mutually exclusive if it is impossible for both events to occur. When two events are mutually exclusive, the Addition Rule for Mutually Exclusive Events can be used to find $P(A \text{ or } B)$. The complement of an event A, denoted A^c, is the event that A does not occur. The Rule of Complements states that $P(A^c)$ is found by subtracting $P(A)$ from 1.

Section 4.3: A conditional probability is a probability that is computed with the knowledge of additional information. Conditional probabilities can be computed with the General Method for computing conditional probabilities. Probabilities of the form $P(A \text{ and } B)$ can be computed with the General Multiplication Rule. If A and B are independent, then $P(A \text{ and } B)$ can be computed with the Multiplication Rule for Independent Events. Two events are independent if the occurrence of one does not affect the probability that the other occurs. When sampling from a population, sampled individuals are independent if the sampling is done with replacement, or if the sample size is less than 5% of the population.

Section 4.4: The Fundamental Principle of Counting states that the total number of ways to perform a sequence of operations is found by multiplying together the numbers of ways of performing each operation. We can compute the number of permutations and combinations of r items chosen from a group of n items. The number of ways that a group of r items can be chosen without regard to order is the number of combinations. The number of ways that a group of r items can be chosen and ordered is the number of permutations.

Some sample spaces consist of the permutations or combinations of r items chosen from a group of n items. When working with these sample spaces, we can use the counting rules to compute probabilities.

Vocabulary and Notation

at least once   174
combination   182
complement   163
compound event   158
conditional probability   167
contingency table   158
dependent events   170
Empirical Method   153
equally likely outcomes   150

event   149
Fundamental Principle of Counting   179
independent events   170
law of large numbers   148
life table   147
mutually exclusive   161
permutation   180
probability   148
probability experiment   148

probability model   150
sample space   149
sampling with replacement   172
sampling without replacement   172
unconditional probability   166
unusual event   153
Venn diagram   161

Important Formulas

General Addition Rule:

$$P(A \text{ or } B) = P(A) + P(B) - P(A \text{ and } B)$$

Multiplication Rule for Independent Events:
$$P(A \text{ and } B) = P(A)P(B)$$

Addition Rule for Mutually Exclusive Events:

$$P(A \text{ or } B) = P(A) + P(B)$$

Rule of Complements:

$$P(A^c) = 1 - P(A)$$

General Method for Computing Conditional Probability:
$$P(B \mid A) = \frac{P(A \text{ and } B)}{P(A)}$$

General Multiplication Rule:
$$P(A \text{ and } B) = P(A)P(B \mid A) = P(B)P(A \mid B)$$

Permutation of r items chosen from n:
$$_nP_r = \frac{n!}{(n-r)!}$$

Combination of r items chosen from n:
$$_nC_r = \frac{n!}{r!(n-r)!}$$

Chapter Quiz

1. Fill in the blank: The probability that a fair coin lands heads is 0.5. Therefore, we can be sure that if we toss a coin repeatedly, the proportion of times it lands heads will _____ .
   i. approach 0.5
   ii. be equal to 0.5
   iii. be greater than 0.5
   iv. be less than 0.5

2. A pollster will draw a simple random sample of voters from a large city to ask whether they support the construction of a new light rail line. Assume that there are one million voters in the city, and that 560,000 of them support this proposition. One voter is sampled at random.
   a. Identify the sample space.
   b. What is the probability that the sampled voter supports the light rail line?

3. State each of the following rules:
   a. General Addition Rule
   b. Addition Rule for Mutually Exclusive Events
   c. Rule of Complements
   d. General Multiplication Rule
   e. Multiplication Rule for Independent Events

4. The following table presents the results of a survey in which 400 college students were asked whether they listen to music while studying.

	Listen	Do Not Listen
Male	121	78
Female	147	54

   a. Find the probability that a randomly selected student does not listen to music while studying.
   b. Find the probability that a randomly selected student listens to music or is male.

5. Which of the following pairs of events are mutually exclusive?
    i. *A*: A randomly chosen student is 18 years old. *B*: The same student is 20 years old.
    ii. *A*: A randomly chosen student owns a red car. *B*: The same student owns a blue car.

6. In a group of 100 teenagers, 61 received their driver's license on their first attempt on the driver's certification exam and 18 received their driver's license on their second attempt. What is the probability that a randomly selected teenager received their driver's license on their first or second attempt?

7. A certain neighborhood has 100 households. Forty-eight households have a dog as a pet. Of these, 32 also have a cat. Given that a household has a dog, what is the probability that it also has a cat?

8. The owner of a bookstore has determined that 80% of people who enter the store will buy a book. Of those who buy a book, 60% will pay with a credit card. Find the probability that a randomly selected person entering the store will buy a book and pay for it using a credit card.

9. A jar contains 4 red marbles, 3 blue marbles, and 5 green marbles. Two marbles are drawn from the jar one at a time without replacement. What is the probability that the second marble is red, given that the first was blue?

10. A student is chosen at random. Which of the following pairs of events are independent?
    i. *A*: The student was born on a Monday. *B*: The student's mother was born on a Monday.
    ii. *A*: The student is above average in height. *B*: The student's mother is above average in height.

11. Individual plays on a slot machine are independent. The probability of winning on any play is 0.38. What is the probability of winning 3 plays in a row?

12. Refer to Problem 11. Suppose that the slot machine is played 5 times in a row. What is the probability of winning at least once?

13. The Roman alphabet (the one used to write English) consists of five vowels (a, e, i, o, u), along with 21 consonants (we are considering y to be a consonant). Gregory needs to make up a computer password containing seven characters. He wants the first six characters to alternate — consonant, vowel, consonant, vowel, consonant, vowel — with repetitions allowed. Then he wants to use a digit for the seventh character.
    a. How many different passwords can he make up?
    b. If he makes up a password at random, what is the probability that his password is banana7?

14. A caterer offers 24 different types of dessert. In how many ways can 5 of them be chosen for a banquet if the order doesn't matter?

15. In a standard game of pool, there are 15 balls labeled 1 through 15.
    a. In how many ways can the 15 balls be ordered?
    b. In how many ways can 3 of the 15 balls be chosen and ordered?

Review Exercises

1. **Colored dice:** A six-sided die has one face painted red, two faces painted white, and three faces painted blue. Each face is equally likely to turn up when the die is rolled.
    a. Construct a sample space for the experiment of rolling this die.
    b. Find the probability that a blue face turns up.

2. **How are your grades?** There were 30 students in last semester's statistics class. Of these, 6 received a grade of A, and 12 received a grade of B. What is the probability that a randomly chosen student received a grade of A or B?

3. **Statistics, anyone?** Let *S* be the event that a randomly selected college student has taken a statistics course, and let *C* be the event that the same student has taken a chemistry course. Suppose $P(S) = 0.4$, $P(C) = 0.3$, and $P(S \text{ and } C) = 0.2$.
    a. Find the probability that a student has taken statistics or chemistry.
    b. Find the probability that a student has taken statistics given that the student has taken chemistry.

4. **Blood types:** Human blood may contain either or both of two antigens, A and B. Blood that contains only the A antigen is called type A, blood that contains only the B antigen is called type B, blood that contains both antigens is called type AB, and blood that contains neither antigen is called type O. A certain blood bank has blood from a total of 1200 donors. Of these, 570 have type O blood, 440 have type A, 125 have type B, and 65 have type AB.
    a. What is the probability that a randomly chosen blood donor is type O?
    b. A recipient with type A blood may safely receive blood from a donor whose blood does not contain the B antigen. What is the probability that a randomly chosen blood donor may donate to a recipient with type A blood?

5. **Start a business:** Suppose that start-up companies in the area of biotechnology have probability 0.2 of becoming profitable, and that those in the area of information technology have probability 0.15 of becoming profitable. A venture capitalist invests in one firm of each type. Assume the companies function independently.
    a. What is the probability that both companies become profitable?
    b. What is the probability that at least one of the two companies becomes profitable?

6. Stop that car: A drag racer has two parachutes, a main and a backup, that are designed to bring the vehicle to a stop at the end of a run. Suppose that the main chute deploys with probability 0.99, and that if the main fails to deploy, the backup deploys with probability 0.98.
   a. What is the probability that one of the two parachutes deploys?
   b. What is the probability that the backup parachute deploys?

7. Defective parts: A process manufactures microcircuits that are used in computers. Twelve percent of the circuits are defective. Assume that three circuits are installed in a computer. Denote a defective circuit by "D" and a good circuit by "G."
   a. List all eight items in the sample space.
   b. What is the probability that all three circuits are good?
   c. The computer will function so long as either two or three of the circuits are good. What is the probability that a computer will function?
   d. If we use a cutoff of 0.05, would it be unusual for all three circuits to be defective?

8. Music to my ears: Jeri is listening to the songs on a new CD in random order. She will listen to two different songs, and will buy the CD if she likes both of them. Assume there are 10 songs on the CD, and that she would like five of them.
   a. What is the probability that she likes the first song?
   b. What is the probability that she likes the second song, given that she liked the first song?
   c. What is the probability that she buys the CD?

9. Female business majors: At a certain university, the probability that a randomly chosen student is female is 0.55, the probability that the student is a business major is 0.20, and the probability that the student is female and a business major is 0.15.
   a. What is the probability that the student is female or a business major?
   b. What is the probability that the student is female given that the student is a business major?
   c. What is the probability that the student is a business major given that the student is female?
   d. Are the events "female" and "business major" independent? Explain.
   e. Are the events "female" and "business major" mutually exclusive? Explain.

10. Heart attack: The following table presents the number of hospitalizations for myocardial infarction (heart attack) for men and women in various age groups.

Age	Male	Female	Total
18–44	26,828	9,265	36,093
45–64	166,340	68,666	235,006
65–84	155,707	124,289	279,996
85 and up	35,524	57,785	93,309
Total	384,399	260,005	644,404

Source: Agency for Healthcare Research and Quality

   a. What is the probability that a randomly chosen patient is a woman?
   b. What is the probability that a randomly chosen patient is aged 45–64?
   c. What is the probability that a randomly chosen patient is a woman and aged 45–64?
   d. What is the probability that a randomly chosen patient is a woman or aged 45–64?
   e. What is the probability that a randomly chosen patient is a woman given that the patient is aged 45–64?
   f. What is the probability that a randomly chosen patient is aged 45–64 given that the patient is a woman?

11. Rainy weekend: Sally is planning to go away for the weekend this coming Saturday and Sunday. At the place she will be going, the probability of rain on any given day is 0.10. Sally says that the probability that it rains on both days is 0.01. She reasons as follows:

$$P(\text{Rain Saturday and Rain Sunday}) = P(\text{Rain Saturday})P(\text{Rain Sunday})$$
$$= (0.1)(0.1)$$
$$= 0.01$$

   a. What assumption is being made in this calculation?
   b. Explain why this assumption is probably not justified in the present case.
   c. Is the probability of 0.01 likely to be too high or too low? Explain.

12. Required courses: A college student must take courses in English, history, mathematics, biology, and physical education. She decides to choose three of these courses to take in her freshman year. In how many ways can this choice be made?

13. Required courses: Refer to Exercise 12. Assume the student chooses three courses at random. What is the probability that she chooses English, mathematics, and biology?

14. Bookshelf: Bart has six books: a novel, a biography, a dictionary, a self-help book, a statistics textbook, and a comic book.
   a. Bart's bookshelf has room for only three of the books. In how many ways can Bart choose and order three books?
   b. In how many ways may the books be chosen and ordered if he does not choose the comic book?

15. Bookshelf: Refer to Exercise 14. Bart chooses three books at random.
 a. What is the probability that the books on his shelf are statistics textbook, dictionary, and comic book, in that order?
 b. What is the probability that the statistics textbook, dictionary, and comic book are the three books chosen, in any order?

Write About It

1. Explain how you could use the law of large numbers to show that a coin is unfair by tossing it many times.

2. When it comes to betting, the chance of winning or losing may be expressed as odds. If there are n equally likely outcomes and m of them result in a win, then the odds of winning are $m:(n - m)$, read "m to $n - m$." For example, suppose that a player rolls a die and wins if the number of dots appearing is either 1 or 2. Since there are two winning outcomes out of six equally likely outcomes, the odds of winning are 2:4.
    Suppose that a pair of dice is rolled and the player wins if it comes up "doubles," that is, if the same number of dots appears on each die. What are the odds of winning?

3. If the odds of an event occurring are 5:8, what is the probability that the event will occur?

4. Explain why the General Addition Rule $P(A \text{ or } B) = P(A) + P(B) - P(A \text{ and } B)$ may be used even when A and B are mutually exclusive events.

5. Sometimes events are in the form "at least" a given number. For example, if a coin is tossed five times, an event could be getting at least two heads. What would be the complement of the event of getting at least two heads?

6. In practice, one must decide whether to treat two events as independent based on an understanding of the process that creates them. For example, in a manufacturing process that produces electronic circuit boards for calculators, assume that the probability that a board is defective is 0.01. You arrive at the manufacturing plant and sample the next two boards that come off the assembly line. Let A be the event that the first board is defective, and let B be the event that the second board is defective. Describe circumstances under which A and B would not be independent.

7. Describe circumstances under which you would use a permutation.

8. Describe circumstances under which you would use a combination.

Case Study: How Likely Are You To Live To Age 100?

The following table is a **life table**, reproduced from the chapter introduction. With an understanding of some basic concepts of probability, one can use the life table to compute the probability that a person of a given age will still be alive a given number of years from now. Life insurance companies use this information to determine how much to charge for life insurance policies.

United States Life Table, Total Population

Age Interval	Proportion Surviving	Age Interval	Proportion Surviving
0–10	0.99123	50–60	0.94010
10–20	0.99613	60–70	0.86958
20–30	0.99050	70–80	0.70938
30–40	0.98703	80–90	0.42164
40–50	0.97150	90–100	0.12248

Source: Centers for Disease Control and Prevention

The column labeled "Proportion Surviving" gives the proportion of people alive at the beginning of an age interval who will still be alive at the end of the age interval. For example, among those currently age 20, the proportion who will still be alive at age 30 is 0.99050, or 99.050%. We will begin by computing the probability that a person lives to any of the ages 10, 20, ..., 100.
    The first number in the column is the probability that a person lives to age 10. So

$$P(\text{Alive at age 10}) = 0.99123$$

The key to using the life table is to realize that the rest of the numbers in the "Proportion Surviving" column are conditional probabilities. They are probabilities that a person is alive at the end of the age interval, given that they were alive at the beginning of the age interval. For example, the row labeled "20–30" contains the conditional probability that someone alive at age 20 will be alive at age 30:

$$P(\text{Alive at age 30} \mid \text{Alive at age 20}) = 0.99050$$

In Exercises 1–5, compute the probability that a person lives to a given age.

1. From the table, find the conditional probability $P(\text{Alive at age 20} \mid \text{Alive at age 10})$.

2. Use the result from Exercise 1 along with the result $P(\text{Alive at age 10}) = 0.99123$ to compute $P(\text{Alive at age 20})$.

3. Use the result from Exercise 2 along with the appropriate number from the table to compute $P(\text{Alive at age 30})$.

4. Use the result from Exercise 3 along with the appropriate number from the table to compute $P(\text{Alive at age 40})$.

5. Compute the probability that a person is alive at ages 50, 60, 70, 80, 90, and 100.

In Exercises 1–5, we computed the probability that a newborn lives to a given age. Now let's compute the probability that a person aged x lives to age y. We'll illustrate this with an example to compute the probability that a person aged 20 lives to age 100. This is the conditional probability that a person lives to age 100, given that the person has lived to age 20.

We want to compute the conditional probability

$$P(\text{Alive at age 100} \mid \text{Alive at age 20})$$

Using the definition of conditional probability, we have

$$P(\text{Alive at age 100} \mid \text{Alive at age 20}) = \frac{P(\text{Alive at age 100 and Alive at age 20})}{P(\text{Alive at age 20})}$$

You computed $P(\text{Alive at age 20})$ in Exercise 2. Now we need to compute $P(\text{Alive at age 100 and Alive at age 20})$. The key is to realize that anyone who is alive at age 100 was also alive at age 20. Therefore,

$$P(\text{Alive at age 100 and Alive at age 20}) = P(\text{Alive at age 100})$$

Therefore,

$$P(\text{Alive at age 100} \mid \text{Alive at age 20}) = \frac{P(\text{Alive at age 100})}{P(\text{Alive at age 20})}$$

In general, for $y > x$,

$$P(\text{Alive at age } y \mid \text{Alive at age } x) = \frac{P(\text{Alive at age } y)}{P(\text{Alive at age } x)}$$

6. Find the probability that a person aged 20 is still alive at age 100.

7. Find the probability that a person aged 50 is still alive at age 70.

8. Which is more probable, that a person aged 20 is still alive at age 50, or that a person aged 50 is still alive at age 60?

9. A life insurance company sells term insurance polices. These policies pay $100,000 if the policyholder dies before age 70, but pay nothing if a person is still alive at age 70. If a person buys a policy at age 40, what is the probability that the insurance company does not have to pay?

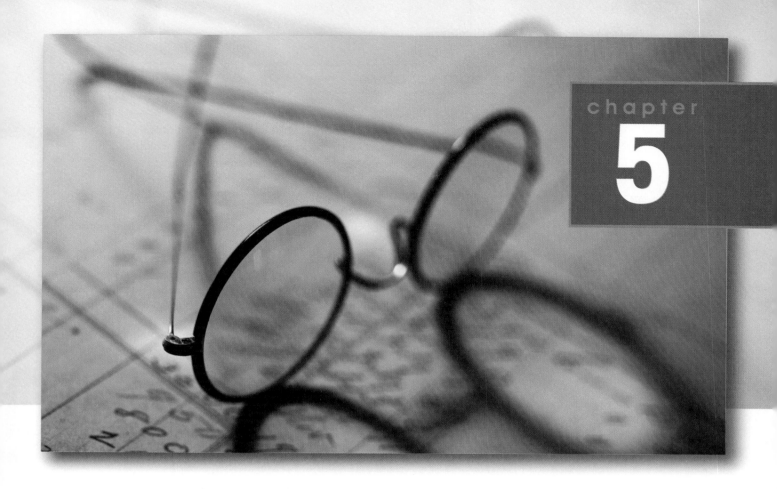

Discrete Probability Distributions

Introduction

How does the Internal Revenue Service detect a fraudulent tax return? One method involves the use of probability in a surprising way. A list of all the amounts claimed as deductions is made. Then a relative frequency distribution is constructed of the first digits of these amounts. This relative frequency distribution is compared to a theoretical distribution, called Benford's law, which gives the probability of each digit. If there is a large discrepancy, the return is suspected of being fraudulent.

The probabilities assigned by Benford's law are given in the following table:

Digit	1	2	3	4	5	6	7	8	9
Probability	0.301	0.176	0.125	0.097	0.079	0.067	0.058	0.051	0.046

Benford's law is an example of a probability distribution. It may be surprising that the first digits of amounts on tax returns are not all equally likely, but in fact the smaller digits occur much more frequently than the larger ones. It turns out that Benford's law describes many data sets that occur naturally. In the case study at the end of the chapter, we will learn more about Benford's law.

SECTION 5.1 | Random Variables

Objectives

1. Distinguish between discrete and continuous random variables
2. Determine a probability distribution for a discrete random variable
3. Describe the connection between probability distributions and populations
4. Construct a probability histogram for a discrete random variable
5. Compute the mean of a discrete random variable
6. Compute the variance and standard deviation of a discrete random variable

If we roll a fair die, the possible outcomes are the numbers 1, 2, 3, 4, 5, and 6, and each of these numbers has probability 1/6. Rolling a die is a probability experiment whose outcomes are numbers. The outcome of such an experiment is called a **random variable**. Thus, rolling a die produces a random variable whose possible values are the numbers 1 through 6, each having probability 1/6.

Mathematicians and statisticians like to use letters to represent numbers. Uppercase letters are often used to represent random variables. Thus, a statistician might say, "Let X be the number that comes up on the next roll of the die."

DEFINITION

A **random variable** is a numerical outcome of a probability experiment.

Notation: Random variables are usually denoted by uppercase letters.

In Section 1.2, we learned that numerical, or quantitative, variables can be discrete or continuous. The same is true for random variables.

Objective 1 Distinguish between discrete and continuous random variables

---

DEFINITION

- **Discrete random variables** are random variables whose possible values can be listed. The list may be infinite — for example, the list of all whole numbers.
- **Continuous random variables** are random variables that can take on any value in an interval. The possible values of a continuous variable are not restricted to any list.

EXAMPLE 5.1 | **Determining whether a random variable is discrete or continuous**

Which of the following random variables are discrete and which are continuous?

   a. The number that comes up on the roll of a die
   b. The height of a randomly chosen college student
   c. The number of siblings a randomly chosen person has

Solution

   a. The number that comes up on a die is discrete. The possible values are 1, 2, 3, 4, 5, and 6.
   b. Height is continuous. A person's height is not restricted to any list of values.
   c. The number of siblings is discrete. The possible values are 0, 1, 2, and so forth.

In this chapter, we will focus on discrete random variables. In the next chapter, we will learn about an important continuous random variable.

Objective 2 Determine a probability distribution for a discrete random variable

> **DEFINITION**
>
> A **probability distribution** for a discrete random variable specifies the probability for each possible value of the random variable.

EXAMPLE 5.2

Determining a probability distribution

A fair coin is tossed twice. Let X be the number of heads that come up. Find the probability distribution of X.

Solution

There are four equally likely outcomes to this probability experiment, listed in Table 5.1. For each outcome, we count the number of heads, which is the value of the random variable X.

Table 5.1

First Toss	Second Toss	X = Number of Heads
H	H	2
H	T	1
T	H	1
T	T	0

There are three possible values for the number of heads: 0, 1, and 2. One of the four outcomes has the value "0," two of the outcomes have the value "1," and one outcome has the value "2." Therefore, the probabilities are

$$P(0) = \frac{1}{4} = 0.25 \qquad P(1) = \frac{2}{4} = 0.50 \qquad P(2) = \frac{1}{4} = 0.25$$

The probability distribution is presented in Table 5.2.

Table 5.2 Probability Distribution of X

x	0	1	2
$P(x)$	0.25	0.50	0.25

Discrete probability distributions satisfy two properties. First, since the values $P(x)$ are probabilities, they must all be between 0 and 1. Second, since the random variable always takes on one of the values in the list, the sum of the probabilities must equal 1.

Explain It Again

Properties of discrete probability distributions: In a probability distribution, each probability must be between 0 and 1, and the sum of all the probabilities must be equal to 1.

> **SUMMARY**
>
> Let $P(x)$ denote the probability that a random variable has the value x. Then
>
> **1.** $0 \le P(x) \le 1$ for every possible value x.
> **2.** $\sum P(x) = 1$

EXAMPLE 5.3

Identifying probability distributions

Which of the following tables represent probability distributions?

a.

x	$P(x)$
1	0.25
2	0.65
3	−0.30
4	0.11

b.

x	$P(x)$
3	0.17
4	0.25
5	0.31
6	0.22
7	0.05

c.

x	$P(x)$
0	1.02
1	0.31
2	0.90
3	0.43

d.

x	$P(x)$
0	0.10
1	0.17
2	0.75
3	0.24

Solution

a. This is not a probability distribution. $P(3)$ is not between 0 and 1.

b. This is a probability distribution. All the probabilities are between 0 and 1, and they add up to 1.

c. This is not a probability distribution. $P(0)$ is not between 0 and 1.

d. This is not a probability distribution. Although all the probabilities are between 0 and 1, they do not add up to 1.

When we are given the probability distribution of a random variable, we can use the rules of probability to compute probabilities involving the random variable. Example 5.4 provides an illustration.

EXAMPLE 5.4 **Computing probabilities**

Four patients have made appointments to have their blood pressure checked at a clinic. Let X be the number of them who have high blood pressure. Based on data from the National Health and Examination Survey, the probability distribution of X is

x	0	1	2	3	4
$P(x)$	0.23	0.41	0.27	0.08	0.01

a. Find $P(2 \text{ or } 3)$.

b. Find $P(\text{More than } 1)$.

c. Find $P(\text{At least one})$.

Recall: The Addition Rule for Mutually Exclusive Events says that if A and B are mutually exclusive, then $P(A \text{ or } B) = P(A) + P(B)$.

Solution

a. The events "2" and "3" are mutually exclusive, since they cannot both happen. We use the Addition Rule for Mutually Exclusive events:

$$P(2 \text{ or } 3) = P(2) + P(3) = 0.27 + 0.08 = 0.35$$

b. "More than 1" means "2 or 3 or 4." Again we use the Addition Rule for Mutually Exclusive events:

$$P(\text{More than } 1) = P(2 \text{ or } 3 \text{ or } 4) = 0.27 + 0.08 + 0.01 = 0.36$$

Recall: The Rule of Complements says that $P(A^c) = 1 - P(A)$.

c. We use the Rule of Complements:

$$P(\text{At least one}) = 1 - P(0) = 1 - 0.23 = 0.77$$

Check Your Understanding

1. A family has three children. If the genders of these children are listed in the order they are born, there are eight possible outcomes: BBB, BBG, BGB, BGG, GBB, GBG, GGB, and GGG. Assume these outcomes are equally likely. Let X represent the number of children that are girls. Find the probability distribution of X.

2. Someone says that the following table shows the probability distribution for the number of boys in a family of four children. Is this possible? Explain why or why not.

x	0	1	2	3	4
$P(x)$	0.12	0.37	0.45	0.25	0.18

3. Which of the following tables represent probability distributions?

a.

x	P(x)
0	0.45
1	0.15
2	0.30
3	0.10

b.

x	P(x)
4	0.27
5	0.15
6	0.11
7	0.34
8	0.25

c.

x	P(x)
1	0.02
2	0.41
3	0.24
4	0.33

4. Following is the probability distribution of a random variable that represents the number of extracurricular activities a college freshman participates in.

x	0	1	2	3	4
P(x)	0.06	0.14	0.45	0.21	0.14

a. Find the probability that a student participates in exactly two activities.
b. Find the probability that a student participates in more than two activities.
c. Find the probability that a student participates in at least one activity.

Answers are on page 208.

Objective 3 Describe the connection between probability distributions and populations

Connection Between Probability Distributions and Populations

Statisticians are interested in studying samples drawn from populations. Random variables are important because when an item is drawn from a population, the value observed is the value of a random variable. The probability distribution of the random variable tells how frequently we can expect each of the possible values of the random variable to turn up in the sample. Example 5.5 presents the idea.

EXAMPLE 5.5 | **Constructing a probability distribution that describes a population**

In a town with a population of 1000 households, 142 of the households have no car, 378 have one car, 423 have two cars, and 57 have three cars. A household is sampled at random. Let X represent the number of cars in the randomly sampled household. Find the probability distribution of X.

Explain It Again

A probability distribution describes a population: We can think of a probability distribution as describing a population. The probability of each value represents the proportion of population items that have that value.

Solution

To find the probability distribution, we must list the possible values of X and then find the probability of each of them. The possible values of X are 0, 1, 2, 3. We find their probabilities:

$$P(0) = \frac{\text{Number of households with 0 cars}}{\text{Total number of households}} = \frac{142}{1000} = 0.142$$

$$P(1) = \frac{\text{Number of households with 1 car}}{\text{Total number of households}} = \frac{378}{1000} = 0.378$$

$$P(2) = \frac{\text{Number of households with 2 cars}}{\text{Total number of households}} = \frac{423}{1000} = 0.423$$

$$P(3) = \frac{\text{Number of households with 3 cars}}{\text{Total number of households}} = \frac{57}{1000} = 0.057$$

The probability distribution is

x	0	1	2	3
P(x)	0.142	0.378	0.423	0.057

5. There are 5000 undergraduates registered at a certain college. Of them, 478 are taking one course, 645 are taking two courses, 568 are taking three courses, 1864 are taking four courses, 1357 are taking five courses, and 88 are taking six courses. Let X be the number of courses taken by a student randomly sampled from this population. Find the probability distribution of X.

Answer is on page 208.

Objective 4 Construct a probability histogram for a discrete random variable

Probability histograms

In Section 2.2, we learned to summarize the data in a sample with a histogram. We can represent discrete probability distributions with histograms as well. A histogram that represents a discrete probability distribution is called a **probability histogram**. Constructing a probability histogram from a probability distribution is just like constructing a relative frequency histogram from a relative frequency distribution for discrete data. For each possible value of the random variable, we draw a rectangle whose height is equal to the probability of that value.

Table 5.3 presents the probability distribution for the number of boys in a family of five children, using the assumption that boys and girls are equally likely and that births are independent events. Figure 5.1 presents a probability histogram for this probability distribution.

> **Explain It Again**
>
> **A probability histogram is like a histogram for a population:** The height of each rectangle in a probability histogram tells us how frequently the value appears in the population.

Table 5.3

x	$P(x)$
0	0.03125
1	0.15625
2	0.31250
3	0.31250
4	0.15625
5	0.03125

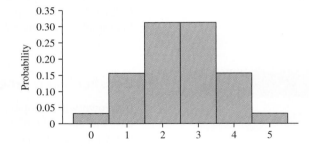

Figure 5.1 Probability histogram for the distribution in Table 5.3

6. Following is a probability histogram for the number of children a woman has. The numbers on the tops of the rectangles are the heights.

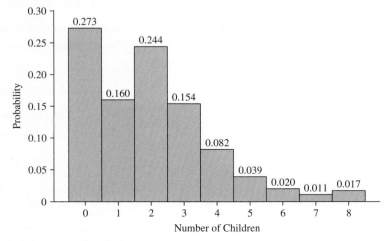

Source: General Social Survey

a. What is the probability that a randomly chosen woman has exactly two children?

b. What is the probability that a randomly chosen woman has fewer than two children?

c. What is the probability that a randomly chosen woman has either four or five children?

Answers are on page 208.

Objective 5 Compute the mean of a discrete random variable

The mean of a random variable

Recall that the mean is a measure of center. The mean of a random variable provides a measure of center for the probability distribution of a random variable.

> **DEFINITION**
>
> To find the **mean** of a discrete random variable, multiply each possible value by its probability, then add the products.
>
> In symbols, $\mu_X = \sum [x \cdot P(x)]$.
>
> Another name for the mean of a random variable is the **expected value**. The notation for the expected value of X is $E(X)$.

EXAMPLE 5.6

Determining the mean of a discrete random variable

A computer monitor is composed of a very large number of points of light called pixels. It is not uncommon for a few of these pixels to be defective. Let X represent the number of defective pixels on a randomly chosen monitor. The probability distribution of X is as follows:

x	0	1	2	3
$P(x)$	0.2	0.5	0.2	0.1

Find the mean number of defective pixels.

Solution
The mean is

$$\mu_X = 0(0.2) + 1(0.5) + 2(0.2) + 3(0.1) = 1.2$$

The mean is 1.2.

The symbol used to represent the mean of a random variable X is μ_X. It is not a coincidence that the mean of a population is also represented by μ. Recall that when we perform a probability experiment to obtain a value of a random variable, it is like sampling an item from a population. The probability distribution of the random variable tells how frequently each of the possible values of the random variable occurs in the population. The mean of the random variable is the same as the mean of the population.

Let's take a closer look at Example 5.6 to see how this is the case. Imagine that we had a population of ten computer monitors. Figure 5.2 presents a visualization of this population, with each monitor labeled with the number of defective pixels it has.

Figure 5.2 Population of ten computer monitors

The probability distribution in Example 5.6 represents this population. If we sample a monitor from this population, the probability that it will have 0 defective pixels is 0.2, the probability that it will have 1 defective pixel is 0.5, and so forth, just as in the probability distribution. Now we'll compute the mean of this population.

$$\mu = \frac{0+0+1+1+1+1+1+2+2+3}{10}$$

$$= \frac{0\cdot2 + 1\cdot5 + 2\cdot2 + 3\cdot1}{10}$$

$$= 0\cdot\frac{2}{10} + 1\cdot\frac{5}{10} + 2\cdot\frac{2}{10} + 3\cdot\frac{1}{10}$$

$$= 0(0.2) + 1(0.5) + 2(0.2) + 3(0.1) = 1.2$$

The mean of the random variable is the same as the mean of the population.

Interpreting the mean of a random variable

In Example 5.6, imagine that we sampled a large number of computer monitors and counted the number of defective pixels on each. We would expect the mean number of defective pixels on our sampled monitors to be close to the population mean of 1.2. This idea provides an interpretation for the mean of a random variable.

Interpretation of the Mean of a Random Variable

If a probability experiment that produces a value of a random variable is repeated over and over again, the average of the values produced will approach the mean of the random variable.

Explain It Again

Law of large numbers for means:
The law of large numbers for means tells us that for a large sample, the sample mean will almost certainly be close to the population mean.

When the probability experiment is sampling from a population, our interpretation of the mean says that as the sample size increases, the sample mean will approach the population mean. This is known as the **law of large numbers for means**.

Law of Large Numbers for Means

If we sample items from a population, then as the sample size grows larger, the sample mean will approach the population mean.

EXAMPLE 5.7   Determining the mean of a discrete random variable

Let X be the number of boys in a family of five children. The probability distribution of X is given in Table 5.4. Find the mean number of boys and interpret the result.

Table 5.4

x	$P(x)$
0	0.03125
1	0.15625
2	0.31250
3	0.31250
4	0.15625
5	0.03125

Solution
The calculations are presented in Table 5.5. We multiply each x by its corresponding $P(x)$, then add the products to obtain the mean. The mean is 2.5. We interpret this by saying that as we sample more and more families with five children, the mean number of boys in the sampled families will approach 2.5.

Table 5.5

x	$P(x)$	$x \cdot P(x)$
0	0.03125	0.00000
1	0.15625	0.15625
2	0.31250	0.62500
3	0.31250	0.93750
4	0.15625	0.62500
5	0.03125	0.15625
		$\sum[x \cdot P(x)] = 2.5$

Check Your Understanding

7. A true–false quiz with ten questions was given to a statistics class. Following is the probability distribution for the score of a randomly chosen student. Find the mean score and interpret the result.

x	5	6	7	8	9	10
$P(x)$	0.04	0.16	0.36	0.24	0.12	0.08

Answer is on page 208.

Objective 6 Compute the variance and standard deviation of a discrete random variable

The variance and standard deviation of a discrete random variable

The variance and standard deviation are measures of spread. The variance and standard deviation of a random variable measure the spread in the probability distribution of the random variable.

DEFINITION

The **variance** of a discrete random variable X is

$$\sigma_X^2 = \sum[(x - \mu_X)^2 \cdot P(x)]$$

An equivalent expression that is often easier when computing by hand is

$$\sigma_X^2 = \sum[x^2 \cdot P(x)] - \mu_X^2$$

The **standard deviation** of X is the square root of the variance:

$$\sigma_X = \sqrt{\sigma_X^2}$$

EXAMPLE 5.8 Computing the variance of a discrete random variable

In Example 5.6, we presented the following probability distribution for the number of defective pixels in a computer monitor. Compute the variance and standard deviation of the number of defective pixels.

x	0	1	2	3
$P(x)$	0.2	0.5	0.2	0.1

Solution

In Example 5.6, we computed $\mu_X = 1.2$. The calculations for the variance σ_X^2 are shown in Table 5.6 on page 202. For each x, we subtract the mean μ_X to obtain $x - \mu_X$. Then we square these quantities and multiply by $P(x)$. We add the products to obtain the variance σ_X^2.

Table 5.6

x	$x - \mu_X$	$(x - \mu_X)^2$	$P(x)$	$(x - \mu_X)^2 \cdot P(x)$
0	-1.2	1.44	0.2	0.288
1	-0.2	0.04	0.5	0.020
2	0.8	0.64	0.2	0.128
3	1.8	3.24	0.1	0.324
				$\sigma_X^2 = \sum[(x - \mu_X)^2 \cdot P(x)] = 0.760$

The variance is $\sigma_X^2 = 0.760$. The standard deviation is

$$\sigma_X = \sqrt{0.760} = 0.872$$

EXAMPLE 5.9

Computing the mean and standard deviation by using technology

Use technology to compute the mean and standard deviation for the probability distribution in Example 5.8.

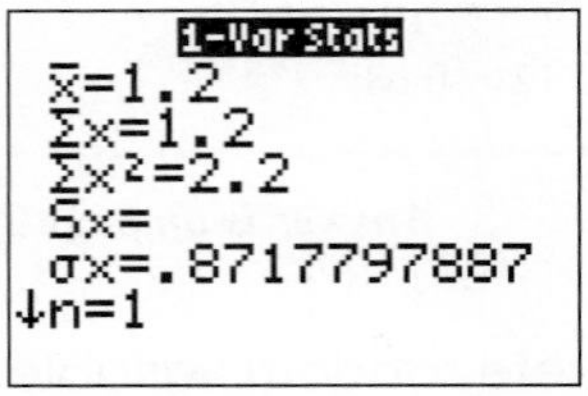

Figure 5.3

Solution

We use the TI-84 Plus calculator. Enter the possible values of the random variable into **L1** and their probabilities into **L2**. Then use the **1 – Var Stats** command. Figure 5.3 presents the calculator display. The mean, μ_X, is denoted by $\bar{x}$. The standard deviation is denoted σx. There is no value for the sample standard deviation Sx because we are not computing the standard deviation of a sample. Step-by-step instructions are presented in the Using Technology section on page 204.

Check Your Understanding

8. Following is the probability distribution for the age of a student at a certain public high school.

x	13	14	15	16	17	18
$P(x)$	0.08	0.24	0.23	0.28	0.14	0.03

  a. Find the variance of the ages.
  b. Find the standard deviation of the ages.

Answers are on page 208.

Applications of the mean

There are many occasions on which people want to predict how much they are likely to gain or lose if they make a certain decision or take a certain action. Often, this is done by computing the mean of a random variable. In such situations, the mean is sometimes called the "expected value." If the expected value is positive, it is an expected gain, and if it is negative, it is an expected loss. Examples 5.10–5.12 provide some illustrations.

Gambling

Probability was invented by mathematicians who were hired by gamblers to help them create games of chance. For this reason, probability is an extremely useful tool to analyze gambling games — this is what it was designed to do. Example 5.10 analyzes the game of roulette.

EXAMPLE 5.10

Find the expected loss at roulette

A Nevada roulette wheel contains 38 pockets, numbered 1 to 36 with a zero (0) and a double-zero (00). Eighteen of the numbers are colored red, eighteen are colored black, and

two (the 0 and the 00) are colored green. Let's say you bet $1 on red. If a red number comes up, you get your dollar back, along with another dollar, so you win $1. If a black or green number comes up, you win −$1 (winning a negative amount is a mathematician's way of saying that you lose). Let X be the amount you win. Find the probability distribution of X and the expected value (mean) of X. Interpret the expected value.

Solution

The possible values of X are 1 and −1. There are 38 outcomes in the sample space, with 18 of them (the red ones) corresponding to 1 and the other 20 corresponding to −1. The probability distribution of X is therefore

x	−1	1
$P(x)$	20/38	18/38

The expected value is the mean of X:

$$\mu_X = (-1)\left(\frac{20}{38}\right) + 1\left(\frac{18}{38}\right) = -\frac{2}{38} = -0.0526$$

Since the expected value is negative, this is an expected loss. We can interpret the expected value by saying that, on the average, you can expect to lose 5.26¢ for every dollar you bet.

Business projections

When making business decisions, executives often use probability distributions to describe the amount of profit or loss that will result.

EXAMPLE 5.11

Computing the expected value of a business decision

A mineral economist estimated that a particular mining venture had probability 0.4 of a $30 million loss, probability 0.5 of a $20 million profit, and probability 0.1 of a $40 million profit. Let X represent the profit, in millions of dollars. Find the probability distribution of the profit and the expected value of the profit. Does this venture represent an expected gain or an expected loss?

Source: *Journal of the Australasian Institute of Mining and Metallurgy* 306:18–22

Solution

The probability distribution of the profit X is as follows:

x	−30	20	40
$P(x)$	0.4	0.5	0.1

The expected value is the mean of X:

$$\mu_X = (-30)(0.4) + 20(0.5) + 40(0.1) = 2.0$$

The expected value is positive, so this is an expected gain of $2 million.

Insurance premiums

Insurance companies must determine a price (called a *premium*) to charge for their policies. Computing an expected value is an important part of this process.

EXAMPLE 5.12

Computing the expected value of an insurance premium

An insurance company sells a one-year term life insurance policy to a 70-year-old man. The man pays a premium of $400. If he dies within one year, the company will pay $10,000 to his beneficiary. According to the U.S. Centers for Disease Control and Prevention, the probability that a 70-year-old man is still alive one year later is 0.9715. Let X be the profit made by the insurance company. Find the probability distribution and the expected value of the profit.

Solution

If the man lives, the insurance company keeps the $400 premium and doesn't have to pay anything. So its profit is $400. If the man dies, the insurance company still keeps the $400, but it must also pay $10,000. So its profit is $400 − $10,000 = −$9600, a loss of $9600. The probability that the man lives is 0.9715 and the probability that he dies is 1 − 0.9715 = 0.0285. The probability distribution is

x	−9600	400
$P(x)$	0.0285	0.9715

The expected value is the mean of X:

$$\mu_X = (-9600)(0.0285) + 400(0.9715) = 115$$

The expected gain for the insurance company is $115. We can interpret this by saying that if the insurance company sells many policies like this, it can expect to earn $115 for each policy, on the average.

USING TECHNOLOGY

We use Example 5.6 to illustrate the technology steps.

TI-84 PLUS

Computing the mean and standard deviation of a discrete random variable

Step 1. Enter the values of the random variable into **L1** in the data editor and the associated probabilities into **L2**. (Figure A).

Step 2. Press **STAT** and highlight the **CALC** menu.

Step 3. Select **1-Var Stats** and enter **L1**, comma, **L2**.

Step 4. Press **ENTER**. (Figure B).

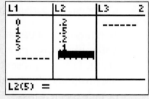

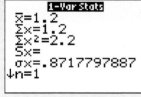

| Figure A | Figure B |

Using the TI-84 PLUS Stat Wizards (see Appendix B for more information)

Step 1. Enter the values of the random variable into **L1** in the data editor and the associated probabilities into **L2**. (Figure A).

Step 2. Press **STAT** and highlight the **CALC** menu.

Step 3. Select **1-Var Stats**. Enter **L1** into the **List** field and **L2** into the **FreqList** field.

Step 4. Select **Calculate** and press **ENTER**. (Figure B).

SECTION 5.1   Exercises

Exercises 1–8 are the Check Your Understanding exercises located within the section.

Understanding the Concepts

In Exercises 9–12, fill in each blank with the appropriate word or phrase.

9. A numerical outcome of a probability experiment is called a _____.

10. The sum of all the probabilities in a discrete probability distribution must be equal to _____.

11. _____ random variables can take on any value in an interval.

12. As the sample size increases, the sample mean approaches the _____ mean.

In Exercises 13–16, determine whether the statement is true or false. If the statement is false, rewrite it as a true statement.

13. To find the mean of a discrete random variable, multiply each possible value of the random variable by its probability, then add the products.

14. The expected value is the mean amount gained or lost.

15. The possible values of a discrete random variable cannot be listed.

16. The standard deviation is found by squaring the variance.

Practicing the Skills

In Exercises 17–26, determine whether the random variable described is discrete or continuous.

17. The number of heads in 100 tosses of a coin

18. The number of people in line at the bank at a randomly chosen time

19. The weight of a randomly chosen student's backpack

20. The amount of rain during the next thunderstorm

21. The number of children absent from school on a randomly chosen day

22. The time it takes to drive to the airport

23. The final exam score of a randomly chosen student from last semester's statistics class

24. The amount of time you wait at a bus stop

25. The height of a randomly chosen college student

26. The number of songs on a randomly chosen iPod

In Exercises 27–32, determine whether the table represents a discrete probability distribution. If not, explain why not.

27.

x	P(x)
1	0.4
2	0.2
3	0.1
4	0.3

28.

x	P(x)
30	0.2
40	0.2
50	0.2
60	0.2
70	0.2

29.

x	P(x)
21	0.1
22	0.1
23	0.1
24	0.1

30.

x	P(x)
55	−0.3
65	0.6
75	0.4
85	0.2

31.

x	P(x)
100	0.2
200	0.3
300	0.5
400	0.4
500	0.1

32.

x	P(x)
2	0.35
4	0.25
6	0.15
8	0.25

In Exercises 33–38, compute the mean and standard deviation of the random variable with the given discrete probability distribution.

33.

x	P(x)
1	0.42
2	0.18
5	0.34
7	0.06

34.

x	P(x)
8	0.15
13	0.23
15	0.25
18	0.27
19	0.10

35.

x	P(x)
4	0.33
6	0.11
7	0.21
9	0.35

36.

x	P(x)
−3	0.10
0	0.17
1	0.56
3	0.17

37.

x	P(x)
15	0.15
17	0.23
19	0.25
22	0.27
26	0.10

38.

x	P(x)
120	0.30
150	0.30
170	0.15
180	0.25

39. Fill in the missing value so that the following table represents a probability distribution.

x	4	5	6	7
P(x)	0.3	?	0.3	0.2

40. Fill in the missing value so that the following table represents a probability distribution.

x	15	25	35	45	55
P(x)	0.25	0.15	?	0.05	0.15

Working with the Concepts

41. **Put some air in your tires:** Let X represent the number of tires with low air pressure on a randomly chosen car. The probability distribution of X is as follows.

x	0	1	2	3	4
P(x)	0.1	0.2	0.4	0.2	0.1

 a. Find $P(1)$.
 b. Find $P(\text{More than } 2)$.
 c. Find the probability that all four tires have low air pressure.
 d. Find the probability that no tires have low air pressure.
 e. Compute the mean μ_X.
 f. Compute the standard deviation σ_X.

42. **Fifteen items or less:** The number of customers in line at a supermarket express checkout counter is a random variable with the following probability distribution.

x	0	1	2	3	4	5
P(x)	0.10	0.25	0.30	0.20	0.10	0.05

 a. Find $P(2)$.
 b. Find $P(\text{No more than } 1)$.
 c. Find the probability that no one is in line.
 d. Find the probability that at least three people are in line.
 e. Compute the mean μ_X.
 f. Compute the standard deviation σ_X.
 g. If each customer takes 3 minutes to check out, what is the probability that it will take more than 6 minutes for all the customers currently in line to check out?

43. **Defective circuits:** The following table presents the probability distribution of the number of defects X in a randomly chosen printed circuit board.

x	0	1	2	3
P(x)	0.5	0.3	0.1	0.1

 a. Find $P(2)$.
 b. Find $P(1 \text{ or more})$.
 c. Find the probability that at least two circuits are defective.
 d. Find the probability that no more than two circuits are defective.
 e. Compute the mean μ_X.
 f. Compute the standard deviation σ_X.
 g. A circuit will function if it has no defects or only one defect. What is the probability that a circuit will function?

44. **Do you carpool?** Let X represent the number of occupants in a randomly chosen car on a certain stretch of highway during morning commute hours. A survey of cars showed that the probability distribution of X is as follows.

x	1	2	3	4	5
P(x)	0.70	0.15	0.10	0.03	0.02

 a. Find $P(2)$.
 b. Find $P(\text{More than } 3)$.

c. Find the probability that a car has only one occupant.

d. Find the probability that a car has fewer than four occupants.

e. Compute the mean μ_X.

f. Compute the standard deviation σ_X.

g. To save energy, a goal is set to have the mean number of occupants be at least two per car. Has this goal been met?

45. Dirty air: The federal government has enacted maximum allowable standards for air pollutants such as ozone. Let X be the number of days per year that the level of air pollution exceeds the standard in a certain city. The probability distribution of X is given by

x	0	1	2	3	4
$P(x)$	0.33	0.38	0.19	0.06	0.04

a. Find $P(1)$.

b. Find $P(3$ or fewer$)$.

c. Find the probability that the standard is exceeded on at least one day.

d. Find the probability that the standard is exceeded on more than two days.

e. Compute the mean μ_X.

f. Compute the standard deviation σ_X.

46. Texting: Five teenagers are selected at random. Let X be the number of them who have sent text messages on their cell phones within the past 30 days. According to a study by the Nielsen Company, the probability distribution of X is as follows:

x	0	1	2	3	4	5
$P(x)$	0.015	0.097	0.258	0.343	0.227	0.060

a. Find $P(2)$.

b. Find $P($More than 1$)$.

c. Find the probability that three or more of the teenagers sent text messages.

d. Find the probability that fewer than two of the teenagers sent text messages.

e. Compute the mean μ_X.

f. Compute the standard deviation σ_X.

47. Relax! The General Social Survey asked 1676 people how many hours per day they were able to relax. The results are presented in the following table.

Number of Hours	Frequency
0	114
1	186
2	336
3	251
4	316
5	231
6	149
7	33
8	60
Total	1676

Consider these 1676 people to be a population. Let X be the number of hours of relaxation for a person sampled at random from this population.

a. Construct the probability distribution of X.

b. Find the probability that a person relaxes more than 4 hours per day.

c. Find the probability that a person doesn't relax at all.

d. Compute the mean μ_X.

e. Compute the standard deviation σ_X.

48. Pain: The General Social Survey asked 827 people how many days they would wait to seek medical treatment if they were suffering pain that interfered with their ability to work. The results are presented in the following table.

Number of Days	Frequency
0	27
1	436
2	263
3	72
4	19
5	10
Total	827

Consider these 827 people to be a population. Let X be the number of days for a person sampled at random from this population.

a. Construct the probability distribution of X.

b. Find the probability that a person would wait for 3 days.

c. Find the probability that a person would wait more than 2 days.

d. Compute the mean μ_X.

e. Compute the standard deviation σ_X.

49. School days: The following table presents the numbers of students enrolled in grades 1 through 8 in public schools in the United States.

Grade	Frequency (in 1000s)
1	3750
2	3640
3	3627
4	3585
5	3601
6	3660
7	3715
8	3765
Total	29,343

Source: *Statistical Abstract of the United States*

Consider these students to be a population. Let X be the grade of a student randomly chosen from this population.

a. Construct the probability distribution of X.
b. Find the probability that the student is in fourth grade.
c. Find the probability that the student is in seventh or eighth grade.
d. Compute the mean μ_X.
e. Compute the standard deviation σ_X.

50. World Cup: The World Cup soccer tournament has been held every four years since 1930, except for 1942 and 1946. The following table presents the number of goals scored by the winning team in each championship game.

Goals	Frequency
1	3
2	4
3	7
4	4
5	1
Total	19

Consider these 19 games to be a population. Let X be the number of goals scored in a game randomly chosen from this population.
a. Construct the probability distribution of X.
b. Find the probability that three goals were scored.
c. Find the probability that fewer than four goals were scored.
d. Compute the mean μ_X.
e. Compute the standard deviation σ_X.

51. Lottery: In the New York State Numbers Lottery, you pay $1 and pick a number from 000 to 999. If your number comes up, you win $500, which is a profit of $499. If you lose, you lose $1. Your probability of winning is 0.001. What is the expected value of your profit? Is it an expected gain or an expected loss?

52. Lottery: In the New York State Numbers Lottery, you pay $1 and can bet that the sum of the numbers that come up is 13. The probability of winning is 0.075, and if you win, you win $6.50, which is a profit of $5.50. If you lose, you lose $1. What is the expected value of your profit? Is it an expected gain or an expected loss?

53. Craps: In the game of craps, two dice are rolled, and people bet on the outcome. For example, you can bet $1 that the dice will total 7. The probability that you win is 1/6, and if you win, your profit is $4. If you lose, you lose $1. What is the expected value of your profit? Is it an expected gain or an expected loss?

54. More craps: Another bet you can make in craps is that the sum of the dice will be 2 (also called "snake eyes"). The probability that you win is 1/36, and if you win, your profit is $30. If you lose, you lose $1. What is the expected value of your profit? Is it an expected gain or an expected loss?

55. SAT: You are trying to answer an SAT multiple choice question. There are five choices. If you get the question right, you gain one point, and if you get it wrong, you lose 1/4 point. Assume you have no idea what the right answer is, so you pick one of the choices at random.
a. What is the expected value of the number of points you get?
b. If you don't answer a question, you get 0 points. The test makers advise you not to answer a question if you have no idea which answer is correct. Do you think this is good advice? Explain.

56. More SAT: Refer to Exercise 55. Assume you can eliminate one of the five choices, and you choose one of the remaining four at random as your answer.
a. What is the expected value of the number of points you get?
b. If you don't answer a question, you get 0 points. The test makers advise you to guess if you can eliminate one or more answers. Do you think this is good advice? Explain.

57. Business projection: An investor is considering a $10,000 investment in a start-up company. She estimates that she has probability 0.25 of a $20,000 loss, probability 0.20 of a $10,000 profit, probability 0.15 of a $50,000 profit, and probability 0.40 of breaking even (a profit of $0). What is the expected value of the profit? Would you advise the investor to make the investment?

58. Insurance: An insurance company sells a one-year term life insurance policy to an 80-year-old woman. The woman pays a premium of $1000. If she dies within one year, the company will pay $20,000 to her beneficiary. According to the U.S. Centers for Disease Control and Prevention, the probability that an 80-year-old woman will be alive one year later is 0.9516. Let X be the profit made by the insurance company. Find the probability distribution and the expected value of the profit.

Extending the Concepts

59. Success and failure: Three components are randomly sampled, one at a time, from a large lot. As each component is selected, it is tested. If it passes the test, a success (S) occurs; if it fails the test, a failure (F) occurs. Assume that 80% of the components in the lot will succeed in passing the test. Let X represent the number of successes among the three sampled components.
a. What are the possible values for X?
b. Find $P(3)$.
c. The event that the first component fails and the next two succeed is denoted by FSS. Find $P(\text{FSS})$.
d. Find $P(\text{SFS})$ and $P(\text{SSF})$.
e. Use the results of parts (c) and (d) to find $P(2)$.
f. Find $P(1)$.
g. Find $P(0)$.
h. Find μ_X.
i. Find σ_X.

Answers to Check Your Understanding Exercises for Section 5.1

1.

x	0	1	2	3
$P(x)$	0.125	0.375	0.375	0.125

2. It is not possible. The probabilities do not add up to 1.

3. (a) and (c)

4. **a.** 0.45 **b.** 0.35 **c.** 0.94

5.

x	1	2	3	4	5	6
$P(x)$	0.0956	0.1290	0.1136	0.3728	0.2714	0.0176

6. **a.** 0.244 **b.** 0.433 **c.** 0.121

7. The mean is 7.48. Interpretation: If we were to give this quiz to more and more students, the mean score for these students would approach 7.48.

8. **a.** 1.6075 **b.** 1.2679

SECTION 5.2 | The Binomial Distribution

Objectives

1. Determine whether a random variable is binomial
2. Determine the probability distribution of a binomial random variable
3. Compute binomial probabilities
4. Compute the mean and variance of a binomial random variable

Your favorite fast-food chain is giving away a coupon with every purchase of a meal. You scratch the coupon to reveal your prize. Twenty percent of the coupons entitle you to a free hamburger, and the rest of them say "better luck next time." You go to this restaurant in a group of ten people, and everyone orders lunch. What is the probability that three of you win a free hamburger? Let X be the number of people out of ten who win a free hamburger. What is the probability distribution of X? In this section, we will learn that X has a distribution called the **binomial distribution**, which is one of the most useful probability distributions.

Objective 1 Determine whether a random variable is binomial

Binomial Random Variables

In the situation just described, we are examining ten coupons. Each time we examine a coupon, we will call it a **trial**, so there are 10 trials. When a coupon is good for a free hamburger, we will call it a "success." The random variable X represents the number of successes in 10 trials.

Under certain conditions, a random variable that represents the number of successes in a series of trials has a probability distribution called the **binomial distribution**. The conditions are:

Conditions for the Binomial Distribution

1. A fixed number of trials are conducted.
2. There are two possible outcomes for each trial. One is labeled "success" and the other is labeled "failure."
3. The probability of success is the same on each trial.
4. The trials are independent. This means that the outcome of one trial does not affect the outcomes of the other trials.
5. The random variable X represents the number of successes that occur.

Notation: The following notation is commonly used:

- The number of trials is denoted by n.
- The probability of success is denoted by p, and the probability of failure is $1 - p$.

It is important to realize that the word *success* does not necessarily refer to a desirable outcome. For example, in medical studies that involve counting the number of people who suffer from a certain disease, the value of p is the probability that someone will come down with the disease. In these studies, disease is a "success," although it is certainly not a desirable outcome.

| EXAMPLE 5.13 | **Determining whether a random variable is binomial** |

Determine which of the following are binomial random variables. For those that are binomial, state the two possible outcomes and specify which is a success. Also state the values of n and p.

  a. A fair coin is tossed ten times. Let X be the number of times the coin lands heads.

  b. Five basketball players each attempt a free throw. Let X be the number of free throws made.

  c. Ten cards are in a box. Five are red and five are green. Three of the cards are drawn at random without replacement. Let X be the number of red cards drawn.

Solution

  a. This is a binomial random variable. Each toss of the coin is a trial. There are two possible outcomes — heads and tails. Since X represents the number of heads, a head counts as a success. The trials are independent, because the outcome of one coin toss does not affect the other tosses. The number of trials is $n = 10$, and the success probability is $p = 0.5$.

  b. This is not a binomial random variable. The probability of success (making a shot) differs from player to player, because they will not all be equally skilled at making free throws.

  c. This is not a binomial random variable because the trials are not independent. If the first card is red, then four of the nine remaining cards will be red, and the probability of a red card on the second draw will be 4/9. If the first card is not red, then five of the nine remaining cards will be red, and the probability of a red card on the second draw will be 5/9. Since the probability of success on the second trial depends on the outcome of the first trial, the trials are not independent.

In part (c) of Example 5.13, the sampling was done without replacement, and the trials were not independent. If the sample is less than 5% of the population, however, then in most cases the lack of replacement will have only a negligible effect, and it is appropriate to consider the trials to be independent. (See the discussion in Section 4.3.) In particular, when a simple random sample is drawn from a population, we will consider the sampled individuals to be independent whenever the sample size is less than 5% of the population size.

> When a simple random sample comprises less than 5% of the population, we will consider the sampled individuals to be independent.

Check Your Understanding

  1. Determine whether X is a binomial random variable.

  a. A fair die is rolled 20 times. Let X be the number of times the die comes up 6.

  b. A standard deck of 52 cards contains four aces. Four cards are dealt without replacement from this deck. Let X be the number that are aces.

  c. A simple random sample of 50 voters is drawn from the residents in a large city. Let X be the number who plan to vote for a proposition to increase spending on public schools.

Answers are on page 218.

Objective 2 Determine the probability distribution of a binomial random variable

The Binomial Probability Distribution
We will determine the probability distribution of a binomial random variable by considering a simple example. A biased coin has probability 0.6 of coming up heads. The coin is tossed three times. Let X be the number of heads that come up. Since X is the number of heads, coming up heads is a success. Then X is binomial, with $n = 3$ trials and success probability $p = 0.6$. We will compute $P(2)$, the probability that exactly two of the tosses are heads.

There are three arrangements of two heads in three tosses of a coin, HHT, HTH, and THH. We first compute the probability of HHT. The event HHT is a sequence of independent events: H on the first toss, H on the second toss, T on the third toss. We know the probabilities of each of these events separately:

$$P(\text{H on the first toss})=0.6, \quad P(\text{H on the second toss})=0.6, \quad P(\text{T on the third toss})=0.4$$

Because the events are independent, the Multiplication Rule for Independent Events tells us that the probability that they all occur is equal to the product of their probabilities. Therefore,

$$P(\text{HHT})=(0.6)(0.6)(0.4)=(0.6)^2(0.4)^1$$

Similarly, $P(\text{HTH})=(0.6)(0.4)(0.6) = (0.6)^2(0.4)^1$, and $P(\text{THH}) = (0.4)(0.6)(0.6) = (0.6)^2(0.4)^1$. We can see that all the different arrangements of two heads and one tail have the same probability. Now

$$P(2) = P(\text{HHT or HTH or THH})$$
$$= P(\text{HHT}) + P(\text{HTH}) + P(\text{THH}) \text{ (Addition Rule for Mutually Exclusive Events)}$$
$$= (0.6)^2(0.4)^1 + (0.6)^2(0.4)^1 + (0.6)^2(0.4)^1$$
$$= 3(0.6)^2(0.4)^1$$

Recall: $_nC_x = \dfrac{n!}{x!(n-x)!}$, where

$n! = n(n-1)\cdots(2)(1)$

Examining this result, we see that the number 3 represents the number of arrangements of two successes (heads) and one failure (tails). In general, this number will be the number of arrangements of x successes in n trials, which is $_nC_x$. The number 0.6 is the success probability, which in general will be p. The exponent 2 is the number of successes, which in general will be x. The number 0.4 is the failure probability, which is $1 - p$, and the exponent 1 is the number of failures, which is $n - x$.

Formula for Binomial Probabilities

For a binomial random variable X that represents the number of successes in n trials with success probability p, the probability of obtaining x successes is

$$P(x) = {_nC_x}\, p^x(1 - p)^{n-x}$$

The possible values of X are $0, 1, ..., n$.

Objective 3 Compute binomial probabilities

Computing Binomial Probabilities

The binomial probability distribution can require tedious calculations. While we can compute simple probabilities by hand, for more involved problems it is better to use a table or technology.

EXAMPLE 5.14   ### Calculating probabilities by using the binomial probability distribution

According to the Nielsen Company, approximately 30% of U.S. households had a digital video recorder (DVR) at the end of the year 2008. Suppose a simple random sample of 15 households is taken. Use the binomial probability distribution to find the following probabilities.

    a. Find the probability that exactly four of the sampled households have a DVR.

    b. Find the probability that fewer than three of the households have a DVR.

    c. Find the probability that more than one household has a DVR.

    d. Find the probability that the number of households that have a DVR is between 1 and 4, inclusive.

Solution

a. We use the binomial probability distribution with $n = 15$, $p = 0.3$, and $x = 4$.

$$P(4) = {}_{15}C_4(0.3)^4(1 - 0.3)^{15-4}$$

$$= \frac{15!}{4!(15 - 4)!}(0.3)^4(0.7)^{11}$$

$$= 1365(0.3)^4(0.7)^{11}$$

$$= 0.219$$

b. The possible numbers of households that are fewer than three are 0, 1, and 2. So we need to find $P(0 \text{ or } 1 \text{ or } 2)$. We use the Addition Rule for Mutually Exclusive Events.

$$P(0 \text{ or } 1 \text{ or } 2) = P(0) + P(1) + P(2)$$

$$= {}_{15}C_0(0.3)^0(1 - 0.3)^{15-0} + {}_{15}C_1(0.3)^1(1 - 0.3)^{15-1}$$

$$+ {}_{15}C_2(0.3)^2(1 - 0.3)^{15-2}$$

$$= 0.0047 + 0.0305 + 0.0916$$

$$= 0.127$$

c. The possible numbers of households that are more than one are 2, 3, 4, and so forth up to 15. We could find $P(\text{More than } 1)$ by adding $P(2) + P(3) + \cdots + P(15)$, but fortunately there is an easier way. We will use the Rule of Complements. The complement of "more than 1" is "1 or fewer," or, equivalently, 0 or 1. We compute the probability of the complement, and subtract from 1.

$$P(0 \text{ or } 1) = P(0) + P(1)$$

$$= {}_{15}C_0(0.3)^0(1 - 0.3)^{15-0} + {}_{15}C_1(0.3)^1(1 - 0.3)^{15-1}$$

$$= 0.0047 + 0.0305$$

$$= 0.035$$

Now we use the Rule of Complements:

$$P(\text{More than } 1) = 1 - P(0 \text{ or } 1) = 1 - 0.035 = 0.965$$

d. Between 1 and 4 inclusive means 1, 2, 3, or 4.

$$P(1 \text{ or } 2 \text{ or } 3 \text{ or } 4) = P(1) + P(2) + P(3) + P(4)$$

$$= {}_{15}C_1(0.3)^1(1 - 0.3)^{15-1} + {}_{15}C_2(0.3)^2(1 - 0.3)^{15-2}$$

$$+ {}_{15}C_3(0.3)^3(1 - 0.3)^{15-3} + {}_{15}C_4(0.3)^4(1 - 0.3)^{15-4}$$

$$= 0.0305 + 0.0916 + 0.1700 + 0.2186$$

$$= 0.511$$

Explain It Again

When can we use a table?
Tables contain only a limited selection of values for n and p. Probabilities involving values not in the table must be computed by hand or with technology.

Using a table to compute binomial probabilities

Table A.1 contains probabilities for the binomial distribution. It can be used to compute binomial probabilities for values of n up to 20 and certain values of p.

EXAMPLE 5.15

Use a table to compute binomial probabilities

According to the Nielsen Company, approximately 30% of U.S. households had a digital video recorder (DVR) at the end of the year 2008. Suppose a simple random sample of 15 households is taken. Use Table A.1 to compute the following probabilities.

a. Find the probability that exactly five of the sampled households have a DVR.

b. Find the probability that fewer than four of the sampled households have a DVR.

c. Find the probability that the number of sampled households that have a DVR is between 6 and 8 inclusive.

Solution

a. We have $n = 15$, so we go to the section of Table A.1 that corresponds to $n = 15$. This is shown in Figure 5.4. We look at the column corresponding to $p = 0.30$. Now for each value in the column labeled "x," the number in the table is the probability $P(x)$. We therefore look in the row corresponding to $x = 5$. The probability that exactly five families have a DVR is $P(5) = 0.206$.

							p							
n	**x**	**0.05**	**0.10**	**0.20**	**0.25**	**0.30**	**0.40**	**0.50**	**0.60**	**0.70**	**0.75**	**0.80**	**0.90**	**0.95**
15	0	0.463	0.206	0.035	0.013	0.005	0.000+	0.000+	0.000+	0.000+	0.000+	0.000+	0.000+	0.000+
	1	0.366	0.343	0.132	0.067	0.031	0.005	0.000+	0.000+	0.000+	0.000+	0.000+	0.000+	0.000+
	2	0.135	0.267	0.231	0.156	0.092	0.022	0.003	0.000+	0.000+	0.000+	0.000+	0.000+	0.000+
	3	0.031	0.129	0.250	0.225	0.170	0.063	0.014	0.002	0.000+	0.000+	0.000+	0.000+	0.000+
	4	0.005	0.043	0.188	0.225	0.219	0.127	0.042	0.007	0.001	0.000+	0.000+	0.000+	0.000+
	5	0.001	0.010	0.103	0.165	0.206	0.186	0.092	0.024	0.003	0.001	0.000+	0.000+	0.000+
	6	0.000+	0.002	0.043	0.092	0.147	0.207	0.153	0.061	0.012	0.003	0.001	0.000+	0.000+
	7	0.000+	0.000+	0.014	0.039	0.081	0.177	0.196	0.118	0.035	0.013	0.003	0.000+	0.000+
	8	0.000+	0.000+	0.003	0.013	0.035	0.118	0.196	0.177	0.081	0.039	0.014	0.000+	0.000+
	9	0.000+	0.000+	0.001	0.003	0.012	0.061	0.153	0.207	0.147	0.092	0.043	0.002	0.000+
	10	0.000+	0.000+	0.000+	0.001	0.003	0.024	0.092	0.186	0.206	0.165	0.103	0.010	0.001
	11	0.000+	0.000+	0.000+	0.000+	0.001	0.007	0.042	0.127	0.219	0.225	0.188	0.043	0.005
	12	0.000+	0.000+	0.000+	0.000+	0.000+	0.002	0.014	0.063	0.170	0.225	0.250	0.129	0.031
	13	0.000+	0.000+	0.000+	0.000+	0.000+	0.000+	0.003	0.022	0.092	0.156	0.231	0.267	0.135
	14	0.000+	0.000+	0.000+	0.000+	0.000+	0.000+	0.000+	0.005	0.031	0.067	0.132	0.343	0.366
	15	0.000+	0.000+	0.000+	0.000+	0.000+	0.000+	0.000+	0.000+	0.005	0.013	0.035	0.206	0.463

Figure 5.4

Explain It Again

Answers using technology may differ: If you find P(Fewer than 4) using technology, your answer will be 0.297 rather than 0.298. This difference isn't large enough to matter.

b. P(Fewer than 4) $= P(0) + P(1) + P(2) + P(3)$. We find these probabilities in Table A.1 and add them. See Figure 5.5.

$$P(\text{Fewer than 4}) = 0.005 + 0.031 + 0.092 + 0.170$$
$$= 0.298$$

							p							
n	**x**	**0.05**	**0.10**	**0.20**	**0.25**	**0.30**	**0.40**	**0.50**	**0.60**	**0.70**	**0.75**	**0.80**	**0.90**	**0.95**
15	0	0.463	0.206	0.035	0.013	0.005	0.000+	0.000+	0.000+	0.000+	0.000+	0.000+	0.000+	0.000+
	1	0.366	0.343	0.132	0.067	0.031	0.005	0.000+	0.000+	0.000+	0.000+	0.000+	0.000+	0.000+
	2	0.135	0.267	0.231	0.156	0.092	0.022	0.003	0.000+	0.000+	0.000+	0.000+	0.000+	0.000+
	3	0.031	0.129	0.250	0.225	0.170	0.063	0.014	0.002	0.000+	0.000+	0.000+	0.000+	0.000+
	4	0.005	0.043	0.188	0.225	0.219	0.127	0.042	0.007	0.001	0.000+	0.000+	0.000+	0.000+
	5	0.001	0.010	0.103	0.165	0.206	0.186	0.092	0.024	0.003	0.001	0.000+	0.000+	0.000+
	6	0.000+	0.002	0.043	0.092	0.147	0.207	0.153	0.061	0.012	0.003	0.001	0.000+	0.000+
	7	0.000+	0.000+	0.014	0.039	0.081	0.177	0.196	0.118	0.035	0.013	0.003	0.000+	0.000+
	8	0.000+	0.000+	0.003	0.013	0.035	0.118	0.196	0.177	0.081	0.039	0.014	0.000+	0.000+
	9	0.000+	0.000+	0.001	0.003	0.012	0.061	0.153	0.207	0.147	0.092	0.043	0.002	0.000+
	10	0.000+	0.000+	0.000+	0.001	0.003	0.024	0.092	0.186	0.206	0.165	0.103	0.010	0.001
	11	0.000+	0.000+	0.000+	0.000+	0.001	0.007	0.042	0.127	0.219	0.225	0.188	0.043	0.005
	12	0.000+	0.000+	0.000+	0.000+	0.000+	0.002	0.014	0.063	0.170	0.225	0.250	0.129	0.031
	13	0.000+	0.000+	0.000+	0.000+	0.000+	0.000+	0.003	0.022	0.092	0.156	0.231	0.267	0.135
	14	0.000+	0.000+	0.000+	0.000+	0.000+	0.000+	0.000+	0.005	0.031	0.067	0.132	0.343	0.366
	15	0.000+	0.000+	0.000+	0.000+	0.000+	0.000+	0.000+	0.000+	0.005	0.013	0.035	0.206	0.463

Figure 5.5

c. P(Between 6 and 8 inclusive) $= P(6) + P(7) + P(8)$. We find these probabilities in Table A.1 and add them. See Figure 5.6.

$$P(\text{Between 6 and 8 inclusive}) = 0.147 + 0.081 + 0.035$$
$$= 0.263$$

| | | p | | | | | | | | | | | | |
n	x	0.05	0.10	0.20	0.25	0.30	0.40	0.50	0.60	0.70	0.75	0.80	0.90	0.95
15	0	0.463	0.206	0.035	0.013	0.005	0.000+	0.000+	0.000+	0.000+	0.000+	0.000+	0.000+	0.000+
	1	0.366	0.343	0.132	0.067	0.031	0.005	0.000+	0.000+	0.000+	0.000+	0.000+	0.000+	0.000+
	2	0.135	0.267	0.231	0.156	0.092	0.022	0.003	0.000+	0.000+	0.000+	0.000+	0.000+	0.000+
	3	0.031	0.129	0.250	0.225	0.170	0.063	0.014	0.002	0.000+	0.000+	0.000+	0.000+	0.000+
	4	0.005	0.043	0.188	0.225	0.219	0.127	0.042	0.007	0.001	0.000+	0.000+	0.000+	0.000+
	5	0.001	0.010	0.103	0.165	0.206	0.186	0.092	0.024	0.003	0.001	0.000+	0.000+	0.000+
	6	0.000+	0.002	0.043	0.092	0.147	0.207	0.153	0.061	0.012	0.003	0.001	0.000+	0.000+
	7	0.000+	0.000+	0.014	0.039	0.081	0.177	0.196	0.118	0.035	0.013	0.003	0.000+	0.000+
	8	0.000+	0.000+	0.003	0.013	0.035	0.118	0.196	0.177	0.081	0.039	0.014	0.000+	0.000+
	9	0.000+	0.000+	0.001	0.003	0.012	0.061	0.153	0.207	0.147	0.092	0.043	0.002	0.000+
	10	0.000+	0.000+	0.000+	0.001	0.003	0.024	0.092	0.186	0.206	0.165	0.103	0.010	0.001
	11	0.000+	0.000+	0.000+	0.000+	0.001	0.007	0.042	0.127	0.219	0.225	0.188	0.043	0.005
	12	0.000+	0.000+	0.000+	0.000+	0.000+	0.002	0.014	0.063	0.170	0.225	0.250	0.129	0.031
	13	0.000+	0.000+	0.000+	0.000+	0.000+	0.000+	0.003	0.022	0.092	0.156	0.231	0.267	0.135
	14	0.000+	0.000+	0.000+	0.000+	0.000+	0.000+	0.000+	0.005	0.031	0.067	0.132	0.343	0.366
	15	0.000+	0.000+	0.000+	0.000+	0.000+	0.000+	0.000+	0.000+	0.005	0.013	0.035	0.206	0.463

Figure 5.6

EXAMPLE 5.16

Using technology to compute binomial probabilities

According to the Nielsen Company, approximately 30% of U.S. households had a digital video recorder (DVR) at the end of the year 2008. Suppose a simple random sample of 15 households is taken. Use technology to compute the following probabilities.

a. Find the probability that exactly four of the sampled households have a DVR.

b. Find the probability that five or fewer of the sampled households have a DVR.

Solution

a. We will use the TI-84 Plus calculator. We use the **binompdf** command. We input 15 for n, .3 for p, and 4 for x. The following display shows the result. Step-by-step instructions are given in the Using Technology section on page 215.

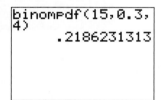

b. We will use MINITAB. The following display shows the result. Step-by-step instructions are given in the Using Technology section on page 215.

```
Binomial with n = 15 and p = 0.3

x   P( X <= x )
5      0.721621
```

Check Your Understanding

2. In June 2009, 20% of video gamers had heard of the game "Modern Warfare 2" (data from GamesBeat). Assume that 18 gamers are randomly sampled.

    a. Use the binomial probability distribution to compute the probability that exactly four of them have heard of "Modern Warfare 2."

    b. Use Table A.1 to find the probability that fewer than three of them have heard of "Modern Warfare 2."

    c. Use any valid method to find the probability that more than three of them have heard of "Modern Warfare 2."

    d. Use any valid method to find the probability that the number who have heard of "Modern Warfare 2" is between 2 and 6 inclusive.

3. The name of "Modern Warfare 2" was originally planned to be "Call to Duty: Modern Warfare 2." In June 2009, 40% of gamers had heard of "Call to Duty: Modern Warfare 2" (data from GamesBeat). Assume that 12 gamers are randomly sampled.

    a. Use the binomial probability distribution to compute the probability that exactly seven of them have heard of "Call to Duty: Modern Warfare 2."

    b. Use Table A.1 to find the probability that fewer than five of them have heard of "Call to Duty: Modern Warfare 2."

    c. Use any valid method to find the probability that more than six of them have heard of "Call to Duty: Modern Warfare 2."

    d. Use any valid method to find the probability that the number who have heard of "Call to Duty: Modern Warfare 2" is between 3 and 5 inclusive.

Answers are on page 218.

Objective 4 Compute the mean and variance of a binomial random variable

Mean and Variance of a Binomial Random Variable

A fair coin has probability 0.5 of landing heads. If we toss a fair coin ten times, we expect to get 5 heads, on the average. The reason is that 5 is half of 10, or, in symbols, $5 = 10 \cdot 0.5$. We can see that the mean number of successes was found by multiplying the number of trials by the success probability. This holds true in general.

The variance and standard deviation of a binomial random variable are straightforward to compute as well, although the reasoning behind them is not so obvious.

Mean, Variance, and Standard Deviation of a Binomial Random Variable

Let X be a binomial random variable with n trials and success probability p. Then the mean of X is

$$\mu_X = np$$

The variance of X is

$$\sigma_X^2 = np(1 - p)$$

The standard deviation of X is

$$\sigma_X = \sqrt{np(1 - p)}$$

EXAMPLE 5.17   Find the mean and standard deviation of a binomial random variable

The probability that a new car of a certain model will require repairs during the warranty period is 0.15. A particular dealership sells 25 such cars. Let X be the number that will require repairs during the warranty period. Find the mean and standard deviation of X.

Solution

There are $n = 25$ trials, with success probability $p = 0.15$. The mean is

$$\mu_X = np = 25 \cdot 0.15 = 3.75$$

The standard deviation is

$$\sigma_X = \sqrt{np(1-p)} = \sqrt{25 \cdot 0.15 \cdot (1-0.15)} = 1.785$$

Check Your Understanding

4. Gregor Mendel discovered the basic laws of heredity by studying pea plants. In one experiment, he produced plants whose parent plants contained genes for both green and yellow pods. Mendel's theory states that the offspring of two such parents has probability 0.75 of having green pods. Assume that 80 such plants are produced.
   a. Find the mean number of plants that have green pods.
   b. Find the variance of the number of plants that have green pods.
   c. Find the standard deviation of the number of plants that have green pods.

Answers are on page 218.

USING TECHNOLOGY

We use Example 5.14 to illustrate the technology steps.

TI-84 PLUS

Computing binomial probabilities of the form $P(x)$ or P(Less than or equal to x)

Step 1. Press **2nd, VARS** to access the **DISTR** menu.

- To compute $P(x)$, select **binompdf** and enter the values for n, p, and x separated by commas and press **ENTER**.

- To compute P(Less than or equal to x), select **binomcdf** and enter the values for n, p, and x separated by commas, and press **ENTER**.

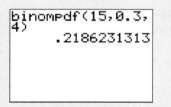

Figure A   **Figure B**

Using the TI-84 PLUS Stat Wizards (see Appendix B for more information)
Step 1. Press **2nd, VARS** to access the **DISTR** menu.

- To compute $P(x)$, select **binompdf** and enter the value for n in the **trials** field, the value for p in the **p** field and the value for x in the **x value** field. Select **Paste** and press **ENTER** to paste the command to the home screen. Press **ENTER** again to run the command.

- To compute $P(x)$, select **binomcdf** and enter the value for n in the **trials** field, the value for p in the **p** field and the value for x in the **x value** field. Select **Paste** and press **ENTER** to paste the command to the home screen. Press **ENTER** again to run the command.

For Example 5.14, $n = 15$ and $p = 0.3$. Figure A displays the result of part (a), which asks for $P(4)$. Figure B displays the result of part (b), which asks for P(Less than or equal to 2).

MINITAB

Computing binomial probabilities of the form $P(x)$ or P(Less than or equal to x)

Step 1. Click **Calc**, then **Probability Distributions**, then **Binomial**.
Step 2. Enter the value for n in the **Number of trials** field and the value for p in the **Probability of success** field.
Step 3. To compute $P(x)$, select the **Probability** option and enter the value for x in the **Input constant** field. To compute P(Less than or equal to x), select the **Cumulative probability** option and enter the value for x in the **Input constant** field.
Step 4. Click **OK**.

Note: Binomial probabilities may be computed for a column of values by entering the column name in the **Input column** field.

EXCEL

Computing binomial probabilities of the form $P(x)$ or $P(\text{Less than or equal to } x)$

Step 1. In an empty cell, select the **Insert Function** icon and highlight **Statistical** in the category field.

Step 2. Click on the **BINOM.DIST** function and press **OK**.

Step 3. Enter the value for x in the **Number_s** field, the value for n in the **Trials** field, and the value for p in the **Probability_s** field.

Step 4. To compute $P(x)$, enter **FALSE** in the **Cumulative** field. To compute $P(\text{Less than or equal to } x)$, enter **TRUE** in the **Cumulative field**.

Step 5. Click **OK**. Figure C illustrates computing $P(4)$ in part (a) of Example 5.14.

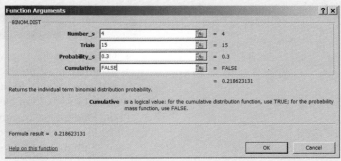

Figure C

SECTION 5.2   Exercises

Exercises 1–4 are the Check Your Understanding exercises located within the section.

Understanding the Concepts

In Exercises 5–7, fill in each blank with the appropriate word or phrase.

5. In a binomial distribution, there are _____ possible outcomes for each trial.

6. To compute a binomial probability, we must know both the success probability and the number n of _____.

7. If X is a binomial random variable with n trials and success probability p, the standard deviation of X is $\sigma_X = $ _____.

In Exercises 8–10, determine whether the statement is true or false. If the statement is false, rewrite it as a true statement.

8. The trials in a binomial distribution are independent.

9. A binomial random variable with n trials can sometimes have a value greater than n.

10. The mean of a binomial random variable is found by multiplying the number of trials by the success probability.

Practicing the Skills

In Exercises 11–16, determine whether the random variable X has a binomial distribution. If it does, state the number of trials n. If it does not, explain why not.

11. Ten students are chosen from a statistics class of 25 students. Let X be the number who got an A in the class.

12. Ten students are chosen from a statistics class of 300 students. Let X be the number who got an A in the class.

13. A coin is tossed seven times. Let X be the number of heads obtained.

14. A die is tossed three times. Let X be the sum of the three numbers obtained.

15. A coin is tossed until a head appears. Let X be the number of tosses.

16. A random sample of 250 voters is chosen from a list of 10,000 registered voters. Let X be the number who support the incumbent mayor for reelection.

In Exercises 17–26, determine the indicated probability for a binomial experiment with the given number of trials n and the given success probability p.

17. $n = 5$, $p = 0.7$, $P(3)$

18. $n = 10$, $p = 0.2$, $P(1)$

19. $n = 20$, $p = 0.6$, $P(8)$

20. $n = 14$, $p = 0.3$, $P(8)$

21. $n = 3$, $p = 0.4$, $P(0)$

22. $n = 6$, $p = 0.8$, $P(6)$

23. $n = 8$, $p = 0.2$, $P(\text{Fewer than 3})$

24. $n = 15$, $p = 0.9$, $P(14 \text{ or more})$

25. $n = 50$, $p = 0.03$, $P(2 \text{ or fewer})$

26. $n = 30$, $p = 0.9$, $P(\text{More than 27})$

Working with the Concepts

27. **Take a guess:** A student takes a true–false test that has 10 questions and guesses randomly at each answer. Let X be the number of questions answered correctly.
    a. Find $P(4)$.
    b. Find $P(\text{Fewer than 3})$.
    c. To pass the test, the student must answer 7 or more questions correctly. Would it be unusual for the student to pass? Explain.

28. **Take another guess:** A student takes a multiple-choice test that has 10 questions. Each question has four choices. The student guesses randomly at each answer.
    a. Find $P(3)$.
    b. Find $P(\text{More than 2})$.

c. To pass the test, the student must answer 7 or more questions correctly. Would it be unusual for the student to pass? Explain.

29. **Your flight has been delayed:** At Denver International Airport, 84% of the flights in January 2010 arrived on time. A sample of 12 flights is studied.
    a. Find the probability that all 12 of the flights were on time.
    b. Find the probability that exactly 10 of the flights were on time.
    c. Find the probability that 10 or more of the flights were on time.
    d. Would it be unusual for 11 or more of the flights to be on time?
    Source: *The Denver Post*

30. **Car inspection:** Of all the registered automobiles in Colorado, 8% fail the state emissions test. Twelve automobiles are selected at random to undergo an emissions test.
    a. Find the probability that exactly three of them fail the test.
    b. Find the probability that fewer than three of them fail the test.
    c. Find the probability that more than two of them fail the test.
    d. Would it be unusual for none of them to fail the test?
    Source: *Air Care Colorado*

31. **Google it:** According to a report of the Nielsen Company, 65% of Internet searches in May 2010 used the Google search engine. Assume that a sample of 25 searches is studied.
    a. What is the probability that exactly 20 of them used Google?
    b. What is the probability that 15 or fewer used Google?
    c. What is the probability that more than 20 of them used Google?
    d. Would it be unusual if fewer than 12 used Google?

32. **Text me:** In 2009, a study from Mediamark Research and Intelligence reported that 57% of teenagers sent a text message on their cell phone during the past 30 days. A sample of 15 teenagers is studied.
    a. What is the probability that six or more of them sent a text message?
    b. What is the probability that fewer than 10 of them sent a text message?

    c. What is the probability that exactly eight of them sent a text message?
    d. Would it be unusual if more than 12 of them had sent a text message?

33. **Blood types:** The blood type O negative is called the "universal donor" type, because it is the only blood type that may safely be transfused into any person. Therefore, when someone needs a transfusion in an emergency and their blood type cannot be determined, they are given type O negative blood. For this reason, donors with this blood type are crucial to blood banks. Unfortunately, this blood type is fairly rare; according to the Red Cross, only 7% of U.S. residents have type O negative blood. Assume that a blood bank has recruited 20 donors.
    a. What is the probability that two or more of them have type O negative blood?
    b. What is the probability that fewer than four of them will have type O negative blood?
    c. Would it be unusual if none of the donors had type O negative blood?
    d. What is the mean number of donors who have type O negative blood?
    e. What is the standard deviation of the number of donors who have type O negative blood?

34. **Coronary bypass surgery:** The Agency for Healthcare Research and Quality reported that 53% of people who had coronary bypass surgery in 2008 were over the age of 65. Fifteen coronary bypass patients are sampled.
    a. What is the probability that exactly 9 of them are over the age of 65?
    b. What is the probability that more than 10 are over the age of 65?
    c. What is the probability that fewer than 8 are over the age of 65?
    d. Would it be unusual if all of them were over the age of 65?
    e. What is the mean number of people over the age of 65 in a sample of 15 coronary bypass patients?
    f. What is the standard deviation of the number of people over the age of 65 in a sample of 15 coronary bypass patients?

35. **College bound:** The *Statistical Abstract of the United States* reported that 67% of students who graduated from high school in 2007 enrolled in college. Thirty high school graduates are sampled.
    a. What is the probability that exactly 18 of them enroll in college?
    b. What is the probability that more than 15 enroll in college?
    c. What is the probability that fewer than 12 enroll in college?
    d. Would it be unusual if more than 25 of them enroll in college?
    e. What is the mean number who enroll in college in a sample of 30 high school graduates?
    f. What is the standard deviation of the number who enroll in college in a sample of 30 high school graduates?

36. **Big babies:** The Centers for Disease Control and Prevention reports that 25% of baby boys 6–8 months old in the United States weigh more than 20 pounds. A sample of 16 babies is studied.

a. What is the probability that exactly 5 of them weigh more than 20 pounds?

b. What is the probability that more than 6 weigh more than 20 pounds?

c. What is the probability that fewer than 3 weigh more than 20 pounds?

d. Would it be unusual if more than 8 of them weigh more than 20 pounds?

e. What is the mean number who weigh more than 20 pounds in a sample of 16 babies aged 6–8 months?

f. What is the standard deviation of the number who weigh more than 20 pounds in a sample of 16 babies aged 6–8 months?

37. **High blood pressure:** The National Health and Nutrition Survey reported that 30% of adults in the United States have hypertension (high blood pressure). A sample of 25 adults is studied.

a. What is the probability that exactly 6 of them have hypertension?

b. What is the probability that more than 8 have hypertension?

c. What is the probability that fewer than 4 have hypertension?

d. Would it be unusual if more than 10 of them have hypertension?

e. What is the mean number who have hypertension in a sample of 25 adults?

f. What is the standard deviation of the number who have hypertension in a sample of 25 adults?

38. **Stress at work:** In a poll conducted by the General Social Survey, 81% of respondents said that their jobs were sometimes or always stressful. Ten workers are chosen at random.

a. What is the probability that exactly 7 of them find their jobs stressful?

b. What is the probability that more than 6 find their jobs stressful?

c. What is the probability that fewer than 5 find their jobs stressful?

d. Would it be unusual if fewer than 4 of them find their jobs stressful?

e. What is the mean number who find their jobs stressful in a sample of 10 workers?

f. What is the standard deviation of the number who find their jobs stressful in a sample of 10 workers?

Extending the Concepts

39. **Recursive computation of binomial probabilities:** Binomial probabilities are often hard to compute by hand, because the computation involves factorials and numbers raised to large powers. It can be shown through algebraic manipulation that if X is a random variable whose distribution is binomial with n trials and success probability p, then

$$P(X = x + 1) = \left(\frac{p}{1-p}\right)\left(\frac{n-x}{x+1}\right) P(X = x)$$

If we know $P(X = x)$, we can use this equation to calculate $P(X = x + 1)$ without computing any factorials or powers.

a. Let X have the binomial distribution with $n = 25$ trials and success probability $p = 0.6$. It can be shown that $P(X = 14) = 0.14651$. Find $P(X = 15)$.

b. Let X have the binomial distribution with $n = 10$ trials and success probability $p = 0.35$. It can be shown that $P(X = 0) = 0.0134627$. Find $P(X = x)$ for $x = 1, 2, ..., 10$.

Answers to Check Your Understanding Exercises for Section 5.2

1. a. X is a binomial random variable.	**2. a.** 0.2153 **b.** 0.2713 **c.** 0.4990 **d.** 0.8496
b. X is not a binomial random variable.	**3. a.** 0.1009 **b.** 0.4382 **c.** 0.1582 **d.** 0.5818
c. X is a binomial random variable.	**4. a.** 60 **b.** 15 **c.** 3.8730

Chapter 5 Summary

Section 5.1: A random variable is a numerical outcome of a probability experiment. Discrete random variables are random variables whose possible values can be listed, whereas continuous random variables can take on any value in some interval. A probability distribution for a discrete random variable specifies the probability for each possible value. A probability histogram is a histogram in which the heights of the rectangles are the probabilities for the possible values of the random variable. A probability histogram can also be thought of as a relative frequency histogram for a population. The law of large numbers for histograms states that as the sample size increases, the relative frequency histogram for the sample approaches the probability histogram.

The mean of a random variable, also called the expected value, measures the center of the distribution. The standard deviation of a random variable measures the spread. The law of large numbers for means states that as the sample size increases, the sample mean approaches the population mean.

Section 5.2: The binomial distribution is an important discrete probability distribution. A random variable has a binomial distribution if it represents the number of successes in a fixed number n of independent trials, all of which have the same success probability p. Binomial probabilities can be found in a table or computed with technology. The mean of a binomial random variable is np, the number of trials multiplied by the success probability. The variance is $np(1 - p)$, and the standard deviation is $\sqrt{np(1 - p)}$.

Vocabulary and Notation

binomial distribution   208
continuous random variable   194
discrete random variable   194
expected value   199

law of large numbers for means   200
mean   199
probability distribution   195

probability histogram   198
random variable   194
trial   208

Important Formulas

Mean of a discrete random variable:
$$\mu_X = \sum[x \cdot P(x)]$$

Variance of a discrete random variable:
$$\sigma_X^2 = \sum[(x - \mu_X)^2 \cdot P(x)] = \sum[x^2 \cdot P(x)] - \mu_X^2$$

Standard deviation of a discrete random variable:
$$\sigma_X = \sqrt{\sigma_X^2}$$

Mean of a binomial random variable:
$$\mu_X = np$$

Variance of a binomial random variable:
$$\sigma_X^2 = np(1 - p)$$

Standard deviation of a binomial random variable:
$$\sigma_X = \sqrt{np(1 - p)}$$

Chapter Quiz

1. Explain why the following is *not* a probability distribution.

x	6	7	8	9	10
$P(x)$	0.32	0.11	0.19	0.28	0.03

2. Find the mean of the random variable X with the following probability distribution.

x	−2	1	4	5
$P(x)$	0.3	0.2	0.1	0.4

3. Refer to Exercise 2.
   a. Find the variance of the random variable X.
   b. Find the standard deviation of the random variable X.

4. Find the missing value that makes the following a valid probability distribution.

x	2	3	5	8	10
$P(x)$	0.23	0.12	0.09	?	0.37

5. The following table presents a probability distribution for the number of pets each family has in a certain neighborhood.

Number of pets	0	1	2	3	4
Probability	0.4	0.2	0.2	0.1	0.1

Construct a probability histogram.

6. Refer to Exercise 5. Find the probability that a randomly selected family has:
   a. 1 or 2 pets
   b. More than 2 pets
   c. No more than 3 pets
   d. At least 1 pet

7. Refer to Exercise 5. Find the mean number of pets.

8. Refer to Exercise 5. Find the standard deviation of the number of pets.

9. At a cell phone battery plant, 5% of cell phone batteries produced are defective. A quality control engineer randomly collects a sample of 50 batteries from a large shipment from this plant and inspects them for defects. Find the probability that
   a. None of the batteries are defective.
   b. At least one of the batteries is defective.
   c. No more than 3 of the batteries are defective.

10. Refer to Exercise 9. Find the mean number of defective batteries in the sample of size 50.

11. Refer to Exercise 9. Find the standard deviation of the number of defective batteries in the sample of 50.

12. A meteorologist states that the probability of rain tomorrow is 0.4 and the probability of rain on the next day is 0.6. Assuming these probabilities are accurate, and that the rain events are independent, find the probability distribution for X, the number of days out of the next two that it rains.

13. At a large clothing store, 20% of all purchased items are returned. A random sample of 12 purchases is selected. Find the probability that
    a. Exactly three of the purchased items were returned.
    b. More than two of the purchased items were returned.
    c. Fewer than two of the purchased items were returned.

14. Refer to Exercise 13. Find the mean number of items returned.

15. Refer to Exercise 13. Find the standard deviation of the number of items returned.

Review Exercises

1. **Which are distributions?** Which of the following tables represent probability distributions?

a.
x	$P(x)$
3	0.35
4	0.20
5	0.18
6	0.09
7	0.18

b.
x	$P(x)$
5	0.27
6	0.45
7	−0.06
8	0.44

c.
x	$P(x)$
0	0.02
1	0.34
2	1.02
3	0.01
4	0.43
5	0.14

d.
x	$P(x)$
2	0.10
3	0.07
4	0.75
5	0.08

2. **Mean, variance, and standard deviation:** A random variable X has the following probability distribution.

x	6	7	8	9	10	11
$P(x)$	0.21	0.12	0.29	0.11	0.01	0.26

a. Find the mean of X.
b. Find the variance of X.
c. Find the standard deviation of X.

3. **AP tests:** Advanced Placement (AP) tests are graded on a scale of 1 (low) through 5 (high). The College Board reported that the distribution of scores on the AP Statistics Exam in 2009 was as follows:

x	1	2	3	4	5
$P(x)$	0.34	0.25	0.18	0.16	0.07

A score of 3 or higher is generally required for college credit. What is the probability that a student scores 3 or higher?

4. **AP tests again:** During the 2008–2009 academic year, approximately 1.7 million students took one or more AP tests. Following is the frequency distribution of the number of AP tests taken by students who took one or more AP tests.

Number of Tests	Frequency (in 1000s)
1	953
2	423
3	194
4	80
5	29
6	9
7	3
8	1
Total	1692

Source: The College Board

Let X represent the number of exams taken by a student who took one or more.
a. Construct the probability distribution for X.
b. Find the probability that a student took exactly one exam.

    c. Compute the mean μ_X.

    d. Compute the standard deviation σ_X.

5. **Lottery tickets:** Several million lottery tickets are sold, and 60% of the tickets are held by women. Five winning tickets will be drawn at random. What is the probability that three or fewer of the winners will be women?

6. **Lottery tickets:** Refer to Exercise 5. What is the probability that three of the winners will be of one gender and two of the winners will be of the other gender?

7. **Genetic disease:** Sickle-cell anemia is a disease that results when a person has two copies of a certain recessive gene. People with one copy of the gene are called carriers. Carriers do not have the disease, but can pass the gene on to their children. A child born to parents who are both carriers has probability 0.25 of having sickle-cell anemia. A medical study samples 18 children in families where both parents are carriers.

    a. What is the probability that four or more of the children have sickle-cell anemia?

    b. What is the probability that fewer than three of the children have sickle-cell anemia?

8. **Craps:** In the game of craps, you may bet $1 that the next roll of the dice will be an 11. If the dice come up 11, your profit is $15. If the dice don't come up 11, you lose $1. The probability that the dice come up 11 is 1/18. What is the expected value of your profit? Is it an expected gain or an expected loss?

9. **Looking for a job:** According to the General Social Survey conducted at the University of Chicago, 59% of employed adults believe that if they lost their job, it would be easy to find another one with a similar salary. Suppose that 10 employed adults are randomly selected.

    a. Find the probability that exactly three of them believe it would be easy to find another job.

    b. Find the probability that more than two of them believe it would be easy to find another job.

10. **Reading tests:** According to the National Center for Education Statistics, 66% of fourth-graders could read at a basic level in 2007. Suppose that eight fourth-graders are randomly selected.

    a. Find the probability that exactly five of them can read at a basic level.

    b. Find the probability that more than six of them can read at a basic level.

11. **Genetic disease:** Refer to Exercise 7. Would it be unusual if none of the 18 children had sickle-cell anemia?

12. **Looking for a job:** Refer to Exercise 9. Would it be unusual if all 10 of them believed it would be easy to find another job?

13. **Reading tests:** Refer to Exercise 10. Would it be unusual if all eight of them could read at a basic level?

14. **Rain, rain, go away:** Let X be the number of days during the next month that it rains. Does X have a binomial distribution? Why or why not?

15. **Survey sample:** In a college with 5000 students, 100 are randomly chosen to complete a survey in which they rate the quality of the cafeteria food. Let X be the number of freshmen who are chosen. Does X have a binomial distribution? Why or why not?

Write About It

1. Provide an example of a discrete random variable and explain why it is discrete.

2. Provide an example of a continuous random variable and explain why it is continuous.

3. If a business decision has an expected gain, is it possible to lose money? Explain.

4. When a population mean is unknown, people will often approximate it with the mean of a large sample. Explain why this is justified.

5. Provide an example of a binomial random variable and explain how each condition for the binomial distribution is fulfilled.

6. Twenty percent of the men in a certain community are more than six feet tall. An anthropologist samples five men from a large family in the community and counts the number X who are more than six feet tall. Explain why the binomial distribution is not appropriate in this situation. Is $P(X = 0)$ likely to be greater than or less than the value predicted by the binomial distribution with $n = 10$ and $p = 0.4$? Explain your reasoning.

Case Study: Benford's Law: Do The Digits 1–9 Occur Equally Often?

One of the most surprising probability distributions found in practice is given by a rule known as Benford's law. This probability distribution concerns the first digits of numbers. The first digit of a number may be any of the digits 1, 2, 3, 4, 5, 6, 7, 8, or 9. It is reasonable to believe that, for most sets of numbers encountered in practice, these digits would occur equally often. In fact, it has been observed that for many naturally occurring data sets, smaller numbers occur more frequently as the first digit than larger numbers do. Benford's law is named for Frank Benford, an engineer at General Electric, who stated it in 1938.

Following are the populations of the 50 states, as of 2003. The first digit of each population number is listed separately.

State	Population	First Digit	State	Population	First Digit	State	Population	First Digit
Alabama	4,557,808	4	Louisiana	4,523,628	4	Ohio	11,464,042	1
Alaska	663,661	6	Maine	1,321,505	1	Oklahoma	3,547,884	3
Arizona	5,939,292	5	Maryland	5,600,388	5	Oregon	3,641,056	3
Arkansas	2,779,154	2	Massachusetts	6,398,743	6	Pennsylvania	12,429,616	1
California	36,132,147	3	Michigan	10,120,860	1	Rhode Island	1,076,189	1
Colorado	4,665,177	4	Minnesota	5,132,799	5	South Carolina	4,255,083	4
Connecticut	3,510,297	3	Mississippi	2,921,088	2	South Dakota	775,933	7
Delaware	843,524	8	Missouri	5,800,310	5	Tennessee	5,962,959	5
Florida	17,789,864	1	Montana	935,670	9	Texas	22,859,968	2
Georgia	9,072,576	9	Nebraska	1,758,787	1	Utah	2,469,585	2
Hawaii	1,275,194	1	Nevada	2,414,807	2	Vermont	623,050	6
Idaho	1,429,096	1	New Hampshire	1,309,940	1	Virginia	7,567,465	7
Illinois	12,763,371	1	New Jersey	8,717,925	8	Washington	6,287,759	6
Indiana	6,271,973	6	New Mexico	1,928,384	1	West Virginia	1,816,856	1
Iowa	2,966,334	2	New York	19,254,630	1	Wisconsin	5,536,201	5
Kansas	2,744,687	2	North Carolina	8,683,242	8	Wyoming	509,294	5
Kentucky	4,173,405	4	North Dakota	636,677	6			

Here is a frequency distribution of the first digits of the state populations:

Digit	Frequency	Digit	Frequency
1	14	6	6
2	7	7	2
3	4	8	3
4	5	9	2
5	7		

For the state populations, the most frequent first digit is 1, with 7, 8, and 9 being the least frequent.

Now here is a table of the closing value of the Dow Jones Industrial Average for each of the years 1974–2008.

Year	Average	First Digit	Year	Average	First Digit
1974	616.24	6	1992	3301.11	3
1975	852.41	8	1993	3754.09	3
1976	1004.65	1	1994	3834.44	3
1977	831.17	8	1995	5117.12	5
1978	805.01	8	1996	6448.27	6
1979	838.74	8	1997	7908.25	7
1980	963.98	9	1998	9181.43	9
1981	875.00	8	1999	11497.12	1
1982	1046.55	1	2000	10786.85	1
1983	1258.64	1	2001	10021.50	1
1984	1211.57	1	2002	8341.63	8
1985	1546.67	1	2003	10453.92	1
1986	1895.95	1	2004	10783.01	1
1987	1938.83	1	2005	10717.50	1
1988	2168.57	2	2006	12463.15	1
1989	2753.20	2	2007	13264.82	1
1990	2633.66	2	2008	8776.39	8
1991	3168.83	3			

Here is a frequency distribution of the first digits of the stock market averages:

Digit	Frequency	Digit	Frequency
1	15	6	2
2	3	7	1
3	4	8	7
4	0	9	2
5	1		

For the stock market averages, the most frequent first digit by far is 1.

The stock market averages give a partial justification for Benford's law. Assume the stock market starts at 1000 and goes up 10% each year. It will take eight years for the average to exceed 2000. Thus, the first eight averages will begin with the digit 1. Now imagine that the average starts at 5000. If it goes up 10% each year, it would take only two years to exceed 6000, so there would be only two years starting with the digit 5. In general, Benford's law applies well to data where increments occur as a result of multiplication rather than addition, and where there is a wide range of values. It does not apply to data sets where the range of values is small.

Here is the probability distribution of digits as predicted by Benford's law:

Digit	Frequency	Digit	Frequency
1	0.301	6	0.067
2	0.176	7	0.058
3	0.125	8	0.051
4	0.097	9	0.046
5	0.079		

The surprising nature of Benford's law makes it a useful tool to detect fraud. When people make up numbers, they tend to make the first digits approximately uniformly distributed; in other words, they have approximately equal numbers of 1s, 2s, and so on. Many tax agencies, including the Internal Revenue Service, use software to detect deviations from Benford's law in tax returns.

Following are results from three hypothetical corporate tax returns. Each purports to be a list of expenditures, in dollars, that the corporation is claiming as deductions. Two of the three are genuine, and one is a fraud. Which one is the fraud?

i.

79,386	17,988
203,374	80,535
11,967	3,037
100,229	132,056
46,428	59,727
7,012	38,354
957,559	137,648
551,284	4,163
97,439	1,279
780,216	91,404
22,443	323,547
1,023	194,288
738,527	24,346
634,814	695,236
850,840	160,546

ii.

1,393	165,648
47,689	601,981
75.854	262,971
5,395	65,407
53,079	6,892
7,791	748,151
93,401	45,054
129,906	83,821
568,823	228,976
4,693	913,337
21,902	252,378
337,122	82,581
162,182	538,342
7,942	99,613
31,121	78,175

iii.

64,888	374,242
1,643	12,338
832,618	14,204
126,811	31,484
13,545	1,818
2,332	104,625
29,288	34,178
81,074	3,684
401,437	11,665
3,040	15,376
244,676	541,894
49,273	65,928
112,111	250,601
56,776	650,316
262,359	90,852

The Normal Distribution

Introduction

Beverage cans are made from a very thin sheet of aluminum, only 1/80 inch thick. Yet they must withstand pressures of up to 90 pounds per square inch (approximately three times the pressure in an automobile tire). Beverage companies often purchase cans in large shipments. To ensure that can failures are rare, quality control inspectors sample several cans from each shipment and test their strength by placing them in testing machines that apply force until the can fails (is punctured or crushed). The testing process destroys the cans, so the number of cans that can be tested is limited.

Assume that a can is considered defective if it fails at a pressure of less than 90 pounds per square inch. The quality control inspectors want the proportion of defective cans to be no more than 0.001, or 1 in 1000. They test 10 cans, with the following results.

Can	1	2	3	4	5	6	7	8	9	10
Pressure at Failure	95	96	98	99	99	100	101	101	103	104

Although none of the 10 cans were defective, this is not enough by itself to determine whether the proportion of defective cans is less than 1 in 1000. To make this determination, we must know something about the probability distribution of the pressures at which cans fail. In this chapter, we will study the **normal distribution**, which is the most important distribution in statistics. In the case study at the end of this chapter, we will show that if the pressures follow a normal distribution, we can estimate the proportion of defective cans.

Objectives

1. Use a probability density curve to describe a population
2. Use a normal curve to describe a normal population
3. Find areas under the standard normal curve
4. Find *z*-scores corresponding to areas under the normal curve

Objective 1 Use a probability density curve to describe a population

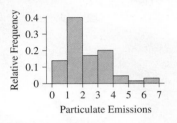

Figure 6.1 Relative frequency histogram for the emissions of a sample of 65 vehicles

Figure 6.1, first shown in Section 2.2, presents a relative frequency histogram for the emissions of a sample of 65 vehicles. The amount of emissions is a continuous variable, because its possible values are not limited to some discrete set. The class intervals are chosen so that each rectangle represents a reasonably large number of vehicles. If the sample were larger, we could make the rectangles narrower. In particular, if we had information on the entire population, containing millions of vehicles, we could make the rectangles extremely narrow. The histogram would then look quite smooth and could be approximated by a curve, which might look like Figure 6.2.

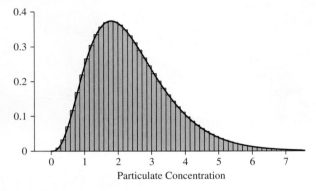

Figure 6.2 The histogram for a large population of vehicles could be drawn with extremely narrow rectangles, and could be represented by a curve.

If a vehicle were chosen at random from this population to have its emissions measured, the emissions level would be a continuous random variable. The curve used to describe the distribution of a continuous random variable is called the **probability density curve** of the random variable. The probability density curve tells us what proportion of the population falls within any given interval. For example, Figure 6.3 illustrates the proportion of the population of vehicles whose emissions levels are between 3 and 4. In general, the area under a probability density curve between any two values *a* and *b* has two interpretations: It represents the proportion of the population whose values are between *a* and *b*, and it also represents the probability that a randomly selected value from the population will be between *a* and *b*.

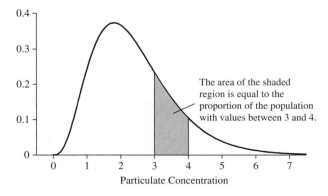

The area of the shaded region is equal to the proportion of the population with values between 3 and 4.

Figure 6.3 The area under a probability density curve between two values is equal to the proportion of the population that falls between the two values.

The region above a single point has zero width, and thus an area of 0. Therefore, when a population is represented with a probability density curve, the probability of obtaining a prespecified value exactly is equal to 0. For this reason, if X is a continuous random variable, then $P(X = a) = 0$ for any number a, and $P(a < X < b) = P(a \leq X \leq b)$ for any numbers a and b. For any probability density curve, the area under the entire curve is equal to 1, because this area represents the entire population.

SUMMARY

- A probability density curve represents the probability distribution of a continuous variable.
- The area under the entire curve is equal to 1.
- The area under the curve between two values a and b has two interpretations:
  1. It is the proportion of the population whose values are between a and b.
  2. It is the probability that a randomly selected individual will have a value between a and b.

EXAMPLE 6.1

Interpret the area under a probability density curve

Following is a probability density curve for a population.

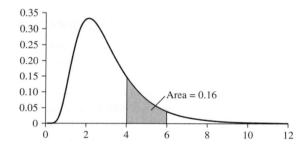

a. What proportion of the population is between 4 and 6?

b. If a value is chosen at random from this population, what is the probability that it will be between 4 and 6?

c. What proportion of the population is not between 4 and 6?

d. If a value is chosen at random from this population, what is the probability that it is not between 4 and 6?

Solution

a. The proportion of the population between 4 and 6 is equal to the area under the curve between 4 and 6, which is 0.16.

b. The probability that a randomly chosen value is between 4 and 6 is equal to the area under the curve between 4 and 6, which is 0.16.

c. The area under the entire curve is equal to 1. Therefore, the proportion that is not between 4 and 6 is equal to $1 - 0.16 = 0.84$.

d. The probability that a randomly chosen value is not between 4 and 6 is equal to the area under the curve that is not between 4 and 6, which is 0.84.

Another way to answer part (d) is to use the Rule of Complements:

$$P(\text{Not between 4 and 6}) = 1 - P(\text{Between 4 and 6}) = 1 - 0.16 = 0.84$$

Recall: The Rule of Complements says that $P(\text{not } A) = 1 - P(A)$.

Check Your Understanding

1. Following is a probability density curve with the area between 0 and 1 and the area between 1 and 2 indicated.

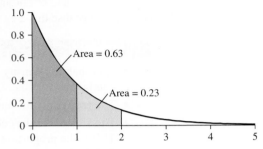

a. What proportion of the population is between 0 and 1?
b. What is the probability that a randomly selected value will be between 1 and 2?
c. What proportion of the population is between 0 and 2?
d. What is the probability that a randomly selected value will be greater than 2?

Answers are on page 240.

Objective 2 Use a normal curve to describe a normal population

The Normal Distribution

Probability density curves come in many varieties, depending on the characteristics of the populations they represent. Remarkably, many important statistical procedures can be carried out using only one type of probability density curve, called a **normal curve**. A population that is represented by a normal curve is said to be **normally distributed**, or to have a **normal distribution**. Figure 6.4 presents some examples of normal curves.

The location and shape of a normal curve reflect the mean and standard deviation of the population. The curve is symmetric around its peak, or mode. Therefore, the mode is equal to the population mean. The population standard deviation measures the spread of the population. Therefore, the normal curve is wide and flat when the population standard deviation is large, and tall and narrow when the population standard deviation is small.

Explain It Again

The mode of a curve: Recall that a peak in a histogram is called a *mode* of the histogram. Similarly, a peak in a probability density curve, such as a normal curve, is called a mode of the curve.

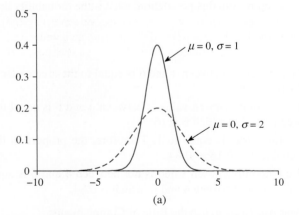

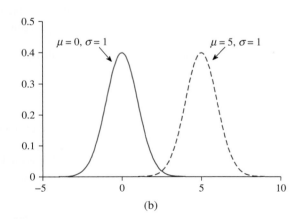

Figure 6.4 (a) Both populations have mean 0. The population with standard deviation 2 is more spread out than the population with standard deviation 1. (b) Both populations have the same spread, because they have the same standard deviation. The curves are centered over the population means.

Properties of Normal Distributions

1. Normal distributions have one mode.

2. Normal distributions are symmetric around the mode.

3. The mean and median of a normal distribution are both equal to the mode. In other words, the mean, median, and mode of a normal distribution are all the same.

4. The normal distribution follows the Empirical Rule (see Figure 6.5):

- Approximately 68% of the population is within one standard deviation of the mean. In other words, approximately 68% of the population is in the interval $\mu - \sigma$ to $\mu + \sigma$.

- Approximately 95% of the population is within two standard deviations of the mean. In other words, approximately 95% of the population is in the interval $\mu - 2\sigma$ to $\mu + 2\sigma$.

- Approximately 99.7% of the population is within three standard deviations of the mean. In other words, approximately 99.7% of the population is in the interval $\mu - 3\sigma$ to $\mu + 3\sigma$.

Recall: The Empirical Rule holds for most unimodal symmetric distributions. See Section 3.2.

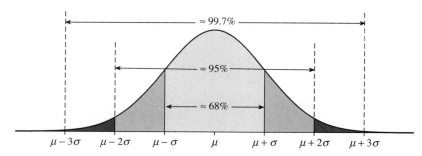

Figure 6.5 Normal curve with mean μ and standard deviation σ

Objective 3 Find areas under the standard normal curve

Finding Areas Under the Standard Normal Curve

A normal distribution can have any mean and any positive standard deviation, but it is only necessary to work with the normal distribution that has mean 0 and standard deviation 1, which is called the **standard normal distribution**. The probability density function for the standard normal distribution is called the **standard normal curve**.

For any interval, the area under a normal curve over the interval represents the proportion of the population that is contained within the interval. Finding an area under a normal curve is a crucial step in many statistical procedures. When finding an area under the standard normal curve, we use the letter z to indicate a value on the horizontal axis (see Figure 6.6). We refer to such a value as a **z-score**. Since the mean of the standard normal distribution, which is located at the mode, is 0, the z-score at the mode of the curve is 0. Points on the horizontal axis to the left of the mode have negative z-scores, and points to the right of the mode have positive z-scores.

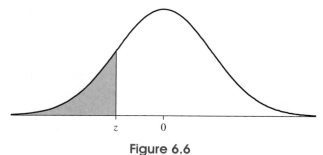

Figure 6.6

SUMMARY

- Points on the horizontal axis to the left of the mode have negative z-scores.
- Points on the horizontal axis to the right of the mode have positive z-scores.
- The mode itself has a z-score of 0.

Finding areas under the standard normal curve by using Table A.2

In general, areas under the standard normal curve can be found by using Table A.2 in Appendix A or by using technology. Table A.2 contains z-scores and areas. Each of the four-digit numbers in the body of the table is the area to the left of a z-score. Examples 6.2–6.4 will show how to use Table A.2.

EXAMPLE 6.2

Finding an area to the left of a z-score

Use Table A.2 to find the area to the left of $z = 1.26$.

Solution

Step 1: Sketch a normal curve, label the point $z = 1.26$, and shade in the area to the left of it. Note that $z = 1.26$ is located to the right of the mode, since it is positive.

Step 2: Consult Table A.2. To look up $z = 1.26$, find the row containing 1.2 and the column containing 0.06. The value in the intersection of the row and column is 0.8962. This is the area to the left of $z = 1.26$ (see Figure 6.7).

z	0.00	0.01	0.02	0.03	0.04	0.05	0.06	0.07	0.08	0.09
⋮	⋮	⋮	⋮	⋮	⋮	⋮	⋮	⋮	⋮	⋮
1.0	.8413	.8438	.8461	.8485	.8508	.8531	.8554	.8577	.8599	.8621
1.1	.8643	.8665	.8686	.8708	.8729	.8749	.8770	.8790	.8810	.8830
1.2	.8849	.8869	.8888	.8907	.8925	.8944	.8962	.8980	.8997	.9015
1.3	.9032	.9049	.9066	.9082	.9099	.9115	.9131	.9147	.9162	.9177
1.4	.9192	.9207	.9222	.9236	.9251	.9265	.9279	.9292	.9306	.9319
⋮	⋮	⋮	⋮	⋮	⋮	⋮	⋮	⋮	⋮	⋮

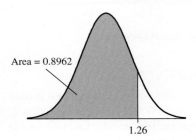

Area = 0.8962

1.26

Figure 6.7

An area to the left of a z-score represents the proportion of a population that is less than a given value. Sometimes we need to know the proportion of a population that is greater than a given value. In these cases we need to find the area to the right of a z-score. Since the area under the entire curve is equal to 1, we can find the area to the right of a z-score by finding the area to the left and subtracting from 1.

EXAMPLE 6.3

Finding an area to the right of a z-score

Use Table A.2 to find the area to the right of $z = -0.58$.

Solution

Step 1: Sketch a normal curve, label the point $z = -0.58$, and shade in the area to the right of it. Note that $z = -0.58$ is located to the left of the mode, since it is negative.

Step 2: Consult Table A.2. To look up $z = -0.58$, find the row containing -0.5 and the column containing 0.08. The value in the intersection of the row and column is

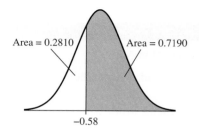

Area = 0.2810   Area = 0.7190

−0.58

Figure 6.8

0.2810. This is the area to the *left* of $z = -0.58$. To find the area to the right, we subtract from 1 (see Figure 6.8):

Area to the right of $z = -0.58 = 1 -$ Area to the left of $z = -0.58$

$$= 1 - 0.2810$$

$$= 0.7190$$

z	0.00	0.01	0.02	0.03	0.04	0.05	0.06	0.07	0.08	0.09
⋮	⋮	⋮	⋮	⋮	⋮	⋮	⋮	⋮	⋮	⋮
−0.7	.2420	.2389	.2358	.2327	.2296	.2266	.2236	.2206	.2177	.2148
−0.6	.2743	.2709	.2676	.2643	.2611	.2578	.2546	.2514	.2483	.2451
−0.5	.3085	.3050	.3015	.2981	.2946	.2912	.2877	.2843	.2810	.2776
−0.4	.3446	.3409	.3372	.3336	.3300	.3264	.3228	.3192	.3156	.3121
−0.3	.3821	.3783	.3745	.3707	.3669	.3632	.3594	.3557	.3520	.3483
⋮	⋮	⋮	⋮	⋮	⋮	⋮	⋮	⋮	⋮	⋮

Sometimes we need to find the proportion of a population that falls between two values. In these cases, we need to find the area between two z-scores. We can do this using Table A.2 by finding the area to the left of each z-score. The area between the z-scores is found by subtracting the smaller area from the larger area.

EXAMPLE 6.4

Finding an area between two z-scores

Find the area between $z = -1.45$ and $z = 0.42$.

Solution

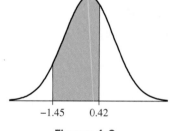

−1.45   0.42

Figure 6.9

Step 1: Sketch a normal curve, label the points $z = -1.45$ and $z = 0.42$, and shade in the area between them. See Figure 6.9.

Step 2: Use Table A.2 to find the areas to the left of $z = -1.45$ and to the left of $z = 0.42$. The area to the left of $z = -1.45$ is 0.0735, and the area to the left of $z = 0.42$ is 0.6628.

Step 3: Subtract the smaller area from the larger area to find the area between the two z-scores:

Area between $z = -1.45$ and $z = 0.42 =$ (Area left of 0.42) − (Area left of −1.45)

$$= 0.6628 - 0.0735$$

$$= 0.5893$$

The area between $z = -1.45$ and $z = 0.42$ is 0.5893. See Figure 6.10.

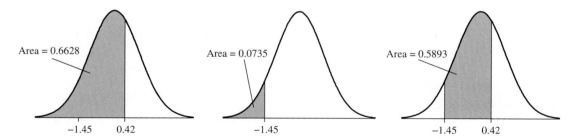

Area = 0.6628   Area = 0.0735   Area = 0.5893

−1.45   0.42   −1.45   −1.45   0.42

Figure 6.10   We start with the area to the left of $z = 0.42$ and subtract the area to the left of $z = -1.45$. This leaves the area between $z = 0.42$ and $z = -1.45$.

SUMMARY

To find an area under the standard normal curve by using Table A.2:

Step 1: Sketch a normal curve, label the z-score or scores, and shade in the area to be found.

Step 2: Look up the area in Table A.2 corresponding to each z-score.

Step 3:
- To find the area to the left of a z-score, use the area in Table A.2.
- To find the area to the right of a z-score, find the area to the left and subtract from 1.
- To find the area between two z-scores, find the area to the left of each, then subtract the smaller area from the larger area.

Check Your Understanding

2. Use Table A.2 to find the area to the left of $z = 0.25$.

3. Use Table A.2 to find the area to the right of $z = 2.31$.

4. Use Table A.2 to find the area between $z = -1.13$ and $z = 2.02$.

Answers are on page 240.

Finding areas under the standard normal curve by using technology

Areas under the standard normal curve can be found by using technology. Examples 6.5 and 6.6 illustrate the method.

EXAMPLE 6.5

Find the area between two z-scores by using technology

In Example 6.4, we found the area between $z = -1.45$ and $z = 0.42$. Find this area by using technology.

Solution

We present results from the TI-84 Plus calculator. The area is found by using the **normalcdf** command. We enter the left endpoint of the interval (-1.45), the right endpoint (0.42), the mean (0), and the standard deviation (1). Step-by-step instructions are given in the Using Technology section on page 236.

```
normalcdf(-1.45,
0.42,0,1)
          .5892279372
```

The TI-84 Plus gives the area as .5892279372. Rounding to four decimal places gives 0.5892.

EXAMPLE 6.6

Find the area to the right of a z-score by using technology

In Example 6.3, we found the area to the right of $z = -0.58$. Find this area by using technology.

Explain It Again

1E99: In Example 6.6, we want to find the area between -0.58 and infinity. Since we can't enter a value of infinity into the calculator, we enter the very large number **1E99** instead.

Solution

We present output from the TI-84 Plus calculator. We use the **normalcdf** command. We enter the left endpoint of the interval (-0.58). Since there is no right endpoint, we enter **1E99**, which represents the very large number that is written with a 1 followed by 99 zeros.

Then we enter the mean (0) and the standard deviation (1). Step-by-step instructions are given in the Using Technology section on page 236.

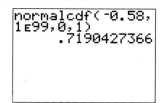

The TI-84 Plus gives the area as .7190427366. Rounding to four decimal places gives 0.7190.

Objective 4 Find z-scores corresponding to areas under the normal curve

Finding a z-Score Corresponding to a Given Area

Often we are given an area and we need to find the z-score that corresponds to an area under the standard normal curve. Examples 6.7–6.11 show how this is done using either Table A.2 or technology. When using the table, it is useful to remember that the mode, $z = 0$, has an area of 0.5 both to its right and to its left.

| EXAMPLE 6.7 |

Finding the z-score corresponding to an area to the left

Use Table A.2 to find the z-score that has an area of 0.26 to its left.

Explain It Again

Finding a z-score corresponding to an area: In Table A.2, the numbers in the body of the table represent *areas*, and numbers down the left-hand column and across the top row represent *z-scores*. When given an area, we find that area in the body of the table, and look at the left-hand column and top row to obtain the z-score.

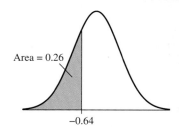

Area = 0.26

−0.64

Figure 6.11

Solution

Step 1: Sketch a normal curve and shade in the given area.

Step 2: In Table A.2, look through the body of the table to find the area closest to 0.26. This value is 0.2611. The values in the left-hand column and top row corresponding to 0.2611 are −0.6 and 0.04. Therefore, the z-score is $z = -0.64$. See Figure 6.11.

z	0.00	0.01	0.02	0.03	0.04	0.05	0.06	0.07	0.08	0.09
⋮	⋮	⋮	⋮	⋮	⋮	⋮	⋮	⋮	⋮	⋮
−0.8	.2119	.2090	.2061	.2033	.2005	.1977	.1949	.1922	.1894	.1867
−0.7	.2420	.2389	.2358	.2327	.2296	.2266	.2236	.2206	.2177	.2148
−0.6	.2743	.2709	.2676	.2643	.2611	.2578	.2546	.2514	.2483	.2451
−0.5	.3085	.3050	.3015	.2981	.2946	.2912	.2877	.2843	.2810	.2776
−0.4	.3446	.3409	.3372	.3336	.3300	.3264	.3228	.3192	.3156	.3121
⋮	⋮	⋮	⋮	⋮	⋮	⋮	⋮	⋮	⋮	⋮

| EXAMPLE 6.8 |

Using technology to find the z-score corresponding to an area to the left

In Example 6.7, we found the z-score that has an area of 0.26 to its left. Use technology to find this z-score.

Solution

We present results from the TI-84 Plus calculator. The z-score is found by using the **invNorm** command. We enter the area to the left (.26), the mean (0), and the standard deviation (1). Step-by-step instructions are given in the Using Technology section on page 237.

```
invNorm(.26,0,1)
            -.6433454021
```

The TI-84 Plus gives $z = -.6433454021$. Rounding to two decimal places gives $z = -0.64$.

EXAMPLE 6.9

Finding the z-score corresponding to an area to the right

Use Table A.2 to find the z-score that has an area of 0.68 to its right.

Solution

Step 1: Sketch a normal curve and shade in the given area.

Step 2: Determine the area to the left of the z-score. Since the area to the right is 0.68, the area to the left is $1 - 0.68 = 0.32$.

Step 3: In Table A.2, look through the body of the table to find the area closest to 0.32. This value is 0.3192. The z-score in Table A.2 corresponding to an area of 0.3192 is $z = -0.47$. See Figure 6.12.

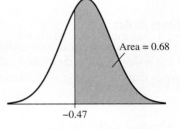

Area = 0.68

−0.47

Figure 6.12

z	0.00	0.01	0.02	0.03	0.04	0.05	0.06	0.07	0.08	0.09
⋮	⋮	⋮	⋮	⋮	⋮	⋮	⋮	⋮	⋮	⋮
−0.6	.2743	.2709	.2676	.2643	.2611	.2578	.2546	.2514	.2483	.2451
−0.5	.3085	.3050	.3015	.2981	.2946	.2912	.2877	.2843	.2810	.2776
−0.4	.3446	.3409	.3372	.3336	.3300	.3264	.3228	.3192	.3156	.3121
−0.3	.3821	.3783	.3745	.3707	.3669	.3632	.3594	.3557	.3520	.3483
−0.2	.4207	.4168	.4129	.4090	.4052	.4013	.3974	.3936	.3897	.3859
⋮	⋮	⋮	⋮	⋮	⋮	⋮	⋮	⋮	⋮	⋮

EXAMPLE 6.10

Using technology to find the z-score corresponding to an area to the right

In Example 6.9, we found the z-score that has an area of 0.68 to its right. Use technology to find this z-score.

Solution

We use the TI-84 Plus calculator. The first two steps are the same as those for using the table. We must first find the area to the *left* of the desired z-score, by subtracting the area to the right from 1. Since the area to the right is 0.68, the area to the left is $1 - 0.68 = 0.32$.

The results are as follows. Step-by-step instructions are given in the Using Technology section on page 237.

```
invNorm(.32,0,1)
           -.4676988012
```

The TI-84 Plus gives $z = -.4676988012$. Rounding to two decimal places gives $z = -0.47$.

Check Your Understanding

5. Use Table A.2 to find the z-score with an area of 0.45 to its left.

6. Use Table A.2 to find the z-score with an area of 0.37 to its right.

7. Use any method to find the z-score with an area of 0.74 to its left.

8. Use any method to find the z-score with an area of 0.09 to its right.

Answers are on page 240.

| EXAMPLE 6.11 | Finding the z-score corresponding to an area in the middle

Use Table A.2 to find the z-scores that bound the middle 95% of the area under the standard normal curve.

Solution

Step 1: Sketch a normal curve and shade in the given area. Label the z-score on the left z_1 and the z-score on the right z_2.

Step 2: Find the area to the left of z_1. Since the area in the middle is 0.95, the area in the two tails combined is 0.05. Half of that area, or 0.025, is to the left of z_1. We conclude that z_1 is the z-score that has an area of 0.025 to its left.

Step 3: In Table A.2, an area of 0.025 corresponds to a z-score of -1.96. Therefore $z_1 = -1.96$.

Step 4: To find z_2, note that the area to the left of z_2 is 0.9750. We can use Table A.2 to determine that $z_2 = 1.96$. Alternatively, note that z_1 and z_2 are equidistant from the mode. Since the normal curve is symmetric, z_1 must be the negative of z_2. Therefore $z_2 = 1.96$. See Figure 6.13.

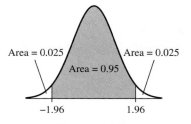

Figure 6.13

The notation z_α

Statisticians have developed a notation for a z-score with a given area to its right.

DEFINITION

Let α be any number between 0 and 1; in other words, $0 < \alpha < 1$. The notation z_α refers to the z-score with an area of α to its right.

| EXAMPLE 6.12 | Finding z_α for a given α

Use Table A.2 to find $z_{0.20}$.

Solution

$z_{0.20}$ is the z-score that has an area of 0.20 to its right. The area to the left is therefore $1 - 0.20 = 0.80$. The closest value to 0.80 in Table A.2 is 0.7995. The z-score corresponding to 0.7995 is $z = 0.84$. Therefore, $z_{0.20} = 0.84$. See Figure 6.14.

Figure 6.14

| EXAMPLE 6.13 | Using technology to find z_α for a given α

In Example 6.12, we used Table A.2 to find $z_{0.20}$. Use technology to find $z_{0.20}$.

Solution

$z_{0.20}$ is the z-score that has an area of 0.20 to its right. The area to the left is therefore $1 - 0.20 = 0.80$.

We use the TI-84 Plus calculator to find the z-score with an area of 0.80 to its left. The result follows. Step-by-step instructions are given in the Using Technology section on page 237.

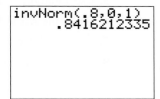

```
invNorm(.8,0,1)
      .8416212335
```

Rounding the answer to two decimal places yields $z_{0.20} = 0.84$.

Check Your Understanding

9. Use Table A.2 to find $z_{0.15}$.

10. Use any method to find $z_{0.25}$.

Answers are on page 240.

USING TECHNOLOGY

TI-84 PLUS

Finding areas under the standard normal curve

The **normalcdf** command is used to calculate area under a normal curve.

Step 1. Press **2nd**, then **VARS** to access the **DISTR** menu. Select **2:normalcdf** (Figure A).

Step 2. Enter the left endpoint, comma, the right endpoint, comma, the mean (**0** for the standard normal), comma, and the standard deviation (**1** for the standard normal).
- When finding the area to the right of a given value, use **1E99** as the right endpoint.
- When finding the area to the left of a given value, use **−1E99** as the left endpoint.

Step 3. Press **ENTER**.

Using the TI-84 PLUS Stat Wizards (see Appendix B for more information)

Step 1. Press **2nd**, then **VARS** to access the **DISTR** menu. Select **2:normalcdf** (Figure A).

Step 2. Enter the left endpoint in the **lower** field, the right endpoint in the **upper** field, the mean in the μ field (**0** for the standard normal), and the standard deviation in the σ field (**1** for the standard normal).
- When finding the area to the right of a given value, use **1E99** as the right endpoint.
- When finding the area to the left of a given value, use **−1E99** as the left endpoint.

Step 3. Select **Paste** and press **ENTER** to paste the command to the home screen. Press **ENTER** again to run the command.

Figure B illustrates finding the area to the left of $z = 1.26$ (Example 6.2).

Figure C illustrates finding the area to the right of $z = -0.58$ (Example 6.3).

Figure D illustrates finding the area between $z = -1.45$ and $z = 0.42$. (Example 6.4).

Note: The quantity 1E99 in the TI-84 PLUS calculator represents a very large number, specifically a 1 followed by 99 zeros.

```
 DISTR DRAW
1:normalpdf(
2:normalcdf(
3:invNorm(
4:invT(
5:tpdf(
6:tcdf(
7↓X²pdf(
```
Figure A

```
normalcdf(-1E99,
1.26,0,1)
      .8961652533
```
Figure B

```
normalcdf(-0.58,
1E99,0,1)
      .7190427366
```
Figure C

```
normalcdf(-1.45,
0.42,0,1)
      .5892279372
```
Figure D

Finding a *z*-score corresponding to a given area

The **invNorm** command is used to calculate the *z*-score corresponding to an *area to the left*.

Step 1. Press **2nd**, then **VARS** to access the **DISTR** menu. Select **3:invNorm** (Figure E).

Step 2. Enter the area to the left of the desired *z*-score, comma, the mean (**0** for the standard normal), comma, and the standard deviation (**1** for the standard normal).

Step 3. Press **ENTER**.

Using the TI-84 PLUS Stat Wizards (see Appendix B for more information)

Step 1. Press **2nd**, then **VARS** to access the **DISTR** menu. Select **3:invNorm** (Figure E).

Step 2. Enter the area to the left of the desired *z*-score in the **area** field, the mean in the μ field (**0** for the standard normal), and the standard deviation in the σ field (**1** for the standard normal).

Step 3. Select **Paste** and press **ENTER** to paste the command to the home screen. Press **ENTER** again to run the command.

Figure F illustrates finding the *z*-score that has an area of 0.26 to its left (Example 6.8).

Figure E

Figure F

MINITAB

Finding areas under the standard normal curve

The following procedure computes the area to the *left* of a given value.

Step 1. Click **Calc**, then **Probability Distributions**, then **Normal**.

Step 2. Select the **Cumulative probability** option.

Step 3. Enter the value for the mean in the **Mean** field (**0** for the standard normal) and the value for the standard deviation in the **Standard deviation** field (**1** for the standard normal).

Step 4. To compute the area to the left of a given *x*, enter the value for *x* in the **Input constant** field.

Step 5. Click **OK**.

Figures G and H illustrate finding the area to the left of *z* = 1.26 (Example 6.2).

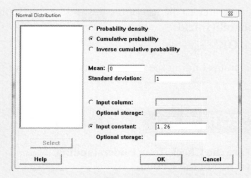

Figure G

Cumulative Distribution Function

Normal with mean = 0 and standard deviation = 1

```
   x   P( X <= x )
1.26     0.896165
```

Figure H

Finding a *z*-score corresponding to a given area

The following procedure is used to calculate the *z*-score corresponding to an *area to the left*.

Step 1. Click **Calc**, then **Probability Distributions**, then **Normal**.

Step 2. Select the **Inverse Cumulative Probability** option.

Step 3. Enter the value for the mean in the **Mean** field (**0** for the standard normal) and the value for the standard deviation in the **Standard deviation** field (**1** for the standard normal).

Step 4. Enter the area to the left of the desired *z*-score in the **Input constant** field and click **OK**.

Figure I illustrates finding the *z*-score that has an area of 0.26 to its left (Example 6.8).

Inverse Cumulative Distribution Function

Normal with mean = 0 and standard deviation = 1

```
P( X <= x )        x
     0.26  -0.643345
```

Figure I

EXCEL

Finding areas under the standard normal curve

The following procedure computes the area to the *left* of a given value.

Step 1. In an empty cell, select the **Insert Function** icon and highlight **Statistical** in the category field.

Step 2. Click on the **NORM.S.DIST** function and press **OK**.

Step 3. To compute the area to the left of a given x, enter the value of x in the **X** field.

Step 4. Enter **TRUE** in the **Cumulative** field and click **OK**.

Figure J illustrates finding the area to the left of $z = 1.26$ (Example 6.2).

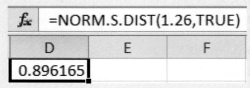

Figure J

Finding a z-score corresponding to a given area

The following procedure is used to calculate the z-score corresponding to an *area to the left*.

Step 1. In an empty cell, select the **Insert Function** icon and highlight **Statistical** in the category field.

Step 2. Click on the **NORM.S.INV** function and press **OK**.

Step 3. Enter the area to the left of the desired z-score in the **Probability** field.

Step 4. Click **OK**.

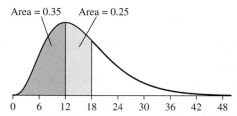

Figure K

Figure K illustrates finding the z-score that has an area of 0.26 to its left (Example 6.8).

SECTION 6.1   Exercises

Exercises 1–10 are the Check Your Understanding exercises located within the section.

Understanding the Concepts

In Exercises 11–16, fill in each blank with the appropriate word or phrase.

11. The proportion of a population that is contained within an interval corresponds to an area under the probability _____ curve.

12. If X is a continuous random variable, then $P(X = a) =$ _____ for any number a.

13. The area under the entire probability density curve is equal to _____.

14. The mean, median, and mode of a normal distribution are _____ to each other.

15. A normal distribution with mean 0 and standard deviation 1 is called the _____ normal distribution.

16. The notation _____ represents a z-score with an area of α to its right.

In Exercises 17–20, determine whether the statement is true or false. If the statement is false, rewrite it as a true statement.

17. The probability that a randomly selected value of a continuous random variable lies between a and b is given by the area under the probability density curve between a and b.

18. A normal curve is symmetric around its mode.

19. A normal curve is wide and flat when the standard deviation is small.

20. The area under the normal curve to the left of the mode is less than 0.5.

Practicing the Skills

21. The following figure is a probability density curve that represents the lifetime, in months, of a certain type of laptop battery.

Area = 0.35   Area = 0.25

0   6   12   18   24   30   36   42   48

a. Find the proportion of batteries with lifetimes between 12 and 18 months.

b. Find the proportion of batteries with lifetimes less than 18 months.

c. What is the probability that a randomly chosen battery lasts more than 18 months?

22. The following figure is a probability density curve that represents the grade point averages (GPA) of the graduating seniors at a large university.

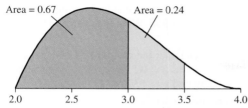

a. Find the proportion of seniors whose GPA is between 3.0 and 3.5.

b. What is the probability that a randomly chosen senior will have a GPA greater than 3.5?

23. Find each of the shaded areas under the standard normal curve.

a.

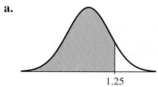

b.

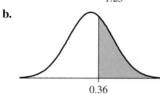

c.

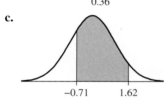

d.

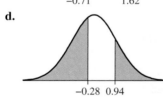

24. Find each of the shaded areas under the standard normal curve.

a.

b.

c.

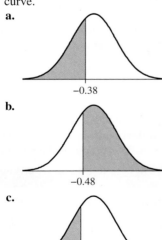

d.

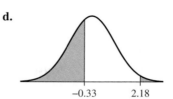

25. Find the area under the standard normal curve to the left of
a. $z = 0.74$
b. $z = -2.16$
c. $z = 1.02$
d. $z = -0.15$

26. Find the area under the standard normal curve to the left of
a. $z = 2.56$
b. $z = 0.53$
c. $z = -0.94$
d. $z = -1.30$

27. Find the area under the standard normal curve to the right of
a. $z = -1.55$
b. $z = 0.32$
c. $z = 3.20$
d. $z = -2.39$

28. Find the area under the standard normal curve to the right of
a. $z = 0.47$
b. $z = -2.91$
c. $z = 2.04$
d. $z = 1.09$

29. Find the area under the standard normal curve that lies between
a. $z = -0.75$ and $z = 1.70$
b. $z = -2.30$ and $z = 1.08$
c. $z = -3.27$ and $z = -1.44$
d. $z = 1.26$ and $z = 2.32$

30. Find the area under the standard normal curve that lies between
a. $z = -1.28$ and $z = 1.36$
b. $z = -0.82$ and $z = -0.42$
c. $z = 1.58$ and $z = 2.06$
d. $z = -2.19$ and $z = 0.07$

31. Find the area under the standard normal curve that lies outside the interval between
a. $z = -0.38$ and $z = 1.02$
b. $z = -1.42$ and $z = 1.78$
c. $z = 0.01$ and $z = 2.67$
d. $z = -2.45$ and $z = -0.34$

32. Find the area under the standard normal curve that lies outside the interval between
a. $z = -1.11$ and $z = 3.21$
b. $z = -1.93$ and $z = 0.59$
c. $z = 0.46$ and $z = 1.75$
d. $z = -2.73$ and $z = -1.39$

33. Find the z-score for which the area to its left is 0.54.

34. Find the z-score for which the area to its left is 0.13.

35. Find the z-score for which the area to its left is 0.93.

36. Find the z-score for which the area to its left is 0.25.

37. Find the z-score for which the area to its right is 0.84.

38. Find the z-score for which the area to its right is 0.14.

39. Find the z-score for which the area to its right is 0.35.

40. Find the z-score for which the area to its right is 0.92.

41. Find the z-scores that bound the middle 50% of the area under the standard normal curve.

42. Find the z-scores that bound the middle 70% of the area under the standard normal curve.

43. Find the z-scores that bound the middle 80% of the area under the standard normal curve.

44. Find the z-scores that bound the middle 98% of the area under the standard normal curve.

45. Find $z_{0.02}$.

46. Find $z_{0.01}$.

47. Find $z_{0.10}$.

48. Find $z_{0.025}$.

Working with the Concepts

49. **Symmetry:** The area under the standard normal curve to the left of $z = -1.75$ is 0.0401. What is the area to the right of $z = 1.75$?

50. **Symmetry:** The area under the standard normal curve to the right of $z = -0.51$ is 0.6950. What is the area to the left of $z = 0.51$?

51. **Symmetry:** The area under the standard normal curve between $z = -1.93$ and $z = 0.59$ is 0.6956. What is the area between $z = -0.59$ and $z = 1.93$?

52. **Symmetry:** The area under the standard normal curve between $z = 1.32$ and $z = 1.82$ is 0.0590. What is the area between $z = -1.82$ and $z = -1.32$?

Extending the Concepts

53. **No table, no technology:** Let a be the number such that the area to the right of $z = a$ is 0.3. Without using a table or technology, find the area to the left of $z = -a$.

54. **No table, no technology:** Let a be the number such that the area to the right of $z = a$ is 0.21. Without using a table or technology, find the area between $z = -a$ and $z = a$.

Answers to Check Your Understanding Exercises for Section 6.1

1. a. 0.63 **b.** 0.23 **c.** 0.86 **d.** 0.14	**6.** 0.33	
2. 0.5987	**7.** 0.64	
3. 0.0104	**8.** 1.34	
4. 0.8491	**9.** 1.04	
5. −0.13	**10.** 0.67	

SECTION 6.2	Applications of the Normal Distribution

Objectives

1. Convert values from a normal distribution to z-scores
2. Find areas under a normal curve
3. Find the value from a normal distribution corresponding to a given proportion

In Section 6.1, we found areas under a standard normal curve, which has mean 0 and standard deviation 1. In this section, we will learn to find areas under normal curves with any mean and standard deviation.

Objective 1 Convert values from a normal distribution to z-scores

Converting Normal Values to z-Scores

Let x be a value from a normal distribution with mean μ and standard deviation σ. We can convert x to a z-score by using a method known as **standardization**. To standardize a value, subtract the mean and divide by the standard deviation. This produces the z-score.

Recall: We first described the method for finding the z-score in Section 3.3.

DEFINITION

Let x be a value from a normal distribution with mean μ and standard deviation σ. The **z-score** of x is

$$z = \frac{x - \mu}{\sigma}$$

The z-score satisfies the following properties.

Properties of the z-Score

1. The z-score follows a standard normal distribution.
2. Values below the mean have negative z-scores, and values above the mean have positive z-scores.
3. The z-score tells how many standard deviations the original value is above or below the mean.

Because the z-score follows a standard normal distribution, we can use the methods of Section 6.1 to find areas under any normal curve, by standardizing to convert the original values to z-scores.

Rounding Off z-Scores

The z-scores in Table A.2 are expressed to two decimal places. For this reason, when converting normal values to z-scores, we will round off the z-scores to two decimal places.

EXAMPLE 6.14   **Finding and interpreting a z-score**

Heights in a certain population of women follow a normal distribution with mean $\mu = 64$ inches and standard deviation $\sigma = 3$ inches.

   a. A randomly selected woman has a height of $x = 67$ inches. Find and interpret the z-score of this value.
   b. Another randomly selected woman has a height of $x = 63$ inches. Find and interpret the z-score of this value.

Solution

   a. The z-score for $x = 67$ is

$$z = \frac{67 - \mu}{\sigma} = \frac{67 - 64}{3} = 1.00$$

We interpret this by saying that a height of 67 inches is 1 standard deviation above the mean height of 64 inches.

   b. The z-score for $x = 63$ is

$$z = \frac{63 - \mu}{\sigma} = \frac{63 - 64}{3} = -0.33$$

We interpret this by saying that a height of 63 inches is 0.33 standard deviation below the mean height of 64 inches.

Explain It Again

Converting x-values to z-scores:
After we convert an x-value to a z-score, we use the standard normal curve. This allows us to find areas under the normal curve by using Table A.2.

Figure 6.15 illustrates the results of Example 6.14. Figure 6.15(a) is the normal curve that represents the heights of the population of women. It has a mean of 64. The heights of the two women are indicated at 63 and 67. Figure 6.15(b) is the standard normal curve. The mean is 0, and the heights are represented by their z-scores of -0.33 and 1.00.

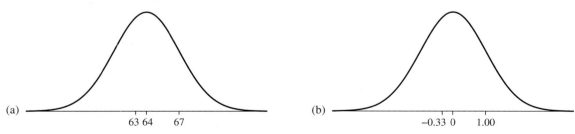

(a)   (b)
          63 64   67   −0.33 0   1.00

Figure 6.15   (a) This is the normal curve with mean 64 and standard deviation 3. It represents the population of heights of women. The heights of 63 and 67 are shown on the x-axis. (b) This is the standard normal curve. It also represents the population of heights of women, by using the z-scores instead of the actual heights. A height of 63 inches is represented by a z-score of -0.33, and a height of 67 inches is represented by a z-score of 1.00.

Check Your Understanding

1. A normal distribution has mean $\mu = 15$ and standard deviation $\sigma = 4$. Find and interpret the z-score for $x = 11$.

2. A normal distribution has mean $\mu = 60$ and standard deviation $\sigma = 20$. Find and interpret the z-score for $x = 75$.

3. Compact fluorescent bulbs are more energy efficient than incandescent bulbs, but they take longer to reach full brightness. The time that it takes for a compact fluorescent bulb to reach full brightness is normally distributed with mean 29.8 seconds and standard deviation 4.5 seconds. A randomly selected bulb takes 28 seconds to reach full brightness. Find and interpret the z-score for $x = 28$.

Answers are on page 251.

Objective 2 Find areas under a normal curve

Finding Areas Under a Normal Curve

In Section 6.1, we used z-scores to compute areas under the standard normal curve. By standardizing, we can use z-scores to compute areas under a normal curve with any mean and standard deviation. An area under a normal curve over an interval can be interpreted in two ways: It represents the proportion of the population that is contained within the interval, and it also represents the probability that a randomly selected individual will have a value within the interval.

EXAMPLE 6.15

Finding an area under a normal curve

A study reported that the length of pregnancy from conception to birth is approximately normally distributed with mean $\mu = 272$ days and standard deviation $\sigma = 9$ days. What proportion of pregnancies last longer than 280 days?

Source: *Singapore Medical Journal* 35:1044–1048

Explain It Again

Probabilities and proportions: The probability that a randomly sampled value falls in a given interval is equal to the proportion of the population that is contained in the interval. So the area under a normal curve represents both probabilities and proportions.

Solution

The proportion of pregnancies lasting longer than 280 days is equal to the area under the normal curve corresponding to values of x greater than 280. We find this area as follows.

Step 1: Find the z-score for $x = 280$.

$$z = \frac{x - \mu}{\sigma} = \frac{280 - 272}{9} = 0.89$$

Step 2: Sketch a normal curve, label the mean, x-value, and z-score, and shade in the area to be found. See Figure 6.16.

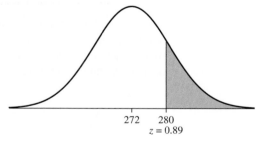

272   280
$z = 0.89$

Figure 6.16

Step 3: Find the area to the right of $z = 0.89$. Using Table A.2, we find the area to the *left* of $z = 0.89$ to be 0.8133. The area to the right is therefore $1 - 0.8133 = 0.1867$. We conclude that the proportion of pregnancies that last longer than 280 days is 0.1867.

> **EXAMPLE 6.16**

Finding an area under a normal curve by using technology

In Example 6.15, we used Table A.2 to compute the proportion of pregnancies that last longer than 280 days. Find this proportion by using technology.

Solution

We present output from the TI-84 Plus calculator. We use the **normalcdf** command. We enter the left endpoint of the interval (280). Since there is no right endpoint, we enter **1E99**, which represents the very large number that is written with a 1 followed by 99 zeros. Then we enter the mean (272) and the standard deviation (9). Step-by-step instructions are given in the Using Technology section on page 246.

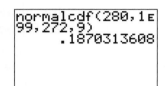

> **Explain It Again**
>
> **Technology and tables can give slightly different answers:** Answers obtained with technology sometimes differ slightly from those obtained by using tables, because the technology is more precise. The differences aren't large enough to matter.

In Example 6.15, we used Table A.2 and found the proportion of pregnancies that last longer than 280 days to be 0.1867. In Example 6.16, the TI-84 Plus calculator found the proportion to be 0.1870. Answers found with technology often differ somewhat from those obtained by using a table. The differences aren't large enough to matter. Whenever the answer obtained from technology differs from the answer obtained by using the table, we will present both answers.

> **EXAMPLE 6.17**

Finding an area under a normal curve between two values

The length of a pregnancy from conception to birth is approximately normally distributed with mean $\mu = 272$ days and standard deviation $\sigma = 9$ days. A pregnancy is considered full-term if it lasts between 252 days and 298 days. What proportion of pregnancies are full-term?

Solution

Step 1: Find the z-scores for $x = 252$ and $x = 298$.

For $x = 252$:
$$z = \frac{252 - 272}{9} = -2.22$$

For $x = 298$:
$$z = \frac{298 - 272}{9} = 2.89$$

Step 2: Sketch a normal curve, label the mean, the x-values, and the z-scores, and shade in the area to be found. See Figure 6.17.

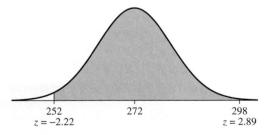

Figure 6.17

Step 3: Using Table A.2, we find that the area to the left of $z = 2.89$ is 0.9981 and the area to the left of $z = -2.22$ is 0.0132. The area between $z = -2.22$ and $z = 2.89$ is therefore $0.9981 - 0.0132 = 0.9849$.

We conclude that the proportion of pregnancies that are full-term is 0.9849.

Check Your Understanding

4. A normal population has mean $\mu = 3$ and standard deviation $\sigma = 1$. Find the proportion of the population that is less than 1.

5. A normal population has mean $\mu = 40$ and standard deviation $\sigma = 10$. Find the probability that a randomly sampled value is greater than 53.

6. A normal population has mean $\mu = 7$ and standard deviation $\sigma = 5$. Find the proportion of the population that is between -2 and 10.

Answers are on page 251.

Objective 3 Find the value from a normal distribution corresponding to a given proportion

Finding the Value from a Normal Distribution Corresponding to a Given Proportion

Sometimes we want to find the value from a normal distribution that has a given proportion of the population above or below it. The method for doing this is the reverse of the method for finding a proportion for a given value. In particular, we need to find the value from the distribution that has a given z-score.

Recall that the z-score tells how many standard deviations a value is above or below the mean. The value of x that corresponds to a given z-score is given by

$$x = \mu + z\sigma$$

EXAMPLE 6.18 **Finding the value from a normal distribution with a given z-score**

Heights in a group of men are normally distributed with mean $\mu = 69$ inches and standard deviation $\sigma = 3$ inches.

a. Find the height whose z-score is 1. Interpret the result.

b. Find the height whose z-score is -2.0. Interpret the result.

c. Find the height whose z-score is 0.6. Interpret the result.

Solution

a. We want the height that is equal to the mean plus one standard deviation. Therefore, $x = \mu + z\sigma = 69 + (1)(3) = 72$. We interpret this by saying that a man 72 inches tall has a height one standard deviation above the mean.

b. We want the height that is equal to the mean minus two standard deviations. Therefore, $x = \mu + z\sigma = 69 + (-2)(3) = 63$. We interpret this by saying that a man 63 inches tall has a height two standard deviations below the mean.

c. We want the height that is equal to the mean plus 0.6 standard deviation. Therefore, $x = \mu + z\sigma = 69 + (0.6)(3) = 70.8$. We interpret this by saying that a man 70.8 inches tall has a height 0.6 standard deviation above the mean.

Explain It Again

$x = \mu + z\sigma$: The z-score tells how many standard deviations x is above or below the mean. Therefore, the value of x that corresponds to a given z-score is equal to the mean (μ) plus z times the standard deviation (σ).

To find the value from a normal distribution that has a given proportion above or below it, we can use either Table A.2 or technology. Following are the steps to find the value that has a given proportion above or below it by using Table A.2.

Finding a Normal Value That Has a Given Proportion Above or Below It by Using Table A.2

Step 1: Sketch a normal curve, label the mean, label the value x to be found, and shade in and label the given area.

Step 2: If the given area is on the right, subtract it from 1 to get the area on the left.

Step 3: Look in the body of Table A.2 to find the area closest to the given area. Find the z-score corresponding to that area.

Step 4: Obtain the value from the normal distribution by computing $x = \mu + z\sigma$.

EXAMPLE 6.19   Finding a normal value corresponding to an area

Mensa is an organization whose membership is limited to people whose IQ is in the top 2% of the population. Assume that scores on an IQ test are normally distributed with mean $\mu = 100$ and standard deviation $\sigma = 15$. What is the minimum score needed to qualify for membership in Mensa?

Solution

Step 1: Figure 6.18 presents a sketch of the normal curve, showing the value x separating the upper 2% from the lower 98%.

Step 2: The area 0.02 is on the right, so we subtract from 1 and work with the area 0.98 on the left.

Step 3: The area closest to 0.98 in Table A.2 is 0.9798, which corresponds to a z-score of 2.05.

Step 4: The IQ score that separates the upper 2% from the lower 98% is

$$x = \mu + z\sigma = 100 + (2.05)(15) = 130.75$$

Since IQ scores are generally whole numbers, we will round this to $x = 131$.

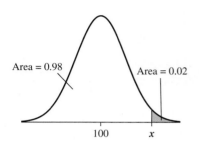

Area = 0.98   Area = 0.02

100   x

Figure 6.18

Finding the normal value corresponding to a given area by using technology

To find the percentile of a normal distribution with technology, follow Steps 1 and 2 of the method for using the table. What is done after that depends on the technology being used. Example 6.20 illustrates the use of the TI-84 Plus calculator.

EXAMPLE 6.20   Finding the normal value corresponding to an area by using technology

IQ scores have a mean of 100 and a standard deviation of 15. Use technology to find the 90th percentile of IQ scores; in other words, find the IQ score that separates the upper 10% from the lower 90%.

Solution

Recall: The pth percentile of a population is the value that separates the lowest p% of the population from the highest $(100 - p)$%.

Step 1: Figure 6.19 presents a sketch of the normal curve, showing the value x separating the upper 10% from the lower 90%.

Step 2: We work with the area 0.90 on the left.

Step 3: For the TI-84 Plus calculator, use the **invNorm** command with area 0.90, mean 100, and standard deviation 15. Step-by-step instructions are given in the Using Technology section on page 246.

Figure 6.20 presents the results from the TI-84 Plus calculator. The IQ score corresponding to the top 10% is 119.

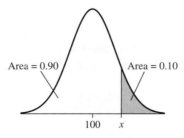

Area = 0.90   Area = 0.10

100   x

Figure 6.19

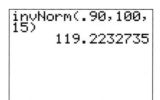

```
invNorm(.90,100,
15)
          119.2232735
```

Figure 6.20

Check Your Understanding

7. A population has mean $\mu = 6.9$ and standard deviation $\sigma = 2.6$. Find the value that has 80% of the population below it (in other words, the 80th percentile).

8. A population has mean $\mu = 53$ and standard deviation $\sigma = 34$. Find the value that has 35% of the population above it.

Answers are on page 251.

USING TECHNOLOGY

TI-84 PLUS

Finding areas under a normal curve

The **normalcdf** command is used to calculate area under a normal curve.

Step 1. Press **2nd**, then **VARS** to access the **DISTR** menu. Select **2:normalcdf** (Figure A).

Step 2. Enter the left endpoint, comma, the right endpoint, comma, the mean, comma, and the standard deviation.
  - When finding the area to the right of a given value, use **1E99** as the right endpoint.
  - When finding the area to the left of a given value, use **−1E99** as the left endpoint.

Step 3. Press **ENTER**.

Figure A

Using the TI-84 PLUS Stat Wizards (see Appendix B for more information)

Step 1. Press **2nd**, then **VARS** to access the **DISTR** menu. Select **2:normalcdf** (Figure A).

Step 2. Enter the left endpoint in the **lower** field, the right endpoint in the **upper** field, the mean in the μ field, and the standard deviation in the σ field.
  - When finding the area to the right of a given value, use **1E99** as the right endpoint.
  - When finding the area to the left of a given value, use **−1E99** as the left endpoint.

Step 3. Select **Paste** and press **ENTER** to paste the command to the home screen. Press **ENTER** again to run the command.

Figure B illustrates finding the area to the right of $x = 280$ with $\mu = 272$ and $\sigma = 9$ (Example 6.15).

```
normalcdf(280,1E
99,272,9)
         .1870313608
```

Figure B

Finding a normal value corresponding to a given area

The **invNorm** command is used to calculate the z-score corresponding to an *area to the left*.

Step 1. Press **2nd**, then **VARS** to access the **DISTR** menu. Select **3:invNorm** (Figure C).

Step 2. Enter the area to the left of the desired normal value, comma, the mean, comma, and the standard deviation.

Step 3. Press **ENTER**.

Figure C

Using the TI-84 PLUS Stat Wizards (see Appendix B for more information)

Step 1. Press **2nd**, then **VARS** to access the **DISTR** menu. Select **3:invNorm** (Figure C).

Step 2. Enter the area to the left of the desired z-score in the **area** field, the mean in the μ field, and the standard deviation in the σ field.

Step 3. Select **Paste** and press **ENTER** to paste the command to the home screen. Press **ENTER** again to run the command.

Figure D illustrates finding the normal value that has an area of 0.98 to its left, where $\mu = 100$ and $\sigma = 15$ (Example 6.19).

```
invNorm(0.98,100
,15)
         130.8062337
```

Figure D

MINITAB

Finding areas under a normal curve

The following procedure computes the area to the *left* of a given value.

Step 1. Click **Calc**, then **Probability Distributions**, then **Normal**.

Step 2. Select the **Cumulative probability** option.

Step 3. Enter the value for the mean in the **Mean** field and the value for the standard deviation in the **Standard deviation** field.

Step 4. To compute the area to the left of a given x, enter the value for x in the **Input constant** field.

Step 5. Click **OK**.

Cumulative Distribution Function

```
Normal with mean = 272 and standard deviation = 9

  x   P( X <= x )
280     0.812969
```

Figure E

Figure E illustrates finding the area to the *left* of $x = 280$ with $\mu = 272$ and $\sigma = 9$. To find the area to the right of $x = 280$, subtract this result from 1 (Example 6.15).

Finding a normal value corresponding to a given area

The following procedure is used to calculate a normal value corresponding to an *area to the left*.

Step 1. Click **Calc**, then **Probability Distributions**, then **Normal**.

Step 2. Select the **Inverse Cumulative Probability** option.

Step 3. Enter the value for the mean in the **Mean** field and the value for the standard deviation in the **Standard deviation** field.

Step 4. Enter the area to the left of the desired normal value and click **OK**.

Inverse Cumulative Distribution Function

```
Normal with mean = 100 and standard deviation = 15

P( X <= x )        x
      0.98   130.806
```

Figure F

Figure F illustrates finding the normal value that has an area of 0.98 to its left, where $\mu = 100$ and $\sigma = 15$ (Example 6.19).

EXCEL

Finding areas under a normal curve

The following procedure computes the area to the *left* of a given value.

Step 1. In an empty cell, select the **Insert Function** icon and highlight **Statistical** in the category field.

Step 2. Click on the **NORM.DIST** function and press **OK**.

Step 3. To compute the area to the left of a given x, enter the value of x in the **X** field.

Step 4. Enter the value for the mean in the **Mean** field and the value for the standard deviation in the **Standard deviation** field.

Step 5. Enter **TRUE** in the **Cumulative** field and click **OK**.

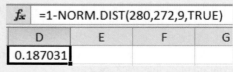

f_x	=1-NORM.DIST(280,272,9,TRUE)		
D	E	F	G
0.187031			

Figure G

Figure G illustrates finding the area to the right of $x = 280$ with $\mu = 272$ and $\sigma = 9$ by subtracting the area on the left from 1 (Example 6.15).

Finding a normal value corresponding to a given area

The following procedure is used to calculate the normal value corresponding to an *area to the left*.

Step 1. In an empty cell, select the **Insert Function** icon and highlight **Statistical** in the category field.

Step 2. Click on the **NORM.INV** function and press **OK**.

Step 3. Enter the area to the left of the desired normal area in the **Probability** field.

Step 4. Enter the value for the mean in the **Mean** field and the value for the standard deviation in the **Standard deviation** field.

Step 5. Click **OK**.

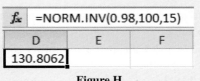

Figure H

Figure H illustrates finding the normal value that has an area of 0.98 to its left, where $\mu = 100$ and $\sigma = 15$ (Example 6.19).

SECTION 6.2 Exercises

Exercises 1–8 are the Check Your Understanding exercises located within the section.

Understanding the Concepts

In Exercises 9–10, fill in each blank with the appropriate word or phrase.

9. The process of converting a value x from a normal distribution to a z-score is known as _____.

10. A value that is two standard deviations below the mean will have a z-score of _____.

In Exercises 11–16, determine whether the statement is true or false. If the statement is false, rewrite it as a true statement.

11. z-scores follow a standard normal distribution.

12. A z-score indicates how many standard deviations a value is above or below the mean.

13. If a normal population has a mean of μ and a standard deviation of σ, then the area to the left of μ is less than 0.5.

14. If a normal population has a mean of μ and a standard deviation of σ, then the area to the right of $\mu + \sigma$ is less than 0.5.

15. If a normal population has a mean of μ and a standard deviation of σ, then $P(X = \mu) = 1$.

16. If a normal population has a mean of μ and a standard deviation of σ, then $P(X = \mu) = 0$.

Practicing the Skills

17. A normal population has mean $\mu = 20$ and standard deviation $\sigma = 4$.
   a. What proportion of the population is less than 18?
   b. What is the probability that a randomly chosen value will be greater than 25?

18. A normal population has mean $\mu = 9$ and standard deviation $\sigma = 6$.
   a. What proportion of the population is less than 20?
   b. What is the probability that a randomly chosen value will be greater than 5?

19. A normal population has mean $\mu = 25$ and standard deviation $\sigma = 11$.
   a. What proportion of the population is greater than 34?
   b. What is the probability that a randomly chosen value will be less than 10?

20. A normal population has mean $\mu = 61$ and standard deviation $\sigma = 16$.
   a. What proportion of the population is greater than 100?
   b. What is the probability that a randomly chosen value will be less than 80?

21. A normal population has mean $\mu = 47$ and standard deviation $\sigma = 3$.
   a. What proportion of the population is between 40 and 50?
   b. What is the probability that a randomly chosen value will be between 50 and 55?

22. A normal population has mean $\mu = 35$ and standard deviation $\sigma = 8$.
   a. What proportion of the population is between 20 and 30?
   b. What is the probability that a randomly chosen value will be between 30 and 40?

23. A normal population has mean $\mu = 12$ and standard deviation $\sigma = 3$. What is the 40th percentile of the population?

24. A normal population has mean $\mu = 56$ and standard deviation $\sigma = 8$. What is the 88th percentile of the population?

25. A normal population has mean $\mu = 46$ and standard deviation $\sigma = 9$. What is the 19th percentile of the population?

26. A normal population has mean $\mu = 71$ and standard deviation $\sigma = 33$. What is the 94th percentile of the population?

Working with the Concepts

27. Check your blood pressure: In a recent study, the Centers for Disease Control and Prevention reported that diastolic blood pressures of adult women in the United States are approximately normally distributed with mean 80.5 and standard deviation 9.9.

a. What proportion of women have blood pressures lower than 70?

b. What proportion of women have blood pressures between 75 and 90?

c. A diastolic blood pressure greater than 90 is classified as hypertension (high blood pressure). What proportion of women have hypertension?

d. Is it unusual for a woman to have a blood pressure lower than 65?

28. Baby weights: According to the 2010 National Health Statistics Reports, the weight of male babies less than 2 months old in the United States is normally distributed with mean 11.5 pounds and standard deviation 2.7 pounds.

a. What proportion of babies weigh more than 13 pounds?

b. What proportion of babies weigh less than 15 pounds?

c. What proportion of babies weigh between 10 and 14 pounds?

d. Is it unusual for a baby to weigh more than 17 pounds?

29. Check your blood pressure: The Centers for Disease Control and Prevention reported that diastolic blood pressures of adult women in the United States are approximately normally distributed with mean 80.5 and standard deviation 9.9.

a. Find the 30th percentile of the blood pressures.

b. Find the 67th percentile of the blood pressures.

c. Find the third quartile of the blood pressures.

30. Baby weights: The weight of male babies less than 2 months old in the United States is normally distributed with mean 11.5 pounds and standard deviation 2.7 pounds.

a. Find the 81st percentile of the baby weights.

b. Find the 10th percentile of the baby weights.

c. Find the first quartile of the baby weights.

31. Fish story: According to a report by the U.S. Fish and Wildlife Service, the mean length of six-year-old rainbow trout in the Arolik River in Alaska is 481 millimeters with a standard deviation of 41 millimeters. Assume these lengths are normally distributed.

a. What proportion of six-year-old rainbow trout are less than 450 millimeters long?

b. What proportion of six-year-old rainbow trout are between 400 and 500 millimeters long?

c. Is it unusual for a six-year-old rainbow trout to be less than 400 millimeters long?

32. Big chickens: According to thepoultrysite.com, the weights of broilers (commercially raised chickens) are approximately normally distributed with mean 1387 grams and standard deviation 161 grams.

a. What proportion of broilers weigh between 1100 and 1200 grams?

b. What is the probability that a randomly selected broiler weighs more than 1500 grams?

c. Is it unusual for a broiler to weigh more than 1550 grams?

33. Fish story: The U.S. Fish and Wildlife Service reported that the mean length of six-year-old rainbow trout in the Arolik River in Alaska is 481 millimeters with a standard deviation of 41 millimeters. Assume these lengths are normally distributed.

a. Find the 58th percentile of the lengths.

b. Find the 76th percentile of the lengths.

c. Find the first quartile of the lengths.

d. A size limit is to be put on trout that are caught. What should the size limit be so that 15% of six-year-old trout have lengths shorter than the limit?

34. Big chickens: A report on thepoultrysite.com stated that the weights of broilers (commercially raised chickens) are approximately normally distributed with mean 1387 grams and standard deviation 161 grams.

a. Find the 22nd percentile of the weights.

b. Find the 93rd percentile of the weights.

c. Find the first quartile of the weights.

d. A chicken farmer wants to provide a money-back guarantee that his broilers will weigh at least a certain amount. What weight should he guarantee so that he will have to give his customers' money back only 1% of the time?

35. Radon: Radon is a naturally occurring radioactive substance that is found in the ground underneath many homes. Radon detectors are often placed in homes to determine whether radon levels are high enough to be dangerous. A radon level less than 4.0 picocuries is considered safe. Because levels fluctuate randomly, the levels measured by detectors are not exactly correct, but are instead normally distributed. It is known from physical theory that when the true level is 4.1 picocuries, the measurement made by a detector over a one-hour period will be normally distributed with mean 4.1 picocuries and standard deviation 0.2 picocurie.

a. If the true level is 4.1, what is the probability that a one-hour measurement will be less than 4.0?

b. If the true level is 4.1, would it be unusual for a one-hour measurement to indicate that the level is safe?

c. If a measurement is made for 24 hours, the mean will still be 4.1 picocuries, but the standard deviation will be only 0.04 picocurie. What is the probability that a 24-hour measurement will be below 4.0?

d. If the true level is 4.1, would it be unusual for a 24-hour measurement to indicate that the level is safe?

36. Electric bills: According to the U.S. Energy Information Administration, the mean monthly household electric bill in the United States in 2007 was $99.70. Assume the amounts are normally distributed with standard deviation $20.00.

a. What proportion of bills are greater than $130?

b. What proportion of bills are between $85 and $140?

c. What is the probability that a randomly selected household had a monthly bill less than $110?

37. Radon: Assume that radon measurements are normally distributed with mean 4.1 picocuries and standard deviation of 0.2.

a. Find the 35th percentile of the measurements.

b. Find the 92nd percentile of the measurements.

c. Find the median of the measurements.

38. Electric bills: The U.S. Energy Information Agency reported that the mean monthly household electric bill in the United States in 2007 was $99.70. Assume the amounts are normally distributed with standard deviation $20.00.

a. Find the 7th percentile of the bill amounts.

b. Find the 62nd percentile of the bill amounts.

c. Find the median of the bill amounts.

39. Tire lifetimes: The lifetime of a certain type of automobile tire (in thousands of miles) is normally distributed with mean $\mu = 40$ and standard deviation $\sigma = 5$.
   a. What is the probability that a randomly chosen tire has a lifetime greater than 48 thousand miles?
   b. What proportion of tires have lifetimes between 38 and 43 thousand miles?
   c. What proportion of tires have lifetimes less than 46 thousand miles?

40. Tree heights: Cherry trees in a certain orchard have heights that are normally distributed with mean $\mu = 112$ inches and standard deviation $\sigma = 14$ inches.
   a. What proportion of trees are more than 120 inches tall?
   b. What proportion of trees are less than 100 inches tall?
   c. What is the probability that a randomly chosen tree is between 90 and 100 inches tall?

41. Tire lifetimes: The lifetime of a certain type of automobile tire (in thousands of miles) is normally distributed with mean $\mu = 40$ and standard deviation $\sigma = 5$.
   a. Find the 12th percentile of the tire lifetimes.
   b. Find the 68th percentile of the tire lifetimes.
   c. Find the first quartile of the tire lifetimes.
   d. The tire company wants to guarantee that its tires will last at least a certain number of miles. What number of miles (in thousands) should the company guarantee so that only 2% of the tires violate the guarantee?

42. Tree heights: Cherry trees in a certain orchard have heights that are normally distributed with mean $\mu = 112$ inches and standard deviation $\sigma = 14$ inches.
   a. Find the 27th percentile of the tree heights.
   b. Find the 88th percentile of the tree heights.
   c. Find the third quartile of the tree heights.
   d. An agricultural scientist wants to study the tallest 1% of the trees to determine whether they have a certain gene that allows them to grow taller. To do this, she needs to study all the trees above a certain height. What height is this?

43. How much is in that can? The volume of beverage in a 12-ounce can is normally distributed with mean 12.05 ounces and standard deviation 0.02 ounce.
   a. What is the probability that a randomly selected can will contain more than 12.06 ounces?
   b. What is the probability that a randomly selected can will contain between 12 and 12.03 ounces?
   c. Is it unusual for a can to be underfilled (contain less than 12 ounces)?

44. How much do you study? A survey among freshmen at a certain university revealed that the number of hours spent studying the week before final exams was normally distributed with mean 25 and standard deviation 7.
   a. What proportion of students studied more than 40 hours?
   b. What is the probability that a randomly selected student spent between 15 and 30 hours studying?
   c. What proportion of students studied less than 30 hours?

45. How much is in that can? The volume of beverage in a 12-ounce can is normally distributed with mean 12.05 ounces and standard deviation 0.02 ounce.
   a. Find the 60th percentile of the volumes.
   b. Find the 4th percentile of the volumes.
   c. Between what two values are the middle 95% of the volumes?

46. How much do you study? A survey among freshmen at a certain university revealed that the number of hours spent studying the week before final exams was normally distributed with mean 25 and standard deviation 7.
   a. Find the 98th percentile of the number of hours studying.
   b. Find the 32nd percentile of the number of hours studying.
   c. Between what two values are the middle 80% of the hours spent studying?

47. Precision manufacturing: A process manufactures ball bearings with diameters that are normally distributed with mean 25.1 millimeters and standard deviation 0.08 millimeter.
   a. What proportion of the diameters are less than 25.0 millimeters?
   b. What proportion of the diameters are greater than 25.4 millimeters?
   c. To meet a certain specification, a ball bearing must have a diameter between 25.0 and 25.3 millimeters. What proportion of the ball bearings meet the specification?

48. Exam grades: Scores on a statistics final in a large class were normally distributed with a mean of 75 and a standard deviation of 8.
   a. What proportion of the scores were above 90?
   b. What proportion of the scores were below 65?
   c. What is the probability that a randomly chosen score is between 70 and 80?

49. Precision manufacturing: A process manufactures ball bearings with diameters that are normally distributed with mean 25.1 millimeters and standard deviation 0.08 millimeter.
   a. Find the 60th percentile of the diameters.
   b. Find the 32nd percentile of the diameters.
   c. A hole is to be designed so that 1% of the ball bearings will fit through it. The bearings that fit through the hole will be melted down and remade. What should the diameter of the hole be?
   d. Between what two values are the middle 50% of the diameters?

50. Exam grades: Scores on a statistics final in a large class were normally distributed with a mean of 75 and a standard deviation of 8.
   a. Find the 40th percentile of the scores.
   b. Find the 65th percentile of the scores.
   c. The instructor wants to give an A to the students whose scores were in the top 10% of the class. What is the minimum score needed to get an A?

d. Between what two values are the middle 60% of the scores?

Extending the Concepts

51. Tall men: Heights of men in a certain city are normally distributed with mean 70 inches. Sixteen percent of the men are more than 73 inches tall. What percentage of the men are between 67 and 70 inches tall?

52. Watch your speed: Speeds of automobiles on a certain stretch of freeway at 11:00 PM are normally distributed with mean 65 mph. Twenty percent of the cars are traveling at speeds between 55 and 65 mph. What percentage of the cars are going faster than 75 mph?

53. Contaminated wells: A study reported that the mean concentration of ammonium in water wells in the state of Iowa was 0.71 milligram per liter, and the standard deviation was 1.09 milligrams per liter. Is it possible to determine whether these concentrations are approximately normally distributed? If so, say whether they are normally distributed, and explain how you know. If not, describe the additional information you would need to determine whether they are normally distributed.

Source: *Water Environment Research* 74:177–186

Answers to Check Your Understanding Exercises for Section 6.2

1. $z = -1$. Interpretation: A value of 11 is one standard deviation below the mean.

2. $z = 0.75$. Interpretation: A value of 75 is 0.75 standard deviation above the mean.

3. $z = -0.4$ Interpretation: The length of time for this bulb is 0.4 standard deviation below the mean.

4. 0.0228

5. 0.0968

6. 0.6898

7. 9.084 [Tech: 9.088]

8. 66.26 [Tech: 66.10]

SECTION 6.3 | Sampling Distributions and the Central Limit Theorem

Objectives

1. Construct the sampling distribution of a sample mean
2. Use the Central Limit Theorem to compute probabilities involving sample means

In Section 6.2, we learned to compute probabilities for a randomly sampled individual from a normal population. In practice, statistical studies involve sampling several, perhaps many, individuals. As discussed in Chapter 3, we often compute numerical summaries of samples, and the most commonly used summary is the sample mean $\bar{x}$.

If several samples are drawn from a population, they are likely to have different values for $\bar{x}$. Because the value of $\bar{x}$ varies each time a sample is drawn, $\bar{x}$ is a random variable, and it has a probability distribution. The probability distribution of $\bar{x}$ is called the **sampling distribution** of $\bar{x}$.

Objective 1 Construct the sampling distribution of a sample mean

An Example of a Sampling Distribution

Tetrahedral dice are four-sided dice, used in role-playing games such as Dungeons & Dragons. They are shaped like a pyramid, with four triangular faces. Each face corresponds to a number between 1 and 4, so that when you toss a tetrahedral die, it comes up with one of the numbers 1, 2, 3, or 4. Tossing a tetrahedral die is like sampling a value from the population

$$\boxed{1}\ \boxed{2}\ \boxed{3}\ \boxed{4}$$

The population mean and variance are:

$$\text{Population mean: } \mu = \frac{1+2+3+4}{4} = 2.5$$

$$\text{Population variance: } \sigma^2 = \frac{(1-2.5)^2 + (2-2.5)^2 + (3-2.5)^2 + (4-2.5)^2}{4} = 1.25$$

Now imagine tossing a tetrahedral die three times. The sequence of three numbers that is observed is a sample of size 3 drawn with replacement from the population just described. There are 64 possible samples, and they are all equally likely. Table 6.1 on page 252 lists them and provides the value of the sample mean $\bar{x}$ for each.

Table 6.1 The 64 Possible Samples of Size 3 and Their Sample Means

Sample	$\bar{x}$	Sample	$\bar{x}$	Sample	$\bar{x}$	Sample	$\bar{x}$
1, 1, 1	1.00	2, 1, 1	1.33	3, 1, 1	1.67	4, 1, 1	2.00
1, 1, 2	1.33	2, 1, 2	1.67	3, 1, 2	2.00	4, 1, 2	2.33
1, 1, 3	1.67	2, 1, 3	2.00	3, 1, 3	2.33	4, 1, 3	2.67
1, 1, 4	2.00	2, 1, 4	2.33	3, 1, 4	2.67	4, 1, 4	3.00
1, 2, 1	1.33	2, 2, 1	1.67	3, 2, 1	2.00	4, 2, 1	2.33
1, 2, 2	1.67	2, 2, 2	2.00	3, 2, 2	2.33	4, 2, 2	2.67
1, 2, 3	2.00	2, 2, 3	2.33	3, 2, 3	2.67	4, 2, 3	3.00
1, 2, 4	2.33	2, 2, 4	2.67	3, 2, 4	3.00	4, 2, 4	3.33
1, 3, 1	1.67	2, 3, 1	2.00	3, 3, 1	2.33	4, 3, 1	2.67
1, 3, 2	2.00	2, 3, 2	2.33	3, 3, 2	2.67	4, 3, 2	3.00
1, 3, 3	2.33	2, 3, 3	2.67	3, 3, 3	3.00	4, 3, 3	3.33
1, 3, 4	2.67	2, 3, 4	3.00	3, 3, 4	3.33	4, 3, 4	3.67
1, 4, 1	2.00	2, 4, 1	2.33	3, 4, 1	2.67	4, 4, 1	3.00
1, 4, 2	2.33	2, 4, 2	2.67	3, 4, 2	3.00	4, 4, 2	3.33
1, 4, 3	2.67	2, 4, 3	3.00	3, 4, 3	3.33	4, 4, 3	3.67
1, 4, 4	3.00	2, 4, 4	3.33	3, 4, 4	3.67	4, 4, 4	4.00

The columns labeled "$\bar{x}$" contain the values of the sample mean for each of the 64 possible samples. Some of these values appear more than once, because several samples have the same mean. The mean of the sampling distribution is the average of these 64 values. The variance of the sampling distribution is the population variance of the 64 sample means, which can be computed by the method presented in Section 3.2. The mean and variance are

$$\text{Mean: } \mu_{\bar{x}} = 2.5 \qquad \text{Variance: } \sigma_{\bar{x}}^2 = 0.4167$$

Comparing the mean and variance of the sampling distribution to the population mean and variance, we see that the mean $\mu_{\bar{x}}$ of the sampling distribution is equal to the population mean μ. The variance $\sigma_{\bar{x}}^2$ of the sampling distribution is 0.4167, which is less than the population variance $\sigma^2 = 1.25$. It is not immediately obvious how these two quantities are related. Note, however, that

$$\sigma_{\bar{x}}^2 = 0.4167 = \frac{1.25}{3} = \frac{\sigma^2}{3}$$

The sample size is $n = 3$, so $\sigma_{\bar{x}}^2 = \dfrac{\sigma^2}{n}$. Now, the standard deviation is the square root of the variance. It follows that the relationship between $\sigma_{\bar{x}}$ and σ is

$$\sigma_{\bar{x}} = \frac{\sigma}{\sqrt{n}}$$

These relationships hold in general. Note that the standard deviation $\sigma_{\bar{x}}$ is sometimes called the **standard error** of the mean.

SUMMARY

Let $\bar{x}$ be the mean of a simple random sample of size n, drawn from a population with mean μ and standard deviation σ.

The mean of the sampling distribution is $\mu_{\bar{x}} = \mu$.

The standard deviation of the sampling distribution is $\sigma_{\bar{x}} = \dfrac{\sigma}{\sqrt{n}}$.

The standard deviation $\sigma_{\bar{x}}$ is sometimes called the **standard error** of the mean.

| EXAMPLE 6.21 | Find the mean and standard deviation of a sampling distribution |

Among students at a certain college, the mean number of hours of television watched per week is $\mu = 10.5$, and the standard deviation is $\sigma = 3.6$. A simple random sample of 16 students is chosen for a study of viewing habits. Let $\bar{x}$ be the mean number of hours of TV watched by the sampled students. Find the mean $\mu_{\bar{x}}$ and the standard deviation $\sigma_{\bar{x}}$ of $\bar{x}$.

Solution
The mean of $\bar{x}$ is

$$\mu_{\bar{x}} = \mu = 10.5$$

The sample size is $n = 16$. Therefore, the standard deviation of $\bar{x}$ is

$$\sigma_{\bar{x}} = \frac{\sigma}{\sqrt{n}} = \frac{3.6}{\sqrt{16}} = 0.9$$

It makes sense that the standard deviation of $\bar{x}$ is less than the population standard deviation σ. In a sample, it is unusual to get all large values or all small values. Samples usually contain both large and small values that cancel each other out when the sample mean is computed. For this reason, the distribution of $\bar{x}$ is less spread out than the population distribution. Therefore, the standard deviation of $\bar{x}$ is less than the population standard deviation.

Check Your Understanding

1. A population has mean $\mu = 6$ and standard deviation $\sigma = 4$. Find $\mu_{\bar{x}}$ and $\sigma_{\bar{x}}$ for samples of size $n = 25$.

2. A population has mean $\mu = 17$ and standard deviation $\sigma = 20$. Find $\mu_{\bar{x}}$ and $\sigma_{\bar{x}}$ for samples of size $n = 100$.

Answers are on page 258.

The probability histogram for the sampling distribution of $\overline{x}$

Consider again the example of the tetrahedral die. Let us compare the probability distribution for the population and the sampling distribution. The population consists of the numbers 1, 2, 3, and 4, each of which is equally likely. The sampling distribution for $\bar{x}$ can be determined from Table 6.1. The probability that the sample mean is 1.00 is 1/64, because out of the 64 possible samples, only one has a sample mean equal to 1.00. Similarly, the probability that $\bar{x} = 1.33$ is 3/64, because there are three samples out of 64 whose sample mean is 1.33. Figure 6.21 presents the probability histogram of the population and Figure 6.22 presents the sampling distribution for $\bar{x}$.

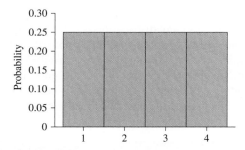

Figure 6.21   Probability histogram for the population

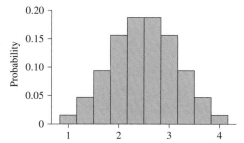

Figure 6.22   Probability histogram for the sampling distribution of $\bar{x}$ for samples of size 3

Note that the probability histogram for the sampling distribution looks a lot like the normal curve, whereas the probability histogram for the population does not. Remarkably, it is true that, for any population, if the sample size is large enough, the sample mean $\bar{x}$ will be approximately normally distributed. For a symmetric population like the one in Figure 6.21, the sample mean is approximately normally distributed even for a small sample size like $n = 3$. For a skewed population, the sample size must be larger for the sample mean to be approximately normal.

Computing the sampling distribution of $\bar{x}$ for a skewed population

For a certain make of car, the number of repairs needed while under warranty has the following probability distribution.

x	$P(x)$
0	0.60
1	0.25
2	0.10
3	0.03
4	0.02

Figure 6.23 presents the probability histogram for this distribution, along with probability histograms for the sampling distribution of $\bar{x}$ for samples of size 3, 10, and 30. The probability histograms for the sampling distributions were created by programming a computer to compute the probability for every possible value of $\bar{x}$.

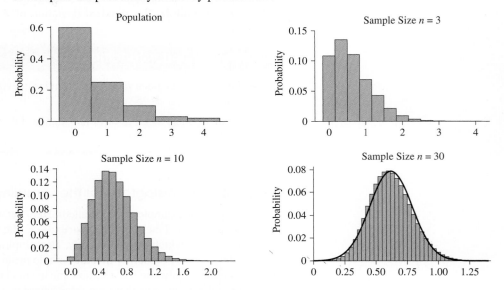

Figure 6.23 The probability histogram for the population distribution is highly skewed. As the sample size increases, the skewness decreases. For a sample size of 30, the probability histogram is reasonably well approximated by a normal curve.

The remarkable fact that the sampling distribution of $\bar{x}$ is approximately normal for a large sample from any distribution is called the **Central Limit Theorem**. The size of the sample needed to obtain approximate normality depends mostly on the skewness of the population. A sample of size $n > 30$ is large enough for most populations encountered in practice. Smaller sample sizes are adequate for distributions that are nearly symmetric. We note that if the population itself is exactly normal, $\bar{x}$ will be exactly normal for any sample size. This fact is of little practical value in most situations, since populations encountered in practice are rarely exactly normal.

The Central Limit Theorem

Let $\bar{x}$ be the mean of a large ($n > 30$) simple random sample from a population with mean μ and standard deviation σ.

Then $\bar{x}$ has an approximately normal distribution, with mean $\mu_{\bar{x}} = \mu$ and standard deviation $\sigma_{\bar{x}} = \dfrac{\sigma}{\sqrt{n}}$.

The Central Limit Theorem is the most important result in statistics, and forms the basis for much of the work that statisticians do.

Computing Probabilities with the Central Limit Theorem

To compute probabilities involving a sample mean $\bar{x}$, use the following procedure:

> ### Procedure for Computing Probabilities with the Central Limit Theorem
>
> **Step 1:** Be sure the sample size is greater than 30. If so, it is appropriate to use the normal curve.
> **Step 2:** Find the mean $\mu_{\bar{x}}$ and standard deviation $\sigma_{\bar{x}}$.
> **Step 3:** Sketch a normal curve and shade in the area to be found.
> **Step 4:** Find the area using Table A.2 or technology.

EXAMPLE 6.22

Using the Central Limit Theorem to compute a probability

Based on data from the U.S. Census, the mean age of college students in 2008 was $\mu = 25$ years, with a standard deviation of $\sigma = 6.8$ years. A simple random sample of 64 students is drawn. What is the probability that the sample mean age of the students is greater than 26 years?

Solution

Step 1: The sample size is 64, which is greater than 30. We may use the normal curve.
Step 2: We compute $\mu_{\bar{x}}$ and $\sigma_{\bar{x}}$.

$$\mu_{\bar{x}} = \mu = 25 \qquad \sigma_{\bar{x}} = \frac{\sigma}{\sqrt{n}} = \frac{6.8}{\sqrt{64}} = 0.85$$

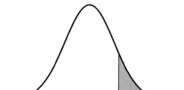

25   26
$z = 1.18$

Figure 6.24

Step 3: Figure 6.24 presents the normal curve with the area of interest shaded.
Step 4: We will use Table A.2. We compute the z-score for 26.

$$z = \frac{x - \mu_{\bar{x}}}{\sigma_{\bar{x}}} = \frac{26 - 25}{0.85} = 1.18$$

> **CAUTION**
>
> When computing the z-score for the distribution of $\bar{x}$, be sure to use the standard deviation $\sigma_{\bar{x}}$, rather than σ.

The table gives the area to the *left* of $z = 1.18$ as 0.8810. The area to the right of $z = 1.18$ is $1 - 0.8810 = 0.1190$. The probability that the sample mean age of the students is greater than 26 years is 0.1190.

EXAMPLE 6.23

Using the Central Limit Theorem to determine whether a given value of $\bar{x}$ is unusual

Hereford cattle are one of the most popular breeds of beef cattle. Based on data from the Hereford Cattle Society, the mean weight of a one-year-old Hereford bull is 1135 pounds, with a standard deviation of 97 pounds. Would it be unusual for the mean weight of 100 head of cattle to be less than 1100 pounds?

Solution

We will compute the probability that the sample mean is less than 1100. We will say that this event is unusual if its probability is less than 0.05.

Step 1: The sample size is 100, which is greater than 30. We may use the normal curve.
Step 2: We compute $\mu_{\bar{x}}$ and $\sigma_{\bar{x}}$.

$$\mu_{\bar{x}} = \mu = 1135 \qquad \sigma_{\bar{x}} = \frac{\sigma}{\sqrt{n}} = \frac{97}{\sqrt{100}} = 9.7$$

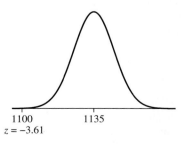

1100   1135
$z = -3.61$

Figure 6.25

Step 3: Figure 6.25 presents the normal curve. We are interested in the area to the left of 1100, which is too small to see.

Step 4: We will use Table A.2. We compute the z-score for 1100.

$$z = \frac{x - \mu_{\bar{x}}}{\sigma_{\bar{x}}} = \frac{1100 - 1135}{9.7} = -3.61$$

The area to the left of $z = -3.61$ is 0.0002. The probability that the sample mean weight is less than 1100 is 0.0002. This probability is less than 0.05, so it would be unusual for the sample mean to be less than 1100.

Check Your Understanding

3. A population has mean $\mu = 10$ and standard deviation $\sigma = 8$. A sample of size 50 is drawn.
  a. Find the probability that $\bar{x}$ is greater than 11.
  b. Would it be unusual for $\bar{x}$ to be less than 8? Explain.

4. A population has mean $\mu = 47.5$ and standard deviation $\sigma = 12.6$. A sample of size 112 is drawn.
  a. Find the probability that $\bar{x}$ is between 45 and 48.
  b. Would it be unusual for $\bar{x}$ to be greater than 48? Explain.

Answers are on page 258.

SECTION 6.3   Exercises

Exercises 1–4 are the Check Your Understanding exercises located within the section.

Understanding the Concepts

In Exercises 5 and 6, fill in each blank with the appropriate word or phrase.

5. The probability distribution of $\bar{x}$ is called a _____ distribution.

6. The _____ states that the sampling distribution of $\bar{x}$ is approximately normal when the sample is large.

In Exercises 7 and 8, determine whether the statement is true or false. If the statement is false, rewrite it as a true statement.

7. If $\bar{x}$ is the mean of a large ($n > 30$) simple random sample from a population with mean μ and standard deviation σ, then $\bar{x}$ is approximately normal with $\sigma_{\bar{x}} = \dfrac{\sigma}{\sqrt{n}}$.

8. As the sample size increases, the sampling distribution of $\bar{x}$ becomes more and more skewed.

Practicing the Skills

9. A sample of size 75 will be drawn from a population with mean 10 and standard deviation 12.
  a. Find the probability that $\bar{x}$ will be between 8 and 14.
  b. Find the 15th percentile of $\bar{x}$.

10. A sample of size 126 will be drawn from a population with mean 26 and standard deviation 3.
  a. Find the probability that $\bar{x}$ will be between 25 and 27.
  b. Find the 55th percentile of $\bar{x}$.

11. A sample of size 68 will be drawn from a population with mean 92 and standard deviation 24.
  a. Find the probability that $\bar{x}$ will be greater than 90.
  b. Find the 90th percentile of $\bar{x}$.

12. A sample of size 284 will be drawn from a population with mean 45 and standard deviation 7.
  a. Find the probability that $\bar{x}$ will be greater than 46.
  b. Find the 75th percentile of $\bar{x}$.

13. A sample of size 91 will be drawn from a population with mean 33 and standard deviation 17.
  a. Find the probability that $\bar{x}$ will be less than 30.
  b. Find the 25th percentile of $\bar{x}$.

14. A sample of size 82 will be drawn from a population with mean 24 and standard deviation 9.
  a. Find the probability that $\bar{x}$ will be less than 26.
  b. Find the 10th percentile of $\bar{x}$.

Working with the Concepts

15. Summer temperatures: Following are the temperatures, in degrees Fahrenheit, in Denver for five days in July 2009:

Date	Temperature
July 21	69
July 22	75
July 23	79
July 24	83
July 25	71

  a. Consider this to be a population. Find the population mean μ and the population standard deviation σ.
  b. List all samples of size 2 drawn with replacement. There are $5 \times 5 = 25$ different samples.

c. Compute the sample mean $\bar{x}$ for each of the 25 samples of size 2. Compute the mean $\mu_{\bar{x}}$ and the standard deviation $\sigma_{\bar{x}}$ of the sample means.

d. Verify that $\mu_{\bar{x}} = \mu$ and $\sigma_{\bar{x}} = \sigma/\sqrt{2}$.

16. Ages of winners: Following are the ages of the Grammy award winners for Best New Artist for the years 2006–2010. (For the Zac Brown Band, the age given is that of the lead singer, Zac Brown.)

Year: Winner	Age
2010: Zac Brown Band	31
2009: Adele	20
2008: Amy Winehouse	25
2007: Carrie Underwood	24
2006: John Legend	27

a. Consider this to be a population. Find the population mean μ and the population standard deviation σ.

b. List all samples of size 2 drawn with replacement. There are $5 \times 5 = 25$ different samples.

c. Compute the sample mean $\bar{x}$ for each of the 25 samples of size 2. Compute the mean $\mu_{\bar{x}}$ and the standard deviation $\sigma_{\bar{x}}$ of the sample means.

d. Verify that $\mu_{\bar{x}} = \mu$ and $\sigma_{\bar{x}} = \sigma/\sqrt{2}$.

17. How's your mileage? The Environmental Protection Agency (EPA) rates the mean highway gas mileage of the 2011 Ford Edge to be 27 miles per gallon. Assume the standard deviation is 3 miles per gallon. A rental car company buys 60 of these cars.

a. What is the probability that the average mileage of the fleet is greater than 26.5 miles per gallon?

b. What is the probability that the average mileage of the fleet is between 26 and 26.8 miles per gallon?

c. Would it be unusual if the average mileage of the fleet were less than 26 miles per gallon?

18. Watch your cholesterol: The National Health and Nutrition Examination Survey (NHANES) reported that in a recent year, the mean serum cholesterol level for U.S. adults was 202, with a standard deviation of 41 (the units are milligrams per deciliter). A simple random sample of 110 adults is chosen.

a. What is the probability that the sample mean cholesterol level is greater than 210?

b. What is the probability that the sample mean cholesterol level is between than 190 and 200?

c. Would it be unusual for the sample mean to be less than 198?

19. TV sets: According to the Nielsen Company, the mean number of TV sets in a U.S. household in 2008 was 2.83. Assume the standard deviation is 1.2. A sample of 85 households is drawn.

a. What is the probability that the sample mean number of TV sets is greater than 3?

b. What is the probability that the sample mean number of TV sets is between 2.5 and 3?

c. Find the 30th percentile of the sample mean.

d. Would it be unusual for the sample mean to be less than 2.5?

e. Would it be unusual for an individual household to have fewer than 2.5 TV sets? Explain.

20. SAT scores: The College Board reports that in 2008, the mean mathematics SAT score was 515, and the standard deviation was 116. A sample of 65 scores is chosen.

a. What is the probability that the sample mean score is less than 500?

b. What is the probability that the sample mean score is between 480 and 520?

c. Find the 80th percentile of the sample mean.

d. Would it be unusual if the sample mean were greater than 550?

e. Do you think it would be unusual for an individual to get a score greater than 550? Explain.

21. Taxes: The Internal Revenue Service reports that the mean federal income tax paid in the year 2007 was $7908. Assume that the standard deviation is $5000. The IRS plans to draw a sample of 1000 tax returns to study the effect of a new tax law.

a. What is the probability that the sample mean tax is less than $8000?

b. What is the probability that the sample mean tax is between $7600 and $7900?

c. Find the 40th percentile of the sample mean.

d. Would it be unusual if the sample mean were less than $7500?

e. Do you think it would be unusual for an individual to pay a tax of less than $7500? Explain.

22. High-rent district: The Real Estate Group NY reports that the mean monthly rent for a one-bedroom apartment without a doorman in Manhattan is $2631. Assume the standard deviation is $500. A real estate firm samples 100 apartments.

a. What is the probability that the sample mean rent is greater than $2700?

b. What is the probability that the sample mean rent is between $2500 and $2600?

c. Find the 60th percentile of the sample mean.

d. Would it be unusual if the sample mean were greater than $2800?

e. Do you think it would be unusual for an individual apartment to have a rent greater than $2800? Explain.

23. Roller coaster ride: A roller coaster is being designed that will accommodate 60 riders. The maximum weight the coaster can hold safely is 12,000 pounds. According to the National Health Statistics Reports, the weights of adult U.S. men have mean 194 pounds and standard deviation 68 pounds, and the weights of adult U.S. women have mean 164 pounds and standard deviation 77 pounds.

a. If 60 people are riding the coaster, and their total weight is 12,000 pounds, what is their average weight?

b. If a random sample of 60 adult men ride the coaster, what is the probability that the maximum safe weight will be exceeded?

c. If a random sample of 60 adult women ride the coaster, what is the probability that the maximum safe weight will be exceeded?

24. Elevator ride: Engineers are designing a large elevator that will accommodate 40 people. The maximum weight the elevator can hold safely is 8120 pounds. According to the National Health Statistics Reports, the weights of adult U.S. men have mean 194 pounds and standard deviation 68 pounds, and the weights of adult U.S. women have mean 164 pounds and standard deviation 77 pounds.
  a. If 40 people are on the elevator, and their total weight is 8120 pounds, what is their average weight?
  b. If a random sample of 40 adult men ride the elevator, what is the probability that the maximum safe weight will be exceeded?
  c. If a random sample of 40 adult women ride the elevator, what is the probability that the maximum safe weight will be exceeded?

25. Annual income: The mean annual income for people in a certain city (in thousands of dollars) is 42, with a standard deviation of 30. A pollster draws a sample of 90 people to interview.
  a. What is the probability that the sample mean income is less than 38?
  b. What is the probability that the sample mean score is between 40 and 45?
  c. Find the 60th percentile of the sample mean.
  d. Would it be unusual for the sample mean to be less than 35?
  e. Do you think it would be unusual for an individual to have an income less than 35? Explain.

26. Going to work: An ABC News report stated that the mean distance that commuters in the United States travel each way to work is 16 miles. Assume the standard deviation is 8 miles. A sample of 75 commuters is chosen.
  a. What is the probability that the sample mean commute distance is greater than 13 miles?
  b. What is the probability that the sample mean commute distance is between 18 and 20 miles?
  c. Find the 10th percentile of the sample mean.
  d. Would it be unusual for the sample mean distance to be greater than 19 miles?

  e. Do you think it would be unusual for an individual to have a commute distance greater than 19 miles? Explain.

Extending the Concepts

27. Eat your cereal: A cereal manufacturer claims that the weight of a box of cereal labeled as weighing 12 ounces has a mean of 12.0 ounces and a standard deviation of 0.1 ounce. You sample 75 boxes and weigh them. Let $\bar{x}$ denote the mean weight of the 75 boxes.
  a. If the claim is true, what is $P(\bar{x} \leq 11.99)$?
  b. Based on the answer to part (a), if the claim is true, is 11.99 ounces an unusually small mean weight for a sample of 75 boxes?
  c. If the mean weight of the boxes were 11.99 ounces, would you be convinced that the claim was false? Explain.
  d. If the claim is true, what is $P(\bar{x} \leq 11.97)$?
  e. Based on the answer to part (d), if the claim is true, is 11.97 ounces an unusually small mean weight for a sample of 75 boxes?
  f. If the mean weight of the boxes were 11.97 ounces, would you be convinced that the claim was false? Explain.

28. Battery life: A battery manufacturer claims that the lifetime of a certain type of battery has a population mean of $\mu = 40$ hours and a standard deviation of $\sigma = 5$ hours. Let $\bar{x}$ represent the mean lifetime of the batteries in a simple random sample of size 100.
  a. If the claim is true, what is $P(\bar{x} \leq 38.5)$?
  b. Based on the answer to part (a), if the claim is true, is a sample mean lifetime of 38.5 hours unusually short?
  c. If the sample mean lifetime of the 100 batteries were 38.5 hours, would you find the manufacturer's claim to be plausible? Explain.
  d. If the claim is true, what is $P(\bar{x} \leq 39.8)$?
  e. Based on the answer to part (d), if the claim is true, is a sample mean lifetime of 39.8 hours unusually short?
  f. If the sample mean lifetime of the 100 batteries were 39.8 hours, would you find the manufacturer's claim to be plausible? Explain.

Answers to Check Your Understanding Exercises for Section 6.3

1. $\mu_{\bar{x}} = 6, \sigma_{\bar{x}} = 0.8$

2. $\mu_{\bar{x}} = 17, \sigma_{\bar{x}} = 2.0$

3. a. 0.1894 [Tech: 0.1884]
  b. The probability that $\bar{x}$ is less than 8 is 0.0384 [Tech: 0.0385]. If we define an event whose probability is less than 0.05 as unusual, then this is unusual.

4. a. 0.6449
  b. The probability that $\bar{x}$ is greater than 48 is 0.3372 [Tech: 0.3373]. This event is not unusual.

SECTION 6.4 The Central Limit Theorem for Proportions

Objectives

1. Construct the sampling distribution for a sample proportion

2. Use the Central Limit Theorem to compute probabilities for sample proportions

A computer retailer wants to estimate the proportion of people in her city who own laptop computers. She cannot survey everyone in the city, so she draws a sample of 100 people and surveys them. It turns out that 35 out of the 100 people in the sample own laptops. The proportion 35/100 is called the **sample proportion** and is denoted $\hat{p}$. The proportion of people in the entire population who own laptops is called the **population proportion** and is denoted p.

DEFINITION

In a population, the proportion who have a certain characteristic is called the **population proportion**.

In a simple random sample of n individuals, let x be the number in the sample who have the characteristic. The **sample proportion** is

$$\hat{p} = \frac{x}{n}$$

Notation:
- The population proportion is denoted by p.
- The sample proportion is denoted by $\hat{p}$.

If several samples are drawn from a population, they are likely to have different values for $\hat{p}$. Because the value of $\hat{p}$ varies each time a sample is drawn, $\hat{p}$ is a random variable, and it has a probability distribution. The probability distribution of $\hat{p}$ is called the **sampling distribution** of $\hat{p}$.

Objective 1 Construct the sampling distribution for a sample proportion

An Example of a Sampling Distribution

To present an example, consider tossing a fair coin five times. This produces a sample of size $n = 5$, where each item in the sample is either a head or a tail. The proportion of times the coin lands heads will be the sample proportion $\hat{p}$. Because the coin is fair, the probability that it lands heads each time is 0.5. Therefore, the population proportion of heads is $p = 0.5$. There are 32 possible samples. Table 6.2 lists them and presents the sample proportion $\hat{p}$ of heads for each.

Table 6.2 The 32 Possible Samples of Size 5 and Their Sample Proportions of Heads

Sample	$\hat{p}$	Sample	$\hat{p}$	Sample	$\hat{p}$	Sample	$\hat{p}$
TTTTT	0.0	THTTT	0.2	HTTTT	0.2	HHTTT	0.4
TTTTH	0.2	THTTH	0.4	HTTTH	0.4	HHTTH	0.6
TTTHT	0.2	THTHT	0.4	HTTHT	0.4	HHTHT	0.6
TTTHH	0.4	THTHH	0.6	HTTHH	0.6	HHTHH	0.8
TTHTT	0.2	THHTT	0.4	HTHTT	0.6	HHHTT	0.6
TTHTH	0.4	THHTH	0.6	HTHTH	0.6	HHHTH	0.8
TTHHT	0.4	THHHT	0.6	HTHHT	0.6	HHHHT	0.8
TTHHH	0.6	THHHH	0.8	HTHHH	0.8	HHHHH	1.0

The columns labeled "$\hat{p}$" contain the values of the sample proportion for each of the 32 possible samples. Some of these values appear more than once, because several samples have the same proportion. The mean of the sampling distribution is the average of these 32 values. The variance of the sampling distribution is the population variance of these 32 values, which can be computed by the method presented in Section 3.2. The mean and variance are

$$\text{Mean: } \mu_{\hat{p}} = 0.5 \qquad \text{Variance: } \sigma_{\hat{p}}^2 = 0.05$$

The values of $\mu_{\hat{p}}$ and $\sigma_{\hat{p}}^2$ are related to the values of the population proportion $p = 0.5$ and the sample size $n = 5$. Specifically,

$$\mu_{\hat{p}} = 0.5 = p$$

The mean of the sample proportion is equal to the population proportion. The relationship among $\sigma_{\hat{p}}^2$, p, and n is less obvious. However, note that

$$\sigma_{\hat{p}}^2 = 0.05 = \frac{(0.5)(1 - 0.5)}{5} = \frac{p(1 - p)}{n}$$

The standard deviation is the square root of the variance. Therefore,

$$\sigma_{\hat{p}} = \sqrt{\frac{p(1 - p)}{n}}$$

These relationships hold in general.

SUMMARY

Let $\hat{p}$ be the sample proportion of a simple random sample of size n, drawn from a population with population proportion p. The mean and standard deviation of the sampling distribution of $\hat{p}$ are

$$\mu_{\hat{p}} = p$$

$$\sigma_{\hat{p}} = \sqrt{\frac{p(1-p)}{n}}$$

EXAMPLE 6.24   Find the mean and standard deviation of a sampling distribution

The soft-drink cups at a certain fast-food restaurant have tickets attached to them. Customers peel off the tickets to see whether they win a prize. The proportion of tickets that are winners is $p = 0.25$. A total of $n = 70$ people purchase soft drinks between noon and 1:00 PM on a certain day. Let $\hat{p}$ be the proportion that win a prize. Find the mean and standard deviation of $\hat{p}$.

Solution

The population proportion is $p = 0.25$ and the sample size is $n = 70$. Therefore,

$$\mu_{\hat{p}} = p = 0.25$$

$$\sigma_{\hat{p}} = \sqrt{\frac{0.25(1-0.25)}{70}} = 0.0518$$

Check Your Understanding

1. Find $\mu_{\hat{p}}$ and $\sigma_{\hat{p}}$ if $n = 20$ and $p = 0.82$.

2. Find $\mu_{\hat{p}}$ and $\sigma_{\hat{p}}$ if $n = 217$ and $p = 0.455$.

Answers are on page 264.

The probability histogram for the sampling distribution of $\hat{p}$

Figure 6.26 presents the probability histogram for the sampling distribution of $\hat{p}$ for the proportion of heads in five tosses of a fair coin, for which $n = 5$ and $p = 0.5$. The distribution is reasonably well approximated by a normal curve. Figure 6.27 presents the probability histogram for the sampling distribution of $\hat{p}$ for the proportion of heads in 50 tosses of a fair coin, for which $n = 50$ and $p = 0.5$. The distribution is very closely approximated by a normal curve.

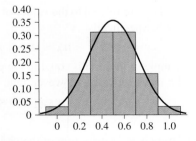

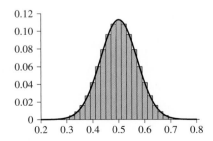

Figure 6.26 The probability histogram for $\hat{p}$ when $n = 5$ and $p = 0.5$. The histogram is reasonably well approximated by a normal curve.

Figure 6.27 The probability histogram for $\hat{p}$ when $n = 50$ and $p = 0.5$. The histogram is very closely approximated by a normal curve.

When $p = 0.5$, the sampling distribution of $\hat{p}$ is somewhat close to normal even for a small sample size like $n = 5$. When p is close to 0 or close to 1, a larger sample size is needed before the distribution of $\hat{p}$ is close to normal. A common rule of thumb is that the distribution may be approximated with a normal curve whenever np and $n(1 - p)$ are both at least 10.

The Central Limit Theorem for Proportions

Let $\hat{p}$ be the sample proportion for a sample size of n and population proportion p. If

$$np \geq 10 \quad \text{and} \quad n(1 - p) \geq 10$$

then the distribution of $\hat{p}$ is approximately normal, with mean and standard deviation

$$\mu_{\hat{p}} = p \quad \text{and} \quad \sigma_{\hat{p}} = \sqrt{\frac{p(1 - p)}{n}}$$

Objective 2 Use the Central Limit Theorem to compute probabilities for sample proportions

Computing Probabilities with the Central Limit Theorem

To compute probabilities involving a sample proportion $\hat{p}$, use the following procedure:

Procedure for Computing Probabilities with the Central Limit Theorem

Step 1: Check to see that the conditions $np \geq 10$ and $n(1 - p) \geq 10$ are both met. If so, it is appropriate to use the normal curve.

Step 2: Find the mean $\mu_{\hat{p}}$ and standard deviation $\sigma_{\hat{p}}$.

Step 3: Sketch a normal curve and shade in the area to be found.

Step 4: Find the area using Table A.2 or technology.

EXAMPLE 6.25

Using the Central Limit Theorem to compute a probability

According to Summit Entertainment, 80% of the audience for the opening weekend of the movie *Twilight: New Moon* was female. If a random sample of $n = 100$ members of the audience were sampled, what is the probability that the sample proportion of females would be greater than 0.85?

Explain It Again

Computing probabilities for sample proportions: Computing probabilities for sample proportions with the Central Limit Theorem is the same as computing probabilities for any normally distributed quantity. Use $\mu_{\hat{p}} = p$ for the mean and $\sigma_{\hat{p}} = \sqrt{p(1 - p)/n}$ for the standard deviation.

Solution

Step 1: $np = (100)(0.8) = 80 \geq 10$, and $n(1 - p) = (100)(1 - 0.8) = 20 \geq 10$. We may use the normal curve.

Step 2: $\mu_{\hat{p}} = p = 0.8$.

$$\sigma_{\hat{p}} = \sqrt{\frac{p(1 - p)}{n}} = \sqrt{\frac{0.8(1 - 0.8)}{100}} = 0.04$$

Step 3: Figure 6.28 presents the normal curve with the area of interest shaded.

Step 4: We will use Table A.2. We compute the z-score for 0.85.

$$z = \frac{\hat{p} - \mu_{\hat{p}}}{\sigma_{\hat{p}}} = \frac{0.85 - 0.80}{0.04} = 1.25$$

Table A.2 gives the area to the *left* of $z = 1.25$ as 0.8944. The area to the right of $z = 1.25$ is $1 - 0.8944 = 0.1056$. The probability that the sample proportion of females is greater than 0.85 is 0.1056.

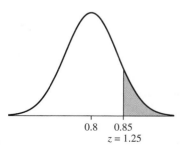

Figure 6.28

EXAMPLE 6.26   Using the Central Limit Theorem to determine whether a given value of $\hat{p}$ is unusual

In the 2008 U.S. presidential election, 53% of voters voted for Barack Obama. If a sample of 75 voters were polled, would it be unusual if less than 40% of them had voted for Barack Obama?

Solution

We will compute the probability that the sample proportion is less than 0.40. If this probability is less than 0.05, we will say that the event is unusual.

Step 1: $np = (75)(0.53) = 39.75 \geq 10$, and $n(1 - p) = (75)(1 - 0.53) = 35.25 \geq 10$. We may use the normal curve.

Step 2: $\mu_{\hat{p}} = p = 0.53$.

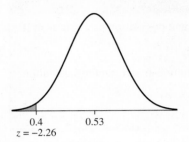

0.4   0.53
$z = -2.26$

Figure 6.29

$$\sigma_{\hat{p}} = \sqrt{\frac{p(1 - p)}{n}} = \sqrt{\frac{0.53(1 - 0.53)}{75}} = 0.057631$$

Step 3: Figure 6.29 presents the normal curve with the area of interest shaded.

Step 4: We will use Table A.2. We compute the z-score for 0.40.

$$z = \frac{\hat{p} - \mu_{\hat{p}}}{\sigma_{\hat{p}}} = \frac{0.40 - 0.53}{0.057631} = -2.26$$

The area to the left of $z = -2.26$ is 0.0119. It would be unusual for the sample proportion to be less than 0.40.

Check Your Understanding

3. The General Social Survey reported that 56% of American adults saw a doctor for an illness during the past year. A sample of 65 adults is drawn.
   a. What is the probability that more than 60% of them saw a doctor?
   b. Would it be unusual if more than 70% of them saw a doctor?

4. For a certain type of computer chip, the proportion of chips that are defective is 0.10. A computer manufacturer receives a shipment of 200 chips.
   a. What is the probability that the proportion of defective chips in the shipment is between 0.08 and 0.15?
   b. Would it be unusual for the proportion of defective chips to be less than 0.075?

Answers are on page 264.

SECTION 6.4   Exercises

Exercises 1–4 are the Check Your Understanding exercises located within the section.

Understanding the Concepts

In Exercises 5 and 6, fill in each blank with the appropriate word or phrase.

5. If n is the sample size and x is the number in the sample who have a certain characteristic, then x/n is called the sample _____.

6. The probability distribution of $\hat{p}$ is called a _____ distribution.

In Exercises 7 and 8, determine whether the statement is true or false. If the statement is false, rewrite it as a true statement.

7. The distribution of $\hat{p}$ is approximately normal if $np \geq 10$ and $n(1 - p) \geq 10$.

8. If n is the sample size, p is the population proportion, and $\hat{p}$ is the sample proportion, then $\sigma_{\hat{p}} = np$.

Practicing the Skills

In Exercises 9–14, n is the sample size, p is the population proportion, and $\hat{p}$ is the sample proportion. Use the Central Limit Theorem to find the indicated probability.

  9. $n = 147$, $p = 0.13$; $P(\hat{p} < 0.11)$

  10. $n = 101$, $p = 0.86$; $P(\hat{p} < 0.80)$

  11. $n = 270$, $p = 0.57$; $P(\hat{p} > 0.61)$

  12. $n = 103$, $p = 0.24$; $P(0.20 < \hat{p} < 0.23)$

  13. $n = 111$, $p = 0.54$; $P(0.46 < \hat{p} < 0.59)$

  14. $n = 234$, $p = 0.75$; $P(0.77 < \hat{p} < 0.81)$

Working with the Concepts

15. Illegal downloads: The International Federation of the Phonographic Industry reported that 95% of music downloads in the year 2008 were illegal. A random sample of 250 downloads is studied.
   a. Find the mean $\mu_{\hat{p}}$.
   b. Find the standard deviation $\sigma_{\hat{p}}$.
   c. Find the probability that more than 97% of the sample downloads are illegal.
   d. Find the probability that the proportion of the sample downloads that are illegal is between 0.93 and 0.96.
   e. Find the probability that less than 96% of the sample downloads are illegal.
   f. Would it be unusual if less than 90% of the sample downloads were illegal?

16. Video gamers: A Pew Research report indicated that in 2008, 48% of teenagers aged 12–17 played video games on their cell phone. A random sample of 150 teenagers is drawn.
   a. Find the mean $\mu_{\hat{p}}$.
   b. Find the standard deviation $\sigma_{\hat{p}}$.
   c. Find the probability that more than 50% of the teenagers in the sample play video games on their cell phone.
   d. Find the probability that the sample proportion who play video games on their cell phone is between 0.45 and 0.55.
   e. Find the probability that less than 55% of the teenagers in the sample play video games on their cell phone.
   f. Would it be unusual if the sample proportion who played video games on their cell phone was less than 0.40?

17. Student loans: The Institute for College Access and Success reported that 67% of college students in 2008 graduated with student loan debt. A random sample of 85 graduates is drawn.
   a. Find the mean $\mu_{\hat{p}}$.
   b. Find the standard deviation $\sigma_{\hat{p}}$.
   c. Find the probability that less than 60% of the people in the sample were in debt.
   d. Find the probability that between 65% and 80% of the people in the sample were in debt.
   e. Find the probability that more than 75% of the people in the sample were in debt.
   f. Would it be unusual if less than 65% of the people in the sample were in debt?

18. High school graduates: The National Center for Educational Statistics reported that 75% of freshmen entering public high schools in the United States in 2005 graduated with their class in 2009. A random sample of 135 freshmen is chosen.
   a. Find the mean $\mu_{\hat{p}}$.
   b. Find the standard deviation $\sigma_{\hat{p}}$.
   c. Find the probability that less than 80% of freshmen in the sample graduated.
   d. Find the probability that the sample proportion of students who graduated is between 0.65 and 0.80.
   e. Find the probability that more than 65% of freshmen in the sample graduated.
   f. Would it be unusual if the sample proportion of students who graduated were more than 0.85?

19. Government workers: The Bureau of Labor Statistics reported in 2010 that 17% of U.S. nonfarm workers are government employees. A random sample of 50 workers is drawn.
   a. Is it appropriate to use the normal approximation to find the probability that less than 20% of the individuals in the sample are government employees? If so, find the probability. If not, explain why not.
   b. A new sample of 90 workers is chosen. Find the probability that more than 20% of workers in this sample are government employees.
   c. Find the probability that the proportion of workers in the sample of 90 who are government employees is between 0.15 and 0.18.
   d. Find the probability that less than 25% of workers in the sample of 90 are government employees.
   e. Would it be unusual if the proportion of government employees in the sample of 90 were greater than 0.25?

20. Working two jobs: The Bureau of Labor Statistics reported in 2010 that 5% of employed adults in the United States held multiple jobs. A random sample of 75 employed adults is chosen.
   a. Is it appropriate to use the normal approximation to find the probability that less than 6.5% of the individuals in the sample hold multiple jobs? If so, find the probability. If not, explain why not.
   b. A new sample of 350 employed adults is chosen. Find the probability that less than 6.5% of the individuals in this sample hold multiple jobs.
   c. Find the probability that more than 6% of the individuals in the sample of 350 hold multiple jobs.
   d. Find the probability that the proportion of individuals in the sample of 350 who hold multiple jobs is between 0.05 and 0.10.
   e. Would it be unusual if less than 4% of the individuals in the sample of 350 held multiple jobs?

21. Future scientists: Education professionals refer to science, technology, engineering, and mathematics as the STEM disciplines. The UCLA Higher Education Research Institute reported that 34% of freshmen entering college in 2009 planned to major in a STEM discipline. A random sample of 85 freshmen is selected.
   a. Is it appropriate to use the normal approximation to find the probability that less than 30% of the freshmen in the sample are planning to major in a STEM discipline? If so, find the probability. If not, explain why not.
   b. A new sample of 150 freshmen is selected. Find the probability that less than 30% of the freshmen in this sample are planning to major in a STEM discipline.

c. Find the probability that the proportion of freshmen in the sample of 150 who plan to major in a STEM discipline is between 0.35 and 0.40.

d. Find the probability that more than 35% of the freshmen in the sample of 150 are planning to major in a STEM discipline.

e. Would it be unusual if more than 40% of the freshmen in the sample of 150 were planning to major in a STEM discipline?

22. **Blood pressure:** High blood pressure has been identified as a risk factor for heart attacks and strokes. The National Health and Nutrition Examination Survey reported that the proportion of U.S. adults with high blood pressure is 0.3. A sample of 38 U.S. adults is chosen.

a. Is it appropriate to use the normal approximation to find the probability that more than 40% of the people in the sample have high blood pressure? If so, find the probability. If not, explain why not.

b. A new sample of 80 adults is drawn. Find the probability that more than 40% of the people in this sample have high blood pressure.

c. Find the probability that the proportion of individuals in the sample of 80 who have high blood pressure is between 0.20 and 0.35.

d. Find the probability that less than 25% of the people in the sample of 80 have high blood pressure.

e. Would it be unusual if more than 45% of the individuals in the sample of 80 had high blood pressure?

23. **Pay your taxes:** According to the Internal Revenue Service, the proportion of federal tax returns for which no tax was paid was $p = 0.326$. As part of a tax audit, tax officials draw a simple random sample of $n = 120$ tax returns.

a. What is the probability that the sample proportion of tax returns for which no tax was paid is less than 0.30?

b. What is the probability that the sample proportion of tax returns for which no tax was paid is between 0.35 and 0.40?

c. What is the probability that the sample proportion of tax returns for which no tax was paid is greater than 0.35?

d. Would it be unusual if the sample proportion of tax returns for which no tax was paid was less than 0.25?

24. **Weekly paycheck:** The Bureau of Labor Statistics reported that in 2009, the median weekly earnings for people employed full time in the United States was $739.

a. What proportion of full-time employees had weekly earnings of more than $739?

b. A sample of 150 full-time employees is chosen. What is the probability that more than 55% of them earned more than $739 per week?

c. What is the probability that less than 60% of the sample of 150 employees earned more than $739 per week?

d. What is the probability that between 45% and 55% of the sample of 150 employees earned more than $739 per week?

e. Would it be unusual if less than 45% of the sample of 150 employees earned more than $739 per week?

25. **Kidney transplants:** The Agency for Healthcare Research and Quality reported that 5% of people who received kidney transplants in 2008 were under the age of 18. How large a sample of kidney transplant patients needs to be drawn so that the sample proportion $\hat{p}$ of those under the age of 18 is approximately normally distributed?

26. **How's your new car?** The General Social Survey reported that 91% of people who bought a car in the past five years were satisfied with their purchase. How large a sample of car buyers needs to be drawn so that the sample proportion $\hat{p}$ who are satisfied is approximately normally distributed?

Extending the Concepts

27. **Flawless tiles:** A new process has been designed to make ceramic tiles. The goal is to have no more than 5% of the tiles be nonconforming due to surface defects. A random sample of 1000 tiles is inspected. Let $\hat{p}$ be the proportion of nonconforming tiles in the sample.

a. If 5% of the tiles produced are nonconforming, what is $P(\hat{p} \geq 0.075)$?

b. Based on the answer to part (a), if 5% of the tiles are nonconforming, is a proportion of 0.075 nonconforming tiles in a sample of 1000 unusually large?

c. If the sample proportion of nonconforming tiles were 0.075, would it be plausible that the goal had been reached? Explain.

d. If 5% of the tiles produced are nonconforming, what is $P(\hat{p} \geq 0.053)$?

e. Based on the answer to part (d), if 5% of the tiles are nonconforming, is a proportion of 0.053 nonconforming tiles in a sample of 1000 unusually large?

f. If the sample proportion of nonconforming tiles were 0.053, would it be plausible that the goal had been reached? Explain.

Answers to Check Your Understanding Exercises for Section 6.4

1. $\mu_{\hat{p}} = 0.82, \sigma_{\hat{p}} = 0.08591$

2. $\mu_{\hat{p}} = 0.455, \sigma_{\hat{p}} = 0.03380$

3. **a.** 0.2578 [Tech: 0.2580]
   b. The probability that $\hat{p}$ is greater than 0.70 is 0.0116 [Tech: 0.0115]. If we define an event whose probability is less than 0.05 as unusual, then this is unusual.

4. **a.** 0.8173 [Tech: 0.8179]
   b. The probability that $\hat{p}$ is less than 0.075 is 0.1190 [Tech: 0.1193]. This event is not unusual.

| **SECTION 6.5** | The Normal Approximation to the Binomial Distribution |

Objectives

1. Use the normal curve to approximate binomial probabilities

Objective 1 Use the normal curve to approximate binomial probabilities

We first introduced binomial random variables in Section 5.2. Recall that a binomial random variable represents the number of successes in a series of independent trials. The sample proportion is found by dividing the number of successes by the number of trials. Since the sample proportion is approximately normally distributed whenever $np \geq 10$ and $n(1 - p) \geq 10$, the number of successes is also approximately normally distributed under these conditions. Therefore, the normal curve can also be used to compute approximate probabilities for the binomial distribution.

We begin by reviewing the conditions under which a random variable has a binomial distribution.

Conditions for the Binomial Distribution

1. A number of trials are conducted.
2. There are two possible outcomes for each trial. One is labeled "success" and the other is labeled "failure."
3. The probability of success is the same on each trial.
4. The trials are independent. This means that the outcome of one trial does not affect the outcomes of the other trials.
5. The random variable X represents the number of successes that occur.

Notation: The following notation is commonly used:

- The number of trials is denoted by n.
- The probability of success is denoted by p, and the probability of failure is $1 - p$.

Mean, Variance, and Standard Deviation of a Binomial Random Variable

Let X be a binomial random variable with n trials and success probability p. Then the mean of X is

$$\mu_X = np$$

The variance of X is

$$\sigma_X^2 = np(1 - p)$$

The standard deviation of X is

$$\sigma_X = \sqrt{np(1 - p)}$$

Explain It Again

Calculating binomial probabilities: Binomial probabilities can be computed exactly by using the methods described in Section 5.2. Using these methods by hand is extremely difficult. The normal approximation provides an easier way to approximate these probabilities when computing by hand.

Binomial probabilities can be very difficult to compute exactly by hand, because many terms have to be calculated and added together. For example, imagine trying to compute the probability that the number of heads is between 75 and 125 when a coin is tossed 200 times. To do this, one would need to compute the following sum:

$$P(X = 75) + P(X = 76) + \cdots + P(X = 124) + P(X = 125)$$

This is nearly impossible to do without technology. Fortunately, probabilities like this can be approximated very closely by using the normal curve. In the days before cheap computing became available, use of the normal curve was the only feasible method for doing these calculations. The normal approximation is somewhat less important now, but is still useful for quick "back of the envelope" calculations.

Recall from Section 6.4 that a sample proportion $\hat{p}$ is approximately normally distributed whenever $np \geq 10$ and $n(1 - p) \geq 10$. Now if X is a binomial random variable representing the number of successes in n trials, the sample proportion is given by $\hat{p} = X/n$. Since $\hat{p}$ is obtained simply by dividing X by the number of trials, it is reasonable to expect that X will be approximately normal whenever $\hat{p}$ is approximately normal. This is in fact the case.

The Normal Approximation to the Binomial

Let X be a binomial random variable with n trials and success probability p. If $np \geq 10$ and $n(1 - p) \geq 10$, then X is approximately normal with mean $\mu_X = np$ and standard deviation $\sigma_X = \sqrt{np(1 - p)}$.

The continuity correction

The binomial distribution is discrete, whereas the normal distribution is continuous. The **continuity correction** is an adjustment, made when approximating a discrete distribution with a continuous one, that can improve the accuracy of the approximation. To see how it works, imagine that a fair coin is tossed 100 times. Let X represent the number of heads. Then X has the binomial distribution with $n = 100$ trials and success probability $p = 0.5$. Imagine that we want to compute the probability that X is between 45 and 55. This probability will differ depending on whether the endpoints, 45 and 55, are included or excluded. Figure 6.30 illustrates the case where the endpoints are included, that is, where we wish to compute $P(45 \leq X \leq 55)$. The exact probability is given by the total area of the rectangles of the binomial probability histogram corresponding to the integers 45 to 55 inclusive. The approximating normal curve is superimposed. To get the best approximation, we should compute the area under the normal curve between 44.5 and 55.5.

In contrast, Figure 6.31 illustrates the case where we wish to compute $P(45 < X < 55)$. Here the endpoints are excluded. The exact probability is given by the total area of the rectangles of the binomial probability histogram corresponding to the integers 46 to 54. The best normal approximation is found by computing the area under the normal curve between 45.5 and 54.5.

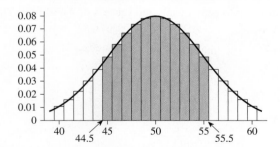

Figure 6.30 To compute $P(45 \leq X \leq 55)$, the areas of the rectangles corresponding to 45 and to 55 should be included. To approximate this probability with the normal curve, compute the area under the curve between 44.5 and 55.5.

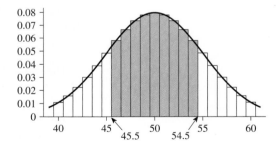

Figure 6.31 To compute $P(45 < X < 55)$, the areas of the rectangles corresponding to 45 and to 55 should be excluded. To approximate this probability with the normal curve, compute the area under the curve between 45.5 and 54.5.

In general, to apply the continuity correction, determine precisely which rectangles of the discrete probability histogram you wish to include, then compute the area under the normal curve corresponding to those rectangles.

EXAMPLE 6.27   Using the continuity correction to compute a probability

Let X be the number of heads that appear when a fair coin is tossed 100 times. Use the normal curve to find $P(45 \leq X \leq 55)$.

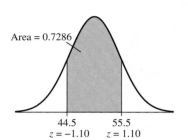

Figure 6.32 Solution to Example 6.27

Solution

This situation is illustrated in Figure 6.30.

Step 1: Check the assumptions: The number of trials is $n = 100$. Since the coin is fair, the success probability is $p = 0.5$. Therefore, $np = (100)(0.5) = 50 \geq 10$ and $n(1 - p) = (100)(1 - 0.5) = 50 \geq 10$. We may use the normal approximation.

Step 2: We compute the mean and standard deviation of X:

$$\mu_X = np = (100)(0.5) = 50 \qquad \sigma_X = \sqrt{np(1 - p)} = \sqrt{(100)(0.5)(1 - 0.5)} = 5$$

Step 3: Because the probability is $P(45 \leq X \leq 55)$, we want to *include* both 45 and 55. Therefore, we set the left endpoint to 44.5 and the right endpoint to 55.5.

Step 4: We sketch a normal curve, label the mean of 50, and the endpoints 44.5 and 55.5.

Step 5: We use Table A.2 to find the area. The z-scores for 44.5 and 55.5 are

$$z = \frac{44.5 - 50}{5} = -1.1 \qquad z = \frac{55.5 - 50}{5} = 1.1$$

From Table A.2, we find that the probability is 0.7286. See Figure 6.32.

In Example 6.27, we used the normal approximation to compute a probability of the form $P(a \leq X \leq b)$. We can also use the normal approximation to compute probabilities of the form $P(X \leq a)$, $P(X \geq a)$, and $P(X = a)$.

EXAMPLE 6.28

Illustrate areas to be found for the continuity correction

A fair coin is tossed 100 times. Let X be the number of heads that appear. Illustrate the area under the normal curve that represents each of the following probabilities.

    a. $P(X \leq 55)$
    b. $P(X \geq 55)$
    c. $P(X = 55)$

Solution

    a. We find the area to the left of 55.5, as illustrated in Figure 6.33.
    b. We find the area to the right of 54.5, as illustrated in Figure 6.34.
    c. We find the area between 54.5 and 55.5, as illustrated in Figure 6.35.

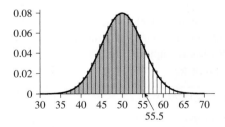

Figure 6.33 To approximate $P(X \leq 55)$, find the area to the left of 55.5.

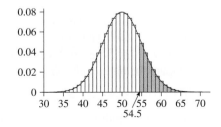

Figure 6.34 To approximate $P(X \geq 55)$, find the area to the right of 54.5.

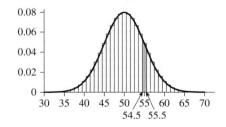

Figure 6.35 To approximate $P(X = 55)$, find the area between 54.5 and 55.5.

SUMMARY

Following are the areas under the normal curve to use when the continuity correction is applied.

$P(a \leq X \leq b)$

Find the area between $a - 0.5$ and $b + 0.5$.

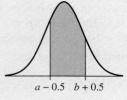

$a - 0.5 \quad b + 0.5$

$P(X \leq b)$

Find the area to the left of $b + 0.5$.

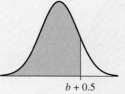

$b + 0.5$

$P(X \geq a)$

Find the area to the right of $a - 0.5$.

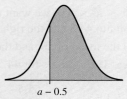

$a - 0.5$

$P(X = a)$

Find the area between $a - 0.5$ and $a + 0.5$.

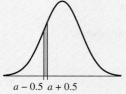

$a - 0.5 \quad a + 0.5$

Use the following steps to compute a binomial probability with the normal approximation.

Explain It Again

We will use Table A.2 when using the normal approximation to the binomial: The normal approximation is useful when computing by hand. If technology is to be used, the exact probability can be calculated, so the normal approximation is less useful.

Procedure for Computing Binomial Probabilities with the Normal Approximation

Step 1: Check to see that the conditions $np \geq 10$ and $n(1 - p) \geq 10$ are both met. If so, it is appropriate to use the normal approximation. If not, the probability must be calculated with the binomial distribution (see Section 5.2).

Step 2: Compute the mean μ_X and the standard deviation σ_X.

Step 3: For each endpoint, determine whether to add 0.5 or subtract 0.5.

Step 4: Sketch a normal curve, label the endpoints, and shade in the area to be found.

Step 5: Find the area using Table A.2 or technology. Note, however, that if you are using technology, you may be able to compute the probability exactly without using the normal approximation.

EXAMPLE 6.29

Using the continuity correction to compute a probability

The *Statistical Abstract of the United States* reported that 67% of students who graduated from high school in 2007 enrolled in college. One hundred high school graduates are sampled. Let X be the number who enrolled in college. Find $P(X \leq 75)$.

Solution

Step 1: Check the assumptions. The number of trials is $n = 100$ and the success probability is $p = 0.67$. Therefore, $np = (100)(0.67) = 67 \geq 10$ and $n(1 - p) = (100)(1 - 0.67) = 33 \geq 10$. We may use the normal approximation.

Step 2: We compute the mean and standard deviation of X:

$$\mu_X = np = (100)(0.67) = 67 \quad \sigma_X = \sqrt{np(1 - p)} = \sqrt{(100)(0.67)(1 - 0.67)} = 4.70213$$

Step 3: Because the probability is $P(X \leq 75)$, we compute the area to the left of 75.5.

Step 4: We sketch a normal curve, and label the mean of 67 and the point 75.5.

Step 5: We use Table A.2 to find the area. The z-score for 75.5 is

$$z = \frac{75.5 - 67}{4.70213} = 1.81$$

From Table A.2, we find that the probability is 0.9649. See Figure 6.36.

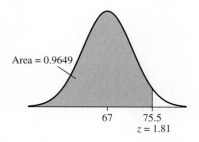

Area = 0.9649

67   75.5
$z = 1.81$

Figure 6.36 Solution to Example 6.29

Sometimes we want to use the normal approximation to compute a probability of the form $P(X < a)$ or $P(X > a)$. One way to do this is by changing the inequality to a form involving $\leq$ or $\geq$. Example 6.30 provides an illustration.

EXAMPLE 6.30

Using the continuity correction to compute a probability

The *Statistical Abstract of the United States* reported that 67% of students who graduated from high school in 2007 enrolled in college. One hundred high school graduates are sampled. Approximate the probability that more than 65 enrolled in college.

Solution

Let X be the number of students in the sample who enrolled in college. We need to find $P(X > 65)$. We change this to an inequality involving $\geq$ by noting that $P(X > 65) = P(X \geq 66)$. We therefore find $P(X \geq 66)$.

Step 1: Check the assumptions. The number of trials is $n = 100$ and the success probability is $p = 0.67$. Therefore, $np = (100)(0.67) = 67 \geq 10$ and $n(1 - p) = (100)(1 - 0.67) = 33 \geq 10$. We may use the normal approximation.

Step 2: We compute the mean and standard deviation of X:

$$\mu_X = np = (100)(0.67) = 67$$
$$\sigma_X = \sqrt{np(1 - p)} = \sqrt{(100)(0.67)(1 - 0.67)} = 4.70213$$

Step 3: Because the probability is $P(X \geq 66)$, we compute the area to the right of 65.5.

Step 4: We sketch a normal curve, and label the mean of 67 and the point 65.5.

Step 5: We use Table A.2 to find the area. The z-score for 65.5 is

$$z = \frac{65.5 - 67}{4.70213} = -0.32$$

From Table A.2, we find that the probability is 0.6255. See Figure 6.37.

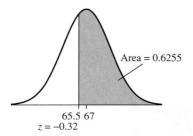

Figure 6.37 Solution to Example 6.30

Area = 0.6255

65.5 67
$z = -0.32$

Check Your Understanding

1. X is a binomial random variable with $n = 50$ and $p = 0.15$. Should the normal approximation be used to find $P(X > 10)$? Why or why not?

2. X is a binomial random variable with $n = 72$ and $p = 0.90$. Should the normal approximation be used to find $P(X \leq 60)$? Why or why not?

3. Let X have a binomial distribution with $n = 64$ and $p = 0.41$. If appropriate, use the normal approximation to find $P(X \leq 20)$. If not, explain why not.

4. Let X have a binomial distribution with $n = 379$ and $p = 0.09$. If appropriate, use the normal approximation to find $P(X > 40)$. If not, explain why not.

Answers are on page 271.

SECTION 6.5   Exercises

Exercises 1–4 are the Check Your Understanding exercises located within the section.

Understanding the Concepts

In Exercises 5 and 6, fill in each blank with the appropriate word or phrase.

5. If X is a binomial random variable and if $np \geq 10$ and $n(1 - p) \geq 10$, then X is approximately normal with $\mu_X =$ _____ and $\sigma_X =$ _____.

6. The adjustment made when approximating a discrete random distribution with a continuous one is called the _____ correction.

In Exercises 7 and 8, determine whether the statement is true or false. If the statement is false, rewrite it as a true statement.

7. If technology is to be used, exact binomial probabilities can be calculated and the normal approximation is not necessary.

8. If X is a binomial random variable with n trials and success probability p, then as n gets larger, the distribution of X becomes more skewed.

Practicing the Skills

In Exercises 9–14, n is the sample size, p is the population proportion of successes, and X is the number of successes in the sample. Use the normal approximation to find the indicated probability.

9. $n = 78$, $p = 0.43$; $P(X > 40)$

10. $n = 538$, $p = 0.86$; $P(X \leq 470)$

11. $n = 99$, $p = 0.57$; $P(X \geq 55)$

12. $n = 442$, $p = 0.54$; $P(X < 243)$

13. $n = 106$, $p = 0.14$; $P(14 < X < 18)$

14. $n = 61$, $p = 0.34$; $P(20 \leq X \leq 24)$

Working with the Concepts

15. Google it: According to a report of the Nielsen Company, 65% of Internet searches in May 2010 used the Google search engine. A sample of 100 searches is studied.
   a. Approximate the probability that more than 70 of the searches used Google.
   b. Approximate the probability that 55 or fewer of the searches used Google.
   c. Approximate the probability that the number of searches that used Google is between 70 and 80 inclusive.

16. Big babies: The Centers for Disease Control and Prevention reports that 25% of baby boys 6–8 months old in the United States weigh more than 20 pounds. A sample of 150 babies is studied.
   a. Approximate the probability that more than 40 weigh more than 20 pounds.
   b. Approximate the probability that 35 or fewer weigh more than 20 pounds.
   c. Approximate the probability that the number who weigh more than 20 pounds is between 30 and 40 exclusive.

17. High blood pressure: The National Health and Nutrition Examination Survey reported that 30% of adults in the United States have hypertension (high blood pressure). A sample of 300 adults is studied.
   a. Approximate the probability that 85 or more have hypertension.
   b. Approximate the probability that fewer than 80 have hypertension.
   c. Approximate the probability that the number who have hypertension is between 75 and 85 exclusive.

18. Stress at work: In a poll conducted by the General Social Survey, 81% of respondents said that their jobs were sometimes or always stressful. Two hundred workers are chosen at random.
   a. Approximate the probability that 160 or fewer find their jobs stressful.
   b. Approximate the probability that more than 150 find their jobs stressful.
   c. Approximate the probability that the number who find their jobs stressful is between 155 and 162 inclusive.

19. What's your opinion? A pollster will interview a sample of 200 voters to ask whether they support a proposal to increase the sales tax to build a new light rail system. Assume that in fact 55% of the voters support the proposal.
   a. Approximate the probability that 100 or fewer of the sampled voters support the proposal.
   b. Approximate the probability that more than 105 voters support the proposal.
   c. Approximate the probability that the number of voters who support the proposal is between 100 and 110 inclusive.

20. Gardening: A gardener buys a package of seeds. Eighty percent of seeds of this type germinate. The gardener plants 90 seeds.
   a. Approximate the probability that fewer than 75 seeds germinate.
   b. Approximate the probability that 80 or more seeds germinate.
   c. Approximate the probability that the number of seeds that germinate is between 67 and 75 exclusive.

21. The car is in the shop: Among automobiles of a certain make, 23% require service during a one-year warranty period. A dealer sells 87 of these vehicles.
   a. Approximate the probability that 25 or fewer of these vehicles require repairs.
   b. Approximate the probability that more than 17 vehicles require repairs.
   c. Approximate the probability that the number of vehicles that require repairs is between 15 and 20 exclusive.

22. Genetics: Pea plants contain two genes for seed color, each of which may be Y (for yellow seeds) or G (for green seeds). Plants that contain one of each type of gene are called heterozygous. According to the Mendelian theory of genetics, if two heterozygous plants are crossed, each of their offspring will have probability 0.75 of having yellow seeds and probability 0.25 of having green seeds. One hundred such offspring are produced.
   a. Approximate the probability that more than 30 have green seeds.
   b. Approximate the probability that 80 or fewer have yellow seeds.
   c. Approximate the probability that the number with green seeds is between 30 and 35 inclusive.

23. Getting bumped: Airlines often sell more tickets for a flight than there are seats, because some ticket holders don't show up for the flight. Assume that an airplane has 100 seats for passengers and that the probability that a person holding a ticket appears for the flight is 0.90. If the airline sells

105 tickets, what is the probability that everyone who appears for the flight will get a seat?

24. **College admissions:** A small college has enough space to enroll 300 new students in its incoming freshman class. From past experience, the admissions office knows that 65% of students who are accepted actually enroll. If the admissions office accepts 450 students, what is the

probability that there will be enough space for all the students who enroll?

Extending the Concepts

25. **Probability of a single number:** A fair coin is tossed 100 times. Use the normal approximation to approximate the probability that the coin comes up heads exactly 50 times.

Answers to Check Your Understanding Exercises for Section 6.5

1. No, $np = 7.5 < 10$.

2. No, $n(1 - p) = 7.2 < 10$.

3. 0.0721 [Tech: 0.0723]

4. 0.1251 [Tech: 0.1257]

SECTION 6.6 | Assessing Normality

Objectives

1. Use dotplots to assess normality
2. Use boxplots to assess normality
3. Use histograms to assess normality
4. Use stem-and-leaf plots to assess normality
5. Use normal quantile plots to assess normality

Many statistical procedures, some of which we will learn about in Chapters 7 and 8, require that we draw a sample from a population whose distribution is approximately normal. Often we don't know whether the population is approximately normal when we draw the sample. So the only way we have to assess whether the population is approximately normal is to examine the sample. In this section, we will describe some ways in which this can be done.

There are three important ideas to remember when assessing normality:

1. We are not trying to determine whether the population is *exactly* normal. No population encountered in practice is *exactly* normal. We are only trying to determine whether the population is *approximately* normal.

2. Assessing normality is more important for small samples than for large samples. When the sample size is large, say $n > 30$, the Central Limit Theorem ensures that $\bar{x}$ is approximately normal. Most statistical procedures designed for large samples rely on the Central Limit Theorem for their validity, so normality of the population is not so important in these cases.

3. Hard-and-fast rules do not work well. They are generally too lenient for very small samples (finding populations to be approximately normal when they are not) or too strict for larger samples (finding populations not to be approximately normal when they are). Informal judgment works as well as or better than hard-and-fast rules.

Recall: An outlier is a data value that is considerably larger or smaller than most of the rest of the data.

When a sample is very small, it is often impossible to be sure whether it came from an approximately normal population. The best we can do is to examine the sample for signs of nonnormality. If no such signs exist, we will treat the population as approximately normal. Because the normal curve is unimodal and symmetric, samples from normal populations rarely have more than one distinct mode, and rarely exhibit a large degree of skewness. In addition, samples from normal populations rarely contain outliers. We summarize the conditions under which we will reject the assumption that a population is approximately normal.

SUMMARY

We will reject the assumption that a population is approximately normal if a sample has *any* of the following features:

1. The sample contains an outlier.
2. The sample exhibits a large degree of skewness.
3. The sample is multimodal; in other words, it has more than one distinct mode.

If the sample has *none* of the preceding features, we will treat the population as being approximately normal.

Many methods have been developed for assessing normality; some of them are quite sophisticated. For our purposes, it will be sufficient to examine dotplots, boxplots, stem-and-leaf plots, and histograms of the sample. We will also describe normal quantile plots, which provide another useful method of assessment.

Objective 1 Use dotplots to assess normality

Dotplots

Dotplots are excellent for detecting outliers and multimodality. They can also be used to detect skewness, although they are not quite as effective as histograms for that purpose.

EXAMPLE 6.31

Recall: Dotplots were introduced in Section 2.3.

Using a dotplot to assess normality

The accuracy of an oven thermostat is being tested. The oven is set to 360°F, and the temperature when the thermostat turns off is recorded. A sample of size 7 yields the following results:

> 358   363   361   355   367   352   368

Is it reasonable to treat this as a sample from an approximately normal population? Explain.

Solution

Figure 6.38 presents a dotplot of the temperatures. The dotplot does not reveal any outliers. The plot does not exhibit a large degree of skewness, and there is no evidence that the population has more than one mode. Therefore, we can treat this as a sample from an approximately normal population.

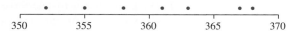

Figure 6.38 The dotplot of the oven temperatures does not reveal any outliers. The plot does not exhibit a large degree of skewness, and there is no evidence that the population has more than one mode. Therefore, we can treat this as a sample from an approximately normal population.

EXAMPLE 6.32

Using a dotplot to assess normality

At a recent health fair, several hundred people had their pulse rates measured. A simple random sample of six records was drawn, and the pulse rates, in beats per minute, were

> 68   71   79   98   67   75

Is it reasonable to treat this as a sample from an approximately normal population? Explain.

Solution

Figure 6.39 presents a dotplot of the pulse rates. It is clear that the value 98 is an outlier. Therefore, we should not treat this as a sample from an approximately normal population.

Figure 6.39 The value 98 is an outlier. Therefore, we should not treat this as a sample from an approximately normal population.

Objective 2 Use boxplots to assess normality

Boxplots

Boxplots are very good for detecting outliers and skewness. They work best for data sets that are not too small. For very small samples, it is just as informative to plot all the points with a dotplot.

EXAMPLE 6.33

Recall: Boxplots were introduced in Section 3.3.

Using a boxplot to assess normality

An insurance adjuster obtains a sample of 20 estimates, in hundreds of dollars, for repairs to cars damaged in collisions. Following are the data.

12.1	15.7	14.2	4.6	8.2	11.6	12.9	11.2	14.9	13.7
6.6	7.2	12.6	9.0	11.9	7.8	9.0	16.2	16.5	12.1

Is it reasonable to treat this as a sample from an approximately normal population? Explain.

Solution

Figure 6.40 presents a boxplot of the repair estimates. There are no outliers. Although the median is not exactly halfway between the quartiles, the skewness is not great. Therefore, we may treat this as a sample from an approximately normal population.

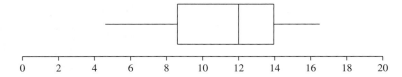

Figure 6.40   There are no outliers, and no evidence of strong skewness. Therefore, we may treat this as a sample from an approximately normal population.

EXAMPLE 6.34

Using a boxplot to assess normality

A recycler determines the amount of recycled newspaper, in cubic feet, collected each week. Following are the results for a sample of 18 weeks.

2129	2853	2530	2054	2075	2011	2162	2285	2668
3194	4834	2469	2380	2567	4117	2337	3179	3157

Is it reasonable to treat this as a sample from an approximately normal population? Explain.

Solution

Figure 6.41 presents a boxplot of the amount of recycled newspaper. The value 4834 is an outlier. In addition, the upper whisker is much longer than the lower one, which indicates fairly strong skewness. Therefore, we should not treat this as a sample from an approximately normal population.

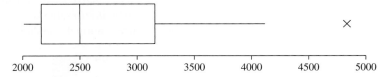

Figure 6.41   The value 4834 is an outlier, and there is evidence of fairly strong skewness as well. Therefore, we should not treat this as a sample from an approximately normal population.

Objective 3 Use histograms to assess normality

Histograms

Histograms are excellent for detecting strong skewness. They are more effective for data sets that are not too small (for very small data sets, a histogram is just like a dotplot with the dots replaced by rectangles).

| EXAMPLE 6.35 | Use a histogram to assess normality |

Recall: Histograms were introduced in Section 2.2.

Diameters were measured, in millimeters, for a simple random sample of 20 grade A eggs from a certain farm. The results were

| 59 | 60 | 60 | 56 | 59 | 56 | 62 | 58 | 60 | 59 |
| 61 | 59 | 61 | 61 | 63 | 60 | 56 | 58 | 63 | 58 |

Construct a histogram for these data. Is it reasonable to treat this as a sample from an approximately normal population? Explain.

Solution

Figure 6.42 presents a relative frequency histogram of the diameters. The histogram does not reveal any outliers, nor does it exhibit a large degree of skewness. There is no evidence that the population has more than one mode. Therefore, we can treat this as a sample from an approximately normal population.

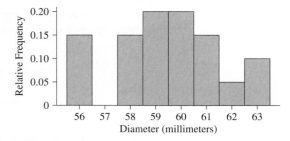

Figure 6.42   The histogram of the egg diameters does not reveal any outliers, nor a large degree of skewness, nor evidence of more than one mode. Therefore, we can treat this as a sample from an approximately normal population.

| EXAMPLE 6.36 | Use a histogram to assess normality |

A shoe manufacturer is testing a new type of leather sole. A simple random sample of 22 people wore shoes with the new sole for a period of four months. The amount of wear on the right shoe was measured for each person. The results, in thousandths of an inch, were

| 24.1 | 2.2 | 11.8 | 2.7 | 4.1 | 13.9 | 33.6 | 2.4 | 36.2 | 16.8 | 5.4 |
| 4.6 | 4.5 | 4.1 | 6.1 | 6.3 | 22.6 | 29.1 | 12.2 | 4.6 | 15.8 | 7.7 |

Construct a histogram for these data. Is it reasonable to treat this as a sample from an approximately normal population? Explain.

Solution

Figure 6.43 presents a relative frequency histogram of the amounts of wear. The histogram reveals that the sample is strongly skewed to the right. We should not treat this as a sample from an approximately normal population.

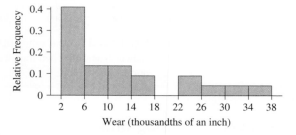

Figure 6.43   The histogram is strongly skewed. Therefore, we should not treat this as a sample from an approximately normal population.

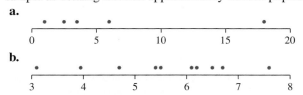

Objective 4 Use stem-and-leaf plots to assess normality

Recall: Stem-and-leaf plots were introduced in Section 2.3.

EXAMPLE 6.37

```
3 | 2
3 | 7
4 | 113
4 | 55889
5 | 223444
5 | 66
6 | 3
6 | 6
```

Figure 6.44 There are no outliers, strong skewness, or multimodality.

Stem-and-Leaf Plots

Stem-and-leaf plots can be used in place of histograms when the number of stems is large enough to provide an idea of the shape of the sample. Like histograms, stem-and-leaf plots are excellent for detecting skewness. They are more useful for data sets that are not too small, so that some of the stems will contain more than one leaf. Stem-and-leaf plots are easier to construct by hand than histograms are, but histograms are sometimes easier to construct with technology. For example, the TI-84 Plus calculator will construct histograms, but cannot construct stem-and-leaf plots.

Use a stem-and-leaf plot to assess normality

A psychologist measures the time it takes for each of 20 rats to run a maze. The times, in seconds, are

54	48	49	54	63	54	66	32	45	52
41	37	56	56	52	53	41	45	48	43

Construct a stem-and-leaf plot for these data. Is it reasonable to treat this as a random sample from an approximately normal population?

Solution

Figure 6.44 presents a stem-and-leaf plot of the times. The stem-and-leaf plot reveals no outliers, strong skewness, or multimodality. We may treat this as a sample from an approximately normal population.

Check Your Understanding

1. For each of the following dotplots, determine whether it is reasonable to treat the sample as coming from an approximately normal population.

   a.

   b.

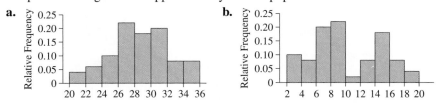

2. For each of the following histograms, determine whether it is reasonable to treat the sample as coming from an approximately normal population.

   a.   b.

3. The following stem-and-leaf plot represents a sample from a population. Is it reasonable to assume that this population is approximately normal?

```
1 | 34579
2 | 0278
3 | 25
4 | 37
5 | 38
6 | 4
7 |
8 | 1
9 | 6
```

4. The following boxplot represents a sample from a population. Is it reasonable to assume that this population is approximately normal?

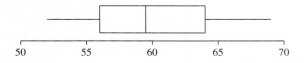

Answers are on page 281.

Objective 5 Use normal quantile plots to assess normality

Normal Quantile Plots

Normal quantile plots are somewhat more complex than dotplots, histograms, and stem-and-leaf plots. We will present the idea behind normal quantile plots with an example. A simple random sample of size $n = 5$ is drawn, and we want to determine whether the population it came from is approximately normal. The five sample values, in increasing order, are

$$3.0 \quad 3.3 \quad 4.8 \quad 5.9 \quad 7.8$$

We proceed by using the following steps:

Step 1: Let n be the number of values in the data set. Spread the n values evenly over the interval from 0 to 1. This is done by assigning the value $1/(2n)$ to the first sample value, $3/(2n)$ to the second, and so forth. The last sample value will be assigned the value $(2n-1)/(2n)$. These values, denoted a_i, represent areas under the normal curve. For $n = 5$, the values are 0.1, 0.3, 0.5, 0.7, and 0.9.

i	x_i	a_i
1	3.0	0.1
2	3.3	0.3
3	4.8	0.5
4	5.9	0.7
5	7.8	0.9

Step 2: The values assigned in Step 1 represent left-tail areas under the normal curve. We now find the z-scores corresponding to each of these areas. The results are shown in the following table.

i	x_i	a_i	z_i
1	3.0	0.1	-1.28
2	3.3	0.3	-0.52
3	4.8	0.5	0.00
4	5.9	0.7	0.52
5	7.8	0.9	1.28

Step 3: Plot the points (x_i, z_i). The plot is shown in Figure 6.45. A straight line has been added to the plot to help in interpreting the results. If the points approximately follow a straight line, then the population may be treated as being approximately normal. If the points deviate substantially from a straight line, the population should not be treated as normal. In this case, the points do approximately follow a straight line, so we may treat this population as approximately normal.

Why do the points on a normal quantile plot tend to follow a straight line when the population is normal? If the population is normal, then, on the average, the values z_i will be close to the actual z-scores of the x_i. Now for any sample, the actual z-scores will follow a straight line when plotted against the x_i. Therefore, if the population is approximately normal, it is likely that the points (x_i, z_i) will approximately follow a straight line.

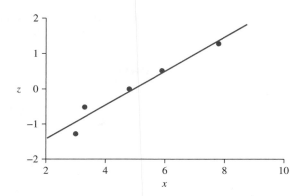

Figure 6.45   The points do not deviate substantially from a straight line. We can treat this population as approximately normal.

In practice, normal quantile plots are always constructed with technology. Figure 6.46 presents the normal quantile plot in Figure 6.45 as drawn by the TI-84 Plus calculator. The calculator does not add a line to the plot. Step-by-step instructions for constructing normal quantile plots with the TI-84 Plus calculator are presented in the Using Technology section on page 278.

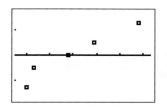

Figure 6.46

| EXAMPLE 6.38 |

Using a normal quantile plot to assess normality

A placement exam is given to each entering freshman at a large university. A simple random sample of 20 exam scores is drawn, with the following results.

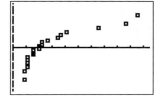

Figure 6.47

| 61 | 60 | 60 | 68 | 63 | 63 | 94 | 66 | 65 | 98 |
| 61 | 71 | 74 | 63 | 66 | 61 | 61 | 65 | 72 | 85 |

Construct a normal probability plot. Is the distribution of exam scores approximately normal?

Solution

We use the TI-84 Plus calculator. The results are shown in Figure 6.47. The points do not closely follow a straight line. The distribution is not approximately normal.

Check Your Understanding

5. Is it reasonable to treat the sample in the following normal quantile plot as coming from an approximately normal population? Explain.

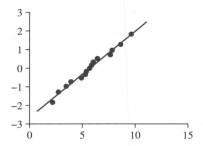

6. Is it reasonable to treat the sample in the following normal quantile plot as coming from an approximately normal population? Explain.

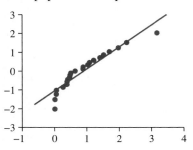

Answers are on page 281.

USING TECHNOLOGY

We use Example 6.38 to illustrate the technology steps.

TI-84 PLUS

Constructing normal quantile plots

Step 1. Enter the data from Example 6.38 into **L1** in the data editor.

Step 2. Press **2nd, Y=** to access the STAT PLOTS menu and select Plot1 by pressing **1**.

Step 3. Select **On** and the normal quantile plot icon.

Step 4. For **Data List**, select **L1**, and for **Data Axis**, choose the **X** option (Figure A).

Step 5. Press **ZOOM** and then **9: ZoomStat** (Figure B).

Figure A

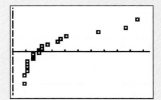

Figure B

MINITAB

Constructing normal quantile plots

Step 1. Enter the data from Example 6.38 into **Column C1**.

Step 2. Click on **Graph** and select **Probability Plot**. Choose the **Single** option and press **OK**.

Step 3. Enter **C1** in the **Graph variables** field.

Step 4. Click **OK** (Figure C).

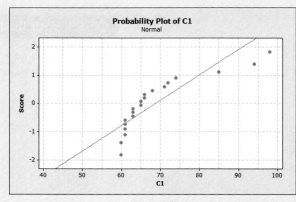

Figure C

SECTION 6.6   Exercises

Exercises 1–6 are the Check Your Understanding exercises located within the section.

Understanding the Concepts

In Exercise 7, fill in each blank with the appropriate word or phrase.

7. A population is rejected as being approximately normal if the sample contains an _____ , if the sample contains a large degree of _____ , or if the sample has more than one distinct _____ .

In Exercise 8, determine whether the statement is true or false. If the statement is false, rewrite it as a true statement.

8. If the points in a normal quantile plot deviate from a straight line, then the population can be treated as approximately normal.

Practicing the Skills

9. The following dotplot illustrates a sample. Is it reasonable to treat this as a sample from an approximately normal population? Explain.

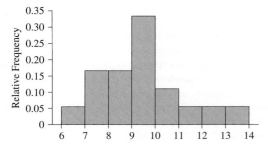

10. The following dotplot illustrates a sample. Is it reasonable to treat this as a sample from an approximately normal population? Explain.

11. The following boxplot illustrates a sample. Is it reasonable to treat this as a sample from an approximately normal population? Explain.

12. The following boxplot illustrates a sample. Is it reasonable to treat this as a sample from an approximately normal population? Explain.

13. The following histogram illustrates a sample. Is it reasonable to treat this as a sample from an approximately normal population? Explain.

14. The following histogram illustrates a sample. Is it reasonable to treat this as a sample from an approximately normal population? Explain.

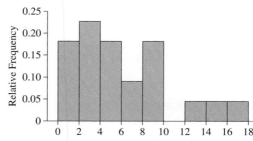

15. The following stem-and-leaf plot illustrates a sample. Is it reasonable to treat this as a sample from an approximately normal population? Explain.

0	35
1	46
2	0022358
3	18
4	3
5	4
6	36
7	19
8	34
9	4
10	
11	8

16. The following stem-and-leaf plot illustrates a sample. Is it reasonable to treat this as a sample from an approximately normal population? Explain.

7	35
8	47
9	024
10	379
11	37
12	34
13	0
14	1

17. The following normal quantile plot illustrates a sample. Is it reasonable to treat this as a sample from an approximately normal population? Explain.

18. The following normal quantile plot illustrates a sample. Is it reasonable to treat this as a sample from an approximately normal population? Explain.

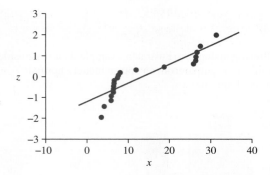

Working with the Concepts

19. Drug concentration: A sample of 10 people ingested a new formulation of a drug. Six hours later, the concentrations in their bloodstreams, in nanograms per milliliter, were as follows.

  2.3 1.4 1.8 2.1 1.0 4.1 1.8 2.9 2.5 2.7

Construct a dotplot for this sample. Is it reasonable to treat the sample as coming from an approximately normal population? Explain.

20. Reading scores: A random sample of eight elementary school children were given a standardized reading test. Following are their scores.

  72 77 65 85 68 83 73 79

Construct a dotplot for this sample. Is it reasonable to treat the sample as coming from an approximately normal population? Explain.

21. Timed task: The number of minutes needed to complete a certain spreadsheet task was measured for 20 clerical workers. The results were as follows.

  4.5 5.8 3.7 4.9 4.3 4.7 5.8 3.2 3.0 5.1
  3.6 4.3 3.6 5.4 4.7 3.0 3.4 4.3 4.4 3.5

Construct a boxplot for this sample. Is it reasonable to treat the sample as coming from an approximately normal population? Explain.

22. Impure cans: A manufacturer of aluminum cans measured the level of impurities in 24 cans. The amounts of impurities, in percent, were as follows.

  2.1 1.5 1.9 1.3 2.7 4.9 2.1 1.8
  1.3 1.0 3.2 4.4 8.0 4.5 2.5 1.6
  2.8 8.2 9.5 3.8 1.9 1.5 2.8 1.6

Construct a boxplot for this sample. Is it reasonable to treat the sample as coming from an approximately normal population? Explain.

23. Defective items: The number of defective items produced on an assembly line during an hour is counted for a random sample of 20 hours. The results are as follows.

  21 16 10 10 11   9 13 12 11 29
  10 14 27 10 11 11 12 19 11   9

Construct a stem-and-leaf plot for this sample. Is it reasonable to treat the sample as coming from an approximately normal population? Explain.

24. Fish weights: A fish hatchery raises trout to stock streams and lakes. The weights, in ounces, of a sample of 18 trout at their time of release are as follows.

  9.9 11.3 11.4   9.0 10.1   8.2   8.9   9.9 10.5
  8.6   7.8 10.8   8.4   9.6   9.9   8.4   9.0   9.1

Construct a stem-and-leaf plot for this sample. Is it reasonable to treat the sample as coming from an approximately normal population? Explain.

25. Timed task: Construct a histogram for the data in Exercise 21. Explain how the histogram shows whether it is appropriate to treat this sample as coming from an approximately normal population.

26. Impure cans: Construct a histogram for the data in Exercise 22. Explain how the histogram shows whether it is appropriate to treat this sample as coming from an approximately normal population.

27. Defective items: Construct a normal quantile plot for the data in Exercise 23. Explain how the plot shows whether it is appropriate to treat this sample as coming from an approximately normal population.

28. Fish weights: Construct a normal quantile plot for the data in Exercise 24. Explain how the plot shows whether it is appropriate to treat this sample as coming from an approximately normal population.

Extending the Concepts

29. Transformation to normality: Consider the following data set:

  2 37 67 108 148 40 1 9 3 237 12 80

a. Show that this data set does not come from an approximately normal population.
b. Take the square root of each value in the data set. This is called a *square-root transformation* of the data. Show that the square roots may be considered to be a sample from an approximately normal population.

30. Transformation to normality: Consider the following data set:

  −0.5 0.8 1.7 −1.0 −10.0 1.7 0.5 0.3 −5.0

a. Show that this data set does not come from an approximately normal population.
b. Take the reciprocal of each value in the data set (the reciprocal of x is $1/x$). This is called a *reciprocal transformation* of the data. Show that the reciprocals may be considered to be a sample from an approximately normal population.

31. Transformation to normality: Consider the following data set:

  4.1 2.7 1.2 10.3 0.9 2.4
  1.5 1.9 2.1 16.1 1.4 1.0

a. Is it reasonable to treat it as a sample from an approximately normal population?
b. Perform a square-root transformation. Is it reasonable to treat the square-root-transformed data as a sample from an approximately normal population?
c. Perform a reciprocal transformation. Is it reasonable to treat the reciprocal-transformed data as a sample from an approximately normal population?

32. Transformation to normality: Consider the following data set:

> 28.0 6.7 8.6 2.3 25.0 12.5 4.4
> 37.3 12.0 48.0 0.7 11.6 0.1

   a. Is it reasonable to treat it as a sample from an approximately normal population?

   b. Perform a square-root transformation. Is it reasonable to treat the square-root-transformed data as a sample from an approximately normal population?

   c. Perform a reciprocal transformation. Is it reasonable to treat the reciprocal-transformed data as a sample from an approximately normal population?

Answers to Check Your Understanding Exercises for Section 6.6

1. a. The plot contains an outlier. The population is not approximately normal.

   b. We may treat this population as approximately normal.

2. a. We may treat this population as approximately normal.

   b. The histogram has more than one mode. The population is not approximately normal.

3. The plot reveals that the sample is strongly skewed. The population is not approximately normal.

4. There are no outliers and no evidence of strong skewness. We may treat this population as approximately normal.

5. The points follow a straight line fairly closely. We may treat this population as approximately normal.

6. The points do not follow a straight line fairly closely. The population is not approximately normal.

Chapter 6 Summary

Section 6.1: Continuous random variables can be described with probability density curves. The area under a probability density curve over an interval can be interpreted in either of two ways. It represents the proportion of the population that is contained in the interval, and it also represents the probability that a randomly chosen value from the population falls within the interval. The normal curve is the most commonly used probability density curve. The standard normal curve represents a normal population with mean 0 and standard deviation 1. We can find areas under the standard normal curve by using Table A.2 or with technology.

Section 6.2: In practice, we need to work with normal distributions with different values for the mean and standard deviation. Technology can be used to compute probabilities for any normal distribution. We can also use Table A.2 to find probabilities for any normal distribution by standardization. Standardization involves computing the z-score by subtracting the mean and dividing by the standard deviation. The z-score has a standard normal distribution, so we can find probabilities by using Table A.2.

Section 6.3: The sampling distribution of a statistic such as a sample mean is the probability distribution of all possible values of the statistic. The Central Limit Theorem states that the sampling distribution of a sample mean is approximately normal so long as the sample size is large enough. Therefore, we can use the normal curve to compute approximate probabilities regarding the sample mean whenever the sample size is sufficiently large. For most populations, samples of size 30 or more are large enough.

Section 6.4: The Central Limit Theorem can also be used to compute approximate probabilities regarding sample proportions. The sampling distribution of a sample proportion is approximately normal so long as the sample size is large enough. The sample size is large enough if both np and $n(1 - p)$ are at least 10.

Section 6.5: A binomial random variable represents the number of successes in a series of independent trials. The number of successes is closely related to the sample proportion, because the sample proportion is found by dividing the number of successes by the number of trials. Since the sample proportion is approximately normally distributed whenever $np \geq 10$ and $n(1 - p) \geq 10$, the number of successes is also approximately normally distributed under these conditions. Therefore, the normal curve can also be used to compute approximate probabilities for the binomial distribution. Because the binomial distribution is discrete, the continuity correction can be used to provide more accurate approximations.

Section 6.6: Many statistical procedures require the assumption that a sample is drawn from a population that is approximately normal. Although it is very difficult to determine whether a small sample comes from such a population, we can examine the sample for outliers, multimodality, and large degrees of skewness. If a sample contains no outliers, is not strongly skewed, and has only one distinct mode, we will treat it as though it came from an approximately normal population. Dotplots, boxplots, histograms, stem-and-leaf plots, and normal quantile plots can be used to assess normality.

Vocabulary and Notation

Central Limit Theorem   254
continuity correction   266
normal approximation to binomial   266
normal curve   228
normal distribution   228

normal quantile plot   276
population proportion   259
probability density curve   226
sample proportion   259
sampling distribution   251

standard error   252
standard normal curve   229
standard normal distribution   229
standardization   240
z-score   229

Important Formulas

z-score:

$$z = \frac{x - \mu}{\sigma}$$

Convert z-score to raw score:

$$x = \mu + z\sigma$$

Standard deviation of the sample mean:

$$\sigma_{\bar{x}} = \frac{\sigma}{\sqrt{n}}$$

z-score for a sample mean:

$$z = \frac{\bar{x} - \mu}{\sigma_{\bar{x}}}$$

Standard deviation of the sample proportion:

$$\sigma_{\hat{p}} = \sqrt{\frac{p(1 - p)}{n}}$$

z-score for a sample proportion:

$$z = \frac{\hat{p} - p}{\sigma_{\hat{p}}}$$

Chapter Quiz

1. Following is a probability density curve for a population.

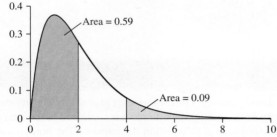

   a. What proportion of the population is between 2 and 4?
   b. If a value is chosen at random from this population, what is the probability that it will be greater than 2?

2. Find the area under the standard normal curve
   a. To the left of $z = 1.77$
   b. To the right of $z = 0.41$
   c. Between $z = -2.12$ and $z = 1.37$

3. Find the z-score that has
   a. An area of 0.33 to its left
   b. An area of 0.79 to its right

4. Find the z-scores that bound the middle 80% of the area under the normal curve.

5. Find $z_{0.15}$.

6. Suppose that salaries of recent graduates from a certain college are normally distributed with mean $\mu = \$42{,}650$ and standard deviation $\sigma = \$3800$. What two salaries bound the middle 50%?

7. A normal population has mean $\mu = 242$ and standard deviation $\sigma = 31$.
   a. What proportion of the population is greater than 233?
   b. What is the probability that a randomly chosen value will be less than 249?

8. Suppose that in a bowling league, the scores among all bowlers are normally distributed with mean $\mu = 182$ points and standard deviation $\sigma = 14$ points. A trophy is given to each player whose score is at or above the 97th percentile. What is the minimum score needed for a bowler to receive a trophy?

9. State the Central Limit Theorem.

10. A population has mean $\mu = 193$ and standard deviation $\sigma = 42$. Compute $\mu_{\bar{x}}$ and $\sigma_{\bar{x}}$ for samples of size $n = 64$.

11. The running time for videos submitted to YouTube in a given week is normally distributed with $\mu = 390$ seconds and standard deviation $\sigma = 148$ seconds.
    a. If a single video is randomly selected, what is the probability that the running time of the video exceeds 6 minutes (360 seconds)?
    b. Suppose that a sample of 40 videos is selected. What is the probability that the mean running time of the sample exceeds 6 minutes?

12. A sample of size $n = 55$ is drawn from a population with proportion $p = 0.34$. Let $\hat{p}$ be the sample proportion.
    a. Find $\mu_{\hat{p}}$ and $\sigma_{\hat{p}}$.
    b. Find $P(\hat{p} > 0.21)$.
    c. Find $P(\hat{p} < 0.40)$.

13. On a certain television channel, 18% of commercials are local advertisers. A sample of 120 commercials is selected.
   a. What is the probability that more than 20% of the commercials in the sample are local advertisers?
   b. Would it be unusual for more than 25% of the commercials to be local advertisers?

14. Let X have a binomial distribution with $n = 240$ and $p = 0.38$. Use the normal approximation to find:
   a. $P(X > 83)$
   b. $P(75 \leq X \leq 95)$
   c. $P(X < 96)$

15. Is it reasonable to treat the following sample as coming from an approximately normal population? Explain.

$$5.5 \quad 8.7 \quad 9.3 \quad 10.1 \quad 15.2 \quad 3.5 \quad 11.9 \quad 7.6 \quad 13.7 \quad 8.7 \quad 14.3 \quad 5.8$$

Review Exercises

1. Find the area: Find the area under the standard normal curve
   a. To the left of $z = 0.35$
   b. To the right of $z = -1.56$
   c. Between $z = 0.35$ and $z = 2.47$

2. Find the z-score: Find the z-score for which the area to its right is 0.89.

3. Your battery is dead: The lifetimes of a certain type of automobile battery are normally distributed with mean 5.9 years and standard deviation 0.4 year. The batteries are guaranteed to last at least 5 years. What proportion of the batteries fail to meet the guarantee?

4. Take your medicine: Medication used to treat a certain condition is administered by syringe. The target dose in a particular application is 10 milligrams. Because of the variations in the syringe, in reading the scale, and in mixing the fluid suspension, the actual dose administered is normally distributed with mean $\mu = 10$ milligrams and standard deviation $\sigma = 1.6$ milligrams.
   a. What is the probability that the dose administered is between 9 and 11.5 milligrams?
   b. Find the 98th percentile of the administered dose.
   c. If a clinical overdose is defined as a dose larger than 15 milligrams, what is the probability that a patient will receive an overdose?

5. Lightbulbs: The lifetime of lightbulbs has a mean of 1500 hours and a standard deviation of 100 hours. A sample of 50 lightbulbs is tested.
   a. What is the probability that the sample mean lifetime is greater than 1520 hours?
   b. What is the probability that the sample mean lifetime is less than 1540 hours?
   c. What is the probability that the sample mean lifetime is between 1490 and 1550 hours?

6. More lightbulbs: Someone claims to have developed a new lightbulb whose mean lifetime is 1800 hours with a standard deviation of 100 hours. A sample of 100 of these bulbs is tested. The sample mean lifetime is 1770 hours.
   a. If the claim is true, what is the probability of obtaining a sample mean that is less than or equal to 1770 hours?
   b. If the claim is true, would it be unusual to obtain a sample mean that is less than or equal to 1770 hours?

7. Pay your taxes: Among all the state income tax forms filed in a particular state, the mean income tax paid was $\mu = \$2000$ and the standard deviation was $\sigma = \$500$. As part of a study of the impact of a new tax law, a sample of 80 income tax returns is examined. Would it be unusual for the sample mean of these 80 returns to be greater than $2150?

8. Safe delivery: A certain delivery truck can safely carry a load of 3400 pounds. The cartons that will be loaded onto the truck have a mean weight of 80 pounds with a standard deviation of 20 pounds. Forty cartons are loaded onto the truck.
   a. If the total weight of the 40 cartons is 3400 pounds, what is the sample mean weight?
   b. What is the probability that the truck can deliver the 40 cartons safely?

9. Elementary school: In a certain elementary school, 52% of the students are girls. A sample of 65 students is drawn.
   a. What is the probability that more than 60% of them are girls?
   b. Would it be unusual for more than 70% of them to be girls?

10. Facebook: Eighty percent of the students at a particular large university have logged on to Facebook at least once in the past week. A sample of 95 students is asked about their Internet habits.
   a. What is the probability that less than 75% of the sampled students have logged on to Facebook within the last week?
   b. What is the probability that more than 78% of the sampled students have logged on to Facebook within the last week?
   c. What is the probability that the proportion of the sampled students who have logged on to Facebook within the last week is between 0.82 and 0.85?

11. It's all politics: A politician in a close election race claims that 52% of the voters support him. A poll is taken in which 200 voters are sampled, and 44% of them support the politician.

    a. If the claim is true, what is the probability of obtaining a sample proportion that is less than or equal to 0.44?

    b. If the claim is true, would it be unusual to obtain a sample proportion less than or equal to 0.44?

    c. If the claim is true, would it be unusual for less than half of the voters in the sample to support the politician?

12. Side effects: A new medical procedure produces side effects in 25% of the patients who receive it. In a clinical trial, 60 people undergo the procedure. What is the probability that 20 or fewer experience side effects?

13. Defective rods: A grinding machine used to manufacture steel rods produces rods, 5% of which are defective. When a customer orders 1000 rods, a package of 1060 rods is shipped, with a guarantee that at least 1000 of the rods are good. What is the probability that a package of 1060 rods contains 1000 or more that are good?

14. Is it normal? Is it reasonable to treat the following sample as though it comes from an approximately normal population? Explain.

2.6 4.2 1.5 2.0 0.6 0.7 6.6 2.2 9.7 1.8 4.2 4.4 0.6

15. Is it normal? Is it reasonable to treat the following sample as though it comes from an approximately normal population? Explain.

8.8 11.2 11.6 6.3 9.3 1.5 14.6 7.5 5.2 9.0 4.3 9.9 7.8 13.1

Write About It

1. Explain why $P(a < X < b)$ is equal to $P(a \le X \le b)$ when X is a continuous random variable.

2. Describe the information you must know to compute the area under the normal curve over a given interval.

3. Describe the information you must know to find the value corresponding to a given proportion of the area under a normal curve.

4. Suppose that in a large class, the instructor announces that the average grade on an exam is 75. Which is more likely to be closer to 75:

    i. The exam grade of a randomly selected student in the class?

    ii. The mean exam grade of a sample of 10 students?

    Explain.

5. Consider the formula for the standard deviation of the sampling distribution of $\hat{p}$ given by $\sigma_{\hat{p}} = \sqrt{\dfrac{p(1-p)}{n}}$. What happens to the standard deviation as n gets larger and larger? Explain what this means in terms of the spread of the sampling distribution.

6. Explain how to decide when it is appropriate to use the normal approximation to the binomial distribution.

7. Describe the effect, if any, that the size of a sample has in assessing the normality of a population.

Case Study: Testing The Strength Of Cans

In the chapter opener, we discussed a method used to determine whether shipments of aluminum cans are strong enough to withstand the pressure of containing a carbonated beverage. Several cans are sampled from a shipment and tested to determine the pressure they can withstand. Based on this small sample, quality inspectors must estimate the proportion of cans that will fail at or below a certain threshold, which we will take to be 90 pounds per square inch.

    The quality control inspectors want the proportion of defective cans to be no more than 0.001, or 1 in 1000. They test 10 cans, with the following results.

Can	1	2	3	4	5	6	7	8	9	10
Pressure at failure	95	96	98	99	99	100	101	101	103	104

None of the cans in the sample were defective; in other words, none of them failed at a pressure of 90 or less. The quality control inspectors want to use these data to estimate the proportion of defective cans in the shipment. If the estimate is to be no more than 0.001, or 1 in 1000, they will accept the shipment; otherwise, they will return it for a refund.

    The following exercises will lead you through the process used by the quality control inspectors. Assume the failure pressures are normally distributed.

1. Compute the sample mean $\bar{x}$ and the sample standard deviation s.

2. Estimate the population mean μ with $\bar{x}$ and the population standard deviation σ with s. In other words, assume that the data are a sample from a normal population with mean $\mu = \bar{x}$ and standard deviation $\sigma = s$. Under this assumption, what proportion of cans will fail at a pressure of 90 or less?

3. The shipment will be accepted if we estimate that the proportion of cans that fail at a pressure of 90 or less is less than 0.001. Will this shipment be accepted?

4. A second shipment of cans is received. Ten randomly sampled cans are tested with the following results.

Can	1	2	3	4	5	6	7	8	9	10
Pressure at failure	96	97	99	100	100	100	101	103	103	120

Explain why the second sample of cans is stronger than the first sample.

5. Compute the sample mean $\bar{x}$ and the sample standard deviation s for the second sample.

6. Using the same method as for the first sample, estimate the proportion of cans that will fail at a pressure of 90 or less.

7. The shipment will be accepted if we estimate that the proportion of cans that fail at a pressure of 90 or less is less than 0.001. Will this shipment be accepted?

8. Make a boxplot of the pressures for the second sample. Is the method appropriate for the second shipment?

Confidence Intervals

Introduction

Air pollution is a serious problem in many places. Particulate matter (PM), which consists of tiny particles in the air, is a form of air pollution that is suspected of causing respiratory illness. PM can come from many sources, such as ash from burning and tiny particles of rubber from automobile and truck tires.

   The town of Libby, Montana, has experienced high levels of PM, especially in the winter. Many houses in Libby are heated by wood stoves, which produce a lot of particulate pollution. In an attempt to reduce the winter levels of air pollution in Libby, a program was undertaken in which almost every wood stove in the town was replaced with a newer, cleaner-burning model. Most stoves were replaced in 2006 or early 2007. Measurements of several air pollutants, including PM, were taken both before and after the stove replacement. To determine PM levels after stoves were replaced, the level was measured on a sample of 20 days in the winter of 2007–2008. The units are micrograms per cubic meter. Following are the results:

| 21.7 | 27.8 | 24.7 | 15.3 | 18.4 | 14.4 | 19.0 | 23.7 | 22.4 | 25.6 |
| 15.0 | 17.0 | 23.2 | 17.7 | 11.1 | 29.8 | 20.0 | 21.6 | 14.8 | 21.0 |

   Clearly, the amount varies from day to day. The sample mean is 20.21 and the sample standard deviation is 4.86. We would like to use this information to estimate the population mean, which is the mean over all days of the winter of 2007–2008. What is the best way to do this? If we had to pick a single number to estimate the population mean, the best choice would be the sample mean, which is 20.21. The estimate 20.21 is called a **point estimate**, because it is a single number. The problem with point estimates is that they are almost never exactly equal to the true values they are estimating. They are almost always off — sometimes by a little, sometimes by a lot. It is unlikely that the mean level of PM for all of 2007–2008 is exactly equal to 20.21; it is somewhat more or less than that. In order for a point estimate to be useful, it is necessary to describe just how close to the true value it is likely to be. To do this, statisticians construct **confidence intervals**. A confidence interval gives a range of values that is likely to contain the true value being estimated.

To construct a confidence interval, we put a plus-or-minus number on the point estimate. So, for example, we might estimate that the population mean is 20.21 ± 2.0 or, equivalently, that the population mean is between 18.21 and 22.21. The interval 20.21 ± 2.0 or, equivalently, (18.21, 22.21), is a confidence interval for the population mean.

One of the benefits of confidence intervals is that they come with a measure of the level of confidence we can have that they actually cover the true value being estimated. For example, we will show that we can be 95% confident that the population mean PM level during the winter of 2007–2008 is in the interval 20.21 ± 2.27 or, equivalently, between 17.94 and 22.48. If we want more confidence, we can widen the interval. For example, we will learn how to show that we can be 99% confident that the population mean PM level is in the interval 20.21 ± 3.11 or, equivalently, between 17.10 and 23.32. In the case study at the end of the chapter, we will use confidence intervals to further study the effects of the Libby stove replacement program.

There are many different situations in which confidence intervals can be constructed. The correct method to use varies from situation to situation. In this chapter, we will describe the methods that are appropriate in several of the most commonly encountered situations.

SECTION 7.1 | Confidence Intervals for a Population Mean, Standard Deviation Known

Objectives

1. Construct and interpret confidence intervals for a population mean when the population standard deviation is known
2. Find critical values for confidence intervals
3. Describe the relationship between the confidence level and the margin of error
4. Find the sample size necessary to obtain a confidence interval of a given width
5. Distinguish between confidence and probability

Objective 1 Construct and interpret confidence intervals for a population mean when the population standard deviation is known

Estimating a Population Mean

How can we measure the reading ability of elementary school students? The No Child Left Behind Act, signed into law in 2002, requires schools to regularly assess the proficiency of students in subjects such as reading and math. In a certain school district, administrators are trying out a new experimental approach to teach reading to fourth-graders. A simple random sample of 100 fourth-graders is selected to take part in the program. At the end of the program, the students are given a standardized reading test. On the basis of past results, it is known that scores on this test have a population standard deviation of $\sigma = 15$.

The sample mean score for the 100 students was $\bar{x} = 67.30$. The administrators want to estimate what the mean score μ would be if the entire population of fourth-graders in the district had enrolled in the program. The best estimate for the population mean is the sample mean, $\bar{x} = 67.30$. The sample mean is a **point estimate**, because it is a single number.

Recall: A parameter is a numerical summary of a population, such as a population mean μ or a population proportion p.

DEFINITION

A **point estimate** is a single number that is used to estimate the value of an unknown parameter.

It is very unlikely that the point estimate $\bar{x}$ is exactly equal to the population mean μ. Therefore, in order for the estimate to be useful, we must describe how close it is likely to be. For example, if we think that $\bar{x} = 67.30$ is likely to be within 1 point of the population mean, we would estimate μ with the interval $66.30 < \mu < 68.30$. This could also be written

Explain It Again

The symbol ±: The symbol ± means to form an interval by adding and subtracting. For example, 67.30 ± 1 means the interval from 67.30 − 1 to 67.30 + 1, or, in other words, from 66.30 to 68.30.

Recall: The quantity $\sigma/\sqrt{n}$ is called the standard error of the mean.

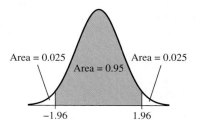

Figure 7.1 95% of the area under the standard normal curve is between $z = -1.96$ and $z = 1.96$.

as 67.30 ± 1. If we think that $\bar{x} = 67.30$ could be off by as much as 10 points from the population mean, we would estimate μ with the interval $57.30 < \mu < 77.30$, which could also be written as 67.30 ± 10. The plus-or-minus number is called the **margin of error**. We need to determine how large to make the margin of error so that the interval is likely to contain the population mean. To do this, we use the sampling distribution of $\bar{x}$.

Because the sample size is large ($n > 30$), the Central Limit Theorem tells us that the sampling distribution of $\bar{x}$ is approximately normal with mean μ and standard deviation (also called the **standard error**) given by

$$\text{Standard error} = \frac{\sigma}{\sqrt{n}} = \frac{15}{\sqrt{100}} = 1.5$$

We will now construct a **95% confidence interval** for μ. We begin with a normal curve, and using the method described in Section 6.1 (Example 6.11), we find the z-scores that bound the middle 95% of the area under the curve. These z-scores are 1.96 and -1.96 (see Figure 7.1). The value 1.96 is called the **critical value**. To obtain the margin of error, we multiply the critical value by the standard error.

$$\text{Margin of error} = \text{Critical value} \cdot \text{Standard error} = (1.96)(1.5) = 2.94$$

A 95% confidence interval for μ is therefore

$$\bar{x} - 2.94 < \mu < \bar{x} + 2.94$$
$$67.30 - 2.94 < \mu < 67.30 + 2.94$$
$$64.36 < \mu < 70.24$$

There are several ways to express this confidence interval. We can write $64.36 < \mu < 70.24$, 67.30 ± 2.94, or $(64.36, 70.24)$. In words, we would say, "We are 95% confident that the population mean is between 64.36 and 70.24."

Figures 7.2 and 7.3 help explain why this interval is called a 95% confidence interval. Figure 7.2 illustrates a sample whose mean $\bar{x}$ is in the middle 95% of its distribution. The 95% confidence interval constructed from this value of $\bar{x}$ covers the true population mean μ.

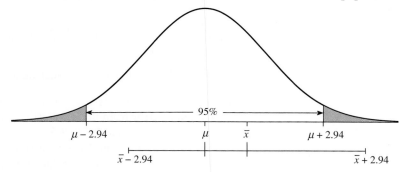

Figure 7.2 The sample mean $\bar{x}$ comes from the middle 95% of the distribution, so the 95% confidence interval $\bar{x} \pm 2.94$ succeeds in covering the population mean μ.

Figure 7.3 illustrates a sample whose mean $\bar{x}$ is in one of the tails of the distribution, outside the middle 95%. The 95% confidence interval constructed from this value of $\bar{x}$ does *not* cover the true population mean μ.

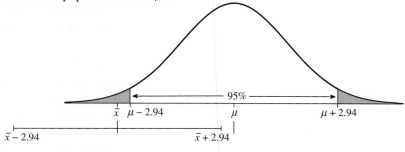

Figure 7.3 The sample mean $\bar{x}$ comes from the outer 5% of the distribution, so the 95% confidence interval $\bar{x} \pm 2.94$ fails to cover the population mean μ.

Now in the long run, 95% of the sample means we observe will be like the one in Figure 7.2. They will be in the middle 95% of the distribution and their confidence intervals will cover the population mean. Therefore, in the long run, 95% of the confidence intervals we construct will cover the population mean. Only 5% of the sample means we observe will be outside the middle 95% of the distribution like the one in Figure 7.3. So in the long run, only 5% of the confidence intervals we construct will fail to cover the population mean.

To summarize, the confidence interval we just constructed is a 95% confidence interval, because the method we used to construct it will cover the population mean μ for 95% of all the possible samples that might be drawn. We can also say that the interval has a **confidence level** of 95%.

DEFINITION

- A **confidence interval** is an interval that is used to estimate the value of a parameter.
- The **confidence level** is a percentage between 0% and 100% that measures the success rate of the method used to construct the confidence interval. If we were to draw many samples and use each one to construct a confidence interval, then in the long run, the percentage of confidence intervals that cover the true value would be equal to the confidence level.

EXAMPLE 7.1

Construct and interpret a 95% confidence interval

A large sample has mean $\bar{x} = 7.1$ and standard error $\sigma/\sqrt{n} = 2.3$. Find the margin of error for a 95% confidence interval. Construct a 95% confidence interval for the population mean μ and explain what it means to say that the confidence level is 95%.

Solution
As shown in Figure 7.1, the critical value for a 95% confidence interval is 1.96. Therefore, the margin of error is

$$\text{Margin of error} = \text{Critical value} \cdot \text{Standard error} = (1.96)(2.3) = 4.5$$

The point estimate of μ is $\bar{x} = 7.1$. To construct a confidence interval, we add and subtract the margin of error from the point estimate. So the 95% confidence interval is 7.1 ± 4.5. We can also write this as $7.1 - 4.5 < \mu < 7.1 + 4.5$, or $2.6 < \mu < 11.6$.

The level of this confidence interval is 95% because if we were to draw many samples and use this method to construct the corresponding confidence intervals, then in the long run, 95% of the intervals would cover the true value of the population mean μ. Unless we were unlucky in the sample we drew, the population mean μ will be between 2.6 and 11.6.

Objective 2 Find critical values for confidence intervals

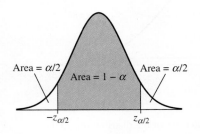

Figure 7.4

Finding the critical value for a given confidence level

Although 95% is the most commonly used confidence level, sometimes we will want to construct a confidence interval with a different level. We can construct a confidence interval with any confidence level between 0% and 100% by finding the appropriate critical value for that level. We have seen that the critical value for a 95% confidence interval is $z = 1.96$, because 95% of the area under a normal curve is between $z = -1.96$ and $z = 1.96$. To find the critical value for a confidence interval with a given level, let $1 - \alpha$ be the confidence level expressed as a decimal. The critical value is then $z_{\alpha/2}$, because the area under the standard normal curve between $-z_{\alpha/2}$ and $z_{\alpha/2}$ is $1 - \alpha$. See Figure 7.4.

The row of Table A.3 labeled "z" presents critical values for several confidence levels. Following is part of that row, which presents critical values for four of the most commonly used confidence levels.

z	$\cdots$	1.645	1.96	2.326	2.576	$\cdots$
	$\cdots$	90%	95%	98%	99%	$\cdots$
			Confidence level			

EXAMPLE 7.2   Construct confidence intervals of various levels

A large sample has mean $\bar{x} = 7.1$ and standard error $\sigma/\sqrt{n} = 2.3$. Construct confidence intervals for the population mean μ with the following levels:
a. 90%   **b.** 98%   **c.** 99%

Solution
The point estimate of μ is $\bar{x} = 7.1$.

    a. From the bottom row of Table A.3, we see that the critical value for a 90% confidence interval is 1.645, so the margin of error is

$$\text{Margin of error} = \text{Critical value} \cdot \text{Standard error} = (1.645)(2.3) = 3.8$$

    The 90% confidence interval is 7.1 ± 3.8. We can also write this as

$$7.1 - 3.8 < \mu < 7.1 + 3.8, \text{ or } 3.3 < \mu < 10.9.$$

    b. From the bottom row of Table A.3, we see that the critical value for a 98% confidence interval is 2.326, so the margin of error is

$$\text{Margin of error} = \text{Critical value} \cdot \text{Standard error} = (2.326)(2.3) = 5.3$$

    The 98% confidence interval is 7.1 ± 5.3. We can also write this as

$$7.1 - 5.3 < \mu < 7.1 + 5.3, \text{ or } 1.8 < \mu < 12.4.$$

    c. From the bottom row of Table A.3, we see that the critical value for a 99% confidence interval is 2.576, so the margin of error is

$$\text{Margin of error} = \text{Critical value} \cdot \text{Standard error} = (2.576)(2.3) = 5.9$$

    The 99% confidence interval is 7.1 ± 5.9. We can also write this as

$$7.1 - 5.9 < \mu < 7.1 + 5.9, \text{ or } 1.2 < \mu < 13.0.$$

Sometimes we may need to find a critical value for a confidence level not given in the last row of Table A.3. We can do this using Table A.2 or with technology, as shown in Example 7.3.

EXAMPLE 7.3   Find a critical value

Find the critical value $z_{\alpha/2}$ for a 92% confidence interval.

Solution
The level is 92%, so we have $1 - \alpha = 0.92$. It follows that $\alpha = 1 - 0.92 = 0.08$, so $\alpha/2 = 0.04$. The critical value is $z_{0.04}$. We now must find the value of $z_{0.04}$. To do this using Table A.2, we find the area to the left of $z_{0.04}$. Since the area to the right of $z_{0.04}$ is 0.04, the area to the left is $1 - 0.04 = 0.96$. See Figure 7.5.

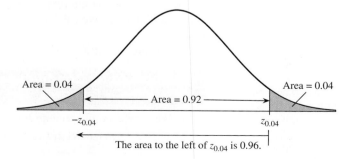

Figure 7.5   The critical value $z_{0.04}$ contains an area of 0.92 under the standard normal curve between $-z_{0.04}$ and $z_{0.04}$.

We now look in the body of Table A.2 (a portion of which is shown in Figure 7.6) to find the closest value to 0.96. This value is 0.9599, and it corresponds to a z-score of 1.75. Therefore, the critical value is $z_{0.04} = 1.75$.

z	0.00	0.01	0.02	0.03	0.04	0.05	0.06	0.07	0.08	0.09
⋮	⋮	⋮	⋮	⋮	⋮	⋮	⋮	⋮	⋮	⋮
1.2	.8849	.8869	.8888	.8907	.8925	.8944	.8962	.8980	.8997	.9015
1.3	.9032	.9049	.9066	.9082	.9099	.9115	.9131	.9147	.9162	.9177
1.4	.9192	.9207	.9222	.9236	.9251	.9265	.9279	.9292	.9306	.9319
1.5	.9332	.9345	.9357	.9370	.9382	.9394	.9406	.9418	.9429	.9441
1.6	.9452	.9463	.9474	.9484	.9495	.9505	.9515	.9525	.9535	.9545
1.7	.9554	.9564	.9573	.9582	.9591	.9599	.9608	.9616	.9625	.9633
1.8	.9641	.9649	.9656	.9664	.9671	.9678	.9686	.9693	.9699	.9706
1.9	.9713	.9719	.9726	.9732	.9738	.9744	.9750	.9756	.9761	.9767
2.0	.9772	.9778	.9783	.9788	.9793	.9798	.9803	.9808	.9812	.9817
2.1	.9821	.9826	.9830	.9834	.9838	.9842	.9846	.9850	.9854	.9857
2.2	.9861	.9864	.9868	.9871	.9875	.9878	.9881	.9884	.9887	.9890
⋮	⋮	⋮	⋮	⋮	⋮	⋮	⋮	⋮	⋮	⋮

Figure 7.6

As an alternative to Table A.2, we can find $z_{0.04}$ with technology, for example, by using the TI-84 Plus calculator. Figure 7.5 shows that the area to the left of $z_{0.04}$ is 0.96. Therefore, we can find $z_{0.04}$ with the command **invNorm(.96,0,1)**. See Figure 7.7.

```
invNorm(.96,0,1)
              1.750686071
```

Figure 7.7

Check Your Understanding

1. Find the critical value $z_{\alpha/2}$ to construct a confidence interval with level

   a. 90%   **b.** 98%   **c.** 99.5%   **d.** 80%

2. Find the levels of the confidence intervals that have the following critical values.

   a. $z_{\alpha/2} = 1.96$ **b.** $z_{\alpha/2} = 2.17$ **c.** $z_{\alpha/2} = 1.28$

   d. $z_{\alpha/2} = 3.28$

3. Find the margin of error given the standard error and the confidence level.

   a. Standard error = 1.2, confidence level 95%

   b. Standard error = 0.4, confidence level 99%

   c. Standard error = 3.5, confidence level 90%

   d. Standard error = 2.75, confidence level 98%

Answers are on page 306.

Assumptions

The method we have described for constructing a confidence interval requires us to assume that the population standard deviation σ is known. In practice, it is more common that σ is not known. The advantage of first learning the method that assumes σ known is that it allows us to use the familiar normal distribution, so we can focus on the basic ideas of confidence intervals. We will learn how to construct confidence intervals when σ is unknown in Section 7.2.

Following are the assumptions for the method we describe.

Explain It Again

$\bar{x}$ **must be approximately normal:** We need assumption 2 to be sure that the sampling distribution of $\bar{x}$ is approximately normal. This allows us to use $z_{\alpha/2}$ as the critical value.

Assumptions for Constructing a Confidence Interval for μ When σ Is Known

   1. We have a simple random sample.

   2. The sample size is large ($n > 30$), or the population is approximately normal.

When these assumptions are met, we can use the following steps to construct a confidence interval for μ when σ is known.

> ## Procedure for Constructing a Confidence Interval for μ When σ Is Known
>
> Check to be sure the assumptions are satisfied. If they are, then proceed with the following steps.
>
> **Step 1:** Find the value of the point estimate $\bar{x}$, if it isn't given.
>
> **Step 2:** Find the critical value $z_{\alpha/2}$ corresponding to the desired confidence level from the last row of Table A.3, from Table A.2, or with technology.
>
> **Step 3:** Find the standard error $\sigma/\sqrt{n}$, and multiply it by the critical value to obtain the margin of error $z_{\alpha/2}\dfrac{\sigma}{\sqrt{n}}$.
>
> **Step 4:** Use the point estimate and the margin of error to construct the confidence interval:
>
> $$\text{Point estimate} \pm \text{Margin of error}$$
>
> $$\bar{x} \pm z_{\alpha/2}\frac{\sigma}{\sqrt{n}}$$
>
> $$\bar{x} - z_{\alpha/2}\frac{\sigma}{\sqrt{n}} < \mu < \bar{x} + z_{\alpha/2}\frac{\sigma}{\sqrt{n}}$$
>
> **Step 5:** Interpret the result.

Rounding off the final result

When constructing a confidence interval for a population mean, you may be given a value for $\bar{x}$, or you may be given the data and have to compute $\bar{x}$ yourself. If you are given the value of $\bar{x}$, round the final result to the same number of decimal places as $\bar{x}$. If you are given data, then round $\bar{x}$ and the final result to one more decimal place than is given in the data.

Although you should round off your final answer, do not round off the calculations you make along the way. Doing so may affect the accuracy of your final answer.

EXAMPLE 7.4

Construct a confidence interval

The mean test score for a simple random sample of $n = 100$ students was $\bar{x} = 67.30$. The population standard deviation of test scores is $\sigma = 15$. Construct a 98% confidence interval for the population mean test score μ.

Solution

First we check the assumptions. The sample is a simple random sample, and the sample size is large ($n > 30$). The assumptions are met, so we may proceed.

Step 1: Find the point estimate. The point estimate is the sample mean $\bar{x} = 67.30$.

Step 2: Find the critical value $z_{\alpha/2}$. The desired confidence level is 98%. We look on the last line of Table A.3 and find that the critical value is $z_{\alpha/2} = 2.326$.

Step 3: Find the standard error and the margin of error. The standard error is

$$\frac{\sigma}{\sqrt{n}} = \frac{15}{\sqrt{100}} = 1.5$$

We multiply the standard error by the critical value to obtain the margin of error:

$$\text{Margin of error} = z_{\alpha/2}\frac{\sigma}{\sqrt{n}} = 2.326(1.5) = 3.489$$

Step 4: Construct the confidence interval. The 98% confidence interval is

$$\bar{x} - z_{\alpha/2}\frac{\sigma}{\sqrt{n}} < \mu < \bar{x} + z_{\alpha/2}\frac{\sigma}{\sqrt{n}}$$

$$67.30 - 3.489 < \mu < 67.30 + 3.489$$

$$63.81 < \mu < 70.79 \quad \text{(rounded to two decimal places, like } \bar{x}\text{)}$$

Step 5: Interpret the result. We are 98% confident that the population mean score μ is between 63.81 and 70.79. Another way to say this is that we are 98% confident that μ is in the interval 67.30 ± 3.49. If we were to draw many different samples and use this method to construct the corresponding confidence intervals, then in the long run, 98% of the intervals would cover the true population mean μ. So unless we were quite unlucky in the sample we drew, the population mean μ will be between 63.81 and 70.79.

Check Your Understanding

4. An IQ test was given to a simple random sample of 75 students at a certain college. The sample mean score was 105.2. Scores on this test are known to have a standard deviation of $\sigma = 10$. It is desired to construct a 90% confidence interval for the mean IQ score of students at this college.
   a. What is the point estimate?
   b. Find the critical value.
   c. Find the standard error.
   d. Find the margin of error.
   e. Construct the 90% confidence interval.
   f. Is it likely that the population mean μ is greater than 100? Explain.

5. The lifetime of a certain type of battery is known to be normally distributed with standard deviation $\sigma = 20$ hours. A sample of 50 batteries had a mean lifetime of 120.1 hours. It is desired to construct a 95% confidence interval for the mean lifetime for this type of battery.
   a. What is the point estimate?
   b. Find the critical value.
   c. Find the standard error.
   d. Find the margin of error.
   e. Construct the 95% confidence interval.
   f. Is it likely that the population mean μ is greater than 130? Explain.

6. In a survey of a simple random sample of students at a certain college, the sample mean time per week spent watching television was 18.3 hours and the margin of error for a 95% confidence interval was 1.2 hours. True or false:
   a. A 95% confidence interval for the mean number of hours per week spent watching television by students at this college is $17.1 < \mu < 19.5$.
   b. Approximately 95% of the students at this university watch between 17.1 and 19.5 hours of television per week.

7. Use the data in Exercise 4 to construct a 95% confidence interval for the mean IQ score.

8. Use the data in Exercise 5 to construct a 98% confidence interval for the mean lifetime for this type of battery.

Answers are on page 306.

Constructing confidence intervals with technology

In Example 7.4, we found a 98% confidence interval for the mean test score, based on a sample size of $n = 100$, a sample mean of $\bar{x} = 67.30$, and a population standard deviation $\sigma = 15$. The following TI-84 Plus display presents the results.

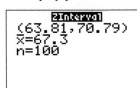

The display presents the confidence interval (63.81, 70.79), along with the values of $\bar{x}$ and n. Note that the confidence level (98%) is not given.

Following is MINITAB output for the same example.

```
The assumed sigma = 15.0000
Variable     N     Mean     StDev     SE Mean          98% CI
Score      100   67.3000   15.0000   1.50000    (63.8105, 70.7895)
```

The output is fairly straightforward. Going from left to right, "N" represents the sample size, "Mean" is the sample mean $\bar{x}$, "StDev" is the population standard deviation σ, and "SE Mean" is the standard error $\sigma/\sqrt{n}$. The lower and upper confidence limits of the 98% confidence interval are given on the right. Note that neither the critical value nor the margin of error is given explicitly in the output.

Step-by-step instructions for constructing confidence intervals with technology are given in the Using Technology section on page 301.

Check Your Understanding

9. To estimate the accuracy of a laboratory scale, a weight known to have a mass of 100 grams is weighed 32 times. The reading of the scale is recorded each time. The following MINITAB output presents a 95% confidence interval for the mean reading of the scale.

```
The assumed sigma = 2.5000
Variable          N      Mean    StDev    SE Mean        95% CI
Scale Reading    32   102.3527   2.5000   0.44194   (101.4865, 103.2189)
```

A scientist claims that the mean reading μ is actually 100 grams. Is it likely that this claim is true?

10. Using the output in Exercise 9:
   a. Find the critical value $z_{\alpha/2}$ for a 99% confidence interval.
   b. Use the critical value along with the information in the output to construct a 99% confidence interval for the mean reading of the scale.

Answers are on page 306.

Objective 3 Describe the relationship between the confidence level and the margin of error

More Confidence Means a Bigger Margin of Error

Other things being equal, it is better to have more confidence than less. We would also rather have a smaller margin of error than a larger one. However, when it comes to confidence intervals, there is a trade-off. If we increase the level of confidence, we must increase the critical value, which in turn increases the margin of error. Examples 7.5 and 7.6 help explain this idea.

EXAMPLE 7.5   Construct a confidence interval

A machine that fills cereal boxes is supposed to put 20 ounces of cereal in each box. A simple random sample of 6 boxes is found to contain a sample mean of 20.25 ounces of cereal. It is known from past experience that the fill weights are normally distributed with a standard deviation of 0.2 ounce. Construct a 90% confidence interval for the mean fill weight.

Solution
We check the assumptions. The sample is a simple random sample, and the population is known to be normal. The assumptions are met, so we may proceed.

Step 1: Find the point estimate. The point estimate is the sample mean $\bar{x} = 20.25$.

Step 2: Find the critical value $z_{\alpha/2}$. The desired confidence level is 90%. We look on the last line of Table A.3 and find that the critical value is $z_{\alpha/2} = 1.645$.

Step 3: Find the standard error and the margin of error. The standard error is

$$\frac{\sigma}{\sqrt{n}} = \frac{0.2}{\sqrt{6}} = 0.08165$$

We multiply the standard error by the critical value to obtain the margin of error:

$$\text{Margin of error} = z_{\alpha/2}\frac{\sigma}{\sqrt{n}} = (1.645)(0.08165) = 0.1343$$

Step 4: Construct the confidence interval. The 90% confidence interval is

$$\bar{x} - z_{\alpha/2}\frac{\sigma}{\sqrt{n}} < \mu < \bar{x} + z_{\alpha/2}\frac{\sigma}{\sqrt{n}}$$

$$20.25 - 0.1343 < \mu < 20.25 + 0.1343$$

$$20.12 < \mu < 20.38 \qquad \text{(rounded to two decimal places, like } \bar{x}\text{)}$$

Step 5: Interpret the result. We are 90% confident that the mean weight μ is between 20.12 and 20.38. Another way to say this is that we are 90% confident that the mean weight μ is in the interval 20.25 ± 0.13. If we were to draw many different samples and use this method to construct the corresponding confidence intervals, then in the long run, 90% of them would cover the true population mean μ. So unless we were somewhat unlucky in the sample we drew, the true mean weight is between 20.12 and 20.38 ounces.

A confidence level of 90% is the lowest level commonly used in practice. In Example 7.6, we will construct a 99% confidence interval.

EXAMPLE 7.6

Construct a confidence interval

Use the data in Example 7.5 to construct a 99% confidence interval for the mean fill weight. Compare the margin of error of this confidence interval to the 90% confidence interval constructed in Example 7.5.

Explain It Again

The relationship between confidence and the margin of error: If we want to increase our confidence that an interval contains the true value, we must increase the critical value. This increases the margin of error, which makes the confidence interval wider.

Solution

As in Example 7.5, the assumptions are met, so we may proceed.

Step 1: Find the point estimate. The point estimate is $\bar{x} = 20.25$.

Step 2: Find the critical value $z_{\alpha/2}$. The desired level is 99%. We look on the last line of Table A.3 and find that $z_{\alpha/2} = 2.576$.

Step 3: Find the standard error and the margin of error. The standard error is

$$\frac{\sigma}{\sqrt{n}} = \frac{0.2}{\sqrt{6}} = 0.08165$$

We multiply the standard error by the critical value to obtain the margin of error:

$$\text{Margin of error} = z_{\alpha/2}\frac{\sigma}{\sqrt{n}} = (2.576)(0.08165) = 0.2103$$

Step 4: Construct the confidence interval. The 99% confidence interval is

$$\bar{x} - z_{\alpha/2}\frac{\sigma}{\sqrt{n}} < \mu < \bar{x} + z_{\alpha/2}\frac{\sigma}{\sqrt{n}}$$

$$20.25 - 0.2103 < \mu < 20.25 + 0.2103$$

$$20.04 < \mu < 20.46 \quad \text{(rounded to two decimal places, like } \bar{x}\text{)}$$

Step 5: Interpret the result. We are 99% confident that the mean weight μ is between 20.04 and 20.46. Another way to say this is that we are 99% confident that the mean weight μ is in the interval 20.25 ± 0.21. If we were to draw many different samples and use this method to construct the corresponding confidence intervals, then in the long run, 99% of them would cover the true population mean μ. So unless we were very unlucky in the sample we drew, the true mean is between 20.04 and 20.46 ounces.

For this 99% confidence interval, the margin of error is 0.2103. For the 90% confidence interval in Example 7.5, the margin of error was only 0.1343. The reason is that for a 90% confidence interval, we used a critical value of 1.645, and for the 99% confidence interval, we must use a larger critical value of 2.576.

We can see that if we want to be more confident that our interval contains the true value, we must increase the critical value, which increases the margin of error. There is a trade-off. We would rather have a higher level of confidence than a lower level, but we would also rather have a smaller margin of error than a larger one. So we have to choose a level of confidence that strikes a good balance. The most common choice is 95%. In some cases where high confidence is very important, a larger confidence level such as 99% may be chosen. In general, intervals with confidence levels less than 90% are not considered to be reliable enough to be used in practical situations.

Figure 7.8 illustrates the trade-off between confidence level and margin of error. One hundred samples were drawn from a population with mean μ. The center diagram presents one hundred 95% confidence intervals, each based on one of these samples. The confidence intervals are all different, because each sample has a different mean $\bar{x}$. The diagram on the left presents 70% confidence intervals based on the same samples. These intervals are narrower because they have a smaller margin of error, but many of them fail to cover the population mean. These intervals are too unreliable to be of any practical value. The figure on the right presents 99.7% confidence intervals. These intervals are very reliable. In the long run, only 3 in 1000 of these intervals will fail to cover the population mean. However, they are wider due to the larger margin of error, so they do not convey as much information.

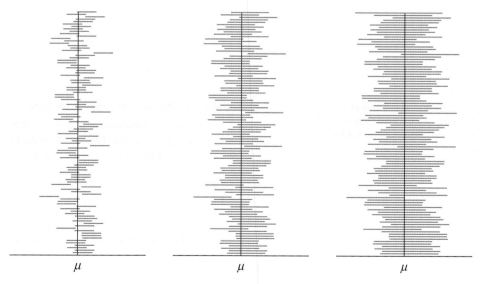

Figure 7.8   *Left:* One hundred 70% confidence intervals for a population mean, each constructed from a different sample. Although their margin of error is small, they cover the population mean only 70% of the time. This low success rate makes the 70% confidence interval unacceptable for practical purposes. *Center:* One hundred 95% confidence intervals constructed from these samples. This represents a good compromise between reliability and margin of error for many purposes. *Right:* One hundred 99.7% confidence intervals constructed from these samples. These intervals cover the population mean 997 times out of 1000. They almost always succeed in covering the population mean, but their margin of error is large.

The confidence level measures the success rate of the method used to construct the confidence interval

The center diagram in Figure 7.8 presents 100 different 95% confidence intervals. When we construct a confidence interval with level 95%, we are essentially getting a look at one of these confidence intervals. However, we don't get to see any of the other confidence intervals, nor do we get to see the vertical line that indicates where the true value μ is. Therefore, we cannot be sure whether we got one of the confidence intervals that covers μ, or whether we were unlucky enough to get one of the unsuccessful ones. What we do know is that our confidence interval was constructed by a method that succeeds 95% of the time. The confidence level describes the success rate of the *method* used to construct a confidence interval, not the success of any particular interval.

Check Your Understanding

11. To determine how well a new method of teaching vocabulary is working in a certain elementary school, education researchers plan to give a vocabulary test to a sample of 100 sixth-graders. It is known that scores on this test have a standard deviation of 8. The researchers plan to compute the sample mean $\bar{x}$, then construct a 95% confidence interval for the population mean test score.
    a. What is the critical value $z_{\alpha/2}$ for this confidence interval?
    b. Find the margin of error for this confidence interval.
    c. Let m represent the margin of error for this confidence interval. For what percentage of all samples will the confidence interval $\bar{x} \pm m$ cover the true population mean?

12. The researchers now plan to construct a 99% confidence interval for the test scores described in Exercise 11.
    a. What is the critical value $z_{\alpha/2}$ for this confidence interval?
    b. Find the margin of error for this confidence interval.
    c. Let m represent the margin of error for this confidence interval. For what percentage of all samples will the confidence interval $\bar{x} \pm m$ cover the true population mean?

Answers are on page 306.

Objective 4 Find the sample size necessary to obtain a confidence interval of a given width

Finding the Necessary Sample Size

We have seen that we can make the margin of error smaller if we are willing to reduce our level of confidence. We can also reduce the margin of error by increasing the sample size. We can see this by looking at the formula for margin of error:

$$m = z_{\alpha/2}\frac{\sigma}{\sqrt{n}}$$

Since the sample size n appears in the denominator, making it larger will make the value of m smaller. We will show how we can manipulate this formula using algebra to express the sample size n in terms of the margin of error m.

$$m = z_{\alpha/2}\frac{\sigma}{\sqrt{n}}$$

$$m\sqrt{n} = \frac{z_{\alpha/2}\cdot\sigma}{\sqrt{n}}\sqrt{n} \qquad \text{(Multiply both sides by } \sqrt{n}\text{)}$$

$$\frac{m\sqrt{n}}{m} = \frac{z_{\alpha/2}\cdot\sigma}{m} \qquad \text{(Divide both sides by } m\text{)}$$

$$n = \left(\frac{z_{\alpha/2}\cdot\sigma}{m}\right)^2 \qquad \text{(Square both sides)}$$

With this formula, if we know how small we want the margin of error to be, we can compute the sample size needed to achieve the desired margin of error.

SUMMARY

Let *m* be the desired margin of error. Let σ be the population standard deviation, and let $z_{\alpha/2}$ be the critical value for a confidence interval. The sample size *n* needed so that the confidence interval will have margin of error *m* is given by

$$n = \left(\frac{z_{\alpha/2} \cdot \sigma}{m}\right)^2$$

If the value of *n* given by the formula is not a whole number, round it *up* to the nearest whole number. By rounding up, we can be sure that the margin of error is no greater than the desired value *m*.

EXAMPLE 7.7 **Finding the necessary sample size**

Scientists want to estimate the mean weight of mice after they have been fed a special diet. From previous studies, it is known that the weight is normally distributed with standard deviation 3 grams. How many mice must be weighed so that a 95% confidence interval will have a margin of error of 0.5 gram?

Solution

Since we want a 95% confidence interval, we use $z_{\alpha/2} = 1.96$. We are also given $\sigma = 3$ and $m = 0.5$. We therefore use the formula as follows:

$$n = \left(\frac{z_{\alpha/2} \cdot \sigma}{m}\right)^2 = \left(\frac{1.96 \cdot 3}{0.5}\right)^2 = 138.30; \quad \text{round up to } 139$$

We must weigh 139 mice in order to obtain a 95% confidence interval with a margin of error of 0.5 gram.

Factors that limit sample size

Since larger sample sizes result in narrower confidence intervals, it is natural to wonder why we don't always collect a large sample when we want to construct a confidence interval. In practice, the size of the sample that is feasible to obtain is often limited. In some cases, an expensive experimental procedure must be repeated each time an observation is made. For example, studies of automobile safety that require the crashing of new cars are not likely to have large sample sizes. Sometimes ethical considerations restrict the sample size. For example, when a new drug is being tested, there is a risk of adverse health effects to the subjects who take the drug. It is important that the sample size not be larger than necessary, to limit the health risk to as few people as possible.

Check Your Understanding

13. A machine used to fill beverage cans is supposed to put exactly 12 ounces of beverage in each can, but the actual amount varies randomly from can to can. The population standard deviation is $\sigma = 0.05$ ounce. A simple random sample of filled cans will have their volumes measured, and a 95% confidence interval for the mean fill volume will be constructed. How many cans must be sampled for the margin of error to be equal to 0.01 ounce?

14. An IQ test is designed to have scores that have a standard deviation of $\sigma = 15$. A simple random sample of students at a large university will be given the test in order to construct a 98% confidence interval for the mean IQ of all students at the university. How many students must be tested so that the margin of error will be equal to 3 points?

Answers are on page 306.

Distinguish Between Confidence and Probability

In Example 7.6, a 99% confidence interval for the population mean weight μ was computed to be $20.04 < \mu < 20.46$. It is tempting to say that the probability is 99% that μ is between 20.04 and 20.46. This, however, is not correct. The term *probability* refers to random events, which can come out differently when experiments are repeated. The numbers 20.04 and 20.46 are fixed, not random. The population mean is also fixed. The population mean weight is either between 20.04 and 20.46 or it is not. There is no randomness involved. Therefore, we say that we have 99% *confidence* (not probability) that the population mean is in this interval.

On the other hand, let's say that we are discussing a *method* used to construct a 99% confidence interval. The method will succeed in covering the population mean 99% of the time, and fail the other 1% of the time. In this case, whether the population mean is covered or not is a random event, because it can vary from experiment to experiment. Therefore it *is* correct to say that a *method* for constructing a 99% confidence interval has probability 99% of covering the population mean.

EXAMPLE 7.8

Interpreting a confidence level

A hospital administrator plans to draw a simple random sample of 100 records of patients who were admitted for cardiac bypass surgery. She will compute the sample mean number of days spent in the hospital, and construct a 95% confidence interval for the population mean, using an appropriate method. She claims that the probability is 0.95 that the confidence interval will cover the population mean. Is she right?

Solution

Yes, she is right. The probability that a 95% confidence interval constructed by an appropriate method will cover the true value is 0.95.

EXAMPLE 7.9

Interpreting a confidence interval

Refer to Example 7.8. After drawing the sample, the hospital administrator constructs the 95% confidence interval, and it turns out to be $7.1 < \mu < 7.5$. The administrator claims that the probability is 0.95 that the population mean is between 7.1 and 7.5. Is she right?

Solution

No, she is not right. Once a specific confidence interval has been constructed, there is no more probability. She should say that she is 95% confident that the population mean is between 7.1 and 7.5.

Check Your Understanding

15. A scientist plans to construct a 95% confidence interval for the mean length of steel rods that are manufactured by a certain process. She will draw a simple random sample of rods and compute the confidence interval using the methods described in this section. She says, "The probability is 95% that the population mean length will be covered by the confidence interval." Is she right? Explain.

16. The scientist in Exercise 15 constructs the 95% confidence interval for the mean length in centimeters, and it turns out to be $25.1 < \mu < 27.2$. She says, "The probability is 95% that the population mean length is between 25.1 and 27.2 centimeters." Is she right? Explain.

Answers are on page 306.

USING TECHNOLOGY

We use Example 7.4 to illustrate the technology steps.

TI-84 PLUS

Constructing a confidence interval for the mean when σ is known

Step 1. Press **STAT** and highlight the **TESTS** menu.

Step 2. Select **ZInterval** and press **ENTER** (Figure A). The **ZInterval** menu appears.

Step 3. For **Inpt**, select the **Stats** option and enter the values of σ, $\bar{x}$, and n. For Example 7.4, we use $\sigma = 15$, $\bar{x} = 67.30$, and $n = 100$.

Step 4. In the **C-Level** field, enter the confidence level. For Example 7.4, we use 0.98 (Figure B).

Step 5. Highlight **Calculate** and press **ENTER** (Figure C).

Note that if the raw data are given, the **ZInterval** command may be used by selecting **Data** as the **Inpt** option and entering the location of the data as the **List** option (Figure D).

Figure A

Figure B

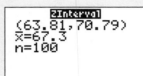

Figure C   **Figure D**

MINITAB

Constructing a confidence interval for the mean when σ is known

Step 1. Click on **Stat**, then **Basic Statistics**, then **1-Sample Z**.

Step 2. Choose one of the following:
- If the summary statistics are given, click **Summarized Data** and enter the **Sample Size** (100), the **Sample Mean** (67.30), and the **Standard Deviation** (15) (Figure E).
- If the raw data are given, click **Samples in Columns** and select the column that contains the data. Enter the **Standard Deviation**.

Step 3. Click **Options** and enter the confidence level in the **Confidence Level** (98) field. Click OK.

Step 4. Click **OK** (Figure F).

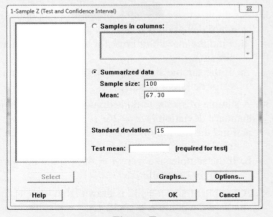

Figure E

One-Sample Z

The assumed standard deviation = 15

N	Mean	SE Mean	98% CI
100	67.3000	1.5000	(63.8105, 70.7895)

Figure F

EXCEL

Constructing a confidence interval for the mean when σ is known

This procedure requires the **MegaStat** EXCEL add-in to be loaded. The **MegaStat** add-in may be downloaded from www.mhhe.com/megastat.

Step 1. Load the **MegaStat** EXCEL add-in.

Step 2. Click on the **MegaStat** menu and select **Confidence Intervals/Sample Size...**

Step 3. Enter the sample mean from Example 7.4 in the **Mean** field (67.30), the standard deviation in the **Std. Dev.** field (15), and the sample size in the **n** field (100). Choose the **z** option for the critical value.

Step 4. In the **Confidence Level** field, enter the confidence level. For Example 7.4, enter **98%** (Figure G).

Step 5. Click **OK** (Figure H).

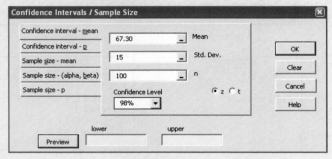

Figure G	**Figure H**

SECTION 7.1 Exercises

Exercises 1–16 are the Check Your Understanding exercises located within the section.

Understanding the Concepts

In Exercises 17–20, fill in each blank with the appropriate word or phrase.

17. A single number that estimates the value of an unknown parameter is called a _____ estimate.

18. The margin of error is the product of the standard error and the _____ .

19. In the confidence interval 24.3 ± 1.2, the quantity 1.2 is called the _____ .

20. If we increase the confidence level and keep the sample size the same, we _____ the margin of error.

In Exercises 21–24, determine whether the statement is true or false. If the statement is false, rewrite it as a true statement.

21. The confidence level is the proportion of all possible samples for which the confidence interval will cover the true value.

22. To construct a confidence interval for a population mean, we add and subtract the critical value from the point estimate.

23. Increasing the sample size while keeping the confidence level the same will result in a narrower confidence interval.

24. If a 95% confidence interval for a population mean is $1.7 < \mu < 2.3$, then the probability is 0.95 that the mean is between 1.7 and 2.3.

Practicing the Skills

In Exercises 25–28, find the critical value $z_{\alpha/2}$ needed to construct a confidence interval with the given level.

25. Level 95%   **26.** Level 85%

27. Level 96%   **28.** Level 99.7%

In Exercises 29–32, find the levels of the confidence intervals that have the given critical values.

29. 2.326   **30.** 2.576   **31.** 2.81   **32.** 1.04

33. A sample of size $n = 49$ is drawn from a population whose standard deviation is $\sigma = 4.8$.

  a. Find the margin of error for a 95% confidence interval for μ.

  b. If the sample size were $n = 60$, would the margin of error be larger or smaller?

34. A sample of size $n = 50$ is drawn from a population whose standard deviation is $\sigma = 26$.

  a. Find the margin of error for a 90% confidence interval for μ.

  b. If the sample size were $n = 40$, would the margin of error be larger or smaller?

35. A sample of size $n = 32$ is drawn from a population whose standard deviation is $\sigma = 12.1$.

  a. Find the margin of error for a 99% confidence interval for μ.

  b. If the confidence level were 90%, would the margin of error be larger or smaller?

36. A sample of size $n = 64$ is drawn from a population whose standard deviation is $\sigma = 24.18$.

  a. Find the margin of error for a 95% confidence interval for μ.

  b. If the confidence level were 98%, would the margin of error be larger or smaller?

37. A sample of size $n = 10$ is drawn from a normal population whose standard deviation is $\sigma = 2.5$. The sample mean is $\bar{x} = 7.92$.

  a. Construct a 95% confidence interval for μ.

  b. If the population were not approximately normal, would the confidence interval constructed in part (a) be valid? Explain.

38. A sample of size $n = 80$ is drawn from a normal population whose standard deviation is $\sigma = 6.8$. The sample mean is $\bar{x} = 40.41$.

  a. Construct a 90% confidence interval for μ.

  b. If the population were not approximately normal, would the confidence interval constructed in part (a) be valid? Explain.

39. A population has standard deviation $\sigma = 21.3$.

  a. How large a sample must be drawn so that a 99% confidence interval for μ will have a margin of error equal to 2.5?

  b. If the required confidence level were 95%, would the necessary sample size be larger or smaller?

40. A population has standard deviation $\sigma = 17.3$.

  a. How large a sample must be drawn so that a 95% confidence interval for μ will have a margin of error equal to 1.4?

  b. If the required confidence level were 98%, would the necessary sample size be larger or smaller?

41. A population has standard deviation $\sigma = 12.7$.

  a. How large a sample must be drawn so that a 96% confidence interval for μ will have a margin of error equal to 2.5?

  b. If the required margin of error were 1.5, would the necessary sample size be larger or smaller?

42. A population has standard deviation $\sigma = 9.2$.

  a. How large a sample must be drawn so that a 92% confidence interval for μ will have a margin of error equal to 0.8?

  b. If the required margin of error were 1.4, would the necessary sample size be larger or smaller?

Working with the Concepts

43. SAT scores: A college admissions officer takes a simple random sample of 100 entering freshmen and computes their mean mathematics SAT score to be 458. Assume the population standard deviation is $\sigma = 116$.

  a. Construct a 99% confidence interval for the mean mathematics SAT score for the entering freshman class.

  b. If the sample size were 75 rather than 100, would the margin of error be larger or smaller than the result in part (a)? Explain.

  c. If the confidence level were 95% rather than 99%, would the margin of error be larger or smaller than the result in part (a)? Explain.

  d. Based on the confidence interval constructed in part (a), is it likely that the mean mathematics SAT score for the entering freshman class is greater than 500?

44. How many computers? In a simple random sample of 150 households, the sample mean number of personal computers was 1.32. Assume the population standard deviation is $\sigma = 0.41$.

  a. Construct a 95% confidence interval for the mean number of personal computers.

  b. If the sample size were 100 rather than 150, would the margin of error be larger or smaller than the result in part (a)? Explain.

  c. If the confidence level were 98% rather than 95%, would the margin of error be larger or smaller than the result in part (a)? Explain.

  d. Based on the confidence interval constructed in part (a), is it likely that the mean number of personal computers is greater than 1.25?

45. Babies: According to the National Health Statistics Reports, a sample of 360 one-year-old baby boys in the United States had a mean weight of 25.5 pounds. Assume the population standard deviation is $\sigma = 5.3$ pounds.

  a. Construct a 95% confidence interval for the mean weight of all one-year-old baby boys in the United States

  b. Should this confidence interval be used to estimate the mean weight of all one-year-old babies in the United States? Explain.

  c. Based on the confidence interval constructed in part (a), is it likely that the mean weight of all one-year-old boys is less than 28 pounds?

46. Watch your cholesterol: A sample of 314 patients between the ages of 38 and 82 were given a combination of the drugs ezetimibe and simvastatin. They achieved a mean reduction in total cholesterol of 0.94 millimole per liter. Assume the population standard deviation is $\sigma = 0.18$.

  a. Construct a 98% confidence interval for the mean reduction in total cholesterol in patients who take this combination of drugs.

  b. Should this confidence interval be used to estimate the mean reduction in total cholesterol for patients over the age of 85? Explain.

  c. Based on the confidence interval constructed in part (a), is it likely that the mean reduction in cholesterol level is less than 0.90?

  Source: *International Journal of Clinical Practice* 58:653–658

47. How smart is your phone? A random sample of 11 BlackBerry Bold 9000 smartphones being sold over the Internet in 2010 had the following prices, in dollars:

230	484	379	300	239	350
300	395	230	410	460	

Assume the population standard deviation is $\sigma = 71$.

a. Explain why it is necessary to check whether the population is approximately normal before constructing a confidence interval.

b. Following is a dotplot of these data. Is it reasonable to assume that the population is approximately normal?

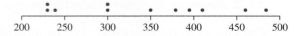

c. If appropriate, construct a 95% confidence interval for the mean price for all phones of this type being sold on the Internet in 2010. If not appropriate, explain why not.

48. Stock prices: The Standard and Poor's (S&P) 500 is a group of 500 of the largest companies traded on the New York Stock Exchange. Following are prices, in dollars, for a random sample of ten stocks on August 2, 2010.

51.02	23.29	211.91	32.84	21.77
20.42	61.93	42.35	16.38	48.69

a. Explain why it is necessary to check whether the population is approximately normal before constructing a confidence interval.

b. Following is a dotplot of these data. Is it reasonable to assume that the population is approximately normal?

```
   •• • •• •                    •
 +----+----+----+----+----+----+
 0    50  100  150  200  250
```

c. If appropriate, construct a 95% confidence interval for the mean price for all S&P 500 stocks on this day. If not appropriate, explain why not.

49. Lifetime of electronics: In a simple random sample of 100 electronic components produced by a certain method, the mean lifetime was 125 hours. Assume that component lifetimes are normally distributed with population standard deviation $\sigma = 20$ hours.

a. Construct a 98% confidence interval for the mean battery life.

b. Find the sample size needed so that a 99% confidence interval will have a margin of error of 3.

50. Efficient manufacturing: Efficiency experts study the processes used to manufacture items in order to make them as efficient as possible. One of the steps used to manufacture a metal clamp involves the drilling of three holes. In a sample of 75 clamps, the mean time to complete this step was 50.1 seconds. Assume that the population standard deviation is $\sigma = 10$ seconds.

a. Construct a 95% confidence interval for the mean time needed to complete this step.

b. Find the sample size needed so that a 98% confidence interval will have margin of error of 1.5.

51. Different levels: Joe and Sally are going to construct confidence intervals from the same simple random sample. Joe's confidence interval will have level 90% and Sally's will have level 95%.

a. Which confidence interval will have the larger margin of error? Or will they both be the same?

b. Which confidence interval is more likely to cover the population mean? Or are they both equally likely to do so?

52. Different levels: Bertha and Todd are going to construct confidence intervals from the same simple random sample. Bertha's confidence interval will have level 98% and Todd's will have level 95%.

a. Which confidence interval will have the larger margin of error? Or will they both be the same?

b. Which confidence interval is more likely to cover the population mean? Or are they both equally likely to do so?

53. Different standard deviations: Maria and Bob are going to construct confidence intervals from different simple random samples. Both confidence intervals will have level 95%. Maria's sample comes from a population with standard deviation $\sigma = 1$, and Bob's comes from a population with $\sigma = 2$. Both sample sizes are the same.

a. Which confidence interval will have the larger margin of error? Or will they both be the same?

b. Which confidence interval is more likely to cover the population mean? Or are they both equally likely to do so?

54. Different standard deviations: Martin and Bianca are going to construct confidence intervals from different simple random samples. Both confidence intervals will have level 99%. Martin's sample comes from a population with standard deviation $\sigma = 25$, and Bianca's comes from a population with $\sigma = 18$. Both sample sizes are the same.

a. Which confidence interval will have the larger margin of error? Or will they both be the same?

b. Which confidence interval is more likely to cover the population mean? Or are they both equally likely to do so?

55. Which interval is which? Sam constructed three confidence intervals, all from the same random sample. The confidence levels are 90%, 95%, and 99%. The confidence intervals are $5.6 < \mu < 14.4$, $7.2 < \mu < 12.8$, and $6.6 < \mu < 13.4$. Unfortunately, Sam has forgotten which confidence interval has which level. Match each confidence interval with its level.

56. Which interval is which? Matilda has constructed three confidence intervals, all from the same random sample. The confidence levels are 95%, 98%, and 99.9%. The confidence intervals are $6.4 < \mu < 12.3$, $5.1 < \mu < 13.6$, and $6.8 < \mu < 11.9$. Unfortunately, Matilda has forgotten which confidence interval has which level. Match each confidence interval with its level.

57. Don't construct a confidence interval: A psychology professor at a certain college gave a test to the students in her class. The test was designed to measure students' attitudes toward school, with higher scores indicating a more positive attitude. There were 30 students in the class, and their mean score was 78. Scores on this test are known to be normally distributed with a standard deviation of 10. Explain why these data should not be used to construct a confidence interval for the mean score for all the students in the college.

58. Don't construct a confidence interval: A college alumni organization sent a survey to all recent graduates to ask their annual income. Twenty percent of the alumni responded, and their mean annual income was $40,000. Assume the population standard deviation is $\sigma = \$10,000$. Explain why these data should not be used to construct a confidence interval for the mean annual income of all recent graduates.

59. Interpret a confidence interval: A dean at a certain college looked up the GPA for a random sample of 85 students. The sample mean GPA was 2.82, and a 95% confidence interval for the mean GPA of all students in the college was $2.76 < \mu < 2.88$. True or false, and explain:
a. We are 95% confident that the mean GPA of all students in the college is between 2.76 and 2.88.
b. We are 95% confident that the mean GPA of all students in the sample is between 2.76 and 2.88.
c. The probability is 0.95 that the mean GPA of all students in the college is between 2.76 and 2.88.
d. 95% of the students in the sample had a GPA between 2.76 and 2.88.

60. Interpret a confidence interval: A survey organization drew a simple random sample of 625 households from a city of 100,000 households. The sample mean number of people in the 625 households was 2.30, and a 99% confidence interval for the mean number of people in the 100,000 households was $2.16 < \mu < 2.44$. True or false, and explain:
a. We are 95% confident that the mean number of people in the 625 households is between 2.16 and 2.44.
b. We are 95% confident that the mean number of people in the 100,000 households is between 2.16 and 2.44.
c. The probability is 0.95 that the mean number of people in the 100,000 households is between 2.16 and 2.44.
d. 95% of the households in the sample contain between 2.16 and 2.44 people.

61. Interpret calculator display: The following display from a TI-84 Plus calculator presents a 95% confidence interval.

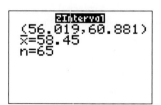

a. Fill in the blanks: We are _____ confident that the population mean is between _____ and _____ .
b. Assume the population is not normally distributed. Is the confidence interval still valid? Explain.

62. Interpret calculator display: The following display from a TI-84 Plus calculator presents a 99% confidence interval.

```
ZInterval
(17.012,20.048)
x̄=18.53
n=15
```

a. Fill in the blanks: We are _____ confident that the population mean is between _____ and _____ .

b. Assume the population is not normally distributed. Is the confidence interval still valid? Explain.

63. Interpret computer output: The following MINITAB output presents a 95% confidence interval.

```
The assumed sigma = 6.5000
Variable   N    Mean    SE Mean      95% CI
     X    23  12.352    1.3553   (9.6956,15.0084)
```

a. Fill in the blanks: We are _____ confident that the population mean is between _____ and _____ .
b. Use the appropriate critical value along with the information in the computer output to construct a 99% confidence interval.
c. Find the sample size needed so that the 95% confidence interval will have a margin of error of 1.5.
d. Find the sample size needed so that the 99% confidence interval will have a margin of error of 1.5.

64. Interpret computer output: The following MINITAB output presents a 98% confidence interval.

```
The assumed sigma = 8.0000
Variable   N    Mean    SE Mean      98% CI
     X    58   2.657    1.0505   (0.2133, 5.1007)
```

a. Fill in the blanks: We are _____ confident that the population mean is between _____ and _____ .
b. Use the appropriate critical value along with the information in the computer output to construct a 95% confidence interval.
c. Find the sample size needed so that the 98% confidence interval will have a margin of error of 1.0.
d. Find the sample size needed so that the 95% confidence interval will have a margin of error of 1.0.

Extending the Concepts

One-sided confidence intervals: A confidence interval provides likely minimum and maximum values for a parameter. In some cases, we are interested only in a maximum or only in a minimum. In these cases, we construct a *one-sided confidence interval*. A one-sided confidence interval can be an *upper confidence bound*, which has the form $\bar{x} + z_\alpha \sigma/\sqrt{n}$, or a *lower confidence bound*, which has the form $\bar{x} - z_\alpha \sigma/\sqrt{n}$. Note that the critical value is z_α rather than $z_{\alpha/2}$.

65. Computers in the classroom: A simple random sample of 50 middle-school children participated in an experimental class designed to introduce them to computer programming. At the end of the class, the students took a final exam to assess their learning. The sample mean score was 78 points, and the population standard deviation is 8 points. Compute a lower 99% confidence bound for the mean score.

66. Charge it: A random sample of 75 charges on a credit card had a mean of $56.85, and the population standard deviation is $21.08. Compute an upper 95% confidence bound for the mean amount charged.

Answers to Check Your Understanding Exercises for Section 7.1

1. **a.** 1.645   **b.** 2.326   **c.** 2.81   **d.** 1.28

2. **a.** 95%   **b.** 97%   **c.** 80%   **d.** 99.9%

3. **a.** 2.352   **b.** 1.030   **c.** 5.758 [Tech: 5.757]   **d.** 6.397

4. **a.** 105.2   **b.** 1.645   **c.** 1.1547   **d.** 1.90

   e. $103.3 < \mu < 107.1$

   f. Yes. We are 90% confident that μ is between 103.3 and 107.1, so it is likely that $\mu > 100$.

5. **a.** 120.1   **b.** 1.96   **c.** 2.8284   **d.** 5.54

   e. $114.6 < \mu < 125.6$

   f. No. We are 95% confident that μ is between 114.6 and 125.6, so it is not likely that $\mu > 130$.

6. **a.** True   **b.** False

7. $102.7 < \mu < 107.3$

8. $113.5 < \mu < 126.7$

9. The confidence interval does not contain the value 100. Therefore, it is not likely that the claim that $\mu = 100$ is true.

10. **a.** 2.576   **b.** $101.2143 < \mu < 103.4911$

11. **a.** 1.96   **b.** 1.568   **c.** 95%

12. **a.** 2.576   **b.** 2.061   **c.** 99%

13. 97

14. 136

15. Yes, the probability that a 95% confidence interval constructed by an appropriate method will cover the true value is 0.95.

16. No. Once a specific confidence interval is constructed, there is no probability attached to it.

SECTION 7.2   Confidence Intervals for a Population Mean, Standard Deviation Unknown

Objectives

1. Describe the properties of the Student's t distribution
2. Construct confidence intervals for a population mean when the population standard deviation is unknown

Objective 1 Describe the properties of the Student's t distribution

The Student's t Distribution

In Section 7.1, we showed how to construct a confidence interval for the mean μ of a normal population when the population standard deviation σ is known. The confidence interval is

$$\bar{x} \pm z_{\alpha/2} \frac{\sigma}{\sqrt{n}}$$

The critical value is $z_{\alpha/2}$ because the quantity

$$\frac{\bar{x} - \mu}{\sigma/\sqrt{n}}$$

has a normal distribution.

In practice, it is more common that σ is unknown. When we don't know the value of σ, we replace it with the sample standard deviation s. However, we cannot then use $z_{\alpha/2}$ as the critical value, because the quantity

$$\frac{\bar{x} - \mu}{s/\sqrt{n}}$$

does not have a normal distribution. One reason is that s is, on the average, a bit smaller than σ, so replacing σ with s tends to increase the magnitude. Another reason is that s is random whereas σ is constant, so replacing σ with s increases the spread.

The distribution of this quantity is called the **Student's t distribution**. It was discovered in 1908 by William Sealy Gosset, a statistician who worked for the Guinness Brewing Company in Dublin, Ireland. The management at Guinness considered the discovery to be proprietary information, and forbade Gosset to publish it. He published it anyway, using the pseudonym "Student."

In fact, there are many different Student's t distributions; they are distinguished by a quantity called the **degrees of freedom**. When using the Student's t distribution to construct a confidence interval for a population mean, the number of degrees of freedom is 1 less than the sample size.

Recall: Degrees of freedom were introduced in Section 3.2.

Degrees of Freedom for the Student's *t* Distribution

When constructing a confidence interval for a population mean, the number of degrees of freedom for the Student's t distribution is 1 less than the sample size n.

$$\text{number of degrees of freedom} = n - 1$$

Figure 7.9 presents t distributions for several different degrees of freedom, along with a standard normal distribution for comparison. The t distributions are symmetric and unimodal, just like the normal distribution. The t distribution is more spread out than the standard normal distribution, because the sample standard deviation s is, on the average, a bit less than σ. When the number of degrees of freedom is small, this tendency is more pronounced, so the t distributions are much more spread out than the normal. When the number of degrees of freedom is large, s tends to be very close to σ, so the t distribution is very close to the normal. Figure 7.9 shows that with 10 degrees of freedom, the difference between the t distribution and the normal is not great. If a t distribution with 30 degrees of freedom were plotted in Figure 7.9, it would be indistinguishable from the normal distribution.

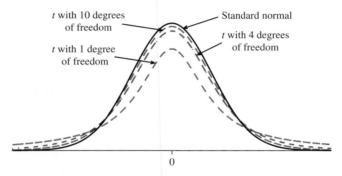

Figure 7.9   Plots of the Student's t distribution for 1, 4, and 10 degrees of freedom. The standard normal distribution is plotted for comparison. The t distributions are more spread out than the normal, but the amount of extra spread decreases as the number of degrees of freedom increases.

SUMMARY

The Student's t distribution has the following properties:

- It is symmetric and unimodal.
- It is more spread out than the standard normal distribution.
- If we increase the number of degrees of freedom, the Student's t curve becomes closer to the standard normal curve.

Finding the critical value

We use the Student's t distribution to construct confidence intervals for μ when σ is unknown. The idea behind the critical value is the same as for the normal distribution. To find the critical value for a confidence interval with a given level, let $1 - \alpha$ be the confidence level expressed as a decimal. The critical value is then $t_{\alpha/2}$, because the area under the Student's t curve between $-t_{\alpha/2}$ and $t_{\alpha/2}$ is $1 - \alpha$. See Figure 7.10. The critical value $t_{\alpha/2}$ can be found in Table A.3, in the row corresponding to the number of degrees of freedom and the column corresponding to the desired confidence level. Example 7.10 shows how to find a critical value.

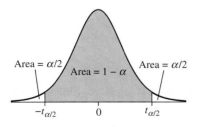

Figure 7.10

EXAMPLE 7.10   Finding a critical value

A simple random sample of size 10 is drawn from a normal population. Find the critical value $t_{\alpha/2}$ for a 95% confidence interval.

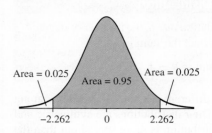

Area = 0.025

Area = 0.95

Area = 0.025

−2.262 0 2.262

Figure 7.11 95% of the area under the Student's t curve with 9 degrees of freedom is between $t = -2.262$ and $t = 2.262$.

Solution

The sample size is $n = 10$, so the number of degrees of freedom is $n - 1 = 9$. We consult Table A.3, looking in the row corresponding to 9 degrees of freedom, and in the column with confidence level 95% (the confidence levels are listed along the bottom of the table). The critical value is $t_{\alpha/2} = 2.262$. See Figure 7.11.

⋮	⋮	⋮	⋮	⋮	⋮	⋮	⋮	⋮	⋮	⋮
4	0.271	0.741	1.533	2.132	2.776	3.747	4.604	5.598	7.173	8.610
5	0.267	0.727	1.476	2.015	2.571	3.365	4.032	4.773	5.893	6.869
6	0.265	0.718	1.440	1.943	2.447	3.143	3.707	4.317	5.208	5.959
7	0.263	0.711	1.415	1.895	2.365	2.998	3.499	4.029	4.785	5.408
8	0.262	0.706	1.397	1.860	2.306	2.896	3.355	3.833	4.501	5.041
9	0.261	0.703	1.383	1.833	**2.262**	2.821	3.250	3.690	4.297	4.781
10	0.260	0.700	1.372	1.812	2.228	2.764	3.169	3.581	4.144	4.587
11	0.260	0.697	1.363	1.796	2.201	2.718	3.106	3.497	4.025	4.437
12	0.259	0.695	1.356	1.782	2.179	2.681	3.055	3.428	3.930	4.318
13	0.259	0.694	1.350	1.771	2.160	2.650	3.012	3.372	3.852	4.221
14	0.258	0.692	1.345	1.761	2.145	2.624	2.977	3.326	3.787	4.140
⋮	⋮	⋮	⋮	⋮	⋮	⋮	⋮	⋮	⋮	⋮
	20%	50%	80%	90%	95%	98%	99%	99.5%	99.8%	99.9%

Confidence Level

What if the number of degrees of freedom isn't in the table?

The largest number of degrees of freedom shown in Table A.3 is 200. If the desired number of degrees of freedom is less than 200 and is not shown in Table A.3, use the next smaller number of degrees of freedom in the table. If the desired number of degrees of freedom is more than 200, use the z-value found in the last row of Table A.3, or use Table A.2. This problem will not arise if a calculator or computer is used to construct a confidence interval, because technology can compute critical values for any number of degrees of freedom.

SUMMARY

If the desired number of degrees of freedom isn't listed in Table A.3, then

- If the desired number is less than 200, use the next smaller number that is in the table.
- If the desired number is greater than 200, use the z-value found in the last row of Table A.3, or use Table A.2.

EXAMPLE 7.11

Finding a critical value

Use Table A.3 to find the critical value for a 99% confidence interval for a sample of size 58.

Solution

Because the sample size is 58, there are 57 degrees of freedom. The number 57 doesn't appear in the degrees of freedom column in Table A.3, so we use the next smaller number that does appear, which is 50. The value of $t_{\alpha/2}$ corresponding to a confidence level of 99% is $t_{\alpha/2} = 2.678$.

Following are the assumptions that are necessary to construct confidence intervals by using the Student's t distribution.

Explain It Again

$\bar{x}$ **must be approximately normal:** We need assumption 2 to be sure that the sampling distribution of $\bar{x}$ is approximately normal.

Assumptions for Constructing a Confidence Interval for μ When σ Is Unknown

1. We have a simple random sample.
2. Either the sample size is large ($n > 30$), *or* the population is approximately normal.

Checking the assumptions

When the sample size is small ($n \leq 30$), we must check to determine whether the sample comes from a population that is approximately normal. This can be done using the methods described in Section 6.6. A simple method is to draw a dotplot or boxplot of the sample. If there are no outliers, and if the sample is not strongly skewed, then it is reasonable to construct a confidence interval using the Student's t distribution.

Check Your Understanding

1. Use Table A.3 to find the critical value $t_{\alpha/2}$ needed to construct a confidence interval of the given level with the given sample size:
   a. Level 95%, sample size 15
   b. Level 99%, sample size 22
   c. Level 90%, sample size 63
   d. Level 95%, sample size 2

2. In each of the following situations, state whether the methods of this section should be used to construct a confidence interval for the population mean. Assume that σ is unknown.
   a. A simple random sample of size 8 is drawn from a distribution that is approximately normal.
   b. A simple random sample of size 15 is drawn from a distribution that is not close to normal.
   c. A simple random sample of size 150 is drawn from a distribution that is not close to normal.
   d. A nonrandom sample is drawn.

Answers are on page 317.

Objective 2 Construct confidence intervals for a population mean when the population standard deviation is unknown

Constructing a Confidence Interval for μ When σ Is Unknown

The ingredients for a confidence interval for a population mean μ when σ is unknown are the point estimate $\bar{x}$, the critical value $t_{\alpha/2}$, and the standard error $s/\sqrt{n}$. The margin of error is $t_{\alpha/2}s/\sqrt{n}$. When the assumptions for the Student's t distribution are met, we can use the following step-by-step procedure for constructing a confidence interval for a population mean.

Procedure for Constructing a Confidence Interval for μ When σ Is Unknown

Check to be sure the assumptions are satisfied. If they are, then proceed with the following steps.

Step 1: Compute the sample mean $\bar{x}$ and sample standard deviation s, if they are not given.

Step 2: Find the number of degrees of freedom $n - 1$ and the critical value $t_{\alpha/2}$.

Step 3: Compute the standard error $s/\sqrt{n}$ and multiply it by the critical value to obtain the margin of error $t_{\alpha/2}\dfrac{s}{\sqrt{n}}$.

Step 4: Use the point estimate and the margin of error to construct the confidence interval:

$$\text{Point estimate} \pm \text{Margin of error}$$

$$\bar{x} \pm t_{\alpha/2}\frac{s}{\sqrt{n}}$$

$$\bar{x} - t_{\alpha/2}\frac{s}{\sqrt{n}} < \mu < \bar{x} + t_{\alpha/2}\frac{s}{\sqrt{n}}$$

Step 5: Interpret the result.

EXAMPLE 7.12

Constructing a confidence interval

The General Social Survey is a survey of opinions and lifestyles of U.S. adults, conducted by the National Opinion Research Center at the University of Chicago. A sample of 123 people aged 18–22 reported the number of hours they spent on the Internet in an average week. The sample mean was 8.20 hours, with a sample standard deviation of 9.84 hours. Assume this is a simple random sample from the population of people aged 18–22 in the United States. Construct a 95% confidence interval for μ, the population mean number of hours per week spent on the Internet by people aged 18–22 in the United States.

Solution

We check the assumptions. We have a simple random sample. Now either the sample size must be greater than 30, or the population must be approximately normal. Since the sample size is $n = 123$, the assumptions are met.

Step 1: Find the sample mean and sample standard deviation. These are given as $\bar{x} = 8.20$ and $s = 9.84$.

Step 2: Find the number of degrees of freedom and the critical value $t_{\alpha/2}$. The number of degrees of freedom is $n - 1 = 123 - 1 = 122$. Since this number of degrees of freedom does not appear in Table A.3, we use the next smaller value in the table, which is 100. The critical value corresponding to a level of 95% is $t_{\alpha/2} = 1.984$.

Step 3: Compute the margin of error. The margin of error is

$$t_{\alpha/2} \frac{s}{\sqrt{n}}$$

We substitute $t_{\alpha/2} = 1.984$, $s = 9.84$, and $n = 123$ to obtain

$$t_{\alpha/2} \frac{s}{\sqrt{n}} = 1.984 \frac{9.84}{\sqrt{123}} = 1.7603$$

Step 4: Construct the confidence interval. The 95% confidence interval is given by

$$\bar{x} - t_{\alpha/2} \frac{s}{\sqrt{n}} < \mu < \bar{x} + t_{\alpha/2} \frac{s}{\sqrt{n}}$$

$$8.20 - 1.7603 < \mu < 8.20 + 1.7603$$

$$6.44 < \mu < 9.96$$

Note that we round the final result to two decimal places, because the value of $\bar{x}$ was given to two decimal places.

Step 5: Interpret the result. We are 95% confident that the mean number of hours per week spent on the Internet by people 18–22 years old is between 6.44 and 9.96.

Note that in Example 7.12, the sample standard deviation of 9.84 is larger than the sample mean of 8.20. Since the minimum possible time to spend on the Internet is 0, the smallest sample value is less than one standard deviation below the mean. This indicates that the sample is fairly skewed. Figure 7.12 confirms this. Even though the sample is skewed, the t statistic is still appropriate, because the sample size of 123 is large.

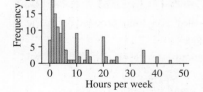

Figure 7.12

Constructing confidence intervals with technology

The following TI-84 Plus display presents the results of Example 7.12.

```
    TInterval
(6.4436,9.9564)
x̄=8.2
Sx=9.84
n=123
```

CAUTION

Confidence intervals constructed using technology may differ from those constructed by hand due to rounding. The differences are never large enough to matter.

The display is fairly straightforward. The quantity Sx is the sample standard deviation s. The TI-84 Plus uses the exact number of degrees of freedom, 122, rather than 100 as we did in the solution to Example 7.12. This does not make a difference when the answer is rounded to two decimal places. Note that the confidence level (95%) is not given in the display.

The following MINITAB output presents the results of the same example.

Variable	N	Mean	StDev	SE Mean	95% CI
Hours	123	8.20000	9.84000	0.88724	(6.44361, 9.95639)

The output is fairly straightforward. Going from left to right, "N" represents the sample size, "Mean" is the sample mean $\bar{x}$, and "StDev" is the sample standard deviation s. The quantity labeled "SE Mean" is the standard error $s/\sqrt{n}$. Note that neither the critical value nor the margin of error is given explicitly in the output. Finally, the lower and upper limits of the 95% confidence interval are given on the right. Like the TI-84 Plus, MINITAB uses 122 degrees of freedom rather than 100 as we did in the solution to the example. This does not make a difference when the answer is rounded to two decimal places.

Step-by-step instructions for constructing confidence intervals with technology are given in the Using Technology section on page 312.

Check Your Understanding

3. A potato chip company wants to evaluate the accuracy of its potato chip bag-filling machine. Bags are labeled as containing 8 ounces of potato chips. A simple random sample of 12 bags had mean weight 8.12 ounces with a sample standard deviation of 0.1 ounce. Construct a 99% confidence interval for the population mean weight of bags of potato chips.

4. A company has developed a new type of lightbulb, and wants to estimate its mean lifetime. A simple random sample of 100 bulbs had a sample mean lifetime of 750.2 hours with a sample standard deviation of 30 hours. Construct a 95% confidence interval for the population mean lifetime of all bulbs manufactured by this new process.

5. The following TI-84 Plus display presents a 95% confidence interval for a population mean.

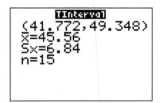

    a. How many degrees of freedom are there?
    b. Find the critical value $t_{\alpha/2}$ for a 99% confidence interval.
    c. Use the critical value along with the information in the display to construct a 99% confidence interval for the population mean.

6. The following MINITAB output presents a confidence interval for a population mean.

Variable	N	Mean	StDev	SE Mean	95% CI
X	10	8.5963	0.11213	0.03546	(8.5161, 8.6765)

a. How many degrees of freedom are there?
b. Find the critical value $t_{\alpha/2}$ for a 99% confidence interval.
c. Use the critical value along with the information in the computer output to construct a 99% confidence interval for the population mean.

Answers are on page 317.

Another way to construct the confidence interval when the sample size is large

When the sample size is large ($n > 30$), some people use $z_{\alpha/2}$ rather than $t_{\alpha/2}$ as the critical value. This is acceptable, because when the number of degrees of freedom is large, there is little difference between $z_{\alpha/2}$ and $t_{\alpha/2}$. Most forms of technology use $t_{\alpha/2}$, however, and since most data analysis is done with technology these days, this means that most confidence intervals with large sample sizes are constructed using $t_{\alpha/2}$. We will follow this practice in this book as well.

USING TECHNOLOGY

We use Example 7.12 to illustrate the technology steps.

TI-84 PLUS

Constructing a confidence interval for the mean when σ is unknown

Step 1. Press **STAT** and highlight the **TESTS** menu.
Step 2. Select **TInterval** and press **ENTER** (Figure A). The **TInterval** menu appears.
Step 3. For **Inpt**, select the **Stats** option and enter the values of $\bar{x}$, s, and n. For Example 7.12, we use $\bar{x} = 8.20$, $s = 9.84$, and $n = 123$.
Step 4. In the **C-Level** field, enter the confidence level. For Example 7.12 we use 0.95 (Figure B).
Step 5. Highlight **Calculate** and press **ENTER** (Figure C).

Note that if the raw data are given, the **TInterval** command may be used by selecting **Data** as the **Inpt** option and entering the location of the data as the **List** option (Figure D).

Figure A

Figure B

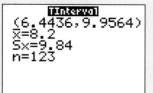

Figure C

Figure D

MINITAB

Constructing a confidence interval for the mean when σ is unknown

Step 1. Click on **Stat**, then **Basic Statistics**, then **1-Sample t**.

Step 2. Choose one of the following:
- If the summary statistics are given, click **Summarized Data** and enter the **Sample Size** (123), the **Mean** (8.20), and the **Standard Deviation** (9.84) (Figure E).
- If the raw data are given, click **Samples** in **Columns** and select the column that contains the data.

Step 3. Click **Options** and enter the confidence level in the **Confidence Level** (95) field. For Example 7.12, enter **95%**. Click **OK**.

Step 4. Click **OK** (Figure F).

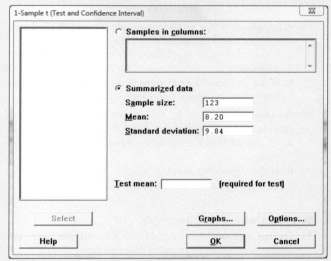

Figure E

One-Sample T

N	Mean	StDev	SE Mean	95% CI
123	8.20000	9.84000	0.88724	(6.44361, 9.95639)

Figure F

EXCEL

Constructing a confidence interval for the mean when σ is unknown

This procedure requires the **MegaStat** EXCEL add-in to be loaded. The **MegaStat** add-in may be downloaded from www.mhhe.com/megastat.

Step 1. Click on the **MegaStat** menu and select **Confidence Intervals/Sample Size...**

Step 2. Enter the sample mean from Example 7.12 in the **Mean** field (8.20), the standard deviation in the **Std. Dev.** field (9.84), and the sample size in the **n** field (123). Choose the **t** option for the critical value.

Step 3. In the **Confidence Level** field, enter the confidence level. For Example 7.12, enter **95%** (Figure G).

Step 4. Click **OK** (Figure H).

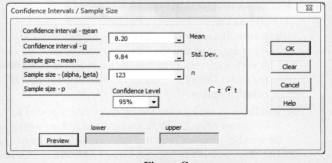

Figure G

Confidence interval - mean

95% confidence level
8.2 mean
9.84 std. dev.
123 n
1.980 t (df = 122)
1.756 half-width
9.956 upper confidence limit
6.444 lower confidence limit

Figure H

SECTION 7.2 Exercises

Exercises 1–6 are the Check Your Understanding exercises located within the section.

Understanding the Concepts

In Exercises 7 and 8, fill in each blank with the appropriate word or phrase.

7. When constructing a confidence interval for a population mean μ from a sample of size 12, the number of degrees of freedom for the critical value $t_{\alpha/2}$ is _____ .

8. When the number of degrees of freedom is large, the Student's t distribution is close to the _____ distribution.

In Exercises 9 and 10, determine whether the statement is true or false. If the statement is false, rewrite it as a true statement.

9. The Student's t curve is less spread out than the standard normal curve.

10. The Student's t distribution should not be used to find a confidence interval for μ if outliers are present in a small sample.

Practicing the Skills

11. Find the critical value $t_{\alpha/2}$ needed to construct a confidence interval of the given level with the given sample size.
    a. Level 95%, sample size 23
    b. Level 90%, sample size 3
    c. Level 98%, sample size 18
    d. Level 99%, sample size 29

12. Find the critical value $t_{\alpha/2}$ needed to construct a confidence interval of the given level with the given sample size.
    a. Level 90%, sample size 6
    b. Level 98%, sample size 12
    c. Level 95%, sample size 32
    d. Level 99%, sample size 10

13. A sample of size $n = 18$ is drawn from a normal population.
    a. Find the critical value $t_{\alpha/2}$ needed to construct a 95% confidence interval.
    b. If the sample size were $n = 25$, would the critical value be smaller or larger?

14. A sample of size $n = 22$ is drawn from a normal population.
    a. Find the critical value $t_{\alpha/2}$ needed to construct a 90% confidence interval.
    b. If the sample size were $n = 15$, would the critical value be smaller or larger?

15. A sample of size $n = 12$ is drawn from a normal population.
    a. Find the critical value $t_{\alpha/2}$ needed to construct a 98% confidence interval.
    b. If the sample size were $n = 50$, would it be necessary for the population to be approximately normal?

16. A sample of size $n = 61$ is drawn.
    a. Find the critical value $t_{\alpha/2}$ needed to construct a 95% confidence interval.
    b. If the sample size were $n = 15$, what additional assumption would need to be made for the confidence interval to be valid?

17. A sample of size $n = 15$ has sample mean $\bar{x} = 2.1$ and sample standard deviation $s = 1.7$.
    a. Construct a 95% confidence interval for the population mean μ.
    b. If the sample size were $n = 25$, would the confidence interval be narrower or wider?

18. A sample of size $n = 44$ has sample mean $\bar{x} = 56.9$ and sample standard deviation $s = 9.1$.
    a. Construct a 98% confidence interval for the population mean μ.
    b. If the sample size were $n = 30$, would the confidence interval be narrower or wider?

19. A sample of size $n = 89$ has sample mean $\bar{x} = 87.2$ and sample standard deviation $s = 5.3$.
    a. Construct a 95% confidence interval for the population mean μ.
    b. If the confidence level were 99%, would the confidence interval be narrower or wider?

20. A sample of size $n = 35$ has sample mean $\bar{x} = 34.85$ and sample standard deviation $s = 17.9$.
    a. Construct a 98% confidence interval for the population mean μ.
    b. If the confidence level were 95%, would the confidence interval be narrower or wider?

Working with the Concepts

21. **Online courses:** A sample of 263 students who were taking online courses were asked to describe their overall impression of online learning on a scale of 1–7, with 7 representing the most favorable impression. The average score was 5.53, and the standard deviation was 0.92.
    a. Construct a 95% confidence interval for the mean score.
    b. Assume that the mean score for students taking traditional courses is 5.55. A college that offers online courses claims that the mean scores for online courses and traditional courses are the same. Does the confidence interval contradict this claim? Explain.
    Source: *Innovations in Education and Teaching International* 45:115–126

22. **Job duration:** In 2008, the General Social Survey asked 846 people how long they had been employed in their present job. The sample mean was 8.51 years with a standard deviation of 8.61 years.
    a. Construct a 98% confidence interval for the mean length of time workers have been employed in their current job.
    b. Data collected in an earlier study suggest that the mean length of time in 2004 was 6.93 years. A sociologist believes that the mean length in 2008 is the same. Does the confidence interval contradict this belief? Explain.

23. **YouTube:** A random sample of 2500 videos posted to YouTube on May 22, 2009, was collected. Two weeks later, the number of times each had been viewed was tabulated. The mean number of viewings was 130.0 with a standard deviation of 835.2.

a. Construct a 90% confidence interval for the mean number of times videos posted to YouTube have been viewed in their first two weeks.

b. Based on the confidence interval, is it reasonable to believe that the mean number of viewings is 100? Explain.

Source: slate.com

24. Let's go to the movies: A random sample of 45 Hollywood movies made since the year 2000 had a mean length of 111.7 minutes, with a standard deviation of 13.8 minutes.

a. Construct a 95% confidence interval for the true mean length of all Hollywood movies made since 2000.

b. As of November 2010, three *Spider-Man* movies have been released, and their mean length is 129 minutes. Someone claims that the mean length of *Spider-Man* movies is actually less than the mean length of all Hollywood movies. Does the confidence interval contradict this claim? Explain.

Based on data from Cox Communications.

25. Hip surgery: In a sample of 123 hip surgeries of a certain type, the average surgery time was 136.9 minutes with a standard deviation of 22.6 minutes.

a. Construct a 95% confidence interval for the mean surgery time for this procedure.

b. If a 99% confidence interval were constructed with these data, would it be wider or narrower than the interval constructed in part (a)? Explain.

Source: *Journal of Engineering in Medicine* 221:699–712

26. Sound it out: Phonics is an instructional method in which children are taught to connect sounds with letters or groups of letters. A sample of 134 first-graders who were learning English were asked to identify as many letter sounds as possible in a period of one minute. The average number of letter sounds identified was 34.06 with a standard deviation of 23.83.

a. Construct a 98% confidence interval for the mean number of letter sounds identified in one minute.

b. If a 95% confidence interval were constructed with these data, would it be wider or narrower than the interval constructed in part (a)? Explain.

Source: *School Psychology Review* 37:5–17

27. Software instruction: A hybrid course is one that contains both online and classroom instruction. In a study performed at Macon State College, a software package was used as the main source of instruction in a hybrid college algebra course. The software tracked the number of hours it took for each student to meet the objectives of the course. In a sample of 45 students, the mean number of hours was 80.5, with a standard deviation of 51.2.

a. Construct a 95% confidence interval for the mean number of hours it takes for a student to meet the course objectives.

b. If a sample of 90 students had been studied, would you expect the confidence interval to be wider or narrower than the interval constructed in part (a)? Explain.

28. Baby talk: In a sample of 77 children, the mean age at which they first began to combine words was 16.51 months, with a standard deviation of 9.59 months.

a. Construct a 95% confidence interval for the mean age at which children first begin to combine words.

b. If a sample of 50 children had been studied, would you expect the confidence interval to be wider or narrower than the interval constructed in part (a)? Explain.

Source: *Proceedings of the 4th International Symposium on Bilingualism*, pp. 58–77

29. Baby weights: Following are weights, in pounds, of 12 two-month-old baby girls. It is reasonable to assume that the population is approximately normal.

12.23	12.32	11.87	12.34	11.48	12.66
8.51	14.13	12.95	10.30	9.34	8.63

a. Construct a 98% confidence interval for the mean weight of two-month-old baby girls.

b. According to the National Health Statistics Reports, the mean weight of two-month-old baby boys is 11.5 pounds. Based on the confidence interval, is it reasonable to believe that the mean weight of two-month-old baby girls may be the same as that of two-month-old baby boys? Explain.

30. Eat your cereal: Boxes of cereal are labeled as containing 14 ounces. Following are the weights, in ounces, of a sample of 12 boxes: It is reasonable to assume that the population is approximately normal.

14.02	13.97	14.11	14.12	14.10	14.02
14.15	13.97	14.05	14.04	14.11	14.12

a. Construct a 98% confidence interval for the mean weight.

b. The quality control manager is concerned that the mean weight is actually less than 14 ounces. Based on the confidence interval, is there a reason to be concerned? Explain.

31. Eat your spinach: Six measurements were made of the mineral content (in percent) of spinach, with the following results. It is reasonable to assume that the population is approximately normal.

$$19.1 \quad 20.8 \quad 20.8 \quad 21.4 \quad 20.5 \quad 19.7$$

a. Construct a 95% confidence interval for the mean mineral content.

b. Based on the confidence interval, is it reasonable to believe that the mean mineral content of spinach may be greater than 21%? Explain.

Source: *Journal of Nutrition* 66:55–66

32. Mortgage rates: Following are interest rates (annual percentage rates) for a 30-year-fixed-rate mortgage from a sample of lenders in Atlanta, Georgia, on August 9, 2010. It is reasonable to assume that the population is approximately normal.

4.327	4.461	4.547	4.398	4.199	4.460
4.531	4.365	4.407	4.639	4.804	4.842

Source: realestate.yahoo.com

a. Construct a 99% confidence interval for the mean rate.

b. One week earlier, the mean rate was 4.803%. A mortgage broker claims that the mean rate is now lower. Based on the confidence interval, is this a reasonable claim? Explain.

33. Hi-def: Following are prices of a random sample of 18 high-definition televisions sold on shopper.cnet.com in 2010 with screen sizes between 45" and 50", along with a dotplot of the data.

698	809	882	968	1005	1099
1179	1230	1299	1393	1499	1604
1790	1999	2110	2249	2329	2490

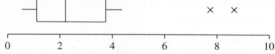

a. Is it reasonable to assume that the conditions for constructing a confidence interval for the mean price are satisfied? Explain.

b. If appropriate, construct a 95% confidence interval for the mean price of all HDTVs in this size range.

34. Big salary for the boss: Following is the total 2009 compensation, in millions of dollars, for chief executive officers at 20 large U.S. corporations, along with a boxplot of the data.

4.03	0.54	1.45	1.25	2.46	3.32	0.69
7.75	0.61	4.05	3.47	1.51	4.37	1.02
2.34	2.77	1.09	2.09	8.66	1.13

a. Is it reasonable to assume that the conditions for constructing a confidence interval for the mean compensation are satisfied? Explain.

b. If appropriate, construct a 95% confidence interval for the mean compensation of a chief executive officer.

35. Pain relief: One of the ways in which doctors try to determine how long a single dose of pain-reliever will provide relief is to measure the drug's half-life, which is the length of time it takes for one-half of the dose to be eliminated from the body. Following are half-lives (in hours) of the pain reliever oxycodone for a sample of 18 individuals, along with a boxplot of the data, based on a report of the National Institutes of Health.

3.3	1.7	2.0	5.0	1.2	2.8	3.7	3.5	4.8
4.7	4.9	2.5	5.1	6.0	3.9	4.3	2.1	3.0

a. Is it reasonable to assume that the conditions for constructing a confidence interval for the mean half-life are satisfied? Explain.

b. If appropriate, construct a 95% confidence interval for the mean half-life.

c. The National Institutes of Health report states that the mean half-life is 3.51 hours. If appropriate, explain whether this confidence interval contradicts this claim.

36. Hummer: Gas mileage, in miles per gallon, was measured for five 2008 Hummer H2 vehicles. Following are the results, along with a dotplot of the data.

14.0   13.4   13.1   12.4   13.0

a. Is it reasonable to assume that the conditions for constructing a confidence interval for the mean gas mileage are satisfied? Explain.

b. If appropriate, construct a 95% confidence interval for the mean gas mileage.

c. Since the Hummer H2 is classified as a Class 3 truck, it does not have an EPA gas mileage rating. Someone suggests that a rating of 13.5 miles per gallon should be assigned. If appropriate, explain whether this may be an appropriate rating, based on the confidence interval.

Source: TrueDelta.com

37. Eat your kale: Kale is a type of cabbage commonly found in salad and used in cooking in many parts of the world. Six measurements were made of the mineral content (in percent) of kale, with the following results.

26.1   17.5   15.4   16.4   15.1   12.8

It turns out that the value 26.1 came from a specimen that the investigator forgot to wash before measuring.

a. The data contain an outlier that is clearly a mistake. Eliminate the outlier, then construct a 95% confidence interval for the mean mineral content from the remaining values.

b. Leave the outlier in and construct the 95% confidence interval. Are the results noticeably different? Explain why it is important to check data for outliers.

Source: *Journal of Nutrition* 66:55–66

38. Sleeping outlier: A simple random sample of eight college freshmen were asked how many hours of sleep they typically got per night. The results were

7.5   8.0   6.5   24   8.5   6.5   7.0   7.5

Notice that one joker said that he sleeps 24 hours a day.

a. The data contain an outlier that is clearly a mistake. Eliminate the outlier, then construct a 95% confidence interval for the mean amount of sleep from the remaining values.

b. Leave the outlier in and construct the 95% confidence interval. Are the results noticeably different? Explain why it is important to check data for outliers.

39. Don't construct a confidence interval: There have been 43 presidents of the United States. Their mean height is 70.8 inches, with a standard deviation of 2.7 inches. Explain why these data should not be used to construct a confidence interval for the mean height of the presidents.

40. Don't construct a confidence interval: As of July 1, 2009, the mean population of the 50 states of the United States was

6.1 million, with a standard deviation of 6.8 million. Explain why these data should not be used to construct a confidence interval for the mean population of the states.

41. Interpret calculator display: The following display from a TI-84 Plus calculator presents a 98% confidence interval.

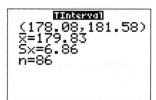

a. Fill in the blanks: We are _____ confident that the population mean is between _____ and _____ .

b. Assume the population is not normally distributed. Is the confidence interval still valid? Explain.

42. Interpret calculator display: The following display from a TI-84 Plus calculator presents a 95% confidence interval.

```
 TInterval
(.85638,2.2836)
x̄=1.57
Sx=.68
n=6
```

a. Fill in the blanks: We are _____ confident that the population mean is between _____ and _____ .

b. Assume the population is not normally distributed. Is the confidence interval still valid? Explain.

43. Interpret computer output: The following MINITAB output presents a confidence interval for a population mean.

Variable	N	Mean	StDev	SE Mean	95% CI
X	15	5.9373	2.0387	0.5264	(4.8083, 7.0663)

a. How many degrees of freedom are there?

b. If the population were not approximately normal, would this confidence interval be valid? Explain.

c. Find the critical value $t_{\alpha/2}$ for a 98% confidence interval.

d. Use the critical value and the information in the output to construct a 98% confidence interval.

44. Interpret computer output: The following MINITAB output presents a confidence interval for a population mean.

Variable	N	Mean	StDev	SE Mean	99% CI
X	71	23.8760	3.9385	0.4674	(22.638, 25.114)

a. How many degrees of freedom are there?

b. If the population were not approximately normal, would this confidence interval be valid? Explain.

c. Find the critical value $t_{\alpha/2}$ for a 95% confidence interval.

d. Use the critical value and the information in the output to construct a 95% confidence interval.

Extending the Concepts

45. Sample of size 1: The concentration of carbon monoxide in parts per million is believed to be normally distributed with a standard deviation $\sigma = 8$. A single measurement of the concentration is made, and its value is 85.

a. Use the methods of Section 7.1 to construct a 95% confidence interval for the mean concentration.

b. Would it be possible to construct a confidence interval using the methods of this section if the population standard deviation were unknown? Explain.

Answers to Check Your Understanding Exercises for Section 7.2

1. a. 2.145   **b.** 2.831   **c.** 1.671   **d.** 12.706

2. a. Yes   **b.** No   **c.** Yes   **d.** No

3. $8.03 < \mu < 8.21$

4. $744.2 < \mu < 756.2$

5. a. 14   **b.** 2.977   **c.** $40.30 < \mu < 50.82$

6. a. 9   **b.** 3.250   **c.** $8.4811 < \mu < 8.7115$

SECTION 7.3   Confidence Intervals for a Population Proportion

Objectives

1. Construct a confidence interval for a population proportion
2. Find the sample size necessary to obtain a confidence interval of a given width
3. Describe a method for constructing confidence intervals with small samples

Objective 1 Construct a confidence interval for a population proportion

Construct a Confidence Interval for a Population Proportion

Are you a Guitar Hero? The music organization Little Kids Rock surveyed 517 music teachers, and 403 of them said that video games like Guitar Hero and Rock Band, in which players try to play music in time with a video image, have a positive effect on music education. Assuming these teachers to be a random sample of U.S. music teachers, we would like to construct a confidence interval for the proportion of music teachers who believe that music video games have a positive effect on music classrooms.

This is an example of a population whose items fall into two categories. In this example, the categories are those teachers who believe that video games have a positive effect, and those who do not. We are interested in the population proportion of those who believe there is a positive effect. We will use the following notation.

NOTATION

- p is the population proportion of individuals who are in a specified category.
- x is the number of individuals in the sample who are in the specified category.
- n is the sample size.
- $\hat{p}$ is the sample proportion of individuals who are in the specified category.
  $\hat{p} = x/n$

To construct a confidence interval, we need a point estimate and a margin of error. The point estimate we use for the population proportion p is the sample proportion

$$\hat{p} = \frac{x}{n}$$

To compute the margin of error, we multiply the standard error of the point estimate by the critical value. The standard error and the critical value are determined by the sampling distribution of $\hat{p}$. In Section 6.4 we found that when the sample size n is large enough, the sample proportion $\hat{p}$ is approximately normal with standard deviation

$$\sqrt{\frac{p(1-p)}{n}}$$

In practice, we don't know the value of p, so we substitute $\hat{p}$ instead to obtain the standard error we use for the confidence interval:

$$\text{Standard error} = \sqrt{\frac{\hat{p}(1-\hat{p})}{n}}$$

Since the point estimate $\hat{p}$ is approximately normal with standard error $\sqrt{\hat{p}(1-\hat{p})/n}$, the appropriate margin of error is

$$\text{Margin of error} = z_{\alpha/2}\sqrt{\frac{\hat{p}(1-\hat{p})}{n}}$$

The confidence interval is

$$\text{Point estimate} \pm \text{Margin of error}$$

$$\hat{p} \pm z_{\alpha/2}\sqrt{\frac{\hat{p}(1-\hat{p})}{n}}$$

The method we have just described requires certain assumptions, which we now state.

Assumptions for Constructing a Confidence Interval for p

1. We have a simple random sample.
2. The population is at least 20 times as large as the sample.
3. The items in the population are divided into two categories.
4. The sample must contain at least 10 individuals in each category.

Following is a step-by-step description of the procedure for constructing a confidence interval for a population proportion p.

Explain It Again

The population proportion and the sample proportion: The population proportion p is unknown. The sample proportion $\hat{p}$ is known, and we use the value of $\hat{p}$ to estimate the unknown value p.

Explain It Again

Reasons for the assumptions: The population must be much larger than the sample (at least 20 times as large), so that the sampled items are independent. The assumption that there are at least 10 items in each category is an approximate check on the assumption that both np and $n(1-p)$ are at least 10, which ensures that the sampling distribution of $\hat{p}$ is approximately normal.

Procedure for Constructing a Confidence Interval for p

Check to be sure the assumptions are satisfied. If they are, then proceed with the following steps.

Step 1: Compute the value of the point estimate $\hat{p}$.

Step 2: Find the critical value $z_{\alpha/2}$ corresponding to the desired confidence level, either from the last line of Table A.3, from Table A.2, or with technology.

Step 3: Compute the standard error $\sqrt{\hat{p}(1-\hat{p})/n}$ and multiply it by the critical value to obtain the margin of error $z_{\alpha/2}\sqrt{\hat{p}(1-\hat{p})/n}$.

Step 4: Use the point estimate and the margin of error to construct the confidence interval:

$$\text{Point estimate} \pm \text{Margin of error}$$

$$\hat{p} \pm z_{\alpha/2}\sqrt{\frac{\hat{p}(1-\hat{p})}{n}}$$

$$\hat{p} - z_{\alpha/2}\sqrt{\frac{\hat{p}(1-\hat{p})}{n}} < p < \hat{p} + z_{\alpha/2}\sqrt{\frac{\hat{p}(1-\hat{p})}{n}}$$

Step 5: Interpret the result.

Explain It Again

Round-off rule: When constructing a confidence interval for a proportion, round the final result to three decimal places.

Rounding off the final result

When constructing confidence intervals for a proportion, we will round the final result to three decimal places. Note that you should round only the final result, and not the calculations you have made along the way.

EXAMPLE 7.13

Construct a confidence interval for a proportion

In a survey of 517 music teachers, 403 said that the video games Guitar Hero and Rock Band have a positive effect on music education.

a. Construct a 95% confidence interval for the proportion of music teachers who believe that these video games have a positive effect.

b. A video game manufacturer claims that 80% of music teachers believe that Guitar Hero and Rock Band have a positive effect. Does the confidence interval contradict this claim?

Solution

a. We begin by checking the assumptions. We have a simple random sample. It is reasonable to believe that the population of music teachers in the United States is at least 20 times as large as the sample. The items in the population can be divided into two categories: those who believe that the games have a positive effect, and those who do not. There are 403 teachers who believe that the games have a positive effect, and $517 - 403 = 114$ who do not, so there are 10 or more items in each category. The assumptions are met.

Step 1: Compute the point estimate $\hat{p}$. The sample size is $n = 517$ and the number who believe that video games have a positive effect is $x = 403$. The point estimate is

$$\hat{p} = \frac{403}{517} = 0.779497$$

Step 2: Find the critical value. The critical value for a 95% confidence interval is $z_{\alpha/2} = 1.96$.

Step 3: Compute the margin of error. The margin of error is

$$z_{\alpha/2}\sqrt{\frac{\hat{p}(1-\hat{p})}{n}}$$

We substitute $z_{\alpha/2} = 1.96$, $\hat{p} = 0.779497$, and $n = 517$ to obtain

$$z_{\alpha/2}\sqrt{\frac{\hat{p}(1 - \hat{p})}{n}} = 1.96\sqrt{\frac{0.779497(1 - 0.779497)}{517}} = 0.035738$$

Step 4: Construct the 95% confidence interval. The point estimate is 0.779497 and the margin of error is 0.035738. The 95% confidence interval is

$$0.779497 - 0.035738 < p < 0.779497 + 0.035738$$
$$0.744 < p < 0.815 \quad \text{(rounded to three decimal places)}$$

Sept 5: Interpret the result. We are 95% confident that the proportion of music teachers who believe that video games have a positive effect is between 0.744 and 0.815.

b. Because the value 0.80 is within the confidence interval, the confidence interval does not contradict the claim.

Constructing confidence intervals with technology

Example 7.13 presented a 95% confidence interval for the proportion of music teachers who believe that video games have a positive effect on music education. The confidence interval obtained was $0.744 < p < 0.815$. Following are the results from a TI-84 Plus calculator.

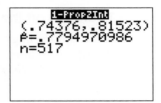

The display presents the confidence interval, followed by the point estimate $\hat{p}$ and the sample size n. Note that the level (95%) is not displayed.

Following is MINITAB output for the same example.

Sample	X	N	Sample p	95% CI
1	403	517	0.779497	(0.743760, 0.815234)

Step-by-step instructions for constructing confidence intervals with technology are presented in the Using Technology section on page 325.

Check Your Understanding

1. A simple random sample of 200 third-graders in a large school district was chosen to participate in an after-school program to improve reading skills. After completing the program, the children were tested, and 142 of them showed improvement in their reading skills.
   a. Find a point estimate for the proportion of third-graders in the school district whose reading scores would improve after completing the program.
   b. Construct a 95% confidence interval for the proportion of third-graders in the school district whose reading scores would improve after completing the program.
   c. Is it reasonable to conclude that more than 60% of the students would improve their reading scores after completing the program? Explain.
   d. The district superintendent wants to construct a confidence interval for the proportion of all elementary school children in the district whose scores would improve. Should the sample of 200 third-graders be used for this purpose? Explain.

Answers are on page 329.

Objective 2 Find the sample size necessary to obtain a confidence interval of a given width

Finding the Necessary Sample Size

If we wish to make the margin of error of a confidence interval smaller while keeping the confidence level the same, we can do this by making the sample size larger. Sometimes we have a specific value m that we would like the margin of error to attain, and we wish to compute a sample size n that is likely to give us a margin of error of that size.

The method for computing the sample size is based on the formula for the margin of error:

$$m = z_{\alpha/2} \sqrt{\frac{\hat{p}(1 - \hat{p})}{n}}$$

By manipulating this formula algebraically, we can solve for n:

$$n = \hat{p}(1 - \hat{p}) \left(\frac{z_{\alpha/2}}{m} \right)^2$$

This formula shows that the sample size n depends not only on the margin of error m but also on the sample proportion $\hat{p}$. Therefore, in order to compute the sample size n, we need a value for $\hat{p}$ as well as a value for m. Now of course we don't know ahead of time what $\hat{p}$ is going to be. The approach, therefore, is to determine a value for $\hat{p}$.

There are two ways to determine a value for $\hat{p}$. One is to use a value that is available from a previously drawn sample. The other is to assume that $\hat{p} = 0.5$. The value $\hat{p} = 0.5$ makes the margin of error as large as possible for any sample size. Therefore, if we assume that $\hat{p} = 0.5$, we will always get a margin of error that is less than or equal to the desired value.

Explain It Again

Computing the sample size: When computing the necessary sample size, use a value of $\hat{p}$ from a previously drawn sample if one is available. Otherwise, use $\hat{p} = 0.5$.

SUMMARY

Let m be the desired margin of error, and let $z_{\alpha/2}$ be the critical value. The sample size n needed so that a confidence interval for a proportion will have margin of error approximately equal to m is

$$n = \hat{p}(1 - \hat{p}) \left(\frac{z_{\alpha/2}}{m} \right)^2 \quad \text{if a value for } \hat{p} \text{ is available}$$

$$n = 0.25 \left(\frac{z_{\alpha/2}}{m} \right)^2 \quad \text{if no value for } \hat{p} \text{ is available}$$

(This is equivalent to assuming that $\hat{p} = 0.5$.)

If the value of n given by the formula is not a whole number, round it *up* to the nearest whole number. By rounding up, we can be sure that the margin of error is no greater than the desired value m.

EXAMPLE 7.14   Find the necessary sample size

Example 7.13 described a sample of 517 music teachers, 403 of whom believe that video games have a positive effect on music education. Estimate the sample size needed so that a 95% confidence interval will have a margin of error of 0.03.

Solution

The desired level is 95%. The critical value is therefore $z_{\alpha/2} = 1.96$. We now compute $\hat{p}$:

$$\hat{p} = \frac{403}{517} = 0.779497$$

The desired margin of error is $m = 0.03$. Since we have a value for $\hat{p}$, we substitute $\hat{p} = 0.779497$, $z_{\alpha/2} = 1.96$, and $m = 0.03$ into the formula

$$n = \hat{p}(1 - \hat{p}) \left(\frac{z_{\alpha/2}}{m} \right)^2$$

and obtain

$$n = (0.779497)(1 - 0.779497)\left(\frac{1.96}{0.03}\right)^2 = 733.67 \quad \text{(round up to 734)}$$

We estimate that we need to sample 734 teachers to obtain a 95% confidence interval with a margin of error of 0.03.

EXAMPLE 7.15

Find the necessary sample size

We plan to sample music teachers in order to construct a 95% confidence interval for the proportion who believe that listening to hip-hop music has a positive effect on music education. We have no value of $\hat{p}$ available. Estimate the sample size needed so that a 95% confidence interval will have a margin of error of 0.03. Explain why the estimated sample size in this example is larger than the one in Example 7.14.

Solution

The desired level is 95%. The critical value is therefore $z_{\alpha/2} = 1.96$. The desired margin of error is $m = 0.03$. Since we have no value of $\hat{p}$, we substitute the values $z_{\alpha/2} = 1.96$ and $m = 0.03$ into the formula

$$n = 0.25\left(\frac{z_{\alpha/2}}{m}\right)^2$$

and obtain

$$n = 0.25\left(\frac{1.96}{0.03}\right)^2 = 1067.1 \quad \text{(round up to 1068)}$$

We estimate that we need to sample 1068 teachers to obtain a 95% confidence interval with a margin of error of 0.03. This estimate is larger than the one in Example 7.14 because we used a value of 0.5 for $\hat{p}$, which provides a sample size large enough to guarantee that the margin of error will be no greater than 0.03 no matter what the true value of p is.

Check Your Understanding

2. In a preliminary study, a simple random sample of 100 computer chips was tested, and 17 of them were found to be defective. Now another sample will be drawn in order to construct a 95% confidence interval for the proportion of chips that are defective. Use the results of the preliminary study to estimate the sample size needed so that the confidence interval will have a margin of error of 0.06.

3. A pollster is going to sample a number of voters in a large city and construct a 98% confidence interval for the proportion who support the incumbent candidate for mayor. Find a sample size so that the margin of error will be no larger than 0.05.

Answers are on page 329.

The margin of error does not depend on the population size

In 2010, there were about 17 million registered voters in the state of California, and about 0.26 million registered voters in the state of Wyoming. A simple random sample of 1000 Wyoming voters is selected to estimate the proportion of voters who favor the Democratic candidate for president. Another simple random sample of 1000 California voters is selected to determine the proportion of Democratic voters in that state. Which estimate has the smaller standard error? Because California has a much larger population of registered voters than does Wyoming, it might seem that a larger sample would be needed in California to produce the same standard error. Surprisingly enough, this is not the case. In fact, the standard errors for the two estimates will be about the same. This is clear from the formula for the standard error: The population size does not enter into the calculation. Since the standard errors are about the same, the margins of error will be about the same if confidence intervals of the same level are constructed for both population proportions.

Intuitively, we can see that population size doesn't matter by considering an analogy with testing the water in a swimming pool. To determine whether the chemical balance is correct, one withdraws a few drops of water to test. As long as the contents of the pool are well mixed, so that the water removed constitutes a simple random sample of molecules from the pool, it doesn't matter how large the pool is. One doesn't need to sample more water from a bigger pool.

EXAMPLE 7.16

The margin of error does not depend on the population size

A pollster has conducted a poll using a sample of 500 drawn from a town with population 25,000. He now wants to conduct the poll in a larger town with population 250,000, and to obtain approximately the same margin of error as in the smaller town. How large a sample must he draw?

Solution
He should draw a sample of 500, just as in the small town. The population size does not affect the margin of error.

Check Your Understanding

4. A pollster is planning to draw a simple random sample of 500 people in Colorado (population 5.0 million). He then will conduct a similar poll in Texas (population 24.7 million). He wants to have approximately the same standard error in both polls. True or false:
   a. The pollster needs a sample in Texas that is about 5 times as large as the one in Colorado.
   b. The pollster needs a sample in Texas that is about the same size as the one in Colorado.

5. A marketing firm in New York City (population 8.4 million) plans to draw a simple random sample of 1000 people to estimate the proportion who have heard about a new product. The firm then plans to take a simple random sample of 500 in Denver (population 610,000) for the same purpose. True or false:
   a. The margin of error for a 95% confidence interval will be larger in New York.
   b. The margin of error for a 95% confidence interval will be larger in Denver.
   c. The margin of error for a 95% confidence interval will be about the same in both cities.

Answers are on page 329.

Objective 3 Describe a method for constructing confidence intervals with small samples

A Method for Constructing Confidence Intervals with Small Samples

The method that we have presented for constructing a confidence interval for a proportion requires that we have at least 10 individuals in each category. When this condition is not met, we can still construct a confidence interval by adjusting the sample proportion a bit. We increase the number of individuals in each category by 2, so that the sample size increases by 4. Thus, instead of using the sample proportion $\hat{p} = x/n$, we use the *adjusted sample proportion*

$$\tilde{p} = \frac{x+2}{n+4}$$

The standard error and critical value are calculated in the same way as in the traditional method, except that we use the adjusted sample proportion $\tilde{p}$ in place of $\hat{p}$, and $n+4$ in place of n.

Constructing Confidence Intervals for a Proportion with Small Samples

If x is the number of individuals in a sample of size n who have a certain characteristic, and p is the population proportion, then:

The adjusted sample proportion is

$$\tilde{p} = \frac{x+2}{n+4}$$

A confidence interval for p is

$$\tilde{p} - z_{\alpha/2}\sqrt{\frac{\tilde{p}(1-\tilde{p})}{n+4}} < p < \tilde{p} + z_{\alpha/2}\sqrt{\frac{\tilde{p}(1-\tilde{p})}{n+4}}$$

Another way to write this is

$$\tilde{p} \pm z_{\alpha/2}\sqrt{\frac{\tilde{p}(1-\tilde{p})}{n+4}}$$

EXAMPLE 7.17

Construct a confidence interval with a small sample

In a random sample of 10 businesses in a certain city, 6 of them had more than 15 employees. Use the small-sample method to construct a 95% confidence interval for the proportion of businesses in this city that have more than 15 employees.

Solution

The adjusted sample proportion is

$$\tilde{p} = \frac{x+2}{n+4} = \frac{6+2}{10+4} = 0.5714$$

The critical value is $z_{\alpha/2} = 1.96$. The 95% confidence interval is therefore

$$\tilde{p} - z_{\alpha/2}\sqrt{\frac{\tilde{p}(1-\tilde{p})}{n+4}} < p < \tilde{p} + z_{\alpha/2}\sqrt{\frac{\tilde{p}(1-\tilde{p})}{n+4}}$$

$$0.5714 - 1.96\sqrt{\frac{0.5714(1-0.5714)}{10+4}} < p < 0.5714 + 1.96\sqrt{\frac{0.5714(1-0.5714)}{10+4}}$$

$$0.312 < p < 0.831$$

Check Your Understanding

6. In a simple random sample of 15 seniors from a certain college, 8 of them had found jobs. Use the small-sample method to construct a 95% confidence interval for the proportion of seniors at that college who have found jobs.

Answer is on page 329.

Using technology to implement the small-sample method

Because the only difference between the small-sample method and the traditional method is the use of $\tilde{p}$ rather than $\hat{p}$, a software package or calculator such as the TI-84 Plus that uses the traditional method can be made to produce a confidence interval using the small-sample method. Simply input $x + 2$ for the number of individuals in the category of interest, and $n + 4$ for the sample size.

The small-sample method is better overall

The small-sample method can be used for any sample size, and recent research has shown that it has two advantages over the traditional method. First, the margin of error is smaller, because we divide by $n + 4$ rather than n. Second, the actual probability that the small-sample confidence interval covers the true population proportion is almost always at least as great as, or greater than, that of the traditional method. This holds for confidence levels of 90% or more, which are the levels commonly used in practice. For more information on this method, see the article "Approximate is Better Than 'Exact' for Interval Estimation of Binomial Proportions" (A. Agresti and B. Coull, *The American Statistician*, 52:119–126).

USING TECHNOLOGY

We use Example 7.13 to illustrate the technology steps.

TI-84 PLUS

Constructing a confidence interval for a proportion

Step 1. Press **STAT** and highlight the **TESTS** menu.

Step 2. Select **1–PropZInt** and press **ENTER** (Figure A). The **1–PropZInt** menu appears.

Step 3. Enter the values of x and n. For Example 7.13, we use $x = 403$ and $n = 517$.

Step 4. In the **C-Level** field, enter the confidence level. For Example 7.13, we use 0.95 (Figure B).

Step 5. Highlight **Calculate** and press **ENTER** (Figure C).

Note: The preceding steps produce the traditional confidence interval. To produce the small-sample interval, enter the value of $x + 2$ for x and the value of $n + 4$ for n.

Figure A

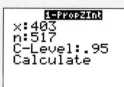

Figure B

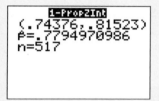

Figure C

MINITAB

Constructing a confidence interval for a proportion

Step 1. Click on **Stat**, then **Basic Statistics**, then **1 Proportion**.

Step 2. Click **Summarized Data** and enter the value of n in the **Number of trials** field and the value of x in the **Number of events** field. For Example 7.13, we use $x = 403$ and $n = 517$ (Figure D).

Step 3. Click **Options** and enter the confidence level in the **Confidence Level** (95) field. Click **OK**.

Step 4. Click **OK** (Figure E).

Note: The preceding steps produce the traditional confidence interval. To produce the small-sample interval, enter the value of $x + 2$ for x and the value of $n + 4$ for n.

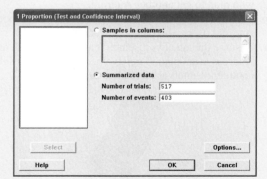

Figure D

Figure E

EXCEL

Constructing a confidence interval for a proportion

This procedure requires the **MegaStat** EXCEL add-in to be loaded. The **MegaStat** add-in may be downloaded from www.mhhe.com/megastat.

Step 1. Click on the **MegaStat** menu and select **Confidence Intervals/Sample Size...**
Step 2. Click on the **Confidence interval – p** option and enter the value of x in the **p** field (note that p automatically changes to x) and the value of n in the **n** field. For Example 7.13, we use $x = 403$ and $n = 517$.
Step 3. In the **Confidence Level** field, enter the confidence level. For Example 7.13, enter **95%** (Figure F).
Step 4. Click **OK** (Figure G).

Note: The preceding steps produce the traditional confidence interval. To produce the small-sample interval, enter the value of $x + 2$ for x and the value of $n + 4$ for n.

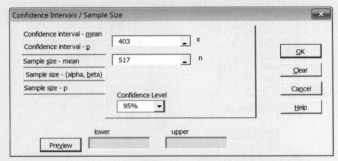

Figure F

Confidence interval - proportion

95%	confidence level
0.779497099	proportion
517	n
1.960	z
0.036	half-width
0.815	upper confidence limit
0.744	lower confidence limit

Figure G

SECTION 7.3 Exercises

Exercises 1–6 are the Check Your Understanding exercises located within the section.

Understanding the Concepts

In Exercises 7 and 8, fill in each blank with the appropriate word or phrase.

7. If $\hat{p}$ is the sample proportion and n is the sample size, then

$$\sqrt{\frac{\hat{p}(1 - \hat{p})}{n}}$$ is the _____ .

8. To estimate the necessary sample size when no value of $\hat{p}$ is available, we use $\hat{p} =$ _____ .

In Exercises 9 and 10, determine whether the statement is true or false. If the statement is false, rewrite it as a true statement.

9. If we estimate the necessary sample size and no value for $\hat{p}$ is available, the estimated sample size will be larger than if a value for $\hat{p}$ were available.

10. The margin of error does not depend on the sample size.

Practicing the Skills

In Exercises 11–14, find the point estimate, the standard error, and the margin of error for the given confidence levels and values of x and n.

11. $x = 146, n = 762$, confidence level 95%

12. $x = 46, n = 97$, confidence level 99%

13. $x = 236, n = 474$, confidence level 90%

14. $x = 29, n = 80$, confidence level 92%

In Exercises 15–18, use the given data to construct a confidence interval of the requested level.

15. $x = 28, n = 64$, confidence level 93%

16. $x = 52, n = 71$, confidence level 97%

17. $x = 125, n = 317$, confidence level 95%

18. $x = 178, n = 531$, confidence level 90%

Working with the Concepts

19. Smart phone: The Nielsen Company surveyed 225 owners of Android phones and found that 160 of them planned to get another Android as their next phone.
  a. Find a point estimate for the proportion of Android users who plan to get another Android.
  b. Construct a 95% confidence interval for the proportion of Android users who plan to get another Android.
  c. Assume that an advertisement claimed that 70% of Android users plan to get another Android. Does the confidence interval contradict this claim?

20. Working at home: According to the U.S. Census Bureau, 43% of men who worked at home were college graduates. In a sample of 500 women who worked at home, 162 were college graduates.

   a. Find a point estimate for the proportion of college graduates among women who work at home.

   b. Construct a 98% confidence interval for the proportion of women who work at home who are college graduates.

   c. Based on the confidence interval, is it reasonable to believe that the proportion of college graduates among women who work at home is the same as the proportion of college graduates among men who work at home? Explain.

21. Sleep apnea: Sleep apnea is a disorder in which there are pauses in breathing during sleep. People with this condition must wake up frequently to breathe. In a sample of 427 people aged 65 and over, 104 of them had sleep apnea.

   a. Find a point estimate for the population proportion of those aged 65 and over who have sleep apnea.

   b. Construct a 99% confidence interval for the proportion of those aged 65 and over who have sleep apnea.

   c. In another study, medical researchers concluded that more than 9% of elderly people have sleep apnea. Based on the confidence interval, does it appear that more than 9% of people aged 65 and over have sleep apnea? Explain.
   Sources: *Sleep* 14:486–495; *Mayo Clinic Proceedings* 76:897–905

22. Internet service: An Internet service provider sampled 540 customers, and finds that 75 of them experienced an interruption in high-speed service during the previous month.

   a. Find a point estimate for the population proportion of all customers who experienced an interruption.

   b. Construct a 90% confidence interval for the proportion of all customers who experienced an interruption.

   c. The company's quality control manager claims that no more than 10% of its customers experienced an interruption during the previous month. Does the confidence interval contradict this claim? Explain.

23. Health insurance: In 2008, the General Social Survey asked 182 people whether they received health insurance as a benefit from their employer. A total of 60 people said they did.

   a. Find a point estimate for the proportion of people who receive health insurance from their employer.

   b. Construct a 95% confidence interval for the proportion of people who receive health insurance from their employer.

   c. An economist states that 50% of employees receive health insurance from their employer. Does the confidence interval contradict this statement? Explain.

24. SAT scores: A college admissions officer sampled 120 entering freshmen and found that 42 of them scored more than 550 on the math SAT.

   a. Find a point estimate for the proportion of all entering freshmen at this college who scored more than 550 on the math SAT.

   b. Construct a 98% confidence interval for the proportion of all entering freshmen at this college who scored more than 550 on the math SAT.

   c. According to the College Board, 39% of all students who took the math SAT in 2009 scored more than 550. The admissions officer believes that the proportion at her university is also 39%. Does the confidence interval contradict this belief? Explain.

25. WOW: In the computer game *World of Warcraft*, some of the strikes are critical strikes, which do more damage. Assume that the probability of a critical strike is the same for every attack, and that attacks are independent. During a particular fight, a character has 242 critical strikes out of 595 attacks.

   a. Construct a 95% confidence interval for the proportion of strikes that are critical strikes.

   b. Construct a 98% confidence interval for the proportion of strikes that are critical strikes.

   c. What is the effect of increasing the level of confidence on the width of the interval?

26. Contaminated water: In a sample of 42 water specimens taken from a construction site, 26 contained detectable levels of lead.

   a. Construct a 90% confidence interval for the proportion of water specimens that contain detectable levels of lead.

   b. Construct a 95% confidence interval for the proportion of water specimens that contain detectable levels of lead.

   c. What is the effect of increasing the level of confidence on the width of the interval?
   Source: *Journal of Environmental Engineering* 128:237–245

27. Call me: A sociologist wants to construct a 95% confidence interval for the proportion of children aged 5–11 living in New York who own a cell phone.

   a. A survey by Mediamark Research and Intelligence estimated the nationwide proportion to be 0.20. Using this estimate, what sample size is needed so that the confidence interval will have a margin of error of 0.02?

   b. Estimate the sample size needed if no estimate of p is available.

   c. If the sociologist wanted to estimate the proportion in the entire United States rather than in New York, would the necessary sample size be larger, smaller, or about the same? Explain.

28. Reading proficiency: An educator wants to construct a 98% confidence interval for the proportion of elementary school children in Colorado who are proficient in reading.

   a. The results of a recent statewide test suggested that the proportion is 0.70. Using this estimate, what sample size is needed so that the confidence interval will have a margin of error of 0.05?

   b. Estimate the sample size needed if no estimate of p is available.

   c. If the educator wanted to estimate the proportion in the entire United States rather than in Colorado, would the necessary sample size be larger, smaller, or about the same? Explain.

29. Surgical complications: A medical researcher wants to construct a 99% confidence interval for the proportion of knee replacement surgeries that result in complications.

   a. An article in the *Journal of Bone and Joint Surgery* suggested that approximately 8% of such operations result in complications. Using this estimate, what sample size is needed so that the confidence interval will have a margin of error of 0.04?

   b. Estimate the sample size needed if no estimate of p is available.

   Source: *Journal of Bone and Joint Surgery* 87:1719–1724

30. **How's the economy?** A pollster wants to construct a 95% confidence interval for the proportion of adults who believe that economic conditions are getting better.

   a. A Gallup poll taken in July 2010 estimates this proportion to be 0.33. Using this estimate, what sample size is needed so that the confidence interval will have a margin of error of 0.03?

   b. Estimate the sample size needed if no estimate of p is available.

31. **Changing jobs:** A sociologist sampled 200 people who work in computer-related jobs, and found that 42 of them have changed jobs in the past 6 months.

   a. Construct a 95% confidence interval for the proportion of those who work in computer-related jobs who have changed jobs in the past six months.

   b. Among the 200 people, 120 of them are under the age of 35. These constitute a simple random sample of workers under the age of 35. If this sample were used to construct a 95% confidence interval for the proportion of workers under the age of 35 who have changed jobs in the past six months, is it likely that the margin of error would be larger, smaller, or about the same as the one in part (a)?

32. **Political polling:** A simple random sample of 300 voters was polled several months before a presidential election. One of the questions asked was: "Are you satisfied with the choice of candidates for president?" A total of 123 of them said that they were not satisfied.

   a. Construct a 99% confidence interval for the proportion of voters who are not satisfied with the choice of candidates.

   b. Among the 300 voters were 158 women. These constitute a simple random sample of women voters. If this sample were used to construct a 99% confidence interval for the proportion of women voters who are satisfied with the choice of candidates for president, is it likely that the margin of error would be larger, smaller, or about the same as the one in part (a)?

33. **Small sample:** Eighteen concrete blocks were sampled and tested for crushing strength in order to estimate the proportion that were sufficiently strong for a certain application. Sixteen of the 18 blocks were sufficiently strong. Use the small-sample method to construct a 95% confidence interval for the proportion of blocks that are sufficiently strong.

34. **Small sample:** During an economic downturn, 20 companies were sampled and asked whether they were planning to
increase their workforce. Only 3 of the 20 companies were planning to increase their workforce. Use the small-sample method to construct a 98% confidence interval for the proportion of companies that are planning to increase their workforce.

35. **Calculator display:** The following TI-84 Plus display presents a 99% confidence interval for a proportion.

```
          1-PropZInt
( .41911,.73714)
p=.578125
n=64
```

   a. Fill in the blanks. We are _____ confident that the population proportion is between _____ and _____ .

   b. Use the information in the display to construct a 95% confidence interval for p.

36. **Calculator display:** The following TI-84 Plus display presents a 95% confidence interval for a proportion.

```
          1-PropZInt
( .19525,.38253)
p=.2888888889
n=90
```

   a. Fill in the blanks. We are _____ confident that the population proportion is between _____ and _____ .

   b. Use the information in the display to construct a 98% confidence interval for p.

37. **Computer output:** The following MINITAB output presents a 98% confidence interval for a proportion.

Sample	X	N	Sample p	98% CI
1	145	181	0.801105	(0.732082, 0.870128)

   a. Fill in the blanks. We are _____ confident that the population proportion is between _____ and _____ .

   b. Use the information in the display to construct a 90% confidence interval for p.

38. **Computer output:** The following MINITAB output presents a 95% confidence interval for a proportion.

Sample	X	N	Sample p	95% CI
1	31	58	0.534483	(0.406111, 0.662854)

   a. Fill in the blanks. We are _____ confident that the population proportion is between _____ and _____ .

   b. Use the information in the display to construct a 99% confidence interval for p.

39. **Don't construct a confidence interval:** In a certain city, it has rained on 72 of the past 365 days. Explain why these data should not be used to construct a confidence interval for the proportion of days that are rainy.

40. Don't construct a confidence interval: At the end of a television documentary on the nature of government, viewers are invited to go to a website and answer the question, "Do you believe that women are more effective at governing than men are?" A total of 2348 viewers answer the question, and 1247 of them answer "Yes." Explain why these data should not be used to construct a confidence interval for the proportion of people who believe that women are more effective at governing than men are.

Extending the Concepts

Wilson's interval: The small-sample method for constructing a confidence interval is a simple approximation of a more complicated interval known as Wilson's interval. Let $\hat{p} = x/n$. Wilson's confidence interval for p is given by

$$\frac{\hat{p} + \frac{z_{\alpha/2}^2}{2n} \pm z_{\alpha/2}\sqrt{\frac{\hat{p}(1-\hat{p})}{n} + \frac{z_{\alpha/2}^2}{4n^2}}}{1 + \frac{z_{\alpha/2}^2}{n}}$$

41. College-bound: In a certain high school, 9 out of 15 tenth-graders said they planned to go to college after graduating. Construct a 95% confidence interval for the proportion of tenth-graders who plan to attend college:
  a. Using Wilson's method

  b. Using the small-sample method
  c. Using the traditional method

42. Comparing the methods: Refer to Exercise 41.
  a. Which of the three confidence intervals is the narrowest?
  b. Does the small-sample method provide a good approximation to Wilson's interval in this case?
  c. Explain why the traditional interval is the widest of the three.

43. Approximation depends on the level: The small-sample method is a good approximation to Wilson's method for all confidence levels commonly used in practice, but is best when $z_{\alpha/2}$ is close to 2. Refer to Exercise 41.
  a. Use Wilson's method to construct a 90% confidence interval, a 95% confidence interval, and a 99% confidence interval for the proportion of tenth-graders who plan to attend college.

  b. Use the small-sample method to construct a 90% confidence interval, a 95% confidence interval, and a 99% confidence interval for the proportion of tenth-graders who plan to attend college.

  c. For which level is the small-sample method the closest to Wilson's method? Explain why this is the case.

Answers to Check Your Understanding Exercises for Section 7.3

1. a. 0.710   **b.** $0.647 < p < 0.773$

  c. Yes. We are 95% confident that the proportion who would improve their scores is between 0.647 and 0.773. Therefore, it is reasonable to conclude that the proportion is greater than 0.60.

  d. No. Because the sample contains only third-graders, it should not be used to construct a confidence interval for all elementary school children.

2. 151

3. 542

4. a. False   **b.** True

5. a. False   **b.** True   **c.** False

6. $0.302 < p < 0.751$

SECTION 7.4 Determining Which Method to Use

Objectives

> 1. Determine which method to use when constructing a confidence interval

Objective 1 Determine which method to use when constructing a confidence interval

One of the challenges in constructing a confidence interval is to determine which method to use. The first step is to determine which type of parameter we are estimating. There are two types of parameters for which we have learned to construct confidence intervals:

- Population mean μ
- Population proportion p

Once you have determined which type of parameter you are estimating, proceed as follows:

- **Population mean:** There are two methods for constructing a confidence interval for a population mean, the z method (Section 7.1) and the t method (Section 7.2). To determine which method to use, we must determine whether the population standard deviation is known, whether the population is approximately normal, and whether the sample size is large ($n > 30$). The following diagram can help you make the correct choice.

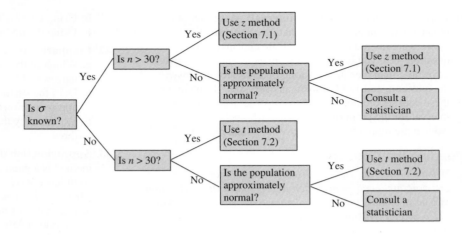

- **Population proportion:** To construct a confidence interval for a population proportion, use the method described in Section 7.3.

EXAMPLE 7.18

Determining which method to use

A random sample of 41 pumpkins harvested from a pumpkin patch has a mean weight of $\bar{x} = 8.53$ pounds with a sample standard deviation of $s = 1.32$ pounds. Construct a 95% confidence interval for the mean weight of pumpkins from this patch. Determine the type of parameter that is to be estimated and construct the confidence interval.

Solution

We are asked to find a confidence interval for the mean weight; this is a population mean. We consult the diagram to determine the correct method. We must first determine whether σ is known. There is no information given about σ, so σ is unknown. We follow the "No" path. Next we must determine whether $n > 30$. There are 41 pumpkins in the sample, so $n > 30$. We follow the "Yes" path, and find that we should use the t method described in Section 7.2.

To construct the confidence interval, there are $41 - 1 = 40$ degrees of freedom. Because the confidence level is 95%, the critical value is $t_{0.025} = 2.021$. The 95% confidence interval is

$$8.53 \pm 2.021 \frac{1.32}{\sqrt{41}}$$

$$8.11 < \mu < 8.95$$

Check Your Understanding

In Exercises 1–4, state which type of parameter is to be estimated, then construct the confidence interval.

1. In a simple random sample of 200 electronic circuits taken from a large shipment, 14 were defective. Construct a 95% confidence interval for the proportion of circuits that are defective.

2. A simple random sample of size 80 has mean $\bar{x} = 7.31$. The population standard deviation is $\sigma = 6.26$. Construct a 99% confidence interval for the population mean.

3. In a simple random sample of 100 children, 22 had reading skills above their grade level. Construct a 99% confidence interval for the proportion of children who have reading skills above their grade level.

4. A simple random sample of size 25 has mean $\bar{x} = 17.4$ and standard deviation $s = 5.3$. The population is approximately normally distributed. Construct a 95% confidence interval for the population mean.

Answers are at bottom of this page.

SECTION 7.4   Exercises

Exercises 1–4 are the Check Your Understanding exercises located within the section.

Practicing the Skills

In Exercises 5–10, state which type of parameter is to be estimated, then construct the confidence interval.

5. A simple random sample of size 18 has mean $\bar{x} = 71.32$ and standard deviation $s = 15.78$. The population is approximately normally distributed. Construct a 95% confidence interval for the population mean.

6. In a simple random sample of 400 voters, 220 said that they were planning to vote for the incumbent mayor in the next election. Construct a 99% confidence interval for the proportion of voters who plan to vote for the incumbent mayor in the next election.

7. In a survey of 250 employed adults, 185 said that they had missed one or more days of work in the past six months. Construct a 95% confidence interval for the proportion of employed adults who missed one or more days of work in the past six months.

8. A simple random sample of size 12 has mean $\bar{x} = 3.37$. The population standard deviation is $\sigma = 1.62$. The population is approximately normally distributed. Construct a 95% confidence interval for the population mean.

9. A simple random sample of size 120 has mean $\bar{x} = 8.45$. The population standard deviation is $\sigma = 4.81$. Construct a 99% confidence interval for the population mean.

10. A simple random sample of size 23 has mean $\bar{x} = 1.48$ and standard deviation $s = 1.32$. The population is approximately normally distributed. Construct a 99% confidence interval for the population mean.

Understanding the Concepts

11. Football players: Following are the weights of 52 randomly selected NFL football players in 2010. The sample mean is $\bar{x} = 256.27$ and the sample standard deviation is $s = 37.90$.

216	318	330	300	245	285	209	250	313
207	200	291	198	200	264	190	252	251
270	239	216	256	315	217	250	225	220
311	212	220	215	330	220	265	320	308
252	255	292	290	299	231	254	266	254
266	261	258	257	261	250	252		

Source: *Chicago Tribune*

Construct a 95% confidence interval for the mean weight of NFL football players in 2010.

12. Ages of students: A simple random sample of 100 U.S. college students had a mean age of 22.68 years. Assume the population standard deviation is $\sigma = 4.74$ years. Construct a 99% confidence interval for the mean age of U.S. college students.

13. Windy place: Mt. Washington, New Hampshire, is one of the windiest places in the United States. Wind speed measurements on a simple random sample of 50 days had a sample mean of 45.01 mph. Assume the population standard deviation is $\sigma = 25.6$ mph. Construct a 95% confidence interval for the mean wind speed on Mt. Washington.

14. Credit card debt: In a survey of 1500 U.S. adults conducted in 2009 by the Financial Industry Regulatory Authority, 810 said they always pay their credit cards in full each month. Construct a 95% confidence interval for the proportion of U.S. adults who pay their credit cards in full each month.

15. Pneumonia: In a simple random sample of 1500 patients admitted to the hospital with pneumonia, 145 were under the age of 18. Construct a 99% confidence interval for the proportion of pneumonia patients who are under the age of 18.

16. College tuition: A simple random sample of 35 colleges and universities in New York State had a mean tuition of $30,577 with a standard deviation of $6,232. Construct a 95% confidence interval for the mean tuition for all colleges and universities in New York State.

Answers to Check Your Understanding Exercises for Section 7.4

1. The parameter is the population proportion. The 95% confidence interval is $0.035 < p < 0.105$.

2. The parameter is the population mean. The 99% confidence interval is $5.51 < \mu < 9.11$.

3. The parameter is the population proportion. The 99% confidence interval is $0.113 < p < 0.327$.

4. The parameter is the population mean. The 95% confidence interval is $15.2 < \mu < 19.6$.

Chapter 7 Summary

Section 7.1: In this section, we presented the basic ideas behind confidence intervals. We learned that a point estimate is a single number that is used to estimate the value of an unknown parameter. For example, the sample mean $\bar{x}$ is a point estimate of the population mean μ. The standard error of a point estimate tells us roughly how far from the true value the point estimate is likely to be. We multiply the standard error by a critical value to obtain the margin of error. By adding and subtracting the margin of error from the point estimate, we obtain a confidence interval. The level of a confidence interval is the proportion of samples for which the confidence interval will contain the true value. If the sample size is large ($n > 30$) or if the population is approximately normal, then the confidence interval for the population mean is $\bar{x} \pm z_{\alpha/2}\sigma/\sqrt{n}$ if the population mean σ is known.

Section 7.2: When the population is approximately normal, or the sample size is large ($n > 30$), we can use the Student's t distribution to construct a confidence interval for a population mean μ when the population standard deviation is unknown. Let s be the sample standard deviation. The confidence interval is $\bar{x} \pm t_{\alpha/2}s/\sqrt{n}$ if σ is unknown.

Section 7.3: In this section, we learned to construct confidence intervals for population proportions. The assumptions are that the individuals in the population can be divided into two categories, that the sample contains at least 10 individuals in each category, and that the population is at least 20 times as large as the sample. We denote the sample size by n and the number of individuals in the sample who fall into the specified category by x. When the assumptions are met, the confidence interval for the population proportion p is $\hat{p} \pm z_{\alpha/2}\sqrt{\hat{p}(1 - \hat{p})/n}$, where $\hat{p} = x/n$. A small-sample method can also be used. In the small-sample method, we define $\tilde{p} = \dfrac{x + 2}{n + 4}$. The confidence interval is $\tilde{p} \pm z_{\alpha/2}\sqrt{\dfrac{\tilde{p}(1 - \tilde{p})}{n + 4}}$. The small-sample confidence interval is actually valid for any sample size.

Section 7.4: We have learned to construct confidence intervals for a population mean and a population proportion. There are two methods for constructing a confidence interval for a population mean, the z method and the t method. The method to use depends on whether the population standard deviation σ is known.

Vocabulary and Notation

confidence interval   290
confidence level   290
critical value   289

degrees of freedom   306
margin of error   289
point estimate   288

standard error   289
Student's t distribution   306

Important Formulas

Confidence interval for a mean, standard deviation known:

$$\bar{x} - z_{\alpha/2}\frac{\sigma}{\sqrt{n}} < \mu < \bar{x} + z_{\alpha/2}\frac{\sigma}{\sqrt{n}}$$

Sample size to construct an interval for μ with margin of error m:

$$n = \left(\frac{z_{\alpha/2} \cdot \sigma}{m}\right)^2$$

Confidence interval for a mean, standard deviation unknown:

$$\bar{x} - t_{\alpha/2}\frac{s}{\sqrt{n}} < \mu < \bar{x} + t_{\alpha/2}\frac{s}{\sqrt{n}}$$

Confidence interval for a proportion:

$$\hat{p} - z_{\alpha/2}\sqrt{\frac{\hat{p}(1 - \hat{p})}{n}} < p < \hat{p} + z_{\alpha/2}\sqrt{\frac{\hat{p}(1 - \hat{p})}{n}}$$

Sample size to construct an interval for p with margin of error m:

$$n = \hat{p}(1 - \hat{p})\left(\frac{z_{\alpha/2}}{m}\right)^2 \quad \text{if a value for } \hat{p} \text{ is available}$$

$$n = 0.25\left(\frac{z_{\alpha/2}}{m}\right)^2 \quad \text{if no value for } \hat{p} \text{ is available}$$

Chapter Quiz

1. Define the following terms:
   a. Point estimate
   b. Confidence interval
   c. Confidence level

2. Find the critical value $t_{\alpha/2}$ needed to construct a 90% confidence interval for a population mean with sample size 27.

3. An owner of a fleet of taxis wants to estimate the mean gas mileage, in miles per gallon, of the cars in the fleet. A random sample of 40 cars is followed for one month, and the sample mean gas mileage is 23.2 with a standard deviation of 5.8. Construct a 90% confidence interval for the mean gas mileage in the fleet.

4. A cookie manufacturer wants to estimate the length of time that her boxes of cookies spend in the store before they are bought. She visits a sample of 15 supermarkets and determines the number of days since manufacture of the oldest box of cookies in the store. The mean is 54.8 days with a standard deviation of 11.3 days. A dotplot of the data indicates that the assumptions for constructing a confidence interval for the mean are satisfied. Construct a 99% confidence interval for the mean number of days.

5. A person selects a random sample of 15 credit cards and determines the annual interest rate, in percent, of each. The sample mean is 12.42 with a sample standard deviation of 1.3. Construct a 95% confidence interval for the mean credit card annual interest rate, assuming that the rates are approximately normally distributed.

6. Find the critical value $z_{\alpha/2}$ needed to construct a confidence interval for a population proportion with confidence level 92%.

7. A water utility wants to take a sample of residences in a city in order to estimate the proportion who have reduced their water consumption during the past year. In the absence of preliminary data, how large a sample must be taken so that a 95% confidence interval will have a margin of error of 0.05?

8. In a sample of 100 residences, 73 had reduced their water consumption. Construct a 95% confidence interval for the proportion of residents who reduced their water consumption.

9. Refer to Exercise 8. How large a sample is needed so that a 95% confidence interval will have a margin of error of 0.05, using this sample proportion for $\hat{p}$?

10. The amount of time that a certain cell phone will keep a charge is known to be normally distributed with standard deviation $\sigma = 16$ hours. A sample of 40 cell phones had a mean time of 141 hours. Let μ represent the population mean time that a cell phone will keep a charge.
    a. What is the point estimate of μ?
    b. What is the standard error of the point estimate?

11. Refer to Exercise 10. Suppose that a 95% confidence interval is to be constructed for the mean time.
    a. What is the critical value?
    b. What is the margin of error?
    c. Construct the 95% confidence interval.

12. Refer to Exercise 10. What sample size is necessary so that a 95% confidence interval will have a margin of error of 1 hour?

13. In a survey of 802 U.S. adult drivers, 265 state that traffic is getting worse in their community. Construct a 99% confidence interval for the proportion of adult drivers who think that traffic is getting worse.

14. Refer to Exercise 13. How large a sample is needed so that a 99% confidence interval will have margin of error of 0.08, using the sample proportion for $\hat{p}$?

15. Refer to Exercise 13. How large a sample is needed so that a 99% confidence interval will have margin of error of 0.08, assuming no estimate of $\hat{p}$ is available?

Review Exercises

1. **Build more parking?** A survey is to be conducted in which a random sample of residents in a certain city will be asked whether they favor or oppose the building of a new parking structure downtown. How many residents should be polled to be sure that a 90% confidence interval for the proportion who favor the construction will have a margin of error no greater than 0.05?

2. **Drill lifetime:** A sample of 50 drills had a mean lifetime of 12.68 holes drilled when drilling a low-carbon steel. Assume the population standard deviation is 6.83.
    a. Construct a 95% confidence interval for the mean lifetime of this type of drill.
    b. The manufacturer of the drills claims that the mean lifetime is greater than 13. Does this confidence interval contradict this claim? Explain.
    c. How large would the sample need to be so that a 95% confidence interval would have a margin of error of 1.0?
    Source: *Journal of Engineering Manufacture* 216:301–305

3. **Cost of environmental restoration:** In a survey of 189 Scottish voters, 61 said they would be willing to pay additional taxes in order to restore the Affric forest.
    a. Assuming that the 189 voters who responded constitute a random sample, construct a 99% confidence interval for the proportion of voters who would be willing to pay to restore the Affric forest.
    b. Use the results from the sample of size 189 to estimate the sample size needed so that the 99% confidence interval will have a margin of error of 0.03.

c. Another survey is planned, in which voters will be asked whether they would be willing to pay in order to restore the Strathsprey forest. At this point, no estimate of this proportion is available. Find an estimate of the sample size needed so that the margin of error of a 99% confidence interval will be 0.03.

Source: *Environmental and Resource Economics* 18:391–410

4. More repairs: A sample of six records for repairs of a component showed the following costs:

93 97 27 79 81 87

a. Construct a 90% confidence interval for the mean cost of a repair for this type of component.
b. Is there any evidence to suggest that this confidence interval may not be reliable? Explain.

5. Automobile pollution: In a random sample of 85 vehicles driven at high altitudes, 21 exceeded a threshold for the amount of particulate pollution. Construct a 99% confidence interval for the proportion of high-altitude vehicles that exceed the threshold for particulate pollution.

6. Contaminated water: Polychlorinated biphenyls (PCBs) are a group of synthetic oil-like chemicals that were at one time widely used as insulation in electrical equipment and were discharged into rivers. They were discovered to be a health hazard, and were banned in the 1970s. Assume that water samples are being drawn from a river in order to estimate the PCB concentration. Suppose that a random sample of size 60 has a sample mean of 1.96 parts per billion (ppb). Assume the population standard deviation is $\sigma = 0.35$ ppb.

a. Construct a 98% confidence interval for the PCB concentration.
b. EPA standards require that the PCB concentration in drinking water be no more than 0.5 ppb. Based on the confidence interval, is it reasonable to believe that this water meets the EPA standard for drinking water? Explain.
c. Estimate the sample size needed so that a 98% confidence interval will have a margin of error of 0.03.

7. Defective electronics: A simple random sample of 200 electronic components was tested, and 17 of them were found to be defective.
a. Construct a 99% confidence interval for the proportion of components that are defective.
b. Use the results from the sample of 200 to estimate the sample size needed so that the 99% confidence interval will have a margin of error equal to 0.04.
c. A simple random sample of a different type of component will be tested. At this point, there is no estimate of the proportion defective. Find a sample size so that the 99% confidence interval will have a margin of error no greater than 0.04.

8. Cost of repairs: A sample of eight repair records for a certain fiber-optic component was drawn, and the cost of each repair, in dollars, was recorded, with the following results:

30 35 19 23 27 22 26 16

a. Construct a dotplot for these data. Are the assumptions for constructing a confidence interval for the mean satisfied? Explain.
b. If appropriate, construct a 98% confidence interval for the mean cost of a repair.

9. High octane: Fifty measurements are taken of the octane rating for a particular type of gasoline. The sample mean rating (in percent) was 85.8 and the sample standard deviation was 1.2. Find a 95% confidence interval for the mean octane rating for this type of gasoline.

10. Super Bowl: A simple random sample of 140 residents in a certain town was polled the week after the Super Bowl, and 75 of them said they had watched the game on television.
a. Construct a 95% confidence interval for the proportion of people in the town who watched the Super Bowl on television.
b. The 2011 Super Bowl between the Green Bay Packers and the Pittsburgh Steelers was the most watched television program in history, with 47.9% of television sets in the United States tuned to the game. Someone claims that the percentage of people who watched the game in this town was less than 47.9%. Does the confidence interval contradict this claim? Explain.
c. Use the results from the sample of 140 to estimate the sample size necessary for a 95% confidence interval to have a margin of error of 0.025.

11. Testing math skills: In order to test the effectiveness of a program to improve mathematical skills, a simple random sample of 45 fifth-graders was chosen to participate in the program. The students were given an exam at the beginning of the program and again at the end. The sample mean increase in the exam score was 12.2 points, with a sample standard deviation of 4.7 points.
a. Construct a 99% confidence interval for the mean increase in score.
b. The developers of the program claim that the program will produce a mean increase of more than 15 points. Does the confidence interval contradict this claim? Explain.

12. Sleep time: In a sample of 87 young adults, the average time per day spent in bed asleep was 7.06 hours. Assume the population sample standard deviation is 1.11 hours.
a. Construct a 99% confidence interval for the mean time spent in bed asleep.
b. Some health experts recommend that people get 8 hours or more of sleep per night. Based on the confidence interval, is it reasonable to believe that the mean number of hours of sleep for young adults is 8 or more? Explain.

c. How large would the sample have to be so that a 99% confidence interval would have a margin of error of 0.1?
   Source: *Behavioral Medicine* 27:71–76

13. **Leaking tanks:** Leakage from underground fuel tanks has been a source of water pollution. In a random sample of 107 gasoline stations, 18 were found to have at least one leaking underground tank.
   a. Find a point estimate for the proportion of gasoline stations with at least one leaking underground tank.
   b. Construct a 95% confidence interval for the proportion of gasoline stations with at least one leaking underground tank.
   c. Use the point estimate computed in part (a) to determine the number of stations that must be sampled so that a 95% confidence interval will have a margin of error of 0.03.

14. **Waist size:** According to the National Health Statistics Reports, a sample of 783 men aged 20–29 years had a mean waist size of 36.9 inches with a standard deviation of 8.8 inches.
   a. Construct a 95% confidence interval for the mean waist size.
   b. The results of another study suggest that the mean waist size for men aged 30–39 is 38.7 inches. Based on the confidence interval, is it reasonable to believe that the mean waist size for men aged 20–29 may be 38.7 inches? Explain.

15. **Don't construct a confidence interval:** A meteorology student examines precipitation records for a certain city and discovers that of the last 365 days, it rained on 46 of them. Explain why these data cannot be used to construct a confidence interval for the proportion of days in this city that are rainy.

Write About It

1. When constructing a confidence interval for μ when σ is known, we assume that we have a simple random sample, that σ is known, and that either the sample size is large or the population is approximately normal. Why is it necessary for these assumptions to be met?

2. What factors can you think of that may affect the width of a confidence interval? In what way does each factor affect the width?

3. Explain the difference between confidence and probability.

   In Exercises 4 and 5, express the following survey results in terms of confidence intervals for p:

4. According to a survey of 1000 American adults, 55% of Americans do not have a will specifying the handling of their estate. The survey's margin of error was plus or minus 3%.
   Source: FindLaw.com

5. In a survey of 5050 U.S. adults, 29% would consider traveling abroad for medical care because of medical costs. The survey's margin of error was plus or minus 2%.
   Source: The Gallup Poll

6. When constructing a confidence interval for μ, how do you decide whether to use the t distribution or the normal distribution? Are there any circumstances when it is acceptable to use either distribution?

7. It is stated in the text that there are many different t distributions. Explain how this is so.

Case Study: Do Newer Wood Stoves Produce Less Pollution?

The town of Libby, Montana, has experienced high levels of air pollution in the winter, because many of the houses in Libby are heated by wood stoves that produce a lot of pollution. In an attempt to reduce the level of air pollution in Libby, a program was undertaken in which almost every wood stove in the town was replaced with a newer, cleaner-burning model. Most stoves were replaced in 2006 and early 2007. Measurements of several air pollutants were taken both before and after the stove replacement. They included particulate matter (PM), total carbon (TC), organic carbon (OC), which is carbon bound in organic molecules, and levoglucosan (LE), which is a compound found in charcoal and is thus an indicator of the amount of wood smoke in the atmosphere.

In order to determine how much the pollution levels were reduced, scientists measured the levels of these pollutants for three winters prior to the replacement. The mean levels over this period of time are referred to as the *baseline* levels. Following are the baseline levels for these pollutants. The units are micrograms per cubic meter.

PM: 27.08   OC: 17.41   TC: 18.87   LE: 2.57

The following table presents values measured on samples of days during the winters of 2007–2008 and 2008–2009.

2007–2008				2008–2009			
PM	OC	TC	LE	PM	OC	TC	LE
21.7	15.6	17.73	1.78	27.0	15.79	19.46	2.06
27.8	15.6	17.87	2.25	24.7	13.61	15.98	3.10
24.7	17.2	18.75	1.98	21.8	12.94	15.79	2.68
15.3	8.3	9.21	0.67	23.2	12.97	16.32	2.80
18.4	11.3	12.46	0.86	23.3	11.19	13.49	2.07
14.4	8.4	9.66	1.93	16.2	9.61	12.44	2.14
19.0	13.2	14.73	1.51	13.4	6.97	8.40	2.32
23.7	11.4	13.23	1.98	13.0	7.96	10.02	2.18
22.4	13.8	17.08	1.69	16.9	8.43	11.08	2.06
25.6	13.2	15.86	2.30	26.3	14.92	21.46	1.94
15.0	15.7	17.27	1.24	31.4	17.15	20.57	1.85
17.0	9.3	10.21	1.44	40.1	15.13	19.64	2.11
23.2	10.5	11.47	1.43	28.0	8.66	10.75	2.50
17.7	14.2	15.64	1.07	4.2	15.95	20.36	2.27
11.1	11.6	13.48	0.59	15.9	11.73	14.59	2.17
29.8	7.0	7.795	2.10	20.5	14.34	17.64	2.74
20.0	19.9	21.20	1.73	23.8	8.99	11.75	2.45
21.6	14.8	15.65	1.56	14.6	10.63	13.12	
14.8	12.6	13.51	1.10	17.8			
21.0	9.1	9.94					

1. For each of the four pollutants, construct a boxplot for the values for the winter of 2007–2008 to verify that the assumptions for constructing a confidence interval are satisfied.
2. Construct a 95% confidence interval for the mean level of each pollutant for the winter of 2007–2008.
3. Is it reasonable to conclude that the mean levels in 2007–2008 were lower than the baseline levels for some or all of the pollutants? Which ones, if any?

The investigators were concerned that the reduction in pollution levels might be only temporary. Specifically, they were concerned that people might use their new stoves carefully at first, thus obtaining the full advantage of their cleaner burning, but then become more casual in their operation, leading to an increase in pollution levels. We will investigate this issue by constructing confidence intervals for the mean levels in 2008–2009.

4. Repeat Exercises 1 and 2 for the 2008–2009 data.
5. Is it reasonable to conclude that the mean levels in 2008–2009 were lower than the baseline levels for some or all of the pollutants? Which ones, if any?

Hypothesis Testing

Introduction

Is global warming real? There is much evidence to suggest that temperatures have been increasing since the early part of the 20th century. Whether the increase is caused by human activity or whether it is part of a natural cycle is a topic of debate. Studies of global warming involve analyzing temperature records. The following table presents the record high and low temperatures in degrees Fahrenheit in Washington, D.C., along with the year in which the record was set, for a selection of days in April through September. The column labeled "More Recent" tells which record, high or low, occurred more recently.

Date	High	Year	Low	Year	More Recent	Date	High	Year	Low	Year	More Recent	Date	High	Year	Low	Year	More Recent
Apr 2	89	1963	23	1907	High	Jun 4	99	1925	46	1929*	Low	Aug 6	106	1918	53	1912	High
9	90	1959	28	1972*	Low	11	101	1911	45	1913	Low	13	101	1881	55	1930*	Low
16	92	2002	29	1928	High	18	97	1944	51	1965*	Low	20	101	1983	50	1896	High
23	95	1960	33	1933*	High	25	100	1997	53	1902	High	27	100	1987	51	1885	High
30	92	1942*	34	1874	High	Jul 2	101	1898	55	1940	Low	Sep 3	98	1953	48	1909*	High
May 7	95	1930	38	1970	Low	9	104	1936	55	1891	High	10	98	1983	44	1883	High
14	93	1956	41	1928	High	16	104	1988	56	1930*	High	17	96	1991	44	1923	High
21	95	1934	41	1907	High	23	101	1991	56	1890	High	24	94	1970	39	1963	High
28	97	1941	42	1961	Low	30	99	1953	56	1914	High						

*Indicates that the record occurred more than once; only the most recent year is given.
Source: National Weather Service

If there were no temperature trend, we would expect that the proportion of days on which the high temperature record was more recent to be about one-half. It would not be surprising if this proportion were somewhat different from one-half, because we would expect to see some difference just by chance. However, we would not expect the proportion to be much different from one-half. If the proportion were much different from one-half, we would conclude that there was a temperature trend.

There are 26 days in the table. Half of 26 is 13. If the record high had been more recent on 13 of the days, there would be no reason to believe there was a warming trend. If the record high had been more recent on 14 or 15 days, this would be slightly more than one-half, but it would seem reasonable to believe that a difference this small was just due to chance.

In fact, the record high temperature was more recent for 18 of the 26 days. The question we need to address is whether this difference from one-half is too large for us to believe that it is simply due to chance. This is the sort of question that hypothesis tests are designed to answer. In this chapter, we will learn to perform hypothesis tests in a variety of commonly occurring situations. In the case study at the end of the chapter, we will study a data set that includes the data in the preceding table, and investigate the possibility of a warming trend in Washington, D.C.

SECTION 8.1   Basic Principles of Hypothesis Testing

Objectives

1. Define the null and alternate hypotheses
2. State conclusions to hypothesis tests
3. Distinguish between Type I and Type II errors

Objective 1 Define the null and alternate hypotheses

The Null Hypothesis and the Alternate Hypothesis

Air pollution has become a serious health problem in many cities. One of the forms of air pollution that health officials are most concerned about is particulate matter (PM), which refers to fine particles that can be trapped in the lungs, increasing the risk of respiratory disease. Some of the PM in the atmosphere comes from car exhaust, so one important way to reduce PM pollution is to design automobile engines that produce less PM. The following example will show how hypothesis testing can play a part in this effort.

A study published in the *Journal of the Air and Waste Management Association* reported that the mean amount of PM produced by cars and light trucks in an urban setting is 35 milligrams of PM per mile of travel. Suppose that a new engine design is proposed that is intended to reduce this level. Now there are two possibilities: either the new design will reduce the level, or it will not. These possibilities are called **hypotheses**. To be specific,

1. The **null hypothesis** says that the new design will not reduce the level, so the mean for the new engines will be $\mu = 35$.
2. The **alternate hypothesis** says that the new design will reduce the level, so $\mu < 35$.

In general, the null hypothesis says that a parameter is equal to a certain value, while the alternate hypothesis says that the parameter differs from this value. Often the null hypothesis is a statement of no change or no difference, while the alternate hypothesis states that a change or difference has occurred.

DEFINITION

- The **null hypothesis** about a parameter states that the parameter is equal to a specific value, for example, H_0: $\mu = 35$. The null hypothesis is denoted H_0.
- The **alternate hypothesis** about a parameter states that the value of the parameter differs from the value specified by the null hypothesis. The alternate hypothesis is denoted H_1.

There are three types of alternate hypothesis, which we now define.

> **DEFINITION**
>
> - A **left-tailed** alternate hypothesis states that the parameter is less than the value specified by the null hypothesis, for example, H_1: $\mu < 35$.
> - A **right-tailed** alternate hypothesis states that the parameter is greater than the value specified by the null hypothesis, for example, H_1: $\mu > 35$.
> - A **two-tailed** alternate hypothesis states that the parameter is not equal to the value specified by the null hypothesis, for example, H_1: $\mu \neq 35$.
>
> Left-tailed and right-tailed hypotheses are called **one-tailed** hypotheses.

EXAMPLE 8.1   State the null and alternate hypotheses

Boxes of a certain kind of cereal are labeled as containing 20 ounces. An inspector thinks that the mean weight may be less than this. State the appropriate null and alternate hypotheses.

Solution

The null hypothesis says that there is no difference, so the null hypothesis is H_0: $\mu = 20$. The inspector thinks that the mean weight may be less than 20, so the alternate hypothesis is H_1: $\mu < 20$.

EXAMPLE 8.2   State the null and alternate hypotheses

Last year, the mean monthly rent for an apartment in a certain city was $800. A real estate agent believes that the mean rent is higher this year. State the appropriate null and alternate hypotheses.

Solution

The null hypothesis says that there is no change, so the null hypothesis is H_0: $\mu = 800$. The real estate agent wants to know whether the mean is higher, so the alternate hypothesis is H_1: $\mu > 800$.

EXAMPLE 8.3   State the null and alternate hypotheses

Scores on a standardized test have a mean of 70. Some modifications are made to the test, and an educator believes that the mean may have changed. State the appropriate null and alternate hypotheses.

Solution

The null hypothesis says that there is no change, so the null hypothesis is H_0: $\mu = 70$. The educator wants to know whether the mean has changed, without specifying whether it has increased or decreased. Therefore, the alternate hypothesis is H_1: $\mu \neq 70$.

Check Your Understanding

1. Last year, the mean amount spent by customers at a certain restaurant was $35. The restaurant owner believes that the mean may be higher this year. State the appropriate null and alternate hypotheses.

2. In a recent year, the mean weight of newborn boys in a certain country was 6.6 pounds. A doctor wants to know whether the mean weight of newborn girls differs from this. State the appropriate null and alternate hypotheses.

3. A certain model of car can be ordered with either a large or small engine. The mean number of miles per gallon for cars with a small engine is 25.5. An automotive

engineer thinks that the mean for cars with the larger engine will be less than this. State the appropriate null and alternate hypotheses.

Answers are on page 343.

A hypothesis test is like a trial

The purpose of a **hypothesis test** is to determine how likely it is that the null hypothesis is true. The idea behind hypothesis testing is the same as the idea behind a criminal trial. At the start of a trial, the defendant is assumed to be innocent. Then the evidence is presented. If the evidence strongly indicates that the defendant is guilty, we abandon the assumption of innocence and find the defendant guilty. In a hypothesis test, the null hypothesis plays the role of the defendant. At the start of a hypothesis test, we assume that the null hypothesis is true. Then we look at the evidence, which comes from data that have been collected. If the data strongly indicate that the null hypothesis is false, we abandon our assumption that it is true and believe the alternate hypothesis instead. This is referred to as **rejecting** the null hypothesis.

> **SUMMARY**
>
> - We begin a hypothesis test by assuming the null hypothesis to be true.
> - If the data provide strong evidence against the null hypothesis, we reject it, and believe the alternate hypothesis.

Objective 2 State conclusions to hypothesis tests

Stating Conclusions

If the null hypothesis is rejected, we conclude that H_1 is true. We can state this conclusion by expressing H_1 in words. We should not simply say "we reject the null hypothesis."

EXAMPLE 8.4

State a conclusion when the null hypothesis is rejected

Boxes of a certain kind of cereal are labeled as containing 20 ounces. An inspector thinks that the mean weight may be less than this, so he performs a test of H_0: $\mu = 20$ versus H_1: $\mu < 20$. He rejects the null hypothesis. State an appropriate conclusion.

Solution

Because the null hypothesis is rejected, we conclude that the alternate hypothesis is true. We express the alternate hypothesis in words: "We conclude that the mean weight of cereal boxes is less than 20 ounces."

If the null hypothesis is rejected, the conclusion is straightforward: We conclude that the null hypothesis is false and the alternate hypothesis is true. However, if the null hypothesis is not rejected, we do *not* conclude that the null hypothesis is true. In our formulation, the null hypothesis says that a parameter, such as μ, is equal to a certain value. Now we can never be sure that a parameter is *exactly* equal to a particular value. Therefore, we can never be sure that the null hypothesis is true. When we do not reject the null hypothesis, this just means that the evidence wasn't strong enough to reject it. An appropriate way to state a conclusion when the null hypothesis is not rejected is to state that there is not sufficient evidence to conclude that H_1 is true.

Explain It Again

The conclusion of a hypothesis test is like the verdict of a jury: Not rejecting H_0 is like a jury verdict of not guilty. A not guilty verdict doesn't mean that the defendant is innocent; it just means that the evidence wasn't strong enough to be sure of guilt. Not rejecting H_0 does not mean that H_0 is true; it just means that the evidence wasn't strong enough to reject it.

> **SUMMARY**
>
> - If there is sufficient evidence to reject the null hypothesis, we conclude that the alternate hypothesis is true.
> - If there is not sufficient evidence to reject the null hypothesis, we conclude that the null hypothesis *might* be true, but we never conclude that the null hypothesis *is* true.

EXAMPLE 8.5

State a conclusion when the null hypothesis is not rejected

Boxes of a certain kind of cereal are labeled as containing 20 ounces. An inspector thinks that the mean weight may be less than this, so he performs a test of $H_0: \mu = 20$ versus $H_1: \mu < 20$. He does not reject the null hypothesis. State an appropriate conclusion.

Solution

The null hypothesis is not rejected, so we do not have sufficient evidence to conclude that the alternate hypothesis is true. We can express this as follows: "There is not enough evidence to conclude that the mean weight of cereal boxes is less than 20 ounces." Another way to state this is: "The mean weight of cereal boxes may be equal to 20 ounces."

Objective 3 Distinguish between Type I and Type II errors

Explain It Again

Type I and Type II errors in a trial:
In a trial, the null hypothesis is that the defendant is innocent. A Type I error occurs if an innocent defendant is found guilty. A Type II error occurs if a guilty defendant is found not guilty.

Type I and Type II Errors

Whenever a decision is made, there is a possibility that it is the wrong decision. There are two ways to make a wrong decision with a hypothesis test. First, if H_0 is true, we might mistakenly reject it. Second, if H_0 is false, we might mistakenly decide not to reject it. These two types of errors have names. Rejecting H_0 when it is true is called a **Type I error**. Failing to reject H_0 when it is false is called a **Type II error**. We summarize the possibilities in the following table.

	Reality	
Decision	H_0 **True**	H_0 **False**
Reject H_0	Type I error	Correct decision
Don't reject H_0	Correct decision	Type II error

EXAMPLE 8.6

Determining which type of error has been made

The dean of a business school wants to determine whether the mean starting salary of graduates of her school is greater than $50,000. She will perform a hypothesis test with the following null and alternate hypotheses:

$$H_0: \mu = \$50,000 \qquad H_1: \mu > \$50,000$$

a. Suppose that the true mean is $\mu = \$50,000$, and the dean rejects H_0. Is this a Type I error, a Type II error, or a correct decision?

b. Suppose that the true mean is $\mu = \$55,000$, and the dean rejects H_0. Is this a Type I error, a Type II error, or a correct decision?

c. Suppose that the true mean is $\mu = \$55,000$, and the dean does not reject H_0. Is this a Type I error, a Type II error, or a correct decision?

Solution

a. The true mean is $\mu = \$50,000$, so H_0 is true. Because the dean rejects H_0, this is a Type I error.

b. The true mean is $\mu = \$55,000$, so H_0 is false. Because the dean rejects H_0, this is a correct decision.

c. The true mean is $\mu = \$55,000$, so H_0 is false. Because the dean does not reject H_0, this is a Type II error.

Check Your Understanding

4. A test is made of $H_0: \mu = 100$ versus $H_1: \mu \neq 100$. The true value of μ is 150, and H_0 is rejected. Is this a Type I error, a Type II error, or a correct decision?

5. A test is made of $H_0: \mu = 18$ versus $H_1: \mu > 18$. The true value of μ is 20, and H_0 is not rejected. Is this a Type I error, a Type II error, or a correct decision?

6. A test is made of H_0: $\mu = 3$ versus H_1: $\mu < 3$. The true value of μ is 3, and H_0 is rejected. Is this a Type I error, a Type II error, or a correct decision?

Answers are on page 343.

SECTION 8.1 Exercises

Exercises 1–6 are the Check Your Understanding exercises located within the section.

Understanding the Concepts

In Exercises 7 and 8, fill in each blank with the appropriate word or phrase.

7. The _____ hypothesis states that a parameter is equal to a certain value while the _____ hypothesis states that the parameter differs from this value.

8. Rejecting H_0 when it is true is called a _____ error, and failing to reject H_0 when it is false is called a _____ error.

In Exercises 9–12, determine whether the statement is true or false. If the statement is false, rewrite it as a true statement.

9. H_1: $\mu > 50$ is an example of a left-tailed alternate hypothesis.

10. If we reject H_0, we conclude that H_0 is false.

11. If we do not reject H_0, then we conclude that H_1 is false.

12. If we do not reject H_0, we conclude that H_0 is true.

Practicing the Skills

In Exercises 13–16, determine whether the alternate hypothesis is left-tailed, right-tailed, or two-tailed.

13. H_0: $\mu = 5$ H_1: $\mu < 5$

14. H_0: $\mu = 10$ H_1: $\mu > 10$

15. H_0: $\mu = 1$ H_1: $\mu \neq 1$

16. H_0: $\mu = 26$ H_1: $\mu \neq 26$

In Exercises 17–20, determine whether the outcome is a Type I error, a Type II error, or a correct decision.

17. A test is made of H_0: $\mu = 20$ versus H_1: $\mu \neq 20$. The true value of μ is 25, and H_0 is rejected.

18. A test is made of H_0: $\mu = 5$ versus H_1: $\mu < 5$. The true value of μ is 5, and H_0 is rejected.

19. A test is made of H_0: $\mu = 63$ versus H_1: $\mu > 63$. The true value of μ is 75, and H_0 is not rejected.

20. A test is made of H_0: $\mu = 45$ versus H_1: $\mu < 45$. The true value of μ is 40, and H_0 is rejected.

Working with the Concepts

21. Fertilizer: A new type of fertilizer is being tested on a plot of land in an orange grove, to see whether it increases the amount of fruit produced. The mean number of pounds of fruit on this plot of land with the old fertilizer was 400 pounds. Agriculture scientists believe that the new fertilizer may increase the yield. State the appropriate null and alternate hypotheses.

22. Big fish: A sample of 100 flounder of a certain species have sample mean weight 21.5 grams. Scientists want to perform a hypothesis test to determine how strong the evidence is that the mean weight differs from 20 grams. State the appropriate null and alternate hypotheses.

23. Check, please: A restaurant owner claims that the mean amount spent by diners at his restaurant is more than $30. A test is made of H_0: $\mu = 30$ versus H_1: $\mu > 30$. The null hypothesis is rejected. State an appropriate conclusion.

24. Coffee: The mean caffeine content per cup of regular coffee served at a certain coffee shop is supposed to be 100 milligrams. A test is made of H_0: $\mu = 100$ versus H_1: $\mu \neq 100$. The null hypothesis is rejected. State an appropriate conclusion.

25. Big dogs: A veterinarian claims that the mean weight of adult German shepherd dogs is 75 pounds. A test is made of H_0: $\mu = 75$ versus H_1: $\mu \neq 75$. The null hypothesis is not rejected. State an appropriate conclusion.

26. Business trips: A sales manager believes that the mean number of days per year her company's sales representatives spend traveling is less than 50. A test is made of H_0: $\mu = 50$ versus H_1: $\mu < 50$. The null hypothesis is not rejected. State an appropriate conclusion.

27. Scales: It is desired to check the calibration of a scale by weighing a standard 10-gram weight 100 times. Let μ be the population mean reading on the scale, so that the scale is in calibration if $\mu = 10$ and out of calibration if $\mu \neq 10$. A test is made of the hypotheses H_0: $\mu = 10$ versus H_1: $\mu \neq 10$. Consider three possible conclusions: (i) The scale is in calibration. (ii) The scale is not in calibration. (iii) The scale might be in calibration.

  a. Which of the three conclusions is best if H_0 is rejected?

  b. Which of the three conclusions is best if H_0 is not rejected?

  c. Assume that the scale is in calibration, but the conclusion is reached that the scale is not in calibration. Which type of error is this?

  d. Assume that the scale is not in calibration. Is it possible to make a Type I error? Explain.

  e. Assume that the scale is not in calibration. Is it possible to make a Type II error? Explain.

28. IQ: Scores on a certain IQ test are known to have a mean of 100. A random sample of 60 students attend a series of coaching classes before taking the test. Let μ be the population mean IQ score that would occur if every student took the coaching classes. The classes are successful if $\mu > 100$. A test is made of the hypotheses H_0: $\mu = 100$ versus H_1: $\mu > 100$. Consider three possible conclusions: (i) The classes are successful. (ii) The classes are not successful. (iii) The classes might not be successful.

a. Which of the three conclusions is best if H_0 is rejected?
b. Which of the three conclusions is best if H_0 is not rejected?
c. Assume that the classes are successful but the conclusion is reached that the classes might not be successful. Which type of error is this?

d. Assume that the classes are not successful. Is it possible to make a Type I error? Explain.
e. Assume that the classes are not successful. Is it possible to make a Type II error? Explain.

Answers to Check Your Understanding Exercises for Section 8.1

1. H_0: $\mu = 35$, H_1: $\mu > 35$

2. H_0: $\mu = 6.6$, H_1: $\mu \neq 6.6$

3. H_0: $\mu = 25.5$, H_1: $\mu < 25.5$

4. Correct decision

5. Type II error

6. Type I error

SECTION 8.2

Hypothesis Tests for a Population Mean, Standard Deviation Known

Objectives

1. Perform hypothesis tests with the critical value method
2. Perform hypothesis tests with the *P*-value method
3. Describe the relationship between hypothesis tests and confidence intervals
4. Describe the relationship between α and the probability of error
5. Report the *P*-value or the test statistic value
6. Distinguish between statistical significance and practical significance

Does coaching improve SAT scores? The College Board reported that the mean math SAT score in 2009 was 515, with a standard deviation of 116. Results of an earlier study (*Preparing for the SAT — An Update*, College Board Report 98–5) suggest that coached students should have a mean SAT score of approximately 530. A teacher who runs an online coaching program thinks that students coached by his method have a higher mean score than this. We will see how to perform a hypothesis test to determine whether the teacher is right.

There are two ways to perform hypothesis tests; both methods produce the same results. The first one we will discuss is called the **critical value method**. Then we will discuss the second method, known as the *P*-value method.

Objective 1 Perform hypothesis tests with the critical value method

The Critical Value Method

In the SAT example, the teacher believes that the mean score for his students is greater than 530. Therefore, the null hypothesis says that the mean μ is equal to 530, and the alternate hypothesis says that μ is greater than 530. In symbols,

$$H_0: \mu = 530 \qquad H_1: \mu > 530$$

Now assume that the teacher draws a random sample of 100 students who are planning to take the SAT, and enrolls them in the online coaching program. After completing the program, their sample mean SAT score is $\bar{x} = 562$. This is higher than 530. Can he reject H_0 and conclude that the mean SAT math score for his students is greater than 530?

The sample mean, $\bar{x} = 562$, differs somewhat from the null hypothesis value for the population mean, $\mu = 530$. The key idea behind a hypothesis test is to measure how large this difference is. If the sample differs from H_0 only slightly, then H_0 may well be true, because slight differences can easily be due to chance. However, if the difference is larger, it is less likely to be due to chance, and H_0 is less likely to be true.

We must now determine how strong the disagreement is between the sample mean $\bar{x} = 562$ and the null hypothesis $\mu = 530$. We do this by calculating the value of a **test statistic**. In this example, the test statistic is the z-score of the sample mean $\bar{x}$. We now show how to compute the z-score.

Recall: The *z*-score tells us how many standard deviations $\bar{x}$ is from μ.

Recall: When the sample size is large ($n > 30$), the sample mean $\bar{x}$ is approximately normally distributed with mean μ and standard deviation $\sigma/\sqrt{n}$.

Recall that in a hypothesis test, we begin by assuming that H_0 is true. We therefore assume that the mean of $\bar{x}$ is $\mu = 530$. Because the sample size is large ($n = 100$), we know that $\bar{x}$ is approximately normally distributed. Suppose the population standard deviation is known to be $\sigma = 116$. The standard deviation of $\bar{x}$ is

$$\frac{\sigma}{\sqrt{n}} = \frac{116}{\sqrt{100}} = 11.6$$

The z-score for $\bar{x}$ is

$$z = \frac{\bar{x} - \mu}{\sigma/\sqrt{n}} = \frac{562 - 530}{116/\sqrt{100}} = 2.76$$

We have found that the value of the test statistic is $z = 2.76$. Does this present strong evidence against H_0? Figure 8.1 presents the distribution of the sample mean under the assumption that H_0 is true. The value $\bar{x} = 562$ that we observed has a z-score of 2.76, which means that our observed mean is 2.76 standard deviations away from the assumed mean of 530. Visually, we can see from Figure 8.1 that our observed value $\bar{x} = 562$ is pretty far out in the tail of the distribution — far from the null hypothesis value $\mu = 530$. Intuitively, therefore, it appears that the evidence against H_0 is fairly strong.

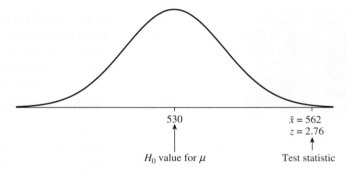

Figure 8.1 If H_0 is true, then the value of $\bar{x}$ is in the tail of the distribution, and far from the null hypothesis mean $\mu = 530$. Visually, it appears that the evidence against H_0 is fairly strong.

The critical value method is based on the idea that we should reject H_0 if the value of the test statistic is unusual when we assume H_0 to be true. In this method, we choose a **critical value**, which forms a boundary between values that are considered unusual and values that are not. The region that contains the unusual values is called the **critical region**. If the value of the test statistic is in the critical region, we reject H_0.

The critical value we choose depends on how small we believe a probability should be for an event to be considered unusual. Let's say that an event with a probability of 0.05 or less is unusual. Figure 8.2 illustrates a critical value of 1.645 and a critical region consisting of z-scores greater than or equal to 1.645. The probability that a z-score is in the critical region is 0.05, so the critical region contains the z-scores that are considered unusual. We have observed a z-score of 2.76, which is in the critical region. Therefore, we reject H_0. We conclude that the mean SAT math score for students completing the online coaching program is greater than 530.

The probability that we use to determine whether an event is unusual is called the **significance level** of the test, and is denoted with the letter α. In Figure 8.2, we used $\alpha = 0.05$. This is the most commonly used value for α, but other values are sometimes used as well. Next to $\alpha = 0.05$, the most commonly used value is $\alpha = 0.01$.

The choice of α is determined by how strong we require the evidence against H_0 to be in order to reject it. The smaller the value of α, the stronger we require the evidence to be. For example, if we choose $\alpha = 0.05$, we will reject H_0 if the test statistic is in the most extreme 5% of its distribution. However, if we choose $\alpha = 0.01$, we will not reject H_0 unless the test statistic is in the most extreme 1% of its distribution.

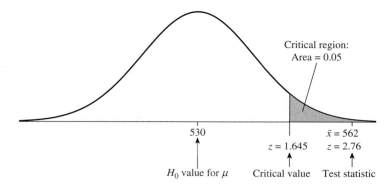

Figure 8.2   The critical value is 1.645. The critical region contains all z-scores greater than or equal to 1.645. The value of our test statistic is $z = 2.76$. This value is in the critical region, so we reject H_0.

DEFINITION

If we reject H_0 after choosing a significance level α, we say that the result is **statistically significant** at the α level.

We also say that $\boldsymbol{H_0}$ **is rejected at the $\boldsymbol{\alpha}$ level**.

In our SAT example, we rejected H_0 at the $\alpha = 0.05$ level, and the result was statistically significant at the $\alpha = 0.05$ level.

Our alternate hypothesis of $\mu > 530$ was a right-tailed alternative. For this reason, the critical region was in the right tail of the distribution. The location of the critical region depends on whether the alternate hypothesis is left-tailed, right-tailed, or two-tailed.

Critical Values for Hypothesis Tests

Let α denote the chosen significance level. The critical value depends on whether the alternate hypothesis is left-tailed, right-tailed, or two-tailed.

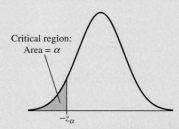 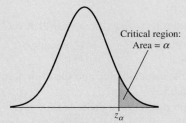 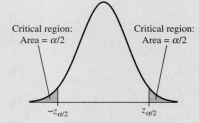

For left-tailed H_1: The critical value is $-z_\alpha$, which has area α to its left. Reject H_0 if $z \leq -z_\alpha$.

For right-tailed H_1: The critical value is z_α, which has area α to its right. Reject H_0 if $z \geq z_\alpha$.

For two-tailed H_1: The critical values are $z_{\alpha/2}$, which has area $\alpha/2$ to its right, and $-z_{\alpha/2}$, which has area $\alpha/2$ to its left. Reject H_0 if $z \geq z_{\alpha/2}$ or $z \leq -z_{\alpha/2}$.

Table 8.1 presents critical values for some commonly used significance levels α.

Table 8.1 Table of Critical Values

	Significance Level α			
H_1	0.10	0.05	0.02	0.01
Left-tailed	−1.282	−1.645	−2.054	−2.326
Right-tailed	1.282	1.645	2.054	2.326
Two-tailed	±1.645	±1.96	±2.326	±2.576

EXAMPLE 8.7 **Find the critical region for a right-tailed alternate hypothesis**

A test is made of H_0: $\mu = 1$ versus H_1: $\mu > 1$. The value of the test statistic is $z = 1.85$.

    a. Is H_0 rejected at the $\alpha = 0.05$ level?
    b. Is H_0 rejected at the $\alpha = 0.01$ level?

Solution

The alternate hypothesis is H_1: $\mu > 1$, so this is a right-tailed test.

    a. From Table 8.1, we see that the critical value for $\alpha = 0.05$ is $z_\alpha = 1.645$. For a right-tailed test, we reject H_0 if $z \geq z_\alpha$. Because $1.85 > 1.645$, we reject H_0 at the $\alpha = 0.05$ level.

    b. The critical value for $\alpha = 0.01$ is 2.326. Because $1.85 < 2.326$, we do not reject H_0 at the $\alpha = 0.01$ level.

Check Your Understanding

1. A test is made of H_0: $\mu = 25$ versus H_1: $\mu < 25$. The value of the test statistic is $z = -1.84$.
    a. Find the critical value and the critical region for a significance level of $\alpha = 0.05$.
    b. Do you reject H_0 at the $\alpha = 0.05$ level?
    c. Find the critical value and the critical region for a significance level of $\alpha = 0.01$.
    d. Do you reject H_0 at the $\alpha = 0.01$ level?

2. A test is made of H_0: $\mu = 7.5$ versus H_1: $\mu > 7.5$. The value of the test statistic is $z = 2.71$.
    a. Find the critical value and the critical region for a significance level of $\alpha = 0.05$.
    b. Do you reject H_0 at the $\alpha = 0.05$ level?
    c. Find the critical value and the critical region for a significance level of $\alpha = 0.01$.
    d. Do you reject H_0 at the $\alpha = 0.01$ level?

3. A test is made of H_0: $\mu = 12$ versus H_1: $\mu \neq 12$. The value of the test statistic is $z = 1.78$.
    a. Find the critical value and the critical region for a significance level of $\alpha = 0.05$.
    b. Do you reject H_0 at the $\alpha = 0.05$ level?
    c. Find the critical value and the critical region for a significance level of $\alpha = 0.01$.
    d. Do you reject H_0 at the $\alpha = 0.01$ level?

Answers are on page 366.

The method we have described requires certain assumptions, which we now state.

Assumptions for Performing a Hypothesis Test About μ When σ Is Known

1. We have a simple random sample.
2. The sample size is large ($n > 30$), or the population is approximately normal.

When these assumptions are met, a hypothesis test may be performed using the following steps.

Performing a Hypothesis Test for a Population Mean with σ Known Using the Critical Value Method

Check to be sure the assumptions are satisfied. If they are, then proceed with the following steps.

Step 1: State the null and alternate hypotheses. The null hypothesis specifies a value for the population mean μ. We will call this value μ_0. So the null hypothesis is of the form H_0: $\mu = \mu_0$. The alternate hypothesis may be stated in one of three ways:

Left-tailed: H_1: $\mu < \mu_0$
Right-tailed: H_1: $\mu > \mu_0$
Two-tailed: H_1: $\mu \neq \mu_0$

Step 2: Choose a significance level α and find the critical value or values.

Step 3: Compute the test statistic $z = \dfrac{\bar{x} - \mu_0}{\sigma/\sqrt{n}}$.

Step 4: Determine whether to reject H_0, as follows:

Left-tailed: H_1: $\mu < \mu_0$ Reject if $z \leq -z_\alpha$.
Right-tailed: H_1: $\mu > \mu_0$ Reject if $z \geq z_\alpha$.
Two-tailed: H_1: $\mu \neq \mu_0$ Reject if $z \geq z_{\alpha/2}$ or $z \leq -z_{\alpha/2}$.

Step 5: State a conclusion.

EXAMPLE 8.8   Performing a hypothesis test with the critical value method

The Energy Information Administration reported that the mean price of a gallon of regular grade gasoline in the city of Los Angeles in July 2010 was $3.15. A recently taken simple random sample of 50 gas stations in Los Angeles had an average price of $3.10 for a gallon of regular grade gasoline. Assume that the standard deviation of prices is $0.15. An economist is interested in determining whether the mean price is less than $3.15. Use the critical value method to perform a hypothesis test at the $\alpha = 0.05$ level of significance.

Solution

We first check the assumptions. We have a simple random sample, the sample size is large ($n > 30$), and the population standard deviation σ is known. The assumptions are satisfied.

Step 1: State H_0 and H_1. The null hypothesis says that the mean price is $3.15. Therefore, we have

$$H_0: \mu = 3.15$$

We are interested in knowing whether the mean price is less than $3.15. Therefore, the alternate hypothesis is

$$H_1: \mu < 3.15$$

At this point, we assume H_0 to be true.

Step 2: Choose a significance level and find the critical value. The significance level is $\alpha = 0.05$. Since the alternate hypothesis is $\mu < 3.15$, this is a left-tailed test. The critical value corresponding to $\alpha = 0.05$ is -1.645.

Step 3: Compute the test statistic. The test statistic is the z-score of the sample mean $\bar{x}$. The population standard deviation is $\sigma = 0.15$. Since we assume H_0 to be true, the population mean is $\mu_0 = 3.15$. The sample size is $n = 50$. Therefore, the test statistic is

$$z = \frac{\bar{x} - \mu_0}{\sigma/\sqrt{n}} = \frac{3.10 - 3.15}{0.15/\sqrt{50}} = -2.36$$

Step 4: Determine whether to reject H_0. This is a left-tailed test, so we reject H_0 if $z < -1.645$. Since $-2.36 < -1.645$, we reject H_0 at the $\alpha = 0.05$ level. See Figure 8.3 on page 348.

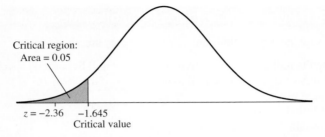

Figure 8.3   The value of the test statistic, $z = -2.36$, is in the level $\alpha = 0.05$ critical region. Therefore, we reject H_0 at the $\alpha = 0.05$ level.

Step 5: State a conclusion. We conclude that the mean price of a gallon of regular gasoline in Los Angeles is less than $3.15.

Check Your Understanding

4. A test is made of H_0: $\mu = 15$ versus H_1: $\mu > 15$. The sample mean is $\bar{x} = 16.5$, the sample size is $n = 50$, and the population standard deviation is $\sigma = 5$.
  a. Find the value of the test statistic z.
  b. Find the critical region for a level $\alpha = 0.05$ test.
  c. Do you reject H_0 at the $\alpha = 0.05$ level?

5. A test is made of H_0: $\mu = 125$ versus H_1: $\mu < 125$. The sample mean is $\bar{x} = 123$, the sample size is $n = 100$, and the population standard deviation is $\sigma = 20$.
  a. Find the value of the test statistic z.
  b. Find the critical region for a level $\alpha = 0.02$ test.
  c. Do you reject H_0 at the $\alpha = 0.02$ level?

6. A test is made of H_0: $\mu = 100$ versus H_1: $\mu \neq 100$. The sample mean is $\bar{x} = 97$, the sample size is $n = 75$, and the population standard deviation is $\sigma = 8$.
  a. Find the value of the test statistic z.
  b. Find the critical region for a level $\alpha = 0.01$ test.
  c. Do you reject H_0 at the $\alpha = 0.01$ level?

Answers are on page 366.

With the critical value method, the value of the test statistic is considered to be unusual if it is in the critical region, and not unusual if it is not in the critical region. We will now describe the ***P*-value method**, which provides more information than the critical value method. Whereas the critical value method tells us only whether the test statistic was unusual or not, the *P*-value method tells us exactly how unusual the test statistic is. For this reason, the *P*-value method is the one more often used in practice. In particular, almost all forms of technology use the *P*-value method.

Objective 2 Perform hypothesis tests with the *P*-value method

The *P*-Value Method

We will introduce the *P*-value method with our SAT example. An online coaching program is supposed to increase the mean SAT math score to a value greater than 530. The null and alternate hypotheses are

$$H_0: \mu = 530 \qquad H_1: \mu > 530$$

Now assume that 100 students are randomly chosen to participate in the program, and their sample mean score is $\bar{x} = 562$. Suppose that the population standard deviation for SAT math scores is known to be $\sigma = 116$. Does this provide strong evidence against the null hypothesis $\mu = 530$?

To measure just how strong the evidence against H_0 is, we compute a quantity called the ***P*-value**. The *P*-value is the probability that a number drawn from the distribution of the sample mean would be as extreme as or more extreme than our observed value of 562. The more extreme the value, the stronger is the evidence against H_0. Because our alternate hypothesis is H_1: $\mu > 530$, this is a right-tailed test, so values of $\bar{x}$ greater than 562 are more extreme than our observed value is. We find the P-value by computing the z-score of our observed sample mean $\bar{x} = 562$. We now explain how to do this.

Recall that we begin by assuming that H_0 is true. We therefore assume that the mean of $\bar{x}$ is $\mu = 530$. The sample size is large ($n = 100$), so we know that $\bar{x}$ is approximately normally distributed. The standard deviation of $\bar{x}$ is

$$\frac{\sigma}{\sqrt{n}} = \frac{116}{\sqrt{100}} = 11.6$$

Therefore, the P-value is the probability that $\bar{x}$ is greater than 562 when μ is assumed to be 530 and the standard deviation is 11.6.

The z-score for $\bar{x}$ is

$$z = \frac{\bar{x} - \mu}{\sigma/\sqrt{n}} = \frac{562 - 530}{116/\sqrt{100}} = 2.76$$

The P-value is therefore the area under the normal curve to the right of $z = 2.76$. Using Table A.2, we see that the area to the *left* of $z = 2.76$ is 0.9971. Therefore, the area to the right of $z = 2.76$ is $1 - 0.9971 = 0.0029$ (see Figure 8.4). Therefore, the P-value for this test is 0.0029.

Recall: When the sample size is large ($n > 30$), the sample mean $\bar{x}$ is approximately normally distributed with mean μ and standard deviation $\sigma/\sqrt{n}$.

Explain It Again

Using technology: The P-value is the area to the right of $\bar{x} = 562$ when the mean is 530 and the standard deviation is 11.6. This area can be found with technology. The following display illustrates the **normalcdf** command on the TI-84 Plus calculator.

```
normalcdf(562,1E
99,530,11.6)
        .0029023496
```

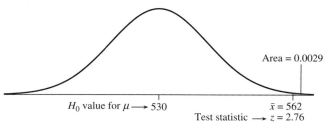

Figure 8.4 If H_0 is true, the probability that $\bar{x}$ takes on a value as extreme as or more extreme than the observed value of 562 is 0.0029. This is the P-value.

This P-value tells us that if H_0 were true, the probability of observing a value of $\bar{x}$ as large as 562 is only 0.0029. Therefore, there are only two possibilities:

- H_0 is false.
- H_0 is true, and we got an unusual sample, whose mean lies in the most extreme 0.0029 of its distribution.

In practice, events in the most extreme 0.0029 of their distributions are very unusual. This means that a P-value as small as 0.0029 is very unlikely to occur if H_0 is true. A P-value of 0.0029 is very strong evidence against H_0.

SUMMARY

- The P-value is the probability, assuming that H_0 is true, of observing a value for the test statistic that is as extreme as or more extreme than the value actually observed.
- The smaller the P-value, the stronger the evidence against H_0.

EXAMPLE 8.9

Find and interpret a P-value

A test is made of H_0: $\mu = 10$ versus H_1: $\mu > 10$. The value of the test statistic is $z = 2.25$. Find the P-value and interpret it.

Solution

The alternate hypothesis is H_1: $\mu > 10$, so this is a right-tailed test. Therefore, values of z greater than our observed value of 2.25 are more extreme than our value is. The P-value is

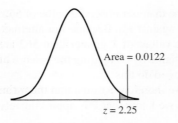

Figure 8.5

the area under the normal curve to the right of the test statistic $z = 2.25$. Using Table A.2, we see that the area to the *left* of $z = 2.25$ is 0.9878. Therefore, the area to the right of $z = 2.25$ is $1 - 0.9878 = 0.0122$. See Figure 8.5.

The P-value of 0.0122 tells us that if H_0 is true, then the probability of observing a test statistic of 2.25 or more is only 0.0122. This result is fairly unusual if we assume H_0 to be true. Therefore, this is fairly strong evidence against H_0.

EXAMPLE 8.10   Find and interpret a *P*-value

A test is made of H_0: $\mu = 5$ versus H_1: $\mu < 5$. The value of the test statistic is $z = -0.63$. Find the P-value and interpret it.

Solution

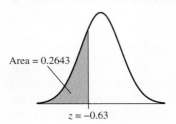

Figure 8.6

The alternate hypothesis is H_1: $\mu < 5$, so this is a left-tailed test. Therefore, values of z less than our value of -0.63 are more extreme than our value is. The P-value is the area under the normal curve to the left of the test statistic $z = -0.63$. Using Table A.2, we see that the area to the left of $z = -0.63$ is 0.2643. See Figure 8.6.

The P-value of 0.2643 tells us that if H_0 is true, then the probability of observing a test statistic of -0.63 or less is 0.2643. This is not particularly unusual, so this is not strong evidence against H_0.

EXAMPLE 8.11   Find and interpret a *P*-value

A test is made of H_0: $\mu = 20$ versus H_1: $\mu \neq 20$. The value of the test statistic is $z = -2.70$. Find the P-value and interpret it.

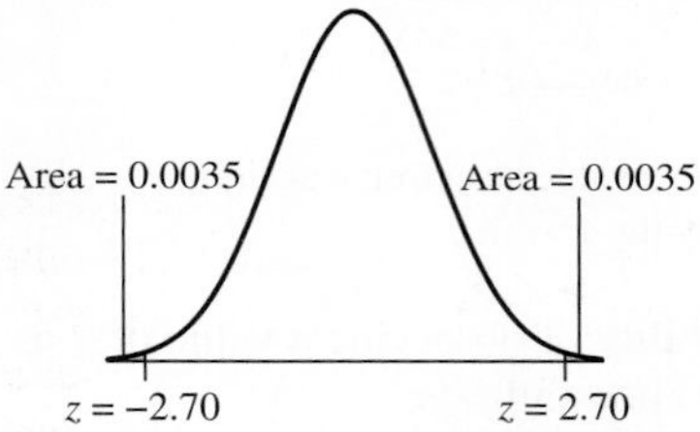

Solution

The alternate hypothesis is H_1: $\mu \neq 20$, so this is a two-tailed test. Therefore, values of z less than our value of -2.70 and values greater than 2.70 are both more extreme than our value is. The P-value is the sum of the areas under the normal curve to the right of $z = 2.70$ and to the left of $z = -2.70$. Using Table A.2, we see that the area to the left of $z = -2.70$ is 0.0035. The area to the right of $z = 2.70$ is also 0.0035. The sum of the areas is therefore $0.0035 + 0.0035 = 0.0070$. See Figure 8.7.

The P-value of 0.0070 tells us that if H_0 is true, then the probability of observing a test statistic greater than 2.70 or less than -2.70 is only 0.0070. This result is quite unusual if we assume H_0 to be true. Therefore, this is very strong evidence against H_0.

Figure 8.7

Check Your Understanding

7. Which provides stronger evidence against H_0: a P-value of 0.05 or a P-value of 0.50?

8. A test is made of H_0: $\mu = 30$ versus H_1: $\mu < 30$. The test statistic is $z = -1.28$. Find and interpret the P-value.

9. A test is made of H_0: $\mu = 6$ versus H_1: $\mu \neq 6$.
   a. The test statistic is $z = 0.75$. Find and interpret the P-value.
   b. The test statistic is $z = -2.20$. Find and interpret the P-value.
   c. Which provides stronger evidence against H_0: $z = 0.75$ or $z = -2.20$?

Answers are on page 366.

The *P*-value is not the probability that *H*₀ is true

Because the P-value is a probability and small P-values indicate that H_0 should be rejected, it is tempting to think that the P-value represents the probability that H_0 is true. This is not the case. The P-value is the probability that a test statistic such as z would take on an extreme value. Probability is used for events that can be different for different samples. Therefore, it makes sense to talk about the probability that the value of z will be more extreme than an observed value, because the value of z can come out differently for different samples. The null hypothesis, however, is either true or not true. The truth of H_0 does not change from sample to sample. For this reason, it does not make sense to talk about the probability that H_0 is true.

SUMMARY

The P-value is the probability, under the assumption that H_0 is true, that the test statistic takes on a value as extreme as or more extreme than the value actually observed.

The P-value is not the probability that the null hypothesis is true.

Check Your Understanding

10. If $P = 0.02$, which is the best conclusion?
    i. The probability that H_0 is true is 0.02.
    ii. If H_0 is true, the probability of obtaining a test statistic more extreme than the one actually observed is 0.02.
    iii. The probability that H_1 is true is 0.02.
    iv. If H_1 is true, the probability of obtaining a test statistic more extreme than the one actually observed is 0.02.

Answer is on page 366.

Choosing a significance level

We have seen that the smaller the P-value, the stronger the evidence against H_0. In practice, people often do not choose a significance level. They simply report the P-value and let the reader decide whether the evidence is strong enough to reject H_0. Sometimes, however, we need to make a firm decision whether to reject H_0. We then choose a significance level α between 0 and 1 before performing the test, and reject H_0 if the P-value is less than or equal to α. The most commonly used value is $\alpha = 0.05$, but other values are sometimes used as well. Next to $\alpha = 0.05$, the most commonly used value is $\alpha = 0.01$.

SUMMARY

To make a decision whether to reject H_0 when using the P-value method:

- Choose a significance level α between 0 and 1.
- Compute the P-value.
- If $P \leq \alpha$, reject H_0. If $P > \alpha$, do not reject H_0.

If $P \leq \alpha$, we say that H_0 is rejected at the α level, or that the result is statistically significant at the α level.

EXAMPLE 8.12   Find the *P*-value

In Example 8.9, the P-value was $P = 0.0122$.
    a. Do you reject H_0 at the $\alpha = 0.05$ level?
    b. Do you reject H_0 at the $\alpha = 0.01$ level?
    c. Is the result statistically significant at the $\alpha = 0.05$ level?
    d. Is the result statistically significant at the $\alpha = 0.01$ level?

Solution

a. Because $P \leq 0.05$, we reject H_0 at the $\alpha = 0.05$ level.

b. Because $P > 0.01$, we do not reject H_0 at the $\alpha = 0.01$ level.

c. We reject H_0 at the $\alpha = 0.05$ level, so the result is statistically significant at the $\alpha = 0.05$ level.

d. We do not reject H_0 at the $\alpha = 0.01$ level, so the result is not statistically significant at the $\alpha = 0.01$ level.

Check Your Understanding

11. A hypothesis test is performed with a significance level of $\alpha = 0.05$.
   a. If the P-value is 0.08, is H_0 rejected?
   b. If the P-value is 0.08, are the results statistically significant at the 0.05 level?
   c. If the P-value is 0.03, is H_0 rejected?
   d. If the P-value is 0.03, are the results statistically significant at the 0.05 level?

12. For each of the following P-values, state whether H_0 will be rejected at the 0.10 level.
   a. $P = 0.12$
   b. $P = 0.07$
   c. $P = 0.05$
   d. $P = 0.20$

13. For each of the following P-values, state whether the result is statistically significant at the 0.10 level.
   a. $P = 0.08$
   b. $P = 0.15$
   c. $P = 0.01$
   d. $P = 0.50$

Answers are on page 366.

The assumptions for using the P-value method are the same as for the critical value method. We repeat these assumptions here.

Assumptions for Performing a Hypothesis Test About μ When σ Is Known

1. We have a simple random sample.

2. The sample size is large ($n > 30$), or the population is approximately normal.

We now summarize the steps in testing a hypothesis with the P-value method.

Performing a Hypothesis Test for a Population Mean with σ Known Using the *P*-Value Method

Check to be sure the assumptions are satisfied. If they are, then proceed with the following steps.

Step 1: State the null and alternate hypotheses. The null hypothesis specifies a value for the population mean μ. We will call this value μ_0. So the null hypothesis is of the form H_0: $\mu = \mu_0$. The alternate hypothesis may be stated in one of three ways:

   Left-tailed: H_1: $\mu < \mu_0$
   Right-tailed: H_1: $\mu > \mu_0$
   Two-tailed: H_1: $\mu \neq \mu_0$

Step 2: If making a decision, choose a significance level α.

Step 3: Compute the test statistic $z = \dfrac{\bar{x} - \mu_0}{\sigma/\sqrt{n}}$.

Step 4: Compute the *P*-value of the test statistic. The *P*-value is the probability, assuming that H_0 is true, of observing a value for the test statistic that is as extreme or more extreme than the value actually observed. The *P*-value is an area under the standard normal curve; it depends on the type of alternate hypothesis. Note that the inequality in the alternate hypothesis points in the direction of the tail that contains the area for the *P*-value.

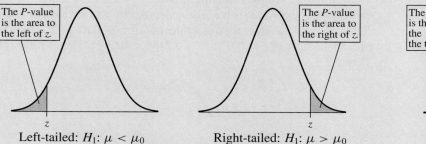

Left-tailed: $H_1: \mu < \mu_0$ Right-tailed: $H_1: \mu > \mu_0$

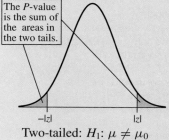

Two-tailed: $H_1: \mu \neq \mu_0$

Step 5: Interpret the *P*-value. If making a decision, reject H_0 if the *P*-value is less than or equal to the significance level α.

Step 6: State a conclusion.

EXAMPLE 8.13   ## Perform a hypothesis test

The National Health and Nutrition Examination Surveys (NHANES) are designed to assess the health and nutritional status of adults and children in the United States. According to a recent NHANES survey, the mean height of adult men in the United States is 69.7 inches, with a standard deviation of 3 inches. A sociologist believes that taller men may be more likely to be promoted to positions of leadership, so the mean height μ of male business executives may be greater than the mean height of the entire male population. A simple random sample of 100 male business executives has a mean height of 69.9 in. Assume that the standard deviation of male executive heights is $\sigma = 3$ inches. Can we conclude that male business executives are taller, on the average, than the general male population at the $\alpha = 0.05$ level?

Solution

We first check the assumptions. We have a simple random sample, the sample size is large ($n > 30$), and the population standard deviation is known. The assumptions are satisfied.

Step 1: State H_0 and H_1. The null hypothesis, H_0, says that there is no difference between the mean heights of executives and others. Therefore, we have

$$H_0: \mu = 69.7$$

We are interested in determining whether the mean height of executives is greater than 69.7. Therefore, we have

$$H_1: \mu > 69.7$$

At this point, we assume that H_0 is true.

Step 2: Choose a level of significance. The level of significance is $\alpha = 0.05$.

Step 3: Compute the test statistic. Because the sample size is large ($n = 100$), the sample mean $\bar{x}$ is approximately normally distributed. The test statistic is the z-score for $\bar{x}$. To find the z-score, we first need to find the mean and standard deviation of $\bar{x}$. Because we are assuming that H_0 is true, we assume that the mean of $\bar{x}$ is $\mu = 69.7$. We know that the population standard deviation is $\sigma = 3$. The standard deviation of $\bar{x}$ is therefore

$$\frac{\sigma}{\sqrt{n}} = \frac{3}{\sqrt{100}} = 0.3$$

It follows that $\bar{x}$ is normally distributed with mean 69.7 and standard deviation 0.3. We observed a value of $\bar{x} = 69.9$. The z-score is

$$z = \frac{\bar{x} - \mu_0}{\sigma/\sqrt{n}} = \frac{69.9 - 69.7}{0.3} = 0.67$$

Step 4: Compute the P-value. Since the alternate hypothesis is $\mu > 69.7$, this is a right-tailed test. The P-value is the area under the curve to the right of $z = 0.67$. Using Table A.2, we see that the area to the *left* of $z = 0.67$ is 0.7486. Therefore, the area to the right of $z = 0.67$ is $1 - 0.7486 = 0.2514$. The P-value is 0.2514. See Figure 8.8.

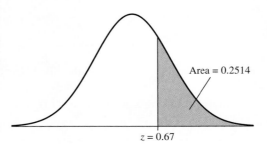

Area = 0.2514

$z = 0.67$

Figure 8.8

Step 5: Interpret the P-value. The P-value of 0.2514 says that if H_0 is true, the probability of observing a test statistic as large or larger than 0.67 is 0.2514. This is not unusual; it will happen for about one out of every four samples. Therefore, this sample does not strongly disagree with H_0. In particular, $P > 0.05$, so we do not reject the null hypothesis at the $\alpha = 0.05$ level.

Step 6: State a conclusion. There is not enough evidence to conclude that male executives have a greater mean height than adult males in general. The mean height of male executives may be the same as the mean height of adult males in general.

Explain It Again

Using technology: In Example 8.13, the P-value is the area to the right of $z = 0.67$. This area can be found with technology. The following display illustrates the **normalcdf** command on the TI-84 Plus calculator. We enter the values $\bar{x} = 69.9$, $\mu_0 = 69.7$, and $\sigma/\sqrt{n} = 0.3$. The result given by the calculator differs slightly from the result found by using Table A.2.

```
normalcdf(69.9,1
E99,69.7,.3)
       .252492467
```

EXAMPLE 8.14

Perform a two-tailed hypothesis test

At a large company, the attitudes of workers are regularly measured with a standardized test. The scores on the test range from 0 to 100, with higher scores indicating greater satisfaction with their jobs. The mean score over all of the company's employees was 74, with a standard deviation of $\sigma = 8$. Some time ago, the company adopted a policy of telecommuting. Under this policy, workers could spend one day per week working from home. After the policy had been in place for some time, a random sample of 80 workers was given the test to determine whether their mean level of satisfaction had changed since the policy was put into effect. The sample mean was 76. Assume the standard deviation is still $\sigma = 8$. Can we conclude that the mean level of satisfaction is different since the policy change at the $\alpha = 0.05$ level?

Solution

We first check the assumptions. We have a simple random sample, the sample size is large ($n > 30$), and the population standard deviation is known. The assumptions are satisfied.

Step 1: State H_0 and H_1. The null hypothesis, H_0, says that there is no difference between the mean level of satisfaction before and after telecommuting. Therefore, we have

$$H_0: \mu = 74$$

We are interested in knowing whether the mean level has changed. We are not specifically interested in whether it went up or down. Therefore, the alternate hypothesis is

$$H_1: \mu \neq 74$$

At this point, we assume that H_0 is true.

Step 2: Choose a level of significance. The level of significance is $\alpha = 0.05$.

Step 3: Compute the test statistic. Since the sample size, $n = 80$, is large, $\bar{x}$ is approximately normally distributed. The test statistic is the z-score for the sample mean $\bar{x}$. The population standard deviation is $\sigma = 8$. Because we assume H_0 to be true, the population mean is $\mu = 74$. Therefore, $\bar{x}$ is normally distributed with mean 74 and standard error

$$\frac{\sigma}{\sqrt{n}} = \frac{8}{\sqrt{80}} = 0.8944$$

We observed a value of $\bar{x} = 76$. The z-score is

$$z = \frac{76 - 74}{0.8944} = 2.24$$

Step 4: Compute the P-value. The alternate hypothesis is $\mu \neq 74$, so this is a two-tailed test. The P-value is thus the sum of two areas: the area to the right of $z = 2.24$ and an equal area to the left of $z = -2.24$. Using Table A.2, we see that the area to the left of $z = -2.24$ is 0.0125. Therefore, the area to the right of $z = 2.24$ is also 0.0125. The P-value is therefore $0.0125 + 0.0125 = 0.0250$. See Figure 8.9.

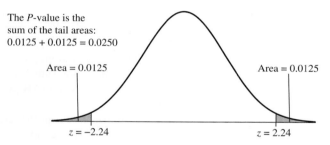

The P-value is the
sum of the tail areas:
$0.0125 + 0.0125 = 0.0250$

Area = 0.0125

Area = 0.0125

$z = -2.24$

$z = 2.24$

Figure 8.9

Step 5: Interpret the P-value. The P-value says that if H_0 is true, then the probability of observing a test statistic as extreme as the one we actually observed is only 0.0250. In practice, this would generally be considered fairly strong evidence against H_0. In particular, $P < 0.05$, so we reject H_0 at the $\alpha = 0.05$ level.

Step 6: State a conclusion. We conclude that the mean score among employees has changed since the adoption of telecommuting.

Check Your Understanding

14. A social scientist suspects that the mean number of years of education μ for adults in a certain large city is greater than 12 years. She will test the null hypothesis $H_0: \mu = 12$ against the alternate hypothesis $H_1: \mu > 12$. She surveys a random sample of 100 adults and finds that the sample mean number of years is $\bar{x} = 12.98$. Assume that the standard deviation for the number of years of education is $\sigma = 3$ years.
   a. Compute the value of the test statistic.
   b. Compute the P-value.
   c. Interpret the P-value.
   d. Is H_0 rejected at the $\alpha = 0.05$ level?
   e. Is H_0 rejected at the $\alpha = 0.01$ level?

Answers are on page 367.

Performing hypothesis tests with technology

Following are the results of Example 8.14, as presented by the TI-84 Plus calculator.

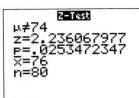

The first line presents the alternate hypothesis, $\mu \neq 74$. Following that are the test statistic (z), the *P*-value (p), the sample mean ($\bar{x}$), and the sample size (n). Note that the *P*-value differs slightly from the value obtained in Example 8.14 by using Table A.2. This is common. Results given by technology are more precise, and therefore often differ slightly from results obtained from tables. The differences are never large enough to matter.

Following are the results of Example 8.14 as presented by MINITAB.

```
Test of mu = 74.0 vs not = 74.0
The assumed standard deviation = 8.0

  N    Mean   SE Mean        95% CI          Z       P
 80   76.00    0.8944   (74.247, 77.753)   2.236   0.025
```

The second line of the output presents both the null and alternate hypotheses. The quantity labeled "SE Mean" is the standard error of the mean, $\sigma/\sqrt{n}$, which is the standard deviation of $\bar{x}$. Notice that MINITAB provides a 95% confidence interval for μ along with the hypothesis test.

Step-by-step instructions for performing hypothesis tests with technology are presented in the Using Technology section on page 361.

Check Your Understanding

15. The following display from a TI-84 Plus calculator presents the results of a hypothesis test for a population mean.

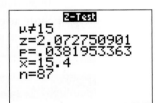

a. What are the null and alternate hypotheses?
b. What is the value of the test statistic?
c. What is the *P*-value?
d. Do you reject H_0 at the $\alpha = 0.05$ level?

16. The following output from MINITAB presents the results of a hypothesis test for a population mean.

```
Test of mu = 53.5 vs not = 53.5
The assumed standard deviation = 2.3634

   N    Mean   SE Mean        95% CI           Z       P
 145   53.246   0.1962   (52.861, 53.631)   -1.29   0.196
```

> **a.** What are the null and alternate hypotheses?
> **b.** What is the value of the test statistic?
> **c.** What is the P-value?
> **d.** Do you reject H_0 at the $\alpha = 0.05$ level?

Answers are on page 367.

Objective 3 Describe the relationship between hypothesis tests and confidence intervals

The Relationship Between Hypothesis Tests and Confidence Intervals

In Example 8.14, we tested the hypotheses H_0: $\mu = 74$ versus H_1: $\mu \neq 74$ and obtained a P-value of 0.025. Because $P < 0.05$, H_0 is rejected at the 0.05 level. Informally, this says that the value 74 is not plausible for μ.

Another way to express information about μ is through a confidence interval. A 95% confidence interval for μ is $74.247 < \mu < 77.753$. (This confidence interval is displayed in the MINITAB output following Example 8.14.) Note that the 95% confidence interval does not contain the null hypothesis value of 74. In this way, the 95% confidence interval agrees with the results of the hypothesis test. Informally, a confidence interval for μ contains all the values that are plausible for μ. Because 74 is not in the confidence interval, 74 is not a plausible value for μ.

This relationship holds for any confidence interval for a population mean, and any two-tailed hypothesis test.

If we test H_0: $\mu = \mu_0$ versus H_1: $\mu \neq \mu_0$, then

- If the 95% confidence interval contains μ_0, then H_0 will not be rejected at the 0.05 level.
- If the 95% confidence interval does not contain μ_0, then H_0 will be rejected at the 0.05 level.

This relationship between hypothesis tests and confidence intervals holds exactly for population means, but only approximately for other parameters such as population proportions. The reason is that the standard error that is used in a hypothesis test for a proportion differs somewhat from the standard error that is used in a confidence interval for a proportion.

Hypothesis tests and confidence intervals address different questions

Although hypothesis tests are closely related to confidence intervals, the two address different questions. A confidence interval provides all of the values that are plausible at a specified level. A hypothesis test tells us about only one value, but it tells us much more precisely how plausible that one value is.

For example, consider the 95% confidence interval $74.247 < \mu < 77.753$ previously mentioned for the mean satisfaction level in Example 8.14. The value $\mu = 74$ is not in the confidence interval, so we can conclude that the hypothesis H_0: $\mu = 74$ will be rejected at the $\alpha = 0.05$ level with a two-tailed test. However, this tells us only that $P < 0.05$. It does not tell us exactly how much less than 0.05 the P-value is. By performing the hypothesis test, we find that $P = 0.025$. This tells us much more precisely just how plausible or implausible the value of 74 is for μ.

SUMMARY

- A confidence interval contains all the values that are plausible at a particular level.
- A hypothesis test tells us precisely how plausible a particular value is.

Check Your Understanding

17. A 95% confidence interval for μ is computed to be (1.75, 3.25). For each of the following hypotheses, state whether H_0 will be rejected at the 0.05 level.
   a. H_0: $\mu = 3$ versus H_1: $\mu \neq 3$
   b. H_0: $\mu = 4$ versus H_1: $\mu \neq 4$
   c. H_0: $\mu = 1.7$ versus H_1: $\mu \neq 1.7$
   d. H_0: $\mu = 3.5$ versus H_1: $\mu \neq 3.5$

18. You want to test H_0: $\mu = 4$ versus H_1: $\mu \neq 4$, so you compute a 95% confidence interval for μ. The 95% confidence interval is $5.1 < \mu < 7.2$.
   a. Do you reject H_0 at the $\alpha = 0.05$ level?
   b. Your friend thinks that $\alpha = 0.01$ is a more appropriate significance level. Can you tell from the confidence interval whether to reject at this level?

Answers are on page 367.

Objective 4 Describe the relationship between α and the probability of error

Table 8.2

	H_0 **true**	H_0 **false**
Reject H_0	Type I error	Correct
Don't reject H_0	Correct	Type II error

The Relationship Between α and the Probability of an Error

Recall that a Type I error occurs if we reject H_0 when it is true, and a Type II error occurs if we do not reject H_0 when it is false (see Table 8.2). When designing a hypothesis test, we would like to make the probabilities of these two errors small. In order to do this, we need to know how to calculate the probabilities of these errors. It is straightforward to find the probability of a Type I error: It is equal to the significance level. So, for example, if we perform a test at a significance level of $\alpha = 0.05$, the probability of a Type I error is 0.05.

> ### SUMMARY
>
> When a test is performed with a significance level α, the probability of a Type I error is α.

The probability of a Type II error is denoted by the letter β. Computing the probability of a Type II error is more difficult than finding the probability of a Type I error. A Type II error occurs when H_0 is false, and a decision is made not to reject. The probability of a Type II error depends on the true value of the parameter being tested.

Because α is the probability of a Type I error, why don't we always choose a very small value for α? The reason is that the smaller a value we choose for α, the larger the value of β, the probability of making a Type II error, becomes (unless we increase the sample size).

> ### SUMMARY
>
> The smaller a value we choose for the significance level α:
>
> - The smaller the probability of a Type I error becomes.
> - The larger the probability of a Type II error becomes.

In general, making a Type I error is more serious than making a Type II error. When a Type I error is much more serious, a smaller value of α is appropriate. When a Type I error is only slightly more serious, a larger value of α can be justified.

Check Your Understanding

19. A hypothesis test is performed at a significance level $\alpha = 0.05$. What is the probability of a Type I error?

20. Charlie will perform a hypothesis test at the $\alpha = 0.05$ level. Felice will perform the same test at the $\alpha = 0.01$ level.
  a. If H_0 is true, who has a greater probability of making a Type I error?
  b. If H_0 is false, who has a greater probability of making a Type II error?

Answers are on page 367.

Report the *P*-Value or the Test Statistic Value

Sometimes people report only that a test result was statistically significant at a certain level, without giving the P-value. It is common, for example, to read that a result was "statistically significant at the 0.05 level" or "statistically significant ($P \leq 0.05$)." It is much better to report the P-value along with the decision whether to reject. There are two reasons for this.

The first reason is that there is a big difference between a P-value that is just barely small enough to reject, say $P = 0.049$, and a P-value that is extremely small, say $P = 0.0001$. If $P = 0.049$, the evidence is just barely strong enough to reject H_0 at the $\alpha = 0.05$ level, whereas if $P = 0.0001$, the evidence against H_0 is overwhelming. Thus, reporting the P-value describes exactly how strong the evidence against H_0 is.

The second reason is that not everyone may agree with your choice of α. For example, let's say you have chosen a significance level of $\alpha = 0.05$. You obtain a P-value of $P = 0.03$. Since $P < 0.05$, you reject H_0. Let's say that you report only that H_0 is rejected at the $\alpha = 0.05$ level, without stating the P-value. Now imagine that the person reading your report believes that a Type I error would be very serious, so that a significance level of $\alpha = 0.01$ would be more appropriate. This reader cannot tell whether to reject H_0 at the $\alpha = 0.01$ level, because you have not reported the P-value. It is much more helpful to report that $P = 0.03$, so that people can decide for themselves whether or not to reject H_0.

When using the critical value method, you should report the value of the test statistic, rather than simply stating whether the test statistic was in the critical region. In this way, the reader can tell whether the value of the test statistic was just barely inside the critical region, or well inside. In addition, reporting the value of the test statistic gives the reader the opportunity to choose a different critical value and determine whether H_0 can be rejected at a different level.

SUMMARY

When presenting the results of a hypothesis test, state the P-value or the value of the test statistic. Don't just state whether or not H_0 was rejected.

Check Your Understanding

21. A test was made of the hypotheses H_0: $\mu = 15$ versus H_1: $\mu > 15$. Four statisticians wrote summaries of the results. For each summary, state whether it contains enough information. If there is not enough information, indicate what needs to be added.
  a. The P-value was 0.02, so we reject H_0 at the $\alpha = 0.05$ level.
  b. The critical value was 1.645. Because $z > 1.645$, we reject H_0 at the $\alpha = 0.05$ level.
  c. The critical value was 1.645. Because $z = 2.05$, we reject H_0 at the $\alpha = 0.05$ level.
  d. Because $P < 0.05$, we reject H_0 at the $\alpha = 0.05$ level.

Answers are on page 367.

Objective 6 Distinguish between statistical significance and practical significance

Statistical Significance Is Not the Same as Practical Significance

When a result has a small P-value, we say that it is "statistically significant." In common usage, the word *significant* means "important." It is therefore tempting to think that statistically significant results must always be important. This is not the case. Sometimes statistically significant results do not have any practical importance. Example 8.15 illustrates the idea.

EXAMPLE 8.15

Determining practical significance

At a large company, employee satisfaction is measured with a standardized test for which scores range from 0 to 100. The mean score on this test was 74. The company then implemented a new policy that allowed telecommuting, so that employees could work from home. After the policy change, the mean score for a sample of employees was 76. In order to determine whether the mean score for all employees, μ, had changed after the new policy was implemented, a hypothesis test was performed of

$$H_0: \mu = 74 \qquad H_1: \mu \neq 74$$

We performed this test in Example 8.14. The standard error of $\bar{x}$ was 0.8944 and the P-value was 0.0250, so we rejected H_0 at the $\alpha = 0.05$ level. We concluded that the mean satisfaction level changed after the new policy was implemented. The human resources manager now writes a report stating that the new policy resulted in a large change in employee satisfaction. Explain why the human resources manager is not interpreting the result correctly.

Solution

The increase in mean score was from 74 to 76. Although this is statistically significant, it is only two points out of 100. It is unlikely that this difference is large enough to matter. The lesson here is that a result can be statistically significant without being large enough to be of practical importance. How can this happen? A difference is statistically significant when it is large compared to its standard error. In the example, a difference of two points was statistically significant because the standard error of $\bar{x}$ was small — only 0.8944. When the standard error is small, even a small difference can be statistically significant.

SUMMARY

When a result is statistically significant, we can only conclude that the true value of the parameter is different from the value specified by H_0. We cannot conclude that the difference is large enough to be important.

Check Your Understanding

22. A certain type of calculator battery has a mean lifetime of 100 hours and a standard deviation of $\sigma = 10$ hours. A company has developed a new battery and claims it has a longer mean life. A random sample of 1000 batteries is tested, and their sample mean lifetime is $\bar{x} = 101$ hours. A test was made of the hypotheses

$$H_0: \mu = 100 \qquad H_1: \mu > 100$$

a. Show that H_0 is rejected at the $\alpha = 0.01$ level.
b. The battery manufacturer says that because the evidence is strong that $\mu > 100$, you should be willing to pay a much higher price for its battery than for the old type of battery. Do you agree? Why or why not?

Answers are on page 367.

USING TECHNOLOGY

We use Example 8.14 to illustrate the technology steps.

TI-84 PLUS

Testing a hypothesis about the population mean when σ is known

Step 1. Press **STAT** and highlight the **TESTS** menu.

Step 2. Select **Z–Test** and press **ENTER** (Figure A). The **Z–Test** menu appears.

Step 3. For **Inpt**, select the **Stats** option and enter the values of μ_0, σ, $\bar{x}$, and n. For Example 8.14, we use $\mu_0 = 74$, $\sigma = 8$, $\bar{x} = 76$, and $n = 80$.

Step 4. Select the form of the alternate hypothesis. For Example 8.14, the alternate hypothesis has the form $\mu \neq \mu_0$ (Figure B).

Step 5. Highlight **Calculate** and press **ENTER** (Figure C).

Note that if the raw data are given, the **Z–Test** command may be used by selecting **Data** as the **Inpt** option and entering the location of the data as the **List** option (Figure D).

Figure A

Figure B

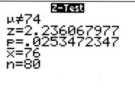

Figure C

Figure D

MINITAB

Testing a hypothesis about the population mean when σ is known

Step 1. Click on **Stat**, then **Basic Statistics**, then **1-Sample Z**.

Step 2. Choose one of the following:
- If the summary statistics are given, click **Summarized Data** and enter the **Sample Size** (80), the **Sample Mean** (76), the **Standard Deviation** (8), and the **Test Mean** (74) (Figure E).
- If the raw data are given, click **Samples in Columns** and select the column that contains the data. Enter the **Standard Deviation**.

Step 3. Click **Options** and select the form of the alternate hypothesis. For Example 8.14, we select **Not Equal**. Given significance level α, enter $100(1 - \alpha)$ as the **Confidence Level**. For Example 8.14, $\alpha = 0.05$ and the confidence level is $100(1 - 0.05) = 95$. Click **OK**.

Step 4. Click **OK** (Figure F).

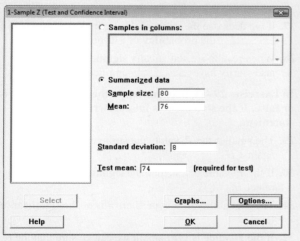

Figure E

```
Test of mu = 74 vs not = 74
The assumed standard deviation = 8


 N     Mean   SE Mean        95% CI           Z       P
80   76.0000   0.8944   (74.2470, 77.7530)   2.24   0.025
```

Figure F

EXCEL

Testing a hypothesis about the population mean when σ is known

This procedure requires the **MegaStat** EXCEL add-in to be loaded. The **MegaStat** add-in may be downloaded from www.mhhe.com/megastat.

Step 1. Load the **MegaStat** EXCEL add-in.

Step 2. Click on the **MegaStat** menu and select **Hypothesis Tests**, then **Mean vs. Hypothesized Value...**

Step 3. Choose one of the following:
- If the summary statistics are given, choose **summary input** and enter the range of the cells that contains, in the following order, the **variable name**, $\bar{x}$, σ, and n. Figure G illustrates the range of cells for Example 8.14 using *Satisfaction* as the variable name.
- If the raw data are given, choose **data input** and select the range of cells that contains the data in the **Input Range** field.

Step 4. Enter the **Hypothesized mean** (74) and select the form of the alternate hypothesis (not equal).

Step 5. Choose the **z-test** option (Figure H).

Step 6. Click **OK** (Figure I).

	A	B
1	Variable	Satisfaction
2	Sample Mean	76
3	Standard Deviation	8
4	Sample Size	80

Figure G

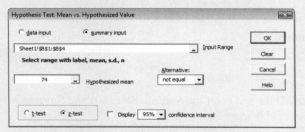

Figure H

Hypothesis Test: Mean vs. Hypothesized Value

74.00 hypothesized value
76.00 mean Satisfaction
8.00 std. dev.
0.89 std. error
80 n

2.24 z
.0253 p-value (two-tailed)

Figure I

SECTION 8.2 Exercises

Exercises 1–22 are the Check Your Understanding exercises located within the section.

Understanding the Concepts

In Exercises 23–28, fill in each blank with the appropriate word or phrase.

23. The _____ is the probability, assuming H_0 is true, of observing a value for the test statistic that is as extreme as or more extreme than the value actually observed.

24. The smaller the P-value is, the stronger the evidence against the _____ hypothesis becomes.

25. When using the critical value method, the region that contains the unusual values is called the _____ region.

26. If we decrease the value of the significance level α, we _____ the probability of a Type I error.

27. If we decrease the value of the significance level α, we _____ the probability of a Type II error.

28. When results are statistically significant, they do not necessarily have _____ significance.

In Exercises 29–34, determine whether the statement is true or false. If the statement is false, rewrite it as a true statement.

29. The smaller the P-value, the stronger the evidence against H_0.

30. If the P-value is less than the significance level, we reject H_0.

31. The probability of a Type II error is α, the significance level.

32. If the P-value is very small, we can be sure that the results have practical significance.

33. The P-value represents the probability that H_0 is true.

34. When presenting the results of a hypothesis test, one should report the P-value or the value of the test statistic.

Practicing the Skills

35. A test is made of H_0: $\mu = 50$ versus H_1: $\mu > 50$. A sample of size $n = 75$ is drawn, and $\bar{x} = 56$. The population standard deviation is $\sigma = 20$.
    a. Compute the value of the test statistic z.
    b. Is H_0 rejected at the $\alpha = 0.05$ level?
    c. Is H_0 rejected at the $\alpha = 0.01$ level?

36. A test is made of H_0: $\mu = 14$ versus H_1: $\mu \neq 14$. A sample of size $n = 48$ is drawn, and $\bar{x} = 12$. The population standard deviation is $\sigma = 6$.
    a. Compute the value of the test statistic z.
    b. Is H_0 rejected at the $\alpha = 0.05$ level?
    c. Is H_0 rejected at the $\alpha = 0.01$ level?

37. A test is made of H_0: $\mu = 130$ versus H_1: $\mu \neq 130$. A sample of size $n = 63$ is drawn, and $\bar{x} = 135$. The population standard deviation is $\sigma = 40$.
    a. Compute the value of the test statistic z.
    b. Is H_0 rejected at the $\alpha = 0.05$ level?
    c. Is H_0 rejected at the $\alpha = 0.01$ level?

38. A test is made of H_0: $\mu = 5$ versus H_1: $\mu < 5$. A sample of size $n = 87$ is drawn, and $\bar{x} = 4.5$. The population standard deviation is $\sigma = 25$.
    a. Compute the value of the test statistic z.
    b. Is H_0 rejected at the $\alpha = 0.05$ level?
    c. Is H_0 rejected at the $\alpha = 0.01$ level?

39. A test of the hypothesis H_0: $\mu = 65$ versus H_1: $\mu \neq 65$ was performed. The P-value was 0.035. Fill in the blank: If $\mu = 65$, then the probability of observing a test statistic as extreme as or more extreme than the one actually observed is _____.

40. A test of the hypothesis H_0: $\mu = 150$ versus H_1: $\mu < 150$ was performed. The P-value was 0.28. Fill in the blank: If $\mu = 150$, then the probability of observing a test statistic as extreme as or more extreme than the one actually observed is _____.

41. True or false: If $P = 0.02$, then
    a. The result is statistically significant at the $\alpha = 0.05$ level.
    b. The result is statistically significant at the $\alpha = 0.01$ level.
    c. The null hypothesis is rejected at the $\alpha = 0.05$ level.
    d. The null hypothesis is rejected at the $\alpha = 0.01$ level.

42. True or false: If $P = 0.08$, then
    a. The result is statistically significant at the $\alpha = 0.05$ level.
    b. The result is statistically significant at the $\alpha = 0.10$ level.
    c. The null hypothesis is rejected at the $\alpha = 0.05$ level.
    d. The null hypothesis is rejected at the $\alpha = 0.10$ level.

43. A test of H_0: $\mu = 17$ versus H_1: $\mu < 17$ is performed using a significance level of $\alpha = 0.01$. The value of the test statistic is $z = -2.68$.
    a. Is H_0 rejected?
    b. If the true value of μ is 17, is the result a Type I error, a Type II error, or a correct decision?
    c. If the true value of μ is 10, is the result a Type I error, a Type II error, or a correct decision?

44. A test of H_0: $\mu = 50$ versus H_1: $\mu \neq 50$ is performed using a significance level of $\alpha = 0.01$. The value of the test statistic is $z = 1.23$.
    a. Is H_0 rejected?
    b. If the true value of μ is 50, is the result a Type I error, a Type II error, or a correct decision?
    c. If the true value of μ is 65, is the result a Type I error, a Type II error, or a correct decision?

45. A test of H_0: $\mu = 0$ versus H_1: $\mu \neq 0$ is performed using a significance level of $\alpha = 0.05$. The P-value is 0.15.
    a. Is H_0 rejected?
    b. If the true value of μ is 1, is the result a Type I error, a Type II error, or a correct decision?
    c. If the true value of μ is 0, is the result a Type I error, a Type II error, or a correct decision?

46. A test of H_0: $\mu = 6$ versus H_1: $\mu > 6$ is performed using a significance level of $\alpha = 0.01$. The P-value is 0.002.
    a. Is H_0 rejected?
    b. If the true value of μ is 8, is the result a Type I error, a Type II error, or a correct decision?
    c. If the true value of μ is 6, is the result a Type I error, a Type II error, or a correct decision?

47. If $P = 0.03$, which of the following is the best conclusion?
    i. If H_0 is true, the probability of obtaining a test statistic as extreme as or more extreme than the one actually observed is 0.03.
    ii. The probability that H_0 is true is 0.03.
    iii. The probability that H_0 is false is 0.03.
    iv. If H_0 is false, the probability of obtaining a test statistic as extreme as or more extreme than the one actually observed is 0.03.

48. If $P = 0.25$, which of the following is the best conclusion?
    i. The probability that H_0 is true is 0.25.
    ii. If H_0 is false, the probability of obtaining a test statistic as extreme as or more extreme than the one actually observed is 0.25.
    iii. If H_0 is true, the probability of obtaining a test statistic as extreme as or more extreme than the one actually observed is 0.25.
    iv. The probability that H_0 is false is 0.25.

Working with the Concepts

49. **Facebook:** A study by the Web metrics firm Hitwise showed that in August 2008, the mean time spent per visit to Facebook was 19.5 minutes. Assume the standard deviation is $\sigma = 8$ minutes. Suppose that a simple random sample of 100 visits in August 2009 has a sample mean of $\bar{x} = 21.5$ minutes. A social scientist is interested in knowing whether the mean time of Facebook visits has increased.
    a. State the appropriate null and alternate hypotheses.
    b. Compute the value of the test statistic.
    c. State a conclusion. Use the $\alpha = 0.05$ level of significance.

50. **Are you smarter than a second-grader?** A random sample of 60 second-graders in a certain school district are given a standardized mathematics skills test. The sample mean score is $\bar{x} = 52$. Assume the standard deviation of test scores is $\sigma = 15$. The nationwide average score on this test is 50.

The school superintendent wants to know whether the second-graders in her school district have greater math skills than the nationwide average.

a. State the appropriate null and alternate hypotheses.

b. Compute the value of the test statistic.

c. State a conclusion. Use the $\alpha = 0.01$ level of significance.

51. **Height and age:** Are older men shorter than younger men? According to the National Health Statistics Reports, the mean height for U.S. men is 69.4 inches. In a sample of 300 men between the ages of 60 and 69, the mean height was $\bar{x} = 69.0$ inches. Public health officials want to determine whether the mean height μ for older men is less than the mean height of all adult men.

a. State the appropriate null and alternate hypotheses.

b. Assume the population standard deviation to be $\sigma = 2.84$ inches. Compute the value of the test statistic.

c. State a conclusion. Use the $\alpha = 0.01$ level of significance.

52. **Calibrating a scale:** Making sure that the scales used by businesses in the United States are accurate is the responsibility of the National Institute for Standards and Technology (NIST) in Washington, D.C. Suppose that NIST technicians are testing a scale by using a weight known to weigh exactly 1000 grams. They weigh this weight on the scale 50 times and read the result each time. The 50 scale readings have a sample mean of $\bar{x} = 1000.6$ grams. The scale is out of calibration if the mean scale reading differs from 1000 grams. The technicians want to perform a hypothesis test to determine whether the scale is out of calibration.

a. State the appropriate null and alternate hypotheses.

b. The standard deviation of scale reading is known to be $\sigma = 2$. Compute the value of the test statistic.

c. State a conclusion. Use the $\alpha = 0.05$ level of significance.

53. **Measuring lung function:** One of the measurements used to determine the health of a person's lungs is the amount of air a person can exhale under force in one second. This is called the forced expiratory volume in one second, and is abbreviated FEV_1. Assume the mean FEV_1 for 10-year-old boys is 2.1 liters and that the population standard deviation is $\sigma = 0.3$. A random sample of 100 10-year-old boys who live in a community with high levels of ozone pollution are found to have a sample mean FEV_1 of 1.95 liters. Can you conclude that the mean FEV_1 in the high-pollution community is less than 2.1 liters? Use the $\alpha = 0.05$ level of significance.

54. **Heavy children:** Are children heavier now than they were in the past? The National Health and Nutrition Examination Survey (NHANES) taken between 1999 and 2002 reported that the mean weight of six-year-old girls in the United States was 49.3 pounds. Another NHANES survey, published in 2008, reported that a sample of 193 six-year-old girls weighed between 2003 and 2006 had an average weight of 51.5 pounds. Assume the population standard deviation is $\sigma = 15$ pounds. Can you conclude that the mean weight of six-year-old girls is higher in 2006 than in 2002? Use the $\alpha = 0.01$ level of significance.

55. **House prices:** Data from the National Association of Realtors indicates that the mean price of a home in Denver, Colorado, in the first three months of 2008 was 225.3 thousand dollars. A random sample of 50 homes sold in 2010 had a mean price of 231 thousand dollars.

a. Assume the population standard deviation is $\sigma = 150$. Can you conclude that the mean price in 2010 differs from the mean price in the first three months of 2008? Use the $\alpha = 0.05$ level of significance.

b. Following is a boxplot of the data. Explain why it is not reasonable to assume that the population is approximately normally distributed.

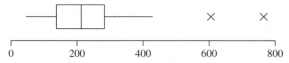

c. Explain why the assumptions for the hypothesis test are satisfied even though the population is not normal.

56. **SAT scores:** The College Board reports that in 2009, the mean score on the math SAT was 516 and the population standard deviation was $\sigma = 116$. A random sample of 20 students who took the test in 2010 had a mean score of 521. Following is a dotplot of the 20 scores.

a. Are the assumptions for a hypothesis test satisfied? Explain.

b. If appropriate, perform a hypothesis test to investigate whether the mean score in 2010 differs from the mean score in 2009. Assume the population standard deviation is $\sigma = 116$. What can you conclude? Use the $\alpha = 0.05$ level of significance.

57. **What are you drinking?** Environmental Protection Agency standards require that the amount of lead in drinking water be less than 15 micrograms per liter. Twelve samples of water from a particular source have the following concentrations, in units of micrograms per liter:

11.4	13.9	11.2	14.5	15.2	8.1
12.4	8.6	10.5	17.1	9.8	15.9

a. Explain why it is necessary to check that the population is approximately normal before performing a hypothesis test.

b. Following is a dotplot of the data. Is it reasonable to assume that the population is approximately normal?

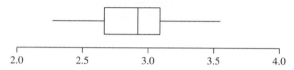

c. Assume that the population standard deviation is $\sigma = 3$. If appropriate, perform a hypothesis test at the $\alpha = 0.01$ level to determine whether you can conclude that the mean concentration of lead meets the EPA standard. What do you conclude?

58. GPA: The mean GPA at a certain university is 2.80. Following are GPAs for a random sample of 16 business students from this university.

2.27	3.05	2.57	3.36	3.10	3.03	3.19	3.08
2.60	2.92	2.77	3.55	2.63	2.79	2.70	2.92

a. Following is a boxplot of the data. Is it reasonable to assume that the population is approximately normal?

b. Assume that the population standard deviation is $\sigma = 0.3$. If appropriate, perform a hypothesis test at the $\alpha = 0.05$ level to determine whether the mean GPA for business students differs from the mean GPA at the whole university. What do you conclude?

59. Interpreting calculator display: The following TI-84 Plus display presents the results of a hypothesis test.

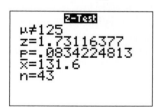

a. What are the null and alternate hypotheses?
b. What is the value of the test statistic?
c. What is the P-value?
d. Do you reject H_0 at the $\alpha = 0.05$ level?
e. Do you reject H_0 at the $\alpha = 0.01$ level?

60. Interpreting calculator display: The following TI-84 Plus display presents the results of a hypothesis test.

```
        Z-Test
µ≠125
z=1.73116377
p=.0834224813
x̄=131.6
n=43
```

a. What are the null and alternate hypotheses?
b. What is the value of the test statistic?
c. What is the P-value?
d. Do you reject H_0 at the $\alpha = 0.05$ level?
e. Do you reject H_0 at the $\alpha = 0.01$ level?

61. Interpreting computer output: The following output from MINITAB presents the results of a hypothesis test.

```
Test of mu = 225.0 vs not = 225.0
The assumed standard deviation = 35.0

 N    Mean    SE Mean         95% CI           Z      P
50   235.32   4.9497   (225.619, 245.021)   2.085   0.037
```

a. What are the null and alternate hypotheses?
b. What is the value of the test statistic?
c. What is the P-value?
d. Do you reject H_0 at the $\alpha = 0.05$ level?
e. Do you reject H_0 at the $\alpha = 0.01$ level?
f. Use the results of the output to compute the value of the test statistic z for a test of H_0: $\mu = 230$ versus H_1: $\mu > 230$.
g. Find the P-value.
h. Do you reject the null hypothesis in part (f) at the $\alpha = 0.05$ level?

62. Interpreting computer output: The following output from MINITAB presents the results of a hypothesis test.

```
Test of mu = 20.0 vs > 20.0
The assumed standard deviation = 6.5

 N    Mean    SE Mean         95% CI           Z      P
45   21.324   0.9690   (19.425, 23.223)   1.366   0.086
```

a. What are the null and alternate hypotheses?
b. What is the value of the test statistic?
c. What is the P-value?
d. Do you reject H_0 at the $\alpha = 0.05$ level?
e. Do you reject H_0 at the $\alpha = 0.01$ level?
f. Use the results of the output to compute the value of the test statistic z for a test of H_0: $\mu = 24$ versus H_0: $\mu \neq 24$.
g. Find the P-value.
h. Do you reject the null hypothesis in part (f) at the $\alpha = 0.05$ level?

63. Statistical or practical significance: A new method of teaching arithmetic to elementary school students was evaluated. The students who were taught by the new method were given a standardized test with a maximum score of 100 points. They scored an average of one point higher than students taught by the old method. A hypothesis test was performed in which the null hypothesis stated that there was no difference between the two groups, and the alternate hypothesis stated that the mean score for the new method was higher. The P-value was 0.001. True or false:
a. Because the P-value is very small, we can conclude that the mean score for students taught by the new method is higher than for students taught by the old method.
b. Because the P-value is very small, we can conclude that the new method represents an important improvement over the old method.

64. Statistical or practical significance: A new method of postoperative treatment was evaluated for patients undergoing a certain surgical procedure. Under the old method, the mean length of hospital stay was 6.3 days. The sample mean for the new method was 6.1 days. A hypothesis

test was performed in which the null hypothesis stated that the mean length of stay was the same for both methods, and the alternate hypothesis stated that the mean stay was lower for the new method. The P-value was 0.002. True or false:
a. Because the P-value is very small, we can conclude that the new method provides an important reduction in the mean length of hospital stay.
b. Because the P-value is very small, we can conclude that the mean length of hospital stay is less for patients treated by the new method than for patients treated by the old method.

65. Test scores: A math teacher has developed a new program to help high school students prepare for the math SAT. A sample of 100 students enroll in the program. They take a math SAT exam before the program starts and again at the end to measure their improvement. The mean number of points improved was $\bar{x} = 2.5$. Assume the standard deviation is $\sigma = 10$. Let μ be the population mean number of points improved. To determine whether the program is effective, a test is made of the hypotheses H_0: $\mu = 0$ versus H_1: $\mu > 0$.
a. Compute the value of the test statistic.
b. Compute the P-value.
c. Do you reject H_0 at the $\alpha = 0.05$ level?
d. Is the result of practical significance? Explain.

66. Weight loss: A doctor has developed a new diet to help people lose weight. A random sample of 500 people went on the diet for six weeks. The mean number of pounds lost was $\bar{x} = 0.5$. Assume the standard deviation is $\sigma = 5$. Let μ be the population mean number of pounds lost. To determine whether the diet is effective, a test is made of the hypotheses H_0: $\mu = 0$ versus H_1: $\mu > 0$.
a. Compute the value of the test statistic.
b. Compute the P-value.
c. Do you reject H_0 at the $\alpha = 0.05$ level?
d. Is the result of practical significance? Explain.

67. Enough information? A test was made of the hypotheses H_0: $\mu = 70$ versus H_1: $\mu \neq 70$. A report of the results stated: "$P < 0.05$, so we reject H_0 at the $\alpha = 0.05$ level." Is there any additional information that should have been included in the report? If so, what is it?

68. Enough information? A test was made of the hypotheses H_0: $\mu = 10$ versus H_1: $\mu > 10$. A report of the results stated: "The critical value was 1.645. Since $z > 1.645$, we reject H_0 at the $\alpha = 0.05$ level." Is there any additional information that should have been included in the report? If so, what is it?

Extending the Concepts

69. Somebody's wrong: Cindy computes a 95% confidence interval for μ and obtains (94.6, 98.3). Luis performs a test of the hypotheses H_0: $\mu = 100$ versus H_1: $\mu \neq 100$ and obtains a P-value of 0.12. Explain why they can't both be right.

70. Large samples and practical significance: A sample of size $n = 100$ is used to test H_0: $\mu = 20$ versus H_1: $\mu > 20$. The value of μ will not have practical significance unless $\mu > 25$. The population standard deviation is $\sigma = 10$. The value of $\bar{x}$ is 21.
a. Assume the sample size is $n = 100$. Compute the P-value. Show that you do not reject H_0 at the $\alpha = 0.05$ level.
b. Assume the sample size is $n = 1000$. Compute the P-value. Show that you reject H_0 at the $\alpha = 0.05$ level.
c. Do you think the difference is likely to be of practical significance? Explain.
d. Explain why a larger sample can be more likely to produce a statistically significant result that is not practically significant.

Answers to Check Your Understanding Exercises for Section 8.2

1. a. Critical value is -1.645, critical region is $z \leq -1.645$.
  b. Yes
  c. Critical value is -2.326, critical region is $z \leq -2.326$.
  d. No

2. a. Critical value is 1.645, critical region is $z \geq 1.645$.
  b. Yes
  c. Critical value is 2.326, critical region is $z \geq 2.326$.
  d. Yes

3. a. Critical values are 1.96 and -1.96, critical region is $z \leq -1.96$ or $z \geq 1.96$.
  b. No
  c. Critical values are 2.576 and -2.576, critical region is $z \leq -2.576$ or $z \geq 2.576$.
  d. No

4. a. $z = 2.12$ **b.** $z \geq 1.645$ **c.** Yes

5. a. $z = -1.00$ **b.** $z \leq -2.054$ **c.** No

6. a. $z = -3.25$ **b.** $z \leq -2.576$ or $z \geq 2.576$ **c.** Yes

7. $P = 0.05$

8. $P = 0.1003$. If H_0 is true, then the probability of observing a test statistic less than or equal to the value we actually observed is 0.1003. This result is not very unusual, so the evidence against H_0 is not strong.

9. a. $P = 0.4532$. If H_0 is true, then the probability of observing a test statistic as extreme as or more extreme than the value we actually observed is 0.4532. This result is not unusual, so the evidence against H_0 is not strong.
  b. $P = 0.0278$. If H_0 is true, then the probability of observing a test statistic as extreme as or more extreme than the value we actually observed is 0.0278. This result is fairly unusual, so the evidence against H_0 is fairly strong.
  c. $z = -2.20$

10. ii

11. a. No **b.** No **c.** Yes **d.** Yes

12. a. No **b.** Yes **c.** Yes **d.** No

13. a. Yes **b.** No **c.** Yes **d.** No

14. a. $z = 3.27$ **b.** $P = 0.0005$
   c. If H_0 is true, then the probability of observing a test
     statistic greater than or equal to the value we actually
     observed is 0.0005. This result is very unusual,
     so the evidence against H_0 is very strong.
   d. Yes   **e.** Yes

15. a. $H_0: \mu = 15$, $H_1: \mu \neq 15$ **b.** $z = 2.072750901$
   c. $P = 0.0381953363$ **d.** Yes

16. a. $H_0: \mu = 53.5$, $H_1: \mu \neq 53.5$ **b.** $z = -1.29$
   c. $P = 0.196$ **d.** No

17. a. No   **b.** Yes   **c.** Yes   **d.** Yes

18. a. Yes   **b.** No

19. 0.05

20. a. Charlie   **b.** Felice

21. a. Contains enough information
   b. The value of the test statistic z needs to be added.
   c. Contains enough information
   d. The P-value needs to be added.

22. a. $z = 3.16$, $P = 0.0008$, so H_0 is rejected at the $\alpha = 0.01$
   level.
   b. No. The difference between $\bar{x} = 101$ and 100 is not
   large enough to be of practical significance.

SECTION 8.3	**Hypothesis Tests for a Population Mean, Standard Deviation Unknown**

Objectives

  1. Test a hypothesis about a mean using the P-value method
  2. Test a hypothesis about a mean using the critical value method

Objective 1 Test a hypothesis about a mean using the P-value method

Do low-fat diets work? The following study was reported in the *Journal of the American Medical Association* (297:969–977). A total of 76 subjects were placed on a low-fat diet. After 12 months, their sample mean weight loss was $\bar{x} = 2.2$ kilograms, with a sample standard deviation of $s = 6.1$ kilograms. How strong is the evidence that people who adhere to this diet will lose weight, on the average?

To answer this question, we need to perform a hypothesis test on a population mean. Assume that the subjects in the study constitute a simple random sample from a population of interest. We are interested in their population mean weight loss μ. We know the sample mean $\bar{x} = 2.2$. We do not know the population standard deviation σ, but we know that the sample standard deviation is $s = 6.1$.

Because we do not know σ, we cannot use the z-score

$$z = \frac{\bar{x} - \mu}{\sigma/\sqrt{n}}$$

as our test statistic. Instead, we replace σ with the sample standard deviation s and use the t statistic

$$t = \frac{\bar{x} - \mu}{s/\sqrt{n}}$$

Recall: When $\bar{x}$ is the mean of a sample from a normal population, the quantity $\frac{\bar{x} - \mu}{s/\sqrt{n}}$ has a Student's t distribution with $n - 1$ degrees of freedom.

When the null hypothesis is true, the t statistic has a Student's t distribution with $n - 1$ degrees of freedom. We described the Student's t distribution in Section 7.2. When we perform a test using the t statistic, we call the test a *t*-test. We can perform a t-test for a population mean whenever the following assumptions are satisfied.

Assumptions for a Test of a Population Mean μ When σ Is Unknown

  1. We have a simple random sample.
  2. The sample size is large ($n > 30$), or the population is approximately normal.

When these assumptions are met, a hypothesis test may be performed. Either the critical value method or the P-value method may be used. Following are the steps for the P-value method.

Performing a Hypothesis Test on a Population Mean with σ Unknown Using the *P*-Value Method

Check to determine whether the assumptions are satisfied. If they are, then proceed with the following steps.

Step 1: State the null and alternate hypotheses. The null hypothesis specifies a value for the population mean μ. We will call this value μ_0. So the null hypothesis is of the form H_0: $\mu = \mu_0$. The alternate hypothesis may be stated in one of three ways:

Left-tailed: H_1: $\mu < \mu_0$

Right-tailed: H_1: $\mu > \mu_0$

Two-tailed: H_1: $\mu \neq \mu_0$

Step 2: If making a decision, choose a significance level α.

Step 3: Compute the test statistic $t = \dfrac{\bar{x} - \mu_0}{s/\sqrt{n}}$.

Step 4: Compute the *P*-value of the test statistic. The *P*-value is the probability, assuming that H_0 is true, of observing a value for the test statistic that disagrees as strongly as or more strongly with H_0 than the value actually observed. The *P*-value is an area under the Student's t curve with $n - 1$ degrees of freedom. The area is in the left tail, the right tail, or in both tails, depending on the type of alternate hypothesis. Note that the inequality points in the direction of the tail that contains the area for the *P*-value.

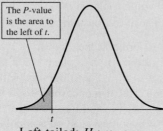

The *P*-value is the area to the left of *t*.

Left-tailed: H_1: $\mu < \mu_0$

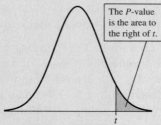

The *P*-value is the area to the right of *t*.

Right-tailed: H_1: $\mu > \mu_0$

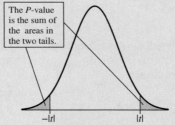

The *P*-value is the sum of the areas in the two tails.

Two-tailed: H_1: $\mu \neq \mu_0$

Step 5: Interpret the *P*-value. If making a decision, reject H_0 if the *P*-value is less than or equal to the significance level α.

Step 6: State a conclusion.

EXAMPLE 8.16

Perform a hypothesis test

In a recent medical study, 76 subjects were placed on a low-fat diet. After 12 months, their sample mean weight loss was $\bar{x} = 2.2$ kilograms, with a sample standard deviation of $s = 6.1$ kilograms. Can we conclude that the mean weight loss is greater than 0? Use the $\alpha = 0.05$ level of significance.

Source: *Journal of the American Medical Association* 297:969–977

Solution

We first check the assumptions. We have a simple random sample. The sample size is 76, so $n > 30$. The assumptions are satisfied.

Step 1: State H_0 and H_1. The issue is whether the mean weight loss μ is greater than 0. So the null and alternate hypotheses are

$$H_0: \mu = 0 \qquad H_1: \mu > 0$$

Note that we have a right-tailed test, because we are particularly interested in whether the diet results in a weight loss.

Step 2: Choose a level of significance. The level of significance is $\alpha = 0.05$.

Step 3: Compute the test statistic. The test statistic is

$$t = \frac{\bar{x} - \mu_0}{s/\sqrt{n}}$$

To compute its value, we note that $\bar{x} = 2.2$, $s = 6.1$, and $n = 76$. We set $\mu_0 = 0$, the value for μ specified by H_0. The value of the test statistic is

$$t = \frac{2.2 - 0}{6.1/\sqrt{76}} = 3.144$$

Step 4: Compute the *P*-value. When H_0 is true, the test statistic t has the Student's t distribution with $n - 1$ degrees of freedom. In this case, the sample size is $n = 76$, so there are $n - 1 = 75$ degrees of freedom. To obtain the P-value, note that the alternate hypothesis is H_1: $\mu > 0$. Therefore, values of the t statistic in the right tail of the Student's t distribution provide evidence against H_0. The P-value is the probability that a value as extreme as or more extreme than the observed value of 3.144 is observed from a t distribution with 75 degrees of freedom. To find the P-value exactly, it is necessary to use technology. The P-value is 0.0012. Figure 8.10 illustrates the P-value as an area under the Student's t curve, and presents the results from the TI-84 Plus calculator. Step-by-step instructions for performing hypothesis tests with technology are given in the Using Technology section on page 376.

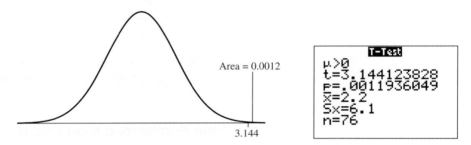

Figure 8.10   The P-value is the area to the right of the observed value of the test statistic, 3.144. The TI-84 Plus display shows that $P = 0.0012$, rounded to four decimal places.

Step 5: Interpret the *P*-value. The P-value is 0.0012. Because $P < 0.05$, we reject H_0.

Step 6: State a conclusion. We conclude that the mean weight loss of people who adhered to this diet for 12 months is greater than 0.

Estimating the *P*-Value from a Table

If no technology is available to compute the P-value, the t table (Table A.3) may be used to provide an approximation. When using a t table, we cannot find the P-value exactly. Instead, we can only specify that P is between two values. We now show how to use Table A.3 to bracket P between two values.

In Example 8.16, there are 75 degrees of freedom. We consult Table A.3 and find that the number 75 does not appear in the degrees of freedom column. We therefore use the next smallest number, which is 60. Now look across the row for two numbers that bracket the observed value 3.144. These are 2.915 and 3.232. The upper-tail probabilities are 0.0025 for 2.915 and 0.001 for 3.232. The P-value must therefore be between 0.001 and 0.0025 (see Figure 8.11 on page 370). We can conclude that the P-value is small enough to reject H_0.

Degrees of freedom	Area in the Right Tail									
	0.40	**0.25**	**0.10**	**0.05**	**0.025**	**0.01**	**0.005**	**0.0025**	**0.001**	**0.0005**
1	0.325	1.000	3.078	6.314	12.706	31.821	63.657	127.321	318.309	636.619
2	0.289	0.816	1.886	2.920	4.303	6.965	9.925	14.089	22.327	31.599
3	0.277	0.765	1.638	2.353	3.182	4.541	5.841	7.453	10.215	12.924
⋮	⋮	⋮	⋮	⋮	⋮	⋮	⋮	⋮	⋮	⋮
38	0.255	0.681	1.304	1.686	2.024	2.429	2.712	2.980	3.319	3.566
39	0.255	0.681	1.304	1.685	2.023	2.426	2.708	2.976	3.313	3.558
40	0.255	0.681	1.303	1.684	2.021	2.423	2.704	2.971	3.307	3.551
50	0.255	0.679	1.299	1.676	2.009	2.403	2.678	2.937	3.261	3.496
60	0.254	0.679	1.296	1.671	2.000	2.390	2.660	2.915	3.232	3.460
80	0.254	0.678	1.292	1.664	1.990	2.374	2.639	2.887	3.195	3.416
100	0.254	0.677	1.290	1.660	1.984	2.364	2.626	2.871	3.174	3.390
200	0.254	0.676	1.289	1.653	1.972	2.345	2.601	2.839	3.131	3.340

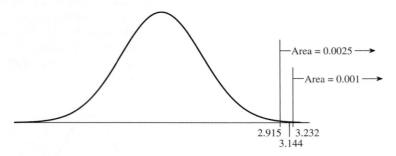

Figure 8.11 The P-value is the area to the right of the observed value of the test statistic, 3.144. The P-value is between 0.001 and 0.0025.

Finding the *P*-value for a two-tailed test from a table

In the previous example, what if the alternate hypothesis were H_1: $\mu \neq 0$? The P-value would be the sum of the areas in two tails. We know that the area in the right tail is 0.0012 (see Figure 8.10). Since the t distribution is symmetric, the sum of the areas in two tails is twice as much: $0.0012 + 0.0012 = 0.0024$. This is shown in Figure 8.12.

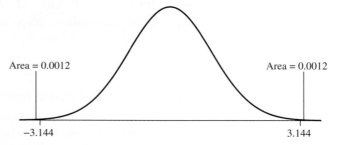

Figure 8.12 The P-value for a two-tailed test is the sum of the areas in the two tails. Each tail has area 0.0012. The P-value is $0.0012 + 0.0012 = 0.0024$.

If we are using Table A.3, we can only specify that P is between two values. We know that the area in one tail is between 0.001 and 0.0025. Therefore, the area in both tails is between $2(0.001) = 0.002$ and $2(0.0025) = 0.005$. This is shown in Figure 8.13.

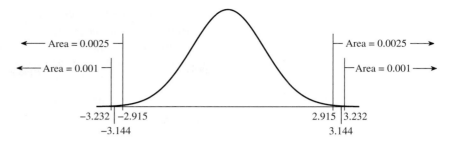

Figure 8.13   The *P*-value for a two-tailed test is the sum of the areas in the two tails. The area in each tail is between 0.001 and 0.0025. The sum of the areas in both tails is therefore between $2(0.001) = 0.002$ and $2(0.0025) = 0.005$.

Check Your Understanding

1. Find the *P*-value for the following values of the test statistic t, sample size n, and alternate hypothesis H_1. If you use Table A.3, you may specify that P is between two values.
   a. $t = 2.584$, $n = 12$, H_1: $\mu > \mu_0$
   b. $t = -1.741$, $n = 21$, H_1: $\mu < \mu_0$
   c. $t = 3.031$, $n = 14$, H_1: $\mu \neq \mu_0$
   d. $t = -2.584$, $n = 31$, H_1: $\mu \neq \mu_0$

2. In Example 8.16, the sample size was $n = 76$, and we observed $\bar{x} = 2.2$ and $s = 6.1$. We tested H_0: $\mu = 0$ versus H_1: $\mu > 0$, and the *P*-value was 0.0012. Assume that the sample size was 41 instead of 76, but that the values of $\bar{x}$ and s were the same.
   a. Find the value of the test statistic t.
   b. How many degrees of freedom are there?
   c. Find the *P*-value.
   d. Is the evidence against H_0 stronger or weaker than the evidence from the sample of 76? Explain.

Answers are on page 380.

| EXAMPLE 8.17 | ## Perform a hypothesis test |

Generic drugs are lower-cost substitutes for brand-name drugs. Before a generic drug can be sold in the United States, it must be tested and found to perform equivalently to the brand-name product. The U.S. Food and Drug Administration is now supervising the testing of a new generic antifungal ointment. The brand-name ointment is known to deliver a mean of 3.5 micrograms of active ingredient to each square centimeter of skin.

As part of the testing, seven subjects apply the ointment. Six hours later, the amount of drug that has been absorbed into the skin is measured. The amounts, in micrograms, are

2.6   3.2   2.1   3.0   3.1   2.9   3.7

How strong is the evidence that the mean amount absorbed differs from 3.5 micrograms? Use the $\alpha = 0.01$ level of significance.

Solution

We first check the assumptions. Because the sample is small, the population must be approximately normal. We check this with a dotplot of the data.

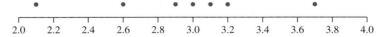

There is no evidence of strong skewness, and no outliers. Therefore, we may proceed.

Step 1:   State the null and alternate hypotheses. The issue is whether the mean μ differs from 3.5. Therefore, the null and alternate hypotheses are

$$H_0\text{: } \mu = 3.5 \qquad H_1\text{: } \mu \neq 3.5$$

Step 2: Choose a significance level α. The significance level is $\alpha = 0.01$.

Step 3: Compute the value of the test statistic t. To compute t, we need to know the sample mean $\bar{x}$, the sample standard deviation s, the null hypothesis mean μ_0, and the sample size n. We compute $\bar{x}$ and s from the sample. The values are

$$\bar{x} = 2.9429 \qquad s = 0.4995$$

The null hypothesis mean is $\mu_0 = 3.5$. The sample size is $n = 7$. The value of the t statistic is

$$
\begin{aligned}
t &= \frac{\bar{x} - \mu_0}{s/\sqrt{n}} \\
&= \frac{2.9429 - 3.5}{0.4995/\sqrt{7}} \\
&= -2.951
\end{aligned}
$$

Step 4: Compute the P-value. The number of degrees of freedom is $n - 1 = 7 - 1 = 6$. The alternate hypothesis is two-tailed, so the P-value is the sum of the area to the left of the observed t statistic -2.951 and the area to the right of 2.951, in a t distribution with 6 degrees of freedom. We can use technology to find that $P = 0.0256$. The following TI-84 Plus display presents the results. Step-by-step instructions for performing hypothesis tests with technology are given in the Using Technology section on page 376.

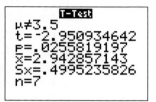

The P-value is given on the third line of the display. Rounding off to four decimal places, we see that $P = 0.0256$.

Alternatively, we can use Table A.3 to specify that the P-value is between two numbers. In the row corresponding to 6 degrees of freedom, the two values closest to 2.951 are 2.612 and 3.143. The area to the right of 2.612 is 0.02, and the area to the right of 3.143 is 0.01. Therefore, the area in the right tail is between 0.01 and 0.02. The P-value is twice the area in the right tail, so we conclude that P is between $2(0.01) = 0.02$ and $2(0.02) = 0.04$. See Figure 8.14.

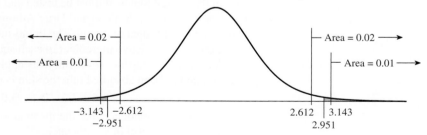

Figure 8.14 The P-value for a two-tailed test is the sum of the areas in the two tails. The area in each tail is between 0.01 and 0.02. The sum of the areas in both tails is therefore between $2(0.01) = 0.02$ and $2(0.02) = 0.04$.

Step 5: Interpret the P-value. The P-value of 0.0256 tells us that if H_0 is true, the probability of observing a value of the test statistic as extreme as or more extreme than the value of -2.951 that we observed is 0.0256. The P-value is small enough to give us doubt about the truth of H_0. However, because $P > 0.01$, we do not reject H_0 at the 0.01 level.

Step 6: State a conclusion. There is not enough evidence to conclude that the mean amount of drug absorbed differs from 3.5 micrograms. The mean may be equal to 3.5 micrograms.

Performing hypothesis tests with technology

The following output (from MINITAB) presents the results of Example 8.17.

```
Test of mu = 3.5 vs not = 3.5

N     Mean    StDev   SE Mean       99% CI          T       P
7    2.9429   0.4995   0.1888   (2.2430, 3.6248)   -2.95   0.026
```

Most of the output is straightforward. The first line specifies the null and alternate hypotheses. The sample size, sample mean, and sample standard deviation are given as "N," "Mean," and "StDev," respectively. The quantity labeled "SE Mean" is the standard error of the mean, which is the quantity $s/\sqrt{n}$ that appears in the denominator of the t statistic. Next, MINITAB provides a 99% confidence interval for μ. Finally, the value of the t statistic and the P-value are given.

The following TI-84 Plus display presents the results of Example 8.17. This display was also shown in the solution to Example 8.17.

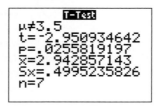

The first line states the alternate hypothesis. The quantity Sx is the sample standard deviation s. Step-by-step instructions for performing hypothesis tests with technology are given in the Using Technology section on page 376.

Check Your Understanding

3. In Example 8.17, the alternate hypothesis was H_1: $\mu \neq 3.5$ and the P-value for the two-tailed test was $P = 0.0256$. What would the P-value be for the alternate hypothesis H_1: $\mu < 3.5$?

4. The following TI-84 Plus display presents the results of a t-test.

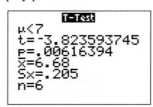

  a. What are the null and alternate hypotheses?
  b. What is the sample size?
  c. How many degrees of freedom are there?
  d. What is the value of $\bar{x}$?
  e. What is the value of s?
  f. What is the value of the test statistic?
  g. What is the P-value?
  h. Do you reject H_0 at the $\alpha = 0.01$ level?

5. Refer to the display in Exercise 4. If the sample mean were 6.80 instead of 6.68, what would the P-value be? If you use Table A.3, you may specify that P is between two values.

Answers are on page 380.

Objective 2 Test a hypothesis about a mean using the critical value method

Testing a Hypothesis About a Population Mean Using the Critical Value Method

The critical value method when σ is unknown is the same as that when σ is known, except that we use the Student's t distribution rather than the normal distribution. The critical value can be found in Table A.3 or with technology. The procedure depends on whether the alternate hypothesis is left-tailed, right-tailed, or two-tailed.

Critical Values for the t Statistic

Let α denote the chosen significance level and let n denote the sample size. The critical value depends on whether the alternate hypothesis is left-tailed, right-tailed, or two-tailed. We use the Student's t distribution with $n - 1$ degrees of freedom.

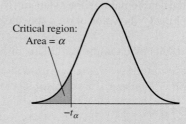

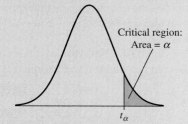

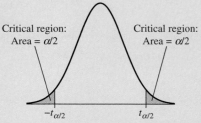

For left-tailed H_1: The critical value is $-t_\alpha$, which has area α to its left. Reject H_0 if $t \leq -t_\alpha$.

For right-tailed H_1: The critical value is t_α, which has area α to its right. Reject H_0 if $t \geq t_\alpha$.

For two-tailed H_1: The critical values are $t_{\alpha/2}$, which has area $\alpha/2$ to its right, and $-t_{\alpha/2}$, which has area $\alpha/2$ to its left. Reject H_0 if $t \geq t_{\alpha/2}$ or $t \leq -t_{\alpha/2}$.

Check Your Understanding

6. Find the critical value or values for the following values of the significance level α, sample size n, and alternate hypothesis H_1.
   a. $\alpha = 0.05$, $n = 3$, $H_1\colon \mu > \mu_0$
   b. $\alpha = 0.01$, $n = 26$, $H_1\colon \mu \neq \mu_0$
   c. $\alpha = 0.10$, $n = 81$, $H_1\colon \mu < \mu_0$
   d. $\alpha = 0.05$, $n = 14$, $H_1\colon \mu \neq \mu_0$

Answers are on page 380.

The assumptions for the critical value method are the same as those for the P-value method. We repeat them here.

Assumptions for a Test of a Population Mean μ When σ Is Unknown

1. We have a simple random sample.
2. The sample size is large ($n > 30$), or the population is approximately normal.

When these assumptions are satisfied, a hypothesis test may be performed using the following steps.

Performing a Hypothesis Test on a Population Mean with σ Unknown Using the Critical Value Method

Check to be sure that the assumptions are satisfied. If they are, then proceed with the following steps:

Step 1: State the null and alternate hypotheses. The null hypothesis specifies a value for the population mean μ. We will call this value μ_0, so the null hypothesis is of the form $H_0\colon \mu = \mu_0$. The alternate hypothesis may be stated in one of three ways:
   Left-tailed: $H_1\colon \mu < \mu_0$
   Right-tailed: $H_1\colon \mu > \mu_0$
   Two-tailed: $H_1\colon \mu \neq \mu_0$

Step 2: Choose a significance level α and find the critical value or values. Use $n - 1$ degrees of freedom, where n is the sample size.

Step 3: Compute the test statistic $t = \dfrac{\bar{x} - \mu_0}{s/\sqrt{n}}$.

Step 4: Determine whether to reject H_0, as follows:

Left-tailed: $H_1: \mu < \mu_0$ Reject if $t \leq -t_\alpha$.

Right-tailed: $H_1: \mu > \mu_0$ Reject if $t \geq t_\alpha$.

Two-tailed: $H_1: \mu \neq \mu_0$ Reject if $t \geq t_{\alpha/2}$ or $t \leq -t_{\alpha/2}$.

Step 5: State a conclusion.

EXAMPLE 8.18   **Test a hypothesis using the critical value method**

A computer software vendor claims that a new version of its operating system will crash fewer than six times per year on average. A system administrator installs the operating system on a random sample of 41 computers. At the end of a year, the sample mean number of crashes is 7.1, with a standard deviation of 3.6. Can you conclude that the vendor's claim is false? Use the $\alpha = 0.05$ significance level.

Solution

We first check the assumptions. We have a large ($n > 30$) random sample, so the assumptions are satisfied.

Step 1: State the null and alternate hypotheses. To conclude that the vendor's claim is false, we must conclude that $\mu > 6$. This is H_1. The hypotheses are $H_0: \mu = 6$ versus $H_1: \mu > 6$.

Step 2: Choose a significance level α and find the critical value. We will use a significance level of $\alpha = 0.05$. We use Table A.3. The number of degrees of freedom is $41 - 1 = 40$. This is a right-tailed test, so the critical value is the t-value with area 0.05 above it in the right tail. Thus, the critical value is $t_\alpha = 1.684$.

Step 3: Compute the test statistic. We have $\bar{x} = 7.1$, $\mu_0 = 6$, $s = 3.6$, and $n = 41$. The test statistic is

$$t = \frac{7.1 - 6}{3.6/\sqrt{41}} = 1.957$$

Step 4: Determine whether to reject H_0. Because this is a right-tailed test, we reject H_0 if $t \geq t_\alpha$. Because $t = 1.957$ and $t_\alpha = 1.684$, we reject H_0. Figure 8.15 illustrates the critical region and the test statistic.

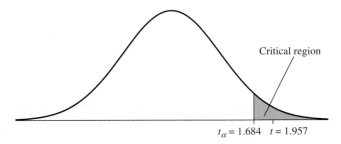

Critical region

$t_\alpha = 1.684$ $t = 1.957$

Figure 8.15

Step 5: State a conclusion. We conclude that the mean number of crashes is greater than six per year.

USING TECHNOLOGY

We use Example 8.17 to illustrate the technology steps.

TI-84 PLUS

Testing a hypothesis about a population mean when σ is unknown

Step 1. Press **STAT** and highlight the **TESTS** menu.

Step 2. Select **T–Test** and press **ENTER** (Figure A). The **T–Test** menu appears.

Step 3. Choose one of the following:
- If the summary statistics are given, select **Stats** as the **Inpt** option and enter μ_0, $\bar{x}$, s, and n.
- If the raw data are given, select **Data** as the **Inpt** option and enter the location of the data as the **List** option. For Example 8.17, the sample has been entered in list **L1**.

Step 4. Select the form of the alternate hypothesis. For Example 8.17, the alternate hypothesis has the form $\neq \mu_0$ (Figure B).

Step 5. Highlight **Calculate** and press **ENTER** (Figure C).

Figure A

Figure B

```
      T-Test
μ≠3.5
t=-2.950934643
P=.0255819197
x̄=2.942857143
Sx=.4995235826
n=7
```

Figure C

MINITAB

Testing a hypothesis about a population mean when σ is unknown

Step 1. Click on **Stat**, then **Basic Statistics**, then **1-Sample t**.

Step 2. Choose one of the following:
- If the summary statistics are given, click **Summarized Data** and enter the **Sample Size**, the **Mean**, and the **Standard Deviation** for the sample.
- If the raw data are given, click **Samples in Columns** and select the column that contains the data. For Example 8.17, the sample has been entered in column **C1**.

Step 3. Enter μ_0 in the **Test Mean** field.

Step 4. Click **Options** and select the form of the alternate hypothesis. For Example 8.17, we select **Not Equal**. Given significance level α, enter $100(1 - \alpha)$ as the **Confidence Level**. For Example 8.17, since $\alpha = 0.01$, the confidence level is $100(1 - 0.01) = 99$. Click **OK**.

Step 5. Click **OK** (Figure D).

```
Test of mu = 3.5 vs not = 3.5


Variable   N     Mean    StDev   SE Mean        99% CI            T      P
C1         7   2.94286  0.49952  0.18880  (2.24289, 3.64283)   -2.95  0.026
```

Figure D

EXCEL

Testing a hypothesis about a population mean when σ is unknown

This procedure requires the **MegaStat** EXCEL add-in to be loaded. The **MegaStat** add-in may be downloaded from www.mhhe.com/megastat.

Step 1. Load the **MegaStat** EXCEL add-in.

Step 2. Click on the **MegaStat** menu and select **Hypothesis Tests**, then **Mean vs. Hypothesized Value...**

Step 3. Choose one of the following:
- If the summary statistics are given, choose **summary input** and enter the range of the cells that contains, in the following order, the **variable name**, $\bar{x}$, s, and n.
- If the raw data are given, choose **data input** and select the range of cells that contains the data in the **Input Range** field. For Example 8.17, the sample has been entered in column **A** (Figure E).

Step 4. Enter the **Hypothesized mean** (3.5) and select the form of the alternate hypothesis (not equal).

Step 5. Choose the **t-test** option (Figure F).

Step 6. Click **OK** (Figure G)

	A
1	**Drug Absorbed**
2	2.6
3	3.2
4	2.1
5	3.0
6	3.1
7	2.9
8	3.7

Figure E

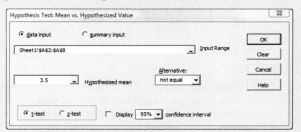

Figure F

Hypothesis Test: Mean vs. Hypothesized Value

3.5000	hypothesized value
2.9429	mean Drug Absorbed
0.4995	std. dev.
0.1888	std. error
7	n
6	df
-2.95	t
.0256	p-value (two-tailed)

Figure G

SECTION 8.3   Exercises

Exercises 1–6 are the Check Your Understanding exercises located within the section.

Understanding the Concepts

In Exercises 7 and 8, fill in each blank with the appropriate word or phrase.

7. To perform a t-test when the sample size is small, the sample must show no evidence of strong _____ and must contain no _____.

8. The number of degrees of freedom for the Student's t-test of a population mean is always 1 less than the _____.

In Exercises 9 and 10, determine whether the statement is true or false. If the statement is false, rewrite it as a true statement.

9. A t-test is used when the population standard deviation is unknown.

10. A t-test is used when the number of degrees of freedom is unknown.

Practicing the Skills

11. Find the P-value for the following values of the test statistic t, sample size n, and alternate hypothesis H_1. If you use Table A.3, you may specify that P is between two values.
   a. $t = 2.336$, $n = 5$, $H_1: \mu > \mu_0$
   b. $t = 1.307$, $n = 18$, $H_1: \mu \neq \mu_0$
   c. $t = -2.864$, $n = 51$, $H_1: \mu < \mu_0$
   d. $t = -2.031$, $n = 3$, $H_1: \mu \neq \mu_0$

12. Find the P-value for the following values of the test statistic t, sample size n, and alternate hypothesis H_1. If you use Table A.3, you may specify that P is between two values.
   a. $t = -1.584$, $n = 19$, $H_1: \mu \neq \mu_0$
   b. $t = -2.473$, $n = 41$, $H_1: \mu < \mu_0$
   c. $t = 1.491$, $n = 30$, $H_1: \mu \neq \mu_0$
   d. $t = 3.635$, $n = 4$, $H_1: \mu > \mu_0$

13. Find the critical value or values for the following values of the significance level α, sample size n, and alternate hypothesis H_1.

a. $\alpha = 0.05$, $n = 27$, H_1: $\mu \neq \mu_0$
b. $\alpha = 0.01$, $n = 61$, H_1: $\mu > \mu_0$
c. $\alpha = 0.10$, $n = 16$, H_1: $\mu \neq \mu_0$
d. $\alpha = 0.05$, $n = 11$, H_1: $\mu < \mu_0$

14. Find the critical value or values for the following values of the significance level α, sample size n, and alternate hypothesis H_1.
a. $\alpha = 0.05$, $n = 39$, H_1: $\mu > \mu_0$
b. $\alpha = 0.01$, $n = 34$, H_1: $\mu < \mu_0$
c. $\alpha = 0.10$, $n = 6$, H_1: $\mu \neq \mu_0$
d. $\alpha = 0.05$, $n = 25$, H_1: $\mu \neq \mu_0$

Working with the Concepts

15. **Is there a doctor in the house?** The Bureau of Labor Statistics reported that in May 2009, the mean annual earnings of all family practitioners in the United States was $168,550. A random sample of 55 family practitioners in Missouri that month had mean earnings of $\bar{x} = \$154,590$ with a standard deviation of $42,750. Do the data provide sufficient evidence to conclude that the mean salary for family practitioners in Missouri is less than the national average?
a. State the null and alternate hypotheses.
b. Compute the value of the t statistic. How many degrees of freedom are there?
c. State your conclusion. Use the $\alpha = 0.05$ level of significance.

16. **College tuition:** The mean annual tuition and fees in the 2009–2010 academic year for a sample of 14 private colleges in California was $30,500 with a standard deviation of $4,500. A dotplot shows that it is reasonable to assume that the population is approximately normal. Can you conclude that the mean tuition and fees for private institutions in California differs from $30,000?
a. State the null and alternate hypotheses.
b. Compute the value of the t statistic. How many degrees of freedom are there?
c. State your conclusion. Use the $\alpha = 0.01$ level of significance.
Based on data from *U.S. News and World Report*

17. **Big babies:** The National Health Statistics Reports described a study in which a sample of 360 one-year-old baby boys were weighed. Their mean weight was 25.5 pounds with standard deviation 5.3 pounds. A pediatrician claims that the mean weight of one-year-old boys is greater than 25 pounds. Do the data provide convincing evidence that the pediatrician's claim is true? Use the $\alpha = 0.01$ level of significance.

18. **Good credit:** The Fair Isaac Corporation (FICO) credit score is used by banks and other lenders to determine whether someone is a good credit risk. Scores range from 300 to 850, with a score of 720 or more indicating that a person is a very good credit risk. An economist wants to determine whether the mean FICO score is lower than the cutoff of 720. She finds that a random sample of 100 people had a mean FICO score of 703 with a standard deviation of 92. Can the economist conclude that the mean FICO score is less than 720? Use the $\alpha = 0.05$ level of significance.

19. **Commuting to work:** A 2007 Gallup poll sampled 1019 people, and asked them how long it took them to commute to work each day. The sample mean one-way commute time was 22.8 minutes with a standard deviation of 17.9 minutes.

A transportation engineer claims that the mean commute time is greater than 20 minutes. Do the data provide convincing evidence that the engineer's claim is true? Use the $\alpha = 0.05$ level of significance.

20. **Watching TV:** In 2008, the General Social Survey asked a sample of 1324 people how much time they spent watching TV each day. The mean number of hours was 2.98 with a standard deviation of 2.66. A sociologist claims that people watch a mean of 3 hours of TV per day. Do the data provide sufficient evidence to disprove the claim? Use the $\alpha = 0.01$ level of significance.

21. **Weight loss:** In a study to determine whether counseling could help people lose weight, a sample of people experienced a group-based behavioral intervention, which involved weekly meetings with a trained interventionist for a period of six months. The following data are the numbers of pounds lost for 14 people, based on means and standard deviations given in the article.

| 18.2 | 24.8 | 3.9 | 20.0 | 17.1 | 8.8 | 13.4 |
| 17.3 | 33.8 | 29.7 | 8.5 | 31.2 | 19.3 | 15.1 |

Source: *Journal of the American Medical Association* 299:1139–1148

a. Following is a boxplot for these data. Is it reasonable to assume that the conditions for performing a hypothesis test are satisfied? Explain.

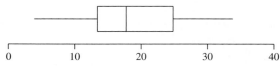

b. If appropriate, perform a hypothesis test to determine whether the mean weight loss is greater than 10 pounds. Use the $\alpha = 0.05$ level of significance. What do you conclude?

22. **How much is in that can?** A machine that fills beverage cans is supposed to put 12 ounces of beverage in each can. Following are the amounts measured in a simple random sample of eight cans.

11.96   12.10   12.04   12.13   11.98   12.05   11.91   12.03

a. Following is a dotplot for these data. Is it reasonable to assume that the conditions for performing a hypothesis test are satisfied? Explain.

b. If appropriate, perform a hypothesis test to determine whether the mean volume differs from 12 ounces. Use the $\alpha = 0.05$ level of significance. What do you conclude?

23. Keep cool: Following are prices, in dollars, of a random sample of ten 7.5-cubic-foot refrigerators.

314	377	330	285	319
274	332	350	299	306

a. Following is a dotplot for these data. Is it reasonable to assume that the conditions for performing a hypothesis test are satisfied? Explain.

b. A consumer organization reports that the mean price of 7.5-cubic-foot refrigerators is greater than $300. Do the data provide convincing evidence of this claim? Use the $\alpha = 0.01$ level of significance.

24. Free dessert: In an attempt to increase business on Monday nights, a restaurant offers a free dessert with every dinner order. Before the offer, the mean number of dinner customers on Monday was 150. Following are the numbers of diners on a random sample of 12 days while the offer was in effect.

206	169	191	152	212	139
142	151	174	220	192	153

a. Following is a boxplot for these data. Is it reasonable to assume that the conditions for performing a hypothesis test are satisfied? Explain.

b. Can you conclude that the mean number of diners increased while the free dessert offer was in effect? Use the $\alpha = 0.01$ level of significance.

25. Effective drugs: When testing a new drug, scientists measure the amount of the active ingredient that is absorbed by the body. In a study done at the Colorado School of Mines, a new antifungal medication that was designed to be applied to the skin was tested. The medication was applied to the skin of eight adult subjects. One hour later, the amount of active ingredient that had been absorbed into the skin was measured for each subject. The results, in micrograms, were

1.28   1.81   2.71   3.13   1.55   2.55   3.36   3.86

a. Construct a boxplot for these data. Is it appropriate to perform a hypothesis test?

b. If appropriate, perform a hypothesis test to determine whether the mean amount absorbed is greater than 2 micrograms. Use the $\alpha = 0.05$ level of significance. What do you conclude?

26. More effective drugs: An antifungal medication was applied to the skin of eight adult subjects. One hour later, the amount of active ingredient that had been absorbed into the skin was measured for each subject. The results, in micrograms, were

2.13   1.88   2.07   1.19   2.51   5.61   2.81   3.05

a. Construct a boxplot for these data. Is it appropriate to perform a hypothesis test?

b. If appropriate, perform a hypothesis test to determine whether the mean amount absorbed is less than

3 micrograms. Use the $\alpha = 0.05$ level of significance. What do you conclude?

27. Interpret calculator display: The following display from a TI-84 Plus calculator presents the results of a hypothesis test for a population mean μ.

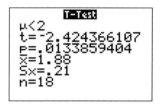

a. State the null and alternate hypotheses.
b. What is the value of $\bar{x}$?
c. What is the value of s?
d. How many degrees of freedom are there?
e. Do you reject H_0 at the 0.05 level? Explain.
f. Someone wants to test the hypothesis H_0: $\mu = 1.8$ versus H_1: $\mu > 1.8$. Use the information in the display to compute the t statistic for this test.
g. Compute the P-value for this test.
h. Can the null hypothesis in part (f) be rejected at the 0.05 level? Explain.

28. Interpret calculator display: The following display from a TI-84 Plus calculator presents the results of a hypothesis test for a population mean μ.

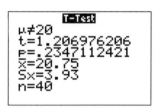

a. State the null and alternate hypotheses.
b. What is the value of $\bar{x}$?
c. What is the value of s?
d. How many degrees of freedom are there?
e. Do you reject H_0 at the 0.05 level? Explain.
f. Someone wants to test the hypothesis H_0: $\mu = 22.5$ versus H_1: $\mu \neq 22.5$. Use the information in the display to compute the t statistic for this test.
g. Compute the P-value for this test.
h. Can the null hypothesis in part (f) be rejected at the 0.05 level? Explain.

29. Interpret computer output: The following computer output (from MINITAB) presents the results of a hypothesis test for a population mean μ.

```
Test of mu = 5.5 vs > 5.5
```

				95% Lower		
N	Mean	StDev	SE Mean	Bound	T	P
5	5.92563	0.15755	0.07046	5.77542	6.04	0.002

a. State the null and alternate hypotheses.
b. What is the value of $\bar{x}$?
c. What is the value of s?
d. How many degrees of freedom are there?
e. Do you reject H_0 at the 0.05 level? Explain.

f. Someone wants to test the hypothesis H_0: $\mu = 6.5$ versus H_1: $\mu < 6.5$. Use the information in the output to compute the t statistic for this test.

g. Compute the P-value for this test.

h. Can the null hypothesis in part (f) be rejected at the 0.05 level? Explain.

30. Interpret computer output: The following computer output (from MINITAB) presents the results of a hypothesis test for a population mean μ.

```
Test of mu = 16 vs not = 16

  N    Mean    StDev   SE Mean      95% CI          T      P
 11  13.2874  6.0989   1.8389   (9.1901, 17.3847)  -1.48  0.171
```

a. State the null and alternate hypotheses.

b. What is the value of $\bar{x}$?

c. What is the value of s?

d. How many degrees of freedom are there?

e. Do you reject H_0 at the 0.05 level? Explain.

f. Someone wants to test the hypothesis H_0: $\mu = 9$ versus H_1: $\mu > 9$. Use the information in the output to compute the t statistic for this test.

g. Compute the P-value for this test.

h. Can the null hypothesis in part (f) be rejected at the 0.05 level? Explain.

31. Does this diet work? In a study of the effectiveness of a certain diet, 100 subjects went on the diet for a period of six months. The sample mean weight loss was 0.5 pound, with a sample standard deviation of 4 pounds.

a. Find the t statistic for testing H_0: $\mu = 0$ versus H_1: $\mu > 0$.

b. Find the P-value for testing H_0: $\mu = 0$ versus H_1: $\mu > 0$.

c. Can you conclude that the diet produces a mean weight loss that is greater than 0? Use the $\alpha = 0.05$ level of significance.

32. Effect of larger sample size: The study described in Exercise 31 is repeated with a larger sample of 1000 subjects. Assume that the sample mean is once again 0.5 pound and the sample standard deviation is once again 4 pounds.

a. Find the t statistic for testing H_0: $\mu = 0$ versus H_1: $\mu > 0$. Is the value of the t statistic greater than or less than the value obtained with a smaller sample of 100?

b. Find the P-value for testing H_0: $\mu = 0$ versus H_1: $\mu > 0$.

c. Can you conclude that the diet produces a mean weight loss that is greater than 0? Use the $\alpha = 0.05$ level of significance.

d. Explain why the mean weight loss is not of practical significance, even though the results are statistically significant at the 0.05 level.

Extending the Concepts

33. Using z instead of t: When the sample size is large, some people treat the sample standard deviation s as if it were the population standard deviation σ, and use the standard normal distribution rather than the Student's t distribution, to find a critical value. Assume that a right-tailed test will be made with a sample of size 100 from a normal population, using the $\alpha = 0.05$ significance level.

a. Find the critical value under the assumption that σ is known.

b. In fact, σ is unknown. How many degrees of freedom should be used for the Student's t distribution?

c. What is the probability of rejecting H_0 when it is true if the critical value in part (a) is used? You will need technology to find the answer.

Answers to Check Your Understanding Exercises for Section 8.3

1. a. P-value is between 0.01 and 0.025 [Tech: 0.0127]
   b. P-value is between 0.025 and 0.05 [Tech: 0.0485]
   c. P-value is between 0.005 and 0.01 [Tech: 0.0096]
   d. P-value is between 0.01 and 0.02 [Tech: 0.0148]

2. a. $t = 2.309$ **b.** 40
   c. Between 0.01 and 0.025 [Tech: 0.0131]
   d. Weaker; the P-value is larger.

3. 0.0128

4. a. H_0: $\mu = 7$, H_1: $\mu < 7$ **b.** 6   **c.** 5   **d.** 6.68
   e. 0.205   **f.** −3.823593745   **g.** 0.00616394   **h.** Yes

5. 0.0312

6. a. 2.920   **b.** −2.787, 2.787
   c. 1.292   **d.** −2.160, 2.160

SECTION 8.4   Hypothesis Tests for Proportions

Objectives

1. Test a hypothesis about a proportion using the P-value method
2. Test a hypothesis about a proportion using the critical value method

Objective 1 Test a hypothesis about a proportion using the P-value method

How cool is Facebook? In the 2009–2010 GenX2Z American College Student Survey, 90% of female college students rated the social network site Facebook as "cool." The other 10% rated it as "lame." Assume that the survey was based on a sample of 500 students. A marketing executive at Facebook wants to advertise the site with the slogan "More than 85% of female college students think Facebook is cool." Before launching the ad campaign, he wants to be confident that the slogan is true. Can he conclude that the proportion of female college students who think Facebook is cool is greater than 0.85?

This is an example of a problem that calls for a hypothesis test about a population proportion. There are two categories, "cool" and "lame." The quantity 0.85 represents the proportion in the "cool" category. To perform the test, we will need some notation, which we summarize as follows.

NOTATION

- p is the population proportion of individuals who are in a specified category.
- p_0 is the population proportion specified by H_0.
- x is the number of individuals in the sample who are in the specified category.
- n is the sample size.
- $\hat{p}$ is the sample proportion of individuals who are in the specified category. $\hat{p} = x/n$.

Explain It Again

Reasons for the assumptions: The population must be much larger than the sample (at least 20 times as large), so that the sampled items are independent. The assumption that both np_0 and $n(1 - p_0)$ are at least 10 ensures that the sampling distribution of $\hat{p}$ is approximately normal when we assume that H_0 is true.

We can perform a test whenever the sample proportion $\hat{p}$ is approximately normally distributed. This will occur when the following assumptions are met.

Assumptions for Performing a Hypothesis Test for a Population Proportion

1. We have a simple random sample.
2. The population is at least 20 times as large as the sample.
3. The individuals in the population are divided into two categories.
4. The values np_0 and $n(1 - p_0)$ are both at least 10.

Either the critical value method or the P-value method may be used to perform a hypothesis test for a population proportion. We will present the steps for the P-value method first.

Performing a Hypothesis Test for a Population Proportion Using the *P*-Value Method

Check to be sure the assumptions are satisfied. If they are, then proceed with the following steps:

Step 1: State the null and alternate hypotheses. The null hypothesis will have the form H_0: $p = p_0$. The alternate hypothesis will be $p < p_0$, $p > p_0$, or $p \neq p_0$.

Step 2: If making a decision, choose a significance level α.

Step 3: Compute the test statistic $z = \dfrac{\hat{p} - p_0}{\sqrt{\dfrac{p_0(1 - p_0)}{n}}}$.

Step 4: Compute the P-value. The P-value is an area under the standard normal curve; it depends on the alternate hypothesis as follows:

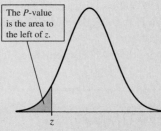

The P-value is the area to the left of z.

Left-tailed: H_1: $p < p_0$

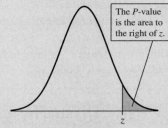

The P-value is the area to the right of z.

Right-tailed: H_1: $p > p_0$

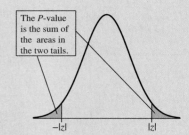

The P-value is the sum of the areas in the two tails.

Two-tailed: H_1: $p \neq p_0$

Step 5: Interpret the P-value. If making a decision, reject H_0 if the P-value is less than or equal to the significance level α.

Step 6: State a conclusion.

EXAMPLE 8.19

Perform a hypothesis test

In the 2009–2010 GenX2Z American College Student Survey, 90% of female college students rated the social network site Facebook as "cool." Assume that the survey was based on a random sample of 500 students. A marketing executive at Facebook wants to advertise the site with the slogan "More than 85% of female college students think Facebook is cool." Can you conclude that the proportion of female college students who think Facebook is cool is greater than 0.85? Use the $\alpha = 0.05$ level of significance.

Solution

We first check the assumptions. We have a simple random sample of students. The members of the population fall into two categories: those who think that Facebook is cool and those who don't. The size of the population of female college students is more than 20 times the sample size of $n = 500$. The proportion specified by the null hypothesis is $p_0 = 0.85$. Now $np_0 = (500)(0.85) = 425 > 10$ and $n(1 - p_0) = (500)(1 - 0.85) = 75 > 10$. The assumptions are satisfied.

Step 1: State H_0 and H_1. We are asked whether we can conclude that the population proportion p is greater than 0.85. The null and alternate hypotheses are therefore

$$H_0: p = 0.85 \qquad H_1: p > 0.85$$

Step 2: Choose a significance level. The significance level is $\alpha = 0.05$.

Step 3: Compute the test statistic. The sample proportion $\hat{p}$ is 0.90. The value of p specified by the null hypothesis is $p_0 = 0.85$. The test statistic is the z-score for $\hat{p}$:

$$z = \frac{\hat{p} - p_0}{\sqrt{\dfrac{p_0(1 - p_0)}{n}}} = \frac{0.90 - 0.85}{\sqrt{\dfrac{0.85(1 - 0.85)}{500}}} = 3.13$$

Step 4: Compute the P-value. The alternate hypothesis is $H_1: \mu > 0.85$, which is right-tailed. The P-value is therefore the area to the right of $z = 3.13$. Using Table A.2, we see that the area to the left of $z = 3.13$ is 0.9991. The area to the right of $z = 3.13$ is therefore $1 - 0.9991 = 0.0009$. The P-value is $P = 0.0009$. See Figure 8.16.

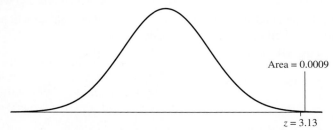

Area = 0.0009

$z = 3.13$

Figure 8.16

Step 5: Interpret the P-value. A P-value of $P = 0.0009$ is very small. This is very strong evidence against H_0. In particular, because $P < 0.05$, we reject H_0 at the $\alpha = 0.05$ level.

Step 6: State a conclusion. We conclude that more than 85% of female college students think Facebook is cool.

Check Your Understanding

1. The Pew Research Center reported in 2008 that only 15% of 18–24-year-olds read a daily newspaper. The publisher of a local newspaper wants to know whether the percentage of newspaper readers among students at a nearby large university differs from the percentage among 18–24-year-olds in general. She surveys a simple random sample of 200 students at the university and finds that 40 of them, or 20%, read a

newspaper each day. Can she conclude that the proportion of students who read a daily newspaper differs from 0.15? Use the $\alpha = 0.05$ level of significance.

a. State the null and alternate hypotheses.
b. Compute the test statistic.
c. Compute the P-value.
d. State a conclusion.

Answers are on page 391.

Performing a hypothesis test with technology

The following computer output (from MINITAB) presents the results of Example 8.19.

```
Test of p = 0.85 vs p > 0.85
                                     95%
                                    Lower
Sample      X      N    Sample p    Bound     Z-Value   P-Value
1         450    500    0.900000   0.877932      3.13     0.001
```

Most of the output is straightforward. The first line specifies the null and alternate hypotheses. The quantity labeled "X" is the number of people in the sample who think Facebook is cool, and N is the sample size. The quantity labeled "Sample p" is the sample proportion $\hat{p}$. The quantity labeled "95% Lower Bound" is a 95% lower confidence bound for the population proportion p. The interpretation of this quantity is that we are 95% confident that the population proportion p is greater than or equal to 0.877932. Next is the value of the test statistic z, labeled "Z-value," and finally at the end of the row is the P-value.

The following display from a TI-84 Plus calculator presents the results of Example 8.19.

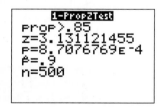

The first line in the display presents the alternate hypothesis. The word "prop" refers to the population proportion p. Note that the letter "p" in the third line is the P-value, not the population proportion. This number is written in scientific notation as 8.7076769E-4. This indicates that we should move the decimal point four places to the left, so $P = 0.00087076769$.

Step-by-step instructions for performing hypothesis tests with technology are presented in the Using Technology section on page 386.

Check Your Understanding

2. The following output from MINITAB presents the results of a hypothesis test.

```
Test of p = 0.60 vs p < 0.60
                                     95%
                                    Upper
Sample      X      N    Sample p    Bound     Z-Value   P-Value
1          72    150    0.480000   0.547097     -3.00     0.001
```

   a. What are the null and alternate hypotheses?
   b. What is the sample size?
   c. What is the value of $\hat{p}$?
   d. What is the value of the test statistic?
   e. Do you reject H_0 at the 0.05 level?
   f. Do you reject H_0 at the 0.01 level?

  3. The following display from a TI-84 Plus calculator presents the results of a hypothesis test.

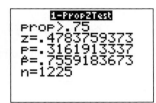

   a. What are the null and alternate hypotheses?
   b. What is the sample size?
   c. What is the value of $\hat{p}$?
   d. What is the value of the test statistic?
   e. Do you reject H_0 at the 0.05 level?
   f. Do you reject H_0 at the 0.01 level?

Answers are on page 391.

Objective 2 Test a hypothesis about a proportion using the critical value method

Testing Hypotheses for a Proportion Using the Critical Value Method

To use the critical value method, compute the test statistic as before. Because the test statistic is a z-score, critical values can be found in Table A.2, in the last line of Table A.3, or with technology. The assumptions for the critical value method are the same as for the P-value method.

Assumptions for Performing a Hypothesis Test for a Population Proportion

1. We have a simple random sample.
2. The population is at least 20 times as large as the sample.
3. The items in the population are divided into two categories.
4. The values np_0 and $n(1 - p_0)$ are both at least 10.

Following are the steps for the critical value method.

Performing a Hypothesis Test for a Proportion Using the Critical Value Method

Check to be sure the assumptions are satisfied. If they are, then proceed with the following steps:

Step 1: State the null and alternate hypotheses. The null hypothesis will have the form H_0: $p = p_0$. The alternate hypothesis will be $p < p_0$, $p > p_0$, or $p \neq p_0$.

Step 2: Choose a significance level α and find the critical value or values.

Step 3: Compute the test statistic $z = \dfrac{\hat{p} - p_0}{\sqrt{\dfrac{p_0(1 - p_0)}{n}}}$.

Step 4: Determine whether to reject H_0, as follows:

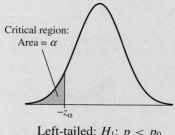

Critical region:
Area $= \alpha$

$-z_\alpha$

Left-tailed: H_1: $p < p_0$
Reject if $z \leq -z_\alpha$.

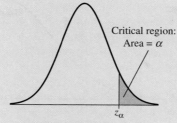

Critical region:
Area $= \alpha$

z_α

Right-tailed: H_1: $p > p_0$
Reject if $z \geq z_\alpha$.

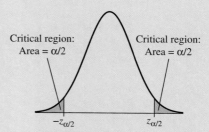

Critical region:
Area $= \alpha/2$

Critical region:
Area $= \alpha/2$

$-z_{\alpha/2}$ $z_{\alpha/2}$

Two-tailed: H_1: $p \neq p_0$
Reject if $z \geq z_{\alpha/2}$ or $z \leq -z_{\alpha/2}$.

Step 5: State a conclusion.

EXAMPLE 8.20

Test a hypothesis about a population proportion using the critical value method

A nationwide survey of working adults indicates that only 50% of them are satisfied with their jobs. The president of a large company believes that more than 50% of employees at his company are satisfied with their jobs. To test his belief, he surveys a random sample of 100 employees, and 54 of them report that they are satisfied with their jobs. Can he conclude that more than 50% of employees at the company are satisfied with their jobs? Use the $\alpha = 0.05$ level of significance.

Solution

We first check the assumptions. We have a simple random sample from the population of employees. Each employee is categorized as being satisfied or not satisfied. The sample size is $n = 100$ and the proportion p_0 specified by H_0 is 0.5. Therefore, we calculate that $np_0 = 100(0.5) = 50 > 10$, and $n(1 - p_0) = 100(1 - 0.5) = 50 > 10$. If the total number of employees in the company is more than 2000, as we shall assume, then the population is more than 20 times as large as the sample. All the assumptions are therefore satisfied.

Step 1: State the null and alternate hypotheses. The issue is whether the proportion of employees that are satisfied with their jobs is more than 0.5. Therefore, the null and alternate hypotheses are

$$H_0\text{: } p = 0.5 \qquad H_1\text{: } p > 0.5$$

Step 2: Choose a significance level and find the critical value. The significance level is $\alpha = 0.05$. The alternate hypothesis is $p > 0.5$, so this is a right-tailed test. The critical value corresponding to $\alpha = 0.05$ is $z_\alpha = 1.645$.

Step 3: Compute the test statistic. The test statistic is

$$z = \frac{\hat{p} - p_0}{\sqrt{\dfrac{p_0(1 - p_0)}{n}}}$$

The value of the sample proportion $\hat{p}$ is

$$\hat{p} = \frac{\text{Number of satisfied employees}}{\text{Sample size}} = \frac{54}{100} = 0.54$$

The quantity p_0 is the value of p specified by H_0, so $p_0 = 0.5$. The sample size is $n = 100$. Therefore, the value of the test statistic is

$$z = \frac{0.54 - 0.5}{\sqrt{\dfrac{0.5(1 - 0.5)}{100}}} = 0.80$$

Step 4: Determine whether to reject H_0. Because this is a right-tailed test, we reject H_0 if $z \geq 1.645$. Because $0.80 < 1.645$, we do not reject H_0. See Figure 8.17.

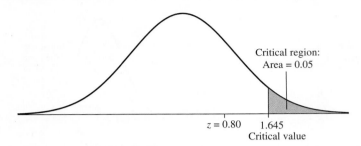

Critical region:
Area = 0.05

$z = 0.80$ 1.645
Critical value

Figure 8.17

Step 5: State a conclusion. There is not enough evidence to conclude that the company president is correct in his belief that the proportion of employees who are satisfied with their jobs is greater than 0.5. The proportion may be equal to 0.5.

Check Your Understanding

4. A Gallup poll taken in December 2009 sampled 1000 adults in the United States. Of these people, 770 said they enjoyed situations in which they competed with other people. Can you conclude that less than 80% of U.S. adults like to compete? Use the critical value method with significance level $\alpha = 0.05$.
   a. State the null and alternate hypotheses.
   b. Compute the test statistic.
   c. Find the critical value.
   d. State a conclusion.

Answers are on page 391.

USING TECHNOLOGY

We use Example 8.20 to illustrate the technology steps.

TI-84 PLUS

Testing a hypothesis about a proportion

Step 1. Press **STAT** and highlight the **TESTS** menu.

Step 2. Select **1–PropZTest** and press **ENTER** (Figure A). The **1-PropZTest** menu appears.

Step 3. Enter the values of p_0, x, and n. For Example 8.20, we use $p_0 = 0.5$, $x = 54$, and $n = 100$.

Step 4. Select the form of the alternate hypothesis. For Example 8.20, the alternate hypothesis has the form $> p_0$ (Figure B).

Step 5. Highlight **Calculate** and press **ENTER** (Figure C).

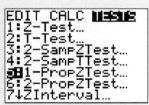

Figure A

Figure B

Figure C

MINITAB

Testing a hypothesis about a proportion

Step 1. Click on **Stat**, then **Basic Statistics**, then **1 Proportion**.

Step 2. Click **Summarized Data**, and enter the value of n in the **Number of Trials** field and the value of x in the **Number of Events** field. For Example 8.20, we use $x = 54$ and $n = 100$ (Figure D).

Step 3. Click **Options**, and enter the value of p_0 in the **Test proportion** field and the form of the alternate hypothesis in the **Alternative** field. For Example 8.20, we enter 0.5 for p_0 and enter **greater than** as the alternate hypothesis.

Step 4. Given significance level α, enter $100(1 - \alpha)$ as the **Confidence Level**. For Example 8.20, $\alpha = 0.05$, so the confidence level is $100(1 - 0.05) = 95$ (Figure E).

Step 5. Check the **Use test and interval based on normal distribution** option and click **OK**.

Step 6. Click **OK** (Figure F).

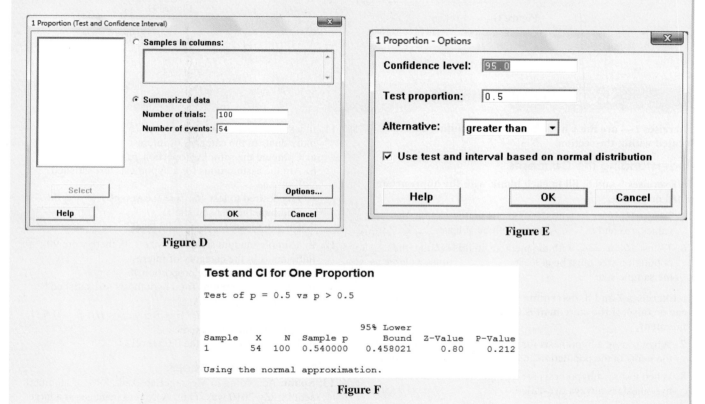

Figure D

Figure E

Test and CI for One Proportion

```
Test of p = 0.5 vs p > 0.5

                            95% Lower
Sample   X    N   Sample p      Bound   Z-Value   P-Value
1        54  100  0.540000   0.458021      0.80     0.212

Using the normal approximation.
```

Figure F

EXCEL

Testing a hypothesis about a proportion

This procedure requires the **MegaStat** EXCEL add-in to be loaded. The **MegaStat** add-in may be downloaded from www.mhhe.com/megastat.

Step 1. Load the **MegaStat** EXCEL add-in.

Step 2. Click on the **MegaStat** menu and select **Hypothesis Tests**, then **Proportion vs. Hypothesized Value...**

Step 3. Under the *Observed* column, enter the value of x in the **p** field (note that p automatically changes to x) and the sample size n in the **n** field. For Example 8.20, we use $x = 54$ and $n = 100$.

Step 4. Under the *Hypothesized* column, enter the value of p_0. We use $p_0 = 0.5$.

Step 5. Select the form of the alternate hypothesis. For Example 8.20, we use **greater than** (Figure G).

Step 6. Click **OK** (Figure H).

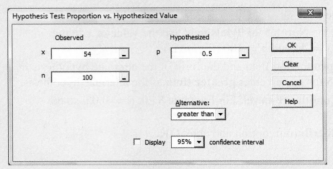

Figure G

Hypothesis test for proportion vs hypothesized value

Observed	Hypothesized	
0.54	0.5	p (as decimal)
54/100	50/100	p (as fraction)
54.	50.	X
100	100	n
	0.05	std. error
	0.80	z
	.2119	p-value (one-tailed, upper)

Figure H

SECTION 8.4 Exercises

Exercises 1–4 are the Check Your Understanding exercises located within the section.

Understanding the Concepts

In Exercises 5 and 6, fill in each blank with the appropriate word or phrase.

5. To test H_0: $p = p_0$ with the methods in this section, the values np_0 and $n(1 - p_0)$ must both be at least _____.

6. To test H_0: $p = p_0$ with the methods in this section, the population size must be at least _____ times as large as the sample size.

In Exercises 7 and 8, determine whether the statement is true or false. If the statement is false, rewrite it as a true statement.

7. When testing a hypothesis for a proportion, we assume that the items in the population are divided into two categories.

8. When testing a hypothesis for a proportion, the alternate hypothesis is always two-tailed.

Practicing the Skills

9. In a simple random sample of size 80, there were 54 individuals in the category of interest.
   a. Compute the sample proportion $\hat{p}$.
   b. Are the assumptions for a hypothesis test satisfied? Explain.
   c. It is desired to test H_0: $p = 0.8$ versus H_1: $p < 0.8$. Compute the test statistic z.
   d. Do you reject H_0 at the 0.05 level?

10. In a simple random sample of size 60, there were 38 individuals in the category of interest.
    a. Compute the sample proportion $\hat{p}$.
    b. Are the assumptions for a hypothesis test satisfied? Explain.
    c. It is desired to test H_0: $p = 0.7$ versus H_1: $p \neq 0.7$. Compute the test statistic z.
    d. Do you reject H_0 at the 0.05 level?

11. In a simple random sample of size 75, there were 42 individuals in the category of interest.
    a. Compute the sample proportion $\hat{p}$.
    b. Are the assumptions for a hypothesis test satisfied? Explain.
    c. It is desired to test H_0: $p = 0.6$ versus H_1: $p \neq 0.6$. Compute the test statistic z.
    d. Do you reject H_0 at the 0.05 level?

12. In a simple random sample of size 150, there were 90 individuals in the category of interest.
    a. Compute the sample proportion $\hat{p}$.
    b. Are the assumptions for a hypothesis test satisfied? Explain.
    c. It is desired to test H_0: $p = 0.5$ versus H_1: $p > 0.5$. Compute the test statistic z.
    d. Do you reject H_0 at the 0.05 level?

Working with the Concepts

13. **Spam:** According to MessageLabs Ltd., 89% of all email sent in July 2010 was spam. A system manager at a large corporation believes that the percentage at his company may be 80%. He examines a random sample of 500 emails received at an email server and finds that 382 of the messages are spam.
    a. State the appropriate null and alternate hypotheses.
    b. Compute the test statistic z.
    c. Using $\alpha = 0.05$, can you conclude that the percentage of emails that are spam differs from 80%?
    d. Using $\alpha = 0.01$, can you conclude that the percentage of emails that are spam differs from 80%?

14. **High salaries for executives:** A Washington Post-ABC News poll conducted in October 2009 surveyed a random sample of 1004 adults in the United States. Of these people, 713 said they would support federal legislation putting limits on the amounts that top executives are paid at companies that receive emergency government loans. One highly paid

executive claims that less than 75% of U.S. adults support limits on the amounts that executives are paid.
  a. State the appropriate null and alternate hypotheses.
  b. Compute the test statistic z.
  c. Using $\alpha = 0.05$, can you conclude that the executive's claim is true?
  d. Using $\alpha = 0.01$, can you conclude that the executive's claim is true?

15. **Kids with cell phones:** A marketing manager for a cell phone company claims that more than 35% of children aged 10–11 have cell phones. In a 2009 survey of 5000 children aged 10–11 by Mediamark Research and Intelligence, 1805 of them had cell phones. Can you conclude that the manager's claim is true? Use the $\alpha = 0.01$ level of significance.

16. **Environment:** In 2008, the General Social Survey asked 1493 U.S. adults to rate their level of interest in environmental issues. Of these, 751 said that they were "very interested." Does the survey provide convincing evidence that more than half of U.S. adults are very interested in environmental issues? Use the $\alpha = 0.05$ level of significance.

17. **Quit smoking:** In a survey of 444 HIV-positive smokers, 170 reported that they had used a nicotine patch to try to quit smoking. Can you conclude that less than half of HIV-positive smokers have used a nicotine patch? Use the $\alpha = 0.05$ level of significance.
Source: *American Journal of Health Behavior* 32:3–15

18. **Mario Kart:** A Pew poll taken in 2008 surveyed 1064 teenagers, and 787 of them said that they play racing video games such as NASCAR, Mario Kart, or Burnout. A sales manager of a video game company claims that more than 70% of teenagers are playing racing games. Does the poll provide convincing evidence that the claim is true? Use the $\alpha = 0.01$ level of significance.

19. **Tattoo:** A Pew poll taken in 2010 surveyed 830 people aged 18–29, and found that 166 of them had one or more tattoos. Can you conclude that the percentage of people aged 18–29 who have a tattoo is less than 25%? Use the $\alpha = 0.01$ level of significance.

20. **Curing diabetes:** Vertical banded gastroplasty is a surgical procedure that reduces the volume of the stomach in order to produce weight loss. In a recent study, 82 patients with Type 2 diabetes underwent this procedure, and 59 of them experienced a recovery from diabetes. Does this study provide convincing evidence that more than 60% of those

with diabetes who undergo this surgery will recover from diabetes? Use the $\alpha = 0.05$ level of significance.
Source: *New England Journal of Medicine* 357:753–761

21. **Facebook for jobs:** The recruiting firm Jobvite, Inc. reported that 78% of U.S. companies use social networks such as Facebook and LinkedIn to recruit job candidates. An economist thinks that the percentage is higher at technology companies. She samples 70 technology companies and finds that 55 of them use social networks. Can she conclude that more than 78% of technology companies use social networks? Use the $\alpha = 0.05$ level of significance.

22. **Google it:** The marketing research company comScore, Inc. reported that 65% of online searches in March 2010 used Google as the search engine. A network administrator wants to determine whether the percentage of searches that use Google is different in his company. He samples 400 searches and finds that 295 of them use Google. Can he conclude that the percentage of searches that use Google in his company differs from 65%? Use the $\alpha = 0.05$ level of significance.

23. **Choosing a doctor:** Which do patients value more when choosing a doctor: interpersonal skills or technical ability? In a recent study, 304 people were asked to choose a physician based on two hypothetical descriptions. One physician was described as having high technical skills and average interpersonal skills, and the other was described as having average technical skills and high interpersonal skills. The physician with high interpersonal skills was chosen by 116 of the people. Can you conclude that less than half of patients prefer a physician with high interpersonal skills? Use the $\alpha = 0.01$ level of significance.
Source: *Health Services Research* 40:957–977

24. **Cable TV choices:** A telecommunications company provided its cable TV subscribers with free access to a new sports channel for a period of one month. It then chose a sample of 400 television viewers and asked them whether they would be willing to pay an extra $10 per month to continue to access the channel. A total of 25 of the 400 replied that they would be willing to pay. The marketing director of the company claims that more than 5% of all its subscribers would pay for the channel. Can you conclude that the director's claim is true? Use the $\alpha = 0.01$ level of significance.

25. **Interpret calculator display:** The following display from a TI-84 Plus calculator presents the results of a hypothesis test for a population proportion p.

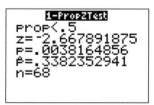

  a. What are the null and alternate hypotheses?
  b. What is the value of the sample proportion $\hat{p}$?
  c. Can H_0 be rejected at the 0.05 level? Explain.
  d. Someone wants to use these data to test H_0: $p = 0.25$ versus H_1: $p \neq 0.25$. Find the test statistic z and use the

method of this section to find the P-value. Do you reject H_0 at the $\alpha = 0.05$ level?

26. Interpret calculator display: The following display from a TI-84 Plus calculator presents the results of a hypothesis test for a population proportion p.

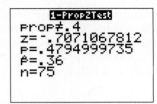

```
      1-PropZTest
Prop≠.4
z=-.7071067812
P=.4794999735
p̂=.36
n=75
```

a. What are the null and alternate hypotheses?
b. What is the value of the sample proportion $\hat{p}$?
c. Can H_0 be rejected at the 0.05 level? Explain.
d. Someone wants to use these data to test H_0: $p = 0.5$ versus H_1: $p < 0.5$. Find the test statistic z and use the method of this section to find the P-value. Do you reject H_0 at the $\alpha = 0.05$ level?

27. Interpret computer output: The following MINITAB output presents the results of a hypothesis test for a population proportion p.

```
Test of p = 0.6 vs p > 0.6

                        95%
                       Lower
   X     N   Sample p   Bound   Z-Value   P-Value
  539   871  0.618829  0.591760   1.13     0.129
```

a. What are the null and alternate hypotheses?
b. What is the value of the sample proportion $\hat{p}$?
c. Can H_0 be rejected at the 0.05 level? Explain.
d. Someone wants to use these data to test H_0: $p = 0.65$ versus H_1: $p < 0.65$. Find the test statistic z and use the method of this section to find the P-value. Do you reject H_0 at the $\alpha = 0.05$ level?

28. Interpret computer output: The following MINITAB output presents the results of a hypothesis test for a population proportion p.

```
Test of p = 0.7 vs p not equal 0.7

 X    N  Sample p        95% CI        Z-Value  P-Value
27   52  0.519231  (0.383432, 0.655029)  -2.84   0.004
```

a. What are the null and alternate hypotheses?
b. What is the value of the sample proportion $\hat{p}$?
c. Can H_0 be rejected at the 0.05 level? Explain.
d. Someone wants to use these data to test H_0: $p = 0.6$ versus H_1: $p \neq 0.6$. Find the test statistic z and use the method of this section to find the P-value. Do you reject H_0 at the $\alpha = 0.05$ level?

29. Satisfied with college? A simple random sample of 500 students at a certain college were surveyed and asked

whether they were satisfied with college life. Two hundred eighty of them replied that they were satisfied. The Dean of Students claims that more than half of the students at the college are satisfied. To test this claim, a test of the hypotheses H_0: $p = 0.5$ versus H_1: $p > 0.5$ is performed.
a. Show that the P-value is 0.004.
b. The P-value is very small, so H_0 is rejected. Someone claims that because P is very small, the population proportion p must be much greater than 0.5. Is this a correct interpretation of the P-value?
c. Someone else claims that because the P-value is very small, we can be fairly certain that the population proportion p is greater than 0.5, but we cannot be certain that it is a lot greater. Is this a correct interpretation of the P-value?

30. Who will you vote for? A simple random sample of 1500 voters were surveyed and asked whether they were planning to vote for the incumbent mayor for re-election. Seven hundred ninety-eight of them replied that they were planning to vote for the mayor. The mayor claims that more than half of all voters are planning to vote for her. To test this claim, a test of the hypotheses H_0: $p = 0.5$ versus H_1: $p > 0.5$ is performed.
a. Show that the P-value is 0.007.
b. The P-value is very small, so H_0 is rejected. A pollster claims that because the P-value is very small, we can be fairly certain that the population proportion p is greater than 0.5, but we cannot be certain that it is a lot greater. Is this a correct interpretation of the P-value?
c. The mayor's campaign manager claims that because the P-value is very small, the population proportion of voters who plan to vote for the mayor must be much greater than 0.5. Is this a correct interpretation of the P-value?

31. Don't perform a test: A few weeks before election day, a TV station broadcast a debate between the two leading candidates for governor. Viewers were invited to visit the station's website after the debate and indicate which candidate they plan to vote for. A total of 3125 people visited the website, and 1800 of them said that they planned to vote for candidate A. Explain why these data should not be used to test the claim that more than half of the voters plan to vote for candidate A.

32. Don't perform a test: Over the past 100 days, the price of a certain stock went up on 60 days and went down on 40 days. Explain why these data should not be used to test the claim that this stock price goes down on less than half of the days.

Extending the Concepts

33. Exact test: When $np_0 < 10$ or $n(1 - p_0) < 10$, we cannot use the normal approximation, but we can use the binomial distribution to perform what is known as an *exact test*. Let p be the probability that a given coin lands heads. The coin is tossed 10 times and comes up heads 9 times. Test H_0: $p = 0.5$ versus H_1: $p > 0.5$, as follows.
a. Let n be the number of tosses and let X denote the number of heads. Find the values of n and X in this example.
b. The distribution of X is binomial. Assuming H_0 is true, find n and p.

c. Because the alternate hypothesis is $p > 0.5$, large values of X support H_1. Find the probability of observing a value of X as extreme as or more extreme than the value actually observed, assuming H_0 to be true. This is the P-value.

d. Do you reject H_0 at the $\alpha = 0.05$ level?

Answers to Check Your Understanding Exercises for Section 8.4

1. a. $H_0: p = 0.15,$ $H_1: p \neq 0.15$ **b.** $z = 1.98$
  c. $P = 0.0478$ [Tech: 0.0477]
  d. We conclude that the proportion of students who read a newspaper differs from 0.15.

2. a. $H_0: p = 0.6,$ $H_1: p < 0.6$ **b.** 150   **c.** 0.48
  d. -3.00 **e.** Yes   **f.** Yes

3. a. $H_0: p = 0.75,$ $H_1: p > 0.75$ **b.** 1225
  c. 0.7559183673   **d.** 0.4783759373   **e.** No   **f.** No

4. a. $H_0: p = 0.80,$ $H_1: p < 0.80$ **b.** $z = -2.37$
  c. -1.645
  d. We conclude that less than 80% of U.S. adults enjoy competing with others.

SECTION 8.5 | Determining Which Method to Use

Objectives

1. Determine which method to use when performing a hypothesis test

Objective 1 Determine which method to use when performing a hypothesis test

One of the challenges in performing a hypothesis test is to determine which method to use. The first step is to determine which type of parameter we are testing. There are two types of parameters about which we have learned to perform hypothesis tests:

- Population mean μ
- Population proportion p

Once you have determined which type of parameter you are testing, proceed as follows:

- **Population mean:** There are two methods for performing a hypothesis test for a population mean, the z-test (Section 8.2) and the t-test (Section 8.3). To determine which method to use, we must determine whether the population is approximately normal, and whether the sample size is large ($n > 30$). The following diagram can help you make the correct choice.

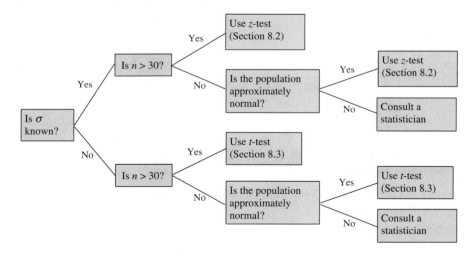

- **Population proportion:** To perform a hypothesis test for a population proportion, use the method described in Section 8.4.

| EXAMPLE 8.21 | **Determining which method to use** |

Starting salaries for a random sample of 51 physicians had a mean of \$103,000. Assume that the population standard deviation is \$10,500. Can you conclude that the mean starting salary for physicians is greater than \$100,000? Determine the type of parameter that is to be tested and perform the hypothesis test. Use the $\alpha = 0.05$ level of significance.

Solution

We are asked to perform a hypothesis test for the mean salary; this is a population mean. We consult the diagram to determine the correct method. We must first determine whether σ is known. We are told that the population standard deviation is \$10,500. Therefore, $\sigma = 10,500$. We follow the "Yes" path. Next we must determine whether $n > 30$. The sample size is 51, so $n > 30$. We follow the "Yes" path, and find that we should use the z-test described in Section 8.2. To perform the test, we compute the value of the test statistic:

$$z = \frac{103,000 - 100,000}{10,500/\sqrt{51}} = 2.04$$

Because the alternate hypothesis is H_1: $\mu > 100,000$, this is a right-tailed test. The P-value is the area under the normal curve to the right of $z = 2.04$. Using Table A.2, we find that the area to the left of $z = 2.04$ is 0.9793. The area to the right is therefore $1 - 0.9793 = 0.0207$. The P-value is 0.0207. Because $P < 0.05$, we conclude that the mean starting salary is greater than \$100,000.

Check Your Understanding

In Exercises 1–4, state which type of parameter is to be tested; then perform the hypothesis test.

1. In a simple random sample of 150 cars undergoing emissions testing, 23 failed the test. Can you conclude that the proportion of cars that fail the test is less than 20%? Use the $\alpha = 0.05$ level of significance.

2. A simple random sample of size 15 has mean $\bar{x} = 27.72$ and standard deviation $s = 8.21$. The population is approximately normally distributed. Can you conclude that the population mean differs from 35? Use the $\alpha = 0.01$ level of significance.

3. In a simple random sample of 300 electronic components, 35 were defective. Can you conclude that more than 10% of components of this type are defective? Use the $\alpha = 0.05$ level of significance.

4. A simple random sample of size 65 has mean $\bar{x} = 38.16$. The population standard deviation is $\sigma = 5.95$. Can you conclude that the mean is less than 40? Use the $\alpha = 0.01$ level of significance.

Answers are on page 393.

| SECTION 8.5 | **Exercises** |

Exercises 1–4 are the Check Your Understanding exercises located within the section.

Practicing the Skills

In Exercises 5–10, state which type of parameter is to be tested; then perform the hypothesis test.

5. A simple random sample of size 13 has mean $\bar{x} = 7.26$ and standard deviation $s = 2.45$. The population is approximately normally distributed. Can you conclude that the population mean differs from 9? Use the $\alpha = 0.01$ level of significance.

6. A simple random sample of size 65 has mean $\bar{x} = 57.3$. The population standard deviation is $\sigma = 12.6$. Can you conclude that the population mean is less than 60? Use the $\alpha = 0.05$ level of significance.

7. In a simple random sample of 95 families, 70 had one or more pets at home. Can you conclude that the proportion of

families with one or more pets differs from 0.6? Use the $\alpha = 0.01$ level of significance.

8. In a simple random sample of 120 law students, 54 were women. Can you conclude that less than half of law students are women? Use the $\alpha = 0.01$ level of significance.

9. A simple random sample of size 23 has mean $\bar{x} = 41.8$. The population standard deviation is $\sigma = 3.72$. Can you conclude that the population mean differs from 40? Use the $\alpha = 0.05$ level of significance.

10. A simple random sample of size 6 has mean $\bar{x} = 5.49$ and standard deviation $s = 2.37$. The population is approximately normally distributed. Can you conclude that the population mean is greater than 4? Use the $\alpha = 0.05$ level of significance.

Working with the Concepts

11. Saving for college: In a survey of 781 U.S. adults with children conducted in 2009 by the Financial Industry Regulatory Authority, 294 said that they had saved money for their children's college education. Can you conclude that more than 33% of U.S. adults with children have saved money for college? Use the $\alpha = 0.05$ level of significance.

12. Big houses: The U.S. Census Bureau reported that the mean area of U.S. homes built in 2009 was 2438 square feet. Assume that a simple random sample of 20 homes built in 2010 had a mean area of 2514 square feet, with a standard deviation of 225 square feet. Can you conclude that the mean area of homes built in 2010 is greater than that of

homes built in 2009? Use the $\alpha = 0.01$ level of significance.

13. Teacher salaries: A random sample of 50 public school teachers in Georgia had a mean annual salary of \$48,300. Assume the population standard deviation is $\sigma = \$8,000$. Can you conclude that the mean salary of public school teachers in Georgia differs from \$50,000? Use the $\alpha = 0.01$ level of significance.

14. Owning a business: The 2008 General Social Survey asked 2021 people whether they owned a business or were self-employed, and 250 said that they did. Can you conclude that less than 15% of people own a business or are self-employed? Use the $\alpha = 0.05$ level of significance.

15. Mercury pollution: Mercury is a toxic metal that is used in many industrial applications. Seven measurements, in milligrams per cubic meter, were taken of the mercury concentration in a lake, with the following results. Assume that the population of measurements is approximately normally distributed.

| 1.02 | 1.23 | 0.91 | 1.29 | 1.01 | 1.35 | 1.43 |

Can you conclude that the mean concentration is greater than 1 milligram per cubic meter? Use the $\alpha = 0.05$ level of significance.

16. Ladies' shoes: A random sample of 100 pairs of ladies' shoes had a mean size of 8.3. Assume the population standard deviation is $\sigma = 1.5$. Can you conclude that the mean size of ladies' shoes differs from 8? Use the $\alpha = 0.01$ level of significance.

Answers to Check Your Understanding Exercises for Section 8.5

1. The parameter is the population proportion. The test statistic is $z = -1.43$. The P-value is 0.0764 [Tech: 0.0765]. Do not reject H_0. There is not enough evidence to conclude that the proportion of cars that fail the test is less than 0.20.

2. The parameter is the population mean. The test statistic is $t = -3.43$. The P-value is $0.002 < P < 0.005$ [Tech: 0.004]. Reject H_0. We conclude that the mean differs from 35.

3. The parameter is the population proportion. The test statistic is $z = 0.96$. The P-value is 0.1685 [Tech: 0.1679]. Do not reject H_0. There is not enough evidence to conclude that more than 10% of components are defective.

4. The parameter is the population mean. The test statistic is $z = -2.49$. The P-value is 0.0064 [Tech: 0.0063]. Reject H_0. We conclude that the population mean is less than 40.

Chapter 8 Summary

Section 8.1: A hypothesis test involves a null hypothesis, H_0, which makes a statement about one or more population parameters, and an alternate hypothesis, which contradicts H_0. We begin by assuming that H_0 is true. If the data provide strong evidence against H_0, we then reject H_0 and believe H_1. A Type I error occurs when a true null hypothesis is rejected. A Type II error occurs when a false H_0 is not rejected.

Section 8.2: We follow one of two methods in performing a hypothesis test. In the critical value method, we choose a significance level α, then find a critical region. We reject H_0 if the test statistic falls inside the critical region. The probability of a Type I error is α, the significance level of the test. In the P-value method, we compute a P-value, which is the probability of observing a value for the test statistic that is as extreme as or more extreme than the value actually observed, under the assumption that H_0 is true. The smaller the P-value, the stronger the evidence against H_0. If we want to make a firm decision about the truth of H_0, we choose a significance level α and reject H_0 if $P \leq \alpha$.

When testing a hypothesis about a population mean with the population standard deviation σ known, the test statistic, z, has a standard normal distribution. If the sample size is not large, the population must be approximately normal. We can check normality with a boxplot or dotplot.

Statistical significance is not the same as practical significance. When a result is statistically significant, we can conclude only that the true value of the parameter is different from the value specified by H_0. We cannot conclude that the difference is large enough to be important.

When presenting the results of a hypothesis test, it is important to state the P-value or the value of the test statistic, so that others can decide for themselves whether to reject H_0. It isn't enough simply to state whether or not H_0 was rejected.

Section 8.3: When testing a hypothesis about a population mean with the population standard deviation σ unknown, the test statistic has a Student's t distribution. The number of degrees of freedom is 1 less than the sample size. The population must be approximately normal, or the sample size must be large ($n > 30$). We can check normality with a boxplot or dotplot.

Section 8.4: When testing a hypothesis about a population proportion, the test statistic is z. The sample proportion must be approximately normal. We check this by requiring that both np_0 and $n(1 - p_0)$ are at least 10.

Section 8.5: We have learned to perform hypothesis tests for a population mean and a population proportion. There are two tests for a population mean, the z-test and the t-test. The test to use depends on whether the population standard deviation σ is known.

Vocabulary and Notation

alternate hypothesis 338	null hypothesis 338	significance level 344
critical region 344	one-tailed hypothesis 339	statistically significant 345
critical value 344	P-value 348	test statistic 343
critical value method 343	P-value method 348	two-tailed hypothesis 339
hypothesis 338	rejecting H_0 340	Type I error 341
hypothesis test 340	right-tailed hypothesis 339	Type II error 341
left-tailed hypothesis 339		

Important Formulas

Test statistic for a mean, standard deviation known:

$$z = \frac{\bar{x} - \mu_0}{\sigma/\sqrt{n}}$$

Test statistic for a mean, standard deviation unknown:

$$t = \frac{\bar{x} - \mu_0}{s/\sqrt{n}}$$

Test statistic for a proportion:

$$z = \frac{\hat{p} - p_0}{\sqrt{\dfrac{p_0(1 - p_0)}{n}}}$$

Chapter Quiz

1. Fill in the blank: A test of the hypotheses H_0: $\mu = 65$ versus H_1: $\mu \neq 65$ was performed. The P-value was 0.035. Fill in the blank: If $\mu = 65$, then the probability of observing a test statistic as extreme as or more extreme than the one actually observed is _____.

2. A hypothesis test results in a P-value of 0.008. Which is the best conclusion?
   i. H_0 is definitely false.
   ii. H_0 is definitely true.
   iii. H_0 is plausible.
   iv. H_0 might be true, but it's very unlikely.
   v. H_0 might be false, but it's very unlikely.

3. True or false: If $P = 0.03$, then
   a. The result is statistically significant at the $\alpha = 0.05$ level.
   b. The result is statistically significant at the $\alpha = 0.01$ level.
   c. The null hypothesis is rejected at the $\alpha = 0.05$ level.
   d. The null hypothesis is rejected at the $\alpha = 0.01$ level.

4. A null hypothesis is rejected at the $\alpha = 0.05$ level. True or false:
   a. The P-value is greater than 0.05.
   b. The P-value is less than or equal to 0.05.
   c. The result is statistically significant at the $\alpha = 0.05$ level.
   d. The result is statistically significant at the $\alpha = 0.10$ level.

5. A sample of size 8 is drawn from a normal population with mean μ, and the population standard deviation is unknown.
   a. Is it appropriate to perform a z-test? Explain.
   b. Is it appropriate to perform a t-test? Explain.

6. A test will be made of H_0: $\mu = 4$ versus H_1: $\mu > 4$, using a sample of size 25. The population standard deviation is unknown. Find the critical value of the test statistic if the significance level is $\alpha = 0.05$.

7. True or false: We never conclude that H_0 is true.

8. In a random sample of 500 people who took their driver's test, 445 passed. Let p be the population proportion who pass. A test will be made of H_0: $p = 0.85$ versus H_1: $p > 0.85$.
   a. Compute the value of the test statistic.
   b. Do you reject H_0 at the $\alpha = 0.05$ level?
   c. State a conclusion.

9. For testing H_0: $\mu = 3$ versus H_1: $\mu < 3$, a P-value of 0.024 is obtained.
   a. If the significance level is $\alpha = 0.05$, would you conclude that $\mu < 3$? Explain.
   b. If the significance level is $\alpha = 0.01$, would you conclude that $\mu < 3$? Explain.

10. True or false: When we reject H_0, we are certain that H_1 is true.

11. The result of a hypothesis test is reported as follows: "We reject H_0 at the $\alpha = 0.05$ level." What additional information should be included?

12. In a test of H_0: $\mu = 5$ versus H_1: $\mu > 5$, the value of the test statistic is $t = 2.96$. There are 17 degrees of freedom. Do you reject H_0 at the $\alpha = 0.05$ level?

13. In a test of H_0: $p = 0.4$ versus H_1: $p \neq 0.4$, the value of the test statistic is $z = -2.13$. Do you reject H_0 at the $\alpha = 0.01$ level?

14. True or false: Sometimes we reject H_0 at the $\alpha = 0.01$ level but not at the $\alpha = 0.05$ level.

15. True or false: Sometimes we reject H_0 at the $\alpha = 0.05$ level but not at the $\alpha = 0.01$ level.

Review Exercises

1. What's the conclusion? A hypothesis test is performed, and $P = 0.02$. Which of the following is the best conclusion?
   i. H_0 is rejected at the 0.05 level.
   ii. H_0 is rejected at the 0.01 level.
   iii. H_1 is rejected at the 0.05 level.
   iv. H_1 is rejected at the 0.01 level.

2. Scoring runs: In 2009, the mean number of runs scored by both teams in a Major League Baseball game was 9.22. Following are the numbers of runs scored in a sample of 24 games in 2010.

2	10	3	9	15	10	7	4	3	7	5	9
5	9	15	15	4	5	13	6	14	11	6	12

   a. Construct a boxplot of the data. Is it appropriate to perform a hypothesis test?
   b. If appropriate, perform a hypothesis test to determine whether the mean number of runs in 2010 is the same as it was in 2009. Use the $\alpha = 0.05$ level.

3. Facebook: A popular blog reports that 60% of college students log in to Facebook on a daily basis. The Dean of Students at a certain university thinks that the proportion may be different at her university. She polls a simple random sample of 200 students, and 134 of them report that they log in to Facebook daily. Can you conclude that the proportion of students who log in to Facebook daily differs from 0.60?
   a. State the null and alternate hypotheses.
   b. Compute the value of the test statistic.
   c. Do you reject H_0? Use the $\alpha = 0.05$ level.
   d. State a conclusion.

4. Playing the market: The Russell 2000 is a group of 2000 small-company stocks. On June 11, 2010, a random sample of 35 of these stocks had a mean price of $21.85, with a standard deviation of $15.82. A stock market analyst predicted that the mean price of all 2000 stocks would be $25.00. Can you conclude that the mean price differs from $25.00?
   a. State the null and alternate hypotheses.
   b. Should we perform a z-test or a t-test? Explain.
   c. Compute the value of the test statistic.
   d. Do you reject H_0? Use the $\alpha = 0.05$ level.
   e. State a conclusion.

5. Treating circulatory disease: A stent is a wire mesh tube that is placed in a blood vessel to keep it open. A total of 1120 patients received a new kind of stent that was coated with a drug designed to prevent a blockage in the blood vessel. Of these, 134 required additional treatment within a year. Can you conclude that less than 15% of patients receiving these stents require additional treatment? Use the $\alpha = 0.05$ level of significance.

6. Contaminated water: The concentration of benzene was measured in units of milligrams per liter for a simple random sample of five specimens of water produced at a gas field. The sample mean was 7.8 with a sample standard deviation of 1.4. Can you conclude that the mean concentration differs from 9 milligrams per liter? Use the $\alpha = 0.01$ level of significance.

7. Household size: For the past several years, the mean number of people in a household has been declining. A social scientist believes that in a certain large city, the mean number of people per household is less than 2.5. To investigate this, she takes a simple random sample of 150 households in the city, and finds that the sample mean number of people is 2.3 with a sample standard deviation of 1.5. Can you conclude that the mean number of people per household is less than 2.5?

a. State the null and alternate hypotheses.
b. Should we perform a z-test or a t-test? Explain.
c. Compute the value of the test statistic.
d. Do you reject H_0? Use the $\alpha = 0.01$ level.
e. State a conclusion.

8. **Job satisfaction:** In 2006, the General Social Survey sampled 1016 employed people and asked them how satisfied they were with their jobs. Of the 1016 people sampled, 568 said that they were completely satisfied or very satisfied with their jobs. Can you conclude that more than 50% of employed people in the United States are completely or very satisfied with their jobs?

a. State the null and alternate hypotheses.
b. Compute the value of the test statistic.
c. Do you reject H_0? Use the $\alpha = 0.01$ level.
d. State a conclusion.

9. **Sugar content:** The sugar content in grams of a syrup used to pack canned fruit is measured for eight cans. The contents are approximately normally distributed. The sample mean is 20.2 and the sample standard deviation is 0.3. Can you conclude that the population mean is greater than 20? Use the $\alpha = 0.01$ level of significance.

10. **Interpret computer output:** The following output from MINITAB presents the results of a hypothesis test.

```
Test of mu = 4.7 vs not = 4.7
The assumed standard deviation = 2.0


  N    Mean    SE Mean        95% CI           Z       P
 35   5.401    0.3381    (4.738, 6.064)    2.074   0.038
```

a. What are the null and alternate hypotheses?
b. What is the value of the test statistic?
c. What is the P-value?
d. Do you reject H_0 at the $\alpha = 0.05$ level?
e. Do you reject H_0 at the $\alpha = 0.01$ level?

11. **Interpret calculator display:** The following TI-84 Plus display presents the results of a hypothesis test.

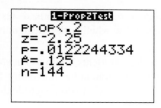

a. Is this a test for a mean, a proportion, or a standard deviation?
b. What are the null and alternate hypotheses?
c. What is the value of the test statistic?
d. What is the P-value?
e. Do you reject H_0 at the $\alpha = 0.05$ level?
f. Do you reject H_0 at the $\alpha = 0.01$ level?

12. **How many TV sets?** A survey organization sampled 60 households in a community and found that the sample mean number of TV sets per household was 3.1. The population standard deviation is $\sigma = 1.5$. Can you conclude that the mean number of TV sets per household is greater than 3?

a. State the null and alternate hypotheses.
b. Should we perform a z-test or a t-test? Explain.
c. Compute the value of the test statistic.
d. Do you reject H_0? Use the $\alpha = 0.01$ level.
e. State a conclusion.

13. **Crackers:** Boxes of crackers are labeled as containing 16 ounces. In a random sample of 100 boxes, 17 of them weighed more than 16.2 ounces. Can you conclude that less than 25% of boxes weigh more than 16.2 ounces? Use the $\alpha = 0.05$ level of significance.

14. **How much rent?** A housing official in a certain city claims that the mean monthly rent for apartments in the city is more than $1000. To verify this claim, a simple random sample of 40 renters in the city was taken, and the sample mean rent paid was $1100 with a sample standard deviation of $300. Can you conclude that the mean monthly rent in the city is greater than $1000?

a. State the null and alternate hypotheses.

b. Should we perform a z-test or a t-test? Explain.

c. Compute the value of the test statistic.

d. Do you reject H_0? Use the $\alpha = 0.05$ level.

e. State a conclusion.

15. **What's the news?** The Pew Research Center reported in 2008 that 36% of 18–24-year-olds watch a cable news channel regularly. The director of media relations at a large university wants to know whether the population proportion of cable news viewers among students at her university is greater than the proportion among 18–24-year-olds in general. She surveys a simple random sample of 200 students at the university and finds that 96 of them watch cable news regularly. Can she conclude that the proportion of students at her university who watch cable news regularly is greater than 0.36?

a. State the null and alternate hypotheses.

b. Compute the value of the test statistic.

c. Do you reject H_0? Use the $\alpha = 0.01$ level.

d. State a conclusion.

Write About It

1. A result is significant at the 0.01 level. Explain why it must also be significant at the 0.05 level.

2. What does the P-value represent?

3. Why is it important to report the P-value or the test statistic when presenting the results of a hypothesis test?

4. Why don't we need to know the population standard deviation when performing a test about a population proportion?

5. In what ways are hypothesis tests for a population mean different from hypothesis tests for a proportion? In what ways are they similar?

Case Study: Is It Getting Warmer In Washington, D.C.?

There is substantial evidence to indicate that temperatures on the surface of the earth have been increasing for the past 100 years or so. We will investigate the possibility of warming trends in one location: Washington, D.C. Table 8.3 presents the record high and low temperatures, along with the year they occurred, for every seventh day at the site of Reagan National Airport in Washington, D.C. The data span the years 1871–2010.

Table 8.3 Dates of Record Temperatures in Washington, D.C.

Date	High	Year	Low	Year	More Recent	Date	High	Year	Low	Year	More Recent	Date	High	Year	Low	Year	More Recent
Jan 1	69	2005	−14	1881	High	May 7	95	1930	38	1970	Low	Sep 3	98	1953	48	1909*	High
8	73	2008	0	1878	High	14	93	1956	41	1928	High	10	98	1983	44	1883	High
15	77	1932	4	1886	High	21	95	1934	41	1907	High	17	96	1991	44	1923	High
22	76	1927	1	1893	High	28	97	1941	42	1961	Low	24	94	1970	39	1963	High
29	76	1975	2	1873	High	Jun 4	99	1925	46	1929*	Low	Oct 1	93	1941*	36	1899	High
Feb 5	70	1991*	−2	1918*	High	11	101	1911	45	1913	Low	8	91	2007	36	1964*	High
12	74	1999	4	1899	High	18	97	1944	51	1965*	Low	15	87	1975	32	1874	High
19	74	1939	4	1903	High	25	100	1997	53	1902	High	22	84	1979*	29	1895	High
26	74	1932	12	1970	Low	Jul 2	101	1898	55	1940	Low	29	82	1918	30	1976*	Low
Mar 5	83	1976	6	1872	High	9	104	1936	55	1891	High	Nov 5	81	2003*	20	1879	High
12	89	1990	11	1900	High	16	104	1988	56	1930*	High	12	77	1912*	24	1926	Low
19	87	1945	12	1876	High	23	101	1991	56	1890	High	19	77	1928	18	1891	High
26	87	1921	23	1955	Low	30	99	1953	56	1914	High	26	74	1979	17	1950	High
Apr 2	89	1963	23	1907	High	Aug 6	106	1918	53	1912	High	Dec 3	70	1950	15	1976	Low
9	90	1959	28	1972*	Low	13	101	1881	55	1930*	Low	10	67	1966*	4	1876	High
16	92	2002	29	1928	High	20	101	1983	50	1896	High	17	64	1984*	10	1876	High
23	95	1960	33	1933*	High	27	100	1987	51	1885	High	24	69	1933	5	1983	Low
30	92	1942*	34	1874	High												

*Indicates that the record occurred more than once; only the most recent year is given.

Source: National Weather Service

1. If there have been no temperature trends over the years, then it will be equally likely for the record high or the record low to be more recent. If there has been a warming trend, it might be more likely for the record high to be more recent. Let p be the probability that the record high occurred more recently than the record low. Use the sample proportion of dates where the high occurred more recently to test H_0: $p = 0.5$ versus H_1: $p > 0.5$. What do you conclude?

2. The following table presents the records for every day in June. The data show that it is common for records to be set on two or more consecutive days in the same year. This is due to hot spells and cold spells in the weather. For example, five consecutive record highs, from June 2 through June 6, occurred in 1925. Explain why using data for every day may violate the assumption, used in Exercise 1, that the data are a simple random sample.

Date	High	Year	Low	Year	Date	High	Year	Low	Year	Date	High	Year	Low	Year
Jun 1	97	1895	45	1938*	Jun 11	101	1911	45	1913	Jun 21	98	1988*	51	1940
2	97	1925*	43	1897	12	95	2002*	50	1907*	22	101	1988	51	1992*
3	99	1925	45	1910	13	96	1954	51	1887	23	98	1988*	51	1918
4	99	1925	46	1929*	14	98	1994	49	1933	24	100	2010	46	1902
5	100	1925	48	1926	15	101	1994	47	1933	25	100	1997	53	1902
6	97	1925	46	1945*	16	99	1994	50	1917	26	101	1952	56	1979
7	98	2008*	47	1894	17	95	1991*	50	1926	27	99	2010	57	1927*
8	98	1999	49	1977*	18	97	1944	51	1965*	28	100	1969	54	1927
9	102	1874	45	1913*	19	99	1994	51	1909	29	101	1934*	54	1888
10	100	1964	46	1913	20	99	1931	54	1926*	30	100	1959	50	1919

*Indicates that the record occurred more than once; only the most recent year is given.

3. We will perform another test to determine whether record highs are more likely to have occurred recently. If a record high is equally likely to occur in any year of observation, the mean year in which a record is observed would occur at the midpoint of the observation period, which is $(1871 + 2010)/2 = 1940.5$. Use the data in Table 8.3 to test the hypothesis that the mean year in which a record high occurred is 1940.5 against the alternative that it is greater. What do you conclude?

4. For some records, marked with a *, the record temperature occurred more than once. In these cases, only the most recent year is listed. Explain how this might cause the mean to be greater than the midpoint of 1940.5, even if records are equally likely to occur in any year.

5. Using the data in Table 8.3, drop the dates in which the record high occurred more than once, and test the hypothesis in Exercise 3 again. Does your conclusion change?

6. Perform a hypothesis test on the record lows, after dropping dates on which the record low occurred more than once, in which the alternate hypothesis is that the mean year is less than 1940.5. What do you conclude?

7. Using the analyses you have performed, write a summary of your findings. Describe how strong you believe the evidence to be that record highs have tended to occur more recently than record lows.

Inferences on Two Samples

Introduction

When a new medical treatment is proposed, a clinical trial is conducted to determine whether the treatment is safe and effective. In a clinical trial, patients are assigned to receive either the new treatment or an existing treatment. If the patients receiving the new treatment tend to have better outcomes, this is evidence that the new treatment represents an improvement over the old one. When assigning patients to treatments, it is important that the two groups be approximately equal with regard to prior health status. If one group is much healthier than the other, this can bias the results of the trial.

An article in the *New England Journal of Medicine* (361:1329–1338) reported the results of a clinical trial to compare the effectiveness of a new type of heart pacemaker in preventing cardiac failure in patients with heart disease. A total of 1820 patients participated, with 1089 receiving the new treatment and 731 receiving the standard treatment. The assignment to treatments was not made by simple random sampling, but instead by an algorithm that was designed to balance the two groups. The following tables present some of the important characteristics of the two groups.

Characteristic	Standard Treatment		New Treatment	
	Mean	**Standard Deviation**	**Mean**	**Standard Deviation**
Age	64	11	65	11
Systolic blood pressure	121	18	124	17
Diastolic blood pressure	71	10	72	10

Characteristic	Standard Treatment	New Treatment
	Percentage with the Characteristic	**Percentage with the Characteristic**
Treatment for hypertension	63.2	63.7
Atrial fibrillation	12.6	11.1
Diabetes	30.6	30.2
Cigarette smoking	12.8	11.4
Coronary bypass surgery	28.5	29.1

There are differences between the two groups in all of these characteristics. This is not surprising, because we would expect to see some differences just by chance. The question is whether the differences are large enough to suggest that they may be due to the assignment procedure, and if so, whether the differences may be large enough to be of concern when evaluating the results of the trial.

In this chapter, we will learn to perform hypothesis tests and construct confidence intervals that will address questions like this. In the case study at the end of the chapter, we will investigate the differences in the table, to determine whether any differences that result from the assignment procedure might be large enough to be of concern.

SECTION 9.1 Inference About the Difference Between Two Means: Independent Samples

Objectives

1. Distinguish between independent and paired samples
2. Perform a hypothesis test for the difference between two means using the *P*-value method
3. Perform a hypothesis test for the difference between two means using the critical value method
4. Construct confidence intervals for the difference between two means

Objective 1 Distinguish between independent and paired samples

How can we tell whether a new drug reduces blood pressure better than an old one? A drug company has developed a new drug that is designed to reduce high blood pressure. The researchers wish to design a study to compare the effectiveness of the new drug to that of the old drug. Here are two ways in which the study can be designed.

Design 1: Two samples of individuals are chosen. One sample is given the old drug and the other sample is given the new drug. After several months, blood pressures of the members of both samples are measured. We compare the blood pressures in the first sample to the blood pressures in the second sample to determine which drug is more effective.

In design 1, we have **independent samples**. This means that the observations in one sample do not influence the observations in the other.

Design 2: A single group of individuals is chosen. They are given the old drug for a month, then their blood pressures are measured. They then switch to the new drug for a month, after which their blood pressures are measured again. This produces two samples of measurements, the first one from the old drug and the second one from the new drug. We compare the blood pressures in the first sample to the blood pressures in the second sample to determine which drug is more effective.

In design 2, we have **paired samples**. Each observation in one sample can be paired with an observation in the second.

SUMMARY

- Two samples are independent if the observations in one sample do not influence the observations in the other.
- Two samples are paired if each observation in one sample can be paired with an observation in the other. Typically the samples consist of pairs of measurements on the same individual, or on pairs of individuals who are related, such as husbands and wives or brothers and sisters.

In this section, we will learn how to perform hypothesis tests and construct confidence intervals from independent samples. In Section 9.3, we will learn how to perform hypothesis tests and construct confidence intervals from paired samples.

Check Your Understanding

1. A sample of students is enrolled in a speed-reading class. Each takes a reading test before and again after the class. The two samples of scores are compared to determine how large an improvement in reading speed occurred. Are these samples independent or paired?

2. A sample of students is enrolled in an online statistics class, and another sample is enrolled in a traditional statistics class. At the end of the semester, the students are given a test. The scores from each sample are compared to determine which class was more effective. Are these samples independent or paired?

Answers are on page 418.

Objective 2 Perform a hypothesis test for the difference between two means using the *P*-value method

Perform a Hypothesis Test for the Difference Between Two Means Using the *P*-Value Method

Do computers help high-school students to learn math? One way to address this question is to give a test to two samples of students — one from the population of students who used computers in their math classes, and another from the population of students who did not. If the difference between the sample mean scores is large enough, we can conclude that there is a real difference between the two populations.

The National Assessment of Educational Progress (NAEP) has been testing students for the past 30 years. Scores on the NAEP mathematics test range from 0 to 500. In a recent year, the sample mean score for students using a computer was 309, with a sample standard deviation of 29. For students not using a computer, the sample mean was 303, with a sample standard deviation of 32. Assume there were 60 students in the computer sample, and 40 students in the sample that didn't use a computer. We can see that the sample mean scores differ by 6 points: $309 - 303 = 6$. Now, we are interested in the difference between the population means, which will not be exactly the same as the difference between the sample means. Is it plausible that the difference between the population means could be 0? How strong is the evidence that the population mean scores are different?

This is an example of a situation in which the data consist of two independent samples. We will describe a method for performing a hypothesis test to determine whether the population means are equal. We will need some notation for the population means, the sample means, the sample standard deviations, and the sample sizes:

We will now describe how to perform the hypothesis test.

The null and alternate hypotheses

The issue is whether the population means μ_1 and μ_2 are equal. The null hypothesis says that the population means are equal:

$$H_0: \mu_1 = \mu_2$$

There are three possibilities for the alternate hypothesis.

$$H_1: \mu_1 < \mu_2 \qquad H_1: \mu_1 > \mu_2 \qquad H_1: \mu_1 \neq \mu_2$$

The test statistic

The test statistic is based on the difference between the two sample means $\bar{x}_1 - \bar{x}_2$. The mean of $\bar{x}_1 - \bar{x}_2$ is $\mu_1 - \mu_2$. The sample means $\bar{x}_1$ and $\bar{x}_2$ have variances σ_1^2/n_1 and σ_2^2/n_2 respectively, where σ_1^2 and σ_2^2 are the population variances. It is a fact that when samples are independent, the variance of the difference $\bar{x}_1 - \bar{x}_2$ is the *sum* of the variances, so

$$\text{Variance of } \bar{x}_1 - \bar{x}_2 = \frac{\sigma_1^2}{n_1} + \frac{\sigma_2^2}{n_2}$$

The standard error of $\bar{x}_1 - \bar{x}_2$ is the square root of the variance. We don't know the values of σ_1^2 and σ_2^2, so we approximate them with the sample variances s_1^2 and s_2^2. The standard error is

$$\text{Standard error of } \bar{x}_1 - \bar{x}_2 = \sqrt{\frac{s_1^2}{n_1} + \frac{s_2^2}{n_2}}$$

The test statistic is

$$t = \frac{(\bar{x}_1 - \bar{x}_2) - (\mu_1 - \mu_2)}{\sqrt{\dfrac{s_1^2}{n_1} + \dfrac{s_2^2}{n_2}}}$$

Under the assumption that H_0 is true, the test statistic has approximately a Student's t distribution. We need to determine the number of degrees of freedom. There are two ways to do this: a simple method that is easier when computing by hand, and a more complicated method that is used by technology. The simple method is:

$$\text{Degrees of freedom} = \text{Smaller of } n_1 - 1 \text{ and } n_2 - 1$$

Performing a hypothesis test requires certain assumptions, which we now state:

Explain It Again

Reason for assumption 3: Assumption 3 is necessary to ensure that the sampling distributions of $\bar{x}_1$ and $\bar{x}_2$ are approximately normal. This justifies the use of the Student's t distribution.

Assumptions for Performing a Hypothesis Test for the Difference Between Two Means with Independent Samples

1. We have simple random samples from two populations.
2. The samples are independent of one another.
3. Each sample size is large ($n > 30$), *or* its population is approximately normal.

We now summarize the steps in testing a hypothesis about the difference between two means with independent samples, using the *P*-value method. Later we will describe the critical value method.

Performing a Hypothesis Test for the Difference Between Two Means Using the *P*-Value Method

Check to be sure the assumptions are satisfied. If they are, then proceed with the following steps.

Step 1: State the null and alternate hypotheses. The null hypothesis specifies that the population means are equal:
$H_0: \mu_1 = \mu_2$. The alternate hypothesis will be $\mu_1 < \mu_2$, $\mu_1 > \mu_2$, or $\mu_1 \neq \mu_2$.

Step 2: If making a decision, choose a significance level α.

Step 3: Compute the test statistic $t = \dfrac{(\bar{x}_1 - \bar{x}_2) - (\mu_1 - \mu_2)}{\sqrt{\dfrac{s_1^2}{n_1} + \dfrac{s_2^2}{n_2}}}$.

Step 4: Compute the *P*-value. The *P*-value is an area under the Student's *t* curve. If using Table A.3, approximate the number of degrees of freedom with the smaller of $n_1 - 1$ and $n_2 - 1$. The *P*-value depends on the alternate hypothesis as follows:

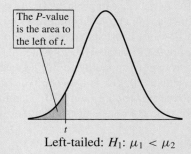
The *P*-value is the area to the left of *t*.

Left-tailed: $H_1: \mu_1 < \mu_2$

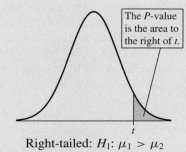
The *P*-value is the area to the right of *t*.

Right-tailed: $H_1: \mu_1 > \mu_2$

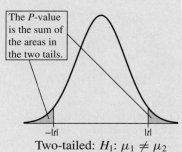
The *P*-value is the sum of the areas in the two tails.

Two-tailed: $H_1: \mu_1 \neq \mu_2$

Step 5: Interpret the *P*-value. If making a decision, reject H_0 if the *P*-value is less than or equal to the significance level α.

Step 6: State a conclusion.

EXAMPLE 9.1

Perform a hypothesis test

The National Assessment of Educational Progress (NAEP) tested a sample of students who had used a computer in their mathematics classes, and another sample of students who had not used a computer. The sample mean score for students using a computer was 309, with a sample standard deviation of 29. For students not using a computer, the sample mean was 303, with a sample standard deviation of 32. Assume there were 60 students in the computer sample, and 40 students in the sample that hadn't used a computer. Can you conclude that the population mean scores differ? Use the $\alpha = 0.05$ level.

Solution

We first check the assumptions. We have two independent random samples. Both sample sizes are larger than 30. The assumptions are satisfied.

Step 1: State the null and alternate hypotheses. We are asked whether we can conclude that the two means differ. Therefore, this is a two-tailed test. The null and alternate hypotheses are

$$H_0: \mu_1 = \mu_2 \qquad H_1: \mu_1 \neq \mu_2$$

Step 2: Choose a significance level. The significance level is $\alpha = 0.05$.

Step 3: Compute the test statistic. The test statistic is

$$t = \frac{(\bar{x}_1 - \bar{x}_2) - (\mu_1 - \mu_2)}{\sqrt{\dfrac{s_1^2}{n_1} + \dfrac{s_2^2}{n_2}}}$$

To help keep track of things, we'll begin by organizing the relevant information in the following table:

	With Computer	**Without Computer**
Sample mean	$\bar{x}_1 = 309$	$\bar{x}_2 = 303$
Sample standard deviation	$s_1 = 29$	$s_2 = 32$
Sample size	$n_1 = 60$	$n_2 = 40$
Population mean	μ_1 (unknown)	μ_2 (unknown)

Under the assumption that H_0 is true, $\mu_1 - \mu_2 = 0$. The value of the test statistic is

$$t = \frac{(309 - 303) - (0)}{\sqrt{\dfrac{29^2}{60} + \dfrac{32^2}{40}}} = 0.953$$

Step 4: Compute the *P*-value. We will approximate the *P*-value by using Table A.3. We begin by finding the number of degrees of freedom. The sample sizes are $n_1 = 60$ and $n_2 = 40$, so the degrees of freedom is $40 - 1 = 39$. The value of the test statistic is $t = 0.953$. This is a two-tailed test, so the *P*-value is the sum of the areas to the right of 0.953 and to the left of -0.953. Figure 9.1 illustrates the *P*-value.

We consult Table A.3 and look at the row corresponding to 39 degrees of freedom. We see that the value of the test statistic, 0.953, is between 0.681 and 1.304. These are the values that correspond to tail areas of 0.25 and 0.10. Therefore, the area in each tail is between 0.10 and 0.25. The *P*-value is the sum of the areas in both tails, so we double these numbers:

$$0.20 < P\text{-value} < 0.50$$

Step 5: Interpret the *P*-value. If H_0 were true, we would expect to observe a value of the test statistic as extreme as or more extreme than our value of 0.953 between 20% and 50% of the time. This is not unusual, so there is no strong evidence against H_0. In particular, $P > 0.05$, so we do not reject H_0 at the $\alpha = 0.05$ level.

Step 6: State a conclusion. There is not enough evidence to conclude that the mean scores differ between those students who use a computer and those who do not. The mean scores may be the same.

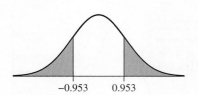

Figure 9.1 The *P*-value for a two-tailed test is the sum of the areas in the two tails. These areas can be approximated by using Table A.3, or found more precisely with technology.

Technology calculates the degrees of freedom differently

If you perform a hypothesis test for the difference between two means with technology, you will usually get a somewhat different answer than you will get using the method we have presented here. The reason is that computers and calculators compute the number of degrees of freedom differently, using a more accurate but rather complicated formula. We present this formula, but you don't need to use it when computing by hand. When computing by hand, it is acceptable just to use the smaller of $n_1 - 1$ and $n_2 - 1$ for the degrees of freedom.

More Accurate Formula for the Degrees of Freedom

Most computer packages compute the degrees of freedom as follows:

$$\text{Degrees of freedom} = \frac{\left[\dfrac{s_1^2}{n_1} + \dfrac{s_2^2}{n_2}\right]^2}{\dfrac{(s_1^2/n_1)^2}{n_1 - 1} + \dfrac{(s_2^2/n_2)^2}{n_2 - 1}}$$

When computing by hand, it is acceptable, and simpler, just to use the smaller of $n_1 - 1$ and $n_2 - 1$ for the degrees of freedom.

Performing a hypothesis test with technology

The following computer output (from MINITAB) presents the results of Example 9.1.

```
Two-sample T for Computer vs No Computer

               N      Mean     StDev     SE Mean
Computer      60      309.0     29.0      3.74388
No computer   40      303.0     32.0      5.05964

Difference = mu (Treatment1) - mu (Treatment2)
Estimate for difference:   6.000
95% CI for difference:    (-6.5333, 18.5333)
T-Test of difference = 0 (vs not =):     T-Value = 0.95
                                         P-Value = 0.343   DF = 77
```

Explain It Again

Results from technology will differ:
Results found with technology will differ from those obtained by hand, because computers and calculators use the more complicated formula for the degrees of freedom.

The output presents the sample sizes (N), the sample means (Mean), and sample standard deviations (StDev). The column labeled "SE Mean" presents the standard errors of $\bar{x}_1$ and $\bar{x}_2$, which are $s_1/\sqrt{n_1}$ and $s_2/\sqrt{n_2}$, respectively. The row labeled "Estimate for difference" presents the difference between the sample means: $\bar{x}_1 - \bar{x}_2$. The next row contains a 95% confidence interval for $\mu_1 - \mu_2$. The row after that specifies that the alternate hypothesis is two-tailed, then presents the value of the test statistic (T-Value), the P-value, and the number of degrees of freedom. The number of degrees of freedom (DF) is 77, which differs from the value of 39 that we used in the solution to Example 9.1. The reason is that MINITAB uses a more complicated formula to compute the number of degrees of freedom, then rounds the value down to the nearest whole number.

The following TI-84 Plus display presents results for Example 9.1.

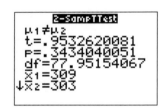

As with the MINITAB output, the results differ somewhat from those we obtained, because the degrees of freedom (labeled "df") have been calculated by the more complicated formula. Note that the degrees of freedom is not a whole number. Unlike MINITAB, the TI-84 Plus does not round the degrees of freedom.

Step-by-step instructions for performing hypothesis tests with technology are presented in the Using Technology section on page 411.

Check Your Understanding

3. A test was made of H_0: $\mu_1 = \mu_2$ versus H_1: $\mu_1 > \mu_2$. Independent random samples were drawn from approximately normal populations. The sample means were $\bar{x}_1 = 6.8$ and $\bar{x}_2 = 4.9$. The sample standard deviations were $s_1 = 1.6$ and $s_2 = 1.3$. The sample sizes were $n_1 = 12$ and $n_2 = 10$.
   a. Find the value of the test statistic t.
   b. Find the number of degrees of freedom for t.
   c. Find the P-value.
   d. Interpret the P-value. Do you reject H_0 at the $\alpha = 0.01$ level?

4. A test was made of H_0: $\mu_1 = \mu_2$ versus H_1: $\mu_1 \neq \mu_2$. Independent random samples were drawn from approximately normal populations. The sample means were

$\bar{x}_1 = 73.9$ and $\bar{x}_2 = 71.8$. The sample standard deviations were $s_1 = 4.2$ and $s_2 = 3.8$. The sample sizes were $n_1 = 23$ and $n_2 = 17$.

a. Find the value of the test statistic t.

b. Find the number of degrees of freedom for t.

c. Find the P-value.

d. Interpret the P-value. Do you reject H_0 at the $\alpha = 0.05$ level?

Answers are on page 418.

Objective 3 Perform a hypothesis test for the difference between two means using the critical value method

Performing Hypothesis Tests Using the Critical Value Method

To use the critical value method, compute the test statistic as before. The procedure for finding the critical value is the same as for hypothesis tests for a mean with σ unknown. The critical value can be found in Table A.3 or with technology. The procedure depends on whether the alternate hypothesis is left-tailed, right-tailed, or two-tailed. The assumptions for the critical value method are the same as for the P-value method.

Following are the steps for the critical value method.

Performing a Hypothesis Test for the Difference Between Two Means Using the Critical Value Method

Check to be sure the assumptions are satisfied. If they are, then proceed with the following steps.

Step 1: State the null and alternate hypotheses. The null hypothesis will have the form $H_0: \mu_1 = \mu_2$. The alternate hypothesis will be $\mu_1 < \mu_2$, $\mu_1 > \mu_2$, or $\mu_1 \neq \mu_2$.

Step 2: Choose a significance level α, and find the critical value or values.

Step 3: Compute the test statistic

$$t = \frac{(\bar{x}_1 - \bar{x}_2) - (\mu_1 - \mu_2)}{\sqrt{\dfrac{s_1^2}{n_1} + \dfrac{s_2^2}{n_2}}}.$$

Step 4: Determine whether to reject H_0, as follows:

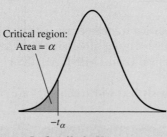

Left-tailed: $H_1: \mu_1 < \mu_2$
Reject H_0 if $t \leq -t_\alpha$.

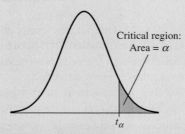

Right-tailed: $H_1: \mu_1 > \mu_2$
Reject H_0 if $t \geq t_\alpha$.

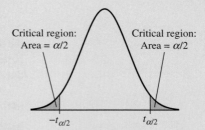

Two-tailed: $H_1: \mu_1 \neq \mu_2$
Reject H_0 if $t \geq t_{\alpha/2}$ or $t \leq -t_{\alpha/2}$.

Step 5: State a conclusion.

EXAMPLE 9.2   Test a hypothesis using the critical value method

Treatment of wastewater is important to reduce the concentration of undesirable pollutants. One such substance is benzene, which is used as an industrial solvent. Two methods of water treatment are being compared. Treatment 1 is applied to five specimens of wastewater, and treatment 2 is applied to seven specimens. The benzene concentrations, in units of milligrams per liter, for each specimen are as follows:

Treatment 1:   7.8   7.6   5.6   6.8   6.4
Treatment 2:   4.1   6.5   3.7   7.7   7.3   4.7   5.9

How strong is the evidence that the mean concentration is less for treatment 2 than for treatment 1? We will test at the $\alpha = 0.05$ significance level.

Solution

We first check the assumptions. Because the samples are small, we must check for strong skewness and outliers. We construct dotplots for each sample.

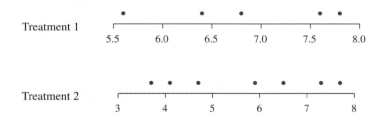

There are no outliers, and no evidence of strong skewness, in either sample. Therefore, we may proceed.

Step 1: State the null and alternate hypotheses. The issue is whether the mean for treatment 2 is less than the mean for treatment 1. Let μ_1 denote the mean for treatment 1 and μ_2 denote the mean for treatment 2. The hypotheses are

$$H_0: \mu_1 = \mu_2 \qquad H_1: \mu_1 > \mu_2$$

Step 2: Choose a significance level and find the critical value. The significance level is $\alpha = 0.05$. We will find the critical value in Table A.3. The sample sizes are $n_1 = 5$ and $n_2 = 7$. For the number of degrees of freedom, we use the smaller of $5 - 1 = 4$ and $7 - 1 = 6$, which is 4. Because the alternate hypothesis, $\mu_1 - \mu_2 > 0$, is right-tailed, the critical value is the value with area 0.05 to its right. We consult Table A.3 with 4 degrees of freedom and find that $t_\alpha = 2.132$.

Step 3: Compute the test statistic. To compute the test statistic, we first compute the sample means and standard deviations. These are

$$\bar{x}_1 = 6.84 \qquad \bar{x}_2 = 5.70 \qquad s_1 = 0.8989 \qquad s_2 = 1.5706$$

The sample sizes are $n_1 = 5$ and $n_2 = 7$. The test statistic is

$$t = \frac{(\bar{x}_1 - \bar{x}_2) - (\mu_1 - \mu_2)}{\sqrt{\dfrac{s_1^2}{n_1} + \dfrac{s_2^2}{n_2}}}$$

Under the assumption that H_0 is true, $\mu_1 - \mu_2 = 0$. The value of the test statistic is

$$t = \frac{(6.84 - 5.70) - 0}{\sqrt{\dfrac{0.8989^2}{5} + \dfrac{1.5706^2}{7}}} = 1.590$$

Step 4: Determine whether to reject H_0. This is a right-tailed test, so we reject H_0 if $t \geq t_\alpha$. Because $t = 1.590$ and $t_\alpha = 2.132$, we do not reject H_0.

Step 5: State a conclusion. There is not enough evidence to conclude that the mean benzene concentration with treatment 1 is greater than that with treatment 2. The concentrations may be the same.

Objective 4 Construct confidence intervals for the difference between two means

Construct Confidence Intervals for the Difference Between Two Means

The most commonly used methods for constructing a confidence interval for the difference between two means is called Welch's method. The assumptions for Welch's method are the same as those for performing a hypothesis test. When these assumptions are satisfied, we can construct a confidence interval by using the following steps.

> ### Procedure for Constructing a Confidence Interval for $\mu_1 - \mu_2$ with Independent Samples (Welch's method)
>
> Check to be sure that the assumptions are satisfied. If they are, then proceed with the following steps.
>
> **Step 1:** Compute the sample means $\bar{x}_1$ and $\bar{x}_2$ if they are not given; then compute the point estimate $\bar{x}_1 - \bar{x}_2$.
>
> **Step 2:** Find the number of degrees of freedom, which is the smaller of $n_1 - 1$ and $n_2 - 1$, and the critical value $t_{\alpha/2}$.
>
> **Step 3:** Compute the sample standard deviations s_1 and s_2 if they are not given, and compute the standard error $\sqrt{\dfrac{s_1^2}{n_1} + \dfrac{s_2^2}{n_2}}$. Multiply the standard error by the critical value to obtain the margin of error: $t_{\alpha/2}\sqrt{\dfrac{s_1^2}{n_1} + \dfrac{s_2^2}{n_2}}$
>
> **Step 4:** Use the point estimate and the margin of error to construct the confidence interval:
>
> Point estimate ± Margin of error
>
> $$\bar{x}_1 - \bar{x}_2 \pm t_{\alpha/2}\sqrt{\frac{s_1^2}{n_1} + \frac{s_2^2}{n_2}}$$
>
> $$\bar{x}_1 - \bar{x}_2 - t_{\alpha/2}\sqrt{\frac{s_1^2}{n_1} + \frac{s_2^2}{n_2}} < \mu_1 - \mu_2 < \bar{x}_1 - \bar{x}_2 + t_{\alpha/2}\sqrt{\frac{s_1^2}{n_1} + \frac{s_2^2}{n_2}}$$
>
> **Step 5:** Interpret the result.

EXAMPLE 9.3   Constructing a confidence interval

A drug company has developed a new drug that is designed to reduce high blood pressure. To test the drug, a sample of 15 patients is recruited to take the drug. Their systolic blood pressures are reduced by an average of 28.3 millimeters, with a standard deviation of 12.0 millimeters. In addition, another sample of 20 patients takes a standard drug. The blood pressures in this group are reduced by an average of 17.1 millimeters with a standard deviation of 9.0 millimeters. Assume that blood pressure reductions are approximately normally distributed. Find a 95% confidence interval for the difference between the population mean reduction for the new drug and that of the standard drug.

Solution

To help us keep track of the relevant information, we present it in the following table:

	New Drug	**Standard Drug**
Sample mean	$\bar{x}_1 = 28.3$	$\bar{x}_2 = 17.1$
Sample standard deviation	$s_1 = 12$	$s_2 = 9$
Sample size	$n_1 = 15$	$n_2 = 20$
Population mean	μ_1 (unknown)	μ_2 (unknown)

We check the assumptions. We have two independent random samples, and the populations are approximately normally distributed. The assumptions are satisfied.

Step 1: Compute the point estimate.

$$\bar{x}_1 - \bar{x}_2 = 28.3 - 17.1 = 11.2$$

Step 2: Find the critical value. In this example, $n_1 = 15$ and $n_2 = 20$, so the degrees of freedom is the smaller of $n_1 - 1 = 14$ and $n_2 - 1 = 19$, which is 14. We look up the critical value $t_{\alpha/2}$ in Table A.3. The value corresponding to 14 degrees of freedom with a confidence level of 95% is $t_{\alpha/2} = 2.145$.

Step 3: Compute the standard error and the margin of error. The standard deviations are $s_1 = 12.0$ and $s_2 = 9.0$. The sample sizes are $n_1 = 15$ and $n_2 = 20$. The standard error is

$$\sqrt{\frac{s_1^2}{n_1} + \frac{s_2^2}{n_2}} = \sqrt{\frac{12.0^2}{15} + \frac{9.0^2}{20}} = 3.6946$$

The margin of error is obtained by multiplying the standard error by the critical value.

$$\text{Margin of error} = t_{\alpha/2}\sqrt{\frac{s_1^2}{n_1} + \frac{s_2^2}{n_2}}$$

In this example, the margin of error is

$$t_{\alpha/2}\sqrt{\frac{s_1^2}{n_1} + \frac{s_2^2}{n_2}} = 2.145\sqrt{\frac{12.0^2}{15} + \frac{9.0^2}{20}} = 7.925$$

Step 4: Construct the confidence interval. The 95% confidence interval is

$$11.2 - 7.925 < \mu_1 - \mu_2 < 11.2 + 7.925$$
$$3.3 < \mu_1 - \mu_2 < 19.1$$

Note that we have rounded the final result to one decimal place, because each of the sample means (28.3 and 17.1) was given to one decimal place.

Step 5: Interpret the result. We are 95% confident that the new drug provides a greater reduction in systolic blood pressure, and that the improvement due to the new drug is between 3.3 and 19.1 millimeters.

Check Your Understanding

5. **Big fish:** A sample of 87 one-year-old spotted flounder had a mean length of 126.31 millimeters with a sample standard deviation of 18.10 millimeters, and a sample of 132 two-year-old spotted flounder had a mean length of 162.41 millimeters with a sample standard deviation of 28.49 millimeters. Construct a 95% confidence interval for the mean length difference between two-year-old flounder and one-year-old flounder.
   Source: *Turkish Journal of Veterinary and Animal Science* 29:1013–1018

6. **Traffic speed:** The mean speed for a sample of 39 cars at a certain intersection was 26.50 kilometers per hour with a standard deviation of 2.37 kilometers per hour, and the mean speed for a sample of 142 motorcycles was 37.14 kilometers per hour with a standard deviation of 3.66 kilometers per hour. Construct a 99% confidence interval for the difference between the mean speeds of motorcycles and cars at this intersection.
   Source: *Journal of Transportation Engineering* 121:317–323

Answers are on page 418.

Constructing confidence intervals with technology

The following TI-84 Plus display presents results for Example 9.3.

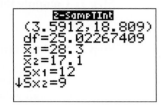

The results differ from those we obtained, because the degrees of freedom (labeled "df") has been calculated by the more accurate formula. Note that the degrees of freedom is not a whole number.

The pooled standard deviation

When the two population variances, σ_1 and σ_2, are known to be equal, there is an alternate method for performing a hypothesis test or computing a confidence interval. This alternate method was widely used in the past, and is still an option in many forms of technology. We recommend against using it, for reasons that we will discuss.

A Method for Testing a Hypothesis About $\mu_1 - \mu_2$ When $\sigma_1 = \sigma_2$ (Not Recommended)

Step 1: Compute the **pooled standard deviation**, s_p, as follows:

$$s_p = \sqrt{\frac{(n_1 - 1)s_1^2 + (n_2 - 1)s_2^2}{n_1 + n_2 - 2}}$$

Step 2: Compute the test statistic:

$$t = \frac{(\bar{x}_1 - \bar{x}_2) - (\mu_1 - \mu_2)}{s_p \sqrt{\dfrac{1}{n_1} + \dfrac{1}{n_2}}}$$

Step 3: Compute the degrees of freedom:

$$\text{Degrees of freedom} = n_1 + n_2 - 2$$

Step 4: Compute the P-value using a Student's t distribution with $n_1 + n_2 - 2$ degrees of freedom.

A Method for Constructing a Confidence Interval When $\sigma_1 = \sigma_2$ (Not Recommended)

Step 1: Compute the **pooled standard deviation**, s_p, as follows:

$$s_p = \sqrt{\frac{(n_1 - 1)s_1^2 + (n_2 - 1)s_2^2}{n_1 + n_2 - 2}}$$

Step 2: Compute the degrees of freedom:

$$\text{Degrees of freedom} = n_1 + n_2 - 2$$

A level $100(1 - \alpha)\%$ confidence interval is

$$\bar{x}_1 - \bar{x}_2 - t_{\alpha/2}s_p\sqrt{\frac{1}{n_1} + \frac{1}{n_2}} < \mu_1 - \mu_2 < \bar{x}_1 - \bar{x}_2 + t_{\alpha/2}s_p\sqrt{\frac{1}{n_1} + \frac{1}{n_2}}$$

The major problem with this method is that the assumption that the population variances are equal is very strict. The method can be quite unreliable if it is used when the population variances are not equal. Now in practice, it is rarely possible to be sure that the variances are equal. Therefore, the best practice is not to use the method that assumes the population variances are equal unless you are very sure that they are.

USING TECHNOLOGY

We use Examples 9.2 and 9.3 to illustrate the technology steps.

TI-84 PLUS

Testing a hypothesis about the difference between means

Step 1. Press **STAT** and highlight the **TESTS** menu.
Step 2. Select **2–SampTTest** and press **ENTER** (Figure A). The **2-SampTTest** menu appears.
Step 3. Choose one of the following:
- If the summary statistics are given, select **Stats** as the **Inpt** option and enter $\bar{x}_1$, s_1, n_1, $\bar{x}_2$, s_2, n_2.
- If the raw data are given, select **Data** as the **Inpt** option and enter the location of the data as the **List1** and **List2** options. For Example 9.2, the sample has been entered in lists **L1** and **L2**.

Step 4. Select the form of the alternate hypothesis. For Example 9.2, the alternate hypothesis has the form $>\mu 2$.
Step 5. Select **No** for the **Pooled** option (Figure B).
Step 6. Highlight **Calculate** and press **ENTER** (Figure C).

Figure A

Figure B

Figure C

TI-84 PLUS

Constructing a confidence interval for the difference between two means

Step 1. Press **STAT** and highlight the **TESTS** menu.
Step 2. Select **2–SampTInt** and press **ENTER** (Figure D). The **2–SampTInt** menu appears.
Step 3. Choose one of the following:
- If the summary statistics are given, select **Stats** as the **Inpt** option and enter $\bar{x}_1$, s_1, n_1, $\bar{x}_2$, s_2, and n_2. For Example 9.3, we use $\bar{x}_1 = 28.3$, $s_1 = 12$, $n_1 = 15$, $\bar{x}_2 = 17.1$, $s_2 = 9$, $n_2 = 20$ (Figure E).
- If the raw data are given, select **Data** as the **Inpt** option and enter the location of the data as the **List1** and **List2** options.

Step 4. In the **C-Level** field, enter the confidence level. For Example 9.3, we use 0.95.
Step 5. Select **No** for the **Pooled** option (Figure F).
Step 6. Highlight **Calculate** and press **ENTER** (Figure G).

Figure D

Figure E

Figure F

Figure G

MINITAB

Testing a hypothesis about the difference between two means

Step 1. Click on **Stat**, then **Basic Statistics**, then **2-Sample t**.

Step 2. Choose one of the following:
- If the summary statistics are given, click **Summarized Data** and enter the **Sample Size**, the **Mean**, and the **Standard Deviation** for each sample.
- If the raw data are given, click **Samples in different columns** and select the columns that contain the data. For Example 9.2, the two samples have been entered in columns **C1** and **C2**.

Step 3. Click **Options**, and enter the difference between the means in the **Test difference** field and select the form of the alternate hypothesis. Given significance level α, enter $100(1 - \alpha)$ as the **Confidence Level**. For Example 9.2, we use **95** as the **Confidence Level**, **0** as the **Test difference**, and **greater than** as the **Alternative**. Click **OK**.

Step 4. Click **OK** (Figure H).

```
Two-sample T for C1 vs C2

     N    Mean   StDev   SE Mean
C1   5   6.840   0.899      0.40
C2   7   5.70    1.57       0.59


Difference = mu (C1) - mu (C2)
Estimate for difference:  1.14000
95% lower bound for difference:  -0.17420
T-Test of difference = 0 (vs >): T-Value = 1.59   P-Value = 0.073   DF = 9
```

Figure H

MINITAB

Constructing a confidence interval for the difference between two means

Step 1. Click on **Stat**, then **Basic Statistics**, then **2-Sample t**.

Step 2. Choose one of the following:
- If the summary statistics are given, click **Summarized Data** and enter the **Sample Size**, the **Mean**, and the **Standard Deviation** for each sample. For Example 9.3, we use $\bar{x}_1 = 28.3$, $s_1 = 12$, $n_1 = 15$, $\bar{x}_2 = 17.1$, $s_2 = 9$, $n_2 = 20$.
- If the raw data are given, click **Samples in different columns** and select the columns that contain the data.

Step 3. Click **Options**, and enter the confidence level in the **Confidence Level** field (95) and choose **not equal** in the **Alternative field**. Click **OK**.

Step 4. Click **OK** (Figure I).

```
Difference = mu (1) - mu (2)
Estimate for difference:  11.2000
95% CI for difference:  (3.5908, 18.8092)
T-Test of difference = 0 (vs not =): T-Value = 3.03   P-Value = 0.006   DF = 25
```

Figure I

EXCEL

Testing a hypothesis about the difference between two means

This procedure requires the **MegaStat** EXCEL add-in to be loaded. The **MegaStat** add-in may be downloaded from www.mhhe.com/megastat.

Step 1. Load the **MegaStat** EXCEL add-in.

Step 2. Click on the **MegaStat** menu and select **Hypothesis Tests**, then **Compare Two Independent Groups...**

Step 3. Choose one of the following:
  - If the summary statistics are given, choose **summary input** and enter the range of the cells that contains, in the following order, the **variable name**, $\bar{x}$, s, and n.
  - If the raw data are given, choose **data input** and select the range of cells that contains the data in the **Input Range** field. For Example 9.2, the samples have been entered in columns **A** and **B** (Figure J).

Step 4. Enter the **Hypothesized difference (0)** and select the form of the alternate hypothesis **(greater than)**.

Step 5. Choose the **t-test (unequal variance)** option (Figure K).

Step 6. Click **OK** (Figure L)

	A	B
1	**Treatment 1**	**Treatment 2**
2	7.8	4.1
3	7.6	6.5
4	5.6	3.7
5	6.8	7.7
6	6.4	7.3
7		4.7
8		5.9

Figure J

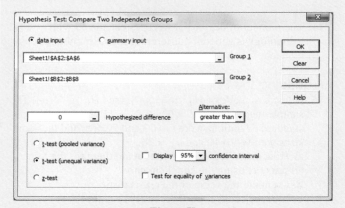

Figure K

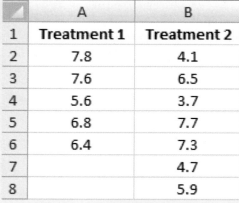

Hypothesis Test: Independent Groups (t-test, unequal variance)

Treatment 1	Treatment 2	
6.840	5.700	mean
0.899	1.571	std. dev.
5	7	n

9 df
1.1400 difference (Treatment 1 - Treatment 2)
0.7169 standard error of difference
0 hypothesized difference

1.59 t
.0731 p-value (one-tailed, upper)

Figure L

EXCEL

Constructing a confidence interval for the difference between two means

This procedure requires the **MegaStat** EXCEL add-in to be loaded. The **MegaStat** add-in may be downloaded from www.mhhe.com/megastat.

Step 1. Click on the **MegaStat** menu, select **Hypothesis Tests**, then **Compare Two Independent Groups...**

Step 2. Choose one of the following:
  - If the summary statistics are given, click **summary input** and select the ranges of cells that contain the data label, the mean, the standard deviation, and the sample size.
  - If the raw data are given, click **data input** and select the ranges of cells for each sample.

Step 3. Enter **0** in the **Hypothesized difference** field and select **not equal** in the **Alternative field**.

Step 4. Choose the **t-test (unequal variance)** option and select the **Display confidence interval** option with the desired confidence level (Figure M).

Step 5. Click **OK** (Figure N).

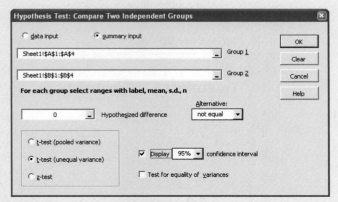

Figure M

Hypothesis Test: Independent Groups (t-test, unequal variance)

	New Drug	Standard Drug	
	28.3	17.1	mean
	12	9	std. dev.
	15	20	n

25 df

3.5908	confidence interval 95.% lower
18.8092	confidence interval 95.% upper
7.6092	margin of error

Figure N

SECTION 9.1   Exercises

Exercises 1–6 are the Check Your Understanding exercises located within the section.

Understanding the Concepts

In Exercises 7–10, fill in each blank with the appropriate word or phrase.

7. To use the methods of this section to test a hypothesis about the difference between two means when the samples are small, the samples must show no evidence of strong _____ and must contain no _____.

8. If each observation in one sample can be paired with an observation in another sample, the samples are said to be _____.

9. If observations in one sample do not influence the observations in another sample, the samples are said to be _____.

10. When determining the number of degrees of freedom by hand with sample sizes n_1 and n_2, we choose the smaller of _____ and _____.

In Exercises 11–14, determine whether the statement is true or false. If the statement is false, rewrite it as a true statement.

11. To use the methods of this section to test a hypothesis about the difference between two means, the population standard deviations must be known.

12. In general, it is not recommended to use a pooled standard deviation when testing a hypothesis for the difference between means.

13. The point estimate for $\mu_1 - \mu_2$ is $\bar{x}_1 + \bar{x}_2$.

14. The number of degrees of freedom calculated with technology is generally different from the number calculated by hand.

Practicing the Skills

15. A test was made of $H_0: \mu_1 = \mu_2$ versus $H_1: \mu_1 < \mu_2$. The sample means were $\bar{x}_1 = 6$ and $\bar{x}_2 = 11$, the sample standard deviations were $s_1 = 3$ and $s_2 = 5$, and the sample sizes were $n_1 = 10$ and $n_2 = 20$.
   a. How many degrees of freedom are there for the test statistic, using the simple method?
   b. Compute the value of the test statistic.
   c. Is H_0 rejected at the 0.05 level? Explain.

16. A test was made of $H_0: \mu_1 = \mu_2$ versus $H_1: \mu_1 \neq \mu_2$. The sample means were $\bar{x}_1 = 10$ and $\bar{x}_2 = 8$, the sample standard deviations were $s_1 = 4$ and $s_2 = 7$, and the sample sizes were $n_1 = 15$ and $n_2 = 27$.
   a. How many degrees of freedom are there for the test statistic, using the simple method?
   b. Compute the value of the test statistic.
   c. Is H_0 rejected at the 0.05 level? Explain.

In Exercises 17–20, construct the confidence interval for the difference $\mu_1 - \mu_2$ for the given level and values of $\bar{x}_1, \bar{x}_2, s_1, s_2, n_1,$ and n_2.

17. Level 90%: $\bar{x}_1 = 104.6, \bar{x}_2 = 92.9, s_1 = 4.8, s_2 = 6.9, n_1 = 26, n_2 = 19$

18. Level 95%: $\bar{x}_1 = 478.81, \bar{x}_2 = 322.49, s_1 = 42.84, s_2 = 25.17, n_1 = 14, n_2 = 16$

19. Level 99%: $\bar{x}_1 = 603.55$, $\bar{x}_2 = 516.63$, $s_1 = 54.7$, $s_2 = 45.2$, $n_1 = 15$, $n_2 = 24$

20. Level 98%: $\bar{x}_1 = 77.3$, $\bar{x}_2 = 72.6$, $s_1 = 9.1$, $s_2 = 8.8$, $n_1 = 12$, $n_2 = 16$

Working with the Concepts

21. More time on the Internet: The General Social Survey polled a sample of 209 people aged 18–30 in the year 2000, asking them how many hours per week they spent on the Internet. The sample mean was 6.75 with a standard deviation of 7.71. A second sample of 541 people aged 18–30 was taken in the year 2006. For this sample, the mean was 7.34 with a standard deviation of 10.93. Assume these are simple random samples from populations of people aged 18–30. Can you conclude that the mean number of hours per week spent on the Internet increased between 2000 and 2006? Use the $\alpha = 0.05$ level.

  a. State the appropriate null and alternate hypotheses.

  b. Compute the test statistic.

  c. How many degrees of freedom are there, using the simple method?

  d. Do you reject H_0? State a conclusion.

22. Low-fat or low-carb? Are low-fat diets or low-carb diets more effective for weight loss? A sample of 77 subjects went on a low-carbohydrate diet for six months. At the end of that time, the sample mean weight loss was 4.7 kilograms with a sample standard deviation of 7.16 kilograms. A second sample of 79 subjects went on a low-fat diet. Their sample mean weight loss was 2.6 kilograms with a standard deviation of 5.90 kilograms. Can you conclude that the mean weight loss differs between the two diets? Use the $\alpha = 0.01$ level.

  a. State the appropriate null and alternate hypotheses.

  b. Compute the test statistic.

  c. How many degrees of freedom are there, using the simple method?

  d. Do you reject H_0? State a conclusion.

  Source: *Journal of the American Medical Association* 297:969–977

23. Are you smarter than your older brother? In a study of birth order and intelligence, IQ tests were given to 18- and 19-year-old men to estimate the size of the difference, if any, between the mean IQs of firstborn sons and secondborn sons. The following data for 10 firstborn sons and 10 secondborn sons are consistent with the means and standard deviations reported in the article. It is reasonable to assume that the samples come from populations that are approximately normal.

Firstborn				
104	82	102	96	129
89	114	107	89	103

Secondborn				
103	103	91	113	102
103	92	90	114	113

Can you conclude that there is a difference in mean IQ between firstborn and secondborn sons? Use the $\alpha = 0.01$ level.

Based on data in *Science* 316:1717

24. Recovering from surgery: A new postsurgical treatment was compared with a standard treatment. Seven subjects received the new treatment, while seven others (the controls) received the standard treatment. The recovery times, in days, are given below.

Treatment:	12	13	15	19	20	21	24
Control:	18	23	24	30	32	35	39

Can you conclude that the mean recovery time for those receiving the new treatment is less than the mean for those receiving the standard treatment? Use the $\alpha = 0.05$ level.

25. Mummy's curse: King Tut was an ancient Egyptian ruler whose tomb was discovered and opened in 1923. Legend has it that the archaeologists who opened the tomb were subject to a "mummy's curse," which would shorten their life spans. A team of scientists conducted an investigation of the mummy's curse. They reported that the 25 people exposed to the curse had a mean life span of 70.0 years with a standard deviation of 12.4 years, while a sample of 11 Westerners in Egypt at the time who were not exposed to the curse had a mean life span of 75.0 years with a standard deviation of 13.6 years. Assume that the populations are approximately normal. Can you conclude that the mean life span of those exposed to the mummy's curse is less than the mean of those not exposed? Use the $\alpha = 0.05$ level.

Source: *British Medical Journal* 325:1482

26. Health inspections: The New York City Department of Health and Mental Hygiene conducts regular inspections of restaurants. Each restaurant receives an inspection score, with lower scores indicating a more satisfactory inspection. Following are scores for the most recent inspection, as of October 2010, for random samples of 25 restaurants in the boroughs of Manhattan and Queens. Boxplots indicate that the samples come from populations that are approximately normal.

Manhattan									
2	22	23	0	40	12	37	43	27	
15	24	8	38	4	17	21	11	18	
13	30	27	19	38	21	4			

Queens									
27	18	14	20	35	8	42	29	0	
12	25	0	19	6	13	22	5	11	
0	10	19	39	2	8	19			

Source: New York City Dept. of Health and Mental Hygiene

Can you conclude that the mean scores differ between the two boroughs? Use the $\alpha = 0.05$ level of significance.

27. Does this diet help? A group of 78 people enrolled in a weight-loss program that involved adhering to a special diet and to a daily exercise program. After six months, their mean weight loss was 25 pounds, with a sample standard deviation of 9 pounds. A second group of 43 people went on the diet but didn't exercise. After six months, their mean weight loss was 14 pounds, with a sample standard deviation of 7 pounds. Construct a 95% confidence interval for the mean difference in weight losses.

28. Contaminated water: The concentration of benzene was measured in units of milligrams per liter for a simple random sample of five specimens of untreated wastewater produced at a gas field. The sample mean was 7.8 with a sample standard deviation of 1.4. Seven specimens of treated wastewater had an average benzene concentration of 3.2 with a standard deviation of 1.7. It is reasonable to assume that both samples come from populations that are approximately normal. Construct a 99% confidence interval for the reduction in benzene concentration after treatment.

29. Fertilizer: In an agricultural experiment, the effects of two fertilizers on the production of oranges were measured. Sixteen randomly selected plots of land were treated with fertilizer A, and 12 randomly selected plots were treated with fertilizer B. The number of pounds of harvested fruit was measured from each plot. Following are the results.

Fertilizer A							
445	523	464	483	441	491	403	466
448	457	437	516	417	420	400	506

Fertilizer B					
362	414	408	398	382	368
393	437	387	373	424	384

a. Explain why it is necessary to check whether the populations are approximately normal before constructing a confidence interval.

b. Following are boxplots of these data. Is it reasonable to assume that the populations are approximately normal?

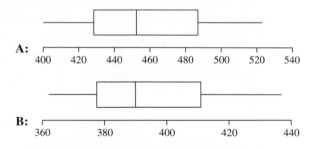

c. If appropriate, construct a 98% confidence interval for the difference between the mean yields for the two types of fertilizer. If not appropriate, explain why not.

30. Computer crashes: A computer system administrator notices that computers running a particular operating system seem to crash more often as the installation of the operating system ages. She measures the time (in minutes) before crash for seven computers one month after installation, and for nine computers seven months after installation. The results are as follows:

One month after installation						
209	230	217	230	221	243	247

Seven months after installation								
85	59	129	201	176	240	149	154	105

a. Explain why it is necessary to check whether the populations are approximately normal before constructing a confidence interval.

b. Following are dotplots of these data. Is it reasonable to assume that the populations are approximately normal?

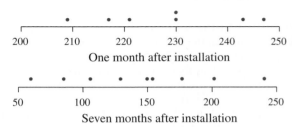

c. If appropriate, construct a 95% confidence interval for the mean difference in time to crash between the first month after installation and the seventh. If not appropriate, explain why not.

31. Boys and girls: The National Health Statistics Reports published in 2008 reported that a sample of 360 one-year-old boys had a mean weight of 25.5 pounds with a standard deviation of 5.3 pounds. In addition, a sample of 328 one-year-old girls had a mean weight of 24.1 pounds with a standard deviation of 4.3 pounds.

a. Construct a 95% confidence interval for the difference between the mean weights.

b. A magazine article states that the mean weight of one-year-old boys is the same as that of one-year-old girls. Does the confidence interval contradict this statement?

32. Body mass index: In a survey of adults with diabetes, the average body mass index (BMI) in a sample of 1924 women was 31.1 with a standard deviation of 0.2. The BMI in a sample of 1559 men was 30.4, with a standard deviation of 0.6.

a. Construct a 99% confidence interval for the difference in the mean BMI between women and men with diabetes.

b. Does the confidence interval contradict the claim that the mean BMI is the same for both men and women with diabetes?

Source: *Journal of Women's Health* 16:1421–1428

33. Interpret calculator display: The following TI-84 Plus calculator display presents the results of a hypothesis test for the difference between two means. The sample sizes are $n_1 = 12$ and $n_2 = 15$.

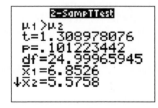

a. Is this a left-tailed test, a right-tailed test, or a two-tailed test?

b. How many degrees of freedom did the calculator use?

c. What is the P-value?

d. Can you reject H_0 at the $\alpha = 0.05$ level?

34. Interpret calculator display: The following TI-84 Plus calculator display presents the results of a hypothesis test for the difference between two means. The sample sizes are $n_1 = 25$ and $n_2 = 28$.

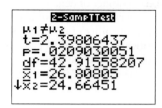

a. Is this a left-tailed test, a right-tailed test, or a two-tailed test?

b. How many degrees of freedom did the calculator use?

c. What is the P-value?

d. Can you reject H_0 at the $\alpha = 0.05$ level?

35. Interpret computer output: The following computer output (from MINITAB) presents the results of a hypothesis test for the difference $\mu_1 - \mu_2$ between two population means:

```
Two-sample T for X1 vs X2

       N    Mean     StDev    SE Mean
X1    58   35.848   10.233    1.3437
X2    36   26.851   15.329    2.5548


Difference = mu (X1) - mu (X2)
Estimate for difference:  8.997
95% CI for difference:  (4.16605, 13.827951)
T-Test of difference = 0 (vs not =):  T-Value = 3.12
                                P-Value = 0.003   DF = 54
```

a. What is the alternate hypothesis?

b. Can H_0 be rejected at the $\alpha = 0.05$ level? Explain.

c. How many degrees of freedom are there for the test statistic?

d. Use the simpler method to compute the degrees of freedom as the smaller of $n_1 - 1$ and $n_2 - 1$.

e. Find the P-value using this value for the degrees of freedom.

36. Interpret computer output: The following computer output (from MINITAB) presents the results of a hypothesis test for the difference $\mu_1 - \mu_2$ between two population means:

```
Two-sample T for X1 vs X2

      N   Mean   StDev   SE Mean
X1   20   3.44   2.65    0.23
X2   25   4.43   2.38    0.18


Difference = mu (X1) - mu (X2)
Estimate for difference:  -0.99
95% upper bound for difference:  0.291437
T-Test of difference = 0 (vs <):  T-Value = -1.30
                             P-Value = 0.100   DF = 38
```

a. What is the alternate hypothesis?

b. Can H_0 be rejected at the $\alpha = 0.05$ level? Explain.

c. How many degrees of freedom are there for the test statistic?

d. Use the simpler method to compute the degrees of freedom as the smaller of $n_1 - 1$ and $n_2 - 1$.

e. Find the P-value using this value for the degrees of freedom.

37. Interpret calculator display: The following TI-84 Plus calculator display presents a 95% confidence interval for the difference between two means. The sample sizes are $n_1 = 7$ and $n_2 = 10$.

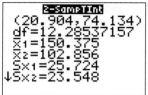

a. Compute the point estimate of $\mu_1 - \mu_2$.

b. How many degrees of freedom did the calculator use?

c. Fill in the blanks: We are 95% confident that the difference between the means is between _____ and _____ .

38. Interpret calculator display: The following TI-84 Plus calculator display presents a 99% confidence interval for the difference between two means. The sample sizes are $n_1 = 50$ and $n_2 = 42$.

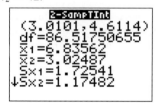

a. Compute the point estimate of $\mu_1 - \mu_2$.

b. How many degrees of freedom did the calculator use?

c. Fill in the blanks: We are 99% confident that the difference between the means is between _____ and _____ .

39. Interpret computer output: The following MINITAB output display presents a 98% confidence interval for the difference between two means.

```
      N     Mean     StDev   SE Mean
A    17   72.9172   10.7134   2.5984
B    25   52.1743    9.1237   1.8247


Difference = mu (A) - mu (B)
Estimate for difference: 20.7429
98% CI for difference:  (12.9408, 28.5450)   DF = 30
```

a. What is the point estimate of $\mu_1 - \mu_2$?

b. How many degrees of freedom did MINITAB use?

c. Fill in the blanks: We are _____ confident that the difference between the means is between _____ and _____ .

40. Interpret computer output: The following MINITAB output display presents a 95% confidence interval for the difference between two means.

```
      N    Mean    StDev   SE Mean
A    48   33.827   8.423   1.2157
B    57   10.372   9.314   1.2337


Difference = mu (A) - mu (B)
Estimate for difference: 23.455
95% CI for difference:  (20.019, 26.891)   DF = 102
```

a. What is the point estimate of $\mu_1 - \mu_2$?

b. How many degrees of freedom did MINITAB use?

c. Fill in the blanks: We are _____ confident that the difference between the means is between _____ and _____.

Extending the Concepts

41. More accurate degrees of freedom: A test will be made of $H_0: \mu_1 = \mu_2$ versus $H_1: \mu_1 > \mu_2$. The sample sizes were $n_1 = 10$ and $n_2 = 20$. The sample standard deviations were $s_1 = 3$ and $s_2 = 8$.

a. Compute the critical value for a level $\alpha = 0.05$ test, using 1 less than the smaller of the two sample sizes for the degrees of freedom.

b. Use the expression given in this section to compute a more accurate number of degrees of freedom.

c. Use the more accurate number of degrees of freedom to compute the probability of rejecting H_0 when it is true when the critical value found in part (a) is used. You will need technology to find the answer.

Answers to Check Your Understanding Exercises for Section 9.1

1. Paired

2. Independent

3. a. 3.073   **b.** 9

   c. The P-value is between 0.005 and 0.01. [Tech: 0.0066] [TI-84 Plus: 0.0030] [MINITAB: 0.0031]

   d. If H_0 is true, the probability of observing a value for the test statistic as extreme as or more extreme than the value actually observed is 0.0066. This is unusual, so the evidence against H_0 is strong. Because $P < 0.01$, we reject H_0 at the $\alpha = 0.01$ level.

4. a. 1.652   **b.** 16

   c. The P-value is between 0.10 and 0.20. [Tech: 0.1180] [TI-84 Plus: 0.1072] [MINITAB: 0.1073]

   d. If H_0 is true, the probability of observing a value for the test statistic as extreme as or more extreme than the value actually observed is 0.1073. This is not very unusual, so the evidence against H_0 is not strong. Because $P > 0.05$, we do not reject H_0 at the $\alpha = 0.05$ level.

5. $29.83 < \mu_1 - \mu_2 < 42.37$ [Tech: $29.89 < \mu_1 - \mu_2 < 42.31$]

6. $9.32 < \mu_1 - \mu_2 < 11.96$ [Tech: $9.36 < \mu_1 - \mu_2 < 11.92$]

SECTION 9.2   Inference About the Difference Between Two Proportions

Objectives

1. Perform a hypothesis test for the difference between two proportions using the *P*-value method
2. Perform a hypothesis test for the difference between two proportions using the critical value method
3. Construct confidence intervals for the difference between two proportions

Objective 1 Perform a hypothesis test for the difference between two proportions using the *P*-value method

Perform a Hypothesis Test for the Difference Between Two Proportions Using the *P*-Value Method

Are more people using computers at work these days? The General Social Survey took a poll to address this question. In the year 2002, they asked 1343 employed people between the ages of 18 and 50 whether they used a computer in their work, and 916 said that they did. In the year 2008, they asked the same question of an independent sample of 615 people, and 465 said that they used a computer at work.

We can compute the sample proportions of people who used a computer at work in each of these years. In 2002, the sample proportion was $916/1343 = 0.682$, and in 2008, the sample proportion was $465/615 = 0.756$. So the sample proportion increased from 2002 to 2008. The question of interest, however, involves the population proportions. There are two populations involved: the population of all employed people at the time the survey was taken in the year 2002, and the population of all employed people at the time the survey was taken in 2008. The question is whether the population proportion of people who used a computer in 2008 is greater than the population proportion in 2002.

This is an example of a situation in which we have two independent samples, with the sample proportion computed for each one. We will describe a method for performing a hypothesis test to determine whether the two population proportions are equal. We will need some notation for the population proportions, the sample proportions, the numbers of individuals in each category, and the sample sizes.

NOTATION

- p_1 and p_2 are the proportions of the category of interest in the two populations.
- $\hat{p}_1$ and $\hat{p}_2$ are the proportions of the category of interest in the two samples.
- x_1 and x_2 are the numbers of individuals in the category of interest in the two samples.
- n_1 and n_2 are the two sample sizes.

We will now describe how to perform the hypothesis test.

The null and alternate hypotheses

The issue is whether the population proportions p_1 and p_2 are equal. The null hypothesis says that they are equal:

$$H_0: p_1 = p_2$$

There are three possibilities for the alternate hypothesis:

$$H_1: p_1 < p_2 \qquad H_1: p_1 > p_2 \qquad H_1: p_1 \neq p_2$$

The test statistic

The test statistic is based on the difference between the sample proportions, $\hat{p}_1 - \hat{p}_2$. When the sample size is large, this difference is approximately normally distributed.

The mean and standard deviation of this distribution are

Recall: Because the samples are independent, the variance of $\hat{p}_1 - \hat{p}_2$ is the sum of the variances of $\hat{p}_1$ and $\hat{p}_2$. The standard deviation is the square root of the variance.

$$\text{Mean} = p_1 - p_2 \qquad \text{Standard deviation} = \sqrt{\frac{p_1(1 - p_1)}{n_1} + \frac{p_2(1 - p_2)}{n_2}}$$

To compute the test statistic, we must find values for the mean and standard deviation. The mean is straightforward: Under the assumption that H_0 is true, $p_1 - p_2 = 0$. The standard deviation is a bit more involved. The standard deviation depends on the population proportions p_1 and p_2, which are unknown. We need to estimate p_1 and p_2. Under H_0, we assume that $p_1 = p_2$. Therefore, we need to estimate p_1 and p_2 with the same value. The value to use is the **pooled proportion**, which we will denote by $\hat{p}$. The pooled proportion is found by treating the two samples as though they were one big sample. We divide the total number of individuals in the category of interest in the two samples by the sum of the two sample sizes:

$$\hat{p} = \frac{x_1 + x_2}{n_1 + n_2}$$

The standard deviation is estimated with the standard error:

$$\text{Standard error} = \sqrt{\frac{\hat{p}(1 - \hat{p})}{n_1} + \frac{\hat{p}(1 - \hat{p})}{n_2}} = \sqrt{\hat{p}(1 - \hat{p})\left(\frac{1}{n_1} + \frac{1}{n_2}\right)}$$

The test statistic is the z-score for $\hat{p}_1 - \hat{p}_2$:

$$z = \frac{(\hat{p}_1 - \hat{p}_2) - (p_1 - p_2)}{\sqrt{\hat{p}(1 - \hat{p})\left(\frac{1}{n_1} + \frac{1}{n_2}\right)}} = \frac{(\hat{p}_1 - \hat{p}_2) - 0}{\sqrt{\hat{p}(1 - \hat{p})\left(\frac{1}{n_1} + \frac{1}{n_2}\right)}} = \frac{\hat{p}_1 - \hat{p}_2}{\sqrt{\hat{p}(1 - \hat{p})\left(\frac{1}{n_1} + \frac{1}{n_2}\right)}}$$

The method just described requires certain assumptions, which we now state:

Explain It Again

Reason for assumption 4: We require that both samples contain at least 10 individuals in each category in order to be sure that $\hat{p}_1$ and $\hat{p}_2$ are both approximately normally distributed.

Assumptions for Performing a Hypothesis Test for the Difference Between Two Proportions

1. There are two simple random samples that are independent of one another.
2. Each population is at least 20 times as large as the sample drawn from it.
3. The individuals in each sample are divided into two categories.
4. Both samples contain at least 10 individuals in each category.

We summarize the steps for testing a hypothesis about the difference between two proportions using the P-value method. Later we will describe the critical value method.

Performing a Hypothesis Test for the Difference Between Two Proportions Using the *P*-Value Method

Check to be sure the assumptions are satisfied. If they are, then proceed with the following steps.

Step 1: State the null and alternate hypotheses. The null hypothesis will have the form H_0: $p_1 = p_2$. The alternate hypothesis will be $p_1 < p_2$, $p_1 > p_2$, or $p_1 \neq p_2$.

Step 2: If making a decision, choose a significance level α.

Step 3: Compute the test statistic $z = \dfrac{\hat{p}_1 - \hat{p}_2}{\sqrt{\hat{p}(1 - \hat{p})\left(\dfrac{1}{n_1} + \dfrac{1}{n_2}\right)}}$

where $\hat{p}$ is the pooled proportion: $\hat{p} = \dfrac{x_1 + x_2}{n_1 + n_2}$

Step 4: Compute the P-value. The P-value is an area under the normal curve. The P-value depends on the alternate hypothesis as follows:

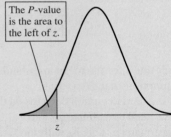

The P-value is the area to the left of z.

Left-tailed: H_1: $p_1 < p_2$

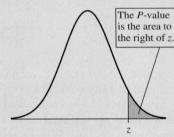

The P-value is the area to the right of z.

Right-tailed: H_1: $p_1 > p_2$

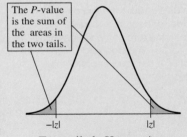

The P-value is the sum of the areas in the two tails.

Two-tailed: H_1: $p_1 \neq p_2$

Step 5: Interpret the P-value. If making a decision, reject H_0 if the P-value is less than or equal to the significance level α.

Step 6: State a conclusion.

EXAMPLE 9.4   Perform a hypothesis test

In the year 2002, the General Social Survey asked 1343 employed people between the ages of 18 and 50 whether they used a computer in their work, and 916 said that they did. In the year 2008, they asked the same question of an independent sample of 615 people, and 465 said that they used a computer at work. Assume these are two random samples from the population of employed people. Can you conclude that the proportion of people who used a computer at work was greater in 2008 than in 2002? Use the $\alpha = 0.05$ level.

Solution

We first check the assumptions. We have two independent random samples, and the populations are more than 20 times as large as the samples. The individuals in each sample are divided into two categories: those who use a computer at work and those who do not.

Finally, each sample contains more than 10 individuals in each category. The assumptions are satisfied.

Step 1: State the null and alternate hypotheses. We'll let p_1 be the population proportion of people who used a computer at work in 2002, and p_2 be the proportion in 2008. The issue is whether the proportions are the same, or whether the 2008 proportion, p_2, is greater than the 2002 proportion, p_1. Therefore, the null and alternate hypotheses are

$$H_0: p_1 = p_2 \qquad H_1: p_1 < p_2$$

Step 2: Choose a significance level. The significance level is $\alpha = 0.05$.

Step 3: Compute the test statistic. We'll begin by summarizing the necessary information in a table:

	2002	**2008**
Sample size	$n_1 = 1343$	$n_2 = 615$
Number of individuals	$x_1 = 916$	$x_2 = 465$
Sample proportion	$\hat{p}_1 = 916/1343 = 0.682055$	$\hat{p}_2 = 465/615 = 0.756098$
Population proportion	p_1 (unknown)	p_2 (unknown)

Next, we compute the pooled proportion $\hat{p}$:

$$\hat{p} = \frac{x_1 + x_2}{n_1 + n_2} = \frac{916 + 465}{1343 + 615} = 0.705312$$

The value of the test statistic is

$$z = \frac{\hat{p}_1 - \hat{p}_2}{\sqrt{\hat{p}(1 - \hat{p})\left(\dfrac{1}{n_1} + \dfrac{1}{n_2}\right)}} = \frac{0.682055 - 0.756098}{\sqrt{0.705312(1 - 0.705312)\left(\dfrac{1}{1343} + \dfrac{1}{615}\right)}}$$
$$= -3.34$$

Step 4: Compute the P-value. The alternate hypothesis, $p_1 < p_2$, is left-tailed. Therefore, the P-value is the area to the left of $z = -3.34$. Using Table A.2, we find this area to be 0.0004. Figure 9.2 illustrates the P-value.

Step 5: Interpret the P-value. The P-value of 0.0004 is less than the significance level $\alpha = 0.05$. Therefore, we reject H_0.

Step 6: State a conclusion. We conclude that the proportion of workers between the ages of 18 and 50 who used a computer at work was greater in 2008 than in 2002.

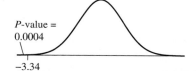

P-value = 0.0004

−3.34

Figure 9.2

Performing a hypothesis test with technology

The following computer output (from MINITAB) presents the results of Example 9.4.

```
Test and CI for Two Proportions: 2002, 2008

Variable        X         N      Sample p
2002          916      1343      0.682055
2008          465       615      0.756097

Difference = p (2002) - p (2008)
Estimate for difference:  -0.074042
95% upper bound for difference: -0.038168
Test for difference = 0 (vs < 0):   Z = -3.34   P-Value = 0.000
```

The numbers of individuals in the category of interest (X), the sample sizes (N), and the sample proportions (Sample p) are given. The quantity "Estimate for difference" is the difference between the sample proportions, $\hat{p}_1 - \hat{p}_2$. The 95% upper bound for the difference is shown next. We can be 95% confident that the difference $p_1 - p_2$ is less than or equal to this value of -0.038168. The last line in the output presents the alternate hypothesis, the value of the test statistic (Z), and the P-value.

Following are the results as presented by the TI-84 Plus calculator:

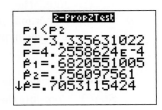

The letter "p" in the fourth line is the P-value.

Step-by-step instructions for performing hypothesis tests with technology are presented in the Using Technology section on page 427.

Check Your Understanding

1. In a clinical trial to compare the effectiveness of two pain relievers, a sample of 100 patients was given drug 1 and an independent sample of 200 patients was given drug 2. Of the patients on drug 1, 76 experienced substantial relief, while of the patients on drug 2, 128 experienced substantial relief. Investigators want to know whether the proportion of patients experiencing substantial relief is greater for drug 1. They will use the $\alpha = 0.05$ level of significance.
   a. Let p_1 be the population proportion of patients experiencing substantial relief from drug 1, and let p_2 be the population proportion of patients experiencing substantial relief from drug 2. State the appropriate null and alternate hypotheses about p_1 and p_2.
   b. Compute the sample proportions $\hat{p}_1$ and $\hat{p}_2$.
   c. Compute the value of the test statistic.
   d. Compute the P-value.
   e. Interpret the P-value.
   f. State a conclusion.

2. A sample of 200 voters over the age of 60 were asked whether they thought Social Security benefits should be increased for people over the age of 65. A total of 95 of them answered yes. A sample of 150 voters aged 18–25 were asked the same question and 63 of them answered yes. A pollster wants to know whether the proportion of voters who support an increase in Social Security benefits is greater among older voters. He will use the $\alpha = 0.05$ level of significance.
   a. Let p_1 be the population proportion of older voters expressing support, and let p_2 be the population proportion of younger voters expressing support. State the appropriate null and alternate hypotheses about p_1 and p_2.
   b. Compute the sample proportions $\hat{p}_1$ and $\hat{p}_2$.
   c. Compute the value of the test statistic.
   d. Compute the P-value.
   e. Interpret the P-value.
   f. State a conclusion.

Answers are on page 433.

Objective 2 Perform a hypothesis test for the difference between two proportions using the critical value method

Using the Critical Value Method

To use the critical value method, compute the test statistic as before. Because the test statistic is a z-score, critical values can be found in Table A.2, in Table 8.1 in Section 8.2, or with technology. The assumptions for the critical value method are the same as for the P-value method.

Following are the steps for the critical value method.

Performing a Hypothesis Test for the Difference Between Two Proportions Using the Critical Value Method

Check to be sure that the assumptions are satisfied. If they are, then proceed with the following steps.

Step 1: State the null and alternate hypotheses. The null hypothesis will have the form H_0: $p_1 = p_2$. The alternate hypothesis will be $p_1 < p_2$, $p_1 > p_2$, or $p_1 \neq p_2$.

Step 2: Choose a significance level α and find the critical value or values.

Step 3: Compute the test statistic $z = \dfrac{\hat{p}_1 - \hat{p}_2}{\sqrt{\hat{p}(1 - \hat{p})\left(\dfrac{1}{n_1} + \dfrac{1}{n_2}\right)}}$

where $\hat{p}$ is the pooled proportion: $\hat{p} = \dfrac{x_1 + x_2}{n_1 + n_2}$

Step 4: Determine whether to reject H_0, as follows:

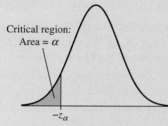

Left-tailed: H_1: $p_1 < p_2$
Reject if $z \leq -z_\alpha$.

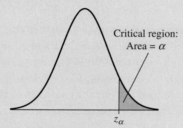

Right-tailed: H_1: $p_1 > p_2$
Reject if $z \geq z_\alpha$.

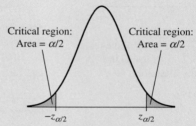

Two-tailed: H_1: $p_1 \neq p_2$
Reject if $z \geq z_{\alpha/2}$ or $z \leq -z_{\alpha/2}$.

Step 5: State a conclusion.

EXAMPLE 9.5   ### Testing a hypothesis using the critical value method

Are younger drivers more likely to have accidents in their driveways? Traffic engineers tabulated types of car accidents by drivers of various ages. Out of a total of 82,486 accidents involving drivers aged 15–24 years, 4243 of them, or 5.1%, occurred in a driveway. Out of a total of 219,170 accidents involving drivers aged 25–64 years, 10,701 of them, or 4.9%, occurred in a driveway. Can you conclude that accidents involving drivers aged 15–24 are more likely to occur in driveways than accidents involving drivers aged 25–64? Use the $\alpha = 0.05$ significance level.

Source: *Journal of Transportation Engineering* 125:502–507

Solution

We first check the assumptions. We have two independent samples, and the individuals in each sample fall into two categories. Each sample contains at least 10 individuals in each category. The assumptions are satisfied.

Step 1: State H_0 and H_1. We are interested in whether the proportion of accidents in driveways is greater among younger drivers. Let p_1 be the population proportion for younger drivers, and let p_2 be the population proportion for older drivers. Then the null and alternate hypotheses are:

$$H_0: p_1 = p_2 \qquad H_1: p_1 > p_2$$

Step 2: Choose a significance level α and find the critical value. We will use $\alpha = 0.05$. Because this is a right-tailed test, the critical value is the value for which the area to the right is 0.05. This value is $z_\alpha = 1.645$.

Step 3: Compute the test statistic. We begin by organizing the available information in a table:

	Ages 15–24	Ages 25–64
Sample size	$n_1 = 82{,}486$	$n_2 = 219{,}170$
Number of individuals	$x_1 = 4{,}243$	$x_2 = 10{,}701$
Sample proportion	$\hat{p}_1 = 4{,}243/82{,}486$ $= 0.051439$	$\hat{p}_2 = 10{,}701/219{,}170$ $= 0.048825$
Population proportion	p_1 (unknown)	p_2 (unknown)

Next, we compute the pooled proportion, $\hat{p}$.

$$\hat{p} = \frac{x_1 + x_2}{n_1 + n_2} = \frac{4{,}243 + 10{,}701}{82{,}486 + 219{,}170} = 0.049540$$

The test statistic is

$$z = \frac{\hat{p}_1 - \hat{p}_2}{\sqrt{\hat{p}(1 - \hat{p})\left(\dfrac{1}{n_1} + \dfrac{1}{n_2}\right)}} = 2.95$$

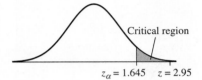

Critical region

$z_\alpha = 1.645$ $z = 2.95$

Figure 9.3 The value of the test statistic, $z = 2.95$, is inside the critical region. Therefore, we reject H_0.

Step 4: Determine whether to reject H_0. This is a right-tailed test, so we reject H_0 if $z > z_\alpha$. Because $z = 2.95$ and $z_\alpha = 1.645$, $z > z_\alpha$. We reject H_0 at the $\alpha = 0.05$ level. Figure 9.3 illustrates the critical region and the test statistic.

Step 5: State a conclusion. We conclude that accidents involving drivers aged 15–24 are more likely to occur in a driveway than accidents involving drivers aged 25–64.

Objective 3 Construct confidence intervals for the difference between two proportions

Confidence Intervals for the Difference Between Two Proportions

We can construct confidence intervals for the difference between two proportions. The assumptions are the same as those for performing a hypothesis test. When these assumptions are met, we can construct a confidence interval for the difference between two proportions by using the following steps.

Procedure for Constructing a Confidence Interval for $p_1 - p_2$

Check to be sure that the assumptions are satisfied. If they are, then proceed with the following steps:

Step 1: Compute the value of the point estimate $\hat{p}_1 - \hat{p}_2$.

Step 2: Find the critical value $z_{\alpha/2}$ corresponding to the desired confidence level from the last line of Table A.3, from Table A.2, or with technology.

Step 3: Compute the standard error

$$\sqrt{\frac{\hat{p}_1(1 - \hat{p}_1)}{n_1} + \frac{\hat{p}_2(1 - \hat{p}_2)}{n_2}}$$

and multiply it by the critical value to obtain the margin of error

$$z_{\alpha/2}\sqrt{\frac{\hat{p}_1(1 - \hat{p}_1)}{n_1} + \frac{\hat{p}_2(1 - \hat{p}_2)}{n_2}}$$

Step 4: Use the point estimate and the margin of error to construct the confidence interval:

Point estimate $\pm$ Margin of error

$$\hat{p}_1 - \hat{p}_2 \pm z_{\alpha/2}\sqrt{\frac{\hat{p}_1(1 - \hat{p}_1)}{n_1} + \frac{\hat{p}_2(1 - \hat{p}_2)}{n_2}}$$

$$\hat{p}_1 - \hat{p}_2 - z_{\alpha/2}\sqrt{\frac{\hat{p}_1(1 - \hat{p}_1)}{n_1} + \frac{\hat{p}_2(1 - \hat{p}_2)}{n_2}} < p_1 - p_2 < \hat{p}_1 - \hat{p}_2 + z_{\alpha/2}\sqrt{\frac{\hat{p}_1(1 - \hat{p}_1)}{n_1} + \frac{\hat{p}_2(1 - \hat{p}_2)}{n_2}}$$

Step 5: Interpret the results.

EXAMPLE 9.6 | Constructing a confidence interval

In a study of the effect of air pollution on lung function, a sample of 50 children living in a community with a high level of ozone pollution had their lung capacities measured, and 14 of them had capacities that were below normal for their size. A second sample of 80 children was drawn from a community with a low level of ozone pollution, and 12 of them had lung capacities that were below normal for their size. Construct a 95% confidence interval for the difference between the proportions of children with lung capacities below normal.

Solution
We begin by summarizing the available information in a table:

	High Pollution	**Low Pollution**
Sample size	$n_1 = 50$	$n_2 = 80$
Number with below-normal lung capacity	$x_1 = 14$	$x_2 = 12$
Population proportion	p_1 (unknown)	p_2 (unknown)

We check the assumptions: We have two independent random samples. The populations of children are more than 20 times as large as the samples. The individuals are divided into two categories. In the first sample, there are 14 children with lung capacity below normal, and $50 - 14 = 36$ whose lung capacity is not below normal. In the second sample, the corresponding numbers are 12 and 68. Therefore, each sample contains at least 10 individuals in each category.

Step 1: Compute the value of the point estimate. The sample proportions are

$$\hat{p}_1 = \frac{14}{50} = 0.280 \qquad \hat{p}_2 = \frac{12}{80} = 0.150$$

The point estimate is

$$\hat{p}_1 - \hat{p}_2 = 0.280 - 0.150 = 0.130$$

Step 2: Find the critical value. The desired confidence level is 95%, so the critical value is $z_{\alpha/2} = 1.96$.

Step 3: Compute the standard error and the margin of error. The standard error is

$$\sqrt{\frac{\hat{p}_1(1 - \hat{p}_1)}{n_1} + \frac{\hat{p}_2(1 - \hat{p}_2)}{n_2}} = \sqrt{\frac{0.280(1 - 0.280)}{50} + \frac{0.150(1 - 0.150)}{80}}$$

$$= 0.075005$$

The margin of error is

$$z_{\alpha/2}\sqrt{\frac{\hat{p}_1(1 - \hat{p}_1)}{n_1} + \frac{\hat{p}_2(1 - \hat{p}_2)}{n_2}} =$$

$$1.96\sqrt{\frac{0.280(1 - 0.280)}{50} + \frac{0.150(1 - 0.150)}{80}} = 0.14701$$

Step 4: Construct the confidence interval. The 95% confidence interval is

$$\text{Point estimate} \pm \text{Margin of error}$$

$$0.130 \pm 0.14701$$

$$0.130 - 0.14701 < p_1 - p_2 < 0.130 + 0.14701$$

$$-0.017 < p_1 - p_2 < 0.277$$

Recall: Some commonly used critical values are shown in the following table:

Level	Critical Value
95%	1.96
98%	2.326
99%	2.576

Step 5: Interpret the results. We are 95% confident that the difference between the proportions is between -0.017 and 0.277. This confidence interval contains 0. Therefore, we cannot be sure that the proportions of children with diminished lung capacity differ between the two communities.

Explain It Again

Round-off rule: When computing a confidence interval for the difference between proportions, round the final result to three decimal places.

In Example 9.6, we rounded the final result to three decimal places. We will follow this rule in general.

Constructing confidence intervals with technology

Example 9.6 presented a 95% confidence interval for the difference between the proportions of children with diminished lung capacity in two communities. We now present the results from a TI-84 Plus calculator and the software package MINITAB.

Following is the TI-84 Plus display.

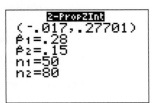

In addition to the confidence interval, the display presents the two sample proportions, $\hat{p}_1$ and $\hat{p}_2$, along with the sample sizes n_1 and n_2.

Following is the MINITAB output.

```
Sample   X   N   Sample p
1       14  50   0.280000
2       12  80   0.150000

Difference = p(1) - p(2)
Estimate for difference:  0.130000
95% CI for difference:  (-0.01701, 0.27701)
```

The MINITAB output is mostly straightforward. The quantities listed under the heading "Sample p" are $\hat{p}_1$ and $\hat{p}_2$. The quantity "Estimate for difference" is $\hat{p}_1 - \hat{p}_2$.

Step-by-step instructions for constructing confidence intervals with technology are given in the Using Technology section on page 427.

Check Your Understanding

3. Teaching methods: A class of 30 computer science students were taught introductory computer programming class with an innovative teaching method that used a graphical interface and drag-and-drop methods of creating computer programs. At the end of the class, 23 of these students said that they felt confident in their ability to write computer programs. Another class of 40 students were taught the same material using a standard method. At the end of class, 25 of these students said they felt confident. Assume that each class contained a simple random sample of students. Construct a 95% confidence interval for the difference between the proportions of students who felt confident.

4. Damp electrical connections: In a test of the effect of dampness on electrical connections, 80 electrical connections were tested under damp conditions and 130 were tested under dry conditions. Twenty of the damp connections failed and only 8 of the dry ones failed. If possible, construct a 90% confidence interval for the difference between the proportions of connections that fail when damp as opposed to dry. If not possible, explain why.

Answers are on page 433.

USING TECHNOLOGY

We use Examples 9.5 and 9.6 to illustrate the technology steps.

TI-84 PLUS

Testing a hypothesis about the difference between two proportions

Step 1. Press **STAT** and highlight the **TESTS** menu.

Step 2. Select **2–PropZTest** and press **ENTER** (Figure A). The **2-PropZTest** menu appears.

Step 3. Enter the values of x_1, n_1, x_2, and n_2. For Example 9.5, we use $x_1 = 4243$, $n_1 = 82486$, $x_2 = 10701$, and $n_2 = 219170$.

Step 4. Select the form of the alternate hypothesis. For Example 9.5, the alternate hypothesis has the form **>p2** (Figure B).

Step 5. Highlight **Calculate** and press **ENTER** (Figure C).

Figure A

Figure B

Figure C

TI-84 PLUS

Constructing a confidence interval for the difference between two proportions

Step 1. Press **STAT** and highlight the **TESTS** menu.

Step 2. Select **2–PropZInt** and press **ENTER** (Figure D). The **2–PropZInt** menu appears.

Step 3. Enter x_1, n_1, x_2, and n_2. For Example 9.6, we use $x_1 = 14$, $n_1 = 50$, $x_2 = 12$, and $n_2 = 80$.

Step 4. In the **C-Level** field, enter the confidence level. For Example 9.6, we use 0.95 (Figure E).

Step 5. Highlight **Calculate** and press **ENTER** (Figure F).

Figure D

Figure E

Figure F

MINITAB

Testing a hypothesis about the difference between two proportions

Step 1. Click on **Stat**, then **Basic Statistics**, then **2 Proportions**.

Step 2. Click **Summarized Data**, and enter the value of n_1 and n_2 in the **Trials** fields in the **First** and **Second** rows. Enter the values of x_1 and x_2 in the **Events** field in the **First** and **Second** rows. For Example 9.5, we use $x_1 = 4243$, $n_1 = 82486$, $x_2 = 10701$, and $n_2 = 219170$ (Figure G).

Step 3. Click **Options**, and enter **0** in the **Test difference** field and select the form of the alternate hypothesis. Given significance level α, enter $100(1 - \alpha)$ as the **Confidence Level**. For Example 9.5, we use **95** as the **Confidence Level**, **0** as the **Test difference**, and **greater than** as the **Alternative**. Check the box for **Use pooled proportion**. Click **OK**.

Step 4. Click **OK** (Figure H).

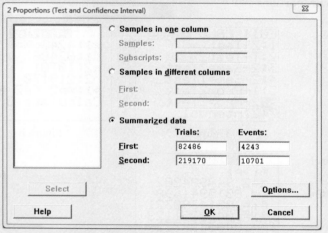

```
Sample       X        N   Sample p
1         4243    82486   0.051439
2        10701   219170   0.048825


Difference = p (1) – p (2)
Estimate for difference:   0.00261392
95% lower bound for difference:  0.00113957
Test for difference = 0 (vs > 0):   Z = 2.95   P-Value = 0.002
```

Figure H

Figure G

MINITAB

Constructing a confidence interval for the difference between two proportions

Step 1. Click on **Stat**, then **Basic Statistics**, then **2-Proportions**.

Step 2. Choose one of the following:
- If the summary statistics are given, click **Summarized Data** and enter the values of n_1 and n_2 in the **Trials** column and the values of x_1 and x_2 in the **Events** column. For Example 9.6, we use $x_1 = 14$, $n_1 = 50$, $x_2 = 12$, and $n_2 = 80$.
- If the raw data are given, click **Samples in different columns** and select the columns that contain the data.

Step 3. Click **Options** and enter the confidence level in the **Confidence Level** field (95) and choose **not equal** in the **Alternative field**. Click **OK**.

Step 4. Click **OK** (Figure I).

```
Sample   X    N   Sample p
1       14   50   0.280000
2       12   80   0.150000


Difference = p (1) – p (2)
Estimate for difference:   0.13
95% CI for difference:   (-0.0170071, 0.277007)
Test for difference = 0 (vs not = 0):   Z = 1.73   P-Value = 0.083
```

Figure I

EXCEL

Testing a hypothesis about the difference between two proportions

This procedure requires the **MegaStat** EXCEL add-in to be loaded. The **MegaStat** add-in may be downloaded from www.mhhe.com/megastat.

Step 1. Load the **MegaStat** EXCEL add-in.

Step 2. Click on the **MegaStat** menu and select **Hypothesis Tests**, then **Compare Two Independent Proportions...**

Step 3. Under the **Group1** column, enter the value of x_1 in the **p** field (note that p automatically changes to x) and the sample size n_1 in the **n** field. Under the **Group2** column, repeat for x_2 and n_2. For Example 9.5, we use $x_1 = 4243$, $n_1 = 82486$, $x_2 = 10701$, and $n_2 = 219170$.

Step 4. Enter the **Hypothesized difference (0)** and select the form of the alternate hypothesis (**greater than**) (Figure J).

Step 5. Click **OK** (Figure K).

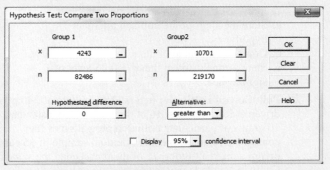

Figure J

Hypothesis test for two independent proportions

p1	p2	p_c	
0.051439	0.048825	0.04954	p (as decimal)
0.051439	0.048825	0.04954	p (as fraction)
4243	10701	14944	X
82486	219170	301656	n

0.002614	difference
0	hypothesized difference
0.000886	std. error
2.948984	z
0.001594	p-value (one-tailed, upper)

Figure K

EXCEL

Constructing a confidence interval for the difference between two proportions

This procedure requires the **MegaStat** EXCEL add-in to be loaded. The **MegaStat** add-in may be downloaded from www.mhhe.com/megastat.

Step 1. Click on the **MegaStat** menu, select **Hypothesis Tests**, then **Compare Two Independent Proportions...**

Step 2. In the **p** field for each group, enter the values of x_1 and x_2 (note that p changes to x). In the **n** field for each group, enter the values of n_1 and n_2. For Example 9.6, we use $x_1 = 14$, $n_1 = 50$, $x_2 = 12$, and $n_2 = 80$.

Step 3. Enter **0** in the **Hypothesized difference** field and select **not equal** in the **Alternative** field.

Step 4. Select the **Display confidence interval** option with the desired confidence level (95) (Figure L).

Step 5. Click **OK** (Figure M).

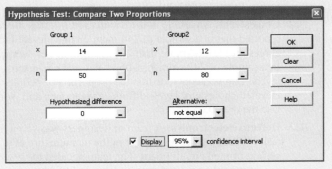

Figure L

Hypothesis test for two independent proportions

p1	p2	p_c	
0.28	0.15	0.2	p (as decimal)
14/50	12/80	26/130	p (as fraction)
14.	12.	26.	X
50	80	130	n

-0.017	confidence interval 95.% lower
0.277	confidence interval 95.% upper
0.147	margin of error

Figure M

SECTION 9.2   Exercises

Exercises 1–4 are the Check Your Understanding exercises located within the section.

Understanding the Concepts

In Exercises 5–8, fill in each blank with the appropriate word or phrase.

5. To use the method of this section to test a hypothesis about the difference between two proportions, each population must be at least _____ times as large as the sample drawn from it.

6. To use the method of this section to test a hypothesis about the difference between two proportions, each sample must contain at least _____ individuals in each category.

7. To construct a confidence interval for $p_1 - p_2$, we must have two _____ samples.

8. When constructing a confidence interval for $p_1 - p_2$, we assume that items in each sample are divided into _____ categories and that there are at least _____ items in each category.

In Exercises 9–12, determine whether the statement is true or false. If the statement is false, rewrite it as a true statement.

9. The individuals in each sample are divided into three or more categories.

10. To compute the test statistic, it is necessary to compute the pooled proportion.

11. The point estimate for $p_1 - p_2$ is $\hat{p}_1 - \hat{p}_2$, where $\hat{p}_1 = x_1/n_1$ and $\hat{p}_2 = x_2/n_2$.

12. The margin of error for $\hat{p}_1 - \hat{p}_2$ is
$$\sqrt{\frac{\hat{p}_1(1 - \hat{p}_1)}{n_1} + \frac{\hat{p}_2(1 - \hat{p}_2)}{n_2}}.$$

Practicing the Skills

13. In a test for the difference between two proportions, the sample sizes were $n_1 = 120$ and $n_2 = 85$, and the numbers of events were $x_1 = 55$ and $x_2 = 45$. A test is made of the hypotheses $H_0: p_1 = p_2$ versus $H_1: p_1 \neq p_2$.
    a. Compute the value of the test statistic.
    b. Can you reject H_0 at the $\alpha = 0.05$ level of significance?
    c. Can you reject H_0 at the $\alpha = 0.01$ level of significance?

14. In a test for the difference between two proportions, the sample sizes were $n_1 = 68$ and $n_2 = 76$, and the numbers of events were $x_1 = 41$ and $x_2 = 25$. A test is made of the hypotheses $H_0: p_1 = p_2$ versus $H_1: p_1 > p_2$.
    a. Compute the value of the test statistic.
    b. Can you reject H_0 at the $\alpha = 0.05$ level of significance?
    c. Can you reject H_0 at the $\alpha = 0.01$ level of significance?

In Exercises 15–18, construct the confidence interval for the difference $p_1 - p_2$ for the given level and values of x_1, n_1, x_2, and n_2.

15. Level 95%: $x_1 = 42$, $n_1 = 80$, $x_2 = 18$, $n_2 = 60$

16. Level 90%: $x_1 = 16$, $n_1 = 30$, $x_2 = 12$, $n_2 = 40$

17. Level 99%: $x_1 = 57$, $n_1 = 147$, $x_2 = 86$, $n_2 = 118$

18. Level 95%: $x_1 = 63$, $n_1 = 106$, $x_2 = 70$, $n_2 = 126$

Working with the Concepts

19. **Childhood obesity:** The National Health and Nutrition Examination Survey (NHANES) weighed a sample of 546 boys aged 6–11 and found that 87 of them were overweight. They weighed a sample of 508 girls aged 6–11 and found that 74 of them were overweight. Can you conclude that the proportion of boys who are overweight differs from the proportion of girls who are overweight?
    a. State the appropriate null and alternate hypotheses.
    b. Compute the value of the test statistic.
    c. State a conclusion at the $\alpha = 0.05$ level of significance.

20. **Pollution and altitude:** In a random sample of 340 cars driven at low altitudes, 46 of them exceeded a standard of 10 grams of particulate pollution per gallon of fuel consumed. In an independent random sample of 85 cars driven at high altitudes, 21 of them exceeded the standard. Can you conclude that the proportion of high-altitude vehicles exceeding the standard is greater than the proportion of low-altitude vehicles exceeding the standard?
    a. State the appropriate null and alternate hypotheses.
    b. Compute the value of the test statistic.
    c. State a conclusion at the $\alpha = 0.01$ level of significance.

21. **Preventing heart attacks:** Medical researchers performed a comparison of two drugs, clopidogrel and ticagrelor, which are designed to reduce the risk of heart attack or stroke in coronary patients. A total of 6676 patients were given clopidogrel, and 6732 were given ticagrelor. Of the clopidogrel patients, 668 suffered a heart attack or stroke within one year, and of the ticagrelor patients, 569 suffered a heart attack or stroke. Can you conclude that the proportion of patients suffering a heart attack or stroke is less for ticagrelor? Use the $\alpha = 0.01$ level.
    Source: *Lancet* 375:283–293

22. **Cholesterol:** An article in the *Archives of Internal Medicine* reported that in a sample of 244 men, 73 had elevated total cholesterol levels (more than 200 milligrams per deciliter). In a sample of 232 women, 44 had elevated cholesterol levels. Can you conclude that the proportion of people with elevated cholesterol levels differs between men and women? Use the $\alpha = 0.05$ level.

23. **Defective electronics:** A team of designers was given the task of reducing the defect rate in the manufacture of a certain printed circuit board. The team decided to reconfigure the cooling system. A total of 973 boards were produced the week before the reconfiguration was implemented, and 254 of these were defective. A total of 847 boards were produced the week after reconfiguration, and 95 of these were defective.

a. Construct a 90% confidence interval for the decrease in the defective rate after the reconfiguration.

b. A quality control engineer claims that the reconfiguration has decreased the proportion of defective parts by more than 0.15. Does the confidence interval contradict this claim?

Source: *The American Statistician* 56:312–315

24. Satisfied? A Pew poll taken in 2010 asked people in the United States whether they were satisfied with the way things were going in the country. Of 830 people aged 18–29, 340 said they were satisfied. Of 1157 people aged 30 and older, 301 said they were satisfied.

a. Construct a 95% confidence interval for the difference between the proportions of adults aged 18–29 and those 30 and older who are satisfied.

b. A sociologist claims that the proportion of people aged 18–29 who are satisfied is greater by more than 0.10 than the proportion of people aged 30 and older who are satisfied. Does the confidence interval contradict this claim?

25. Cancer prevention: Colonoscopy is a medical procedure that is designed to find and remove precancerous lesions in the colon before they become cancerous. In a sample of 51,460 people without colorectal cancer, 5043 had previously had a colonoscopy, and in a sample of 10,292 people diagnosed with colorectal cancer, 720 had previously had a colonoscopy.

a. Construct a 95% confidence interval for the difference in the proportions of people who had colonoscopies between those who were diagnosed with colorectal cancer and those who were not.

b. Does the confidence interval contradict the claim that the proportion of people who have had colonoscopies is the same among those with colorectal cancer and those without?

Source: *Annals of Internal Medicine* 150:1–8

26. Kids and cell phones: The MediaMark Research and Intelligence Survey American Kids study conducted in 2005 found that out of 5000 children aged 5–11, 595 had cell phones. The study was repeated in 2009, and 1000 out of 5000 children had cell phones.

a. Construct a 95% confidence interval for the increase in the proportion of children with cell phones between 2005 and 2009.

b. A cell phone marketing executive claims that the proportion of children aged 5–11 who have cell phones increased by more than 0.10 between 2005 and 2009. Does the confidence interval contradict this claim?

27. Don't perform a hypothesis test: In a certain year, there was measurable snowfall on 80 out of 365 days in Denver, and 63 out of 365 days in Chicago. A meteorologist proposes to perform a test of the hypothesis that the proportions of days with snow are equal in the two cities. Explain why this cannot be done using the method presented in this section.

28. Don't perform a hypothesis test: A new reading program is being tested. Parents are asked whether they would like to enroll their children, and 50 children are enrolled in the program. There are 45 children whose parents do not choose to enroll their children. At the end of the school year, the children are tested. Of the 50 children who participated in the program, 38 are found to be reading at grade level. Of the 45 children who did not participate, 24 were reading at grade level. Explain why these data should not be used to test the hypothesis that the proportion of children reading at grade level is higher for those who participate in the program.

29. Interpret calculator display: The following TI-84 Plus calculator display presents the results of a hypothesis test for the difference between two proportions. The sample sizes are $n_1 = 165$ and $n_2 = 152$.

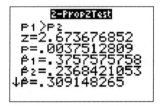

a. Is this a left-tailed test, a right-tailed test, or a two-tailed test?

b. What is the P-value?

c. Can you reject H_0 at the $\alpha = 0.05$ level?

30. Interpret calculator display: The following TI-84 Plus calculator display presents the results of a hypothesis test for the difference between two proportions. The sample sizes are $n_1 = 71$ and $n_2 = 62$.

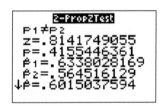

a. Is this a left-tailed test, a right-tailed test, or a two-tailed test?

b. What is the P-value?

c. Can you reject H_0 at the $\alpha = 0.05$ level?

31. Interpret computer output: The following computer output (from MINITAB) presents the results of a hypothesis test on the difference between two proportions.

```
Test and CI for Two Proportions: P1, P2

Variable    X    N   Sample p
P1         22   43   0.511628
P2         55   93   0.591398

Difference = p (P1) - p (P2)
Estimate for difference:  -0.079770
95% upper bound for difference: 0.071079
Test for difference = 0 (vs < 0):  Z = -0.87  P-Value = 0.192
```

a. Is this a left-tailed test, a right-tailed test, or a two-tailed test?

b. What is the P-value?

c. Can H_0 be rejected at the 0.05 level? Explain.

32. Interpret computer output: The following computer output (from MINITAB) presents the results of a hypothesis test on the difference between two proportions.

```
Test and CI for Two Proportions: P1, P2

Variable    X    N    Sample p
P1        405  577   0.701906
P2        363  578   0.628028

Difference = p (P1) - p (P2)
Estimate for difference:  0.073879
95% CI for difference: (0.0194191, 0.127827)
Test for difference = 0 (vs not = 0): Z = -2.66 P-Value = 0.008
```

  a. Is this a left-tailed test, a right-tailed test, or a two-tailed test?
  b. What is the P-value?
  c. Can H_0 be rejected at the 0.05 level? Explain.

33. Interpret calculator display: The following TI-84 Plus calculator display presents a 95% confidence interval for the difference between two proportions.

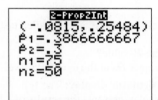

  a. Compute the point estimate of $p_1 - p_2$.
  b. Fill in the blanks: We are 95% confident that the difference between the proportions is between _____ and _____.

34. Interpret calculator display: The following TI-84 Plus calculator display presents a 99% confidence interval for the difference between two proportions.

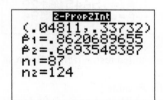

  a. Compute the point estimate of $p_1 - p_2$.
  b. Fill in the blanks: We are 99% confident that the difference between the proportions is between _____ and _____.

35. Interpret computer output: The following MINITAB output presents a confidence interval for the difference between two proportions.

```
Sample    X    N    Sample p
1        32   59   0.542373
2        23   63   0.365079

Difference = p(1) - p(2)
Estimate for difference:  0.177294
99% CI for difference:  (-0.051451, 0.406038)
```

  a. What is the point estimate of $p_1 - p_2$?
  b. Fill in the blanks: We are _____ confident that the difference between the proportions is between _____ and _____.

36. Interpret computer output: The following MINITAB output presents a confidence interval for the difference between two proportions.

```
Sample    X    N    Sample p
1        16  546   0.029304
2        18  935   0.019251

Difference = p(1) - p(2)
Estimate for difference:  0.010053
95% CI for difference:  (-0.006612, 0.026717)
```

  a. What is the point estimate of $p_1 - p_2$?
  b. Fill in the blanks: We are _____ confident that the difference between the proportions is between _____ and _____.

Extending the Concepts

Null difference other than 0: *Occasionally someone may wish to test a hypothesis of the form H_0: $p_1 - p_2 = p_d$, where $p_d \neq 0$. In this situation, the null hypothesis says that the population proportions are unequal, so we do not compute the pooled proportion, which assumes the population proportions are equal. One approach to testing this hypothesis is to use the test statistic*

$$z = \frac{(p_1 - p_2) - p_d}{\sqrt{\dfrac{\hat{p}_1(1 - \hat{p}_1)}{n_1} + \dfrac{\hat{p}_2(1 - \hat{p}_2)}{n_2}}}$$

When the assumptions of this section are met, this statistic has approximately a standard normal distribution when H_0 is true.

37. Computer chips: A computer manufacturer has a choice of two machines, a less expensive one and a more expensive one, to manufacture a particular computer chip. Out of 500 chips manufactured on the less expensive machine, 70 were defective. Out of 400 chips manufactured on the more expensive machine, only 20 were defective. The manufacturer will buy the more expensive machine if he is convinced that the proportion of defectives is more than 5% less than on the less expensive machine. Let p_1 represent the proportion of defectives produced by the less expensive machine, and let p_2 represent the proportion of defectives produced by the more expensive machine.

  a. State appropriate null and alternate hypotheses.
  b. Compute the value of the test statistic.
  c. Can you reject H_0 at the $\alpha = 0.05$ level?
  d. Which machine should the manufacturer buy?

Answers to Check Your Understanding Exercises for Section 9.2

1. a. H_0: $p_1 = p_2$, H_1: $p_1 > p_2$

  b. $\hat{p}_1 = 0.76$, $\hat{p}_2 = 0.64$ **c.** $z = 2.10$ **d.** $P = 0.0179$

  e. If H_0 is true, the probability of observing a value for the test statistic as extreme as or more extreme than the value actually observed is 0.0179. This is unusual, so the evidence against H_0 is strong. Because $P < 0.05$, we reject H_0 at the $\alpha = 0.05$ level.

  f. We conclude that the proportion of patients experiencing substantial relief is greater for drug 1.

2. a. H_0: $p_1 = p_2$, H_1: $p_1 > p_2$

  b. $\hat{p}_1 = 0.475$, $\hat{p}_2 = 0.420$ **c.** $z = 1.02$

  d. $P = 0.1539$ [Tech: 0.1531]

e. If H_0 is true, the probability of observing a value for the test statistic as extreme as or more extreme than the value actually observed is 0.1539. This is not unusual, so the evidence against H_0 is not strong. Because $P > 0.05$, we do not reject H_0 at the $\alpha = 0.05$ level.

f. We conclude that the proportions of younger and older voters that support an increase in Social Security benefits may be the same.

3. $-0.071 < p_1 - p_2 < 0.355$

4. It is not possible to construct a confidence interval, because the sample of dry connections contains fewer than 10 that failed.

SECTION 9.3 | **Inference About the Difference Between Two Means: Paired Samples**

Objectives

1. Perform a hypothesis test with matched pairs using the P-value method
2. Perform a hypothesis test with matched pairs using the critical value method
3. Construct confidence intervals with paired samples

Objective 1 Perform a hypothesis test with matched pairs using the P-value method

Hypothesis Tests with Matched Pairs Using the P-Value Method

Does tuning a car engine improve the gas mileage? A sample of eight automobiles were run to determine their mileage, in miles per gallon. Then each car was given a tune-up, and run again to measure the mileage a second time. The results are presented in Table 9.1.

Table 9.1 Gas Mileage Before and After Tune-up for Eight Automobiles

	Automobile								
	1	**2**	**3**	**4**	**5**	**6**	**7**	**8**	**Sample Mean**
After Tune-up	35.44	35.17	31.07	31.57	26.48	23.11	25.18	32.39	30.05125
Before Tune-up	33.76	34.30	29.55	30.90	24.92	21.78	24.30	31.25	28.84500
Difference	1.68	0.87	1.52	0.67	1.56	1.33	0.88	1.14	1.20625

The sample mean mileage was higher after tune-up. We would like to determine how strong the evidence is that the population mean mileage is higher after tune-up.

We have two samples, a sample of gas mileages before tune-up and a sample after tune-up. These are paired samples, because each value in one sample can be paired with the value from the same automobile in the other sample. For example, the first pair is (35.44, 33.76), which are the two values from automobile 1. These pairs are called **matched pairs**. The bottom row of Table 9.1 contains the differences between the values in each matched pair. These differences are a sample from the population of differences. We can compute the means of the two original samples, along with the mean of the sample of differences. Denote the means of the original samples by $\bar{x}_1$ and $\bar{x}_2$. Denote the mean of the sample of differences by $\bar{d}$. The sample means are presented in the rightmost column of Table 9.1. They are

$$\bar{x}_1 = 30.05125 \qquad \bar{x}_2 = 28.845 \qquad \bar{d} = 1.20625$$

Simple arithmetic shows that the mean of the differences is the same as the difference between the sample means. In other words, $\bar{d} = \bar{x}_1 - \bar{x}_2$. The same relationship holds for the population means. If we denote the population means by μ_1 and μ_2, and denote the population mean of the differences by μ_d, then $\mu_d = \mu_1 - \mu_2$. This is a very useful fact. It means that a confidence interval for the mean μ_d is also a confidence interval for the difference $\mu_1 - \mu_2$. The matched pairs reduce the two-sample problem to a one-sample problem.

The data show that the sample mean gas mileage increased after tune-up. We would like to perform a hypothesis test for the population mean increase μ_d. The method for performing a hypothesis test for μ_d is the usual method for performing a hypothesis test for a population mean. This method was presented in Section 8.3. We now list the assumptions for this method, when applied to matched pairs.

Assumptions for Performing a Hypothesis Test Using Matched Pairs

1. We have two paired random samples.
2. Either the sample size is large ($n > 30$), *or* the differences between the matched pairs come from a population that is approximately normal.

Notation:

- $\bar{d}$ is the sample mean of the differences between the values in the matched pairs.
- s_d is the sample standard deviation of the differences between the values in the matched pairs.
- μ_d is the population mean difference for the matched pairs.

When these assumptions are satisfied, a hypothesis test may be performed in the same way as for a test for a population mean, using the following steps.

Performing a Hypothesis Test with Matched-Pair Data Using the *P*-Value Method

Check to be sure the assumptions are satisfied. If they are, then proceed with the following steps.

Step 1: State the null and alternate hypotheses. The null hypothesis will have the form $H_0: \mu_d = \mu_0$. The alternate hypothesis will be of the form $\mu_d < \mu_0$, $\mu_d > \mu_0$, or $\mu_d \neq \mu_0$.

Step 2: If making a decision, choose a significance level α.

Step 3: Compute the test statistic $t = \dfrac{\bar{d} - \mu_0}{s_d / \sqrt{n}}$.

Step 4: Compute the *P*-value. The *P*-value is an area under the *t* curve with $n - 1$ degrees of freedom. The *P*-value depends on the alternate hypothesis as follows:

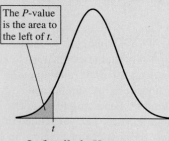

The *P*-value is the area to the left of *t*.

Left-tailed: $H_1: \mu_d < \mu_0$

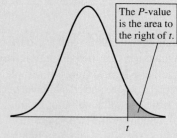

The *P*-value is the area to the right of *t*.

Right-tailed: $H_1: \mu_d > \mu_0$

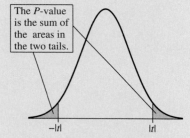

The *P*-value is the sum of the areas in the two tails.

Two-tailed: $H_1: \mu_d \neq \mu_0$

Step 5: Interpret the *P*-value. If making a decision, reject H_0 if the *P*-value is less than or equal to the significance level α.

Step 6: State a conclusion.

EXAMPLE 9.7 Test a hypothesis with matched-pair data

Test $H_0: \mu_d = 0$ versus $H_1: \mu_d > 0$, using the data in Table 9.1. Use the $\alpha = 0.01$ significance level.

Solution

We first check the assumptions. We have a simple random sample of differences. Because the sample size is small ($n = 8$), we must check for signs of strong skewness or outliers. Following is a dotplot of the differences.

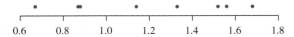

The dotplot does not reveal any outliers or strong skewness. Therefore, we may proceed.

Step 1: State H_0 and H_1. The issue is whether the mileage is greater after tune-up, so the null and alternate hypotheses are

$$H_0\text{: } \mu_d = 0 \qquad H_1\text{: } \mu_d > 0$$

Step 2: Choose a significance level. We will use $\alpha = 0.01$.

Step 3: Compute the test statistic. First we compute the sample mean and sample standard deviation of the differences. These are

$$\bar{d} = 1.20625 \qquad s_d = 0.37317$$

The test statistic is

$$t = \frac{\bar{d} - \mu_0}{s_d/\sqrt{n}}$$

Under the assumption that H_0 is true, $\mu_d = \mu_0 = 0$. The value of the test statistic is therefore

$$t = \frac{\bar{d} - \mu_0}{s_d/\sqrt{n}} = \frac{1.20625 - 0}{0.37317/\sqrt{8}} = 9.1427$$

Step 4: Compute the P-value. Under the assumption that H_0 is true, the test statistic has a t distribution. The number of degrees of freedom is $n - 1 = 8 - 1 = 7$. The alternate hypothesis is $\mu_d > 0$, so the P-value is the area to the right of the observed value of 9.1427. Technology gives $P = 0.0000193$.

Step 5: Interpret the P-value. The P-value is nearly 0. If H_0 were true, there would be virtually no chance of observing a test statistic as extreme as the value of 9.1427 that we observed. Because $P < 0.01$, we reject H_0 at the $\alpha = 0.01$ level.

Step 6: State a conclusion. We conclude that the gas mileage increased after a tune-up.

Performing hypothesis tests with technology

The following computer output (from MINITAB) presents the results of the hypothesis test performed in Example 9.7.

```
Paired T for After - Before

                N      Mean      StDev      SE Mean
After           8   30.05125   4.60928     1.62963
Before          8   28.84500   4.63519     1.63879
Difference      8    1.20625   0.37317     0.13194


99% lower bound for mean difference: 0.81071
T-Test of mean difference = 0 (vs > 0): T-Value = 9.14   P-Value = 0.000
```

The column labeled "SE Mean" presents the standard errors for the means of the two samples, and for the mean of the differences. The standard error is the standard deviation divided by the square root of the sample size. Note that the sample standard deviation of the differences is much smaller than the sample standard deviations of the original samples. This is the case for most matched-pair data, and is the reason that tests based on matched pairs have more power than tests based on independent samples.

Following are the results of Example 9.7 as displayed on a TI-84 Plus calculator.

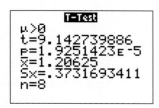

```
         T-Test
μ>0
t=9.142739886
P=1.9251423E-5
x̄=1.20625
Sx=.3731693411
n=8
```

The second line states the alternate hypothesis. This is followed by the value of the test statistic t, and the P-value. The quantity $\bar{x}$ is the sample mean of the differences $\bar{d}$, and the quantity Sx is the sample standard deviation of the differences, s_d.

Step-by-step instructions for performing hypothesis tests with technology are presented in the Using Technology section on page 440.

Check Your Understanding

1. A sample of five third-graders took a reading test. They then participated in a reading improvement program, and took the test again to determine whether their reading ability had improved. Following are the test scores for each of the students both before and after the program. Can you conclude that the mean reading score increased after the program?

	1	2	3	4	5
After	67	68	78	75	84
Before	59	63	81	74	78

   a. Let μ_d denote the population mean difference After − Before. State the appropriate null and alternate hypotheses about μ_d.
   b. Compute the differences After − Before.
   c. Compute the value of the test statistic.
   d. Compute the P-value.
   e. Do you reject H_0 at the $\alpha = 0.05$ level?
   f. State a conclusion.

2. Following are the annual amounts of rainfall, in inches, in six randomly chosen cities for two consecutive years. Can you conclude that the mean rainfall was greater in year 2 than in year 1?

	1	2	3	4	5	6
Year 2	34.6	18.7	42.6	41.3	60.6	29.9
Year 1	25.1	15.3	46.4	31.2	51.7	24.2

   a. Let μ_d denote the population mean difference Year 2 − Year 1. State the appropriate null and alternate hypotheses about μ_d.
   b. Compute the differences Year 2 − Year 1.
   c. Compute the value of the test statistic.
   d. Compute the P-value.
   e. Do you reject H_0 at the $\alpha = 0.05$ level?
   f. State a conclusion.

Answers are on page 446.

Objective 2 Perform a hypothesis test with matched pairs using the critical value method

Testing a Hypothesis with Matched-Pair Data Using the Critical Value Method

The critical value method for matched-pair data is essentially the same as that for a population mean with σ unknown. We can find the critical value in Table A.3 or with technology. The assumptions for the critical value method are the same as for the P-value method. When the assumptions are satisfied, a hypothesis test may be performed using the following steps.

Performing a Hypothesis Test with Matched-Pair Data Using the Critical Value Method

Check to be sure the assumptions are satisfied. If they are, then proceed with the following steps.

Step 1: State the null and alternate hypotheses. The null hypothesis will have the form $H_0: \mu_d = \mu_0$. The alternate hypothesis will be of the form $\mu_d < \mu_0$, $\mu_d > \mu_0$, or $\mu_d \neq \mu_0$.

Step 2: Choose a significance level α and find the critical value or values.

Step 3: Compute the test statistic $t = \dfrac{\bar{d} - \mu_0}{s_d/\sqrt{n}}$.

Step 4: Determine whether to reject H_0, as follows:

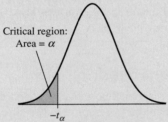

Critical region:
Area = α

Left-tailed: $H_1: \mu_d < \mu_0$

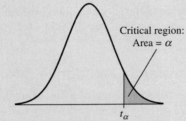

Critical region:
Area = α

Right-tailed: $H_1: \mu_d > \mu_0$

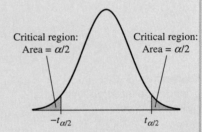

Critical region:
Area = $\alpha/2$

Critical region:
Area = $\alpha/2$

Two-tailed: $H_1: \mu_d \neq \mu_0$

Step 5: State a conclusion.

EXAMPLE 9.8

Testing hypotheses with the critical value method

For a sample of nine automobiles, the mileage (in 1000s of miles) at which the original front brake pads were worn to 10% of their original thickness was measured, as was the mileage at which the original rear brake pads were worn to 10% of their original thickness. The results are given below.

	Automobile								
	1	**2**	**3**	**4**	**5**	**6**	**7**	**8**	**9**
Rear	42.7	36.7	46.1	46.0	39.9	51.7	51.6	46.1	47.3
Front	32.8	26.6	35.6	36.4	29.2	40.9	40.9	34.8	36.6
Difference	9.9	10.1	10.5	9.6	10.7	10.8	10.7	11.3	10.7

The differences in the last line of the table are Rear $-$ Front. Can you conclude that the mean time for the rear brake pads to wear out is longer than the mean time for the front pads? Use the $\alpha = 0.05$ significance level.

Solution

We first check the assumptions. Because the sample size is small, we will construct a dotplot.

The dotplot shows no evidence of outliers or extreme skewness, so we may proceed.

Step 1: State the null and alternate hypotheses. We are interested in determining whether the mean time for the rear pads is longer than for the front. Therefore, the hypotheses are

$$H_0: \mu_d = 0 \qquad H_1: \mu_d > 0$$

Step 2: Choose a significance level α and find the critical value. We will use $\alpha = 0.05$. Because this is a right-tailed test, the critical value is the value for which the area to the right is 0.05. The sample size is $n = 9$, so there are $9 - 1 = 8$ degrees of freedom. The critical value is $t_\alpha = 1.860$.

Step 3: Compute the test statistic. The sample size is $n = 9$. We compute the sample mean and standard deviation of the differences:

$$\bar{d} = 10.478 \qquad s_d = 0.5215$$

The test statistic is

$$t = \frac{\bar{d} - 0}{s_d/\sqrt{n}} = \frac{10.478 - 0}{0.5215/\sqrt{9}} = 60.28$$

Step 4: Determine whether to reject H_0. This is a right-tailed test, so we reject H_0 if $t \geq t_\alpha$. Because $t = 60.28$ and $t_\alpha = 1.860$, we reject H_0 at the $\alpha = 0.05$ level.

Step 5: State a conclusion. We conclude that the mean time for rear brake pads to wear out is longer than the mean time for front brake pads.

Objective 3 Construct confidence intervals with paired samples

Construct Confidence Intervals with Paired Samples

Does drinking a small amount of alcohol reduce reaction time noticeably? Sixteen volunteers were given a test in which they had to push a button in response to the appearance of an image on a screen. Their reaction times were measured. Then the subjects consumed enough alcohol to raise their blood alcohol level to 0.05%. (In most states, a person is not considered to be "under the influence" until the blood alcohol level reaches 0.08%.) They then took the reaction time test again. Their reaction times, in milliseconds, are presented in Table 9.2. The row labeled "Difference" is the increase in reaction time after consuming alcohol. A negative difference occurs when the reaction time after consuming alcohol is less.

Table 9.2 Reaction Times Before and After Consuming Alcohol

	1	2	3	4	5	6	7	8	9	10	11	12	13	14	15	16	Sample Mean
Blood alcohol 0.05%	102	100	77	61	85	50	95	115	64	98	107	44	47	92	70	94	81.3
Blood alcohol 0	103	99	69	50	96	26	71	109	53	89	103	27	50	100	66	86	74.8
Difference	−1	1	8	11	−11	24	24	6	11	9	4	17	−3	−8	4	8	6.5

The data in Table 9.2 are matched pairs. When the sample size is large ($n > 30$) or the differences come from a population that is approximately normal, we can construct a confidence interval for the population mean difference as follows.

Constructing a Confidence Interval Using Matched Pairs

Let $\bar{d}$ be the sample mean of the differences between matched pairs, and let s_d be the sample standard deviation. Let μ_d be the population mean difference between matched pairs.

A level $100(1 - \alpha)\%$ confidence interval for μ_d is

$$\bar{d} - t_{\alpha/2}\frac{s_d}{\sqrt{n}} < \mu_d < \bar{d} + t_{\alpha/2}\frac{s_d}{\sqrt{n}}$$

Another way to write this is

$$\bar{d} \pm t_{\alpha/2}\frac{s_d}{\sqrt{n}}$$

EXAMPLE 9.9

Construct a confidence interval

Use the data in Table 9.2 to construct a 95% confidence for μ_d, the mean difference in reaction times.

We check the assumptions. Because the sample size is small ($n = 16$), we construct a boxplot for the differences to check for outliers or strong skewness.

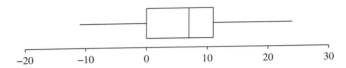

There are no outliers and no evidence of strong skewness, so we may proceed.

Step 1: Compute the sample mean difference $\bar{d}$, and the sample standard deviation of the differences s_d. The sample mean and standard deviation are

$$\bar{d} = 6.500 \qquad s_d = 9.93311$$

Step 2: Compute the critical value. We use the t statistic. The sample size is $n = 16$, so the degrees of freedom is $16 - 1 = 15$. The confidence level is 95%. From Table A.3, we find the critical value to be

$$t_{\alpha/2} = 2.131$$

Step 3: Compute the standard error and the margin of error. The standard error is

$$\frac{s_d}{\sqrt{n}} = \frac{9.93311}{\sqrt{16}} = 2.48328$$

The margin of error is

$$t_{\alpha/2}\frac{s_d}{\sqrt{n}} = 2.131(2.48328) = 5.292$$

Step 4: Construct the confidence interval. The 95% confidence interval is

$$\text{Point estimate} \pm \text{Margin of error}$$

$$6.5 - 5.292 < \mu_d < 6.5 + 5.292$$

$$1.2 < \mu_d < 11.8$$

Note that we have rounded the final result to one decimal place, because the original data (the differences) were given as whole numbers (no places after the decimal point).

Step 5: Interpret the result. We are 95% confident that the mean difference is between 1.2 and 11.8. In particular, the confidence interval does not contain 0, and all the values in the confidence interval are positive. We can be fairly certain that the mean reaction time is greater when the blood alcohol level is 0.05%.

Check Your Understanding

3. **High blood pressure:** A group of five individuals with high blood pressure were given a new drug that was designed to lower blood pressure. Systolic blood pressure was measured before and after treatment for each individual. The results follow. Construct a 95% confidence interval for the mean reduction in systolic blood pressure.

	Individual				
	1	**2**	**3**	**4**	**5**
Before	170	164	168	158	183
After	145	132	129	135	145

4. Extra help: The statistics department at a large university instituted a program in which students could get extra help with statistics in the evening. The following table presents scores for tests taken before and after the program for a random sample of six students. Construct a 99% confidence interval for the mean increase in test score.

	Student					
	1	2	3	4	5	6
Before	67	58	78	61	75	80
After	73	66	85	69	80	82

Answers are on page 446.

Constructing confidence intervals with technology

The following TI-84 Plus display presents results for Example 9.9.

```
TInterval
(1.207,11.793)
x̄=6.5
Sx=9.933109617
n=16
```

The following output from MINITAB presents the results for Example 9.9.

	N	Mean	StDev	SE Mean
Difference	16	6.50000	9.93311	2.48328

95% CI for mean difference: (1.20702, 11.79298)

Most of the output is straightforward. The quantity labeled "StDev" is the standard deviation of the differences, s_d, and the quantity labeled "SE Mean" is $s_d/\sqrt{n}$, which is the standard error.

Step-by-step instructions for constructing confidence intervals with technology are given in the Using Technology section on this page.

USING TECHNOLOGY

We use Examples 9.7 and 9.9 to illustrate the technology steps.

TI-84 PLUS

Testing a hypothesis about a difference using matched pairs

Step 1. Enter the data for into **L1** and **L2** in the data editor. On the home screen, enter **(L1 – L2) STO L3** to assign the differences in list **L3** (Figure A).

Step 2. Press **STAT** and highlight the **TESTS** menu.

Step 3. Select **T–Test** and press **ENTER** (Figure B). The **T–Test** menu appears.

Step 4. For **Inpt**, select the **Data** option and enter **L3** as the **List** option.

Step 5. Enter the null hypothesis mean for μ_0 and select the form of the alternate hypothesis. For Example 9.7, we have $\mu_0 = 0$ and the alternate hypothesis has the form $> \mu 0$ (Figure C).

Step 6. Highlight **Calculate** and press **ENTER** (Figure D).

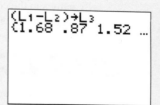

Figure A

Figure B

Figure C

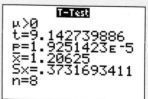

Figure D

TI-84 PLUS

Constructing a confidence interval for the difference using matched pairs

Step 1. Enter the data into **L1** and **L2** in the data editor. On the home screen, enter **(L1 - L2)** STO **L3** to assign the differences in list **L3** (Figure E).

Step 2. Press **STAT** and highlight the **TESTS** menu.

Step 3. Select **TInterval** and press **ENTER** (Figure F). The **TInterval** menu appears.

Step 4. For **Inpt**, select the **Data** option and enter **L3** as the **List** option.

Step 5. In the **C-Level** field, enter the confidence level. For Example 9.9, we use 0.95 (Figure G).

Step 6. Highlight **Calculate** and press **ENTER** (Figure H).

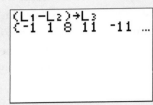

Figure E

Figure F

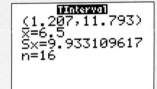

Figure G

Figure H

MINITAB

Testing a hypothesis about a difference using matched pairs

Step 1. Enter the data from Example 9.7 into **Columns C1** and **C2**.

Step 2. Click on **Stat**, then **Basic Statistics**, then **Paired t**.

Step 3. Select Samples in **Columns**, and enter **C1** in the **First Sample** field and **C2** in the **Second Sample** field.

Step 4. Click **Options**, and enter the null hypothesis difference between the means in the **Test difference** field and select the form of the alternate hypothesis. Given significance level α, enter $100(1 - \alpha)$ as the **Confidence Level**. For Example 9.7, we use **99** as the **Confidence Level**, **0** as the **Test difference**, and **greater than** as the **Alternative**. Click **OK**.

Step 5. Click **OK** (Figure I).

```
Paired T for C1 - C2

             N     Mean    StDev   SE Mean
C1           8   30.0513   4.6093   1.6296
C2           8   28.8450   4.6352   1.6388
Difference   8   1.20625  0.37317  0.13194


99% lower bound for mean difference: 0.81071
T-Test of mean difference = 0 (vs > 0): T-Value = 9.14   P-Value = 0.000
```

Figure I

MINITAB

Constructing a confidence interval for a difference using matched pairs

Step 1. Enter the data from Example 9.9 into **Columns C1** and **C2**.

Step 2. Click on **Stat**, then **Basic Statistics**, then **Paired t**.

Step 3. Select **Samples in Columns** and enter **C1** in the **First Sample** field and **C2** in the **Second Sample** field.

Step 4. Click **Options** and enter the confidence level in the **Confidence Level** (95) field. Enter **0** in the **Test Mean** field and choose **not equal** in the **Alternative** field. Click **OK** (Figure J).

Step 5. Click **OK** (Figure K).

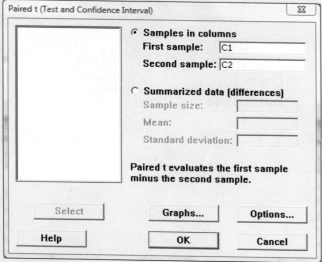

Figure J

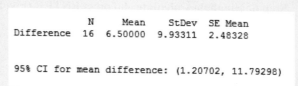

```
             N    Mean    StDev   SE Mean
Difference   16  6.50000  9.93311  2.48328

95% CI for mean difference: (1.20702, 11.79298)
```

Figure K

EXCEL

Testing a hypothesis about a difference using matched pairs

This procedure requires the **MegaStat** EXCEL add-in to be loaded. The **MegaStat** add-in may be downloaded from www.mhhe.com/megastat.

Step 1. Enter the data from Example 9.7 into **Columns A** and **B** in the worksheet.

Step 2. Click on the **MegaStat** menu, select **Hypothesis Tests**, then **Paired Observations...**

Step 3. Select the **data input** option, and enter the range of cells for the first sample in the **Group 1** field and the range of cells for the second sample in the **Group 2** field.

Step 4. Enter **0** in the **Hypothesized difference** field and select **greater than** in the **Alternative** field.

Step 5. Choose the **t-test** option (Figure L).

Step 6. Click **OK** (Figure M).

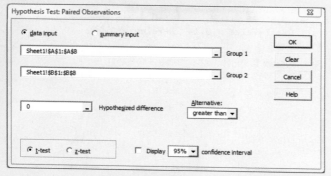

Figure L

Hypothesis Test: Paired Observations

```
 0.00000  hypothesized value
30.05125  mean Group 1
28.84500  mean Group 2
 1.20625  mean difference  (Group 1 - Group 2)
 0.37317  std. dev.
 0.13194  std. error
      8   n
      7   df

    9.14   t
1.93E-05   p-value (one-tailed, upper)
```

Figure M

EXCEL

Constructing a confidence interval for a difference using matched pairs

This procedure requires the **MegaStat** EXCEL add-in to be loaded. The **MegaStat** add-in may be downloaded from www.mhhe.com/megastat.

Step 1. Enter the data from Example 9.9 into **Columns A** and **B** in the worksheet.

Step 2. Click on the **MegaStat** menu, select **Hypothesis Tests**, then **Paired Observations...**

Step 3. Select the **data input** option and enter the range of cells for the first sample in the **Group 1** field and the range of cells for the second sample in the **Group 2** field.

Step 4. Enter **0** in the **Hypothesized difference** field and select **not equal** in the **Alternative** field.

Step 5. Choose the **t-test (unequal variances)** option and select the **Display confidence interval** option with the desired confidence level (Figure N).

Step 6. Click **OK** (Figure O).

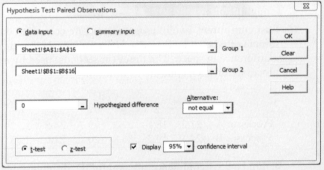

Figure N

Hypothesis Test: Paired Observations

1.207	confidence interval 95.% lower
11.793	confidence interval 95.% upper
5.293	margin of error

Figure O

SECTION 9.3   Exercises

Exercises 1–4 are the Check Your Understanding exercises located within the section.

Understanding the Concepts

In Exercises 5 and 6, fill in each blank with the appropriate word or phrase.

5. If the sample size is small, the differences between the items in the matched pairs must show no evidence of strong _____ and must contain no _____.

6. With matched pairs, the test for the difference between population means is the same as the test for a single population _____.

In Exercises 7 and 8, determine whether the statement is true or false. If the statement is false, rewrite it as a true statement.

7. Paired data are data for which each value in one sample can be matched with a corresponding value in another sample.

8. To compute the test statistic for a test with matched pairs, we must compute the standard deviations of the samples.

Practicing the Skills

9. Following is a sample of five matched pairs.

Sample 1	19	15	16	23	24
Sample 2	18	19	10	14	17

Let μ_1 and μ_2 represent the population means and let $\mu_d = \mu_1 - \mu_2$. A test will be made of the hypotheses H_0: $\mu_d = 0$ versus H_1: $\mu_d > 0$.

a. Compute the differences.

b. Compute the test statistic.

c. Can you reject H_0 at the $\alpha = 0.05$ level of significance?

d. Can you reject H_0 at the $\alpha = 0.01$ level of significance?

10. Following is a sample of ten matched pairs.

Sample 1	28	29	22	25	26	29	27	24	27	28
Sample 2	34	30	31	26	31	30	31	32	29	37

Let μ_1 and μ_2 represent the population means and let $\mu_d = \mu_1 - \mu_2$. A test will be made of the hypotheses H_0: $\mu_d = 0$ versus H_1: $\mu_d \neq 0$.

a. Compute the differences.

b. Compute the test statistic.

c. Can you reject H_0 at the $\alpha = 0.05$ level of significance?

d. Can you reject H_0 at the $\alpha = 0.01$ level of significance?

Working with the Concepts

11. Crossover trial: A crossover trial is a type of experiment used to compare two drugs. Subjects take one drug for a period of time, then switch to the other. The responses of the subjects are then compared using matched-pair methods. In an experiment to compare two pain relievers, seven subjects took one pain reliever for two weeks, then switched to the other. They rated their pain level from 1 to 10, with larger numbers representing higher levels of pain. The results were:

Subject							
	1	2	3	4	5	6	7
Drug A	6	3	4	5	7	1	4
Drug B	5	1	5	5	5	2	2

Can you conclude that the mean pain level is less with drug B?
a. State the null and alternate hypotheses.
b. Compute the test statistic.
c. State a conclusion. Use the $\alpha = 0.05$ level of significance.

12. **Comparing scales:** In an experiment to determine whether there is a systematic difference between the weights obtained with two different scales, 10 rock specimens were weighed, in grams, on each scale. The following data were obtained:

Specimen	Weight on Scale 1	Weight on Scale 2
1	11.23	11.27
2	14.36	14.41
3	8.33	8.35
4	10.50	10.52
5	23.42	23.41
6	9.15	9.17
7	13.47	13.52
8	6.47	6.46
9	12.40	12.45
10	19.38	19.35

Can you conclude that the mean weight differs between the scales?
a. State the null and alternate hypotheses.
b. Compute the test statistic.
c. State a conclusion. Use the $\alpha = 0.01$ level of significance.

13. **Strength of concrete:** The compressive strength, in kilopascals, was measured for concrete blocks from five different batches of concrete, both three and six days after pouring. The data are as follows:

	Block				
	1	2	3	4	5
After 3 days	1341	1316	1352	1355	1327
After 6 days	1376	1373	1366	1384	1358

Can you conclude that the mean strength after three days differs from the mean strength after six days?
a. State the null and alternate hypotheses.
b. Compute the test statistic.
c. State a conclusion. Use the $\alpha = 0.05$ level of significance.

14. **Truck pollution:** In an experiment to determine the effect of ambient temperature on the emissions of oxides of nitrogen (NO_x) of diesel trucks, ten trucks were run at temperatures of 40°F and 80°F. The emissions, in parts per billion, are presented in the following table.

Truck	40°F	80°F
1	834.7	815.2
2	753.2	765.2
3	855.7	842.6
4	901.2	797.1
5	785.4	764.3
6	862.9	819.5
7	882.7	783.6
8	740.3	694.5
9	748.0	772.9
10	848.6	794.7

Can you conclude that the mean emissions are higher at 40°?
a. State the null and alternate hypotheses.
b. Compute the test statistic.
c. State a conclusion. Use the $\alpha = 0.05$ level of significance.

15. **Fast computer:** Two microprocessors are compared on a sample of 6 benchmark codes to determine whether there is a difference in speed. The times (in seconds) used by each processor on each code are as follows:

	Code					
	1	2	3	4	5	6
Processor A	27.2	18.1	27.2	19.7	24.5	22.1
Processor B	24.1	19.3	26.8	20.1	27.6	29.8

a. Find a 95% confidence interval for the difference between the mean speeds.
b. A computer scientist claims that the mean speed is the same for both processors. Does the confidence interval contradict this claim?

16. **Brake wear:** For a sample of 9 automobiles, the mileage (in 1000s of miles) at which the original front brake pads were worn to 10% of their original thickness was measured, as was the mileage at which the original rear brake pads were worn to 10% of their original thickness. The results were as follows:

Car	Rear	Front
1	41.2	32.5
2	35.8	26.5
3	46.6	35.6
4	46.9	36.2
5	39.2	29.8
6	51.5	40.9
7	51.0	40.7
8	46.0	34.5
9	47.3	36.5

a. Construct a 99% confidence interval for the difference in mean lifetime between the front and rear brake pads.
b. An automotive engineer claims that the mean lifetime for rear brake pads is more than 10,000 miles more than the mean lifetime for front brake pads. Does the confidence interval contradict this claim?

17. **High cholesterol:** A group of eight individuals with high cholesterol levels were given a new drug that was designed to lower cholesterol levels. Cholesterol levels, in milligrams

per deciliter, were measured before and after treatment for each individual, with the following results:

Individual	Before	After
1	283	215
2	299	206
3	274	187
4	284	212
5	248	178
6	275	212
7	293	192
8	277	196

a. Construct a 90% confidence interval for the mean reduction in cholesterol level.

b. A physician claims that the mean reduction in cholesterol level is more than 80 milligrams per deciliter. Does the confidence interval contradict this claim?

18. **Tires and fuel economy:** A tire manufacturer is interested in testing the fuel economy for two different tread patterns. Tires of each tread type were driven for 1000 miles on each of nine different cars. The mileages, in miles per gallon, were as follows:

Car	Tread A	Tread B
1	24.7	20.3
2	22.5	19.0
3	24.0	22.5
4	26.9	23.1
5	22.5	20.9
6	23.5	23.6
7	22.7	21.4
8	19.7	18.2
9	27.5	25.9

a. Construct a 95% confidence interval for the mean difference in fuel economy.

b. Based on the confidence interval, is it reasonable to believe that the mean mileage may be the same for both types of tread?

19. **Interpret calculator display:** The following TI-84 Plus calculator display presents the results of a hypothesis test for the mean difference between matched pairs.

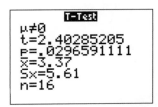

a. Is this a left-tailed test, a right-tailed test, or a two-tailed test?

b. How many degrees of freedom are there?

c. What is the P-value?

d. Can H_0 be rejected at the 0.05 level? Explain.

20. **Interpret calculator display:** The following TI-84 Plus calculator display presents the results of a hypothesis test for the mean difference between matched pairs.

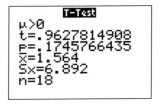

a. Is this a left-tailed test, a right-tailed test, or a two-tailed test?

b. How many degrees of freedom are there?

c. What is the P-value?

d. Can H_0 be rejected at the 0.05 level? Explain.

21. **Interpret computer output:** The following MINITAB output presents the results of a hypothesis test for a mean difference.

```
Paired T for X - Y

                N     Mean    StDev   SE Mean
X              12  134.233   68.376    19.739
Y              12  100.601   94.583    27.304
Difference     12  33.6316   59.511    17.179

95% lower bound for mean difference: 2.7793
T-Test of mean difference = 0 (vs > 0): T-Value = 1.96
                                       P-Value = 0.038
```

a. Is this a left-tailed test, a right-tailed test, or a two-tailed test?

b. Can H_0 be rejected at the 0.05 level? Explain.

c. Can H_0 be rejected at the 0.01 level? Explain.

22. **Interpret computer output:** The following MINITAB output presents the results of a hypothesis test for a mean difference.

```
Paired T for X - Y

               N     Mean    StDev   SE Mean
X              7   21.4236   10.145    3.8344
Y              7   19.2587    8.4049   3.1767
Difference     7    2.16485   5.3707   2.0299

95% CI for mean difference: (-2.802239, 7.131933)
T-Test of mean difference = 0 (vs not = 0): T-Value = 1.07
                                           P-Value = 0.327
```

a. Is this a left-tailed test, a right-tailed test, or a two-tailed test?

b. Can H_0 be rejected at the 0.05 level? Explain.

c. Can H_0 be rejected at the 0.01 level? Explain.

23. **Interpret calculator display:** The following TI-84 Plus calculator display presents a 95% confidence interval for the mean difference between matched pairs.

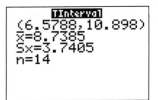

a. What is the point estimate of μ_d?
b. How many degrees of freedom are there?
c. Fill in the blanks: We are 95% confident that the mean difference is between _____ and _____ .

24. Interpret calculator display: The following TI-84 Plus calculator display presents a 99% confidence interval for the mean difference between matched pairs.

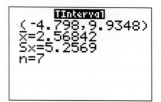

```
        TInterval
 (-4.798,9.9348)
 x̄=2.56842
 Sx=5.2569
 n=7
```

a. What is the point estimate of μ_d?
b. How many degrees of freedom are there?
c. Fill in the blanks: We are 99% confident that the mean difference is between _____ and _____ .

25. Interpret computer output: The following output from MINITAB presents a confidence interval for the mean difference between matched pairs.

	N	Mean	StDev	SE Mean
Difference	6	2.5324	3.6108	1.47410

99% CI for mean difference: (-3.411394, 8.476194)

a. What is the point estimate of μ_d?
b. How many degrees of freedom are there?
c. Fill in the blanks: We are _____ confident that the mean difference is between _____ and _____ .

26. Interpret computer output: The following output from MINITAB presents a confidence interval for the mean difference between matched pairs.

	N	Mean	StDev	SE Mean
Difference	12	16.412	3.626	1.04674

95% CI for mean difference: (14.10815, 18.71585)

a. What is the point estimate of μ_d?
b. How many degrees of freedom are there?
c. Fill in the blanks: We are _____ confident that the mean difference is between _____ and _____ .

Extending the Concepts

27. Refer to Exercise 14. Assume you did not know that the two samples were paired, so you used the methods of Section 9.1 to perform the test.
a. What is the P-value?
b. Explain why the P-value is greater when the methods of Section 9.1 are used.

Answers to Check Your Understanding Exercises for Section 9.3

1. a. H_0: $\mu_d = 0$, H_1: $\mu_d > 0$ **b.** $8, 5, -3, 1, 6$
c. $t = 1.731$
d. P-value is between 0.05 and 0.10 [Tech: 0.0793].
e. If H_0 is true, the probability of observing a value for the test statistic as extreme as or more extreme than the value actually observed is 0.0793. This is somewhat unusual, so there is some evidence against H_0. However, because $P > 0.05$, we do not reject H_0 at the $\alpha = 0.05$ level.
f. We conclude that the mean reading score may have remained the same after the reading program.

2. a. H_0: $\mu_d = 0$, H_1: $\mu_d > 0$

b. $9.5, 3.4, -3.8, 10.1, 8.9, 5.7$ **c.** $t = 2.612$
d. P-value is between 0.01 and 0.025 [Tech: 0.0238].
e. If H_0 is true, the probability of observing a value for the test statistic as extreme as or more extreme than the value actually observed is 0.0238. This is fairly unusual, so there is fairly strong evidence against H_0. In particular, because $P < 0.05$, we reject H_0 at the $\alpha = 0.05$ level.
f. We conclude that the mean rainfall was greater in year 2 than in year 1.

3. $22.3 < \mu_d < 40.5$
4. $2.2 < \mu_d < 9.8$

Chapter 9 Summary

Section 9.1: When we want to estimate the difference between two population means, we may use either independent samples or paired samples. Two samples are independent if the observations in one sample do not influence the observations in the other. Two samples are paired if each observation can be paired with an observation in the other. We can test hypotheses about the difference between two population means. The test statistic has a Student's t distribution. The number of degrees of freedom can be taken to be 1 less than the smaller sample size. A more complicated formula, used by technology, provides a greater number of degrees of freedom. The assumptions that are necessary for one-sample tests must hold for both populations. Welch's method can be used to construct confidence intervals for the difference between two means when the samples are independent.

Section 9.2: We can test hypotheses about the difference between two proportions. The test statistic has a standard normal distribution. The assumptions that are necessary for tests involving a single proportion must hold for both populations. We can also construct confidence intervals for the difference between two proportions. The assumptions necessary to construct a confidence interval for a single proportion must hold for both populations.

Section 9.3: When the data consist of matched pairs, we can test hypotheses about the difference between the population means by computing the difference between the values in each pair, then following the procedure for hypotheses about a single population mean. The assumptions required for a test of a population mean must hold for the population of differences. We can also construct confidence intervals for the difference between two population means using matched pairs.

Vocabulary and Notation

independent samples   400

matched pairs   433

paired samples   401

pooled proportion   419

pooled standard deviation   410

Welch's method   408

Important Formulas

Test statistic for the difference between two means, independent samples:

$$t = \frac{(\bar{x}_1 - \bar{x}_2) - (\mu_1 - \mu_2)}{\sqrt{\dfrac{s_1^2}{n_1} + \dfrac{s_2^2}{n_2}}}$$

Test statistic for the difference between two proportions:

$$z = \frac{\hat{p}_1 - \hat{p}_2}{\sqrt{\hat{p}(1 - \hat{p})\left(\dfrac{1}{n_1} + \dfrac{1}{n_2}\right)}}$$

where $\hat{p}$ is the pooled proportion $\hat{p} = \dfrac{x_1 + x_2}{n_1 + n_2}$

Confidence interval for the difference between two means, independent samples:

$$\bar{x}_1 - \bar{x}_2 - t_{\alpha/2}\sqrt{\dfrac{s_1^2}{n_1} + \dfrac{s_2^2}{n_2}} < \mu_1 - \mu_2 < \bar{x}_1 - \bar{x}_2 + t_{\alpha/2}\sqrt{\dfrac{s_1^2}{n_1} + \dfrac{s_2^2}{n_2}}$$

Confidence interval for the difference between two proportions:

$$\hat{p}_1 - \hat{p}_2 - z_{\alpha/2}\sqrt{\dfrac{\hat{p}_1(1 - \hat{p}_1)}{n_1} + \dfrac{\hat{p}_2(1 - \hat{p}_2)}{n_2}} < p_1 - p_2 < \hat{p}_1 - \hat{p}_2 + z_{\alpha/2}\sqrt{\dfrac{\hat{p}_1(1 - \hat{p}_1)}{n_1} + \dfrac{\hat{p}_2(1 - \hat{p}_2)}{n_2}}$$

Test statistic for the difference between two means, matched pairs:

$$t = \frac{\bar{d} - \mu_0}{s_d/\sqrt{n}}$$

Confidence interval for the difference between two means, matched pairs:

$$\bar{d} - t_{\alpha/2}\frac{s_d}{\sqrt{n}} < \mu_d < \bar{d} + t_{\alpha/2}\frac{s_d}{\sqrt{n}}$$

Chapter Quiz

In Exercises 1 and 2, determine whether the samples described are paired or independent.

1. A sample of 15 weight lifters is tested to see how much weight they can bench press. They then follow a special training program for three weeks, after which they are tested again. The samples are the amounts of weights that were lifted before and after the training program.

2. A sample of 20 weight lifters is tested to see how much weight they can bench press. Ten of them are chosen at random as the treatment group. They participate in a special training program for three weeks. The remaining 10 are the control group. They follow their usual program. At the end of three weeks, all 20 weight lifters are tested again and the increases in the amounts they can lift are recorded. The two samples are the increases in the amounts lifted by the treatment group and the control group.

3. A fleet of 100 taxis is divided into two groups of 50 cars each to determine whether premium gasoline reduces maintenance costs. Premium unleaded fuel is used in group A, while regular unleaded fuel is used in group B. The total maintenance cost for each vehicle during a one-year period is recorded. The question of interest is whether the mean maintenance cost is less for vehicles using premium fuel. To address this question, which of the following is the most appropriate type of hypothesis test?
    i. A test for the difference between two population means using independent samples
    ii. A test for the difference between two population proportions
    iii. A test for the difference between two population means using matched pairs

4. A simple random sample of 75 people is given a new drug that is designed to relieve pain. After taking this drug for a month, they switch to a standard drug. The question of interest is whether the proportion of people who experienced relief is greater when taking the new drug. To address this question, which of the following is the most appropriate type of hypothesis test?

   i. A test for the difference between two population means using independent samples

   ii. A test for the difference between two population proportions

   iii. A test for the difference between two population means using matched pairs

5. In a test of H_0: $p_1 = p_2$ versus H_1: $p_1 \neq p_2$, the value of the test statistic is $z = -1.21$. What do you conclude about the difference $p_1 - p_2$ at the $\alpha = 0.05$ level of significance?

6. For a test of H_0: $\mu_1 = \mu_2$ versus H_1: $\mu_1 \neq \mu_2$, the sample sizes were $n_1 = 15$ and $n_2 = 25$. How many degrees of freedom are there for the test statistic? Use the simple method.

7. In a set of 12 matched pairs, the mean difference was $\bar{d} = 18$ and the standard deviation of the differences was $s_d = 4$. Find the value of the test statistic for testing H_0: $\mu_d = 15$ versus H_1: $\mu_d > 15$. Can you reject H_0 at the $\alpha = 0.05$ level?

8. Two suppliers of machine parts delivered large shipments. A simple random sample of 150 parts was chosen from each shipment. For supplier A, 12 of the 150 parts were defective. For supplier B, 28 of the 150 parts were defective. The question of interest is whether the proportion of defective parts is greater for supplier B than for supplier A. Let p_1 be the population proportion of defective parts for supplier A, and let p_2 be the population proportion of defective parts for supplier B. State appropriate null and alternate hypotheses.

9. Refer to Exercise 8. Can you reject H_0 at the $\alpha = 0.01$ level? State a conclusion.

10. A simple random sample of 17 business majors from a certain university had a mean GPA of 2.81 with a standard deviation of 0.27. A simple random sample of 23 psychology majors was selected from the same university, and their mean GPA was 2.97 with a standard deviation of 0.23. Boxplots show that it is reasonable to assume that the populations are approximately normal. The question of interest is whether the mean GPAs differ between business majors and psychology majors. Let μ_1 be the population mean GPA for business majors, and let μ_2 be the population mean GPA for psychology majors. State the null and alternate hypotheses.

11. Refer to Exercise 10. Can you reject H_0 at the $\alpha = 0.05$ level? State a conclusion.

12. In a survey of 300 randomly selected female and 240 male holiday shoppers, 87 of the females and 98 of the males stated that they will wait until the last week before Christmas to finish buying gifts. Let p_1 be the population proportion of males who will wait until the last week and let p_2 be the population proportion of females. Compute a point estimate for the difference $p_1 - p_2$.

13. Eight students in a particular college course are given a pretest at the beginning of the semester and are then given the same exam at the end to test what they have learned. The exam scores at the beginning and at the end are given in the following table.

	Student							
	1	**2**	**3**	**4**	**5**	**6**	**7**	**8**
End	83	71	79	95	84	72	69	78
Beginning	72	58	76	81	69	63	71	77

Let μ_d be the mean difference End $-$ Beginning. Construct a 99% confidence interval for the difference μ_d.

14. A random sample of 76 residents in a small town had a mean annual income of $34,214, with a sample standard deviation of $2171. In a neighboring town, a random sample of 88 residents had a mean annual income of $31,671 with a sample standard deviation of $3279. Let μ_1 be the population mean annual income in the first town, and let μ_2 be the population mean annual income in the neighboring town. Construct a 90% confidence interval for the difference $\mu_1 - \mu_2$.

15. In a poll of 100 voters, 57 said they were planning to vote for the incumbent governor, and 48 said they were planning to vote for the incumbent mayor. Explain why these data should not be used to construct a confidence interval for the difference between the proportions of voters who plan to vote for the governor and those who plan to vote for the mayor.

Review Exercises

1. Sick days: A large company is considering a policy of flextime, in which employees can choose their own work schedules within broad limits. The company is interested to determine whether this policy would reduce the number of sick days taken. They chose two simple random samples of 100 employees each. The employees in one sample were allowed to choose their own schedules. The other sample was a control group. Employees in that sample were required to come to work according to a schedule set by management. At the end of one year, the employees in the flextime group had a sample mean of 4.7 days missed, with a sample standard deviation of 3.1 days. The employees in the control group had a sample mean of 5.9 days missed, with a sample standard deviation of 3.9 days. Perform a hypothesis test to measure the strength of the evidence that the mean number of days missed is less in the flextime group. State the null and alternate hypotheses, find the P-value, and state your conclusion. Use the $\alpha = 0.01$ level of significance.

2. Political polling: In a certain state, a referendum is being held to determine whether the transportation authority should issue additional highway bonds. A sample of 500 voters is taken in county A, and 285 say that they favor the bond proposal. A sample of

600 voters is taken in county B, and 305 say that they favor the bond issue. Perform a hypothesis test to measure the strength of the evidence that the proportion of voters who favor the proposal is greater in county A than in county B. State the null and alternate hypotheses, find the P-value, and state your conclusion. Use the $\alpha = 0.05$ level of significance.

3. **Sales commissions:** A company studied two programs for compensating its sales staff. Nine salespeople participated in the study. In program A, salespeople were paid a higher salary, plus a small commission for each item they sold. In program B, they were paid a lower salary with a larger commission. Following are the amounts sold, in thousands of dollars, for each salesperson on each program.

	Salesperson								
Program	**1**	**2**	**3**	**4**	**5**	**6**	**7**	**8**	**9**
A	55	22	34	22	25	61	55	36	68
B	53	24	36	28	31	61	58	38	72

Can you conclude that the mean sales differ between the two programs? Use the $\alpha = 0.05$ level of significance.

4. **Interpret calculator display:** The following TI-84 Plus calculator display presents the results of a hypothesis test for the difference between two means. The sample sizes are $n_1 = 18$ and $n_2 = 16$.

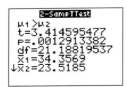

a. Is this a left-tailed test, a right-tailed test, or a two-tailed test?
b. How many degrees of freedom did the calculator use?
c. What is the P-value?
d. Can you reject H_0 at the $\alpha = 0.05$ level?

5. **Interpret computer output:** The following MINITAB output presents a 95% confidence interval for the difference between two means.

```
Two-sample T for Population1 vs Population2

              N      Mean      StDev    SE Mean
Population1   55   16.48435   10.23430  1.52564
Population2   47   18.32197    8.38450  1.22301


Difference = mu (Treatment1) - mu (Treatment2)
Estimate for difference:  -1.83762
95% upper bound for difference:  2.22314
T-Test of difference = 0 (vs < 0): T-Value = -0.997  P-Value = 0.161  DF = 99
```

a. Is this a left-tailed test, a right-tailed test, or a two-tailed test?
b. How many degrees of freedom did MINITAB use?
c. What is the P-value?
d. Can you reject H_0 at the $\alpha = 0.05$ level?

6. **Interpret calculator display:** The following TI-84 Plus calculator display presents the results of a hypothesis test for the difference between two proportions. The sample sizes are $n_1 = 125$ and $n_2 = 150$.

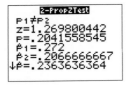

a. Is this a left-tailed test, a right-tailed test, or a two-tailed test?
b. What is the P-value?
c. Can you reject H_0 at the $\alpha = 0.05$ level?

7. Interpret computer output: The following MINITAB output presents the results of a hypothesis test for the difference between two proportions.

```
Test and CI for Two Proportions: A, B

Variable      X       N     Sample p
A            31      45     0.688889
B            23      58     0.396552

Difference = p (A) - p (B)
Estimate for difference:  0.292337
95% Lower Bound for difference: 0.128108
Test for difference = 0 (vs > 0):  Z = 2.95  P-Value = 0.003
```

    a. Is this a left-tailed test, a right-tailed test, or a two-tailed test?
    b. What is the P-value?
    c. Can you reject H_0 at the $\alpha = 0.05$ level?

8. Exercise and heart rate: A simple random sample of seven people embarked on a program of regular aerobic exercise. Their heart rates, in beats per minute, were measured before and after, with the following results:

	\multicolumn{7}{c}{**Person**}					
	1	**2**	**3**	**4**	**5**	**6**	**7**
Before	81	84	79	85	79	84	87
After	73	77	73	78	71	75	80

Construct a 95% confidence interval for the mean reduction in heart rate.

9. Recovery time from surgery: A new postsurgical treatment is being compared with a standard treatment. Seven subjects receive the new treatment, while seven others (the controls) receive the standard treatment. The recovery times, in days, are given below.

    Control: 18 23 24 30 32 35 39   Treatment: 12 13 15 19 20 21 24

Construct a 98% confidence interval for the reduction in the mean recovery times associated with treatment.

10. Polling results: A simple random sample of 400 voters in the town of East Overshoe was polled, and 242 said they planned to vote in favor of a bond issue to raise money for elementary schools. A simple random sample of 300 voters in West Overshoe was polled, and 161 said they were in favor. Construct a 98% confidence interval for the difference between the proportions of voters in the two towns who favor the bond issue.

11. Treating bean plants: In a study to measure the effect of an herbicide on the phosphate content of bean plants, a sample of 75 plants treated with the herbicide had a mean phosphate concentration (in percent) of 3.52 with a standard deviation of 0.41, and 100 untreated plants had a mean phosphate concentration of 5.82 with a standard deviation of 0.52. Construct a 95% confidence interval for the difference in mean phosphate concentration between treated and untreated plants.

12. Interpret calculator display: The following TI-84 Plus calculator display presents a 95% confidence interval for the difference between two means. The sample sizes are $n_1 = 85$ and $n_2 = 71$.

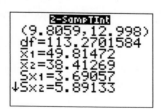

    a. Find the point estimate of $\mu_1 - \mu_2$.
    b. How many degrees of freedom did the calculator use?
    c. Fill in the blanks: We are 95% confident that the difference between the means is between _____ and _____.

13. Interpret computer output: The following MINITAB output display presents a 95% confidence interval for the difference between two means.

```
        N      Mean    StDev   SE Mean
A      12     9.5713   1.025   0.2959
B       8     7.2198   5.173   1.8289


Difference = mu (A) - mu (B)
Estimate for difference: 2.3515
95% CI for difference:   (-2.02947, 6.73247)    DF = 7
```

a. Find the point estimate of $\mu_1 - \mu_2$.

b. How many degrees of freedom did MINITAB use?

c. Fill in the blanks: We are _____ confident that the difference between the means is between _____ and _____.

14. **Interpret calculator display:** The following TI-84 Plus calculator display presents a 95% confidence interval for the mean difference between matched pairs.

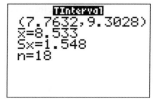

a. Find the point estimate of μ_d.

b. How many degrees of freedom are there?

c. Fill in the blanks: We are 95% confident that the mean difference is between _____ and _____.

15. **Interpret computer output:** The following output from MINITAB presents a confidence interval for the mean difference between matched pairs.

```
                N      Mean    StDev    SE Mean
Difference     15     9.8612   3.7149   0.95918


95% CI for mean difference:   (7.803957, 11.918443)
```

a. Find the point estimate of μ_d.

b. How many degrees of freedom are there?

c. Fill in the blanks: We are _____ confident that the mean difference is between _____ and _____.

Write About It

1. Provide an example, real or imagined, of a hypothesis test for the difference between two means.

2. Describe under what circumstances a hypothesis test for the difference between two proportions would be performed. Provide an example.

3. Describe the differences between performing a hypothesis test for $\mu_1 - \mu_2$ with paired samples and performing the same test for independent samples.

4. Why is it necessary for all values in the confidence interval to be positive to conclude that $\mu_1 > \mu_2$? What would have to be true to conclude that $\mu_1 < \mu_2$?

5. In what ways is the procedure for constructing a confidence interval for the difference between two proportions similar to constructing a confidence interval for one proportion? In what ways is it different?

6. Provide an example of two samples that are independent. Explain why these samples are independent.

7. Provide an example of two samples that are paired. Explain why these samples are paired.

Case Study: Evaluating The Assignment Of Subjects In A Clinical Trial

In the chapter opener, we described a study in which patients were assigned to receive either a new treatment or a standard treatment for the prevention of heart failure. A total of 1820 patients participated, with 1089 receiving the new treatment and 731 receiving the standard treatment. The assignment was not made by simple random sampling; instead, an algorithm was used that was designed to produce balance between the groups. The following table presents summary statistics describing several health characteristics of the people in each group.

Characteristic	Standard Treatment		New Treatment	
	Mean	**Standard Deviation**	**Mean**	**Standard Deviation**
Age	64	11	65	11
Systolic blood pressure	121	18	124	17
Diastolic blood pressure	71	10	72	10

Characteristic	Standard Treatment	New Treatment
	Percentage with the Characteristic	**Percentage with the Characteristic**
Treatment for hypertension	63.2	63.7
Atrial fibrillation	12.6	11.1
Diabetes	30.6	30.2
Cigarette smoking	12.8	11.4
Coronary bypass surgery	28.5	29.1

1. For each health characteristic, perform a test of the null hypothesis that the group means or group proportions are equal versus the alternative that they are not equal. State the P-value for each test.

2. Based on the P-values computed in Exercise 1, for which health characteristics does it appear that the assignment to groups is not balanced? Use the 0.05 level of significance.

3. For each health characteristic, construct a 95% confidence interval for the difference between the group means or group proportions.

4. Based on the confidence intervals in Exercise 3, for which health characteristics does it appear that the assignment to groups is not balanced?

5. Are the answers to Exercises 2 and 4 the same? Explain.

6. Based on the confidence intervals in Exercise 3, does it appear that the imbalance is large enough to be of concern? Explain.

Tests with Qualitative Data

Introduction

Do graduate schools discriminate against women? This issue was addressed in a famous study carried out at the University of California at Berkeley. The following table presents the numbers of male and female applicants to six of the most popular departments at the University of California at Berkeley. Out of 2691 male applicants, 1198, or 44.5%, were accepted. Out of 1835 female applicants, only 557, or 30.4%, were accepted. Is this difference due to discrimination against women? In the case study at the end of the chapter, we will use the methods presented in this chapter to determine the real reason for this difference.

Gender	Accept	Reject	Total
Male	1198	1493	2691
Female	557	1278	1835
Total	1755	2771	4526

SECTION 10.1   Testing Goodness of Fit

Objectives

1. Find critical values of the chi-square distribution
2. Perform goodness-of-fit tests

Objective 1 Find critical values of the chi-square distribution

Recall: Qualitative data classify individuals into categories.

The Chi-Square Distribution

In this chapter, we will introduce hypothesis tests for qualitative data, also called categorical data. These tests are based on the **chi-square distribution**. The test statistic used for these tests is called the **chi-square statistic**, denoted χ^2. The symbol χ is the Greek letter chi (pronounced "kigh"; rhymes with sky). We find critical values for this statistic by using the chi-square distribution. We will begin by reviewing the features of this distribution.

There are actually many different chi-square distributions, each with a different number of degrees of freedom. Figure 10.1 presents chi-square distributions for several different degrees of freedom. There are two important points to notice.

- The chi-square distribution is not symmetric. It is skewed to the right.
- Values of the χ^2 statistic are always greater than or equal to 0. They are never negative.

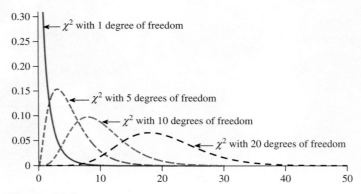

Figure 10.1 Chi-square distributions with various degrees of freedom

Finding critical values for the chi-square distribution

We find right-tail critical values for the chi-square distribution. These values can be found using Table A.4.

EXAMPLE 10.1

Find a critical value

Find the $\alpha = 0.05$ critical value for the chi-square distribution with 12 degrees of freedom.

Solution

The critical value is found at the intersection of the row corresponding to 12 degrees of freedom and the column corresponding to $\alpha = 0.05$. The critical value is 21.026.

Degrees of Freedom	Area in Right Tail									
	0.995	0.99	0.975	0.95	0.90	0.10	0.05	0.025	0.01	0.005
⋮	⋮	⋮	⋮	⋮	⋮	⋮	⋮	⋮	⋮	⋮
10	2.156	2.558	3.247	3.940	4.865	15.987	18.307	20.483	23.209	25.188
11	2.603	3.053	3.816	4.575	5.578	17.275	19.675	21.920	24.725	26.757
12	3.074	3.571	4.404	5.226	6.304	18.549	21.026	23.337	26.217	28.300
13	3.565	4.107	5.009	5.892	7.042	19.812	22.362	24.736	27.688	29.819
14	4.075	4.660	5.629	6.571	7.790	21.064	23.685	26.119	29.141	31.319
15	4.601	5.229	6.262	7.261	8.547	22.307	24.996	27.488	30.578	32.801
⋮	⋮	⋮	⋮	⋮	⋮	⋮	⋮	⋮	⋮	⋮

Figure 10.2 presents the chi-square distribution with 12 degrees of freedom, with the $\alpha = 0.05$ critical value labeled.

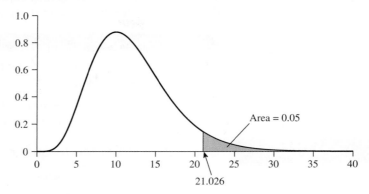

Figure 10.2 The area to the right of 21.026 is 0.05, so 21.026 is the $\alpha = 0.05$ critical value.

Check Your Understanding

1. Find the $\alpha = 0.05$ critical value for the chi-square distribution with 18 degrees of freedom.

2. Find the $\alpha = 0.10$ critical value for the chi-square distribution with 4 degrees of freedom.

3. Find the area to the right of 29.141 under the chi-square distribution with 14 degrees of freedom.

4. Find the area to the right of 46.979 under the chi-square distribution with 30 degrees of freedom.

Answers are on page 462.

Objective 2 Perform goodness-of-fit tests

Goodness-of-Fit Tests

Imagine that you want to determine whether a coin is fair. You could toss the coin a number of times, and compute the sample proportion $\hat{p}$ of heads. You could then use a test for a population proportion (Section 8.4) to test the hypotheses H_0: $p = 0.5$ versus H_1: $p \neq 0.5$. The test for a population proportion is designed for an experiment with two possible outcomes, such as the toss of a coin. Sometimes we work with experiments that have more than two possible outcomes. For example, imagine that a gambler wants to test a die to determine whether it is fair. The roll of a die has six possible outcomes: 1, 2, 3, 4, 5, and 6; and the die is fair if each of these outcomes is equally likely. The gambler rolls the die 60 times, and counts the number of times each number comes up. These counts, which are called the **observed frequencies**, are presented in Table 10.1.

Table 10.1 Observed Frequencies for 60 Rolls of a Die

Outcome	1	2	3	4	5	6
Observed	12	7	14	15	4	8

Explain It Again

Hypotheses for goodness-of-fit tests: The null hypothesis always specifies a probability for each category. The alternate hypothesis says that some or all of these probabilities differ from the true probabilities of the categories.

The gambler wants to perform a hypothesis test to determine whether the die is fair. The null hypothesis for this test says that the die is fair; in other words, it says that each of the six outcomes has probability 1/6 of occurring. Let p_1 be the probability of rolling a 1, p_2 be the probability of rolling a 2, and so on. Then the null hypothesis is

$$H_0: p_1 = p_2 = p_3 = p_4 = p_5 = p_6 = 1/6$$

The alternate hypothesis says that the roll of a die does not follow the distribution specified by H_0; in other words, it states that not all of the p_i are equal to 1/6.

Computing expected frequencies

To test H_0, we begin by computing **expected frequencies**. The expected frequencies are the mean counts that would occur if H_0 were true.

> **DEFINITION**
>
> If the probabilities specified by H_0 are p_1, p_2, ..., and the total number of trials is n, the expected frequencies are
>
> $$E_1 = np_1, \quad E_2 = np_2, \quad \text{and so on}$$

EXAMPLE 10.2

Computing expected frequencies

Compute the expected frequencies for the die example.

Solution

The probabilities specified by H_0 are $p_1 = p_2 = \cdots = p_6 = 1/6$. The total number of trials is $n = 60$. Therefore, the expected frequencies are

$$E_1 = E_2 = E_3 = E_4 = E_5 = E_6 = (60)(1/6) = 10$$

Table 10.2 presents both observed and expected frequencies for the die example.

Table 10.2 Observed and Expected Frequencies

Outcome	1	2	3	4	5	6
Observed	12	7	14	15	4	8
Expected	10	10	10	10	10	10

Explain It Again

The expected frequency: The expected value of a binomial random variable is $E = np$. Here n is the total number of trials, and p is the probability of a particular outcome.

Check Your Understanding

5. A researcher wants to determine whether children are more likely to be born on certain days of the week. She will sample 350 births and record the day of the week for each. The null hypothesis is that a birth is equally likely to occur on any day of the week. Compute the expected frequencies.

6. A researcher wants to test the hypothesis that births are more likely to occur on weekdays. The null hypothesis is that 17% of births occur on each of the days Monday through Friday, 10% occur on Saturday, and 5% occur on Sunday. If 350 births are sampled, find the expected frequencies.

Answers are on page 462.

If H_0 is true, the observed and expected frequencies should be fairly close. The larger the differences are between the observed and expected frequencies, the stronger the evidence is against H_0. We compute a test statistic that measures how large these differences are. As mentioned previously, the statistic is called the chi-square statistic, denoted χ^2.

> **DEFINITION**
>
> Let k be the number of categories, let O_1, ..., O_k be the observed frequencies, and let E_1, ..., E_k be the expected frequencies. The chi-square statistic is
>
> $$\chi^2 = \sum \frac{(O - E)^2}{E}$$

When H_0 is true, the chi-square statistic has approximately a chi-square distribution, provided that all the expected frequencies are 5 or more.

When H_0 is true, the statistic

$$\chi^2 = \sum \frac{(O - E)^2}{E}$$

has a chi-square distribution with $k - 1$ degrees of freedom, where k is the number of categories, provided that all the expected frequencies are greater than or equal to 5.

We will first describe how to perform a hypothesis test using the critical value method and Table A.4. Then we will describe how to use the P-value method with technology.

Performing a Goodness-of-Fit Test

Step 1: State the null and alternate hypotheses. The null hypothesis specifies a probability for each category. The alternate hypothesis says that some or all of the actual probabilities differ from those specified by H_0.

Step 2: Compute the expected frequencies and check to be sure that all of them are 5 or more. If they are, then proceed.

Step 3: Choose a significance level α.

Step 4: Compute the test statistic $\chi^2 = \sum \dfrac{(O - E)^2}{E}$.

Step 5: Find the critical value from Table A.4, using $k - 1$ degrees of freedom, where k is the number of categories. If χ^2 is greater than or equal to the critical value, reject H_0. Otherwise, do not reject H_0.

Step 6: State a conclusion.

EXAMPLE 10.3 Perform a goodness-of-fit test

Table 10.3 presents the observed frequencies for the die example. Can you conclude at the $\alpha = 0.05$ level that the die is not fair?

Table 10.3

Category	Observed
1	12
2	7
3	14
4	15
5	4
6	8

Table 10.4

Category	Observed	Expected
1	12	10
2	7	10
3	14	10
4	15	10
5	4	10
6	8	10

Solution

Step 1: State the null and alternate hypotheses. The null hypothesis says that the die is fair, and the alternate hypothesis says that the die is not fair, so we have

H_0: $p_1 = p_2 = p_3 = p_4 = p_5 = p_6 = 1/6$ $\qquad$ H_1: Some or all of the p_i differ from $1/6$

Step 2: Compute the expected frequencies. The expected frequencies were computed in Example 10.2. We present them in Table 10.4. They are all greater than 5, so we proceed.

Step 3: Choose a level of significance. We will use $\alpha = 0.05$.

Step 4: Compute the value of the test statistic. The following table presents the calculations.

Category	O	E	$O - E$	$(O-E)^2$	$\dfrac{(O-E)^2}{E}$
1	12	10	2	4	0.4
2	7	10	−3	9	0.9
3	14	10	4	16	1.6
4	15	10	5	25	2.5
5	4	10	−6	36	3.6
6	8	10	−2	4	0.4

$$\chi^2 = \sum \frac{(O - E)^2}{E} = 9.4$$

The value of the test statistic is $\chi^2 = 9.4$.

Step 5: Find the critical value. There are six categories, so there are $6 - 1 = 5$ degrees of freedom. From Table A.4, we find that the $\alpha = 0.05$ critical value for 5 degrees of freedom is 11.070. The value of the test statistic is $\chi^2 = 9.4$. Because $9.4 < 11.070$, we do not reject H_0.

Step 6: State a conclusion. There is not enough evidence to conclude that the die is unfair.

| EXAMPLE 10.4 | Perform a goodness-of-fit test using technology |

The following TI-84 Plus display presents the results of Example 10.3.

```
χ²GOF-Test
χ²=9.4
P=.0941343839
df=5
CNTRB={.4 .9 1...
```

Most of the output is straightforward. The first, second, and third lines present the value of the χ^2 statistic, the P-value, and the degrees of freedom, respectively. The last line, labeled "CNTRB," presents the quantities $\dfrac{(O - E)^2}{E}$ for the first two categories.

The P-value is 0.0941. Because $P > 0.05$, we do not reject H_0 at the $\alpha = 0.05$ level. This conclusion is the same as the one we reached when we used the critical value method in Example 10.3.

Step-by-step instructions for using technology are presented in the Using Technology section on page 459.

| EXAMPLE 10.5 | Perform a goodness-of-fit test |

A poll conducted by the General Social Survey asked 1155 people whether they thought that people with high incomes should pay a greater or smaller percentage of their income in tax than low-income people. The results are presented in the following table.

Category	Observed
Pay much more	218
Pay somewhat more	497
Pay the same	425
Pay less	15

Five years earlier, it was determined that 18.5% believed that the rich should pay much more, 39.2% believed they should pay somewhat more, 41.2% believed they should pay the same, and 1.1% believed they should pay less. Can we conclude that the current percentages differ from these? Use the $\alpha = 0.05$ level of significance.

Solution

Step 1: State the null and alternate hypotheses. The null hypothesis is H_0: $p_1 = 0.185$, $p_2 = 0.392$, $p_3 = 0.412$, $p_4 = 0.011$. The alternate hypothesis states that some of the probabilities are not equal to the values specified by H_0.

Step 2: Compute the expected frequencies. The number of trials is $n = 1155$. The expected frequencies are

$$E_1 = np_1 = (1155)(0.185) = 213.675 \qquad E_2 = np_2 = (1155)(0.392) = 452.76$$

$$E_3 = np_3 = (1155)(0.412) = 475.86 \qquad E_4 = np_4 = (1155)(0.011) = 12.705$$

All the expected frequencies are 5 or more, so we proceed.

Step 3: Choose a significance level. We will use $\alpha = 0.05$.

Step 4: Compute the test statistic. Using the observed and expected frequencies, we compute the value of the test statistic to be

$$\chi^2 = \frac{(218 - 213.675)^2}{213.675} + \frac{(497 - 452.76)^2}{452.76} + \frac{(425 - 475.86)^2}{475.86} + \frac{(15 - 12.705)^2}{12.705} = 10.261$$

Step 5: Find the critical value. There are four categories, so there are $4 - 1 = 3$ degrees of freedom. From Table A.4, we find that the $\alpha = 0.05$ critical value for 3 degrees of freedom is 7.815. The value of the test statistic is $\chi^2 = 10.261$. Because $10.261 > 7.815$, we reject H_0.

Step 6: State a conclusion. We conclude that the distribution of opinions on this issue changed during the 5 years prior to the survey.

Check Your Understanding

7. Following are observed frequencies for five categories:

Category	1	2	3	4	5
Observed	25	14	23	6	2

   a. Compute the expected frequencies for testing
      H_0: $p_1 = 0.3$, $p_2 = 0.25$, $p_3 = 0.2$, $p_4 = 0.15$, $p_5 = 0.1$.
   b. One of the observed frequencies is less than 5. Is the chi-square test appropriate?
   c. Compute the value of χ^2.
   d. How many degrees of freedom are there?
   e. Find the level $\alpha = 0.05$ critical value.
   f. Do you reject H_0 at the 0.05 level?
   g. Find the level $\alpha = 0.01$ critical value.
   h. Do you reject H_0 at the 0.01 level?

8. For the data in Exercise 7:
   a. Compute the expected frequencies for testing
      H_0: $p_1 = 0.4$, $p_2 = 0.3$, $p_3 = 0.1$, $p_4 = 0.15$, $p_5 = 0.05$.
   b. Is it appropriate to perform a chi-square test for the hypothesis in part (a)? Explain.

Answers are on page 462.

USING TECHNOLOGY

We use Example 10.3 to illustrate the technology steps.

TI-84 PLUS

Testing goodness of fit

Step 1. Enter observed frequencies into **L1** in the data editor and expected frequencies into **L2**. Figure A illustrates this for Example 10.3.

Step 2. Press **STAT** and highlight the **TESTS** menu. Select χ^2**GOF-Test** and press **ENTER** (Figure B). The χ^2**GOF-Test** menu appears.

Step 3. In the **Observed** field, enter **L1**, and in the **Expected** field, enter **L2**.

Step 4. Enter the degrees of freedom in the **df** field. For Example 10.3, there are 5 degrees of freedom (Figure C).

Step 5. Highlight **Calculate** and press **ENTER** (Figure D).

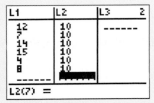

Figure A

Figure B

Figure C

Figure D

EXCEL

Testing goodness of fit

This procedure requires the **MegaStat** EXCEL add-in to be loaded. The **MegaStat** add-in may be downloaded from www.mhhe.com/megastat.

Step 1. Enter the observed frequencies from Example 10.3 into **Column A** and the expected frequencies into **Column B** (Figure E).

Step 2. Click on the **MegaStat** menu, select **Chi-Square/Crosstab**, then **Goodness of Fit Test...**

Step 3. Enter the range of cells for the observed frequencies in the **Observed values** field and the range of cells for the expected frequencies in the **Expected values** field (Figure F).

Step 4. Click **OK** (Figure G).

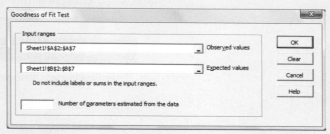

Figure F

Goodness of Fit Test

	A	B
1	**Observed**	**Expected**
2	12	10
3	7	10
4	14	10
5	15	10
6	4	10
7	8	10

Figure E

observed	expected	O - E	(O - E)²/ E	% of chisq
12	10.000	2.000	0.400	4.26
7	10.000	-3.000	0.900	9.57
14	10.000	4.000	1.600	17.02
15	10.000	5.000	2.500	26.60
4	10.000	-6.000	3.600	38.30
8	10.000	-2.000	0.400	4.26
60	60.000	0.000	9.400	100.00

9.40 chi-square
5 df
.0941 p-value

Figure G

SECTION 10.1 Exercises

Exercises 1–8 are the Check Your Understanding exercises located within the section.

Understanding the Concepts

In Exercises 9 and 10, fill in each blank with the appropriate word or phrase.

9. For the goodness-of-fit test to be valid, each of the _____ frequencies must be at least 5.

10. In a goodness-of-fit test, we reject H_0 if the _____ frequencies are much different from the expected frequencies.

In Exercises 11 and 12, determine whether the statement is true or false. If the statement is false, rewrite it as a true statement.

11. The chi-square distribution is symmetric.

12. The alternate hypothesis for a goodness-of-fit test says that some of the probabilities differ from those specified by the null hypothesis.

Practicing the Skills

13. Find the $\alpha = 0.05$ critical value for the chi-square statistic with 14 degrees of freedom.

14. Find the $\alpha = 0.01$ critical value for the chi-square statistic with 5 degrees of freedom.

15. Find the area to the right of 24.725 under the chi-square distribution with 11 degrees of freedom.

16. Find the area to the right of 40.256 under the chi-square distribution with 30 degrees of freedom.

17. For the following observed and expected frequencies:

Observed	9	22	53	9	7
Expected	15	20	40	15	10

a. Compute the value of χ^2.
b. How many degrees of freedom are there?
c. Test the hypothesis that the distribution of the observed frequencies is as given by the expected frequencies. Use the $\alpha = 0.05$ level of significance.

18. For the following observed and expected frequencies:

Observed	43	42	31	19	34	32
Expected	44	44	33	15	36	29

a. Compute the value of χ^2.
b. How many degrees of freedom are there?
c. Test the hypothesis that the distribution of the observed frequencies is as given by the expected frequencies. Use the $\alpha = 0.01$ level of significance.

19. Following are observed frequencies. The null hypothesis is H_0: $p_1 = 0.5$, $p_2 = 0.3$, $p_3 = 0.15$, $p_4 = 0.05$.

Category	1	2	3	4
Observed	106	64	24	6

a. Compute the expected frequencies.
b. Compute the value of χ^2.
c. How many degrees of freedom are there?
d. Test the hypothesis that the distribution of the observed frequencies is as given by the null hypothesis. Use the $\alpha = 0.01$ level of significance.

20. Following are observed frequencies. The null hypothesis is H_0: $p_1 = 0.4$, $p_2 = 0.25$, $p_3 = 0.05$, $p_4 = 0.1$, $p_5 = 0.2$.

Category	1	2	3	4	5
Observed	50	51	14	12	23

a. Compute the expected frequencies.
b. Compute the value of χ^2.
c. How many degrees of freedom are there?
d. Test the hypothesis that the distribution of the observed frequencies is as given by the null hypothesis. Use the $\alpha = 0.05$ level of significance.

Working with the Concepts

21. Is the lottery fair? Powerball is a multistate lottery in which players try to guess the numbers that will turn up in a drawing of numbered balls. One of the balls drawn is the "Powerball." Matching the number drawn on the Powerball increases one's winnings. From 2005 through 2008, the Powerball was drawn from a collection of 42 balls numbered 1 through 42. A total of 350 drawings were held. For the purposes of this exercise, we grouped the numbers into six categories: 1–7, 8–14, and so on. If the lottery is fair, then the winning number is equally likely to occur in any category. Following are the observed frequencies.

Category	1–7	8–14	15–21	22–28	29–35	36–42
Observed	60	71	68	49	52	50

Source: powerball.com

a. Compute the expected frequencies.
b. Compute the value of χ^2.
c. How many degrees of freedom are there?
d. Test the hypothesis that each of the categories is equally likely. Use the $\alpha = 0.05$ level of significance.

22. Grade distribution: A statistics teacher claims that, on the average, 20% of her students get a grade of A, 35% get a B, 25% get a C, 10% get a D, and 10% get an F. The grades of a random sample of 100 students were recorded. The following table presents the results.

Grade	A	B	C	D	F
Observed	29	42	20	5	4

a. How many of the students in the sample got an A? How many got an F?
b. Compute the expected frequencies.
c. Which grades were given more often than expected? Which grades were given less often than expected?
d. What is the value of χ^2?
e. How many degrees of freedom are there?
f. Test the hypothesis that the grades follow the distribution claimed by the teacher. Use the 0.05 level of significance.

23. False alarm: The numbers of false fire alarms were counted each month at a number of sites. The results are given in the following table.

Month	Number of Alarms
January	32
February	15
March	37
April	38
May	45
June	48
July	46
August	42
September	34
October	36
November	28
December	26

Source: *Journal of Architectural Engineering* 5:62–65

Test the hypothesis that false alarms are equally likely to occur in any month. Use the $\alpha = 0.01$ level of significance.

24. Crime rates: The U.S. Census Bureau computed the proportion of violent crimes in the United States in 2007 falling into each of four categories. A simple random sample of 500 violent crimes committed in California during 2007 were categorized in the same way. The following table presents the results.

Category	U.S. Proportion	California Frequency
Murder	0.012	6
Forcible rape	0.064	21
Robbery	0.317	177
Aggravated assault	0.607	296

Can you conclude that the proportions of crimes in the various categories in California differ from those in the United States as a whole? Use the 0.05 level of significance.

25. Where do you live? The U.S. Census Bureau computed the proportion of U.S. residents who lived in each of four geographic regions in 1990. Then a simple random sample was drawn of 300 people living in the United States in 2006. The following table presents the results.

Region	1990 Proportion	2006 Frequency
Northeast	0.204	54
Midwest	0.240	57
South	0.344	108
West	0.212	81

Can you conclude that the proportions of people living in the various regions changed between 1990 and 2006? Use the 0.05 level of significance.

26. **Abortion policy:** A CBS News/New York Times poll taken on November 16, 2009, asked 1167 adult Americans to state their opinion on the availability of abortions. The following table presents the results, along with the proportions of people who held these views in 1995.

Opinion	1995 Proportion	2009 Frequency
Generally available	0.37	397
Available with limits	0.41	467
Should not be permitted	0.20	268
Don't know/No answer	0.02	35

Can you conclude that the proportions of people giving the various responses changed between 1995 and 2009? Use the 0.01 level of significance.

27. **Economic future:** In 2010, the economy in many parts of the world, including the United States, was going through difficult times. A poll taken on February 10, 2010, obtained responses from 1061 adult Americans to the question, "Do you think the economy is getting better, getting worse, or staying about the same?" The following table presents the results, along with the proportions of people who gave these responses in 2009.

View	2009 Proportion	2010 Frequency
Better	0.24	260
Same	0.48	487
Worse	0.28	314

Source: CBS News/New York Times poll

Can you conclude that the proportions of people giving the various responses changed between 2009 and 2010? Use the

0.01 level of significance. Do these results suggest that Americans were more pessimistic about their economic future in 2010 than in 2009?

28. **Guess the answer:** A statistics instructor gave a four-question true–false quiz to his class of 150 students. The results were as follows.

Number correct	0	1	2	3	4
Observed	2	13	29	71	35

The instructor thinks that the students may have answered the questions by guessing, so that the probability that any given answer is correct is 0.5. Under this null hypothesis, the number of correct answers has a binomial distribution with 4 trials and success probability 0.5. Perform a chi-square test of this hypothesis. Can you reject H_0 at the $\alpha = 0.05$ level?

Extending the Concepts

29. **Fair die?** A gambler rolls a die 600 times to determine whether or not it is fair. Following are the results.

Outcome	1	2	3	4	5	6
Observed	113	101	106	81	108	91

a. Let p_1 be the probability that the die comes up 1, let p_2 be the probability that the die comes up 2, and so on. Use the chi-square distribution to test the null hypothesis, at the $\alpha = 0.05$ level of significance, that the die is fair:

b. The gambler decides to use the test for proportions (discussed in Section 8.4) to test H_0: $p_i = 1/6$ for each p_i. Find the P-values for each of these tests.

c. Show that the hypothesis H_0: $p_4 = 1/6$ is rejected at level 0.05.

Answers to Check Your Understanding Exercises for Section 10.1

1. 28.869

2. 7.779

3. 0.01

4. 0.025

5.
Sunday	Monday	Tuesday	Wednesday	Thursday	Friday	Saturday
50	50	50	50	50	50	50

6.
Sunday	Monday	Tuesday	Wednesday	Thursday	Friday	Saturday
17.5	59.5	59.5	59.5	59.5	59.5	35.0

7. a.
1	2	3	4	5
21.0	17.5	14.0	10.5	7.0

b. Yes, because all the expected frequencies are 5 or more.

c. 12.748   d. 4   e. 9.488   f. Yes

g. 13.277   h. No

8. a.
1	2	3	4	5
28.0	21.0	7.0	10.5	3.5

b. No, one of the expected frequencies is less than 5.

SECTION 10.2   Tests for Independence and Homogeneity

Objectives

1. Interpret contingency tables
2. Perform tests of independence
3. Perform tests of homogeneity

Objective 1 Interpret
contingency tables

Contingency Tables

Do some college majors require more studying than others? The 2009 National Survey of Student Engagement asked a number of college freshmen what their major was and how many hours per week they spent studying, on average. A sample of 1000 of these students was chosen, and the numbers of students in each category are presented in Table 10.5.

Table 10.5 Observed Frequencies

Hours Studying Per Week	Major			
	Humanities	Social Science	Business	Engineering
0–10	68	106	131	40
11–20	119	103	127	81
More Than 20	70	52	51	52

Table 10.5 is called a **contingency table**. A contingency table relates two qualitative variables. One of the variables, called the **row variable**, has one category for each row of the table. The other variable, called the **column variable**, has one category for each column of the table. In Table 10.5, hours studying is the row variable and major is the column variable. In general, it does not matter which variable is the row variable and which is the column variable. We could just as well have made major the row variable and hours studying the column variable. The intersection of a row and a column is called a **cell**. For example, the number 68 appears in the upper left cell, which tells us that 68 students were humanities majors who study 0–10 hours per week.

Objective 2 Perform tests of
independence

Performing a Test of Independence

We are interested in determining whether the distribution of one variable differs, depending on the value of the other variable. If so, the variables are *dependent*. If the distribution of one variable is the same for all the values of the other variable, the variables are *independent*. For Table 10.5, the null and alternate hypotheses are

H_0: Hours studying and major are independent.

H_1: Hours studying and major are not independent.

We will use the chi-square statistic to test the null hypothesis that major and hours studying are independent. If we reject H_0, we will conclude that the variables are dependent. The values in Table 10.5 are the observed frequencies. To compute the value of χ^2, we must compute the expected frequencies.

Computing the expected frequencies

The first step in computing the expected frequencies is to compute the row and column totals. For example, the total in the first row is

Total number of students studying 0–10 hours $= 68 + 106 + 131 + 40 = 345$

The total in the first column is

Total number of humanities majors $= 68 + 119 + 70 = 257$

Table 10.6 on page 464 presents Table 10.5 with the row and column totals included. The total number of individuals in the table, 1000, is included as well. This total is often called the **grand total**.

As with any hypothesis test, we begin by assuming the null hypothesis to be true. The null hypothesis says that hours studying and major are independent. We can now use the Multiplication Rule for Independent Events to compute the expected frequencies. For example,

P(Study 0–10 hours and Humanities major) $= P$(Study 0–10 hours)P(Humanities major)

Explain It Again

Independence: If hours studied and major are independent, then the distribution of hours studied will be the same for all majors, and the distribution of majors will be the same for all categories of hours studied.

Recall: The Multiplication Rule for Independent Events says that if events *E* and *F* are independent, then $P(E \text{ and } F) = P(E) \cdot P(F)$.

Table 10.6 Observed Frequencies with Row and Column Totals

Hours Studying Per Week	Major				Row Total
	Humanities	Social Science	Business	Engineering	
0–10	68	106	131	40	345
11–20	119	103	127	81	430
More Than 20	70	52	51	52	225
Column Total	257	261	309	173	1000

Now out of a total of 1000 students, 345 studied 0–10 hours per week. Therefore,

$$P(\text{Study 0–10 hours}) = \frac{345}{1000}$$

Out of a total of 1000 students, 257 were humanities majors. Therefore,

$$P(\text{Humanities major}) = \frac{257}{1000}$$

The Multiplication Rule for Independent Events tells us that if H_0 is true, then

$$P(\text{Study 0–10 hours and Humanities major}) = \left(\frac{345}{1000}\right)\left(\frac{257}{1000}\right)$$

We obtain the expected frequency for those who study 0–10 hours and are humanities majors by multiplying this probability by the grand total, which is 1000.

$$\text{Expected frequency} = 1000\left(\frac{345}{1000}\right)\left(\frac{257}{1000}\right)$$

Before calculating this quantity, simplify it as follows:

$$\text{Expected frequency} = \cancel{1000}\left(\frac{345}{\cancel{1000}}\right)\left(\frac{257}{1000}\right) = \frac{345 \cdot 257}{1000} = 88.665$$

We see that the expected frequency can be computed as

$$\text{Expected frequency} = \frac{\text{Row total} \cdot \text{Column total}}{\text{Grand total}}$$

SUMMARY

To find the expected frequency for a cell, multiply the row total by the column total, then divide by the grand total.

$$E = \frac{\text{Row total} \cdot \text{Column total}}{\text{Grand total}}$$

The expected frequency for a cell represents the number of individuals we would expect to find in that cell under the assumption that the two variables are independent. If the differences between the observed and expected frequencies tend to be large, we will reject the null hypothesis of independence.

Check Your Understanding

1. The following contingency table presents observed frequencies. Compute the expected frequencies.

	1	2	3
A	13	8	27
B	18	21	35
C	19	13	15
D	20	17	27

Answer is on page 473.

Recall: We can use the chi-square statistic whenever the expected frequencies are all at least 5.

Once the expected frequencies are computed, we check to determine whether all of them are at least 5. If so, we use the chi-square statistic as a test statistic. The number of degrees of freedom is $(r - 1)(c - 1)$, where r is the number of rows and c is the number of columns. We will first describe how to perform a hypothesis test using the critical value method and Table A.4. Then we will describe how to use the P-value method with technology.

Performing a Test of Independence

Step 1: State the null and alternate hypotheses. The null hypothesis says that the row and column variables are independent. The alternate hypothesis says that they are not independent.

Step 2: Compute the row and column totals.

Step 3: Compute the expected frequencies:

$$E = \frac{\text{Row total} \cdot \text{Column total}}{\text{Grand total}}$$

Check to be sure that all the expected frequencies are at least 5.

Step 4: Choose a level of significance α, and compute the test statistic:

$$\chi^2 = \sum \frac{(O - E)^2}{E}$$

Step 5: Find the critical value from Table A.4, using $(r - 1)(c - 1)$ degrees of freedom, where r is the number of rows and c is the number of columns. If χ^2 is greater than or equal to the critical value, reject H_0. Otherwise, do not reject H_0.

Step 6: State a conclusion.

EXAMPLE 10.6   Perform a test of independence

Perform a test of the null hypothesis that major and hours studying are independent, using the data in Table 10.6. Use $\alpha = 0.01$.

Solution

Step 1: State the null and alternate hypotheses. The hypotheses are

H_0: Major and hours studying are independent.

H_1: Major and hours studying are not independent.

Step 2: Compute the row and column totals. These are shown in Table 10.6.

Step 3: Compute the expected frequencies. As an example, we compute the expected frequency for the cell corresponding to business major, studying 11–20 hours. The row total is 430, the column total is 309, and the grand total is 1000. The expected frequency is

$$E = \frac{430 \cdot 309}{1000} = 132.87$$

Table 10.7 on page 466 presents the expected frequencies. All the expected frequencies are at least 5, so we may proceed.

Step 4: Choose a level of significance and compute the test statistic. We will use the $\alpha = 0.01$ level of significance. To compute the test statistic, we use the observed frequencies in Table 10.6 and the expected frequencies in Table 10.7:

$$\chi^2 = \frac{(68 - 88.665)^2}{88.665} + \cdots + \frac{(52 - 38.925)^2}{38.925} = 34.638$$

Table 10.7 Expected Frequencies

Hours Studying Per Week	Major			
	Humanities	Social Science	Business	Engineering
0–10	88.665	90.045	106.605	59.685
11–20	110.510	112.230	132.870	74.390
More Than 20	57.825	58.725	69.525	38.925

Step 5: Find the critical value. There are $r = 3$ rows and $c = 4$ columns, so the number of degrees of freedom is $(3 - 1)(4 - 1) = 6$. From Table A.4, we find that the critical value corresponding to 6 degrees of freedom and $\alpha = 0.01$ is 16.812. The value of the test statistic is 34.638. Because $34.638 > 16.812$, we reject H_0.

Step 6: State a conclusion. We conclude that the choice of major and the number of hours spent studying are not independent. The numbers of hours that students study varies among majors.

Check Your Understanding

2. The following contingency table presents observed frequencies.

	Observed		
	1	**2**	**3**
A	8	13	14
B	18	1	15
C	16	17	15
D	19	19	8

a. Compute the expected frequencies.
b. One of the observed frequencies is less than 5. Is it appropriate to perform a test of independence? Explain.
c. Compute the value of the test statistic.
d. How many degrees of freedom are there?
e. Do you reject H_0 at the $\alpha = 0.05$ level?

Answers are on page 473.

EXAMPLE 10.7 **Perform a test of independence with technology**

Use technology to test the hypothesis of independence of major and hours studied.

Solution
We present the results from MINITAB.

In the MINITAB output, each cell (intersection of row and column) contains three numbers. The top number is the observed frequency, the middle number is the expected frequency, and the bottom number is the contribution $\frac{(O - E)^2}{E}$ to the chi-square statistic from that cell. The P-value is given as 0.000. This means that the P-value is less than 0.0005, so when rounded to three decimal places, the value is 0.000.

Because $P < 0.01$, we reject H_0 at the $\alpha = 0.01$ level, and conclude that the choice of major and the number of hours studying are not independent. This conclusion is the same as the one we reached in Example 10.6 using the critical value method.

Step-by-step instructions for using technology are presented in the Using Technology section on page 469.

```
Chi-Square Test: Humanities, Science, Business, Engineering

Expected counts are printed below observed counts
Chi-Square contributions are printed below expected counts

          Humanities   Science   Business   Engineering   Total
    1          68         106        131           40       345
             88.67       90.05     106.61        59.69
             4.816       2.827      5.582        6.492

    2         119         103        127           81       430
            110.51      112.23     132.87        74.39
             0.652       0.759      0.259        0.587

    3          70          52         51           52       225
             57.83       58.73      69.53        38.93
             2.563       0.770      4.936        4.392

  Total       257         261        309          173      1000

Chi-Sq = 34.638, DF = 6, P-Value = 0.000
```

Objective 3 Perform tests of homogeneity

Tests of Homogeneity

In the contingency tables we have seen so far, the individuals in the table were sampled from a single population. For each individual, the values of both the row and column variables were random. In some cases, values of one of the variables (say, the row variable) are assigned by the investigator, and are not random. In these cases, we consider the rows as representing separate populations, and we are interested in testing the hypothesis that the distribution of the column variable is the same for each row. This is known as a **test of homogeneity**. Following is an example.

The drugs telmisartan and ramipril are designed to reduce high blood pressure. In a clinical trial to compare the effectiveness of these drugs in preventing heart attacks, 25,620 patients were divided into three groups. One group took one telmisartan tablet each day, another took one ramipril tablet each day, and the third group took one tablet of each drug each day. The patients were followed for 56 months, and the numbers who suffered fatal and nonfatal heart attacks were counted. Table 10.8 presents the results.

Table 10.8

	Fatal Heart Attack	Nonfatal Heart Attack	No Heart Attack
Telmisartan only	598	431	7513
Ramipril only	603	400	7573
Both drugs	620	424	7458

Source: www.clinicaltrials.gov

In this table, the patients were assigned a row category, so only the column variable is random. We are interested in performing a test of homogeneity, to test the hypothesis that the distribution of outcomes is the same for each row. We have already seen the method for performing a test of homogeneity. It is the same as the method for performing a test of independence.

The method for performing a test of homogeneity is identical to the method for performing a test of independence.

EXAMPLE 10.8

Perform a test of homogeneity

Explain It Again

Interpretation of a test of homogeneity: If we reject the null hypothesis, we conclude that the distributions are not all the same, but we cannot tell which ones are different.

Refer to Table 10.8. Test the hypothesis that the distribution of outcomes is the same for all three treatment groups. Use the $\alpha = 0.05$ level.

Solution

We follow the same steps as for a test of independence.

Step 1: State the null and alternate hypotheses. The null hypothesis says that the distribution of outcomes (fatal heart attack, nonfatal heart attack, no heart attack) is the same for all the drug treatments. The alternate hypothesis says that the distribution of outcomes is not the same for all the treatments.

Step 2: Compute the row and column totals. These are shown in the following table.

	Fatal Heart Attack	Nonfatal Heart Attack	No Heart Attack	Row Total
Telmisartan only	598	431	7513	8542
Ramipril only	603	400	7573	8576
Both drugs	620	424	7458	8502
Column Total	1821	1255	22,544	25,620

Step 3: Compute the expected frequencies. As an example, we compute the expected frequency for the cell corresponding to Telmisartan, Fatal heart attack. The row total is 8542, the column total is 1821, and the grand total is 25,620. The expected frequency is

$$\frac{8542 \cdot 1821}{25,620} = 607.14$$

The following table presents the expected frequencies. All the expected frequencies are at least 5, so we may proceed.

	Fatal Heart Attack	Nonfatal Heart Attack	No Heart Attack
Telmisartan only	607.14	418.43	7516.43
Ramipril only	609.56	420.10	7546.34
Both drugs	604.30	416.47	7481.23

Step 4: Choose a level of significance and compute the test statistic. We will use the $\alpha = 0.05$ level of significance. The test statistic is

$$\chi^2 = \frac{(598 - 607.14)^2}{607.14} + \cdots + \frac{(8502 - 7481.23)^2}{7481.23} = 2.259$$

Step 5: Find the critical value. There are $r = 3$ rows and $c = 3$ columns, so the number of degrees of freedom is $(3 - 1)(3 - 1) = 4$. From Table A.4, we find that the critical value corresponding to 4 degrees of freedom and $\alpha = 0.05$ is 9.488. The value of the test statistic is 2.259. Since $2.259 < 9.488$, we do not reject H_0.

Step 6: State a conclusion. There is not enough evidence to conclude that the distribution of outcomes is different for different drug treatments.

USING TECHNOLOGY

We use Table 10.5 to illustrate the technology steps.

TI-84 PLUS

Testing for independence

Step 1. Press **2nd**, then **MATRIX** to access the Matrix menu. Highlight **EDIT** and press **ENTER**. Select **1:[A]**.

Step 2. To input the data from Table 10.5, enter the size of the matrix as **3 × 4**. Enter each of the data values (Figure A; note that the last column does not show).

Step 3. Press **STAT** and highlight the **TESTS** menu. Select χ^2–**Test** and press **ENTER** (Figure B). The χ^2–**Test** menu appears.

Step 4. Enter **[A]** in the **Observed** field. The default value for the **Expected** field is **[B]** (Figure C).

Step 5. Highlight **Calculate** and press **ENTER** (Figure D).

Note: The expected frequencies may be viewed by accessing matrix **[B]** from the Matrix menu.

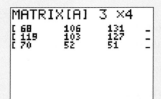

Figure A

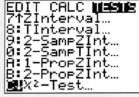

Figure B

Figure C

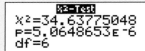

Figure D

MINITAB

Testing for independence

Step 1. Enter the data from Table 10.5 as shown in Figure E.

Step 2. Click on **Stat**, then **Tables**, then **Chi-Square Test**.

Step 3. Select all columns (**Humanities–Engineering**) in the **Columns containing the table** field (Figure F).

Step 4. Click **OK** (Figure G).

↓	C1	C2	C3	C4
	Humanities	Social Science	Business	Engineering
1	68	106	131	40
2	119	103	127	81
3	70	52	51	52

Figure E

Chi-Square Test (Table in Worksheet)

C1	Humanities
C2	Social Scie
C3	Business
C4	Engineering

Columns containing the table:

Humanities-Engineering

Select

Help   OK   Cancel

Figure F

Chi-Square Test: Humanities, Social Science, Business, Engineering

Expected counts are printed below observed counts
Chi-Square contributions are printed below expected counts

	Humanities	Social Science	Business	Engineering	Total
1	68	106	131	40	345
	88.67	90.05	106.61	59.69	
	4.816	2.827	5.582	6.492	
2	119	103	127	81	430
	110.51	112.23	132.87	74.39	
	0.652	0.759	0.259	0.587	
3	70	52	51	52	225
	57.83	58.73	69.53	38.93	
	2.563	0.770	4.936	4.392	
Total	257	261	309	173	1000

Chi-Sq = 34.638, DF = 6, P-Value = 0.000

Figure G

EXCEL

Testing for independence

This procedure requires the **MegaStat** EXCEL add-in to be loaded. The **MegaStat** add-in may be downloaded from www.mhhe.com/megastat.

Step 1. Enter the data from Table 10.5 as shown in Figure H.

Step 2. Click on the **MegaStat** menu, select **Chi-Square/Crosstab**, then **Contingency Table...**

Step 3. Enter the range of cells for the data (including labels) in the **Input range** field and choose the **chi-square** option (Figure I).

Step 4. Click **OK** (Figure J).

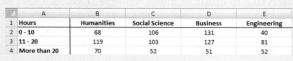

	A	B	C	D	E
1	Hours	Humanities	Social Science	Business	Engineering
2	0 - 10	68	106	131	40
3	11 - 20	119	103	127	81
4	More than 20	70	52	51	52

Figure H

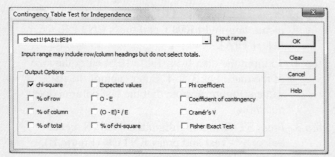

Figure I

Chi-square Contingency Table Test for Independence

	Humanities	Social Science	Business	Engineering	Total
0 - 10	68	106	131	40	345
11 - 20	119	103	127	81	430
More than 20	70	52	51	52	225
Total	257	261	309	173	1000

34.64 chi-square
6 df
5.06E-06 p-value

Figure J

SECTION 10.2   Exercises

Exercises 1 and 2 are the Check Your Understanding exercises located within the section.

Understanding the Concepts

In Exercises 3–5, fill in each blank with the appropriate word or phrase.

3. To calculate the expected frequencies, we must know the row totals, the column totals, and the _____ total.

4. We reject H_0 if the value of the test statistic is _____ the critical value.

5. In the test for _____, the null hypothesis is that the distribution of the column variable is the same in each row.

In Exercises 6–8, determine whether the statement is true or false. If the statement is false, rewrite it as a true statement.

6. A contingency table containing observed values has three rows and four columns. The number of degrees of freedom for the chi-square statistic is 7.

7. In a test of homogeneity, the alternate hypothesis says that the distributions in the rows are the same.

8. The procedure for testing homogeneity is the same as the procedure for testing independence.

Practicing the Skills

9. For the given table of observed frequencies:

	1	2	3
A	15	10	12
B	3	11	11
C	9	14	12

   a. Compute the row totals, the column totals, and the grand total.
   b. Construct the corresponding table of expected frequencies.
   c. Compute the value of the chi-square statistic.
   d. How many degrees of freedom are there?
   e. If appropriate, perform a test of independence, using the $\alpha = 0.05$ level of significance. If not appropriate, explain why.

10. For the given table of observed frequencies:

	1	2	3
A	25	4	11
B	3	3	4
C	42	3	5

   a. Compute the row totals, the column totals, and the grand total.
   b. Construct the corresponding table of expected frequencies.

c. Compute the value of the chi-square statistic.
d. How many degrees of freedom are there?
e. If appropriate, perform a test of independence, using the $\alpha = 0.05$ level of significance. If not appropriate, explain why.

Working with the Concepts

11. Carbon monoxide: A recent study examined the effects of carbon monoxide exposure on a group of construction workers. The following table presents the numbers of workers who reported various symptoms, along with the shift (morning, evening, or night) that they worked.

	Shift		
	Morning	**Evening**	**Night**
Influenza	16	13	18
Headache	24	33	6
Weakness	11	16	5
Shortness of Breath	7	9	9

Source: *Journal of Environmental Science and Health* A39:1129–1139

a. Compute the expected frequencies under the null hypothesis.
b. Compute the value of the chi-square statistic.
c. How many degrees of freedom are there?
d. Test the hypothesis of independence. Use the $\alpha = 0.05$ level of significance. What do you conclude?

12. Beryllium disease: Beryllium is an extremely lightweight metal that is used in many industries, such as aerospace and electronics. Long-term exposure to beryllium can cause people to become sensitized. Once an individual is sensitized, continued exposure can result in chronic beryllium disease, which involves scarring of the lungs. In a study of the effects of exposure to beryllium, workers were categorized by their duration of exposure (in years) and by their disease status (diseased, sensitized, or normal). The results were as follows:

	Duration of Exposure		
	< 1	**1 to < 5**	**≥ 5**
Diseased	10	8	23
Sensitized	9	19	11
Normal	70	136	206

Source: *Environmental Health Perspectives* 113:1366–1372

a. Compute the expected frequencies under the null hypothesis.
b. Compute the value of the chi-square statistic.
c. How many degrees of freedom are there?
d. Test the hypothesis of independence. Use the $\alpha = 0.01$ level of significance. What do you conclude?

13. No smoking: The General Social Survey conducted a poll of 668 adults in which the subjects were asked whether they agree that the government should prohibit smoking in public places. In addition, each was asked how many people lived in his or her household. The results are summarized in the following contingency table.

	Household Size				
	1	**2**	**3**	**4**	**5**
Agree	73	109	48	37	37
No Opinion	31	52	29	20	18
Disagree	42	71	38	40	23

a. Compute the expected frequencies.
b. Compute the value of the test statistic.
c. How many degrees of freedom are there?
d. Test the hypothesis of independence. Use the $\alpha = 0.01$ level of significance. What do you conclude?

14. How big is your family? The General Social Survey asked a sample of 2780 adults how many children they had, and also how many siblings (brothers and sisters) they had. The results are summarized in the following contingency table.

	Number of Children					
Siblings	**0**	**1**	**2**	**3**	**4**	**More Than 4**
0	60	19	34	15	10	6
1	189	97	163	63	29	12
2	179	98	137	81	41	20
3	124	85	132	83	31	16
4	85	53	88	61	32	22
More Than 4	128	121	175	156	77	58

a. Compute the expected frequencies.
b. Compute the value of the test statistic.
c. How many degrees of freedom are there?
d. Test the hypothesis of independence. Use the $\alpha = 0.05$ level of significance. What do you conclude?

15. Age discrimination: The following table presents the numbers of employees, by age group, who were promoted, or not promoted, in a sample drawn from a certain industry during the past year.

	Age			
	Under 30	**30–39**	**40–49**	**50 and Over**
Promoted	16	22	26	15
Not Promoted	38	39	45	38

Can you conclude that the people in some age groups are more likely to be promoted than those in other age groups? Use the $\alpha = 0.05$ level of significance.

16. Schools and museums: Do people who are interested in educational issues visit museums more often than people who are not? In 2008, the General Social Survey asked 1499 people how interested they were in educational issues, and how often they had visited a science museum in the past year. The following table presents the results.

	Number of Visits		
	None	**One**	**More Than One**
Very Interested	512	138	58
Moderately Interested	460	98	34
Not Interested	163	21	14

Can you conclude that the number of visits to a science museum is related to interest in educational issues? Use the $\alpha = 0.01$ level of significance.

17. Genes: At a certain genetic locus on a chromosome, each individual has one of three different DNA sequences (alleles). The three alleles are denoted A, B, C. At another genetic locus on the same chromosome, each organism has one of three alleles, denoted 1, 2, 3. Each individual therefore has one of nine possible allele pairs: A1, A2, A3, B1, B2, B3, C1, C2, or C3. These allele pairs are called *haplotypes*. The loci are said to be in *linkage equilibrium* if the two alleles in an individual's haplotype are independent. Haplotypes were determined for 316 individuals. The following MINITAB output presents the results of a chi-square test for independence.

```
Chi-Square Test: A, B, C

Expected counts are printed below observed counts
Chi-Square contributions are printed below expected counts

              A       B       C   Total
    1        66      44      34     144
          61.06   47.39   35.54
          0.399   0.243   0.067

    2        36      38      20      94
          39.86   30.94   23.20
          0.374   1.613   0.442

    3        32      22      24      78
          33.08   25.67   19.25
          0.035   0.525   1.170

Total      134     104      78     316

Chi-Sq = 4.868, DF = 4, P-Value = 0.301
```

a. How many individuals were observed to have the haplotype B3?
b. What is the expected number of individuals with the haplotype A2?
c. Which of the nine haplotypes was least frequently observed?
d. Which of the nine haplotypes has the smallest expected count?
e. What is the *P*-value?
f. Can you conclude at the $\alpha = 0.05$ level that the loci are not in linkage equilibrium (i.e., not independent)? Explain.
g. Can you conclude that the loci are in linkage equilibrium (i.e., independent)? Explain.

18. **Product rating:** A firm that is planning to market a new cleaning product surveyed 1268 users of the leading competitor's product. Each person rated the product as fair, good, or excellent. In addition, each person stated whether they use the product rarely (1), occasionally (2), or frequently (3). The firm is interested in determining whether the rating given to the product is independent of the frequency with which the product is used. The following MINITAB output presents the results of a chi-square test for independence.

```
Chi-Square Test: Fair, Good, Excellent

Expected counts are printed below observed counts
Chi-Square contributions are printed below expected counts

             Fair     Good  Excellent  Total
    1          97      136         92    325
            79.97   141.23     103.81
            3.627    0.193      1.343

    2         128      234        155    517
           127.21   224.66     165.13
            0.005    0.388      0.621

    3          87      181        158    426
           104.82   185.12     136.06
            3.030    0.091      3.536

Total       312      551        405   1268

Chi-Sq = 12.835, DF = 4, P-Value = 0.012
```

a. How many individuals who rarely use the product rated it good?
b. What is the expected number of individuals who used the product occasionally and rated it excellent?
c. Which of the nine combinations was least frequently observed?
d. Which of the nine combinations has the smallest expected count?
e. What is the *P*-value?
f. Can you conclude at the $\alpha = 0.05$ level that rating and frequency of use are not independent? Explain.

Extending the Concepts

19. **Degrees of freedom:** In the following contingency table, the row and column totals are presented, but the data for one row and one column have been omitted. Thus, there are data for only $r - 1$ rows and $c - 1$ columns. Show that you can calculate the missing values.

	1	2	3	4	Row Total
A	10	52	29	—	98
B	25	38	10	—	92
C	—	—	—	—	147
Column Total	65	117	83	72	

Conclude that if $(r - 1)(c - 1)$ entries in the table are known, the remaining ones are automatically determined, so there are no degrees of freedom left.

20. **Are you an optimist?** The General Social Survey asked 1373 men and 993 women in the United States whether they agreed that they were generally optimistic about the future. The results are presented in the following table.

	Male	Female
Optimistic	1148	815
Pessimistic	225	178

a. Compute the value of the χ^2 statistic for testing the hypothesis that the opinion on optimism is independent of gender.

b. Compute the proportion of men who were optimistic.

c. Compute the proportion of women who were optimistic.

d. Compute the test statistic z for testing the null hypothesis that the two proportions are equal versus the alternative that they are not equal.

e. Show that $\chi^2 = z^2$.

f. Use technology to find the P-value for each test. Show that the P-values are equal.

g. Conclude that when a contingency table has two rows and two columns, the chi-square test is equivalent to the test for the difference between proportions.

Answers to Check Your Understanding Exercises for Section 10.2

1.

	1	2	3
A	14.421	12.155	21.425
B	22.232	18.738	33.030
C	14.120	11.901	20.979
D	19.227	16.206	28.567

2. a.

	1	2	3
A	13.098	10.736	11.166
B	12.724	10.429	10.847
C	17.963	14.724	15.313
D	17.215	14.110	14.675

b. Yes, because all the expected frequencies are 5 or more.

c. 20.973   **d.** 6   **e.** Yes

Chapter 10 Summary

Section 10.1: In this section, we introduced the chi-square test for goodness of fit. This test is based on the chi-square statistic. The data consist of observed frequencies in several categories. The null hypothesis specifies a distribution, which consists of a probability for each category. The chi-square statistic is used to test this null hypothesis. The degrees of freedom is 1 less than the number of categories. We reject H_0 if the value of the test statistic is greater than or equal to the critical value.

Section 10.2: In this section, we studied contingency tables. A contingency table relates the values of two qualitative variables. When both row and column totals are random, we test the hypothesis that the two variables are independent. When one of the variables is assigned, and the other is random, we test the hypothesis of homogeneity. The procedure is the same for both tests. The test statistic is the chi-square statistic with $(r-1)(c-1)$ degrees of freedom, where r is the number of rows and c is the number of columns. We reject H_0 if the value of the test statistic is greater than or equal to the critical value.

Vocabulary and Notation

chi-square distribution   454
chi-square statistic   454
cell   463
column variable   463

contingency table   463
expected frequency   456
goodness-of-fit test   455
grand total   463

observed frequency   455
row variable   463
test of independence   463
test of homogeneity   467

Important Formulas

Chi-square statistic:
$$\chi^2 = \sum \frac{(O-E)^2}{E}$$

Expected frequency for goodness-of-fit:
$$E = np$$

Expected frequency for independence or homogeneity:
$$E = \frac{\text{Row total} \cdot \text{Column total}}{\text{Grand total}}$$

Chapter Quiz

1. A contingency table containing observed values has four rows and five columns. The value of the chi-square statistic for testing independence is 22.87. Is H_0 rejected at the $\alpha = 0.05$ level?

2. A goodness-of-fit test is performed to test the null hypothesis that each of the six faces on a die has probability 1/6 of coming up. The null hypothesis is rejected. True or false: We can conclude that the probability that a 6 comes up is not equal to 1/6.

3. A test of homogeneity is performed and the null hypothesis is rejected. True or false: We can conclude that the distributions are not the same in every row.

Exercises 4–9 refer to the following data:

Electric motors are assembled on four different production lines. Random samples of motors are taken from each line and inspected. The numbers that pass and that fail the inspection are counted for each line, with the following results:

	Line			
	1	**2**	**3**	**4**
Pass	482	467	458	404
Fail	57	59	37	47

4. State the appropriate null and alternate hypotheses for determining whether to conclude that the failure rates differ among the four lines.

5. Compute the expected frequencies.

6. Compute the value of the chi-square statistic.

7. How many degrees of freedom are there?

8. Find the critical value for the $\alpha = 0.05$ level of significance.

9. State a conclusion.

Exercises 10–15 refer to the following data:

Anthropologists can estimate the birthrate of an ancient society by studying the age distribution of skeletons found in ancient cemeteries. An article in the journal *Current Anthropology* presented the following numbers of skeletons of various ages found at two such sites.

	Ages of Skeletons		
Site	**0–4 Years**	**5–19 Years**	**20 Years or More**
Casa da Moura	27	61	126
Wandersleben	38	60	118

Source: *Current Anthropology* 43:637–650

10. State the appropriate null and alternate hypotheses for determining whether to conclude that the age distributions differ between the two sites.

11. Compute the expected frequencies.

12. Compute the value of the chi-square statistic.

13. How many degrees of freedom are there?

14. Find the critical value for the $\alpha = 0.01$ level of significance.

15. State a conclusion.

Review Exercises

Exercises 1–3 refer to the following data:

A hypothetical sample of 200 families, each with four children, was selected, and the number of boys was recorded for each. The results are presented in the following table.

Number of boys	0	1	2	3	4
Observed	10	57	80	38	15

1. **Null hypothesis:** Let p_0 be the probability that a family with four children has no boys, p_1 be the probability that a family has one boy, and so on. The null hypothesis is that the number of boys in a four-child family follows a binomial distribution with $n = 4$ and $p = 0.5$. State the null hypothesis in terms of p_0, p_1, p_2, p_3, and p_4.

2. **Expected frequencies:** Compute the expected frequencies.

3. **State a conclusion:** Can you conclude that the distribution of boys differs from the binomial with $p = 0.5$? Use the $\alpha = 0.05$ level of significance.

Exercises 4–6 refer to the following data:

The General Social Survey polled 1280 men and 1531 women to determine their level of education. The results are presented in the following table.

	Educational Level				
	No High School Diploma	High School Diploma	Associate's Degree	Bachelor's Degree	Graduate Degree
Men	178	608	96	248	150
Women	186	827	128	259	131

4. **Expected frequencies:** Compute the expected frequencies under the null hypothesis of independence.

5. **Test statistic:** Compute the value of the chi-square statistic.

6. **State a conclusion:** Can you conclude that education level is independent of gender? Use the $\alpha = 0.01$ level of significance.

Exercises 7–9 refer to the following data:

At an assembly plant for light trucks, routine monitoring of the quality of welds yielded the following data.

	Number of Welds		
	High Quality	Moderate Quality	Low Quality
Day Shift	467	191	42
Evening Shift	445	171	34
Night Shift	254	129	17

7. **Expected frequencies:** Compute the expected frequencies under the null hypothesis of homogeneity.

8. **Test statistic:** Compute the value of the chi-square statistic.

9. **State a conclusion:** Can you conclude that the quality varies among shifts? Use the $\alpha = 0.01$ level of significance.

Exercises 10–15 refer to the following data:

In a hypothetical study, four hospitals were compared with regard to the outcome of a particular type of surgery. For each patient at each hospital, the outcome was classified as Substantial improvement, Some improvement, or No improvement. The results are presented in the following contingency table.

	Outcome		
Hospital	Substantial Improvement	Some Improvement	No Improvement
A	114	64	22
B	132	52	16
C	100	64	36
D	126	56	18

10. **Expected frequencies:** Compute the expected frequencies under the null hypothesis of homogeneity.

11. **Test statistic:** Compute the value of the chi-square statistic.

12. **State a conclusion:** Can you conclude that the distribution of outcomes differs among the hospitals? Use the $\alpha = 0.05$ level of significance.

13. **Can't read the numbers:** Because of printer failure, none of the observed frequencies in the following table were printed, but some of the row and column totals were. Is it possible to construct the corresponding table of expected frequencies from the information given? If so, construct it. If not, describe the additional information you would need.

	Observed			
	1	2	3	Total
A	—	—	—	25
B	—	—	—	—
C	—	—	—	40
D	—	—	—	75
Total	50	20	—	150

14. **Lottery:** Powerball is a multistate lottery in which players try to guess the numbers that will turn up in a drawing of numbered balls. One of the balls drawn is the "Powerball." Matching the number drawn on the Powerball increases one's winnings. From 2005 to

2008, the Powerball was drawn from a collection of 42 balls numbered 1 through 42. A total of 350 drawings were held. Following are the observed frequencies.

Number	Frequency	Number	Frequency	Number	Frequency
1	10	15	9	29	9
2	13	16	8	30	8
3	11	17	13	31	8
4	2	18	13	32	10
5	11	19	9	33	6
6	10	20	10	34	4
7	3	21	6	35	7
8	9	22	3	36	10
9	10	23	10	37	13
10	9	24	12	38	8
11	9	25	5	39	5
12	8	26	11	40	4
13	9	27	3	41	5
14	17	28	5	42	5

Source: powerball.com

Perform a test of the null hypothesis that each of the numbers is equally likely to come up. Use the $\alpha = 0.05$ level.

15. **Absent from school:** Following are the total numbers of absences on each day of the week for the academic year 2008–2009 at a Montana elementary school.

Monday	Tuesday	Wednesday	Thursday	Friday
844	909	781	795	837

Test the null hypothesis that absences are equally likely to occur on any day of the week. Use the $\alpha = 0.05$ level of significance.

Write About It

1. Why do large values of χ^2 provide evidence against H_0? Why don't small values of χ^2 provide evidence against H_0?

2. Explain what the expected frequencies represent in a goodness-of-fit test.

3. If the row variable and column variable are interchanged, how are the expected frequencies affected? Is the value of the chi-square statistic affected? Is the number of degrees of freedom affected?

4. Explain what the expected frequencies represent in a test of independence.

Case Study: Gender Bias In Graduate Admissions

The chapter opener described a famous study carried out at the University of California at Berkeley in the 1970s, regarding what appeared to be a case of gender discrimination in admissions to graduate school. The information in this case study was taken from the article "Sex Bias in Graduate Admissions Data from Berkeley," which appeared in *Science* magazine.

Table 10.9 presents the numbers of male and female applicants to six of the most popular departments at the University of California at Berkeley. Out of 2691 male applicants, 1198, or 44.5%, were accepted. Out of 1835 female applicants, only 557, or 30.4%, were accepted.

Table 10.9

Gender	Accept	Reject	Total
Male	1198	1493	2691
Female	557	1278	1835
Total	1755	2771	4526

In graduate school, each department conducts its own admissions process. Table 10.10 presents the numbers of applicants accepted and rejected by each of the six departments.

Table 10.10

Department	A	B	C	D	E	F	Total
Accept	601	370	322	269	147	46	1755
Reject	332	215	596	523	437	668	2771
Total	933	585	918	792	584	714	4526

University policy does not allow these departments to be identified by name.

Table 10.11 presents the numbers of men and women who applied to each of the six departments.

Table 10.11

Department	A	B	C	D	E	F	Total
Male	825	560	325	417	191	373	2691
Female	108	25	593	375	393	341	1835
Total	933	585	918	792	584	714	4526

University policy does not allow these departments to be identified by name.

1. Use the data in Table 10.9 to test the null hypothesis that acceptance to graduate school is independent of gender. Show that this hypothesis is rejected at the $\alpha = 0.01$ level.

2. Use the data in Table 10.10 to test the null hypothesis that acceptance to graduate school is independent of department. Show that this hypothesis is rejected at the $\alpha = 0.01$ level.

3. Use the data in Table 10.11 to test the null hypothesis that gender is independent of department. Show that this hypothesis is rejected at the $\alpha = 0.01$ level.

   We conclude that department is associated with both gender and admissions. Therefore, department is a confounder for the relationship between gender and admissions. This means that it is possible that the differences in admissions rates between men and women may be due to differences in the departments they apply to, rather than to gender. To determine whether this is the case, we must look at the admissions rates for men and women in each department separately. The following six tables present these data.

Department A			
Gender	Accept	Reject	Total
Male	512	313	825
Female	89	19	108
Total	601	332	933

Department B			
Gender	Accept	Reject	Total
Male	353	207	560
Female	17	8	25
Total	370	215	585

Department C			
Gender	Accept	Reject	Total
Male	120	205	325
Female	202	391	593
Total	322	596	918

Department D			
Gender	Accept	Reject	Total
Male	138	279	417
Female	131	244	375
Total	269	523	792

Department E			
Gender	Accept	Reject	Total
Male	53	138	191
Female	94	299	393
Total	147	437	584

Department F			
Gender	Accept	Reject	Total
Male	22	351	373
Female	24	317	341
Total	46	668	714

4. For each department, test the hypothesis that gender and admissions are independent. Use the $\alpha = 0.01$ level of significance. Show that the only department for which this hypothesis is rejected is department A. Show that, in fact, the admissions rate for women in department A is significantly higher than the rate for men.

5. For each department, compute the proportion of all applicants who are accepted.

6. For each department, compute the proportion of all applicants who are men.

7. In general, do the departments with the higher acceptance proportions tend to have the higher proportions of male applicants?

8. Which of the following is the best explanation for the fact that the graduate admissions rate is lower for women than for men?
   i. The admissions process discriminates against women.
  ii. Women tend to apply to departments that are harder to get into.

The data set in this case study provides an example of a result known as *Simpson's Paradox*. Simpson's Paradox occurs when two variables in a contingency table are dependent, but the dependence vanishes or reverses when separate tables are made for each level of a confounder. The lesson to be learned is that lack of independence is not the same as causation. When we reject the null hypothesis of independence in an observational study, it is possible that the result may be due to confounding. To determine whether a certain variable is a confounder, it is necessary to make a separate table for each value of the confounder.

Correlation and Regression

Introduction

Inflation and unemployment are measures of the health of the economy. Inflation is the percentage increase in prices over the course of a year, and unemployment is the percentage of the labor force that is out of work. The following table presents levels of inflation and unemployment, as reported by the Bureau of Labor Statistics, for the years 1981 through 2008.

Year	Inflation	Unemployment	Year	Inflation	Unemployment
1981	8.9	7.6	1995	2.5	5.6
1982	3.8	9.7	1996	3.3	5.4
1983	3.8	9.6	1997	1.7	4.9
1984	3.9	7.5	1998	1.6	4.5
1985	3.8	7.2	1999	2.7	4.2
1986	1.1	7.0	2000	3.4	4.0
1987	4.4	6.2	2001	1.6	4.7
1988	4.4	5.5	2002	2.4	5.8
1989	4.6	5.3	2003	1.9	6.0
1990	6.1	5.6	2004	3.3	5.5
1991	3.1	6.8	2005	3.4	5.1
1992	2.9	7.5	2006	2.5	4.6
1993	2.7	6.9	2007	4.1	4.6
1994	2.7	6.1	2008	0.1	5.8

Economists have long studied the relationship between inflation and unemployment. One theory states that inflation and unemployment follow a pattern called "the Phillips curve," in which higher inflation leads to lower unemployment, while lower inflation leads to higher unemployment. This theory is now widely regarded as too simple, and economists continue to study data, looking for more complex relationships. In the case study at the end of this chapter, we will examine some methods for predicting unemployment.

Questions about relationships between variables arise frequently in science, business, public policy, and other areas where informed decisions need to be made. For example, how does a person's level of education affect his or her income? How does the amount of time spent studying for an exam affect an exam score? Data used to study questions like these consist of **ordered pairs**. An ordered pair consists of values of two variables for each individual in the data set. In the preceding table, the ordered pairs are (inflation rate, unemployment rate). To study the relationship between education and income, the ordered pair might be (number of years of education, annual income).

Data that consist of ordered pairs are called **bivariate data**. The basic graphical tool used to study bivariate data is the **scatterplot**, in which each ordered pair is plotted as a point. In many cases, the points on a scatterplot tend to cluster around a straight line. In these cases, the summary statistic most often used to measure the closeness of the relationship between the two variables is the **correlation coefficient**, which we will study in Section 11.1. When two variables are closely related to each other, it is often of interest to try to predict the value of one of them when given the value of the other. This is done with the equation of the **least-squares regression line**, which we will study in Section 11.2.

SECTION 11.1 | Correlation

Objectives

1. Construct scatterplots for bivariate data
2. Compute the correlation coefficient
3. Interpret the correlation coefficient
4. Understand that correlation is not the same as causation

Objective 1 Construct scatterplots for bivariate data

Scatterplots

A real estate agent wants to study the relationship between the size of a house and its selling price. Table 11.1 presents the size in square feet and the selling price in thousands of dollars, for a sample of houses in a suburban Denver neighborhood.

Table 11.1 Size and Selling Price for a Sample of Houses

Size (square feet)	Selling Price ($1000s)
2521	400
2555	426
2735	428
2846	435
3028	469
3049	475
3198	488
3198	455

Source: Sue Bays Realty

It is reasonable to suspect that the selling price is related to the size of the house. Specifically, we expect that houses with larger sizes are more likely to have higher selling prices. A good way to visualize a relationship like this is with a **scatterplot**. In a scatterplot, each individual in the data set contributes an ordered pair of numbers, and each ordered pair is plotted on a set of axes.

EXAMPLE 11.1

Construct a scatterplot

Construct a scatterplot for the data in Table 11.1.

Solution

Each of the eight houses in Table 11.1 contributes an ordered pair of numbers. We will take the size as the first number and selling price as the second number. So the ordered pairs to be plotted are (2521, 400), (2555, 426), and so on. Figure 11.1 presents the scatterplot. We can see that houses with larger sizes tend to have larger selling prices, and houses with smaller sizes tend to have smaller (lower) selling prices.

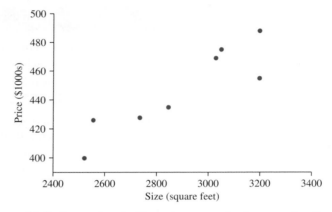

Figure 11.1 Scatterplot of selling price versus size for a sample of houses

Let's take a closer look at Figure 11.1. We have observed that larger sizes tend to be associated with larger prices, and smaller sizes tend to be associated with smaller prices. We refer to this as a **positive association** between size and selling price. In addition, the points tend to cluster around a straight line from lower left to upper right. We describe this by saying that the relationship between the two variables is **linear**. Therefore, we can say that the scatterplot in Figure 11.1 exhibits a positive linear association between size and selling price.

In some cases, large values of one variable are associated with small values of another. An example is the weight of a car and its gas mileage. Large weights are associated with small gas mileages, and small weights are associated with large gas mileages. Therefore, we say that weight and gas mileage have a **negative association**.

Figure 11.2 presents examples of scatterplots that exhibit various kinds of association.

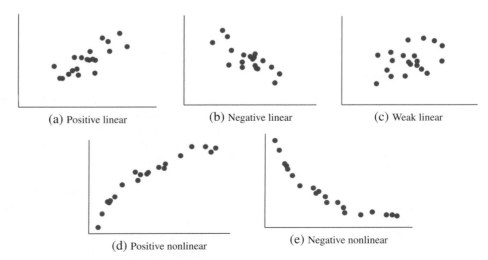

Figure 11.2 Scatterplots exhibiting various types of association

SUMMARY

- Two variables are **positively associated** if large values of one variable are associated with large values of the other.
- Two variables are **negatively associated** if large values of one variable are associated with small values of the other.
- Two variables have a **linear relationship** if the data tend to cluster around a straight line when plotted on a scatterplot.

Check Your Understanding

1. Fill in the blank: If large values of one variable are associated with small values of another, then the two variables have a _____ association.

2. Fill in the blank: If two variables have a positive association, then large values of one variable are associated with _____ values of the other.

3. For each of the following scatterplots, state the type of association that is exhibited: *Choices: positive linear, negative linear, positive nonlinear, negative nonlinear, weak linear.*

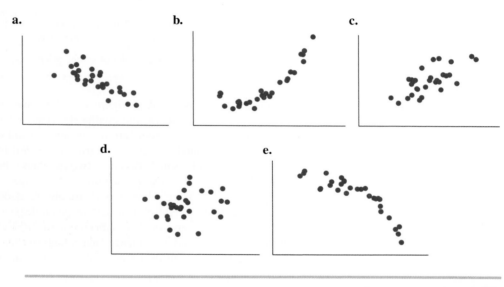

Answers are on page 492.

Objective 2 Compute the correlation coefficient

Explain It Again

Appearances can be misleading: The appearance of a scatterplot depends on the scales chosen for the axes. To get a reliable measure of the strength of a linear relationship, we must compute the correlation coefficient.

The Correlation Coefficient

When two variables have a linear relationship, we want to measure how strong the relationship is. It isn't enough to look at the scatterplot, because the visual impression can be affected by the scales on the axes. Figure 11.3 presents two scatterplots of the house data presented in Table 11.1. The plots differ only in the scale used on the y-axis, yet the plot on the left appears to show a strong linear relationship while the plot on the right appears to show a weak one.

We need a numerical measure of the strength of the linear relationship between two variables that is not affected by the scale of a plot. The appropriate quantity is the **correlation coefficient**. The formula for the correlation coefficient is a bit complicated, although calculating it does not involve much more than calculating sample means and standard deviations as was done in Chapter 3.

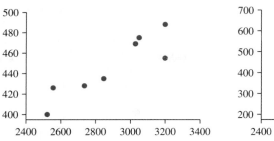 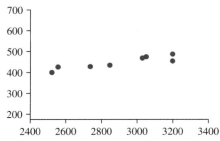

Figure 11.3 Both plots present the same data, yet the plot on the left appears to show a stronger linear relationship than the plot on the right. The reason is that the scales on the y-axis are different.

The Correlation Coefficient

Given ordered pairs (x, y), with sample means $\bar{x}$ and $\bar{y}$, sample standard deviations s_x and s_y, and sample size n, the correlation coefficient r is given by

$$r = \frac{1}{n-1} \sum \left(\frac{x - \bar{x}}{s_x}\right) \left(\frac{y - \bar{y}}{s_y}\right)$$

We often refer to r as the correlation between x and y.

Not surprisingly, most people nowadays use technology to compute the correlation coefficient. Procedures for the TI-84 Plus calculator, MINITAB, and Excel are presented in the Using Technology section on pages 487–488.

The correlation coefficient has several important properties, which we list.

Properties of the Correlation Coefficient

- The correlation coefficient is always between -1 and 1, inclusive. In other words, $-1 \leq r \leq 1$.
- The value of the correlation coefficient does not depend on the units of the variables. If we measure x and y in different units, the correlation will still be the same.
- It does not matter which variable is x and which is y.
- The correlation coefficient measures only the strength of the *linear* relationship between variables, and can be misleading when the relationship is nonlinear.
- The correlation coefficient is sensitive to outliers, and can be misleading when outliers are present.

EXAMPLE 11.2

Compute the correlation coefficient

Use the data in Table 11.1 to compute the correlation between size and selling price.

Solution

We will denote size by x and selling price by y. We compute the correlation coefficient using the following steps:

Step 1: Compute the sample means and standard deviations. We obtain $\bar{x} = 2891.25$, $\bar{y} = 447.0$, $s_x = 269.49357$, $s_y = 29.68405$.

Step 2: Compute the quantities $\dfrac{x - \bar{x}}{s_x}$ and $\dfrac{y - \bar{y}}{s_y}$.

Step 3: Compute the products $\left(\dfrac{x - \bar{x}}{s_x}\right) \left(\dfrac{y - \bar{y}}{s_y}\right)$.

Step 4: Add the products computed in Step 3, and divide the sum by $n - 1$.

The calculations in Steps 2–4 are summarized in the following table.

x	y	$\dfrac{x - \bar{x}}{s_x}$	$\dfrac{y - \bar{y}}{s_y}$	$\left(\dfrac{x - \bar{x}}{s_x}\right)\left(\dfrac{y - \bar{y}}{s_y}\right)$
2521	400	−1.3738732	−1.5833419	2.1753110
2555	426	−1.2477106	−0.7074506	0.8826936
2735	428	−0.5797912	−0.6400744	0.3711095
2846	435	−0.1679075	−0.4042575	0.0678779
3028	469	0.5074333	0.7411387	0.3760785
3049	475	0.5853572	0.9432675	0.5521484
3198	488	1.1382461	1.3812131	1.5721604
3198	455	1.1382461	0.2695050	0.3067630

$$\frac{\sum\left(\dfrac{x - \bar{x}}{s_x}\right)\left(\dfrac{y - \bar{y}}{s_y}\right)}{n - 1} = \frac{6.3041423}{7}$$
$$= 0.9005918$$

We round our final answer to three decimal places. The correlation coefficient is $r = 0.901$.

> **CAUTION**
>
> Do not round the intermediate values used to calculate the correlation coefficient. Round only the final result.

In general, we will round the correlation coefficient to three decimal places when it is the final result.

Objective 3 Interpret the correlation coefficient

Interpreting the correlation coefficient

The correlation coefficient measures the strength of the *linear* relationship between two variables. For this reason, it is meaningful only when the variables are linearly related. It can be misleading in other situations.

Interpreting the Correlation Coefficient

When two variables have a linear relationship, the correlation coefficient can be interpreted as follows:

- If r is positive, the two variables have a positive linear association.
- If r is negative, the two variables have a negative linear association.
- If r is close to 0, the linear association is weak.
- The closer r is to 1, the more strongly positive the linear association is.
- The closer r is to −1, the more strongly negative the linear association is.
- If $r = 1$, then the points lie exactly on a straight line with positive slope; in other words, the variables have a perfect positive linear association.
- If $r = -1$, then the points lie exactly on a straight line with negative slope; in other words, the variables have a perfect negative linear association.

When two variables are not linearly related, the correlation coefficient does not provide a reliable description of the relationship between the variables.

> **CAUTION**
>
> Be sure that the relationship is linear before interpreting the correlation coefficient.

In Example 11.2, the two variables do have a linear relationship, as verified by the scatterplot in Figure 11.1. The value of the correlation coefficient is $r = 0.901$, which indicates a strong positive linear association.

Check Your Understanding

4. The National Assessment for Educational Progress (NAEP) is a U.S. government organization that assesses the performance of students and schools at all levels across the United States. The following table presents the percentage of eighth-grade students who were found to be proficient in mathematics, and the percentage who were found to be proficient in reading in each of the ten most populous states.

State	Percentage Proficient in Reading	Percentage Proficient in Mathematics
California	60	59
Texas	73	78
New York	75	70
Florida	66	68
Illinois	75	70
Pennsylvania	79	77
Ohio	79	76
Michigan	73	66
Georgia	67	64
North Carolina	71	73

Source: National Assessment for Educational Progress

a. Construct a scatterplot with reading proficiency on the horizontal axis and math proficiency on the vertical axis. Is there a linear relationship?

b. Compute the correlation between reading proficiency and math proficiency. Is the linear association positive or negative? Weak or strong?

Answers are on page 492.

The correlation coefficient is not resistant

Recall: A statistic is resistant if its value is not affected much by extreme data values.

Figure 11.4 presents a scatterplot of the amount of farmland (including ranches) plotted against the total land area, for a selection of U.S. states. It is reasonable to suspect that states with larger land area would tend to have more farmland, and the scatterplot shows that, in general, this is true.

Recall: An outlier is a point that is detached from the main bulk of the data.

There is an outlier in the lower right corner of the plot, corresponding to the state of Alaska. Alaska is an outlier because it has a huge land area but very little farming. The correlation coefficient for the scatterplot in Figure 11.4 is $r = -0.119$. This suggests that there is actually a weak *negative* association between the total land area and the area of farmland. If we ignore the Alaska point and compute the correlation coefficient for the remaining points, we get $r = 0.710$, a big difference.

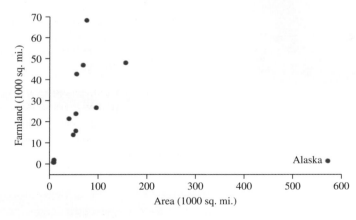

Figure 11.4   Area of farmland versus total land area for a selection of U.S. states. Alaska is an outlier. Because of the outlier, the correlation coefficient for this plot is -0.119, which is misleading. If the outlier is removed, the correlation coefficient for the remaining points is $r = 0.710$.

With the Alaska outlier in the plot, the correlation is misleading. For the states other than Alaska, there is a strong positive association between total land area and farmland area. Because Alaska is such a big exception to this rule, it throws the correlation coefficient way off.

SUMMARY

The correlation coefficient is not resistant. It may be misleading when outliers are present.

Check Your Understanding

5. For which of the following scatterplots is the correlation coefficient an appropriate summary?

(a)

(b)

(c)

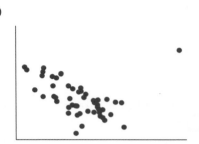

Answer is on page 492.

Objective 4 Understand that correlation is not the same as causation

Correlation Is Not Causation

A group of elementary school children took a vocabulary test. It turned out that children with larger shoe sizes tended to get higher scores on the test, and those with smaller shoe sizes tended to get lower scores. As a result, there was a large positive correlation between vocabulary and shoe size. Does this mean that learning new words causes one's feet to grow, or that growing feet cause one's vocabulary to increase? Obviously not. There is a third factor — age — that is related to both shoe size and vocabulary. Individuals with larger ages tend to have larger shoe sizes. Individuals with larger ages also tend to have larger vocabularies. It follows that individuals with larger shoe sizes will tend to have larger vocabularies.

Age is a confounder in this example. Age is related to both shoe size and vocabulary, which makes it appear as if shoe size and vocabulary are related to each other. The fact that shoe size and vocabulary are correlated does not mean that changing one variable will cause the other to change.

SUMMARY

Correlation is not the same as causation. In general, when two variables are correlated, we cannot conclude that changing the value of one variable will cause a change in the value of the other.

Check Your Understanding

6. An economist discovers that over the past several years, both the salaries of U.S. college professors and the amount of beer consumed in the United States have gone up. Thus, there is a positive correlation between the average salary of college professors and the amount of beer consumed. The economist concludes that the increase in beer consumption must be caused by professors spending their additional money on beer. Explain why this conclusion is not necessarily true.

Answer is on page 492.

USING TECHNOLOGY

We use the data in Table 11.1 to illustrate the technology steps.

TI-84 PLUS

Constructing a scatterplot

Step 1. Enter the x-values from Table 11.1 into **L1** and the y-values into **L2**.

Step 2. Press **2nd, Y=** to access the STAT PLOTS menu and select Plot1 by pressing **1**.

Step 3. Select **On** and the scatterplot icon (Figure A).

Step 4. Press **ZOOM** and then **9: ZoomStat** (Figure B).

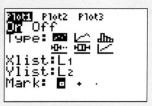

Figure A

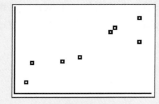

Figure B

Computing the correlation coefficient

The correlation coefficient is calculated as part of the procedure for computing the least-squares regression line and is presented at the end of Section 11.2 on page 499.

MINITAB

Constructing a scatterplot

Step 1. Enter the x-values from Table 11.1 into **Column C1** and the y-values into **Column C2**.

Step 2. Click on **Graph** and select **Scatterplot**. Choose the **Simple** option and press **OK**.

Step 3. Enter **C2** in the **Y variables** field and **C1** in the **X variables** field.

Step 4. Click **OK** (Figure C).

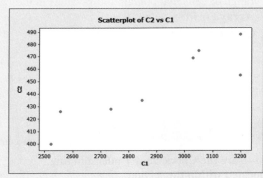

Figure C

Computing the correlation coefficient

Step 1. Enter the x-values from Table 11.1 into **Column C1** and the y-values into **Column C2**.

Step 2. Click on **Stat**, then **Basic Statistics**, then **Correlation**.

Step 3. Double-click **C1** and **C2** to enter these variables in the **Variables** field.

Step 4. Click **OK** (Figure D).

Correlations: C1, C2

Pearson correlation of C1 and C2 = 0.901

Figure D

EXCEL

Constructing a scatterplot

Step 1. Enter the *x*-values from Table 11.1 into **Column A** and the *y*-values into **Column B**.
Step 2. Highlight all values in **Columns A** and **B**.
Step 3. Click on **Insert** and then **Scatter**.
Step 4. Click **OK** (Figure E).

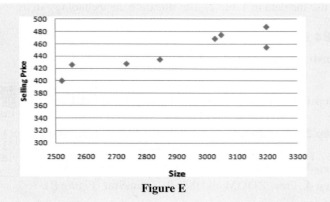

Figure E

Computing the correlation coefficient

Step 1. Enter the data from Table 11.1 into the worksheet.
Step 2. In an empty cell, select the **Insert Function** icon and highlight **Statistical** in the category field.
Step 3. Click on the **CORREL** function and press **OK**.
Step 4. Enter the range of cells that contain the *x*-values from Table 11.1 in the **Array1** field, and enter the range of cells that contain the *y*-values in the **Array2** field.
Step 5. Click **OK** (Figure F).

	C2			fx	=CORREL(A2:A9,B2:B9)	
	A	**B**	**C**		**D**	
1	**Size**	**Selling Price**	**Correlation**			
2	2521	400	0.900591753			
3	2555	426				
4	2735	428				
5	2846	435				
6	3028	469				
7	3049	475				
8	3198	488				
9	3198	455				

Figure F

SECTION 11.1   Exercises

Exercises 1–6 are the Check Your Understanding exercises located within the section.

Understanding the Concepts

In Exercises 7–10, fill in each blank with the appropriate word or phrase.

7. Bivariate data consist of ordered _____.

8. In a _____, ordered pairs are plotted on a set of axes.

9. Two variables have a _____ relationship if the data tend to cluster around a straight line.

10. The correlation coefficient measures only the strength of the _____ relationship between variables.

In Exercises 11–14, determine whether the statement is true or false. If the statement is false, rewrite it as a true statement.

11. Two variables are negatively associated if large values of one variable are associated with large values of the other.

12. If the correlation coefficient *r* equals 1, then the points on a scatterplot lie exactly on a straight line.

13. The correlation coefficient is not resistant.

14. When two variables are correlated, changing the value of one variable will cause a change in value of the other variable.

Practicing the Skills

In Exercises 15–18, compute the correlation coefficient.

15.

x	1	2	3	4	5		
y	2	1	4	3	7		

16.

x	24	13	8	81	63	36	5
y	44	52	42	5	1	48	15

17.

x	5.5	4.2	4.7	5.6	6.0	3.9	6.3	5.7
y	4.9	4.8	4.8	4.7	5.5	5.1	5.8	6.5

18.

x	5	−8	−2	6	9	−10	13	7
y	−1	−3	−6	−7	−1	5	13	22

In Exercises 20–22, determine whether the correlation coefficient is an appropriate summary for the scatterplot and explain your reasoning.

19.

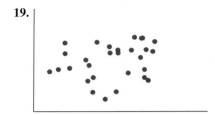

20.

21.

22.

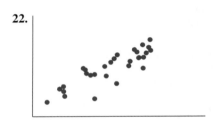

Working with the Concepts

23. Price of eggs and milk: The following table presents the average price in dollars for a dozen eggs and a gallon of milk for each month from March through December 2008.

Dozen Eggs	Gallon of Milk
2.07	3.80
1.93	3.76
1.92	3.77
2.01	3.96
1.85	3.89
1.98	3.77
1.86	3.66
1.84	3.73
1.83	3.68
1.85	3.58

Source: Bureau of Labor Statistics

a. Construct a scatterplot of the price of milk (y) versus the price of eggs (x).

b. Compute the correlation coefficient between the price of eggs and the price of milk.

c. In a month where the price of eggs is above average, would you expect the price of milk to be above average or below average? Explain.

d. Which of the following is the best interpretation of the correlation coefficient?

    i. When the price of eggs rises, it causes the price of milk to rise.

    ii. When the price of milk rises, it causes the price of eggs to rise.

    iii. Changes in the price of eggs or milk do not cause changes in the price of the other; the correlation indicates that the prices of milk and eggs tend to go up and down together.

24. Government funding: The following table presents the budget (in millions of dollars) for selected organizations that received U.S. government funding for arts and culture in both 2004 and 2006.

Organization	2004	2006
Smithsonian Institution	489	517
Corporation for Public Broadcasting	377	460
Institute of Museum and Library Services	262	247
National Endowment for the Humanities	135	142
National Endowment for the Arts	121	124
National Gallery of Art	88	95
Kennedy Center for the Performing Arts	17	18
Commission of Fine Arts	8	2
Advisory Council on Historic Preservation	4	5

Source: National Endowment for the Arts

a. Construct a scatterplot of the funding in 2006 (y) versus the funding in 2004 (x).

b. Compute the correlation coefficient between the funding in 2004 and the funding in 2006.

c. For an organization whose funding in 2004 was above the average, would you expect their funding in 2006 to be above or below average? Explain.

d. Which of the following is the best interpretation of the correlation coefficient?

    i. If we increase the funding for an organization in 2004, this will cause the funding in 2006 to increase.

    ii. If we increase the funding for an organization in 2006, this will cause the funding in 2004 to increase.

    iii. Some organizations get more funding than others, and those that were more highly funded in 2004 were generally more highly funded in 2006 as well.

25. Pass the ball: The following table lists the heights (inches) and weights (pounds) of 14 National Football League quarterbacks in the 2009 season.

Name	Height	Weight
Peyton Manning	77	230
Tom Brady	76	225
Ben Roethlisberger	77	241
Drew Brees	72	209
Eli Manning	76	225
Carson Palmer	77	235
Phillip Rivers	77	228
Kurt Warner	74	214
Donovan McNabb	74	240
Jay Cutler	75	233
Tony Romo	74	225
Matt Ryan	76	220
Brett Favre	74	222
Kyle Orton	76	225

Source: *The Chicago Tribune*

a. Construct a scatterplot of the weight (y) versus the height (x).
b. Compute the correlation coefficient between the height and weight of the quarterbacks.
c. If a quarterback is below average in height, would you expect him to be above average or below average in weight? Explain.
d. Which of the following is the best interpretation of the correlation coefficient?
   i. If a quarterback gains weight, he will grow taller.
   ii. Given two quarterbacks, the taller one is likely to be heavier than the shorter one.
   iii. Given two quarterbacks, the heavier one is likely to be shorter than the lighter one.

26. Carbon footprint: Carbon dioxide (CO_2) is produced by burning fossil fuels such as oil and natural gas, and has been connected to global warming. The following table presents the average amounts (in metric tons) of CO_2 emissions for the years 1990–2006 per person in the United States and per person in the rest of the world.

Year	Non-U.S.	U.S.
1990	3.6	19.2
1991	3.6	19.0
1992	3.5	18.8
1993	3.3	19.7
1994	3.3	19.8
1995	3.3	19.5
1996	3.4	19.7
1997	3.4	20.0
1998	3.3	19.5
1999	3.2	19.6
2000	3.3	20.0
2001	3.3	19.6
2002	3.3	19.6
2003	3.5	19.4
2004	3.7	19.6
2005	3.8	19.5
2006	3.7	19.0

Source: World Bank

a. Construct a scatterplot of U.S. carbon dioxide emissions (y) versus non-U.S. emissions (x).
b. Compute the correlation coefficient between U.S. carbon dioxide emissions and non-U.S. emissions.
c. In a year when U.S. emissions are above average, would you expect emissions in the rest of the world to be above average or below average? Explain.
d. As developing countries modernize, their use of fossil fuels increases. Countries that are already developed strive to reduce emissions. How does this fact explain the relationship between U.S. and non-U.S. emissions?

27. Foot temperatures: Foot ulcers are a common problem for people with diabetes. Higher skin temperatures on the foot indicate an increased risk of ulcers. In a study performed at the Colorado School of Mines, skin temperatures on both feet were measured, in degrees Fahrenheit, for 18 diabetic patients. The results are presented in the following table.

Left Foot	Right Foot	Left Foot	Right Foot
80	80	76	81
85	85	89	86
75	80	87	82
88	86	78	78
89	87	80	81
87	82	87	82
78	78	86	85
88	89	76	80
89	90	88	89

Source: Kimberly Anderson, M.S. thesis, Colorado School of Mines

a. Construct a scatterplot of the right foot temperature (y) versus the left foot temperature (x).
b. Compute the correlation coefficient between the temperatures of the left and right feet.
c. If a patient's left foot is cooler than the average, would you expect the patient's right foot to be warmer or cooler than average? Explain.
d. Which of the following is the best interpretation of the correlation coefficient?
   i. Some patients have warmer feet than others. Those who have warmer left feet generally have warmer right feet as well.
   ii. If we warm a patient's left foot, the patient's right foot will become warmer.
   iii. If we cool a patient's left foot, the patient's right foot will become warmer.

28. Mortgage payments: The following table presents interest rates, in percent, for 30-year and 15-year fixed-rate mortgages, for June 2009 through May 2010.

30-Year	15-Year	30-Year	15-Year
5.42	4.90	4.88	4.36
5.22	4.69	5.05	4.46
5.19	4.61	4.99	4.37
5.06	4.49	4.97	4.33
4.95	4.39	5.10	4.42
4.88	4.34	4.89	4.28

Source: Freddie Mac

a. Construct a scatterplot of the 15-year rate (y) versus the 30-year rate (x).
b. Compute the correlation coefficient between 30-year and 15-year rates.
c. When the 30-year rate is below average, would you expect the 15-year rate to be above or below average? Explain.
d. Which of the following is the best interpretation of the correlation coefficient?
   i. When a bank increases the 30-year rate, that causes the 15-year rate to rise as well.
   ii. Interest rates are determined by economic conditions. When economic conditions cause 30-year rates to increase, these same conditions cause 15-year rates to increase as well.
   iii. When a bank increases the 15-year rate, that causes the 30-year rate to rise as well.

29. Blood pressure: A blood pressure measurement consists of two numbers: the systolic pressure, which is the maximum pressure taken when the heart is contracting, and the diastolic pressure, which is the minimum pressure taken at the beginning of the heartbeat. Blood pressures were measured, in millimeters, for a sample of 16 adults. The following table presents the results.

Systolic	Diastolic	Systolic	Diastolic
134	87	133	91
115	83	112	75
113	77	107	71
123	77	110	74
119	69	108	69
118	88	105	66
130	76	157	103
116	70	154	94

Based on results published in the *Journal of Human Hypertension*

a. Construct a scatterplot of the diastolic blood pressure (y) versus the systolic blood pressure (x).
b. Compute the correlation coefficient between systolic and diastolic blood pressure.
c. If someone's diastolic pressure is above average, would you expect that person's systolic pressure to be above or below average? Explain.

30. Butterfly wings: Do larger butterflies live longer? The wingspan (in millimeters) and the lifespan in the adult state (in days) were measured for 22 species of butterfly. Following are the results.

Wingspan	Lifespan	Wingspan	Lifespan
35.5	19.8	25.9	32.5
30.6	17.3	31.3	27.5
30.0	27.5	23.0	31.0
32.3	22.4	26.3	37.4
23.9	40.7	23.7	22.6
27.7	18.3	27.1	23.1
28.8	25.9	28.1	18.5
35.9	23.1	25.9	32.3
25.4	24.0	28.8	29.1
24.6	38.8	31.4	37.0
28.1	36.5	28.5	33.7

Source: *Oikos Journal of Ecology* 105:41–54

a. Construct a scatterplot of the lifespan (y) versus the wingspan (x).
b. Compute the correlation coefficient between wingspan and lifespan.
c. Do larger butterflies tend to live for a longer or shorter time than smaller butterflies? Explain.

31. Police and crime: In a survey of cities in the United States, it is discovered that there is a positive correlation between the number of police officers hired by the city and the number of crimes committed. Do you believe that increasing the number of police officers causes the crime rate to increase? Why or why not?

32. Age and education: A survey of U.S. adults showed that there is a negative correlation between age and education level. Does this mean that people become less educated as they become older? Why or why not?

33. What's the correlation? In a sample of adults, would the correlation between age and year graduated from high school be closest to -1, -0.5, 0, 0.5, or 1? Explain.

34. What's the correlation? In a sample of adults, would the correlation between year of birth and year graduated from high school be closest to -1, -0.5, 0, 0.5, or 1? Explain.

Extending the Concepts

35. Changing means and standard deviations: A small company has five employees. The following table presents the number of years each has been employed (x) and the hourly wage in dollars (y).

x (years)	0.5	1.0	1.75	2.5	3.0
y (dollars)	9.51	8.23	10.95	12.70	12.75

a. Compute $\bar{x}$, $\bar{y}$, s_x, and s_y.
b. Compute the correlation coefficient between years of service and hourly wage.
c. Each employee is given a raise of $1.00 per hour, so each y-value is increased by 1. Using these new y-values, compute the sample mean $\bar{y}$ and the sample standard deviation s_y.
d. In part (c), each y-value was increased by 1. What was the effect on $\bar{y}$? What was the effect on s_y?
e. Compute the correlation coefficient between years of service and the increased hourly wage. Explain why the correlation coefficient is unchanged even though the y-values have changed.
f. Convert x to months by multiplying each x-value by 12. So the new x-values are 6, 12, 21, 30, and 36. Compute the sample mean $\bar{x}$ and the sample standard deviation s_x.
g. In part (f), each x-value was multiplied by 12. What was the effect on $\bar{x}$ and s_x?
h. Compute the correlation coefficient between months of service and hourly wage in dollars. Explain why the correlation coefficient is unchanged even though the x-values, $\bar{x}$, and s_x have changed.
i. Use the results of parts (a)–(h) to fill in the blank: If a constant is added to each x-value or to each y-value, the correlation coefficient is _____.
j. Use the results of parts (a)–(h) to fill in the blank: If each x-value or each y-value is multiplied by a positive constant, the correlation coefficient is _____.

Answers to Check Your Understanding Exercises for Section 11.1

1. negative

2. large

3. a. Negative linear
 b. Positive nonlinear   **c.** Positive linear
 d. Weak linear
 e. Negative nonlinear

4. a.

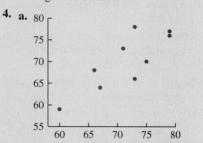

The scatterplot shows a linear relationship.

b. $r = 0.809$. The linear relationship is positive and fairly strong.

5. Scatterplot (a) is the only one for which the correlation coefficient is an appropriate summary.

6. Correlation is not causation. It is possible that the college professors are drinking the same amount of beer as before, while people other than college professors are drinking more beer.

<table>
<tr><td>**SECTION 11.2**</td><td>**The Least-Squares Regression Line**</td></tr>
</table>

Objectives

1. Compute the least-squares regression line
2. Use the least-squares regression line to make predictions
3. Interpret predicted values, the slope, and the y-intercept of the least-squares regression line

Objective 1 Compute the least-squares regression line

The Least-Squares Regression Line

Table 11.2 presents the size in square feet and selling price in thousands of dollars for a sample of houses. These data were first presented in Section 11.1. A scatterplot of these data showed that they tend to cluster around a line, and we computed the correlation to be 0.901. We concluded that there is a strong positive linear association between size and price.

Table 11.2 Size and Selling Price for a Sample of Houses

Size (square feet)	Selling Price ($1000s)
2521	400
2555	426
2735	428
2846	435
3028	469
3049	475
3198	488
3198	455

Source: Sue Bays Realty

We can use these data to predict the selling price of a house based on its size. The key is to summarize the data with a straight line. We want to find the line that fits the data best. We now explain what we mean by "best." Figure 11.5 presents scatterplots of the data in Table 11.2, each with a different line superimposed. For each line, we have drawn the vertical distances from the points to the line. It is clear that the line in Figure 11.5(a) fits better than the line in Figure 11.5(b). The reason is that the vertical distances are, on the whole, smaller for the line in Figure 11.5(a). We determine exactly how well a line fits the data by squaring the vertical

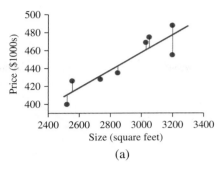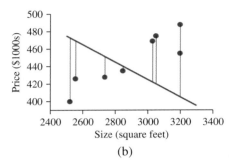

(a)   (b)

Figure 11.5   The line in (a) fits better than the line in (b), because the vertical distances are generally smaller.

distances and adding them up. The line that fits best is the line for which this sum of squared distances is as small as possible. This line is called the **least-squares regression line**.

Fortunately, we don't have to worry about vertical distances when we calculate the least-squares regression line. We can use the following formula.

Equation of the Least-Squares Regression Line

Given ordered pairs (x, y), with sample means $\bar{x}$ and $\bar{y}$, sample standard deviations s_x and s_y, and correlation coefficient r, the equation of the least-squares regression line for predicting y from x is

$$\hat{y} = b_0 + b_1 x$$

where $b_1 = r\dfrac{s_y}{s_x}$ is the **slope** and $b_0 = \bar{y} - b_1\bar{x}$ is the **y-intercept**.

> ### Explain It Again
>
> **Explanatory variable and outcome variable:** The explanatory variable is used to explain or predict the value of the outcome variable.

In general, the variable we want to predict (in this case, selling price) is called the **outcome variable**, or **response variable**, and the variable we are given is called the **explanatory variable**, or **predictor variable**. In the equation of the least-squares regression line, x represents the explanatory variable and y represents the outcome variable.

> **EXAMPLE 11.3**

Compute the least-squares regression line

Use the data in Table 11.2 to compute the least-squares regression line for predicting price from size.

Solution

We first find $\bar{x}$, $\bar{y}$, s_x, s_y, and r. We computed these quantities in Section 11.1:

$$\bar{x} = 2891.25, \quad \bar{y} = 447.0, \quad s_x = 269.49357, \quad s_y = 29.68405, \quad r = 0.9005918.$$

The slope of the least-squares regression line is

$$b_1 = r\frac{s_y}{s_x} = (0.9005918)\frac{29.68405}{269.49357} = 0.09919796$$

We use the value of b_1 just found to compute b_0, the y-intercept of the least-squares regression line:

$$b_0 = \bar{y} - b_1\bar{x} = 447.0 - (0.09919796)(2891.25) = 160.1939$$

The equation of the least-squares regression line is $\hat{y} = 160.1939 + 0.0992x$.

> ### CAUTION
>
> When computing the least-squares regression line, be sure that x represents the variable you are given (the explanatory variable), and y represents the variable you want to predict (the outcome variable).

> ### CAUTION
>
> We don't round the value of r in this calculation because it is an intermediate value.

> ### CAUTION
>
> Do not confuse the slope b_1 of the least-squares regression line with the correlation coefficient r. In most cases, they are not equal.

In general, we will round the slope and y-intercept values to four decimal places.

Figure 11.6 on page 494 presents a scatterplot of the data in Table 11.2 with the least-squares regression line superimposed. It can be seen that the points tend to cluster around the least-squares regression line.

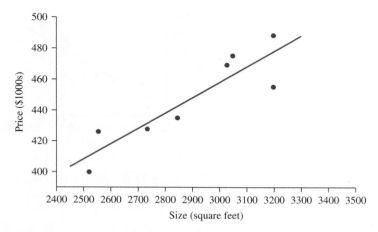

Figure 11.6   Scatterplot of the data in Table 11.2 with the least-squares regression line superimposed. The points tend to cluster around the least-squares regression line.

Computing the least-squares regression line with technology

Nowadays, least-squares regression lines are usually computed with technology rather than by hand. Figure 11.7 shows the least-squares regression line for predicting house price from house size, as presented by the TI-84 Plus calculator. There are four numbers in the output, labeled a, b, r^2, and r. Of these, a is the y-intercept of the least-squares regression line and b is the slope. The calculator provides many more digits than are generally necessary for these quantities. If you round a and b, you will get a = 160.1939 and b = 0.0992, which agree with the results calculated by hand in Example 11.3. The last quantity, r, is the correlation coefficient. When rounded, this value is 0.901, which agrees with the value computed by hand in Example 11.2. Finally, the value r^2 is computed by squaring the correlation coefficient r.

Step-by-step instructions for using the TI-84 Plus calculator to compute the least-squares line and correlation coefficient are presented in the Using Technology section on page 499.

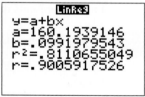

Figure 11.7   The least-squares regression line as presented by the TI-84 Plus calculator. The y-intercept is denoted by a, and the slope of the line is denoted by b. The value r, in the last line, is the correlation coefficient.

Following is MINITAB output for the least-squares regression line for predicting house price from house size. The equation is given near the top of the output as `Selling Price = 160.19 + 0.09920 Size`. In the table below that, the values of the slope and intercept are presented again in the column labeled `Coef`.

Step-by-step instructions for using MINITAB to compute the least-squares line are presented in the Using Technology section on page 499.

```
The regression equation is
Selling Price = 160.19 + 0.09920 Size

Predictor     Coef    SE Coef      T      P
Constant    160.19      56.73   2.82  0.030
Size        0.09920    0.01955   5.08  0.002
```

Finally, we present the output from Excel for this least-squares regression line. The slope and intercept are found in the column labeled Coefficients. The slope is labeled X Variable 1. Step-by-step instructions for using EXCEL to compare the least-squares line are presented in the Using Technology section on page 499.

	Coefficients	Standard Error	t Stat	P-value
Intercept	160.1939146	56.72636198	2.823976525	0.030195859
X Variable 1	0.099197954	0.019545859	5.075139241	0.00227642

Check Your Understanding

1. The following table presents the percentage of students who tested proficient in reading and the percentage who tested proficient in math for each of the ten most populous states in the United States. Compute the least-squares regression line for predicting math proficiency from reading proficiency.

State	Percent Proficient in Reading	Percent Proficient in Mathematics
California	60	59
Texas	73	78
New York	75	70
Florida	66	68
Illinois	75	70
Pennsylvania	79	77
Ohio	79	76
Michigan	73	66
Georgia	67	64
North Carolina	71	73

Source: National Assessment for Educational Progress

Answer is on page 503.

Objective 2 Use the least-squares regression line to make predictions

Using the Least-Squares Regression Line for Prediction

We can use the least-squares regression line to predict the value of the outcome variable if we are given the value of the explanatory variable. Simply substitute the value of the explanatory value for x in the equation of the least-squares regression line. The value of $\hat{y}$ that is computed is the **predicted value**.

EXAMPLE 11.4

Use the least-squares regression line for prediction

Use the least-squares regression line computed in Example 11.3 to predict the selling price of a house of size 2800 square feet.

Solution
The equation of the least-squares regression line is $\hat{y} = 160.1939 + 0.0992x$. Substituting 2800 for x yields

$$\hat{y} = 160.1939 + 0.0992(2800) = 438.0$$

We predict that the selling price of the house will be 438.0 thousand dollars, or $438,000.

We will round predicted values to one more decimal place than the outcome variable.

Figure 11.8 on page 496 presents a scatterplot of the data with the point for the prediction added. The given value for the explanatory variable was $x = 2800$, and the predicted price is the y-value on the least-squares regression line corresponding to $x = 2800$.

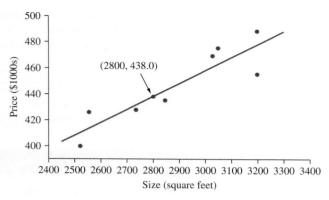

Figure 11.8   The predicted price for a house with size $x = 2800$ is 438.0, which is the y-value on the least-squares regression line.

The least-squares regression line goes through the point of averages

In the house data, the average size is $\bar{x} = 2891.25$ and the average selling price is $\bar{y} = 447.0$. What selling price do we predict for a house of average size? We substitute 2891.25 for x in the equation of the least-squares regression line to obtain

$$\hat{y} = 160.1939 + 0.0992(2891.25) = 447.0$$

For a house of average size, we predict that the selling price will be the average selling price. In general, when the explanatory variable x is equal to $\bar{x}$, the predicted value $\hat{y}$ is equal to $\bar{y}$.

> **SUMMARY**
>
> The least-squares regression line goes through the **point of averages** $(\bar{x}, \bar{y})$.

It makes sense that the least-squares regression line goes through $(\bar{x}, \bar{y})$. For example, if the correlation coefficient is positive, then above-average values of x are associated with above-average values of y, and below-average values of x are associated with below-average values of y. It follows that the value of x equal to its average would be associated with the average value of y.

Objective 3 Interpret predicted values, the slope, and the y-intercept of the least-squares regression line

Interpreting the Least-Squares Regression Line

The least-squares regression line has slope b_1 and y-intercept b_0. We use the least-squares regression line to compute a predicted value $\hat{y}$. We explain how to interpret these quantities.

Interpreting the predicted value $\widehat{y}$

The predicted value $\hat{y}$ can be used to estimate the average outcome for a given value of the explanatory variable x. For any given value of x, the value $\hat{y}$ is an estimate of the average y-value for all points with that x-value.

EXAMPLE 11.5   Use the least-squares regression line to estimate the average outcome

Use the least-squares regression line computed in Example 11.3 to estimate the average price of all houses whose size is 3000 square feet.

Solution

The equation of the least-squares regression line is $\hat{y} = 160.1939 + 0.0992x$. Given $x = 3000$, we predict

$$\hat{y} = 160.1939 + 0.0992(3000) = 457.8$$

We estimate the average price for a house of 3000 square feet to be 457.8 thousand dollars, or \$457,800.

Interpreting the *y*-intercept b_0

The *y*-intercept b_0 is the point where the line crosses the *y*-axis. This has a practical interpretation only when the data contain both positive and negative values of *x* — in other words, only when the scatterplot contains points on both sides of the *y*-axis.

- If the data contain both positive and negative *x*-values, then the *y*-intercept is the estimated outcome when the value of the explanatory variable *x* is 0.
- If the *x*-values are all positive or all negative, then the *y*-intercept b_0 does not have a useful interpretation.

Interpreting the slope b_1

If the *x*-values of two points on a line differ by 1, their *y*-values will differ by an amount equal to the slope of the line. For example, if a line has a slope of 4, then two points whose *x*-values differ by 1 will have *y*-values that differ by 4. This fact enables us to interpret the slope b_1 of the least-squares regression line. If the values of the explanatory variable for two individuals differ by 1, their predicted values will differ by b_1. If the values of the explanatory variable differ by an amount *d*, then their predicted values will differ by $b_1 \cdot d$.

EXAMPLE 11.6

Compute the predicted difference in outcomes

Two houses differ in size by 150 square feet. By how much should we predict their prices to differ?

Solution
The slope of the least-squares regression line is $b_1 = 0.0992$. We predict the prices to differ by $(0.0992)(150) = 14.9$ thousand dollars, or \$14,900.

Check Your Understanding

2. At the final exam in a statistics class, the professor asks each student to indicate how many hours he or she studied for the exam. After grading the exam, the professor computes the least-squares regression line for predicting the final exam score from the number of hours studied. The equation of the line is $\hat{y} = 50 + 5x$.
   a. Antoine studied for 6 hours. What do you predict his exam score to be?
   b. Emma studied for 3 hours longer than Jeremy did. How much higher do you predict Emma's score to be?

3. For each of the following plots, interpret the *y*-intercept of the least-squares regression line if possible. If not possible, explain why not.
   a. The least-squares regression line is $\hat{y} = 1.98 + 0.039x$, where *x* is the temperature in a freezer in degrees Fahrenheit, and *y* is the time it takes to freeze a certain amount of water into ice.

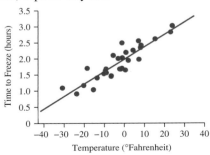

b. The least-squares regression line is $\hat{y} = -13.586 + 4.340x$, where x represents the age of an elementary school student and y represents the score on a standardized test.

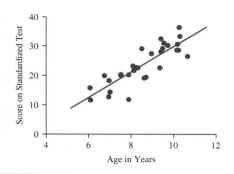

Answers are on page 503.

The least-squares regression line does not predict the effect of changing the explanatory variable

We have worded the interpretation of the slope of the least-squares regression line very carefully. The slope is the estimated difference in y-values for *two different* individuals whose x-values differ by 1. This does *not* mean that changing the value of x for a particular individual will cause that individual's y-value to change. The following example will help make this clear.

EXAMPLE 11.7

The least-squares regression line doesn't predict the result of changing the explanatory variable

A study is done in which a sample of men were weighed, and then each man was tested to see how much weight he could lift. The explanatory variable (x) was the man's weight, and the outcome (y) was the amount he could lift. The least-squares regression line was computed to be $\hat{y} = 50 + 0.6x$.

Joe is a weightlifter. After looking at the equation of the least-squares regression line, he reasons as follows: "The slope of the least-squares regression line is 0.6. Therefore, if I gain 10 pounds, I'll be able to lift 6 pounds more, because $(0.6)(10) = 6$." Is he right?

Solution

No, he is not right. You can't improve your weightlifting ability simply by putting on weight. What the slope of 0.6 tells us is that if two men have weights that differ by 10 pounds, then, on the average, the heavier man will be able to lift 6 pounds more than the lighter man. This does not mean that an individual man can increase his weightlifting ability by increasing his weight.

Check Your Understanding

4. The Sanchez family wants to sell their house, which is 2800 square feet in size. Mr. Sanchez notices that the slope of the least-squares regression line for predicting price from size is 0.0992. He says that if they put a 250-square-foot addition on their house, the selling price will increase by $(0.0992)(250) = 24.8$ thousand dollars, or $24,800. Is this necessarily a good prediction? Explain.

Answer is on page 503.

USING TECHNOLOGY

We use the data in Table 11.2 to illustrate the technology steps.

TI-84 PLUS

Computing the least-squares regression line

Note: Before computing the least-squares regression line, a one-time calculator setting should be modified to correctly configure the calculator to display the correlation coefficient. The following steps describe how to do this.

Step 1. Press **2nd, 0** to access the calculator catalog.
Step 2. Scroll down and select **DiagnosticOn**.
Step 3. Press **Enter** and then **Enter**.

The following steps describe how to compute the least-squares regression line.

Step 1. Enter the *x*-values from Table 11.2 into **L1** and the *y*-values into **L2**.
Step 2. Press **STAT** and then the right arrow key to access the **CALC** menu.
Step 3. Select **8: LinReg(a+bx)** (Figure A) and press **ENTER** (Figure B).

Using the TI-84 PLUS Stat Wizards (see Appendix B for more information)

Step 1. Enter the *x*-values from Table 11.2 into **L1** and the *y*-values into **L2**.
Step 2. Press **STAT** and then the right arrow key to access the **CALC** menu.
Step 3. Select **8:LinReg(a+bx)** (Figure A). Enter **L1** in the **Xlist** field and **L2** in the **Ylist** field. Select **Calculate** and press **ENTER** (Figure B).

Figure A

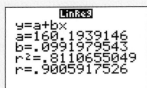

Figure B

MINITAB

Computing the least-squares regression line

Step 1. Enter the *x*-values from Table 11.2 into **Column C1** and the *y*-values into **Column C2**.
Step 2. Click **STAT**, then **Regression**, then **Regression**.
Step 3. Select the *y*-variable (**C2**) as the **Response variable** and the *x*-variable (**C1**) as the **Predictor** and click **OK** (Figure C).

Regression Analysis: C2 versus C1

The regression equation is
C2 = 160 + 0.0992 C1

Figure C

EXCEL

Computing the least-squares regression line

Step 1. Enter the *x*-values from Table 11.2 into **Column A** and the *y*-values into **Column B**.
Step 2. Select **Data**, then **Data Analysis**. Highlight **Regression** and press **OK**.
Step 3. Enter the range of cells that contain the *x*-values in the **Input X Range** field and the range of cells that contain the *y*-values in the **Input Y Range** field.
Step 4. Click **OK** (Figure D).

	Coefficients
Intercept	160.1939146
X Variable 1	0.099197954

Figure D

The least-squares regression line is given by
$$\hat{y} = (\textbf{X Variable 1})x + \textbf{Intercept}$$

Exercises 1–4 are the Check Your Understanding exercises located within the section.

Understanding the Concepts

In Exercises 5–7, fill in each blank with the appropriate word or phrase.

5. When we are given the value of the _____ variable, we can use the least-squares regression line to predict the value of the _____ variable.

6. If the correlation coefficient is equal to 0, the slope of the least-squares regression line will be equal to _____.

7. If the least-squares regression line has slope $b_1 = 5$, and two x-values differ by 3, the predicted difference in the y-values is _____.

In Exercises 8–12, determine whether the statement is true or false. If the statement is false, rewrite it as a true statement.

8. Substituting the value of the explanatory variable for x in the equation of the least-squares regression line results in a prediction for y.

9. The least-squares regression line passes through the point of averages $(\bar{x}, \bar{y})$.

10. In general, the slope of the least-squares regression line is equal to the correlation coefficient.

11. The least-squares regression line predicts the result of changing the value of the explanatory variable.

12. The y-intercept b_0 of a least-squares regression line has a useful interpretation only if the x-values are either all positive or all negative.

Practicing the Skills

In Exercises 13–16, compute the least-squares regression line for the given data set.

13.

x	1	2	3	4	5
y	5	6	9	8	7

14.

x	9	5	7	13	−8	−2	6	−10
y	3	3	31	36	0	3	−2	−14

15.

x	42	36	14	18	23	36	17
y	72	68	25	31	42	65	32

16.

x	5.7	4.1	6.2	4.4	6.5	5.8	4.9
y	1.9	4.8	0.8	3.9	1.2	1.7	3.0

17. Compute the least-squares regression line for predicting y from x given the following summary statistics:
$$\bar{x} = 5 \qquad s_x = 2 \qquad \bar{y} = 1350$$
$$s_y = 100 \qquad r = 0.70$$

18. Compute the least-squares regression line for predicting y from x given the following summary statistics:
$$\bar{x} = 8.1 \qquad s_x = 1.2 \qquad \bar{y} = 30.4$$
$$s_y = 1.9 \qquad r = -0.85$$

19. In a hypothetical study of the relationship between the income of parents (x) and the IQs of their children (y), the following summary statistics were obtained:

$$\bar{x} = 45,000 \qquad s_x = 20,000 \qquad \bar{y} = 100$$
$$s_y = 15 \qquad r = 0.40$$

Find the equation of the least-squares regression line for predicting IQ from income.

20. Assume that in a study of educational level in years (x) and income (y), the following summary statistics were obtained:
$$\bar{x} = 12.8 \qquad s_x = 2.3 \qquad \bar{y} = 41,000$$
$$s_y = 15,000 \qquad r = 0.60$$
Find the equation of the least-squares regression line for predicting income from educational level.

Working with the Concepts

21. **Price of eggs and milk:** The following table presents the average price in dollars for a dozen eggs and a gallon of milk for each month from March through December 2008.

Dozen Eggs	Gallon of Milk
2.07	3.80
1.93	3.76
1.92	3.77
2.01	3.96
1.85	3.89
1.98	3.77
1.86	3.66
1.84	3.73
1.83	3.68
1.85	3.58

Source: Bureau of Labor Statistics

  a. Compute the least-squares regression line for predicting the price of milk from the price of eggs.

  b. If the price of eggs differs by $0.25 from one month to the next, by how much would you expect the price of milk to differ?

  c. Predict the price of milk in a month when the price of eggs is $1.95.

22. **Government funding:** The following table presents the budget (in millions) for selected organizations that received U.S. government funding for arts and culture in both 2004 and 2006.

Organization	2004	2006
Smithsonian Institution	489	517
Corporation for Public Broadcasting	377	460
Institute of Museum and Library Services	262	247
National Endowment for the Humanities	135	142
National Endowment for the Arts	121	124
National Gallery of Art	88	95
Kennedy Center for the Performing Arts	17	18
Commission of Fine Arts	8	2
Advisory Council on Historic Preservation	4	5

Source: National Endowment for the Arts

  a. Compute the least-squares regression line for predicting the 2006 budget from the 2004 budget.

  b. If two institutions have budgets that differ by 10 million dollars in 2004, by how much would you predict their budgets to differ in 2006?

c. Predict the 2006 budget for an organization whose 2004 budget was 200 million dollars.

23. **Pass the ball:** The following table lists the heights (inches) and weights (pounds) of 14 National Football League quarterbacks in the 2009 season.

Name	Height	Weight
Peyton Manning	77	230
Tom Brady	76	225
Ben Roethlisberger	77	241
Drew Brees	72	209
Eli Manning	76	225
Carson Palmer	77	235
Phillip Rivers	77	228
Kurt Warner	74	214
Donovan McNabb	74	240
Jay Cutler	75	233
Tony Romo	74	225
Matt Ryan	76	220
Brett Favre	74	222
Kyle Orton	76	225

Source: *The Chicago Tribune*

a. Compute the least-squares regression line for predicting weight from height.
b. Is it possible to interpret the y-intercept? Explain.
c. If two quarterbacks differ in height by two inches, by how much would you predict their weights to differ?
d. Predict the weight of a quarterback who is 74.5 inches tall.
e. Tom Brady is 76 inches tall and weighs 225 pounds. Does he weigh more or less than the weight predicted by the least-squares regression line?

24. **Carbon footprint:** Carbon dioxide (CO_2) is produced by burning fossil fuels such as oil and natural gas, and has been connected to global warming. The following table presents the average amounts (in metric tons) of CO_2 emissions for the years 1990–2006 per person in the United States and per person in the rest of the world.

Year	Non-U.S.	U.S.
1990	3.6	19.2
1991	3.6	19.0
1992	3.5	18.8
1993	3.3	19.7
1994	3.3	19.8
1995	3.3	19.5
1996	3.4	19.7
1997	3.4	20.0
1998	3.3	19.5
1999	3.2	19.6
2000	3.3	20.0
2001	3.3	19.6
2002	3.3	19.6
2003	3.5	19.4
2004	3.7	19.6
2005	3.8	19.5
2006	3.7	19.0

Source: World Bank

a. Compute the least-squares regression line for predicting U.S. emissions from non-U.S. emissions.

b. If the non-U.S. emissions differ by 0.2 from one year to the next, by how much would you predict the U.S. emissions to differ?
c. Predict the U.S. emissions for a year when the non-U.S. emissions level is 3.4.

25. **Foot temperatures:** Foot ulcers are a common problem for people with diabetes. Higher skin temperatures on the foot indicate an increased risk of ulcers. In a study carried out at the Colorado School of Mines, skin temperatures on both feet were measured, in degrees Fahrenheit, for 18 diabetic patients. The results are presented in the following table.

Left Foot	Right Foot	Left Foot	Right Foot
80	80	76	81
85	85	89	86
75	80	87	82
88	86	78	78
89	87	80	81
87	82	87	82
78	78	86	85
88	89	76	80
89	90	88	89

Source: Kimberly Anderson, M.S. thesis, Colorado School of Mines

a. Compute the least-squares regression line for predicting the right foot temperature from the left foot temperature.
b. Construct a scatterplot of the right foot temperature (y) versus the left foot temperature (x). Graph the least-squares regression line on the same axes.
c. If the left foot temperatures of two patients differ by 2 degrees, by how much would you predict their right foot temperatures to differ?
d. Predict the right foot temperature for a patient whose left foot temperature is 81 degrees.

26. **Mortgage payments:** The following table presents interest rates, in percent, for 30-year and 15-year fixed-rate mortgages, for June 2009 through May 2010.

30-Year	15-Year	30-Year	15-Year
5.42	4.90	4.88	4.36
5.22	4.69	5.05	4.46
5.19	4.61	4.99	4.37
5.06	4.49	4.97	4.33
4.95	4.39	5.10	4.42
4.88	4.34	4.89	4.28

Source: Freddie Mac

a. Compute the least-squares regression line for predicting the 15-year rate from the 30-year rate.

b. Construct a scatterplot of the 15-year rate (y) versus the 30-year rate (x). Graph the least-squares regression line on the same axes.

c. Is it possible to interpret the y-intercept? Explain.

d. If the 30-year rate differs by 0.3 percent from one month to the next, by how much would you predict the 15-year rate to differ?

e. Predict the 15-year rate for a month when the 30-year rate is 5.25 percent.

27. Blood pressure: A blood pressure measurement consists of two numbers: the systolic pressure, which is the maximum pressure taken when the heart is contracting, and the diastolic pressure, which is the minimum pressure taken at the beginning of the heartbeat. Blood pressures were measured, in millimeters, for a sample of 16 adults. The following table presents the results.

Systolic	Diastolic	Systolic	Diastolic
134	87	133	91
115	83	112	75
113	77	107	71
123	77	110	74
119	69	108	69
118	88	105	66
130	76	157	103
116	70	154	94

Based on results published in the *Journal of Human Hypertension*

a. Compute the least-squares regression line for predicting the diastolic pressure from the systolic pressure.

b. Is it possible to interpret the y-intercept? Explain.

c. If the systolic pressures of two patients differ by 10 millimeters, by how much would you predict their diastolic pressures to differ?

d. Predict the diastolic pressure for a patient whose systolic pressure is 125 millimeters.

28. Butterfly wings: Do larger butterflies live longer? The wingspan (in millimeters) and the lifespan in the adult state (in days) were measured for 22 species of butterfly. Following are the results.

Wingspan	Lifespan	Wingspan	Lifespan
35.5	19.8	25.9	32.5
30.6	17.3	31.3	27.5
30.0	27.5	23.0	31.0
32.3	22.4	26.3	37.4
23.9	40.7	23.7	22.6
27.7	18.3	27.1	23.1
28.8	25.9	28.1	18.5
35.9	23.1	25.9	32.3
25.4	24.0	28.8	29.1
24.6	38.8	31.4	37.0
28.1	36.5	28.5	33.7

Source: *Oikos Journal of Ecology* 105:41–54

a. Compute the least-squares regression line for predicting the lifespan from the wingspan.

b. Is it possible to interpret the y-intercept? Explain.

c. If the wingspans of two butterflies differ by 2 millimeters, by how much would you predict their lifespans to differ?

d. Predict the lifespan for a butterfly whose wingspan is 28.5 millimeters.

29. Interpreting technology: The following display from the TI-84 Plus calculator presents the least-squares regression line for predicting a student's score on a statistics exam (y) from the number of hours spent studying (x).

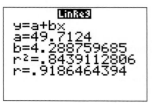

a. Write the equation of the least-squares regression line.

b. What is the correlation between the score and the time spent studying?

c. Predict the score for a student who studies for 10 hours.

30. Interpreting technology: The following display from the TI-84 Plus calculator presents the least-squares regression line for predicting the price of a certain stock (y) from the prime interest rate in percent (x).

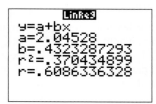

a. Write the equation of the least-squares regression line.

b. What is the correlation between the interest rate and the yield of the stock?

c. Predict the price when the prime interest rate is 5%.

31. Interpreting technology: The following MINITAB output presents the least-squares regression line for predicting the concentration of ozone in the atmosphere from the concentration of oxides of nitrogen (NOx).

```
The regression equation is
Ozone = 33.8127 + 1.21015 NOx

Predictor      Coef      SE Coef         T        P
Constant    33.8127      1.06035     31.89    0.000
NOx         1.21015      0.09047     12.38    0.000
```

a. Write the equation of the least-squares regression line.

b. Predict the ozone concentration when the NOx concentration is 21.4.

32. Interpreting technology: The following MINITAB output presents the least-squares regression line for predicting the score on a final exam from the score on a midterm exam.

```
The regression equation is
Final = 23.7789 + 0.71384 Midterm

Predictor      Coef      SE Coef         T        P
Constant    23.7789      4.46723     5.323    0.000
Midterm     0.71384      0.13507     5.285    0.000
```

a. Write the equation of the least-squares regression line.
b. Predict the final exam score for a student who scored 75 on the midterm.

33. **Interpreting technology:** A business school professor computed a least-squares regression line for predicting the salary in $1000s for a graduate from the number of years of experience. The results are presented in the following Excel output.

	Coefficients
Intercept	55.91275257
Experience	2.58289361

a. Write the equation of the least-squares regression line.
b. Predict the salary for a graduate with 5 years of experience.

34. **Interpreting technology:** A biologist computed a least-squares regression line for predicting the brain weight in grams of a bird from its body weight in grams. The results are presented in the following Excel output.

	Coefficients
Intercept	3.79229595
Body weight	0.08063922

a. Write the equation of the least-squares regression line.
b. Predict the brain weight for a bird whose body weight is 300 grams.

Extending the Concepts

35. **Least-squares regression line for z-scores:** The following table presents math and verbal SAT scores for six freshmen.

Verbal (x)	428	386	653	316	438	323
Math (y)	373	571	686	319	607	440

a. Compute the correlation coefficient between math and verbal SAT score.
b. Compute the mean $\bar{x}$ and the standard deviation s_x for the verbal scores.
c. Compute the mean $\bar{y}$ and the standard deviation s_y for the math scores.
d. Compute the least-squares regression line for predicting math score from verbal score.
e. Compute the z-score for each x-value:
$$z_x = \frac{x - \bar{x}}{s_x}$$
f. Compute the z-score for each y-value:
$$z_y = \frac{y - \bar{y}}{s_y}$$
g. Compute the correlation coefficient r between z_x and z_y. Is it the same as the correlation between math and verbal SAT scores?
h. Compute the least-squares regression line for predicting z_y from z_x. Explain why the equation of the line is $\hat{z}_y = r\, z_x$.

Answers to Check Your Understanding Exercises for Section 11.2

1. $\hat{y} = 11.0358 + 0.8226x$
2. a. 80   b. 15 points higher
3. a. The length of time it takes to freeze water in a freezer set to 0°F
   b. No interpretation

4. No. The least-squares line does not predict the effect of changing the explanatory variable.

SECTION 11.3   Inference on the Slope of the Regression Line

Objectives

1. State the assumptions of the linear model
2. Check the assumptions of the linear model
3. Construct confidence intervals for the slope
4. Test hypotheses about the slope

Objective 1 State the assumptions of the linear model

The Linear Model

In Sections 11.1 and 11.2, we discussed bivariate data — data that are in the form of ordered pairs. We learned to construct scatterplots, and we found that, in many cases, the points on a scatterplot tend to cluster around a straight line. We learned to summarize a scatterplot by computing the least-squares regression line.

When the points on a scatterplot are a random sample from a population, we can imagine plotting every point in the population on a scatterplot. Then, if certain assumptions are met, we say that the population follows a **linear model**. The intercept b_0 and the slope b_1 of the least-squares regression line are then estimates of a population intercept β_0 and a population slope β_1. We cannot determine the exact values of β_0 and β_1, because we cannot observe the entire population. However, we can use the sample points to construct confidence intervals and test hypotheses about β_0 and β_1. We will focus on β_1.

The assumptions for a linear model are illustrated in Figure 11.9, which presents a hypothetical scatterplot of an entire population. The scatterplot is divided up into narrow vertical strips, so that the points within each strip have approximately the same x-value. The following three conditions hold:

Assumptions for the Linear Model

1. The mean of the y-values within a strip is denoted $\mu_{y|x}$. As x varies, the values of $\mu_{y|x}$ follow a straight line: $\mu_{y|x} = \beta_0 + \beta_1 x$.

2. The amount of vertical spread is approximately the same in each strip, except perhaps near the ends.

3. The y-values within a strip are approximately normally distributed. (This is not obvious from the scatterplot.) This assumption is not necessary if the sample size is large ($n > 30$).

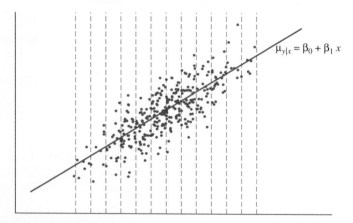

Figure 11.9 A scatterplot of a population that follows the linear model

When the assumptions of the linear model hold, the points (x, y) satisfy the following linear model equation:

$$y = \beta_0 + \beta_1 x + \varepsilon$$

In this equation, β_0 is the y-intercept, β_1 is the slope of the line that summarizes the entire population, and ε is a random error. The y-intercept b_0 and the slope b_1 of the least-squares line are estimates of β_0 and β_1.

We will illustrate the ideas in this section with a data set based on a nutritional analysis of more than 350 fast-food products conducted by the United States Department of Agriculture in 2010. Table 11.3 presents the number of calories and number of grams of fat per 100 grams of product for a sample of 18 fast-food products.

We use technology to find the least-squares regression line for the data in Table 11.3. The following TI-84 Plus display (Figure 11.10) shows that the equation of the least-squares regression line is $\hat{y} = 130.251662 + 10.00792114x$.

Figure 11.10

Table 11.3 Grams of Fat and Number of Calories per 100 Grams of Product

Product	Fat (x)	Calories (y)
Burger King Chicken Tenders	16.67	289
Burger King Croissan'wich with Sausage and Cheese	25.45	376
Domino's Cheese Pizza, Thin Crust	16.82	315
Kentucky Fried Chicken Xtra Crispy	16.55	268
Kentucky Fried Chicken Original Recipe	12.03	221
Little Caesar's Cheese Pizza Thin Crust	16.99	309
McDonald's Big and Tasty	13.68	226
McDonald's Biscuit	16.01	344
McDonald's Chocolate Triple Shake	4.51	163
McDonald's Deluxe Cinnamon Roll	16.24	367
McDonald's Hot Caramel Sundae	4.89	188
Papa John's Pepperoni Pizza Original Crust	11.86	275
Popeye's Biscuit	24.53	408
Popeye's Fried Chicken	35.39	460
Taco Bell Burrito Supreme with Beef	8.05	189
Taco Bell Nachos	22.17	366
Wendy's Chicken Nuggets	23.17	334
Wendy's Classic Double	14.20	241

Source: USDA National Nutrient Database for Standard Reference, Release 21 (2010)

Figure 11.11 presents a scatterplot of the data, from MINITAB, with the least-squares regression line superimposed.

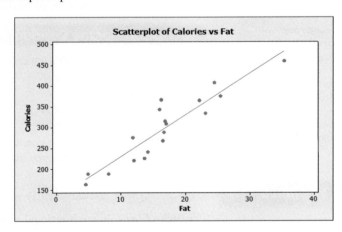

Figure 11.11   A scatterplot of the data in Table 11.3. The least-squares regression line is superimposed.

In the remainder of this section, we will describe how to check the assumptions of the linear model and how to construct confidence intervals and perform hypothesis tests when these assumptions are met. The computations are rather lengthy, and technology is almost always used in practice. We will present the hand calculations first, to illustrate the ideas behind the methods, and then we will present examples using technology.

Objective 2 Check the assumptions of the linear model

Checking Assumptions

Before we can compute confidence intervals and perform hypothesis tests, we must check that the assumptions of the linear model are satisfied. In practice, we do not see the entire population, so we must use the sample to do the checking.

We check the assumptions by computing quantities called *residuals* and plotting them in a *residual plot*. We now define these terms.

> ### DEFINITION
>
> Given a point (x, y) and the least-squares regression line $\hat{y} = b_0 + b_1 x$, the **residual** for the point (x, y) is the difference between the observed value y and the predicted value $\hat{y}$:
>
> $$\text{Residual} = y - \hat{y}$$
>
> A **residual plot** is a plot in which the residuals are plotted against the values of the explanatory variable x. In other words, the points on the residual plot are $(x, \; y - \hat{y})$.

Figure 11.12 presents the residual plot, as drawn by MINITAB, for the data in Table 11.3.

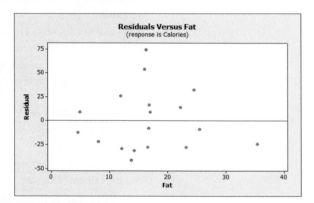

Figure 11.12 Residual plot for the data in Table 11.3

When the linear model assumptions are satisfied, the residual plot will not show any obvious pattern. In particular, the residual plot must satisfy the following conditions.

Conditions for the Residual Plot

1. The residual plot must not exhibit an obvious pattern.
2. The vertical spread of the points in the residual plot must be roughly the same across the plot.
3. There must be no outliers.

Figure 11.12 satisfies all three conditions, so we may assume that the linear model is valid, and we may construct confidence intervals and test hypotheses.

Explain It Again

Reasons for the conditions:
Condition 1 checks that $\mu_{y|x}$ follows a straight line. Condition 2 checks that the variance of the y-values is the same for every x-value. Condition 3 checks that the y-values corresponding to a given x are approximately normally distributed.

EXAMPLE 11.8

Checking the assumptions with a residual plot

For each of the following residual plots, determine whether the assumptions of the linear model are satisfied. If they are not, specify which assumptions are violated.

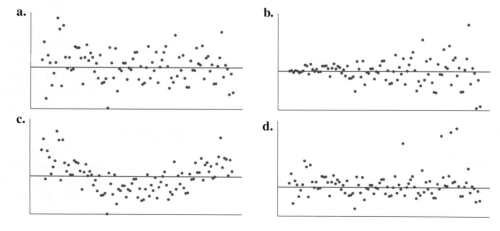

Solution

    a. The plot shows no obvious pattern. The assumptions of the linear model are satisfied.

    b. The vertical spread varies. The linear model is not valid.

    c. The plot shows an obvious curved pattern. The linear model is not valid.

    d. The plot contains outliers. The linear model is not valid.

Check Your Understanding

1. For each of the following residual plots, determine whether the assumptions of the linear model are satisfied. If they are not, specify which assumptions are violated.

a.
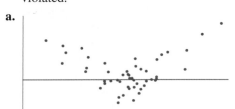

b.
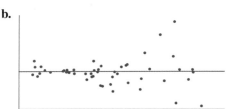

c.
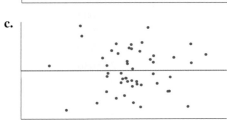

d.
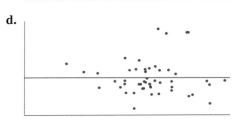

Answers are on page 519.

Objective 3 Construct confidence intervals for the slope

Constructing Confidence Intervals for the Slope

The slope b_1 of the least-squares regression line is a point estimate of the population slope β_1. When the assumptions of the linear model are satisfied, we can construct a confidence interval for β_1. To form a confidence interval, we need a point estimate, a standard error, and a critical value. The point estimate for β_1 is b_1.

The standard error of b_1

To compute the standard error of b_1, we first compute a quantity called the **residual standard deviation**. This quantity, denoted s_e, measures the spread of the points on the scatterplot around the least-squares regression line. The formula for s_e is

$$s_e = \sqrt{\frac{\sum(y - \hat{y})^2}{n - 2}}$$

To understand this formula, note that the predicted value $\hat{y}$ is an estimate of the mean of y. The residual $y - \hat{y}$ estimates the deviation between the observed data value y and its mean. The formula for s_e is similar to the formula for the sample standard deviation, in that we square the deviations and sum them. We divide by $n - 2$ rather than $n - 1$ because the predicted values involve the estimation of two parameters, β_0 and β_1.

EXAMPLE 11.9 Compute the residual standard deviation

Compute the residual standard deviation for the data in Table 11.3.

Solution

We have computed the equation of the least-squares line to be $\hat{y} = 130.251662 + 10.00792114x$ (see Figure 11.10 on page 504).

Step 1: Compute the residuals $y - \hat{y}$, and the sum of squared residuals $\sum(y - \hat{y})^2$. Table 11.4 illustrates the calculations. We obtain $\sum(y - \hat{y})^2 = 17205.3433$.

Step 2: Substitute the number of points $n = 18$, and the value $\sum(y - \hat{y})^2 = 17205.3433$ into the formula for s_e:

$$s_e = \sqrt{\frac{\sum(y - \hat{y})^2}{n - 2}} = \sqrt{\frac{17205.3433}{18 - 2}} = 32.792285$$

Table 11.4

x	y	Predicted Value $\hat{y} = 130.251662 + 10.00792114x$	Residual $y - \hat{y}$	Residual^2 $(y - \hat{y})^2$
16.67	289	297.083707	−8.083707	65.34631886
25.45	376	384.953255	−8.953255	80.16077510
16.82	315	298.584896	16.415104	269.45563933
16.55	268	295.882757	−27.882757	777.44813792
12.03	221	250.646953	−29.646953	878.94182218
16.99	309	300.286242	8.713758	75.92957848
13.68	226	267.160023	−41.160023	1694.14749336
16.01	344	290.478479	53.521521	2864.55321015
4.51	163	175.387386	−12.387386	153.44733191
16.24	367	292.780301	74.219699	5508.56371965
4.89	188	179.190396	8.809604	77.60912264
11.86	275	248.945607	26.054393	678.83139460
24.53	408	375.745968	32.254032	1040.32258026
35.39	460	484.431991	−24.431991	596.92218422
8.05	189	210.815427	−21.815427	475.91285519
22.17	366	352.127274	13.872726	192.45252667
23.17	334	362.135195	−28.135195	791.58919769
14.20	241	272.364142	−31.364142	983.70940340

$$\sum(y - \hat{y})^2 = 17205.3433$$

Explain It Again

Relationship between $\sum(x - \bar{x})^2$ and the sample variance: We can compute $\sum(x - \bar{x})^2$ as $\sum(x - \bar{x})^2 = (n-1)s_x^2$, where s_x^2 is the sample variance of the x-values.

Once we have computed s_e, we divide it by the quantity $\sqrt{\sum(x - \bar{x})^2}$ to obtain the standard error of b_1. The quantity $\sum(x - \bar{x})^2$ is called the **sum of squares for x**. The standard error of b_1 is

$$s_b = \frac{s_e}{\sqrt{\sum(x - \bar{x})^2}}$$

EXAMPLE 11.10

Compute the standard error of b_1

Compute the standard error s_b for the fast-food data in Table 11.3.

Solution

Step 1: Compute s_e, the residual standard deviation. We did this in Example 11.9, and obtained $s_e = 32.792285$.

Step 2: Compute $\sum(x - \bar{x})^2$. The calculations are presented in Table 11.5. We obtain $\sum(x - \bar{x})^2 = 983.1712$.

Table 11.5

x	$x-\bar{x}$	$(x-\bar{x})^2$
16.67	0.04722222	0.002230
25.45	8.82722222	77.919852
16.82	0.19722222	0.038897
16.55	−0.07277778	0.005297
12.03	−4.59277778	21.093608
16.99	0.36722222	0.134852
13.68	−2.94277778	8.659941
16.01	−0.61277778	0.375497
4.51	−12.11277778	146.719385
16.24	−0.38277778	0.146519
4.89	−11.73277778	137.658074
11.86	−4.76277778	22.684052
24.53	7.90722222	62.524163
35.39	18.76722222	352.20863
8.05	−8.57277778	73.492519
22.17	5.54722222	30.771674
23.17	6.54722222	42.866119
14.20	−2.42277778	5.869852

$$\bar{x} = \frac{\sum x}{n} = 16.622778 \qquad\qquad \sum(x-\bar{x})^2 = 983.1712$$

We now compute the standard error s_b:

$$s_b = \frac{s_e}{\sqrt{\sum(x-\bar{x})^2}} = \frac{32.792285}{\sqrt{983.1712}} = 1.0458$$

The critical value and the margin of error

Under the assumptions of the linear model, the quantity

$$\frac{b_1 - \beta_1}{s_b}$$

has a Student's t distribution with $n - 2$ degrees of freedom. Therefore, the critical value for a level $100(1 - \alpha)\%$ confidence interval is the value $t_{\alpha/2}$ for which the area under the t curve with $n - 2$ degrees of freedom between $-t_{\alpha/2}$ and $t_{\alpha/2}$ is $1 - \alpha$.

The margin of error for a level $100(1 - \alpha)\%$ confidence interval is

$$\text{Margin of error} = t_{\alpha/2} \cdot s_b$$

A level $100(1 - \alpha)\%$ confidence interval for β_1 is

$$b_1 \pm t_{\alpha/2} \cdot s_b$$

$$b_1 - t_{\alpha/2} \cdot s_b < \beta_1 < b_1 + t_{\alpha/2} \cdot s_b$$

The steps for constructing a confidence interval for β_1 are as follows:

Constructing a Confidence Interval for β_1

Step 1: Compute the least-squares regression line $\hat{y} = b_0 + b_1 x$.

Step 2: Compute the residuals and construct a residual plot to be sure the assumptions of the linear model are satisfied.

Step 3: Compute the residual standard deviation: $s_e = \sqrt{\dfrac{\sum(y - \hat{y})^2}{n - 2}}$.

Step 4: Compute the standard error of b_1: $s_b = \dfrac{s_e}{\sqrt{\sum(x - \bar{x})^2}}$.

Continued on page 510

Step 5: Find the critical value $t_{\alpha/2}$ from the Student's t curve with $n - 2$ degrees of freedom and multiply it by the standard error to obtain the margin of error $t_{\alpha/2} \cdot s_b$.

Step 6: Use the point estimate b_1 and the margin of error $t_{\alpha/2} \cdot s_b$ to compute the confidence interval.

$$\text{Point estimate} \pm \text{Margin of error}$$
$$b_1 \pm t_{\alpha/2} \cdot s_b$$
$$b_1 - t_{\alpha/2} \cdot s_b < \beta_1 < b_1 + t_{\alpha/2} \cdot s_b$$

Step 7: Interpret the result.

EXAMPLE 11.11   Construct a confidence interval

Construct a 95% confidence interval for the slope β_1 for the fast-food data.

Solution

Step 1: Compute the least-squares regression line. We computed the equation of the least-squares regression line (Figure 11.10) and obtained $\hat{y} = 130.251662 + 10.007921x$.

Step 2: Compute the residuals and construct a residual plot to be sure the assumptions of the linear model are satisfied. The residual plot was presented in Figure 11.12. The assumptions of the linear model are satisfied.

Step 3: Compute the residual standard deviation. We computed the residual standard deviation in Example 11.9, and obtained $s_e = 32.792285$.

Step 4: Compute the standard error of b_1. We computed the standard error of b_1 in Example 11.10, and obtained $s_b = 1.0458$.

Step 5: Find the critical value $t_{\alpha/2}$ from the Student's t curve with $n - 2$ degrees of freedom and multiply it by the standard error to obtain the margin of error $t_{\alpha/2} \cdot s_b$. There are $n - 2 = 18 - 2 = 16$ degrees of freedom for the Student's t distribution. From Table A.3, we find that the critical value for a 95% confidence interval is $t_{\alpha/2} = 2.120$. The margin of error is therefore

$$\text{Margin of error} = t_{\alpha/2} \cdot s_b = 2.120 \cdot 1.0458 = 2.2171$$

Step 6: Use the point estimate b_1 and the margin of error to construct the confidence interval. The point estimate is $b_1 = 10.007921$. The margin of error is 2.2171. The 95% confidence interval is

$$\text{Point estimate} \pm \text{Margin of error}$$
$$10.007921 \pm 2.2171$$
$$7.791 < \beta_1 < 12.225$$

Step 7: Interpret the result. We are 95% confident that the mean difference in calories for food items that differ by 1 gram in fat content is between 7.791 and 12.225.

EXAMPLE 11.12   Interpreting a confidence interval

Nutritionists have found that a gram of fat contains 9 calories. Is the confidence interval constructed in Example 11.11 consistent with this finding?

Solution

The parameter β_1 represents the mean difference in calories corresponding to a difference of one gram of fat. The confidence interval constructed in Example 11.11 is $7.791 < \beta_1 < 12.225$. This confidence interval contains 9, so it is consistent with the finding.

Construct confidence intervals with technology

Construct a confidence interval with technology

Use the TI-84 Plus calculator to construct the confidence interval in Example 11.11.

Solution
The TI-84 Plus display is as follows:

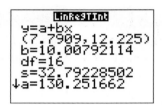

```
LinRegTInt
y=a+bx
(7.7909,12.225)
b=10.00792114
df=16
s=32.79228502
↓a=130.251662
```

The confidence interval is shown on the second line of the display. Step-by-step instructions for constructing confidence intervals with technology are presented in the Using Technology section on page 515.

Check Your Understanding

2. A certain data set contains 27 points. The least-squares regression line is computed, with the following results: $b_1 = 5.78$, $s_e = 1.35$, and $\sum(x - \bar{x})^2 = 3.4$. Construct a 95% confidence interval for β_1.

3. Following is a TI-84 Plus display showing a 95% confidence interval for β_1.

```
LinRegTInt
y=a+bx
(.17354,.2208)
b=.1971681416
df=10
s=.3254404775
↓a=1.077522124
```

    a. What is the slope of the least-squares regression line?
    b. How many degrees of freedom are there?
    c. How many points are in the data set?
    d. What is the 95% confidence interval for β_1?

Answers are on page 519.

Objective 4 Test hypotheses about the slope

Testing Hypotheses About the Slope

We can use the values of b_1 and s_b to test hypotheses about the population slope β_1. If $\beta_1 = 0$, then there is no linear relationship between the explanatory variable x and the outcome variable y. For this reason, the null hypothesis most often tested is $H_0: \beta_1 = 0$. If this null hypothesis is rejected, we conclude that there is a linear relationship between x and y, and that the explanatory variable x is useful in predicting the outcome variable y.

Recall that the quantity

$$\frac{b_1 - \beta_1}{s_b}$$

Explain It Again

$\beta_1 = 0$ **means no linear relationship:** If $\beta_1 = 0$, then the mean of the outcome variable is $\mu_{y|x} = \beta_0$ for every value of x. Therefore, no matter what the value of x, the mean of y stays the same.

has a Student's t distribution with $n - 2$ degrees of freedom. We construct the test statistic for testing H_0: $\beta_1 = 0$ by setting $\beta_1 = 0$. The test statistic is

$$t = \frac{b_1}{s_b}$$

When H_0 is true, the test statistic has a Student's t distribution with $n - 2$ degrees of freedom. If the assumptions of the linear model are satisfied, a test of the hypothesis $\beta_1 = 0$ can be performed. The steps are as follows:

Testing H_0: $\beta_1 = 0$

Step 1: Compute the least-squares regression line. Verify that the assumptions of the linear model are satisfied.

Step 2: State the null and alternate hypotheses. The null hypothesis is H_0: $\beta_1 = 0$. The alternate hypothesis may be stated in any of three ways:

Left-tailed: H_1: $\beta_1 < 0$
Right-tailed: H_1: $\beta_1 > 0$
Two-tailed: H_1: $\beta_1 \neq 0$

Step 3: If making a decision, choose a significance level α.

Step 4: Compute the standard error of the slope s_b.

Step 5: Compute the value of the test statistic $t = \dfrac{b_1}{s_b}$ and the number of degrees of freedom $n - 2$.

The P-Value Method

Step 6: Compute the P-value of the test statistic.

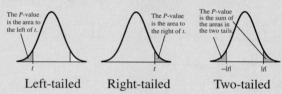

The P-value is the area to the left of t. The P-value is the area to the right of t. The P-value is the sum of the areas in the two tails.

Left-tailed   Right-tailed   Two-tailed

Step 7: Interpret the P-value. If making a decision, reject H_0 if the P-value is less than or equal to the significance level α.

Step 8: State a conclusion.

The Critical Value Method

Step 6: Find the critical value.

Step 7: Determine whether to reject H_0, as follows:

Left-tailed: H_1: $\beta_1 < 0$ Reject if $t \leq -t_\alpha$.
Right-tailed: H_1: $\beta_1 > 0$ Reject if $t \geq t_\alpha$.
Two-tailed: H_1: $\beta_1 \neq 0$ Reject if $t \geq t_{\alpha/2}$ or $t \leq -t_{\alpha/2}$.

Step 8: State a conclusion.

EXAMPLE 11.14 **Test a hypothesis about the slope**

For the data in Table 11.3, perform a test of H_0: $\beta_1 = 0$ versus H_1: $\beta_1 > 0$. Use the $\alpha = 0.05$ level of significance.

Solution

Step 1: **Compute the least-squares regression line and verify that the assumptions of the linear model are satisfied.** We computed the least-squares regression line (Figure 11.10) and obtained $b_1 = 10.0079$. The assumptions were verified in Figure 11.12.

Step 2: **State the null and alternate hypotheses.** The hypotheses are

$$H_0: \beta_1 = 0 \qquad H_1: \beta_1 > 0$$

Step 3: **Choose a significance level.** We will choose $\alpha = 0.05$.

Step 4: **Compute s_b.** In Example 11.10, we computed $s_b = 1.0458$.

Step 5: Compute the value of the test statistic. In Example 11.10, we computed $s_b = 1.0458$. The point estimate is $b_1 = 10.0079$. We compute

$$t = \frac{b_1}{s_b} = \frac{10.0079}{1.0458} = 9.57$$

Because the sample size is $n = 18$, the number of degrees of freedom is $n - 2 = 16$.

_P_-Value Method

Step 6: Compute the _P_-value of the test statistic. We use technology to compute the _P_-value. The following TI-84 Plus calculator display presents the _P_-value in scientific notation. The notation **E-8** indicates that the decimal point should be moved eight places to the left. Thus, the _P_-value is $P = 0.0000000252$.

Step 7: Interpret the _P_-value. Because $P < 0.05$, we reject H_0. We conclude that $\beta_1 > 0$.

Step 8: State a conclusion. There is a linear relationship between the amount of fat and the number of calories in fast-food products. Because we conclude that $\beta_1 > 0$, we conclude that products with more fat tend to have more calories.

Critical Value Method

Step 6: Find the critical value. This is a right-tailed test, so the critical value is the value t_α for which the area to the right is $\alpha = 0.05$. We use Table A.3 with 16 degrees of freedom. The critical value is $t_\alpha = 1.746$.

Step 7: Determine whether to reject H_0. The value of the test statistic is $t = 9.57$. Because $t > t_\alpha$, we reject H_0. We conclude that $\beta_1 > 0$.

Step 8: State a conclusion. There is a linear relationship between the amount of fat and the number of calories in fast-food products. Because we conclude that $\beta_1 > 0$, we conclude that products with more fat tend to have more calories.

Testing the correlation

In Section 11.1, we introduced the sample correlation coefficient r, which is computed from a sample. If we knew the entire population and computed the correlation from it, we would obtain the **population correlation**, which is denoted with the Greek letter ρ (rho). The correlation measures the strength of the linear relationship between two variables. The population correlation ρ and the population slope β_1 always have the same sign. In particular, whenever one of them is equal to 0, the other is equal to 0 as well. For this reason, a test of the hypothesis $\beta_1 = 0$ is also a test of the hypothesis $\rho = 0$. A specialized test of H_0: $\rho = 0$ is available, but it always produces the same result as the test of H_0: $\beta_1 = 0$ that we have presented.

EXAMPLE 11.15 **Test a hypothesis with technology**

For the data in Table 11.3, perform a test of H_0: $\beta_1 = 0$ versus H_1: $\beta_1 > 0$. Use the $\alpha = 0.05$ level of significance.

Solution
The following TI-84 Plus display was presented in Example 11.14. We explain it in more detail.

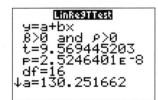

The second line specifies the alternate hypothesis. The third line presents the value of the test statistic, and the fourth line shows the P-value. As explained in Example 11.14, the symbol **E−8** means that the decimal point should be moved over eight places to the left.

Now we will present the results from MINITAB.

```
Regression Analysis: Calories versus Fat

The regression equation is
Calories = 130 + 10.0 Fat

Predictor       Coef      SE Coef       T        P
Constant      130.25        19.03    6.85    0.000
Fat           10.008         1.046   9.57    0.000
```

The P-value is given in the column headed "P," in the row labeled "Fat."

Check Your Understanding

4. For a given data set containing 18 points, the assumptions of the linear model are satisfied. The following values are computed: $b_1 = 5.58$ and $s_b = 4.42$. Perform a test of the hypothesis $H_0: \beta_1 = 0$ versus $H_1: \beta_1 \neq 0$. Use the $\alpha = 0.05$ level of significance. Can you conclude that the explanatory variable is useful in predicting the outcome variable? Explain.

5. For a given data set containing 26 points, the assumptions of the linear model are satisfied. The following values are computed: $b_1 = 46.8$ and $s_b = 15.2$. Perform a test of the hypothesis $H_0: \beta_1 = 0$ versus $H_1: \beta_1 > 0$. Use the $\alpha = 0.01$ level of significance. Can you conclude that the explanatory variable is useful in predicting the outcome variable? Explain.

6. The following TI-84 Plus display presents the results of a test of the null hypothesis $H_0: \beta_1 = 0$.

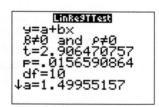

a. What is the alternate hypothesis?
b. What is the value of the test statistic?
c. How many degrees of freedom are there?
d. What is the P-value?
e. Can you conclude that the explanatory variable is useful in predicting the outcome variable? Answer this question using the $\alpha = 0.05$ significance level.

Answers are on page 519.

USING TECHNOLOGY

We use the data in Table 11.3 and Examples 11.11 and 11.14 to illustrate the technology steps.

TI-84 PLUS

Constructing a confidence interval for the slope of the least-squares regression line

Step 1. Enter the x-values from Table 11.3 into **L1** and the y-values into **L2** (Figure A).

Step 2. Press **STAT** and highlight the **TESTS** menu. Select **LinRegTInt** and press **ENTER** (Figure B). The **LinRegTInt** menu appears.

Step 3. Enter **L1** in the **Xlist** field and **L2** in the **Ylist** field.

Step 4. Enter the confidence level in the **C-Level** field. For Example 11.11, we enter **.95** (Figure C).

Step 5. Highlight **Calculate** and press **ENTER** (Figure D).

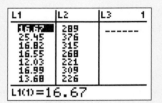

Figure A

Figure B

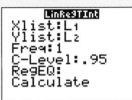

Figure C

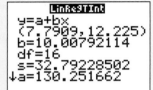

Figure D

Testing a hypothesis about the slope of the least-squares regression line

Step 1. Enter the x-values from Table 11.3 into **L1** and the y-values into **L2** (Figure E).

Step 2. Press **STAT** and highlight the **TESTS** menu. Select **LinRegTTest** and press **ENTER** (Figure F). The **LinRegTTest** menu appears.

Step 3. Enter **L1** in the **Xlist** field and **L2** in the **Ylist** field.

Step 4. Select the form of the alternate hypothesis. For Example 11.14, the alternate hypothesis has the form **>0** (Figure G).

Step 5. Highlight **Calculate** and press **ENTER** (Figure H).

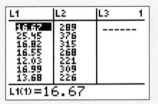

Figure E

Figure F

Figure G

Figure H

MINITAB

Testing a hypothesis about the slope of the least-squares regression line

Step 1. Label **Column C1** as **Fat** and **Column C2** as **Calories**. Enter the x-values from Table 11.3 into the **Fat** column and the y-values into the **Calories** column.

Step 2. Click on **Stat**, then **Regression**, then **Regression**.

Step 3. Select the y-variable (**Calories**) as the **Response variable** and the x-variable as the **Predictor (Fat)**.

Step 4. Click **OK** (Figure I).

```
The regression equation is
Calories = 130 + 10.0 Fat

Predictor      Coef     SE Coef       T       P
Constant     130.25       19.03    6.85   0.000
Fat          10.008        1.046   9.57   0.000
```

Figure I

Note: MINITAB presents the P-value for a two-tailed test by default. For a one-tailed test, divide this value by 2.

EXCEL

Constructing a confidence interval and testing a hypothesis for the slope of the least-squares regression line

This procedure requires the **MegaStat** EXCEL add-in to be loaded. The **MegaStat** add-in may be downloaded from www.mhhe.com/megastat.

Step 1. Enter the x-values from Table 11.3 into **Column A** and the y-values into **Column B**.

Step 2. Click on the **MegaStat** menu, select **Correlation/Regression**, then **Regression Analysis...**

Step 3. Enter the range of cells containing the x-values in the **X, Independent variable(s)** field and the range of cells containing the y-values in the **Y, Dependent variable** field. To find the confidence interval, enter the confidence level in the **Confidence Level** field. For Example 11.11, we use **95%** (Figure J).

Step 4. Click **OK** (Figure K).

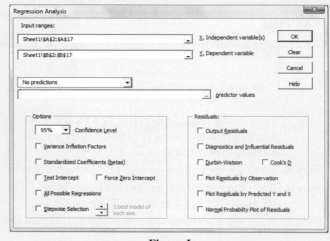

Figure J

Regression output					confidence interval	
variables	coefficients	std. error	t (df=16)	p-value	95% lower	95% upper
Intercept	130.2517					
Fat	10.0079	1.0458	9.569	5.05E-08	7.7909	12.2250

Figure K

Note: EXCEL presents the P-value for a two-tailed test by default. For a one-tailed test, divide this value by 2.

SECTION 11.3   Exercises

Exercises 1–6 are the Check Your Understanding exercises located within the section.

Understanding the Concepts

In Exercises 7 and 8, fill in each blank with the appropriate word or phrase.

7. If there are 20 pairs (x, y) in a data set, then the number of degrees of freedom for the critical value is _____ .

8. Under the assumptions of the linear model, the values of $\mu_{y|x}$ follow a _____ .

In Exercises 9 and 10, determine whether the statement is true or false. If the statement is false, rewrite it as a true statement.

9. Under the assumptions of the linear model, the residual plot will exhibit a linear pattern.

10. Under the assumptions of the linear model, the vertical spread in a residual plot will be about the same across the plot.

Practicing the Skills

11. The summary statistics for a certain set of points are: $n = 30$, $s_e = 3.975$, $\sum(x - \bar{x})^2 = 15.425$, and $b_1 = 1.212$. Assume the conditions of the linear model hold. A 95% confidence interval for β_1 will be constructed.
    a. How many degrees of freedom are there for the critical value?
    b. What is the critical value?
    c. What is the margin of error?
    d. Construct the 95% confidence interval.

12. The summary statistics for a certain set of points are: $n = 20$, $s_e = 4.65$, $\sum(x - \bar{x})^2 = 118.26$, and $b_1 = 1.62$. Assume the conditions of the linear model hold. A 99% confidence interval for β_1 will be constructed.
    a. How many degrees of freedom are there for the critical value?
    b. What is the critical value?
    c. What is the margin of error?
    d. Construct the 99% confidence interval.

13. Use the summary statistics in Exercise 11 to test the null hypothesis $H_0: \beta_1 = 0$ versus $H_1: \beta_1 \neq 0$. Use the $\alpha = 0.01$ level of significance.

14. Use the summary statistics in Exercise 12 to test the null hypothesis $H_0: \beta_1 = 0$ versus $H_1: \beta_1 > 0$. Use the $\alpha = 0.05$ level of significance.

In Exercises 15–18, use the given set of points to
    a. Compute b_1.
    b. Compute the residual standard deviation s_e.
    c. Compute the sum of squares for x, $\sum(x - \bar{x})^2$.
    d. Compute the standard error of b_1, s_b.
    e. Find the critical value for a 95% confidence interval for β_1.
    f. Compute the margin of error for a 95% confidence interval for β_1.
    g. Construct a 95% confidence interval for β_1.
    h. Test the null hypothesis $H_0: \beta_1 = 0$ versus $H_1: \beta_1 \neq 0$. Use the $\alpha = 0.05$ level of significance.

15.

x	12	21	27	27	10	15
y	52	90	113	111	45	65

16.

x	12	17	3	17	16	11	14	9
y	13	14	16	13	14	14	13	14

17.

x	18	20	17	12	10
y	71	77	68	52	46

18.

x	12	13	15	13	12	14	13
y	18	19	18	16	16	15	20

Working with the Concepts

19. Calories and protein: The following table presents the number of grams of protein and the number of calories per 100 grams for each of 18 fast-food products.

Protein	Calories	Protein	Calories
17.25	289	5.62	367
13.73	376	3.58	188
12.96	315	11.97	275
21.24	268	5.84	408
22.54	221	12.22	460
16.23	309	8.05	189
10.64	226	5.15	366
6.16	344	15.93	334
3.69	163	16.52	241

Source: United States Department of Agriculture

a. Compute the least-squares regression line for predicting calories (y) from protein (x).
b. Construct a 95% confidence interval for the slope.
c. Test H_0: $\beta_1 = 0$ versus H_1: $\beta_1 \neq 0$. Can you conclude that the amount of protein is useful in predicting the number of calories? Use the $\alpha = 0.05$ level of significance.

20. Like father, like son: In 1906, the statistician Karl Pearson measured the heights of 1078 pairs of fathers and sons. The following table presents a sample of 16 pairs, with height measured in inches, simulated from the distribution specified by Pearson.

Father's height	Son's height	Father's height	Son's height
70.8	69.8	72.4	69.1
65.4	66.0	65.7	65.3
65.7	70.9	69.1	71.8
69.0	69.1	70.7	71.0
73.6	74.9	72.3	71.9
66.7	68.8	73.6	76.5
70.1	73.3	69.3	71.4
68.3	68.3	64.5	68.5

a. Compute the least-squares regression line for predicting son's height (y) from father's height (x).
b. Construct a 95% confidence interval for the slope.
c. Test H_0: $\beta_1 = 0$ versus H_1: $\beta_1 \neq 0$. Can you conclude that father's height is useful in predicting son's height? Use the $\alpha = 0.05$ level of significance.

21. Butterfly wings: Do larger butterflies live longer? The wingspan (in millimeters) and the lifespan in the adult state (in days) were measured for 22 species of butterfly. Following are the results.

Wingspan	Lifespan	Wingspan	Lifespan
35.5	19.8	25.9	32.5
30.6	17.3	31.3	27.5
30.0	27.5	23.0	31.0
32.3	22.4	26.3	37.4
23.9	40.7	23.7	22.6
27.7	18.3	27.1	23.1
28.8	25.9	28.1	18.5
35.9	23.1	25.9	32.3
25.4	24.0	28.8	29.1
24.6	38.8	31.4	37.0
28.1	36.5	28.5	33.7

Source: *Oikos Journal of Ecology* 105:41–54

a. Compute the least-squares regression line for predicting lifespan (y) from wingspan (x).
b. Construct a 99% confidence interval for the slope.
c. Test H_0: $\beta_1 = 0$ versus H_1: $\beta_1 < 0$. Can you conclude that wingspan is useful in predicting lifespan? Use the $\alpha = 0.05$ level of significance.
d. Do larger butterflies tend to live for a longer or shorter time than smaller butterflies? Explain.

22. Blood pressure: A blood pressure measurement consists of two numbers: the systolic pressure, which is the maximum pressure taken when the heart is contracting, and the diastolic pressure, which is the minimum pressure taken at the beginning of the heartbeat. Blood pressures were measured, in millimeters, for a sample of 16 adults. The following table presents the results.

Systolic	Diastolic	Systolic	Diastolic
134	87	133	91
115	83	112	75
113	77	107	71
123	77	110	74
119	69	108	69
118	88	105	66
130	76	157	103
116	70	154	94

Based on results published in the *Journal of Hypertension* 26:199–209

a. Compute the least-squares regression line for predicting diastolic pressure (y) from systolic pressure (x).
b. Construct a 99% confidence interval for the slope.
c. Test H_0: $\beta_1 = 0$ versus H_1: $\beta_1 > 0$. Can you conclude that systolic blood pressure is useful in predicting diastolic blood pressure? Use the $\alpha = 0.01$ level of significance.
d. Do people with higher diastolic pressure tend to have higher or lower systolic pressures? Explain.

23. Noisy streets: How much noisier are streets where cars travel faster? The following table presents noise levels in decibels and average speed in kilometers per hour for a sample of roads.

Speed	Noise
28.26	78.1
36.22	79.6
38.73	81.0
29.07	78.7
30.28	78.6
30.25	78.5
29.03	78.4
33.17	79.6

Source: *Journal of Transportation Engineering* 125:152–159

a. Compute the least-squares regression line for predicting noise level (y) from speed (x).
b. Construct a 95% confidence interval for the slope.
c. Test H_0: $\beta_1 = 0$ versus H_1: $\beta_1 \neq 0$. Can you conclude that speed is useful in predicting noise level? Use the $\alpha = 0.01$ level of significance.

24. **Fast reactions:** In a study of reaction times, the time to respond to a visual stimulus (x) and the time to respond to an auditory stimulus (y) were recorded for each of 10 subjects. Times were measured in thousandths of a second. The results are presented in the following table.

Visual	Auditory
161	159
203	206
235	241
176	163
201	197
188	193
228	209
211	189
191	169
178	201

a. Compute the least-squares regression line for predicting auditory response time (y) from visual response time (x).
b. Construct a 95% confidence interval for the slope.
c. Test H_0: $\beta_1 = 0$ versus H_1: $\beta_1 \neq 0$. Can you conclude that visual response is useful in predicting auditory response? Use the $\alpha = 0.01$ level of significance.

25. **Getting bigger:** Concrete expands both horizontally and vertically over time. Measurements of horizontal and vertical expansion (in units of parts per hundred thousand) were made at several locations on a bridge in Quebec City in Canada. The results are presented in the following table.

Horizontal	Vertical
20	58
15	58
43	55
5	80
18	58
24	68
32	57
10	69
21	63

Source: *Canadian Journal of Civil Engineering* 32:463–479

a. Compute the least-squares line for predicting vertical expansion (y) from horizontal expansion (x).
b. Construct a 95% confidence interval for the slope β_1.
c. Test H_0: $\beta_1 = 0$ versus H_1: $\beta_1 \neq 0$. Can you conclude that horizontal expansion is useful in predicting vertical expansion? Use the $\alpha = 0.05$ level of significance.

26. **Dry up:** In a study to determine the relationship between ambient outdoor temperature and the rate of evaporation of water from soil, measurements of average daytime temperature in °C and evaporation in millimeters per day were taken for 10 days. The results are shown in the following table.

Temperature	Evaporation
11.8	2.4
21.5	4.4
16.5	5.0
23.6	4.1
19.1	6.0
21.6	5.9
31.0	4.8
18.9	3.0
24.2	7.1
19.1	1.6

a. Compute the least-squares line for predicting evaporation (y) from temperature (x).
b. Construct a 99% confidence interval for β_1.
c. Test H_0: $\beta_1 = 0$ versus H_1: $\beta_1 \neq 0$. Can you conclude that temperature is useful in predicting evaporation? Use the $\alpha = 0.05$ level of significance.

27. **Calculator display:** The following TI-84 Plus display presents the results of a test of the null hypothesis H_0: $\beta_1 = 0$.

```
   LinRegTTest
y=a+bx
β≠0 and ρ≠0
t=3.143104276
P=.0199889322
df=6
↓a=1.544316997
```

a. What is the alternate hypothesis?
b. What is the value of the test statistic?
c. How many degrees of freedom are there?
d. What is the P-value?
e. Can you conclude that the explanatory variable is useful in predicting the outcome variable? Answer this question using the $\alpha = 0.05$ level of significance.

28. **Calculator display:** The following TI-84 Plus display presents the results of a test of the null hypothesis H_0: $\beta_1 = 0$.

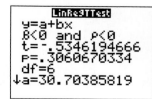

```
   LinRegTTest
y=a+bx
β<0 and ρ<0
t=-.5346194666
P=.3060670334
df=6
↓a=30.70385819
```

a. What is the alternate hypothesis?
b. What is the value of the test statistic?
c. How many degrees of freedom are there?
d. What is the P-value?
e. Can you conclude that the explanatory variable is useful in predicting the outcome variable? Answer this question using the $\alpha = 0.05$ level of significance.

29. **Air pollution:** Ozone is a major component of air pollution in many cities. Atmospheric ozone levels are influenced by many factors, including weather. In one study, the mean percent relative humidity (x) and the ozone levels (y) were measured for 120 days in a western city. Ozone levels were measured in parts per billion. The following MINITAB output describes the fit of a linear model to these data. Assume that the assumptions of the linear model are satisfied.

```
The regression equation is
Ozone = 88.761 - 0.7524 Humidity

Predictor      Coef     SE Coef        T        P
Constant     88.761       7.288    12.18    0.000
Humidity    -0.7524     0.13024    -5.78    0.000
```

a. What are the slope and intercept of the least-squares regression line?
b. Can you conclude that relative humidity is useful in predicting ozone levels? Answer this question using the $\alpha = 0.05$ level of significance.

30. **Cholesterol:** Serum cholesterol levels (y) and age in years (x) were recorded for several men in a medical center.

Cholesterol levels were measured in milligrams per deciliter. The following MINITAB output describes the fit of a linear model to these data. Assume that the assumptions of the linear model are satisfied.

```
The regression equation is
Cholesterol = 162.15 + 1.2499 Age

Predictor      Coef     SE Coef        T        P
Constant     162.15      16.439    9.863    0.000
Age          1.2499     0.38708    3.772    0.007
```

a. What are the slope and intercept of the least-squares regression line?
b. Can you conclude that age is useful in predicting cholesterol levels? Answer this question using the $\alpha = 0.05$ level of significance.

Extending the Concepts

31. **Confidence interval for the conditional mean:** In Example 11.11, we constructed a 95% confidence interval for the slope β_1 in the model to predict the number of calories from the number of grams of fat. The 95% confidence interval is $7.791 < \beta_1 < 12.225$. Let $\mu_{y|15}$ be the mean number of calories for food products containing 15 grams of fat, and let $\mu_{y|20}$ be the mean number of calories for food products containing 20 grams of fat. Construct a 95% confidence interval for the difference $\mu_{y|20} - \mu_{y|15}$.

Answers to Check Your Understanding Exercises for Section 11.3

1. a. Not satisfied; plot exhibits a pattern.
   b. Not satisfied; vertical spread varies.
   c. Satisfied
   d. Not satisfied; plot contains outliers.
2. $4.27 < \beta_1 < 7.29$
3. a. 0.1971681416   b. 10   c. 12
   d. $0.17354 < \beta_1 < 0.2208$

4. No. $P > 0.05$, so we do not reject H_0. It is possible that $\beta_1 = 0$ so that the explanatory variable is not helpful in predicting the outcome variable.
5. Yes. $P < 0.01$, so we reject H_0. We conclude that $\beta_1 > 0$, so the explanatory variable is helpful in predicting the outcome variable.
6. a. $\beta_1 \neq 0$ b. $t = 2.906470757$ c. 10
   d. 0.0156590864   e. Yes

SECTION 11.4   Inference About the Response

Objectives

1. Construct confidence intervals for the mean response
2. Construct prediction intervals for an individual response

Objective 1 Construct confidence intervals for the mean response

Confidence Intervals for the Mean Response

In Section 11.3, we learned how to construct confidence intervals for the slope in a linear model that was used to predict the number of calories in a fast-food product from the number of grams of fat. The least-squares regression line was $\hat{y} = 130.251662 + 10.00792114x$.

In this section, we will consider two further problems.

1. Given that the number of grams of fat is x, estimate the mean number of calories for all fast-food products whose fat content is x.
2. Given that the number of grams of fat is x, predict the number of calories for a particular fast-food product whose fat content is x.

Figure 11.13 presents an intuitive picture of these two problems. Imagine that this figure represents the entire population of fast-food products. Each point represents a particular product. The x-value of the point represents the fat content, and the y-value of the point represents the number of calories. The vertical strip contains all the points for which the fat content is x. We can visualize the two problems by looking at this figure.

1. The mean number of calories for all the products whose fat content is x is the value $\mu_{y|x}$. This is the y-value of the line $\mu_{y|x} = \beta_0 + \beta_1 x$ through the middle of the vertical strip.

2. The number of calories in a particular fast-food product whose fat content is x is the y-value of a randomly chosen point in the vertical strip.

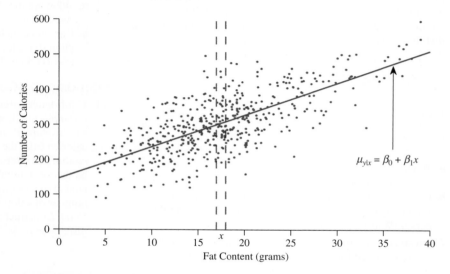

Figure 11.13 Imagine that this scatterplot represents the entire population of fast-food products. The vertical strip contains all the products for which the fat content is x.

The point estimate is the same for both of these problems. The point estimate is the y-value on the least-squares regression line: $\hat{y} = 130.251662 + 10.00792114x$. However, if we want to construct intervals around these point estimates, the interval for the predicted number of calories in a particular product will have a larger margin of error than the interval for the estimated mean number of calories of all the products. The reason is that there is less variation in the mean of all the values in a vertical strip than in the distribution of the individual points.

Constructing a confidence interval for the mean response

The mean y-value corresponding to a given x-value is called the **mean response**. We show how to construct a confidence interval for the mean response.

CAUTION

Be sure that the assumptions of the linear model are satisfied before constructing a confidence interval for the mean response.

Constructing a Confidence Interval for the Mean Response

Let x^* be a value of the explanatory variable x, let $\hat{y} = b_0 + b_1 x^*$ be the predicted value corresponding to x^*, and let n be the sample size. A level $100(1 - \alpha)\%$ confidence interval for the mean response is

$$\hat{y} \pm t_{\alpha/2} \cdot s_e \sqrt{\frac{1}{n} + \frac{(x^* - \bar{x})^2}{\sum (x - \bar{x})^2}}$$

The critical value $t_{\alpha/2}$ is based on $n - 2$ degrees of freedom.

EXAMPLE 11.16 | **Constructing a confidence interval for the mean response**

Construct a 95% confidence interval for the mean number of calories for fast-food products containing 18 grams of fat.

Solution
The least-squares regression line is $\hat{y} = 130.251662 + 10.00792114x$. To obtain the point estimate $\hat{y}$, we replace x with $x^* = 18$ to obtain

$$\hat{y} = 130.251662 + 10.00792114(18) = 310.39424$$

The sample size is $n = 18$, so there are 16 degrees of freedom. The critical value is $t_{\alpha/2} = 2.120$.

To obtain the margin of error, recall that we computed $\bar{x} = 16.622778$, $s_e = 32.792285$, and $\sum(x - \bar{x})^2 = 983.1712$ in Example 11.10 in Section 11.3. The margin of error is therefore

Recall: The quantity s_e is the residual standard deviation:

$$s_e = \sqrt{\frac{\sum(y - \hat{y})^2}{n - 2}}$$

$$t_{\alpha/2} \cdot s_e \sqrt{\frac{1}{n} + \frac{(x^* - \bar{x})^2}{\sum(x - \bar{x})^2}} = 2.120 \cdot 32.792285 \sqrt{\frac{1}{18} + \frac{(18 - 16.622778)^2}{983.1712}} = 16.66802$$

The 95% confidence interval is

$$310.39424 \pm 16.66802$$

$$293.73 < \text{Mean response} < 327.06$$

We are 95% confident that the mean number of calories for fast-food products containing 18 grams of fat is between 293.73 and 327.06.

EXAMPLE 11.17 | **Interpreting a confidence interval**

In Example 11.16, we found that we are 95% confident that the mean number of calories for fast-food products containing 18 grams of fat is between 293.73 and 327.06. You are planning to purchase a particular product that contains 18 grams of fat. Can you be 95% confident that the number of calories in your particular product will be between 293.73 and 327.06? Explain why or why not.

Solution
No, you cannot be 95% confident that the number of calories in your particular product will be between 293.73 and 327.06. The confidence interval for the mean response provides information about the mean number of calories for all fast-food products with 18 grams of fat. To estimate the number of calories in a particular product, we need a prediction interval for an **individual response**. The prediction interval will have a larger margin of error than the confidence interval for the mean response. We will learn to construct prediction intervals later in this section.

Check Your Understanding

1. For a sample of size $n = 20$, the following values were obtained: $b_0 = 1.05$, $b_1 = 4.50$, $s_e = 0.54$, $\sum(x - \bar{x})^2 = 10.9$, $\bar{x} = 8.52$. Construct a 95% confidence interval for the mean response when $x = 10$.

Answer is on page 525.

Objective 2 Construct prediction intervals for an individual response

Prediction Intervals for an Individual Response
Following is the method for constructing a **prediction interval**.

Constructing a Prediction Interval

Let x^* be a value of the explanatory variable x, let $\hat{y} = b_0 + b_1 x^*$ be the predicted value corresponding to x^*, and let n be the sample size. A level $100(1-\alpha)\%$ prediction interval for an individual response is

$$\hat{y} \pm t_{\alpha/2} \cdot s_e \sqrt{1 + \frac{1}{n} + \frac{(x^* - \bar{x})^2}{\sum (x - \bar{x})^2}}$$

The critical value $t_{\alpha/2}$ is based on $n - 2$ degrees of freedom.

Note that the standard error for the prediction interval is similar to the one for the confidence interval for a mean response. The difference is that the standard error for prediction has a "1" added to the quantity under the square root. This reflects the extra variability in the prediction interval.

EXAMPLE 11.18

Constructing a prediction interval

A particular fast-food product has a fat content of 18 grams. Construct a 95% prediction interval for the number of calories in this product.

Solution
The least-squares regression line is $\hat{y} = 130.251662 + 10.00792114x$. To obtain the point estimate $\hat{y}$, we replace x with $x^* = 18$ to obtain

$$\hat{y} = 130.251662 + 10.00792114(18) = 310.39424$$

The sample size is $n = 18$, so there are 16 degrees of freedom. The critical value is $t_{\alpha/2} = 2.120$.

To obtain the margin of error, recall that we computed $\bar{x} = 16.622778$, $s_e = 32.792285$, and $\sum (x - \bar{x})^2 = 983.1712$ in Example 11.10 in Section 11.3. The margin of error is therefore

$$t_{\alpha/2} \cdot s_e \sqrt{1 + \frac{1}{n} + \frac{(x^* - \bar{x})^2}{\sum (x - \bar{x})^2}} = 2.120 \cdot 32.792285 \sqrt{1 + \frac{1}{18} + \frac{(18 - 16.622778)^2}{983.1712}}$$

$$= 71.49$$

The 95% prediction interval is

$$310.39 \pm 71.49$$

$$238.90 < \text{Number of calories} < 381.88$$

We are 95% confident that a particular fast-food product with a fat content of 18 grams will have between 238.90 and 381.88 calories.

EXAMPLE 11.19

Interpret a prediction interval

Refer to Example 11.18. You are planning to eat lunch at a fast-food restaurant, and you want to consume less than 400 calories. If you choose an item that contains 18 grams of fat, can you be reasonably sure that it will contain less than 400 calories?

Solution
Yes. We are 95% confident that a particular fast-food product with a fat content of 18 grams will have between 238.90 and 381.88 calories. Therefore, we can be reasonably sure that it will contain less than 400 calories.

Check Your Understanding

2. For a sample of size $n = 15$, the following values were obtained: $b_0 = 3.71$, $b_1 = 8.38$, $s_e = 1.13$, $\sum(x - \bar{x})^2 = 7.71$, $\bar{x} = 13.16$. Construct a 95% prediction interval for an individual response when $x = 8$.

Answer is on page 525.

EXAMPLE 11.20   ## Constructing intervals with technology

Use technology to construct a 95% confidence interval for the mean number of calories for fast-food products containing 18 grams of fat, and to construct a 95% prediction interval for the number of calories in a particular fast-food product that contains 18 grams of fat.

Solution
We will use MINITAB. The output is as follows.

Fit	StDev Fit	95.0% CI	95.0% PI
310.79	7.86	(293.73, 327.06)	(238.91, 381.88)

The 95% confidence interval and the 95% prediction interval are shown. The prediction interval constructed with technology differs slightly from the one computed by hand in Example 11.18 because MINITAB uses a more precise critical value. Step-by-step instructions for constructing confidence intervals for the mean response and prediction intervals are given in the Using Technology section that follows.

USING TECHNOLOGY

We use the data in Table 11.3 and Example 11.18 to illustrate the technology steps.

MINITAB

Constructing confidence and prediction intervals

Step 1. Follow Steps 1–3 in the MINITAB procedure described on page 515 in Section 11.3.

Step 2. Click **Options...** and enter the response value in the **Prediction intervals for new observations** field. For Example 11.18, we use **18**.

Step 3. Enter the confidence level in the **Confidence level** field. We use **95**. Click **OK**.

Step 4. Click **OK** (Figure A).

Fit	StDev Fit	95.0% CI	95.0% PI
310.79	7.86	(293.73, 327.06)	(238.91, 381.88)

Figure A

EXCEL

Constructing confidence and prediction intervals

Step 1. Follow Steps 1–3 in the EXCEL procedure described on page 516 in Section 11.3.

Step 2. Select **Type in predictor values** from the pull-down menu and enter the response value in the **predictor values** field. For Example 11.18, we use **18**.

Step 3. Click **OK** (Figure B).

Predicted values for: Fat

Calories	Predicted	95% Confidence Interval lower	upper	95% Prediction Interval lower	upper
18	310.394	293.727	327.062	238.908	381.881

Figure B

SECTION 11.4   **Exercises**

Exercises 1 and 2 are the Check Your Understanding exercises located within the section.

Understanding the Concepts

In Exercises 3 and 4, fill in each blank with the appropriate word or phrase.

3. A _____ interval estimates the mean y-value for all individuals with a given x-value.

4. A _____ interval estimates the y-value for a particular individual with a given x-value.

In Exercises 5 and 6, determine whether the statement is true or false. If the statement is false, rewrite it as a true statement.

5. For a given x-value, the 95% confidence interval for the mean response will always be wider than the 95% prediction interval.

6. For a given x-value, the point estimate for a 95% confidence interval for the mean response is the same as the one for the 95% prediction interval.

Practicing the Skills

7. For a sample of size 25, the following values were obtained: $b_0 = 3.25$, $b_1 = 2.32$, $s_e = 3.53$, $\sum(x - \bar{x})^2 = 224.05$, and $\bar{x} = 0.98$.
   a. Construct a 95% confidence interval for the mean response when $x = 2$.
   b. Construct a 95% prediction interval for an individual response when $x = 2$.

8. For a sample of size 18, the following values were obtained: $b_0 = 2.27$, $b_1 = -1.46$, $s_e = 5.72$, $\sum(x - \bar{x})^2 = 360.26$, and $\bar{x} = 1.95$.
   a. Construct a 99% confidence interval for the mean response when $x = 2$.
   b. Construct a 99% prediction interval for an individual response when $x = 2$.

In Exercises 9 and 10, use the given set of points to
   a. Compute b_0 and b_1.
   b. Compute the predicted value $\hat{y}$ for the given value of x.
   c. Compute the residual standard deviation s_e.
   d. Compute the sum of squares for x, $\sum(x - \bar{x})^2$.
   e. Find the critical value for a 95% confidence or prediction interval.
   f. Construct a 95% confidence interval for the mean response for the given value of x.
   g. Construct a 95% prediction interval for an individual response for the given value of x.

9.

x	15	11	17	15	11	16
y	30	15	33	27	22	37

$x = 12$

10.

x	23	16	17	19	30	19	18	27
y	51	22	56	34	67	59	55	25

$x = 25$

Working with the Concepts

11. **Calories and protein:** Use the data in Exercise 19 in Section 11.3 for the following:
   a. Compute a point estimate for the mean number of calories in fast-food products that contain 15 grams of protein.
   b. Construct a 95% confidence interval for the mean number of calories in fast-food products that contain 15 grams of protein.
   c. Predict the number of calories in a particular product that contains 15 grams of protein.
   d. Construct a 95% prediction interval for the number of calories in a particular product that contains 15 grams of protein.

12. **Like father, like son:** Use the data in Exercise 20 in Section 11.3 for the following.
   a. Compute a point estimate of the mean height of sons whose fathers are 70 inches tall.
   b. Construct a 95% confidence interval for the mean height of sons whose fathers are 70 inches tall.
   c. Predict the height of a particular son whose father is 70 inches tall.
   d. Construct a 95% prediction interval for the height of a particular son whose father is 70 inches tall.

13. **Butterfly wings:** Use the data in Exercise 21 in Section 11.3 for the following.
   a. Compute a point estimate of the mean lifespan of butterflies with a wingspan of 30 millimeters.
   b. Construct a 95% confidence interval for the mean lifespan of butterflies with a wingspan of 30 millimeters.
   c. Predict the lifespan of a particular butterfly whose wingspan is 30 millimeters.
   d. Construct a 95% prediction interval for the lifespan of a particular butterfly whose wingspan is 30 millimeters.

14. **Blood pressure:** Use the data in Exercise 22 in Section 11.3 for the following.
   a. Compute a point estimate of the mean diastolic pressure for people whose systolic pressure is 120.
   b. Construct a 95% confidence interval for the mean diastolic pressure for people whose systolic pressure is 120.
   c. Predict the diastolic pressure of a particular person whose systolic pressure is 120.
   d. Construct a 95% prediction interval for the diastolic pressure of a particular person whose systolic pressure is 120.

15. **Noisy streets:** Use the data in Exercise 23 in Section 11.3 for the following.
   a. Compute a point estimate for the mean noise level for streets with a mean speed of 35 kilometers per hour.
   b. Construct a 99% confidence interval for the mean noise level for streets with a mean speed of 35 kilometers per hour.
   c. Predict the noise level for a particular street with a mean speed of 35 kilometers per hour.
   d. Construct a 99% prediction interval for the noise level of a particular street with a mean speed of 35 kilometers per hour.

16. Fast reactions: Use the data in Exercise 24 in Section 11.3 for the following.

a. Compute a point estimate for the mean auditory response time for subjects with a visual response time of 200.

b. Construct a 99% confidence interval for the mean auditory response time for subjects with a visual response time of 200.

c. Predict the auditory response time for a particular subject whose visual response time is 200.

d. Construct a 99% prediction interval for the auditory response time for a particular subject whose visual response time is 200.

17. Getting bigger: Use the data in Exercise 25 in Section 11.3 for the following.

a. Compute a point estimate for the mean vertical expansion at locations where the horizontal expansion is 25.

b. Construct a 99% confidence interval for the mean vertical expansion at locations where the horizontal expansion is 25.

c. Predict the vertical expansion at a particular location where the horizontal expansion is 25.

d. Construct a 99% prediction interval for the vertical expansion at a particular location where the horizontal expansion is 25.

18. Dry up: Use the data in Exercise 26 in Section 11.3 for the following.

a. Compute a point estimate for the mean evaporation rate when the temperature is 20°C.

b. Construct a 99% confidence interval for the mean evaporation rate for all days with a temperature of 20°C.

c. Predict the evaporation rate when the temperature is 20°C.

d. Construct a 99% prediction interval for the evaporation rate on a given day with a temperature of 20°C.

19. Air pollution: The following MINITAB output presents a 95% confidence interval for the mean ozone level on days when the relative humidity is 60%, and a 95% prediction interval for the ozone level on a particular day when the relative humidity is 60%. The units of ozone are parts per billion.

```
Predicted Values for New Observations

New Obs    Fit    SE Fit      95.0% CI          95.0% PI
1         43.62    1.20    (41.23, 46.00)    (20.86, 66.37)

Values of Predictors for New Observations

New Obs    Humidity
1             60.0
```

a. What is the point estimate for the mean ozone level for days when the relative humidity is 60%?

b. What is the 95% confidence interval for the mean ozone level for days when the relative humidity is 60%?

c. Predict the ozone level for a day when the relative humidity is 60%.

d. Upon learning that the relative humidity on a certain day is 60%, someone predicts that the ozone level that day will be 80 parts per billion. Is this a reasonable prediction? If so, explain why. If not, give a reasonable range of predicted values.

20. Cholesterol: The following MINITAB output presents a 95% confidence interval for the mean cholesterol levels for men aged 50 years, and a 95% prediction interval for an individual man aged 50. The units of cholesterol are milligrams per deciliter.

```
Predicted Values for New Observations

New Obs    Fit    SE Fit       95.0% CI            95.0% PI
1        224.64    6.08    (211.40, 237.89)    (182.66, 266.42)

Values of Predictors for New Observations

New Obs    Age
1          50.0
```

a. What is the point estimate for the mean cholesterol level for men aged 50?

b. What is the 95% confidence interval for the mean cholesterol level for men aged 50?

c. Predict the cholesterol level for a man aged 50.

d. Upon learning that a man is 50 years old, someone predicts that his cholesterol level is 160. Is this a reasonable prediction? If so, explain why. If not, give a reasonable range of predicted values.

Extending the Concepts

21. Several 95% confidence intervals for the mean response will be constructed, based on a data set for which the sample mean value for the explanatory variable is $\bar{x} = 10$. The values of x^* for which the confidence intervals will be constructed are $x^* = 9$, $x^* = 12$, and $x^* = 14$.

a. For which of these values of x^* will the margin of error be the smallest?

b. For which of these values of x^* will the margin of error be the largest?

c. If one wanted to construct a 95% confidence interval with the smallest possible margin of error, which value of x^* would one use?

Answers to Check Your Understanding Exercises for Section 11.4

1. 45.482 < Mean response < 46.618

2. 65.561 < Individual response < 75.939

Chapter 11 Summary

Section 11.1: Bivariate data are data that consist of ordered pairs. A scatterplot provides a good graphical summary for bivariate data. When large values of one variable are associated with large values of the other, the variables are said to have a positive association. When large values of one variable are associated with small values of the other, the variables are said to have a negative association. When the points on a scatterplot tend to cluster around a straight line, the relationship is said to be linear.

The correlation coefficient r measures the strength of a linear relationship. The value of r is always between -1 and 1. Positive values of r indicate a positive linear association, while negative values of r indicate a negative linear association. Values near 1 or -1 indicate a strong linear association, while values near 0 indicate a weak linear association. The correlation coefficient should not be used when the relationship is not linear.

Correlation is not the same as causation. Even when two variables are highly correlated, it is not necessarily the case that changing the value of one of them will cause a change in the other.

Section 11.2: When two variables have a linear relationship, the points on a scatterplot tend to cluster around a straight line called the least-squares regression line. Given a value of the explanatory variable x, we can predict a value $\hat{y}$ for the outcome variable by substituting the value of x into the equation of the least-squares regression line. The slope of the least-squares regression line predicts the difference between the y-values for two points whose x-values differ by 1. The intercept of the least-squares regression line predicts the y-value of a point whose x-value is 0. The intercept can be interpreted only when the data set contains both positive and negative x-values.

Section 11.3: When the assumptions of the linear model are satisfied, the intercept b_0 and slope b_1 of the least-squares regression line are estimates of a true intercept β_0 and a true slope β_1. The linear model assumptions can be checked by constructing a residual plot. When the residual plot exhibits no obvious pattern, the vertical spread is approximately the same across the plot, and there are no outliers, we may conclude that the assumptions of the linear model are satisfied. We may then compute confidence intervals and test hypotheses about β_1. If we reject H_0: $\beta_1 = 0$, we may conclude that the explanatory variable is useful to help predict the value of the outcome variable.

Section 11.4: When the assumptions of the linear model are satisfied, we may construct confidence intervals for the mean response and prediction intervals for an individual response. A confidence interval for the mean response is an interval that is likely to contain the mean value of the response variable y for a given value of the explanatory variable x. A prediction interval for an individual response is an interval that is likely to contain the value of the response variable y for a randomly chosen individual whose value of the explanatory variable is x.

Vocabulary and Notation

bivariate data 480	mean response 520	prediction interval 521
correlation coefficient r 482	negative association 481	residual 506
explanatory variable (predictor variable) 493	outcome variable (response variable) 493	residual plot 506
individual response 521	ordered pairs 480	residual standard deviation 507
least-squares regression line 493	population correlation 513	scatterplot 480
linear 481	positive association 481	slope b_1 493
linear model 503	point of averages 496	sum of squares for x: $\sum(x - \bar{x})^2$ 508
linear relationship 482	predicted value 495	y-intercept b_0 493

Important Formulas

Correlation coefficient:

$$r = \frac{1}{n-1} \sum \left(\frac{x - \bar{x}}{s_x} \right) \left(\frac{y - \bar{y}}{s_y} \right)$$

Equation of least-squares regression line:
$$\hat{y} = b_0 + b_1 x$$

Slope of least-squares regression line:
$$b_1 = r \frac{s_y}{s_x}$$

y-intercept of least-squares regression line:
$$b_0 = \bar{y} - b_1 \bar{x}$$

Residual standard deviation:
$$s_e = \sqrt{\frac{\sum(y - \hat{y})^2}{n-2}}$$

Standard error for b_1:

$$s_b = \frac{s_e}{\sqrt{\sum(x - \bar{x})^2}}$$

Confidence interval for slope:
$$b_1 - t_{\alpha/2} \cdot s_b < \beta_1 < b_1 + t_{\alpha/2} \cdot s_b$$

Test statistic for slope b_1:
$$t = \frac{b_1}{s_b}$$

Confidence interval for the mean response:

$$\hat{y} \pm t_{\alpha/2} \cdot s_e \sqrt{\frac{1}{n} + \frac{(x^* - \bar{x})^2}{\sum(x - \bar{x})^2}}$$

Prediction interval for an individual response:

$$\hat{y} \pm t_{\alpha/2} \cdot s_e \sqrt{1 + \frac{1}{n} + \frac{(x^* - \bar{x})^2}{\sum(x - \bar{x})^2}}$$

Chapter Quiz

1. Compute the correlation coefficient for the following data set.

x	2	5	6	7	11
y	15	9	6	4	1

2. The number of theaters showing the movie *Night at the Museum: Battle of the Smithsonian x* days after opening are presented in the following table.

x	Number of Theaters
10	4101
17	3807
24	3365
31	2962
33	2409
36	2250

Source: http://www.the-numbers.com

Construct a scatterplot with number of days on the horizontal axis and number of theaters on the vertical axis.

3. Use the data in Exercise 2 to compute the correlation between the number of days after the opening of the movie and the number of theaters showing the movie. Is the association positive or negative? Weak or strong?

4. A scatterplot has a correlation of $r = -1$. Describe the pattern of the points.

5. In a survey of U.S. cities, it is discovered that there is a positive correlation between the number of paved streets in the city and the number of registered cars. Does this mean that paving more streets in the city will result in an increase in the number of registered cars? Explain.

6. The following table presents the average delay in minutes for departures and arrivals of domestic flights in the United States for selected years.

Year	Average Delay in Departures	Average Delay in Arrivals
2004	50.3	53.0
2005	55.8	61.3
2006	51.4	56.5
2007	54.0	58.3
2008	55.3	59.4
2009	56.4	59.0

Source: Bureau of Transportation Statistics. Data for 2009 are May 2008–April 2009.

Compute the least-squares regression line for predicting the delay in arrival time from the delay in departure time.

7. Use the least-squares regression line computed in Exercise 6 to predict the average delay in arrival time in a year when the average delay in departure time is 53.5 minutes.

8. Refer to Exercise 6. If the average delay in departure times differs by 2 minutes from one year to the next, by how much would you predict the average delay in arrival times to change?

9. Compute the least-squares regression line for the following data set.

x	0	1	3	4	7	9
y	7	5	4	3	2	1

10. A confidence interval for β_1 is to be constructed from a sample of 20 points. How many degrees of freedom are there for the critical value?

11. A confidence interval for a mean response and a prediction interval for an individual response are to be constructed from the same data. True or false: The number of degrees of freedom for the critical value is the same for both intervals.

12. True or false: If we fail to reject the null hypothesis $H_0: \beta_1 = 0$, we can conclude that there is no linear relationship between the explanatory variable and the outcome variable.

13. True or false: When the sample size is large, confidence intervals and hypothesis tests for β_1 are valid even when the assumptions of the linear model are not met.

14. A statistics student has constructed a confidence interval for the mean height of daughters whose mothers are 66 inches tall, and a prediction interval for the height of a particular daughter whose mother is 66 inches tall. One of the intervals is (65.3, 68.2) and the other is (63.8, 69.7). Unfortunately, the student has forgotten which interval is which. Can you tell which is the confidence interval and which is the prediction interval? Explain.

15. For the following the data set:

x	25	13	16	19	29	19	16	30
y	40	20	33	30	50	37	34	37

a. Compute the point estimates b_0 and b_1.
b. Construct a 95% confidence interval for β_1.
c. Test the hypotheses $H_0: \beta_1 = 0$ versus $H_1: \beta_1 \neq 0$. Use the $\alpha = 0.01$ level of significance.
d. Construct a 95% confidence interval for the mean response when $x = 20$.
e. Construct a 95% prediction interval for an individual response when $x = 20$.

Review Exercises

1. Predicting height: The heights (y) and lengths of forearms (x) were measured in inches for a sample of men. The following summary statistics were obtained:

$$\bar{x} = 10.1 \quad s_x = 0.8 \quad \bar{y} = 70.1 \quad s_y = 2.5 \quad r = 0.81$$

a. Compute the least-squares regression line for predicting height from forearm length.
b. Joe's forearm is 1 inch longer than Sam's. How much taller than Sam do you predict Joe to be?
c. Predict the height of a man whose forearm is 9.5 inches long.

2. How much wood is in that tree? For a sample of 12 trees, the volume of lumber (y) (in cubic meters) and the diameter (x) (in centimeters) at a fixed height above ground level was measured. The following summary statistics were obtained:

$$\bar{x} = 36.1 \quad s_x = 8.8 \quad \bar{y} = 0.86 \quad s_y = 0.49 \quad r = 0.94$$

a. Compute the least-squares regression line for predicting volume from diameter.
b. If the diameters of two trees differ by 8 centimeters, by how much do you predict their volumes to differ?
c. Predict the volume for a tree whose diameter is 44 centimeters.

3. How's your mileage? Weight (in tons) and fuel economy (in mpg) were measured for a sample of seven diesel trucks. The results are presented in the following table.

Weight	8.00	24.50	27.00	14.50	28.50	12.75	21.25
Mileage	7.69	4.97	4.56	6.49	4.34	6.24	4.45

Source: Janet Yanowitz, Ph.D. thesis, Colorado School of Mines

a. Compute the least-squares regression line for predicting mileage from weight.
b. Construct a residual plot. Verify that a linear model is appropriate.
c. If two trucks differ in weight by 5 tons, by how much would you predict their mileages to differ?
d. Predict the mileage for trucks with a weight of 15 tons.

4. Energy efficiency: A sample of 10 households was monitored for one year. The household income (in $1000s) and the amount of energy consumed (in 10^{10} joules) were determined. The results follow.

Income	31	40	28	48	195	96	70	100	145	78
Energy	16	40	30	46	185	98	94	77	115	67

a. Compute the least-squares regression line for predicting energy consumption from income.
b. Construct a residual plot. Verify that a linear model is appropriate.
c. If two families differ in income by $12,000, by how much would you predict their energy consumptions to differ?
d. Predict the energy consumption for a family whose income is $50,000.

5. Pigskin: In football, a turnover occurs when a team loses possession of the ball due to a fumble or an interception. Turnovers are bad when they happen to your team, but good when they happen to your opponent. The turnover margin for a team is the difference (Turnovers by opponent − Turnovers by team). The following table presents the turnover margin and the total number of wins for each team in the Southeastern Conference (SEC) in the 2008 season.

Team	Turnover Margin	Wins	Team	Turnover Margin	Wins
Florida	22	13	S. Carolina	−11	7
Alabama	6	12	Vanderbilt	9	7
Georgia	−3	10	Arkansas	−9	5
Ole Miss	−2	9	Auburn	−8	5
LSU	−1	8	Tennessee	2	5
Kentucky	5	7	Miss. State	−4	4

Source: www.secsports.com

a. Compute the least-squares regression line for predicting team wins from turnover margin.
b. Construct a residual plot. Verify that a linear model is appropriate.
c. Which teams won more games than would be predicted from their turnover margin?

6. **SAT scores:** The following table presents the number of years of study in English and language arts and the average SAT writing score for students who took the 2008 SAT exam.

Years of Study	0.5	1.0	2.0	3.0	4.0
SAT Score	418	427	455	459	498

Source: The College Board

a. Compute the least-squares regression line for predicting mean SAT score from years of study.
b. Construct a residual plot. Verify that a linear model is appropriate.
c. Predict the mean SAT score for students with 2.5 years of study.

7. **Watching paint dry:** In tests designed to measure the effect of the concentration (in percent) of a certain additive on the drying time (in hours) of paint, the following data were obtained.

Concentration of Additive	Drying Time
4.0	8.7
4.2	8.8
4.4	8.3
4.6	8.7
4.8	8.1
5.0	8.0
5.2	8.1
5.4	7.7
5.6	7.5
5.8	7.2

a. Compute the least-squares regression line for predicting drying time (y) from concentration (x).
b. Construct a 95% confidence interval for the slope.
c. Test $H_0: \beta_1 = 0$ versus $H_1: \beta_1 < 0$. Can you conclude that concentration is useful in predicting drying time? Use the $\alpha = 0.05$ level of significance.

8. **Watching paint dry:** Use the data in Exercise 7 for the following.
a. Compute a point estimate for the mean drying time for paint with a concentration of 5.1.
b. Construct a 95% confidence interval for the mean drying time for paint whose concentration is 5.1.
c. Predict the mean drying time for a particular can of paint with a concentration of 5.1.
d. Construct a 95% prediction interval for the drying time of a particular can of paint whose concentration is 5.1.

9. **Energy use:** A sample of 10 households was monitored for one year. The household income (in $1000s) and the amount of energy consumed (in 10^{10} joules) were determined. The results follow.

Income	Energy	Income	Energy
31	16.0	96	98.3
40	40.2	70	93.8
28	29.8	100	77.1
48	45.6	145	114.8
195	184.6	78	67.0

a. Compute the least-squares line for predicting energy consumption (y) from income (x).
b. Compute a 95% confidence interval for the slope.
c. Test $H_0: \beta_1 = 0$ versus $H_1: \beta_1 > 0$. Can you conclude that income is useful in predicting energy consumption? Use the $\alpha = 0.01$ level of significance.

10. **Energy use:** Use the data in Exercise 9 for the following.
a. Compute a point estimate for the mean energy use for families with an income of $50,000.
b. Construct a 95% confidence interval for the mean energy use for families with an income of $50,000.
c. Predict the energy use for a particular family with an income of $50,000.
d. Construct a 95% prediction interval for the energy use for a particular family with an income of $50,000.

11. **Interpret technology:** The following display from the TI-84 Plus calculator presents the results from computing a least-squares regression line.

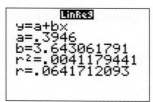

a. Write the equation of the least-squares regression line.
b. Predict the value of y when the x-value is 10.
c. What is the correlation between x and y?
d. Is the linear relationship between x and y strong or weak? Explain.

12. **Interpret technology:** The following display from the TI-84 Plus calculator presents the results from computing a least-squares regression line.

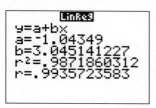

a. Write the equation of the least-squares regression line.
b. Predict the value of y when the x-value is 50.
c. What is the correlation between x and y?
d. Is the linear relationship between x and y strong or weak? Explain.

13. **Interpret technology:** The following output from MINITAB presents the results from computing a least-squares regression line.

```
The regression equation is
Y = 4.99971 + 0.20462 X

Predictor        Coef      SE Coef          T          P
Constant      4.99971      0.02477     201.81      0.000
X             0.20462      0.01115      18.36      0.000
```

a. Write the equation of the least-squares regression line.
b. Predict the value of y when the x-value is 25.

14. **Interpret technology:** The following TI-84 Plus display presents the results of a test of the null hypothesis $H_0: \beta_1 = 0$.

a. What is the alternate hypothesis?
b. What is the value of the test statistic?
c. How many degrees of freedom are there?
d. What is the P-value?
e. Can you conclude that the explanatory variable is useful in predicting the outcome variable? Answer this question using the $\alpha = 0.01$ level of significance.

15. **Interpret technology:** The following MINITAB output presents the results of a test of the null hypothesis H_0: $\beta_1 = 0$.

```
Regression Analysis: Y versus X

The regression equation is
Y = 1.9167 + 5.5582 X

Predictor        Coef     SE Coef        T        P
Constant       1.9167      0.1721    11.14    0.000
X              5.5582      2.1158     2.63    0.006
```

a. What are the slope and intercept of the least-squares regression line?

b. Can you conclude that x is useful for predicting y? Use the $\alpha = 0.05$ level of significance.

Write About It

1. Describe an example in which two variables are strongly correlated, but changes in one do not cause changes in the other.

2. Two variables x and y have a positive association if large values of x are associated with large values of y. Write an equivalent definition that describes what small values of x are associated with. Then write a definition for negatively associated random variables that describes what small values of y are associated with.

3. Explain why the predicted value $\hat{y}$ is always equal to $\bar{y}$ when $r = 0$.

4. If the slope of the least-squares regression line is negative, can the correlation coefficient be positive? Explain why or why not.

5. Describe conditions under which the slope of the least-squares line will be equal to the correlation coefficient.

6. The quantity $\sum(x - \bar{x})^2$ measures the spread in the x-values. Explain why using x-values that are more spread out will result in a narrower confidence interval for β_1.

7. Suppose you are planning to buy a car that weighs 3500 pounds, and you have a linear model that predicts gas mileage (y) given the weight of the car (x). Which do you think would be more appropriate, a confidence interval for the mean gas mileage of cars that weigh 3500 pounds, or a prediction interval for the mileage of a particular car that weighs 3500 pounds? Explain.

Case Study: How Are Inflation And Unemployment Related?

The following table, reproduced from the chapter introduction, presents the inflation rate and unemployment rate, both in percent, for the years 1981–2008.

Year	Inflation	Unemployment	Year	Inflation	Unemployment
1981	8.9	7.6	1995	2.5	5.6
1982	3.8	9.7	1996	3.3	5.4
1983	3.8	9.6	1997	1.7	4.9
1984	3.9	7.5	1998	1.6	4.5
1985	3.8	7.2	1999	2.7	4.2
1986	1.1	7.0	2000	3.4	4.0
1987	4.4	6.2	2001	1.6	4.7
1988	4.4	5.5	2002	2.4	5.8
1989	4.6	5.3	2003	1.9	6.0
1990	6.1	5.6	2004	3.3	5.5
1991	3.1	6.8	2005	3.4	5.1
1992	2.9	7.5	2006	2.5	4.6
1993	2.7	6.9	2007	4.1	4.6
1994	2.7	6.1	2008	0.1	5.8

Source: Bureau of Labor Statistics

We will investigate some methods for predicting unemployment. First, we will try to predict the unemployment rate from the inflation rate.

1. Construct a scatterplot of unemployment (y) versus inflation (x). Do you detect any strong nonlinearity?

2. Compute the least-squares line for predicting unemployment from inflation.

3. Predict the unemployment in a year when inflation is 3.0%.
4. Compute the correlation coefficient between inflation and unemployment.

The relationship between inflation and unemployment is not very strong. However, if we are interested in predicting unemployment, we would probably want to predict next year's unemployment from this year's inflation. We can construct an equation to do this by matching each year's inflation with the next year's unemployment, as shown in the following table.

Year	This Year's Inflation	Next Year's Unemployment	Year	This Year's Inflation	Next Year's Unemployment
1981	8.9	9.7	1995	2.5	5.4
1982	3.8	9.6	1996	3.3	4.9
1983	3.8	7.5	1997	1.7	4.5
1984	3.9	7.2	1998	1.6	4.2
1985	3.8	7.0	1999	2.7	4.0
1986	1.1	6.2	2000	3.4	4.7
1987	4.4	5.5	2001	1.6	5.8
1988	4.4	5.3	2002	2.4	6.0
1989	4.6	5.6	2003	1.9	5.5
1990	6.1	6.8	2004	3.3	5.1
1991	3.1	7.5	2005	3.4	4.6
1992	2.9	6.9	2006	2.5	4.6
1993	2.7	6.1	2007	4.1	5.8
1994	2.7	5.6			

Source: Bureau of Labor Statistics

5. Compute the least-squares line for predicting next year's unemployment from this year's inflation.
6. Predict next year's unemployment if this year's inflation is 3.0%.
7. Compute the correlation coefficient between this year's inflation and next year's unemployment.

If we are going to use data from this year to predict unemployment next year, why not use this year's unemployment to predict next year's unemployment? A model like this, in which previous values of a variable are used to predict future values of the same variable, is called an *autoregressive* model. The following table presents the data needed to fit this model.

Year	This Year's Unemployment	Next Year's Unemployment	Year	This Year's Unemployment	Next Year's Unemployment
1981	7.6	9.7	1995	5.6	5.4
1982	9.7	9.6	1996	5.4	4.9
1983	9.6	7.5	1997	4.9	4.5
1984	7.5	7.2	1998	4.5	4.2
1985	7.2	7.0	1999	4.2	4.0
1986	7.0	6.2	2000	4.0	4.7
1987	6.2	5.5	2001	4.7	5.8
1988	5.5	5.3	2002	5.8	6.0
1989	5.3	5.6	2003	6.0	5.5
1990	5.6	6.8	2004	5.5	5.1
1991	6.8	7.5	2005	5.1	4.6
1992	7.5	6.9	2006	4.6	4.6
1993	6.9	6.1	2007	4.6	5.8
1994	6.1	5.6			

Source: Bureau of Labor Statistics

8. Compute the least-squares line for predicting next year's unemployment from this year's unemployment.
9. Predict next year's unemployment if this year's unemployment is 5.0%.
10. Compute the correlation coefficient between this year's unemployment and next year's unemployment.
11. Which of the three models do you think provides the best prediction of unemployment, the one using inflation in the same year, the one using inflation in the previous year, or the one using unemployment in the previous year? Explain.

Tables

- **Table A.1** Binomial Probabilities
- **Table A.2** Cumulative Normal Distribution
- **Table A.3** Critical Values for the Student's t Distribution
- **Table A.4** Critical Values for the χ^2 Distribution

Table A.1 Binomial Probabilities

$$P(x) = \frac{n!}{x!(n-x)!} p^x (1-p)^{(n-x)}$$

								p						
n	x	0.05	0.10	0.20	0.25	0.30	0.40	0.50	0.60	0.70	0.75	0.80	0.90	0.95
2	0	0.903	0.810	0.640	0.563	0.490	0.360	0.250	0.160	0.090	0.063	0.040	0.010	0.003
	1	0.095	0.180	0.320	0.375	0.420	0.480	0.500	0.480	0.420	0.375	0.320	0.180	0.095
	2	0.003	0.010	0.040	0.063	0.090	0.160	0.250	0.360	0.490	0.563	0.640	0.810	0.903
3	0	0.857	0.729	0.512	0.422	0.343	0.216	0.125	0.064	0.027	0.016	0.008	0.001	0.000+
	1	0.135	0.243	0.384	0.422	0.441	0.432	0.375	0.288	0.189	0.141	0.096	0.027	0.007
	2	0.007	0.027	0.096	0.141	0.189	0.288	0.375	0.432	0.441	0.422	0.384	0.243	0.135
	3	0.000+	0.001	0.008	0.016	0.027	0.064	0.125	0.216	0.343	0.422	0.512	0.729	0.857
4	0	0.815	0.656	0.410	0.316	0.240	0.130	0.063	0.026	0.008	0.004	0.002	0.000+	0.000+
	1	0.171	0.292	0.410	0.422	0.412	0.346	0.250	0.154	0.076	0.047	0.026	0.004	0.000+
	2	0.014	0.049	0.154	0.211	0.265	0.346	0.375	0.346	0.265	0.211	0.154	0.049	0.014
	3	0.000+	0.004	0.026	0.047	0.076	0.154	0.250	0.346	0.412	0.422	0.410	0.292	0.171
	4	0.000+	0.000+	0.002	0.004	0.008	0.026	0.063	0.130	0.240	0.316	0.410	0.656	0.815
5	0	0.774	0.590	0.328	0.237	0.168	0.078	0.031	0.010	0.002	0.001	0.000+	0.000+	0.000+
	1	0.204	0.328	0.410	0.396	0.360	0.259	0.156	0.077	0.028	0.015	0.006	0.000+	0.000+
	2	0.021	0.073	0.205	0.264	0.309	0.346	0.313	0.230	0.132	0.088	0.051	0.008	0.001
	3	0.001	0.008	0.051	0.088	0.132	0.230	0.313	0.346	0.309	0.264	0.205	0.073	0.021
	4	0.000+	0.000+	0.006	0.015	0.028	0.077	0.156	0.259	0.360	0.396	0.410	0.328	0.204
	5	0.000+	0.000+	0.000+	0.001	0.002	0.010	0.031	0.078	0.168	0.237	0.328	0.590	0.774
6	0	0.735	0.531	0.262	0.178	0.118	0.047	0.016	0.004	0.001	0.000+	0.000+	0.000+	0.000+
	1	0.232	0.354	0.393	0.356	0.303	0.187	0.094	0.037	0.010	0.004	0.002	0.000+	0.000+
	2	0.031	0.098	0.246	0.297	0.324	0.311	0.234	0.138	0.060	0.033	0.015	0.001	0.000+
	3	0.002	0.015	0.082	0.132	0.185	0.276	0.313	0.276	0.185	0.132	0.082	0.015	0.002
	4	0.000+	0.001	0.015	0.033	0.060	0.138	0.234	0.311	0.324	0.297	0.246	0.098	0.031
	5	0.000+	0.000+	0.002	0.004	0.010	0.037	0.094	0.187	0.303	0.356	0.393	0.354	0.232
	6	0.000+	0.000+	0.000+	0.000+	0.001	0.004	0.016	0.047	0.118	0.178	0.262	0.531	0.735
7	0	0.698	0.478	0.210	0.133	0.082	0.028	0.008	0.002	0.000+	0.000+	0.000+	0.000+	0.000+
	1	0.257	0.372	0.367	0.311	0.247	0.131	0.055	0.017	0.004	0.001	0.000+	0.000+	0.000+
	2	0.041	0.124	0.275	0.311	0.318	0.261	0.164	0.077	0.025	0.012	0.004	0.000+	0.000+
	3	0.004	0.023	0.115	0.173	0.227	0.290	0.273	0.194	0.097	0.058	0.029	0.003	0.000+
	4	0.000+	0.003	0.029	0.058	0.097	0.194	0.273	0.290	0.227	0.173	0.115	0.023	0.004
	5	0.000+	0.000+	0.004	0.012	0.025	0.077	0.164	0.261	0.318	0.311	0.275	0.124	0.041
	6	0.000+	0.000+	0.000+	0.001	0.004	0.017	0.055	0.131	0.247	0.311	0.367	0.372	0.257
	7	0.000+	0.000+	0.000+	0.000+	0.000+	0.002	0.008	0.028	0.082	0.133	0.210	0.478	0.698
8	0	0.663	0.430	0.168	0.100	0.058	0.017	0.004	0.001	0.000+	0.000+	0.000+	0.000+	0.000+
	1	0.279	0.383	0.336	0.267	0.198	0.090	0.031	0.008	0.001	0.000+	0.000+	0.000+	0.000+
	2	0.051	0.149	0.294	0.311	0.296	0.209	0.109	0.041	0.010	0.004	0.001	0.000+	0.000+
	3	0.005	0.033	0.147	0.208	0.254	0.279	0.219	0.124	0.047	0.023	0.009	0.000+	0.000+
	4	0.000+	0.005	0.046	0.087	0.136	0.232	0.273	0.232	0.136	0.087	0.046	0.005	0.000+
	5	0.000+	0.000+	0.009	0.023	0.047	0.124	0.219	0.279	0.254	0.208	0.147	0.033	0.005
	6	0.000+	0.000+	0.001	0.004	0.010	0.041	0.109	0.209	0.296	0.311	0.294	0.149	0.051
	7	0.000+	0.000+	0.000+	0.000+	0.001	0.008	0.031	0.090	0.198	0.267	0.336	0.383	0.279
	8	0.000+	0.000+	0.000+	0.000+	0.000+	0.001	0.004	0.017	0.058	0.100	0.168	0.430	0.663
9	0	0.630	0.387	0.134	0.075	0.040	0.010	0.002	0.000+	0.000+	0.000+	0.000+	0.000+	0.000+
	1	0.299	0.387	0.302	0.225	0.156	0.060	0.018	0.004	0.000+	0.000+	0.000+	0.000+	0.000+
	2	0.063	0.172	0.302	0.300	0.267	0.161	0.070	0.021	0.004	0.001	0.000+	0.000+	0.000+
	3	0.008	0.045	0.176	0.234	0.267	0.251	0.164	0.074	0.021	0.009	0.003	0.000+	0.000+
	4	0.001	0.007	0.066	0.117	0.172	0.251	0.246	0.167	0.074	0.039	0.017	0.001	0.000+
	5	0.000+	0.001	0.017	0.039	0.074	0.167	0.246	0.251	0.172	0.117	0.066	0.007	0.001
	6	0.000+	0.000+	0.003	0.009	0.021	0.074	0.164	0.251	0.267	0.234	0.176	0.045	0.008
	7	0.000+	0.000+	0.000+	0.001	0.004	0.021	0.070	0.161	0.267	0.300	0.302	0.172	0.063
	8	0.000+	0.000+	0.000+	0.000+	0.000+	0.004	0.018	0.060	0.156	0.225	0.302	0.387	0.299
	9	0.000+	0.000+	0.000+	0.000+	0.000+	0.000+	0.002	0.010	0.040	0.075	0.134	0.387	0.630

A value of 0.000+ indicates that the probability is 0.000 when rounded to three decimal places. The actual probability is slightly greater than 0.

Table A.1 Binomial Probabilities (continued)

n	x	0.05	0.10	0.20	0.25	0.30	0.40	0.50	0.60	0.70	0.75	0.80	0.90	0.95
10	0	0.599	0.349	0.107	0.056	0.028	0.006	0.001	0.000+	0.000+	0.000+	0.000+	0.000+	0.000+
	1	0.315	0.387	0.268	0.188	0.121	0.040	0.010	0.002	0.000+	0.000+	0.000+	0.000+	0.000+
	2	0.075	0.194	0.302	0.282	0.233	0.121	0.044	0.011	0.001	0.000+	0.000+	0.000+	0.000+
	3	0.010	0.057	0.201	0.250	0.267	0.215	0.117	0.042	0.009	0.003	0.001	0.000+	0.000+
	4	0.001	0.011	0.088	0.146	0.200	0.251	0.205	0.111	0.037	0.016	0.006	0.000+	0.000+
	5	0.000+	0.001	0.026	0.058	0.103	0.201	0.246	0.201	0.103	0.058	0.026	0.001	0.000+
	6	0.000+	0.000+	0.006	0.016	0.037	0.111	0.205	0.251	0.200	0.146	0.088	0.011	0.001
	7	0.000+	0.000+	0.001	0.003	0.009	0.042	0.117	0.215	0.267	0.250	0.201	0.057	0.010
	8	0.000+	0.000+	0.000+	0.000+	0.001	0.011	0.044	0.121	0.233	0.282	0.302	0.194	0.075
	9	0.000+	0.000+	0.000+	0.000+	0.000+	0.002	0.010	0.040	0.121	0.188	0.268	0.387	0.315
	10	0.000+	0.000+	0.000+	0.000+	0.000+	0.000+	0.001	0.006	0.028	0.056	0.107	0.349	0.599
11	0	0.569	0.314	0.086	0.042	0.020	0.004	0.000+	0.000+	0.000+	0.000+	0.000+	0.000+	0.000+
	1	0.329	0.384	0.236	0.155	0.093	0.027	0.005	0.001	0.000+	0.000+	0.000+	0.000+	0.000+
	2	0.087	0.213	0.295	0.258	0.200	0.089	0.027	0.005	0.001	0.000+	0.000+	0.000+	0.000+
	3	0.014	0.071	0.221	0.258	0.257	0.177	0.081	0.023	0.004	0.001	0.000+	0.000+	0.000+
	4	0.001	0.016	0.111	0.172	0.220	0.236	0.161	0.070	0.017	0.006	0.002	0.000+	0.000+
	5	0.000+	0.002	0.039	0.080	0.132	0.221	0.226	0.147	0.057	0.027	0.010	0.000+	0.000+
	6	0.000+	0.000+	0.010	0.027	0.057	0.147	0.226	0.221	0.132	0.080	0.039	0.002	0.000+
	7	0.000+	0.000+	0.002	0.006	0.017	0.070	0.161	0.236	0.220	0.172	0.111	0.016	0.001
	8	0.000+	0.000+	0.000+	0.001	0.004	0.023	0.081	0.177	0.257	0.258	0.221	0.071	0.014
	9	0.000+	0.000+	0.000+	0.000+	0.001	0.005	0.027	0.089	0.200	0.258	0.295	0.213	0.087
	10	0.000+	0.000+	0.000+	0.000+	0.000+	0.001	0.005	0.027	0.093	0.155	0.236	0.384	0.329
	11	0.000+	0.000+	0.000+	0.000+	0.000+	0.000+	0.000+	0.004	0.020	0.042	0.086	0.314	0.569
12	0	0.540	0.282	0.069	0.032	0.014	0.002	0.000+	0.000+	0.000+	0.000+	0.000+	0.000+	0.000+
	1	0.341	0.377	0.206	0.127	0.071	0.017	0.003	0.000+	0.000+	0.000+	0.000+	0.000+	0.000+
	2	0.099	0.230	0.283	0.232	0.168	0.064	0.016	0.002	0.000+	0.000+	0.000+	0.000+	0.000+
	3	0.017	0.085	0.236	0.258	0.240	0.142	0.054	0.012	0.001	0.000+	0.000+	0.000+	0.000+
	4	0.002	0.021	0.133	0.194	0.231	0.213	0.121	0.042	0.008	0.002	0.001	0.000+	0.000+
	5	0.000+	0.004	0.053	0.103	0.158	0.227	0.193	0.101	0.029	0.011	0.003	0.000+	0.000+
	6	0.000+	0.000+	0.016	0.040	0.079	0.177	0.226	0.177	0.079	0.040	0.016	0.000+	0.000+
	7	0.000+	0.000+	0.003	0.011	0.029	0.101	0.193	0.227	0.158	0.103	0.053	0.004	0.000+
	8	0.000+	0.000+	0.001	0.002	0.008	0.042	0.121	0.213	0.231	0.194	0.133	0.021	0.002
	9	0.000+	0.000+	0.000+	0.000+	0.001	0.012	0.054	0.142	0.240	0.258	0.236	0.085	0.017
	10	0.000+	0.000+	0.000+	0.000+	0.000+	0.002	0.016	0.064	0.168	0.232	0.283	0.230	0.099
	11	0.000+	0.000+	0.000+	0.000+	0.000+	0.000+	0.003	0.017	0.071	0.127	0.206	0.377	0.341
	12	0.000+	0.000+	0.000+	0.000+	0.000+	0.000+	0.000+	0.002	0.014	0.032	0.069	0.282	0.540
13	0	0.513	0.254	0.055	0.024	0.010	0.001	0.000+	0.000+	0.000+	0.000+	0.000+	0.000+	0.000+
	1	0.351	0.367	0.179	0.103	0.054	0.011	0.002	0.000+	0.000+	0.000+	0.000+	0.000+	0.000+
	2	0.111	0.245	0.268	0.206	0.139	0.045	0.010	0.001	0.000+	0.000+	0.000+	0.000+	0.000+
	3	0.021	0.100	0.246	0.252	0.218	0.111	0.035	0.006	0.001	0.000+	0.000+	0.000+	0.000+
	4	0.003	0.028	0.154	0.210	0.234	0.184	0.087	0.024	0.003	0.001	0.000+	0.000+	0.000+
	5	0.000+	0.006	0.069	0.126	0.180	0.221	0.157	0.066	0.014	0.005	0.001	0.000+	0.000+
	6	0.000+	0.001	0.023	0.056	0.103	0.197	0.209	0.131	0.044	0.019	0.006	0.000+	0.000+
	7	0.000+	0.000+	0.006	0.019	0.044	0.131	0.209	0.197	0.103	0.056	0.023	0.001	0.000+
	8	0.000+	0.000+	0.001	0.005	0.014	0.066	0.157	0.221	0.180	0.126	0.069	0.006	0.000+
	9	0.000+	0.000+	0.000+	0.001	0.003	0.024	0.087	0.184	0.234	0.210	0.154	0.028	0.003
	10	0.000+	0.000+	0.000+	0.000+	0.001	0.006	0.035	0.111	0.218	0.252	0.246	0.100	0.021
	11	0.000+	0.000+	0.000+	0.000+	0.000+	0.001	0.010	0.045	0.139	0.206	0.268	0.245	0.111
	12	0.000+	0.000+	0.000+	0.000+	0.000+	0.000+	0.002	0.011	0.054	0.103	0.179	0.367	0.351
	13	0.000+	0.000+	0.000+	0.000+	0.000+	0.000+	0.000+	0.001	0.010	0.024	0.055	0.254	0.513
14	0	0.488	0.229	0.044	0.018	0.007	0.001	0.000+	0.000+	0.000+	0.000+	0.000+	0.000+	0.000+
	1	0.359	0.356	0.154	0.083	0.041	0.007	0.001	0.000+	0.000+	0.000+	0.000+	0.000+	0.000+
	2	0.123	0.257	0.250	0.180	0.113	0.032	0.006	0.001	0.000+	0.000+	0.000+	0.000+	0.000+
	3	0.026	0.114	0.250	0.240	0.194	0.085	0.022	0.003	0.000+	0.000+	0.000+	0.000+	0.000+
	4	0.004	0.035	0.172	0.220	0.229	0.155	0.061	0.014	0.001	0.000+	0.000+	0.000+	0.000+
	5	0.000+	0.008	0.086	0.147	0.196	0.207	0.122	0.041	0.007	0.002	0.000+	0.000+	0.000+
	6	0.000+	0.001	0.032	0.073	0.126	0.207	0.183	0.092	0.023	0.008	0.002	0.000+	0.000+
	7	0.000+	0.000+	0.009	0.028	0.062	0.157	0.209	0.157	0.062	0.028	0.009	0.000+	0.000+
	8	0.000+	0.000+	0.002	0.008	0.023	0.092	0.183	0.207	0.126	0.073	0.032	0.001	0.000+
	9	0.000+	0.000+	0.000+	0.002	0.007	0.041	0.122	0.207	0.196	0.147	0.086	0.008	0.000+
	10	0.000+	0.000+	0.000+	0.000+	0.001	0.014	0.061	0.155	0.229	0.220	0.172	0.035	0.004
	11	0.000+	0.000+	0.000+	0.000+	0.000+	0.003	0.022	0.085	0.194	0.240	0.250	0.114	0.026
	12	0.000+	0.000+	0.000+	0.000+	0.000+	0.001	0.006	0.032	0.113	0.180	0.250	0.257	0.123
	13	0.000+	0.000+	0.000+	0.000+	0.000+	0.000+	0.001	0.007	0.041	0.083	0.154	0.356	0.359
	14	0.000+	0.000+	0.000+	0.000+	0.000+	0.000+	0.000+	0.001	0.007	0.018	0.044	0.229	0.488

A value of 0.000+ indicates that the probability is 0.000 when rounded to three decimal places. The actual probability is slightly greater than 0.

Table A.1 Binomial Probabilities (continued)

n	x	0.05	0.10	0.20	0.25	0.30	0.40	0.50	0.60	0.70	0.75	0.80	0.90	0.95
15	0	0.463	0.206	0.035	0.013	0.005	0.000+	0.000+	0.000+	0.000+	0.000+	0.000+	0.000+	0.000+
	1	0.366	0.343	0.132	0.067	0.031	0.005	0.000+	0.000+	0.000+	0.000+	0.000+	0.000+	0.000+
	2	0.135	0.267	0.231	0.156	0.092	0.022	0.003	0.000+	0.000+	0.000+	0.000+	0.000+	0.000+
	3	0.031	0.129	0.250	0.225	0.170	0.063	0.014	0.002	0.000+	0.000+	0.000+	0.000+	0.000+
	4	0.005	0.043	0.188	0.225	0.219	0.127	0.042	0.007	0.001	0.000+	0.000+	0.000+	0.000+
	5	0.001	0.010	0.103	0.165	0.206	0.186	0.092	0.024	0.003	0.001	0.000+	0.000+	0.000+
	6	0.000+	0.002	0.043	0.092	0.147	0.207	0.153	0.061	0.012	0.003	0.001	0.000+	0.000+
	7	0.000+	0.000+	0.014	0.039	0.081	0.177	0.196	0.118	0.035	0.013	0.003	0.000+	0.000+
	8	0.000+	0.000+	0.003	0.013	0.035	0.118	0.196	0.177	0.081	0.039	0.014	0.000+	0.000+
	9	0.000+	0.000+	0.001	0.003	0.012	0.061	0.153	0.207	0.147	0.092	0.043	0.002	0.000+
	10	0.000+	0.000+	0.000+	0.001	0.003	0.024	0.092	0.186	0.206	0.165	0.103	0.010	0.001
	11	0.000+	0.000+	0.000+	0.000+	0.001	0.007	0.042	0.127	0.219	0.225	0.188	0.043	0.005
	12	0.000+	0.000+	0.000+	0.000+	0.000+	0.002	0.014	0.063	0.170	0.225	0.250	0.129	0.031
	13	0.000+	0.000+	0.000+	0.000+	0.000+	0.000+	0.003	0.022	0.092	0.156	0.231	0.267	0.135
	14	0.000+	0.000+	0.000+	0.000+	0.000+	0.000+	0.000+	0.005	0.031	0.067	0.132	0.343	0.366
	15	0.000+	0.000+	0.000+	0.000+	0.000+	0.000+	0.000+	0.000+	0.005	0.013	0.035	0.206	0.463
16	0	0.440	0.185	0.028	0.010	0.003	0.000+	0.000+	0.000+	0.000+	0.000+	0.000+	0.000+	0.000+
	1	0.371	0.329	0.113	0.053	0.023	0.003	0.000+	0.000+	0.000+	0.000+	0.000+	0.000+	0.000+
	2	0.146	0.275	0.211	0.134	0.073	0.015	0.002	0.000+	0.000+	0.000+	0.000+	0.000+	0.000+
	3	0.036	0.142	0.246	0.208	0.146	0.047	0.009	0.001	0.000+	0.000+	0.000+	0.000+	0.000+
	4	0.006	0.051	0.200	0.225	0.204	0.101	0.028	0.004	0.000+	0.000+	0.000+	0.000+	0.000+
	5	0.001	0.014	0.120	0.180	0.210	0.162	0.067	0.014	0.001	0.000+	0.000+	0.000+	0.000+
	6	0.000+	0.003	0.055	0.110	0.165	0.198	0.122	0.039	0.006	0.001	0.000+	0.000+	0.000+
	7	0.000+	0.000+	0.020	0.052	0.101	0.189	0.175	0.084	0.019	0.006	0.001	0.000+	0.000+
	8	0.000+	0.000+	0.006	0.020	0.049	0.142	0.196	0.142	0.049	0.020	0.006	0.000+	0.000+
	9	0.000+	0.000+	0.001	0.006	0.019	0.084	0.175	0.189	0.101	0.052	0.020	0.000+	0.000+
	10	0.000+	0.000+	0.000+	0.001	0.006	0.039	0.122	0.198	0.165	0.110	0.055	0.003	0.000+
	11	0.000+	0.000+	0.000+	0.000+	0.001	0.014	0.067	0.162	0.210	0.180	0.120	0.014	0.001
	12	0.000+	0.000+	0.000+	0.000+	0.000+	0.004	0.028	0.101	0.204	0.225	0.200	0.051	0.006
	13	0.000+	0.000+	0.000+	0.000+	0.000+	0.001	0.009	0.047	0.146	0.208	0.246	0.142	0.036
	14	0.000+	0.000+	0.000+	0.000+	0.000+	0.000+	0.002	0.015	0.073	0.134	0.211	0.275	0.146
	15	0.000+	0.000+	0.000+	0.000+	0.000+	0.000+	0.000+	0.003	0.023	0.053	0.113	0.329	0.371
	16	0.000+	0.000+	0.000+	0.000+	0.000+	0.000+	0.000+	0.000+	0.003	0.010	0.028	0.185	0.440
17	0	0.418	0.167	0.023	0.008	0.002	0.000+	0.000+	0.000+	0.000+	0.000+	0.000+	0.000+	0.000+
	1	0.374	0.315	0.096	0.043	0.017	0.002	0.000+	0.000+	0.000+	0.000+	0.000+	0.000+	0.000+
	2	0.158	0.280	0.191	0.114	0.058	0.010	0.001	0.000+	0.000+	0.000+	0.000+	0.000+	0.000+
	3	0.041	0.156	0.239	0.189	0.125	0.034	0.005	0.000+	0.000+	0.000+	0.000+	0.000+	0.000+
	4	0.008	0.060	0.209	0.221	0.187	0.080	0.018	0.002	0.000+	0.000+	0.000+	0.000+	0.000+
	5	0.001	0.017	0.136	0.191	0.208	0.138	0.047	0.008	0.001	0.000+	0.000+	0.000+	0.000+
	6	0.000+	0.004	0.068	0.128	0.178	0.184	0.094	0.024	0.003	0.001	0.000+	0.000+	0.000+
	7	0.000+	0.001	0.027	0.067	0.120	0.193	0.148	0.057	0.009	0.002	0.000+	0.000+	0.000+
	8	0.000+	0.000+	0.008	0.028	0.064	0.161	0.185	0.107	0.028	0.009	0.002	0.000+	0.000+
	9	0.000+	0.000+	0.002	0.009	0.028	0.107	0.185	0.161	0.064	0.028	0.008	0.000+	0.000+
	10	0.000+	0.000+	0.000+	0.002	0.009	0.057	0.148	0.193	0.120	0.067	0.027	0.001	0.000+
	11	0.000+	0.000+	0.000+	0.001	0.003	0.024	0.094	0.184	0.178	0.128	0.068	0.004	0.000+
	12	0.000+	0.000+	0.000+	0.000+	0.001	0.008	0.047	0.138	0.208	0.191	0.136	0.017	0.001
	13	0.000+	0.000+	0.000+	0.000+	0.000+	0.002	0.018	0.080	0.187	0.221	0.209	0.060	0.008
	14	0.000+	0.000+	0.000+	0.000+	0.000+	0.000+	0.005	0.034	0.125	0.189	0.239	0.156	0.041
	15	0.000+	0.000+	0.000+	0.000+	0.000+	0.000+	0.001	0.010	0.058	0.114	0.191	0.280	0.158
	16	0.000+	0.000+	0.000+	0.000+	0.000+	0.000+	0.000+	0.002	0.017	0.043	0.096	0.315	0.374
	17	0.000+	0.000+	0.000+	0.000+	0.000+	0.000+	0.000+	0.000+	0.002	0.008	0.023	0.167	0.418

A value of 0.000+ indicates that the probability is 0.000 when rounded to three decimal places. The actual probability is slightly greater than 0.

Table A.1 Binomial Probabilities (continued)

n	x	0.05	0.10	0.20	0.25	0.30	0.40	0.50	0.60	0.70	0.75	0.80	0.90	0.95
18	0	0.397	0.150	0.018	0.006	0.002	0.000+	0.000+	0.000+	0.000+	0.000+	0.000+	0.000+	0.000+
	1	0.376	0.300	0.081	0.034	0.013	0.001	0.000+	0.000+	0.000+	0.000+	0.000+	0.000+	0.000+
	2	0.168	0.284	0.172	0.096	0.046	0.007	0.001	0.000+	0.000+	0.000+	0.000+	0.000+	0.000+
	3	0.047	0.168	0.230	0.170	0.105	0.025	0.003	0.000+	0.000+	0.000+	0.000+	0.000+	0.000+
	4	0.009	0.070	0.215	0.213	0.168	0.061	0.012	0.001	0.000+	0.000+	0.000+	0.000+	0.000+
	5	0.001	0.022	0.151	0.199	0.202	0.115	0.033	0.004	0.000+	0.000+	0.000+	0.000+	0.000+
	6	0.000+	0.005	0.082	0.144	0.187	0.166	0.071	0.015	0.001	0.000+	0.000+	0.000+	0.000+
	7	0.000+	0.001	0.035	0.082	0.138	0.189	0.121	0.037	0.005	0.001	0.000+	0.000+	0.000+
	8	0.000+	0.000+	0.012	0.038	0.081	0.173	0.167	0.077	0.015	0.004	0.001	0.000+	0.000+
	9	0.000+	0.000+	0.003	0.014	0.039	0.128	0.185	0.128	0.039	0.014	0.003	0.000+	0.000+
	10	0.000+	0.000+	0.001	0.004	0.015	0.077	0.167	0.173	0.081	0.038	0.012	0.000+	0.000+
	11	0.000+	0.000+	0.000+	0.001	0.005	0.037	0.121	0.189	0.138	0.082	0.035	0.001	0.000+
	12	0.000+	0.000+	0.000+	0.000+	0.001	0.015	0.071	0.166	0.187	0.144	0.082	0.005	0.000+
	13	0.000+	0.000+	0.000+	0.000+	0.000+	0.004	0.033	0.115	0.202	0.199	0.151	0.022	0.001
	14	0.000+	0.000+	0.000+	0.000+	0.000+	0.001	0.012	0.061	0.168	0.213	0.215	0.070	0.009
	15	0.000+	0.000+	0.000+	0.000+	0.000+	0.000+	0.003	0.025	0.105	0.170	0.230	0.168	0.047
	16	0.000+	0.000+	0.000+	0.000+	0.000+	0.000+	0.001	0.007	0.046	0.096	0.172	0.284	0.168
	17	0.000+	0.000+	0.000+	0.000+	0.000+	0.000+	0.000+	0.001	0.013	0.034	0.081	0.300	0.376
	18	0.000+	0.000+	0.000+	0.000+	0.000+	0.000+	0.000+	0.000+	0.002	0.006	0.018	0.150	0.397
19	0	0.377	0.135	0.014	0.004	0.001	0.000+	0.000+	0.000+	0.000+	0.000+	0.000+	0.000+	0.000+
	1	0.377	0.285	0.068	0.027	0.009	0.001	0.000+	0.000+	0.000+	0.000+	0.000+	0.000+	0.000+
	2	0.179	0.285	0.154	0.080	0.036	0.005	0.000+	0.000+	0.000+	0.000+	0.000+	0.000+	0.000+
	3	0.053	0.180	0.218	0.152	0.087	0.017	0.002	0.000+	0.000+	0.000+	0.000+	0.000+	0.000+
	4	0.011	0.080	0.218	0.202	0.149	0.047	0.007	0.001	0.000+	0.000+	0.000+	0.000+	0.000+
	5	0.002	0.027	0.164	0.202	0.192	0.093	0.022	0.002	0.000+	0.000+	0.000+	0.000+	0.000+
	6	0.000+	0.007	0.095	0.157	0.192	0.145	0.052	0.008	0.001	0.000+	0.000+	0.000+	0.000+
	7	0.000+	0.001	0.044	0.097	0.153	0.180	0.096	0.024	0.002	0.000+	0.000+	0.000+	0.000+
	8	0.000+	0.000+	0.017	0.049	0.098	0.180	0.144	0.053	0.008	0.002	0.000+	0.000+	0.000+
	9	0.000+	0.000+	0.005	0.020	0.051	0.146	0.176	0.098	0.022	0.007	0.001	0.000+	0.000+
	10	0.000+	0.000+	0.001	0.007	0.022	0.098	0.176	0.146	0.051	0.020	0.005	0.000+	0.000+
	11	0.000+	0.000+	0.000+	0.002	0.008	0.053	0.144	0.180	0.098	0.049	0.017	0.000+	0.000+
	12	0.000+	0.000+	0.000+	0.000+	0.002	0.024	0.096	0.180	0.153	0.097	0.044	0.001	0.000+
	13	0.000+	0.000+	0.000+	0.000+	0.001	0.008	0.052	0.145	0.192	0.157	0.095	0.007	0.000+
	14	0.000+	0.000+	0.000+	0.000+	0.000+	0.002	0.022	0.093	0.192	0.202	0.164	0.027	0.002
	15	0.000+	0.000+	0.000+	0.000+	0.000+	0.001	0.007	0.047	0.149	0.202	0.218	0.080	0.011
	16	0.000+	0.000+	0.000+	0.000+	0.000+	0.000+	0.002	0.017	0.087	0.152	0.218	0.180	0.053
	17	0.000+	0.000+	0.000+	0.000+	0.000+	0.000+	0.000+	0.005	0.036	0.080	0.154	0.285	0.179
	18	0.000+	0.000+	0.000+	0.000+	0.000+	0.000+	0.000+	0.001	0.009	0.027	0.068	0.285	0.377
	19	0.000+	0.000+	0.000+	0.000+	0.000+	0.000+	0.000+	0.000+	0.001	0.004	0.014	0.135	0.377
20	0	0.358	0.122	0.012	0.003	0.001	0.000++	0.000++	0.000++	0.000++	0.000++	0.000++	0.000++	0.000++
	1	0.377	0.270	0.058	0.021	0.007	0.000+	0.000+	0.000+	0.000+	0.000+	0.000+	0.000+	0.000+
	2	0.189	0.285	0.137	0.067	0.028	0.003	0.000+	0.000+	0.000+	0.000+	0.000+	0.000+	0.000+
	3	0.060	0.190	0.205	0.134	0.072	0.012	0.001	0.000+	0.000+	0.000+	0.000+	0.000+	0.000+
	4	0.013	0.090	0.218	0.190	0.130	0.035	0.005	0.000+	0.000+	0.000+	0.000+	0.000+	0.000+
	5	0.002	0.032	0.175	0.202	0.179	0.075	0.015	0.001	0.000+	0.000+	0.000+	0.000+	0.000+
	6	0.000+	0.009	0.109	0.169	0.192	0.124	0.037	0.005	0.000+	0.000+	0.000+	0.000+	0.000+
	7	0.000+	0.002	0.055	0.112	0.164	0.166	0.074	0.015	0.001	0.000+	0.000+	0.000+	0.000+
	8	0.000+	0.000+	0.022	0.061	0.114	0.180	0.120	0.035	0.004	0.001	0.000+	0.000+	0.000+
	9	0.000+	0.000+	0.007	0.027	0.065	0.160	0.160	0.071	0.012	0.003	0.000+	0.000+	0.000+
	10	0.000+	0.000+	0.002	0.010	0.031	0.117	0.176	0.117	0.031	0.010	0.002	0.000+	0.000+
	11	0.000+	0.000+	0.000+	0.003	0.012	0.071	0.160	0.160	0.065	0.027	0.007	0.000+	0.000+
	12	0.000+	0.000+	0.000+	0.001	0.004	0.035	0.120	0.180	0.114	0.061	0.022	0.000+	0.000+
	13	0.000+	0.000+	0.000+	0.000+	0.001	0.015	0.074	0.166	0.164	0.112	0.055	0.002	0.000+
	14	0.000+	0.000+	0.000+	0.000+	0.000+	0.005	0.037	0.124	0.192	0.169	0.109	0.009	0.000+
	15	0.000+	0.000+	0.000+	0.000+	0.000+	0.001	0.015	0.075	0.179	0.202	0.175	0.032	0.002
	16	0.000+	0.000+	0.000+	0.000+	0.000+	0.000+	0.005	0.035	0.130	0.190	0.218	0.090	0.013
	17	0.000+	0.000+	0.000+	0.000+	0.000+	0.000+	0.001	0.012	0.072	0.134	0.205	0.190	0.060
	18	0.000+	0.000+	0.000+	0.000+	0.000+	0.000+	0.000+	0.003	0.028	0.067	0.137	0.285	0.189
	19	0.000+	0.000+	0.000+	0.000+	0.000+	0.000+	0.000+	0.000+	0.007	0.021	0.058	0.270	0.377
	20	0.000+	0.000+	0.000+	0.000+	0.000+	0.000+	0.000+	0.000+	0.001	0.003	0.012	0.122	0.358

A value of 0.000+ indicates that the probability is 0.000 when rounded to three decimal places. The actual probability is slightly greater than 0.

Table A.2 Cumulative Normal Distribution

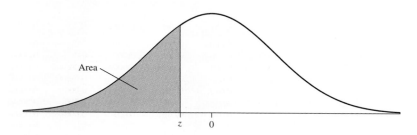

z	0.00	0.01	0.02	0.03	0.04	0.05	0.06	0.07	0.08	0.09
−3.7 or less	.0001									
−3.6	.0002	.0002	.0001	.0001	.0001	.0001	.0001	.0001	.0001	.0001
−3.5	.0002	.0002	.0002	.0002	.0002	.0002	.0002	.0002	.0002	.0002
−3.4	.0003	.0003	.0003	.0003	.0003	.0003	.0003	.0003	.0003	.0002
−3.3	.0005	.0005	.0005	.0004	.0004	.0004	.0004	.0004	.0004	.0003
−3.2	.0007	.0007	.0006	.0006	.0006	.0006	.0006	.0005	.0005	.0005
−3.1	.0010	.0009	.0009	.0009	.0008	.0008	.0008	.0008	.0007	.0007
−3.0	.0013	.0013	.0013	.0012	.0012	.0011	.0011	.0011	.0010	.0010
−2.9	.0019	.0018	.0018	.0017	.0016	.0016	.0015	.0015	.0014	.0014
−2.8	.0026	.0025	.0024	.0023	.0023	.0022	.0021	.0021	.0020	.0019
−2.7	.0035	.0034	.0033	.0032	.0031	.0030	.0029	.0028	.0027	.0026
−2.6	.0047	.0045	.0044	.0043	.0041	.0040	.0039	.0038	.0037	.0036
−2.5	.0062	.0060	.0059	.0057	.0055	.0054	.0052	.0051	.0049	.0048
−2.4	.0082	.0080	.0078	.0075	.0073	.0071	.0069	.0068	.0066	.0064
−2.3	.0107	.0104	.0102	.0099	.0096	.0094	.0091	.0089	.0087	.0084
−2.2	.0139	.0136	.0132	.0129	.0125	.0122	.0119	.0116	.0113	.0110
−2.1	.0179	.0174	.0170	.0166	.0162	.0158	.0154	.0150	.0146	.0143
−2.0	.0228	.0222	.0217	.0212	.0207	.0202	.0197	.0192	.0188	.0183
−1.9	.0287	.0281	.0274	.0268	.0262	.0256	.0250	.0244	.0239	.0233
−1.8	.0359	.0351	.0344	.0336	.0329	.0322	.0314	.0307	.0301	.0294
−1.7	.0446	.0436	.0427	.0418	.0409	.0401	.0392	.0384	.0375	.0367
−1.6	.0548	.0537	.0526	.0516	.0505	.0495	.0485	.0475	.0465	.0455
−1.5	.0668	.0655	.0643	.0630	.0618	.0606	.0594	.0582	.0571	.0559
−1.4	.0808	.0793	.0778	.0764	.0749	.0735	.0721	.0708	.0694	.0681
−1.3	.0968	.0951	.0934	.0918	.0901	.0885	.0869	.0853	.0838	.0823
−1.2	.1151	.1131	.1112	.1093	.1075	.1056	.1038	.1020	.1003	.0985
−1.1	.1357	.1335	.1314	.1292	.1271	.1251	.1230	.1210	.1190	.1170
−1.0	.1587	.1562	.1539	.1515	.1492	.1469	.1446	.1423	.1401	.1379
−0.9	.1841	.1814	.1788	.1762	.1736	.1711	.1685	.1660	.1635	.1611
−0.8	.2119	.2090	.2061	.2033	.2005	.1977	.1949	.1922	.1894	.1867
−0.7	.2420	.2389	.2358	.2327	.2296	.2266	.2236	.2206	.2177	.2148
−0.6	.2743	.2709	.2676	.2643	.2611	.2578	.2546	.2514	.2483	.2451
−0.5	.3085	.3050	.3015	.2981	.2946	.2912	.2877	.2843	.2810	.2776
−0.4	.3446	.3409	.3372	.3336	.3300	.3264	.3228	.3192	.3156	.3121
−0.3	.3821	.3783	.3745	.3707	.3669	.3632	.3594	.3557	.3520	.3483
−0.2	.4207	.4168	.4129	.4090	.4052	.4013	.3974	.3936	.3897	.3859
−0.1	.4602	.4562	.4522	.4483	.4443	.4404	.4364	.4325	.4286	.4247
−0.0	.5000	.4960	.4920	.4880	.4840	.4801	.4761	.4721	.4681	.4641

Table A.2 Cumulative Normal Distribution (continued)

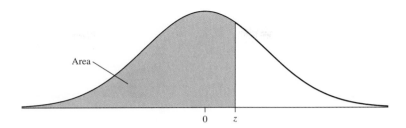

z	0.00	0.01	0.02	0.03	0.04	0.05	0.06	0.07	0.08	0.09
0.0	.5000	.5040	.5080	.5120	.5160	.5199	.5239	.5279	.5319	.5359
0.1	.5398	.5438	.5478	.5517	.5557	.5596	.5636	.5675	.5714	.5753
0.2	.5793	.5832	.5871	.5910	.5948	.5987	.6026	.6064	.6103	.6141
0.3	.6179	.6217	.6255	.6293	.6331	.6368	.6406	.6443	.6480	.6517
0.4	.6554	.6591	.6628	.6664	.6700	.6736	.6772	.6808	.6844	.6879
0.5	.6915	.6950	.6985	.7019	.7054	.7088	.7123	.7157	.7190	.7224
0.6	.7257	.7291	.7324	.7357	.7389	.7422	.7454	.7486	.7517	.7549
0.7	.7580	.7611	.7642	.7673	.7704	.7734	.7764	.7794	.7823	.7852
0.8	.7881	.7910	.7939	.7967	.7995	.8023	.8051	.8078	.8106	.8133
0.9	.8159	.8186	.8212	.8238	.8264	.8289	.8315	.8340	.8365	.8389
1.0	.8413	.8438	.8461	.8485	.8508	.8531	.8554	.8577	.8599	.8621
1.1	.8643	.8665	.8686	.8708	.8729	.8749	.8770	.8790	.8810	.8830
1.2	.8849	.8869	.8888	.8907	.8925	.8944	.8962	.8980	.8997	.9015
1.3	.9032	.9049	.9066	.9082	.9099	.9115	.9131	.9147	.9162	.9177
1.4	.9192	.9207	.9222	.9236	.9251	.9265	.9279	.9292	.9306	.9319
1.5	.9332	.9345	.9357	.9370	.9382	.9394	.9406	.9418	.9429	.9441
1.6	.9452	.9463	.9474	.9484	.9495	.9505	.9515	.9525	.9535	.9545
1.7	.9554	.9564	.9573	.9582	.9591	.9599	.9608	.9616	.9625	.9633
1.8	.9641	.9649	.9656	.9664	.9671	.9678	.9686	.9693	.9699	.9706
1.9	.9713	.9719	.9726	.9732	.9738	.9744	.9750	.9756	.9761	.9767
2.0	.9772	.9778	.9783	.9788	.9793	.9798	.9803	.9808	.9812	.9817
2.1	.9821	.9826	.9830	.9834	.9838	.9842	.9846	.9850	.9854	.9857
2.2	.9861	.9864	.9868	.9871	.9875	.9878	.9881	.9884	.9887	.9890
2.3	.9893	.9896	.9898	.9901	.9904	.9906	.9909	.9911	.9913	.9916
2.4	.9918	.9920	.9922	.9925	.9927	.9929	.9931	.9932	.9934	.9936
2.5	.9938	.9940	.9941	.9943	.9945	.9946	.9948	.9949	.9951	.9952
2.6	.9953	.9955	.9956	.9957	.9959	.9960	.9961	.9962	.9963	.9964
2.7	.9965	.9966	.9967	.9968	.9969	.9970	.9971	.9972	.9973	.9974
2.8	.9974	.9975	.9976	.9977	.9977	.9978	.9979	.9979	.9980	.9981
2.9	.9981	.9982	.9982	.9983	.9984	.9984	.9985	.9985	.9986	.9986
3.0	.9987	.9987	.9987	.9988	.9988	.9989	.9989	.9989	.9990	.9990
3.1	.9990	.9991	.9991	.9991	.9992	.9992	.9992	.9992	.9993	.9993
3.2	.9993	.9993	.9994	.9994	.9994	.9994	.9994	.9995	.9995	.9995
3.3	.9995	.9995	.9995	.9996	.9996	.9996	.9996	.9996	.9996	.9997
3.4	.9997	.9997	.9997	.9997	.9997	.9997	.9997	.9997	.9997	.9998
3.5	.9998	.9998	.9998	.9998	.9998	.9998	.9998	.9998	.9998	.9998
3.6	.9998	.9998	.9999	.9999	.9999	.9999	.9999	.9999	.9999	.9999
3.7 or more	.9999									

Table A.3 Critical Values for the Student's *t* Distribution

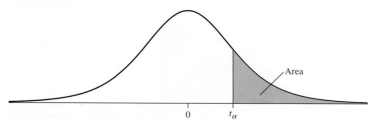

Degrees of Freedom	Area in Right Tail									
	0.40	**0.25**	**0.10**	**0.05**	**0.025**	**0.01**	**0.005**	**0.0025**	**0.001**	**0.0005**
1	0.325	1.000	3.078	6.314	12.706	31.821	63.657	127.321	318.309	636.619
2	0.289	0.816	1.886	2.920	4.303	6.965	9.925	14.089	22.327	31.599
3	0.277	0.765	1.638	2.353	3.182	4.541	5.841	7.453	10.215	12.924
4	0.271	0.741	1.533	2.132	2.776	3.747	4.604	5.598	7.173	8.610
5	0.267	0.727	1.476	2.015	2.571	3.365	4.032	4.773	5.893	6.869
6	0.265	0.718	1.440	1.943	2.447	3.143	3.707	4.317	5.208	5.959
7	0.263	0.711	1.415	1.895	2.365	2.998	3.499	4.029	4.785	5.408
8	0.262	0.706	1.397	1.860	2.306	2.896	3.355	3.833	4.501	5.041
9	0.261	0.703	1.383	1.833	2.262	2.821	3.250	3.690	4.297	4.781
10	0.260	0.700	1.372	1.812	2.228	2.764	3.169	3.581	4.144	4.587
11	0.260	0.697	1.363	1.796	2.201	2.718	3.106	3.497	4.025	4.437
12	0.259	0.695	1.356	1.782	2.179	2.681	3.055	3.428	3.930	4.318
13	0.259	0.694	1.350	1.771	2.160	2.650	3.012	3.372	3.852	4.221
14	0.258	0.692	1.345	1.761	2.145	2.624	2.977	3.326	3.787	4.140
15	0.258	0.691	1.341	1.753	2.131	2.602	2.947	3.286	3.733	4.073
16	0.258	0.690	1.337	1.746	2.120	2.583	2.921	3.252	3.686	4.015
17	0.257	0.689	1.333	1.740	2.110	2.567	2.898	3.222	3.646	3.965
18	0.257	0.688	1.330	1.734	2.101	2.552	2.878	3.197	3.610	3.922
19	0.257	0.688	1.328	1.729	2.093	2.539	2.861	3.174	3.579	3.883
20	0.257	0.687	1.325	1.725	2.086	2.528	2.845	3.153	3.552	3.850
21	0.257	0.686	1.323	1.721	2.080	2.518	2.831	3.135	3.527	3.819
22	0.256	0.686	1.321	1.717	2.074	2.508	2.819	3.119	3.505	3.792
23	0.256	0.685	1.319	1.714	2.069	2.500	2.807	3.104	3.485	3.768
24	0.256	0.685	1.318	1.711	2.064	2.492	2.797	3.091	3.467	3.745
25	0.256	0.684	1.316	1.708	2.060	2.485	2.787	3.078	3.450	3.725
26	0.256	0.684	1.315	1.706	2.056	2.479	2.779	3.067	3.435	3.707
27	0.256	0.684	1.314	1.703	2.052	2.473	2.771	3.057	3.421	3.690
28	0.256	0.683	1.313	1.701	2.048	2.467	2.763	3.047	3.408	3.674
29	0.256	0.683	1.311	1.699	2.045	2.462	2.756	3.038	3.396	3.659
30	0.256	0.683	1.310	1.697	2.042	2.457	2.750	3.030	3.385	3.646
31	0.256	0.682	1.309	1.696	2.040	2.453	2.744	3.022	3.375	3.633
32	0.255	0.682	1.309	1.694	2.037	2.449	2.738	3.015	3.365	3.622
33	0.255	0.682	1.308	1.692	2.035	2.445	2.733	3.008	3.356	3.611
34	0.255	0.682	1.307	1.691	2.032	2.441	2.728	3.002	3.348	3.601
35	0.255	0.682	1.306	1.690	2.030	2.438	2.724	2.996	3.340	3.591
36	0.255	0.681	1.306	1.688	2.028	2.434	2.719	2.990	3.333	3.582
37	0.255	0.681	1.305	1.687	2.026	2.431	2.715	2.985	3.326	3.574
38	0.255	0.681	1.304	1.686	2.024	2.429	2.712	2.980	3.319	3.566
39	0.255	0.681	1.304	1.685	2.023	2.426	2.708	2.976	3.313	3.558
40	0.255	0.681	1.303	1.684	2.021	2.423	2.704	2.971	3.307	3.551
50	0.255	0.679	1.299	1.676	2.009	2.403	2.678	2.937	3.261	3.496
60	0.254	0.679	1.296	1.671	2.000	2.390	2.660	2.915	3.232	3.460
80	0.254	0.678	1.292	1.664	1.990	2.374	2.639	2.887	3.195	3.416
100	0.254	0.677	1.290	1.660	1.984	2.364	2.626	2.871	3.174	3.390
200	0.254	0.676	1.286	1.653	1.972	2.345	2.601	2.839	3.131	3.340
z	0.253	0.674	1.282	1.645	1.960	2.326	2.576	2.807	3.090	3.291
	20%	50%	80%	90%	95%	98%	99%	99.5%	99.8%	99.9%
					Confidence Level					

Table A.4 Critical Values for the χ^2 Distribution

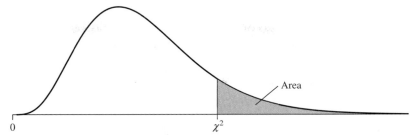

Degrees of Freedom	Area in Right Tail									
	0.995	**0.99**	**0.975**	**0.95**	**0.90**	**0.10**	**0.05**	**0.025**	**0.01**	**0.005**
1	0.000	0.000	0.001	0.004	0.016	2.706	3.841	5.024	6.635	7.879
2	0.010	0.020	0.051	0.103	0.211	4.605	5.991	7.378	9.210	10.597
3	0.072	0.115	0.216	0.352	0.584	6.251	7.815	9.348	11.345	12.838
4	0.207	0.297	0.484	0.711	1.064	7.779	9.488	11.143	13.277	14.860
5	0.412	0.554	0.831	1.145	1.610	9.236	11.070	12.833	15.086	16.750
6	0.676	0.872	1.237	1.635	2.204	10.645	12.592	14.449	16.812	18.548
7	0.989	1.239	1.690	2.167	2.833	12.017	14.067	16.013	18.475	20.278
8	1.344	1.646	2.180	2.733	3.490	13.362	15.507	17.535	20.090	21.955
9	1.735	2.088	2.700	3.325	4.168	14.684	16.919	19.023	21.666	23.589
10	2.156	2.558	3.247	3.940	4.865	15.987	18.307	20.483	23.209	25.188
11	2.603	3.053	3.816	4.575	5.578	17.275	19.675	21.920	24.725	26.757
12	3.074	3.571	4.404	5.226	6.304	18.549	21.026	23.337	26.217	28.300
13	3.565	4.107	5.009	5.892	7.042	19.812	22.362	24.736	27.688	29.819
14	4.075	4.660	5.629	6.571	7.790	21.064	23.685	26.119	29.141	31.319
15	4.601	5.229	6.262	7.261	8.547	22.307	24.996	27.488	30.578	32.801
16	5.142	5.812	6.908	7.962	9.312	23.542	26.296	28.845	32.000	34.267
17	5.697	6.408	7.564	8.672	10.085	24.769	27.587	30.191	33.409	35.718
18	6.265	7.015	8.231	9.390	10.865	25.989	28.869	31.526	34.805	37.156
19	6.844	7.633	8.907	10.117	11.651	27.204	30.144	32.852	36.191	38.582
20	7.434	8.260	9.591	10.851	12.443	28.412	31.410	34.170	37.566	39.997
21	8.034	8.897	10.283	11.591	13.240	29.615	32.671	35.479	38.932	41.401
22	8.643	9.542	10.982	12.338	14.041	30.813	33.924	36.781	40.289	42.796
23	9.260	10.196	11.689	13.091	14.848	32.007	35.172	38.076	41.638	44.181
24	9.886	10.856	12.401	13.848	15.659	33.196	36.415	39.364	42.980	45.559
25	10.520	11.524	13.120	14.611	16.473	34.382	37.652	40.646	44.314	46.928
26	11.160	12.198	13.844	15.379	17.292	35.563	38.885	41.923	45.642	48.290
27	11.808	12.879	14.573	16.151	18.114	36.741	40.113	43.195	46.963	49.645
28	12.461	13.565	15.308	16.928	18.939	37.916	41.337	44.461	48.278	50.993
29	13.121	14.256	16.047	17.708	19.768	39.087	42.557	45.722	49.588	52.336
30	13.787	14.953	16.791	18.493	20.599	40.256	43.773	46.979	50.892	53.672
31	14.458	15.655	17.539	19.281	21.434	41.422	44.985	48.232	52.191	55.003
32	15.134	16.362	18.291	20.072	22.271	42.585	46.194	49.480	53.486	56.328
33	15.815	17.074	19.047	20.867	23.110	43.745	47.400	50.725	54.776	57.648
34	16.501	17.789	19.806	21.664	23.952	44.903	48.602	51.966	56.061	58.964
35	17.192	18.509	20.569	22.465	24.797	46.059	49.802	53.203	57.342	60.275
36	17.887	19.233	21.336	23.269	25.643	47.212	50.998	54.437	58.619	61.581
37	18.586	19.96	22.106	24.075	26.492	48.363	52.192	55.668	59.893	62.883
38	19.289	20.691	22.878	24.884	27.343	49.513	53.384	56.896	61.162	64.181
39	19.996	21.426	23.654	25.695	28.196	50.660	54.572	58.120	62.428	65.476
40	20.707	22.164	24.433	26.509	29.051	51.805	55.758	59.342	63.691	66.766
41	21.421	22.906	25.215	27.326	29.907	52.949	56.942	60.561	64.950	68.053
42	22.138	23.650	25.999	28.144	30.765	54.090	58.124	61.777	66.206	69.336
43	22.859	24.398	26.785	28.965	31.625	55.230	59.304	62.990	67.459	70.616
44	23.584	25.148	27.575	29.787	32.487	56.369	60.481	64.201	68.710	71.893
45	24.311	25.901	28.366	30.612	33.350	57.505	61.656	65.410	69.957	73.166
50	27.991	29.707	32.357	34.764	37.689	63.167	67.505	71.420	76.154	79.490
60	35.534	37.485	40.482	43.188	46.459	74.397	79.082	83.298	88.379	91.952
70	43.275	45.442	48.758	51.739	55.329	85.527	90.531	95.023	100.425	104.215
80	51.172	53.540	57.153	60.391	64.278	96.578	101.879	106.629	112.329	116.321
90	59.196	61.754	65.647	69.126	73.291	107.565	113.145	118.136	124.116	128.299
100	67.328	70.065	74.222	77.929	82.358	118.498	124.342	129.561	135.807	140.169

TI-84 PLUS Stat Wizards

Stat Wizards is a feature on TI-84 PLUS calculators running operating system OS 2.55 MP or higher. This feature provides a wizard interface for selected commands and functions. The latest operatng system may be downloaded from http://education.ti.com/calculators/downloads/.

The Stat Wizards may be turned on or off through an option on the **MODE** screen. The **MATHPRINT/CLASSIC** options affect the appearance of the calculator output. These options also appear on this screen. The screenshots in this text are generated using the **CLASSIC** setting.

Wizards are available for all commands in the **[STAT] CALC** menu and the **DISTR** menu.

1-Var Stats

The **1-Var Stats** wizard is accessed by selecting the **1-Var Stats** option under the **[STAT] CALC** menu. **L1** is the default setting for the **List** field. **FreqList** is an optional argument. **FreqList** accepts list names only. To run the command, select **Calculate** and press ⏎.

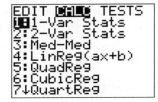

LinReg(a + bx)

The **LinReg(a + bx)** wizard is accessed by selecting the **LinReg(a + bx)** option under the [**STAT**] **CALC** menu. **L1** and **L2** are the default settings for the **Xlist** and **Ylist** fields. **FreqList** is an optional argument. A function name such as **Y1** may be entered in the **Store RegEQ** field as a location to store the regression equation. To run the command, select **Calculate** and press ⏎.

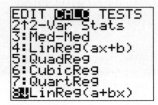
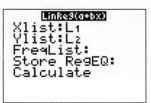

binompdf/binomcdf

The wizards for **binompdf** or **binomcdf** are accessed by selecting either the **binompdf** or **binomcdf** option under the **DISTR** menu. After entering the values for n, p, and x in the **trials**, **p**, and **x value** fields, select **Paste** and press [ENTER] to paste the command on the home screen.

normalcdf

The **normalcdf** wizard is accessed by selecting the **normalcdf** option under the **DISTR** menu. The lower and upper endpoints are entered in the **lower** and **upper** fields. The default for the **lower** field is -1E99. The mean and standard deviation are entered in the μ and σ fields. The default for the μ field is 0 and the default for the σ field is 1. After entering all values, select **Paste** and press [ENTER] to paste the command on the home screen.

invNorm

The **invNorm** wizard is accessed by selecting the **invNorm** option under the **DISTR** menu. The area to the left of the desired value is entered in the **area** field. The mean and standard deviation are entered in the μ and σ fields. The default for the μ field is 0 and the default for the σ field is 1. After entering all values, select **Paste** and press [ENTER] to paste the command on the home screen.

Answers to Odd-Numbered Exercises

CHAPTER 1

Section 1.1

Exercises 1–6 are the Check Your Understanding exercises for this section. Answers to these exercises are on page 12.

7. population

9. simple random sample

11. cluster

13. False

15. True

17. Statistic

19. Parameter

21. Answers will vary.

23. Answers will vary. Cluster sample

25. Stratified sample

27. Sample of convenience

29. Voluntary response sample

31. Sample of convenience

33. Stratified sample

35. Simple random sample

37. It will be necessary to draw a sample of convenience. There is no list of all headache sufferers from which to draw a simple random sample.

39. Answers will vary. A simple random sample could be drawn from a list of all registered voters in the town.

41. Answers will vary. A stratified sample, consisting of simple random samples of 100 men and 100 women, could be drawn.

43. Answers will vary.

Section 1.2

Exercises 1–4 are the Check Your Understanding exercises for this section. Answers to these exercises are on page 18.

5. variables

7. Quantitative

9. discrete

11. False

13. True

15. Qualitative

17. Quantitative

19. Quantitative

21. Qualitative

23. Qualitative

25. Ordinal

27. Ordinal

29. Nominal

31. Nominal

33. Continuous

35. Discrete

37. Continuous

39. Ordinal

41. Ordinal

43. Nominal

45. **a.** Game title, Publisher
    b. Percentage of gaming audience, Average minutes played per week
    c. Publisher **d.** Game title

47. **a.** Ordinal
    b. Yes, it reflects a more favorable opinion of the construction of a new shopping mall.
    c. No, we cannot say that Jason's opinion is twice as favorable.
    d. Quantitative
    e. Yes, Brenda's answer reflects the ownership of more cars, and specifically, the ownership of twice as many cars.
    f. Nominal
    g. No, Brenda's answer reflects neither more of something nor twice as much of something.

Section 1.3

Exercises 1–4 are the Check Your Understanding exercises for this section. Answers to these exercises are on page 26.

5. randomized

7. observational

9. prospective

11. True

13. False

15. True

17. **a.** Randomized experiment
    b. Yes, because the assignment to treatments is made at random, there is no systematic difference between the groups other than the drug taken that can explain the difference in pain relief.

19. **a.** Randomized experiment
    b. Yes, because the assignment to treatments is made at random, there is no systematic difference between the groups other than the amount of exercise that can explain the difference in blood pressure.

21. An observational study will be necessary, because one can't assign people to live in areas with high pollution levels.

23. The result may be due to confounding. Areas with denser populations may have both more crime and more taxicabs.

25. a. False   **b.** True

27. a. Heart rate   **b.** Maternal smoking
   c. Cohort   **d.** Prospective
   e. Yes. The level of prenatal care may differ between smoking and nonsmoking mothers.

29. a. Yes, because the subjects were randomly assigned to treatment
   b. If a doctor knew whether a child had received the vaccine, it might influence the diagnosis.
   c. It could be due to confounding. The children who received the placebo were more likely to be middle- or upper-income than those who did not participate, and this may be the reason that the rate of polio was higher.

Section 1.4

Exercises 1 and 2 are the Check Your Understanding exercises for this section. Answers to these exercises are on page 29.

3. Voluntary response surveys

5. population

7. True

9. Nonresponse bias

11. Self-interest bias

13. Voluntary response bias

15. Nonresponse bias

17. a. No
   b. No. Both questions are leading. The first question leads to a "yes" response, and the second leads to a "no" response.

19. Yes. People who do not have landline phones may tend to have different opinions on some issues than people who do have landline phones.

21. a. The poll oversampled higher-income people.
   b. Nonresponse bias. The response rate was low—only 23%. This results in nonresponse bias.
   c. A sample that is not drawn by a valid method can produce misleading results, even when it is large.

CHAPTER 1 Quiz

1. Answers will vary.

2. Qualitative

3. True

4. Continuous

5. False

6. Stratified sample

7. acceptable

8. Sample of convenience

9. True

10. Observational study

11. Randomized experiment

12. differences in treatment

13. Seniors may be more likely to have better preparation for the class than sophomores.

14. True

15. Not reliable. This is a voluntary response survey, so the people who respond tend to hold stronger opinions than others.

CHAPTER 1 Review Exercises

1. Quantitative

2. Nominal

3. Continuous

4. a. True   **b.** True   **c.** False

5. Stratified sample

6. Voluntary response sample

7. Cluster sample

8. Simple random sample

9. a. Observational study
   b. Yes. People who live in areas with fluoridated water may have different dental habits than those who live in areas without fluoridated water.

10. a. Randomized experiment
   b. Because this is a randomized experiment, the results are unlikely to be due to confounding.

11. a. Observational study
   b. Yes. People who talk on cell phones while driving may be more careless in general than those who do not.

12. a. Randomized experiment
   b. Because this is a randomized experiment, the results are unlikely to be due to confounding.

13. The sample is a voluntary response sample.

14. Nonresponse bias; living people not included. People who are still alive are not included in the sample.

15. There is a considerable level of nonresponse bias.

CHAPTER 1 Case Study

1. 450

2. 41

3. 9.1%

4. 43

5. 2

6. 4.7%

7. Yes

8. The high-exposure people and the school-return people are the same people.

9. The low-exposure people and the mail-return people are the same people.

10. People who respond by mail will be responding during a period of lower PM.

11. People with symptoms may tend to respond earlier; therefore, people with symptoms are more likely to be school-return people.

12. There would be no tendency for people with symptoms to respond earlier.

CHAPTER 2

Section 2.1

Exercises 1–4 are the Check Your Understanding exercises for this section. Answers to these exercises are on pages 47–48.

5. frequency

7. Pareto chart

9. False

11. True

13. a. Meat, poultry, fish, and eggs   **b.** False   **c.** True

15. a.

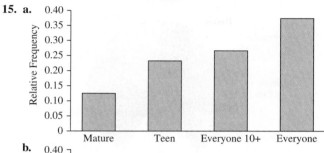

b.

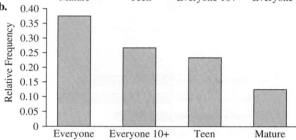

c. Everyone (E)   **d.** False   **e.** True

17. a.

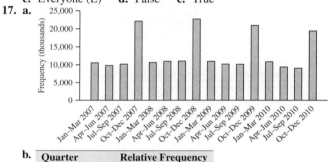

b.

Quarter	Relative Frequency
Jan.–Mar. 2007	0.050
Apr.–Jun. 2007	0.047
Jul.–Sep. 2007	0.049
Oct.–Dec. 2007	0.106
Jan.–Mar. 2008	0.051
Apr.–Jun. 2008	0.053
Jul.–Sep. 2008	0.053
Oct.–Dec. 2008	0.109
Jan.–Mar. 2009	0.053
Apr.–Jun. 2009	0.049
Jul.–Sep. 2009	0.049
Oct.–Dec. 2009	0.100
Jan.–Mar. 2010	0.052
Apr.–Jun. 2010	0.045
Jul.–Sep. 2010	0.043
Oct.–Dec. 2010	0.093

c.

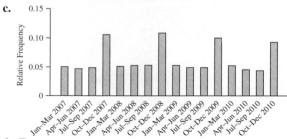

d. True

19. a.

Quarter	Frequency (thousands)
Jan–Mar	43,091
Apr–Jun	40,451
Jul–Sep	40,479
Oct–Dec	85,264

b.

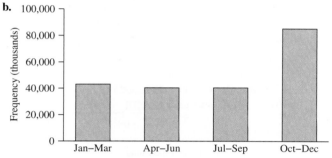

c.

Quarter	Relative Frequency
Jan–Mar	0.206
Apr–Jun	0.193
Jul–Sep	0.193
Oct–Dec	0.407

d.

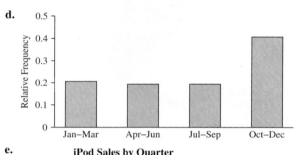

e.

iPod Sales by Quarter

f. False

21. a.

	Frequency
Congestive heart failure	
Coronary atherosclerosis	
Heart attack	
Infant birth	
Pneumonia	

b.

Reason	Relative Frequency
Congestive heart failure	0.122
Coronary atherosclerosis	0.172
Heart attack	0.091
Infant birth	0.467
Pneumonia	0.148

c.

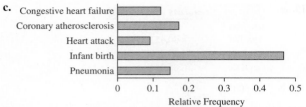

d.

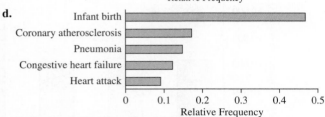

e.   **Hospital Admissions**

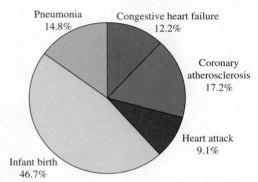

f. True

23. a.

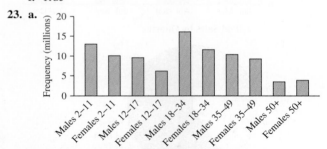

b.

Gender and Age Group	Relative Frequency
Males 2–11	0.139
Females 2–11	0.108
Males 12–17	0.102
Females 12–17	0.066
Males 18–34	0.172
Females 18–34	0.124
Males 35–49	0.111
Females 35–49	0.099
Males 50+	0.037
Females 50+	0.042

c.

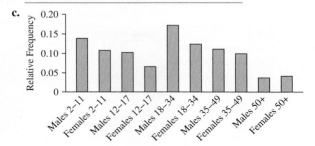

d.   **Gender and Age of Video Game Players**

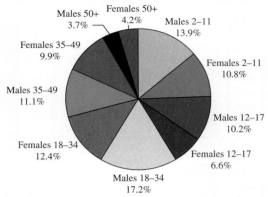

e. True   **f.** True   **g.** 0.289

25. a.

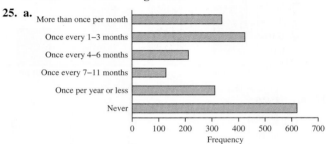

b.

Response	Relative Frequency
More than once per month	0.166
Once every 1–3 months	0.209
Once every 4–6 months	0.104
Once every 7–11 months	0.063
Once per year or less	0.153
Never	0.305

c.

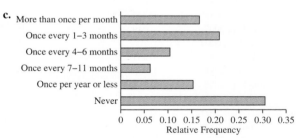

d.   **Frequency of Backups**

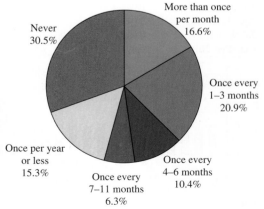

e. True   **f.** False

27. a.

Type of Music	Relative Frequency
CD	0.284
Download single	0.450
Mobile	0.201
Other	0.065

b.

Type of Music	Relative Frequency
CD	0.213
Download single	0.572
Mobile	0.187
Other	0.028

c.

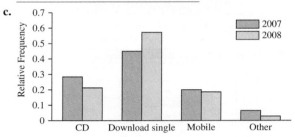

d. True

29. a.

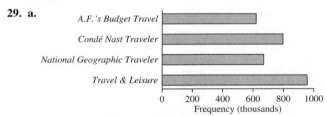

b.

Magazine	Relative Frequency
A.F.'s Budget Travel	0.204
Condé Nast Traveler	0.262
National Geographic Traveler	0.220
Travel & Leisure	0.314

c.

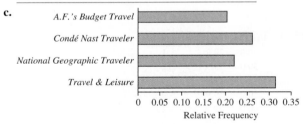

d.

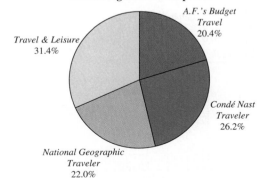

e. 0.314

31. a.

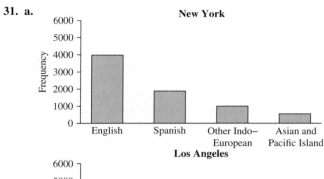

b.

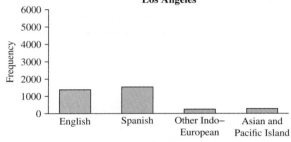

c.

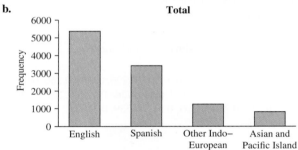

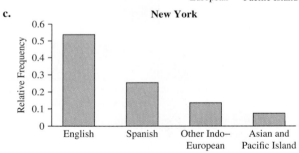

d.

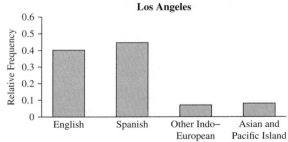

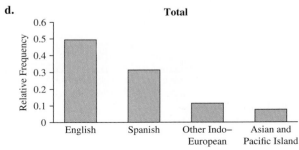

e. The total frequency is equal to the sum of the frequencies for the two cities.

f. The total relative frequency is the total frequency divided by the sum of all total frequencies. The relative frequency for each city is the frequency for that city divided by the sum of the frequencies for that city. Since the sum of the frequencies for each city is not the same as the sum of the total frequencies, the total relative frequency is not the sum of the relative frequencies for the two cities.

Section 2.2

Exercises 1–4 are the Check Your Understanding exercises for this section. Answers to these exercises are on page 63.

5. symmetric

7. bimodal

9. False

11. True

13. Skewed to the left

15. Approximately symmetric

17. Bimodal

19. **a.** 11   **b.** 1   **c.** 70–71
   d. 9%   **e.** Approximately symmetric

21. **a.** 9   **b.** 0.020
   c. Lower limits: 0.180, 0.200, 0.220, 0.240, 0.260, 0.280, 0.300, 0.320, 0.340. Upper limits: 0.199, 0.219, 0.239, 0.259, 0.279, 0.299, 0.319, 0.339, 0.359.
   d.

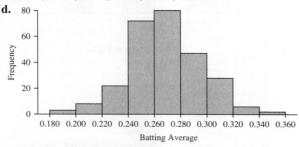

Batting Average	Relative Frequency
0.180–0.199	0.011
0.200–0.219	0.030
0.220–0.239	0.082
0.240–0.259	0.269
0.260–0.279	0.299
0.280–0.299	0.175
0.300–0.319	0.104
0.320–0.339	0.022
0.340–0.359	0.007

e.

f.

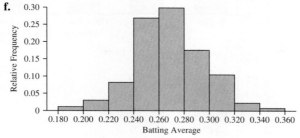

g. 13.4%   **h.** 4.1%

23. **a.** 10   **b.** 3.0
   c. Lower limits: 1.0, 4.0, 7.0, 10.0, 13.0, 16.0, 19.0, 22.0, 25.0, 28.0. Upper limits: 3.9, 6.9, 9.9, 12.9, 15.9, 18.9, 21.9, 24.9, 27.9, 30.9.
   d.

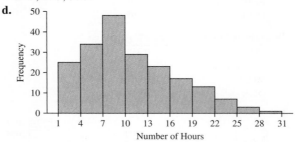

Number of Hours	Relative Frequency
1.0 – 3.9	0.125
4.0 – 6.9	0.170
7.0 – 9.9	0.240
10.0 – 12.9	0.145
13.0 – 15.9	0.115
16.0 – 18.9	0.085
19.0 – 21.9	0.065
22.0 – 24.9	0.035
25.0 – 27.9	0.015
28.0 – 30.9	0.005

e.

f.

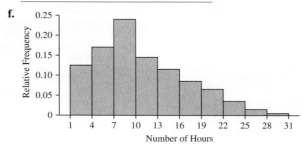

g. 53.5%   **h.** 12.0%

25. **a.**

Price ($1000s)	Frequency
20.0 – 29.9	1
30.0 – 39.9	12
40.0 – 49.9	11
50.0 – 59.9	9
60.0 – 69.9	2
70.0 – 79.9	3
80.0 – 89.9	2
90.0 – 99.9	0
100.0 – 109.9	2
110.0 – 119.9	1
120.0 – 129.9	1

b.

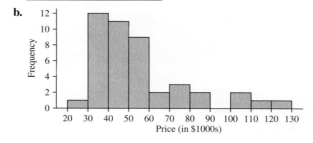

c.

Price ($1000s)	Relative Frequency
20.0 – 29.9	0.023
30.0 – 39.9	0.273
40.0 – 49.9	0.250
50.0 – 59.9	0.205
60.0 – 69.9	0.045
70.0 – 79.9	0.068
80.0 – 89.9	0.045
90.0 – 99.9	0.000
100.0 – 109.9	0.045
110.0 – 119.9	0.023
120.0 – 129.9	0.023

d.

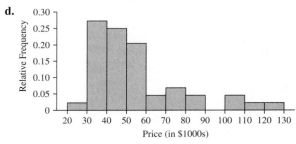

e. Unimodal

f.

Price ($1000s)	Frequency
20 – 39.9	13
40 – 59.9	20
60 – 79.9	5
80 – 99.9	2
100 – 119.9	3
120 – 139.9	1

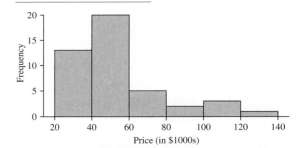

Price ($1000s)	Relative Frequency
20 – 39.9	0.295
40 – 59.9	0.455
60 – 79.9	0.114
80 – 99.9	0.045
100 – 119.9	0.068
120 – 139.9	0.023

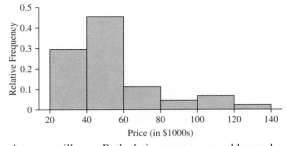

g. Answers will vary. Both choices seem reasonably good.

27. a. Answers will vary. Here is one possibility:

Number of Words	Frequency
0–1999	25
2000–3999	25
4000–5999	5
6000–7999	0
8000–9999	1

b.

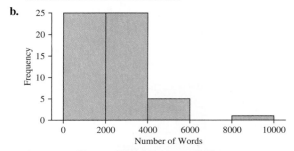

c. Answers will vary. Here is one possibility:

Number of Words	Relative Frequency
0–1999	0.446
2000–3999	0.446
4000–5999	0.089
6000–7999	0.000
8000–9999	0.018

d.

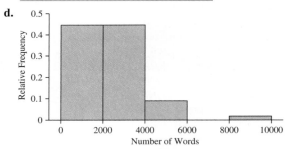

e. Skewed to the right

f. Answers will vary. Here is one possibility:

Number of Words	Frequency
0 – 999	5
1000 – 1999	20
2000 – 2999	18
3000 – 3999	7
4000 – 4999	4
5000 – 5999	1
6000 – 6999	0
7000 – 7999	0
8000 – 8999	1

g.

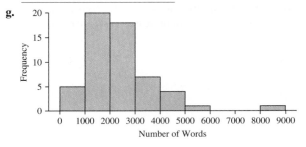

Answers will vary. Here is one possibility:

Number of Words	Relative Frequency
0 – 999	0.089
1000 – 1999	0.357
2000 – 2999	0.321
3000 – 3999	0.125
4000 – 4999	0.071
5000 – 5999	0.018
6000 – 6999	0.000
7000 – 7999	0.000
8000 – 8999	0.018

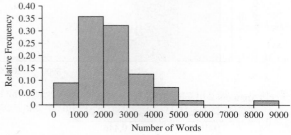

h. Answers will vary.

29. a.

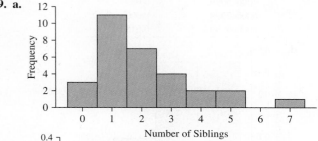

b.

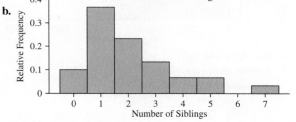

c. Skewed to the right

31. It is not possible to construct a histogram for this data set because the last class is open-ended.

33. 0.15

Section 2.3

Exercises 1 and 2 are the Check Your Understanding exercises for this section. Answers to these exercises are on page 74.

3. leaf

5. time-series plot

7. True

9. True

11.

1	1225566
2	0012779
3	19
4	556
5	02578

13. The list is: 30, 30, 31, 32, 35, 36, 37, 37, 39, 42, 43, 44, 45, 46, 47, 47, 47, 47, 48, 48, 49, 50, 51, 51, 51, 52, 52, 52, 52, 54, 56, 57, 58, 58, 59, 61, 63

15.

```
    ••   ••    •      •        •        ••
   ••   ••    •••    •  •   •      ••   • •  •  ••
   |-----|-----|-----|-----|-----|
  10    20    30    40    50    60
```

17. a.

2	9
3	335556677999
4	111334567
5	00022344579
6	35
7	77
8	044
9	
10	06
11	5
12	4

b.

2	
2	9
3	33
3	5556677999
4	111334
4	567
5	00022344
5	579
6	3
6	5
7	
7	77
8	044
8	
9	
9	
10	0
10	6
11	
11	5
12	4
12	

c. Answers will vary. The plot with the split stems has more detail than is needed for stems of 6 and higher.

19. a.

0	3
0	55669999
1	01111112222333344
1	555666889
2	11124
2	556777
3	0111334
3	555678
4	02
4	6
5	
5	9
6	
6	66

b. Answers will vary. The split stem-and-leaf plot provides more detail in the range 0–39, where there is a lot of data. It is more spread out than necessary for values greater than 40, where the data are sparse.

21. a.

Wimbledon		Master's
	1	
87	1	
4444433322222222221111110	2	33
99877776665555	2	566777888899
110	3	011112222233333
	3	5567888999
	4	123
	4	6

b. The Wimbledon champions are generally younger than the Master's champions.

23.

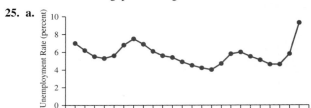

There are several gaps. The largest is between 63 and 67.

25. a.

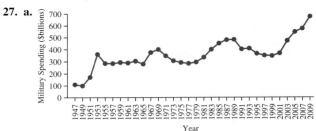

b. Increasing: 1989–1992, 2000–2003, 2007–2009. Decreasing: 1986–1989, 1992–2000, 2003–2007.

27. a.

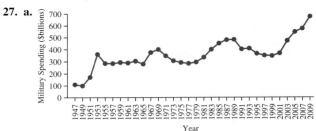

b. Increased: 1950s, 1960s, 1980s, 2000s. Decreased: 1970s, 1990s.

c. Spending increased greatly.

d. Spending increased from 1965 to 1969, then decreased through 1975.

29. a. Approximately $600 billion

b. Approximately $300 billion

c. True   **d.** True

31. a. Approximately 115 inches   **b.** 1910   **c.** Less than

d. True   **e.** False

33. a.

0	3333333344444
0	5555556667777788999
1	0000111123
1	5557
2	11
2	7
3	1
3	4
4	
4	
5	
5	5

b.

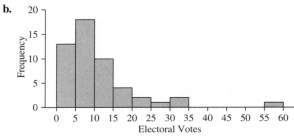

c. Each line of the stem-and-leaf plot corresponds to a class for the histogram.

Section 2.4

Exercises 1 and 2 are the Check Your Understanding exercises for this section. Answers to these exercises are on page 80.

3. zero

5. (i). Graph (A) presents an accurate picture, because the baseline is at zero. Graph (B) exaggerates the decline, because the baseline is above zero.

7. Graph (B) presents the more accurate picture. The baseline is at zero, and the bars are of equal width. The dollar bill graphic does not follow the area principle. The length and width of the smaller image are about 40% less than the length and width of the larger image, so the area of the smaller image is about 64% less than that of the larger image. This exaggerates the difference.

9. It presents an accurate picture of the increase, because the baseline is at zero.

11. a. The bars appear shorter than they really are.

b. Answers may vary. The following bar graph presents an accurate picture.

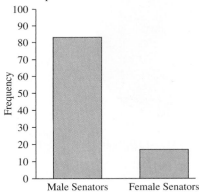

13. a.

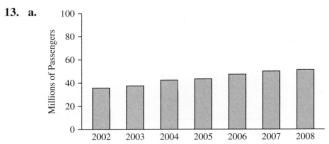

b. It makes the differences look smaller, because the scale on the y-axis extends much farther than the largest bar height.

c. Answers will vary. Figure 2.19 has the baseline at zero, and the scale on the *y*-axis is appropriate for the maximum bar height.

CHAPTER 2 Quiz

1.

Grade	Frequency
A	9
B	5
C	6
D	3
F	4

2.

Grade	Relative Frequency
A	0.333
B	0.185
C	0.222
D	0.111
F	0.148

3.

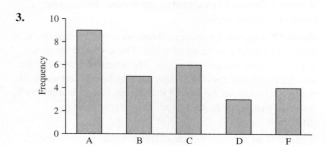

4.

Grades in Algebra Class

F 14.8%
A 33.3%
D 11.1%
C 22.2%
B 18.5%

5. 5.0–7.9, 8.0–10.9, 11.0–13.9, 14.0–16.9, 17.0–19.9. The class width is 3.

6. True

7.

8.

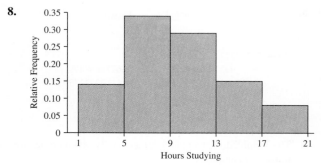

9. The list is: 11, 11, 15, 15, 19, 19, 19, 22, 22, 23, 25, 27, 28, 30, 30, 38, 44, 45, 47, 48, 50, 51, 53, 53, 55, 56, 58

10.

1	9
2	22889
3	579
4	1
5	
6	8

11.

2	5
3	01
4	0
5	006
6	5
7	07
8	
9	99

12.

Espresso Makers		Coffee Makers
	1	9
5	2	22889
10	3	579
0	4	1
600	5	
5	6	8
70	7	
	8	
99	9	

13.

14.

15. Twice

CHAPTER 2 Review Exercises

1. a. Somewhat   **b.** True   **c.** False   **d.** True

2. a.

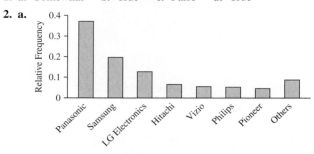

b.   **Market Share for TV Vendors**

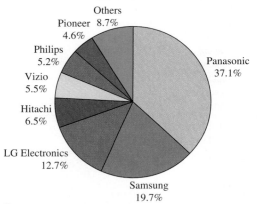

c. True

3. a.

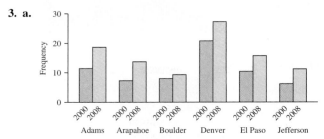

b. True

c. Adams

4. a.

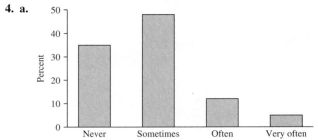

b.   **Failure to Complete Assignments**

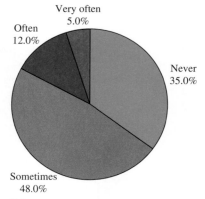

c. False

5. a. 7   **b.** 10   **c.** 10%   **d.** Unimodal

6. a. 8   **b.** 20

c. 20–39, 40–59, 60–79, 80–99, 100–119, 120–139, 140–159, 160–179.

d.

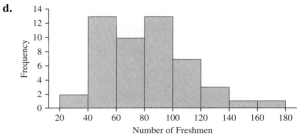

e.

Number of Freshmen	Relative Frequency
20 – 39	0.040
40 – 59	0.260
60 – 79	0.200
80 – 99	0.260
100 – 119	0.140
120 – 139	0.060
140 – 159	0.020
160 – 179	0.020

f.

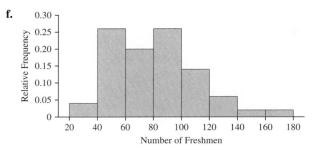

7. a. 24%   **b.** 30%

8. a.

Age	Frequency
10–19	2
20–29	1
30–39	3
40–49	10
50–59	9
60–69	9
70–79	4
80–89	2

b.

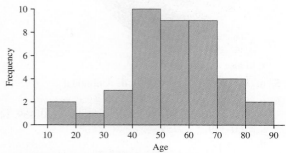

c.

Age	Relative Frequency
10–19	0.050
20–29	0.025
30–39	0.075
40–49	0.250
50–59	0.225
60–69	0.225
70–79	0.100
80–89	0.050

d.

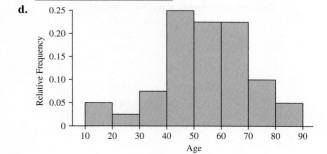

9.

1	25
2	8
3	235
4	0012368999
5	124566889
6	457777889
7	0167
8	11

10. a.

Age	Frequency
45–49	2
50–54	1
55–59	4
60–64	6
65–69	6
70–74	6
75–79	4
80–84	3
85–89	2
90–94	4

b.

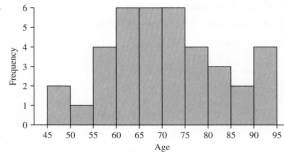

c.

Age	Relative Frequency
45–49	0.053
50–54	0.026
55–59	0.105
60–64	0.158
65–69	0.158
70–74	0.158
75–79	0.105
80–84	0.079
85–89	0.053
90–94	0.105

d.

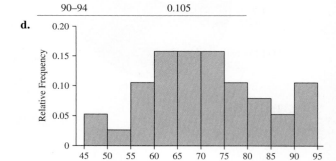

11. a.

Presidents		Monarchs
	1	25
	2	8
	3	235
96	4	0012368999
87763	5	124566889
877765443300	6	457777889
9887432110	7	0167
85310	8	11
3300	9	

b.

Presidents		Monarchs
	1	2
	1	5
	2	
	2	8
	3	23
	3	5
	4	00123
96	4	68999
3	5	124
8776	5	566889
443300	6	4
877765	6	57777889
432110	7	01
9887	7	67
310	8	11
85	8	
3300	9	
	9	

c. Answers will vary. The split stem-and-leaf plot provides a more appropriate level of detail.

12. a.

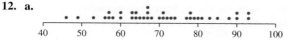

13. a.

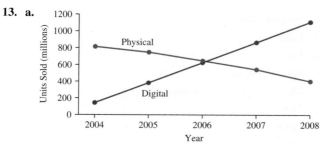

b. Digital sales are increasing; physical sales are decreasing.

14. a.

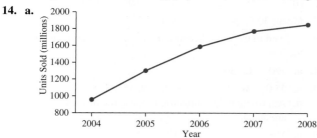

b.

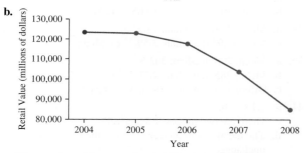

c. The number of inexpensive download singles has been increasing, while the number of expensive CDs has been decreasing. The total number of units has been increasing, but because the number of CDs has been decreasing, the total retail value has been decreasing.

15. (ii). The birth rate rose slightly between 2001 and 2007. The plot on the left is misleading, because the baseline is not at zero.

CHAPTER 2 Case Study

1.

Mileage	Frequency
16.0–16.9	1
17.0–17.9	0
18.0–18.9	0
19.0–19.9	0
20.0–20.9	0
21.0–21.9	3
22.0–22.9	0
23.0–23.9	3
24.0–24.9	3
25.0–25.9	0
26.0–26.9	3
27.0–27.9	9
28.0–28.9	8
29.0–29.9	3
30.0–30.9	6
31.0–31.9	6
32.0–32.9	3
33.0–33.9	4
34.0–34.9	3
35.0–35.9	1
36.0–36.9	1
37.0–37.9	1
38.0–38.9	3
39.0–39.9	0
40.0–40.9	1

2. There are 24 classes, which is too many for a data set with only 62 values.

3.

Mileage	Frequency	Relative Frequency
15.0–16.9	1	0.016
17.0–18.9	0	0.000
19.0–20.9	0	0.000
21.0–22.9	3	0.048
23.0–24.9	6	0.097
25.0–26.9	3	0.048
27.0–28.9	17	0.274
29.0–30.9	9	0.145
31.0–32.9	9	0.145
33.0–34.9	7	0.113
35.0–36.9	2	0.032
37.0–38.9	4	0.065
39.0–40.9	1	0.016

4.

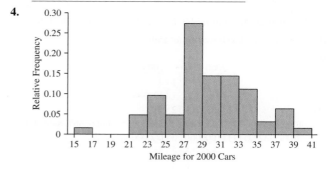

The histogram is unimodal. There is little skewness.

5. Answers will vary. Here is a frequency distribution with a class width of 2.

Mileage	Relative Frequency
14.0–15.9	2
16.0–17.9	3
18.0–19.9	5
20.0–21.9	2
22.0–23.9	1
24.0–25.9	10
26.0–27.9	9
28.0–29.9	9
30.0–31.9	7
32.0–33.9	2
34.0–35.9	5

6. Answers will vary. Here is a relative frequency distribution with a class width of 2.

Mileage	Relative Frequency
14.0–15.9	0.036
16.0–17.9	0.055
18.0–19.9	0.091
20.0–21.9	0.036
22.0–23.9	0.018
24.0–25.9	0.182
26.0–27.9	0.164
28.0–29.9	0.164
30.0–31.9	0.127
32.0–33.9	0.036
34.0–35.9	0.091

7. Answers will vary. Here is a histogram with a class width of 2.

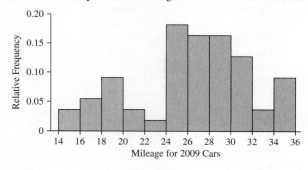

The histogram is unimodal and slightly skewed to the left.

8. 2000 cars tend to have higher mileage.

9.

2000 Cars		2009 Cars
	1	4
6	1	577788889
444333111	2	112
99988888888777777777666	2	55555555556666666778888899999
4443333222111111000000	3	00000013344
888765	3	555
0	4	

Answers will vary. The back-to-back stem-and-leaf plots seem to show more clearly that the 2000 cars tend to have higher mileage than the 2009 cars.

CHAPTER 3
Section 3.1

Exercises 1–6 are the Check Your Understanding exercises for this section. Answers to these exercises are on page 104.

7. mean

9. extreme values

11. False

13. False

15. Mean: 23.4; median: 26; mode: 27

17. Mean: 5.5; median: 14; mode: 28

19. 24.6

21. 145.0

23. (ii)

25. (i)

27. Mean: 30.4; median: 29; mode: 27

29. Skewed to the right, because the mean is greater than the median.

31. a. 290   **b.** 300

33. a. 35.0   **b.** 35   **c.** 23, 25, 29, 35, 38, 47
    d. Approximately symmetric because the mean and median are equal.

35. a. Mean: 13.39; median: 12
    b. Mean: 10.76; median: 10.05   **c.** Yes

37. a. Mean: 2.307; median: 2.02
    b. Mean: 3.968; median: 3.59   **c.** Mean

39. a. Mean: 296; median: 302.5
    b. Mean: 285.5; median: 285
    c. Offensive linemen are somewhat heavier.

41. a. 1.73   **b.** 1.4
    c. There are two modes: 1.2 and 1.4.
    d. The mean would increase to 4.61; the median would be unchanged.

43. a. 35.2
    b. Too small, because the average age within the first class is greater than the midpoint.

45. a. 37.5   **b.** 36   **c.** Skewed to the right
    d. Answers will vary. Here is one possibility:

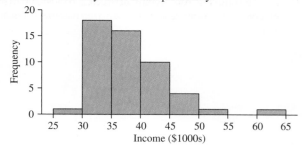

The results agree with the expectation.

47. Fiction

49. a. 13   **b.** 12

51. 208

53. a. 220,600   **b.** 20,000
    c. The mean is more appropriate, because it better reflects the amount of money the family now has.

55. Answers will vary.

57. Answers will vary.

59. No. If the largest or smallest value is an outlier, the value of the midrange will be strongly affected.

61. a. 68.4 **b.** 68 **c.** 5.417, 6.000, 5.667, 5.583, 5.833
 d. 5.7; yes **e.** 5.667; yes

63. a. They are both equal to 5.
 b. The median: The mean increases to 6, and the median increases to 8.
 c. The mean: The mean increases to 9.5, and the median increases to 8.
 d. As the value becomes more extreme, the mean steadily increases, but the median stays the same. At some point, the mean becomes greater than the median.

Section 3.2

Exercises 1–8 are the Check Your Understanding exercises for this section. Answers to these exercises are on page 123.

9. zero

11. 68%

13. False

15. False

17. Variance is 100; standard deviation is 10.

19. Variance is 49; standard deviation is 7.

21. Variance is 289; standard deviation is 17.

23. Variance is approximately 228.41; standard deviation is approximately 15.11.

25. Variance is approximately 5680; standard deviation is approximately 76.37.

27. a. 68% **b.** 20 and 44 **c.** 75%

29. a. 95% **b.** 140 and 212 **c.** 88.9%

31. a. 0.931 **b.** 1.626 **c.** Yes

33. a. 26.8 **b.** 23.2 **c.** Offensive

35. a. 3.13 **b.** 2.36 **c.** 1997–1998: 11.5; 2007–2008: 7.9
 d. Decrease **e.** Decrease

37. a. 14.615 **b.** 18.905 **c.** July

39. a. 7.58 **b.** 2.75

41. a. Almost all **b.** 68% **c.** 71.2 and 82.0

43. a. 422 **b.** 590

45. Not appropriate; histogram is skewed.

47. Approximately 68%

49. At least 75% of the days had temperatures between 56.2°F and 68.6°F.

51. a. Impossible **b.** Possible **c.** Impossible **d.** Possible

53. a. Yes. Answers will vary

55. a. 0.045 **b.** 0.351 **c.** Weight

57. a. 4.8 **b.**

x	$x - \bar{x}$	$(x - \bar{x})^2$	$|x - \bar{x}|$
1	−3.8	14.44	3.8
3	−1.8	3.24	1.8
4	−0.8	0.64	0.8
7	2.2	4.84	2.2
9	4.2	17.64	4.2

 c. SD = 3.1937; MAD = 2.56 **d.** SD = 10.677; MAD = 7
 e. The MAD is more resistant. Its value changed less when the outlier was added to the data set.

Section 3.3

Exercises 1–4 are the Check Your Understanding exercises for this section. Answers to these exercises are on page 139.

5. Quartiles

7. interquartile range

9. False

11. False

13. a. −1 **b.** 1.5 **c.** 11

15. The outlier is 4.91. It seems certain to be an error.

17. a. $Q_1 = 20$; $Q_3 = 44$ **b.** 24
 c. Lower: −16; upper: 80 **d.** 82 is the only outlier.

19. a. 34 **b.** 14 **c.** 40 **d.** 8

21. a. 0.78 **b.** 1.16 **c.** SAT **d.** 31 **e.** 341

23. a. 19 **b.** Lower: 79.5; upper: 155.5 **c.** No

25. a. $Q_1 = 11$; $Q_3 = 32$ **b.** 15
 c. Lower: −20.5; upper: 63.5
 d. 67, 86, 97, 97, 116
 e.
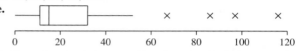
 f. Skewed to the right **g.** 12 **h.** 49 **i.** 55th percentile

27. a. $Q_1 = 19$; $Q_3 = 22$ **b.** 21
 c. Lower: 14.5; upper: 26.5 **d.** 31, 36, 38, 39
 e.

 f. Skewed to the right **g.** 17 **h.** 26 **i.** 90th percentile

29. a. $Q_1 = 14$; $Q_3 = 41$ **b.** 27
 c. Lower: −26.5; upper: 81.5 **d.** No
 e. No, neither is an outlier.
 f.
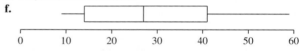
 g. Approximately symmetric **h.** 24 **i.** 39
 j. 66th percentile

31. a. $Q_1 = 25$; $Q_3 = 42.5$ **b.** 35
 c. Lower: −1.25; upper: 68.75 **d.** No outliers
 e.
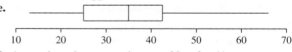
 f. Approximately symmetric **g.** 29 **h.** 41
 i. 43rd percentile

33. No, only 25% of the class scored lower than Ed.

35. a. Median: 1.4; $Q_1 = 0.44$; $Q_3 = 6$
 b. Median: 2.45; $Q_1 = 0.41$; $Q_3 = 13$
 c. Lower: −7.9; upper: 14.34
 d. Lower: −18.475; upper: 31.885
 e.
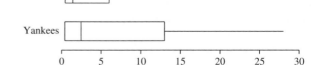

Both sets of salaries are skewed to the right. The Yankees have more high salaries than the Phillies.

37. a. $Q_1 = 20$; $Q_3 = 60$; IQR $= 40$
  b. Upper outlier boundary is $60 + 1.5 \cdot 40 = 120$. Since
    $150 > 120$, 150 is an outlier.
  c. $Q_1 = 25$; $Q_3 = 105$; IQR $= 80$ **d.** No
  e. Both the third quartile and the IQR increased.

39. a. Computation   **b.** $z = \dfrac{0 - 3.749}{3.5808} = -1.05$
  c. $z = \dfrac{7.5 - 3.749}{3.5808} = 1.05$ **d.** 2.4%   **e.** 19%
  f. Less extreme
  g. The right tail extends out farther than the left tail, so there
    are more data to the right of $z = 1.05$ than to the left of
    $z = -1.05$.

CHAPTER 3 Quiz

1. The mode
2. Mean: 520; median: 550; mode: 550
3. The mean
4. mean, median
5. **a.** 9.76   **b.** 4.51
6. 4
7. 3.96, 2.28
8. 95%
9. 75
10. 0.5
11. 0.037
12. False
13. 44
14. **a.** $Q_1 = 22$; $Q_3 = 39$
    b. Outlier boundaries are -3.5 and 64.5.
    c. 68 is the only outlier.
15.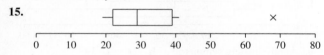

CHAPTER 3 Review Exercises

1. **a.** 100.84   **b.** 101.0
2. **a.** 9.83   **b.** 12   **c.** Skewed to the left
3. **a.** Mean of process 1 is 92.87; mean of process 2 is 91.46.
   b. Median of process 1 is 92.2; median of process 2 is 93.3.
   c. They are about the same.
4. **a.** Variance of process 1 is 9.40; variance of process 2 is 53.36.
   b. Standard deviation of process 1 is 3.07; standard deviation
     of process 2 is 7.30.
   c. Process 1 produces a more uniform thickness.
5. **a.** Mean in September is 24.595; median in September
     is 24.61.
   b. Mean in October is 25.182; median in October is 25.23.
   c. They are about the same.
6. **a.** 0.513   **b.** 0.696   **c.** Greater in October
7. **a.** A: 2.87; B: 0.75
   b. Method A. Estimating by eye is less precise than measuring
     with a ruler.
   c. It is better to have a smaller standard deviation. With a small
     standard deviation, there is less need to remeasure,

since all measurements will be reasonably close to the
first one.

8. 153 and 172.6
9. 25%
10. 68%
11. At least 8/9 of the rents are between $350 and $1250.
12. **a.** 7.78   **b.** 7.8   **c.** 5.31   **d.** 2.30   **e.** 6   **f.** 8.6
    g. 6.65   **h.** 8.4
13. **a.** (3)   **b.** (1)   **c.** (4)   **d.** (2)
14. **a.** $Q_1 = 14.6$; $Q_3 = 17.4$ **b.** 16.2
    c. Lower: 10.4; upper: 21.6   **d.** No outliers
    e.

15. **a.** $Q_1 = 6.2$; $Q_3 = 15.3$ **b.** 12
    c. Lower: -7.45; upper: 28.95   **d.** $-38.7, 40.6$
    e.
    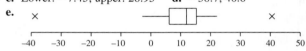

CHAPTER 3 Case Study

1.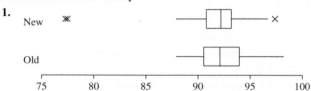
2. For the recycled wafers, 77.3, 77.5, and 97.4 are outliers. There
   are no outliers for the new wafers.
3. The outliers 77.3 and 77.5 should be deleted, because they
   resulted from an error.
   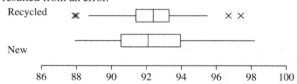
4. For the recycled wafers, 87.9, 88.0, 96.7, and 97.4 are outliers.
   There are no outliers for the new wafers. No outliers should be
   deleted, because they do not result from errors.
5. Approximately symmetric
6. New: 92.33; recycled: 92.31
7. New: 92.1; recycled: 92.4
8. New: 2.36; recycled: 2.21
9. Answers will vary. The interquartile range is more useful,
   because the standard deviation is not resistant to outliers.

CHAPTER 4

Section 4.1

**Exercises 1–4 are the Check Your Understanding exercises for
this section. Answers to these exercises are on page 157.**

5. 0
7. sample space
9. True
11. False

13. 1/6

15. 1/3

17. 0

19. a. No   **b.** No   **c.** Yes

21. No. The probabilities do not add up to 1.

23. Yes. The probabilities are all between 0 and 1, and they add up to 1.

25. a. ii   **b.** vi   **c.** iv   **d.** i
e. iii   **f.** vii   **g.** v   **h.** vii

27. a. $275/500 = 0.55$
b. We estimate that 55% of all voters plan to vote to reelect the mayor.

29. a. {TTTT, TTTF, TTFT, TTFF, TFTT, TFTF, TFFT, TFFF, FTTT, FTTF, FTFT, FTFF, FFTT, FFTF, FFFT, FFFF}
b. 1/8   **c.** 1/4   **d.** 3/8

31. $180/400 = 0.45$

33. a. $1912/2825 = 0.6768$ **b.** $685/2825 = 0.2425$

35. a. $7792/11,217 = 0.6947$ **b.** $10,270/11,217 = 0.9156$

37. a. $18/38 = 0.4737$
b. The law of large numbers says that in the long run, the percentage of the time you win will approach 47.37%.

39. a. 0.8674   **b.** 0.3118   **c.** No

41. a. 0.1944   **b.** 0.2378   **c.** Yes

43.

(1, 1)	(1, 2)	(1, 3)	(1, 4)	(1, 5)	(1, 6)
(2, 1)	(2, 2)	(2, 3)	(2, 4)	(2, 5)	(2, 6)
(3, 1)	(3, 2)	(3, 3)	(3, 4)	(3, 5)	(3, 6)
(4, 1)	(4, 2)	(4, 3)	(4, 4)	(4, 5)	(4, 6)
(5, 1)	(5, 2)	(5, 3)	(5, 4)	(5, 5)	(5, 6)
(6, 1)	(6, 2)	(6, 3)	(6, 4)	(6, 5)	(6, 6)

45. 1/6

47. {(3, 1), (3, 2), (3, 3), (3, 4), (3, 5), (3, 6)}

49. 1/6; yes

Section 4.2

Exercises 1–4 are the Check Your Understanding exercises for this section. Answers to these exercises are on page 166.

5. $P(A \text{ and } B)$

7. complement

9. True

11. False

13. 0.9

15. 0.7

17. Yes

19. 0.65

21. 0.73

23. 1

25. Not mutually exclusive

27. Mutually exclusive

29. Not mutually exclusive.

31. a. 200 or fewer of them use Google as their primary search engine.
b. Fewer than 200 of them use Google as their primary search engine.

c. At least 200 of them use Google as their primary search engine.
d. The number that use Google as their primary search engine is not equal to 200.

33. a. {RR, RY, RG, YR, YY, YG, GR, GY, GG}
b. {RR, YY, GG}
c. {RY, RG, YR, YG, GR, GY}
d. {RG, YG, GR, GY}
e. Yes; they have no outcomes in common.
f. No; they both contain the event GG.

35. a. 0.11   **b.** 0.90

37. a. $336/800 = 0.42$ **b.** $734/800 = 0.9175$

39. a. 0.226   **b.** 0.854

41. a. $18/25 = 0.72$ **b.** $10/25 = 0.4$ **c.** 0.88   **d.** 0.12

43. a. 0.42   **b.** 0.56   **c.** 0.47   **d.** 0.53
e. 0.51   **f.** 0.02   **g.** 0.53

45. Answers will vary.

Section 4.3

Exercises 1–6 are the Check Your Understanding exercises for this section. Answers to these exercises are on page 178.

7. conditional

9. 5

11. False

13. False

15. 0.12

17. 0.18

19. 0.16

21. 0.28

23. $1/16 = 0.0625$

25. $1/216 = 0.0046$

27. Mutually exclusive

29. Neither

31. a. Yes; $P(A \text{ and } B) = P(A)P(B)$ **b.** 0.55
c. No; $P(A \text{ and } B) \neq 0$

33. a. 0.3   **b.** No; $P(A \text{ or } B) \neq P(A) + P(B)$
c. No; $P(A \text{ and } B) \neq P(A)P(B)$

35. $91/216 = 0.4213$

37. $1/42 = 0.0238$

39. a. 0.5660   **b.** 0.2333   **c.** 0.7391
d. 0.2537   **e.** 0.8113

41. a. 0.8   **b.** 0.7   **c.** 0.7   **d.** Yes

43. a. 0.5123   **b.** 0.0555   **c.** 0.0316
d. 0.0617   **e.** 0.5691

45. 0.0125

47. 0.05

49. a. 0.15   **b.** 0.05

51. a. $3/10 = 0.3$ **b.** $2/9 = 0.2222$ **c.** $1/15 = 0.0667$
d. No; if the first component is defective, the second component is less likely to be defective.

53. 0.7903

55. 0.98

57. $1/3 = 0.3333$

59. Since $P(A) = P(B) = 0$, $P(A \text{ and } B) = 0$. Therefore, A and B are independent because $P(A \text{ and } B) = P(A)P(B)$. Also, A and B are mutually exclusive, because $P(A \text{ and } B) = 0$.

61. No. If A and B are mutually exclusive, then $P(A \text{ and } B) = 0$. But since $P(A) > 0$ and $P(B) > 0$, $P(A)P(B) > 0$. Therefore, $P(A \text{ and } B) \neq P(A)P(B)$, so A and B are not independent.

Section 4.4

Exercises 1–6 are the Check Your Understanding exercises for this section. Answers to these exercises are on page 186.

7. mn

9. False

11. 362,880

13. 1

15. 1

17. 210

19. 1190

21. 1

23. 126

25. 2300

27. 1

29. 48

31. a. 336   **b.** 56

33. a. $10^4 \cdot 26^3 = 175{,}760{,}000$ **b.** $10^4 = 10{,}000$
    c. $1/26^3 = 0.0000569$

35. a. $_{12}C_8 = 495$ **b.** 0.0303   **c.** 0.9697

37. a. $4^3 = 64$ **b.** $_4P_3 = 24$ **c.** 8
    d. $24/64 = 0.375$ **e.** $1/8 = 0.125$

39. a. 1326   **b.** $_4C_2 = 6$ **c.** $6/1326 = 0.00452$

41. $\dfrac{1}{_{39}C_5} = 0.00000174$

43. a. 8   **b.** $2/8 = 0.25$

CHAPTER 4 Quiz

1. (i)

2. a. The sample space is the population of one million voters.
    b. 0.56

3. a. $P(A \text{ or } B) = P(A) + P(B) - P(A \text{ and } B)$
    b. $P(A \text{ or } B) = P(A) + P(B)$
    c. $P(A^c) = 1 - P(A)$
    d. $P(A \text{ and } B) = P(A)P(B \mid A)$ or
        $P(A \text{ and } B) = P(B)P(A \mid B)$
    e. $P(A \text{ and } B) = P(A)P(B)$

4. a. $132/400 = 0.33$ **b.** 0.865

5. (i)

6. $79/100 = 0.79$

7. $2/3 = 0.6667$

8. 0.48

9. $4/11 = 0.3636$

10. (i)

11. $0.38^3 = 0.0549$

12. 0.9084

13. a. $21^3 \cdot 5^3 \cdot 10 = 11{,}576{,}250$
    b. $1/11{,}576{,}250 = 0.0000000864$

14. $_{24}C_5 = 42{,}504$

15. a. $15! = 1.308 \times 10^{12}$ **b.** $_{15}P_3 = 2730$

CHAPTER 4 Review Problems

1. a. {R, W, W, B, B, B}   **b.** 1/2

2. $18/30 = 0.6$

3. a. 0.5   **b.** 0.6667

4. a. $570/1200 = 0.475$ **b.** $1010/1200 = 0.8417$

5. a. 0.03   **b.** 0.32

6. a. 0.9998   **b.** 0.0098

7. a. {DDD, DDG, DGD, DGG, GDD, GDG, GGD, GGG}
    b. 0.6815   **c.** 0.9603   **d.** Yes

8. a. $5/10 = 0.5$ **b.** $4/9 = 0.4444$ **c.** 0.2222

9. a. 0.6   **b.** 0.75   **c.** 0.2727
    d. No; $P(\text{Female and Business major}) \neq$
        $P(\text{Female})P(\text{Business major})$
    e. No; $P(\text{Female and Business major}) \neq 0$

10. a. 0.4035   **b.** 0.3647   **c.** 0.1066   **d.** 0.6616
    e. 0.2922   **f.** 0.2641

11. a. That the two days are independent with regard to rain
    b. If it rains on Saturday, it is more likely that it will rain on Sunday.
    c. Too low. In the equation, $P(\text{Rain Sunday})$ should be $P(\text{Rain Sunday} \mid \text{Rain Saturday})$, which is greater than 0.1.

12. $_5C_3 = 10$

13. $1/10 = 0.1$

14. a. $_6P_3 = 120$ **b.** $_5P_3 = 60$

15. a. $1/120 = 0.00833$ **b.** $1/20 = 0.05$

CHAPTER 4 Case Study

1. 0.99613

2. 0.98739

3. 0.97801

4. 0.96533

5. 50: 0.93782; 60: 0.88164; 70: 0.76666; 80: 0.54385; 90: 0.22931; 100: 0.02809

6. 0.028444

7. 0.81749

8. The probability that a person aged 20 is still alive at age 50 is 0.94979. The probability that a person aged 50 is still alive at age 60 is 0.94010. It is more probable that a person aged 20 will still be alive at age 50.

9. 0.79419

CHAPTER 5

Section 5.1

Exercises 1–8 are the Check Your Understanding exercises for this section. Answers to these exercises are on page 208.

9. random variable

11. Continuous

13. True

15. False

17. Discrete

19. Continuous

21. Discrete

23. Discrete

25. Continuous

27. Represents a probability distribution

29. Does not represent a probability distribution; probabilities do not add up to 1.

31. Does not represent a probability distribution; probabilities do not add up to 1.

33. Mean: 2.9; standard deviation: 2.042

35. Mean: 6.6; standard deviation: 2.078

37. Mean: 19.45; standard deviation: 3.232

39. 0.2

41. a. 0.2　**b.** 0.3　**c.** 0.1　**d.** 0.1　**e.** 2　**f.** 1.095

43. a. 0.1　**b.** 0.5　**c.** 0.2　**d.** 0.9　**e.** 0.8
　f. 0.980　**g.** 0.8

45. a. 0.38　**b.** 0.96　**c.** 0.67　**d.** 0.10　**e.** 1.1　**f.** 1.054

47. a.

x	$P(x)$
0	0.0680
1	0.1110
2	0.2005
3	0.1498
4	0.1885
5	0.1378
6	0.0889
7	0.0197
8	0.0358

　b. 0.282　**c.** 0.068　**d.** 3.36　**e.** 1.97

49. a.

x	$P(x)$
1	0.1278
2	0.1241
3	0.1236
4	0.1222
5	0.1227
6	0.1247
7	0.1266
8	0.1283

　b. 0.122　**c.** 0.255　**d.** 4.51　**e.** 2.31

51. −$0.50, an expected loss

53. −1/6 = −$0.17, an expected loss

55. a. 0

　b. Answers will vary. If you don't answer a question, your score is the same as the expected value of a random guess.

57. $4500. It would be wise to make the investment.

59. a. 0, 1, 2, 3　**b.** 0.512　**c.** 0.128
　d. $P(\text{SFS}) = P(\text{SSF}) = 0.128$　**e.** 0.384　**f.** 0.096
　g. 0.008　**h.** 2.4　**i.** 0.6928

Section 5.2

Exercises 1–4 are the Check Your Understanding exercises for this section. Answers to these exercises are on page 218.

5. two

7. $\sqrt{np(1 - p)}$

9. False

11. Does not have a binomial distribution because the sample is more than 5% of the population.

13. Has a binomial distribution with 7 trials.

15. Does not have a binomial distribution because it is not the number of successes in independent trials.

17. 0.3087

19. 0.0355

21. 0.2160

23. 0.7969

25. 0.8108

27. a. 0.2051　**b.** 0.0547　**c.** No, $P(7 \text{ or more}) = 0.1719$.

29. a. 0.1234　**b.** 0.2955　**c.** 0.7010
　d. No, $P(11 \text{ or more}) = 0.4055$.

31. a. 0.0506　**b.** 0.3697　**c.** 0.0320
　d. Yes, $P(\text{Fewer than } 12) = 0.0255$.

33. a. 0.4131　**b.** 0.9529　**c.** No, $P(0) = 0.2342$.
　d. 1.4　**e.** 1.1411

35. a. 0.1068　**b.** 0.9601　**c.** 0.00064
　d. Yes, $P(\text{More than } 25) = 0.0134$.　**e.** 20.1　**f.** 2.5755

37. a. 0.1472　**b.** 0.3231　**c.** 0.0332
　d. No, $P(\text{More than } 10) = 0.0978$.　**e.** 7.5　**f.** 2.2913

39. a. 0.16116
　b.

x	$P(x)$
0	0.0134627
1	0.0724915
2	0.1756524
3	0.2522188
4	0.2376677
5	0.1535699
6	0.0689096
7	0.0212029
8	0.0042814
9	0.0005123
10	0.0000276

CHAPTER 5 Quiz

1. The probabilities do not add up to 1.

2. 2

3. a. 9　**b.** 3

4. 0.19

5.

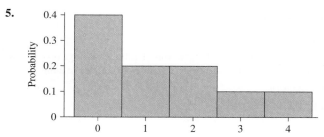

6. a. 0.4   **b.** 0.2   **c.** 0.9   **d.** 0.6

7. 1.3

8. 1.3454

9. a. 0.0769   **b.** 0.9231   **c.** 0.7604

10. 2.5

11. 1.5411

12.

x	P(x)
0	0.24
1	0.52
2	0.24

13. a. 0.2362   **b.** 0.4417   **c.** 0.2749

14. 2.4

15. 1.3856

CHAPTER 5 Review Exercises

1. a. Yes   **b.** No   **c.** No   **d.** Yes

2. a. 8.37   **b.** 3.3131   **c.** 1.8202

3. 0.41

4. a.

x	P(x)
1	0.5632
2	0.2500
3	0.1147
4	0.0473
5	0.0171
6	0.0053
7	0.0018
8	0.0006

   b. 0.5632   **c.** 1.731   **d.** 1.049

5. 0.6630

6. 0.5760

7. a. 0.6943   **b.** 0.1353

8. −$0.11, an expected loss

9. a. 0.0480   **b.** 0.9854

10. a. 0.2756   **b.** 0.1844

11. Yes, $P(0) = 0.00564$.

12. Yes, $P(10) = 0.00511$.

13. Yes, $P(8) = 0.0360$.

14. No, the trials are not independent. If it rains on one day, it is more likely to rain the next day.

15. Yes; because the sample size is less than 5% of the population, X may be considered to have a binomial distribution.

CHAPTER 5 Case Study

List (ii) is the fraud.

CHAPTER 6

Section 6.1

Exercises 1–10 are the Check Your Understanding exercises for this section. Answers to these exercises are on page 240.

11. density

13. 1

15. standard

17. True

19. False

21. a. 0.25   **b.** 0.6   **c.** 0.4

23. a. 0.8944   **b.** 0.3594   **c.** 0.7085   **d.** 0.5633

25. a. 0.7704   **b.** 0.0154   **c.** 0.8461   **d.** 0.4404

27. a. 0.9394   **b.** 0.3745   **c.** 0.0007   **d.** 0.9916

29. a. 0.7288   **b.** 0.8492   **c.** 0.0744   **d.** 0.0936

31. a. 0.5059   **b.** 0.1153   **c.** 0.5078   **d.** 0.6402

33. 0.10

35. 1.48

37. −0.99

39. 0.39

41. −0.67 and 0.67

43. −1.28 and 1.28

45. 2.05

47. 1.28

49. 0.0401

51. 0.6956

53. 0.3

Section 6.2

Exercises 1–8 are the Check Your Understanding exercises for this section. Answers to these exercises are on page 251.

9. standardization

11. True

13. False

15. False

17. a. 0.3085   **b.** 0.1056

19. a. 0.2061 [Tech: 0.2066]   **b.** 0.0869 [Tech: 0.0863]

21. a. 0.8314 [Tech: 0.8315]   **b.** 0.1549 [Tech: 0.1548]

23. 11.25 [Tech: 11.24]

25. 38.08 [Tech: 38.10]

27. a. 0.1446 [Tech: 0.1444]   **b.** 0.5438 [Tech: 0.5421]
   c. 0.1685 [Tech: 0.1686]
   d. 0.0582 [Tech: 0.0587]; not unusual

29. a. 75.35 [Tech: 75.31]   **b.** 84.86   **c.** 87.13 [Tech: 87.18]

31. a. 0.2236 [Tech: 0.2248]   **b.** 0.6533 [Tech: 0.6544]
   c. Yes, $P(\text{Less than } 400) = 0.0239$ [Tech: 0.0241]

33. a. 489.20 [Tech: 489.28]   **b.** 510.11 [Tech: 509.96]
   c. 453.53 [Tech: 453.35]   **d.** 438.36 [Tech: 438.51]

35. a. 0.3085   **b.** No   **c.** 0.0062   **d.** Yes

37. a. 4.022 [Tech: 4.023]   **b.** 4.382 [Tech: 4.381]   **c.** 4.1

39. a. 0.0548   **b.** 0.3811 [Tech: 0.3812]   **c.** 0.8849

41. a. 34.15 [Tech: 34.13]   **b.** 42.35 [Tech: 42.34]
   c. 36.65 [Tech: 36.63]   **d.** 29.75 [Tech: 29.73]

43. a. 0.3085   **b.** 0.1525 [Tech: 0.1524]
   c. Yes, $P(\text{Less than } 12) = 0.0062$.

45. a. 12.055   **b.** 12.015   **c.** 12.011 and 12.089

47. a. 0.1056   **b.** 0.0001   **c.** 0.8882 [Tech: 0.8881]

49. a. 25.1200 [Tech: 25.1203]   **b.** 25.0624 [Tech: 25.0626]
c. 24.9136 [Tech: 24.9138]
d. 25.0464 and 25.1536 [Tech: 25.0460 and 25.1540]

51. 34%

53. They are not approximately normal. If they were normally distributed, approximately 26% of the wells would have negative concentrations, which is impossible.

Section 6.3

Exercises 1–4 are the Check Your Understanding exercises for this section. Answers to these exercises are on page 258.

5. sampling

7. True

9. a. 0.9232 [Tech: 0.9236]   **b.** 8.56

11. a. 0.7549 [Tech: 0.7540]   **b.** 95.73

13. a. 0.0465 [Tech: 0.0461]   **b.** 31.81 [Tech: 31.80]

15. a. $\mu = 75.4, \sigma = 5.1225$
b. (69, 69), (69, 75), (69, 79), (69, 83), (69, 71), (75, 69), (75, 75), (75, 79), (75, 83), (75, 71), (79, 69), (79, 75), (79, 79), (79, 83), (79, 71), (83, 69), (83, 75), (83, 79), (83, 83), (83, 71), (71, 69), (71, 75), (71, 79), (71, 83), (71, 71)
c. $\mu_{\bar{x}} = 75.4, \sigma_{\bar{x}} = 3.62215$
d. $\mu_{\bar{x}} = 75.4 = \mu; \sigma_{\bar{x}} = 3.62215 = \sigma/\sqrt{2}$

17. a. 0.9015 [Tech: 0.9016]   **b.** 0.2966 [Tech: 0.2979]
c. Yes, P(Less than 26) = 0.0049.

19. a. 0.0951 [Tech: 0.0958]   **b.** 0.8994 [Tech: 0.8986]
c. 2.76   **d.** Yes, P(Less than 2.5) = 0.0055 [Tech: 0.0056].
e. No, the Central Limit Theorem applies only to the sample mean, not to individual values.

21. a. 0.7190 [Tech: 0.7197]   **b.** 0.4545 [Tech: 0.4541]
c. 7868.47 [Tech: 7867.94]
d. Yes, P(Less than 7500) = 0.0049.
e. No, the Central Limit Theorem applies only to the sample mean, not to individual values.

23. a. 200 pounds   **b.** 0.2483 [Tech: 0.2472]   **c.** 0.0001

25. a. 0.1038 [Tech: 0.1030]   **b.** 0.5646 [Tech: 0.5651]
c. 42.79 [Tech: 42.80]
d. Yes, P(Less than 35) = 0.0136 [Tech: 0.0134].
e. No, the Central Limit Theorem applies only to the sample mean, not to individual values.

27. a. 0.1922 [Tech: 0.1932]   **b.** No
c. No, because this result would not be unusual if the claim were true.
d. 0.0047   **e.** Yes
f. Yes, because this result would be unusual if the claim were true.

Section 6.4

Exercises 1–4 are the Check Your Understanding exercises for this section. Answers to these exercises are on page 264.

5. proportion

7. True

9. 0.2358 [Tech: 0.2354]

11. 0.0918 [Tech: 0.0922]

13. 0.8099 [Tech: 0.8093]

15. a. 0.95   **b.** 0.0138   **c.** 0.0735 [Tech: 0.0734]
d. 0.6938 [Tech: 0.6925]   **e.** 0.7673 [Tech: 0.7659]
f. Yes, P(Less than 90%) = 0.0001.

17. a. 0.67   **b.** 0.05100   **c.** 0.0853 [Tech: 0.0850]
d. 0.6463 [Tech: 0.6471]   **e.** 0.0582 [Tech: 0.0584]
f. No, P(Less than 65%) = 0.3483 [Tech: 0.3475].

19. a. No, because $np = 8.5$, which is less than 10.
b. 0.2236 [Tech: 0.2243]   **c.** 0.2937 [Tech: 0.2930]
d. 0.9783   **e.** Yes, P(Greater than 0.25) = 0.0217.

21. a. Yes, because $np = 28.9$, which is greater than 10. The probability is 0.2177 [Tech: 0.2181].
b. 0.1515 [Tech: 0.1505]   **c.** 0.3368 [Tech: 0.3376]
d. 0.3974 [Tech: 0.3980]
e. No, P(More than 40%) = 0.0606 [Tech: 0.0604].

23. a. 0.2709 [Tech: 0.2717]   **b.** 0.2459 [Tech: 0.2456]
c. 0.2877 [Tech: 0.2874]
d. Yes, P(Less than 0.25) = 0.0375 [Tech: 0.0379].

25. 200

27. a. 0.0001   **b.** Yes
c. No, because a sample proportion of 0.075 would be unusual if the goal had been reached.
d. 0.3300 [Tech: 0.3317]   **e.** No
f. Yes, because a sample proportion of 0.053 would not be unusual if the goal had been reached.

Section 6.5

Exercises 1–4 are the Check Your Understanding exercises for this section. Answers to these exercises are on page 271.

5. $np, \sqrt{np(1-p)}$

7. True

9. 0.0559 [Tech using normal approximation: 0.0557; tech using binomial: 0.0563]

11. 0.6517 [Tech using normal approximation: 0.6524; tech using binomial: 0.6538]

13. 0.3102 [Tech using normal approximation: 0.3097; tech using binomial: 0.3008]

15. a. 0.1251 [Tech using normal approximation: 0.1244; tech using binomial: 0.1236]
b. 0.0233 [Tech using normal approximation: 0.0232; tech using binomial: 0.0246]
c. 0.1730 [Tech using normal approximation: 0.1721; tech using binomial: 0.1727]

17. a. 0.7549 [Tech using normal approximation: 0.7558; tech using binomial: 0.7544]
b. 0.0934 [Tech using normal approximation: 0.0929; tech using binomial: 0.0918]
c. 0.2115 [Tech using normal approximation: 0.2103; tech using binomial: 0.2133]

19. a. 0.0885 [Tech using binomial: 0.0887]
b. 0.7389 [Tech using normal approximation: 0.7388; tech using binomial: 0.7392]
c. 0.4598 [Tech using normal approximation: 0.4605; tech using binomial: 0.4593]

21. a. 0.9192 [Tech using normal approximation: 0.9190; tech using binomial: 0.9163]
b. 0.7389 [Tech using normal approximation: 0.7387; tech using binomial: 0.7341]

c. 0.3232 [Tech using normal approximation: 0.3230; tech using binomial: 0.3340]

23. 0.9744 [Tech using normal approximation: 0.9745; tech using binomial: 0.9833]

25. 0.0796 [Tech using normal approximation: 0.0797]

Section 6.6

Exercises 1–6 are the Check Your Understanding exercises for this section. Answers to these exercises are on page 281.

7. outlier, skewness, mode

9. No. The sample is strongly skewed to the right.

11. Yes. There are no outliers, no strong skewness, and no evidence of multiple modes.

13. Yes. There are no outliers, no strong skewness, and no evidence of multiple modes.

15. No. The sample is strongly skewed to the right.

17. Yes. The points approximately follow a straight line.

19.

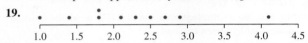

No. The data contain an outlier.

21.

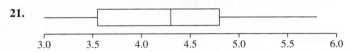

Yes. There are no outliers, no strong skewness, and no evidence of multiple modes.

23. Answers will vary. Here is one possibility.

```
0 |
0 | 99
1 | 0000111112234
1 | 69
2 | 1
2 | 79
```

The data are skewed to the right. It is not appropriate to treat this sample as coming from an approximately normal population.

25. Answers will vary. Here is one possibility.

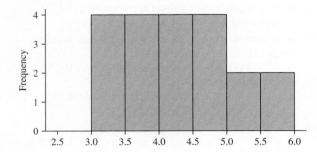

There are no outliers, no strong skewness, and no evidence of multiple modes. It is appropriate to treat this sample as coming from an approximately normal population.

27.

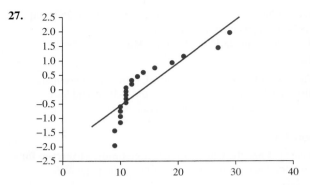

The points do not follow a straight line, so it is not appropriate to treat this sample as coming from an approximately normal population.

29. a. The following boxplot shows that the data do not come from an approximately normal population.

b. The following boxplot shows that the square-root-transformed data come from an approximately normal population.

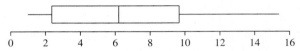

31. a. The following boxplot shows that the data do not come from an approximately normal population.

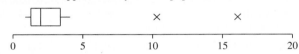

b. The following boxplot shows that the square-root-transformed data do not come from an approximately normal population.

c. The following boxplot shows that the reciprocal-transformed data come from an approximately normal population.

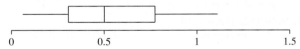

CHAPTER 6 Quiz

1. a. 0.32   **b.** 0.41

2. a. 0.9616   **b.** 0.3409   **c.** 0.8977

3. a. −0.44   **b.** 0.81

4. $z = -1.28$ and $z = 1.28$

5. 1.04

6. $40,104 and $45,196 [Tech: $40,087 and $45,213]

7. a. 0.6141 [Tech: 0.6142]   **b.** 0.5910 [Tech: 0.5893]

8. 208.32 [Tech: 208.33]; because bowling scores are whole numbers, this can be rounded up to 209.

9. Let $\bar{x}$ be the mean of a large ($n > 30$) simple random sample from a population with mean μ and standard deviation σ. Then $\bar{x}$ has an approximately normal distribution, with mean $\mu_{\bar{x}} = \mu$ and standard deviation $\sigma_{\bar{x}} = \dfrac{\sigma}{\sqrt{n}}$.

10. $\mu_{\bar{x}} = 193$, $\sigma_{\bar{x}} = 5.25$

11. a. 0.5793 [Tech: 0.5803]   **b.** 0.8997 [Tech: 0.9001]

12. a. $\mu_{\hat{p}} = 0.34$, $\sigma_{\hat{p}} = 0.063875$ **b.** 0.9793 [Tech: 0.9791]
   c. 0.8264 [Tech: 0.8262]

13. a. 0.2843 [Tech: 0.2842]
   b. Yes, $P[\text{More than } 0.25] = 0.0228$ [Tech: 0.0230].

14. a. 0.8461 [Tech: 0.8471]   **b.** 0.7025 [Tech: 0.7031]
   c. 0.7157 [Tech: 0.7163]

15. The following boxplot shows that the data come from an approximately normal population.

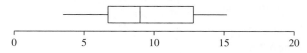

CHAPTER 6 Review Exercises

1. a. 0.6368   **b.** 0.9406   **c.** 0.3564

2. -1.23

3. 0.0122

4. a. 0.5621 [Tech: 0.5598]   **b.** 13.280 [Tech: 13.286]
   c. 0.0009

5. a. 0.0793 [Tech: 0.0786]   **b.** 0.9977
   c. 0.7609 [Tech: 0.7600]

6. a. 0.0013   **b.** Yes

7. Yes, $P(\text{Greater than } \$2150) = 0.0037$ [Tech: 0.0036].

8. a. 85 pounds   **b.** 0.9429 [Tech: 0.9431]

9. a. 0.0985 [Tech: 0.0984]
   b. Yes, $P[\text{More than } 70\%] = 0.0019$ [Tech: 0.0018]

10. a. 0.1112 [Tech: 0.1115]   **b.** 0.6879 [Tech: 0.6870]
   c. 0.2009 [Tech: 0.2015]

11. a. 0.0119 [Tech: 0.0118]   **b.** Yes
   c. No, $P[\text{Less than half}] = 0.2843$ [Tech: 0.2856].

12. 0.9495

13. 0.8554 [Tech: 0.8547]

14. The following boxplot shows that the data do not come from an approximately normal population.

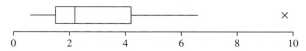

15. The following boxplot shows that the data come from an approximately normal population.

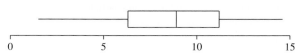

CHAPTER 6 Case Study

1. $\bar{x} = 99.6$, $s = 2.8363$

2. 0.0004

3. Yes

4. If the cans in each sample are arranged in increasing order of strength, each can in the second sample is stronger than the corresponding can in the first sample.

5. $\bar{x} = 101.9$, $s = 6.7404$

6. 0.0384 [Tech: 0.0387]

7. No

8. The following boxplot shows that the data do not come from an approximately normal population. For this reason, the method is not appropriate for the second shipment.

CHAPTER 7
Section 7.1

Exercises 1–16 are the Check Your Understanding exercises for this section. Answers to these exercises are on page 306.

17. point

19. margin of error

21. True

23. True

25. 1.96

27. 2.05

29. 98%

31. 99.5%

33. a. 1.344   **b.** Smaller, because the sample size is larger.

35. a. 5.510   **b.** Smaller, because the confidence level is lower.

37. a. $6.37 < \mu < 9.47$
   b. No, because the sample size is less than 30.

39. a. 482   **b.** Smaller, because the confidence level is lower.

41. a. 109   **b.** Larger, because the margin of error is smaller.

43. a. $428 < \mu < 488$
   b. Larger, because the sample size is smaller.
   c. Smaller, because the confidence level is lower.
   d. No, because the values in the confidence interval are all less than 500.

45. a. $25.0 < \mu < 26.0$
   b. No, because the sample consisted entirely of boys.
   c. Yes, because all the values in the confidence interval are less than 28.

47. a. The sample size is small ($n \le 30$).
   b. Yes   **c.** $301.4 < \mu < 385.3$

49. a. $120 < \mu < 130$ **b.** 295

51. a. Sally's confidence interval will have the larger margin of error because the confidence level is higher.
   b. Sally's confidence interval is more likely to cover the population mean because the confidence level is higher.

53. a. Bob's confidence interval will have the larger margin of error because the standard error will be larger.
   b. Both are equally likely to cover the population mean because they both have the same confidence level.

55. The 90% confidence interval is $7.2 < \mu < 12.8$, the 95% confidence interval is $6.6 < \mu < 13.4$, and the 99% confidence interval is $5.6 < \mu < 14.4$.

57. The students in the class are not a simple random sample of the students in the college.

59. a. True; this is the appropriate interpretation of a confidence interval.

    b. False; the confidence interval is for the population mean, not the sample mean.

    c. False; the confidence level is not the probability that the interval contains the true value.

    d. False; the confidence level is about the population mean, not the proportion of the population contained in the interval.

61. a. 95%, 56.019, 60.881

    b. Yes, because the sample size is large ($n > 30$).

63. a. 95%, 9.6956, 15.0084

    b. $8.861 < \mu < 15.843$ **c.** 73   **d.** 125

65. 75.4

Section 7.2

Exercises 1–6 are the Check Your Understanding exercises for this section. Answers to these exercises are on page 317.

7. 11

9. False

11. a. 2.074   **b.** 2.920   **c.** 2.567   **d.** 2.763

13. a. 2.110   **b.** Smaller

15. a. 2.718   **b.** No

17. a. $1.2 < \mu < 3.0$ **b.** Narrower

19. a. $86.1 < \mu < 88.3$ **b.** Wider

21. a. $5.42 < \mu < 5.64$

    b. No, because 5.55 is contained in the confidence interval.

23. a. $102.5 < \mu < 157.5$

    b. No, because 100 is not contained in the confidence interval.

25. a. $132.9 < \mu < 140.9$

    b. Wider, because the confidence level is higher.

27. a. $65.1 < \mu < 95.9$

    b. Narrower, because the sample size is greater.

29. a. $9.986 < \mu < 12.808$

    b. Yes, because 11.5 is contained in the confidence interval.

31. a. $19.50 < \mu < 21.26$

    b. Yes, it is reasonable to believe that the mean mineral content may be as high as 21.3%.

33. a. Yes; there are no outliers, and no strong skewness.

    b. $1200.4 < \mu < 1758.7$

35. a. Yes; there are no outliers, and no strong skewness.

    b. $2.91 < \mu < 4.26$

    c. It does not contradict the claim, because the value 3.51 is contained in the confidence interval.

37. a. $13.27 < \mu < 17.61$

    b. $12.36 < \mu < 22.07$. The results are noticeably different. It is important to check for outliers in order to avoid misleading results.

39. We have data on the whole population of presidents, not just a sample. We know that the population mean is 70.8, so we don't need to construct a confidence interval.

41. a. 98%, 178.08, 181.58

    b. Yes, because the sample is large ($n > 30$).

43. a. 14   **b.** No, because the sample is small ($n \le 30$).

    c. 2.624

    d. $4.5561 < \mu < 7.3185$ [Tech: $4.5558 < \mu < 7.3188$]

45. a. $69.3 < \mu < 100.7$

    b. No, because we can't compute a sample standard deviation from a sample of size 1.

Section 7.3

Exercises 1–6 are the Check Your Understanding exercises for this section. Answers to these exercises are on page 329.

7. standard error

9. True

11. Point estimate: 0.1916; standard error: 0.01426; margin of error $= 0.02794$

13. Point estimate: 0.4979; standard error: 0.02297; margin of error $= 0.0378$

15. $0.325 < p < 0.550$

17. $0.341 < p < 0.448$

19. a. 0.711

    b. $0.652 < p < 0.770$

    c. No, because 0.70 is contained in the confidence interval.

21. a. 0.244

    b. $0.190 < p < 0.297$

    c. Yes, because all the values in the confidence interval are greater than 0.09.

23. a. 0.330

    b. $0.261 < p < 0.398$

    c. Yes, because all the values in the confidence interval are less than 0.50.

25. a. $0.367 < p < 0.446$

    b. $0.360 < p < 0.454$

    c. Increasing the confidence level makes the interval wider.

27. a. 1537

    b. 2401

    c. About the same. The necessary sample size does not depend on the size of the population.

29. a. 306   **b.** 1037

31. a. $0.154 < p < 0.266$

    b. Larger, because the sample size is smaller.

33. $0.657 < p < 0.979$

35. a. 99%, 0.41911, 0.73714   **b.** $0.457 < p < 0.699$

37. a. 98%, 0.732082, 0.870128   **b.** $0.752 < p < 0.850$

39. The 365 days are not independent trials. If it rains on one day, it is more likely to rain the next day.

41. a. $0.357 < p < 0.802$ **b.** $0.357 < p < 0.801$

   c. $0.352 < p < 0.848$

43. a. 90%: $0.392 < p < 0.777$; 95%: $0.357 < p < 0.802$; 99%: $0.296 < p < 0.842$

   b. 90%: $0.393 < p < 0.765$; 95%: $0.357 < p < 0.801$; 99%: $0.287 < p < 0.871$

   c. The 95% confidence interval. The reason is that $z_{\alpha/2} = 1.96$ for the 95% confidence interval, which is very close to 2.

Section 7.4

Exercises 1–4 are the Check Your Understanding exercises for this section. Answers to these exercises are on page 331.

5. Population mean; $63.47 < \mu < 79.17$

7. Population proportion, $0.686 < p < 0.794$

9. Population mean, $7.32 < \mu < 9.58$

11. $245.71 < \mu < 266.83$ [Tech: $245.72 < \mu < 266.82$]

13. $37.91 < \mu < 52.11$

15. $0.077 < p < 0.116$

CHAPTER 7 Quiz

1. a. A single number that is used to estimate the value of a parameter

   b. An interval that is used to estimate the value of a parameter

   c. The percentage of confidence intervals that will cover the true value of the parameter in the long run

2. 1.706

3. $21.7 < \mu < 24.7$

4. $46.1 < \mu < 63.5$

5. $11.70 < \mu < 13.14$

6. 1.75 [Tech: 1.751]

7. 385

8. $0.643 < p < 0.817$

9. 303

10. a. 141 **b.** 2.53

11. a. 1.96 **b.** 4.958 **c.** $136 < \mu < 146$

12. 984

13. $0.288 < p < 0.373$

14. 230

15. 260

CHAPTER 7 Review Exercises

1. 271

2. a. $10.79 < \mu < 14.57$

   b. No, because the value 13 is contained in the confidence interval.

   c. 180

3. a. $0.235 < p < 0.410$ **b.** 1612 **c.** 1844

4. a. $56.3 < \mu < 98.4$

   b. Yes, the value 27 is an outlier.

5. $0.126 < \overset{.}{p} < 0.368$

6. a. $1.85 < \mu < 2.07$

   b. No, because all the values in the confidence interval are greater than 0.5.

   c. 737

7. a. $0.034 < p < 0.136$ **b.** 323 **c.** 1037

8. a.

   Yes. There are no outliers, no strong skewness, and no evidence of multiple modes.

   b. $18.3 < \mu < 31.2$

9. $85.5 < \mu < 86.1$

10. a. $0.453 < p < 0.618$

   b. No, because the value 0.479 is contained in the confidence interval.

   c. 1529

11. a. $10.3 < \mu < 14.1$

   b. Yes, because all the values in the confidence interval are less than 15.

12. a. $6.75 < \mu < 7.37$

   b. No, because all the values in the confidence interval are less than 8.

   c. 818

13. a. 0.168 **b.** $0.097 < p < 0.239$ **c.** 598

14. a. $36.3 < \mu < 37.5$

   b. No, because the value 38.7 is not contained in the confidence interval.

15. The days are not independent trials. If it rains on one day, it is more likely to rain the next day.

CHAPTER 7 Case Study

1.

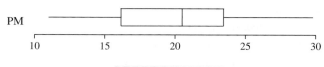

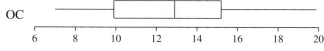

2. PM: $17.94 < \mu < 22.48$; OC: $11.08 < \mu < 14.19$; TC: $12.428 < \mu < 15.847$; LE: $1.291 < \mu < 1.784$

3. It is reasonable to conclude that the mean levels were lower than the baseline for all the pollutants, because all the values in the confidence intervals are less than the corresponding baselines.

4.

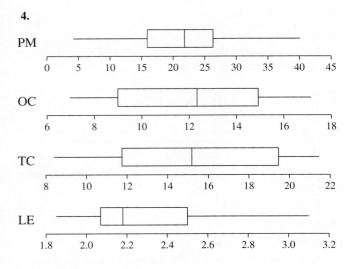

95% Confidence intervals:
PM: $17.33 < \mu < 25.00$;   OC: $10.493 < \mu < 13.615$;
TC: $13.149 < \mu < 17.169$;   LE: $2.143 < \mu < 2.496$

5. It is reasonable to conclude that the mean levels were lower than the baseline for all the pollutants, because all the values in the confidence intervals are less than the corresponding baselines.

CHAPTER 8
Section 8.1

Exercises 1–6 are the Check Your Understanding exercises for this section. Answers to these exercises are on page 343.

7. null, alternate

9. False

11. False

13. Left-tailed

15. Two-tailed

17. Correct decision

19. Type II error

21. H_0: $\mu = 400$, H_1: $\mu > 400$

23. The mean amount spent by diners is greater than \$30.

25. There is not enough evidence to conclude that the mean weight of adult German shepherd dogs differs from 75 pounds.

27. a. (ii)   **b.** (iii)   **c.** Type I error
d. No, a Type I error occurs if H_0 is rejected when it is true. Therefore, a Type I error cannot occur when H_0 is false.
e. Yes, if H_0 is not rejected, a Type II error will occur.

Section 8.2

Exercises 1–22 are the Check Your Understanding exercises for this section. Answers to these exercises are on pages 366–367.

23. P-value

25. critical

27. increase

29. True

31. False

33. False

35. a. $z = 2.60$
b. Critical value: 1.645, P-value: 0.0047; H_0 is rejected.
c. Critical value: 2.326, P-value: 0.0047; H_0 is rejected.

37. a. $z = 0.99$
b. Critical values: -1.96, 1.96, P-value: 0.3222 [Tech: 0.3211]; H_0 is not rejected.
c. Critical values: -2.576, 2.576, P-value: 0.3222 [Tech: 0.3211]; H_0 is not rejected.

39. 0.035

41. a. True   **b.** False   **c.** True   **d.** False

43. a. Yes   **b.** Type I error   **c.** Correct decision

45. a. No   **b.** Type II error   **c.** Correct decision

47. i

49. a. H_0: $\mu = 19.5$, H_1: $\mu > 19.5$ **b.** $z = 2.50$
c. Critical value: 1.645, P-value: 0.0062. Reject H_0. We conclude that the mean time of Facebook visits has increased.

51. a. H_0: $\mu = 69.4$, H_1: $\mu < 69.4$ **b.** $z = -2.44$
c. Critical value: -2.326, P-value: 0.0073 [Tech: 0.0074]. Reject H_0. We conclude that the mean height of men aged 60–69 is less than the mean height of all U.S. men.

53. H_0: $\mu = 2.1$, H_1: $\mu < 2.1$; $z = -5.00$; Critical value: -1.645, P-value: 0.0001 [Tech: 0.000000287]. Reject H_0. We conclude that the mean FEV_1 in the high-pollution community is less than 2.1 liters.

55. a. H_0: $\mu = 225.3$, H_1: $\mu \neq 225.3$; Test statistic: $z = 0.27$; Critical values: -1.96, 1.96, P-value: 0.7872 [Tech: 0.7882]. Do not reject H_0. There is not enough evidence to conclude that the mean price of homes differs between 2008 and 2010.
b. There are two outliers.
c. The sample size is greater than 30.

57. a. The sample is small ($n \leq 30$).
b. Yes, there are no outliers and no evidence of strong skewness.
c. H_0: $\mu = 15$, H_1: $\mu < 15$; Test statistic: $z = -3.02$; Critical value: -2.326, P-value: 0.0013. Reject H_0. We conclude that the mean concentration meets the EPA standard.

59. a. H_0: $\mu = 45$, H_1: $\mu \neq 45$ **b.** $z = 3.094063348$
c. 0.0019744896   **d.** Yes   **e.** Yes

61. a. H_0: $\mu = 225$, H_1: $\mu \neq 225$ **b.** $z = 2.085$ **c.** 0.037
d. Yes   **e.** No   **f.** $z = 1.07$ **g.** 0.1423 [Tech: 0.1412]
h. No

63. a. True   **b.** False

65. a. $z = 2.50$ **b.** 0.0062   **c.** Yes
d. No, an increase of 2.5 points on the SAT is small.

67. Yes, the actual P-value should have been given, rather than just saying "$P < 0.05$."

69. If the value of 100 specified by the null hypothesis is not contained in the 95% confidence interval, then the P-value must be less than 0.05.

Section 8.3

Exercises 1–6 are the Check Your Understanding exercises for this section. Answers to these exercises are on page 380.

7. skewness, outliers

11. a. Proportion   **b.** H_0: $p = 0.2$, H_1: $p < 0.2$
 c. $z = -2.25$ **d.** P-value is 0.0122244334   **e.** Yes
 f. No

12. a. H_0: $\mu = 3$, H_1: $\mu > 3$
 b. We should perform a z-test, because the population standard deviation is known.
 c. $z = 0.52$
 d. Critical value: 2.326, P-value: 0.3015 [Tech: 0.3028]. Do not reject H_0.
 e. There is not enough evidence to conclude that the mean number of TV sets per household is greater than 3.

13. H_0: $p = 0.25$, H_1: $p < 0.25$, Test statistic: $z = -1.85$, Critical value: -1.645, P-value: 0.0322 [Tech: 0.0323]. Reject H_0. We conclude that less than 25% of the boxes weigh more than 16.2 ounces.

14. a. H_0: $\mu = 1000$, H_1: $\mu > 1000$
 b. We should perform a t-test, because the population standard deviation is unknown.
 c. $t = 2.108$
 d. Critical value: 1.685, P-value is between 0.01 and 0.025 [Tech: 0.0207]. Reject H_0.
 e. We conclude that the mean monthly rent is greater than $1000.

15. a. H_0: $p = 0.36$, H_1: $p > 0.36$
 b. $z = 3.54$
 c. Critical value: 2.326, P-value: 0.0002. Reject H_0.
 d. We conclude that the proportion of students at the director's university who watch cable news regularly is greater than 0.36.

CHAPTER 8 Case Study

1. Test statistic: $z = 3.33$, P-value: 0.0004, H_0 is rejected at any reasonable level, including $\alpha = 0.05$ and $\alpha = 0.01$. We conclude that the probability is greater than 0.5 that a record high occurred more recently than a record low.

2. Answers will vary. The days are not independent and thus do not constitute a simple random sample.

3. Test statistic: $t = 3.964$, P-value is less than 0.0005 [Tech: 0.00012]. H_0 is rejected at any reasonable level, including $\alpha = 0.05$ and $\alpha = 0.01$. We conclude that the probability is greater than 0.5 that the mean year of record high is greater than 1940.5.

4. Answers will vary. When two years are both record highs, only the later one counts.

5. Test statistic: $t = 3.347$, P-value is between 0.001 and 0.0005 [Tech: 0.00085]. H_0 is rejected at any reasonable level, including $\alpha = 0.05$ and $\alpha = 0.01$. The conclusion does not change. We conclude that the probability is greater than 0.5 that the mean year of record high is greater than 1940.5.

6. Test statistic: $t = -6.148$, P-value is less than 0.0005 [Tech: 0.00000013]. H_0 is rejected at any reasonable level, including $\alpha = 0.05$ and $\alpha = 0.01$. We conclude that the probability is greater than 0.5 that the mean year of record low is less than 1940.5.

7. Answers will vary.

CHAPTER 9
Section 9.1

Exercises 1–6 are the Check Your Understanding exercises for this section. Answers to these exercises are on page 418.

7. skewness, outliers

9. independent

11. False

13. False

15. a. 9   **b.** $t = -3.41$
 c. Critical value: -1.833, P-value is between 0.0025 and 0.005 [Tech: 0.0039] [TI-84 Plus: 0.0010] [MINITAB: 0.0011]. Reject H_0.

17. $8.5 < \mu_1 - \mu_2 < 14.9$ [Tech: $8.6 < \mu_1 - \mu_2 < 14.8$]

19. $36.70 < \mu_1 - \mu_2 < 137.14$
 [TI-84 Plus: $39.99 < \mu_1 - \mu_2 < 133.85$]
 [MINITAB: $39.90 < \mu_1 - \mu_2 < 133.94$]

21. a. H_0: $\mu_1 = \mu_2$, H_1: $\mu_1 < \mu_2$ **b.** $t = -0.830$
 c. 208 [TI-84 Plus: 532.68] [MINITAB: 532]
 d. Critical value: -1.645, P-value is between 0.10 and 0.25 [Tech: 0.2033] [TI-84 Plus: $P = 0.2034$] [MINITAB: $P = 0.2034$]. Do not reject H_0. There is not enough evidence to conclude that the mean number of hours per week increased between 2000 and 2006.

23. H_0: $\mu_1 = \mu_2$, H_1: $\mu_1 \neq \mu_2$, Test statistic: $t = -0.173$, Critical values: -3.250, 3.250, P-value is greater than 0.80 [Tech: 0.8662] [TI-84 Plus: $P = 0.8646$] [MINITAB: $P = 0.8647$]. Do not reject H_0. There is not enough evidence to conclude that there is a difference in mean IQ between firstborn and secondborn sons.

25. H_0: $\mu_1 = \mu_2$, H_1: $\mu_1 < \mu_2$, Test statistic: $t = -1.043$, Critical value: -1.812, P-value is between 0.10 and 0.25 [Tech: 0.1607] [TI-84 Plus: $P = 0.1554$] [MINITAB: $P = 0.1557$]. Do not reject H_0. There is not enough evidence to conclude that the mean life span of those exposed to the mummy's curse is less than the mean of those not exposed.

27. $8.0 < \mu_1 - \mu_2 < 14.0$ [Tech: $8.1 < \mu_1 - \mu_2 < 13.9$]

29. a. The sample sizes are small ($n \leq 30$).
 b. Yes; there are no outliers and no evidence of strong skewness.
 c. $31.4 < \mu_1 - \mu_2 < 94.9$
 [TI-84 Plus: $34.1 < \mu_1 - \mu_2 < 92.2$]
 [MINITAB: $34.0 < \mu_1 - \mu_2 < 92.3$]

31. a. $0.7 < \mu_1 - \mu_2 < 2.1$
 b. Because the confidence interval does not contain 0, it contradicts the claim that the mean weight is the same for both boys and girls.

33. a. Right-tailed   **b.** 24.99965945   **c.** 0.101223442
 d. No

35. a. H_1: $\mu_1 \neq \mu_2$ **b.** Yes, the P-value is 0.003.
 c. 54   **d.** 35
 e. The P-value is between 0.002 and 0.005 [Tech: 0.0036].

37. a. 47.519   **b.** 12.28537157   **c.** 20.904, 74.134

39. a. 20.7429   **b.** 30   **c.** 98%, 12.9408, 28.5450

41. a. 1.833   **b.** 26.727   **c.** 0.039

Section 9.2

Exercises 1–4 are the Check Your Understanding exercises for this section. Answers to these exercises are on page 433.

5. 20

7. independent

9. False

11. True

13. a. $z = -1.00$ **b.** No   **c.** No

15. $0.066 < p_1 - p_2 < 0.384$

17. $-0.489 < p_1 - p_2 < -0.193$

19. a. H_0: $p_1 = p_2$, H_1: $p_1 \neq p_2$ **b.** $z = 0.62$

  c. Critical values: -1.96, 1.96, P-value is 0.5352 [Tech: 0.5376]. Do not reject H_0. There is not enough evidence to conclude that the proportion of boys who are overweight differs from the proportion of girls who are overweight.

21. H_0: $p_1 = p_2$, H_1: $p_1 > p_2$, Test statistic: $z = 3.11$, Critical value: 2.326, P-value is 0.0009. Reject H_0. We conclude that the proportion of patients suffering a heart attack or stroke is less for ticagrelor.

23. a. $0.120 < p_1 - p_2 < 0.178$

  b. No, it does not contradict the claim. It is reasonable to believe that the proportion of defective parts may have decreased by as much as 17.8%.

25. a. $0.022 < p_1 - p_2 < 0.034$

  b. Because the confidence interval does not contain 0, it contradicts the claim that the proportion of patients who have had colonoscopies is the same for those with and without colorectal cancer.

27. These are not independent samples.

29. a. Right-tailed   **b.** 0.0037512809   **c.** Yes

31. a. Left-tailed   **b.** 0.192

  c. No, because the P-value is greater than 0.05.

33. a. 0.086666667   **b.** -0.0815, 0.25484

35. a. 0.177294   **b.** 99%, -0.051451, 0.406038

37. a. H_0: $p_1 - p_2 = 0.05$, H_1: $p_1 - p_2 > 0.05$ **b.** $z = 2.11$

  c. Critical value: 1.645, P-value is 0.0174 [Tech: 0.0175]. Reject H_0.

  d. The more expensive machine

Section 9.3

Exercises 1–4 are the Check Your Understanding exercises for this section. Answers to these exercises are on page 446.

5. skewness, outliers

7. True

9. a. 1, -4, 6, 9, 7   **b.** $t = 1.614$

  c. Critical value: 2.132, P-value is between 0.05 and 0.10 [Tech: 0.0909]. Do not reject H_0.

  d. Critical value: 3.747, P-value is between 0.05 and 0.10 [Tech: 0.0909]. Do not reject H_0.

11. a. H_0: $\mu_d = 0$, H_1: $\mu_d > 0$ **b.** $t = 1.369$

  c. Critical value: 1.943, P-value is between 0.10 and 0.25 [Tech: 0.1100]. Do not reject H_0. There is not enough evidence to conclude that the mean pain level is less with drug B.

13. a. H_0: $\mu_d = 0$, H_1: $\mu_d \neq 0$ **b.** $t = -4.790$

  c. Critical values: -2.776, 2.776, P-value is between 0.005 and 0.01 [Tech: 0.0087]. Reject H_0. We conclude that the mean strength after three days differs from the mean strength after six days.

15. a. $-5.33 < \mu_d < 2.36$

  b. Because the confidence interval contains 0, it does not contradict the claim that the mean speeds of the processors are the same.

17. a. $70.4 < \mu_d < 88.3$

  b. No; it is reasonable to believe that the difference may be as large as 88.3.

19. a. Two-tailed   **b.** 15   **c.** 0.0296591111

  d. Yes, because the P-value is less than 0.05.

21. a. Right-tailed

  b. Yes, because the P-value is less than 0.05.

  c. No, because the P-value is greater than 0.01.

23. a. 8.7385   **b.** 13   **c.** 6.5788, 10.898

25. a. 2.5324   **b.** 5   **c.** 99%, -3.411394, 8.476194

27. a. P-value is between 0.05 and 0.10 [Tech: 0.0726] [TI-84 Plus: 0.0653] [MINITAB: 0.0658].

  b. The P-value is greater because the standard error is larger.

CHAPTER 9 Quiz

1. Paired

2. Independent

3. i

4. iii

5. Do not reject H_0. The difference $p_1 - p_2$ may be equal to 0.

6. 14

7. Test statistic is 2.598. Critical value is 1.796, P-value is between 0.01 and 0.025 [Tech: 0.0124]. Reject H_0.

8. H_0: $p_1 = p_2$, H_1: $p_1 < p_2$

9. Critical value: -2.326, P-value is 0.0033. Reject H_0.

10. H_0: $\mu_1 = \mu_2$, H_1: $\mu_1 \neq \mu_2$

11. Critical values: -2.120, 2.120, P-value is between 0.05 and 0.10 [Tech: 0.0662] [TI-84 Plus: 0.0576] [MINITAB: 0.0577]. Do not reject H_0.

12. 0.1183

13. $-0.02 < \mu_d < 16.02$

14. $1825.8 < \mu_1 - \mu_2 < 3260.2$ [Tech: $1832.7 < \mu_1 - \mu_2 < 3253.3$]

15. These are not independent samples.

CHAPTER 9 Review Exercises

1. H_0: $\mu_1 = \mu_2$, H_1: $\mu_1 < \mu_2$. Test statistic: $t = -2.409$, Critical value: -2.374, P-value is between 0.005 and 0.01 [Tech: 0.0089] [TI-84 Plus: 0.0085] [MINITAB: 0.0085]. Reject H_0.